Zane Grey's Westerns (Volume 1)

By

Zane Grey

Cover Photograph: Mark Gunn

ISBN: 978-1-78139-478-6

Contents

THE LAST OF THE PLAINSMEN

THE HERITAGE OF THE DESERT

THE YOUNG FORESTER

RIDERS OF THE PURPLE SAGE

KEN WARD IN THE JUNGLE

DESERT GOLD

THE RUSTLERS OF PECOS COUNTY

THE LAST OF THE PLAINSMEN

PREFATORY NOTE

Buffalo Jones needs no introduction to American sportsmen, but to these of my readers who are unacquainted with him a few words may not be amiss.

He was born sixty-two years ago on the Illinois prairie, and he has devoted practically all of his life to the pursuit of wild animals. It has been a pursuit which owed its unflagging energy and indomitable purpose to a singular passion, almost an obsession, to capture alive, not to kill. He has caught and broken the will of every well-known wild beast native to western North America. Killing was repulsive to him. He even disliked the sight of a sporting rifle, though for years necessity compelled him to earn his livelihood by supplying the meat of buffalo to the caravans crossing the plains. At last, seeing that the extinction of the noble beasts was inevitable, he smashed his rifle over a wagon wheel and vowed to save the species. For ten years he labored, pursuing, capturing and taming buffalo, for which the West gave him fame, and the name Preserver of the American Bison.

As civilization encroached upon the plains Buffalo Jones ranged slowly westward; and to-day an isolated desert-bound plateau on the north rim of the Grand Canyon of Arizona is his home. There his buffalo browse with the mustang and deer, and are as free as ever they were on the rolling plains.

In the spring of 1907 I was the fortunate companion of the old plainsman on a trip across the desert, and a hunt in that wonderful country of yellow crags, deep canyons and giant pines. I want to tell about it. I want to show the color and beauty of those painted cliffs and the long, brown-matted bluebell-dotted aisles in the grand forests; I want to give a suggestion of the tang of the dry, cool air; and particularly I want to throw a little light upon the life and nature of that strange character and remarkable man, Buffalo Jones.

Happily in remembrance a writer can live over his experiences, and see once more the moonblanched silver mountain peaks against the dark blue sky; hear the lonely sough of the night wind through the pines; feel the dance of wild expectation in the quivering pulse; the stir, the thrill, the joy of hard action in perilous moments; the mystery of man's yearning for the unattainable.

As a boy I read of Boone with a throbbing heart, and the silent moccasined, vengeful Wetzel I loved.

I pored over the deeds of later men—Custer and Carson, those heroes of the plains. And as a man I came to see the wonder, the tragedy of their lives, and to

write about them. It has been my destiny—what a happy fulfillment of my dreams of border spirit!—to live for a while in the fast-fading wild environment which produced these great men with the last of the great plainsmen.
ZANE GREY.

CHAPTER 1. THE ARIZONA DESERT

One afternoon, far out on the sun-baked waste of sage, we made camp near a clump of withered pinyon trees. The cold desert wind came down upon us with the sudden darkness. Even the Mormons, who were finding the trail for us across the drifting sands, forgot to sing and pray at sundown. We huddled round the campfire, a tired and silent little group. When out of the lonely, melancholy night some wandering Navajos stole like shadows to our fire, we hailed their advent with delight. They were good-natured Indians, willing to barter a blanket or bracelet; and one of them, a tall, gaunt fellow, with the bearing of a chief, could speak a little English.

"How," said he, in a deep chest voice.

"Hello, Noddlecoddy," greeted Jim Emmett, the Mormon guide.

"Ugh!" answered the Indian.

"Big paleface—Buffalo Jones—-big chief—buffalo man," introduced Emmett, indicating Jones.

"How." The Navajo spoke with dignity, and extended a friendly hand.

"Jones big white chief—rope buffalo—tie up tight," continued Emmett, making motions with his arm, as if he were whirling a lasso.

"No big—heap small buffalo," said the Indian, holding his hand level with his knee, and smiling broadly.

Jones, erect, rugged, brawny, stood in the full light of the campfire. He had a dark, bronzed, inscrutable face; a stern mouth and square jaw, keen eyes, half-closed from years of searching the wide plains; and deep furrows wrinkling his cheeks. A strange stillness enfolded his feature the tranquility earned from a long life of adventure.

He held up both muscular hands to the Navajo, and spread out his fingers.

"Rope buffalo—heap big buffalo—heap many—one sun."

The Indian straightened up, but kept his friendly smile.

"Me big chief," went on Jones, "me go far north—Land of Little Sticks—Naza! Naza! rope musk-ox; rope White Manitou of Great Slave Naza! Naza!"

"Naza!" replied the Navajo, pointing to the North Star; "no—no."

"Yes me big paleface—me come long way toward setting sun—go cross Big Water—go Buckskin—Siwash—chase cougar."

The cougar, or mountain lion, is a Navajo god and the Navajos hold him in as much fear and reverence as do the Great Slave Indians the musk-ox.

"No kill cougar," continued Jones, as the Indian's bold features hardened. "Run cougar horseback—run long way—dogs chase cougar long time—chase cougar up tree! Me big chief—me climb tree—climb high up—lasso cougar—rope cougar—tie cougar all tight."

The Navajo's solemn face relaxed

"White man heap fun. No."

"Yes," cried Jones, extending his great arms. "Me strong; me rope cougar—me tie cougar; ride off wigwam, keep cougar alive."

"No," replied the savage vehemently.

"Yes," protested Jones, nodding earnestly.

"No," answered the Navajo, louder, raising his dark head.

"Yes!" shouted Jones.

"BIG LIE!" the Indian thundered.

Jones joined good-naturedly in the laugh at his expense. The Indian had crudely voiced a skepticism I had heard more delicately hinted in New York, and singularly enough, which had strengthened on our way West, as we met ranchers, prospectors and cowboys. But those few men I had fortunately met, who really knew Jones, more than overbalanced the doubt and ridicule cast upon him. I recalled a scarred old veteran of the plains, who had talked to me in true Western bluntness:

"Say, young feller, I heerd yer couldn't git acrost the Canyon fer the deep snow on the north rim. Wal, ye're lucky. Now, yer hit the trail fer New York, an' keep goin'! Don't ever tackle the desert, 'specially with them Mormons. They've got water on the brain, wusser 'n religion. It's two hundred an' fifty miles from Flagstaff to Jones range, an' only two drinks on the trail. I know this hyar Buffalo Jones. I knowed him way back in the seventies, when he was doin' them ropin' stunts thet made him famous as the preserver of the American bison. I know about that crazy trip of his'n to the Barren Lands, after musk-ox. An' I reckon I kin guess what he'll do over there in the Siwash. He'll rope cougars—sure he will—an' watch 'em jump. Jones would rope the devil, an' tie him down if the lasso didn't burn. Oh! he's hell on ropin' things. An' he's wusser 'n hell on men, an' hosses, an' dogs."

All that my well-meaning friend suggested made me, of course, only the more eager to go with Jones. Where I had once been interested in the old buffalo hunter, I was now fascinated. And now I was with him in the desert and seeing him as he was, a simple, quiet man, who fitted the mountains and the silences, and the long reaches of distance.

"It does seem hard to believe—all this about Jones," remarked Judd, one of Emmett's men.

"How could a man have the strength and the nerve? And isn't it cruel to keep wild animals in captivity? it against God's word?"

CHAPTER 1. THE ARIZONA DESERT

Quick as speech could flow, Jones quoted: "And God said, 'Let us make man in our image, and give him dominion over the fish of the sea, the fowls of the air, over all the cattle, and over every creeping thing that creepeth upon the earth'!"

"Dominion—over all the beasts of the field!" repeated Jones, his big voice rolling out. He clenched his huge fists, and spread wide his long arms. "Dominion! That was God's word!" The power and intensity of him could be felt. Then he relaxed, dropped his arms, and once more grew calm. But he had shown a glimpse of the great, strange and absorbing passion of his life. Once he had told me how, when a mere child, he had hazarded limb and neck to capture a fox squirrel, how he had held on to the vicious little animal, though it bit his hand through; how he had never learned to play the games of boyhood; that when the youths of the little Illinois village were at play, he roamed the prairies, or the rolling, wooded hills, or watched a gopher hole. That boy was father of the man: for sixty years an enduring passion for dominion over wild animals had possessed him, and made his life an endless pursuit.

Our guests, the Navajos, departed early, and vanished silently in the gloom of the desert. We settled down again into a quiet that was broken only by the low chant-like song of a praying Mormon. Suddenly the hounds bristled, and old Moze, a surly and aggressive dog, rose and barked at some real or imaginary desert prowler. A sharp command from Jones made Moze crouch down, and the other hounds cowered close together.

"Better tie up the dogs," suggested Jones. "Like as not coyotes run down here from the hills."

The hounds were my especial delight. But Jones regarded them with considerable contempt. When all was said, this was no small wonder, for that quintet of long-eared canines would have tried the patience of a saint. Old Moze was a Missouri hound that Jones had procured in that State of uncertain qualities; and the dog had grown old over coon-trails. He was black and white, grizzled and battlescarred; and if ever a dog had an evil eye, Moze was that dog. He had a way of wagging his tail—an indeterminate, equivocal sort of wag, as if he realized his ugliness and knew he stood little chance of making friends, but was still hopeful and willing. As for me, the first time he manifested this evidence of a good heart under a rough coat, he won me forever.

To tell of Moze's derelictions up to that time would take more space than would a history of the whole trip; but the enumeration of several incidents will at once stamp him as a dog of character, and will establish the fact that even if his progenitors had never taken any blue ribbons, they had at least bequeathed him fighting blood. At Flagstaff we chained him in the yard of a livery stable. Next morning we found him hanging by his chain on the other side of an eight-foot fence. We took him down, expecting to have the sorrowful duty of burying him; but Moze shook himself, wagged his tail and then pitched into the livery stable dog. As a matter of fact, fighting was his forte. He whipped all of the dogs in Flagstaff; and when our blood hounds came on from California, he put three of them hors de combat at once, and subdued the pup with a savage growl. His crowning feat, however, made even the stoical Jones open his mouth in amaze. We had taken Moze to the El Tovar at the Grand Canyon, and finding it impossible to get over to the north rim, we left him with one of Jones's men, called Rust, who was working on the Canyon trail. Rust's instructions were to bring Moze to Flagstaff in two weeks. He brought the dog a little ahead time, and roared his appreciation of the relief it to get the responsibility off his hands. And he related many strange things, most striking of which was how Moze had broken his chain and plunged into the raging Colorado River, and tried to swim it just above the terrible Sockdolager Rapids. Rust and his fellow-workmen watched the dog disappear in the yellow, wrestling, turbulent whirl of waters, and had heard his knell in the booming roar of the falls. Nothing but a fish could live in that current; nothing but a bird could scale those perpendicular marble walls. That night, however, when the men crossed on the tramway, Moze met them with a wag of his tail. He had crossed the river, and he had come back!

To the four reddish-brown, high-framed bloodhounds I had given the names of Don, Tige, Jude and Ranger; and by dint of persuasion, had succeeded in establishing some kind of family relation between them and Moze. This night I tied up the bloodhounds, after bathing and salving their sore feet; and I left Moze free, for he grew fretful and surly under restraint.

The Mormons, prone, dark, blanketed figures, lay on the sand. Jones was crawling into his bed. I walked a little way from the dying fire, and faced the north, where the desert stretched, mysterious and illimitable. How solemn and still it was! I drew in a great breath of the cold air, and thrilled with a nameless sensation. Something was there, away to the northward; it called to me from out of the dark and gloom; I was going to meet it.

I lay down to sleep with the great blue expanse open to my eyes. The stars were very large, and wonderfully bright, yet they seemed so much farther off than I had ever seen them. The wind softly sifted the sand. I hearkened to the tinkle of the cowbells on the hobbled horses. The last thing I remembered was old Moze creeping close to my side, seeking the warmth of my body.

When I awakened, a long, pale line showed out of the dun-colored clouds in the east. It slowly lengthened, and tinged to red. Then the morning broke, and the slopes of snow on the San Francisco peaks behind us glowed a delicate pink. The Mormons were up and doing with the dawn. They were stalwart men, rather silent, and all workers. It was interesting to see them pack for the day's journey. They traveled with wagons and mules, in the most primitive way, which Jones assured me was exactly as their fathers had crossed the plains fifty years before, on the trail to Utah.

All morning we made good time, and as we descended into the desert, the air became warmer, the scrubby cedar growth began to fail, and the bunches of sage were few and far between. I turned often to gaze back at the San Francisco peaks. The snowcapped tips glistened and grew higher, and stood out in startling relief. Some one said they could be seen two hundred miles across the desert, and were a landmark and a fascination to all travelers thitherward.

CHAPTER 1. THE ARIZONA DESERT

I never raised my eyes to the north that I did not draw my breath quickly and grow chill with awe and bewilderment with the marvel of the desert. The scaly red ground descended gradually; bare red knolls, like waves, rolled away northward; black buttes reared their flat heads; long ranges of sand flowed between them like streams, and all sloped away to merge into gray, shadowy obscurity, into wild and desolate, dreamy and misty nothingness.

"Do you see those white sand dunes there, more to the left?" asked Emmett. "The Little Colorado runs in there. How far does it look to you?"

"Thirty miles, perhaps," I replied, adding ten miles to my estimate.

"It's seventy-five. We'll get there day after to-morrow. If the snow in the mountains has begun to melt, we'll have a time getting across."

That afternoon, a hot wind blew in my face, carrying fine sand that cut and blinded. It filled my throat, sending me to the water cask till I was ashamed. When I fell into my bed at night, I never turned. The next day was hotter; the wind blew harder; the sand stung sharper.

About noon the following day, the horses whinnied, and the mules roused out of their tardy gait. "They smell water," said Emmett. And despite the heat, and the sand in my nostrils, I smelled it, too. The dogs, poor foot-sore fellows, trotted on ahead down the trail. A few more miles of hot sand and gravel and red stone brought us around a low mesa to the Little Colorado.

It was a wide stream of swiftly running, reddish-muddy water. In the channel, cut by floods, little streams trickled and meandered in all directions. The main part of the river ran in close to the bank we were on. The dogs lolled in the water; the horses and mules tried to run in, but were restrained; the men drank, and bathed their faces. According to my Flagstaff adviser, this was one of the two drinks I would get on the desert, so I availed myself heartily of the opportunity. The water was full of sand, but cold and gratefully thirst-quenching.

The Little Colorado seemed no more to me than a shallow creek; I heard nothing sullen or menacing in its musical flow.

"Doesn't look bad, eh?" queried Emmett, who read my thought. "You'd be surprised to learn how many men and Indians, horses, sheep and wagons are buried under that quicksand."

The secret was out, and I wondered no more. At once the stream and wet bars of sand took on a different color. I removed my boots, and waded out to a little bar. The sand seemed quite firm, but water oozed out around my feet; and when I stepped, the whole bar shook like jelly. I pushed my foot through the crust, and the cold, wet sand took hold, and tried to suck me down.

"How can you ford this stream with horses?" I asked Emmett.

"We must take our chances," replied he. "We'll hitch two teams to one wagon, and run the horses. I've forded here at worse stages than this. Once a team got stuck, and I had to leave it; another time the water was high, and washed me downstream."

Emmett sent his son into the stream on a mule. The rider lashed his mount, and plunging, splashing, crossed at a pace near a gallop. He returned in the same manner, and reported one bad place near the other side.

Jones and I got on the first wagon and tried to coax up the dogs, but they would not come. Emmett had to lash the four horses to start them; and other Mormons riding alongside, yelled at them, and used their whips. The wagon bowled into the water with a tremendous splash. We were wet through before we had gone twenty feet. The plunging horses were lost in yellow spray; the stream rushed through the wheels; the Mormons yelled. I wanted to see, but was lost in a veil of yellow mist. Jones yelled in my ear, but I could not hear what he said. Once the wagon wheels struck a stone or log, almost lurching us overboard. A muddy splash blinded me. I cried out in my excitement, and punched Jones in the back. Next moment, the keen exhilaration of the ride gave way to horror. We seemed to drag, and almost stop. Some one roared: "Horse down!" One instant of painful suspense, in which imagination pictured another tragedy added to the record of this deceitful river—a moment filled with intense feeling, and sensation of splash, and yell, and fury of action; then the three able horses dragged their comrade out of the quicksand. He regained his feet, and plunged on. Spurred by fear, the horses increased their efforts, and amid clouds of spray, galloped the remaining distance to the other side.

Jones looked disgusted. Like all plainsmen, he hated water. Emmett and his men calmly unhitched. No trace of alarm, or even of excitement showed in their bronzed faces.

"We made that fine and easy," remarked Emmett.

So I sat down and wondered what Jones and Emmett, and these men would consider really hazardous. I began to have a feeling that I would find out; that experience for me was but in its infancy; that far across the desert the something which had called me would show hard, keen, perilous life. And I began to think of reserve powers of fortitude and endurance.

The other wagons were brought across without mishap; but the dogs did not come with them. Jones called and called. The dogs howled and howled. Finally I waded out over the wet bars and little streams to a point several hundred yards nearer the dogs. Moze was lying down, but the others were whining and howling in a state of great perturbation. I called and called. They answered, and even ran into the water, but did not start across.

"Hyah, Moze! hyah, you Indian!" I yelled, losing my patience. "You've already swum the Big Colorado, and this is only a brook. Come on!"

This appeal evidently touched Moze, for he barked, and plunged in. He made the water fly, and when carried off his feet, breasted the current with energy and power. He made shore almost even with me, and wagged his tail. Not to be outdone, Jude, Tige and Don followed suit, and first one and then another was swept off his feet and carried downstream. They landed below me. This left Ranger, the pup, alone on the other shore. Of all the pitiful yelps ever uttered by a frightened and lonely puppy, his were the most forlorn I had ever heard. Time after time he plunged in, and with many bitter howls of distress, went back. I kept calling, and at last, hoping to make him come by a show of indifference, I started away. This broke his heart. Putting up his head, he let out a long, melancholy wail, which for aught I knew might have been a prayer, and then consigned himself to the yellow current. Ranger swam like a boy learning. He seemed to be afraid to get wet. His forefeet were continually pawing the air in front of his nose. When he struck the swift place, he went downstream like a flash, but still kept swimming valiantly. I tried to follow along the sand-bar, but found it impossible. I encouraged him by yelling. He drifted far below, stranded on an island, crossed it, and plunged in again, to make shore almost out of my sight. And when at last I got to dry sand, there was Ranger, wet and disheveled, but consciously proud and happy.

After lunch we entered upon the seventy-mile stretch from the Little to the Big Colorado.

Imagination had pictured the desert for me as a vast, sandy plain, flat and monotonous. Reality showed me desolate mountains gleaming bare in the sun, long lines of red bluffs, white sand dunes, and hills of blue clay, areas of level ground—in all, a many-hued, boundless world in itself, wonderful and beautiful, fading all around into the purple haze of deceiving distance.

Thin, clear, sweet, dry, the desert air carried a languor, a dreaminess, tidings of far-off things, and an enthralling promise. The fragrance of flowers, the beauty and grace of women, the sweetness of music, the mystery of life—all seemed to float on that promise. It was the air breathed by the lotus-eaters, when they dreamed, and wandered no more.

Beyond the Little Colorado, we began to climb again. The sand was thick; the horses labored; the drivers shielded their faces. The dogs began to limp and lag. Ranger had to be taken into a wagon; and then, one by one, all of the other dogs except Moze. He refused to ride, and trotted along with his head down.

Far to the front the pink cliffs, the ragged mesas, the dark, volcanic spurs of the Big Colorado stood up and beckoned us onward. But they were a far hundred miles across the shifting sands, and baked day, and ragged rocks. Always in the rear rose the San Francisco peaks, cold and pure, startlingly clear and close in the rare atmosphere.

We camped near another water hole, located in a deep, yellow-colored gorge, crumbling to pieces, a ruin of rock, and silent as the grave. In the bottom of the canyon was a pool of water, covered with green scum. My thirst was effectually quenched by the mere sight of it. I slept poorly, and lay for hours watching the great stars. The silence was painfully oppressive. If Jones had not begun to give a respectable imitation of the exhaust pipe on a steamboat, I should have been compelled to shout aloud, or get up; but this snoring would have dispelled anything. The morning came gray and cheerless. I got up stiff and sore, with a tongue like a rope.

All day long we ran the gauntlet of the hot, flying sand. Night came again, a cold, windy night. I slept well until a mule stepped on my bed, which was conducive to restlessness. At dawn, cold, gray clouds tried to blot out the rosy east. I could hardly get up. My lips were cracked; my tongue swollen to twice its natural size; my eyes smarted and burned. The barrels and kegs of water were exhausted. Holes that had been dug in the dry sand of a dry streambed the night before in the morning yielded a scant supply of muddy alkali water, which went to the horses.

Only twice that day did I rouse to anything resembling enthusiasm. We came to a stretch of country showing the wonderful diversity of the desert land. A long range of beautifully rounded clay stones bordered the trail. So symmetrical were they that I imagined them works of sculptors. Light blue, dark blue, clay blue, marine blue, cobalt blue—every shade of blue was there, but no other color. The other time that I awoke to sensations from without was when we came to the top of a ridge. We had been passing through red-lands. Jones called the place a strong, specific word which really was illustrative of the heat amid those scaling red ridges. We came out where the red changed abruptly to gray. I seemed always to see things first, and I cried out: "Look! here are a red lake and trees!"

"No, lad, not a lake," said old Jim, smiling at me; "that's what haunts the desert traveler. It's only mirage!"

So I awoke to the realization of that illusive thing, the mirage, a beautiful lie, false as stairs of sand. Far northward a clear rippling lake sparkled in the sunshine. Tall, stately trees, with waving green foliage, bordered the water. For a long moment it lay there, smiling in the sun, a thing almost tangible; and then it faded. I felt a sense of actual loss. So real had been the illusion that I could not believe I was not soon to drink and wade and dabble in the cool waters. Disappointment was keen. This is what maddens the prospector or sheep-herder lost in the desert. Was it not a terrible thing to be dying of thirst, to see sparkling water, almost to smell it and then realize suddenly that all was only a lying track of the desert, a lure, a delusion? I ceased to wonder at the Mormons, and their search for water, their talk of water. But I had not realized its true significance. I had not known what water was. I had never appreciated it. So it was my destiny to learn that water is the greatest thing on earth. I hung over a three-foot hole in a dry stream-bed, and watched it ooze and seep through the sand, and fill up—oh, so slowly; and I felt it loosen my parched tongue, and steal through all my dry body with strength and life. Water is said to constitute three fourths of the universe. However that may be, on the desert it is the whole world, and all of life.

Two days passed by, all hot sand and wind and glare. The Mormons sang no more at evening; Jones was silent; the dogs were limp as rags.

At Moncaupie Wash we ran into a sandstorm. The horses turned their backs to it, and bowed their heads patiently. The Mormons covered themselves. I wrapped a blanket round my head and hid behind a sage bush. The wind, carrying the sand, made a strange hollow roar. All was enveloped in a weird yellow opacity. The sand seeped through the sage bush and swept by with a soft, rustling sound, not unlike the wind in the rye. From time to time I raised a corner of my blanket and peeped out. Where my feet had stretched was an enormous mound of sand. I felt the blanket, weighted down, slowly settle over me.

CHAPTER 1. THE ARIZONA DESERT

Suddenly as it had come, the sandstorm passed. It left a changed world for us. The trail was covered; the wheels hub-deep in sand; the horses, walking sand dunes. I could not close my teeth without grating harshly on sand.

We journeyed onward, and passed long lines of petrified trees, some a hundred feet in length, lying as they had fallen, thousands of years before. White ants crawled among the ruins. Slowly climbing the sandy trail, we circled a great red bluff with jagged peaks, that had seemed an interminable obstacle. A scant growth of cedar and sage again made its appearance. Here we halted to pass another night. Under a cedar I heard the plaintive, piteous bleat of an animal. I searched, and presently found a little black and white lamb, scarcely able to stand. It came readily to me, and I carried it to the wagon.

"That's a Navajo lamb," said Emmett. "It's lost. There are Navajo Indians close by."

"Away in the desert we heard its cry," quoted one of the Mormons.

Jones and I climbed the red mesa near camp to see the sunset. All the western world was ablaze in golden glory. Shafts of light shot toward the zenith, and bands of paler gold, tinging to rose, circled away from the fiery, sinking globe. Suddenly the sun sank, the gold changed to gray, then to purple, and shadows formed in the deep gorge at our feet. So sudden was the transformation that soon it was night, the solemn, impressive night of the desert. A stillness that seemed too sacred to break clasped the place; it was infinite; it held the bygone ages, and eternity.

More days, and miles, miles, miles! The last day's ride to the Big Colorado was unforgettable. We rode toward the head of a gigantic red cliff pocket, a veritable inferno, immeasurably hot, glaring, awful. It towered higher and higher above us. When we reached a point of this red barrier, we heard the dull rumbling roar of water, and we came out, at length, on a winding trail cut in the face of a blue overhanging the Colorado River. The first sight of most famous and much-heralded wonders of nature is often disappointing; but never can this be said of the blood-hued Rio Colorado. If it had beauty, it was beauty that appalled. So riveted was my gaze that I could hardly turn it across the river, where Emmett proudly pointed out his lonely home—an oasis set down amidst beetling red cliffs. How grateful to the eye was the green of alfalfa and cottonwood! Going round the bluff trail, the wheels had only a foot of room to spare; and the sheer descent into the red, turbid, congested river was terrifying.

I saw the constricted rapids, where the Colorado took its plunge into the box-like head of the Grand Canyon of Arizona; and the deep, reverberating boom of the river, at flood height, was a fearful thing to hear. I could not repress a shudder at the thought of crossing above that rapid.

The bronze walls widened as we proceeded, and we got down presently to a level, where a long wire cable stretched across the river. Under the cable ran a rope. On the other side was an old scow moored to the bank.

"Are we going across in that?" I asked Emmett, pointing to the boat.

"We'll all be on the other side before dark," he replied cheerily.

I felt that I would rather start back alone over the desert than trust myself in such a craft, on such a river. And it was all because I had had experience with bad rivers, and thought I was a judge of dangerous currents. The Colorado slid with a menacing roar out of a giant split in the red wall, and whirled, eddied, bulged on toward its confinement in the iron-ribbed canyon below.

In answer to shots fired, Emmett's man appeared on the other side, and rode down to the ferry landing. Here he got into a skiff, and rowed laboriously upstream for a long distance before he started across, and then swung into the current. He swept down rapidly, and twice the skiff whirled, and completely turned round; but he reached our bank safely. Taking two men aboard he rowed upstream again, close to the shore, and returned to the opposite side in much the same manner in which he had come over.

The three men pushed out the scow, and grasping the rope overhead, began to pull. The big craft ran easily. When the current struck it, the wire cable sagged, the water boiled and surged under it, raising one end, and then the other. Nevertheless, five minutes were all that were required to pull the boat over.

It was a rude, oblong affair, made of heavy planks loosely put together, and it leaked. When Jones suggested that we get the agony over as quickly as possible, I was with him, and we embarked together. Jones said he did not like the looks of the tackle; and when I thought of his by no means small mechanical skill, I had not added a cheerful idea to my consciousness. The horses of the first team had to be dragged upon the scow, and once on, they reared and plunged.

When we started, four men pulled the rope, and Emmett sat in the stern, with the tackle guys in hand. As the current hit us, he let out the guys, which maneuver caused the boat to swing stern downstream. When it pointed obliquely, he made fast the guys again. I saw that this served two purposes: the current struck, slid alongside, and over the stern, which mitigated the danger, and at the same time helped the boat across.

To look at the river was to court terror, but I had to look. It was an infernal thing. It roared in hollow, sullen voice, as a monster growling. It had voice, this river, and one strangely changeful. It moaned as if in pain—it whined, it cried. Then at times it would seem strangely silent. The current as complex and mutable as human life. It boiled, beat and bulged. The bulge itself was an incompressible thing, like a roaring lift of the waters from submarine explosion. Then it would smooth out, and run like oil. It shifted from one channel to another, rushed to the center of the river, then swung close to one shore or the other. Again it swelled near the boat, in great, boiling, hissing eddies.

"Look! See where it breaks through the mountain!" yelled Jones in my ear.

I looked upstream to see the stupendous granite walls separated in a gigantic split that must have been made by a terrible seismic disturbance; and from this gap poured the dark, turgid, mystic flood.

I was in a cold sweat when we touched shore, and I jumped long before the boat was properly moored.

Emmett was wet to the waist where the water had surged over him. As he sat rearranging some tackle I remarked to him that of course he must be a splendid swimmer, or he would not take such risks.

"No, I can't swim a stroke," he replied; "and it wouldn't be any use if I could. Once in there a man's a goner."

"You've had bad accidents here?" I questioned.

"No, not bad. We only drowned two men last year. You see, we had to tow the boat up the river, and row across, as then we hadn't the wire. Just above, on this side, the boat hit a stone, and the current washed over her, taking off the team and two men."

"Didn't you attempt to rescue them?" I asked, after waiting a moment.

"No use. They never came up."

"Isn't the river high now?" I continued, shuddering as I glanced out at the whirling logs and drifts.

"High, and coming up. If I don't get the other teams over to-day I'll wait until she goes down. At this season she rises and lowers every day or so, until June then comes the big flood, and we don't cross for months."

I sat for three hours watching Emmett bring over the rest of his party, which he did without accident, but at the expense of great effort. And all the time in my ears dinned the roar, the boom, the rumble of this singularly rapacious and purposeful river—a river of silt, a red river of dark, sinister meaning, a river with terrible work to perform, a river which never gave up its dead.

CHAPTER 2. THE RANGE

After a much-needed rest at Emmett's, we bade good-by to him and his hospitable family, and under the guidance of his man once more took to the wind-swept trail. We pursued a southwesterly course now, following the lead of the craggy red wall that stretched on and on for hundreds of miles into Utah. The desert, smoky and hot, fell away to the left, and in the foreground a dark, irregular line marked the Grand Canyon cutting through the plateau.

The wind whipped in from the vast, open expanse, and meeting an obstacle in the red wall, turned north and raced past us. Jones's hat blew off, stood on its rim, and rolled. It kept on rolling, thirty miles an hour, more or less; so fast, at least, that we were a long time catching up to it with a team of horses. Possibly we never would have caught it had not a stone checked its flight. Further manifestation of the power of the desert wind surrounded us on all sides. It had hollowed out huge stones from the cliffs, and tumbled them to the plain below; and then, sweeping sand and gravel low across the desert floor, had cut them deeply, until they rested on slender pedestals, thus sculptoring grotesque and striking monuments to the marvelous persistence of this element of nature.

Late that afternoon, as we reached the height of the plateau, Jones woke up and shouted: "Ha! there's Buckskin!"

Far southward lay a long, black mountain, covered with patches of shining snow. I could follow the zigzag line of the Grand Canyon splitting the desert plateau, and saw it disappear in the haze round the end of the mountain. From this I got my first clear impression of the topography of the country surrounding our objective point. Buckskin mountain ran its blunt end eastward to the Canyon—in fact, formed a hundred miles of the north rim. As it was nine thousand feet high it still held the snow, which had occasioned our lengthy desert ride to get back of the mountain. I could see the long slopes rising out of the desert to meet the timber.

As we bowled merrily down grade I noticed that we were no longer on stony ground, and that a little scant silvery grass had made its appearance. Then little branches of green, with a blue flower, smiled out of the clayish sand.

All of a sudden Jones stood up, and let out a wild Comanche yell. I was more startled by the yell than by the great hand he smashed down on my shoulder, and for the moment I was dazed.

CHAPTER 2. THE RANGE

"There! look! look! the buffalo! Hi! Hi! Hi!"

Below us, a few miles on a rising knoll, a big herd of buffalo shone black in the gold of the evening sun. I had not Jones's incentive, but I felt enthusiasm born of the wild and beautiful picture, and added my yell to his. The huge, burly leader of the herd lifted his head, and after regarding us for a few moments calmly went on browsing.

The desert had fringed away into a grand rolling pastureland, walled in by the red cliffs, the slopes of Buckskin, and further isolated by the Canyon. Here was a range of twenty-four hundred square miles without a foot of barb-wire, a pasture fenced in by natural forces, with the splendid feature that the buffalo could browse on the plain in winter, and go up into the cool foothills of Buckskin in summer.

From another ridge we saw a cabin dotting the rolling plain, and in half an hour we reached it. As we climbed down from the wagon a brown and black dog came dashing out of the cabin, and promptly jumped at Moze. His selection showed poor discrimination, for Moze whipped him before I could separate them. Hearing Jones heartily greeting some one, I turned in his direction, only to be distracted by another dog fight. Don had tackled Moze for the seventh time. Memory rankled in Don, and he needed a lot of whipping, some of which he was getting when I rescued him.

Next moment I was shaking hands with Frank and Jim, Jones's ranchmen. At a glance I liked them both. Frank was short and wiry, and had a big, ferocious mustache, the effect of which was softened by his kindly brown eyes. Jim was tall, a little heavier; he had a careless, tidy look; his eyes were searching, and though he appeared a young man, his hair was white.

"I shore am glad to see you all," said Jim, in slow, soft, Southern accent.

"Get down, get down," was Frank's welcome—a typically Western one, for we had already gotten down; "an' come in. You must be worked out. Sure you've come a long way." He was quick of speech, full of nervous energy, and beamed with hospitality.

The cabin was the rudest kind of log affair, with a huge stone fireplace in one end, deer antlers and coyote skins on the wall, saddles and cowboys' traps in a corner, a nice, large, promising cupboard, and a table and chairs. Jim threw wood on a smoldering fire, that soon blazed and crackled cheerily.

I sank down into a chair with a feeling of blessed relief. Ten days of desert ride behind me! Promise of wonderful days before me, with the last of the old plainsmen. No wonder a sweet sense of ease stole over me, or that the fire seemed a live and joyously welcoming thing, or that Jim's deft maneuvers in preparation of supper roused in me a rapt admiration.

"Twenty calves this spring!" cried Jones, punching me in my sore side. "Ten thousand dollars worth of calves!"

He was now altogether a changed man; he looked almost young; his eyes danced, and he rubbed his big hands together while he plied Frank with questions. In strange surroundings—that is, away from his Native Wilds, Jones had been a silent man; it had been almost impossible to get anything out of him. But now I saw that I should come to know the real man. In a very few moments he had talked more than on all the desert trip, and what he said, added to the little I had already learned, put me in possession of some interesting information as to his buffalo.

Some years before he had conceived the idea of hybridizing buffalo with black Galloway cattle; and with the characteristic determination and energy of the man, he at once set about finding a suitable range. This was difficult, and took years of searching. At last the wild north rim of the Grand Canyon, a section unknown except to a few Indians and mustang hunters, was settled upon. Then the gigantic task of transporting the herd of buffalo by rail from Montana to Salt Lake was begun. The two hundred and ninety miles of desert lying between the home of the Mormons and Buckskin Mountain was an obstacle almost insurmountable. The journey was undertaken and found even more trying than had been expected. Buffalo after buffalo died on the way. Then Frank, Jones's right-hand man, put into execution a plan he had been thinking of—namely, to travel by night. It succeeded. The buffalo rested in the day and traveled by easy stages by night, with the result that the big herd was transported to the ideal range.

Here, in an environment strange to their race, but peculiarly adaptable, they thrived and multiplied. The hybrid of the Galloway cow and buffalo proved a great success. Jones called the new species "Cattalo." The cattalo took the hardiness of the buffalo, and never required artificial food or shelter. He would face the desert storm or blizzard and stand stock still in his tracks until the weather cleared. He became quite domestic, could be easily handled, and grew exceedingly fat on very little provender. The folds of his stomach were so numerous that they digested even the hardest and flintiest of corn. He had fourteen ribs on each side, while domestic cattle had only thirteen; thus he could endure rougher work and longer journeys to water. His fur was so dense and glossy that it equaled that of the unplucked beaver or otter, and was fully as valuable as the buffalo robe. And not to be overlooked by any means was the fact that his meat was delicious.

Jones had to hear every detail of all that had happened since his absence in the East, and he was particularly inquisitive to learn all about the twenty cattalo calves. He called different buffalo by name; and designated the calves by descriptive terms, such as "Whiteface" and "Crosspatch." He almost forgot to eat, and kept Frank too busy to get anything into his own mouth. After supper he calmed down.

"How about your other man—Mr. Wallace, I think you said?" asked Frank.

"We expected to meet him at Grand Canyon Station, and then at Flagstaff. But he didn't show up. Either he backed out or missed us. I'm sorry; for when we get up on Buckskin, among the wild horses and cougars, we'll be likely to need him."

"I reckon you'll need me, as well as Jim," said Frank dryly, with a twinkle in his eye. "The buffs are in good shape an' can get along without me for a while."

"That'll be fine. How about cougar sign on the mountain?"

"Plenty. I've got two spotted near Clark Spring. Comin' over two weeks ago I tracked them in the snow along the trail for miles. We'll ooze over that way, as it's goin' toward the Siwash. The Siwash breaks of the Canyon—there's the place for lions. I met a wild-horse wrangler not long back, an' he was tellin' me about Old Tom an' the colts he'd killed this winter."

Naturally, I here expressed a desire to know more of Old Tom.

"He's the biggest cougar ever known of in these parts. His tracks are bigger than a horse's, an' have been seen on Buckskin for twelve years. This wrangler—his name is Clark—said he'd turned his saddle horse out to graze near camp, an' Old Tom sneaked in an' downed him. The lions over there are sure a bold bunch. Well, why shouldn't they be? No one ever hunted them. You see, the mountain is hard to get at. But now you're here, if it's big cats you want we sure can find them. Only be easy, be easy. You've all the time there is. An' any job on Buckskin will take time. We'll look the calves over, an' you must ride the range to harden up. Then we'll ooze over toward Oak. I expect it'll be boggy, an' I hope the snow melts soon."

"The snow hadn't melted on Greenland point," replied Jones. "We saw that with a glass from the El Tovar. We wanted to cross that way, but Rust said Bright Angel Creek was breast high to a horse, and that creek is the trail."

"There's four feet of snow on Greenland," said Frank. "It was too early to come that way. There's only about three months in the year the Canyon can be crossed at Greenland."

"I want to get in the snow," returned Jones. "This bunch of long-eared canines I brought never smelled a lion track. Hounds can't be trained quick without snow. You've got to see what they're trailing, or you can't break them."

Frank looked dubious. "'Pears to me we'll have trouble gettin' a lion without lion dogs. It takes a long time to break a hound off of deer, once he's chased them. Buckskin is full of deer, wolves, coyotes, and there's the wild horses. We couldn't go a hundred feet without crossin' trails."

"How's the hound you and Jim fetched in las' year? Has he got a good nose? Here he is—I like his head. Come here, Bowser—what's his name?"

"Jim named him Sounder, because he sure has a voice. It's great to hear him on a trail. Sounder has a nose that can't be fooled, an' he'll trail anythin'; but I don't know if he ever got up a lion."

Sounder wagged his bushy tail and looked up affectionately at Frank. He had a fine head, great brown eyes, very long ears and curly brownish-black hair. He was not demonstrative, looked rather askance at Jones, and avoided the other dogs.

"That dog will make a great lion-chaser," said Jones, decisively, after his study of Sounder. "He and Moze will keep us busy, once they learn we want lions."

"I don't believe any dog-trainer could teach them short of six months," replied Frank. "Sounder is no spring chicken; an' that black and dirty white cross between a cayuse an' a barb-wire fence is an old dog. You can't teach old dogs new tricks."

Jones smiled mysteriously, a smile of conscious superiority, but said nothing.

"We'll shore hev a storm to-morrow," said Jim, relinquishing his pipe long enough to speak. He had been silent, and now his meditative gaze was on the west, through the cabin window, where a dull afterglow faded under the heavy laden clouds of night and left the horizon dark.

I was very tired when I lay down, but so full of excitement that sleep did not soon visit my eyelids. The talk about buffalo, wild-horse hunters, lions and dogs, the prospect of hard riding and unusual adventure; the vision of Old Tom that had already begun to haunt me, filled my mind with pictures and fancies. The other fellows dropped off to sleep, and quiet reigned. Suddenly a succession of queer, sharp barks came from the plain, close to the cabin. Coyotes were paying us a call, and judging from the chorus of yelps and howls from our dogs, it was not a welcome visit. Above the medley rose one big, deep, full voice that I knew at once belonged to Sounder. Then all was quiet again. Sleep gradually benumbed my senses. Vague phrases dreamily drifted to and fro in my mind: "Jones's wild range—Old Tom—Sounder—great name—great voice—Sounder! Sounder! Sounder—"

Next morning I could hardly crawl out of my sleeping-bag. My bones ached, my muscles protested excruciatingly, my lips burned and bled, and the cold I had contracted on the desert clung to me. A good brisk walk round the corrals, and then breakfast, made me feel better.

"Of course you can ride?" queried Frank.

My answer was not given from an overwhelming desire to be truthful. Frank frowned a little, as it wondering how a man could have the nerve to start out on a jaunt with Buffalo Jones without being a good horseman. To be unable to stick on the back of a wild mustang, or a cayuse, was an unpardonable sin in Arizona. My frank admission was made relatively, with my mind on what cowboys held as a standard of horsemanship.

The mount Frank trotted out of the corral for me was a pure white, beautiful mustang, nervous, sensitive, quivering. I watched Frank put on the saddle, and when he called me I did not fail to catch a covert twinkle in his merry brown eyes. Looking away toward Buckskin Mountain, which was coincidentally in the direction of home, I said to myself: "This may be where you get on, but most certainly it is where you get off!"

Jones was already riding far beyond the corral, as I could see by a cloud of dust; and I set off after him, with the painful consciousness that I must have looked to Frank and Jim much as Central Park equestrians had often looked to me. Frank shouted after me that he would catch up with us out on the range. I was not in any great hurry to overtake Jones, but evidently my horse's inclinations differed from mine; at any rate, he made the dust fly, and jumped the little sage bushes.

Jones, who had tarried to inspect one of the pools—formed of running water from the corrals—greeted me as I came up with this cheerful observation.

CHAPTER 2. THE RANGE

"What in thunder did Frank give you that white nag for? The buffalo hate white horses—anything white. They're liable to stampede off the range, or chase you into the canyon."

I replied grimly that, as it was certain something was going to happen, the particular circumstance might as well come off quickly.

We rode over the rolling plain with a cool, bracing breeze in our faces. The sky was dull and mottled with a beautiful cloud effect that presaged wind. As we trotted along Jones pointed out to me and descanted upon the nutritive value of three different kinds of grass, one of which he called the Buffalo Pea, noteworthy for a beautiful blue blossom. Soon we passed out of sight of the cabin, and could see only the billowy plain, the red tips of the stony wall, and the black-fringed crest of Buckskin. After riding a while we made out some cattle, a few of which were on the range, browsing in the lee of a ridge. No sooner had I marked them than Jones let out another Comanche yell.

"Wolf!" he yelled; and spurring his big bay, he was off like the wind.

A single glance showed me several cows running as if bewildered, and near them a big white wolf pulling down a calf. Another white wolf stood not far off. My horse jumped as if he had been shot; and the realization darted upon me that here was where the certain something began. Spot—the mustang had one black spot in his pure white—snorted like I imagined a blooded horse might, under dire insult. Jones's bay had gotten about a hundred paces the start. I lived to learn that Spot hated to be left behind; moreover, he would not be left behind; he was the swiftest horse on the range, and proud of the distinction. I cast one unmentionable word on the breeze toward the cabin and Frank, then put mind and muscle to the sore task of remaining with Spot. Jones was born on a saddle, and had been taking his meals in a saddle for about sixty-three years, and the bay horse could run. Run is not a felicitous word—he flew. And I was rendered mentally deranged for the moment to see that hundred paces between the bay and Spot materially lessen at every jump. Spot lengthened out, seemed to go down near the ground, and cut the air like a high-geared auto. If I had not heard the fast rhythmic beat of his hoofs, and had not bounced high into the air at every jump, I would have been sure I was riding a bird. I tried to stop him. As well might I have tried to pull in the Lusitania with a thread. Spot was out to overhaul that bay, and in spite of me, he was doing it. The wind rushed into my face and sang in my ears. Jones seemed the nucleus of a sort of haze, and it grew larger and larger. Presently he became clearly defined in my sight; the violent commotion under me subsided; I once more felt the saddle, and then I realized that Spot had been content to stop alongside of Jones, tossing his head and champing his bit.

"Well, by George! I didn't know you were in the stretch," cried my companion. "That was a fine little brush. We must have come several miles. I'd have killed those wolves if I'd brought a gun. The big one that had the calf was a bold brute. He never let go until I was within fifty feet of him. Then I almost rode him down. I don't think the calf was much hurt. But those blood-thirsty devils will return, and like as not get the calf. That's the worst of cattle raising. Now, take the buffalo.

Do you suppose those wolves could have gotten a buffalo calf out from under the mother? Never. Neither could a whole band of wolves. Buffalo stick close together, and the little ones do not stray. When danger threatens, the herd closes in and faces it and fights. That is what is grand about the buffalo and what made them once roam the prairies in countless, endless droves."

From the highest elevation in that part of the range we viewed the surrounding ridges, flats and hollows, searching for the buffalo. At length we spied a cloud of dust rising from behind an undulating mound, then big black dots hove in sight.

"Frank has rounded up the herd, and is driving it this way. We'll wait," said Jones.

Though the buffalo appeared to be moving fast, a long time elapsed before they reached the foot of our outlook. They lumbered along in a compact mass, so dense that I could not count them, but I estimated the number at seventy-five. Frank was riding zigzag behind them, swinging his lariat and yelling. When he espied us he reined in his horse and waited. Then the herd slowed down, halted and began browsing.

"Look at the cattalo calves," cried Jones, in ecstatic tones. "See how shy they are, how close they stick to their mothers."

The little dark-brown fellows were plainly frightened. I made several unsuccessful attempts to photograph them, and gave it up when Jones told me not to ride too close and that it would be better to wait till we had them in the corral.

He took my camera and instructed me to go on ahead, in the rear of the herd. I heard the click of the instrument as he snapped a picture, and then suddenly heard him shout in alarm: "Look out! look out! pull your horse!"

Thundering hoof-beats pounding the earth accompanied his words. I saw a big bull, with head down, tail raised, charging my horse. He answered Frank's yell of command with a furious grunt. I was paralyzed at the wonderfully swift action of the shaggy brute, and I sat helpless. Spot wheeled as if he were on a pivot and plunged out of the way with a celerity that was astounding. The buffalo stopped, pawed the ground, and angrily tossed his huge head. Frank rode up to him, yelled, and struck him with the lariat, whereupon he gave another toss of his horns, and then returned to the herd.

"It was that darned white nag," said Jones. "Frank, it was wrong to put an inexperienced man on Spot. For that matter, the horse should never be allowed to go near the buffalo."

"Spot knows the buffs; they'd never get to him," replied Frank. But the usual spirit was absent from his voice, and he glanced at me soberly. I knew I had turned white, for I felt the peculiar cold sensation on my face.

"Now, look at that, will you?" cried Jones. "I don't like the looks of that."

He pointed to the herd. They stopped browsing, and were uneasily shifting to and fro. The bull lifted his head; the others slowly grouped together.

"Storm! Sandstorm!" exclaimed Jones, pointing desert-ward. Dark yellow clouds like smoke were rolling, sweeping, bearing down upon us. They expanded, blossoming out like gigantic roses, and whirled and merged into one another, all the time rolling on and blotting out the light.

"We've got to run. That storm may last two days," yelled Frank to me. "We've had some bad ones lately. Give your horse free rein, and cover your face."

A roar, resembling an approaching storm at sea, came on puffs of wind, as the horses got into their stride. Long streaks of dust whipped up in different places; the silver-white grass bent to the ground; round bunches of sage went rolling before us. The puffs grew longer, steadier, harder. Then a shrieking blast howled on our trail, seeming to swoop down on us with a yellow, blinding pall. I shut my eyes and covered my face with a handkerchief. The sand blew so thick that it filled my gloves, pebbles struck me hard enough to sting through my coat.

Fortunately, Spot kept to an easy swinging lope, which was the most comfortable motion for me. But I began to get numb, and could hardly stick on the saddle. Almost before I had dared to hope, Spot stopped. Uncovering my face, I saw Jim in the doorway of the lee side of the cabin. The yellow, streaky, whistling clouds of sand split on the cabin and passed on, leaving a small, dusty space of light.

"Shore Spot do hate to be beat," yelled Jim, as he helped me off. I stumbled into the cabin and fell upon a buffalo robe and lay there absolutely spent. Jones and Frank came in a few minutes apart, each anathematizing the gritty, powdery sand.

All day the desert storm raged and roared. The dust sifted through the numerous cracks in the cabin burdened our clothes, spoiled our food and blinded our eyes. Wind, snow, sleet and rainstorms are discomforting enough under trying circumstances; but all combined, they are nothing to the choking stinging, blinding sandstorm.

"Shore it'll let up by sundown," averred Jim. And sure enough the roar died away about five o'clock, the wind abated and the sand settled.

Just before supper, a knock sounded heavily o the cabin door. Jim opened it to admit one of Emmett's sons and a very tall man whom none of us knew. He was a sand-man. All that was not sand seemed a space or two of corduroy, a big bone-handled knife, a prominent square jaw and bronze cheek and flashing eyes.

"Get down—get down, an' come in, stranger, said Frank cordially.

"How do you do, sir," said Jones.

"Colonel Jones, I've been on your trail for twelve days," announced the stranger, with a grim smile. The sand streamed off his coat in little white streak. Jones appeared to be casting about in his mind.

"I'm Grant Wallace," continued the newcomer. "I missed you at the El Tovar, at Williams and at Flagstaff, where I was one day behind. Was half a day late at the Little Colorado, saw your train cross Moncaupie Wash, and missed you because of the sandstorm there. Saw you from the other side of the Big Colorado as you rode out from Emmett's along the red wall. And here I am. We've never met till now, which obviously isn't my fault."

The Colonel and I fell upon Wallace's neck. Frank manifested his usual alert excitation, and said: "Well, I guess he won't hang fire on a long cougar chase." And Jim—slow, careful Jim, dropped a plate with the exclamation: "Shore it do beat hell!" The hounds sniffed round Wallace, and welcomed him with vigorous tails.

Supper that night, even if we did grind sand with our teeth, was a joyous occasion. The biscuits were flaky and light; the bacon fragrant and crisp. I produced a jar of blackberry jam, which by subtle cunning I had been able to secrete from the Mormons on that dry desert ride, and it was greeted with acclamations of pleasure. Wallace, divested of his sand guise, beamed with the gratification of a hungry man once more in the presence of friends and food. He made large cavities in Jim's great pot of potato stew, and caused biscuits to vanish in a way that would not have shamed a Hindoo magician. The Grand Canyon he dug in my jar of jam, however, could not have been accomplished by legerdemain.

Talk became animated on dogs, cougars, horses and buffalo. Jones told of our experience out on the range, and concluded with some salient remarks.

"A tame wild animal is the most dangerous of beasts. My old friend, Dick Rock, a great hunter and guide out of Idaho, laughed at my advice, and got killed by one of his three-year-old bulls. I told him they knew him just well enough to kill him, and they did. My friend, A. H. Cole, of Oxford, Nebraska, tried to rope a Weetah that was too tame to be safe, and the bull killed him. Same with General Bull, a member of the Kansas Legislature, and two cowboys who went into a corral to tie up a tame elk at the wrong time. I pleaded with them not to undertake it. They had not studied animals as I had. That tame elk killed all of them. He had to be shot in order to get General Bull off his great antlers. You see, a wild animal must learn to respect a man. The way I used to teach the Yellowstone Park bears to be respectful and safe neighbors was to rope them around the front paw, swing them up on a tree clear of the ground, and whip them with a long pole. It was a dangerous business, and looks cruel, but it is the only way I could find to make the bears good. You see, they eat scraps around the hotels and get so tame they will steal everything but red-hot stoves, and will cuff the life out of those who try to shoo them off. But after a bear mother has had a licking, she not only becomes a good bear for the rest of her life, but she tells all her cubs about it with a good smack of her paw, for emphasis, and teaches them to respect peaceable citizens generation after generation.

"One of the hardest jobs I ever tackled was that of supplying the buffalo for Bronx Park. I rounded up a magnificent 'king' buffalo bull, belligerent enough to fight a battleship. When I rode after him the cowmen said I was as good as killed. I made a lance by driving a nail into the end of a short pole and sharpening it. After he had chased me, I wheeled my broncho, and hurled the lance into his back, ripping a wound as long as my hand. That put the fear of Providence into him and took the fight all out of him. I drove him uphill and down, and across canyons at a dead run for eight miles single handed, and loaded him on a freight car; but he came near getting me once or twice, and only quick broncho work and lance play saved me.

"In the Yellowstone Park all our buffaloes have become docile, excepting the huge bull which led them. The Indians call the buffalo leader the 'Weetah,' the master of the herd. It was sure death to go near this one. So I shipped in another Weetah, hoping that he might whip some of the fight out of old Manitou, the Mighty. They came together head on, like a railway collision, and ripped up over a square mile of landscape, fighting till night came on, and then on into the night.

"I jumped into the field with them, chasing them with my biograph, getting a series of moving pictures of that bullfight which was sure the real thing. It was a ticklish thing to do, though knowing that neither bull dared take his eyes off his adversary for a second, I felt reasonably safe. The old Weetah beat the new champion out that night, but the next morning they were at it again, and the new buffalo finally whipped the old one into submission. Since then his spirit has remained broken, and even a child can approach him safely—but the new Weetah is in turn a holy terror.

"To handle buffalo, elk and bear, you must get into sympathy with their methods of reasoning. No tenderfoot stands any show, even with the tame animals of the Yellowstone."

The old buffalo hunter's lips were no longer locked. One after another he told reminiscences of his eventful life, in a simple manner; yet so vivid and gripping were the unvarnished details that I was spellbound.

"Considering what appears the impossibility of capturing a full-grown buffalo, how did you earn the name of preserver of the American bison?" inquired Wallace.

"It took years to learn how, and ten more to capture the fifty-eight that I was able to keep. I tried every plan under the sun. I roped hundreds, of all sizes and ages. They would not live in captivity. If they could not find an embankment over which to break their necks, they would crush their skulls on stones. Failing any means like that, they would lie down, will themselves to die, and die. Think of a savage wild nature that could will its heart to cease beating! But it's true. Finally I found I could keep only calves under three months of age. But to capture them so young entailed time and patience. For the buffalo fight for their young, and when I say fight, I mean till they drop. I almost always had to go alone, because I could neither coax nor hire any one to undertake it with me. Sometimes I would be weeks getting one calf. One day I captured eight—eight little buffalo calves! Never will I forget that day as long as I live!"

"Tell us about it," I suggested, in a matter of fact, round-the-campfire voice. Had the silent plainsman ever told a complete and full story of his adventures? I doubted it. He was not the man to eulogize himself.

A short silence ensued. The cabin was snug and warm; the ruddy embers glowed; one of Jim's pots steamed musically and fragrantly. The hounds lay curled in the cozy chimney corner.

Jones began to talk again, simply and unaffectedly, of his famous exploit; and as he went on so modestly, passing lightly over features we recognized as wonderful, I allowed the fire of my imagination to fuse for myself all the toil, patience, endurance, skill, herculean strength and marvelous courage and unfathomable passion which he slighted in his narrative.

CHAPTER 3. THE LAST HERD

Over gray No-Man's-Land stole down the shadows of night. The undulating prairie shaded dark to the western horizon, rimmed with a fading streak of light. Tall figures, silhouetted sharply against the last golden glow of sunset, marked the rounded crest of a grassy knoll.

"Wild hunter!" cried a voice in sullen rage, "buffalo or no, we halt here. Did Adams and I hire to cross the Staked Plains? Two weeks in No-Man's-Land, and now we're facing the sand! We've one keg of water, yet you want to keep on. Why, man, you're crazy! You didn't tell us you wanted buffalo alive. And here you've got us looking death in the eye!"

In the grim silence that ensued the two men unhitched the team from the long, light wagon, while the buffalo hunter staked out his wiry, lithe-limbed racehorses. Soon a fluttering blaze threw a circle of light, which shone on the agitated face of Rude and Adams, and the cold, iron-set visage of their brawny leader.

"It's this way," began Jones, in slow, cool voice; "I engaged you fellows, and you promised to stick by me. We've had no luck. But I've finally found sign—old sign, I'll admit the buffalo I'm looking for—the last herd on the plains. For two years I've been hunting this herd. So have other hunters. Millions of buffalo have been killed and left to rot. Soon this herd will be gone, and then the only buffalo in the world will be those I have given ten years of the hardest work in capturing. This is the last herd, I say, and my last chance to capture a calf or two. Do you imagine I'd quit? You fellows go back if you want, but I keep on."

"We can't go back. We're lost. We'll have to go with you. But, man, thirst is not the only risk we run. This is Comanche country. And if that herd is in here the Indians have it spotted."

"That worries me some," replied the plainsman, "but we'll keep on it."

They slept. The night wind swished the grasses; dark storm clouds blotted out the northern stars; the prairie wolves mourned dismally.

Day broke cold, wan, threatening, under a leaden sky. The hunters traveled thirty miles by noon, and halted in a hollow where a stream flowed in wet season. Cottonwood trees were bursting into green; thickets of prickly thorn, dense and matted, showed bright spring buds.

"What is it?" suddenly whispered Rude.

The plainsman lay in strained posture, his ear against the ground.

"Hide the wagon and horses in the clump of cottonwoods," he ordered, tersely. Springing to his feet, he ran to the top of the knoll above the hollow, where he again placed his ear to the ground.

Jones's practiced ear had detected the quavering rumble of far-away, thundering hoofs. He searched the wide waste of plain with his powerful glass. To the southwest, miles distant, a cloud of dust mushroomed skyward. "Not buffalo," he muttered, "maybe wild horses." He watched and waited. The yellow cloud rolled forward, enlarging, spreading out, and drove before it a darkly indistinct, moving mass. As soon as he had one good look at this he ran back to his comrades.

"Stampede! Wild horses! Indians! Look to your rifles and hide!"

Wordless and pale, the men examined their Sharps, and made ready to follow Jones. He slipped into the thorny brake and, flat on his stomach, wormed his way like a snake far into the thickly interlaced web of branches. Rude and Adams crawled after him. Words were superfluous. Quiet, breathless, with beating hearts, the hunters pressed close to the dry grass. A long, low, steady rumble filled the air, and increased in volume till it became a roar. Moments, endless moments, passed. The roar filled out like a flood slowly released from its confines to sweep down with the sound of doom. The ground began to tremble and quake: the light faded; the smell of dust pervaded the thicket, then a continuous streaming roar, deafening as persistent roll of thunder, pervaded the hiding place. The stampeding horses had split round the hollow. The roar lessened. Swiftly as a departing snow-squall rushing on through the pines, the thunderous thud and tramp of hoofs died away.

The trained horses hidden in the cottonwoods never stirred. "Lie low! lie low!" breathed the plainsman to his companions.

Throb of hoofs again became audible, not loud and madly pounding as those that had passed, but low, muffled, rhythmic. Jones's sharp eye, through a peephole in the thicket, saw a cream-colored mustang bob over the knoll, carrying an Indian. Another and another, then a swiftly following, close-packed throng appeared. Bright red feathers and white gleamed; weapons glinted; gaunt, bronzed savage leaned forward on racy, slender mustangs.

The plainsman shrank closer to the ground. "Apache!" he exclaimed to himself, and gripped his rifle. The band galloped down to the hollow, and slowing up, piled single file over the bank. The leader, a short, squat chief, plunged into the brake not twenty yards from the hidden men. Jones recognized the cream mustang; he knew the somber, sinister, broad face. It belonged to the Red Chief of the Apaches.

"Geronimo!" murmured the plainsman through his teeth.

Well for the Apache that no falcon savage eye discovered aught strange in the little hollow! One look at the sand of the stream bed would have cost him his life. But the Indians crossed the thicket too far up; they cantered up the slope and disappeared. The hoof-beats softened and ceased.

"Gone?" whispered Rude.

"Gone. But wait," whispered Jones. He knew the savage nature, and he knew how to wait. After a long time, he cautiously crawled out of the thicket and searched the surroundings with a plainsman's eye. He climbed the slope and saw the clouds of dust, the near one small, the far one large, which told him all he needed to know.

"Comanches?" queried Adams, with a quaver in his voice. He was new to the plains.

"Likely," said Jones, who thought it best not to tell all he knew. Then he added to himself: "We've no time to lose. There's water back here somewhere. The Indians have spotted the buffalo, and were running the horses away from the water."

The three got under way again, proceeding carefully, so as not to raise the dust, and headed due southwest. Scantier and scantier grew the grass; the hollows were washes of sand; steely gray dunes, like long, flat, ocean swells, ribbed the prairie. The gray day declined. Late into the purple night they traveled, then camped without fire.

In the gray morning Jones climbed a high ride and scanned the southwest. Low dun-colored sandhills waved from him down and down, in slow, deceptive descent. A solitary and remote waste reached out into gray infinitude. A pale lake, gray as the rest of that gray expanse, glimmered in the distance.

"Mirage!" he muttered, focusing his glass, which only magnified all under the dead gray, steely sky. "Water must be somewhere; but can that be it? It's too pale and elusive to be real. No life—a blasted, staked plain! Hello!"

A thin, black, wavering line of wild fowl, moving in beautiful, rapid flight, crossed the line of his vision. "Geese flying north, and low. There's water here," he said. He followed the flock with his glass, saw them circle over the lake, and vanish in the gray sheen.

"It's water." He hurried back to camp. His haggard and worn companions scorned his discovery. Adams siding with Rude, who knew the plains, said: "Mirage! the lure of the desert!" Yet dominated by a force too powerful for them to resist, they followed the buffalo-hunter. All day the gleaming lake beckoned them onward, and seemed to recede. All day the drab clouds scudded before the cold north wind. In the gray twilight, the lake suddenly lay before them, as if it had opened at their feet. The men rejoiced, the horses lifted their noses and sniffed the damp air.

The whinnies of the horses, the clank of harness, and splash of water, the whirl of ducks did not blur out of Jones's keen ear a sound that made him jump. It was the thump of hoofs, in a familiar beat, beat, beat. He saw a shadow moving up a ridge. Soon, outlined black against the yet light sky, a lone buffalo cow stood like a statue. A moment she held toward the lake, studying the danger, then went out of sight over the ridge.

Jones spurred his horse up the ascent, which was rather long and steep, but he mounted the summit in time to see the cow join eight huge, shaggy buffalo. The hunter reined in his horse, and standing high in his stirrups, held his hat at arms' length over his head. So he thrilled to a moment he had sought for two years. The last herd of American bison was near at hand. The cow would not venture far from the main herd; the eight stragglers were the old broken-down bulls that had been expelled, at this season, from the herd by younger and more vigorous bulls. The old monarchs saw the hunter at the same time his eyes were gladdened by sight of them, and lumbered away after the cow, to disappear in the gathering darkness. Frightened buffalo always make straight for their fellows; and this knowledge contented Jones to return to the lake, well satisfied that the herd would not be far away in the morning, within easy striking distance by daylight.

At dark the storm which had threatened for days, broke in a fury of rain, sleet and hail. The hunters stretched a piece of canvas over the wheels of the north side of the wagon, and wet and shivering, crawled under it to their blankets. During the night the storm raged with unabated strength.

Dawn, forbidding and raw, lightened to the whistle of the sleety gusts. Fire was out of the question. Chary of weight, the hunters had carried no wood, and the buffalo chips they used for fuel were lumps of ice. Grumbling, Adams and Rude ate a cold breakfast, while Jones, munching a biscuit, faced the biting blast from the crest of the ridge. The middle of the plain below held a ragged, circular mass, as still as stone. It was the buffalo herd, with every shaggy head to the storm. So they would stand, never budging from their tracks, till the blizzard of sleet was over.

Jones, though eager and impatient, restrained himself, for it was unwise to begin operations in the storm. There was nothing to do but wait. Ill fared the hunters that day. Food had to be eaten uncooked. The long hours dragged by with the little group huddled under icy blankets. When darkness fell, the sleet changed to drizzling rain. This blew over at midnight, and a colder wind, penetrating to the very marrow of the sleepless men, made their condition worse. In the after part of the night, the wolves howled mournfully.

With a gray, misty light appearing in the east, Jones threw off his stiff, ice-incased blanket, and crawled out. A gaunt gray wolf, the color of the day and the sand and the lake, sneaked away, looking back. While moving and threshing about to warm his frozen blood, Jones munched another biscuit. Five men crawled from under the wagon, and made an unfruitful search for the whisky. Fearing it, Jones had thrown the bottle away. The men cursed. The patient horses drooped sadly, and shivered in the lee of the improvised tent. Jones kicked the inch-thick casing of ice from his saddle. Kentuck, his racer, had been spared on the whole trip for this day's work. The thoroughbred was cold, but as Jones threw the saddle over him, he showed that he knew the chase ahead, and was eager to be off. At last, after repeated efforts with his benumbed fingers, Jones got the girths tight. He tied a bunch of soft cords to the saddle and mounted.

"Follow as fast as you can," he called to his surly men. "The buffs will run north against the wind. This is the right direction for us; we'll soon leave the sand. Stick to my trail and come a-humming."

From the ridge he met the red sun, rising bright, and a keen northeasterly wind that lashed like a whip. As he had anticipated, his quarry had moved northward.

Kentuck let out into a swinging stride, which in an hour had the loping herd in sight. Every jump now took him upon higher ground, where the sand failed, and the grass grew thicker and began to bend under the wind.

In the teeth of the nipping gale Jones slipped close upon the herd without alarming even a cow. More than a hundred little reddish-black calves leisurely loped in the rear. Kentuck, keen to his work, crept on like a wolf, and the hunter's great fist clenched the coiled lasso. Before him expanded a boundless plain. A situation long cherished and dreamed of had become a reality. Kentuck, fresh and strong, was good for all day. Jones gloated over the little red bulls and heifers, as a miser gloats over gold and jewels. Never before had he caught more than two in one day, and often it had taken days to capture one. This was the last herd, this the last opportunity toward perpetuating a grand race of beasts. And with born instinct he saw ahead the day of his life.

At a touch, Kentuck closed in, and the buffalo, seeing him, stampeded into the heaving roll so well known to the hunter. Racing on the right flank of the herd, Jones selected a tawny heifer and shot the lariat after her. It fell true, but being stiff and kinky from the sleet, failed to tighten, and the quick calf leaped through the loop to freedom.

Undismayed the pursuer quickly recovered his rope. Again he whirled and sent the loop. Again it circled true, and failed to close; again the agile heifer bounded through it. Jones whipped the air with the stubborn rope. To lose a chance like that was worse than boy's work.

The third whirl, running a smaller loop, tightened the coil round the frightened calf just back of its ears. A pull on the bridle brought Kentuck to a halt in his tracks, and the baby buffalo rolled over and over in the grass. Jones bounced from his seat and jerked loose a couple of the soft cords. In a twinkling; his big knee crushed down on the calf, and his big hands bound it helpless.

Kentuck neighed. Jones saw his black ears go up. Danger threatened. For a moment the hunter's blood turned chill, not from fear, for he never felt fear, but because he thought the Indians were returning to ruin his work. His eye swept the plain. Only the gray forms of wolves flitted through the grass, here, there, all about him. Wolves! They were as fatal to his enterprise as savages. A trooping pack of prairie wolves had fallen in with the herd and hung close on the trail, trying to cut a calf away from its mother. The gray brutes boldly trotted to within a few yards of him, and slyly looked at him, with pale, fiery eyes. They had already scented his captive. Precious time flew by; the situation, critical and baffling, had never before been met by him. There lay his little calf tied fast, and to the north ran many others, some of which he must—he would have. To think quickly had meant the solving of many a plainsman's problem. Should he stay with his prize to save it, or leave it to be devoured?

"Ha! you old gray devils!" he yelled, shaking his fist at the wolves. "I know a trick or two." Slipping his hat between the legs of the calf, he fastened it securely. This done, he vaulted on Kentuck, and was off with never a backward glance.

Certain it was that the wolves would not touch anything, alive or dead, that bore the scent of a human being.

The bison scoured away a long half-mile in the lead, sailing northward like a cloud-shadow over the plain. Kentuck, mettlesome, over-eager, would have run himself out in short order, but the wary hunter, strong to restrain as well as impel, with the long day in his mind, kept the steed in his easy stride, which, springy and stretching, overhauled the herd in the course of several miles.

A dash, a swirl, a shock, a leap, horse and hunter working in perfect accord, and a fine big calf, bellowing lustily, struggled desperately for freedom under the remorseless knee. The big hands toyed with him; and then, secure in the double knots, the calf lay still, sticking out his tongue and rolling his eyes, with the coat of the hunter tucked under his bonds to keep away the wolves.

The race had but begun; the horse had but warmed to his work; the hunter had but tasted of sweet triumph. Another hopeful of a buffalo mother, negligent in danger, truant from his brothers, stumbled and fell in the enmeshing loop. The hunter's vest, slipped over the calf's neck, served as danger signal to the wolves. Before the lumbering buffalo missed their loss, another red and black baby kicked helplessly on the grass and sent up vain, weak calls, and at last lay still, with the hunter's boot tied to his cords.

Four! Jones counted them aloud, add in his mind, and kept on. Fast, hard work, covering upward of fifteen miles, had begun to tell on herd, horse and man, and all slowed down to the call for strength. The fifth time Jones closed in on his game, he encountered different circumstances such as called forth his cunning.

The herd had opened up; the mothers had fallen back to the rear; the calves hung almost out of sight under the shaggy sides of protectors. To try them out Jones darted close and threw his lasso. It struck a cow. With activity incredible in such a huge beast, she lunged at him. Kentuck, expecting just such a move, wheeled to safety. This duel, ineffectual on both sides, kept up for a while, and all the time, man and herd were jogging rapidly to the north.

Jones could not let well enough alone; he acknowledged this even as he swore he must have five. Emboldened by his marvelous luck, and yielding headlong to the passion within, he threw caution to the winds. A lame old cow with a red calf caught his eye; in he spurred his willing horse and slung his rope. It stung the haunch of the mother. The mad grunt she vented was no quicker than the velocity with which she plunged and reared. Jones had but time to swing his leg over the saddle when the hoofs beat down. Kentuck rolled on the plain, flinging his rider from him. The infuriated buffalo lowered her head for the fatal charge on the horse, when the plainsman, jerking out his heavy Colts, shot her dead in her tracks.

Kentuck got to his feet unhurt, and stood his ground, quivering but ready, showing his steadfast courage. He showed more, for his ears lay back, and his eyes had the gleam of the animal that strikes back.

The calf ran round its mother. Jones lassoed it, and tied it down, being compelled to cut a piece from his lasso, as the cords on the saddle had given out. He left his other boot with baby number five. The still heaving, smoking body of the victim called forth the stern, intrepid hunter's pity for a moment. Spill of blood he had not wanted. But he had not been able to avoid it; and mounting again with close-shut jaw and smoldering eye, he galloped to the north.

Kentuck snorted; the pursuing wolves shied off in the grass; the pale sun began to slant westward. The cold iron stirrups froze and cut the hunter's bootless feet.

When once more he came hounding the buffalo, they were considerably winded. Short-tufted tails, raised stiffly, gave warning. Snorts, like puffs of escaping steam, and deep grunts from cavernous chests evinced anger and impatience that might, at any moment, bring the herd to a defiant stand.

He whizzed the shortened noose over the head of a calf that was laboring painfully to keep up, and had slipped down, when a mighty grunt told him of peril. Never looking to see whence it came, he sprang into the saddle. Fiery Kentuck jumped into action, then hauled up with a shock that almost threw himself and rider. The lasso, fast to the horse, and its loop end round the calf, had caused the sudden check.

A maddened cow bore down on Kentuck. The gallant horse straightened in a jump, but dragging the calf pulled him in a circle, and in another moment he was running round and round the howling, kicking pivot. Then ensued a terrible race, with horse and bison describing a twenty-foot circle. Bang! Bang! The hunter fired two shots, and heard the spats of the bullets. But they only augmented the frenzy of the beast. Faster Kentuck flew, snorting in terror; closer drew the dusty, bouncing pursuer; the calf spun like a top; the lasso strung tighter than wire. Jones strained to loosen the fastening, but in vain. He swore at his carelessness in dropping his knife by the last calf he had tied. He thought of shooting the rope, yet dared not risk the shot. A hollow sound turned him again, with the Colts leveled. Bang! Dust flew from the ground beyond the bison.

The two charges left in the gun were all that stood between him and eternity. With a desperate display of strength Jones threw his weight in a backward pull, and hauled Kentuck up. Then he leaned far back in the saddle, and shoved the Colts out beyond the horse's flank. Down went the broad head, with its black, glistening horns. Bang! She slid forward with a crash, plowing the ground with hoofs and nose—spouted blood, uttered a hoarse cry, kicked and died.

Kentuck, for once completely terrorized, reared and plunged from the cow, dragging the calf. Stern command and iron arm forced him to a standstill. The calf, nearly strangled, recovered when the noose was slipped, and moaned a feeble protest against life and captivity. The remainder of Jones's lasso went to bind number six, and one of his socks went to serve as reminder to the persistent wolves.

"Six! On! On! Kentuck! On!" Weakening, but unconscious of it, with bloody hands and feet, without lasso, and with only one charge in his revolver, hatless, coatless, vestless, bootless, the wild hunter urged on the noble horse. The herd had gained miles in the interval of the fight. Game to the backbone, Kentuck lengthened out to overhaul it, and slowly the rolling gap lessened and lessened. A long hour thumped away, with the rumble growing nearer.

Once again the lagging calves dotted the grassy plain before the hunter. He dashed beside a burly calf, grasped its tail, stopped his horse, and jumped. The calf went down with him, and did not come up. The knotted, blood-stained hands, like claws of steel, bound the hind legs close and fast with a leathern belt, and left between them a torn and bloody sock.

"Seven! On! Old Faithfull! We MUST have another! the last! This is your day."

The blood that flecked the hunter was not all his own.

The sun slanted westwardly toward the purpling horizon; the grassy plain gleamed like a ruffled sea of glass; the gray wolves loped on.

When next the hunter came within sight of the herd, over a wavy ridge, changes in its shape and movement met his gaze. The calves were almost done; they could run no more; their mothers faced the south, and trotted slowly to and fro; the bulls were grunting, herding, piling close. It looked as if the herd meant to stand and fight.

This mattered little to the hunter who had captured seven calves since dawn. The first limping calf he reached tried to elude the grasping hand and failed. Kentuck had been trained to wheel to the right or left, in whichever way his rider leaned; and as Jones bent over and caught an upraised tail, the horse turned to strike the calf with both front hoofs. The calf rolled; the horse plunged down; the rider sped beyond to the dust. Though the calf was tired, he still could bellow, and he filled the air with robust bawls.

Jones all at once saw twenty or more buffalo dash in at him with fast, twinkling, short legs. With the thought of it, he was in the air to the saddle. As the black, round mounds charged from every direction, Kentuck let out with all there was left in him. He leaped and whirled, pitched and swerved, in a roaring, clashing, dusty melee. Beating hoofs threw the turf, flying tails whipped the air, and everywhere were dusky, sharp-pointed heads, tossing low. Kentuck squeezed out unscathed. The mob of bison, bristling, turned to lumber after the main herd. Jones seized his opportunity and rode after them, yelling with all his might. He drove them so hard that soon the little fellows lagged paces behind. Only one or two old cows straggled with the calves.

Then wheeling Kentuck, he cut between the herd and a calf, and rode it down. Bewildered, the tously little bull bellowed in great affright. The hunter seized the stiff tail, and calling to his horse, leaped off. But his strength was far spent and the buffalo, larger than his fellows, threshed about and jerked in terror. Jones threw it again and again. But it struggled up, never once ceasing its loud demands for help. Finally the hunter tripped it up and fell upon it with his knees.

Above the rumble of retreating hoofs, Jones heard the familiar short, quick, jarring pound on the turf. Kentuck neighed his alarm and raced to the right. Bearing down on the hunter, hurtling through the air, was a giant furry mass, instinct with fierce life and power—a buffalo cow robbed of her young.

With his senses almost numb, barely able to pull and raise the Colt, the plainsman willed to live, and to keep his captive. His leveled arm wavered like a leaf in a storm.

Bang! Fire, smoke, a shock, a jarring crash, and silence!

The calf stirred beneath him. He put out a hand to touch a warm, furry coat. The mother had fallen beside him. Lifting a heavy hoof, he laid it over the neck of the calf to serve as additional weight. He lay still and listened. The rumble of the herd died away in the distance.

The evening waned. Still the hunter lay quiet. From time to time the calf struggled and bellowed. Lank, gray wolves appeared on all sides; they prowled about with hungry howls, and shoved black-tipped noses through the grass. The sun sank, and the sky paled to opal blue. A star shone out, then another, and another. Over the prairie slanted the first dark shadow of night.

Suddenly the hunter laid his ear to the ground, and listened. Faint beats, like throbs of a pulsing heart, shuddered from the soft turf. Stronger they grew, till the hunter raised his head. Dark forms approached; voices broke the silence; the creaking of a wagon scared away the wolves.

"This way!" shouted the hunter weakly.

"Ha! here he is. Hurt?" cried Rude, vaulting the wheel.

"Tie up this calf. How many—did you find?" The voice grew fainter.

"Seven—alive, and in good shape, and all your clothes."

But the last words fell on unconscious ears.

CHAPTER 4. THE TRAIL

"Frank, what'll we do about horses?" asked Jones. "Jim'll want the bay, and of course you'll want to ride Spot. The rest of our nags will only do to pack the outfit."

"I've been thinkin'," replied the foreman. "You sure will need good mounts. Now it happens that a friend of mine is just at this time at House Rock Valley, an outlyin' post of one of the big Utah ranches. He is gettin' in the horses off the range, an' he has some crackin' good ones. Let's ooze over there—it's only thirty miles—an' get some horses from him."

We were all eager to act upon Frank's suggestion. So plans were made for three of us to ride over and select our mounts. Frank and Jim would follow with the pack train, and if all went well, on the following evening we would camp under the shadow of Buckskin.

Early next morning we were on our way. I tried to find a soft place on Old Baldy, one of Frank's pack horses. He was a horse that would not have raised up at the trumpet of doom. Nothing under the sun, Frank said, bothered Old Baldy but the operation of shoeing. We made the distance to the outpost by noon, and found Frank's friend a genial and obliging cowboy, who said we could have all the horses we wanted.

While Jones and Wallace strutted round the big corral, which was full of vicious, dusty, shaggy horses and mustangs, I sat high on the fence. I heard them talking about points and girth and stride, and a lot of terms that I could not understand. Wallace selected a heavy sorrel, and Jones a big bay; very like Jim's. I had observed, way over in the corner of the corral, a bunch of cayuses, and among them a clean-limbed black horse. Edging round on the fence I got a closer view, and then cried out that I had found my horse. I jumped down and caught him, much to my surprise, for the other horses were wild, and had kicked viciously. The black was beautifully built, wide-chested and powerful, but not heavy. His coat glistened like sheeny black satin, and he had a white face and white feet and a long mane.

"I don't know about giving you Satan—that's his name," said the cowboy. "The foreman rides him often. He's the fastest, the best climber, and the best dispositioned horse on the range.

"But I guess I can let you have him," he continued, when he saw my disappointed face.

"By George!" exclaimed Jones. "You've got it on us this time."

"Would you like to trade?" asked Wallace, as his sorrel tried to bite him. "That black looks sort of fierce."

I led my prize out of the corral, up to the little cabin nearby, where I tied him, and proceeded to get acquainted after a fashion of my own. Though not versed in horse-lore, I knew that half the battle was to win his confidence. I smoothed his silky coat, and patted him, and then surreptitiously slipped a lump of sugar from my pocket. This sugar, which I had purloined in Flagstaff, and carried all the way across the desert, was somewhat disreputably soiled, and Satan sniffed at it disdainfully. Evidently he had never smelled or tasted sugar. I pressed it into his mouth. He munched it, and then looked me over with some interest. I handed him another lump. He took it and rubbed his nose against me. Satan was mine!

Frank and Jim came along early in the afternoon. What with packing, changing saddles and shoeing the horses, we were all busy. Old Baldy would not be shod, so we let him off till a more opportune time. By four o'clock we were riding toward the slopes of Buckskin, now only a few miles away, standing up higher and darker.

"What's that for?" inquired Wallace, pointing to a long, rusty, wire-wrapped, double-barreled blunderbuss of a shotgun, stuck in the holster of Jones's saddle.

The Colonel, who had been having a fine time with the impatient and curious hounds, did not vouchsafe any information on that score. But very shortly we were destined to learn the use of this incongruous firearm. I was riding in advance of Wallace, and a little behind Jones. The dogs—excepting Jude, who had been kicked and lamed—were ranging along before their master. Suddenly, right before me, I saw an immense jack-rabbit; and just then Moze and Don caught sight of it. In fact, Moze bumped his blunt nose into the rabbit. When it leaped into scared action, Moze yelped, and Don followed suit. Then they were after it in wild, clamoring pursuit. Jones let out the stentorian blast, now becoming familiar, and spurred after them. He reached over, pulled the shotgun out of the holster and fired both barrels at the jumping dogs.

I expressed my amazement in strong language, and Wallace whistled.

Don came sneaking back with his tail between his legs, and Moze, who had cowered as if stung, circled round ahead of us. Jones finally succeeded in gettin him back.

"Come in hyah! You measly rabbit dogs! What do you mean chasing off that way? We're after lions. Lions! understand?"

Don looked thoroughly convinced of his error, but Moze, being more thick-headed, appeared mystified rather than hurt or frightened.

"What size shot do you use?" I asked.

"Number ten. They don't hurt much at seventy five yards," replied our leader. "I use them as sort of a long arm. You see, the dogs must be made to know what we're after. Ordinary means would never do in a case like this. My idea is to break them of coyotes, wolves and deer, and when we cross a lion trail, let them go. I'll teach them sooner than you'd think. Only we must get where we can see what they're trailing. Then I can tell whether to call then back or not."

The sun was gilding the rim of the desert rampart when we began the ascent of the foothills of Buckskin. A steep trail wound zigzag up the mountain We led our horses, as it was a long, hard climb. From time to time, as I stopped to catch my breath I gazed away across the growing void to the gorgeous Pink Cliffs, far above and beyond the red wall which had seemed so high, and then out toward the desert. The irregular ragged crack in the plain, apparently only a thread of broken ground, was the Grand Canyon. How unutterably remote, wild, grand was that world of red and brown, of purple pall, of vague outline!

Two thousand feet, probably, we mounted to what Frank called Little Buckskin. In the west a copper glow, ridged with lead-colored clouds, marked where the sun had set. The air was very thin and icy cold. At the first clump of pinyon pines, we made dry camp. When I sat down it was as if I had been anchored. Frank solicitously remarked that I looked "sort of beat." Jim built a roaring fire and began getting supper. A snow squall came on the rushing wind. The air grew colder, and though I hugged the fire, I could not get warm. When I had satisfied my hunger, I rolled out my sleeping-bag and crept into it. I stretched my aching limbs and did not move again. Once I awoke, drowsily feeling the warmth of the fire, and I heard Frank say: "He's asleep, dead to the world!"

"He's all in," said Jones. "Riding's what did it You know how a horse tears a man to pieces."

"Will he be able to stand it?" asked Frank, with as much solicitude as if he were my brother. "When you get out after anythin'—well, you're hell. An' think of the country we're goin' into. I know you've never seen the breaks of the Siwash, but I have, an' it's the worst an' roughest country I ever saw. Breaks after breaks, like the ridges on a washboard, headin' on the south slope of Buckskin, an' runnin' down, side by side, miles an' miles, deeper an' deeper, till they run into that awful hole. It will be a killin' trip on men, horses an' dogs. Now, Mr. Wallace, he's been campin' an' roughin' with the Navajos for months; he's in some kind of shape, but—"

Frank concluded his remark with a doubtful pause.

"I'm some worried, too," replied Jones. "But he would come. He stood the desert well enough; even the Mormons said that."

In the ensuing silence the fire sputtered, the glare fitfully merged into dark shadows under the weird pinyons, and the wind moaned through the short branches.

"Wal," drawled a slow, soft voice, "shore I reckon you're hollerin' too soon. Frank's measly trick puttin' him on Spot showed me. He rode out on Spot, an' he rode in on Spot. Shore he'll stay."

It was not all the warmth of the blankets that glowed over me then. The voices died away dreamily, and my eyelids dropped sleepily tight. Late in the night I sat up suddenly, roused by some unusual disturbance. The fire was dead; the wind swept with a rush through the pinyons. From the black darkness came the staccato chorus of coyotes. Don barked his displeasure; Sounder made the welkin ring, and old Moze growled low and deep, grumbling like muttered thunder. Then all was quiet, and I slept.

Dawn, rosy red, confronted me when I opened my eyes. Breakfast was ready; Frank was packing Old Baldy; Jones talked to his horse as he saddled him; Wallace came stooping his giant figure under the pinyons; the dogs, eager and soft-eyed, sat around Jim and begged. The sun peeped over the Pink Cliffs; the desert still lay asleep, tranced in a purple and golden-streaked mist.

"Come, come!" said Jones, in his big voice. "We're slow; here's the sun."

"Easy, easy," replied Frank, "we've all the time there is."

When Frank threw the saddle over Satan I interrupted him and said I would care for my horse henceforward. Soon we were under way, the horses fresh, the dogs scenting the keen, cold air.

The trail rolled over the ridges of pinyon and scrubby pine. Occasionally we could see the black, ragged crest of Buckskin above us. From one of these ridges I took my last long look back at the desert, and engraved on my mind a picture of the red wall, and the many-hued ocean of sand. The trail, narrow and indistinct, mounted the last slow-rising slope; the pinyons failed, and the scrubby pines became abundant. At length we reached the top, and entered the great arched aisles of Buckskin Forest. The ground was flat as a table. Magnificent pine trees, far apart, with branches high and spreading, gave the eye glad welcome. Some of these monarchs were eight feet thick at the base and two hundred feet high. Here and there one lay, gaunt and prostrate, a victim of the wind. The smell of pitch pine was sweetly overpowering.

"When I went through here two weeks ago, the snow was a foot deep, an' I bogged in places," said Frank. "The sun has been oozin' round here some. I'm afraid Jones won't find any snow on this end of Buckskin."

Thirty miles of winding trail, brown and springy from its thick mat of pine needles, shaded always by the massive, seamy-barked trees, took us over the extremity of Buckskin. Then we faced down into the head of a ravine that ever grew deeper, stonier and rougher. I shifted from side to side, from leg to leg in my saddle, dismounted and hobbled before Satan, mounted again, and rode on. Jones called the dogs and complained to them of the lack of snow. Wallace sat his horse comfortably, taking long pulls at his pipe and long gazes at the shaggy sides of the ravine. Frank, energetic and tireless, kept the pack-horses in the trail. Jim jogged on silently. And so we rode down to Oak Spring.

The spring was pleasantly situated in a grove of oaks and Pinyons, under the shadow of three cliffs. Three ravines opened here into an oval valley. A rude cabin of rough-hewn logs stood near the spring.

"Get down, get down," sang out Frank. "We'll hang up here. Beyond Oak is No-Man's-Land. We take our chances on water after we leave here."

When we had unsaddled, unpacked, and got a fire roaring on the wide stone hearth of the cabin, it was once again night.

CHAPTER 4. THE TRAIL

"Boys," said Jones after supper, "we're now on the edge of the lion country. Frank saw lion sign in here only two weeks ago; and though the snow is gone, we stand a show of finding tracks in the sand and dust. To-morrow morning, before the sun gets a chance at the bottom of these ravines, we'll be up and doing. We'll each take a dog and search in different directions. Keep the dog in leash, and when he opens up, examine the ground carefully for tracks. If a dog opens on any track that you are sure isn't lion's, punish him. And when a lion-track is found, hold the dog in, wait and signal. We'll use a signal I have tried and found far-reaching and easy to yell. Waa-hoo! That's it. Once yelled it means come. Twice means comes quickly. Three times means come—danger!"

In one corner of the cabin was a platform of poles, covered with straw. I threw the sleeping-bag on this, and was soon stretched out. Misgivings as to my strength worried me before I closed my eyes. Once on my back, I felt I could not rise; my chest was sore; my cough deep and rasping. It seemed I had scarcely closed my eyes when Jones's impatient voice recalled me from sweet oblivion.

"Frank, Frank, it's daylight. Jim—boys!" he called.

I tumbled out in a gray, wan twilight. It was cold enough to make the fire acceptable, but nothing like the morning before on Buckskin.

"Come to the festal board," drawled Jim, almost before I had my boots laced.

"Jones," said Frank, "Jim an' I'll ooze round here to-day. There's lots to do, an' we want to have things hitched right before we strike for the Siwash. We've got to shoe Old Baldy, an' if we can't get him locoed, it'll take all of us to do it."

The light was still gray when Jones led off with Don, Wallace with Sounder and I with Moze. Jones directed us to separate, follow the dry stream beds in the ravines, and remember his instructions given the night before.

The ravine to the right, which I entered, was choked with huge stones fallen from the cliff above, and pinyons growing thick; and I wondered apprehensively how a man could evade a wild animal in such a place, much less chase it. Old Moze pulled on his chain and sniffed at coyote and deer tracks. And every time he evinced interest in such, I cut him with a switch, which, to tell the truth, he did not notice. I thought I heard a shout, and holding Moze tight, I waited and listened.

"Waa-hoo—waa-hoo!" floated on the air, rather deadened as if it had come from round the triangular cliff that faced into the valley. Urging and dragging Moze, I ran down the ravine as fast as I could, and soon encountered Wallace coming from the middle ravine. "Jones," he said excitedly, "this way—there's the signal again." We dashed in haste for the mouth of the third ravine, and came suddenly upon Jones, kneeling under a pinyon tree. "Boys, look!" he exclaimed, as he pointed to the ground. There, clearly defined in the dust, was a cat track as big as my spread hand, and the mere sight of it sent a chill up my spine. "There's a lion track for you; made by a female, a two-year-old; but can't say if she passed here last night. Don won't take the trail. Try Moze."

I led Moze to the big, round imprint, and put his nose down into it. The old hound sniffed and sniffed, then lost interest.

"Cold!" ejaculated Jones. "No go. Try Sounder. Come, old boy, you've the nose for it."

He urged the reluctant hound forward. Sounder needed not to be shown the trail; he stuck his nose in it, and stood very quiet for a long moment; then he quivered slightly, raised his nose and sought the next track. Step by step he went slowly, doubtfully. All at once his tail wagged stiffly.

"Look at that!" cried Jones in delight. "He's caught a scent when the others couldn't. Hyah, Moze, get back. Keep Moze and Don back; give him room."

Slowly Sounder paced up the ravine, as carefully as if he were traveling on thin ice. He passed the dusty, open trail to a scaly ground with little bits of grass, and he kept on.

We were electrified to hear him give vent to a deep bugle-blast note of eagerness.

"By George, he's got it, boys!" exclaimed Jones, as he lifted the stubborn, struggling hound off the trail. "I know that bay. It means a lion passed here this morning. And we'll get him up as sure as you're alive. Come, Sounder. Now for the horses."

As we ran pell-mell into the little glade, where Jim sat mending some saddle trapping, Frank rode up the trail with the horses.

"Well, I heard Sounder," he said with his genial smile. "Somethin's comin' off, eh? You'll have to ooze round some to keep up with that hound."

I saddled Satan with fingers that trembled in excitement, and pushed my little Remington automatic into the rifle holster.

"Boys, listen," said our leader. "We're off now in the beginning of a hunt new to you. Remember no shooting, no blood-letting, except in self-defense. Keep as close to me as you can. Listen for the dogs, and when you fall behind or separate, yell out the signal cry. Don't forget this. We're bound to lose each other. Look out for the spikes and branches on the trees. If the dogs split, whoever follows the one that trees the lion must wait there till the rest come up. Off now! Come, Sounder; Moze, you rascal, hyah! Come, Don, come, Puppy, and take your medicine."

Except Moze, the hounds were all trembling and running eagerly to and fro. When Sounder was loosed, he led them in a bee-line to the trail, with us cantering after. Sounder worked exactly as before, only he followed the lion tracks a little farther up the ravine before he bayed. He kept going faster and faster, occasionally letting out one deep, short yelp. The other hounds did not give tongue, but eager, excited, baffled, kept at his heels. The ravine was long, and the wash at the bottom, up which the lion had proceeded, turned and twisted round boulders large as houses, and led through dense growths of some short, rough shrub. Now and then the lion tracks showed plainly in the sand. For five miles or more Sounder led us up the ravine, which began to contract and grow steep. The dry stream bed got to be full of thickets of branchless saplings, about the poplar—tall, straight, size of a man's arm, and growing so close we had to press them aside to let our horses through.

CHAPTER 4. THE TRAIL

Presently Sounder slowed up and appeared at fault. We found him puzzling over an open, grassy patch, and after nosing it for a little while, he began skirting the edge.

"Cute dog!" declared Jones. "That Sounder will make a lion chaser. Our game has gone up here somewhere."

Sure enough, Sounder directly gave tongue from the side of the ravine. It was climb for us now. Broken shale, rocks of all dimensions, pinyons down and pinyons up made ascending no easy problem. We had to dismount and lead the horses, thus losing ground. Jones forged ahead and reached the top of the ravine first. When Wallace and I got up, breathing heavily, Jones and the hounds were out of sight. But Sounder kept voicing his clear call, giving us our direction. Off we flew, over ground that was still rough, but enjoyable going compared to the ravine slopes. The ridge was sparsely covered with cedar and pinyon, through which, far ahead, we pretty soon spied Jones. Wallace signaled, and our leader answered twice. We caught up with him on the brink of another ravine deeper and craggier than the first, full of dead, gnarled pinyon and splintered rocks.

"This gulch is the largest of the three that head in at Oak Spring," said Jones. "Boys, don't forget your direction. Always keep a feeling where camp is, always sense it every time you turn. The dogs have gone down. That lion is in here somewhere. Maybe he lives down in the high cliffs near the spring and came up here last night for a kill he's buried somewhere. Lions never travel far. Hark! Hark! There's Sounder and the rest of them! They've got the scent; they've all got it! Down, boys, down, and ride!"

With that he crashed into the cedar in a way that showed me how impervious he was to slashing branches, sharp as thorns, and steep descent and peril.

Wallace's big sorrel plunged after him and the rolling stones cracked. Suffering as I was by this time, with cramp in my legs, and torturing pain, I had to choose between holding my horse in or falling off; so I chose the former and accordingly got behind.

Dead cedar and pinyon trees lay everywhere, with their contorted limbs reaching out like the arms of a devil-fish. Stones blocked every opening. Making the bottom of the ravine after what seemed an interminable time, I found the tracks of Jones and Wallace. A long "Waa-hoo!" drew me on; then the mellow bay of a hound floated up the ravine. Satan made up time in the sandy stream bed, but kept me busily dodging overhanging branches. I became aware, after a succession of efforts to keep from being strung on pinyons, that the sand before me was clean and trackless. Hauling Satan up sharply, I waited irresolutely and listened. Then from high up the ravine side wafted down a medley of yelps and barks.

"Waa-hoo, waa-hoo!" ringing down the slope, pealed against the cliff behind me, and sent the wild echoes flying. Satan, of his own accord, headed up the incline. Surprised at this, I gave him free rein. How he did climb! Not long did it take me to discover that he picked out easier going than I had. Once I saw Jones crossing a ledge far above me, and I yelled our signal cry. The answer returned clear and sharp; then its echo cracked under the hollow cliff, and crossing and recrossing the ravine, it died at last far away, like the muffled peal of a bell-buoy. Again I heard the blended yelping of the hounds, and closer at hand. I saw a long, low cliff above, and decided that the hounds were running at the base of it. Another chorus of yelps, quicker, wilder than the others, drew a yell from me. Instinctively I knew the dogs had jumped game of some kind. Satan knew it as well as I, for he quickened his pace and sent the stones clattering behind him.

I gained the base of the yellow cliff, but found no tracks in the dust of ages that had crumbled in its shadow, nor did I hear the dogs. Considering how close they had seemed, this was strange. I halted and listened. Silence reigned supreme. The ragged cracks in the cliff walls could have harbored many a watching lion, and I cast an apprehensive glance into their dark confines. Then I turned my horse to get round the cliff and over the ridge. When I again stopped, all I could hear was the thumping of my heart and the labored panting of Satan. I came to a break in the cliff, a steep place of weathered rock, and I put Satan to it. He went up with a will. From the narrow saddle of the ridge-crest I tried to take my bearings. Below me slanted the green of pinyon, with the bleached treetops standing like spears, and uprising yellow stones. Fancying I heard a gunshot, I leaned a straining ear against the soft breeze. The proof came presently in the unmistakable report of Jones's blunderbuss. It was repeated almost instantly, giving reality to the direction, which was down the slope of what I concluded must be the third ravine. Wondering what was the meaning of the shots, and chagrined because I was out of the race, but calmer in mind, I let Satan stand.

Hardly a moment elapsed before a sharp bark tingled in my ears. It belonged to old Moze. Soon I distinguished a rattling of stones and the sharp, metallic clicks of hoofs striking rocks. Then into a space below me loped a beautiful deer, so large that at first I took it for an elk. Another sharp bark, nearer this time, told the tale of Moze's dereliction. In a few moments he came in sight, running with his tongue out and his head high.

"Hyah, you old gladiator! hyah! hyah!" I yelled and yelled again. Moze passed over the saddle on the trail of the deer, and his short bark floated back to remind me how far he was from a lion dog.

Then I divined the meaning of the shotgun reports. The hounds had crossed a fresher trail than that of the lion, and our leader had discovered it. Despite a keen appreciation of Jones's task, I gave way to amusement, and repeated Wallace's paradoxical formula: "Pet the lions and shoot the hounds."

So I headed down the ravine, looking for a blunt, bold crag, which I had descried from camp. I found it before long, and profiting by past failures to judge of distance, gave my first impression a great stretch, and then decided that I was more than two miles from Oak.

Long after two miles had been covered, and I had begun to associate Jim's biscuits with a certain soft seat near a ruddy fire, I was apparently still the same distance from my landmark crag. Suddenly a slight noise brought me to a halt. I listened intently. Only an indistinct rattling of small rocks disturbed the impressive stillness. It might have been the weathering that goes on constantly, and it might have been an animal. I inclined to the former idea till I saw Satan's ears go up. Jones had told me to watch the ears of my horse, and short as had been my acquaintance with Satan, I had learned that he always discovered things more quickly than I. So I waited patiently.

From time to time a rattling roll of pebbles, almost musical, caught my ear. It came from the base of the wall of yellow cliff that barred the summit of all those ridges. Satan threw up his head and nosed the breeze. The delicate, almost stealthy sounds, the action of my horse, the waiting drove my heart to extra work. The breeze quickened and fanned my cheek, and borne upon it came the faint and far-away bay of a hound. It came again and again, each time nearer. Then on a stronger puff of wind rang the clear, deep, mellow call that had given Sounder his beautiful name. Never it seemed had I heard music so blood-stirring. Sounder was on the trail of something, and he had it headed my way. Satan heard, shot up his long ears, and tried to go ahead; but I restrained and soothed him into quiet.

Long moments I sat there, with the poignant consciousness of the wildness of the scene, of the significant rattling of the stones and of the bell-tongued hound baying incessantly, sending warm joy through my veins, the absorption in sensations new, yielding only to the hunting instinct when Satan snorted and quivered. Again the deep-toned bay rang into the silence with its stirring thrill of life. And a sharp rattling of stones just above brought another snort from Satan.

Across an open space in the pinyons a gray form flashed. I leaped off Satan and knelt to get a better view under the trees. I soon made out another deer passing along the base of the cliff. Mounting again, I rode up to the cliff to wait for Sounder.

A long time I had to wait for the hound. It proved that the atmosphere was as deceiving in regard to sound as to sight. Finally Sounder came running along the wall. I got off to intercept him. The crazy fellow—he had never responded to my overtures of friendship—uttered short, sharp yelps of delight, and actually leaped into my arms. But I could not hold him. He darted upon the trail again and paid no heed to my angry shouts. With a resolve to overhaul him, I jumped on Satan and whirled after the hound.

The black stretched out with such a stride that I was at pains to keep my seat. I dodged the jutting rocks and projecting snags; felt stinging branches in my face and the rush of sweet, dry wind. Under the crumbling walls, over slopes of weathered stone and droppings of shelving rock, round protruding noses of cliff, over and under pinyons Satan thundered. He came out on the top of the ridge, at the narrow back I had called a saddle. Here I caught a glimpse of Sounder far below, going down into the ravine from which I had ascended some time before. I called to him, but I might as well have called to the wind.

Weary to the point of exhaustion, I once more turned Satan toward camp. I lay forward on his neck and let him have his will. Far down the ravine I awoke to strange sounds, and soon recognized the cracking of iron-shod hoofs against stone; then voices. Turning an abrupt bend in the sandy wash, I ran into Jones and Wallace.

"Fall in! Line up in the sad procession!" said Jones. "Tige and the pup are faithful. The rest of the dogs are somewhere between the Grand Canyon and the Utah desert."

I related my adventures, and tried to spare Moze and Sounder as much as conscience would permit.

"Hard luck!" commented Jones. "Just as the hounds jumped the cougar—Oh! they bounced him out of the rocks all right—don't you remember, just under that cliff wall where you and Wallace came up to me? Well, just as they jumped him, they ran right into fresh deer tracks. I saw one of the deer. Now that's too much for any hounds, except those trained for lions. I shot at Moze twice, but couldn't turn him. He has to be hurt, they've all got to be hurt to make them understand."

Wallace told of a wild ride somewhere in Jones's wake, and of sundry knocks and bruises he had sustained, of pieces of corduroy he had left decorating the cedars and of a most humiliating event, where a gaunt and bare pinyon snag had penetrated under his belt and lifted him, mad and kicking, off his horse.

"These Western nags will hang you on a line every chance they get," declared Jones, "and don't you overlook that. Well, there's the cabin. We'd better stay here a few days or a week and break in the dogs and horses, for this day's work was apple pie to what we'll get in the Siwash."

I groaned inwardly, and was remorselessly glad to see Wallace fall off his horse and walk on one leg to the cabin. When I got my saddle off Satan, had given him a drink and hobbled him, I crept into the cabin and dropped like a log. I felt as if every bone in my body was broken and my flesh was raw. I got gleeful gratification from Wallace's complaints, and Jones's remark that he had a stitch in his back. So ended the first chase after cougars.

CHAPTER 5. OAK SPRING

Moze and Don and Sounder straggled into camp next morning, hungry, footsore and scarred; and as they limped in, Jones met them with characteristic speech: "Well, you decided to come in when you got hungry and tired? Never thought of how you fooled me, did you? Now, the first thing you get is a good licking."

He tied them in a little log pen near the cabin and whipped them soundly. And the next few days, while Wallace and I rested, he took them out separately and deliberately ran them over coyote and deer trails. Sometimes we heard his stentorian yell as a forerunner to the blast from his old shotgun. Then again we heard the shots unheralded by the yell. Wallace and I waxed warm under the collar over this peculiar method of training dogs, and each of us made dire threats. But in justice to their implacable trainer, the dogs never appeared to be hurt; never a spot of blood flecked their glossy coats, nor did they ever come home limping. Sounder grew wise, and Don gave up, but Moze appeared not to change.

"All hands ready to rustle," sang out Frank one morning. "Old Baldy's got to be shod."

This brought us all, except Jones, out of the cabin, to see the object of Frank's anxiety tied to a nearby oak. At first I failed to recognize Old Baldy. Vanished was the slow, sleepy, apathetic manner that had characterized him; his ears lay back on his head; fire flashed from his eyes. When Frank threw down a kit-bag, which emitted a metallic clanking, Old Baldy sat back on his haunches, planted his forefeet deep in the ground and plainly as a horse could speak, said "No!"

"Sometimes he's bad, and sometimes worse," growled Frank.

"Shore he's plumb bad this mornin'," replied Jim.

Frank got the three of us to hold Baldy's head and pull him up, then he ventured to lift a hind foot over his line. Old Baldy straightened out his leg and sent Frank sprawling into the dirt. Twice again Frank patiently tried to hold a hind leg, with the same result; and then he lifted a forefoot. Baldy uttered a very intelligible snort, bit through Wallace's glove, yanked Jim off his feet, and scared me so that I let go his forelock. Then he broke the rope which held him to the tree. There was a plunge, a scattering of men, though Jim still valiantly held on to Baldy's head, and a thrashing of scrub pinyon, where Baldy reached out vigorously with his hind feet. But for Jim, he would have escaped.

"What's all the row?" called Jones from the cabin. Then from the door, taking in the situation, he yelled: "Hold on, Jim! Pull down on the ornery old cayuse!"

He leaped into action with a lasso in each hand, one whirling round his head. The slender rope straightened with a whiz and whipped round Baldy's legs as he kicked viciously. Jones pulled it tight, then fastened it with nimble fingers to the tree.

"Let go! let go! Jim!" he yelled, whirling the other lasso. The loop flashed and fell over Baldy's head and tightened round his neck. Jones threw all the weight of his burly form on the lariat, and Baldy crashed to the ground, rolled, tussled, screamed, and then lay on his back, kicking the air with three free legs. "Hold this," ordered Jones, giving the tight rope to Frank. Whereupon he grabbed my lasso from the saddle, roped Baldy's two forefeet, and pulled him down on his side. This lasso he fastened to a scrub cedar.

"He's chokin'!" said Frank.

"Likely he is," replied Jones shortly. "It'll do him good." But with his big hands he drew the coil loose and slipped it down over Baldy's nose, where he tightened it again.

"Now, go ahead," he said, taking the rope from Frank.

It had all been done in a twinkling. Baldy lay there groaning and helpless, and when Frank once again took hold of the wicked leg, he was almost passive. When the shoeing operation had been neatly and quickly attended to and Baldy released from his uncomfortable position he struggled to his feet with heavy breaths, shook himself, and looked at his master.

"How'd you like being hog-tied?" queried his conqueror, rubbing Baldy's nose. "Now, after this you'll have some manners."

Old Baldy seemed to understand, for he looked sheepish, and lapsed once more into his listless, lazy unconcern.

"Where's Jim's old cayuse, the pack-horse?" asked our leader.

"Lost. Couldn't find him this morning, an' had a deuce of a time findin' the rest of the bunch. Old Baldy was cute. He hid in a bunch of pinyons an' stood quiet so his bell wouldn't ring. I had to trail him."

"Do the horses stray far when they are hobbled?" inquired Wallace.

"If they keep jumpin' all night they can cover some territory. We're now on the edge of the wild horse country, and our nags know this as well as we. They smell the mustangs, an' would break their necks to get away. Satan and the sorrel were ten miles from camp when I found them this mornin'. An' Jim's cayuse went farther, an' we never will get him. He'll wear his hobbles out, then away with the wild horses. Once with them, he'll never be caught again."

On the sixth day of our stay at Oak we had visitors, whom Frank introduced as the Stewart brothers and Lawson, wild-horse wranglers. They were still, dark men, whose facial expression seldom varied; tall and lithe and wiry as the mustangs they rode. The Stewarts were on their way to Kanab, Utah, to arrange for the sale of a drove of horses they had captured and corraled in a narrow canyon back in the Siwash. Lawson said he was at our service, and was promptly hired to look after our horses.

"Any cougar signs back in the breaks?" asked Jones.

"Wal, there's a cougar on every deer trail," replied the elder Stewart, "An' two for every pinto in the breaks. Old Tom himself downed fifteen colts fer us this spring."

"Fifteen colts! That's wholesale murder. Why don't you kill the butcher?"

"We've tried more'n onct. It's a turrible busted up country, them brakes. No man knows it, an' the cougars do. Old Tom ranges all the ridges and brakes, even up on the slopes of Buckskin; but he lives down there in them holes, an' Lord knows, no dog I ever seen could follow him. We tracked him in the snow, an' had dogs after him, but none could stay with him, except two as never cum back. But we've nothin' agin Old Tom like Jeff Clarke, a hoss rustler, who has a string of pintos corraled north of us. Clarke swears he ain't raised a colt in two years."

"We'll put that old cougar up a tree," exclaimed Jones.

"If you kill him we'll make you all a present of a mustang, an' Clarke, he'll give you two each," replied Stewart. "We'd be gettin' rid of him cheap."

"How many wild horses on the mountain now?"

"Hard to tell. Two or three thousand, mebbe. There's almost no ketchin' them, an' they regrowin' all the time We ain't had no luck this spring. The bunch in corral we got last year."

"Seen anythin' of the White Mustang?" inquired Frank. "Ever get a rope near him?"

"No nearer'n we hev fer six years back. He can't be ketched. We seen him an' his band of blacks a few days ago, headin' fer a water-hole down where Nail Canyon runs into Kanab Canyon. He's so cunnin' he'll never water at any of our trap corrals. An' we believe he can go without water fer two weeks, unless mebbe he hes a secret hole we've never trailed him to."

"Would we have any chance to see this White Mustang and his band?" questioned Jones.

"See him? Why, thet'd be easy. Go down Snake Gulch, camp at Singin' Cliffs, go over into Nail Canyon, an' wait. Then send some one slippin' down to the water-hole at Kanab Canyon, an' when the band cums in to drink—which I reckon will be in a few days now—hev them drive the mustangs up. Only be sure to hev them get ahead of the White Mustang, so he'll hev only one way to cum, fer he sure is knowin'. He never makes a mistake. Mebbe you'll get to see him cum by like a white streak. Why, I've heerd thet mustang's hoofs ring like bells on the rocks a mile away. His hoofs are harder'n any iron shoe as was ever made. But even if you don't get to see him, Snake Gulch is worth seein'."

I learned later from Stewart that the White Mustang was a beautiful stallion of the wildest strain of mustang blue blood. He had roamed the long reaches between the Grand Canyon and Buckskin toward its southern slope for years; he had been the most sought-for horse by all the wranglers, and had become so shy and experienced that nothing but a glimpse was ever obtained of him. A singular fact was that he never attached any of his own species to his band, unless they were coal black. He had been known to fight and kill other stallions, but he kept out of the well-wooded and watered country frequented by other bands, and ranged the brakes of the Siwash as far as he could range. The usual method, indeed the only successful way to capture wild horses, was to build corrals round the waterholes. The wranglers lay out night after night watching. When the mustangs came to drink—which was always after dark—the gates would be closed on them. But the trick had never even been tried on the White Mustang, for the simple reason that he never approached one of these traps.

"Boys," said Jones, "seeing we need breaking in, we'll give the White Mustang a little run."

This was most pleasurable news, for the wild horses fascinated me. Besides, I saw from the expression on our leader's face that an uncapturable mustang was an object of interest for him.

Wallace and I had employed the last few warm sunny afternoons in riding up and down the valley, below Oak, where there was a fine, level stretch. Here I wore out my soreness of muscle, and gradually overcame my awkwardness in the saddle. Frank's remedy of maple sugar and red pepper had rid me of my cold, and with the return of strength, and the coming of confidence, full, joyous appreciation of wild environment and life made me unspeakably happy. And I noticed that my companions were in like condition of mind, though self-contained where I was exuberant. Wallace galloped his sorrel and watched the crags; Jones talked more kindly to the dogs; Jim baked biscuits indefatigably, and smoked in contented silence; Frank said always: "We'll ooze along easy like, for we've all the time there is." Which sentiment, whether from reiterated suggestion, or increasing confidence in the practical cowboy, or charm of its free import, gradually won us all.

"Boys," said Jones, as we sat round the campfire, "I see you're getting in shape. Well, I've worn off the wire edge myself. And I have the hounds coming fine. They mind me now, but they're mystified. For the life of them they can't understand what I mean. I don't blame them. Wait till, by good luck, we get a cougar in a tree. When Sounder and Don see that, we've lion dogs, boys! we've lion dogs! But Moze is a stubborn brute. In all my years of animal experience, I've never discovered any other way to make animals obey than by instilling fear and respect into their hearts. I've been fond of buffalo, horses and dogs, but sentiment never ruled me. When animals must obey, they must—that's all, and no mawkishness! But I never trusted a buffalo in my life. If I had I wouldn't be here to-night. You all know how many keepers of tame wild animals get killed. I could tell you dozens of tragedies. And I've often thought, since I got back from New York, of that woman I saw with her troop of African lions. I dream about those lions, and see them leaping over her head. What a grand sight that was! But the public is fooled. I read somewhere that she trained those lions by love. I don't believe it. I saw her use a whip and a steel spear. Moreover, I saw many things that escaped most observers—how she entered the cage, how she maneuvered among them, how she kept a compelling gaze on them! It was an admirable, a great piece of work. Maybe she loves those huge yellow brutes, but her life was in danger every moment while she was in that cage, and she knew it. Some day, one of her pets likely the King of Beasts she pets the most will rise up and kill her. That is as certain as death."

CHAPTER 6. THE WHITE MUSTANG

For thirty miles down Nail Canyon we marked, in every dusty trail and sandy wash, the small, oval, sharply defined tracks of the White Mustang and his band.

The canyon had been well named. It was long, straight and square sided; its bare walls glared steel-gray in the sun, smooth, glistening surfaces that had been polished by wind and water. No weathered heaps of shale, no crumbled piles of stone obstructed its level floor. And, softly toning its drab austerity, here grew the white sage, waving in the breeze, the Indian Paint Brush, with vivid vermilion flower, and patches of fresh, green grass.

"The White King, as we Arizona wild-hoss wranglers calls this mustang, is mighty pertickler about his feed, an' he ranged along here last night, easy like, browsin' on this white sage," said Stewart. Inflected by our intense interest in the famous mustang, and ruffled slightly by Jones's manifest surprise and contempt that no one had captured him, Stewart had volunteered to guide us. "Never knowed him to run in this way fer water; fact is, never knowed Nail Canyon had a fork. It splits down here, but you'd think it was only a crack in the wall. An' thet cunnin' mustang hes been foolin' us fer years about this water-hole."

The fork of Nail Canyon, which Stewart had decided we were in, had been accidentally discovered by Frank, who, in search of our horses one morning had crossed a ridge, to come suddenly upon the blind, box-like head of the canyon. Stewart knew the lay of the ridges and run of the canyons as well as any man could know a country where, seemingly, every rod was ridged and bisected, and he was of the opinion that we had stumbled upon one of the White Mustang's secret passages, by which he had so often eluded his pursuers.

Hard riding had been the order of the day, but still we covered ten more miles by sundown. The canyon apparently closed in on us, so camp was made for the night. The horses were staked out, and supper made ready while the shadows were dropping; and when darkness settled thick over us, we lay under our blankets.

Morning disclosed the White Mustang's secret passage. It was a narrow cleft, splitting the canyon wall, rough, uneven, tortuous and choked with fallen rocks—no more than a wonderful crack in solid stone, opening into another canyon. Above us the sky seemed a winding, flowing stream of blue. The walls were so close in places that a horse with pack would have been blocked, and a rider had to pull his legs up over the saddle. On the far side, the passage fell very suddenly for several hundred feet to the floor of the other canyon. No hunter could have seen it, or suspected it from that side.

"This is Grand Canyon country, an' nobody knows what he's goin' to find," was Frank's comment.

"Now we're in Nail Canyon proper," said Stewart; "An' I know my bearin's. I can climb out a mile below an' cut across to Kanab Canyon, an' slip up into Nail Canyon agin, ahead of the mustangs, an' drive 'em up. I can't miss 'em, fer Kanab Canyon is impassable down a little ways. The mustangs will hev to run this way. So all you need do is go below the break, where I climb out, an' wait. You're sure goin' to get a look at the White Mustang. But wait. Don't expect him before noon, an' after thet, any time till he comes. Mebbe it'll be a couple of days, so keep a good watch."

Then taking our man Lawson, with blankets and a knapsack of food, Stewart rode off down the canyon.

We were early on the march. As we proceeded the canyon lost its regularity and smoothness; it became crooked as a rail fence, narrower, higher, rugged and broken. Pinnacled cliffs, cracked and leaning, menaced us from above. Mountains of ruined wall had tumbled into fragments.

It seemed that Jones, after much survey of different corners, angles and points in the canyon floor, chose his position with much greater care than appeared necessary for the ultimate success of our venture—which was simply to see the White Mustang, and if good fortune attended us, to snap some photographs of this wild king of horses. It flashed over me that, with his ruling passion strong within him, our leader was laying some kind of trap for that mustang, was indeed bent on his capture.

Wallace, Frank and Jim were stationed at a point below the break where Stewart had evidently gone up and out. How a horse could have climbed that streaky white slide was a mystery. Jones's instructions to the men were to wait until the mustangs were close upon them, and then yell and shout and show themselves.

He took me to a jutting corner of cliff, which hid us from the others, and here he exercised still more care in scrutinizing the lay of the ground. A wash from ten to fifteen feet wide, and as deep, ran through the canyon in a somewhat meandering course. At the corner which consumed so much of his attention, the dry ditch ran along the cliff wall about fifty feet out; between it and the wall was good level ground, on the other side huge rocks and shale made it hummocky, practically impassable for a horse. It was plain the mustangs, on their way up, would choose the inside of the wash; and here in the middle of the passage, just round the jutting corner, Jones tied our horses to good, strong bushes. His next act was significant. He threw out his lasso and, dragging every crook out of it, carefully recoiled it, and hung it loose over the pommel of his saddle.

"The White Mustang may be yours before dark," he said with the smile that came so seldom. "Now I placed our horses there for two reasons. The mustangs won't see them till they're right on them. Then you'll see a sight and have a chance for a great picture. They will halt; the stallion will prance, whistle and snort for a fight, and then they'll see the saddles and be off. We'll hide across the wash, down a little way, and at the right time we'll shout and yell to drive them up."

By piling sagebrush round a stone, we made a hiding-place. Jones was extremely cautious to arrange the bunches in natural positions. "A Rocky Mountain Big Horn is the only four-footed beast," he said, "that has a better eye than a wild horse. A cougar has an eye, too; he's used to lying high up on the cliffs and looking down for his quarry so as to stalk it at night; but even a cougar has to take second to a mustang when it comes to sight."

The hours passed slowly. The sun baked us; the stones were too hot to touch; flies buzzed behind our ears; tarantulas peeped at us from holes. The afternoon slowly waned.

At dark we returned to where we had left Wallace and the cowboys. Frank had solved the problem of water supply, for he had found a little spring trickling from a cliff, which, by skillful management, produced enough drink for the horses. We had packed our water for camp use.

"You take the first watch to-night," said Jones to me after supper. "The mustangs might try to slip by our fire in the night and we must keep a watch or them. Call Wallace when your time's up. Now, fellows, roll in."

When the pink of dawn was shading white, we were at our posts. A long, hot day—interminably long, deadening to the keenest interest—passed, and still no mustangs came. We slept and watched again, in the grateful cool of night, till the third day broke.

The hours passed; the cool breeze changed to hot; the sun blazed over the canyon wall; the stones scorched; the flies buzzed. I fell asleep in the scant shade of the sage bushes and awoke, stifled and moist. The old plainsman, never weary, leaned with his back against a stone and watched, with narrow gaze, the canyon below. The steely walls hurt my eyes; the sky was like hot copper. Though nearly wild with heat and aching bones and muscles and the long hours of wait—wait—wait, I was ashamed to complain, for there sat the old man, still and silent. I routed out a hairy tarantula from under a stone and teased him into a frenzy with my stick, and tried to get up a fight between him and a scallop-backed horned-toad that blinked wonderingly at me. Then I espied a green lizard on a stone. The beautiful reptile was about a foot in length, bright green, dotted with red, and he had diamonds for eyes. Nearby a purple flower blossomed, delicate and pale, with a bee sucking at its golden heart. I observed then that the lizard had his jewel eyes upon the bee; he slipped to the edge of the stone, flicked out a long, red tongue, and tore the insect from its honeyed perch. Here were beauty, life and death; and I had been weary for something to look at, to think about, to distract me from the wearisome wait!

"Listen!" broke in Jones's sharp voice. His neck was stretched, his eyes were closed, his ear was turned to the wind.

With thrilling, reawakened eagerness, I strained my hearing. I caught a faint sound, then lost it.

CHAPTER 6. THE WHITE MUSTANG

"Put your ear to the ground," said Jones. I followed his advice, and detected the rhythmic beat of galloping horses.

"The mustangs are coming, sure as you're born!" exclaimed Jones.

"There I see the cloud of dust!" cried he a minute later.

In the first bend of the canyon below, a splintered ruin of rock now lay under a rolling cloud of dust. A white flash appeared, a line of bobbing black objects, and more dust; then with a sharp pounding of hoofs, into clear vision shot a dense black band of mustangs, and well in front swung the White King.

"Look! Look! I never saw the beat of that—never in my born days!" cried Jones. "How they move! yet that white fellow isn't half-stretched out. Get your picture before they pass. You'll never see the beat of that."

With long manes and tails flying, the mustangs came on apace and passed us in a trampling roar, the white stallion in the front. Suddenly a shrill, whistling blast, unlike any sound I had ever heard, made the canyon fairly ring. The white stallion plunged back, and his band closed in behind him. He had seen our saddle horses. Then trembling, whinnying, and with arched neck and high-poised head, bespeaking his mettle, he advanced a few paces, and again whistled his shrill note of defiance. Pure creamy white he was, and built like a racer. He pranced, struck his hoofs hard and cavorted; then, taking sudden fright, he wheeled.

It was then, when the mustangs were pivoting, with the white in the lead, that Jones jumped upon the stone, fired his pistol and roared with all his strength. Taking his cue, I did likewise. The band huddled back again, uncertain and frightened, then broke up the canyon.

Jones jumped the ditch with surprising agility, and I followed close at his heels. When we reached our plunging horses, he shouted: "Mount, and hold this passage. Keep close in by that big stone at the turn so they can't run you down, or stampede you. If they head your way, scare them back."

Satan quivered, and when I mounted, reared and plunged. I had to hold him in hard, for he was eager to run. At the cliff wall I was at some pains to check him. He kept champing his bit and stamping his feet.

From my post I could see the mustangs flying before a cloud of dust. Jones was turning in his horse behind a large rock in the middle of the canyon, where he evidently intended to hide. Presently successive yells and shots from our comrades blended in a roar which the narrow box-canyon augmented and echoed from wall to wall. High the White Mustang reared, and above the roar whistled his snort of furious terror. His band wheeled with him and charged back, their hoofs ringing like hammers on iron.

The crafty old buffalo-hunter had hemmed the mustangs in a circle and had left himself free in the center. It was a wily trick, born of his quick mind and experienced eye.

The stallion, closely crowded by his followers, moved swiftly I saw that he must pass near the stone. Thundering, crashing, the horses came on. Away beyond them I saw Frank and Wallace. Then Jones yelled to me: "Open up! open up!"

I turned Satan into the middle of the narrow passage, screaming at the top of my voice and discharging my revolver rapidly.

But the wild horses thundered on. Jones saw that they would not now be balked, and he spurred his bay directly in their path. The big horse, courageous as his intrepid master, dove forward.

Then followed confusion for me. The pound of hoofs, the snorts, a screaming neigh that was frightful, the mad stampede of the mustangs with a whirling cloud of dust, bewildered and frightened me so that I lost sight of Jones. Danger threatened and passed me almost before I was aware of it. Out of the dust a mass of tossing manes, foam-flecked black horses, wild eyes and lifting hoofs rushed at me. Satan, with a presence of mind that shamed mine, leaped back and hugged the wall. My eyes were blinded by dust; the smell of dust choked me. I felt a strong rush of wind and a mustang grazed my stirrup. Then they had passed, on the wings of the dust-laden breeze.

But not all, for I saw that Jones had, in some inexplicable manner, cut the White Mustang and two of his blacks out of the band. He had turned them back again and was pursuing them. The bay he rode had never before appeared to much advantage, and now, with his long, lean, powerful body in splendid action, imbued with the relentless will of his rider, what a picture he presented! How he did run! With all that, the White Mustang made him look dingy and slow. Nevertheless, it was a critical time in the wild career of that king of horses. He had been penned in a space two hundred by five hundred yards, half of which was separated from him by a wide ditch, a yawning chasm that he had refused, and behind him, always keeping on the inside, wheeled the yelling hunter, who savagely spurred his bay and whirled a deadly lasso. He had been cut off and surrounded; the very nature of the rocks and trails of the canyon threatened to end his freedom or his life. Certain it was he preferred to end the latter, for he risked death from the rocks as he went over them in long leaps.

Jones could have roped either of the two blacks, but he hardly noticed them. Covered with dust and splotches of foam, they took their advantage, turned on the circle toward the passage way and galloped by me out of sight. Again Wallace, Frank and Jim let out strings of yells and volleys. The chase was narrowing down. Trapped, the White Mustang King had no chance. What a grand spirit he showed! Frenzied as I was with excitement, the thought occurred to me that this was an unfair battle, that I ought to stand aside and let him pass. But the blood and lust of primitive instinct held me fast. Jones, keeping back, met his every turn. Yet always with lithe and beautiful stride the stallion kept out of reach of the whirling lariat.

"Close in!" yelled Jones, and his voice, powerful with a note of triumph, bespoke the knell of the king's freedom.

The trap closed in. Back and forth at the upper end the White Mustang worked; then rendered desperate by the closing in, he circled round nearer to me. Fire shone in his wild eyes. The wily Jones was not to be outwitted; he kept in the middle, always on the move, and he yelled to me to open up.

CHAPTER 6. THE WHITE MUSTANG

I lost my voice again, and fired my last shot. Then the White Mustang burst into a dash of daring, despairing speed. It was his last magnificent effort. Straight for the wash at the upper end he pointed his racy, spirited head, and his white legs stretched far apart, twinkled and stretched again. Jones galloped to cut him off, and the yells he emitted were demoniacal. It was a long, straight race for the mustang, a short curve for the bay.

That the white stallion gained was as sure as his resolve to elude capture, and he never swerved a foot from his course. Jones might have headed him, but manifestly he wanted to ride with him, as well as to meet him, so in case the lasso went true, a terrible shock might be averted.

Up went Jones's arm as the space shortened, and the lasso ringed his head. Out it shot, lengthened like a yellow, striking snake, and fell just short of the flying white tail.

The White Mustang, fulfilling his purpose in a last heroic display of power, sailed into the air, up and up, and over the wide wash like a white streak. Free! the dust rolled in a cloud from under his hoofs, and he vanished.

Jones's superb horse, crashing down on his haunches, just escaped sliding into the hole.

I awoke to the realization that Satan had carried me, in pursuit of the thrilling chase, all the way across the circle without my knowing it.

Jones calmly wiped the sweat from his face, calmly coiled his lasso, and calmly remarked:

"In trying to capture wild animals a man must never be too sure. Now what I thought my strong point was my weak point—the wash. I made sure no horse could ever jump that hole."

CHAPTER 7. SNAKE GULCH

Not far from the scene of our adventure with the White Streak as we facetious and appreciatively named the mustang, deep, flat cave indented the canyon wall. By reason of its sandy floor and close proximity to Frank's trickling spring, we decided to camp in it. About dawn Lawson and Stewart straggled in on spent horse and found awaiting them a bright fire, a hot supper and cheery comrades.

"Did yu fellars git to see him?" was the ranger's first question.

"Did we get to see him?" echoed five lusty voice as one. "We did!"

It was after Frank, in his plain, blunt speech had told of our experience, that the long Arizonian gazed fixedly at Jones.

"Did yu acktully tech the hair of thet mustang with a rope?"

In all his days Jones never had a greater complement. By way of reply, he moved his big hand to button of his coat, and, fumbling over it, unwound a string of long, white hairs, then said: "I pulled these out of his tail with my lasso; it missed his left hind hoof about six inches."

There were six of the hairs, pure, glistening white, and over three feet long. Stewart examined then in expressive silence, then passed them along; and when they reached me, they stayed.

The cave, lighted up by a blazing fire, appeared to me a forbidding, uncanny place. Small, peculiar round holes, and dark cracks, suggestive of hidden vermin, gave me a creepy feeling; and although not over-sensitive on the subject of crawling, creeping things, I voiced my disgust.

"Say, I don't like the idea of sleeping in this hole. I'll bet it's full of spiders, snakes and centipedes and other poisonous things."

Whatever there was in my inoffensive declaration to rouse the usually slumbering humor of the Arizonians, and the thinly veiled ridicule of Colonel Jones, and a mixture of both in my once loyal California friend, I am not prepared to state. Maybe it was the dry, sweet, cool air of Nail Canyon; maybe my suggestion awoke ticklish associations that worked themselves off thus; maybe it was the first instance of my committing myself to a breach of camp etiquette. Be that as it may, my innocently expressed sentiment gave rise to bewildering dissertations on entomology, and most remarkable and startling tales from first-hand experience.

"Like as not," began Frank in matter-of-fact tone. "Them's tarantuler holes all right. An' scorpions, centipedes an' rattlers always rustle with tarantulers. But we never mind them—not us fellers! We're used to sleepin' with them. Why, I often wake up in the night to see a big tarantuler on my chest, an' see him wink. Ain't thet so, Jim?"

"Shore as hell," drawled faithful, slow Jim.

"Reminds me how fatal the bite of a centipede is," took up Colonel Jones, complacently. "Once I was sitting in camp with a hunter, who suddenly hissed out: 'Jones, for God's sake don't budge! There's a centipede on your arm!' He pulled his Colt, and shot the blamed centipede off as clean as a whistle. But the bullet hit a steer in the leg; and would you believe it, the bullet carried so much poison that in less than two hours the steer died of blood poisoning. Centipedes are so poisonous they leave a blue trail on flesh just by crawling over it. Look there!"

He bared his arm, and there on the brown-corded flesh was a blue trail of something, that was certain. It might have been made by a centipede.

"This is a likely place for them," put in Wallace, emitting a volume of smoke and gazing round the cave walls with the eye of a connoisseur. "My archaeological pursuits have given me great experience with centipedes, as you may imagine, considering how many old tombs, caves and cliff-dwellings I have explored. This Algonkian rock is about the right stratum for centipedes to dig in. They dig somewhat after the manner of the fluviatile long-tailed decapod crustaceans, of the genera Thoracostraca, the common crawfish, you know. From that, of course, you can imagine, if a centipede can bite rock, what a biter he is."

I began to grow weak, and did not wonder to see Jim's long pipe fall from his lips. Frank looked queer around the gills, so to speak, but the gaunt Stewart never batted an eye.

"I camped here two years ago," he said, "An' the cave was alive with rock-rats, mice, snakes, horned-toads, lizards an' a big Gila monster, besides bugs, scorpions' rattlers, an' as fer tarantulers an' centipedes—say! I couldn't sleep fer the noise they made fightin'."

"I seen the same," concluded Lawson, as nonchalant as a wild-horse wrangler well could be. "An' as fer me, now I allus lays perfickly still when the centipedes an' tarantulers begin to drop from their holes in the roof, same as them holes up there. An' when they light on me, I never move, nor even breathe fer about five minutes. Then they take a notion I'm dead an' crawl off. But sure, if I'd breathed I'd been a goner!"

All of this was playfully intended for the extinction of an unoffending and impressionable tenderfoot.

With an admiring glance at my tormentors, I rolled out my sleeping-bag and crawled into it, vowing I would remain there even if devil-fish, armed with pikes, invaded our cave.

Late in the night I awoke. The bottom of the canyon and the outer floor of our cave lay bathed in white, clear moonlight. A dense, gloomy black shadow veiled the opposite canyon wall. High up the pinnacles and turrets pointed toward a resplendent moon. It was a weird, wonderful scene of beauty entrancing, of breathless, dreaming silence that seemed not of life. Then a hoot-owl lamented dismally, his call fitting the scene and the dead stillness; the echoes resounded from cliff to cliff, strangely mocking and hollow, at last reverberating low and mournful in the distance.

How long I lay there enraptured with the beauty of light and mystery of shade, thrilling at the lonesome lament of the owl, I have no means to tell; but I was awakened from my trance by the touch of something crawling over me. Promptly I raised my head. The cave was as light as day. There, sitting sociably on my sleeping-bag was a great black tarantula, as large as my hand.

For one still moment, notwithstanding my contempt for Lawson's advice, I certainly acted upon it to the letter. If ever I was quiet, and if ever I was cold, the time was then. My companions snored in blissful ignorance of my plight. Slight rustling sounds attracted my wary gaze from the old black sentinel on my knee. I saw other black spiders running to and fro on the silver, sandy floor. A giant, as large as a soft-shell crab, seemed to be meditating an assault upon Jones's ear. Another, grizzled and shiny with age or moonbeams I could not tell which—pushed long, tentative feelers into Wallace's cap. I saw black spots darting over the roof. It was not a dream; the cave was alive with tarantulas!

Not improbably my strong impression that the spider on my knee deliberately winked at me was the result of memory, enlivening imagination. But it sufficed to bring to mind, in one rapid, consoling flash, the irrevocable law of destiny—that the deeds of the wicked return unto them again.

I slipped back into my sleeping-bag, with a keen consciousness of its nature, and carefully pulled the flap in place, which almost hermetically sealed me up.

"Hey! Jones! Wallace! Frank! Jim!" I yelled, from the depths of my safe refuge.

Wondering cries gave me glad assurance that they had awakened from their dreams.

"The cave's alive with tarantulas!" I cried, trying to hide my unholy glee.

"I'll be durned if it ain't!" ejaculated Frank.

"Shore it beats hell!" added Jim, with a shake of his blanket.

"Look out, Jones, there's one on your pillow!" shouted Wallace.

Whack! A sharp blow proclaimed the opening of hostilities.

Memory stamped indelibly every word of that incident; but innate delicacy prevents the repetition of all save the old warrior's concluding remarks: "! ! ! place I was ever in! Tarantulas by the million—centipedes, scorpions, bats! Rattlesnakes, too, I'll swear. Look out, Wallace! there, under your blanket!"

From the shuffling sounds which wafted sweetly into my bed, I gathered that my long friend from California must have gone through motions creditable to a contortionist. An ensuing explosion from Jones proclaimed to the listening world that Wallace had thrown a tarantula upon him. Further fearful language suggested the thought that Colonel Jones had passed on the inquisitive spider to Frank. The reception accorded the unfortunate tarantula, no doubt scared out of its wits, began with a wild yell from Frank and ended in pandemonium.

CHAPTER 7. SNAKE GULCH

While the confusion kept up, with whacks and blows and threshing about, with language such as never before had disgraced a group of old campers, I choked with rapture, and reveled in the sweetness of revenge.

When quiet reigned once more in the black and white canyon, only one sleeper lay on the moon-silvered sand of the cave.

At dawn, when I opened sleepy eyes, Frank, Slim, Stewart and Lawson had departed, as pre-arranged, with the outfit, leaving the horses belonging to us and rations for the day. Wallace and I wanted to climb the divide at the break, and go home by way of Snake Gulch, and the Colonel acquiesced with the remark that his sixty-three years had taught him there was much to see in the world. Coming to undertake it, we found the climb—except for a slide of weathered rock—no great task, and we accomplished it in half an hour, with breath to spare and no mishap to horses.

But descending into Snake Gulch, which was only a mile across the sparsely cedared ridge, proved to be tedious labor. By virtue of Satan's patience and skill, I forged ahead; which advantage, however, meant more risk for me because of the stones set in motion above. They rolled and bumped and cut into me, and I sustained many a bruise trying to protect the sinewy slender legs of my horse. The descent ended without serious mishap.

Snake Gulch had a character and sublimity which cast Nail Canyon into the obscurity of forgetfulness. The great contrast lay in the diversity of structure. The rock was bright red, with parapet of yellow, that leaned, heaved, bulged outward. These emblazoned cliff walls, two thousand feet high, were cracked from turret to base; they bowled out at such an angle that we were afraid to ride under them. Mountains of yellow rock hung balanced, ready to tumble down at the first angry breath of the gods. We rode among carved stones, pillars, obelisks and sculptured ruined walls of a fallen Babylon. Slides reaching all the way across and far up the canyon wall obstructed our passage. On every stone silent green lizards sunned themselves, gliding swiftly as we came near to their marble homes.

We came into a region of wind-worn caves, of all sizes and shapes, high and low on the cliffs; but strange to say, only on the north side of the canyon they appeared with dark mouths open and uninviting. One, vast and deep, though far off, menaced us as might the cave of a tawny-maned king of beasts; yet it impelled, fascinated and drew us on.

"It's a long, hard climb," said Wallace to the Colonel, as we dismounted.

"Boys, I'm with you," came the reply. And he was with us all the way, as we clambered over the immense blocks and threaded a passage between them and pulled weary legs up, one after the other. So steep lay the jumble of cliff fragments that we lost sight of the cave long before we got near it. Suddenly we rounded a stone, to halt and gasp at the thing looming before us.

The dark portal of death or hell might have yawned there. A gloomy hole, large enough to admit a church, had been hollowed in the cliff by ages of nature's chiseling.

"Vast sepulcher of Time's past, give up thy dead!" cried Wallace, solemnly.

"Oh! dark Stygian cave forlorn!" quoted I, as feelingly as my friend.

Jones hauled us down from the clouds.

"Now, I wonder what kind of a prehistoric animal holed in here?" said he.

Forever the one absorbing interest! If he realized the sublimity of this place, he did not show it.

The floor of the cave ascended from the very threshold. Stony ridges circled from wall to wall. We climbed till we were two hundred feet from the opening, yet we were not half-way to the dome.

Our horses, browsing in the sage far below, looked like ants. So steep did the ascent become that we desisted; for if one of us had slipped on the smooth incline, the result would have been terrible. Our voices rang clear and hollow from the walls. We were so high that the sky was blotted out by the overhanging square, cornice-like top of the door; and the light was weird, dim, shadowy, opaque. It was a gray tomb.

"Waa-hoo!" yelled Jones with all the power of his wide, leather lungs.

Thousands of devilish voices rushed at us, seemingly on puffs of wind. Mocking, deep echoes bellowed from the ebon shades at the back of the cave, and the walls, taking them up, hurled them on again in fiendish concatenation.

We did not again break the silence of that tomb, where the spirits of ages lay in dusty shrouds; and we crawled down as if we had invaded a sanctuary and invoked the wrath of the gods.

We all proposed names: Montezuma's Amphitheater being the only rival of Jones's selection, Echo cave, which we finally chose.

Mounting our horses again, we made twenty miles of Snake Gulch by noon, when we rested for lunch. All the way up we had played the boy's game of spying for sights, with the honors about even. It was a question if Snake Gulch ever before had such a raking over. Despite its name, however, we discovered no snakes.

From the sandy niche of a cliff where we lunched Wallace espied a tomb, and heralded his discovery with a victorious whoop. Digging in old ruins roused in him much the same spirit that digging in old books roused in me. Before we reached him, he had a big bowie-knife buried deep in the red, sandy floor of the tomb.

This one-time sealed house of the dead had been constructed of small stones, held together by a cement, the nature of which, Wallace explained, had never become clear to civilization. It was red in color and hard as flint, harder than the rocks it glued together. The tomb was half-round in shape, and its floor was a projecting shelf of cliff rock. Wallace unearthed bits of pottery, bone and finely braided rope, all of which, to our great disappointment, crumbled to dust in our fingers. In the case of the rope, Wallace assured us, this was a sign of remarkable antiquity.

In the next mile we traversed, we found dozens of these old cells, all demolished except a few feet of the walls, all despoiled of their one-time possessions. Wallace thought these depredations were due to Indians of our own time. Suddenly we came upon Jones, standing under a cliff, with his neck craned to a desperate angle.

"Now, what's that?" demanded he, pointing upward.

High on the cliff wall appeared a small, round protuberance. It was of the unmistakably red color of the other tombs; and Wallace, more excited than he had been in the cougar chase, said it was a sepulcher, and he believed it had never been opened.

From an elevated point of rock, as high up as I could well climb, I decided both questions with my glass. The tomb resembled nothing so much as a mud-wasp's nest, high on a barn wall. The fact that it had never been broken open quite carried Wallace away with enthusiasm.

"This is no mean discovery, let me tell you that," he declared. "I am familiar with the Aztec, Toltec and Pueblo ruins, and here I find no similarity. Besides, we are out of their latitude. An ancient race of people—very ancient indeed lived in this canyon. How long ago, it is impossible to tell."

"They must have been birds," said the practical Jones. "Now, how'd that tomb ever get there? Look at it, will you?"

As near as we could ascertain, it was three hundred feet from the ground below, five hundred from the rim wall above, and could not possibly have been approached from the top. Moreover, the cliff wall was as smooth as a wall of human make.

"There's another one," called out Jones.

"Yes, and I see another; no doubt there are many of them," replied Wallace. "In my mind, only one thing possible accounts for their position. You observe they appear to be about level with each other. Well, once the Canyon floor ran along that line, and in the ages gone by it has lowered, washed away by the rains."

This conception staggered us, but it was the only one conceivable. No doubt we all thought at the same time of the little rainfall in that arid section of Arizona.

"How many years?" queried Jones.

"Years! What are years?" said Wallace. "Thousands of years, ages have passed since the race who built these tombs lived."

Some persuasion was necessary to drag our scientific friend from the spot, where obviously helpless to do anything else, he stood and gazed longingly at the isolated tombs. The canyon widened as we proceeded; and hundreds of points that invited inspection, such as overhanging shelves of rock, dark fissures, caverns and ruins had to be passed by, for lack of time.

Still, a more interesting and important discovery was to come, and the pleasure and honor of it fell to me. My eyes were sharp and peculiarly farsighted—the Indian sight, Jones assured me; and I kept them searching the walls in such places as my companions overlooked. Presently, under a large, bulging bluff, I saw a dark spot, which took the shape of a figure. This figure, I recollected, had been presented to my sight more than once, and now it stopped me. The hard climb up the slippery stones was fatiguing, but I did not hesitate, for I was determined to know. Once upon the ledge, I let out a yell that quickly set my companions in my direction. The figure I had seen was a dark, red devil, a painted image, rude, unspeakably wild, crudely executed, but painted by the hand of man. The whole surface of the cliff wall bore figures of all shapes—men, mammals, birds and strange devices, some in red paint, mostly in yellow. Some showed the wear of time; others were clear and sharp.

Wallace puffed up to me, but he had wind enough left for another whoop. Jones puffed up also, and seeing the first thing a rude sketch of what might have been a deer or a buffalo, he commented thus: "Darn me if I ever saw an animal like that? Boys, this is a find, sure as you're born. Because not even the Piutes ever spoke of these figures. I doubt if they know they're here. And the cowboys and wranglers, what few ever get by here in a hundred years, never saw these things. Beats anything I ever saw on the Mackenzie, or anywhere else."

The meaning of some devices was as mystical as that of others was clear. Two blood-red figures of men, the larger dragging the smaller by the hair, while he waved aloft a blood-red hatchet or club, left little to conjecture. Here was the old battle of men, as old as life. Another group, two figures of which resembled the foregoing in form and action, battling over a prostrate form rudely feminine in outline, attested to an age when men were as susceptible as they are in modern times, but more forceful and original. An odd yellow Indian waved aloft a red hand, which striking picture suggested the idea that he was an ancient Macbeth, listening to the knocking at the gate. There was a character representing a great chief, before whom many figures lay prostrate, evidently slain or subjugated. Large red paintings, in the shape of bats, occupied prominent positions, and must have represented gods or devils. Armies of marching men told of that blight of nations old or young—war. These, and birds unnamable, and beasts unclassable, with dots and marks and hieroglyphics, recorded the history of a bygone people. Symbols they were of an era that had gone into the dim past, leaving only these marks, {Symbols recording the history of a bygone people.} forever unintelligible; yet while they stood, century after century, ineffaceable, reminders of the glory, the mystery, the sadness of life.

"How could paint of any kind last so long? asked Jones, shaking his head doubtfully.

"That is the unsolvable mystery," returned Wallace. "But the records are there. I am absolutely sure the paintings are at least a thousand years old. I have never seen any tombs or paintings similar to them. Snake Gulch is a find, and I shall some day study its wonders."

Sundown caught us within sight of Oak Spring, and we soon trotted into camp to the welcoming chorus of the hounds. Frank and the others had reached the cabin some hours before. Supper was steaming on the hot coals with a delicious fragrance.

Then came the pleasantest time of the day, after a long chase or jaunt—the silent moments, watching the glowing embers of the fire; the speaking moments when a red-blooded story rang clear and true; the twilight moments, when the wood-smoke smelled sweet.

CHAPTER 7. SNAKE GULCH

Jones seemed unusually thoughtful. I had learned that this preoccupation in him meant the stirring of old associations, and I waited silently. By and by Lawson snored mildly in a corner; Jim and Frank crawled into their blankets, and all was still. Wallace smoked his Indian pipe and hunted in firelit dreams.

"Boys," said our leader finally, "somehow the echoes dying away in that cave reminded me of the mourn of the big white wolves in the Barren Lands."

Wallace puffed huge clouds of white smoke, and I waited, knowing that I was to hear at last the story of the Colonel's great adventure in the Northland.

CHAPTER 8. NAZA! NAZA! NAZA!

It was a waiting day at Fort Chippewayan. The lonesome, far-northern Hudson's Bay Trading Post seldom saw such life. Tepees dotted the banks of the Slave River and lines of blanketed Indians paraded its shores. Near the boat landing a group of chiefs, grotesque in semi-barbaric, semicivilized splendor, but black-browed, austere-eyed, stood in savage dignity with folded arms and high-held heads. Lounging on the grassy bank were white men, traders, trappers and officials of the post.

All eyes were on the distant curve of the river where, as it lost itself in a fine-fringed bend of dark green, white-glinting waves danced and fluttered. A June sky lay blue in the majestic stream; ragged, spear-topped, dense green trees massed down to the water; beyond rose bold, bald-knobbed hills, in remote purple relief.

A long Indian arm stretched south. The waiting eyes discerned a black speck on the green, and watched it grow. A flatboat, with a man standing to the oars, bore down swiftly.

Not a red hand, nor a white one, offered to help the voyager in the difficult landing. The oblong, clumsy, heavily laden boat surged with the current and passed the dock despite the boatman's efforts. He swung his craft in below upon a bar and roped it fast to a tree. The Indians crowded above him on the bank. The boatman raised his powerful form erect, lifted a bronzed face which seemed set in craggy hardness, and cast from narrow eyes a keen, cool glance on those above. The silvery gleam in his fair hair told of years.

Silence, impressive as it was ominous, broke only to the rattle of camping paraphernalia, which the voyager threw to a level, grassy bench on the bank. Evidently this unwelcome visitor had journeyed from afar, and his boat, sunk deep into the water with its load of barrels, boxes and bags, indicated that the journey had only begun. Significant, too, were a couple of long Winchester rifles shining on a tarpaulin.

The cold-faced crowd stirred and parted to permit the passage of a tall, thin, gray personage of official bearing, in a faded military coat.

"Are you the musk-ox hunter?" he asked, in tones that contained no welcome.

The boatman greeted this peremptory interlocutor with a cool laugh—a strange laugh, in which the muscles of his face appeared not to play.

"Yes, I am the man," he said.

CHAPTER 8. NAZA! NAZA! NAZA!

"The chiefs of the Chippewayan and Great Slave tribes have been apprised of your coming. They have held council and are here to speak with you."

At a motion from the commandant, the line of chieftains piled down to the level bench and formed a half-circle before the voyager. To a man who had stood before grim Sitting Bull and noble Black Thunder of the Sioux, and faced the falcon-eyed Geronimo, and glanced over the sights of a rifle at gorgeous-feathered, wild, free Comanches, this semi-circle of savages—lords of the north—was a sorry comparison. Bedaubed and betrinketed, slouchy and slovenly, these low-statured chiefs belied in appearance their scorn-bright eyes and lofty mien. They made a sad group.

One who spoke in unintelligible language, rolled out a haughty, sonorous voice over the listening multitude. When he had finished, a half-breed interpreter, in the dress of a white man, spoke at a signal from the commandant.

"He says listen to the great orator of the Chippewayan. He has summoned all the chiefs of the tribes south of Great Slave Lake. He has held council. The cunning of the pale-face, who comes to take the musk-oxen, is well known. Let the pale-face hunter return to his own hunting-grounds; let him turn his face from the north. Never will the chiefs permit the white man to take musk-oxen alive from their country. The Ageter, the Musk-ox, is their god. He gives them food and fur. He will never come back if he is taken away, and the reindeer will follow him. The chiefs and their people would starve. They command the pale-face hunter to go back. They cry Naza! Naza! Naza!"

"Say, for a thousand miles I've heard that word Naza!" returned the hunter, with mingled curiosity and disgust. "At Edmonton Indian runners started ahead of me, and every village I struck the redskins would crowd round me and an old chief would harangue at me, and motion me back, and point north with Naza! Naza! Naza! What does it mean?"

"No white man knows; no Indian will tell," answered the interpreter. "The traders think it means the Great Slave, the North Star, the North Spirit, the North Wind, the North Lights and the musk-ox god."

"Well, say to the chiefs to tell Ageter I have been four moons on the way after some of his little Ageters, and I'm going to keep on after them."

"Hunter, you are most unwise," broke in the commandant, in his officious voice. "The Indians will never permit you to take a musk-ox alive from the north. They worship him, pray to him. It is a wonder you have not been stopped."

"Who'll stop me?"

"The Indians. They will kill you if you do not turn back."

"Faugh! to tell an American plainsman that!" The hunter paused a steady moment, with his eyelids narrowing over slits of blue fire. "There is no law to keep me out, nothing but Indian superstition and Naza! And the greed of the Hudson's Bay people. I am an old fox, not to be fooled by pretty baits. For years the officers of this fur-trading company have tried to keep out explorers. Even Sir John Franklin, an Englishman, could not buy food of them. The policy of the company is to side with the Indians, to keep out traders and trappers. Why? So they can keep on cheating the poor savages out of clothing and food by trading a few trinkets and blankets, a little tobacco and rum for millions of dollars worth of furs. Have I failed to hire man after man, Indian after Indian, not to know why I cannot get a helper? Have I, a plainsman, come a thousand miles alone to be scared by you, or a lot of craven Indians? Have I been dreaming of musk-oxen for forty years, to slink south now, when I begin to feel the north? Not I."

Deliberately every chief, with the sound of a hissing snake, spat in the hunter's face. He stood immovable while they perpetrated the outrage, then calmly wiped his cheeks, and in his strange, cool voice, addressed the interpreter.

"Tell them thus they show their true qualities, to insult in council. Tell them they are not chiefs, but dogs. Tell them they are not even squaws, only poor, miserable starved dogs. Tell them I turn my back on them. Tell them the paleface has fought real chiefs, fierce, bold, like eagles, and he turns his back on dogs. Tell them he is the one who could teach them to raise the musk-oxen and the reindeer, and to keep out the cold and the wolf. But they are blinded. Tell them the hunter goes north."

Through the council of chiefs ran a low mutter, as of gathering thunder.

True to his word, the hunter turned his back on them. As he brushed by, his eye caught a gaunt savage slipping from the boat. At the hunter's stern call, the Indian leaped ashore, and started to run. He had stolen a parcel, and would have succeeded in eluding its owner but for an unforeseen obstacle, as striking as it was unexpected.

A white man of colossal stature had stepped in the thief's passage, and laid two great hands on him. Instantly the parcel flew from the Indian, and he spun in the air to fall into the river with a sounding splash. Yells signaled the surprise and alarm caused by this unexpected incident. The Indian frantically swam to the shore. Whereupon the champion of the stranger in a strange land lifted a bag, which gave forth a musical clink of steel, and throwing it with the camp articles on the grassy bench, he extended a huge, friendly hand.

"My name is Rea," he said, in deep, cavernous tones.

"Mine is Jones," replied the hunter, and right quickly did he grip the proffered hand. He saw in Rea a giant, of whom he was but a stunted shadow. Six and one-half feet Rea stood, with yard-wide shoulders, a hulk of bone and brawn. His ponderous, shaggy head rested on a bull neck. His broad face, with its low forehead, its close-shut mastiff under jaw, its big, opaque eyes, pale and cruel as those of a jaguar, marked him a man of terrible brute force.

"Free-trader!" called the commandant "Better think twice before you join fortunes with the musk-ox hunter."

"To hell with you an' your rantin', dog-eared redskins!" cried Rea. "I've run agin a man of my own kind, a man of my own country, an' I'm goin' with him."

With this he thrust aside some encroaching, gaping Indians so unconcernedly and ungently that they sprawled upon the grass.

Slowly the crowd mounted and once more lined the bank.

CHAPTER 8. NAZA! NAZA! NAZA!

Jones realized that by some late-turning stroke of fortune, he had fallen in with one of the few free-traders of the province. These free-traders, from the very nature of their calling, which was to defy the fur company, and to trap and trade on their own account—were a hardy and intrepid class of men. Rea's worth to Jones exceeded that of a dozen ordinary men. He knew the ways of the north, the language of the tribes, the habits of animals, the handling of dogs, the uses of food and fuel. Moreover, it soon appeared that he was a carpenter and blacksmith.

"There's my kit," he said, dumping the contents of his bag. It consisted of a bunch of steel traps, some tools, a broken ax, a box of miscellaneous things such as trappers used, and a few articles of flannel. "Thievin' redskins," he added, in explanation of his poverty. "Not much of an outfit. But I'm the man for you. Besides, I had a pal onct who knew you on the plains, called you 'Buff' Jones. Old Jim Bent he was."

"I recollect Jim," said Jones. "He went down in Custer's last charge. So you were Jim's pal. That'd be a recommendation if you needed one. But the way you chucked the Indian overboard got me."

Rea soon manifested himself as a man of few words and much action. With the planks Jones had on board he heightened the stern and bow of the boat to keep out the beating waves in the rapids; he fashioned a steering-gear and a less awkward set of oars, and shifted the cargo so as to make more room in the craft.

"Buff, we're in for a storm. Set up a tarpaulin an' make a fire. We'll pretend to camp to-night. These Indians won't dream we'd try to run the river after dark, and we'll slip by under cover."

The sun glazed over; clouds moved up from the north; a cold wind swept the tips of the spruces, and rain commenced to drive in gusts. By the time it was dark not an Indian showed himself. They were housed from the storm. Lights twinkled in the teepees and the big log cabins of the trading company. Jones scouted round till pitchy black night, when a freezing, pouring blast sent him back to the protection of the tarpaulin. When he got there he found that Rea had taken it down and awaited him. "Off!" said the free-trader; and with no more noise than a drifting feather the boat swung into the current and glided down till the twinkling fires no longer accentuated the darkness.

By night the river, in common with all swift rivers, had a sullen voice, and murmured its hurry, its restraint, its menace, its meaning. The two boat-men, one at the steering gear, one at the oars, faced the pelting rain and watched the dim, dark line of trees. The craft slid noiselessly onward into the gloom.

And into Jones's ears, above the storm, poured another sound, a steady, muffled rumble, like the roll of giant chariot wheels. It had come to be a familiar roar to him, and the only thing which, in his long life of hazard, had ever sent the cold, prickling, tight shudder over his warm skin. Many times on the Athabasca that rumble had presaged the dangerous and dreaded rapids.

"Hell Bend Rapids!" shouted Rea. "Bad water, but no rocks."

The rumble expanded to a roar, the roar to a boom that charged the air with heaviness, with a dreamy burr. The whole indistinct world appeared to be moving to the lash of wind, to the sound of rain, to the roar of the river. The boat shot down and sailed aloft, met shock on shock, breasted leaping dim white waves, and in a hollow, unearthly blend of watery sounds, rode on and on, buffeted, tossed, pitched into a black chaos that yet gleamed with obscure shrouds of light. Then the convulsive stream shrieked out a last defiance, changed its course abruptly to slow down and drown the sound of rapids in muffling distance. Once more the craft swept on smoothly, to the drive of the wind and the rush of the rain.

By midnight the storm cleared. Murky cloud split to show shining, blue-white stars and a fitful moon, that silvered the crests of the spruces and sometimes hid like a gleaming, black-threaded peak behind the dark branches.

Jones, a plainsman all his days, wonderingly watched the moon-blanched water. He saw it shade and darken under shadowy walls of granite, where it swelled with hollow song and gurgle. He heard again the far-off rumble, faint on the night. High cliff banks appeared, walled out the mellow, light, and the river suddenly narrowed. Yawning holes, whirlpools of a second, opened with a gurgling suck and raced with the boat.

On the craft flew. Far ahead, a long, declining plane of jumping frosted waves played dark and white with the moonbeams. The Slave plunged to his freedom, down his riven, stone-spiked bed, knowing no patient eddy, and white-wreathed his dark shiny rocks in spume and spray.

CHAPTER 9. THE LAND OF THE MUSK-OX

A far cry it was from bright June at Port Chippewayan to dim October on Great Slave Lake.

Two long, laborious months Rea and Jones threaded the crooked shores of the great inland sea, to halt at the extreme northern end, where a plunging rivulet formed the source of a river. Here they found a stone chimney and fireplace standing among the darkened, decayed ruins of a cabin.

"We mustn't lose no time," said Rea. "I feel the winter in the wind. An' see how dark the days are gettin' on us."

"I'm for hunting musk-oxen," replied Jones.

"Man, we're facin' the northern night; we're in the land of the midnight sun. Soon we'll be shut in for seven months. A cabin we want, an' wood, an' meat."

A forest of stunted spruce trees edged on the lake, and soon its dreary solitudes rang to the strokes of axes. The trees were small and uniform in size. Black stumps protruded, here and there, from the ground, showing work of the steel in time gone by. Jones observed that the living trees were no larger in diameter than the stumps, and questioned Rea in regard to the difference in age.

"Cut twenty-five, mebbe fifty years ago," said the trapper.

"But the living trees are no bigger."

"Trees an' things don't grow fast in the north land."

They erected a fifteen-foot cabin round the stone chimney, roofed it with poles and branches of spruce and a layer of sand. In digging near the fireplace Jones unearthed a rusty file and the head of a whisky keg, upon which was a sunken word in unintelligible letters.

"We've found the place," said Rea. "Frank built a cabin here in 1819. An' in 1833 Captain Back wintered here when he was in search of Captain Ross of the vessel Fury. It was those explorin' parties thet cut the trees. I seen Indian sign out there, made last winter, I reckon; but Indians never cut down no trees."

The hunters completed the cabin, piled cords of firewood outside, stowed away the kegs of dried fish and fruits, the sacks of flour, boxes of crackers, canned meats and vegetables, sugar, salt, coffee, tobacco—all of the cargo; then took the boat apart and carried it up the bank, which labor took them less than a week.

Jones found sleeping in the cabin, despite the fire, uncomfortably cold, because of the wide chinks between the logs. It was hardly better than sleeping under the swaying spruces. When he essayed to stop up the crack, a task by no means easy, considering the lack of material—Rea laughed his short "Ho! Ho!" and stopped him with the word, "Wait." Every morning the green ice extended farther out into the lake; the sun paled dim and dimmer; the nights grew colder. On October 8th the thermometer registered several degrees below zero; it fell a little more next night and continued to fall.

"Ho! Ho!" cried Rea. "She's struck the toboggan, an' presently she'll commence to slide. Come on, Buff, we've work to do."

He caught up a bucket, made for their hole in the ice, rebroke a six-inch layer, the freeze of a few hours, and filling his bucket, returned to the cabin. Jones had no inkling of the trapper's intention, and wonderingly he soused his bucket full of water and followed.

By the time he had reached the cabin, a matter of some thirty or forty good paces, the water no longer splashed from his pail, for a thin film of ice prevented. Rea stood fifteen feet from the cabin, his back to the wind, and threw the water. Some of it froze in the air, most of it froze on the logs. The simple plan of the trapper to incase the cabin with ice was easily divined. All day the men worked, easing only when the cabin resembled a glistening mound. It had not a sharp corner nor a crevice. Inside it was warm and snug, and as light as when the chinks were open.

A slight moderation of the weather brought the snow. Such snow! A blinding white flutter of grey flakes, as large as feathers! All day they rustle softly; all night they swirled, sweeping, seeping brushing against the cabin. "Ho! Ho!" roared Rea. "'Tis good; let her snow, an' the reindeer will migrate. We'll have fresh meat." The sun shone again, but not brightly. A nipping wind came down out of the frigid north and crusted the snows. The third night following the storm, when the hunters lay snug under their blankets, a commotion outside aroused them.

"Indians," said Rea, "come north for reindeer."

Half the night, shouting and yelling, barking dogs, hauling of sleds and cracking of dried-skin tepees murdered sleep for those in the cabin. In the morning the level plain and edge of the forest held an Indian village. Caribou hides, strung on forked poles, constituted tent-like habitations with no distinguishable doors. Fires smoked in the holes in the snow. Not till late in the day did any life manifest itself round the tepees, and then a group of children, poorly clad in ragged pieces of blankets and skins, gaped at Jones. He saw their pinched, brown faces, staring, hungry eyes, naked legs and throats, and noted particularly their dwarfish size. When he spoke they fled precipitously a little way, then turned. He called again, and all ran except one small lad. Jones went into the cabin and came out with a handful of sugar in square lumps.

"Yellow Knife Indians," said Rea. "A starved tribe! We're in for it."

CHAPTER 9. THE LAND OF THE MUSK-OX

Jones made motions to the lad, but he remained still, as if transfixed, and his black eyes stared wonderingly.

"Molar nasu (white man good)," said Rea.

The lad came out of his trance and looked back at his companions, who edged nearer. Jones ate a lump of sugar, then handed one to the little Indian. He took it gingerly, put it into his mouth and immediately jumped up and down.

"Hoppiesharnpoolie! Hoppiesharnpoolie!" he shouted to his brothers and sisters. They came on the run.

"Think he means sweet salt," interpreted Rea. "Of course these beggars never tasted sugar."

The band of youngsters trooped round Jones, and after tasting the white lumps, shrieked in such delight that the braves and squaws shuffled out of the tepees.

In all his days Jones had never seen such miserable Indians. Dirty blankets hid all their person, except straggling black hair, hungry, wolfish eyes and moccasined feet. They crowded into the path before the cabin door and mumbled and stared and waited. No dignity, no brightness, no suggestion of friendliness marked this peculiar attitude.

"Starved!" exclaimed Rea. "They've come to the lake to invoke the Great Spirit to send the reindeer. Buff, whatever you do, don't feed them. If you do, we'll have them on our hands all winter. It's cruel, but, man, we're in the north!"

Notwithstanding the practical trapper's admonition Jones could not resist the pleading of the children. He could not stand by and see them starve. After ascertaining there was absolutely nothing to eat in the tepees, he invited the little ones into the cabin, and made a great pot of soup, into which he dropped compressed biscuits. The savage children were like wildcats. Jones had to call in Rea to assist him in keeping the famished little aborigines from tearing each other to pieces. When finally they were all fed, they had to be driven out of the cabin.

"That's new to me," said Jones. "Poor little beggars!"

Rea doubtfully shook his shaggy head.

Next day Jones traded with the Yellow Knives. He had a goodly supply of baubles, besides blankets, gloves and boxes of canned goods, which he had brought for such trading. He secured a dozen of the large-boned, white and black Indian dogs, huskies, Rea called them—two long sleds with harness and several pairs of snowshoes. This trade made Jones rub his hands in satisfaction, for during all the long journey north he had failed to barter for such cardinal necessities to the success of his venture.

"Better have doled out the grub to them in rations," grumbled Rea.

Twenty-four hours sufficed to show Jones the wisdom of the trapper's words, for in just that time the crazed, ignorant savages had glutted the generous store of food, which should have lasted them for weeks. The next day they were begging at the cabin door. Rea cursed and threatened them with his fists, but they returned again and again.

Days passed. All the time, in light and dark, the Indians filled the air with dismal chant and doleful incantations to the Great Spirit, and the tum! tum! tum! tum! of tomtoms, a specific feature of their wild prayer for food.

But the white monotony of the rolling land and level lake remained unbroken. The reindeer did not come. The days became shorter, dimmer, darker. The mercury kept on the slide.

Forty degrees below zero did not trouble the Indians. They stamped till they dropped, and sang till their voices vanished, and beat the tomtoms everlastingly. Jones fed the children once each day, against the trapper's advice.

One day, while Rea was absent, a dozen braves succeeded in forcing an entrance, and clamored so fiercely, and threatened so desperately, that Jones was on the point of giving them food when the door opened to admit Rea.

With a glance he saw the situation. He dropped the bucket he carried, threw the door wide open and commenced action. Because of his great bulk he seemed slow, but every blow of his sledge-hammer fist knocked a brave against the wall, or through the door into the snow. When he could reach two savages at once, by way of diversion, he swung their heads together with a crack. They dropped like dead things. Then he handled them as if they were sacks of corn, pitching them out into the snow. In two minutes the cabin was clear. He banged the door and slipped the bar in place.

"Buff, I'm goin' to get mad at these thievin' red, skins some day," he said gruffly. The expanse of his chest heaved slightly, like the slow swell of a calm ocean, but there was no other indication of unusual exertion.

Jones laughed, and again gave thanks for the comradeship of this strange man.

Shortly afterward, he went out for wood, and as usual scanned the expanse of the lake. The sun shone mistier and warmer, and frost feathers floated in the air. Sky and sun and plain and lake—all were gray. Jones fancied he saw a distant moving mass of darker shade than the gray background. He called the trapper.

"Caribou," said Rea instantly. "The vanguard of the migration. Hear the Indians! Hear their cry: "Aton! Aton!" they mean reindeer. The idiots have scared the herd with their infernal racket, an' no meat will they get. The caribou will keep to the ice, an' man or Indian can't stalk them there."

For a few moments his companion surveyed the lake and shore with a plainsman's eye, then dashed within, to reappear with a Winchester in each hand. Through the crowd of bewailing, bemoaning Indians; he sped, to the low, dying bank. The hard crust of snow upheld him. The gray cloud was a thousand yards out upon the lake and moving southeast. If the caribou did not swerve from this course they would pass close to a projecting point of land, a half-mile up the lake. So, keeping a wary eye upon them, the hunter ran swiftly. He had not hunted antelope and buffalo on the plains all his life without learning how to approach moving game. As long as the caribou were in action, they could not tell whether he moved or was motionless. In order to tell if an object was inanimate or not, they must stop to see, of which fact the keen hunter took advantage. Suddenly he saw the gray mass slow down and bunch up. He stopped running, to stand like a stump. When the reindeer moved again, he moved, and when they slackened again, he stopped and became motionless. As they kept to their course, he worked gradually closer and closer. Soon he distinguished gray, bobbing heads. When the leader showed signs of halting in his slow trot the hunter again became a statue. He saw they were easy to deceive; and, daringly confident of success, he encroached on the ice and closed up the gap till not more than two hundred yards separated him from the gray, bobbing, antlered mass.

Jones dropped on one knee. A moment only his eyes lingered admiringly on the wild and beautiful spectacle; then he swept one of the rifles to a level. Old habit made the little beaded sight cover first the stately leader. Bang! The gray monarch leaped straight forward, forehoofs up, antlered head back, to fall dead with a crash. Then for a few moments the Winchester spat a deadly stream of fire, and when emptied was thrown down for the other gun, which in the steady, sure hands of the hunter belched death to the caribou.

The herd rushed on, leaving the white surface of the lake gray with a struggling, kicking, bellowing heap. When Jones reached the caribou he saw several trying to rise on crippled legs. With his knife he killed these, not without some hazard to himself. Most of the fallen ones were already dead, and the others soon lay still. Beautiful gray creatures they were, almost white, with wide-reaching, symmetrical horns.

A medley of yells arose from the shore, and Rea appeared running with two sleds, with the whole tribe of Yellow Knives pouring out of the forest behind him.

"Buff, you're jest what old Jim said you was," thundered Rea, as he surveyed the gray pile. "Here's winter meat, an' I'd not have given a biscuit for all the meat I thought you'd get."

"Thirty shots in less than thirty seconds," said Jones, "An' I'll bet every ball I sent touched hair. How many reindeer?"

"Twenty! twenty! Buff, or I've forgot how to count. I guess mebbe you can't handle them shootin' arms. Ho! here comes the howlin' redskins."

Rea whipped out a bowie knife and began disemboweling the reindeer. He had not proceeded far in his task when the crazed savages were around him. Every one carried a basket or receptacle, which he swung aloft, and they sang, prayed, rejoiced on their knees. Jones turned away from the sickening scenes that convinced him these savages were little better than cannibals. Rea cursed them, and tumbled them over, and threatened them with the big bowie. An altercation ensued, heated on his side, frenzied on theirs. Thinking some treachery might befall his comrade, Jones ran into the thick of the group.

"Share with them, Rea, share with them."

Whereupon the giant hauled out ten smoking carcasses. Bursting into a babel of savage glee and tumbling over one another, the Indians pulled the caribou to the shore.

"Thievin' fools," growled Rea, wiping the sweat from his brow. "Said they'd prevailed on the Great Spirit to send the reindeer. Why, they'd never smelled warm meat but for you. Now, Buff, they'll gorge every hair, hide an' hoof of their share in less than a week. Thet's the last we do for the damned cannibals. Didn't you see them eatin' of the raw innards?—faugh! I'm calculatin' we'll see no more reindeer. It's late for the migration. The big herd has driven southward. But we're lucky, thanks to your prairie trainin'. Come on now with the sleds, or we'll have a pack of wolves to fight."

By loading three reindeer on each sled, the hunters were not long in transporting them to the cabin. "Buff, there ain't much doubt about them keepin' nice and cool," said Rea. "They'll freeze, an' we can skin them when we want."

That night the starved wolf dogs gorged themselves till they could not rise from the snow. Likewise the Yellow Knives feasted. How long the ten reindeer might have served the wasteful tribe, Rea and Jones never found out. The next day two Indians arrived with dog-trains, and their advent was hailed with another feast, and a pow-wow that lasted into the night.

"Guess we're goin' to get rid of our blasted hungry neighbors," said Rea, coming in next morning with the water pail, "An' I'll be durned, Buff, if I don't believe them crazy heathen have been told about you. Them Indians was messengers. Grab your gun, an' let's walk over and see."

The Yellow Knives were breaking camp, and the hunters were at once conscious of the difference in their bearing. Rea addressed several braves, but got no reply. He laid his broad hand on the old wrinkled chief, who repulsed him, and turned his back. With a growl, the trapper spun the Indian round, and spoke as many words of the language as he knew. He got a cold response, which ended in the ragged old chief starting up, stretching a long, dark arm northward, and with eyes fixed in fanatical subjection, shouting: "Naza! Naza! Naza!"

"Heathen!" Rea shook his gun in the faces of the messengers. "It'll go bad with you to come Nazain' any longer on our trail. Come, Buff, clear out before I get mad."

When they were once more in the cabin, Rea told Jones that the messengers had been sent to warn the Yellow Knives not to aid the white hunters in any way. That night the dogs were kept inside, and the men took turns in watching. Morning showed a broad trail southward. And with the going of the Yellow Knives the mercury dropped to fifty, and the long, twilight winter night fell.

So with this agreeable riddance and plenty of meat and fuel to cheer them, the hunters sat down in their snug cabin to wait many months for daylight.

Those few intervals when the wind did not blow were the only times Rea and Jones got out of doors. To the plainsman, new to the north, the dim gray world about him was of exceeding interest. Out of the twilight shone a wan, round, lusterless ring that Rea said was the sun. The silence and desolation were heart-numbing.

"Where are the wolves?" asked Jones of Rea.

"Wolves can't live on snow. They're farther south after caribou, or farther north after musk-ox."

In those few still intervals Jones remained out as long as he dared, with the mercury sinking to -sixty degrees. He turned from the wonder of the unreal, remote sun, to the marvel in the north—Aurora borealis—ever-present, ever-changing, ever-beautiful! and he gazed in rapt attention.

"Polar lights," said Rea, as if he were speaking of biscuits. "You'll freeze. It's gettin' cold."

Cold it became, to the matter of -seventy degrees. Frost covered the walls of the cabin and the roof, except just over the fire. The reindeer were harder than iron. A knife or an ax or a steel-trap burned as if it had been heated in fire, and stuck to the hand. The hunters experienced trouble in breathing; the air hurt their lungs.

The months dragged. Rea grew more silent day by day, and as he sat before the fire his wide shoulders sagged lower and lower. Jones, unaccustomed to the waiting, the restraint, the barrier of the north, worked on guns, sleds, harness, till he felt he would go mad. Then to save his mind he constructed a windmill of caribou hides and pondered over it trying to invent, to put into practical use an idea he had once conceived.

Hour after hour he lay under his blankets unable to sleep, and listened to the north wind. Sometimes Rea mumbled in his slumbers; once his giant form started up, and he muttered a woman's name. Shadows from the fire flickered on the walls, visionary, spectral shadows, cold and gray, fitting the north. At such times he longed with all the power of his soul to be among those scenes far southward, which he called home. For days Rea never spoke a word, only gazed into the fire, ate and slept. Jones, drifting far from his real self, feared the strange mood of the trapper and sought to break it, but without avail. More and more he reproached himself, and singularly on the one fact that, as he did not smoke himself, he had brought only a small store of tobacco. Rea, inordinate and inveterate smoker, had puffed away all the weed in clouds of white, then had relapsed into gloom.

CHAPTER 10. SUCCESS AND FAILURE

At last the marvel in the north dimmed, the obscure gray shade lifted, the hope in the south brightened, and the mercury climbed reluctantly, with a tyrant's hate to relinquish power.

Spring weather at twenty-five below zero! On April 12th a small band of Indians made their appearance. Of the Dog tribe were they, an offcast of the Great Slaves, according to Rea, and as motley, starring and starved as the Yellow Knives. But they were friendly, which presupposed ignorance of the white hunters, and Rea persuaded the strongest brave to accompany them as guide northward after musk-oxen.

On April 16th, having given the Indians several caribou carcasses, and assuring them that the cabin was protected by white spirits, Rea and Jones, each with sled and train of dogs, started out after their guide, who was similarly equipped, over the glistening snow toward the north. They made sixty miles the first day, and pitched their Indian tepee on the shores of Artillery Lake. Traveling northeast, they covered its white waste of one hundred miles in two days. Then a day due north, over rolling, monotonously snowy plain; devoid of rock, tree or shrub, brought them into a country of the strangest, queerest little spruce trees, very slender, and none of them over fifteen feet in height. A primeval forest of saplings.

"Ditchen Nechila," said the guide.

"Land of Sticks Little," translated Rea.

An occasional reindeer was seen and numerous foxes and hares trotted off into the woods, evincing more curiosity than fear. All were silver white, even the reindeer, at a distance, taking the hue of the north. Once a beautiful creature, unblemished as the snow it trod, ran up a ridge and stood watching the hunters. It resembled a monster dog, only it was inexpressibly more wild looking.

"Ho! Ho! there you are!" cried Rea, reaching for his Winchester. "Polar wolf! Them's the white devils we'll have hell with."

As if the wolf understood, he lifted his white, sharp head and uttered a bark or howl that was like nothing so much as a haunting, unearthly mourn. The animal then merged into the white, as if he were really a spirit of the world whence his cry seemed to come.

CHAPTER 10. SUCCESS AND FAILURE

In this ancient forest of youthful appearing trees, the hunters cut firewood to the full carrying capacity of the sleds. For five days the Indian guide drove his dogs over the smooth crust, and on the sixth day, about noon, halting in a hollow, he pointed to tracks in the snow and called out: "Ageter! Ageter! Ageter!"

The hunters saw sharply defined hoof-marks, not unlike the tracks of reindeer, except that they were longer. The tepee was set up on the spot and the dogs unharnessed.

The Indian led the way with the dogs, and Rea and Jones followed, slipping over the hard crust without sinking in and traveling swiftly. Soon the guide, pointing, again let out the cry: "Ageter!" at the same moment loosing the dogs.

Some few hundred yards down the hollow, a number of large black animals, not unlike the shaggy, humpy buffalo, lumbered over the snow. Jones echoed Rea's yell, and broke into a run, easily distancing the puffing giant.

The musk-oxen squared round to the dogs, and were soon surrounded by the yelping pack. Jones came up to find six old bulls uttering grunts of rage and shaking ram-like horns at their tormentors. Notwithstanding that for Jones this was the cumulation of years of desire, the crowning moment, the climax and fruition of long-harbored dreams, he halted before the tame and helpless beasts, with joy not unmixed with pain.

"It will be murder!" he exclaimed. "It's like shooting down sheep."

Rea came crashing up behind him and yelled, "Get busy. We need fresh meat, an' I want the skins."

The bulls succumbed to well-directed shots, and the Indian and Rea hurried back to camp with the dogs to fetch the sleds, while Jones examined with warm interest the animals he had wanted to see all his life. He found the largest bull approached within a third of the size of a buffalo. He was of a brownish-black color and very like a large, woolly ram. His head was broad, with sharp, small ears; the horns had wide and flattened bases and lay flat on the head, to run down back of the eyes, then curve forward to a sharp point. Like the bison, the musk ox had short, heavy limbs, covered with very long hair, and small, hard hoofs with hairy tufts inside the curve of bone, which probably served as pads or checks to hold the hoof firm on ice. His legs seemed out of proportion to his body.

Two musk-oxen were loaded on a sled and hauled to camp in one trip. Skinning them was but short work for such expert hands. All the choice cuts of meat were saved. No time was lost in broiling a steak, which they found sweet and juicy, with a flavor of musk that was disagreeable.

"Now, Rea, for the calves," exclaimed Jones, "And then we're homeward bound."

"I hate to tell this redskin," replied Rea. "He'll be like the others. But it ain't likely he'd desert us here. He's far from his base, with nothin' but thet old musket." Rea then commanded the attention of the brave, and began to mangle the Great Slave and Yellow Knife languages. Of this mixture Jones knew but few words. "Ageter nechila," which Rea kept repeating, he knew, however, meant "musk-oxen little."

The guide stared, suddenly appeared to get Rea's meaning, then vigorously shook his head and gazed at Jones in fear and horror. Following this came an action as singular as inexplicable. Slowly rising, he faced the north, lifted his hand, and remained statuesque in his immobility. Then he began deliberately packing his blankets and traps on his sled, which had not been unhitched from the train of dogs.

"Jackoway ditchen hula," he said, and pointed south.

"Jackoway ditchen hula," echoed Rea. "The damned Indian says 'wife sticks none.' He's goin' to quit us. What do you think of thet? His wife's out of wood. Jackoway out of wood, an' here we are two days from the Arctic Ocean. Jones, the damned heathen don't go back!"

The trapper coolly cocked his rifle. The savage, who plainly saw and understood the action, never flinched. He turned his breast to Rea, and there was nothing in his demeanor to suggest his relation to a craven tribe.

"Good heavens, Rea, don't kill him!" exclaimed Jones, knocking up the leveled rifle.

"Why not, I'd like to know?" demanded Rea, as if he were considering the fate of a threatening beast. "I reckon it'd be a bad thing for us to let him go."

"Let him go," said Jones. "We are here on the ground. We have dogs and meat. We'll get our calves and reach the lake as soon as he does, and we might get there before."

"Mebbe we will," growled Rea.

No vacillation attended the Indian's mood. From friendly guide, he had suddenly been transformed into a dark, sullen savage. He refused the musk-ox meat offered by Jones, and he pointed south and looked at the white hunters as if he asked them to go with him. Both men shook their heads in answer. The savage struck his breast a sounding blow and with his index finger pointed at the white of the north, he shouted dramatically: "Naza! Naza! Naza!"

He then leaped upon his sled, lashed his dogs into a run, and without looking back disappeared over a ridge.

The musk-ox hunters sat long silent. Finally Rea shook his shaggy locks and roared. "Ho! Ho! Jackoway out of wood! Jackoway out of wood! Jackoway out of wood!"

On the day following the desertion, Jones found tracks to the north of the camp, making a broad trail in which were numerous little imprints that sent him flying back to get Rea and the dogs. Muskoxen in great numbers had passed in the night, and Jones and Rea had not trailed the herd a mile before they had it in sight. When the dogs burst into full cry, the musk-oxen climbed a high knoll and squared about to give battle.

"Calves! Calves! Calves!" cried Jones.

"Hold back! Hold back! Thet's a big herd, an' they'll show fight."

As good fortune would have it, the herd split up into several sections, and one part, hard pressed by the dogs, ran down the knoll, to be cornered under the lee of a bank. The hunters, seeing this small number, hurried upon them to find three cows and five badly frightened little calves backed against the bank of snow, with small red eyes fastened on the barking, snapping dogs.

To a man of Jones's experience and skill, the capturing of the calves was a ridiculously easy piece of work. The cows tossed their heads, watched the dogs, and forgot their young. The first cast of the lasso settled over the neck of a little fellow. Jones hauled him out over the slippery snow and laughed as he bound the hairy legs. In less time than he had taken to capture one buffalo calf, with half the escort, he had all the little musk-oxen bound fast. Then he signaled this feat by pealing out an Indian yell of victory.

"Buff, we've got 'em," cried Rea; "An' now for the hell of it gettin' 'em home. I'll fetch the sleds. You might as well down thet best cow for me. I can use another skin."

Of all Jones's prizes of captured wild beasts—which numbered nearly every species common to western North America—he took greatest pride in the little musk-oxen. In truth, so great had been his passion to capture some of these rare and inaccessible mammals, that he considered the day's world the fulfillment of his life's purpose. He was happy. Never had he been so delighted as when, the very evening of their captivity, the musk-oxen, evincing no particular fear of him, began to dig with sharp hoofs into the snow for moss. And they found moss, and ate it, which solved Jones's greatest problem. He had hardly dared to think how to feed them, and here they were picking sustenance out of the frozen snow.

"Rea, will you look at that! Rea, will you look at that!" he kept repeating. "See, they're hunting, feed."

And the giant, with his rare smile, watched him play with the calves. They were about two and a half feet high, and resembled long-haired sheep. The ears and horns were undiscernible, and their color considerably lighter than that of the matured beasts.

"No sense of fear of man," said the life-student of animals. "But they shrink from the dogs."

In packing for the journey south, the captives were strapped on the sleds. This circumstance necessitated a sacrifice of meat and wood, which brought grave, doubtful shakes of Rea's great head.

Days of hastening over the icy snow, with short hours for sleep and rest, passed before the hunters awoke to the consciousness that they were lost. The meat they had packed had gone to feed themselves and the dogs. Only a few sticks of wood were left.

"Better kill a calf, an' cook meat while we've got little wood left," suggested Rea.

"Kill one of my calves? I'd starve first!" cried Jones.

The hungry giant said no more.

They headed southwest. All about them glared the grim monotony of the arctics. No rock or bush or tree made a welcome mark upon the hoary plain Wonderland of frost, white marble desert, infinitude of gleaming silences!

Snow began to fall, making the dogs flounder, obliterating the sun by which they traveled. They camped to wait for clearing weather. Biscuits soaked in tea made their meal. At dawn Jones crawled out of the tepee. The snow had ceased. But where were the dogs? He yelled in alarm. Then little mounds of white, scattered here and there became animated, heaved, rocked and rose to dogs. Blankets of snow had been their covering.

Rea had ceased his "Jackoway out of wood," for a reiterated question: "Where are the wolves?"

"Lost," replied Jones in hollow humor.

Near the close of that day, in which they had resumed travel, from the crest of a ridge they descried a long, low, undulating dark line. It proved to be the forest of "Little sticks," where, with grateful assurance of fire and of soon finding their old trail, they made camp.

"We've four biscuits left, an' enough tea for one drink each," said Rea. "I calculate we're two hundred miles from Great Slave Lake. Where are the wolves?"

At that moment the night wind wafted through the forest a long, haunting mourn. The calves shifted uneasily; the dogs raised sharp noses to sniff the air, and Rea, settling back against a tree, cried out: "Ho! Ho!" Again the savage sound, a keen wailing note with the hunger of the northland in it, broke the cold silence. "You'll see a pack of real wolves in a minute," said Rea. Soon a swift pattering of feet down a forest slope brought him to his feet with a curse to reach a brawny hand for his rifle. White streaks crossed the black of the tree trunks; then indistinct forms, the color of snow, swept up, spread out and streaked to and fro. Jones thought the great, gaunt, pure white beasts the spectral wolves of Rea's fancy, for they were silent, and silent wolves must belong to dreams only.

"Ho! Ho!" yelled Rea. "There's green-fire eyes for you, Buff. Hell itself ain't nothin' to these white devils. Get the calves in the tepee, an' stand ready to loose the dogs, for we've got to fight."

Raising his rifle he opened fire upon the white foe. A struggling, rustling sound followed the shots. But whether it was the threshing about of wolves dying in agony, or the fighting of the fortunate ones over those shot, could not be ascertained in the confusion.

Following his example Jones also fired rapidly on the other side of the tepee. The same inarticulate, silently rustling wrestle succeeded this volley.

"Wait!" cried Rea. "Be sparin' of cartridges."

The dogs strained at their chains and bravely bayed the wolves. The hunters heaped logs and brush on the fire, which, blazing up, sent a bright light far into the woods. On the outer edge of that circle moved the white, restless, gliding forms.

"They're more afraid of fire than of us," said Jones.

So it proved. When the fire burned and crackled they kept well in the background. The hunters had a long respite from serious anxiety, during which time they collected all the available wood at hand. But at midnight, when this had been mostly consumed, the wolves grew bold again.

CHAPTER 10. SUCCESS AND FAILURE

"Have you any shots left for the 45-90, besides what's in the magazine?" asked Rea.

"Yes, a good handful."

"Well, get busy."

With careful aim Jones emptied the magazine into the gray, gliding, groping mass. The same rustling, shuffling, almost silent strife ensued.

"Rea, there's something uncanny about those brutes. A silent pack of wolves!"

"Ho! Ho!" rolled the giant's answer through the woods.

For the present the attack appeared to have been effectually checked. The hunters, sparingly adding a little of their fast diminishing pile of fuel to the fire, decided to lie down for much needed rest, but not for sleep. How long they lay there, cramped by the calves, listening for stealthy steps, neither could tell; it might have been moments and it might have been hours. All at once came a rapid rush of pattering feet, succeeded by a chorus of angry barks, then a terrible commingling of savage snarls, growls, snaps and yelps.

"Out!" yelled Rea. "They're on the dogs!"

Jones pushed his cocked rifle ahead of him and straightened up outside the tepee. A wolf, large as a panther and white as the gleaming snow, sprang at him. Even as he discharged his rifle, right against the breast of the beast, he saw its dripping jaws, its wicked green eyes, like spurts of fire and felt its hot breath. It fell at his feet and writhed in the death struggle. Slender bodies of black and white, whirling and tussling together, sent out fiendish uproar. Rea threw a blazing stick of wood among them, which sizzled as it met the furry coats, and brandishing another he ran into the thick of the fight. Unable to stand the proximity of fire, the wolves bolted and loped off into the woods.

"What a huge brute!" exclaimed Jones, dragging the one he had shot into the light. It was a superb animal, thin, supple, strong, with a coat of frosty fur, very long and fine. Rea began at once to skin it, remarking that he hoped to find other pelts in the morning.

Though the wolves remained in the vicinity of camp, none ventured near. The dogs moaned and whined; their restlessness increased as dawn approached, and when the gray light came, Jones founds that some of them had been badly lacerated by the fangs of the wolves. Rea hunted for dead wolves and found not so much as a piece of white fur.

Soon the hunters were speeding southward. Other than a disposition to fight among themselves, the dogs showed no evil effects of the attack. They were lashed to their best speed, for Rea said the white rangers of the north would never quit their trail. All day the men listened for the wild, lonesome, haunting mourn. But it came not.

A wonderful halo of white and gold, that Rea called a sun-dog, hung in the sky all afternoon, and dazzlingly bright over the dazzling world of snow circled and glowed a mocking sun, brother of the desert mirage, beautiful illusion, smiling cold out of the polar blue.

The first pale evening star twinkled in the east when the hunters made camp on the shore of Artilery Lake. At dusk the clear, silent air opened to the sound of a long, haunting mourn.

"Ho! Ho!" called Rea. His hoarse, deep voice rang defiance to the foe.

While he built a fire before the tepee, Jones strode up and down, suddenly to whip out his knife and make for the tame little musk-oxen, now digging the snow. Then he wheeled abruptly and held out the blade to Rea.

"What for?" demanded the giant.

"We've got to eat," said Jones. "And I can't kill one of them. I can't, so you do it."

"Kill one of our calves?" roared Rea. "Not till hell freezes over! I ain't commenced to get hungry. Besides, the wolves are going to eat us, calves and all."

Nothing more was said. They ate their last biscuit. Jones packed the calves away in the tepee, and turned to the dogs. All day they had worried him; something was amiss with them, and even as he went among them a fierce fight broke out. Jones saw it was unusual, for the attacked dogs showed craven fear, and the attacking ones a howling, savage intensity that surprised him. Then one of the vicious brutes rolled his eyes, frothed at the mouth, shuddered and leaped in his harness, vented a hoarse howl and fell back shaking and retching.

"My God! Rea!" cried Jones in horror. "Come here! Look! That dog is dying of rabies! Hydrophobia! The white wolves have hydrophobia!"

"If you ain't right!" exclaimed Rea. "I seen a dog die of thet onct, an' he acted like this. An' thet one ain't all. Look, Buff! look at them green eyes! Didn't I say the white wolves was hell? We'll have to kill every dog we've got."

Jones shot the dog, and soon afterward three more that manifested signs of the disease. It was an awful situation. To kill all the dogs meant simply to sacrifice his life and Rea's; it meant abandoning hope of ever reaching the cabin. Then to risk being bitten by one of the poisoned, maddened brutes, to risk the most horrible of agonizing deaths—that was even worse.

"Rea, we've one chance," cried Jones, with pale face. "Can you hold the dogs, one by one, while muzzle them?"

"Ho! Ho!" replied the giant. Placing his bowie knife between his teeth, with gloved hands he seized and dragged one of the dogs to the campfire. The animal whined and protested, but showed no ill spirit. Jones muzzled his jaws tightly with strong cords. Another and another were tied up, then one which tried to snap at Jones was nearly crushed by the giant's grip. The last, a surly brute, broke out into mad ravings the moment he felt the touch of Jones's hands, and writhing, frothing, he snapped Jones's sleeve. Rea jerked him loose and held him in the air with one arm, while with the other he swung the bowie. They hauled the dead dogs out on the snow, and returning to the fire sat down to await the cry they expected.

Presently, as darkness fastened down tight, it came—the same cry, wild, haunting, mourning. But for hours it was not repeated.

"Better rest some," said Rea; "I'll call you if they come."

Jones dropped to sleep as he touched his blankets. Morning dawned for him, to find the great, dark, shadowy figure of the giant nodding over the fire.

"How's this? Why didn't you call me?" demanded Jones.

"The wolves only fought a little over the dead dogs."

On the instant Jones saw a wolf skulking up the bank. Throwing up his rifle, which he had carried out of the tepee, he took a snap-shot at the beast. It ran off on three legs, to go out of sight over the hank. Jones scrambled up the steep, slippery place, and upon arriving at the ridge, which took several moments of hard work, he looked everywhere for the wolf. In a moment he saw the animal, standing still some hundred or more paces down a hollow. With the quick report of Jones's second shot, the wolf fell and rolled over. The hunter ran to the spot to find the wolf was dead. Taking hold of a front paw, he dragged the animal over the snow to camp. Rea began to skin the animal, when suddenly he exclaimed:

"This fellow's hind foot is gone!"

"That's strange. I saw it hanging by the skin as the wolf ran up the bank. I'll look for it."

By the bloody trail on the snow he returned to the place where the wolf had fallen, and thence back to the spot where its leg had been broken by the bullet. He discovered no sign of the foot.

"Didn't find it, did you?" said Rea.

"No, and it appears odd to me. The snow is so hard the foot could not have sunk."

"Well, the wolf ate his foot, thet's what," returned Rea. "Look at them teeth marks!"

"Is it possible?" Jones stared at the leg Rea held up.

"Yes, it is. These wolves are crazy at times. You've seen thet. An' the smell of blood, an' nothin' else, mind you, in my opinion, made him eat his own' foot. We'll cut him open."

Impossible as the thing seemed to Jones—and he could not but believe further evidence of his own' eyes—it was even stranger to drive a train of mad dogs. Yet that was what Rea and he did, and lashed them, beat them to cover many miles in the long day's journey. Rabies had broken out in several dogs so alarmingly that Jones had to kill them at the end of the run. And hardly had the sound of the shots died when faint and far away, but clear as a bell, bayed on the wind the same haunting mourn of a trailing wolf.

"Ho! Ho! where are the wolves?" cried Rea.

A waiting, watching, sleepless night followed. Again the hunters faced the south. Hour after hour, riding, running, walking, they urged the poor, jaded, poisoned dogs. At dark they reached the head of Artillery Lake. Rea placed the tepee between two huge stones. Then the hungry hunters, tired, grim, silent, desperate, awaited the familiar cry.

It came on the cold wind, the same haunting mourn, dreadful in its significance.

Absence of fire inspirited the wary wolves. Out of the pale gloom gaunt white forms emerged, agile and stealthy, slipping on velvet-padded feet, closer, closer, closer. The dogs wailed in terror.

"Into the tepee!" yelled Rea.

Jones plunged in after his comrade. The despairing howls of the dogs, drowned in more savage, frightful sounds, knelled one tragedy and foreboded a more terrible one. Jones looked out to see a white mass, like leaping waves of a rapid.

"Pump lead into thet!" cried Rea.

Rapidly Jones emptied his rifle into the white fray. The mass split; gaunt wolves leaped high to fall back dead; others wriggled and limped away; others dragged their hind quarters; others darted at the tepee.

"No more cartridges!" yelled Jones.

The giant grabbed the ax, and barred the door of the tepee. Crash! the heavy iron cleaved the skull of the first brute. Crash! it lamed the second. Then Rea stood in the narrow passage between the rocks, waiting with uplifted ax. A shaggy, white demon, snapping his jaws, sprang like a dog. A sodden, thudding blow met him and he slunk away without a cry. Another rabid beast launched his white body at the giant. Like a flash the ax descended. In agony the wolf fell, to spin round and round, running on his hind legs, while his head and shoulders and forelegs remained in the snow. His back was broken.

Jones crouched in the opening of the tepee, knife in hand. He doubted his senses. This was a nightmare. He saw two wolves leap at once. He heard the crash of the ax; he saw one wolf go down and the other slip under the swinging weapon to grasp the giant's hip. Jones's heard the rend of cloth, and then he pounced like a cat, to drive his knife into the body of the beast. Another nimble foe lunged at Rea, to sprawl broken and limp from the iron. It was a silent fight. The giant shut the way to his comrade and the calves; he made no outcry; he needed but one blow for every beast; magnificent, he wielded death and faced it—silent. He brought the white wild dogs of the north down with lightning blows, and when no more sprang to the attack, down on the frigid silence he rolled his cry: "Ho! Ho!"

"Rea! Rea! how is it with you?" called Jones, climbing out.

"A torn coat—no more, my lad."

Three of the poor dogs were dead; the fourth and last gasped at the hunters and died.

The wintry night became a thing of half-conscious past, a dream to the hunters, manifesting its reality only by the stark, stiff bodies of wolves, white in the gray morning.

"If we can eat, we'll make the cabin," said Rea. "But the dogs an' wolves are poison."

"Shall I kill a calf?" asked Jones.

"Ho! Ho! when hell freezes over—if we must!"

CHAPTER 10. SUCCESS AND FAILURE

Jones found one 45-90 cartridge in all the outfit, and with that in the chamber of his rifle, once more struck south. Spruce trees began to show on the barrens and caribou trails roused hope in the hearts of the hunters.

"Look in the spruces," whispered Jones, dropping the rope of his sled. Among the black trees gray objects moved.

"Caribou!" said Rea. "Hurry! Shoot! Don't miss!"

But Jones waited. He knew the value of the last bullet. He had a hunter's patience. When the caribou came out in an open space, Jones whistled. It was then the rifle grew set and fixed; it was then the red fire belched forth.

At four hundred yards the bullet took some fraction of time to strike. What a long time that was! Then both hunters heard the spiteful spat of the lead. The caribou fell, jumped up, ran down the slope, and fell again to rise no more.

An hour of rest, with fire and meat, changed the world to the hunters; still glistening, it yet had lost its bitter cold its deathlike clutch.

"What's this?" cried Jones.

Moccasin tracks of different sizes, all toeing north, arrested the hunters.

"Pointed north! Wonder what thet means?" Rea plodded on, doubtfully shaking his head.

Night again, clear, cold, silver, starlit, silent night! The hunters rested, listening ever for the haunting mourn. Day again, white, passionless, monotonous, silent day. The hunters traveled on—on—on, ever listening for the haunting mourn.

Another dusk found them within thirty miles of their cabin. Only one more day now.

Rea talked of his furs, of the splendid white furs he could not bring. Jones talked of his little muskoxen calves and joyfully watched them dig for moss in the snow.

Vigilance relaxed that night. Outworn nature rebelled, and both hunters slept.

Rea awoke first, and kicking off the blankets, went out. His terrible roar of rage made Jones fly to his side.

Under the very shadow of the tepee, where the little musk-oxen had been tethered, they lay stretched out pathetically on crimson snow—stiff stone-cold, dead. Moccasin tracks told the story of the tragedy.

Jones leaned against his comrade.

The giant raised his huge fist.

"Jackoway out of wood! Jackoway out of wood!"

Then he choked.

The north wind, blowing through the thin, dark, weird spruce trees, moaned and seemed to sigh, "Naza! Naza! Naza!"

CHAPTER 11. ON TO THE SIWASH

"Who all was doin' the talkin' last night?" asked Frank next morning, when we were having a late breakfast. "Cause I've a joke on somebody. Jim he talks in his sleep often, an' last night after you did finally get settled down, Jim he up in his sleep an' says: 'Shore he's windy as hell! Shore he's windy as hell'!"

At this cruel exposure of his subjective wanderings, Jim showed extreme humiliation; but Frank's eyes fairly snapped with the fun he got out of telling it. The genial foreman loved a joke. The week's stay at Oak, in which we all became thoroughly acquainted, had presented Jim as always the same quiet character, easy, slow, silent, lovable. In his brother cowboy, however, we had discovered in addition to his fine, frank, friendly spirit, an overwhelming fondness for playing tricks. This boyish mischievousness, distinctly Arizonian, reached its acme whenever it tended in the direction of our serious leader.

Lawson had been dispatched on some mysterious errand about which my curiosity was all in vain. The order of the day was leisurely to get in readiness, and pack for our journey to the Siwash on the morrow. I watered my horse, played with the hounds, knocked about the cliffs, returned to the cabin, and lay down on my bed. Jim's hands were white with flour. He was kneading dough, and had several low, flat pans on the table. Wallace and Jones strolled in, and later Frank, and they all took various positions before the fire. I saw Frank, with the quickness of a sleight-of-hand performer, slip one of the pans of dough on the chair Jones had placed by the table. Jim did not see the action; Jones's and Wallace's backs were turned to Frank, and he did not know I was in the cabin. The conversation continued on the subject of Jones's big bay horse, which, hobbles and all, had gotten ten miles from camp the night before.

"Better count his ribs than his tracks," said Frank, and went on talking as easily and naturally as if he had not been expecting a very entertaining situation.

But no one could ever foretell Colonel Jones's actions. He showed every intention of seating himself in the chair, then walked over to his pack to begin searching for something or other. Wallace, however, promptly took the seat; and what began to be funnier than strange, he did not get up. Not unlikely this circumstance was owing to the fact that several of the rude chairs had soft layers of old blanket tacked on them. Whatever were Frank's internal emotions, he presented a remarkably placid and commonplace exterior; but when Jim began to search for the missing pan of dough, the joker slowly sagged in his chair.

"Shore that beats hell!" said Jim. "I had three pans of dough. Could the pup have taken one?"

Wallace rose to his feet, and the bread pan clattered to the floor, with a clang and a clank, evidently protesting against the indignity it had suffered. But the dough stayed with Wallace, a great white conspicuous splotch on his corduroys. Jim, Frank and Jones all saw it at once.

"Why—Mr. Wal—lace—you set—in the dough!" exclaimed Frank, in a queer, strangled voice. Then he exploded, while Jim fell over the table.

It seemed that those two Arizona rangers, matured men though they were, would die of convulsions. I laughed with them, and so did Wallace, while he brought his one-handled bowie knife into novel use. Buffalo Jones never cracked a smile, though he did remark about the waste of good flour.

Frank's face was a study for a psychologist when Jim actually apologized to Wallace for being so careless with his pans. I did not betray Frank, but I resolved to keep a still closer watch on him. It was partially because of this uneasy sense of his trickiness in the fringe of my mind that I made a discovery. My sleeping-bag rested on a raised platform in one corner, and at a favorable moment I examined the bag. It had not been tampered with, but I noticed a string turning out through a chink between the logs. I found it came from a thick layer of straw under my bed, and had been tied to the end of a flatly coiled lasso. Leaving the thing as it was, I went outside and carelessly chased the hounds round the cabin. The string stretched along the logs to another chink, where it returned into the cabin at a point near where Frank slept. No great power of deduction was necessary to acquaint me with full details of the plot to spoil my slumbers. So I patiently awaited developments.

Lawson rode in near sundown with the carcasses of two beasts of some species hanging over his saddle. It turned out that Jones had planned a surprise for Wallace and me, and it could hardly have been a more enjoyable one, considering the time and place. We knew he had a flock of Persian sheep on the south slope of Buckskin, but had no idea it was within striking distance of Oak. Lawson had that day hunted up the shepherd and his sheep, to return to us with two sixty-pound Persian lambs. We feasted at suppertime on meat which was sweet, juicy, very tender and of as rare a flavor as that of the Rocky Mountain sheep.

My state after supper was one of huge enjoyment and with intense interest I awaited Frank's first spar for an opening. It came presently, in a lull of the conversation.

"Saw a big rattler run under the cabin to-day," he said, as if he were speaking of one of Old Baldy's shoes. "I tried to get a whack at him, but he oozed away too quick."

"Shore I seen him often," put in Jim. Good, old, honest Jim, led away by his trickster comrade! It was very plain. So I was to be frightened by snakes.

"These old canyon beds are ideal dens for rattle snakes," chimed in my scientific California friend. "I have found several dens, but did not molest them as this is a particularly dangerous time of the year to meddle with the reptiles. Quite likely there's a den under the cabin."

While he made this remarkable statement, he had the grace to hide his face in a huge puff of smoke. He, too, was in the plot. I waited for Jones to come out with some ridiculous theory or fact concerning the particular species of snake, but as he did not speak, I concluded they had wisely left him out of the secret. After mentally debating a moment, I decided, as it was a very harmless joke, to help Frank into the fulfillment of his enjoyment.

"Rattlesnakes!" I exclaimed. "Heavens! I'd die if I heard one, let alone seeing it. A big rattler jumped at me one day, and I've never recovered from the shock."

Plainly, Frank was delighted to hear of my antipathy and my unfortunate experience, and he proceeded to expatiate on the viciousness of rattlesnakes, particularly those of Arizona. If I had believed the succeeding stories, emanating from the fertile brains of those three fellows, I should have made certain that Arizona canyons were Brazilian jungles. Frank's parting shot, sent in a mellow, kind voice, was the best point in the whole trick. "Now, I'd be nervous if I had a sleepin' bag like yours, because it's just the place for a rattler to ooze into."

In the confusion and dim light of bedtime I contrived to throw the end of my lasso over the horn of a saddle hanging on the wall, with the intention of augmenting the noise I soon expected to create; and I placed my automatic rifle and .38 S. and W. Special within easy reach of my hand. Then I crawled into my bag and composed myself to listen. Frank soon began to snore, so brazenly, so fictitiously, that I wondered at the man's absorbed intensity in his joke; and I was at great pains to smother in my breast a violent burst of riotous merriment. Jones's snores, however, were real enough, and this made me enjoy the situation all the more; because if he did not show a mild surprise when the catastrophe fell, I would greatly miss my guess. I knew the three wily conspirators were wide-awake. Suddenly I felt a movement in the straw under me and a faint rustling. It was so soft, so sinuous, that if I had not known it was the lasso, I would assuredly have been frightened. I gave a little jump, such as one will make quickly in bed. Then the coil ran out from under the straw. How subtly suggestive of a snake! I made a slight outcry, a big jump, paused a moment for effectiveness in which time Frank forgot to snore—then let out a tremendous yell, grabbed my guns, sent twelve thundering shots through the roof and pulled my lasso.

Crash! the saddle came down, to be followed by sounds not on Frank's programme and certainly not calculated upon by me. But they were all the more effective. I gathered that Lawson, who was not in the secret, and who was a nightmare sort of sleeper anyway, had knocked over Jim's table, with its array of pots and pans and then, unfortunately for Jones had kicked that innocent person in the stomach.

CHAPTER 11. ON TO THE SIWASH

As I lay there in my bag, the very happiest fellow in the wide world, the sound of my mirth was as the buzz of the wings of a fly to the mighty storm. Roar on roar filled the cabin.

When the three hypocrites recovered sufficiently from the startling climax to calm Lawson, who swore the cabin had been attacked by Indians; when Jones stopped roaring long enough to hear it was only a harmless snake that had caused the trouble, we hushed to repose once more—not, however, without hearing some trenchant remarks from the boiling Colonel anent fun and fools, and the indubitable fact that there was not a rattlesnake on Buckskin Mountain.

Long after this explosion had died away, I heard, or rather felt, a mysterious shudder or tremor of the cabin, and I knew that Frank and Jim were shaking with silent laughter. On my own score, I determined to find if Jones, in his strange make-up, had any sense of humor, or interest in life, or feeling, or love that did not center and hinge on four-footed beasts. In view of the rude awakening from what, no doubt, were pleasant dreams of wonderful white and green animals, combining the intelligence of man and strength of brutes—a new species creditable to his genius—I was perhaps unjust in my conviction as to his lack of humor. And as to the other question, whether or not he had any real human feeling for the creatures built in his own image, that was decided very soon and unexpectedly.

The following morning, as soon as Lawson got in with the horses, we packed and started. Rather sorry was I to bid good-by to Oak Spring. Taking the back trail of the Stewarts, we walked the horses all day up a slowly narrowing, ascending canyon. The hounds crossed coyote and deer trails continually, but made no break. Sounder looked up as if to say he associated painful reminiscences with certain kinds of tracks. At the head of the canyon we reached timber at about the time dusk gathered, and we located for the night. Being once again nearly nine thousand feet high, we found the air bitterly cold, making a blazing fire most acceptable.

In the haste to get supper we all took a hand, and some one threw upon our tarpaulin tablecloth a tin cup of butter mixed with carbolic acid—a concoction Jones had used to bathe the sore feet of the dogs. Of course I got hold of this, spread a generous portion on my hot biscuit, placed some red-hot beans on that, and began to eat like a hungry hunter. At first I thought I was only burned. Then I recognized the taste and burn of the acid and knew something was wrong. Picking up the tin, I examined it, smelled the pungent odor and felt a queer numb sense of fear. This lasted only for a moment, as I well knew the use and power of the acid, and had not swallowed enough to hurt me. I was about to make known my mistake in a matter-of-fact way, when it flashed over me the accident could be made to serve a turn.

"Jones!" I cried hoarsely. "What's in this butter?"

"Lord! you haven't eaten any of that. Why, I put carbolic acid in it."

"Oh—oh—oh—I'm poisoned! I ate nearly all of it! Oh—I'm burning up! I'm dying!" With that I began to moan and rock to and fro and hold my stomach.

Consternation preceded shock. But in the excitement of the moment, Wallace—who, though badly scared, retained his wits made for me with a can of condensed milk. He threw me back with no gentle hand, and was squeezing the life out of me to make me open my mouth, when I gave him a jab in his side. I imagined his surprise, as this peculiar reception of his first-aid-to-the-injured made him hold off to take a look at me, and in this interval I contrived to whisper to him: "Joke! Joke! you idiot! I'm only shamming. I want to see if I can scare Jones and get even with Frank. Help me out! Cry! Get tragic!"

From that moment I shall always believe that the stage lost a great tragedian in Wallace. With a magnificent gesture he threw the can of condensed milk at Jones, who was so stunned he did not try to dodge. "Thoughtless man! Murderer! it's too late!" cried Wallace, laying me back across his knees. "It's too late. His teeth are locked. He's far gone. Poor boy! poor boy! Who's to tell his mother?"

I could see from under my hat-brim that the solemn, hollow voice had penetrated the cold exterior of the plainsman. He could not speak; he clasped and unclasped his big hands in helpless fashion. Frank was as white as a sheet. This was simply delightful to me. But the expression of miserable, impotent distress on old Jim's sun-browned face was more than I could stand, and I could no longer keep up the deception. Just as Wallace cried out to Jones to pray—I wished then I had not weakened so soon—I got up and walked to the fire.

"Jim, I'll have another biscuit, please."

His under jaw dropped, then he nervously shoveled biscuits at me. Jones grabbed my hand and cried out with a voice that was new to me: "You can eat? You're better? You'll get over it?"

"Sure. Why, carbolic acid never phases me. I've often used it for rattlesnake bites. I did not tell you, but that rattler at the cabin last night actually bit me, and I used carbolic to cure the poison."

Frank mumbled something about horses, and faded into the gloom. As for Jones, he looked at me rather incredulously, and the absolute, almost childish gladness he manifested because I had been snatched from the grave, made me regret my deceit, and satisfied me forever on one score.

On awakening in the morning I found frost half an inch thick covered my sleeping-bag, whitened the ground, and made the beautiful silver spruce trees silver in hue as well as in name.

We were getting ready for an early start, when two riders, with pack-horses jogging after them, came down the trail from the direction of Oak Spring. They proved to be Jeff Clarke, the wild-horse wrangler mentioned by the Stewarts, and his helper. They were on the way into the breaks for a string of pintos. Clarke was a short, heavily bearded man, of jovial aspect. He said he had met the Stewarts going into Fredonia, and being advised of our destination, had hurried to come up with us. As we did not know, except in a general way, where we were making for, the meeting was a fortunate event.

Our camping site had been close to the divide made by one of the long, wooded ridges sent off by Buckskin Mountain, and soon we were descending again.

CHAPTER 11. ON TO THE SIWASH

We rode half a mile down a timbered slope, and then out into a beautiful, flat forest of gigantic pines. Clarke informed us it was a level bench some ten miles long, running out from the slopes of Buckskin to face the Grand Canyon on the south, and the 'breaks of the Siwash on the west. For two hours we rode between the stately lines of trees, and the hoofs of the horses gave forth no sound. A long, silvery grass, sprinkled with smiling bluebells, covered the ground, except close under the pines, where soft red mats invited lounging and rest. We saw numerous deer, great gray mule deer, almost as large as elk. Jones said they had been crossed with elk once, which accounted for their size. I did not see a stump, or a burned tree, or a windfall during the ride.

Clarke led us to the rim of the canyon. Without any preparation—for the giant trees hid the open sky—we rode right out to the edge of the tremendous chasm. At first I did not seem to think; my faculties were benumbed; only the pure sensorial instinct of the savage who sees, but does not feel, made me take note of the abyss. Not one of our party had ever seen the canyon from this side, and not one of us said a word. But Clarke kept talking.

"Wild place this is hyar," he said. "Seldom any one but horse wranglers gits over this far. I've hed a bunch of wild pintos down in a canyon below fer two years. I reckon you can't find no better place fer camp than right hyar. Listen. Do you hear thet rumble? Thet's Thunder Falls. You can only see it from one place, an' thet far off, but thar's brooks you can git at to water the hosses. Fer thet matter, you can ride up the slopes an' git snow. If you can git snow close, it'd be better, fer thet's an all-fired bad trail down fer water."

"Is this the cougar country the Stewarts talked about?" asked Jones.

"Reckon it is. Cougars is as thick in hyar as rabbits in a spring-hole canyon. I'm on the way now to bring up my pintos. The cougars hev cost me hundreds I might say thousands of dollars. I lose hosses all the time; an' damn me, gentlemen, I've never raised a colt. This is the greatest cougar country in the West. Look at those yellow crags! Thar's where the cougars stay. No one ever hunted 'em. It seems to me they can't be hunted. Deer and wild hosses by the thousand browse hyar on the mountain in summer, an' down in the breaks in winter. The cougars live fat. You'll find deer and wild-hoss carcasses all over this country. You'll find lions' dens full of bones. You'll find warm deer left for the coyotes. But whether you'll find the cougars, I can't say. I fetched dogs in hyar, an' tried to ketch Old Tom. I've put them on his trail an' never saw hide nor hair of them again. Jones, it's no easy huntin' hyar."

"Well, I can see that," replied our leader. "I never hunted lions in such a country, and never knew any one who had. We'll have to learn how. We've the time and the dogs, all we need is the stuff in us."

"I hope you fellars git some cougars, an' I believe you will. Whatever you do, kill Old Tom."

"We'll catch him alive. We're not on a hunt to kill cougars," said Jones.

"What!" exclaimed Clarke, looking from Jones to us. His rugged face wore a half-smile.

"Jones ropes cougars, an' ties them up," replied Frank.

"I'm — — if he'll ever rope Old Tom," burst out Clarke, ejecting a huge quid of tobacco. "Why, man alive! it'd be the death of you to git near thet old villain. I never seen him, but I've seen his tracks fer five years. They're larger than any hoss tracks you ever seen. He'll weigh over three hundred, thet old cougar. Hyar, take a look at my man's hoss. Look at his back. See them marks? Wal, Old Tom made them, an' he made them right in camp last fall, when we were down in the canyon."

The mustang to which Clarke called our attention was a sleek cream and white pinto. Upon his side and back were long regular scars, some an inch wide, and bare of hair.

"How on earth did he get rid of the cougar?" asked Jones.

"I don't know. Perhaps he got scared of the dogs. It took thet pinto a year to git well. Old Tom is a real lion. He'll kill a full-grown hoss when he wants, but a yearlin' colt is his especial likin'. You're sure to run acrost his trail, an' you'll never miss it. Wal, if I find any cougar sign down in the canyon, I'll build two fires so as to let you know. Though no hunter, I'm tolerably acquainted with the varmints. The deer an' hosses are rangin' the forest slopes now, an' I think the cougars come up over the rim rock at night an' go back in the mornin'. Anyway, if your dogs can follow the trails, you've got sport, an' more'n sport comin' to you. But take it from me—don't try to rope Old Tom."

After all our disappointments in the beginning of the expedition, our hardship on the desert, our trials with the dogs and horses, it was real pleasure to make permanent camp with wood, water and feed at hand, a soul-stirring, ever-changing picture before us, and the certainty that we were in the wild lairs of the lions—among the Lords of the Crags!

While we were unpacking, every now and then I would straighten up and gaze out beyond. I knew the outlook was magnificent and sublime beyond words, but as yet I had not begun to understand it. The great pine trees, growing to the very edge of the rim, received their full quota of appreciation from me, as did the smooth, flower-decked aisles leading back into the forest.

The location we selected for camp was a large glade, fifty paces or more from the precipice far enough, the cowboys averred, to keep our traps from being sucked down by some of the whirlpool winds, native to the spot. In the center of this glade stood a huge gnarled and blasted old pine, that certainly by virtue of hoary locks and bent shoulders had earned the right to stand aloof from his younger companions. Under this tree we placed all our belongings, and then, as Frank so felicitously expressed it, we were free to "ooze round an' see things."

I believe I had a sort of subconscious, selfish idea that some one would steal the canyon away from me if I did not hurry to make it mine forever; so I sneaked off, and sat under a pine growing on the very rim. At first glance, I saw below me, seemingly miles away, a wild chaos of red and buff mesas rising out of dark purple clefts. Beyond these reared a long, irregular tableland, running south almost to the extent of my vision, which I remembered Clarke had called Powell's Plateau. I remembered, also, that he had said it was twenty miles distant, was almost that many miles long, was connected to the mainland of Buckskin Mountain by a very narrow wooded dip of land called the Saddle, and that it practically shut us out of a view of the Grand Canyon proper. If that was true, what, then, could be the name of the canyon at my feet? Suddenly, as my gaze wandered from point to point, it was attested by a dark, conical mountain, white-tipped, which rose in the notch of the Saddle. What could it mean? Were there such things as canyon mirages? Then the dim purple of its color told of its great distance from me; and then its familiar shape told I had come into my own again—I had found my old friend once more. For in all that plateau there was only one snow-capped mountain—the San Francisco Peak; and there, a hundred and fifty, perhaps two hundred miles away, far beyond the Grand Canyon, it smiled brightly at me, as it had for days and days across the desert.

Hearing Jones yelling for somebody or everybody, I jumped up to find a procession heading for a point farther down the rim wall, where our leader stood waving his arms. The excitement proved to have been caused by cougar signs at the head of the trail where Clarke had started down.

"They're here, boys, they're here," Jones kept repeating, as he showed us different tracks. "This sign is not so old. Boys, to-morrow we'll get up a lion, sure as you're born. And if we do, and Sounder sees him, then we've got a lion-dog! I'm afraid of Don. He has a fine nose; he can run and fight, but he's been trained to deer, and maybe I can't break him. Moze is still uncertain. If old Jude only hadn't been lamed! She would be the best of the lot. But Sounder is our hope. I'm almost ready to swear by him."

All this was too much for me, so I slipped off again to be alone, and this time headed for the forest. Warm patches of sunlight, like gold, brightened the ground; dark patches of sky, like ocean blue, gleamed between the treetops. Hardly a rustle of wind in the fine-toothed green branches disturbed the quiet. When I got fully out of sight of camp, I started to run as if I were a wild Indian. My running had no aim; just sheer mad joy of the grand old forest, the smell of pine, the wild silence and beauty loosed the spirit in me so it had to run, and I ran with it till the physical being failed.

While resting on a fragrant bed of pine needles, endeavoring to regain control over a truant mind, trying to subdue the encroaching of the natural man on the civilized man, I saw gray objects moving under the trees. I lost them, then saw them, and presently so plainly that, with delight on delight, I counted seventeen deer pass through an open arch of dark green. Rising to my feet, I ran to get round a low mound. They saw me and bounded away with prodigiously long leaps. Bringing their forefeet together, stiff-legged under them, they bounced high, like rubber balls, yet they were graceful.

The forest was so open that I could watch them for a long way; and as I circled with my gaze, a glimpse of something white arrested my attention. A light, grayish animal appeared to be tearing at an old stump. Upon nearer view, I recognized a wolf, and he scented or sighted me at the same moment, and loped off into the shadows of the trees. Approaching the spot where I had marked him I found he had been feeding from the carcass of a horse. The remains had been only partly eaten, and were of an animal of the mustang build that had evidently been recently killed. Frightful lacerations under the throat showed where a lion had taken fatal hold. Deep furrows in the ground proved how the mustang had sunk his hoofs, reared and shaken himself. I traced roughly defined tracks fifty paces to the lee of a little bank, from which I concluded the lion had sprung.

I gave free rein to my imagination and saw the forest dark, silent, peopled by none but its savage denizens, The lion crept like a shadow, crouched noiselessly down, then leaped on his sleeping or browsing prey. The lonely night stillness split to a frantic snort and scream of terror, and the stricken mustang with his mortal enemy upon his back, dashed off with fierce, wild love of life. As he went he felt his foe crawl toward his neck on claws of fire; he saw the tawny body and the gleaming eyes; then the cruel teeth snapped with the sudden bite, and the woodland tragedy ended.

On the spot I conceived an antipathy toward lions. It was born of the frightful spectacle of what had once been a glossy, prancing mustang, of the mute, sickening proof of the survival of the fittest, of the law that levels life.

Upon telling my camp-fellows about my discovery, Jones and Wallace walked out to see it, while Jim told me the wolf I had seen was a "lofer," one of the giant buffalo wolves of Buckskin; and if I would watch the carcass in the mornings and evenings, I would "shore as hell get a plunk at him."

White pine burned in a beautiful, clear blue flame, with no smoke; and in the center of the campfire left a golden heart. But Jones would not have any sitting up, and hustled us off to bed, saying we would be "blamed" glad of it in about fifteen hours. I crawled into my sleeping-bag, made a hood of my Navajo blanket, and peeping from under it, watched the fire and the flickering shadows. The blaze burned down rapidly. Then the stars blinked. Arizona stars would be moons in any other State! How serene, peaceful, august, infinite and wonderfully bright! No breeze stirred the pines. The clear tinkle of the cowbells on the hobbled horses rang from near and distant parts of the forest. The prosaic bell of the meadow and the pasture brook, here, in this environment, jingled out different notes, as clear, sweet, musical as silver bells.

CHAPTER 12. OLD TOM

At daybreak our leader routed us out. The frost mantled the ground so heavily that it looked like snow, and the rare atmosphere bit like the breath of winter. The forest stood solemn and gray; the canyon lay wrapped in vapory slumber.

Hot biscuits and coffee, with a chop or two of the delicious Persian lamb meat, put a less Spartan tinge on the morning, and gave Wallace and me more strength—we needed not incentive to leave the fire, hustle our saddles on the horses and get in line with our impatient leader. The hounds scampered over the frost, shoving their noses at the tufts of grass and bluebells. Lawson and Jim remained in camp; the rest of us trooped southwest.

A mile or so in that direction, the forest of pine ended abruptly, and a wide belt of low, scrubby old trees, breast high to a horse, fringed the rim of the canyon and appeared to broaden out and grow wavy southward. The edge of the forest was as dark and regular as if a band of woodchoppers had trimmed it. We threaded our way through this thicket, all peering into the bisecting deer trails for cougar tracks in the dust.

"Bring the dogs! Hurry!" suddenly called Jones from a thicket.

We lost no time complying, and found him standing in a trail, with his eyes on the sand. "Take a look, boys. A good-sized male cougar passed here last night. Hyar, Sounder, Don, Moze, come on!"

It was a nervous, excited pack of hounds. Old Jude got to Jones first, and she sang out; then Sounder opened with his ringing bay, and before Jones could mount, a string of yelping dogs sailed straight for the forest.

"Ooze along, boys!" yelled Frank, wheeling Spot.

With the cowboy leading, we strung into the pines, and I found myself behind. Presently even Wallace disappeared. I almost threw the reins at Satan, and yelled for him to go. The result enlightened me. Like an arrow from a bow, the black shot forward. Frank had told me of his speed, that when he found his stride it was like riding a flying feather to be on him. Jones, fearing he would kill me, had cautioned me always to hold him in, which I had done. Satan stretched out with long graceful motions; he did not turn aside for logs, but cleared them with easy and powerful spring, and he swerved only slightly to the trees. This latter, I saw at once, made the danger for me. It became a matter of saving my legs and dodging branches. The imperative need of this came to me with convincing force. I dodged a branch on one tree, only to be caught square in the middle by a snag on another. Crack! If the snag had not broken, Satan would have gone on riderless, and I would have been left hanging, a pathetic and drooping monition to the risks of the hunt. I kept ducking my head, now and then falling flat over the pommel to avoid a limb that would have brushed me off, and hugging the flanks of my horse with my knees. Soon I was at Wallace's heels, and had Jones in sight. Now and then glimpses of Frank's white horse gleamed through the trees.

We began to circle toward the south, to go up and down shallow hollows, to find the pines thinning out; then we shot out of the forest into the scrubby oak. Riding through this brush was the cruelest kind of work, but Satan kept on close to the sorrel. The hollows began to get deeper, and the ridges between them narrower. No longer could we keep a straight course.

On the crest of one of the ridges we found Jones awaiting us. Jude, Tige and Don lay panting at his feet. Plainly the Colonel appeared vexed.

"Listen," he said, when we reined in.

We complied, but did not hear a sound.

"Frank's beyond there some place," continued Jones, "but I can't see him, nor hear the hounds anymore. Don and Tige split again on deer trails. Old Jude hung on the lion track, but I stopped her here. There's something I can't figure. Moze held a beeline southwest, and he yelled seldom. Sounder gradually stopped baying. Maybe Frank can tell us something."

Jones's long drawn-out signal was answered from the direction he expected, and after a little time, Frank's white horse shone out of the gray-green of a ledge a mile away.

This drew my attention to our position. We were on a high ridge out in the open, and I could see fifty miles of the shaggy slopes of Buckskin. Southward the gray, ragged line seemed to stop suddenly, and beyond it purple haze hung over a void I knew to be the canyon. And facing west, I came, at last, to understand perfectly the meaning of the breaks in the Siwash. They were nothing more than ravines that headed up on the slopes and ran down, getting steeper and steeper, though scarcely wider, to break into the canyon. Knife-crested ridges rolled westward, wave on wave, like the billows of a sea. I appreciated that these breaks were, at their sources, little washes easy to jump across, and at their mouths a mile deep and impassable. Huge pine trees shaded these gullies, to give way to the gray growth of stunted oak, which in turn merged into the dark green of pinyon. A wonderful country for deer and lions, it seemed to me, but impassable, all but impossible for a hunter.

Frank soon appeared, brushing through the bending oaks, and Sounder trotted along behind him.

"Where's Moze?" inquired Jones.

"The last I heard of Moze he was out of the brush, goin' across the pinyon flat, right for the canyon. He had a hot trail."

"Well, we're certain of one thing; if it was a deer, he won't come back soon, and if it was a lion, he'll tree it, lose the scent, and come back. We've got to show the hounds a lion in a tree. They'd run a hot trail, bump into a tree, and then be at fault. What was wrong with Sounder?"

"I don't know. He came back to me."

"We can't trust him, or any of them yet. Still, maybe they're doing better than we know."

The outcome of the chase, so favorably started was a disappointment, which we all felt keenly. After some discussion, we turned south, intending to ride down to the rim wall and follow it back to camp. I happened to turn once, perhaps to look again at the far-distant pink cliffs of Utah, or the wave-like dome of Trumbull Mountain, when I saw Moze trailing close behind me. My yell halted the Colonel.

"Well, I'll be darned!" ejaculated he, as Moze hove in sight. "Come hyar, you rascal!"

He was a tired dog, but had no sheepish air about him, such as he had worn when lagging in from deer chases. He wagged his tail, and flopped down to pant and pant, as if to say: "What's wrong with you guys?"

"Boys, for two cents I'd go back and put Jude on that trail. It's just possible that Moze treed a lion. But—well, I expect there's more likelihood of his chasing the lion over the rim; so we may as well keep on. The strange thing is that Sounder wasn't with Moze. There may have been two lions. You see we are up a tree ourselves. I have known lions to run in pairs, and also a mother keep four two-year-olds with her. But such cases are rare. Here, in this country, though, maybe they run round and have parties."

As we left the breaks behind we got out upon a level pinyon flat. A few cedars grew with the pinyons. Deer runways and trails were thick.

"Boys, look at that," said Jones. "This is great lion country, the best I ever saw."

He pointed to the sunken, red, shapeless remain of two horses, and near them a ghastly scattering of bleached bones. "A lion-lair right here on the flat. Those two horses were killed early this spring, and I see no signs of their carcasses having been covered with brush and dirt. I've got to learn lion lore over again, that's certain."

As we paused at the head of a depression, which appeared to be a gap in the rim wall, filled with massed pinyons and splintered piles of yellow stone, caught Sounder going through some interesting moves. He stopped to smell a bush. Then he lifted his head, and electrified me with a great, deep sounding bay.

"Hi! there, listen to that!" yelled Jones "What's Sounder got? Give him room—don't run him down. Easy now, old dog, easy, easy!"

Sounder suddenly broke down a trail. Moze howled, Don barked, and Tige let out his staccato yelp. They ran through the brush here, there, every where. Then all at once old Jude chimed in with her mellow voice, and Jones tumbled off his horse.

"By the Lord Harry! There's something here."

"Here, Colonel, here's the bush Sounder smelt and there's a sandy trail under it," I called.

"There go Don an' Tige down into the break!" cried Frank. "They've got a hot scent!"

Jones stooped over the place I designated, to jerk up with reddening face, and as he flung himself into the saddle roared out: "After Sounder! Old Tom! Old Tom! Old Tom!"

We all heard Sounder, and at the moment of Jones's discovery, Moze got the scent and plunged ahead of us.

"Hi! Hi! Hi! Hi!" yelled the Colonel. Frank sent Spot forward like a white streak. Sounder called to us in irresistible bays, which Moze answered, and then crippled Jude bayed in baffled impotent distress.

The atmosphere was charged with that lion. As if by magic, the excitation communicated itself to all, and men, horses and dogs acted in accord. The ride through the forest had been a jaunt. This was a steeplechase, a mad, heedless, perilous, glorious race. And we had for a pacemaker a cowboy mounted on a tireless mustang.

Always it seemed to me, while the wind rushed, the brush whipped, I saw Frank far ahead, sitting his saddle as if glued there, holding his reins loosely forward. To see him ride so was a beautiful sight. Jones let out his Comanche yell at every dozen jumps and Wallace sent back a thrilling "Waa-hoo-o!" In the excitement I had again checked my horse, and when Jones remembered, and loosed the bridle, how the noble animal responded! The pace he settled into dazed me; I could hardly distinguish the deer trail down which he was thundering. I lost my comrades ahead; the pinyons blurred in my sight; I only faintly heard the hounds. It occurred to me we were making for the breaks, but I did not think of checking Satan. I thought only of flying on faster and faster.

"On! On! old fellow! Stretch out! Never lose this race! We've got to be there at the finish!" I called to Satan, and he seemed to understand and stretched lower, farther, quicker.

The brush pounded my legs and clutched and tore my clothes; the wind whistled; the pinyon branches cut and whipped my face. Once I dodged to the left, as Satan swerved to the right, with the result that I flew out of the saddle, and crashed into a pinyon tree, which marvelously brushed me back into the saddle. The wild yells and deep bays sounded nearer. Satan tripped and plunged down, throwing me as gracefully as an aerial tumbler wings his flight. I alighted in a bush, without feeling of scratch or pain. As Satan recovered and ran past, I did not seek to make him stop, but getting a good grip on the pommel, I vaulted up again. Once more he raced like a wild mustang. And from nearer and nearer in front pealed the alluring sounds of the chase.

Satan was creeping close to Wallace and Jones, with Frank looming white through the occasional pinyons. Then all dropped out of sight, to appear again suddenly. They had reached the first break. Soon I was upon it. Two deer ran out of the ravine, almost brushing my horse in the haste. Satan went down and up in a few giant strides. Only the narrow ridge separated us from another break. It was up and down then for Satan, a work to which he manfully set himself. Occasionally I saw Wallace and Jones, but heard them oftener. All the time the breaks grew deeper, till finally Satan had to zigzag his way down and up. Discouragement fastened on me, when from the summit of the next ridge I saw Frank far down the break, with Jones and Wallace not a quarter of a mile away from him. I sent out a long, exultant yell as Satan crashed into the hard, dry wash in the bottom of the break.

I knew from the way he quickened under me that he intended to overhaul somebody. Perhaps because of the clear going, or because my frenzy had cooled to a thrilling excitement which permitted detail, I saw clearly and distinctly the speeding horsemen down the ravine. I picked out the smooth pieces of ground ahead, and with the slightest touch of the rein on his neck, guided Satan into them. How he ran! The light, quick beats of his hoofs were regular, pounding. Seeing Jones and Wallace sail high into the air, I knew they had jumped a ditch. Thus prepared, I managed to stick on when it yawned before me; and Satan, never slackening, leaped up and up, giving me a new swing.

Dust began to settle in little clouds before me; Frank, far ahead, had turned his mustang up the side of the break; Wallace, within hailing distance, now turned to wave me a hand. The rushing wind fairly sang in my ears; the walls of the break were confused blurs of yellow and green; at every stride Satan seemed to swallow a rod of the white trail.

Jones began to scale the ravine, heading up obliquely far on the side of where Frank had vanished, and as Wallace followed suit, I turned Satan. I caught Wallace at the summit, and we raced together out upon another flat of pinyon. We heard Frank and Jones yelling in a way that caused us to spur our horses frantically. Spot, gleaming white near a clump of green pinyons, was our guiding star. That last quarter of a mile was a ringing run, a ride to remember.

As our mounts crashed back with stiff forelegs and haunches, Wallace and I leaped off and darted into the clump of pinyons, whence issued a hair-raising medley of yells and barks. I saw Jones, then Frank, both waving their arms, then Moze and Sounder running wildly, airlessly about.

"Look there!" rang in my ear, and Jones smashed me on the back with a blow, which at any ordinary time would have laid me flat.

In a low, stubby pinyon tree, scarce twenty feet from us, was a tawny form. An enormous mountain lion, as large as an African lioness, stood planted with huge, round legs on two branches; and he faced us gloomily, neither frightened nor fierce. He watched the running dogs with pale, yellow eyes, waved his massive head and switched a long, black tufted tail.

"It's Old Tom! sure as you're born! It's Old Tom!" yelled Jones. "There's no two lions like that in one country. Hold still now. Jude is here, and she'll see him, she'll show him to the other hounds. Hold still!"

We heard Jude coming at a fast pace for a lame dog, and we saw her presently, running with her nose down for a moment, then up. She entered the clump of trees, and bumped her nose against the pinyon Old Tom was in, and looked up like a dog that knew her business. The series of wild howls she broke into quickly brought Sounder and Moze to her side. They, too, saw the big lion, not fifteen feet over their heads.

We were all yelling and trying to talk at once, in some such state as the dogs.

"Hyar, Moze! Come down out of that!" hoarsely shouted Jones.

Moze had begun to climb the thick, many-branched, low pinyon tree. He paid not the slightest attention to Jones, who screamed and raged at him.

"Cover the lion!" cried he to me. "Don't shoot unless he crouches to jump on me."

The little beaded front-sight wavered slightly as I held my rifle leveled at the grim, snarling face, and out of the corner of my eye, as it were, I saw Jones dash in under the lion and grasp Moze by the hind leg and haul him down. He broke from Jones and leaped again to the first low branch. His master then grasped his collar and carried him to where we stood and held him choking.

"Boys, we can't keep Tom up there. When he jumps, keep out of his way. Maybe we can chase him up a better tree."

Old Tom suddenly left the branches, swinging violently; and hitting the ground like a huge cat on springs, he bounded off, tail up, in a most ludicrous manner. His running, however, did not lack speed, for he quickly outdistanced the bursting hounds.

A stampede for horses succeeded this move. I had difficulty in closing my camera, which I had forgotten until the last moment, and got behind the others. Satan sent the dust flying and the pinyon branches crashing. Hardly had I time to bewail my ill-luck in being left, when I dashed out of a thick growth of trees to come upon my companions, all dismounted on the rim of the Grand Canyon.

"He's gone down! He's gone down!" raged Jones, stamping the ground. "What luck! What miserable luck! But don't quit; spread along the rim, boys, and look for him. Cougars can't fly. There's a break in the rim somewhere."

The rock wall, on which we dizzily stood, dropped straight down for a thousand feet, to meet a long, pinyon-covered slope, which graded a mile to cut off into what must have been the second wall. We were far west of Clarke's trail now, and faced a point above where Kanab Canyon, a red gorge a mile deep, met the great canyon. As I ran along the rim, looking for a fissure or break, my gaze seemed impellingly drawn by the immensity of this thing I could not name, and for which I had as yet no intelligible emotion.

Two "Waa-hoos" in the rear turned me back in double-quick time, and hastening by the horses, I found the three men grouped at the head of a narrow break.

"He went down here. Wallace saw him round the base of that tottering crag."

The break was wedge-shaped, with the sharp end off toward the rim, and it descended so rapidly as to appear almost perpendicular. It was a long, steep slide of small, weathered shale, and a place that no man in his right senses would ever have considered going down. But Jones, designating Frank and me, said in his cool, quick voice:

CHAPTER 12. OLD TOM

"You fellows go down. Take Jude and Sounder in leash. If you find his trail below along the wall, yell for us. Meanwhile, Wallace and I will hang over the rim and watch for him."

Going down, in one sense, was much easier than had appeared, for the reason that once started we moved on sliding beds of weathered stone. Each of us now had an avalanche for a steed. Frank forged ahead with a roar, and then seeing danger below, tried to get out of the mass. But the stones were like quicksand; every step he took sunk him in deeper. He grasped the smooth cliff, to find holding impossible. The slide poured over a fall like so much water. He reached and caught a branch of a pinyon, and lifting his feet up, hung on till the treacherous area of moving stones had passed.

While I had been absorbed in his predicament, my avalanche augmented itself by slide on slide, perhaps loosened by his; and before I knew it, I was sailing down with ever-increasing momentum. The sensation was distinctly pleasant, and a certain spirit, before restrained in me, at last ran riot. The slide narrowed at the drop where Frank had jumped, and the stones poured over in a stream. I jumped also, but having a rifle in one hand, failed to hold, and plunged down into the slide again. My feet were held this time, as in a vise. I kept myself upright and waited. Fortunately, the jumble of loose stone slowed and stopped, enabling me to crawl over to one side where there was comparatively good footing. Below us, for fifty yards was a sheet of rough stone, as bare as washed granite well could be. We slid down this in regular schoolboy fashion, and had reached another restricted neck in the fissure, when a sliding crash above warned us that the avalanches had decided to move of their own free will. Only a fraction of a moment had we to find footing along the yellow cliff, when, with a cracking roar, the mass struck the slippery granite. If we had been on that slope, our lives would not have been worth a grain of the dust flying in clouds above us. Huge stones, that had formed the bottom of the slides, shot ahead, and rolling, leaping, whizzed by us with frightful velocity, and the remainder groaned and growled its way down, to thunder over the second fall and die out in a distant rumble.

The hounds had hung back, and were not easily coaxed down to us. From there on, down to the base of the gigantic cliff, we descended with little difficulty.

"We might meet the old gray cat anywheres along here," said Frank.

The wall of yellow limestone had shelves, ledges, fissures and cracks, any one of which might have concealed a lion. On these places I turned dark, uneasy glances. It seemed to me events succeeded one another so rapidly that I had no time to think, to examine, to prepare. We were rushed from one sensation to another.

"Gee! look here," said Frank; "here's his tracks. Did you ever see the like of that?"

Certainly I had never fixed my eyes on such enormous cat-tracks as appeared in the yellow dust at the base of the rim wall. The mere sight of them was sufficient to make a man tremble.

"Hold in the dogs, Frank," I called. "Listen. I think I heard a yell."

From far above came a yell, which, though thinned out by distance, was easily recognized as Jones's. We returned to the opening of the break, and throwing our heads back, looked up the slide to see him coming down.

"Wait for me! Wait for me! I saw the lion go in a cave. Wait for me!"

With the same roar and crack and slide of rocks as had attended our descent, Jones bore down on us. For an old man it was a marvelous performance. He walked on the avalanches as though he wore seven-league boots, and presently, as we began to dodge whizzing bowlders, he stepped down to us, whirling his coiled lasso. His jaw bulged out; a flash made fire in his cold eyes.

"Boys, we've got Old Tom in a corner. I worked along the rim north and looked over every place I could. Now, maybe you won't believe it, but I heard him pant. Yes, sir, he panted like the tired lion he is. Well, presently I saw him lying along the base of the rim wall. His tongue was hanging out. You see, he's a heavy lion, and not used to running long distances. Come on, now. It's not far. Hold in the dogs. You there with the rifle, lead off, and keep your eyes peeled."

Single file, we passed along in the shadow of the great cliff. A wide trail had been worn in the dust.

"A lion run-way," said Jones. "Don't you smell the cat?"

Indeed, the strong odor of cat was very pronounced; and that, without the big fresh tracks, made the skin on my face tighten and chill. As we turned a jutting point in the wall, a number of animals, which I did not recognize, plunged helter-skelter down the canyon slope.

"Rocky Mountain sheep!" exclaimed Jones. "Look! Well, this is a discovery. I never heard of a bighorn in the Canyon."

It was indicative of the strong grip Old Tom had on us that we at once forgot the remarkable fact of coming upon those rare sheep in such a place.

Jones halted us presently before a deep curve described by the rim wall, the extreme end of which terminated across the slope in an impassable projecting corner.

"See across there, boys. See that black hole. Old Tom's in there."

"What's your plan?" queried the cowboy sharply.

"Wait. We'll slip up to get better lay of the land."

We worked our way noiselessly along the rim-wall curve for several hundred yards and came to a halt again, this time with a splendid command of the situation. The trail ended abruptly at the dark cave, so menacingly staring at us, and the corner of the cliff had curled back upon itself. It was a box-trap, with a drop at the end, too great for any beast, a narrow slide of weathered stone running down, and the rim wall trail. Old Tom would plainly be compelled to choose one of these directions if he left his cave.

"Frank, you and I will keep to the wall and stop near that scrub pinyon, this side of the hole. If I rope him, I can use that tree."

Then he turned to me:

"Are you to be depended on here?"

"I? What do you want me to do?" I demanded, and my whole breast seemed to sink in.

"You cut across the head of this slope and take up your position in the slide below the cave, say just by that big stone. From there you can command the cave, our position and your own. Now, if it is necessary to kill this lion to save me or Frank, or, of course, yourself, can you be depended upon to kill him?"

I felt a queer sensation around my heart and a strange tightening of the skin upon my face! What a position for me to be placed in! For one instant I shook like a quivering aspen leaf. Then because of the pride of a man, or perhaps inherited instincts cropping out at this perilous moment, I looked up and answered quietly:

"Yes. I will kill him!"

"Old Tom is cornered, and he'll come out. He can run only two ways: along this trail, or down that slide. I'll take my stand by the scrub pinyon there so I can get a hitch if I rope him. Frank, when I give the word, let the dogs go. Grey, you block the slide. If he makes at us, even if I do get my rope on him, kill him! Most likely he'll jump down hill—then you'll HAVE to kill him! Be quick. Now loose the hounds. Hi! Hi! Hi! Hi!"

I jumped into the narrow slide of weathered stone and looked up. Jones's stentorian yell rose high above the clamor of the hounds. He whirled his lasso.

A huge yellow form shot over the trail and hit the top of the slide with a crash. The lasso streaked out with arrowy swiftness, circled, and snapped viciously close to Old Tom's head. "Kill him! Kill him!" roared Jones. Then the lion leaped, seemingly into the air above me. Instinctively I raised my little automatic rifle. I seemed to hear a million bellowing reports. The tawny body, with its grim, snarling face, blurred in my sight. I heard a roar of sliding stones at my feet. I felt a rush of wind. I caught a confused glimpse of a whirling wheel of fur, rolling down the slide.

Then Jones and Frank were pounding me, and yelling I know not what. From far above came floating down a long "Waa-hoo!" I saw Wallace silhouetted against the blue sky. I felt the hot barrel of my rifle, and shuddered at the bloody stones below me—then, and then only, did I realize, with weakening legs, that Old Tom had jumped at me, and had jumped to his death.

CHAPTER 13. SINGING CLIFFS

Old Tom had rolled two hundred yards down the canyon, leaving a red trail and bits of fur behind him. When I had clambered down to the steep slide where he had lodged, Sounder and Jude had just decided he was no longer worth biting, and were wagging their tails. Frank was shaking his head, and Jones, standing above the lion, lasso in hand, wore a disconsolate face.

"How I wish I had got the rope on him!"

"I reckon we'd be gatherin' up the pieces of you if you had," said Frank, dryly.

We skinned the old king on the rocky slope of his mighty throne, and then, beginning to feel the effects of severe exertion, we cut across the slope for the foot of the break. Once there, we gazed up in disarray. That break resembled a walk of life—how easy to slip down, how hard to climb! Even Frank, inured as he was to strenuous toil, began to swear and wipe his sweaty brow before we had made one-tenth of the ascent. It was particularly exasperating, not to mention the danger of it, to work a few feet up a slide, and then feel it start to move. We had to climb in single file, which jeopardized the safety of those behind the leader. Sometimes we were all sliding at once, like boys on a pond, with the difference that we were in danger. Frank forged ahead, turning to yell now and then for us to dodge a cracking stone. Faithful old Jude could not get up in some places, so laying aside my rifle, I carried her, and returned for the weapon. It became necessary, presently, to hide behind cliff projections to escape the avalanches started by Frank, and to wait till he had surmounted the break. Jones gave out completely several times, saying the exertion affected his heart. What with my rifle, my camera and Jude, I could offer him no assistance, and was really in need of that myself. When it seemed as if one more step would kill us, we reached the rim, and fell panting with labored chests and dripping skins. We could not speak. Jones had worn a pair of ordinary shoes without thick soles and nails, and it seemed well to speak of them in the past tense. They were split into ribbons and hung on by the laces. His feet were cut and bruised.

On the way back to camp, we encountered Moze and Don coming out of the break where we had started Sounder on the trail. The paws of both hounds were yellow with dust, which proved they had been down under the rim wall. Jones doubted not in the least that they had chased a lion.

CHAPTER 13. SINGING CLIFFS

Upon examination, this break proved to be one of the two which Clarke used for trails to his wild horse corral in the canyon. According to him, the distance separating them was five miles by the rim wall, and less than half that in a straight line. Therefore, we made for the point of the forest where it ended abruptly in the scrub oak. We got into camp, a fatigued lot of men, horses and dogs. Jones appeared particularly happy, and his first move, after dismounting, was to stretch out the lion skin and measure it.

"Ten feet, three inches and a half!" he sang out.

"Shore it do beat hell!" exclaimed Jim in tones nearer to excitement than any I had ever heard him use.

"Old Tom beats, by two inches, any cougar I ever saw," continued Jones. "He must have weighed more than three hundred. We'll set about curing the hide. Jim, stretch it well on a tree, and we'll take a hand in peeling off the fat."

All of the party worked on the cougar skin that afternoon. The gristle at the base of the neck, where it met the shoulders, was so tough and thick we could not scrape it thin. Jones said this particular spot was so well protected because in fighting, cougars were most likely to bite and claw there. For that matter, the whole skin was tough, tougher than leather; and when it dried, it pulled all the horseshoe nails out of the pine tree upon which we had it stretched.

About time for the sun to set, I strolled along the rim wall to look into the canyon. I was beginning to feel something of its character and had growing impressions. Dark purple smoke veiled the clefts deep down between the mesas. I walked along to where points of cliff ran out like capes and peninsulas, all seamed, cracked, wrinkled, scarred and yellow with age, with shattered, toppling ruins of rocks ready at a touch to go thundering down. I could not resist the temptation to crawl out to the farthest point, even though I shuddered over the yard-wide ridges; and when once seated on a bare promontory, two hundred feet from the regular rim wall, I felt isolated, marooned.

The sun, a liquid red globe, had just touched its under side to the pink cliffs of Utah, and fired a crimson flood of light over the wonderful mountains, plateaus, escarpments, mesas, domes and turrets or the gorge. The rim wall of Powell's Plateau was a thin streak of fire; the timber above like grass of gold; and the long slopes below shaded from bright to dark. Point Sublime, bold and bare, ran out toward the plateau, jealously reaching for the sun. Bass's Tomb peeped over the Saddle. The Temple of Vishnu lay bathed in vapory shading clouds, and the Shinumo Altar shone with rays of glory.

The beginning of the wondrous transformation, the dropping of the day's curtain, was for me a rare and perfect moment. As the golden splendor of sunset sought out a peak or mesa or escarpment, I gave it a name to suit my fancy; and as flushing, fading, its glory changed, sometimes I rechristened it. Jupiter's Chariot, brazen wheeled, stood ready to roll into the clouds. Semiramis's Bed, all gold, shone from a tower of Babylon. Castor and Pollux clasped hands over a Stygian river. The Spur of Doom, a mountain shaft as red as hell, and inaccessible, insurmountable, lured with strange light. Dusk, a bold, black dome, was shrouded by the shadow of a giant mesa. The Star of Bethlehem glittered from the brow of Point Sublime. The Wraith, fleecy, feathered curtain of mist, floated down among the ruins of castles and palaces, like the ghost of a goddess. Vales of Twilight, dim, dark ravines, mystic homes of specters, led into the awful Valley of the Shadow, clothed in purple night.

Suddenly, as the first puff of the night wind fanned my cheek, a strange, sweet, low moaning and sighing came to my ears. I almost thought I was in a dream. But the canyon, now blood-red, was there in overwhelming reality, a profound, solemn, gloomy thing, but real. The wind blew stronger, and then I was to a sad, sweet song, which lulled as the wind lulled. I realized at once that the sound was caused by the wind blowing into the peculiar formations of the cliffs. It changed, softened, shaded, mellowed, but it was always sad. It rose from low, tremulous, sweetly quavering sighs, to a sound like the last woeful, despairing wail of a woman. It was the song of the sea sirens and the music of the waves; it had the soft sough of the night wind in the trees, and the haunting moan of lost spirits.

With reluctance I turned my back to the gorgeously changing spectacle of the canyon and crawled in to the rim wall. At the narrow neck of stone I peered over to look down into misty blue nothingness.

That night Jones told stories of frightened hunters, and assuaged my mortification by saying "buck-fever" was pardonable after the danger had passed, and especially so in my case, because of the great size and fame of Old Tom.

"The worst case of buck-fever I ever saw was on a buffalo hunt I had with a fellow named Williams," went on Jones. "I was one of the scouts leading a wagon-train west on the old Santa Fe trail. This fellow said he was a big hunter, and wanted to kill buffalo, so I took him out. I saw a herd making over the prairie for a hollow where a brook ran, and by hard work, got in ahead of them. I picked out a position just below the edge of the bank, and we lay quiet, waiting. From the direction of the buffalo, I calculated we'd be just about right to get a shot at no very long range. As it was, I suddenly heard thumps on the ground, and cautiously raising my head, saw a huge buffalo bull just over us, not fifteen feet up the bank. I whispered to Williams: 'For God's sake, don't shoot, don't move!' The bull's little fiery eyes snapped, and he reared. I thought we were goners, for when a bull comes down on anything with his forefeet, it's done for. But he slowly settled back, perhaps doubtful. Then, as another buffalo came to the edge of the bank, luckily a little way from us, the bull turned broadside, presenting a splendid target. Then I whispered to Williams: 'Now's your chance. Shoot!' I waited for the shot, but none came. Looking at Williams, I saw he was white and trembling. Big drops of sweat stood out on his brow his teeth chattered, and his hands shook. He had forgotten he carried a rifle."

"That reminds me," said Frank. "They tell a story over at Kanab on a Dutchman named Schmitt. He was very fond of huntin', an' I guess had pretty good success after deer an' small game. One winter he was out in the Pink Cliffs with a Mormon named Shoonover, an' they run into a lammin' big grizzly track, fresh an' wet. They trailed him to a clump of chaparral, an' on goin' clear round it, found no tracks leadin' out. Shoonover said Schmitt commenced to sweat. They went back to the place where the trail led in, an' there they were, great big silver tip tracks, bigger'n hoss-tracks, so fresh thet water was oozin' out of 'em. Schmitt said: 'Zake, you go in und ged him. I hef took sick right now.'"

Happy as we were over the chase of Old Tom, and our prospects for Sounder, Jude and Moze had seen a lion in a tree—we sought our blankets early. I lay watching the bright stars, and listening to the roar of the wind in the pines. At intervals it lulled to a whisper, and then swelled to a roar, and then died away. Far off in the forest a coyote barked once. Time and time again, as I was gradually sinking into slumber, the sudden roar of the wind startled me. I imagined it was the crash of rolling, weathered stone, and I saw again that huge outspread flying lion above me.

I awoke sometime later to find Moze had sought the warmth of my side, and he lay so near my arm that I reached out and covered him with an end of the blanket I used to break the wind. It was very cold and the time must have been very late, for the wind had died down, and I heard not a tinkle from the hobbled horses. The absence of the cowbell music gave me a sense of loneliness, for without it the silence of the great forest was a thing to be felt.

This oppressiveness, however, was broken by a far-distant cry, unlike any sound I had ever heard. Not sure of myself, I freed my ears from the blanketed hood and listened. It came again, a wild cry, that made me think first of a lost child, and then of the mourning wolf of the north. It must have been a long distance off in the forest. An interval of some moments passed, then it pealed out again, nearer this time, and so human that it startled me. Moze raised his head and growled low in his throat and sniffed the keen air.

"Jones, Jones," I called, reaching over to touch the old hunter.

He awoke at once, with the clear-headedness of the light sleeper.

"I heard the cry of some beast," I said, "And it was so weird, so strange. I want to know what it was."

Such a long silence ensued that I began to despair of hearing the cry again, when, with a suddenness which straightened the hair on my head, a wailing shriek, exactly like a despairing woman might give in death agony, split the night silence. It seemed right on us.

"Cougar! Cougar! Cougar!" exclaimed Jones.

"What's up?" queried Frank, awakened by the dogs.

Their howling roused the rest of the party, and no doubt scared the cougar, for his womanish screech was not repeated. Then Jones got up and gatherered his blankets in a roll.

"Where you oozin' for now?" asked Frank, sleepily.

"I think that cougar just came up over the rim on a scouting hunt, and I'm going to go down to the head of the trail and stay there till morning. If he returns that way, I'll put him up a tree."

With this, he unchained Sounder and Don, and stalked off under the trees, looking like an Indian. Once the deep bay of Sounder rang out; Jones's sharp command followed, and then the familiar silence encompassed the forest and was broken no more.

When I awoke all was gray, except toward the canyon, where the little bit of sky I saw through the pines glowed a delicate pink. I crawled out on the instant, got into my boots and coat, and kicked the smoldering fire. Jim heard me, and said:

"Shore you're up early."

"I'm going to see the sunrise from the north rim of the Grand Canon," I said, and knew when I spoke that very few men, out of all the millions of travelers, had ever seen this, probably the most surpassingly beautiful pageant in the world. At most, only a few geologists, scientists, perhaps an artist or two, and horse wranglers, hunters and prospectors have ever reached the rim on the north side; and these men, crossing from Bright Angel or Mystic Spring trails on the south rim, seldom or never get beyond Powell's Plateau.

The frost cracked under my boots like frail ice, and the bluebells peeped wanly from the white. When I reached the head of Clarke's trail it was just daylight; and there, under a pine, I found Jones rolled in his blankets, with Sounder and Moze asleep beside him. I turned without disturbing him, and went along the edge of the forest, but back a little distance from the rim wall.

I saw deer off in the woods, and tarrying, watched them throw up graceful heads, and look and listen. The soft pink glow through the pines deepened to rose, and suddenly I caught a point of red fire. Then I hurried to the place I had named Singing Cliffs, and keeping my eyes fast on the stone beneath me, trawled out to the very farthest point, drew a long, breath, and looked eastward.

The awfulness of sudden death and the glory of heaven stunned me! The thing that had been mystery at twilight, lay clear, pure, open in the rosy hue of dawn. Out of the gates of the morning poured a light which glorified the palaces and pyramids, purged and purified the afternoon's inscrutable clefts, swept away the shadows of the mesas, and bathed that broad, deep world of mighty mountains, stately spars of rock, sculptured cathedrals and alabaster terraces in an artist's dream of color. A pearl from heaven had burst, flinging its heart of fire into this chasm. A stream of opal flowed out of the sun, to touch each peak, mesa, dome, parapet, temple and tower, cliff and cleft into the new-born life of another day.

I sat there for a long time and knew that every second the scene changed, yet I could not tell how. I knew I sat high over a hole of broken, splintered, barren mountains; I knew I could see a hundred miles of the length of it, and eighteen miles of the width of it, and a mile of the depth of it, and the shafts and rays of rose light on a million glancing, many-hued surfaces at once; but that knowledge was no help to me. I repeated a lot of meaningless superlatives to myself, and I found words inadequate and superfluous. The spectacle was too elusive and too great. It was life and death, heaven and hell.

I tried to call up former favorite views of mountain and sea, so as to compare them with this; but the memory pictures refused to come, even with my eyes closed. Then I returned to camp, with unsettled, troubled mind, and was silent, wondering at the strange feeling burning within me.

Jones talked about our visitor of the night before, and said the trail near where he had slept showed only one cougar track, and that led down into the canyon. It had surely been made, he thought, by the beast we had heard. Jones signified his intention of chaining several of the hounds for the next few nights at the head of this trail; so if the cougar came up, they would scent him and let us know. From which it was evident that to chase a lion bound into the canyon and one bound out were two different things.

The day passed lazily, with all of us resting on the warm, fragrant pine-needle beds, or mending a rent in a coat, or working on some camp task impossible of commission on exciting days.

About four o'clock, I took my little rifle and walked off through the woods in the direction of the carcass where I had seen the gray wolf. Thinking it best to make a wide detour, so as to face the wind, I circled till I felt the breeze was favorable to my enterprise, and then cautiously approached the hollow were the dead horse lay. Indian fashion, I slipped from tree to tree, a mode of forest travel not without its fascination and effectiveness, till I reached the height of a knoll beyond which I made sure was my objective point. On peeping out from behind the last pine, I found I had calculated pretty well, for there was the hollow, the big windfall, with its round, starfish-shaped roots exposed to the bright sun, and near that, the carcass. Sure enough, pulling hard at it, was the gray-white wolf I recognized as my "lofer."

But he presented an exceedingly difficult shot. Backing down the ridge, I ran a little way to come up behind another tree, from which I soon shifted to a fallen pine. Over this I peeped, to get a splendid view of the wolf. He had stopped tugging at the horse, and stood with his nose in the air. Surely he could not have scented me, for the wind was strong from him to me; neither could he have heard my soft footfalls on the pine needles; nevertheless, he was suspicious. Loth to spoil the picture he made, I risked a chance, and waited. Besides, though I prided myself on being able to take a fair aim, I had no great hope that I could hit him at such a distance. Presently he returned to his feeding, but not for long. Soon he raised his long, fine-pointed head, and trotted away a few yards, stopped to sniff again, then went back to his gruesome work.

At this juncture, I noiselessly projected my rifle barrel over the log. I had not, however, gotten the sights in line with him, when he trotted away reluctantly, and ascended the knoll on his side of the hollow. I lost him, and had just begun sourly to call myself a mollycoddle hunter, when he reappeared. He halted in an open glade, on the very crest of the knoll, and stood still as a statue wolf, a white, inspiriting target, against a dark green background. I could not stifle a rush of feeling, for I was a lover of the beautiful first, and a hunter secondly; but I steadied down as the front sight moved into the notch through which I saw the black and white of his shoulder.

Spang! How the little Remington sang! I watched closely, ready to send five more missiles after the gray beast. He jumped spasmodically, in a half-curve, high in the air, with loosely hanging head, then dropped in a heap. I yelled like a boy, ran down the hill, up the other side of the hollow, to find him stretched out dead, a small hole in his shoulder where the bullet had entered, a great one where it had come out.

The job I made of skinning him lacked some hundred degrees the perfection of my shot, but I accomplished it, and returned to camp in triumph.

"Shore I knowed you'd plunk him," said Jim very much pleased. "I shot one the other day same way, when he was feedin' off a dead horse. Now thet's a fine skin. Shore you cut through once or twice. But he's only half lofer, the other half in plain coyote. Thet accounts fer his feedin' on dead meat."

My naturalist host and my scientific friend both remarked somewhat grumpily that I seemed to get the best of all the good things. I might have retaliated that I certainly had gotten the worst of all the bad jokes; but, being generously happy over my prize, merely remarked: "If you want fame or wealth or wolves, go out and hunt for them."

Five o'clock supper left a good margin of day, in which my thoughts reverted to the canyon. I watched the purple shadows stealing out of their caverns and rolling up about the base of the mesas. Jones came over to where I stood, and I persuaded him to walk with me along the rim wall. Twilight had stealthily advanced when we reached the Singing Cliffs, and we did not go out upon my promontory, but chose a more comfortable one nearer the wall.

The night breeze had not sprung up yet, so the music of the cliffs was hushed.

"You cannot accept the theory of erosion to account for this chasm?" I asked my companion, referring to a former conversation.

"I can for this part of it. But what stumps me is the mountain range three thousand feet high, crossing the desert and the canyon just above where we crossed the river. How did the river cut through that without the help of a split or earthquake?"

"I'll admit that is a poser to me as well as to you. But I suppose Wallace could explain it as erosion. He claims this whole western country was once under water, except the tips of the Sierra Nevada mountains. There came an uplift of the earth's crust, and the great inland sea began to run out, presumably by way of the Colorado. In so doing it cut out the upper canyon, this gorge eighteen miles wide. Then came a second uplift, giving the river a much greater impetus toward the sea, which cut out the second, or marble canyon. Now as to the mountain range crossing the canyon at right angles. It must have come with the second uplift. If so, did it dam the river back into another inland sea, and then wear down into that red perpendicular gorge we remember so well? Or was there a great break in the fold of granite, which let the river continue on its way? Or was there, at that particular point, a softer stone, like this limestone here, which erodes easily?"

"You must ask somebody wiser than I."

"Well, let's not perplex our minds with its origin. It is, and that's enough for any mind. Ah! listen! Now you will hear my Singing Cliffs."

From out of the darkening shadows murmurs rose on the softly rising wind. This strange music had a depressing influence; but it did not fill the heart with sorrow, only touched it lightly. And when, with the dying breeze, the song died away, it left the lonely crags lonelier for its death.

The last rosy gleam faded from the tip of Point Sublime; and as if that were a signal, in all the clefts and canyons below, purple, shadowy clouds marshaled their forces and began to sweep upon the battlements, to swing colossal wings into amphitheaters where gods might have warred, slowly to enclose the magical sentinels. Night intervened, and a moving, changing, silent chaos pulsated under the bright stars.

"How infinite all this is! How impossible to understand!" I exclaimed.

"To me it is very simple," replied my comrade. "The world is strange. But this canyon—why, we can see it all! I can't make out why people fuss so over it. I only feel peace. It's only bold and beautiful, serene and silent."

With the words of this quiet old plainsman, my sentimental passion shrank to the true appreciation of the scene. Self passed out to the recurring, soft strains of cliff song. I had been reveling in a species of indulgence, imagining I was a great lover of nature, building poetical illusions over storm-beaten peaks. The truth, told by one who had lived fifty years in the solitudes, among the rugged mountains, under the dark trees, and by the sides of the lonely streams, was the simple interpretation of a spirit in harmony with the bold, the beautiful, the serene, the silent.

He meant the Grand Canyon was only a mood of nature, a bold promise, a beautiful record. He meant that mountains had sifted away in its dust, yet the canyon was young. Man was nothing, so let him be humble. This cataclysm of the earth, this playground of a river was not inscrutable; it was only inevitable—as inevitable as nature herself. Millions of years in the bygone ages it had lain serene under a half moon; it would bask silent under a rayless sun, in the onward edge of time.

It taught simplicity, serenity, peace. The eye that saw only the strife, the war, the decay, the ruin, or only the glory and the tragedy, saw not all the truth. It spoke simply, though its words were grand: "My spirit is the Spirit of Time, of Eternity, of God. Man is little, vain, vaunting. Listen. To-morrow he shall be gone. Peace! Peace!"

CHAPTER 14. ALL HEROES BUT ONE

As we rode up the slope of Buckskin, the sunrise glinted red-gold through the aisles of frosted pines, giving us a hunter's glad greeting.

With all due respect to, and appreciation of, the breaks of the Siwash, we unanimously decided that if cougars inhabited any other section of canyon country, we preferred it, and were going to find it. We had often speculated on the appearance of the rim wall directly across the neck of the canyon upon which we were located. It showed a long stretch of breaks, fissures, caves, yellow crags, crumbled ruins and clefts green with pinyon pine. As a crow flies, it was only a mile or two straight across from camp, but to reach it, we had to ascend the mountain and head the canyon which deeply indented the slope.

A thousand feet or more above the level bench, the character of the forest changed; the pines grew thicker, and interspersed among them were silver spruces and balsams. Here in the clumps of small trees and underbrush, we began to jump deer, and in a few moments a greater number than I had ever seen in all my hunting experiences loped within range of my eye. I could not look out into the forest where an aisle or lane or glade stretched to any distance, without seeing a big gray deer cross it. Jones said the herds had recently come up from the breaks, where they had wintered. These deer were twice the size of the Eastern species, and as fat as well-fed cattle. They were almost as tame, too. A big herd ran out of one glade, leaving behind several curious does, which watched us intently for a moment, then bounded off with the stiff, springy bounce that so amused me.

Sounder crossed fresh trails one after another; Jude, Tige and Ranger followed him, but hesitated often, barked and whined; Don started off once, to come sneaking back at Jones's stern call. But surly old Moze either would not or could not obey, and away he dashed. Bang! Jones sent a charge of fine shot after him. He yelped, doubled up as if stung, and returned as quickly as he had gone.

"Hyar, you white and black coon dog," said Jones, "get in behind, and stay there."

We turned to the right after a while and got among shallow ravines. Gigantic pines grew on the ridges and in the hollows, and everywhere bluebells shone blue from the white frost. Why the frost did not kill these beautiful flowers was a mystery to me. The horses could not step without crushing them.

CHAPTER 14. ALL HEROES BUT ONE

Before long, the ravines became so deep that we had to zigzag up and down their sides, and to force our horses through the aspen thickets in the hollows. Once from a ridge I saw a troop of deer, and stopped to watch them. Twenty-seven I counted outright, but there must have been three times that number. I saw the herd break across a glade, and watched them until they were lost in the forest. My companions having disappeared, I pushed on, and while working out of a wide, deep hollow, I noticed the sunny patches fade from the bright slopes, and the golden streaks vanish among the pines. The sky had become overcast, and the forest was darkening. The "Waa-hoo," I cried out returned in echo only. The wind blew hard in my face, and the pines began to bend and roar. An immense black cloud enveloped Buckskin.

Satan had carried me no farther than the next ridge, when the forest frowned dark as twilight, and on the wind whirled flakes of snow. Over the next hollow, a white pall roared through the trees toward me. Hardly had I time to get the direction of the trail, and its relation to the trees nearby, when the storm enfolded me. Of his own accord Satan stopped in the lee of a bushy spruce. The roar in the pines equaled that of the cave under Niagara, and the bewildering, whirling mass of snow was as difficult to see through as the tumbling, seething waterfall.

I was confronted by the possibility of passing the night there, and calming my fears as best I could, hastily felt for my matches and knife. The prospect of being lost the next day in a white forest was also appalling, but I soon reassured myself that the storm was only a snow squall, and would not last long. Then I gave myself up to the pleasure and beauty of it. I could only faintly discern the dim trees; the limbs of the spruce, which partially protected me, sagged down to my head with their burden; I had but to reach out my hand for a snowball. Both the wind and snow seemed warm. The great flakes were like swan feathers on a summer breeze. There was something joyous in the whirl of snow and roar of wind. While I bent over to shake my holster, the storm passed as suddenly as it had come. When I looked up, there were the pines, like pillars of Parian marble, and a white shadow, a vanishing cloud fled, with receding roar, on the wings of the wind. Fast on this retreat burst the warm, bright sun.

I faced my course, and was delighted to see, through an opening where the ravine cut out of the forest, the red-tipped peaks of the canyon, and the vaulted dome I had named St. Marks. As I started, a new and unexpected after-feature of the storm began to manifest itself. The sun being warm, even to melt the snow, and under the trees a heavy rain fell, and in the glades and hollows a fine mist blew. Exquisite rainbows hung from white-tipped branches and curved over the hollows. Glistening patches of snow fell from the pines, and broke the showers.

In a quarter of an hour, I rode out of the forest to the rim wall on dry ground. Against the green pinyons Frank's white horse stood out conspicuously, and near him browsed the mounts of Jim and Wallace. The boys were not in evidence. Concluding they had gone down over the rim, I dismounted and kicked off my chaps, and taking my rifle and camera, hurried to look the place over.

To my surprise and interest, I found a long section of rim wall in ruins. It lay in a great curve between the two giant capes; and many short, sharp, projecting promontories, like the teeth of a saw, overhung the canyon. The slopes between these points of cliff were covered with a deep growth of pinyon, and in these places descent would be easy. Everywhere in the corrugated wall were rents and rifts; cliffs stood detached like islands near a shore; yellow crags rose out of green clefts; jumble of rocks, and slides of rim wall, broken into blocks, massed under the promontories.

The singular raggedness and wildness of the scene took hold of me, and was not dispelled until the baying of Sounder and Don roused action in me. Apparently the hounds were widely separated. Then I heard Jim's yell. But it ceased when the wind lulled, and I heard it no more. Running back from the point, I began to go down. The way was steep, almost perpendicular; but because of the great stones and the absence of slides, was easy. I took long strides and jumps, and slid over rocks, and swung on pinyon branches, and covered distance like a rolling stone. At the foot of the rim wall, or at a line where it would have reached had it extended regularly, the slope became less pronounced. I could stand up without holding on to a support. The largest pinyons I had seen made a forest that almost stood on end. These trees grew up, down, and out, and twisted in curves, and many were two feet in thickness. During my descent, I halted at intervals to listen, and always heard one of the hounds, sometimes several. But as I descended for a long time, and did not get anywhere or approach the dogs, I began to grow impatient.

A large pinyon, with a dead top, suggested a good outlook, so I climbed it, and saw I could sweep a large section of the slope. It was a strange thing to look down hill, over the tips of green trees. Below, perhaps four hundred yards, was a slide open for a long way; all the rest was green incline, with many dead branches sticking up like spars, and an occasional crag. From this perch I heard the hounds; then followed a yell I thought was Jim's, and after it the bellowing of Wallace's rifle. Then all was silent. The shots had effectually checked the yelping of the hounds. I let out a yell. Another cougar that Jones would not lasso! All at once I heard a familiar sliding of small rocks below me, and I watched the open slope with greedy eyes.

Not a bit surprised was I to see a cougar break out of the green, and go tearing down the slide. In less than six seconds, I had sent six steel-jacketed bullets after him. Puffs of dust rose closer and closer to him as each bullet went nearer the mark and the last showered him with gravel and turned him straight down the canyon slope.

I slid down the dead pinyon and jumped nearly twenty feet to the soft sand below, and after putting a loaded clip in my rifle, began kangaroo leaps down the slope. When I reached the point where the cougar had entered the slide, I called the hounds, but they did not come nor answer me. Notwithstanding my excitement, I appreciated the distance to the bottom of the slope before I reached it. In my haste, I ran upon the verge of a precipice twice as deep as the first rim wall, but one glance down sent me shatteringly backward.

With all the breath I had left I yelled: "Waa-hoo! Waa-hoo!" From the echoes flung at me, I imagined at first that my friends were right on my ears. But no real answer came. The cougar had probably passed along this second rim wall to a break, and had gone down. His trail could easily be taken by any of the hounds. Vexed and anxious, I signaled again and again. Once, long after the echo had gone to sleep in some hollow canyon, I caught a faint "Wa-a-ho-o-o!" But it might have come from the clouds. I did not hear a hound barking above me on the slope; but suddenly, to my amazement, Sounder's deep bay rose from the abyss below. I ran along the rim, called till I was hoarse, leaned over so far that the blood rushed to my head, and then sat down. I concluded this canyon hunting could bear some sustained attention and thought, as well as frenzied action.

Examination of my position showed how impossible it was to arrive at any clear idea of the depth or size, or condition of the canyon slopes from the main rim wall above. The second wall—a stupendous, yellow-faced cliff two thousand feet high—curved to my left round to a point in front of me. The intervening canyon might have been a half mile wide, and it might have been ten miles. I had become disgusted with judging distance. The slope above this second wall facing me ran up far above my head; it fairly towered, and this routed all my former judgments, because I remembered distinctly that from the rim this yellow and green mountain had appeared an insignificant little ridge. But it was when I turned to gaze up behind me that I fully grasped the immensity of the place. This wall and slope were the first two steps down the long stairway of the Grand Canyon, and they towered over me, straight up a half-mile in dizzy height. To think of climbing it took my breath away.

Then again Sounder's bay floated distinctly to me, but it seemed to come from a different point. I turned my ear to the wind, and in the succeeding moments I was more and more baffled. One bay sounded from below and next from far to the right; another from the left. I could not distinguish voice from echo. The acoustic properties of the amphitheater beneath me were too wonderful for my comprehension.

As the bay grew sharper, and correspondingly more significant, I became distracted, and focused a strained vision on the canyon deeps. I looked along the slope to the notch where the wall curved and followed the base line of the yellow cliff. Quite suddenly I saw a very small black object moving with snail-like slowness. Although it seemed impossible for Sounder to be so small, I knew it was he. Having something now to judge distance from, I conceived it to be a mile, without the drop. If I could hear Sounder, he could hear me, so I yelled encouragement. The echoes clapped back at me like so many slaps in the face. I watched the hound until he disappeared among broken heaps of stone, and long after that his bay floated to me.

Having rested, I essayed the discovery of some of my lost companions or the hounds, and began to climb. Before I started, however, I was wise enough to study the rim wall above, to familiarize myself with the break so I would have a landmark. Like horns and spurs of gold the pinnacles loomed up. Massed closely together, they were not unlike an astounding pipe-organ. I had a feeling of my littleness, that I was lost, and should devote every moment and effort to the saving of my life. It did not seem possible I could be hunting. Though I climbed diagonally, and rested often, my heart pumped so hard I could hear it. A yellow crag, with a round head like an old man's cane, appealed to me as near the place where I last heard from Jim, and toward it I labored. Every time I glanced up, the distance seemed the same. A climb which I decided would not take more than fifteen minutes, required an hour.

While resting at the foot of the crag, I heard more baying of hounds, but for my life I could not tell whether the sound came from up or down, and I commenced to feel that I did not much care. Having signaled till I was hoarse, and receiving none but mock answers, I decided that if my companions had not toppled over a cliff, they were wisely withholding their breath.

Another stiff pull up the slope brought me under the rim wall, and there I groaned, because the wall was smooth and shiny, without a break. I plodded slowly along the base, with my rifle ready. Cougar tracks were so numerous I got tired of looking at them, but I did not forget that I might meet a tawny fellow or two among those narrow passes of shattered rock, and under the thick, dark pinyons. Going on in this way, I ran point-blank into a pile of bleached bones before a cave. I had stumbled on the lair of a lion and from the looks of it one like that of Old Tom. I flinched twice before I threw a stone into the dark-mouthed cave. What impressed me as soon as I found I was in no danger of being pawed and clawed round the gloomy spot, was the fact of the bones being there. How did they come on a slope where a man could hardly walk? Only one answer seemed feasible. The lion had made his kill one thousand feet above, had pulled his quarry to the rim and pushed it over. In view of the theory that he might have had to drag his victim from the forest, and that very seldom two lions worked together, the fact of the location of the bones as startling. Skulls of wild horses and deer, antlers and countless bones, all crushed into shapelessness, furnished indubitable proof that the carcasses had fallen from a great height. Most remarkable of all was the skeleton of a cougar lying across that of a horse. I believed—I could not help but believe that the cougar had fallen with his last victim.

Not many rods beyond the lion den, the rim wall split into towers, crags and pinnacles. I thought I had found my pipe organ, and began to climb toward a narrow opening in the rim. But I lost it. The extraordinarily cut-up condition of the wall made holding to one direction impossible. Soon I realized I was lost in a labyrinth. I tried to find my way down again, but the best I could do was to reach the verge of a cliff, from which I could see the canyon. Then I knew where I was, yet I did not know, so I plodded wearily back. Many a blind cleft did I ascend in the maze of crags. I could hardly crawl along, still I kept at it, for the place was conducive to dire thoughts. A tower of Babel menaced me with tons of loose shale. A tower that leaned more frightfully than the Tower of Pisa threatened to build my tomb. Many a lighthouse-shaped crag sent down little scattering rocks in ominous notice.

After toiling in and out of passageways under the shadows of these strangely formed cliffs, and coming again and again to the same point, a blind pocket, I grew desperate. I named the baffling place Deception Pass, and then ran down a slide. I knew if I could keep my feet I could beat the avalanche. More by good luck than management I outran the roaring stones and landed safely. Then rounding the cliff below, I found myself on a narrow ledge, with a wall to my left, and to the right the tips of pinyon trees level with my feet.

Innocently and wearily I passed round a pillar-like corner of wall, to come face to face with an old lioness and cubs. I heard the mother snarl, and at the same time her ears went back flat, and she crouched. The same fire of yellow eyes, the same grim snarling expression so familiar in my mind since Old Tom had leaped at me, faced me here.

My recent vow of extermination was entirely forgotten and one frantic spring carried me over the ledge.

Crash! I felt the brushing and scratching of branches, and saw a green blur. I went down straddling limbs and hit the ground with a thump. Fortunately, I landed mostly on my feet, in sand, and suffered no serious bruise. But I was stunned, and my right arm was numb for a moment. When I gathered myself together, instead of being grateful the ledge had not been on the face of Point Sublime—from which I would most assuredly have leaped—I was the angriest man ever let loose in the Grand Canyon.

Of course the cougars were far on their way by that time, and were telling neighbors about the brave hunter's leap for life; so I devoted myself to further efforts to find an outlet. The niche I had jumped into opened below, as did most of the breaks, and I worked out of it to the base of the rim wall, and tramped a long, long mile before I reached my own trail leading down. Resting every five steps, I climbed and climbed. My rifle grew to weigh a ton; my feet were lead; the camera strapped to my shoulder was the world. Soon climbing meant trapeze work—long reach of arm, and pull of weight, high step of foot, and spring of body. Where I had slid down with ease, I had to strain and raise myself by sheer muscle. I wore my left glove to tatters and threw it away to put the right one on my left hand. I thought many times I could not make another move; I thought my lungs would burst, but I kept on. When at last I surmounted the rim, I saw Jones, and flopped down beside him, and lay panting, dripping, boiling, with scorched feet, aching limbs and numb chest.

"I've been here two hours," he said, "and I knew things were happening below; but to climb up that slide would kill me. I am not young any more, and a steep climb like this takes a young heart. As it was I had enough work. Look!" He called my attention to his trousers. They had been cut to shreds, and the right trouser leg was missing from the knee down. His shin was bloody. "Moze took a lion along the rim, and I went after him with all my horse could do. I yelled for the boys, but they didn't come. Right here it is easy to go down, but below, where

Moze started this lion, it was impossible to get over the rim. The lion lit straight out of the pinyons. I lost ground because of the thick brush and numerous trees. Then Moze doesn't bark often enough. He treed the lion twice. I could tell by the way he opened up and bayed. The rascal coon-dog climbed the trees and chased the lion out. That's what Moze did! I got to an open space and saw him, and was coming up fine when he went down over a hollow which ran into the canyon. My horse tripped and fell, turning clear over with me before he threw me into the brush. I tore my clothes, and got this bruise, but wasn't much hurt. My horse is pretty lame."

I began a recital of my experience, modestly omitting the incident where I bravely faced an old lioness. Upon consulting my watch, I found I had been almost four hours climbing out. At that moment, Frank poked a red face over the rim. He was in shirt sleeves, sweating freely, and wore a frown I had never seen before. He puffed like a porpoise, and at first could hardly speak.

"Where were—you—all?" he panted. "Say! but mebbe this hasn't been a chase! Jim and Wallace an' me went tumblin' down after the dogs, each one lookin' out for his perticilar dog, an' darn me if I don't believe his lion, too. Don took one oozin' down the canyon, with me hot-footin' it after him. An' somewhere he treed thet lion, right below me, in a box canyon, sort of an offshoot of the second rim, an' I couldn't locate him. I blamed near killed myself more'n once. Look at my knuckles! Barked em slidin' about a mile down a smooth wall. I thought once the lion had jumped Don, but soon I heard him barkin' again. All thet time I heard Sounder, an' once I heard the pup. Jim yelled, an' somebody was shootin'. But I couldn't find nobody, or make nobody hear me. Thet canyon is a mighty deceivin' place. You'd never think so till you go down. I wouldn't climb up it again for all the lions in Buckskin. Hello, there comes Jim oozin' up."

Jim appeared just over the rim, and when he got up to us, dusty, torn and fagged out, with Don, Tige and Ranger showing signs of collapse, we all blurted out questions. But Jim took his time.

"Shore thet canyon is one hell of a place," he began finally. "Where was everybody? Tige and the pup went down with me an' treed a cougar. Yes, they did, an' I set under a pinyon holdin' the pup, while Tige kept the cougar treed. I yelled an' yelled. After about an hour or two, Wallace came poundin' down like a giant. It was a sure thing we'd get the cougar; an' Wallace was takin' his picture when the blamed cat jumped. It was embarrassin', because he wasn't polite about how he jumped. We scattered some, an' when Wallace got his gun, the cougar was humpin' down the slope, an' he was goin' so fast an' the pinyons was so thick thet Wallace couldn't get a fair shot, an' missed. Tige an' the pup was so scared by the shots they wouldn't take the trail again. I heard some one shoot about a million times, an' shore thought the cougar was done for. Wallace went plungin' down the slope an' I followed. I couldn't keep up with him—he shore takes long steps—an' I lost him. I'm reckonin' he went over the second wall. Then I made tracks for the top. Boys, the way you can see an' hear things down in thet canyon, an' the way you can't hear an' see things is pretty funny."

CHAPTER 14. ALL HEROES BUT ONE

"If Wallace went over the second rim wall, will he get back to-day?" we all asked.

"Shore, there's no tellin'."

We waited, lounged, and slept for three hours, and were beginning to worry about our comrade when he hove in sight eastward, along the rim. He walked like a man whose next step would be his last. When he reached us, he fell flat, and lay breathing heavily for a while.

"Somebody once mentioned Israel Putnam's ascent of a hill," he said slowly. "With all respect to history and a patriot, I wish to say Putnam never saw a hill!"

"Ooze for camp," called out Frank.

Five o'clock found us round a bright fire, all casting ravenous eyes at a smoking supper. The smell of the Persian meat would have made a wolf of a vegetarian. I devoured four chops, and could not have been counted in the running. Jim opened a can of maple syrup which he had been saving for a grand occasion, and Frank went him one better with two cans of peaches. How glorious to be hungry—to feel the craving for food, and to be grateful for it, to realize that the best of life lies in the daily needs of existence, and to battle for them!

Nothing could be stronger than the simple enumeration and statement of the facts of Wallace's experience after he left Jim. He chased the cougar, and kept it in sight, until it went over the second rim wall. Here he dropped over a precipice twenty feet high, to alight on a fan-shaped slide which spread toward the bottom. It began to slip and move by jerks, and then started off steadily, with an increasing roar. He rode an avalanche for one thousand feet. The jar loosened bowlders from the walls. When the slide stopped, Wallace extricated his feet and began to dodge the bowlders. He had only time to jump over the large ones or dart to one side out of their way. He dared not run. He had to watch them coming. One huge stone hurtled over his head and smashed a pinyon tree below.

When these had ceased rolling, and he had passed down to the red shale, he heard Sounder baying near, and knew a cougar had been treed or cornered. Hurdling the stones and dead pinyons, Wallace ran a mile down the slope, only to find he had been deceived in the direction. He sheered off to the left. Sounder's illusive bay came up from a deep cleft. Wallace plunged into a pinyon, climbed to the ground, skidded down a solid slide, to come upon an impassable the obstacle in the form of a solid wall of red granite. Sounder appeared and came to him, evidently having given up the chase.

Wallace consumed four hours in making the ascent. In the notch of the curve of the second rim wall, he climbed the slippery steps of a waterfall. At one point, if he had not been six feet five inches tall he would have been compelled to attempt retracing his trail—an impossible task. But his height enabled him to reach a root, by which he pulled himself up. Sounder he lassoed a la Jones, and hauled up. At another spot, which Sounder climbed, he lassoed a pinyon above, and walked up with his feet slipping from under him at every step. The knees of his corduroy trousers were holes, as were the elbows of his coat. The sole of his left boot, which he used most in climbing—was gone, and so was his hat.

CHAPTER 15. JONES ON COUGARS

The mountain lion, or cougar, of our Rocky Mountain region, is nothing more nor less than the panther. He is a little different in shape, color and size, which vary according to his environment. The panther of the Rockies is usually light, taking the grayish hue of the rocks. He is stockier and heavier of build, and stronger of limb than the Eastern species, which difference comes from climbing mountains and springing down the cliffs after his prey.

In regions accessible to man, or where man is encountered even rarely, the cougar is exceedingly shy, seldom or never venturing from cover during the day. He spends the hours of daylight high on the most rugged cliffs, sleeping and basking in the sunshine, and watching with wonderfully keen sight the valleys below. His hearing equals his sight, and if danger threatens, he always hears it in time to skulk away unseen. At night he steals down the mountain side toward deer or elk he has located during the day. Keeping to the lowest ravines and thickets, he creeps upon his prey. His cunning and ferocity are keener and more savage in proportion to the length of time he has been without food. As he grows hungrier and thinner, his skill and fierce strategy correspondingly increase. A well-fed cougar will creep upon and secure only about one in seven of the deer, elk, antelope or mountain sheep that he stalks. But a starving cougar is another animal. He creeps like a snake, is as sure on the scent as a vulture, makes no more noise than a shadow, and he hides behind a stone or bush that would scarcely conceal a rabbit. Then he springs with terrific force, and intensity of purpose, and seldom fails to reach his victim, and once the claws of a starved lion touch flesh, they never let go.

A cougar seldom pursues his quarry after he has leaped and missed, either from disgust or failure, or knowledge that a second attempt would be futile. The animal making the easiest prey for the cougar is the elk. About every other elk attacked falls a victim. Deer are more fortunate, the ratio being one dead to five leaped at. The antelope, living on the lowlands or upland meadows, escapes nine times out of ten; and the mountain sheep, or bighorn, seldom falls to the onslaught of his enemy.

Once the lion gets a hold with the great forepaw, every movement of the struggling prey sinks the sharp, hooked claws deeper. Then as quickly as is possible, the lion fastens his teeth in the throat of his prey and grips till it is dead. In this way elk have carried lions for many rods. The lion seldom tears the skin of the neck, and never, as is generally supposed, sucks the blood of its victim; but he cuts into the side, just behind the foreshoulder, and eats the liver first. He rolls the skin back as neatly and tightly as a person could do it. When he has gorged himself, he drags the carcass into a ravine or dense thicket, and rakes leaves, sticks or dirt over it to hide it from other animals. Usually he returns to his cache on the second night, and after that the frequency of his visits depends on the supply of fresh prey. In remote regions, unfrequented by man, the lion will guard his cache from coyote and buzzards.

In sex there are about five female lions to one male. This is caused by the jealous and vicious disposition of the male. It is a fact that the old Toms kill every young lion they can catch. Both male and female of the litter suffer alike until after weaning time, and then only the males. In this matter wise animal logic is displayed by the Toms. The domestic cat, to some extent, possesses the same trait. If the litter is destroyed, the mating time is sure to come about regardless of the season. Thus this savage trait of the lions prevents overproduction, and breeds a hardy and intrepid race. If by chance or that cardinal feature of animal life—the survival of the fittest—a young male lion escapes to the weaning time, even after that he is persecuted. Young male lions have been killed and found to have had their flesh beaten until it was a mass of bruises and undoubtedly it had been the work of an old Tom. Moreover, old males and females have been killed, and found to be in the same bruised condition. A feature, and a conclusive one, is the fact that invariably the female is suckling her young at this period, and sustains the bruises in desperately defending her litter.

It is astonishing how cunning, wise and faithful an old lioness is. She seldom leaves her kittens. From the time they are six weeks old she takes them out to train them for the battles of life, and the struggle continues from birth to death. A lion hardly ever dies naturally. As soon as night descends, the lioness stealthily stalks forth, and because of her little ones, takes very short steps. The cubs follow, stepping in their mother's tracks. When she crouches for game, each little lion crouches also, and each one remains perfectly still until she springs, or signals them to come. If she secures the prey, they all gorge themselves. After the feast the mother takes her back trail, stepping in the tracks she made coming down the mountain. And the cubs are very careful to follow suit, and not to leave marks of their trail in the soft snow. No doubt this habit is practiced to keep their deadly enemies in ignorance of their existence. The old Toms and white hunters are their only foes. Indians never kill a lion. This trick of the lions has fooled many a hunter, concerning not only the direction, but particularly the number.

The only successful way to hunt lions is with trained dogs. A good hound can trail them for several hours after the tracks have been made, and on a cloudy or wet day can hold the scent much longer. In snow the hound can trail for three or four days after the track has been made.

When Jones was game warden of the Yellowstone National Park, he had unexampled opportunities to hunt cougars and learn their habits. All the cougars in that region of the Rockies made a rendezvous of the game preserve. Jones soon procured a pack of hounds, but as they had been trained to run deer, foxes and coyotes he had great trouble. They would break on the trail of these animals, and also on elk and antelope just when this was farthest from his wish. He soon realized that to train the hounds was a sore task. When they refused to come back at his call, he stung them with fine shot, and in this manner taught obedience. But obedience was not enough; the hounds must know how to follow and tree a lion. With this in mind, Jones decided to catch a lion alive and give his dogs practical lessons.

A few days after reaching this decision, he discovered the tracks of two lions in the neighborhood of Mt. Everett. The hounds were put on the trail and followed it into an abandoned coal shaft. Jones recognized this as his opportunity, and taking his lasso and an extra rope, he crawled into the hole. Not fifteen feet from the opening sat one of the cougars, snarling and spitting. Jones promptly lassoed it, passed his end of the lasso round a side prop of the shaft, and out to the soldiers who had followed him. Instructing them not to pull till he called, he cautiously began to crawl by the cougar, with the intention of getting farther back and roping its hind leg, so as to prevent disaster when the soldiers pulled it out. He accomplished this, not without some uneasiness in regard to the second lion, and giving the word to his companions, soon had his captive hauled from the shaft and tied so tightly it could not move.

Jones took the cougar and his hounds to an open place in the park, where there were trees, and prepared for a chase. Loosing the lion, he held his hounds back a moment, then let them go. Within one hundred yards the cougar climbed a tree, and the dogs saw the performance. Taking a forked stick, Jones mounted up to the cougar, caught it under the jaw with the stick, and pushed it out. There was a fight, a scramble, and the cougar dashed off to run up another tree. In this manner, he soon trained his hounds to the pink of perfection.

Jones discovered, while in the park, that the cougar is king of all the beasts of North America. Even a grizzly dashed away in great haste when a cougar made his appearance. At the road camp, near Mt. Washburn, during the fall of 1904, the bears, grizzlies and others, were always hanging round the cook tent. There were cougars also, and almost every evening, about dusk, a big fellow would come parading past the tent. The bears would grunt furiously and scamper in every direction. It was easy to tell when a cougar was in the neighborhood, by the peculiar grunts and snorts of the bears, and the sharp, distinct, alarmed yelps of coyotes. A lion would just as lief kill a coyote as any other animal and he would devour it, too. As to the fighting of cougars and grizzlies, that was a mooted question, with the credit on the side of the former.

The story of the doings of cougars, as told in the snow, was intensely fascinating and tragic! How they stalked deer and elk, crept to within springing distance, then crouched flat to leap, was as easy to read as if it had been told in print. The leaps and bounds were beyond belief. The longest leap on a level measured eighteen and one-half feet. Jones trailed a half-grown cougar, which in turn was trailing a big elk. He found where the cougar had struck his game, had clung for many rods, to be dashed off by the low limb of a spruce tree. The imprint of the body of the cougar was a foot deep in the snow; blood and tufts of hair covered the place. But there was no sign of the cougar renewing the chase.

In rare cases cougars would refuse to run, or take to trees. One day Jones followed the hounds, eight in number, to come on a huge Tom holding the whole pack at bay. He walked to and fro, lashing his tail from side to side, and when Jones dashed up, he coolly climbed a tree. Jones shot the cougar, which, in falling, struck one of the hounds, crippling him. This hound would never approach a tree after this incident, believing probably that the cougar had sprung upon him.

Usually the hounds chased their quarry into a tree long before Jones rode up. It was always desirable to kill the animal with the first shot. If the cougar was wounded, and fell or jumped among the dogs, there was sure to be a terrible fight, and the best dogs always received serious injuries, if they were not killed outright. The lion would seize a hound, pull him close, and bite him in the brain.

Jones asserted that a cougar would usually run from a hunter, but that this feature was not to be relied upon. And a wounded cougar was as dangerous as a tiger. In his hunts Jones carried a shotgun, and shells loaded with ball for the cougar, and others loaded with fine shot for the hounds. One day, about ten miles from the camp, the hounds took a trail and ran rapidly, as there were only a few inches of snow. Jones found a large lion had taken refuge in a tree that had fallen against another, and aiming at the shoulder of the beast, he fired both barrels. The cougar made no sign he had been hit. Jones reloaded and fired at the head. The old fellow growled fiercely, turned in the tree and walked down head first, something he would not have been able to do had the tree been upright. The hounds were ready for him, but wisely attacked in the rear. Realizing he had been shooting fine shot at the animal, Jones began a hurried search for a shell loaded with ball. The lion made for him, compelling him to dodge behind trees. Even though the hounds kept nipping the cougar, the persistent fellow still pursued the hunter. At last Jones found the right shell, just as the cougar reached for him. Major, the leader of the hounds, darted bravely in, and grasped the leg of the beast just in the nick of time. This enabled Jones to take aim and fire at close range, which ended the fight. Upon examination, it was discovered the cougar had been half-blinded by the fine shot, which accounted for the ineffectual attempts he had made to catch Jones.

The mountain lion rarely attacks a human being for the purpose of eating. When hungry he will often follow the tracks of people, and under favorable circumstances may ambush them. In the park where game is plentiful, no one has ever known a cougar to follow the trail of a person; but outside the park lions have been known to follow hunters, and particularly stalk little children. The Davis family, living a few miles north of the park, have had children pursued to the very doors of their cabin. And other families relate similar experiences. Jones heard of only one fatality, but he believes that if the children were left alone in the woods, the cougars would creep closer and closer, and when assured there was no danger, would spring to kill.

Jones never heard the cry of a cougar in the National Park, which strange circumstance, considering the great number of the animals there, he believed to be on account of the abundance of game. But he had heard it when a boy in Illinois, and when a man all over the West, and the cry was always the same, weird and wild, like the scream of a terrified woman. He did not understand the significance of the cry, unless it meant hunger, or the wailing mourn of a lioness for her murdered cubs.

The destructiveness of this savage species was murderous. Jones came upon one old Tom's den, where there was a pile of nineteen elk, mostly yearlings. Only five or six had been eaten. Jones hunted this old fellow for months, and found that the lion killed on the average three animals a week. The hounds got him up at length, and chased him to the Yellowstone River, which he swam at a point impassable for man or horse. One of the dogs, a giant bloodhound named Jack, swam the swift channel, kept on after the lion, but never returned. All cougars have their peculiar traits and habits, the same as other creatures, and all old Toms have strongly marked characteristics, but this one was the most destructive cougar Jones ever knew.

During Jones's short sojourn as warden in the park, he captured numerous cougars alive, and killed seventy-two.

CHAPTER 16. KITTY

It seemed my eyelids had scarcely touched when Jones's exasperating, yet stimulating, yell aroused me. Day was breaking. The moon and stars shone with wan luster. A white, snowy frost silvered the forest. Old Moze had curled close beside me, and now he gazed at me reproachfully and shivered. Lawson came hustling in with the horses. Jim busied himself around the campfire. My fingers nearly froze while I saddled my horse.

At five o'clock we were trotting up the slope of Buckskin, bound for the section of ruined rim wall where we had encountered the convention of cougars. Hoping to save time, we took a short cut, and were soon crossing deep ravines.

The sunrise coloring the purple curtain of cloud over the canyon was too much for me, and I lagged on a high ridge to watch it, thus falling behind my more practical companions. A far-off "Waa-hoo!" brought me to a realization of the day's stern duty and I hurried Satan forward on the trail.

I came suddenly upon our leader, leading his horse through the scrub pinyon on the edge of the canyon, and I knew at once something had happened, for he was closely scrutinizing the ground.

"I declare this beats me all hollow!" began Jones. "We might be hunting rabbits instead of the wildest animals on the continent. We jumped a bunch of lions in this clump of pinyon. There must have been at least four. I thought first we'd run upon an old lioness with cubs, but all the trails were made by full-grown lions. Moze took one north along the rim, same as the other day, but the lion got away quick. Frank saw one lion. Wallace is following Sounder down into the first hollow. Jim has gone over the rim wall after Don. There you are! Four lions playing tag in broad daylight on top of this wall! I'm inclined to believe Clarke didn't exaggerate. But confound the luck! the hounds have split again. They're doing their best, of course, and it's up to us to stay with them. I'm afraid we'll lose some of them. Hello! I hear a signal. That's from Wallace. Waa-hoo! Waa-hoo! There he is, coming out of the hollow."

The tall Californian reached us presently with Sounder beside him. He reported that the hound had chased a lion into an impassable break. We then joined Frank on a jutting crag of the canyon wall.

"Waa-hoo!" yelled Jones. There was no answer except the echo, and it rolled up out of the chasm with strange, hollow mockery.

"Don took a cougar down this slide," said Frank. "I saw the brute, an' Don was makin' him hump. A—ha! There! Listen to thet!"

From the green and yellow depths soared the faint yelp of a hound.

"That's Don! that's Don!" cried Jones. "He's hot on something. Where's Sounder? Hyar, Sounder! By George! there he goes down the slide. Hear him! He's opened up! Hi! Hi! Hi!"

The deep, full mellow bay of the hound came ringing on the clear air.

"Wallace, you go down. Frank and I will climb out on that pointed crag. Grey, you stay here. Then we'll have the slide between us. Listen and watch!"

From my promontory I watched Wallace go down with his gigantic strides, sending the rocks rolling and cracking; and then I saw Jones and Frank crawl out to the end of a crumbling ruin of yellow wall which threatened to go splintering and thundering down into the abyss.

I thought, as I listened to the penetrating voice of the hound, that nowhere on earth could there be a grander scene for wild action, wild life. My position afforded a commanding view over a hundred miles of the noblest and most sublime work of nature. The rim wall where I stood sheered down a thousand feet, to meet a long wooded slope which cut abruptly off into another giant precipice; a second long slope descended, and jumped off into what seemed the grave of the world. Most striking in that vast void were the long, irregular points of rim wall, protruding into the Grand Canyon. From Point Sublime to the Pink Cliffs of Utah there were twelve of these colossal capes, miles apart, some sharp, some round, some blunt, all rugged and bold. The great chasm in the middle was full of purple smoke. It seemed a mighty sepulcher from which misty fumes rolled upward. The turrets, mesas, domes, parapets and escarpments of yellow and red rock gave the appearance of an architectural work of giant hands. The wonderful river of silt, the blood-red, mystic and sullen Rio Colorado, lay hidden except in one place far away, where it glimmered wanly. Thousands of colors were blended before my rapt gaze. Yellow predominated, as the walls and crags lorded it over the lower cliffs and tables; red glared in the sunlight; green softened these two, and then purple and violet, gray, blue and the darker hues shaded away into dim and distinct obscurity.

Excited yells from my companions on the other crag recalled me to the living aspect of the scene. Jones was leaning far down in a niche, at seeming great hazard of life, yelling with all the power of his strong lungs. Frank stood still farther out on a cracked point that made me tremble, and his yell reenforced Jones's. From far below rolled up a chorus of thrilling bays and yelps, and Jim's call, faint, but distinct on that wonderfully thin air, with its unmistakable note of warning.

Then on the slide I saw a lion headed for the rim wall and climbing fast. I added my exultant cry to the medley, and I stretched my arms wide to that illimitable void and gloried in a moment full to the brim of the tingling joy of existence. I did not consider how painful it must have been to the toiling lion. It was only the spell of wild environment, of perilous yellow crags, of thin, dry air, of voice of man and dog, of the stinging expectation of sharp action, of life.

CHAPTER 16. KITTY

I watched the lion growing bigger and bigger. I saw Don and Sounder run from the pinyon into the open slide, and heard their impetuous burst of wild yelps as they saw their game. Then Jones's clarion yell made me bound for my horse. I reached him, was about to mount, when Moze came trotting toward me. I caught the old gladiator. When he heard the chorus from below, he plunged like a mad bull. With both arms round him I held on. I vowed never to let him get down that slide. He howled and tore, but I held on. My big black horse with ears laid back stood like a rock.

I heard the pattering of little sliding rocks below; stealthy padded footsteps and hard panting breaths, almost like coughs; then the lion passed out of the slide not twenty feet away. He saw us, and sprang into the pinyon scrub with the leap of a scared deer.

Samson himself could no longer have held Moze. Away he darted with his sharp, angry bark. I flung myself upon Satan and rode out to see Jones ahead and Frank flashing through the green on the white horse.

At the end of the pinyon thicket Satan overhauled Jones's bay, and we entered the open forest together. We saw Frank glinting across the dark pines.

"Hi! Hi!" yelled the Colonel.

No need was there to whip or spur those magnificent horses. They were fresh; the course was open, and smooth as a racetrack, and the impelling chorus of the hounds was in full blast. I gave Satan a loose rein, and he stayed neck and neck with the bay. There was not a log, nor a stone, nor a gully. The hollows grew wider and shallower as we raced along, and presently disappeared altogether. The lion was running straight from the canyon, and the certainty that he must sooner or later take to a tree, brought from me a yell of irresistible wild joy.

"Hi! Hi! Hi!" answered Jones.

The whipping wind with its pine-scented fragrance, warm as the breath of summer, was intoxicating as wine. The huge pines, too kingly for close communion with their kind, made wide arches under which the horses stretched out long and low, with supple, springy, powerful strides. Frank's yell rang clear as a bell. We saw him curve to the right, and took his yell as a signal for us to cut across. Then we began to close in on him, and to hear more distinctly the baying of the hounds.

"Hi! Hi! Hi! Hi!" bawled Jones, and his great trumpet voice rolled down the forest glades.

"Hi! Hi! Hi! Hi!" I screeched, in wild recognition of the spirit of the moment.

Fast as they were flying, the bay and the black responded to our cries, and quickened, strained and lengthened under us till the trees sped by in blurs.

There, plainly in sight ahead ran the hounds, Don leading, Sounder next, and Moze not fifty yards, behind a desperately running lion.

There are all-satisfying moments of life. That chase through the open forest, under the stately pines, with the wild, tawny quarry in plain sight, and the glad staccato yelps of the hounds filling my ears and swelling my heart, with the splendid action of my horse carrying me on the wings of the wind, was glorious answer and fullness to the call and hunger of a hunter's blood.

But as such moments must be, they were brief. The lion leaped gracefully into the air, splintering the bark from a pine fifteen feet up, and crouched on a limb. The hounds tore madly round the tree.

"Full-grown female," said Jones calmly, as we dismounted, "and she's ours. We'll call her Kitty."

Kitty was a beautiful creature, long, slender, glossy, with white belly and black-tipped ears and tail. She did not resemble the heavy, grim-faced brute that always hung in the air of my dreams. A low, brooding menacing murmur, that was not a snarl nor a growl, came from her. She watched the dogs with bright, steady eyes, and never so much as looked at us.

The dogs were worth attention, even from us, who certainly did not need to regard them from her personally hostile point of view. Don stood straight up, with his forepaws beating the air; he walked on his hind legs like the trained dog in the circus; he yelped continuously, as if it agonized him to see the lion safe out of his reach. Sounder had lost his identity. Joy had unhinged his mind and had made him a dog of double personality. He had always been unsocial with me, never responding to my attempts to caress him, but now he leaped into my arms and licked my face. He had always hated Jones till that moment, when he raised his paws to his master's breast. And perhaps more remarkable, time and time again he sprang up at Satan's nose, whether to bite him or kiss him, I could not tell. Then old Moze, he of Grand Canyon fame, made the delirious antics of his canine fellows look cheap. There was a small, dead pine that had fallen against a drooping branch of the tree Kitty had taken refuge in, and up this narrow ladder Moze began to climb. He was fifteen feet up, and Kitty had begun to shift uneasily, when Jones saw him.

"Hyar! you wild coon hyar! Git out of that! Come down! Come down!"

But Jones might have been in the bottom of the canyon for all Moze heard or cared. Jones removed his coat, carefully coiled his lasso, and began to go hand and knee up the leaning pine.

"Hyar! dad-blast you, git down!" yelled Jones, and he kicked Moze off. The persistent hound returned, and followed Jones to a height of twenty feet, where again he was thrust off.

"Hold him, one of you!" called Jones.

"Not me," said Frank, "I'm lookin' out for myself."

"Same here," I cried, with a camera in one hand and a rifle in the other. "Let Moze climb if he likes."

Climb he did, to be kicked off again. But he went back. It was a way he had. Jones at last recognized either his own waste of time or Moze's greatness, for he desisted, allowing the hound to keep close after him.

The cougar, becoming uneasy, stood up, reached for another limb, climbed out upon it, and peering down, spat hissingly at Jones. But he kept steadily on with Moze close on his heels. I snapped my camera on them when Kitty was not more than fifteen feet above them. As Jones reached the snag which upheld the leaning tree, she ran out on her branch, and leaped into an adjoining pine. It was a good long jump, and the weight of the animal bent the limb alarmingly.

Jones backed down, and laboriously began to climb the other tree. As there were no branches low down, he had to hug the trunk with arms and legs as a boy climbs. His lasso hampered his progress. When the slow ascent was accomplished up to the first branch, Kitty leaped back into her first perch. Strange to say Jones did not grumble; none of his characteristic impatience manifested itself. I supposed with him all the exasperating waits, vexatious obstacles, were little things preliminary to the real work, to which he had now come. He was calm and deliberate, and slid down the pine, walked back to the leaning tree, and while resting a moment, shook his lasso at Kitty. This action fitted him, somehow; it was so compatible with his grim assurance.

To me, and to Frank, also, for that matter, it was all new and startling, and we were as excited as the dogs. We kept continually moving about, Frank mounted, and I afoot, to get good views of the cougar. When she crouched as if to leap, it was almost impossible to remain under the tree, and we kept moving.

Once more Jones crept up on hands and knees. Moze walked the slanting pine like a rope performer. Kitty began to grow restless. This time she showed both anger and impatience, but did not yet appear frightened. She growled low and deep, opened her mouth and hissed, and swung her tufted tail faster and faster.

"Look out, Jones! look out!" yelled Frank warningly.

Jones, who had reached the trunk of the tree, halted and slipped round it, placing it between him and Kitty. She had advanced on her limb, a few feet above Jones, and threateningly hung over.

Jones backed down a little till she crossed to another branch, then he resumed his former position.

"Watch below," called he.

Hardly any doubt was there as to how we watched. Frank and I were all eyes, except very high and throbbing hearts. When Jones thrashed the lasso at Kitty we both yelled. She ran out on the branch and jumped. This time she fell short of her point, clutched a dead snag, which broke, letting her through a bushy branch from where she hung head downward. For a second she swung free, then reaching toward the tree caught it with front paws, ran down like a squirrel, and leaped off when thirty feet from the ground. The action was as rapid as it was astonishing.

Like a yellow rubber ball she bounded up, and fled with the yelping hounds at her heels. The chase was short. At the end of a hundred yards Moze caught up with her and nipped her. She whirled with savage suddenness, and lunged at Moze, but he cunningly eluded the vicious paws. Then she sought safety in another pine.

Frank, who was as quick as the hounds, almost rode them down in his eagerness. While Jones descended from his perch, I led the two horses down the forest.

This time the cougar was well out on a low spreading branch. Jones conceived the idea of raising the loop of his lasso on a long pole, but as no pole of sufficient length could be found, he tried from the back of his horse. The bay walked forward well enough; when, however, he got under the beast and heard her growl, he reared and almost threw Jones. Frank's horse could not be persuaded to go near the tree. Satan evinced no fear of the cougar, and without flinching carried Jones directly beneath the limb and stood with ears back and forelegs stiff.

"Look at that! look at that!" cried Jones, as the wary cougar pawed the loop aside. Three successive times did Jones have the lasso just ready to drop over her neck, when she flashed a yellow paw and knocked the noose awry. Then she leaped far out over the waiting dogs, struck the ground with a light, sharp thud, and began to run with the speed of a deer. Frank's cowboy training now stood us in good stead. He was off like a shot and turned the cougar from the direction of the canyon. Jones lost not a moment in pursuit, and I, left with Jones's badly frightened bay, got going in time to see the race, but not to assist. For several hundred yards Kitty made the hounds appear slow. Don, being swiftest, gained on her steadily toward the close of the dash, and presently was running under her upraised tail. On the next jump he nipped her. She turned and sent him reeling. Sounder came flying up to bite her flank, and at the same moment fierce old Moze closed in on her. The next instant a struggling mass whirled on the ground. Jones and Frank, yelling like demons, almost rode over it. The cougar broke from her assailants, and dashing away leaped on the first tree. It was a half-dead pine with short snags low down and a big branch extending out over a ravine.

"I think we can hold her now," said Jones. The tree proved to be a most difficult one to climb. Jones made several ineffectual attempts before he reached the first limb, which broke, giving him a hard fall. This calmed me enough to make me take notice of Jones's condition. He was wet with sweat and covered with the black pitch from the pines; his shirt was slit down the arm, and there was blood on his temple and his hand. The next attempt began by placing a good-sized log against the tree, and proved to be the necessary help. Jones got hold of the second limb and pulled himself up.

As he kept on, Kitty crouched low as if to spring upon him. Again Frank and I sent warning calls to him, but he paid no attention to us or to the cougar, and continued to climb. This worried Kitty as much as it did us. She began to move on the snags, stepping from one to the other, every moment snarling at Jones, and then she crawled up. The big branch evidently took her eye. She tried several times to climb up to it, but small snags close together made her distrustful. She walked uneasily out upon two limbs, and as they bent with her weight she hurried back. Twice she did this, each time looking up, showing her desire to leap to the big branch. Her distress became plainly evident; a child could have seen that she feared she would fall. At length, in desperation, she spat at Jones, then ran out and leaped. She all but missed the branch, but succeeded in holding to it and swinging to safety. Then she turned to her tormentor, and gave utterance to most savage sounds. As she did not intimidate her pursuer, she retreated out on the branch, which sloped down at a deep angle, and crouched on a network of small limbs.

CHAPTER 16. KITTY

When Jones had worked up a little farther, he commanded a splendid position for his operations. Kitty was somewhat below him in a desirable place, yet the branch she was on joined the tree considerably above his head. Jones cast his lasso. It caught on a snag. Throw after throw he made with like result. He recoiled and recast nineteen times, to my count, when Frank made a suggestion.

"Rope those dead snags an' break them off."

This practical idea Jones soon carried out, which left him a clear path. The next fling of the lariat caused the cougar angrily to shake her head. Again Jones sent the noose flying. She pulled it off her back and bit it savagely.

Though very much excited, I tried hard to keep sharp, keen faculties alert so as not to miss a single detail of the thrilling scene. But I must have failed, for all of a sudden I saw how Jones was standing in the tree, something I had not before appreciated. He had one hand hold, which he could not use while recoiling the lasso, and his feet rested upon a precariously frail-appearing, dead snag. He made eleven casts of the lasso, all of which bothered Kitty, but did not catch her. The twelfth caught her front paw. Jones jerked so quickly and hard that he almost lost his balance, and he pulled the noose off. Patiently he recoiled the lasso.

"That's what I want. If I can get her front paw she's ours. My idea is to pull her off the limb, let her hang there, and then lasso her hind legs."

Another cast, the unlucky thirteenth, settled the loop perfectly round her neck. She chewed on the rope with her front teeth and appeared to have difficulty in holding it.

"Easy! Easy! Ooze thet rope! Easy!" yelled the cowboy.

Cautiously Jones took up the slack and slowly tightened the nose, then with a quick jerk, fastened it close round her neck.

We heralded this achievement with yells of triumph that made the forest ring.

Our triumph was short-lived. Jones had hardly moved when the cougar shot straight out into the air. The lasso caught on a branch, hauling her up short, and there she hung in mid-air, writhing, struggling and giving utterance to sounds terribly human. For several seconds she swung, slowly descending, in which frenzied time I, with ruling passion uppermost, endeavored to snap a picture of her.

The unintelligible commands Jones was yelling to Frank and me ceased suddenly with a sharp crack of breaking wood. Then crash! Jones fell out of the tree. The lasso streaked up, ran over the limb, while the cougar dropped pell-mell into the bunch of waiting, howling dogs.

The next few moments it was impossible for me to distinguish what actually transpired. A great flutter of leaves whirled round a swiftly changing ball of brown and black and yellow, from which came a fiendish clamor.

Then I saw Jones plunge down the ravine and bounce here and there in mad efforts to catch the whipping lasso. He was roaring in a way that made all his former yells merely whispers. Starting to run, I tripped on a root, fell prone on my face into the ravine, and rolled over and over until I brought up with a bump against a rock.

What a tableau rivited my gaze! It staggered me so I did not think of my camera. I stood transfixed not fifteen feet from the cougar. She sat on her haunches with body well drawn back by the taut lasso to which Jones held tightly. Don was standing up with her, upheld by the hooked claws in his head. The cougar had her paws outstretched; her mouth open wide, showing long, cruel, white fangs; she was trying to pull the head of the dog to her. Don held back with all his power, and so did Jones. Moze and Sounder were tussling round her body. Suddenly both ears of the dog pulled out, slit into ribbons. Don had never uttered a sound, and once free, he made at her again with open jaws. One blow sent him reeling and stunned. Then began again that wrestling whirl.

"Beat off the dogs! Beat off the dogs!" roared Jones. "She'll kill them! She'll kill them!"

Frank and I seized clubs and ran in upon the confused furry mass, forgetful of peril to ourselves. In the wild contagion of such a savage moment the minds of men revert wholly to primitive instincts. We swung our clubs and yelled; we fought all over the bottom of the ravine, crashing through the bushes, over logs and stones. I actually felt the soft fur of the cougar at one fleeting instant. The dogs had the strength born of insane fighting spirit. At last we pulled them to where Don lay, half-stunned, and with an arm tight round each, I held them while Frank turned to help Jones.

The disheveled Jones, bloody, grim as death, his heavy jaw locked, stood holding to the lasso. The cougar, her sides shaking with short, quick pants, crouched low on the ground with eyes of purple fire.

"For God's sake, get a half-hitch on the saplin'!" called the cowboy.

His quick grasp of the situation averted a tragedy. Jones was nearly exhausted, even as he was beyond thinking for himself or giving up. The cougar sprang, a yellow, frightful flash. Even as she was in the air, Jones took a quick step to one side and dodged as he threw his lasso round the sapling. She missed him, but one alarmingly outstretched paw grazed his shoulder. A twist of Jones's big hand fastened the lasso—and Kitty was a prisoner. While she fought, rolled, twisted, bounded, whirled, writhed with hissing, snarling fury, Jones sat mopping the sweat and blood from his face.

Kitty's efforts were futile; she began to weaken from the choking. Jones took another rope, and tightening a noose around her back paws, which he lassoed as she rolled over, he stretched her out. She began to contract her supple body, gave a savage, convulsive spring, which pulled Jones flat on the ground, then the terrible wrestling started again. The lasso slipped over her back paws. She leaped the whole length of the other lasso. Jones caught it and fastened it more securely; but this precaution proved unnecessary, for she suddenly sank down either exhausted or choked, and gasped with her tongue hanging out. Frank slipped the second noose over her back paws, and Jones did likewise with a third lasso over her right front paw. These lassoes Jones tied to different saplings.

"Now you are a good Kitty," said Jones, kneeling by her. He took a pair of clippers from his hip pocket, and grasping a paw in his powerful fist he calmly clipped the points of the dangerous claws. This done, he called to me to get the collar and chain that were tied to his saddle. I procured them and hurried back. Then the old buffalo hunter loosened the lasso which was round her neck, and as soon as she could move her head, he teased her to bite a club. She broke two good sticks with her sharp teeth, but the third, being solid, did not break. While she was chewing it Jones forced her head back and placed his heavy knee on the club. In a twinkling he had strapped the collar round her neck. The chain he made fast to the sapling. After removing the club from her mouth he placed his knee on her neck, and while her head was in this helpless position he dexterously slipped a loop of thick copper wire over her nose, pushed it back and twisted it tight Following this, all done with speed and precision, he took from his pocket a piece of steel rod, perhaps one-quarter of an inch thick, and five inches long. He pushed this between Kitty's jaws, just back of her great white fangs, and in front of the copper wire. She had been shorn of her sharp weapons; she was muzzled, bound, helpless, an object to pity.

Lastly Jones removed the three lassoes. Kitty slowly gathered her lissom body in a ball and lay panting, with the same brave wildfire in her eyes. Jones stroked her black-tipped ears and ran his hand down her glossy fur. All the time he had kept up a low monotone, talking to her in the strange language he used toward animals. Then he rose to his feet.

"We'll go back to camp now, and get a pack, saddle and horse," he said. "She'll be safe here. We'll rope her again, tie her up, throw her over a pack-saddle, and take her to camp."

To my utter bewilderment the hounds suddenly commenced fighting among themselves. Of all the vicious bloody dog-fights I ever saw that was the worst. I began to belabor them with a club, and Frank sprang to my assistance. Beating had no apparent effect. We broke a dozen sticks, and then Frank grappled with Moze and I with Sounder. Don kept on fighting either one till Jones secured him. Then we all took a rest, panting and weary.

"What's it mean?" I ejaculated, appealing to Jones.

"Jealous, that's all. Jealous over the lion."

We all remained seated, men and hounds, a sweaty, dirty, bloody, ragged group. I discovered I was sorry for Kitty. I forgot all the carcasses of deer and horses, the brutality of this species of cat; and even forgot the grim, snarling yellow devil that had leaped at me. Kitty was beautiful and helpless. How brave she was, too! No sign of fear shone in her wonderful eyes, only hate, defiance, watchfulness.

On the ride back to camp Jones expressed himself thus: "How happy I am that I can keep this lion and the others we are going to capture, for my own. When I was in the Yellowstone Park I did not get to keep one of the many I captured. The military officials took them from me."

When we reached camp Lawson was absent, but fortunately Old Baldy browsed near at hand, and was easily caught. Frank said he would rather take Old

Baldy for the cougar than any other horse we had. Leaving me in camp, he and Jones rode off to fetch Kitty.

About five o'clock they came trotting up through the forest with Jim, who had fallen in with them on the way. Old Baldy had remained true to his fame—nothing, not even a cougar bothered him. Kitty, evidently no worse for her experience, was chained to a pine tree about fifty feet from the campfire.

Wallace came riding wearily in, and when he saw the captive, he greeted us with an exultant yell. He got there just in time to see the first special features of Kitty's captivity. The hounds surrounded her, and could not be called off. We had to beat them. Whereupon the six jealous canines fell to fighting among themselves, and fought so savagely as to be deaf to our cries and insensible to blows. They had to be torn apart and chained.

About six o'clock Lawson loped in with the horses. Of course he did not know we had a cougar, and no one seemed interested enough to inform him. Perhaps only Frank and I thought of it; but I saw a merry snap in Frank's eyes, and kept silent. Kitty had hidden behind the pine tree. Lawson, astride Jones' pack horse, a crochety animal, reined in just abreast of the tree, and leisurely threw his leg over the saddle. Kitty leaped out to the extent of her chain, and fairly exploded in a frightful cat-spit.

Lawson had stated some time before that he was afraid of cougars, which was a weakness he need not have divulged in view of what happened. The horse plunged, throwing him ten feet, and snorting in terror, stampeded with the rest of the bunch and disappeared among the pines.

"Why the hell didn't you tell a feller?" reproachfully growled the Arizonian. Frank and Jim held each other upright, and the rest of us gave way to as hearty if not as violent mirth.

We had a gay supper, during which Kitty sat her pine and watched our every movement.

"We'll rest up for a day or two," said Jones "Things have commenced to come our way. If I'm not mistaken we'll bring an old Tom alive into camp. But it would never do for us to get a big Tom in the fix we had Kitty to-day. You see, I wanted to lasso her front paw, pull her off the limb, tie my end of the lasso to the tree, and while she hung I'd go down and rope her hind paws. It all went wrong to-day, and was as tough a job as I ever handled."

Not until late next morning did Lawson corral all the horses. That day we lounged in camp mending broken bridles, saddles, stirrups, lassoes, boots, trousers, leggins, shirts and even broken skins.

During this time I found Kitty a most interesting study. She reminded me of an enormous yellow kitten. She did not appear wild or untamed until approached. Then she slowly sank down, laid back her ears, opened her mouth and hissed and spat, at the same time throwing both paws out viciously. Kitty may have rested, but did not sleep. At times she fought her chain, tugging and straining at it, and trying to bite it through. Everything in reach she clawed, particularly the bark of the tree. Once she tried to hang herself by leaping over a low limb. When any one walked by her she crouched low, evidently imagining herself unseen. If one of us walked toward her, or looked at her, she did not crouch. At other times, noticeably when no one was near, she would roll on her back and extend all four paws in the air. Her actions were beautiful, soft, noiseless, quick and subtle.

The day passed, as all days pass in camp, swiftly and pleasantly, and twilight stole down upon us round the ruddy fire. The wind roared in the pines and lulled to repose; the lonesome, friendly coyote barked; the bells on the hobbled horses jingled sweetly; the great watch stars blinked out of the blue.

The red glow of the burning logs lighted up Jones's calm, cold face. Tranquil, unalterable and peaceful it seemed; yet beneath the peace I thought I saw a suggestion of wild restraint, of mystery, of unslaked life.

Strangely enough, his next words confirmed my last thought.

"For forty years I've had an ambition. It's to get possession of an island in the Pacific, somewhere between Vancouver and Alaska, and then go to Siberia and capture a lot of Russian sables. I'd put them on the island and cross them with our silver foxes. I'm going to try it next year if I can find the time."

The ruling passion and character determine our lives. Jones was sixty-three years old, yet the thing that had ruled and absorbed his mind was still as strong as the longing for freedom in Kitty's wild heart.

Hours after I had crawled into my sleeping-bag, in the silence of night I heard her working to get free. In darkness she was most active, restless, intense. I heard the clink of her chain, the crack of her teeth, the scrape of her claws. How tireless she was. I recalled the wistful light in her eyes that saw, no doubt, far beyond the campfire to the yellow crags, to the great downward slopes, to freedom. I slipped my elbow out of the bag and raised myself. Dark shadows were hovering under the pines. I saw Kitty's eyes gleam like sparks, and I seemed to see in them the hate, the fear, the terror she had of the clanking thing that bound her!

I shivered, perhaps from the cold night wind which moaned through the pines; I saw the stars glittering pale and far off, and under their wan light the still, set face of Jones, and blanketed forms of my other companions.

The last thing I remembered before dropping into dreamless slumber was hearing a bell tinkle in the forest, which I recognized as the one I had placed on Satan.

CHAPTER 17. CONCLUSION

Kitty was not the only cougar brought into camp alive. The ensuing days were fruitful of cougars and adventure. There were more wild rides to the music of the baying hounds, and more heart-breaking canyon slopes to conquer, and more swinging, tufted tails and snarling savage faces in the pinyons. Once again, I am sorry to relate, I had to glance down the sights of the little Remington, and I saw blood on the stones. Those eventful days sped by all too soon.

When the time for parting came it took no little discussion to decide on the quickest way of getting me to a railroad. I never fully appreciated the inaccessibility of the Siwash until the question arose of finding a way out. To return on our back trail would require two weeks, and to go out by the trail north to Utah meant half as much time over the same kind of desert. Lawson came to our help, however, with the information that an occasional prospector or horse hunter crossed the canyon from the Saddle, where a trail led down to the river.

"I've heard the trail is a bad one," said Lawson, "an' though I never seen it, I reckon it could be found. After we get to the Saddle we'll build two fires on one of the high points an' keep them burnin' well after dark. If Mr. Bass, who lives on the other side, sees the fires he'll come down his trail next mornin' an' meet us at the river. He keeps a boat there. This is takin' a chance, but I reckon it's worth while."

So it was decided that Lawson and Frank would try to get me out by way of the canyon; Wallace intended to go by the Utah route, and Jones was to return at once to his range and his buffalo.

That night round the campfire we talked over the many incidents of the hunt. Jones stated he had never in his life come so near getting his "everlasting" as when the big bay horse tripped on a canyon slope and rolled over him. Notwithstanding the respect with which we regarded his statement we held different opinions. Then, with the unfailing optimism of hunters, we planned another hunt for the next year.

"I'll tell you what," said Jones. "Up in Utah there's a wild region called Pink Cliffs. A few poor sheep-herders try to raise sheep in the valleys. They wouldn't be so poor if it was not for the grizzly and black bears that live on the sheep. We'll go up there, find a place where grass and water can be had, and camp. We'll notify the sheep-herders we are there for business. They'll be only too glad to hustle in with news of a bear, and we can get the hounds on the trail by sun-up. I'll have a dozen hounds then, maybe twenty, and all trained. We'll put every black bear we chase up a tree, and we'll rope and tie him. As to grizzlies—well, I'm not saying so much. They can't climb trees, and they are not afraid of a pack of hounds. If we rounded up a grizzly, got him cornered, and threw a rope on him—there'd be some fun, eh, Jim?"

"Shore there would," Jim replied.

On the strength of this I stored up food for future thought and thus reconciled myself to bidding farewell to the purple canyons and shaggy slopes of Buckskin Mountain.

At five o'clock next morning we were all stirring. Jones yelled at the hounds and untangled Kitty's chain. Jim was already busy with the biscuit dough. Frank shook the frost off the saddles. Wallace was packing. The merry jangle of bells came from the forest, and presently Lawson appeared driving in the horses. I caught my black and saddled him, then realizing we were soon to part I could not resist giving him a hug.

An hour later we all stood at the head of the trail leading down into the chasm. The east gleamed rosy red. Powell's Plateau loomed up in the distance, and under it showed the dark-fringed dip in the rim called the Saddle. Blue mist floated round the mesas and domes.

Lawson led the way down the trail. Frank started Old Baldy with the pack.

"Come," he called, "be oozin' along."

I spoke the last good-by and turned Satan into the narrow trail. When I looked back Jones stood on the rim with the fresh glow of dawn shining on his face. The trail was steep, and claimed my attention and care, but time and time again I gazed back. Jones waved his hand till a huge jutting cliff walled him from view. Then I cast my eyes on the rough descent and the wonderful void beneath me. In my mind lingered a pleasing consciousness of my last sight of the old plainsman. He fitted the scene; he belonged there among the silent pines and the yellow crags.

THE HERITAGE OF THE DESERT

I. THE SIGN OF THE SUNSET

"BUT the man's almost dead."

The words stung John Hare's fainting spirit into life. He opened his eyes. The desert still stretched before him, the appalling thing that had overpowered him with its deceiving purple distance. Near by stood a sombre group of men.

"Leave him here," said one, addressing a gray-bearded giant. "He's the fellow sent into southern Utah to spy out the cattle thieves. He's all but dead. Dene's outlaws are after him. Don't cross Dene."

The stately answer might have come from a Scottish Covenanter or a follower of Cromwell.

"Martin Cole, I will not go a hair's-breadth out of my way for Dene or any other man. You forget your religion. I see my duty to God."

"Yes, August Naab, I know," replied the little man, bitterly. "You would cast the Scriptures in my teeth, and liken this man to one who went down from Jerusalem to Jericho and fell among thieves. But I've suffered enough at the hands of Dene."

The formal speech, the Biblical references, recalled to the reviving Hare that he was still in the land of the Mormons. As he lay there the strange words of the Mormons linked the hard experience of the last few days with the stern reality of the present.

"Martin Cole, I hold to the spirit of our fathers," replied Naab, like one reading from the Old Testament. "They came into this desert land to worship and multiply in peace. They conquered the desert; they prospered with the years that brought settlers, cattle-men, sheep-herders, all hostile to their religion and their livelihood. Nor did they ever fail to succor the sick and unfortunate. What are our toils and perils compared to theirs? Why should we forsake the path of duty, and turn from mercy because of a cut-throat outlaw? I like not the sign of the times, but I am a Mormon; I trust in God."

"August Naab, I am a Mormon too," returned Cole, "but my hands are stained with blood. Soon yours will be if you keep your water-holes and your cattle. Yes, I know. You're strong, stronger than any of us, far off in your desert oasis, hemmed in by walls, cut off by canyons, guarded by your Navajo friends. But Holderness is creeping slowly on you. He'll ignore your water rights and drive your stock. Soon Dene will steal cattle under your very eyes. Don't make them enemies."

"I can't pass by this helpless man," rolled out August Naab's sonorous voice.

Suddenly, with livid face and shaking hand, Cole pointed westward. "There! Dene and his band! See, under the red wall; see the dust, not ten miles away. See them?"

The desert, gray in the foreground, purple in the distance, sloped to the west. Eyes keen as those of hawks searched the waste, and followed the red mountain rampart, which, sheer in bold height and processional in its craggy sweep, shut out the north. Far away little puffs of dust rose above the white sage, and creeping specks moved at a snail's pace.

"See them? Ah! then look, August Naab, look in the heavens above for my prophecy," cried Cole, fanatically. "The red sunset—the sign of the times—blood!"

A broad bar of dense black shut out the April sky, except in the extreme west, where a strip of pale blue formed background for several clouds of striking color and shape. They alone, in all that expanse, were dyed in the desert's sunset crimson. The largest projected from behind the dark cloud-bank in the shape of a huge fist, and the others, small and round, floated below. To Cole it seemed a giant hand, clutching, with inexorable strength, a bleeding heart. His terror spread to his companions as they stared.

Then, as light surrendered to shade, the sinister color faded; the tracing of the closed hand softened; flush and glow paled, leaving the sky purple, as if mirroring the desert floor. One golden shaft shot up, to be blotted out by sudden darkening change, and the sun had set.

"That may be God's will," said August Naab. "So be it. Martin Cole, take your men and go."

There was a word, half oath, half prayer, and then rattle of stirrups, the creak of saddles, and clink of spurs, followed by the driving rush of fiery horses. Cole and his men disappeared in a pall of yellow dust.

A wan smile lightened John Hare's face as he spoke weakly: "I fear your—generous act—can't save me... may bring you harm. I'd rather you left me—seeing you have women in your party."

"Don't try to talk yet," said August Naab. "You're faint. Here—drink." He stooped to Hare, who was leaning against a sage-bush, and held a flask to his lips. Rising, he called to his men: "Make camp, sons. We've an hour before the outlaws come up, and if they don't go round the sand-dune we'll have longer."

Hare's flagging senses rallied, and he forgot himself in wonder. While the bustle went on, unhitching of wagon-teams, hobbling and feeding of horses, unpacking of camp-supplies, Naab appeared to be lost in deep meditation or prayer. Not once did he glance backward over the trail on which peril was fast approaching. His gaze was fastened on a ridge to the east where desert line, fringed by stunted cedars, met the pale-blue sky, and for a long time he neither spoke nor stirred. At length he turned to the camp-fire; he raked out red coals, and placed the iron pots in position, by way of assistance to the women who were preparing the evening meal.

A cool wind blew in from the desert, rustling the sage, sifting the sand, fanning the dull coals to burning opals. Twilight failed and night fell; one by one great stars shone out, cold and bright. From the zone of blackness surrounding the camp burst the short bark, the hungry whine, the long-drawn-out wail of desert wolves.

"Supper, sons," called Naab, as he replenished the fire with an armful of grease-wood.

Naab's sons had his stature, though not his bulk. They were wiry, rangy men, young, yet somehow old. The desert had multiplied their years. Hare could not have told one face from another, the bronze skin and steel eye and hard line of each were so alike. The women, one middle-aged, the others young, were of comely, serious aspect.

"Mescal," called the Mormon.

A slender girl slipped from one of the covered wagons; she was dark, supple, straight as an Indian.

August Naab dropped to his knees, and, as the members of his family bowed their heads, he extended his hands over them and over the food laid on the ground.

"Lord, we kneel in humble thanksgiving. Bless this food to our use. Strengthen us, guide us, keep us as Thou hast in the past. Bless this stranger within our gates. Help us to help him. Teach us Thy ways, O Lord—Amen."

Hare found himself flushing and thrilling, found himself unable to control a painful binding in his throat. In forty-eight hours he had learned to hate the Mormons unutterably; here, in the presence of this austere man, he felt that hatred wrenched from his heart, and in its place stirred something warm and living. He was glad, for if he had to die, as he believed, either from the deed of evil men, or from this last struggle of his wasted body, he did not want to die in bitterness. That simple prayer recalled the home he had long since left in Connecticut, and the time when he used to tease his sister and anger his father and hurt his mother while grace was being said at the breakfast-table. Now he was alone in the world, sick and dependent upon the kindness of these strangers. But they were really friends—it was a wonderful thought.

"Mescal, wait on the stranger," said August Naab, and the girl knelt beside him, tendering meat and drink. His nerveless fingers refused to hold the cup, and she put it to his lips while he drank. Hot coffee revived him; he ate and grew stronger, and readily began to talk when the Mormon asked for his story.

"There isn't much to tell. My name is Hare. I am twenty-four. My parents are dead. I came West because the doctors said I couldn't live in the East. At first I got better. But my money gave out and work became a necessity. I tramped from place to place, ending up ill in Salt Lake City. People were kind to me there. Some one got me a job with a big cattle company, and sent me to Marysvale, southward over the bleak plains. It was cold; I was ill when I reached Lund. Before I even knew what my duties were for at Lund I was to begin work—men called me a spy. A fellow named Chance threatened me. An innkeeper led me out the back way, gave me bread and water, and said: 'Take this road to Bane; it's sixteen miles. If you make it some one'll give you a lift North.' I walked all night, and all the next day. Then I wandered on till I dropped here where you found me."

"You missed the road to Bane," said Naab. "This is the trail to White Sage. It's a trail of sand and stone that leaves no tracks, a lucky thing for you. Dene wasn't in Lund while you were there—else you wouldn't be here. He hasn't seen you, and he can't be certain of your trail. Maybe he rode to Bane, but still we may find a way—"

One of his sons whistled low, causing Naab to rise slowly, to peer into the darkness, to listen intently.

"Here, get up," he said, extending a hand to Hare. "Pretty shaky, eh? Can you walk? Give me a hold—there.... Mescal, come." The slender girl obeyed, gliding noiselessly like a shadow. "Take his arm." Between them they led Hare to a jumble of stones on the outer edge of the circle of light.

"It wouldn't do to hide," continued Naab, lowering his voice to a swift whisper, "that might be fatal. You're in sight from the camp-fire, but indistinct. By-and-by the outlaws will get here, and if any of them prowl around close, you and Mescal must pretend to be sweethearts. Understand? They'll pass by Mormon love-making without a second look. Now, lad, courage... Mescal, it may save his life."

Naab returned to the fire, his shadow looming in gigantic proportions on the white canopy of a covered wagon. Fitful gusts of wind fretted the blaze; it roared and crackled and sputtered, now illuminating the still forms, then enveloping them in fantastic obscurity. Hare shivered, perhaps from the cold air, perhaps from growing dread. Westward lay the desert, an impenetrable black void; in front, the gloomy mountain wall lifted jagged peaks close to the stars; to the right rose the ridge, the rocks and stunted cedars of its summit standing in weird relief. Suddenly Hare's fugitive glance descried a dark object; he watched intently as it moved and rose from behind the summit of the ridge to make a bold black figure silhouetted against the cold clearness of sky. He saw it distinctly, realized it was close, and breathed hard as the wind-swept mane and tail, the lean, wild shape and single plume resolved themselves into the unmistakable outline of an Indian mustang and rider.

"Look!" he whispered to the girl. "See, a mounted Indian, there on the ridge—there, he's gone—no, I see him again. But that's another. Look! there are more." He ceased in breathless suspense and stared fearfully at a line of mounted Indians moving in single file over the ridge to become lost to view in the intervening blackness. A faint rattling of gravel and the peculiar crack of unshod hoof on stone gave reality to that shadowy train.

"Navajos," said Mescal.

"Navajos!" he echoed. "I heard of them at Lund; 'desert hawks' the men called them, worse than Piutes. Must we not alarm the men?—You—aren't you afraid?

"No."

"But they are hostile."

"Not to him." She pointed at the stalwart figure standing against the firelight.

"Ah! I remember. The man Cole spoke of friendly Navajos. They must be close by. What does it mean?"

"I'm not sure. I think they are out there in the cedars, waiting."

"Waiting! For what?"

"Perhaps for a signal."

"Then they were expected?"

"I don't know; I only guess. We used to ride often to White Sage and Lund; now we go seldom, and when we do there seem to be Navajos near the camp at night, and riding the ridges by day. I believe Father Naab knows."

"Your father's risking much for me. He's good. I wish I could show my gratitude."

"I call him Father Naab, but he is not my father."

"A niece or granddaughter, then?"

"I'm no relation. Father Naab raised me in his family. My mother was a Navajo, my father a Spaniard."

"Why!" exclaimed Hare. "When you came out of the wagon I took you for an Indian girl. But the moment you spoke—you talk so well—no one would dream—"

"Mormons are well educated and teach the children they raise," she said, as he paused in embarrassment.

He wanted to ask if she were a Mormon by religion, but the question seemed curious and unnecessary. His interest was aroused; he realized suddenly that he had found pleasure in her low voice; it was new and strange, unlike any woman's voice he had ever heard; and he regarded her closely. He had only time for a glance at her straight, clean-cut profile, when she turned startled eyes on him, eyes black as the night. And they were eyes that looked through and beyond him. She held up a hand, slowly bent toward the wind, and whispered:

"Listen."

Hare heard nothing save the barking of coyotes and the breeze in the sage. He saw, however, the men rise from round the camp-fire to face the north, and the women climb into the wagon, and close the canvas flaps. And he prepared himself, with what fortitude he could command for the approach of the outlaws. He waited, straining to catch a sound. His heart throbbed audibly, like a muffled drum, and for an endless moment his ears seemed deadened to aught else. Then a stronger puff of wind whipped in, banging the rhythmic beat of flying hoofs. Suspense ended. Hare felt the easing of a weight upon him. Whatever was to be his fate, it would be soon decided. The sound grew into a clattering roar. A black mass hurled itself over the border of opaque circle, plunged into the light, and halted.

August Naab deliberately threw a bundle of grease-wood upon the camp-fire. A blaze leaped up, sending abroad a red flare. "Who comes?" he called.

"Friends, Mormons, friends," was the answer.

"Get down—friends—and come to the fire."

Three horsemen advanced to the foreground; others, a troop of eight or ten, remained in the shadow, a silent group.

Hare sank back against the stone. He knew the foremost of those horsemen though he had never seen him.

"Dene," whispered Mescal, and confirmed his instinctive fear.

Hare was nervously alive to the handsome presence of the outlaw. Glimpses that he had caught of "bad" men returned vividly as he noted the clean-shaven face, the youthful, supple body, the cool, careless mien. Dene's eyes glittered as he pulled off his gauntlets and beat the sand out of them; and but for that quick fierce glance his leisurely friendly manner would have disarmed suspicion.

"Are you the Mormon Naab?" he queried.

"August Naab, I am."

"Dry camp, eh? Hosses tired, I reckon. Shore it's a sandy trail. Where's the rest of you fellers?"

"Cole and his men were in a hurry to make White Sage to-night. They were travelling light; I've heavy wagons."

"Naab, I reckon you shore wouldn't tell a lie?"

"I have never lied."

"Heerd of a young feller thet was in Lund—pale chap—lunger, we'd call him back West?"

"I heard that he had been mistaken for a spy at Lund and had fled toward Bane."

"Hadn't seen nothin' of him this side of Lund?"

"No."

"Seen any Navvies?"

"Yes."

The outlaw stared hard at him. Apparently he was about to speak of the Navajos, for his quick uplift of head at Naab's blunt affirmative suggested the impulse. But he checked himself and slowly drew on his gloves.

"Naab, I'm shore comin' to visit you some day. Never been over thet range. Heerd you hed fine water, fine cattle. An' say, I seen thet little Navajo girl you have, an' I wouldn't mind seein' her again."

August Naab kicked the fire into brighter blaze. "Yes fine range," he presently replied, his gaze fixed on Dene. "Fine water, fine cattle, fine browse. I've a fine graveyard, too; thirty graves, and not one a woman's. Fine place for graves, the canyon country. You don't have to dig. There's one grave the Indians never named; it's three thousand feet deep."

"Thet must be in hell," replied Dene, with a smile, ignoring the covert meaning. He leisurely surveyed Naab's four sons, the wagons and horses, till his eye fell upon Hare and Mescal. With that he swung in his saddle as if to dismount.

"I shore want a look around."

"Get down, get down," returned the Mormon. The deep voice, unwelcoming, vibrant with an odd ring, would have struck a less suspicious man than Dene. The outlaw wrung his leg back over the pommel, sagged in the saddle, and appeared to be pondering the question. Plainly he was uncertain of his ground. But his indecision was brief.

"Two-Spot, you look 'em over," he ordered.

The third horseman dismounted and went toward the wagons.

Hare, watching this scene, became conscious that his fear had intensified with the recognition of Two-Spot as Chance, the outlaw whom he would not soon forget. In his excitement he moved against Mescal and felt her trembling violently.

"Are you afraid?" he whispered.

"Yes, of Dene."

The outlaw rummaged in one of the wagons, pulled aside the canvas flaps of the other, laughed harshly, and then with clinking spurs tramped through the camp, kicking the beds, overturning a pile of saddles, and making disorder generally, till he spied the couple sitting on the stone in the shadow.

As the outlaw lurched that way, Hare, with a start of recollection, took Mescal in his arms and leaned his head against hers. He felt one of her hands lightly brush his shoulder and rest there, trembling.

Shuffling footsteps scraped the sand, sounded nearer and nearer, slowed and paused.

"Sparkin'! Dead to the world. Ham! Haw! Haw!"

The coarse laugh gave place to moving footsteps. The rattling clink of stirrup and spur mingled with the restless stamp of horse. Chance had mounted. Dene's voice drawled out: "Good-bye, Naab, I shore will see you all some day." The heavy thuds of many hoofs evened into a roar that diminished as it rushed away.

In unutterable relief Hare realized his deliverance. He tried to rise, but power of movement had gone from him.

He was fainting, yet his sensations were singularly acute. Mescal's hand dropped from his shoulder; her cheek, that had been cold against his, grew hot; she quivered through all her slender length. Confusion claimed his senses. Gratitude and hope flooded his soul. Something sweet and beautiful, the touch of this desert girl, rioted in his blood; his heart swelled in exquisite agony. Then he was whirling in darkness; and he knew no more.

II. WHITE SAGE

THE night was as a blank to Hare; the morning like a drifting of hazy clouds before his eyes. He felt himself moving; and when he awakened clearly to consciousness he lay upon a couch on the vine-covered porch of a cottage. He saw August Naab open a garden gate to admit Martin Cole. They met as friends; no trace of scorn marred August's greeting, and Martin was not the same man who had shown fear on the desert. His welcome was one of respectful regard for his superior.

"Elder, I heard you were safe in," he said, fervently. "We feared—I know not what. I was distressed till I got the news of your arrival. How's the young man?"

"He's very ill. But while there's life there's hope."

"Will the Bishop administer to him?"

"Gladly, if the young man's willing. Come, let's go in."

"Wait, August," said Cole. "Did you know your son Snap was in the village?"

"My son here!" August Naab betrayed anxiety. "I left him home with work. He shouldn't have come. Is—is he—"

"He's drinking and in an ugly mood. It seems he traded horses with Jeff Larsen, and got the worst of the deal. There's pretty sure to be a fight."

"He always hated Larsen."

"Small wonder. Larsen is mean; he's as bad as we've got and that's saying a good deal. Snap has done worse things than fight with Larsen. He's doing a worse thing now, August—he's too friendly with Dene."

"I've heard—I've heard it before. But, Martin, what can I do?"

"Do? God knows. What can any of us do? Times have changed, August. Dene is here in White Sage, free, welcome in many homes. Some of our neighbors, perhaps men we trust, are secret members of this rustler's band."

"You're right, Cole. There are Mormons who are cattle-thieves. To my eternal shame I confess it. Under cover of night they ride with Dene, and here in our midst they meet him in easy tolerance. Driven from Montana he comes here to corrupt our young men. God's mercy!"

"August, some of our young men need no one to corrupt them. Dene had no great task to win them. He rode in here with a few outlaws and now he has a strong band. We've got to face it. We haven't any law, but he can be killed. Some one must kill him. Yet bad as Dene is, he doesn't threaten our living as Holderness does. Dene steals a few cattle, kills a man here and there. Holderness reaches out and takes our springs. Because we've no law to stop him, he steals the blood of our life—water—water—God's gift to the desert! Some one must kill Holderness, too!"

"Martin, this lust to kill is a fearful thing. Come in, you must pray with the Bishop."

"No, it's not prayer I need, Elder," replied Cole, stubbornly. "I'm still a good Mormon. What I want is the stock I've lost, and my fields green again."

August Naab had no answer for his friend. A very old man with snow-white hair and beard came out on the porch.

"Bishop, brother Martin is railing again," said Naab, as Cole bared his head.

"Martin, my son, unbosom thyself," rejoined the Bishop.

"Black doubt and no light," said Cole, despondently. "I'm of the younger generation of Mormons, and faith is harder for me. I see signs you can't see. I've had trials hard to bear. I was rich in cattle, sheep, and water. These Gentiles, this rancher Holderness and this outlaw Dene, have driven my cattle, killed my sheep, piped my water off my fields. I don't like the present. We are no longer in the old days. Our young men are drifting away, and the few who return come with ideas opposed to Mormonism. Our girls and boys are growing up influenced by the Gentiles among us. They intermarry, and that's a death-blow to our creed."

"Martin, cast out this poison from your heart. Return to your faith. The millennium will come. Christ will reign on earth again. The ten tribes of Israel will be restored. The Book of Mormon is the Word of God. The creed will live. We may suffer here and die, but our spirits will go marching on; and the City of Zion will be builded over our graves."

Cole held up his hands in a meekness that signified hope if not faith.

August Naab bent over Hare. "I would like to have the Bishop administer to you," he said.

"What's that?" asked Hare.

"A Mormon custom, 'the laying on of hands.' We know its efficacy in trouble and illness. A Bishop of the Mormon Church has the gift of tongues, of prophecy, of revelation, of healing. Let him administer to you. It entails no obligation. Accept it as a prayer."

"I'm willing," replied the young man.

Thereupon Naab spoke a few low words to some one through the open door. Voices ceased; soft footsteps sounded without; women crossed the threshold, followed by tall young men and rosy-checked girls and round-eyed children. A white-haired old woman came forward with solemn dignity. She carried a silver bowl which she held for the Bishop as he stood close by Hare's couch. The Bishop put his hands into the bowl, anointing them with fragrant oil; then he placed them on the young man's head, and offered up a brief prayer, beautiful in its simplicity and tremulous utterance.

The ceremony ended, the onlookers came forward with pleasant words on their lips, pleasant smiles on their faces. The children filed by his couch, bashful yet sympathetic; the women murmured, the young men grasped his hand. Mescal flitted by with downcast eye, with shy smile, but no word.

"Your fever is gone," said August Naab, with his hand on Hare's cheek.

"It comes and goes suddenly," replied Hare. "I feel better now, only I'm oppressed. I can't breathe freely. I want air, and I'm hungry."

"Mother Mary, the lad's hungry. Judith, Esther, where are your wits? Help your mother. Mescal, wait on him, see to his comfort."

Mescal brought a little table and a pillow, and the other girls soon followed with food and drink; then they hovered about, absorbed in caring for him.

"They said I fell among thieves," mused Hare, when he was once more alone. "I've fallen among saints as well." He felt that he could never repay this August Naab. "If only I might live!" he ejaculated. How restful was this cottage garden! The green sward was a balm to his eyes. Flowers new to him, though of familiar springtime hue, lifted fresh faces everywhere; fruit-trees, with branches intermingling, blended the white and pink of blossoms. There was the soft laughter of children in the garden. Strange birds darted among the trees. Their notes were new, but their song was the old delicious monotone—the joy of living and love of spring. A green-bowered irrigation ditch led by the porch and unseen water flowed gently, with gurgle and tinkle, with music in its hurry. Innumerable bees murmured amid the blossoms.

Hare fell asleep. Upon returning drowsily to consciousness he caught through half-open eyes the gleam of level shafts of gold sunlight low down in the trees; then he felt himself being carried into the house to be laid upon a bed. Some one gently unbuttoned his shirt at the neck, removed his shoes, and covered him with a blanket. Before he had fully awakened he was left alone, and quiet settled over the house. A languorous sense of ease and rest lulled him to sleep again. In another moment, it seemed to him, he was awake; bright daylight streamed through the window, and a morning breeze stirred the faded curtain.

The drag in his breathing which was always a forerunner of a coughing-spell warned him now; he put on coat and shoes and went outside, where his cough attacked him, had its sway, and left him.

"Good-morning," sang out August Naab's cheery voice. "Sixteen hours of sleep, my lad!"

"I did sleep, didn't I? No wonder I feel well this morning. A peculiarity of my illness is that one day I'm down, the next day up."

"With the goodness of God, my lad, we'll gradually increase the days up. Go in to breakfast. Afterward I want to talk to you. This'll be a busy day for me, shoeing the horses and packing supplies. I want to start for home to-morrow."

Hare pondered over Naab's words while he ate. The suggestion in them, implying a relation to his future, made him wonder if the good Mormon intended to take him to his desert home. He hoped so, and warmed anew to this friend. But he had no enthusiasm for himself; his future seemed hopeless.

Naab was waiting for him on the porch, and drew him away from the cottage down the path toward the gate.

"I want you to go home with me."

"You're kind—I'm only a sort of beggar—I've no strength left to work my way. I'll go—though it's only to die."

"I haven't the gift of revelation—yet somehow I see that you won't die of this illness. You will come home with me. It's a beautiful place, my Navajo oasis. The Indians call it the Garden of Eschtah. If you can get well anywhere it'll be there."

"I'll go but I ought not. What can I do for you?"

"No man can ever tell what he may do for another. The time may come—well, John, is it settled?" He offered his huge broad hand.

"It's settled—I—" Hare faltered as he put his hand in Naab's. The Mormon's grip straightened his frame and braced him. Strength and simplicity flowed from the giant's toil-hardened palm. Hare swallowed his thanks along with his emotion, and for what he had intended to say he substituted: "No one ever called me John. I don't know the name. Call me Jack."

"Very well, Jack, and now let's see. You'll need some things from the store. Can you come with me? It's not far."

"Surely. And now what I need most is a razor to scrape the alkali and stubble off my face."

The wide street, bordered by cottages peeping out of green and white orchards, stretched in a straight line to the base of the ascent which led up to the Pink Cliffs. A green square enclosed a gray church, a school-house and public hall. Farther down the main thoroughfare were several weather-boarded whitewashed stores. Two dusty men were riding along, one on each side of the wildest, most vicious little horse Hare had ever seen. It reared and bucked and kicked, trying to escape from two lassoes. In front of the largest store were a number of mustangs all standing free, with bridles thrown over their heads and trailing on the ground. The loungers leaning against the railing and about the doors were lank brown men very like Naab's sons. Some wore sheepskin "chaps," some blue overalls; all wore boots and spurs, wide soft hats, and in their belts, far to the back, hung large Colt's revolvers.

"We'll buy what you need, just as if you expected to ride the ranges for me to-morrow," said Naab. "The first thing we ask a new man is, can he ride? Next, can he shoot?"

"I could ride before I got so weak. I've never handled a revolver, but I can shoot a rifle. Never shot at anything except targets, and it seemed to come natural for me to hit them."

"Good. We'll show you some targets—lions, bears, deer, cats, wolves. There's a fine forty-four Winchester here that my friend Abe has been trying to sell. It has a long barrel and weighs eight pounds. Our desert riders like the light carbines that go easy on a saddle. Most of the mustangs aren't weight-carriers. This rifle has a great range; I've shot it, and it's just the gun for you to use on wolves and coyotes. You'll need a Colt and a saddle, too."

"By-the-way," he went on, as they mounted the store steps, "here's the kind of money we use in this country." He handed Hare a slip of blue paper, a written check for a sum of money, signed, but without register of bank or name of firm. "We don't use real money," he added. "There's very little coin or currency in southern Utah. Most of the Gentiles lately come in have money, and some of us Mormons have a bag or two of gold, but scarcely any of it gets into circulation. We use these checks, which go from man to man sometimes for six months. The roundup of a check means sheep, cattle, horses, grain, merchandise or labor. Every man gets his real money's value without paying out an actual cent."

"Such a system at least means honest men," said Hare, laughing his surprise.

They went into a wide door to tread a maze of narrow aisles between boxes and barrels, stacks of canned vegetables, and piles of harness and dry goods; they entered an open space where several men leaned on a counter.

"Hello, Abe," said Naab; "seen anything of Snap?"

"Hello, August. Yes, Snap's inside. So's Holderness. Says he rode in off the range on purpose to see you." Abe designated an open doorway from which issued loud voices. Hare glanced into a long narrow room full of smoke and the fumes of rum. Through the haze he made out a crowd of men at a rude bar. Abe went to the door and called out: "Hey, Snap, your dad wants you. Holderness, here's August Naab."

A man staggered up the few steps leading to the store and swayed in. His long face had a hawkish cast, and it was gray, not with age, but with the sage-gray of the desert. His eyes were of the same hue, cold yet burning with little fiery flecks in their depths. He appeared short of stature because of a curvature of the spine, but straightened up he would have been tall. He wore a blue flannel shirt, and blue overalls; round his lean hips was a belt holding two Colt's revolvers, their heavy, dark butts projecting outward, and he had on high boots with long, cruel spurs.

"Howdy, father?" he said.

"I'm packing to-day," returned August Naab. "We ride out to-morrow. I need your help."

"All-l right. When I get my pinto from Larsen."

"Never mind Larsen. If he got the better of you let the matter drop."

"Jeff got my pinto for a mustang with three legs. If I hadn't been drunk I'd never have traded. So I'm looking for Jeff."

He bit out the last words with a peculiar snap of his long teeth, a circumstance which caused Hare instantly to associate the savage clicking with the name he had heard given this man. August Naab looked at him with gloomy eyes and stern shut mouth, an expression of righteous anger, helplessness and grief combined, the look of a man to whom obstacles had been nothing, at last confronted with crowning defeat. Hare realized that this son was Naab's first-born, best-loved, a thorn in his side, a black sheep.

"Say, father, is that the spy you found on the trail?" Snap's pale eyes gleamed on Hare and the little flames seemed to darken and leap.

"This is John Hare, the young man I found. But he's not a spy."

"You can't make any one believe that. He's down as a spy. Dene's spy! His name's gone over the ranges as a counter of unbranded stock. Dene has named him and Dene has marked him. Don't take him home, as you've taken so many sick and hunted men before. What's the good of it? You never made a Mormon of one of them yet. Don't take him—unless you want another grave for your cemetery. Ha! Ha!"

Hare recoiled with a shock. Snap Naab swayed to the door, and stepped down, all the time with his face over his shoulder, his baleful glance on Hare; then the blue haze swallowed him.

The several loungers went out; August engaged the storekeeper in conversation, introducing Hare and explaining their wants. They inspected the various needs of a range-rider, selecting, in the end, not the few suggested by Hare, but the many chosen by Naab. The last purchase was the rifle Naab had talked about. It was a beautiful weapon, finely polished and carved, entirely out of place among the plain coarse-sighted and coarse-stocked guns in the rack.

"Never had a chance to sell it," said Abe. "Too long and heavy for the riders. I'll let it go cheap, half price, and the cartridges also, two thousand."

"Taken," replied Naab, quickly, with a satisfaction which showed he liked a bargain.

"August, you must be going to shoot some?" queried Abe. "Something bigger than rabbits and coyotes. Its about time—even if you are an Elder. We Mormons must—" he broke off, continuing in a low tone: "Here's Holderness now."

Hare wheeled with the interest that had gathered with the reiteration of this man's name. A new-comer stooped to get in the door. He out-topped even Naab in height, and was a superb blond-bearded man, striding with the spring of a mountaineer.

"Good-day to you, Naab," he said. "Is this the young fellow you picked up?"

"Yes. Jack Hare," rejoined Naab.

"Well, Hare, I'm Holderness. You'll recall my name. You were sent to Lund by men interested in my ranges. I expected to see you in Lund, but couldn't get over."

Hare met the proffered hand with his own, and as he had recoiled from Snap Naab so now he received another shock, different indeed but impelling in its power, instinctive of some great portent. Hare was impressed by an indefinable subtlety, a nameless distrust, as colorless as the clear penetrating amber lightness of the eyes that bent upon him.

"Holderness, will you right the story about Hare?" inquired Naab.

"You mean about his being a spy? Well, Naab, the truth is that was his job. I advised against sending a man down here for that sort of work. It won't do. These Mormons will steal each other's cattle, and they've got to get rid of them; so they won't have a man taking account of stock, brands, and all that. If the Mormons would stand for it the rustlers wouldn't. I'll take Hare out to the ranch and give him work, if he wants. But he'd do best to leave Utah."

"Thank you, no," replied Hare, decidedly.

"He's going with me," said August Naab.

Holderness accepted this with an almost imperceptible nod, and he swept Hare with eyes that searched and probed for latent possibilities. It was the keen intelligence of a man who knew what development meant on the desert; not in any sense an interest in the young man at present. Then he turned his back.

Hare, feeling that Holderness wished to talk with Naab, walked to the counter, and began assorting his purchases, but he could not help hearing what was said.

"Lungs bad?" queried Holderness.

"One of them," replied Naab.

"He's all in. Better send him out of the country. He's got the name of Dene's spy and he'll never get another on this desert. Dene will kill him. This isn't good judgment, Naab, to take him with you. Even your friends don't like it, and it means trouble for you."

"We've settled it," said Naab, coldly.

"Well, remember, I've warned you. I've tried to be friendly with you, Naab, but you won't have it. Anyway, I've wanted to see you lately to find out how we stand."

"What do you mean?"

"How we stand on several things—to begin with, there Mescal."

"You asked me several times for Mescal, and I said no."

"But I never said I'd marry her. Now I want her, and I will marry her."

"No," rejoined Naab, adding brevity to his coldness.

"Why not?" demanded Holderness. "Oh, well, I can't take that as an insult. I know there's not enough money in Utah to get a girl away from a Mormon.... About the offer for the water-rights—how do we stand? I'll give you ten thousand dollars for the rights to Seeping Springs and Silver Cup."

"Ten thousand!" ejaculated Naab. "Holderness, I wouldn't take a hundred thousand. You might as well ask to buy my home, my stock, my range, twenty years of toil, for ten thousand dollars!"

"You refuse? All right. I think I've made you a fair proposition," said Holderness, in a smooth, quick tone. "The land is owned by the Government, and though your ranges are across the Arizona line they really figure as Utah land. My company's spending big money, and the Government won't let you have a monopoly. No one man can control the water-supply of a hundred miles of range. Times are changing. You want to see that. You ought to protect yourself before it's too late."

"Holderness, this is a desert. No men save Mormons could ever have made it habitable. The Government scarcely knows of its existence. It'll be fifty years before man can come in here to take our water."

"Why can't he? The water doesn't belong to any one. Why can't he?"

"Because of the unwritten law of the desert. No Mormon would refuse you or your horse a drink, or even a reasonable supply for your stock. But you can't come in here and take our water for your own use, to supplant us, to parch our stock. Why, even an Indian respects desert law!"

"Bah! I'm not a Mormon or an Indian. I'm a cattleman. It's plain business with me. Once more I make you the offer."

Naab scorned to reply. The men faced each other for a silent moment, their glances scintillating. Then Holderness whirled on his heel, jostling into Hare.

"Get out of my way," said the rancher, in the disgust of intense irritation. He swung his arm, and his open hand sent Hare reeling against the counter.

"Jack," said Naab, breathing hard, "Holderness showed his real self to-day. I always knew it, yet I gave him the benefit of the doubt.... For him to strike you! I've not the gift of revelation, but I see—let us go."

On the return to the Bishop's cottage Naab did not speak once; the transformation which had begun with the appearance of his drunken son had reached a climax of gloomy silence after the clash with Holderness. Naab went directly to the Bishop, and presently the quavering voice of the old minister rose in prayer.

Hare dropped wearily into the chair on the porch; and presently fell into a doze, from which he awakened with a start. Naab's sons, with Martin Cole and several other men, were standing in the yard. Naab himself was gently crowding the women into the house. When he got them all inside he closed the door and turned to Cole.

"Was it a fair fight?"

"Yes, an even break. They met in front of Abe's. I saw the meeting. Neither was surprised. They stood for a moment watching each other. Then they drew—only Snap was quicker. Larsen's gun went off as he fell. That trick you taught Snap saved his life again. Larsen was no slouch on the draw."

"Where's Snap now?"

"Gone after his pinto. He was sober. Said he'd pack at once. Larsen's friends are ugly. Snap said to tell you to hurry out of the village with young Hare, if you want to take him at all. Dene has ridden in; he swears you won't take Hare away."

"We're all packed and ready to hitch up," returned Naab. "We could start at once, only until dark I'd rather take chances here than out on the trail."

"Snap said Dene would ride right into the Bishop's after Hare."

"No. He wouldn't dare."

"Father!" Dave Naab spoke sharply from where he stood high on a grassy bank. "Here's Dene now, riding up with Culver, and some man I don't know. They're coming in. Dene's jumped the fence! Look out!"

A clatter of hoofs and rattling of gravel preceded the appearance of a black horse in the garden path. His rider bent low to dodge the vines of the arbor, and reined in before the porch to slip out of the saddle with the agility of an Indian. It was Dene, dark, smiling, nonchalant.

"What do you seek in the house of a Bishop?" challenged August Naab, planting his broad bulk square before Hare.

"Dene's spy!"

"What do you seek in the house of a Bishop?" repeated Naab.

"I shore want to see the young feller you lied to me about," returned Dene, his smile slowly fading.

"No speech could be a lie to an outlaw."

"I want him, you Mormon preacher!"

"You can't have him."

"I'll shore get him."

In one great stride Naab confronted and towered over Dene.

The rustler's gaze shifted warily from Naab to the quiet Mormons and back again. Then his right hand quivered and shot downward. Naab's act was even quicker. A Colt gleamed and whirled to the grass, and the outlaw cried as his arm cracked in the Mormon's grasp.

Dave Naab leaped off the bank directly in front of Dene's approaching companions, and faced them, alert and silent, his hand on his hip.

August Naab swung the outlaw against the porch-post and held him there with brawny arm.

"Whelp of an evil breed!" he thundered, shaking his gray head. "Do you think we fear you and your gunsharp tricks? Look! See this!" He released Dene and stepped back with his hand before him. Suddenly it moved, quicker than sight, and a Colt revolver lay in his outstretched palm. He dropped it back into the holster. "Let that teach you never to draw on me again." He doubled his huge fist and shoved it before Dene's eyes. "One blow would crack your skull like an egg-shell. Why don't I deal it? Because, you mindless hell-hound, because there's a higher law than man's—God's law—Thou shalt not kill! Understand that if you can. Leave me and mine alone from this day. Now go!"

He pushed Dene down the path into the arms of his companions.

"Out with you!" said Dave Naab. "Hurry! Get your horse. Hurry! I'm not so particular about God as Dad is!"

III. THE TRAIL OF THE RED WALL

AFTER the departure of Dene and his comrades Naab decided to leave White Sage at nightfall. Martin Cole and the Bishop's sons tried to persuade him to remain, urging that the trouble sure to come could be more safely met in the village. Naab, however, was obdurate, unreasonably so, Cole said, unless there were some good reason why he wished to strike the trail in the night. When twilight closed in Naab had his teams ready and the women shut in the canvas-covered wagons. Hare was to ride in an open wagon, one that Naab had left at White Sage to be loaded with grain. When it grew so dark that objects were scarcely discernible a man vaulted the cottage fence.

"Dave, where are the boys?" asked Naab.

"Not so loud! The boys are coming," replied Dave in a whisper. "Dene is wild. I guess you snapped a bone in his arm. He swears he'll kill us all. But Chance and the rest of the gang won't be in till late. We've time to reach the Coconina Trail, if we hustle."

"Any news of Snap?"

"He rode out before sundown."

Three more forms emerged from the gloom.

"All right, boys. Go ahead, Dave, you lead."

Dave and George Naab mounted their mustangs and rode through the gate; the first wagon rolled after them, its white dome gradually dissolving in the darkness; the second one started; then August Naab stepped to his seat on the third with a low cluck to the team. Hare shut the gate and climbed over the tail-board of the wagon.

A slight swish of weeds and grasses brushing the wheels was all the sound made in the cautious advance. A bare field lay to the left; to the right low roofs and sharp chimneys showed among the trees; here and there lights twinkled. No one hailed; not a dog barked.

Presently the leaders turned into a road where the iron hoofs and wheels cracked and crunched the stones.

Hare thought he saw something in the deep shade of a line of poplar-trees; he peered closer, and made out a motionless horse and rider, just a shade blacker than the deepest gloom. The next instant they vanished, and the rapid clatter of hoofs down the road told Hare his eyes had not deceived him.

"Getup," growled Naab to his horses. "Jack, did you see that fellow?"

"Yes. What was he doing there?"

"Watching the road. He's one of Dene's scouts."

"Will Dene—"

One of Naab's sons came trotting back. "Think that was Larsen's pal. He was laying in wait for Snap."

"I thought he was a scout for Dene," replied August.

"Maybe he's that too."

"Likely enough. Hurry along and keep the gray team going lively. They've had a week's rest."

Hare watched the glimmering lights of the village vanish one by one, like Jack-o'-lanterns. The horses kept a steady, even trot on into the huge windy hall of the desert night. Fleecy clouds veiled the stars, yet transmitted a wan glow. A chill crept over Hare. As he crawled under the blankets Naab had spread for him his hand came into contact with a polished metal surface cold as ice. It was his rifle. Naab had placed it under the blankets. Fingering the rifle Hare found the spring opening on the right side of the breech, and, pressing it down, he felt the round head of a cartridge. Naab had loaded the weapon, he had placed it where Hare's hand must find it, yet he had not spoken of it. Hare did not stop to reason with his first impulse. Without a word, with silent insistence, disregarding his shattered health, August Naab had given him a man's part to play. The full meaning lifted Hare out of his self-abasement; once more he felt himself a man.

Hare soon yielded to the warmth of the blankets; a drowsiness that he endeavored in vain to throw off smothered his thoughts; sleep glued his eyelids tight. They opened again some hours later. For a moment he could not realize where he was; then the whip of the cold wind across his face, the woolly feel and smell of the blankets, and finally the steady trot of horses and the clink of a chain swinging somewhere under him, recalled the actuality of the night ride. He wondered how many miles had been covered, how the drivers knew the direction and kept the horses in the trail, and whether the outlaws were in pursuit. When Naab stopped the team and, climbing down, walked back some rods to listen, Hare felt sure that Dene was coming. He listened, too, but the movements of the horses and the rattle of their harness were all the sounds he could hear. Naab returned to his seat; the team started, now no longer in a trot; they were climbing. After that Hare fell into a slumber in which he could hear the slow grating whirr of wheels, and when it ceased he awoke to raise himself and turn his ear to the back trail. By-and-by he discovered that the black night had changed to gray; dawn was not far distant; he dozed and awakened to clear light. A rose-red horizon lay far below and to the eastward; the intervening descent was like a rolling sea with league-long swells.

"Glad you slept some," was Naab's greeting. "No sign of Dene yet. If we can get over the divide we're safe. That's Coconina there, Fire Mountain in Navajo meaning. It's a plateau low and narrow at this end, but it runs far to the east and rises nine thousand feet. It forms a hundred miles of the north rim of the Grand Canyon. We're across the Arizona line now."

III. THE TRAIL OF THE RED WALL

Hare followed the sweep of the ridge that rose to the eastward, but to his inexperienced eyes its appearance carried no sense of its noble proportions.

"Don't form any ideas of distance and size yet a while," said Naab, reading Hare's expression. "They'd only have to be made over as soon as you learn what light and air are in this country. It looks only half a mile to the top of the divide; well, if we make it by midday we're lucky. There, see a black spot over this way, far under the red wall? Look sharp. Good! That's Holderness's ranch. It's thirty miles from here. Nine Mile Valley heads in there. Once it belonged to Martin Cole. Holderness stole it. And he's begun to range over the divide."

The sun rose and warmed the chill air. Hare began to notice the increased height and abundance of the sagebrush, which was darker in color. The first cedar-tree, stunted in growth, dead at the top, was the half-way mark up the ascent, so Naab said; it was also the forerunner of other cedars which increased in number toward the summit. At length Hare, tired of looking upward at the creeping white wagons, closed his eyes. The wheels crunched on the stones; the horses heaved and labored; Naab's "Getup" was the only spoken sound; the sun beamed down warm, then hot; and the hours passed. Some unusual noise roused Hare out of his lethargy. The wagon was at a standstill. Naab stood on the seat with outstretched arm. George and Dave were close by their mustangs, and Snap Naab, mounted on a cream-colored pinto, reined him under August's arm, and faced the valley below.

"Maybe you'll make them out," said August. "I can't, and I've watched those dust-clouds for hours. George can't decide, either."

Hare, looking at Snap, was attracted by the eyes from which his father and brothers expected so much. If ever a human being had the eyes of a hawk Snap Naab had them. The little brown flecks danced in clear pale yellow. Evidently Snap had not located the perplexing dust-clouds, for his glance drifted. Suddenly the remarkable vibration of his pupils ceased, and his glance grew fixed, steely, certain.

"That's a bunch of wild mustangs," he said.

Hare gazed till his eyes hurt, but could see neither clouds of dust nor moving objects. No more was said. The sons wheeled their mustangs and rode to the fore; August Naab reseated himself and took up the reins; the ascent proceeded.

But it proceeded leisurely, with more frequent rests. At the end of an hour the horses toiled over the last rise to the summit and entered a level forest of cedars; in another hour they were descending gradually.

"Here we are at the tanks," said Naab.

Hare saw that they had come up with the other wagons. George Naab was leading a team down a rocky declivity to a pool of yellow water. The other boys were unharnessing and unsaddling.

"About three," said Naab, looking at the sun. "We're in good time. Jack, get out and stretch yourself. We camp here. There's the Coconina Trail where the Navajos go in after deer."

It was not a pretty spot, this little rock-strewn glade where the white hard trail forked with the road. The yellow water with its green scum made Hare sick. The horses drank with loud gulps. Naab and his sons drank of it. The women filled a pail and portioned it out in basins and washed their faces and hands with evident pleasure. Dave Naab whistled as he wielded an axe vigorously on a cedar. It came home to Hare that the tension of the past night and morning had relaxed. Whether to attribute that fact to the distance from White Sage or to the arrival at the water-hole he could not determine. But the certainty was shown in August's cheerful talk to the horses as he slipped bags of grain over their noses, and in the subdued laughter of the women. Hare sent up an unspoken thanksgiving that these good Mormons had apparently escaped from the dangers incurred for his sake. He sat with his back to a cedar and watched the kindling of fires, the deft manipulating of biscuit dough in a basin, and the steaming of pots. The generous meal was spread on a canvas cloth, around which men and women sat cross-legged, after the fashion of Indians. Hare found it hard to adapt his long legs to the posture, and he wondered how these men, whose legs were longer than his, could sit so easily. It was the crown of a cheerful dinner after hours of anxiety and abstinence to have Snap Naab speak civilly to him, and to see him bow his head meekly as his father asked the blessing. Snap ate as though he had utterly forgotten that he had recently killed a man; to hear the others talk to him one would suppose that they had forgotten it also.

All had finished eating, except Snap and Dave Naab, when one of the mustangs neighed shrilly. Hare would not have noticed it but for looks exchanged among the men. The glances were explained a few minutes later when a pattering of hoofs came from the cedar forest, and a stream of mounted Indians poured into the glade.

The ugly glade became a place of color and action. The Navajos rode wiry, wild-looking mustangs and drove ponies and burros carrying packs, most of which consisted of deer-hides. Each Indian dismounted, and unstrapping the blanket which had served as a saddle headed his mustang for the water-hole and gave him a slap. Then the hides and packs were slipped from the pack-train, and soon the pool became a kicking, splashing melee. Every cedar-tree circling the glade and every branch served as a peg for deer meat. Some of it was in the haunch, the bulk in dark dried strips. The Indians laid their weapons aside. Every sagebush and low stone held a blanket. A few of these blankets were of solid color, most of them had bars of white and gray and red, the last color predominating. The mustangs and burros filed out among the cedars, nipping at the sage and the scattered tufts of spare grass. A group of fires, sending up curling columns of blue smoke, and surrounded by a circle of lean, half-naked, bronze-skinned Indians, cooking and eating, completed a picture which afforded Hare the satisfying fulfilment of boyish dreams. What a contrast to the memory of a camp-site on the Connecticut shore, with boy friends telling tales in the glow of the fire, and the wash of the waves on the beach!

III. THE TRAIL OF THE RED WALL

The sun sank low in the west, sending gleams through the gnarled branches of the cedars, and turning the green into gold. At precisely the moment of sunset, the Mormon women broke into soft song which had the element of prayer; and the lips of the men moved in silent harmony. Dave Naab, the only one who smoked, removed his pipe for the moment's grace to dying day.

This simple ceremony over, one of the boys put wood on the fire, and Snap took a jews'-harp out of his pocket and began to extract doleful discords from it, for which George kicked at him in disgust, finally causing him to leave the circle and repair to the cedars, where he twanged with supreme egotism.

"Jack," said August Naab, "our friends the Navajo chiefs, Scarbreast and Eschtah, are coming to visit us. Take no notice of them at first. They've great dignity, and if you entered their hogans they'd sit for some moments before appearing to see you. Scarbreast is a war-chief. Eschtah is the wise old chief of all the Navajos on the Painted Desert. It may interest you to know he is Mescal's grandfather. Some day I'll tell you the story."

Hare tried very hard to appear unconscious when two tall Indians stalked into the circle of Mormons; he set his eyes on the white heart of the camp-fire and waited. For several minutes no one spoke or even moved. The Indians remained standing for a time; then seated themselves. Presently August Naab greeted them in the Navajo language. This was a signal for Hare to use his eyes and ears. Another interval of silence followed before they began to talk. Hare could see only their blanketed shoulders and black heads.

"Jack, come round here," said Naab at length. "I've been telling them about you. These Indians do not like the whites, except my own family. I hope you'll make friends with them."

"How do?" said the chief whom Naab had called Eschtah, a stately, keen-eyed warrior, despite his age.

The next Navajo greeted him with a guttural word. This was a warrior whose name might well have been Scarface, for the signs of conflict were there. It was a face like a bronze mask, cast in the one expression of untamed desert fierceness.

Hare bowed to each and felt himself searched by burning eyes, which were doubtful, yet not unfriendly.

"Shake," finally said Eschtah, offering his hand.

"Ugh!" exclaimed Scarbreast, extending a bare silver-braceleted arm.

This sign of friendship pleased Naab. He wished to enlist the sympathies of the Navajo chieftains in the young man's behalf. In his ensuing speech, which was plentifully emphasized with gestures, he lapsed often into English, saying "weak—no strong" when he placed his hand on Hare's legs, and "bad" when he touched the young man's chest, concluding with the words "sick—sick."

Scarbreast regarded Hare with great earnestness, and when Naab had finished he said: "Chineago—ping!" and rubbed his hand over his stomach.

"He says you need meat—lots of deer-meat," translated Naab.

"Sick," repeated Eschtah, whose English was intelligible. He appeared to be casting about in his mind for additional words to express his knowledge of the white man's tongue, and, failing, continued in Navajo: "Tohodena—moocha—malocha."

Hare was nonplussed at the roar of laughter from the Mormons. August shook like a mountain in an earthquake.

"Eschtah says, 'you hurry, get many squaws—many wives.'"

Other Indians, russet-skinned warriors, with black hair held close by bands round their foreheads, joined the circle, and sitting before the fire clasped their knees and talked. Hare listened awhile, and then, being fatigued, he sought the cedar-tree where he had left his blankets. The dry mat of needles made an odorous bed. He placed a sack of grain for a pillow, and doubling up one blanket to lie upon, he pulled the others over him. Then he watched and listened. The cedar-wood burned with a clear flame, and occasionally snapped out a red spark. The voices of the Navajos, scarcely audible, sounded "toa's" and "taa's"—syllables he soon learned were characteristic and dominant—in low, deep murmurs. It reminded Hare of something that before had been pleasant to his ear. Then it came to mind: a remembrance of Mescal's sweet voice, and that recalled the kinship between her and the Navajo chieftain. He looked about, endeavoring to find her in the ring of light, for he felt in her a fascination akin to the charm of this twilight hour. Dusky forms passed to and fro under the trees; the tinkle of bells on hobbled mustangs rang from the forest; coyotes had begun their night quest with wild howls; the camp-fire burned red, and shadows flickered on the blanketed Indians; the wind now moaned, now lulled in the cedars.

Hare lay back in his blankets and saw lustrous stars through the network of branches. With their light in his face and the cold wind waving his hair on his brow he thought of the strangeness of it all, of its remoteness from anything ever known to him before, of its inexpressible wildness. And a rush of emotion he failed wholly to stifle proved to him that he could have loved this life if—if he had not of late come to believe that he had not long to live. Still Naab's influence exorcised even that one sad thought; and he flung it from him in resentment.

Sleep did not come so readily; he was not very well this night; the flush of fever was on his cheek, and the heat of feverish blood burned his body. He raised himself and, resolutely seeking for distraction, once more stared at the camp-fire. Some time must have passed during his dreaming, for only three persons were in sight. Naab's broad back was bowed and his head nodded. Across the fire in its ruddy flicker sat Eschtah beside a slight, dark figure. At second glance Hare recognized Mescal. Surprise claimed him, not more for her presence there than for the white band binding her smooth black tresses. She had not worn such an ornament before. That slender band lent her the one touch which made her a Navajo. Was it worn in respect to her aged grandfather? What did this mean for a girl reared with Christian teaching? Was it desert blood? Hare had no answers for these questions. They only increased the mystery and romance. He fell asleep with the picture in his mind of Eschtah and Mescal, sitting in the glow of the fire, and of August Naab, nodding silently.

III. THE TRAIL OF THE RED WALL

"Jack, Jack, wake up." The words broke dully into his slumbers; wearily he opened his eyes. August Naab bent over him, shaking him gently.

"Not so well this morning, eh? Here's a cup of coffee. We're all packed and starting. Drink now, and climb aboard. We expect to make Seeping Springs to-night."

Hare rose presently and, laboring into the wagon, lay down on the sacks. He had one of his blind, sickening headaches. The familiar lumbering of wheels began, and the clanking of the wagon-chain. Despite jar and jolt he dozed at times, awakening to the scrape of the wheel on the leathern brake. After a while the rapid descent of the wagon changed to a roll, without the irritating rattle. He saw a narrow valley; on one side the green, slow-swelling cedar slope of the mountain; on the other the perpendicular red wall, with its pinnacles like spears against the sky. All day this backward outlook was the same, except that each time he opened aching eyes the valley had lengthened, the red wall and green slope had come closer together in the distance. By and by there came a halt, the din of stamping horses and sharp commands, the bustle and confusion of camp. Naab spoke kindly to him, but he refused any food, lay still and went to sleep.

Daylight brought him the relief of a clear head and cooled blood. The camp had been pitched close under the red wall. A lichen-covered cliff, wet with dripping water, overhung a round pool. A ditch led the water down the ridge to a pond. Cattle stood up to their knees drinking; others lay on the yellow clay, which was packed as hard as stone; still others were climbing the ridge and passing down on both sides.

"You look as if you enjoyed that water," remarked Naab, when Hare presented himself at the fire. "Well, it's good, only a little salty. Seeping Springs this is, and it's mine. This ridge we call The Saddle; you see it dips between wall and mountain and separates two valleys. This valley we go through to-day is where my cattle range. At the other end is Silver Cup Spring, also mine. Keep your eyes open now, my lad."

How different was the beginning of this day! The sky was as blue as the sea; the valley snuggled deep in the embrace of wall and mountain. Hare took a place on the seat beside Naab and faced the descent. The line of Navajos, a graceful straggling curve of color on the trail, led the way for the white-domed wagons.

Naab pointed to a little calf lying half hidden under a bunch of sage. "That's what I hate to see. There's a calf, just born; its mother has gone in for water. Wolves and lions range this valley. We lose hundreds of calves that way."

As far as Hare could see red and white and black cattle speckled the valley.

"If not overstocked, this range is the best in Utah," said Naab. "I say Utah, but it's really Arizona. The Grand Canyon seems to us Mormons to mark the line. There's enough browse here to feed a hundred thousand cattle. But water's the thing. In some seasons the springs go almost dry, though Silver Cup holds her own well enough for my cattle."

Hare marked the tufts of grass lying far apart on the yellow earth; evidently there was sustenance enough in every two feet of ground to support only one tuft.

"What's that?" he asked, noting a rolling cloud of dust with black bobbing borders.

"Wild mustangs," replied Naab. "There are perhaps five thousand on the mountain, and they are getting to be a nuisance. They're almost as bad as sheep on the browse; and I should tell you that if sheep pass over a range once the cattle will starve. The mustangs are getting too plentiful. There are also several bands of wild horses."

"What's the difference between wild horses and mustangs?"

"I haven't figured that out yet. Some say the Spaniards left horses in here three hundred years ago. Wild? They are wilder than any naturally wild animal that ever ran on four legs. Wait till you get a look at Silvermane or Whitefoot."

"What are they?"

"Wild stallions. Silvermane is an iron gray, with a silver mane, the most beautiful horse I ever saw. Whitefoot's an old black shaggy demon, with one white foot. Both stallions ought to be killed. They fight my horses and lead off the mares. I had a chance to shoot Silvermane on the way over this trip, but he looked so splendid that I just laid down my rifle."

"Can they run?" asked Hare eagerly, with the eyes of a man who loved a horse.

"Run? Whew! Just you wait till you see Silvermane cover ground! He can look over his shoulder at you and beat any horse in this country. The Navajos have given up catching him as a bad job. Why—here! Jack! quick, get out your rifle—coyotes!"

Naab pulled on the reins, and pointed to one side. Hare discerned three grayish sharp-nosed beasts sneaking off in the sage, and he reached back for the rifle. Naab whistled, stopping the coyotes; then Hare shot. The ball cut a wisp of dust above and beyond them. They loped away into the sage.

"How that rifle spangs!" exclaimed Naab. "It's good to hear it. Jack, you shot high. That's the trouble with men who have never shot at game. They can't hold low enough. Aim low, lower than you want. Ha! There's another—this side—hold ahead of him and low, quick!—too high again."

It was in this way that August and Hare fell far behind the other wagons. The nearer Naab got to his home the more genial he became. When he was not answering Hare's queries he was giving information of his own accord, telling about the cattle and the range, the mustangs, the Navajos, and the desert. Naab liked to talk; he had said he had not the gift of revelation, but he certainly had the gift of tongues.

The sun was in the west when they began to climb a ridge. A short ascent, and a long turn to the right brought them under a bold spur of the mountain which shut out the northwest. Camp had been pitched in a grove of trees of a species new to Hare. From under a bowlder gushed the sparkling spring, a grateful sight and sound to desert travellers. In a niche of the rock hung a silver cup.

"Jack, no man knows how old this cup is, or anything about it. We named the spring after it—Silver Cup. The strange thing is that the cup has never been lost nor stolen. But—could any desert man, or outlaw, or Indian, take it away, after drinking here?"

The cup was nicked and battered, bright on the sides, moss-green on the bottom. When Hare drank from it he understood.

That evening there was rude merriment around the campfire. Snap Naab buzzed on his jews'-harp and sang. He stirred some of the younger braves to dancing, and they stamped and swung their arms, singing, "hoya-heeya-howya," as they moved in and out of the firelight.

Several of the braves showed great interest in Snap's jews'-harp and repeatedly asked him for it. Finally the Mormon grudgingly lent it to a curious Indian, who in trying to play it went through such awkward motions and made such queer sounds that his companions set upon him and fought for possession of the instrument. Then Snap, becoming solicitous for its welfare, jumped into the fray. They tussled for it amid the clamor of a delighted circle. Snap, passing from jest to earnest, grew so strenuous in his efforts to regain the harp that he tossed the Navajos about like shuttle-cocks. He got the harp and, concealing it, sought to break away. But the braves laid hold upon him, threw him to the ground, and calmly sat astride him while they went through his pockets. August Naab roared his merriment and Hare laughed till he cried. The incident was as surprising to him as it was amusing. These serious Mormons and silent Navajos were capable of mirth.

Hare would have stayed up as late as any of them, but August's saying to him, "Get to bed: to-morrow will be bad!" sent him off to his blankets, where he was soon fast asleep. Morning found him well, hungry, eager to know what the day would bring.

"Wait," said August, soberly.

They rode out of the gray pocket in the ridge and began to climb. Hare had not noticed the rise till they were started, and then, as the horses climbed steadily he grew impatient at the monotonous ascent. There was nothing to see; frequently it seemed that they were soon to reach the summit, but still it rose above them. Hare went back to his comfortable place on the sacks.

"Now, Jack," said August.

Hare gasped. He saw a red world. His eyes seemed bathed in blood. Red scaly ground, bare of vegetation, sloped down, down, far down to a vast irregular rent in the earth, which zigzagged through the plain beneath. To the right it bent its crooked way under the brow of a black-timbered plateau; to the left it straightened its angles to find a V-shaped vent in the wall, now uplifted to a mountain range. Beyond this earth-riven line lay something vast and illimitable, a far-reaching vision of white wastes, of purple plains, of low mesas lost in distance. It was the shimmering dust-veiled desert.

"Here we come to the real thing," explained Naab. "This is Windy Slope; that black line is the Grand Canyon of Arizona; on the other side is the Painted Desert where the Navajos live; Coconina Mountain shows his flat head there to the right, and the wall on our left rises to the Vermillion Cliffs. Now, look while you can, for presently you'll not be able to see."

"Why?"

"Wind, sand, dust, gravel, pebbles—watch out for your eyes!"

Naab had not ceased speaking when Hare saw that the train of Indians trailing down the slope was enveloped in red clouds. Then the white wagons disappeared. Soon he was struck in the back by a gust which justified Naab's warning. It swept by; the air grew clear again; once more he could see. But presently a puff, taking him unawares, filled his eyes with dust difficult of removal. Whereupon he turned his back to the wind.

The afternoon grew apace; the sun glistened on the white patches of Coconina Mountain; it set; and the wind died.

"Five miles of red sand," said Naab. "Here's what kills the horses. Getup."

There was no trail. All before was red sand, hollows, slopes, levels, dunes, in which the horses sank above their fetlocks. The wheels ploughed deep, and little red streams trailed down from the tires. Naab trudged on foot with the reins in his hands. Hare essayed to walk also, soon tired, and floundered behind till Naab ordered him to ride again. Twilight came with the horses still toiling.

"There! thankful I am when we get off that strip! But, Jack, that trailless waste prevents a night raid on my home. Even the Navajos shun it after dark. We'll be home soon. There's my sign. See? Night or day we call it the Blue Star."

High in the black cliff a star-shaped, wind-worn hole let the blue sky through.

There was cheer in Naab's "Getup," now, and the horses quickened with it. Their iron-shod hoofs struck fire from the rosy road. "Easy, easy—soho!" cried Naab to his steeds. In the pitchy blackness under the shelving cliff they picked their way cautiously, and turned a corner. Lights twinkled in Hare's sight, a fresh breeze, coming from water, dampened his cheek, and a hollow rumble, a long roll as of distant thunder, filled his ears.

"What's that?" he asked.

"That, my lad, is what I always love to hear. It means I'm home. It's the roar of the Colorado as she takes her first plunge into the Canyon."

IV. THE OASIS

AUGUST NAAB'S oasis was an oval valley, level as a floor, green with leaf and white with blossom, enclosed by a circle of colossal cliffs of vivid vermilion hue. At its western curve the Colorado River split the red walls from north to south. When the wind was west a sullen roar, remote as of some far-off driving mill, filled the valley; when it was east a dreamy hollow hum, a somnolent song, murmured through the cottonwoods; when no wind stirred, silence reigned, a silence not of serene plain or mountain fastness, but shut in, compressed, strange, and breathless. Safe from the storms of the elements as well as of the world was this Garden of Eschtah.

Naab had put Hare to bed on the unroofed porch of a log house, but routed him out early, and when Hare lifted the blankets a shower of cotton-blossoms drifted away like snow. A grove of gray-barked trees spread green canopy overhead, and through the intricate web shone crimson walls, soaring with resistless onsweep up and up to shut out all but a blue lake of sky.

"I want you to see the Navajos cross the river," said Naab.

Hare accompanied him out through the grove to a road that flanked the first rise of the red wall; they followed this for half a mile, and turning a corner came into an unobstructed view. A roar of rushing waters had prepared Hare, but the river that he saw appalled him. It was red and swift; it slid onward like an enormous slippery snake; its constricted head raised a crest of leaping waves, and disappeared in a dark chasm, whence came a bellow and boom.

"That opening where she jumps off is the head of the Grand Canyon," said Naab. "It's five hundred feet deep there, and thirty miles below it's five thousand. Oh, once in, she tears in a hurry! Come, we turn up the bank here."

Hare could find no speech, and he felt immeasurably small. All that he had seen in reaching this isolated spot was dwarfed in comparison. This "Crossing of the Fathers," as Naab called it, was the gateway of the desert. This roar of turbulent waters was the sinister monotone of the mighty desert symphony of great depths, great heights, great reaches.

On a sandy strip of bank the Navajos had halted. This was as far as they could go, for above the wall jutted out into the river. From here the head of the Canyon was not visible, and the roar of the rapids was accordingly lessened in volume. But even in this smooth water the river spoke a warning.

"The Navajos go in here and swim their mustangs across to that sand bar," explained Naab. "The current helps when she's high, and there's a three-foot raise on now."

"I can't believe it possible. What danger they must run—those little mustangs!" exclaimed Hare.

"Danger? Yes, I suppose so," replied Naab, as if it were a new idea. "My lad, the Mormons crossed here by the hundreds. Many were drowned. This trail and crossing were unknown except to Indians before the Mormon exodus."

The mustangs had to be driven into the water. Scarbreast led, and his mustang, after many kicks and reluctant steps, went over his depth, wetting the stalwart chief to the waist. Bare-legged Indians waded in and urged their pack-ponies. Shouts, shrill cries, blows mingled with snorts and splashes.

Dave and George Naab in flat boats rowed slowly on the down-stream side of the Indians. Presently all the mustangs and ponies were in, the procession widening out in a triangle from Scarbreast, the leader. The pack-ponies appeared to swim better than the mounted mustangs, or else the packs of deer-pelts made them more buoyant. When one-third way across the head of the swimming train met the current, and the line of progress broke. Mustang after mustang swept down with a rapidity which showed the power of the current. Yet they swam steadily with flanks shining, tails sometimes afloat, sometimes under, noses up, and riders holding weapons aloft. But the pack-ponies labored when the current struck them, and whirling about, they held back the Indians who were leading them, and blocked those behind. The orderly procession of the start became a broken line, and then a rout. Here and there a Navajo slipped into the water and swam, leading his mustang; others pulled on pack-ponies and beat their mounts; strong-swimming mustangs forged ahead; weak ones hung back, and all obeyed the downward will of the current.

While Hare feared for the lives of some of the Navajos, and pitied the laden ponies, he could not but revel in the scene, in its vivid action and varying color, in the cries and shrill whoops of the Indians, and the snorts of the frightened mustangs, in Naab's hoarse yells to his sons, and the ever-present menacing roar from around the bend. The wildness of it all, the necessity of peril and calm acceptance of it, stirred within Hare the call, the awakening, the spirit of the desert.

August Naab's stentorian voice rolled out over the river. "Ho! Dave—the yellow pinto—pull him loose—George, back this way—there's a pack slipping—down now, downstream, turn that straggler in—Dave, in that tangle—quick! There's a boy drowning—his foot's caught—he's been kicked—Hurry! Hurry!—pull him in the boat—There's a pony under—Too late, George, let that one go—let him go, I tell you!"

So the crossing of the Navajos proceeded, never an instant free from danger in that churning current. The mustangs and ponies floundered somewhat on the sand-bar and then parted the willows and appeared on a trail skirting the red wall. Dave Naab moored his boat on that side of the river, and returned with George.

IV. THE OASIS

"We'll look over my farm," said August, as they retraced their steps. He led Hare through fields of alfalfa, in all stages of growth, explaining that it yielded six crops a year. Into one ten-acre lot pigs and cows had been turned to feed at will. Everywhere the ground was soggy; little streams of water trickled down ditches. Next to the fields was an orchard, where cherries were ripe, apricots already large, plum-trees shedding their blossoms, and apple-trees just opening into bloom. Naab explained that the products of his oasis were abnormal; the ground was exceedingly rich and could be kept always wet; the reflection of the sun from the walls robbed even winter of any rigor, and the spring, summer, and autumn were tropical. He pointed to grape-vines as large as a man's thigh and told of bunches of grapes four feet long; he showed sprouting plants on which watermelons and pumpkins would grow so large that one man could not lift them; he told of one pumpkin that held a record of taking two men to roll it.

"I can raise any kind of fruit in such abundance that it can't be used. My garden is prodigal. But we get little benefit, except for our own use, for we cannot transport things across the desert."

The water which was the prime factor in all this richness came from a small stream which Naab, by making a dam and tunnelling a corner of cliff, had diverted from its natural course into his oasis.

Between the fence and the red wall there was a wide bare plain which stretched to the house. At its farthest end was a green enclosure, which Hare recognized as the cemetery mentioned by Snap. Hare counted thirty graves, a few with crude monuments of stone, the others marked by wooden head-pieces.

"I've the reputation of doctoring the women, and letting the men die," said Naab, with a smile. "I hardly think it's fair. But the fact is no women are buried here. Some graves are of men I fished out of the river; others of those who drifted here, and who were killed or died keeping their secrets. I've numbered those unknown graves and have kept a description of the men, so, if the chance ever comes, I may tell some one where a father or brother lies buried. Five sons of mine, not one of whom died a natural death, found graves here—God rest them! Here's the grave of Mescal's father, a Spaniard. He was an adventurer. I helped him over in Nevada when he was ill; he came here with me, got well, and lived nine years, and he died without speaking one word of himself or telling his name."

"What strange ends men come to!" mused Hare. Well, a grave was a grave, wherever it lay. He wondered if he would come to rest in that quiet nook, with its steady light, its simple dignity of bare plain graves fitting the brevity of life, the littleness of man.

"We break wild mustangs along this stretch," said Naab, drawing Hare away. "It's a fine run. Wait till you see Mescal on Black Bolly tearing up the dust! She's a Navajo for riding."

Three huge corrals filled a wide curved space in the wall. In one corral were the teams that had hauled the wagons from White Sage; in another upward of thirty burros, drooping, lazy little fellows half asleep; in the third a dozen or more mustangs and some horses which delighted Hare. Snap Naab's cream pinto, a bay, and a giant horse of mottled white attracted him most.

"Our best stock is out on the range," said Naab. "The white is Charger, my saddle-horse. When he was a yearling he got away and ran wild for three years. But we caught him. He's a weight-carrier and he can run some. You're fond of a horse—I can see that."

"Yes," returned Hare, "but I—I'll never ride again." He said it brightly, smiling the while; still the look in his eyes belied the cheerful resignation.

"I've not the gift of revelation, yet I seem to see you on a big gray horse with a shining mane." Naab appeared to be gazing far away.

The cottonwood grove, at the western curve of the oasis, shaded the five log huts where August's grown sons lived with their wives, and his own cabin, which was of considerable dimensions. It had a covered porch on one side, an open one on the other, a shingle roof, and was a roomy and comfortable habitation.

Naab was pointing out the school-house when he was interrupted by childish laughter, shrieks of glee, and the rush of little feet.

"It's recess-time," he said.

A frantic crowd of tousled-headed little ones were running from the log school-house to form a circle under the trees. There were fourteen of them, from four years of age up to ten or twelve. Such sturdy, glad-eyed children Hare had never seen. In a few moments, as though their happy screams were signals, the shady circle was filled with hounds, and a string of puppies stepping on their long ears, and ruffling turkey-gobblers, that gobbled and gobbled, and guinea-hens with their shrill cries, and cackling chickens, and a lame wild goose that hobbled along alone. Then there were shiny peafowls screeching clarion calls from the trees overhead, and flocks of singing blackbirds, and pigeons hovering over and alighting upon the house. Last to approach were a woolly sheep that added his baa-baa to the din, and a bald-faced burro that walked in his sleep. These two became the centre of clamor. After many tumbles four chubby youngsters mounted the burro; and the others, with loud acclaim, shouting, "Noddle, Noddle, getup! getup!" endeavored to make him go. But Noddle nodded and refused to awaken or budge. Then an ambitious urchin of six fastened his hands in the fur of the sheep and essayed to climb to his back. Willing hands assisted him. "Ride him, Billy, ride him. Getup, Navvy, getup!"

Navvy evidently had never been ridden, for he began a fair imitation of a bucking bronco. Billy held on, but the smile vanished and the corners of his mouth drew down.

"Hang on, Billy, hang on," cried August Naab, in delight. Billy hung on a moment longer, and then Navvy, bewildered by the pestering crowd about him, launched out and, butting into Noddle, spilled the four youngsters and Billy also into a wriggling heap.

This recess-time completed Hare's introduction to the Naabs. There were Mother Mary, and Judith and Esther, whom he knew, and Mother Ruth and her two daughters very like their sisters. Mother Ruth, August's second wife, was younger than Mother Mary, more comely of face, and more sad and serious of expression. The wives of the five sons, except Snap Naab's frail bride, were stalwart women, fit to make homes and rear children.

"Now, Jack, things are moving all right," said August. "For the present you must eat and rest. Walk some, but don't tire yourself. We'll practice shooting a little every day; that's one thing I'll spare time for. I've a trick with a gun to teach you. And if you feel able, take a burro and ride. Anyway, make yourself at home."

Hare found eating and resting to be matters of profound enjoyment. Before he had fallen in with these good people it had been a year since he had sat down to a full meal; longer still since he had eaten wholesome food. And now he had come to a "land overflowing with milk and honey," as Mother Ruth smilingly said. He could not choose between roast beef and chicken, and so he waived the question by taking both; and what with the biscuits and butter, apple-sauce and blackberry jam, cherry pie and milk like cream, there was danger of making himself ill. He told his friends that he simply could not help it, which shameless confession brought a hearty laugh from August and beaming smiles from his women-folk.

For several days Hare was remarkably well, for an invalid. He won golden praise from August at the rifle practice, and he began to take lessons in the quick drawing and rapid firing of a Colt revolver. Naab was wonderfully proficient in the use of both firearms; and his skill in drawing the smaller weapon, in which his movement was quicker than the eye, astonished Hare. "My lad," said August, "it doesn't follow because I'm a Christian that I don't know how to handle a gun. Besides, I like to shoot."

In these few days Hare learned what conquering the desert made of a man. August Naab was close to threescore years; his chest was wide as a door, his arm like the branch of an oak. He was a blacksmith, a mechanic, a carpenter, a cooper, a potter. At his forge and in his shop, everywhere, were crude tools, wagons, farming implements, sets of buckskin harness, odds and ends of nameless things, eloquent and pregnant proof of the fact that necessity is the mother of invention. He was a mason; the levee that buffeted back the rage of the Colorado in flood, the wall that turned the creek, the irrigation tunnel, the zigzag trail cut on the face of the cliff—all these attested his eye for line, his judgment of distance, his strength in toil. He was a farmer, a cattle man, a grafter of fruit-trees, a breeder of horses, a herder of sheep, a preacher, a physician. Best and strangest of all in this wonderful man was the instinct and the heart to heal. "I don't combat the doctrine of the Mormon church," he said, "but I administer a little medicine with my healing. I learned that from the Navajos." The children ran to him with bruised heads, and cut fingers, and stubbed toes; and his blacksmith's hands were as gentle as a woman's. A mustang with a lame leg claimed his serious attention; a sick sheep gave him an anxious look; a steer with a gored skin sent him running for a bucket of salve. He could not pass by a crippled quail. The farm was overrun by Navajo sheep which he had found strayed and lost on the desert. Anything hurt or helpless had in August Naab a friend. Hare found himself looking up to a great and luminous figure, and he loved this man.

As the days passed Hare learned many other things. For a while illness confined him to his bed on the porch. At night he lay listening to the roar of the river, and watching the stars. Twice he heard a distant crash and rumble, heavy as thunder, and he knew that somewhere along the cliffs avalanches were slipping. By day he watched the cotton snow down upon him, and listened to the many birds, and waited for the merry show at recess-time. After a short time the children grew less shy and came readily to him. They were the most wholesome children he had ever known. Hare wondered about it, and decided it was not so much Mormon teaching as isolation from the world. These children had never been out of their cliff-walled home, and civilization was for them as if it were not. He told them stories, and after school hours they would race to him and climb on his bed, and beg for more.

He exhausted his supply of fairy-stories and animal stories; and had begun to tell about the places and cities which he had visited when the eager-eyed children were peremptorily called within by Mother Mary. This pained him and he was at a loss to understand it. Enlightenment came, however, in the way of an argument between Naab and Mother Mary which he overheard. The elder wife said that the stranger was welcome to the children, but she insisted that they hear nothing of the outside world, and that they be kept to the teachings of the Mormon geography—which made all the world outside Utah an untrodden wilderness. August Naab did not hold to the letter of the Mormon law; he argued that if the children could not be raised as Mormons with a full knowledge of the world, they would only be lost in the end to the Church.

Other developments surprised Hare. The house of this good Mormon was divided against itself. Precedence was given to the first and elder wife—Mother Mary; Mother Ruth's life was not without pain. The men were out on the ranges all day, usually two or more of them for several days at a time, and this left the women alone. One daughter taught the school, the other daughters did all the chores about the house, from feeding the stock to chopping wood. The work was hard, and the girls would rather have been in White Sage or Lund. They disliked Mescal, and said things inspired by jealousy. Snap Naab's wife was vindictive, and called Mescal "that Indian!"

It struck him on hearing this gossip that he had missed Mescal. What had become of her? Curiosity prompting him, he asked little Billy about her.

"Mescal's with the sheep," piped Billy.

That she was a shepherdess pleased Hare, and he thought of her as free on the open range, with the wind blowing her hair.

One day when Hare felt stronger he took his walk round the farm with new zest. Upon his return to the house he saw Snap's cream pinto in the yard, and Dave's mustang cropping the grass near by. A dusty pack lay on the ground. Hare walked down the avenue of cottonwoods and was about to turn the corner of the old forge when he stopped short.

"Now mind you, I'll take a bead on this white-faced spy if you send him up there."

IV. THE OASIS

It was Snap Naab's voice, and his speech concluded with the click of teeth characteristic of him in anger.

"Stand there!" August Naab exclaimed in wrath. "Listen. You have been drinking again or you wouldn't talk of killing a man. I warned you. I won't do this thing you ask of me till I have your promise. Why won't you leave the bottle alone?"

"I'll promise," came the sullen reply.

"Very well. Then pack and go across to Bitter Seeps."

"That job'll take all summer," growled Snap.

"So much the better. When you come home I'll keep my promise."

Hare moved away silently; the shock of Snap's first words had kept him fast in his tracks long enough to hear the conversation. Why did Snap threaten him? Where was August Naab going to send him? Hare had no means of coming to an understanding of either question. He was disturbed in mind and resolved to keep out of Snap's way. He went to the orchard, but his stay of an hour availed nothing, for on his return, after threading the maze of cottonwoods, he came face to face with the man he wanted to avoid.

Snap Naab, at the moment of meeting, had a black bottle tipped high above his lips.

With a curse he threw the bottle at Hare, missing him narrowly. He was drunk. His eyes were bloodshot.

"If you tell father you saw me drinking I'll kill you!" he hissed, and rattling his Colt in its holster, he walked away.

Hare walked back to his bed, where he lay for a long time with his whole inner being in a state of strife. It gradually wore off as he strove for calm. The playground was deserted; no one had seen Snap's action, and for that he was glad. Then his attention was diverted by a clatter of ringing hoofs on the road; a mustang and a cloud of dust were approaching.

"Mescal and Black Bolly!" he exclaimed, and sat up quickly. The mustang turned in the gate, slid to a stop, and stood quivering, restive, tossing its thoroughbred head, black as a coal, with freedom and fire in every line. Mescal leaped off lightly. A gray form flashed in at the gate, fell at her feet and rose to leap about her. It was a splendid dog, huge in frame, almost white, wild as the mustang.

This was the Mescal whom he remembered, yet somehow different. The sombre homespun garments had given place to fringed and beaded buckskin.

"I've come for you," she said.

"For me?" he asked, wonderingly, as she approached with the bridle of the black over her arm.

"Down, Wolf!" she cried to the leaping dog. "Yes. Didn't you know? Father Naab says you're to help me tend the sheep. Are you better? I hope so— You're quite pale."

"I—I'm not so well," said Hare.

He looked up at her, at the black sweep of her hair under the white band, at her eyes, like jet; and suddenly realized, with a gladness new and strange to him, that he liked to look at her, that she was beautiful.

V. BLACK SAGE AND JUNIPER

AUGUST NAAB appeared on the path leading from his fields.

"Mescal, here you are," he greeted. "How about the sheep?"

"Piute's driving them down to the lower range. There are a thousand coyotes hanging about the flock."

"That's bad," rejoined August. "Jack, there's evidently some real shooting in store for you. We'll pack to-day and get an early start to-morrow. I'll put you on Noddle; he's slow, but the easiest climber I ever owned. He's like riding... What's the matter with you? What's happened to make you angry?"

One of his long strides spanned the distance between them.

"Oh, nothing," said Hare, flushing.

"Lad, I know of few circumstances that justify a lie. You've met Snap."

Hare might still have tried to dissimulate; but one glance at August's stern face showed the uselessness of it. He kept silent.

"Drink makes my son unnatural," said Naab. He breathed heavily as one in conflict with wrath. "We'll not wait till to-morrow to go up on the plateau; we'll go at once."

Then quick surprise awakened for Hare in the meaning in Mescal's eyes; he caught only a fleeting glimpse, a dark flash, and it left him with a glow of an emotion half pleasure, half pain.

"Mescal," went on August, "go into the house, and keep out of Snap's way. Jack, watch me pack. You need to learn these things. I could put all this outfit on two burros, but the trail is narrow, and a wide pack might bump a burro off. Let's see, I've got all your stuff but the saddle; that we'll leave till we get a horse for you. Well, all's ready."

Mescal came at his call and, mounting Black Bolly, rode out toward the cliff wall, with Wolf trotting before her. Hare bestrode Noddle. August, waving goodbye to his women-folk, started the train of burros after Mescal.

How they would be able to climb the face of that steep cliff puzzled Hare. Upon nearer view he discovered the yard-wide trail curving upward in cork-screw fashion round a projecting corner of cliff. The stone was a soft red shale, and the trail had been cut in it at a steep angle. It was so steep that the burros appeared to be climbing straight up. Noddle pattered into it, dropped his head and his long ears and slackened his pace to patient plodding. August walked in the rear.

The first thing that struck Hare was the way the burros in front of him stopped at the curves in the trail, and turned in a space so small that their four feet were close together; yet as they swung their packs they scarcely scraped the wall. At every turn they were higher than he was, going in the opposite direction, yet he could reach out and touch them. He glanced up to see Mescal right above him, leaning forward with her brown hands clasping the pommel. Then he looked out and down; already the green cluster of cottonwoods lay far below. After that sensations pressed upon him. Round and round, up and up, steadily, surely, the beautiful mustang led the train; there were sounds of rattling stones, and click of hoofs, and scrape of pack. On one side towered the iron-stained cliff, not smooth or glistening at close range, but of dull, dead, rotting rock. The trail changed to a zigzag along a seamed and cracked buttress where ledges leaned outward waiting to fall. Then a steeper incline, where the burros crept upward warily, led to a level ledge heading to the left.

Mescal halted on a promontory. She, with her windblown hair, the gleam of white band about her head, and a dash of red along the fringed leggings, gave inexpressible life and beauty to that wild, jagged point of rock, sharp against the glaring sky.

"This is Lookout Point," said Naab. "I keep an Indian here all the time during daylight. He's a peon, a Navajo slave. He can't talk, as he was born without a tongue, or it was cut out, but he has the best eyes of any Indian I know. You see this point commands the farm, the crossing, the Navajo Trail over the river, the Echo Cliffs opposite, where the Navajos signal to me, and also the White Sage Trail."

The oasis shone under the triangular promontory; the river with its rising roar wound in bold curve from the split in the cliffs. To the right white-sloped Coconina breasted the horizon. Forward across the Canyon line opened the many-hued desert.

"With this peon watching here I'm not likely to be surprised," said Naab. "That strip of sand protects me at night from approach, and I've never had anything to fear from across the river."

Naab's peon came from a little cave in the wall; and grinned the greeting he could not speak. To Hare's uneducated eye all Indians resembled each other. Yet this one stood apart from the others, not differing in blanketed leanness, or straggling black hair, or bronze skin, but in the bird-of-prey cast of his features and the wildness of his glittering eyes. Naab gave him a bag from one of the packs, spoke a few words in Navajo, and then slapped the burros into the trail.

The climb thenceforth was more rapid because less steep, and the trail now led among broken fragments of cliff. The color of the stones had changed from red to yellow, and small cedars grew in protected places. Hare's judgment of height had such frequent cause for correction that he gave up trying to estimate the altitude. The ride had begun to tell on his strength, and toward the end he thought he could not manage to stay longer upon Noddle. The air had grown thin and cold, and though the sun was yet an hour high, his fingers were numb.

"Hang on, Jack," cheered August. "We're almost up."

At last Black Bolly disappeared, likewise the bobbing burros, one by one, then Noddle, wagging his ears, reached a level. Then Hare saw a gray-green cedar forest, with yellow crags rising in the background, and a rush of cold wind smote his face. For a moment he choked; he could not get his breath. The air was thin and rare, and he inhaled deeply trying to overcome the suffocation. Presently he realized that the trouble was not with the rarity of the atmosphere, but with the bittersweet penetrating odor it carried. He was almost stifled. It was not like the smell of pine, though it made him think of pine-trees.

"Ha! that's good!" said Naab, expanding his great chest. "That's air for you, my lad. Can you taste it? Well, here's camp, your home for many a day, Jack. There's Piute—how do? how're the sheep?"

A short, squat Indian, good-humored of face, shook his black head till the silver rings danced in his ears, and replied: "Bad—damn coyotee!"

"Piute—shake with Jack. Him shoot coyote—got big gun," said Naab.

"How-do-Jack?" replied Piute, extending his hand, and then straightway began examining the new rifle. "Damn—heap big gun!"

"Jack, you'll find this Indian one you can trust, for all he's a Piute outcast," went on August. "I've had him with me ever since Mescal found him on the Coconina Trail five years ago. What Piute doesn't know about this side of Coconina isn't worth learning."

In a depression sheltered from the wind lay the camp. A fire burned in the centre; a conical tent, like a tepee in shape, hung suspended from a cedar branch and was staked at its four points; a leaning slab of rock furnished shelter for camp supplies and for the Indian, and at one end a spring gushed out. A gray-sheathed cedar-tree marked the entrance to this hollow glade, and under it August began preparing Hare's bed.

"Here's the place you're to sleep, rain or shine or snow," he said. "Now I've spent my life sleeping on the ground, and mother earth makes the best bed. I'll dig out a little pit in this soft mat of needles; that's for your hips. Then the tarpaulin so; a blanket so. Now the other blankets. Your feet must be a little higher than your head; you really sleep down hill, which breaks the wind. So you never catch cold. All you need do is to change your position according to the direction of the wind. Pull up the blankets, and then the long end of the tarpaulin. If it rains or snows cover your head, and sleep, my lad, sleep to the song of the wind!"

From where Hare lay, resting a weary body, he could see down into the depression which his position guarded. Naab built up the fire; Piute peeled potatoes with deliberate care; Mescal, on her knees, her brown arms bare, kneaded dough in a basin; Wolf crouched on the ground, and watched his mistress; Black Bolly tossed her head, elevating the bag on her nose so as to get all the grain.

Naab called him to supper, and when Hare set to with a will on the bacon and eggs, and hot biscuits, he nodded approvingly. "That's what I want to see," he said approvingly. "You must eat. Piute will get deer, or you may shoot them yourself;

eat all the venison you can. Remember what Scarbreast said. Then rest. That's the secret. If you eat and rest you will gain strength."

The edge of the wall was not a hundred paces from the camp; and when Hare strolled out to it after supper, the sun had dipped the under side of its red disc behind the desert. He watched it sink, while the golden-red flood of light grew darker and darker. Thought seemed remote from him then; he watched, and watched, until he saw the last spark of fire die from the snow-slopes of Coconina. The desert became dimmer and dimmer; the oasis lost its outline in a bottomless purple pit, except for a faint light, like a star.

The bleating of sheep aroused him and he returned to camp. The fire was still bright. Wolf slept close to Mescal's tent; Piute was not in sight; and Naab had rolled himself in blankets. Crawling into his bed, Hare stretched aching legs and lay still, as if he would never move again. Tired as he was, the bleating of the sheep, the clear ring of the bell on Black Bolly, and the faint tinkle of lighter bells on some of the rams, drove away sleep for a while. Accompanied by the sough of the wind through the cedars the music of the bells was sweet, and he listened till he heard no more.

A thin coating of frost crackled on his bed when he awakened; and out from under the shelter of the cedar all the ground was hoar-white. As he slipped from his blankets the same strong smell of black sage and juniper smote him, almost like a blow. His nostrils seemed glued together by some rich piny pitch; and when he opened his lips to breathe a sudden pain, as of a knife-thrust, pierced his lungs. The thought following was as sharp as the pain. Pneumonia! What he had long expected! He sank against the cedar, overcome by the shock. But he rallied presently, for with the reestablishment of the old settled bitterness, which had been forgotten in the interest of his situation, he remembered that he had given up hope. Still, he could not get back at once to his former resignation. He hated to acknowledge that the wildness of this desert canyon country, and the spirit it sought to instil in him, had wakened a desire to live. For it meant only more to give up. And after one short instant of battle he was himself again. He put his hand under his flannel shirt and felt of the soreness of his lungs. He found it not at the apex of the right lung, always the one sensitive spot, but all through his breast. Little panting breaths did not hurt; but the deep inhalation, which alone satisfied him filled his whole chest with thousands of pricking needles. In the depth of his breast was a hollow that burned.

When he had pulled on his boots and coat, and had washed himself in the runway of the spring, his hands were so numb with cold they refused to hold his comb and brush; and he presented himself at the roaring fire half-frozen, dishevelled, trembling, but cheerful. He would not tell Naab. If he had to die to-day, tomorrow or next week, he would lie down under a cedar and die; he could not whine about it to this man.

"Up with the sun!" was Naab's greeting. His cheerfulness was as impelling as his splendid virility. Following the wave of his hand Hare saw the sun, a pale-pink globe through a misty blue, rising between the golden crags of the eastern wall.

Mescal had a shy "good-morning" for him, and Piute a broad smile, and familiar "how-do"; the peon slave, who had finished breakfast and was about to depart, moved his lips in friendly greeting that had no sound.

"Did you hear the coyotes last night?" inquired August. "No! Well, of all the choruses I ever heard. There must be a thousand on the bench. Jack, I wish I could spare the time to stay up here with you and shoot some. You'll have practice with the rifle, but don't neglect the Colt. Practice particularly the draw I taught you. Piute has a carbine, and he shoots at the coyotes, but who ever saw an Indian that could hit anything?"

"Damn—gun no good!" growled Piute, who evidently understood English pretty well. Naab laughed, and while Hare ate breakfast he talked of the sheep. The flock he had numbered three thousand. They were a goodly part of them Navajo stock: small, hardy sheep that could live on anything but cactus, and needed little water. This flock had grown from a small number to its present size in a few years. Being remarkably free from the diseases and pests which retard increase in low countries, the sheep had multiplied almost one for one for every year. But for the ravages of wild beasts Naab believed he could raise a flock of many thousands and in a brief time be rich in sheep alone. In the winter he drove them down into the oasis; the other seasons he herded them on the high ranges where the cattle could not climb. There was grass enough on this plateau for a million sheep. After the spring thaw in early March, occasional snows fell till the end of May, and frost hung on until early summer; then the July rains made the plateau a garden.

"Get the forty-four," concluded Naab, "and we'll go out and break it in."

With the long rifle in the hollow of his arm Jack forgot that he was a sick man. When he came within gunshot of the flock the smell of sheep effectually smothered the keen, tasty odor of black sage and juniper. Sheep ranged everywhere under the low cedars. They browsed with noses in the frost, and from all around came the tinkle of tiny bells on the curly-horned rams, and an endless variety of bleats.

"They're spread now," said August. "Mescal drives them on every little while and Piute goes ahead to pick out the best browse. Watch the dog, Jack; he's all but human. His mother was a big shepherd dog that I got in Lund. She must have had a strain of wild blood. Once while I was hunting deer on Coconina she ran off with timber wolves and we thought she was killed. But she came back, and had a litter of three puppies. Two were white, the other black. I think she killed the black one. And she neglected the others. One died, and Mescal raised the other. We called him Wolf. He loves Mescal, and loves the sheep, and hates a wolf. Mescal puts a bell on him when she is driving, and the sheep know the bell. I think it would be a good plan for her to tie something red round his neck—a scarf, so as to keep you from shooting him for a wolf."

Nimble, alert, the big white dog was not still a moment. His duty was to keep the flock compact, to head the stragglers and turn them back; and he knew his part perfectly. There was dash and fire in his work. He never barked. As he circled the flock the small Navajo sheep, edging ever toward forbidden ground, bleated their way back to the fold, the larger ones wheeled reluctantly, and the old belled rams squared themselves, lowering their massive horns as if to butt him. Never, however, did they stand their ground when he reached them, for there was a decision about Wolf which brooked no opposition. At times when he was working on one side a crafty sheep on the other would steal out into the thicket. Then Mescal called and Wolf flashed back to her, lifting his proud head, eager, spirited, ready to take his order. A word, a wave of her whip sufficed for the dog to rout out the recalcitrant sheep and send him bleating to his fellows.

"He manages them easily now," said Naab, "but when the lambs come they can't be kept in. The coyotes and wolves hang out in the thickets and pick up the stragglers. The worst enemy of sheep, though, is the old grizzly bear. Usually he is grouchy, and dangerous to hunt. He comes into the herd, kills the mother sheep, and eats the milk-bag—no more! He will kill forty sheep in a night. Piute saw the tracks of one up on the high range, and believes this bear is following the flock. Let's get off into the woods some little way, into the edge of the thickets—for Piute always keeps to the glades—and see if we can pick off a few coyotes."

August cautioned Jack to step stealthily, and slip from cedar to cedar, to use every bunch of sage and juniper to hide his advance.

"Watch sharp, Jack. I've seen two already. Look for moving things. Don't try to see one quiet, for you can't till after your eye catches him moving. They are gray, gray as the cedars, the grass, the ground. Good! Yes, I see him, but don't shoot. That's too far. Wait. They sneak away, but they return. You can afford to make sure. Here now, by that stone—aim low and be quick."

In the course of a mile, without keeping the sheep near at hand, they saw upward of twenty coyotes, five of which Jack killed in as many shots.

"You've got the hang of it," said Naab, rubbing his hands. "You'll kill the varmints. Piute will skin and salt the pelts. Now I'm going up on the high range to look for bear sign. Go ahead, on your own hook."

Hare was regardless of time while he stole under the cedars and through the thickets, spying out the cunning coyotes. Then Naab's yell pealing out claimed his attention; he answered and returned. When they met he recounted his adventures in mingled excitement and disappointment.

"Are you tired?" asked Naab.

"Tired? No," replied Jack.

"Well, you mustn't overdo the very first day. I've news for you. There are some wild horses on the high range. I didn't see them, but found tracks everywhere. If they come down here you send Piute to close the trail at the upper end of the bench, and you close the one where we came up. There are only two trails where even a deer can get off this plateau, and both are narrow splits in the wall, which can be barred by the gates. We made the gates to keep the sheep in, and they'll serve a turn. If you get the wild horses on the bench send Piute for me at once."

They passed the Indian herding the sheep into a corral built against an uprising ridge of stone. Naab dispatched him to look for the dead coyotes. The three burros were in camp, two wearing empty pack-saddles, and Noddle, for once not asleep, was eating from Mescal's hand.

"Mescal, hadn't I better take Black Bolly home?" asked August.

"Mayn't I keep her?"

"She's yours. But you run a risk. There are wild horses on the range. Will you keep her hobbled?"

"Yes," replied Mescal, reluctantly. "Though I don't believe Bolly would run off from me."

"Look out she doesn't go, hobbles and all. Jack, here's the other bit of news I have for you. There's a big grizzly camping on the trail of our sheep. Now what I want to know is—shall I leave him to you, or put off work and come up here to wait for him myself?"

"Why—" said Jack, slowly, "whatever you say. If you think you can safely leave him to me—I'm willing."

"A grizzly won't be pleasant to face. I never knew one of those sheep-killers that wouldn't run at a man, if wounded."

"Tell me what to do."

"If he comes down it's more than likely to be after dark. Don't risk hunting him then. Wait till morning, and put Wolf on his trail. He'll be up in the rocks, and by holding in the dog you may find him asleep in a cave. However, if you happen to meet him by day do this. Don't waste any shots. Climb a ledge or tree if one be handy. If not, stand your ground. Get down on your knee and shoot and let him come. Mind you, he'll grunt when he's hit, and start for you, and keep coming till he's dead. Have confidence in yourself and your gun, for you can kill him. Aim low, and shoot steady. If he keeps on coming there's always a fatal shot, and that is when he rises. You'll see a bare spot on his breast. Put a forty-four into that, and he'll go down."

August had spoken so easily, quite as if he were explaining how to shear a yearling sheep, that Jack's feelings fluctuated between amazement and laughter. Verily this desert man was stripped of all the false fears of civilization.

"Now, Jack, I'm off. Good-bye and good luck. Mescal, look out for him.... So-ho! Noddle! Getup! Biscuit!" And with many a cheery word and slap he urged the burros into the forest, where they and his tall form soon disappeared among the trees.

Piute came stooping toward camp so burdened with coyotes that he could scarcely be seen under the gray pile. With a fervent "damn" he tumbled them under a cedar, and trotted back into the forest for another load. Jack insisted on assuming his share of the duties about camp; and Mescal assigned him to the task of gathering firewood, breaking red-hot sticks of wood into small pieces, and raking them into piles of live coals. Then they ate, these two alone. Jack did not do justice to the supper; excitement had robbed him of appetite. He told Mescal how he had crept upon the coyotes, how so many had eluded him, how he had missed a gray wolf. He plied her with questions about the sheep, and wanted to know if there would be more wolves, and if she thought the "silvertip" would come. He was quite carried away by the events of the day.

The sunset drew him to the rim. Dark clouds were mantling the desert like rolling smoke from a prairie-fire. He almost stumbled over Mescal, who sat with her back to a stone. Wolf lay with his head in her lap, and he growled.

"There's a storm on the desert," she said. "Those smoky streaks are flying sand. We may have snow to-night. It's colder, and the wind is north. See, I've a blanket. You had better get one."

He thanked her and went for it. Piute was eating his supper, and the peon had just come in. The bright campfire was agreeable, yet Hare did not feel cold. But he wrapped himself in a blanket and returned to Mescal and sat beside her. The desert lay indistinct in the foreground, inscrutable beyond; the canyon lost its line in gloom. The solemnity of the scene stilled his unrest, the strange freedom of longings unleashed that day. What had come over him? He shook his head; but with the consciousness of self returned a feeling of fatigue, the burning pain in his chest, the bitter-sweet smell of black sage and juniper.

"You love this outlook?" he asked.

"Yes."

"Do you sit here often?"

"Every evening."

"Is it the sunset that you care for, the roar of the river, just being here high above it all?"

"It's that last, perhaps; I don't know."

"Haven't you been lonely?"

"No."

"You'd rather be here with the sheep than be in Lund, or Salt Lake City, as Esther and Judith want to be?"

"Yes."

Any other reply from her would not have been consistent with the impression she was making on him. As yet he had hardly regarded her as a young girl; she had been part of this beautiful desert-land. But he began to see in her a responsive being, influenced by his presence. If the situation was wonderful to him what must it be for her? Like a shy, illusive creature, unused to men, she was troubled by questions, fearful of the sound of her own voice. Yet in repose, as she watched the lights and shadows, she was serene, unconscious; her dark, quiet glance was dreamy and sad, and in it was the sombre, brooding strength of the desert.

Twilight and falling dew sent them back to the camp. Piute and Peon were skinning coyotes by the blaze of the fire. The night wind had not yet risen; the sheep were quiet; there was no sound save the crackle of burning cedar sticks. Jack began to talk; he had to talk, so, addressing Piute and the dumb peon, he struck at random into speech, and words flowed with a rush. Piute approved, for he said "damn" whenever his intelligence grasped a meaning, and the peon twisted his lips and fixed his diamond eyes upon Hare in rapt gaze. The sound of a voice was welcome to the sentinels of that lonely sheep-range. Jack talked of cities, of ships, of people, of simple things in the life he had left, and he discovered that Mescal listened. Not only did she listen; she became absorbed; it was romance to her, fulfilment of her vague dreams. Nor did she seek her tent till he ceased; then with a startled "good-night" she was gone.

From under the snugness of his warm blankets Jack watched out the last wakeful moments of that day of days. A star peeped through the fringe of cedar foliage. The wind sighed, and rose steadily, to sweep over him with breath of ice, with the fragrance of juniper and black sage and a tang of cedar.

But that day was only the beginning of eventful days, of increasing charm, of forgetfulness of self, of time that passed unnoted. Every succeeding day was like its predecessor, only richer. Every day the hoar-frost silvered the dawn; the sheep browsed; the coyotes skulked in the thickets; the rifle spoke truer and truer. Every sunset Mescal's changing eyes mirrored the desert. Every twilight Jack sat beside her in the silence; every night, in the camp-fire flare, he talked to Piute and the peon.

The Indians were appreciative listeners, whether they understood Jack or not, but his talk with them was only a presence. He wished to reveal the outside world to Mescal, and he saw with pleasure that every day she grew more interested.

One evening he was telling of New York City, of the monster buildings where men worked, and of the elevated railways, for the time was the late seventies and they were still a novelty. Then something unprecedented occurred, inasmuch as Piute earnestly and vigorously interrupted Jack, demanding to have this last strange story made more clear. Jack did his best in gesture and speech, but he had to appeal to Mescal to translate his meaning to the Indian. This Mescal did with surprising fluency. The result, however, was that Piute took exception to the story of trains carrying people through the air. He lost his grin and regarded Jack with much disfavor. Evidently he was experiencing the bitterness of misplaced trust.

"Heap damn lie!" he exclaimed with a growl, and stalked off into the gloom.

Piute's expressive doubt discomfited Hare, but only momentarily, for Mescal's silvery peal of laughter told him that the incident had brought them closer together. He laughed with her and discovered a well of joyousness behind her reserve. Thereafter he talked directly to Mescal. The ice being broken she began to ask questions, shyly at first, yet more and more eagerly, until she forgot herself in the desire to learn of cities and people; of women especially, what they wore and how they lived, and all that life meant to them.

The sweetest thing which had ever come to Hare was the teaching of this desert girl. How naive in her questions and how quick to grasp she was! The reaching out of her mind was like the unfolding of a rose. Evidently the Mormon restrictions had limited her opportunities to learn.

But her thought had striven to escape its narrow confines, and now, liberated by sympathy and intelligence, it leaped forth.

Lambing-time came late in May, and Mescal, Wolf, Piute and Jack knew no rest. Night-time was safer for the sheep than the day, though the howling of a thousand coyotes made it hideous for the shepherds. All in a day, seemingly, the little fleecy lambs came, as if by magic, and filled the forest with piping bleats. Then they were tottering after their mothers, gamboling at a day's growth, wilful as youth—and the carnage began. Boldly the coyotes darted out of thicket and bush, and many lambs never returned to their mothers. Gaunt shadows hovered always near; the great timber-wolves waited in covert for prey. Piute slept not at all, and the dog's jaws were flecked with blood morning and night. Jack hung up fifty-four coyotes the second day; the third he let them lie, seventy in number. Many times the rifle-barrel burned his hands. His aim grew unerring, so that running brutes in range dropped in their tracks. Many a gray coyote fell with a lamb in his teeth.

One night when sheep and lambs were in the corral, and the shepherds rested round the camp-fire, the dog rose quivering, sniffed the cold wind, and suddenly bristled with every hair standing erect.

"Wolf!" called Mescal.

The sheep began to bleat. A rippling crash, a splintering of wood, told of an irresistible onslaught on the corral fence.

"Chus—chus!" exclaimed Piute.

Wolf, not heeding Mescal's cry, flashed like lightning under the cedars. The rush of the sheep, pattering across the corral was succeeded by an uproar.

"Bear! Bear!" cried Mescal, with dark eyes on Jack. He seized his rifle.

"Don't go," she implored, her hand on his arm. "Not at night—remember Father Naab said not."

"Listen! I won't stand that. I'll go. Here, get in the tree—quick!"

"No—no—"

"Do as I say!" It was a command. The girl wavered. He dropped the rifle, and swung her up. "Climb!"

"No—don't go—Jack!"

With Piute at his heels he ran out into the darkness.

VI. THE WIND IN THE CEDARS

PIUTE'S Indian sense of the advantage of position in attack stood Jack in good stead; he led him up the ledge which overhung one end of the corral. In the pale starlight the sheep could be seen running in bands, massing together, crowding the fence; their cries made a deafening din.

The Indian shouted, but Jack could not understand him. A large black object was visible in the shade of the ledge. Piute fired his carbine. Before Jack could bring his rifle up the black thing moved into startlingly rapid flight. Then spouts of red flame illumined the corral. As he shot, Jack got fleeting glimpses of the bear moving like a dark streak against a blur of white. For all he could tell no bullet took effect.

When certain that the visitor had departed Jack descended into the corral. He and Piute searched for dead sheep, but, much to their surprise, found none. If the grizzly had killed one he must have taken it with him; and estimating his strength from the gap he had broken in the fence, he could easily have carried off a sheep. They repaired the break and returned to camp.

"He's gone, Mescal. Come down," called Jack into the cedar. "Let me help you—there! Wasn't it lucky? He wasn't so brave. Either the flashes from the guns or the dog scared him. I was amazed to see how fast he could run."

Piute found woolly brown fur hanging from Wolf's jaws.

"He nipped the brute, that's sure," said Jack. "Good dog! Maybe he kept the bear from— Why Mescal! you're white—you're shaking. There's no danger. Piute and I'll take turns watching with Wolf."

Mescal went silently into her tent.

The sheep quieted down and made no further disturbance that night. The dawn broke gray, with a cold north wind. Dun-colored clouds rolled up, hiding the tips of the crags on the upper range, and a flurry of snow whitened the cedars. After breakfast Jack tried to get Wolf to take the track of the grizzly, but the scent had cooled.

Next day Mescal drove the sheep eastward toward the crags, and about the middle of the afternoon reached the edge of the slope. Grass grew luxuriantly and it was easy to keep the sheep in. Moreover, that part of the forest had fewer trees, and scarcely any sage or thickets, so that the lambs were safer, barring danger which might lurk in the seamed and cracked cliffs overshadowing the open grassy plots. Piute's task at the moment was to drag dead coyotes to the rim, near at hand, and throw them over. Mescal rested on a stone, and Wolf reclined at her feet.

Jack presently found a fresh deer track, and trailed it into the cedars, then up the slope to where the huge rocks massed.

Suddenly a cry from Mescal halted him; another, a piercing scream of mortal fright, sent him flying down the slope. He bounded out of the cedars into the open.

The white, well-bunched flock had spread, and streams of jumping sheep fled frantically from an enormous silver-backed bear.

As the bear struck right and left, a brute-engine of destruction, Jack sent a bullet into him at long range. Stung, the grizzly whirled, bit at his side, and then reared with a roar of fury.

But he did not see Jack. He dropped down and launched his huge bulk for Mescal. The blood rushed back to Jack's heart, and his empty veins seemed to freeze.

The grizzly hurdled the streams of sheep. Terror for Mescal dominated Jack; if he had possessed wings he could not have flown quickly enough to head the bear. Checking himself with a suddenness that fetched him to his knees, he levelled the rifle. It waved as if it were a stick of willow. The bead-sight described a blurred curve round the bear. Yet he shot—in vain—again—in vain.

Above the bleat of sheep and trample of many hoofs rang out Mescal's cry, despairing.

She had turned, her hands over her breast. Wolf spread his legs before her and crouched to spring, mane erect, jaws wide.

By some lightning flash of memory, August Naab's words steadied Jack's shaken nerves. He aimed low and ahead of the running bear. Down the beast went in a sliding sprawl with a muffled roar of rage. Up he sprang, dangling a useless leg, yet leaping swiftly forward. One blow sent the attacking dog aside. Jack fired again. The bear became a wrestling, fiery demon, death-stricken, but full of savage fury. Jack aimed low and shot again.

Slowly now the grizzly reared, his frosted coat blood-flecked, his great head swaying. Another shot. There was one wide sweep of the huge paw, and then the bear sank forward, drooping slowly, and stretched all his length as if to rest.

Mescal, recalled to life, staggered backward. Between her and the outstretched paw was the distance of one short stride.

Jack, bounding up, made sure the bear was dead before he looked at Mescal. She was faint. Wolf whined about her. Piute came running from the cedars. Her eyes were still fixed in a look of fear.

"I couldn't run—I couldn't move," she said, shuddering. A blush drove the white from her cheeks as she raised her face to Jack. "He'd soon have reached me."

Piute added his encomium: "Damn—heap big bear— Jack kill um—big chief!"

VI. THE WIND IN THE CEDARS

Hare laughed away his own fear and turned their attention to the stampeded sheep. It was dark before they got the flock together again, and they never knew whether they had found them all. Supper-time was unusually quiet that night. Piute was jovial, but no one appeared willing to talk save the peon, and he could only grimace. The reaction of feeling following Mescal's escape had robbed Jack of strength of voice; he could scarcely whisper. Mescal spoke no word; her black lashes hid her eyes; she was silent, but there was that in her silence which was eloquent. Wolf, always indifferent save to Mescal, reacted to the subtle change, and as if to make amends laid his head on Jack's knees. The quiet hour round the camp-fire passed, and sleep claimed them. Another day dawned, awakening them fresh, faithful to their duties, regardless of what had gone before.

So the days slipped by. June came, with more leisure for the shepherds, better grazing for the sheep, heavier dews, lighter frosts, snow-squalls half rain, and bursting blossoms on the prickly thorns, wild-primrose patches in every shady spot, and bluebells lifting wan azure faces to the sun.

The last snow-storm of June threatened all one morning; hung menacing over the yellow crags, in dull lead clouds waiting for the wind. Then like ships heaving anchor to a single command they sailed down off the heights; and the cedar forest became the centre of a blinding, eddying storm. The flakes were as large as feathers, moist, almost warm. The low cedars changed to mounds of white; the sheep became drooping curves of snow; the little lambs were lost in the color of their own pure fleece. Though the storm had been long in coming it was brief in passing. Wind-driven toward the desert, it moaned its last in the cedars, and swept away, a sheeted pall. Out over the Canyon it floated, trailing long veils of white that thinned out, darkened, and failed far above the golden desert. The winding columns of snow merged into straight lines of leaden rain; the rain flowed into vapory mist, and the mist cleared in the gold-red glare of endless level and slope. No moisture reached the parched desert.

Jack marched into camp with a snowy burden over his shoulder. He flung it down, disclosing a small deer; then he shook the white mantle from his coat, and whistling, kicked the fire-logs, and looked abroad at the silver cedars, now dripping under the sun, at the rainbows in the settling mists, at the rapidly melting snow on the ground.

"Got lost in that squall. Fine! Fine!" he exclaimed, and threw wide his arms.

"Jack!" said Mescal. "Jack!" Memory had revived some forgotten thing. The dark olive of her skin crimsoned; her eyes dilated and shadowed with a rare change of emotion.

"Jack," she repeated.

"Well?" he replied, in surprise.

"To look at you!—I never dreamed—I'd forgotten—"

"What's the matter with me?" demanded Jack.

Wonderingly, her mind on the past, she replied: "You were dying when we found you at White Sage."

He drew himself up with a sharp catch in his breath, and stared at her as if he saw a ghost.

"Oh—Jack! You're going to get well!"

Her lips curved in a smile.

For an instant Jack Hare spent his soul in searching her face for truth. While waiting for death he had utterly forgotten it; he remembered now, when life gleamed in the girl's dark eyes. Passionate joy flooded his heart.

"Mescal—Mescal!" he cried, brokenly. The eyes were true that shed this sudden light on him; glad and sweet were the lips that bade him hope and live again. Blindly, instinctively he kissed them—a kiss unutterably grateful; then he fled into the forest, running without aim.

That flight ended in sheer exhaustion on the far rim of the plateau. The spreading cedars seemed to have eyes; and he shunned eyes in this hour. "God! to think I cared so much," he whispered. "What has happened?" With time relief came to limbs, to labored breast and lungs, but not to mind. In doubt that would not die, he looked at himself. The leanness of arms, the flat chest, the hollows were gone. He did not recognize his own body. He breathed to the depths of his lungs. No pain—only exhilaration! He pounded his chest—no pain! He dug his trembling fingers into the firm flesh over the apex of his right lung—the place of his torture—no pain!

"I wanted to live!" he cried. He buried his face in the fragrant juniper; he rolled on the soft brown mat of earth and hugged it close; he cooled his hot cheeks in the primrose clusters. He opened his eyes to new bright green of cedar, to sky of a richer blue, to a desert, strange, beckoning, enthralling as life itself. He counted backward a month, two months, and marvelled at the swiftness of time. He counted time forward, he looked into the future, and all was beautiful—long days, long hunts, long rides, service to his friend, freedom on the wild steppes, blue-white dawns upon the eastern crags, red-gold sunsets over the lilac mountains of the desert. He saw himself in triumphant health and strength, earning day by day the spirit of this wilderness, coming to fight for it, to live for it, and in far-off time, when he had won his victory, to die for it.

Suddenly his mind was illumined. The lofty plateau with its healing breath of sage and juniper had given back strength to him; the silence and solitude and strife of his surroundings had called to something deep within him; but it was Mescal who made this wild life sweet and significant. It was Mescal, the embodiment of the desert spirit. Like a man facing a great light Hare divined his love. Through all the days on the plateau, living with her the natural free life of Indians, close to the earth, his unconscious love had ripened. He understood now her charm for him; he knew now the lure of her wonderful eyes, flashing fire, desert-trained, like the falcon eyes of her Indian grandfather. The knowledge of what she had become to him dawned with a mounting desire that thrilled all his blood.

Twilight had enfolded the plateau when Hare traced his way back to camp. Mescal was not there. His supper awaited him; Piute hummed a song; the peon sat grimacing at the fire. Hare told them to eat, and moved away toward the rim.

VI. THE WIND IN THE CEDARS

Mescal was at her favorite seat, with the white dog beside her; and she watched the desert where the last glow of sunset gilded the mesas. How cold and calm was her face! How strange to him in this new character!

"Mescal, I didn't know I loved you—then—but I know it now."

Her face dropped quickly from its level poise, hiding the brooding eyes; her hand trembled on Wolf's head.

"You spoke the truth. I'll get well. I'd rather have had it from your lips than from any in the world. I mean to live my life here where these wonderful things have come to me. The friendship of the good man who saved me, this wild, free desert, the glory of new hope, strength, life—and love."

He took her hand in his and whispered, "For I love you. Do you care for me? Mescal! It must be complete. Do you care—a little?"

The wind blew her dusky hair; he could not see her face; he tried gently to turn her to him. The hand he had taken lay warm and trembling in his, but it was not withdrawn. As he waited, in fear, in hope, it became still. Her slender form, rigid within his arm, gradually relaxed, and yielded to him; her face sank on his breast, and her dark hair loosened from its band, covered her, and blew across his lips. That was his answer.

The wind sang in the cedars. No longer a sigh, sad as thoughts of a past forever flown, but a song of what had come to him, of hope, of life, of Mescal's love, of the things to be!

VII. SILVERMANE

LITTLE dew fell on the night of July first; the dawn brightened without mists; a hot sun rose; the short summer of the plateau had begun.

As Hare rose, refreshed and happy from his breakfast, his whistle was cut short by the Indian.

"Ugh!" exclaimed Piute, lifting a dark finger. Black Bolly had thrown her nose-bag and slipped her halter, and she moved toward the opening in the cedars, her head high, her black ears straight up.

"Bolly!" called Mescal. The mare did not stop.

"What the deuce?" Hare ran forward to catch her.

"I never knew Bolly to act that way," said Mescal. "See—she didn't eat half the oats. Well, Bolly—Jack! look at Wolf!"

The white dog had risen and stood warily shifting his nose. He sniffed the wind, turned round and round, and slowly stiffened with his head pointed toward the eastern rise of the plateau.

"Hold, Wolf, hold!" called Mescal, as the dog appeared to be about to dash away.

"Ugh!" grunted Piute.

"Listen, Jack; did you hear?" whispered the girl.

"Hear what?"

"Listen."

The warm breeze came down in puffs from the crags; it rustled in the cedars and blew fragrant whiffs of camp-fire smoke into his face; and presently it bore a low, prolonged whistle. He had never before heard its like. The sound broke the silence again, clearer, a keen, sharp whistle.

"What is it?" he queried, reaching for his rifle.

"Wild mustangs," said Mescal.

"No," corrected Piute, vehemently shaking his head. "Clea, Clea."

"Jack, he says 'horse, horse.' It's a wild horse."

A third time the whistle rang down from the ridge, splitting the air, strong and trenchant, the fiery, shrill challenge of a stallion.

Black Bolly reared straight up.

Jack ran to the rise of ground above the camp, and looked over the cedars. "Oh!" he cried, and beckoned for Mescal. She ran to him, and Piute, tying Black

Bolly, hurried after. "Look! look!" cried Jack. He pointed to a ridge rising to the left of the yellow crags. On the bare summit stood a splendid stallion clearly silhouetted against the ruddy morning sky. He was an iron-gray, wild and proud, with long silver-white mane waving in the wind.

"Silvermane! Silvermane!" exclaimed Mescal.

"What a magnificent animal!" Jack stared at the splendid picture for the moment before the horse moved back along the ridge and disappeared. Other horses, blacks and bays, showed above the sage for a moment, and they, too, passed out of sight.

"He's got some of his band with him," said Jack, thrilled with excitement. "Mescal, they're down off the upper range, and grazing along easy. The wind favors us. That whistle was just plain fight, judging from what Naab told me of wild stallions. He came to the hilltop, and whistled down defiance to any horse, wild or tame, that might be below. I'll slip round through the cedars, and block the trail leading up to the other range, and you and Piute close the gate of our trail at this end. Then send Piute down to tell Naab we've got Silvermane."

Jack chose the lowest edge of the plateau rim where the cedars were thickest for his detour to get behind the wild band; he ran from tree to tree, avoiding the open places, taking advantage of the thickets, keeping away from the ridge. He had never gone so far as the gate, but, knowing where the trail led into a split in the crags, he climbed the slope, and threaded a way over masses of fallen cliff, until he reached the base of the wall. The tracks of the wildhorse band were very fresh and plain in the yellow trail. Four stout posts guarded the opening, and a number of bars lay ready to be pushed into place. He put them up, making a gate ten feet high, an impregnable barrier. This done, he hurried back to camp.

"Jack, Bolly will need more watching to-day than the sheep, unless I let her loose. Why, she pulls and strains so she'll break that halter."

"She wants to go with the band; isn't that it?"

"I don't like to think so. But Father Naab doesn't trust Bolly, though she's the best mustang he ever broke."

"Better keep her in," replied Jack, remembering Naab's warning. "I'll hobble her, so if she does break loose she can't go far."

When Mescal and Jack drove in the sheep that afternoon, rather earlier than usual, Piute had returned with August Naab, Dave, and Billy, a string of mustangs and a pack-train of burros.

"Hello, Mescal," cheerily called August, as they came into camp. "Well Jack—bless me! Why, my lad, how fine and brown—and yes, how you've filled out!" He crushed Jack's hand in his broad palm, and his gray eyes beamed. "I've not the gift of revelation—but, Jack, you're going to get well."

"Yes, I—" He had difficulty with his enunciation, but he thumped his breast significantly and smiled.

"Black sage and juniper!" exclaimed August. "In this air if a man doesn't go off quickly with pneumonia, he'll get well. I never had a doubt for you, Jack—and thank God!"

He questioned Piute and Mescal about the sheep, and was greatly pleased with their report. He shook his head when Jack spread out the grizzly-pelt, and asked for the story of the killing. Jack made a poor showing with the tale and slighted his share in it, but Mescal told it as it actually happened. And Naab's great hand resounded from Jack's shoulder. Then, catching sight of the pile of coyote skins under the stone shelf, he gave vent to his surprise and delight. Then he came back to the object of his trip upon the plateau.

"So you've corralled Silvermane? Well, Jack, if he doesn't jump over the cliff he's ours. He can't get off any other way. How many horses with him?"

"We had no chance to count. I saw at least twelve."

"Good! He's out with his picked band. Weren't they all blacks and bays?"

"Yes."

"Jack, the history of that stallion wouldn't make you proud of him. We've corralled him by a lucky chance. If I don't miss my guess he's after Bolly. He has been a lot of trouble to ranchers all the way from the Nevada line across Utah. The stallions he's killed, the mares he's led off! Well, Dave, shall we thirst him out, or line up a long corral?"

"Better have a look around to-morrow," replied Dave. "It'll take a lot of chasing to run him down, but there's not a spring on the bench where we can throw up a trap-corral. We'll have to chase him."

"Mescal, has Bolly been good since Silvermane came down?"

"No, she hasn't," declared Mescal, and told of the circumstance.

"Bolly's all right," said Billy Naab. "Any mustang will do that. Keep her belled and hobbled."

"Silvermane would care a lot about that, if he wanted Bolly, wouldn't he?" queried Dave in quiet scorn. "Keep her roped and haltered, I say."

"Dave's right," said August. "You can't trust a wild mustang any more than a wild horse."

August was right. Black Bolly broke her halter about midnight and escaped into the forest, hobbled as she was. The Indian heard her first, and he awoke August, who aroused the others.

"Don't make any noise," he said, as Jack came up, throwing on his coat. "There's likely to be some fun here presently. Bolly's loose, broke her rope, and I think Silvermane is close. Listen sharp now."

The slight breeze favored them, the camp-fire was dead, and the night was clear and starlit. They had not been quiet many moments when the shrill neigh of a mustang rang out. The Naabs raised themselves and looked at one another in the starlight.

"Now what do you think of that?" whispered Billy.

"No more than I expected. It was Bolly," replied Dave.

"Bolly it was, confound her black hide!" added August. "Now, boys, did she whistle for Silvermane, or to warn him, which?"

"No telling," answered Billy. "Let's lie low, and take a chance on him coming close. It proves one thing—you can't break a wild mare. That spirit may sleep in her blood, maybe for years, but some time it'll answer to—"

"Shut up—listen," interrupted Dave.

Jack strained his hearing, yet caught no sound, except the distant yelp of a coyote. Moments went by.

"There!" whispered Dave.

From the direction of the ridge came the faint rattling of stones.

"They're coming," put in Billy.

Presently sharp clicks preceded the rattles, and the sounds began to merge into a regular rhythmic tramp. It softened at intervals, probably when the horses were under the cedars, and strengthened as they came out on the harder ground of the open.

"I see them," whispered Dave.

A black, undulating line wound out of the cedars, a line of horses approaching with drooping heads, hurrying a little as they neared the spring.

"Twenty-odd, all blacks and bays," said August, "and some of them are mustangs. But where's Silvermane?—hark!"

Out among the cedars rose the peculiar halting thump of a hobbled horse trying to cover ground, followed by snorts and crashings of brush and the pound of plunging hoofs. The long black line stopped short and began to stamp. Then into the starlit glade below moved two shadows, the first a great gray horse with snowy mane; the second, a small, shiny, black mustang.

"Silvermane and Bolly!" exclaimed August, "and now she's broken her hobbles."

The stallion, in the fulfilment of a conquest such as had made him king of the wild ranges, was magnificent in action. Wheeling about her, neighing, and plunging, he arched his splendid neck and pushed his head against her. His action was that of a master. Suddenly Black Bolly snorted and whirled down the glade. Silvermane whistled one blast of anger or terror and thundered after her. They vanished in the gloom of the cedars, and the band of frightened horses and mustangs clattered after them.

"It's one on me," remarked Billy. "That little mare played us at the finish. Caught when she was a yearling, broken better than any mustang we ever had, she has helped us run down many a stallion, and now she runs off with that big white-maned brute!"

"They'll make a team, and if they get out of here we'll have to chase them to the Great Salt Basin," replied Dave.

"Mescal, that's a well-behaved mustang of yours," said August; "not only did she break loose, but she whistled an alarm to Silvermane and his band. Well, roll in now, everybody, and sleep."

At breakfast the following day the Naabs fell into a discussion upon the possibility of there being other means of exit from the plateau than the two trails already closed. They had never run any mustangs on the plateau, and in the case of a wild horse like Silvermane, who would take desperate chances, it was advisable to know the ground exactly. Billy and Dave taking their mounts from the sheep-corral, where they had put them up for the night, rode in opposite directions around the rim of the plateau. It was triangular in shape, and some six or seven miles in circumference; and the brothers rode around it in less than an hour.

"Corralled," said Dave, laconically.

"Good! Did you see him? What kind of a bunch has he with him?" asked his father.

"If we get the pick of the lot it will be worth two weeks' work," replied Dave. "I saw him, and Bolly, too. I believe we can catch her easily. She was off from the bunch, and it looks as though the mares were jealous. I think we can run her into a cove under the wall, and get her. Then Mescal can help us run down the stallion. And you can look out on this end for the best level stretch to drop the line of cedars and make our trap."

The brothers, at their father's nod, rode off into the forest. Naab had detained the peon, and now gave him orders and sent him off.

"To-night you can stand on the rim here, and watch him signal across to the top of Echo Cliffs to the Navajos," explained August to Jack. "I've sent for the best breaker of wild mustangs on the desert. Dave can break mustangs, and Piute is very good; but I want the best man in the country, because this is a grand horse, and I intend to give him to you."

"To me!" exclaimed Hare.

"Yes, and if he's broken right at the start, he'll serve you faithfully, and not try to bite your arm off every day, or kick your brains out. No white man can break a wild mustang to the best advantage."

"Why is that?"

"I don't know. To be truthful, I have an idea it's bad temper and lack of patience. Just wait till you see this Navajo go at Silvermane!"

After Mescal and Piute drove down the sheep, Jack accompanied Naab to the corral.

"I've brought up your saddle," said Naab, "and you can put it on any mustang here."

What a pleasure it was to be in the saddle again, and to feel strength to remain there! He rode with August all over the western end of the plateau. They came at length to a strip of ground, higher than the bordering forest, which was comparatively free of cedars and brush; and when August had surveyed it once he slapped his knee with satisfaction.

"Fine, better than I hoped for! This stretch is about a mile long, and narrow at this end. Now, Jack, you see the other side faces the rim, this side the forest, and at the end here is a wall of rock; luckily it curves in a half circle, which will save us work. We'll cut cedars, drag them in line, and make a big corral against the rock. From the opening in the corral we'll build two fences of trees; then we'll chase Silvermane till he's done, run him down into this level, and turn him inside the fence. No horse can break through a close line of cedars. He'll run till he's in the corral, and then we'll rope him."

"Great!" said Jack, all enthusiasm. "But isn't it going to take a lot of work?"

"Rather," said August, dryly. "It'll take a week to cut and drag the cedars, let alone to tire out that wild stallion. When the finish comes you want to be on that ledge where we'll have the corral."

They returned to camp and prepared supper. Mescal and Piute soon arrived, and, later, Dave and Billy on jaded mustangs. Black Bolly limped behind, stretching a long halter, an unhappy mustang with dusty, foam-stained coat and hanging head.

"Not bad," said August, examining the lame leg. "She'll be fit in a few days, long before we need her to help run down Silvermane. Bring the liniment and a cloth, one of you, and put her in the sheep-corral to-night."

Mescal's love for the mustang shone in her eyes while she smoothed out the crumpled mane, and petted the slender neck.

"Bolly, to think you'd do it!" And Bolly dropped her head as though really ashamed.

When darkness fell they gathered on the rim to watch the signals. A fire blazed out of the black void below, and as they waited it brightened and flamed higher.

"Ugh!" said Piute, pointing across to the dark line of cliffs.

"Of course he'd see it first," laughed Naab. "Dave, have you caught it yet? Jack, see if you can make out a fire over on Echo Cliffs."

"No, I don't see any light, except that white star. Have you seen it?"

"Long ago," replied Naab. "Here, sight along my finger, and narrow your eyes down."

"I believe I see it—yes, I'm sure."

"Good. How about you, Mescal?"

"Yes," she replied.

Jack was amused, for Dave insisted that he had been next to the Indian, and Billy claimed priority to all of them. To these men bred on the desert keen sight was preeminently the chief of gifts.

"Jack, look sharp!" said August. "Peon is blanketing his fire. See the flicker? One, two—one, two—one. Now for the answer."

Jack peered out into the shadowy space, star-studded above, ebony below. Far across the depths shone a pinpoint of steady light. The Indian grunted again, August vented his "ha!" and then Jack saw the light blink like a star, go out for a second, and blink again.

"That's what I like to see," said August. "We're answered. Now all's over but the work."

Work it certainly was, as Jack discovered next day. He helped the brothers cut down cedars while August hauled them into line with his roan. What with this labor and the necessary camp duties nearly a week passed, and in the mean time Black Bolly recovered from her lameness.

Twice the workers saw Silvermane standing on open high ridges, restive and suspicious, with his silver mane flying, and his head turned over his shoulder, watching, always watching.

"It'd be worth something to find out how long that stallion could go without water," commented Dave. "But we'll make his tongue hang out to-morrow. It'd serve him right to break him with Black Bolly."

Daylight came warm and misty; veils unrolled from the desert; a purple curtain lifted from the eastern crags; then the red sun burned.

Dave and Billy Naab mounted their mustangs, and each led another mount by a halter.

"We'll go to the ridge, cut Silvermane out of his band and warm him up; then we'll drive him down to this end."

Hare, in his eagerness, found the time very tedious while August delayed about camp, punching new holes in his saddle-girth, shortening his stirrups, and smoothing kinks out of his lasso. At last he saddled the roan, and also Black Bolly. Mescal came out of her tent ready for the chase; she wore a short skirt of buckskin, and leggings of the same material. Her hair, braided, and fastened at the back, was bound by a double band closely fitting her black head. Hare walked, leading two mustangs by the halters, and Naab and Mescal rode, each of them followed by two other spare mounts. August tied three mustangs at one point along the level stretch, and three at another. Then he led Mescal and Jack to the top of the stone wall above the corral, where they had good view of a considerable part of the plateau.

The eastern rise of ground, a sage and juniper slope, was in plain sight. Hare saw a white flash; then Silvermane broke out of the cedars into the sage. One of the brothers raced him half the length of the slope, and then the other coming out headed him off down toward the forest. Soon the pounding of hoofs sounded through the trees nearer and nearer. Silvermane came out straight ahead on the open level. He was running easily.

"He hasn't opened up yet," said August.

Hare watched the stallion with sheer fascination; He ran seemingly without effort. What a stride he had. How beautifully his silver mane waved in the wind! He veered off to the left, out of sight in the brush, while Dave and Billy galloped up to the spot where August had tied the first three mustangs. Here they dismounted, changed saddles to fresh horses, and were off again.

The chase now was close and all down-hill for the watchers. Silvermane twinkled in and out among the cedars, and suddenly stopped short on the rim. He wheeled and coursed away toward the crags, and vanished. But soon he reappeared, for Billy had cut across and faced him about. Again he struck the level stretch. Dave was there in front of him. He shot away to the left, and flashed through the glades beyond. The brothers saved their steeds, content to keep him cornered in that end of the plateau. Then August spurred his roan into the scene of action. Silvermane came out on the one piece of rising ground beyond the level, and stood looking backward toward the brothers. When the great roan crashed through the thickets into his sight he leaped as if he had been stung, and plunged away.

The Naabs had hemmed him in a triangle, Dave and Billy at the broad end, August at the apex, and now the real race began. August chased him up and down, along the rim, across to the long line of cedars, always in the end heading him for the open stretch. Down this he fled with flying mane, only to be checked by the relentless brothers. To cover this broad end of the open required riding the like of which Hare had never dreamed of. The brothers, taking advantage of the brief periods when the stallion was going toward August, changed their tired mustangs for fresh ones.

"Ho! Mescal!" rolled out August's voice. That was the call for Mescal to put Black Bolly after Silvermane. Her fleetness made the other mustangs seem slow. All in a flash she was round the corral, with Silvermane between her and the long fence of cedars. Uttering a piercing snort of terror the gray stallion lunged out, for the first time panic-stricken, and lengthened his stride in a wonderful way. He raced down the stretch with his head over his shoulder watching the little black. Seeing her gaining, he burst into desperate headlong flight. He saved nothing; he had found his match; he won that first race down the level but it had cost him his best. If he had been fresh he might have left Black Bolly far behind, but now he could not elude her.

August Naab let him run this time, and Silvermane, keeping close to the fence, passed the gate, ran down to the rim, and wheeled. The black mustang was on him again, holding him in close to the fence, driving him back down the stretch.

The brothers remorselessly turned him, and now Mescal, forcing the running, caught him, lashed his haunches with her whip, and drove him into the gate of the corral.

August and his two sons were close behind, and blocked the gate. Silvermane's race was nearly run.

"Hold here, boys," said August. "I'll go in and drive him round and round till he's done, then, when I yell, you stand aside and rope him as he comes out."

Silvermane ran round the corral, tore at the steep scaly walls, fell back and began his weary round again and yet again. Then as sense and courage yielded gradually to unreasoning terror, he ran blindly; every time he passed the guarded gateway his eyes were wilder, and his stride more labored.

"Now!" yelled August Naab.

Mescal drew out of the opening, and Dave and Billy pulled away, one on each side, their lassoes swinging loosely.

Silvermane sprang for the opening with something of his old speed. As he went through, yellow loops flashed in the sun, circling, narrowing, and he seemed to run straight into them. One loop whipped close round his glossy neck; the other caught his head. Dave's mustang staggered under the violent shock, went to his knees, struggled up and held firmly. Bill's mount slid on his haunches and spilled his rider from the saddle. Silvermane seemed to be climbing into the air. Then August Naab, darting through the gate in a cloud of dust, shot his lasso, catching the right foreleg. Silvermane landed hard, his hoofs striking fire from the stones; and for an instant strained in convulsive struggle; then fell heaving and groaning. In a twinkling Billy loosened his lasso over a knot, making of it a halter, and tied the end to a cedar stump.

The Naabs stood back and gazed at their prize.

Silvermane was badly spent; he was wet with foam, but no fleck of blood marred his mane; his superb coat showed scratches, but none cut into the flesh. After a while he rose, panting heavily, and trembling in every muscle. He was a beaten horse; the noble head was bowed; yet he showed no viciousness, only the fear of a trapped animal. He eyed Black Bolly and then the halter, as though he had divined the fatal connection between them.

VIII. THE BREAKER OF WILD MUSTANGS

FOR a few days after the capture of Silvermane, a time full to the brim of excitement for Hare, he had no word with Mescal, save for morning and evening greetings. When he did come to seek her, with a purpose which had grown more impelling since August Naab's arrival, he learned to his bewilderment that she avoided him. She gave him no chance to speak with her alone; her accustomed resting-place on the rim at sunset knew her no more; early after supper she retired to her tent.

Hare nursed a grievance for forty-eight hours, and then, taking advantage of Piute's absence on an errand down to the farm, and of the Naabs' strenuous day with four vicious wild horses in the corral at one time, he walked out to the pasture where Mescal shepherded the flock.

"Mescal, why are you avoiding me?" he asked. "What has happened?"

She looked tired and unhappy, and her gaze, instead of meeting his, wandered to the crags.

"Nothing," she replied.

"But there must be something. You have given me no chance to talk to you, and I wanted to know if you'd let me speak to Father Naab."

"To Father Naab? Why—what about?"

"About you, of course—and me—that I love you and want to marry you."

She turned white. "No—no!"

Hare paused blankly, not so much at her refusal as at the unmistakable fear in her face.

"Why—not?" he asked presently, with an odd sense of trouble. There was more here than Mescal's habitual shyness.

"Because he'll be terribly angry."

"Angry—I don't understand. Why angry?"

The girl did not answer, and looked so forlorn that Hare attempted to take her in his arms. She resisted and broke from him.

"You must never—never do that again."

Hare drew back sharply.

"Why not? What's wrong? You must tell me, Mescal."

"I remembered." She hung her head.

"Remembered—what?"

"I am pledged to marry Father Naab's eldest son."

For a moment Hare did not understand. He stared at her unbelievingly.

"What did you say?" he asked, slowly.

Mescal repeated her words in a whisper.

"But—but Mescal—I love you. You let me kiss you," said Hare stupidly, as if he did not grasp her meaning. "You let me kiss you," he repeated.

"Oh, Jack, I forgot," she wailed. "It was so new, so strange, to have you up here. It was like a kind of dream. And after—after you kissed me I—I found out—"

"What, Mescal?"

Her silence answered him.

"But, Mescal, if you really love me you can't marry any one else," said Hare. It was the simple persistence of a simple swain.

"Oh, you don't know, you don't know. It's impossible!"

"Impossible!" Hare's anger flared up. "You let me believe I had won you. What kind of a girl are you? You were not true. Your actions were lies."

"Not lies," she faltered, and turned her face from him.

With no gentle hand he grasped her arm and forced her to look at him. But the misery in her eyes overcame him, and he roughly threw his arms around her and held her close.

"It can't be a lie. You do care for me—love me. Look at me." He drew her head back from his breast. Her face was pale and drawn; her eyes closed tight, with tears forcing a way out under the long lashes; her lips were parted. He bowed to their sweet nearness; he kissed them again and again, while the shade of the cedars seemed to whirl about him. "I love you, Mescal. You are mine—I will have you—I will keep you—I will not let him have you!"

She vibrated to that like a keen strung wire under a strong touch. All in a flash the trembling, shame-stricken girl was transformed. She leaned back in his arms, supple, pliant with quivering life, and for the first time gave him wide-open level eyes, in which there were now no tears, no shyness, no fear, but a dark smouldering fire.

"You do love me, Mescal?"

"I—I couldn't help it."

There was a pause, tense with feeling.

"Mescal, tell me—about your being pledged," he said, at last.

"I gave him my promise because there was nothing else to do. I was pledged to—to him in the church at White Sage. It can't be changed. I've got to marry—Father Naab's eldest son."

"Eldest son?" echoed Jack, suddenly mindful of the implication. "Why! that's Snap Naab. Ah! I begin to see light. That—Mescal—"

"I hate him."

"You hate him and you're pledged to marry him!... God! Mescal, I'd utterly forgotten Snap Naab already has a wife."

"You've also forgotten that we're Mormons."

"Are you a Mormon?" he queried bluntly.

"I've been raised as one."

"That's not an answer. Are you one? Do you believe any man under God's sky ought to have more than one wife at a time?"

"No. But I've been taught that it gave woman greater glory in heaven. There have been men here before you, men who talked to me, and I doubted before I ever saw you. And afterward—I knew."

"Would not Father Naab release you?"

"Release me? Why, he would have taken me as a wife for himself but for Mother Mary. She hates me. So he pledged me to Snap."

"Does August Naab love you?"

"Love me? No. Not in the way you mean—perhaps as a daughter. But Mormons teach duty to church first, and say such love comes—to the wives—afterward. But it doesn't—not in the women I've seen. There's Mother Ruth—her heart is broken. She loves me, and I can tell."

"When was this—this marriage to be?"

"I don't know. Father Naab promised me to his son when he came home from the Navajo range. It would be soon if they found out that you and I—Jack, Snap Naab would kill you!"

The sudden thought startled the girl. Her eyes betrayed her terror.

"I mightn't be so easy to kill," said Hare, darkly. The words came unbidden, his first answer to the wild influences about him. "Mescal, I'm sorry—maybe I've brought you unhappiness."

"No. No. To be with you has been like sitting there on the rim watching the desert, the greatest happiness I have ever known. I used to love to be with the children, but Mother Mary forbade. When I am down there, which is seldom, I'm not allowed to play with the children any more."

"What can I do?" asked Hare, passionately.

"Don't speak to Father Naab. Don't let him guess. Don't leave me here alone," she answered low. It was not the Navajo speaking in her now. Love had sounded depths hitherto unplumbed; a quick, soft impulsiveness made the contrast sharp and vivid.

"How can I help but leave you if he wants me on the cattle ranges?"

"I don't know. You must think. He has been so pleased with what you've done. He's had Mormons up here, and two men not of his Church, and they did nothing. You've been ill, besides you're different. He will keep me with the sheep as long as he can, for two reasons—because I drive them best, he says, and because Snap Naab's wife must be persuaded to welcome me in her home."

"I'll stay, if I have to get a relapse and go down on my back again," declared Jack. "I hate to deceive him, but Mescal, pledged or not—I love you, and I won't give up hope."

Her hands flew to her face again and tried to hide the dark blush.

VII. SILVERMANE

"Mescal, there's one question I wish you'd answer. Does August Naab think he'll make a Mormon of me? Is that the secret of his wonderful kindness?"

"Of course he believes he'll make a Mormon of you. That's his religion. He's felt that way over all the strangers who ever came out here. But he'd be the same to them without his hopes. I don't know the secret of his kindness, but I think he loves everybody and everything. And Jack, he's so good. I owe him all my life. He would not let the Navajos take me; he raised me, kept me, taught me. I can't break my promise to him. He's been a father to me, and I love him."

"I think I love him, too," replied Hare, simply.

With an effort he left her at last and mounted the grassy slope and climbed high up among the tottering yellow crags; and there he battled with himself. Whatever the charm of Mescal's surrender, and the insistence of his love, stern hammer-strokes of fairness, duty, honor, beat into his brain his debt to the man who had saved him. It was a long-drawn-out battle not to be won merely by saying right was right. He loved Mescal, she loved him; and something born in him with his new health, with the breath of this sage and juniper forest, with the sight of purple canyons and silent beckoning desert, made him fiercely tenacious of all that life had come to mean for him. He could not give her up—and yet—

Twilight forced Hare from his lofty retreat, and he trod his way campward, weary and jaded, but victorious over himself. He thought he had renounced his hope of Mescal; he returned with a resolve to be true to August, and to himself; bitterness he would not allow himself to feel. And yet he feared the rising in him of a new spirit akin to that of the desert itself, intractable and free.

"Well, Jack, we rode down the last of Silvermane's band," said August, at supper. "The Navajos came up and helped us out. To-morrow you'll see some fun, when we start to break Silvermane. As soon as that's done I'll go, leaving the Indians to bring the horses down when they're broken."

"Are you going to leave Silvermane with me?" asked Jack.

"Surely. Why, in three days, if I don't lose my guess, he'll be like a lamb. Those desert stallions can be made into the finest kind of saddle-horses. I've seen one or two. I want you to stay up here with the sheep. You're getting well, you'll soon be a strapping big fellow. Then when we drive the sheep down in the fall you can begin life on the cattle ranges, driving wild steers. There's where you'll grow lean and hard, like an iron bar. You'll need that horse, too, my lad."

"Why—because he's fast?" queried Jack, quickly answering to the implied suggestion.

August nodded gloomily. "I haven't the gift of revelation, but I've come to believe Martin Cole. Holderness is building an outpost for his riders close to Seeping Springs. He has no water. If he tries to pipe my water—" The pause was not a threat; it implied the Mormon's doubt of himself. "Then Dene is on the march this way. He's driven some of Marshall's cattle from the range next to mine. Dene got away with about a hundred head. The barefaced robber sold them in Lund to a buying company from Salt Lake."

"Is he openly an outlaw, a rustler?" inquired Hare.

"Everybody knows it, and he's finding White Sage and vicinity warmer than it was. Every time he comes in he and his band shoot up things pretty lively. Now the Mormons are slow to wrath. But they are awakening. All the way from Salt Lake to the border outlaws have come in. They'll never get the power on this desert that they had in the places from which they've been driven. Men of the Holderness type are more to be dreaded. He's a rancher, greedy, unscrupulous, but hard to corner in dishonesty. Dene is only a bad man, a gun-fighter. He and all his ilk will get run out of Utah. Did you ever hear of Plummer, John Slade, Boone Helm, any of those bad men?"

"No."

"Well, they were men to fear. Plummer was a sheriff in Idaho, a man high in the estimation of his townspeople, but he was the leader of the most desperate band of criminals ever known in the West; and he instigated the murder of, or killed outright, more than one hundred men. Slade was a bad man, fatal on the draw. Helm was a killing machine. These men all tried Utah, and had to get out. So will Dene have to get out. But I'm afraid there'll be warm times before that happens. When you get in the thick of it you'll appreciate Silvermane."

"I surely will. But I can't see that wild stallion with a saddle and a bridle, eating oats like any common horse, and being led to water."

"Well, he'll come to your whistle, presently, if I'm not greatly mistaken. You must make him love you, Jack. It can be done with any wild creature. Be gentle, but firm. Teach him to obey the slightest touch of rein, to stand when you throw your bridle on the ground, to come at your whistle. Always remember this. He's a desert-bred horse; he can live on scant browse and little water. Never break him of those best virtues in a horse. Never feed him grain if you can find a little patch of browse; never give him a drink till he needs it. That's one-tenth as often as a tame horse. Some day you'll be caught in the desert, and with these qualities of endurance Silvermane will carry you out."

Silvermane snorted defiance from the cedar corral next morning when the Naabs, and Indians, and Hare appeared. A half-naked sinewy Navajo with a face as changeless as a bronze mask sat astride August's blindfolded roan, Charger. He rode bareback except for a blanket strapped upon the horse; he carried only a long, thick halter, with a loop and a knot. When August opened the improvised gate, with its sharp bayonet-like branches of cedar, the Indian rode into the corral. The watchers climbed to the knoll. Silvermane snorted a blast of fear and anger. August's huge roan showed uneasiness; he stamped, and shook his head, as if to rid himself of the blinders.

Into the farthest corner of densely packed cedar boughs Silvermane pressed himself and watched. The Indian rode around the corral, circling closer and closer, yet appearing not to see the stallion. Many rounds he made; closer he got, and always with the same steady gait. Silvermane left his corner and tried another. The old unwearying round brought Charger and the Navajo close by him. Silvermane pranced out of his thicket of boughs; he whistled; he wheeled with his shiny hoofs lifting. In an hour the Indian was edging the outer circle of the corral, with the stallion pivoting in the centre, ears laid back, eyes shooting sparks, fight in every line of him. And the circle narrowed inward.

Suddenly the Navajo sent the roan at Silvermane and threw his halter. It spread out like a lasso, and the loop went over the head of the stallion, slipped to the knot and held fast, while the rope tightened. Silvermane leaped up, forehoofs pawing the air, and his long shrill cry was neither whistle, snort, nor screech, but all combined. He came down, missing Charger with his hoofs, sliding off his haunches. The Indian, his bronze muscles rippling, close-hauled on the rope, making half hitches round his bony wrist.

In a whirl of dust the roan drew closer to the gray, and Silvermane began a mad race around the corral. The roan ran with him nose to nose. When Silvermane saw he could not shake him, he opened his jaws, rolled back his lip in an ugly snarl, his white teeth glistening, and tried to bite. But the Indian's moccasined foot shot up under the stallion's ear and pressed him back. Then the roan hugged Silvermane so close that half the time the Navajo virtually rode two horses. But for the rigidity of his arms, and the play and sudden tension of his leg-muscles, the Indian's work would have appeared commonplace, so dexterous was he, so perfectly at home in his dangerous seat. Suddenly he whooped and August Naab hauled back the gate, and the two horses, neck and neck, thundered out upon the level stretch.

"Good!" cried August. "Let him rip now, Navvy. All over but the work, Jack. I feared Silvermane would spear himself on some of those dead cedar spikes in the corral. He's safe now."

Jack watched the horses plunge at breakneck speed down the stretch, circle at the forest edge, and come tearing back. Silvermane was pulling the roan faster than he had ever gone in his life, but the dark Indian kept his graceful seat. The speed slackened on the second turn, and decreased as, mile after mile, the imperturbable Indian held roan and gray side to side and let them run.

The time passed, but Hare's interest in the breaking of the stallion never flagged. He began to understand the Indian, and to feel what the restraint and drag must be to the horse. Never for a moment could Silvermane elude the huge roan, the tight halter, the relentless Navajo. Gallop fell to trot, and trot to jog, and jog to walk; and hour by hour, without whip or spur or word, the breaker of desert mustangs drove the wild stallion. If there were cruelty it was in his implacable slow patience, his farsighted purpose. Silvermane would have killed himself in an hour; he would have cut himself to pieces in one headlong dash, but that steel arm suffered him only to wear himself out. Late that afternoon the Navajo led a dripping, drooping, foam-lashed stallion into the corral, tied him with the halter, and left him.

Later Silvermane drank of the water poured into the corral trough, and had not the strength or spirit to resent the Navajo's caressing hand on his mane.

Next morning the Indian rode again into the corral on blindfolded Charger. Again he dragged Silvermane out on the level and drove him up and down with remorseless, machine-like persistence. At noon he took him back, tied him up, and roped him fast. Silvermane tried to rear and kick, but the saddle went on, strapped with a flash of the dark-skinned hands. Then again Silvermane ran the level stretch beside the giant roan, only he carried a saddle now. At the first, he broke out with free wild stride as if to run forever from under the hateful thing. But as the afternoon waned he crept weariedly back to the corral.

On the morning of the third day the Navajo went into the corral without Charger, and roped the gray, tied him fast, and saddled him. Then he loosed the lassoes except the one around Silvermane's neck, which he whipped under his foreleg to draw him down. Silvermane heaved a groan which plainly said he never wanted to rise again. Swiftly the Indian knelt on the stallion's head; his hands flashed; there was a scream, a click of steel on bone; and proud Silvermane jumped to his feet with a bit between his teeth.

The Navajo, firmly in the saddle, rose with him, and Silvermane leaped through the corral gate, and out upon the stretch, lengthening out with every stride, and settling into a wild, despairing burst of speed. The white mane waved in the wind; the half-naked Navajo swayed to the motion. Horse and rider disappeared in the cedars.

They were gone all day. Toward night they appeared on the stretch. The Indian rode into camp and, dismounting, handed the bridle-rein to Naab. He spoke no word; his dark impassiveness invited no comment. Silvermane was dust-covered and sweat-stained. His silver crest had the same proud beauty, his neck still the splendid arch, his head the noble outline, but his was a broken spirit.

"Here, my lad," said August Naab, throwing the bridle-rein over Hare's arm. "What did I say once about seeing you on a great gray horse? Ah! Well, take him and know this: you've the swiftest horse in this desert country."

IX. THE SCENT OF DESERT-WATER

SOON the shepherds were left to a quiet unbroken by the whistle of wild mustangs, the whoop of hunters, the ring of iron-shod hoofs on the stones. The scream of an eagle, the bleating of sheep, the bark of a coyote were once more the only familiar sounds accentuating the silence of the plateau. For Hare, time seemed to stand still. He thought but little; his whole life was a matter of feeling from without. He rose at dawn, never failing to see the red sun tip the eastern crags; he glowed with the touch of cold spring-water and the morning air; he trailed Silvermane under the cedars and thrilled when the stallion, answering his call, thumped the ground with hobbled feet and came his way, learning day by day to be glad at sight of his master. He rode with Mescal behind the flock; he hunted hour by hour, crawling over the fragrant brown mats of cedar, through the sage and juniper, up the grassy slopes. He rode back to camp beside Mescal, drove the sheep, and put Silvermane to his fleetest to beat Black Bolly down the level stretch where once the gray, even with freedom at stake, had lost to the black. Then back to camp and fire and curling blue smoke, a supper that testified to busy Piute's farmward trips, sunset on the rim, endless changing desert, the wind in the cedars, bright stars in the blue, and sleep—so time stood still.

Mescal and Hare were together, or never far apart, from dawn to night. Until the sheep were in the corral, every moment had its duty, from camp-work and care of horses to the many problems of the flock, so that they earned the rest on the rim-wall at sundown. Only a touch of hands bridged the chasm between them. They never spoke of their love, of Mescal's future, of Jack's return to hearth; a glance and a smile, scarcely sad yet not altogether happy, was the substance of their dream. Where Jack had once talked about the canyon and desert, he now seldom spoke at all. From watching Mescal he had learned that to see was enough. But there were moments when some association recalled the past and the strangeness of the present faced him. Then he was wont to question Mescal.

"What are you thinking of?" he asked, curiously, interrupting their silence. She leaned against the rocks and kept a changeless, tranquil, unseeing gaze on the desert. The level eyes were full of thought, of sadness, of mystery; they seemed to look afar.

Then she turned to him with puzzled questioning look and enigmatical reply. "Thinking?" asked her eyes. "I wasn't thinking," were her words.

"I fancied—I don't know exactly what," he went on. "You looked so earnest. Do you ever think of going to the Navajos?"

"No."

"Or across that Painted Desert to find some place you seem to know, or see?"

"No."

"I don't know why, but, Mescal, sometimes I have the queerest ideas when I catch your eyes watching, watching. You look at once happy and sad. You see something out there that I can't see. Your eyes are haunted. I've a feeling that if I'd look into them I'd see the sun setting, the clouds coloring, the twilight shadows changing; and then back of that the secret of it all—of you—Oh! I can't explain, but it seems so."

"I never had a secret, except the one you know," she answered. "You ask me so often what I think about, and you always ask me when we're here." She was silent for a pause. "I don't think at all till you make me. It's beautiful out there. But that's not what it is to me. I can't tell you. When I sit down here all within me is—is somehow stilled. I watch—and it's different from what it is now, since you've made me think. Then I watch, and I see, that's all."

It came to Hare afterward with a little start of surprise that Mescal's purposeless, yet all-satisfying, watchful gaze had come to be part of his own experience. It was inscrutable to him, but he got from it a fancy, which he tried in vain to dispel, that something would happen to them out there on the desert.

And then he realized that when they returned to the camp-fire they seemed freed from this spell of the desert. The blaze-lit circle was shut in by the darkness; and the immensity of their wild environment, because for the hour it could not be seen, lost its paralyzing effect. Hare fell naturally into a talkative mood. Mescal had developed a vivacity, an ambition which contrasted strongly with her silent moods; she became alive and curious, human like the girls he had known in the East, and she fascinated him the more for this complexity.

The July rains did not come; the mists failed; the dews no longer freshened the grass, and the hot sun began to tell on shepherds and sheep. Both sought the shade. The flowers withered first—all the blue-bells and lavender patches of primrose, and pale-yellow lilies, and white thistle-blossoms. Only the deep magenta of cactus and vermilion of Indian paint-brush, flowers of the sun, survived the heat. Day by day the shepherds scanned the sky for storm-clouds that did not appear. The spring ran lower and lower. At last the ditch that carried water to the corral went dry, and the margin of the pool began to retreat. Then Mescal sent Piute down for August Naab.

He arrived at the plateau the next day with Dave and at once ordered the breaking up of camp.

"It will rain some time," he said, "but we can't wait any longer. Dave, when did you last see the Blue Star waterhole?"

"On the trip in from Silver Cup, ten days ago. The waterhole was full then."

"Will there be water enough now?"

"We've got to chance it. There's no water here, and no springs on the upper range where we can drive sheep; we've got to go round under the Star."

"That's so," replied August. His fears needed confirmation, because his hopes always influenced his judgment till no hope was left. "I wish I had brought Zeke and George. It'll be a hard drive, though we've got Jack and Mescal to help."

Hot as it was August Naab lost no time in the start. Piute led the train on foot, and the flock, used to following him, got under way readily. Dave and Mescal rode along the sides, and August with Jack came behind, with the pack-burros bringing up the rear. Wolf circled them all, keeping the flanks close in, heading the lambs that strayed, and, ever vigilant, made the drive orderly and rapid.

The trail to the upper range was wide and easy of ascent, the first of it winding under crags, the latter part climbing long slopes. It forked before the summit, where dark pine trees showed against the sky, one fork ascending, the other, which Piute took, beginning to go down. It admitted of no extended view, being shut in for the most part on the left, but there were times when Hare could see a curving stream of sheep on half a mile of descending trail. Once started down the flock could not be stopped, that was as plain as Piute's hard task. There were times when Hare could have tossed a pebble on the Indian just below him, yet there were more than three thousand sheep, strung out in line between them. Clouds of dust rolled up, sheets of gravel and shale rattled down the inclines, the clatter, clatter, clatter of little hoofs, the steady baa-baa-baa filled the air. Save for the crowding of lambs off the trail, and a jamming of sheep in the corners, the drive went on without mishap. Hare was glad to see the lambs scramble back bleating for their mothers, and to note that, though peril threatened at every steep turn, the steady down-flow always made space for the sheep behind. He was glad, too, when through a wide break ahead his eye followed the face of a vast cliff down to the red ground below, and he knew the flock would soon be safe on the level.

A blast as from a furnace smote Hare from this open break in the wall. The air was dust-laden, and carried besides the smell of dust and the warm breath of desert growths, a dank odor that was unpleasant.

The sheep massed in a flock on the level, and the drivers spread to their places. The route lay under projecting red cliffs, between the base and enormous sections of wall that had broken off and fallen far out. There was no weathering slope; the wind had carried away the smaller stones and particles, and had cut the huge pieces of pinnacle and tower into hollowed forms. This zone of rim merged into another of strange contrast, the sloping red stream of sand which flowed from the wall of the canyon.

Piute swung the flock up to the left into an amphitheatre, and there halted. The sheep formed a densely packed mass in the curve of the wall. Dave Naab galloped back toward August and Hare, and before he reached them shouted out: "The waterhole's plugged!"

"What?" yelled his father.

"Plugged, filled with stone and sand."

"Was it a cave-in?"

"I reckon not. There's been no rain."

August spurred his roan after Dave, and Hare kept close behind them, till they reined in on a muddy bank. What had once been a waterhole was a red and yellow heap of shale, fragments of stones, gravel, and sand. There was no water, and the sheep were bleating. August dismounted and climbed high above the hole to examine the slope; soon he strode down with giant steps, his huge fists clinched, shaking his gray mane like a lion.

"I've found the tracks! Somebody climbed up and rolled the stones, started the cave-in. Who?"

"Holderness's men. They did the same for Martin Cole's waterhole at Rocky Point. How old are the tracks?"

"Two days, perhaps. We can't follow them. What can be done?"

"Some of Holderness's men are Mormons, and others are square fellows. They wouldn't stand for such work as this, and somebody ought to ride in there and tell them."

"And get shot up by the men paid to do the dirty work. No. I won't hear of it. This amounts to nothing; we seldom use this hole, only twice a year when driving the flock. But it makes me fear for Silver Cup and Seeping Springs."

"It makes me fear for the sheep, if this wind doesn't change."

"Ah! I had forgotten the river scent. It's not strong to-night. We might venture if it wasn't for the strip of sand. We'll camp here and start the drive at dawn."

The sun went down under a crimson veil; a dull glow spread, fan-shaped, upward; twilight faded to darkness with the going down of the wind. August Naab paced to and fro before his tired and thirsty flock.

"I'd like to know," said Hare to Dave, "why those men filled up this waterhole."

"Holderness wants to cut us off from Silver Cup Spring, and this was a halfway waterhole. Probably he didn't know we had the sheep upland, but he wouldn't have cared. He's set himself to get our cattle range and he'll stop at nothing. Prospects look black for us. Father never gives up. He doesn't believe yet that we can lose our water. He prays and hopes, and sees good and mercy in his worst enemies."

"If Holderness works as far as Silver Cup, how will he go to work to steal another man's range and water?"

"He'll throw up a cabin, send in his men, drive in ten thousand steers."

"Well, will his men try to keep you away from your own water, or your cattle?"

"Not openly. They'll pretend to welcome us, and drive our cattle away in our absence. You see there are only five of us to ride the ranges, and we'd need five times five to watch all the stock."

"Then you can't stop this outrage?"

"There's only one way," said Dave, significantly tapping the black handle of his Colt. "Holderness thinks he pulls the wool over our eyes by talking of the cattle company that employs him. He's the company himself, and he's hand and glove with Dene."

"And I suppose, if your father and you boys were to ride over to Holderness's newest stand, and tell him to get off there would be a fight."

"We'd never reach him now, that is, if we went together. One of us alone might get to see him, especially in White Sage. If we all rode over to his ranch we'd have to fight his men before we reached the corrals. You yourself will find it pretty warm when you go out with us on the ranges, and if you make White Sage you'll find it hot. You're called 'Dene's spy' there, and the rustlers are still looking for you. I wouldn't worry about it, though."

"Why not, I'd like to know?" inquired Hare, with a short laugh.

"Well, if you're like the other Gentiles who have come into Utah you won't have scruples about drawing on a man. Father says the draw comes natural to you, and you're as quick as he is. Then he says you can beat any rifle shot he ever saw, and that long-barrelled gun you've got will shoot a mile. So if it comes to shooting—why, you can shoot. If you want to run—who's going to catch you on that white-maned stallion? We talked about you, George and I; we're mighty glad you're well and can ride with us."

Long into the night Jack Hare thought over this talk. It opened up a vista of the range-life into which he was soon to enter. He tried to silence the voice within that cried out, eager and reckless, for the long rides on the windy open. The years of his illness returned in fancy, the narrow room with the lamp and the book, and the tears over stories and dreams of adventure never to be for such as he. And now how wonderful was life! It was, after all, to be full for him. It was already full. Already he slept on the ground, open to the sky. He looked up at a wild black cliff, mountain-high, with its windworn star of blue; he felt himself on the threshold of the desert, with that subtle mystery waiting; he knew himself to be close to strenuous action on the ranges, companion of these sombre Mormons, exposed to their peril, making their cause his cause, their life his life. What of their friendship, their confidence? Was he worthy? Would he fail at the pinch? What a man he must become to approach their simple estimate of him! Because he had found health and strength, because he could shoot, because he had the fleetest horse on the desert, were these reasons for their friendship? No, these were only reasons for their trust. August Naab loved him. Mescal loved him; Dave and George made of him a brother. "They shall have my life," he muttered.

The bleating of the sheep heralded another day. With the brightening light began the drive over the sand. Under the cliff the shade was cool and fresh; there was no wind; the sheep made good progress. But the broken line of shade crept inward toward the flock, and passed it. The sun beat down, and the wind arose. A red haze of fine sand eddied about the toiling sheep and shepherds. Piute trudged ahead leading the king-ram, old Socker, the leader of the flock; Mescal and Hare rode at the right, turning their faces from the sand-filled puffs of wind; August and Dave drove behind; Wolf, as always, took care of the stragglers. An hour went by without signs of distress; and with half the five-mile trip at his back August Naab's voice gathered cheer. The sun beat hotter. Another hour told a different story—the sheep labored; they had to be forced by urge of whip, by knees of horses, by Wolf's threatening bark. They stopped altogether during the frequent hot sand-blasts, and could not be driven. So time dragged. The flock straggled out to a long irregular line; rams refused to budge till they were ready; sheep lay down to rest; lambs fell. But there was an end to the belt of sand, and August Naab at last drove the lagging trailers out upon the stony bench.

The sun was about two hours past the meridian; the red walls of the desert were closing in; the V-shaped split where the Colorado cut through was in sight. The trail now was wide and unobstructed and the distance short, yet August Naab ever and anon turned to face the canyon and shook his head in anxious foreboding.

It quickly dawned upon Hare that the sheep were behaving in a way new and singular to him. They packed densely now, crowding forward, many raising their heads over the haunches of others and bleating. They were not in their usual calm pattering hurry, but nervous, excited, and continually facing west toward the canyon, noses up.

On the top of the next little ridge Hare heard Silvermane snort as he did when led to drink. There was a scent of water on the wind. Hare caught it, a damp, muggy smell. The sheep had noticed it long before, and now under its nearer, stronger influence began to bleat wildly, to run faster, to crowd without aim.

"There's work ahead. Keep them packed and going. Turn the wheelers," ordered August.

What had been a drive became a flight. And it was well so long as the sheep headed straight up the trail. Piute had to go to the right to avoid being run down. Mescal rode up to fill his place. Hare took his cue from Dave, and rode along the flank, crowding the sheep inward. August cracked his whip behind. For half a mile the flock kept to the trail, then, as if by common consent, they sheered off to the right. With this move August and Dave were transformed from quiet almost to frenzy. They galloped to the fore, and into the very faces of the turning sheep, and drove them back. Then the rear-guard of the flock curved outward.

"Drive them in!" roared August.

Hare sent Silvermane at the deflecting sheep and frightened them into line.

Wolf no longer had power to chase the stragglers; they had to be turned by a horse. All along the flank noses pointed outward; here and there sheep wilder than the others leaped forward to lead a widening wave of bobbing woolly backs. Mescal engaged one point, Hare another, Dave another, and August Naab's roan thundered up and down the constantly broken line. All this while as the shepherds fought back the sheep, the flight continued faster eastward, farther canyonward. Each side gained, but the flock gained more toward the canyon than the drivers gained toward the oasis.

By August's hoarse yells, by Dave's stern face and ceaseless swift action, by the increasing din, Hare knew terrible danger hung over the flock; what it was he could not tell. He heard the roar of the river rapids, and it seemed that the sheep heard it with him. They plunged madly; they had gone wild from the scent and sound of water. Their eyes gleamed red; their tongues flew out. There was no aim to the rush of the great body of sheep, but they followed the leaders and the leaders followed the scent. And the drivers headed them off, rode them down, ceaselessly, riding forward to check one outbreak, wheeling backward to check another.

The flight became a rout. Hare was in the thick of dust and din, of the terror-stricken jumping mob, of the ever-starting, ever-widening streams of sheep; he rode and yelled and fired his Colt. The dust choked him, the sun burned him, the flying pebbles cut his cheek. Once he had a glimpse of Black Bolly in a melee of dust and sheep; Dave's mustang blurred in his sight; August's roan seemed to be double. Then Silvermane, of his own accord, was out before them all.

The sheep had almost gained the victory; their keen noses were pointed toward the water; nothing could stop their flight; but still the drivers dashed at them, ever fighting, never wearying, never ceasing.

At the last incline, where a gentle slope led down to a dark break in the desert, the rout became a stampede. Left and right flanks swung round, the line lengthened, and round the struggling horses, knee-deep in woolly backs, split the streams to flow together beyond in one resistless river of sheep. Mescal forced Bolly out of danger; Dave escaped the right flank, August and Hare swept on with the flood, till the horses, sighting the dark canyon, halted to stand like rocks.

"Will they run over the rim?" yelled Hare, horrified. His voice came to him as a whisper. August Naab, sweat-stained in red dust, haggard, gray locks streaming in the wind, raised his arms above his head, hopeless.

The long nodding line of woolly forms, lifting like the crest of a yellow wave, plunged out and down in rounded billow over the canyon rim. With din of hoofs and bleats the sheep spilled themselves over the precipice, and an awful deafening roar boomed up from the river, like the spreading thunderous crash of an avalanche.

How endless seemed that fatal plunge! The last line of sheep, pressing close to those gone before, and yet impelled by the strange instinct of life, turned their eyes too late on the brink, carried over by their own momentum.

The sliding roar ceased; its echo, muffled and hollow, pealed from the cliffs, then rumbled down the canyon to merge at length in the sullen, dull, continuous sound of the rapids.

Hare turned at last from that narrow iron-walled cleft, the depth of which he had not seen, and now had no wish to see; and his eyes fell upon a little Navajo lamb limping in the trail of the flock, headed for the canyon, as sure as its mother in purpose. He dismounted and seized it to find, to his infinite wonder and gladness, that it wore a string and bell round its neck. It was Mescal's pet.

X. RIDING THE RANGES

THE shepherds were home in the oasis that evening, and next day the tragedy of the sheep was a thing of the past. No other circumstance of Hare's four months with the Naabs had so affected him as this swift inevitable sweeping away of the flock; nothing else had so vividly told him the nature of this country of abrupt heights and depths. He remembered August Naab's magnificent gesture of despair; and now the man was cheerful again; he showed no sign of his great loss. His tasks were many, and when one was done, he went on to the next. If Hare had not had many proofs of this Mormon's feeling he would have thought him callous. August Naab trusted God and men, loved animals, did what he had to do with all his force, and accepted fate. The tragedy of the sheep had been only an incident in a tragical life—that Hare divined with awe.

Mescal sorrowed, and Wolf mourned in sympathy with her, for their occupation was gone, but both brightened when August made known his intention to cross the river to the Navajo range, to trade with the Indians for another flock. He began his preparations immediately. The snow-freshets had long run out of the river, the water was low, and he wanted to fetch the sheep down before the summer rains. He also wanted to find out what kept his son Snap so long among the Navajos.

"I'll take Billy and go at once. Dave, you join George and Zeke out on the Silver Cup range. Take Jack with you. Brand all the cattle you can before the snow flies. Get out of Dene's way if he rides over, and avoid Holderness's men. I'll have no fights. But keep your eyes sharp for their doings."

It was a relief to Hare that Snap Naab had not yet returned to the oasis, for he felt a sense of freedom which otherwise would have been lacking. He spent the whole of a long calm summer day in the orchard and the vineyard. The fruit season was at its height. Grapes, plums, pears, melons were ripe and luscious. Midsummer was vacationtime for the children, and they flocked into the trees like birds. The girls were picking grapes; Mother Ruth enlisted Jack in her service at the pear-trees; Mescal came, too, and caught the golden pears he threw down, and smiled up at him; Wolf was there, and Noddle; Black Bolly pushed her black nose over the fence, and whinnied for apples; the turkeys strutted, the peafowls preened their beautiful plumage, the guinea-hens ran like quail. Save for those frowning red cliffs Hare would have forgotten where he was; the warm sun, the yellow fruit, the merry screams of children, the joyous laughter of girls, were pleasant reminders of autumn picnic days long gone. But, in the face of those dominating wind-scarred walls, he could not forget.

That night Hare endeavored to see Mescal alone for a few moments, to see her once more with unguarded eyes, to whisper a few words, to say good-bye; but it was impossible.

On the morrow he rode out of the red cliff gate with Dave and the pack-horses, a dull ache in his heart; for amid the cheering crowd of children and women who bade them good-bye he had caught the wave of Mescal's hand and a look of her eyes that would be with him always. What might happen before he returned, if he ever did return! For he knew now, as well as he could feel Silvermane's easy stride, that out there under the white glare of desert, the white gleam of the slopes of Coconina, was wild life awaiting him. And he shut his teeth, and narrowed his eyes, and faced it with an eager joy that was in strange contrast to the pang in his breast.

That morning the wind dipped down off the Vermillion Cliffs and whipped west; there was no scent of river-water, and Hare thought of the fatality of the sheep-drive, when, for one day out of the year, a moistened dank breeze had met the flock on the narrow bench. Soon the bench lay far behind them, and the strip of treacherous sand, and the maze of sculptured cliff under the Blue Star, and the hummocky low ridges beyond, with their dry white washes. Silvermane kept on in front. Already Hare had learned that the gray would have no horse before him. His pace was swift, steady, tireless. Dave was astride his Navajo mount, an Indian-bred horse, half mustang, which had to be held in with a firm rein. The pack train strung out far behind, trotting faithfully along, with the white packs, like the humps of camels, nodding up and down. Jack and Dave slackened their gait at the foot of the stony divide. It was an ascent of miles, so long that it did not appear steep. Here the pack-train caught up, and thereafter hung at the heels of the riders.

From the broad bare summit Jack saw the Silver Cup valley-range with eyes which seemed to magnify the winding trail, the long red wall, the green slopes, the dots of sage and cattle. Then he made allowance for months of unobstructed vision; he had learned to see; his eyes had adjusted themselves to distance and dimensions.

Silver Cup Spring lay in a bright green spot close under a break in the rocky slope that soon lost its gray cliff in the shaggy cedared side of Coconina.

The camp of the brothers was situated upon this cliff in a split between two sections of wall. Well sheltered from the north and west winds was a grassy plot which afforded a good survey of the valley and the trails. Dave and Jack received glad greetings from Zeke and George, and Silvermane was an object of wonder and admiration. Zeke, who had often seen the gray and chased him too, walked round and round him, stroking the silver mane, feeling the great chest muscles, slapping his flanks.

"Well, well, Silvermane, to think I'd live to see you wearing a saddle and bridle! He's even bigger than I thought. There's a horse, Hare! Never will be another like him in this desert. If Dene ever sees that horse he'll chase him to the Great Salt Basin. Dene's crazy about fast horses. He's from Kentucky, somebody said, and knows a horse when he sees one."

"How are things?" queried Dave.

"We can't complain much," replied Zeke, "though we've wasted some time on old Whitefoot. He's been chasing our horses. It's been pretty hot and dry. Most of the cattle are on the slopes; fair browse yet. There's a bunch of steers gone up on the mountain, and some more round toward the Saddle or the canyon."

"Been over Seeping Springs way?"

"Yes. No change since your trip. Holderness's cattle are ranging in the upper valley. George found tracks near the spring. We believe somebody was watching there and made off when we came up."

"We'll see Holderness's men when we get to riding out," put in George. "And some of Dene's too. Zeke met Two-Spot Chance and Culver below at the spring one day, sort of surprised them."

"What day was that?"

"Let's see, this's Friday. It was last Monday."

"What were they doing over here?"

"Said they were tracking a horse that had broken his hobbles. But they seemed uneasy, and soon rode off."

"Did either of them ride a horse with one shoe shy?"

"Now I think of it, yes. Zeke noticed the track at the spring."

"Well, Chance and Culver had been out our way," declared Dave. "I saw their tracks, and they filled up the Blue Star waterhole—and cost us three thousand sheep."

Then he related the story of the drive of the sheep, the finding of the plugged waterhole, the scent of the Colorado, and the plunge of the sheep into the canyon.

"We've saved one, Mescal's belled lamb," he concluded.

Neither Zeke nor George had a word in reply. Hare thought their silence unnatural. Neither did the mask-like stillness of their faces change. But Hare saw in their eyes a pointed clear flame, vibrating like a compass-needle, a mere glimmering spark.

"I'd like to know," continued Dave, calmly poking the fire, "who hired Dene's men to plug the waterhole. Dene couldn't do that. He loves a horse, and any man who loves a horse couldn't fill a waterhole in this desert."

Hare entered upon his new duties as a range-rider with a zeal that almost made up for his lack of experience; he bade fair to develop into a right-hand man for Dave, under whose watchful eye he worked. His natural qualifications were soon shown; he could ride, though his seat was awkward and clumsy compared to that of the desert rangers, a fault that Dave said would correct itself as time fitted him close to the saddle and to the swing of his horse. His sight had become extraordinarily keen for a new-comer on the ranges, and when experience had taught him the land-marks, the trails, the distances, the difference between smoke and dust and haze, when he could distinguish a band of mustangs from cattle, and range-riders from outlaws or Indians; in a word, when he had learned to know what it was that he saw, to trust his judgment, he would have acquired the basic feature of a rider's training. But he showed no gift for the lasso, that other essential requirement of his new calling.

"It's funny," said Dave, patiently, "you can't get the hang of it. Maybe it's born in a fellow. Now handling a gun seems to come natural for some fellows, and you're one of them. If only you could get the rope away as quick as you can throw your gun!"

Jack kept faithfully at it, unmindful of defeats, often chagrined when he missed some easy opportunity. Not improbably he might have failed altogether if he had been riding an ordinary horse, or if he had to try roping from a fiery mustang. But Silvermane was as intelligent as he was beautiful and fleet. The horse learned rapidly the agile turns and sudden stops necessary, and as for free running he never got enough. Out on the range Silvermane always had his head up and watched; his life had been spent in watching; he saw cattle, riders, mustangs, deer, coyotes, every moving thing. So that Hare, in the chasing of a cow, had but to start Silvermane, and then he could devote himself to the handling of his rope. It took him ten times longer to lasso the cow than it took Silvermane to head the animal. Dave laughed at some of Jack's exploits, encouraged him often, praised his intent if not his deed; and always after a run nodded at Silvermane in mute admiration.

Branding the cows and yearlings and tame steers which watered at Silver Cup, and never wandered far away, was play according to Dave's version. "Wait till we get after the wild steers up on the mountain and in the canyons," he would say when Jack dropped like a log at supper. Work it certainly was for him. At night he was so tired that he could scarcely crawl into bed; his back felt as if it were broken; his legs were raw, and his bones ached. Many mornings he thought it impossible to arise, but always he crawled out, grim and haggard, and hobbled round the camp-fire to warm his sore and bruised muscles. Then when Zeke and George rode in with the horses the day's work began. During these weeks of his "hardening up," as Dave called it, Hare bore much pain, but he continued well and never missed a day. At the most trying time when for a few days he had to be helped on and off Silvermane—for he insisted that he would not stay in camp—the brothers made his work as light as possible. They gave him the branding outfit to carry, a running-iron and a little pot with charcoal and bellows; and with these he followed the riders at a convenient distance and leisurely pace.

Some days they branded one hundred cattle. By October they had August Naab's crudely fashioned cross on thousands of cows and steers. Still the stock kept coming down from the mountain, driven to the valley by cold weather and snow-covered grass. It was well into November before the riders finished at Silver Cup, and then arose a question as to whether it would be advisable to go to Seeping Springs or to the canyons farther west along the slope of Coconina. George favored the former, but Dave overruled him.

"Father's orders," he said. "He wants us to ride Seeping Springs last because he'll be with us then, and Snap too. We're going to have trouble over there."

"How's this branding stock going to help the matter any, I'd like to know?" inquired George. "We Mormons never needed it."

"Father says we'll all have to come to it. Holderness's stock is branded. Perhaps he's marked a good many steers of ours. We can't tell. But if we have our own branded we'll know what's ours. If he drives our stock we'll know it; if Dene steals, it can be proved that he steals."

"Well, what then? Do you think he'll care for that, or Holderness either?"

"No, only it makes this difference: both things will then be barefaced robbery. We've never been able to prove anything, though we boys know; we don't need any proof. Father gives these men the benefit of a doubt. We've got to stand by him. I know, George, your hand's begun to itch for your gun. So does mine. But we've orders to obey."

Many gullies and canyons headed up on the slope of Coconina west of Silver Cup, and ran down to open wide on the flat desert. They contained plots of white sage and bunches of rich grass and cold springs. The steers that ranged these ravines were wild as wolves, and in the tangled thickets of juniper and manzanita and jumbles of weathered cliff they were exceedingly difficult to catch.

Well it was that Hare had received his initiation and had become inured to rough, incessant work, for now he came to know the real stuff of which these Mormons were made. No obstacle barred them. They penetrated the gullies to the last step; they rode weathered slopes that were difficult for deer to stick upon; they thrashed the bayonet-guarded manzanita copses; they climbed into labyrinthine fastnesses, penetrating to every nook where a steer could hide. Miles of sliding slope and marble-bottomed streambeds were ascended on foot, for cattle could climb where a horse could not. Climbing was arduous enough, yet the hardest and most perilous toil began when a wild steer was cornered. They roped the animals on moving slopes of weathered stone, and branded them on the edges of precipices.

The days and weeks passed, how many no one counted or cared. The circle of the sun daily lowered over the south end of Coconina; and the black snow-clouds crept down the slopes. Frost whitened the ground at dawn, and held half the day in the shade. Winter was close at the heels of the long autumn.

As for Hare, true to August Naab's assertion, he had lost flesh and suffered, and though the process was heartbreaking in its severity, he hung on till he hardened into a leather lunged, wire-muscled man, capable of keeping pace with his companions.

He began his day with the dawn when he threw off the frost-coated tarpaulin; the icy water brought him a glow of exhilaration; he drank in the spiced cold air, and there was the spring of the deer-hunter in his step as he went down the slope for his horse. He no longer feared that Silvermane would run away. The gray's bell could always be heard near camp in the mornings, and when Hare whistled there came always the answering thump of hobbled feet. When Silvermane saw him striding through the cedars or across the grassy belt of the valley he would neigh his gladness. Hare had come to love Silvermane and talked to him and treated him as if he were human.

When the mustangs were brought into camp the day's work began, the same work as that of yesterday, and yet with endless variety, with ever-changing situations that called for quick wits, steel arms, stout hearts, and unflagging energies. The darkening blue sky and the sun-tipped crags of Vermillion Cliffs were signals to start for camp. They ate like wolves, sat for a while around the camp-fire, a ragged, weary, silent group; and soon lay down, their dark faces in the shadow of the cedars.

In the beginning of this toil-filled time Hare had resolutely set himself to forget Mescal, and he had succeeded at least for a time, when he was so sore and weary that he scarcely thought at all. But she came back to him, and then there was seldom an hour that was not hers. The long months which seemed years since he had seen her, the change in him wrought by labor and peril, the deepening friendship between him and Dave, even the love he bore Silvermane—these, instead of making dim the memory of the dark-eyed girl, only made him tenderer in his thought of her.

Snow drove the riders from the canyon-camp down to Silver Cup, where they found August Naab and Snap, who had ridden in the day before.

"Now you couldn't guess how many cattle are back there in the canyons," said Dave to his father.

"I haven't any idea," answered August, dubiously.

"Five thousand head."

"Dave!" His father's tone was incredulous.

"Yes. You know we haven't been back in there for years. The stock has multiplied rapidly in spite of the lions and wolves. Not only that, but they're safe from the winter, and are not likely to be found by Dene or anybody else."

"How do you make that out?"

"The first cattle we drove in used to come back here to Silver Cup to winter. Then they stopped coming, and we almost forgot them. Well, they've got a trail round under the Saddle, and they go down and winter in the canyon. In summer they head up those rocky gullies, but they can't get up on the mountain. So it isn't likely any one will ever discover them. They are wild as deer and fatter than any stock on the ranges."

"Good! That's the best news I've had in many a day. Now, boys, we'll ride the mountain slope toward Seeping Springs, drive the cattle down, and finish up this branding. Somebody ought to go to White Sage. I'd like to know what's going on, what Holderness is up to, what Dene is doing, if there's any stock being driven to Lund."

"I told you I'd go," said Snap Naab.

"I don't want you to," replied his father. "I guess it can wait till spring, then we'll all go in. I might have thought to bring you boys out some clothes and boots.

You're pretty ragged. Jack there, especially, looks like a scarecrow. Has he worked as hard as he looks?"

"Father, he never lost a day," replied Dave, warmly, "and you know what riding is in these canyons."

August Naab looked at Hare and laughed. "It'd be funny, wouldn't it, if Holderness tried to slap you now? I always knew you'd do, Jack, and now you're one of us, and you'll have a share with my sons in the cattle."

But the generous promise failed to offset the feeling aroused by the presence of Snap Naab. With the first sight of Snap's sharp face and strange eyes Hare became conscious of an inward heat, which he had felt before, but never as now, when there seemed to be an actual flame within his breast. Yet Snap seemed greatly changed; the red flush, the swollen lines no longer showed in his face; evidently in his absence on the Navajo desert he had had no liquor; he was good-natured, lively, much inclined to joking, and he seemed to have entirely forgotten his animosity toward Hare. It was easy for Hare to see that the man's evil nature was in the ascendancy only when he was under the dominance of drink. But he could not forgive; he could not forget. Mescal's dark, beautiful eyes haunted him. Even now she might be married to this man. Perhaps that was why Snap appeared to be in such cheerful spirits. Suspense added its burdensome insistent question, but he could not bring himself to ask August if the marriage had taken place. For a day he fought to resign himself to the inevitability of the Mormon custom, to forget Mescal, and then he gave up trying. This surrender he felt to be something crucial in his life, though he could not wholly understand it. It was the darkening of his spirit; the death of boyish gentleness; the concluding step from youth into a forced manhood. The desert regeneration had not stopped at turning weak lungs, vitiated blood, and flaccid muscles into a powerful man; it was at work on his mind, his heart, his soul. They answered more and more to the call of some outside, ever-present, fiercely subtle thing.

Thenceforth he no longer vexed himself by trying to forget Mescal; if she came to mind he told himself the truth, that the weeks and months had only added to his love. And though it was bitter-sweet there was relief in speaking the truth to himself. He no longer blinded himself by hoping, striving to have generous feelings toward Snap Naab; he called the inward fire by its real name—jealousy—and knew that in the end it would become hatred.

On the third morning after leaving Silver Cup the riders were working slowly along the slope of Coconina; and Hare having driven down a bunch of cattle, found himself on an open ridge near the temporary camp. Happening to glance up the valley he saw what appeared to be smoke hanging over Seeping Springs.

"That can't be dust," he soliloquized. "Looks blue to me."

He studied the hazy bluish cloud for some time, but it was so many miles away that he could not be certain whether it was smoke or not, so he decided to ride over and make sure. None of the Naabs was in camp, and there was no telling when they would return, so he set off alone. He expected to get back before dark, but it was of little consequence whether he did or not, for he had his blanket under the saddle, and grain for Silvermane and food for himself in the saddle-bags.

Long before Silvermane's easy trot had covered half the distance Hare recognized the cloud that had made him curious. It was smoke. He thought that range-riders were camping at the springs, and he meant to see what they were about. After three hours of brisk travel he reached the top of a low rolling knoll that hid Seeping Springs. He remembered the springs were up under the red wall, and that the pool where the cattle drank was lower down in a clump of cedars. He saw smoke rising in a column from the cedars, and he heard the lowing of cattle.

"Something wrong here," he muttered. Following the trail, he rode through the cedars to come upon the dry hole where the pool had once been. There was no water in the flume. The bellowing cattle came from beyond the cedars, down the other side of the ridge. He was not long in reaching the open, and then one glance made all clear.

A new pool, large as a little lake, shone in the sunlight, and round it a jostling horned mass of cattle were pressing against a high corral. The flume that fed water to the pool was fenced all the way up to the springs.

Jack slowly rode down the ridge with eyes roving under the cedars and up to the wall. Not a man was in sight.

When he got to the fire he saw that it was not many hours old and was surrounded by fresh boot and horse tracks in the dust. Piles of slender pine logs, trimmed flat on one side, were proof of somebody's intention to erect a cabin. In a rage he flung himself from the saddle. It was not many moments' work for him to push part of the fire under the fence, and part of it against the pile of logs. The pitch-pines went off like rockets, driving the thirsty cattle back.

"I'm going to trail those horse-tracks," said Hare.

He tore down a portion of the fence enclosing the flume, and gave Silvermane a drink, then put him to a fast trot on the white trail. The tracks he had resolved to follow were clean-cut. A few inches of snow had fallen in the valley, and melting, had softened the hard ground. Silvermane kept to his gait with the tirelessness of a desert horse. August Naab had once said fifty miles a day would be play for the stallion. All the afternoon Hare watched the trail speed toward him and the end of Coconina rise above him. Long before sunset he had reached the slope of the mountain and had begun the ascent. Half way up he came to the snow and counted the tracks of three horses. At twilight he rode into the glade where August Naab had waited for his Navajo friends. There, in a sheltered nook among the rocks, he unsaddled Silvermane, covered and fed him, built a fire, ate sparingly of his meat and bread, and rolling up in his blanket, was soon asleep.

He was up and off before sunrise, and he came out on the western slope of Coconina just as the shadowy valley awakened from its misty sleep into daylight. Soon the Pink Cliffs leaned out, glimmering and vast, to change from gloomy gray to rosy glow, and then to brighten and to redden in the morning sun.

The snow thinned and failed, but the iron-cut horsetracks showed plainly in the trail. At the foot of the mountain the tracks left the White Sage trail and led off to the north toward the cliffs. Hare searched the red sage-spotted waste for Holderness's ranch. He located it, a black patch on the rising edge of the valley under the wall, and turned Silvermane into the tracks that pointed straight toward it.

The sun cleared Coconina and shone warm on his back; the Pink Cliffs lifted higher and higher before him. From the ridge-tops he saw the black patch grow into cabins and corrals. As he neared the ranch he came into rolling pasture-land where the bleached grass shone white and the cattle were ranging in the thousands. This range had once belonged to Martin Cole, and Hare thought of the bitter Mormon as he noted the snug cabins for the riders, the rambling, picturesque ranch-house, the large corrals, and the long flume that ran down from the cliff. There was a corral full of shaggy horses, and another full of steers, and two lines of cattle, one going into a pond-corral, and one coming out. The air was gray with dust. A bunch of yearlings were licking at huge lumps of brown rock-salt. A wagonful of cowhides stood before the ranch-house.

Hare reined in at the door and helloed.

A red-faced ranger with sandy hair and twinkling eyes appeared.

"Hello, stranger, get down an' come in," he said.

"Is Holderness here?" asked Hare.

"No. He's been to Lund with a bunch of steers. I reckon he'll be in White Sage by now. I'm Snood, the foreman. Is it a job ridin' you want?"

"No."

"Say! thet hoss—" he exclaimed. His gaze of friendly curiosity had moved from Hare to Silvermane. "You can corral me if it ain't thet Sevier range stallion!"

"Yes," said Hare.

Snood's whoop brought three riders to the door, and when he pointed to the horse, they stepped out with good-natured grins and admiring eyes.

"I never seen him but onc't," said one.

"Lordy, what a hoss!" Snood walked round Silvermane. "If I owned this ranch I'd trade it for that stallion. I know Silvermane. He an' I hed some chases over in Nevada. An', stranger, who might you be?"

"I'm one of August Naab's riders."

"Dene's spy!" Snood looked Hare over carefully, with much interest, and without any show of ill-will. "I've heerd of you. An' what might one of Naab's riders want of Holderness?"

"I rode in to Seeping Springs yesterday," said Hare, eying the foreman. "There was a new pond, fenced in. Our cattle couldn't drink. There were a lot of trimmed logs. Somebody was going to build a cabin. I burned the corrals and logs—and I trailed fresh tracks from Seeping Springs to this ranch."

"The h—l you did!" shouted Snood, and his face flamed. "See here, stranger, you're the second man to accuse some of my riders of such dirty tricks. That's enough for me. I was foreman of this ranch till this minute. I was foreman, but there were things gain' on thet I didn't know of. I kicked on thet deal with Martin Cole. I quit. I steal no man's water. Is thet good with you?"

Snood's query was as much a challenge as a question. He bit savagely at his pipe. Hare offered his hand.

"Your word goes. Dave Naab said you might be Holderness's foreman, but you weren't a liar or a thief. I'd believe it even if Dave hadn't told me."

"Them fellers you tracked rode in here yesterday. They're gone now. I've no more to say, except I never hired them."

"I'm glad to hear it. Good-day, Snood, I'm in something of a hurry."

With that Hare faced about in the direction of White Sage. Once clear of the corrals he saw the village closer than he had expected to find it. He walked Silvermane most of the way, and jogged along the rest, so that he reached the village in the twilight. Memory served him well. He rode in as August Naab had ridden out, and arrived at the Bishop's barn-yard, where he put up his horse. Then he went to the house. It was necessary to introduce himself for none of the Bishop's family recognized in him the young man they had once befriended. The old Bishop prayed and reminded him of the laying on of hands. The women served him with food, the young men brought him new boots and garments to replace those that had been worn to tatters. Then they plied him with questions about the Naabs, whom they had not seen for nearly a year. They rejoiced at his recovered health; they welcomed him with warm words.

Later Hare sought an interview alone with the Bishop's sons, and he told them of the loss of the sheep, of the burning of the new corrals, of the tracks leading to Holderness's ranch. In turn they warned him of his danger, and gave him information desired by August Naab. Holderness's grasp on the outlying ranges and water-rights had slowly and surely tightened; every month he acquired new territory; he drove cattle regularly to Lund, and it was no secret that much of the stock came from the eastern slope of Coconina. He could not hire enough riders to do his work. A suspicion that he was not a cattle-man but a rustler had slowly gained ground; it was scarcely hinted, but it was believed. His friendship with Dene had become offensive to the Mormons, who had formerly been on good footing with him. Dene's killing of Martin Cole was believed to have been at Holderness's instigation. Cole had threatened Holderness. Then Dene and Cole had met in the main street of White Sage. Cole's death ushered in the bloody time that he had prophesied. Dene's band had grown; no man could say how many men he had or who they were. Chance and Culver were openly his lieutenants, and whenever they came into the village there was shooting. There were ugly rumors afloat in regard to their treatment of Mormon women. The wives and daughters of once peaceful White Sage dared no longer venture out-of-doors after nightfall. There was more money in coin and more whiskey than ever before in the village. Lund and the few villages northward were terrorized as well as White Sage. It was a bitter story.

The Bishop and his sons tried to persuade Hare next morning to leave the village without seeing Holderness, urging the futility of such a meeting.

"I will see him," said Hare. He spent the morning at the cottage, and when it came time to take his leave he smiled into the anxious faces. "If I weren't able to take care of myself August Naab would never have said so."

Had Hare asked himself what he intended to do when he faced Holderness he could not have told. His feelings were pent-in, bound, but at the bottom something rankled. His mind seemed steeped in still thunderous atmosphere.

How well he remembered the quaint wide street, the gray church! As he rode many persons stopped to gaze at Silvermane. He turned the corner into the main thoroughfare. A new building had been added to the several stores. Mustangs stood, bridles down, before the doors; men lounged along the railings.

As he dismounted he heard the loungers speak of his horse, and he saw their leisurely manner quicken. He stepped into the store to meet more men, among them August Naab's friend Abe. Hare might never have been in White Sage for all the recognition he found, but he excited something keener than curiosity. He asked for spurs, a clasp-knife and some other necessaries, and he contrived, when momentarily out of sight behind a pile of boxes, to whisper his identity to Abe. The Mormon was dumbfounded. When he came out of his trance he showed his gladness, and at a question of Hare's he silently pointed toward the saloon.

Hare faced the open door. The room had been enlarged; it was now on a level with the store floor, and was blue with smoke, foul with the fumes of rum, and noisy with the voices of dark, rugged men.

A man in the middle of the room was dancing a jig.

"Hello, who's this?" he said, straightening up.

It might have been the stopping of the dance or the quick spark in Hare's eyes that suddenly quieted the room. Hare had once vowed to himself that he would never forget the scarred face; it belonged to the outlaw Chance.

The sight of it flashed into the gulf of Hare's mind like a meteor into black night. A sudden madness raced through his veins.

"Hello, Don't you know me?" he said, with a long step that brought him close to Chance.

The outlaw stood irresolute. Was this an old friend or an enemy? His beady eyes scintillated and twitched as if they sought to look him over, yet dared not because it was only in the face that intention could be read.

The stillness of the room broke to a hoarse whisper from some one.

"Look how he packs his gun."

Another man answering whispered: "There's not six men in Utah who pack a gun thet way."

Chance heard these whispers, for his eye shifted downward the merest fraction of a second. The brick color of his face turned a dirty white.

"Do you know me?" demanded Hare.

Chance's answer was a spasmodic jerking of his hand toward his hip. Hare's arm moved quicker, and Chance's Colt went spinning to the floor.

"Too slow," said Hare. Then he flung Chance backward and struck him blows that sent his head with sodden thuds against the log wall. Chance sank to the floor in a heap.

Hare kicked the outlaw's gun out of the way, and wheeled to the crowd. Holderness stood foremost, his tall form leaning against the bar, his clear eyes shining like light on ice.

"Do you know me?" asked Hare, curtly.

Holderness started slightly. "I certainly don't," he replied.

"You slapped my face once." Hare leaned close to the rancher. "Slap it now—you rustler!"

In the slow, guarded instant when Hare's gaze held Holderness and the other men, a low murmuring ran through the room.

"Dene's spy!" suddenly burst out Holderness.

Hare slapped his face. Then he backed a few paces with his right arm held before him almost as high as his shoulder, the wrist rigid, the fingers quivering.

"Don't try to draw, Holderness. Thet's August Naab's trick with a gun," whispered a man, hurriedly.

"Holderness, I made a bonfire over at Seeping Springs," said Hare. "I burned the new corrals your men built, and I tracked them to your ranch. Snood threw up his job when he heard it. He's an honest man, and no honest man will work for a water-thief, a cattle-rustler, a sheep-killer. You're shown up, Holderness. Leave the country before some one kills you—understand, before some one kills you!"

Holderness stood motionless against the bar, his eyes fierce with passionate hate.

Hare backed step by step to the outside door, his right hand still high, his look holding the crowd bound to the last instant. Then he slipped out, scattered the group round Silvermane, and struck hard with the spurs.

The gray, never before spurred, broke down the road into his old wild speed.

Men were crossing from the corner of the green square. One, a compact little fellow, swarthy, his dark hair long and flowing, with jaunty and alert air, was Dene, the outlaw leader. He stopped, with his companions, to let the horse cross.

Hare guided the thundering stallion slightly to the left. Silvermane swerved and in two mighty leaps bore down on the outlaw. Dene saved himself by quickly leaping aside, but even as he moved Silvermane struck him with his left fore-leg, sending him into the dust.

At the street corner Hare glanced back. Yelling men were rushing from the saloon and some of them fired after him. The bullets whistled harmlessly behind Hare. Then the corner house shut off his view.

Silvermane lengthened out and stretched lower with his white mane flying and his nose pointed level for the desert.

XI. THE DESERT-HAWK

TOWARD the close of the next day Jack Hare arrived at Seeping Springs. A pile of gray ashes marked the spot where the trimmed logs had lain. Round the pool ran a black circle hard packed into the ground by many hoofs. Even the board flume had been burned to a level with the glancing sheet of water. Hare was slipping Silvermane's bit to let him drink when he heard a halloo. Dave Naab galloped out of the cedars, and presently August Naab and his other sons appeared with a pack-train.

"Now you've played bob!" exclaimed Dave. He swung out of his saddle and gripped Hare with both hands. "I know what you've done; I know where you've been. Father will be furious, but don't you care."

The other Naabs trotted down the slope and lined their horses before the pool. The sons stared in blank astonishment; the father surveyed the scene slowly, and then fixed wrathful eyes on Hare.

"What does this mean?" he demanded, with the sonorous roll of his angry voice.

Hare told all that had happened.

August Naab's gloomy face worked, and his eagle-gaze had in it a strange far-seeing light; his mind was dwelling upon his mystic power of revelation.

"I see—I see," he said haltingly.

"Ki—yi-i-i!" yelled Dave Naab with all the power of his lungs. His head was back, his mouth wide open, his face red, his neck corded and swollen with the intensity of his passion.

"Be still—boy!" ordered his father. "Hare, this was madness—but tell me what you learned."

Briefly Hare repeated all that he had been told at the Bishop's, and concluded with the killing of Martin Cole by Dene.

August Naab bowed his head and his giant frame shook under the force of his emotion. Martin Cole was the last of his life-long friends.

"This—this outlaw—you say you ran him down?" asked Naab, rising haggard and shaken out of his grief.

"Yes. He didn't recognize me or know what was coming till Silvermane was on him. But he was quick, and fell sidewise. Silvermane's knee sent him sprawling."

XI. THE DESERT-HAWK

"What will it all lead to?" asked August Naab, and in his extremity he appealed to his eldest son.

"The bars are down," said Snap Naab, with a click of his long teeth.

"Father," began Dave Naab earnestly, "Jack has done a splendid thing. The news will fly over Utah like wildfire. Mormons are slow. They need a leader. But they can follow and they will. We can't cure these evils by hoping and praying. We've got to fight!"

"Dave's right, dad, it means fight," cried George, with his fist clinched high.

"You've been wrong, father, in holding back," said Zeke Naab, his lean jaw bulging. "This Holderness will steal the water and meat out of our children's mouths. We've got to fight!"

"Let's ride to White Sage," put in Snap Naab, and the little flecks in his eyes were dancing. "I'll throw a gun on Dene. I can get to him. We've been tolerable friends. He's wanted me to join his band. I'll kill him."

He laughed as he raised his right hand and swept it down to his left side; the blue Colt lay on his outstretched palm. Dene's life and Holderness's, too, hung in the balance between two deadly snaps of this desert-wolf's teeth. He was one of the Naabs, and yet apart from them, for neither religion, nor friendship, nor life itself mattered to him.

August Naab's huge bulk shook again, not this time with grief, but in wrestling effort to withstand the fiery influence of this unholy fighting spirit among his sons.

"I am forbidden."

His answer was gentle, but its very gentleness breathed of his battle over himself, of allegiance to something beyond earthly duty. "We'll drive the cattle to Silver Cup," he decided, "and then go home. I give up Seeping Springs. Perhaps this valley and water will content Holderness."

When they reached the oasis Hare was surprised to find that it was the day before Christmas. The welcome given the long-absent riders was like a celebration. Much to Hare's disappointment Mescal did not appear; the homecoming was not joyful to him because it lacked her welcoming smile.

Christmas Day ushered in the short desert winter; ice formed in the ditches and snow fell, but neither long resisted the reflection of the sun from the walls. The early morning hours were devoted to religious services. At midday dinner was served in the big room of August Naab's cabin. At one end was a stone fireplace where logs blazed and crackled.

In all his days Hare had never seen such a bountiful board. Yet he was unable to appreciate it, to share in the general thanksgiving. Dominating all other feeling was the fear that Mescal would come in and take a seat by Snap Naab's side. When Snap seated himself opposite with his pale little wife Hare found himself waiting for Mescal with an intensity that made him dead to all else. The girls, Judith, Esther, Rebecca, came running gayly in, clad in their best dresses, with bright ribbons to honor the occasion. Rebecca took the seat beside Snap, and Hare gulped with a hard contraction of his throat. Mescal was not yet a Mormon's wife!

He seemed to be lifted upward, to grow light-headed with the blessed assurance. Then Mescal entered and took the seat next to him. She smiled and spoke, and the blood beat thick in his ears.

That moment was happy, but it was as nothing to its successor. Under the table-cover Mescal's hand found his, and pressed it daringly and gladly. Her hand lingered in his all the time August Naab spent in carving the turkey—lingered there even though Snap Naab's hawk eyes were never far away. In the warm touch of her hand, in some subtle thing that radiated from her Hare felt a change in the girl he loved. A few months had wrought in her some indefinable difference, even as they had increased his love to its full volume and depth. Had his absence brought her to the realization of her woman's heart?

In the afternoon Hare left the house and spent a little while with Silvermane; then he wandered along the wall to the head of the oasis, and found a seat on the fence. The next few weeks presented to him a situation that would be difficult to endure. He would be near Mescal, but only to have the truth forced cruelly home to him every sane moment—that she was not for him. Out on the ranges he had abandoned himself to dreams of her; they had been beautiful; they had made the long hours seem like minutes; but they had forged chains that could not be broken, and now he was hopelessly fettered.

The clatter of hoofs roused him from a reverie which was half sad, half sweet. Mescal came tearing down the level on Black Bolly. She pulled in the mustang and halted beside Hare to hold out shyly a red scarf embroidered with Navajo symbols in white and red beads.

"I've wanted a chance to give you this," she said, "a little Christmas present."

For a few seconds Hare could find no words.

"Did you make it for me, Mescal?" he finally asked. "How good of you! I'll keep it always."

"Put it on now—let me tie it—there!"

"But, child. Suppose he—they saw it?"

"I don't care who sees it."

She met him with clear, level eyes. Her curt, crisp speech was full of meaning. He looked long at her, with a yearning denied for many a day. Her face was the same, yet wonderfully changed; the same in line and color, but different in soul and spirit. The old sombre shadow lay deep in the eyes, but to it had been added gleam of will and reflection of thought. The whole face had been refined and transformed.

"Mescal! What's happened? You're not the same. You seem almost happy. Have you—has he—given you up?"

"Don't you know Mormons better than that? The thing is the same—so far as they're concerned."

"But Mescal—are you going to marry him? For God's sake, tell me."

"Never." It was a woman's word, instant, inflexible, desperate. With a deep breath Hare realized where the girl had changed.

"Still you're promised, pledged to him! How'll you get out of it?"

"I don't know how. But I'll cut out my tongue, and be dumb as my poor peon before I'll speak the word that'll make me Snap Naab's wife."

There was a long silence. Mescal smoothed out Bolly's mane, and Hare gazed up at the walls with eyes that did not see them.

Presently he spoke. "I'm afraid for you. Snap watched us to-day at dinner."

"He's jealous."

"Suppose he sees this scarf?"

Mescal laughed defiantly. It was bewildering for Hare to hear her.

"He'll—Mescal, I may yet come to this." Hare's laugh echoed Mescal's as he pointed to the enclosure under the wall, where the graves showed bare and rough.

Her warm color fled, but it flooded back, rich, mantling brow and cheek and neck.

"Snap Naab will never kill you," she said impulsively.

"Mescal."

She swiftly turned her face away as his hand closed on hers.

"Mescal, do you love me?"

The trembling of her fingers and the heaving of her bosom lent his hope conviction. "Mescal," he went on, "these past months have been years, years of toiling, thinking, changing, but always loving. I'm not the man you knew. I'm wild— I'm starved for a sight of you. I love you! Mescal, my desert flower!"

She raised her free hand to his shoulder and swayed toward him. He held her a moment, clasped tight, and then released her.

"I'm quite mad!" he exclaimed, in a passion of self-reproach. "What a risk I'm putting on you! But I couldn't help it. Look at me— Just once—please— Mescal, just one look.... Now go."

The drama of the succeeding days was of absorbing interest. Hare had liberty; there was little work for him to do save to care for Silvermane. He tried to hunt foxes in the caves and clefts; he rode up and down the broad space under the walls; he sought the open desert only to be driven in by the bitter, biting winds. Then he would return to the big living-room of the Naabs and sit before the burning logs. This spacious room was warm, light, pleasant, and was used by every one in leisure hours. Mescal spent most of her time there. She was engaged upon a new frock of buckskin, and over this she bent with her needle and beads. When there was a chance Hare talked with her, speaking one language with his tongue, a far different one with his eyes. When she was not present he looked into the glowing red fire and dreamed of her.

In the evenings when Snap came in to his wooing and drew Mescal into a corner, Hare watched with covert glance and smouldering jealousy. Somehow he had come to see all things and all people in the desert glass, and his symbol for Snap Naab was the desert-hawk. Snap's eyes were as wild and piercing as those of a hawk; his nose and mouth were as the beak of a hawk; his hands resembled the claws of a hawk; and the spurs he wore, always bloody, were still more significant of his ruthless nature. Then Snap's courting of the girl, the cool assurance, the unhastening ease, were like the slow rise, the sail, and the poise of a desert-hawk before the downward lightning-swift swoop on his quarry.

It was intolerable for Hare to sit there in the evenings, to try to play with the children who loved him, to talk to August Naab when his eye seemed ever drawn to the quiet couple in the corner, and his ear was unconsciously strained to catch a passing word. That hour was a miserable one for him, yet he could not bring himself to leave the room. He never saw Snap touch her; he never heard Mescal's voice; he believed that she spoke very little. When the hour was over and Mescal rose to pass to her room, then his doubt, his fear, his misery, were as though they had never been, for as Mescal said good-night she would give him one look, swift as a flash, and in it were womanliness and purity, and something beyond his comprehension. Her Indian serenity and mysticism veiled yet suggested some secret, some power by which she might yet escape the iron band of this Mormon rule. Hare could not fathom it. In that good-night glance was a meaning for him alone, if meaning ever shone in woman's eyes, and it said: "I will be true to you and to myself!"

Once the idea struck him that as soon as spring returned it would be an easy matter, and probably wise, for him to leave the oasis and go up into Utah, far from the desert-canyon country. But the thought refused to stay before his consciousness a moment. New life had flushed his veins here. He loved the dreamy, sleepy oasis with its mellow sunshine always at rest on the glistening walls; he loved the cedar-scented plateau where hope had dawned, and the wind-swept sand-strips, where hard out-of-door life and work had renewed his wasting youth; he loved the canyon winding away toward Coconina, opening into wide abyss; and always, more than all, he loved the Painted Desert, with its ever-changing pictures, printed in sweeping dust and bare peaks and purple haze. He loved the beauty of these places, and the wildness in them had an affinity with something strange and untamed in him. He would never leave them. When his blood had cooled, when this tumultuous thrill and swell had worn themselves out, happiness would come again.

Early in the winter Snap Naab had forced his wife to visit his father's house with him; and she had remained in the room, white-faced, passionately jealous, while he wooed Mescal. Then had come a scene. Hare had not been present, but he knew its results. Snap had been furious, his father grave, Mescal tearful and ashamed. The wife found many ways to interrupt her husband's lovemaking. She sent the children for him; she was taken suddenly ill; she discovered that the corral gate was open and his cream-colored pinto, dearest to his heart, was running loose; she even set her cottage on fire.

One Sunday evening just before twilight Hare was sitting on the porch with August Naab and Dave, when their talk was interrupted by Snap's loud calling for his wife. At first the sounds came from inside his cabin. Then he put his head out of a window and yelled. Plainly he was both impatient and angry. It was nearly time for him to make his Sunday call upon Mescal.

"Something's wrong," muttered Dave.

"Hester! Hester!" yelled Snap.

Mother Ruth came out and said that Hester was not there.

"Where is she?" Snap banged on the window-sill with his fists. "Find her, somebody—Hester!"

"Son, this is the Sabbath," called Father Naab, gravely. "Lower your voice. Now what's the matter?"

"Matter!" bawled Snap, giving way to rage. "When I was asleep Hester stole all my clothes. She's hid them—she's run off—there's not a d—n thing for me to put on! I'll—"

The roar of laughter from August and Dave drowned the rest of the speech. Hare managed to stifle his own mirth. Snap pulled in his head and slammed the window shut.

"Jack," said August, "even among Mormons the course of true love never runs smooth."

Hare finally forgot his bitter humor in pity for the wife. Snap came to care not at all for her messages and tricks, and he let nothing interfere with his evening beside Mescal. It was plain that he had gone far on the road of love. Whatever he had been in the beginning of the betrothal, he was now a lover, eager, importunate. His hawk's eyes were softer than Hare had ever seen them; he was obliging, kind, gay, an altogether different Snap Naab. He groomed himself often, and wore clean scarfs, and left off his bloody spurs. For eight months he had not touched the bottle. When spring approached he was madly in love with Mescal. And the marriage was delayed because his wife would not have another woman in her home.

Once Hare heard Snap remonstrating with his father.

"If she don't come to time soon I'll keep the kids and send her back to her father."

"Don't be hasty, son. Let her have time," replied August. "Women must be humored. I'll wager she'll give in before the cottonwood blows, and that's not long."

It was Hare's habit, as the days grew warmer, to walk a good deal, and one evening, as twilight shadowed the oasis and grew black under the towering walls, he strolled out toward the fields. While passing Snap's cottage Hare heard a woman's voice in passionate protest and a man's in strident anger. Later as he stood with his arm on Silvermane, a woman's scream, at first high-pitched, then suddenly faint and smothered, caused him to grow rigid, and his hand clinched tight. When he went back by the cottage a low moaning confirmed his suspicion.

That evening Snap appeared unusually bright and happy; and he asked his father to name the day for the wedding. August did so in a loud voice and with evident relief. Then the quaint Mormon congratulations were offered to Mescal. To Hare, watching the strange girl with the distressingly keen intuition of an unfortunate lover, she appeared as pleased as any of them that the marriage was settled. But there was no shyness, no blushing confusion. When Snap bent to kiss her—his first kiss—she slightly turned her face, so that his lips brushed her cheek, yet even then her self-command did not break for an instant. It was a task for Hare to pretend to congratulate her; nevertheless he mumbled something. She lifted her long lashes, and there, deep beneath the shadows, was unutterable anguish. It gave him a shock. He went to his room, convinced that she had yielded; and though he could not blame her, and he knew she was helpless, he cried out in reproach and resentment. She had failed him, as he had known she must fail. He tossed on his bed and thought; he lay quiet, wide-open eyes staring into the darkness, and his mind burned and seethed. Through the hours of that long night he learned what love had cost him.

With the morning light came some degree of resignation. Several days went slowly by, bringing the first of April, which was to be the wedding-day. August Naab had said it would come before the cottonwoods shed their white floss; and their buds had just commenced to open. The day was not a holiday, and George and Zeke and Dave began to pack for the ranges, yet there was an air of jollity and festivity. Snap Naab had a springy step and jaunty mien. Once he regarded Hare with a slow smile.

Piute prepared to drive his new flock up on the plateau. The women of the household were busy and excited; the children romped.

The afternoon waned into twilight, and Hare sought the quiet shadows under the wall near the river trail. He meant to stay there until August Naab had pronounced his son and Mescal man and wife. The dull roar of the rapids borne on a faint puff of westerly breeze was lulled into a soothing murmur. A radiant white star peeped over the black rim of the wall. The solitude and silence were speaking to Hare's heart, easing his pain, when a soft patter of moccasined feet brought him bolt upright.

A slender form rounded the corner wall. It was Mescal. The white dog Wolf hung close by her side. Swiftly she reached Hare.

"Mescal!" he exclaimed.

"Hush! Speak softly," she whispered fearfully. Her hands were clinging to his.

"Jack, do you love me still?"

More than woman's sweetness was in the whisper; the portent of indefinable motive made Hare tremble like a shaking leaf.

"Good heavens! You are to be married in a few minutes—What do you mean? Where are you going? this buckskin suit—and Wolf with you—Mescal!"

"There's no time—only a word—hurry—do you love me still?" she panted, with great shining eyes close to his.

"Love you? With all my soul!"

"Listen," she whispered, and leaned against him. A fresh breeze bore the boom of the river. She caught her breath quickly: "I love you!—I love you!—Good-bye!"

She kissed him and broke from his clasp. Then silently, like a shadow, with the white dog close beside her, she disappeared in the darkness of the river trail.

XI. THE DESERT-HAWK

She was gone before he came out of his bewilderment. He rushed down the trail; he called her name. The gloom had swallowed her, and only the echo of his voice made answer.

XII. ECHO CLIFFS

WHEN thought came clearly to him he halted irresolute. For Mescal's sake he must not appear to have had any part in her headlong flight, or any knowledge of it.

With stealthy footsteps he reached the cottonwoods, stole under the gloomy shade, and felt his way to a point beyond the twinkling lights. Then, peering through the gloom until assured he was safe from observation, and taking the dark side of the house, he gained the hall, and his room. He threw himself on his bed, and endeavored to compose himself, to quiet his vibrating nerves, to still the triumphant bell-beat of his heart. For a while all his being swung to the palpitating consciousness of joy—Mescal had taken her freedom. She had escaped the swoop of the hawk.

While Hare lay there, trying to gather his shattered senses, the merry sound of voices and the music of an accordion hummed from the big living-room next to his. Presently heavy boots thumped on the floor of the hall; then a hand rapped on his door.

"Jack, are you there?" called August Naab.

"Yes."

"Come along then."

Hare rose, opened the door and followed August. The room was bright with lights; the table was set, and the Naabs, large and small, were standing expectantly. As Hare found a place behind them Snap Naab entered with his wife. She was as pale as if she were in her shroud. Hare caught Mother Ruth's pitying subdued glance as she drew the frail little woman to her side. When August Naab began fingering his Bible the whispering ceased.

"Why don't they fetch her?" he questioned.

"Judith, Esther, bring her in," said Mother Mary, calling into the hallway.

Quick footsteps, and the girls burst in impetuously, exclaiming: "Mescal's not there!"

"Where is she, then?" demanded August Naab, going to the door. "Mescal!" he called.

Succeeding his authoritative summons only the cheery sputter of the wood-fire broke the silence.

"She hadn't put on her white frock," went on Judith.

"Her buckskins aren't hanging where they always are," continued Esther.

August Naab laid his Bible on the table. "I always feared it," he said simply.

"She's gone!" cried Snap Naab. He ran into the hall, into Mescal's room, and returned trailing the white wedding-dress. "The time we thought she spent to put this on she's been—"

He choked over the words, and sank into a chair, face convulsed, hands shaking, weak in the grip of a grief that he had never before known. Suddenly he flung the dress into the fire. His wife fell to the floor in a dead faint. Then the desert-hawk showed his claws. His hands tore at the close scarf round his throat as if to liberate a fury that was stifling him; his face lost all semblance to anything human. He began to howl, to rave, to curse; and his father circled him with iron arm and dragged him from the room.

The children were whimpering, the wives lamenting. The quiet men searched the house and yard and corrals and fields. But they found no sign of Mescal. After long hours the excitement subsided and all sought their beds.

Morning disclosed the facts of Mescal's flight. She had dressed for the trail; a knapsack was missing and food enough to fill it; Wolf was gone; Noddle was not in his corral; the peon slave had not slept in his shack; there were moccasin-tracks and burro-tracks and dog-tracks in the sand at the river crossing, and one of the boats was gone. This boat was not moored to the opposite shore. Questions arose. Had the boat sunk? Had the fugitives crossed safely or had they drifted into the canyon? Dave Naab rode out along the river and saw the boat, a mile below the rapids, bottom side up and lodged on a sand-bar.

"She got across, and then set the boat loose," said August. "That's the Indian of her. If she went up on the cliffs to the Navajos maybe we'll find her. If she went into the Painted Desert—" a grave shake of his shaggy head completed his sentence.

Morning also disclosed Snap Naab once more in the clutch of his demon, drunk and unconscious, lying like a log on the porch of his cottage.

"This means ruin to him," said his father. "He had one chance; he was mad over Mescal, and if he had got her, he might have conquered his thirst for rum."

He gave orders for the sheep to be driven up on the plateau, and for his sons to ride out to the cattle ranges. He bade Hare pack and get in readiness to accompany him to the Navajo cliffs, there to search for Mescal.

The river was low, as the spring thaws had not yet set in, and the crossing promised none of the hazard so menacing at a later period. Billy Naab rowed across with the saddle and packs. Then August had to crowd the lazy burros into the water. Silvermane went in with a rush, and Charger took to the river like an old duck. August and Jack sat in the stern of the boat, while Billy handled the oars. They crossed swiftly and safely. The three burros were then loaded, two with packs, the other with a heavy water-bag.

"See there," said August, pointing to tracks in the sand. The imprints of little moccasins reassured Hare, for he had feared the possibility suggested by the upturned boat. "Perhaps it'll be better if I never find her," continued Naab. "If I bring her back Snap's as likely to kill her as to marry her. But I must try to find her. Only what to do with her—"

"Give her to me," interrupted Jack.

"Hare!"

"I love her!"

Naab's stern face relaxed. "Well, I'm beat! Though I don't see why you should be different from all the others. It was that time you spent with her on the plateau. I thought you too sick to think of a woman!"

"Mescal cares for me," said Hare.

"Ah! That accounts. Hare, did you play me fair?"

"We tried to, though we couldn't help loving."

"She would have married Snap but for you."

"Yes. But I couldn't help that. You brought me out here, and saved my life. I know what I owe you. Mescal meant to marry your son when I left for the range last fall. But she's a true woman and couldn't. August Naab, if we ever find her will you marry her to him—now?"

"That depends. Did you know she intended to run?"

"I never dreamed of it. I learned it only at the last moment. I met her on the river trail."

"You should have stopped her."

Hare maintained silence.

"You should have told me," went on Naab.

"I couldn't. I'm only human."

"Well, well, I'm not blaming you, Hare. I had hot blood once. But I'm afraid the desert will not be large enough for you and Snap. She's pledged to him. You can't change the Mormon Church. For the sake of peace I'd give you Mescal, if I could. Snap will either have her or kill her. I'm going to hunt this desert in advance of him, because he'll trail her like a hound. It would be better to marry her to him than to see her dead."

"I'm not so sure of that."

"Hare, your nose is on a blood scent, like a wolf's. I can see—I've always seen—well, remember, it's man to man between you now."

During this talk they were winding under Echo Cliffs, gradually climbing, and working up to a level with the desert, which they presently attained at a point near the head of the canyon. The trail swerved to the left following the base of the cliffs. The tracks of Noddle and Wolf were plainly visible in the dust. Hare felt that if they ever led out into the immense airy space of the desert all hope of finding Mescal must be abandoned.

They trailed the tracks of the dog and burro to Bitter Seeps, a shallow spring of alkali, and there lost all track of them. The path up the cliffs to the Navajo ranges was bare, time-worn in solid rock, and showed only the imprint of age. Desertward the ridges of shale, the washes of copper earth, baked in the sun, gave no sign of the fugitives' course. August Naab shrugged his broad shoulders and pointed his horse to the cliff. It was dusk when they surmounted it.

XII. ECHO CLIFFS

They camped in the lee of an uplifting crag. When the wind died down the night was no longer unpleasantly cool; and Hare, finding August Naab uncommunicative and sleepy, strolled along the rim of the cliff, as he had been wont to do in the sheep-herding days. He could scarcely dissociate them from the present, for the bitter-sweet smell of tree and bush, the almost inaudible sigh of breeze, the opening and shutting of the great white stars in the blue dome, the silence, the sense of the invisible void beneath him—all were thought-provoking parts of that past of which nothing could ever be forgotten. And it was a silence which brought much to the ear that could hear. It was a silence penetrated by faint and distant sounds, by mourning wolf, or moan of wind in a splintered crag. Weird and low, an inarticulate voice, it wailed up from the desert, winding along the hollow trail, freeing itself in the wide air, and dying away. He had often heard the scream of lion and cry of wildcat, but this was the strange sound of which August Naab had told him, the mysterious call of canyon and desert night.

Daylight showed Echo Cliffs to be of vastly greater range than the sister plateau across the river. The roll of cedar level, the heave of craggy ridge, the dip of white-sage valley gave this side a diversity widely differing from the two steps of the Vermillion tableland. August Naab followed a trail leading back toward the river. For the most part thick cedars hid the surroundings from Hare's view; occasionally, however, he had a backward glimpse from a high point, or a wide prospect below, where the trail overlooked an oval hemmed-in valley.

About midday August Naab brushed through a thicket, and came abruptly on a declivity. He turned to his companion with a wave of his hand.

"The Navajo camp," he said. "Eschtah has lived there for many years. It's the only permanent Navajo camp I know. These Indians are nomads. Most of them live wherever the sheep lead them. This plateau ranges for a hundred miles, farther than any white man knows, and everywhere, in the valleys and green nooks, will be found Navajo hogans. That's why we may never find Mescal."

Hare's gaze travelled down over the tips of cedar and crag to a pleasant vale, dotted with round mound-like white-streaked hogans, from which lazy floating columns of blue smoke curled upward. Mustangs and burros and sheep browsed on the white patches of grass. Bright-red blankets blazed on the cedar branches. There was slow colorful movement of Indians, passing in and out of their homes. The scene brought irresistibly to Hare the thought of summer, of long warm afternoons, of leisure that took no stock of time.

On the way down the trail they encountered a flock of sheep driven by a little Navajo boy on a brown burro. It was difficult to tell which was the more surprised, the long-eared burro, which stood stock-still, or the boy, who first kicked and pounded his shaggy steed, and then jumped off and ran with black locks flying. Farther down Indian girls started up from their tasks, and darted silently into the shade of the cedars. August Naab whooped when he reached the valley, and Indian braves appeared, to cluster round him, shake his hand and Hare's, and lead them toward the centre of the encampment.

The hogans where these desert savages dwelt were all alike; only the chief's was larger. From without it resembled a mound of clay with a few white logs, half imbedded, shining against the brick red. August Naab drew aside a blanket hanging over a door, and entered, beckoning his companion to follow. Inured as Hare had become to the smell and smart of wood-smoke, for a moment he could not see, or scarcely breathe, so thick was the atmosphere. A fire, the size of which attested the desert Indian's love of warmth, blazed in the middle of the hogan, and sent part of its smoke upward through a round hole in the roof. Eschtah, with blanket over his shoulders, his lean black head bent, sat near the fire. He noted the entrance of his visitors, but immediately resumed his meditative posture, and appeared to be unaware of their presence.

Hare followed August's example, sitting down and speaking no word. His eyes, however, roved discreetly to and fro. Eschtah's three wives presented great differences in age and appearance. The eldest was a wrinkled, parchment-skinned old hag who sat sightless before the fire; the next was a solid square squaw, employed in the task of combing a naked boy's hair with a comb made of stiff thin roots tied tightly in a round bunch. Judging from the youngster's actions and grimaces, this combing process was not a pleasant one. The third wife, much younger, had a comely face, and long braids of black hair, of which, evidently, she was proud. She leaned on her knees over a flat slab of rock, and holding in her hands a long oval stone, she rolled and mashed corn into meal. There were young braves, handsome in their bronze-skinned way, with bands binding their straight thick hair, silver rings in their ears, silver bracelets on their wrists, silver buttons on their moccasins. There were girls who looked up from their blanket-weaving with shy curiosity, and then turned to their frames strung with long threads. Under their nimble fingers the wool-carrying needles slipped in and out, and the colored stripes grew apace. Then there were younger boys and girls, all bright-eyed and curious; and babies sleeping on blankets. Where the walls and ceiling were not covered with buckskin garments, weapons and blankets, Hare saw the white wood-ribs of the hogan structure. It was a work of art, this circular house of forked logs and branches, interwoven into a dome, arched and strong, and all covered and cemented with clay.

At a touch of August's hand Hare turned to the old chief; and awaited his speech. It came with the uplifting of Eschtah's head, and the offering of his hand in the white man's salute. August's replies were slow and labored; he could not speak the Navajo language fluently, but he understood it.

"The White Prophet is welcome," was the chief's greeting. "Does he come for sheep or braves or to honor the Navajo in his home?"

"Eschtah, he seeks the Flower of the Desert," replied August Naab. "Mescal has left him. Her trail leads to the bitter waters under the cliff, and then is as a bird's."

"Eschtah has waited, yet Mescal has not come to him."

"She has not been here?"

"Mescal's shadow has not gladdened the Navajo's door."

"She has climbed the crags or wandered into the canyons. The white father loves her; he must find her."

"Eschtah's braves and mustangs are for his friend's use. The Navajo will find her if she is not as the grain of drifting sand. But is the White Prophet wise in his years? Let the Flower of the Desert take root in the soil of her forefathers."

"Eschtah's wisdom is great, but he thinks only of Indian blood. Mescal is half white, and her ways have been the ways of the white man. Nor does Eschtah think of the white man's love."

"The desert has called. Where is the White Prophet's vision? White blood and red blood will not mix. The Indian's blood pales in the white man's stream; or it burns red for the sun and the waste and the wild. Eschtah's forefathers, sleeping here in the silence, have called the Desert Flower."

"It is true. But the white man is bound; he cannot be as the Indian; he does not content himself with life as it is; he hopes and prays for change; he believes in the progress of his race on earth. Therefore Eschtah's white friend smelts Mescal; he has brought her up as his own; he wants to take her home, to love her better, to trust to the future."

"The white man's ways are white man's ways. Eschtah understands. He remembers his daughter lying here. He closed her dead eyes and sent word to his white friend. He named this child for the flower that blows in the wind of silent places. Eschtah gave his granddaughter to his friend. She has been the bond between them. Now she is flown and the White Father seeks the Navajo. Let him command. Eschtah has spoken."

Eschtah pressed into Naab's service a band of young braves, under the guidance of several warriors who knew every trail of the range, every waterhole, every cranny where even a wolf might hide. They swept the river-end of the plateau, and working westward, scoured the levels, ridges, valleys, climbed to the peaks, and sent their Indian dogs into the thickets and caves. From Eschtah's encampment westward the hogans diminished in number till only one here and there was discovered, hidden under a yellow wall, or amid a clump of cedars. All the Indians met with were sternly questioned by the chiefs, their dwellings were searched, and the ground about their waterholes was closely examined. Mile after mile the plateau was covered by these Indians, who beat the brush and penetrated the fastnesses with a hunting instinct that left scarcely a rabbit-burrow unrevealed. The days sped by; the circle of the sun arched higher; the patches of snow in high places disappeared; and the search proceeded westward. They camped where the night overtook them, sometimes near water and grass, sometimes in bare dry places. To the westward the plateau widened. Rugged ridges rose here and there, and seared crags split the sky like sharp sawteeth. And after many miles of wild up-ranging they reached a divide which marked the line of Eschtah's domain.

Naab's dogged persistence and the Navajos' faithfulness carried them into the country of the Moki Indians, a tribe classed as slaves by the proud race of Eschtah. Here they searched the villages and ancient tombs and ruins, but of Mescal there was never a trace.

Hare rode as diligently and searched as indefatigably as August, but he never had any real hope of finding the girl. To hunt for her, however, despite its hopelessness, was a melancholy satisfaction, for never was she out of his mind.

Nor was the month's hard riding with the Navajos without profit. He made friends with the Indians, and learned to speak many of their words. Then a whole host of desert tricks became part of his accumulating knowledge. In climbing the crags, in looking for water and grass, in loosing Silvermane at night and searching for him at dawn, in marking tracks on hard ground, in all the sight and feeling and smell of desert things he learned much from the Navajos. The whole outward life of the Indian was concerned with the material aspect of Nature—dust, rock, air, wind, smoke, the cedars, the beasts of the desert. These things made up the Indians' day. The Navajos were worshippers of the physical; the sun was their supreme god. In the mornings when the gray of dawn flushed to rosy red they began their chant to the sun. At sunset the Navajos were watchful and silent with faces westward. The Moki Indians also, Hare observed, had their morning service to the great giver of light. In the gloom of early dawn, before the pink appeared in the east, and all was whitening gray, the Mokis emerged from their little mud and stone huts and sat upon the roofs with blanketed and drooping heads.

One day August Naab showed in few words how significant a factor the sun was in the lives of desert men.

"We've got to turn back," he said to Hare. "The sun's getting hot and the snow will melt in the mountains. If the Colorado rises too high we can't cross."

They were two days in riding back to the encampment. Eschtah received them in dignified silence, expressive of his regret. When their time of departure arrived he accompanied them to the head of the nearest trail, which started down from Saweep Peak, the highest point of Echo Cliffs. It was the Navajos' outlook over the Painted Desert.

"Mescal is there," said August Naab. "She's there with the slave Eschtah gave her. He leads Mescal. Who can follow him there?"

The old chieftain reined in his horse, beside the time-hollowed trail, and the same hand that waved his white friend downward swept up in slow stately gesture toward the illimitable expanse. It was a warrior's salute to an unconquered world. Hare saw in his falcon eyes the still gleam, the brooding fire, the mystical passion that haunted the eyes of Mescal.

"The slave without a tongue is a wolf. He scents the trails and the waters. Eschtah's eyes have grown old watching here, but he has seen no Indian who could follow Mescal's slave. Eschtah will lie there, but no Indian will know the path to the place of his sleep. Mescal's trail is lost in the sand. No man may find it. Eschtah's words are wisdom. Look!"

To search for any living creatures in that borderless domain of colored dune, of shifting cloud of sand, of purple curtain shrouding mesa and dome, appeared the vainest of all human endeavors. It seemed a veritable rainbow realm of the sun. At first only the beauty stirred Hare—he saw the copper belt close under the cliffs, the white beds of alkali and washes of silt farther out, the wind-ploughed canyons and dust-encumbered ridges ranging west and east, the scalloped slopes of the flat tableland rising low, the tips of volcanic peaks leading the eye beyond to veils and vapors hovering over blue clefts and dim line of level lanes, and so on, and on, out to the vast unknown. Then Hare grasped a little of its meaning. It was a sun-painted, sun-governed world. Here was deep and majestic Nature eternal and unchangeable. But it was only through Eschtah's eyes that he saw its parched slopes, its terrifying desolateness, its sleeping death.

When the old chieftain's lips opened Hare anticipated the austere speech, the import that meant only pain to him, and his whole inner being seemed to shrink.

"The White Prophet's child of red blood is lost to him," said Eschtah. "The Flower of the Desert is as a grain of drifting sand."

XIII. THE SOMBRE LINE

AUGUST NAAB hoped that Mescal might have returned in his absence; but to Hare such hope was vain. The women of the oasis met them with gloomy faces presaging bad news, and they were reluctant to tell it. Mescal's flight had been forgotten in the sterner and sadder misfortune that had followed.

Snap Naab's wife lay dangerously ill, the victim of his drunken frenzy. For days after the departure of August and Jack the man had kept himself in a stupor; then his store of drink failing, he had come out of his almost senseless state into an insane frenzy. He had tried to kill his wife and wreck his cottage, being prevented in the nick of time by Dave Naab, the only one of his brothers who dared approach him. Then he had ridden off on the White Sage trail and had not been heard from since.

The Mormon put forth all his skill in surgery and medicine to save the life of his son's wife, but he admitted that he had grave misgivings as to her recovery. But these in no manner affected his patience, gentleness, and cheer. While there was life there was hope, said August Naab. He bade Hare, after he had rested awhile, to pack and ride out to the range, and tell his sons that he would come later.

It was a relief to leave the oasis, and Hare started the same day, and made Silver Cup that night. As he rode under the low-branching cedars toward the bright camp-fire he looked about him sharply. But not one of the four faces ruddy in the glow belonged to Snap Naab.

"Hello, Jack," called Dave Naab, into the dark. "I knew that was you. Silvermane sure rings bells when he hoofs it down the stones. How're you and dad? and did you find Mescal? I'll bet that desert child led you clear to the Little Colorado."

Hare told the story of the fruitless search.

"It's no more than we expected," said Dave. "The man doesn't live who can trail the peon. Mescal's like a captured wild mustang that's slipped her halter and gone free. She'll die out there on the desert or turn into a stalk of the Indian cactus for which she's named. It's a pity, for she's a good girl, too good for Snap."

"What's your news?" inquired Hare.

"Oh, nothing much," replied Dave, with a short laugh. "The cattle wintered well. We've had little to do but hang round and watch. Zeke and I chased old Whitefoot one day, and got pretty close to Seeping Springs. We met Joe Stube, a rider who was once a friend of Zeke's. He's with Holderness now, and he said that Holderness had rebuilt the corrals at the spring; also he has put up a big cabin, and he has a dozen riders there. Stube told us Snap had been shooting up White Sage. He finished up by killing Snood. They got into an argument about you."

"About me!"

"Yes, it seems that Snood took your part, and Snap wouldn't stand for it. Too bad! Snood was a good fellow. There's no use talking, Snap's going too far—he is—" Dave did not conclude his remark, and the silence was more significant than any utterance.

"What will the Mormons in White Sage say about Snap's killing Snood?"

"They've said a lot. This even-break business goes all right among gun-fighters, but the Mormons call killing murder. They've outlawed Culver, and Snap will be outlawed next."

"Your father hinted that Snap would find the desert too small for him and me?"

"Jack, you can't be too careful. I've wanted to speak to you about it. Snap will ride in here some day and then—" Dave's pause was not reassuring.

And it was only on the third day after Dave's remark that Hare, riding down the mountain with a deer he had shot, looked out from the trail and saw Snap's cream pinto trotting toward Silver Cup. Beside Snap rode a tall man on a big bay. When Hare reached camp he reported to George and Zeke what he had seen, and learned in reply that Dave had already caught sight of the horsemen, and had gone down to the edge of the cedars. While they were speaking Dave hurriedly ran up the trail.

"It's Snap and Holderness," he called out, sharply. "What's Snap doing with Holderness? What's he bringing him here for?"

"I don't like the looks of it," replied Zeke, deliberately.

"Jack, what'll you do?" asked Dave, suddenly.

"Do? What can I do? I'm not going to run out of camp because of a visit from men who don't like me."

"It might be wisest."

"Do you ask me to run to avoid a meeting with your brother?"

"No." The dull red came to Dave's cheek. "But will you draw on him?"

"Certainly not. He's August Naab's son and your brother."

"Yes, and you're my friend, which Snap won't think of. Will you draw on Holderness, then?"

"For the life of me, Dave, I can't tell you," replied Hare, pacing the trail. "Something must break loose in me before I can kill a man. I'd draw, I suppose, in self-defence. But what good would it do me to pull too late? Dave, this thing is what I've feared. I'm not afraid of Snap or Holderness, not that way. I mean I'm not ready. Look here, would either of them shoot an unarmed man?"

"Lord, I hope not; I don't think so. But you're packing your gun."

Hare unbuckled his cartridge-belt, which held his Colt, and hung it over the pommel of his saddle; then he sat down on one of the stone seats near the camp-fire.

"There they come," whispered Zeke, and he rose to his feet, followed by George.

"Steady, you fellows," said Dave, with a warning glance. "I'll do the talking."

Holderness and Snap appeared among the cedars, and trotting out into the glade reined in their mounts a few paces from the fire. Dave Naab stood directly before Hare, and George and Zeke stepped aside.

"Howdy, boys?" called out Holderness, with a smile, which was like a gleam of light playing on a frozen lake. His amber eyes were steady, their gaze contracted into piercing yellow points. Dave studied the cattle-man with cool scorn, but refusing to speak to him, addressed his brother.

"Snap, what do you mean by riding in here with this fellow?"

"I'm Holderness's new foreman. We're just looking round," replied Snap. The hard lines, the sullen shade, the hawk-beak cruelty had returned tenfold to his face and his glance was like a living, leaping flame.

"New foreman!" exclaimed Dave. His jaw dropped and he stared in amazement. "No—you can't mean that—you're drunk!"

"That's what I said," growled Snap.

"You're a liar!" shouted Dave, a crimson blot blurring with the brown on his cheeks. He jumped off the ground in his fury.

"It's true, Naab; he's my new foreman," put in Holderness, suavely. "A hundred a month—in gold—and I've got as good a place for you."

"Well, by G—d!" Dave's arms came down and his face blanched to his lips. "Holderness!"

"I know what you'd say," interrupted the ranchman.

"But stop it. I know you're game. And what's the use of fighting? I'm talking business. I'll—"

"You can't talk business or anything else to me," said Dave Naab, and he veered sharply toward his brother. "Say it again, Snap Naab. You've hired out to ride for this man?"

"That's it."

"You're going against your father, your brothers, your own flesh and blood?"

"I can't see it that way."

"Then you're a drunken, easily-led fool. This man's no rancher. He's a rustler. He ruined Martin Cole, the father of your first wife. He's stolen our cattle; he's jumped our water-rights. He's trying to break us. For God's sake, ain't you a man?"

"Things have gone bad for me," replied Snap, sullenly, shifting in his saddle. "I reckon I'll do better to cut out alone for myself."

"You crooked cur! But you're only my half-brother, after all. I always knew you'd come to something bad, but I never thought you'd disgrace the Naabs and break your father's heart. Now then, what do you want here? Be quick. This's our range and you and your boss can't ride here. You can't even water your horses. Out with it!"

At this, Hare, who had been so absorbed as to forget himself, suddenly felt a cold tightening of the skin of his face, and a hard swell of his breast. The dance of Snap's eyes, the downward flit of his hand seemed instantaneous with a red flash and loud report. Instinctively Hare dodged, but the light impact of something like a puff of air gave place to a tearing hot agony. Then he slipped down, back to the stone, with a bloody hand fumbling at his breast.

Dave leaped with tigerish agility, and knocking up the levelled Colt, held Snap as in a vise. George Naab gave Holderness's horse a sharp kick which made the mettlesome beast jump so suddenly that his rider was nearly unseated. Zeke ran to Hare and laid him back against the stone.

"Cool down, there!" ordered Zeke. "He's done for."

"My God—my God!" cried Dave, in a broken voice. "Not—not dead?"

"Shot through the heart!"

Dave Naab flung Snap backward, almost off his horse. "D—n you! run, or I'll kill you. And you, Holderness! Remember! If we ever meet again—you draw!" He tore a branch from a cedar and slashed both horses. They plunged out of the glade, and clattering over the stones, brushing the cedars, disappeared. Dave groped blindly back toward his brothers.

"Zeke, this's awful. Another murder by Snap! And my friend!... Who's to tell father?"

Then Hare sat up, leaning against the stone, his shirt open and his bare shoulder bloody; his face was pale, but his eyes were smiling. "Cheer up, Dave. I'm not dead yet."

"Sure he's not," said Zeke. "He ducked none too soon, or too late, and caught the bullet high up in the shoulder."

Dave sat down very quietly without a word, and the hand he laid on Hare's knee shook a little.

"When I saw George go for his gun," went on Zeke, "I knew there'd be a lively time in a minute if it wasn't stopped, so I just said Jack was dead."

"Do you think they came over to get me?" asked Hare.

"No doubt," replied Dave, lifting his face and wiping the sweat from his brow. "I knew that from the first, but I was so dazed by Snap's going over to Holderness that I couldn't keep my wits, and I didn't mark Snap edging over till too late."

"Listen, I hear horses," said Zeke, looking up from his task over Hare's wound.

"It's Billy, up on the home trail," added George. "Yes, and there's father with him. Good Lord, must we tell him about Snap?"

"Some one must tell him," answered Dave.

"That'll be you, then. You always do the talking."

August Naab galloped into the glade, and swung himself out of the saddle. "I heard a shot. What's this? Who's hurt?—Hare! Why—lad—how is it with you?"

"Not bad," rejoined Hare.

"Let me see," August thrust Zeke aside. "A bullet-hole—just missed the bone—not serious. Tie it up tight. I'll take him home to-morrow.... Hare, who's been here?"

"Snap rode in and left his respects."

"Snap! Already? Yet I knew it—I saw it. You had Providence with you, lad, for this wound is not bad. Snap surprised you, then?"

"No. I knew it was coming."

"Jack hung his belt and gun on Silvermane's saddle," said Dave. "He didn't feel as if he could draw on either Snap or Holderness—"

"Holderness!"

"Yes. Snap rode in with Holderness. Hare thought if he was unarmed they wouldn't draw. But Snap did."

"Was he drunk?"

"No. They came over to kill Hare." Dave went on to recount the incident in full. "And—and see here, dad—that's not all. Snap's gone to the bad."

Dave Naab hid his face while he told of his brother's treachery; the others turned away, and Hare closed his eyes.

For long moments there was silence broken only by the tramp of the old man as he strode heavily to and fro. At last the footsteps ceased, and Hare opened his eyes to see Naab's tall form erect, his arms uplifted, his shaggy head rigid.

"Hare," began August, presently. "I'm responsible for this cowardly attack on you. I brought you out here. This is the second one. Beware of the third! I see—but tell me, do you remember that I said you must meet Snap as man to man?"

"Yes."

"Don't you want to live?"

"Of course."

"You hold to no Mormon creed?"

"Why, no," Hare replied, wonderingly.

"What was the reason I taught you my trick with a gun?"

"I suppose it was to help me to defend myself."

"Then why do you let yourself be shot down in cold blood? Why did you hang up your gun? Why didn't you draw on Snap? Was it because of his father, his brothers, his family?"

"Partly, but not altogether," replied Hare, slowly. "I didn't know before what I know now. My flesh sickened at the thought of killing a man, even to save my own life; and to kill—your son—"

"No son of mine!" thundered Naab. "Remember that when next you meet. I don't want your blood on my hands. Don't stand to be killed like a sheep! If you have felt duty to me, I release you."

Zeke finished bandaging the wound. Making a bed of blankets he lifted Hare into it, and covered him, cautioning him to lie still. Hare had a sensation of extreme lassitude, a deep drowsiness which permeated even to his bones. There were intervals of oblivion, then a time when the stars blinked in his eyes; he heard the wind, Silvermane's bell, the murmur of voices, yet all seemed remote from him, intangible as things in a dream.

He rode home next day, drooping in the saddle and fainting at the end of the trail, with the strong arm of August Naab upholding him. His wound was dressed and he was put to bed, where he lay sleeping most of the time, brooding the rest.

In three weeks he was in the saddle again, riding out over the red strip of desert toward the range. During his convalescence he had learned that he had come to the sombre line of choice. Either he must deliberately back away, and show his unfitness to survive in the desert, or he must step across into its dark wilds. The stern question haunted him. Yet he knew a swift decision waited on the crucial moment.

He sought lonely rides more than ever, and, like Silvermane, he was always watching and listening. His duties carried him half way to Seeping Springs, across the valley to the red wall, up the slope of Coconina far into the forest of stately pines. What with Silvermane's wonderful scent and sight, and his own constant watchfulness, there were never range-riders or wild horses nor even deer near him without his knowledge.

The days flew by; spring had long since given place to summer; the blaze of sun and blast of flying sand were succeeded by the cooling breezes from the mountain; October brought the flurries of snow and November the dark storm-clouds.

Hare was the last of the riders to be driven off the mountain. The brothers were waiting for him at Silver Cup, and they at once packed and started for home.

August Naab listened to the details of the range-riding since his absence, with silent surprise. Holderness and Snap had kept away from Silver Cup after the supposed killing of Hare. Occasionally a group of horsemen rode across the valley or up a trail within sight of Dave and his followers, but there was never a meeting. Not a steer had been driven off the range that summer and fall; and except for the menace always hanging in the blue smoke over Seeping Springs the range-riding had passed without unusual incident.

So for Hare the months had gone by swiftly; though when he looked back afterward they seemed years. The winter at the oasis he filled as best he could, with the children playing in the yard, with Silvermane under the sunny lee of the great red wall, with any work that offered itself. It was during the long evenings, when he could not be active, that time oppressed him, and the memories of the past hurt him. A glimpse of the red sunset through the cliff-gate toward the west would start the train of thought; he both loved and hated the Painted Desert. Mescal was there in the purple shadows. He dreamed of her in the glowing embers of the log-fire. He saw her on Black Bolly with hair flying free to the wind. And he could not shut out the picture of her sitting in the corner of the room, silent, with bowed head, while the man to whom she was pledged hung close over her. That memory had a sting. It was like a spark of fire dropped on the wound in his breast where the desert-hawk had struck him. It was like a light gleaming on the sombre line he was waiting to cross.

XIV. WOLF

ON the anniversary of the night Mescal disappeared the mysterious voice which had called to Hare so often and so strangely again pierced his slumber, and brought him bolt upright in his bed shuddering and listening. The dark room was as quiet as a tomb. He fell back into his blankets trembling with emotion. Sleep did not close his eyes again that night; he lay in a fever waiting for the dawn, and when the gray gloom lightened he knew what he must do.

After breakfast he sought August Naab. "May I go across the river?" he asked.

The old man looked up from his carpenter's task and fastened his glance on Hare. "Mescal?"

"Yes."

"I saw it long ago." He shook his head and spread his great hands. "There's no use for me to say what the desert is. If you ever come back you'll bring her. Yes, you may go. It's a man's deed. God keep you!"

Hare spoke to no other person; he filled one saddle-bag with grain, another with meat, bread, and dried fruits, strapped a five-gallon leather water-sack back of Silvermane's saddle, and set out toward the river. At the crossing-bar he removed Silvermane's equipments and placed them in the boat. At that moment a long howl, as of a dog baying the moon, startled him from his musings, and his eyes sought the river-bank, up and down, and then the opposite side. An animal, which at first he took to be a gray timber-wolf, was running along the sand-bar of the landing.

"Pretty white for a wolf," he muttered. "Might be a Navajo dog."

The beast sat down on his haunches and, lifting a lean head, sent up a doleful howl. Then he began trotting along the bar, every few paces stepping to the edge of the water. Presently he spied Hare, and he began to bark furiously.

"It's a dog all right; wants to get across," said Hare. "Where have I seen him?"

Suddenly he sprang to his feet, almost upsetting the boat. "He's like Mescal's Wolf!" He looked closer, his heart beginning to thump, and then he yelled: "Ki-yi! Wolf! Hyer! Hyer!"

The dog leaped straight up in the air, and coming down, began to dash back and forth along the sand with piercing yelps.

"It's Wolf! Mescal must be near," cried Hare. A veil obscured his sight, and every vein was like a hot cord. "Wolf! Wolf! I'm coming!"

XIV. WOLF

With trembling hands he tied Silvermane's bridle to the stern seat of the boat and pushed off. In his eagerness he rowed too hard, dragging Silvermane's nose under water, and he had to check himself. Time and again he turned to call to the dog. At length the bow grated on the sand, and Silvermane emerged with a splash and a snort.

"Wolf, old fellow!" cried Hare. "Where's Mescal? Wolf, where is she?" He threw his arms around the dog. Wolf whined, licked Hare's face, and breaking away, ran up the sandy trail, and back again. But he barked no more; he waited to see if Hare was following.

"All right, Wolf—coming." Never had Hare saddled so speedily, nor mounted so quickly. He sent Silvermane into the willow-skirted trail close behind the dog, up on the rocky bench, and then under the bulging wall. Wolf reached the level between the canyon and Echo Cliffs, and then started straight west toward the Painted Desert. He trotted a few rods and turned to see if the man was coming.

Doubt, fear, uncertainty ceased for Hare. With the first blast of dust-scented air in his face he knew Wolf was leading him to Mescal. He knew that the cry he had heard in his dream was hers, that the old mysterious promise of the desert had at last begun its fulfilment. He gave one sharp exultant answer to that call. The horizon, ever-widening, lay before him, and the treeless plains, the sun-scorched slopes, the sandy stretches, the massed blocks of black mesas, all seemed to welcome him; his soul sang within him.

For Mescal was there. Far away she must be, a mere grain of sand in all that world of drifting sands, perhaps ill, perhaps hurt, but alive, waiting for him, calling for him, crying out with a voice that no distance could silence. He did not see the sharp peaks as pitiless barriers, nor the mesas and domes as black-faced death, nor the moisture-drinking sands as life-sucking foes to plant and beast and man. That painted wonderland had sheltered Mescal for a year. He had loved it for its color, its change, its secrecy; he loved it now because it had not been a grave for Mescal, but a home. Therefore he laughed at the deceiving yellow distances in the foreground of glistening mesas, at the deceiving purple distances of the far-off horizon. The wind blew a song in his ears; the dry desert odors were fragrance in his nostrils; the sand tasted sweet between his teeth, and the quivering heat-waves, veiling the desert in transparent haze, framed beautiful pictures for his eyes.

Wolf kept to the fore for some thirty paces, and though he had ceased to stop, he still looked back to see if the horse and man were following. Hare had noted the dog occasionally in the first hours of travel, but he had given his eyes mostly to the broken line of sky and desert in the west, to the receding contour of Echo Cliffs, to the spread and break of the desert near at hand. Here and there life showed itself in a gaunt coyote sneaking into the cactus, or a horned toad huddling down in the dust, or a jewel-eyed lizard sunning himself upon a stone. It was only when his excited fancy had cooled that Hare came to look closely at Wolf. But for the dog's color he could not have been distinguished from a real wolf. His head and ears and tail drooped, and he was lame in his right front paw.

Hare halted in the shade of a stone, dismounted and called the dog to him. Wolf returned without quickness, without eagerness, without any of the old-time friendliness of shepherding days. His eyes were sad and strange. Hare felt a sudden foreboding, but rejected it with passionate force. Yet a chill remained. Lifting Wolf's paw he discovered that the ball of the foot was worn through; whereupon he called into service a piece of buckskin, and fashioning a rude moccasin he tied it round the foot. Wolf licked his hand, but there was no change in the sad light of his eyes. He turned toward the west as if anxious to be off.

"All right, old fellow," said Hare, "only go slow. From the look of that foot I think you've turned back on a long trail."

Again they faced the west, dog leading, man following, and addressed themselves to a gradual ascent. When it had been surmounted Hare realized that his ride so far had brought him only through an anteroom; the real portal now stood open to the Painted Desert. The immensity of the thing seemed to reach up to him with a thousand lines, ridges, canyons, all ascending out of a purple gulf. The arms of the desert enveloped him, a chill beneath their warmth.

As he descended into the valley, keeping close to Wolf, he marked a straight course in line with a volcanic spur. He was surprised when the dog, though continually threading jumbles of rock, heading canyons, crossing deep washes, and going round obstructions, always veered back to this bearing as true as a compass-needle to its magnet.

Hare felt the air growing warmer and closer as he continued the descent. By mid-afternoon, when he had travelled perhaps thirty miles, he was moist from head to foot, and Silvermane's coat was wet. Looking backward Hare had a blank feeling of loss; the sweeping line of Echo Cliffs had retreated behind the horizon. There was no familiar landmark left.

Sunset brought him to a standstill, as much from its sudden glorious gathering of brilliant crimsons splashed with gold, as from its warning that the day was done. Hare made his camp beside a stone which would serve as a wind-break. He laid his saddle for a pillow and his blanket for a bed. He gave Silvermane a nose-bag full of water and then one of grain; he fed the dog, and afterward attended to his own needs. When his task was done the desert brightness had faded to gray; the warm air had blown away on a cool breeze, and night approached. He scooped out a little hollow in the sand for his hips, took a last look at Silvermane haltered to the rock, and calling Wolf to his side stretched himself to rest. He was used to lying on the ground, under the open sky, out where the wind blew and the sand seeped in, yet all these were different on this night. He was in the Painted Desert; Wolf crept close to him; Mescal lay somewhere under the blue-white stars.

He awakened and arose before any color of dawn hinted of the day. While he fed his four-footed companions the sky warmed and lightened. A tinge of rose gathered in the east. The air was cool and transparent. He tried to cheer Wolf out of his sad-eyed forlornness, and failed.

XIV. WOLF

Hare vaulted into the saddle. The day had its possibilities, and while he had sobered down from his first unthinking exuberance, there was still a ring in his voice as he called to the dog:

"On, Wolf, on, old boy!"

Out of the east burst the sun, and the gray curtain was lifted by shafts of pink and white and gold, flashing westward long trails of color.

When they started the actions of the dog showed Hare that Wolf was not tracking a back-trail, but travelling by instinct. There were draws which necessitated a search for a crossing, and areas of broken rock which had to be rounded, and steep flat mesas rising in the path, and strips of deep sand and canyons impassable for long distances. But the dog always found a way and always came back to a line with the black spur that Hare had marked. It still stood in sharp relief, no nearer than before, receding with every step, an illusive landmark, which Hare began to distrust.

Then quite suddenly it vanished in the ragged blue mass of the Ghost Mountains. Hare had seen them several times, though never so distinctly. The purple tips, the bold rock-ribs, the shadowed canyons, so sharp and clear in the morning light—how impossible to believe that these were only the deceit of the desert mirage! Yet so they were; even for the Navajos they were spirit-mountains.

The splintered desert-floor merged into an area of sand. Wolf slowed his trot, and Silvermane's hoofs sunk deep. Dismounting Hare labored beside him, and felt the heat steal through his boots and burn the soles of his feet. Hare plodded onward, stopping once to tie another moccasin on Wolf's worn paw, this time the left one; and often he pulled the stopper from the water-bag and cooled his parching lips and throat. The waves of the sand-dunes were as the waves of the ocean. He did not look backward, dreading to see what little progress he had made. Ahead were miles on miles of graceful heaps, swelling mounds, crested ridges, all different, yet regular and rhythmical, drift on drift, dune on dune, in endless waves. Wisps of sand were whipped from their summits in white ribbons and wreaths, and pale clouds of sand shrouded little hollows. The morning breeze, rising out of the west, approached in a rippling lines like the crest of an inflowing tide.

Silvermane snorted, lifted his ears and looked westward toward a yellow pall which swooped up from the desert.

"Sand-storm," said Hare, and calling Wolf he made for the nearest rock that was large enough to shelter them. The whirling sand-cloud mushroomed into an enormous desert covering, engulfing the dunes, obscuring the light. The sunlight failed; the day turned to gloom. Then an eddying fog of sand and dust enveloped Hare. His last glimpse before he covered his face with a silk handkerchief was of sheets of sand streaming past his shelter. The storm came with a low, soft, hissing roar, like the sound in a sea-shell magnified. Breathing through the handkerchief Hare avoided inhaling the sand which beat against his face, but the finer dust particles filtered through and stifled him. At first he felt that he would suffocate, and he coughed and gasped; but presently, when the thicker sand-clouds had passed, he managed to get air enough to breathe. Then he waited patiently while the steady seeping rustle swept by, and the band of his hat sagged heavier, and the load on his shoulders had to be continually shaken off, and the weighty trap round his feet crept upward. When the light, fine touch ceased he removed the covering from his face to see himself standing nearly to his knees in sand, and Silvermane's back and the saddle burdened with it. The storm was moving eastward, a dull red now with the sun faintly showing through it like a ball of fire.

"Well, Wolf, old boy, how many storms like that will we have to weather?" asked Hare, in a cheery tone which he had to force. He knew these sand-storms were but vagaries of the desert-wind. Before the hour closed he had to seek the cover of a stone and wait for another to pass. Then he was caught in the open, with not a shelter in sight. He was compelled to turn his back to a third storm, the worst of all, and to bear as best he could the heavy impact of the first blow, and the succeeding rush and flow of sand. After that his head drooped and he wearily trudged beside Silvermane, dreading the interminable distance he must cover before once more gaining hard ground. But he discovered that it was useless to try to judge distance on the desert. What had appeared miles at his last look turned out to be only rods.

It was good to get into the saddle again and face clear air. Far away the black spur again loomed up, now surrounded by groups of mesas with sage-slopes tinged with green. That surely meant the end of this long trail; the faint spots of green lent suggestion of a desert waterhole; there Mescal must be, hidden in some shady canyon. Hare built his hopes anew.

So he pressed on down a plain of bare rock dotted by huge bowlders; and out upon a level floor of scant sage and greasewood where a few living creatures, a desert-hawk sailing low, lizards darting into holes, and a swiftly running ground-bird, emphasized the lack of life in the waste. He entered a zone of clay-dunes of violet and heliotrope hues; and then a belt of lava and cactus. Reddish points studded the desert, and here and there were meagre patches of white grass. Far away myriads of cactus plants showed like a troop of distorted horsemen. As he went on the grass failed, and streams of jagged lava flowed downward. Beds of cinders told of the fury of a volcanic fire. Soon Hare had to dismount to make moccasins for Wolf's hind feet; and to lead Silvermane carefully over the cracked lava. For a while there were strips of ground bare of lava and harboring only an occasional bunch of cactus, but soon every foot free of the reddish iron bore a projecting mass of fierce spikes and thorns. The huge barrel-shaped cacti, and thickets of slender dark-green rods with bayonet points, and broad leaves with yellow spines, drove Hare and his sore-footed fellow-travellers to the lava.

Hare thought there must be an end to it some time, yet it seemed as though he were never to cross that black forbidding inferno. Blistered by the heat, pierced by the thorns, lame from long toil on the lava, he was sorely spent when once more he stepped out upon the bare desert. On pitching camp he made the grievous discovery that the water-bag had leaked or the water had evaporated, for there was only enough left for one more day. He ministered to thirsty dog and horse in silence, his mind revolving the grim fact of his situation.

His little fire of greasewood threw a wan circle into the surrounding blackness. Not a sound hinted of life. He longed for even the bark of a coyote. Silvermane stooped motionless with tired head. Wolf stretched limply on the sand. Hare rolled into his blanket and stretched out with slow aching relief.

He dreamed he was a boy roaming over the green hills of the old farm, wading through dewy clover-fields, and fishing in the Connecticut River. It was the long vacationtime, an endless freedom. Then he was at the swimming-hole, and playmates tied his clothes in knots, and with shouts of glee ran up the bank leaving him there to shiver.

When he awakened the blazing globe of the sun had arisen over the eastern horizon, and the red of the desert swathed all the reach of valley.

Hare pondered whether he should use his water at once or dole it out. That ball of fire in the sky, a glazed circle, like iron at white heat, decided for him. The sun would be hot and would evaporate such water as leakage did not claim, and so he shared alike with Wolf, and gave the rest to Silvermane.

For an hour the mocking lilac mountains hung in the air and then paled in the intense light. The day was soundless and windless, and the heat-waves rose from the desert like smoke. For Hare the realities were the baked clay flats, where Silvermane broke through at every step; the beds of alkali, which sent aloft clouds of powdered dust; the deep gullies full of round bowlders; thickets of mesquite and prickly thorn which tore at his legs; the weary detour to head the canyons; the climb to get between two bridging mesas; and always the haunting presence of the sad-eyed dog. His unrealities were the shimmering sheets of water in every low place; the baseless mountains floating in the air; the green slopes rising close at hand; beautiful buttes of dark blue riding the open sand, like monstrous barks at sea; the changing outlines of desert shapes in pink haze and veils of purple and white lustre—all illusions, all mysterious tricks of the mirage.

In the heat of midday Hare yielded to its influence and reined in his horse under a slate-bank where there was shade. His face was swollen and peeling, and his lips had begun to dry and crack and taste of alkali. Then Wolf pattered on; Silvermane kept at his heels; Hare dozed in the saddle. His eyes burned in their sockets from the glare, and it was a relief to shut out the barren reaches. So the afternoon waned.

Silvermane stumbled, jolting Hare out of his stupid lethargy. Before him spread a great field of bowlders with not a slope or a ridge or a mesa or an escarpment. Not even a tip of a spur rose in the background. He rubbed his sore eyes. Was this another illusion?

When Silvermane started onward Hare thought of the Navajos' custom to trust horse and dog in such an emergency. They were desert-bred; beyond human understanding were their sight and scent. He was at the mercy now of Wolf's instinct and Silvermane's endurance. Resignation brought him a certain calmness of soul, cold as the touch of an icy hand on fevered cheek. He remembered the desert secret in Mescal's eyes; he was about to solve it. He remembered August Naab's words: "It's a man's deed!" If so, he had achieved the spirit of it, if not the letter. He remembered Eschtah's tribute to the wilderness of painted wastes: "There is the grave of the Navajo, and no one knows the trail to the place of his sleep!" He remembered the something evermore about to be, the unknown always subtly calling; now it was revealed in the stone-fettering grip of the desert. It had opened wide to him, bright with its face of danger, beautiful with its painted windows, inscrutable with its alluring call. Bidding him enter, it had closed behind him; now he looked upon it in its iron order, its strange ruins racked by fire, its inevitable remorselessness.

XV. DESERT NIGHT

THE gray stallion, finding the rein loose on his neck, trotted forward and overtook the dog, and thereafter followed at his heels. With the setting of the sun a slight breeze stirred, and freshened as twilight fell, rolling away the sultry atmosphere. Then the black desert night mantled the plain.

For a while this blackness soothed the pain of Hare's sun-blinded eyes. It was a relief to have the unattainable horizon line blotted out. But by-and-by the opaque gloom brought home to him, as the day had never done, the reality of his solitude. He was alone in this immense place of barrenness, and his dumb companions were the world to him. Wolf pattered onward, a silent guide; and Silvermane followed, never lagging, sure-footed in the dark, faithful to his master. All the love Hare had borne the horse was as nothing to that which came to him on this desert night. In and out, round and round, ever winding, ever zigzagging, Silvermane hung close to Wolf, and the sandy lanes between the bowlders gave forth no sound. Dog and horse, free to choose their trail, trotted onward miles and miles into the night.

A pale light in the east turned to a glow, then to gold, and the round disc of the moon silhouetted the black bowlders on the horizon. It cleared the dotted line and rose, an oval orange-hued strange moon, not mellow nor silvery nor gloriously brilliant as Hare had known it in the past, but a vast dead-gold melancholy orb, rising sadly over the desert. To Hare it was the crowning reminder of lifelessness; it fitted this world of dull gleaming stones.

Silvermane went lame and slackened his trot, causing Hare to rein in and dismount. He lifted the right forefoot, the one the horse had favored, and found a stone imbedded tightly in the cloven hoof. He pried it out with his knife and mounted again. Wolf shone faintly far ahead, and presently he uttered a mournful cry which sent a chill to the rider's heart. The silence had been oppressive before; now it was terrible. It was not a silence of life. It had been broken suddenly by Wolf's howl, and had closed sharply after it, without echo; it was a silence of death.

Hare took care not to fall behind Wolf again, he had no wish to hear that cry repeated. The dog moved onward with silent feet; the horse wound after him with hoofs padded in the sand; the moon lifted and the desert gleamed; the bowlders grew larger and the lanes wider. So the night wore on, and Hare's eyelids grew heavy, and his whole weary body cried out for rest and forgetfulness. He nodded until he swayed in the saddle; then righted himself, only to doze again. The east gave birth to the morning star. The whitening sky was the harbinger of day. Hare could not bring himself to face the light and heat, and he stopped at a wind-worn cave under a shelving rock. He was asleep when he rolled out on the sand-strewn floor. Once he awoke and it was still day, for his eyes quickly shut upon the glare. He lay sweltering till once more slumber claimed him. The dog awakened him, with cold nose and low whine. Another twilight had fallen. Hare crawled out, stiff and sore, hungry and parching with thirst. He made an attempt to eat, but it was a failure. There was a dry burning in his throat, a dizzy feeling in his brain, and there were red flashes before his eyes. Wolf refused meat, and Silvermane turned from the grain, and lowered his head to munch a few blades of desert grass.

Then the journey began, and the night fell black. A cool wind blew from the west, the white stars blinked, the weird moon rose with its ghastly glow. Huge bowlders rose before him in grotesque shapes, tombs and pillars and statues of Nature's dead, carved by wind and sand. But some had life in Hare's disordered fancy. They loomed and towered over him, and stalked abroad and peered at him with deep-set eyes.

Hare fought with all his force against this mood of gloom. Wolf was not a phantom; he trotted forward with unerring instinct; and he would find water, and that meant life. Silvermane, desert-steeled, would travel to the furthermost corner of this hell of sand-swept stone. Hare tried to collect all his spirit, all his energies, but the battle seemed to be going against him. All about him was silence, breathless silence, insupportable silence of ages. Desert spectres danced in the darkness. The worn-out moon gleamed golden over the worn-out waste. Desolation lurked under the sable shadows.

Hare rode on into the night, tumbled from his saddle in the gray of dawn to sleep, and stumbled in the twilight to his drooping horse. His eyes were blind now to the desert shapes, his brain burned and his tongue filled his mouth. Silvermane trod ever upon Wolf's heels; he had come into the kingdom of his desert-strength; he lifted his drooping head and lengthened his stride; weariness had gone and he snorted his welcome to something on the wind. Then he passed the limping dog and led the way.

Hare held to the pommel and bent dizzily forward in the saddle. Silvermane was going down, step by step, with metallic clicks upon flinty rock. Whether he went down or up was all the same to Hare; he held on with closed eyes and whispered to himself. Down and down, step by step, cracking the stones with iron-shod hoofs, the gray stallion worked his perilous way, sure-footed as a mountain-sheep. Then he stopped with a great slow heave and bent his head.

The black bulge of a canyon rim blurred in Hare's hot eyes. A trickling sound penetrated his tired brain. His ears had grown like his eyes—false. Only another delusion! As he had been tortured with the sight of lake and stream now he was to be tortured with the sound of running water. Yet he listened, for it was sweet even in its mockery. What a clear musical tinkle, like silver bells tossing on the wind! He listened. Soft murmuring flow, babble and gurgle, little hollow fall and splash!

Suddenly Silvermane, lifting his head, broke the silence of the canyon with a great sigh of content. It pierced the dull fantasy of Hare's mind; it burst the gloomy spell. The sigh and the snort which followed were Silvermane's triumphant signals when he had drunk his fill.

Hare fell from the saddle. The gray dog lay stretched low in the darkness. Hare crawled beside him and reached out with his hot hands. Smooth cool marble rock, growing slippery, then wet, led into running water. He slid forward on his face and wonderful cold thrills quivered over his burning skin. He drank and drank until he could drink no more. Then he lay back upon the rock; the madness of his brain went out with the light of the stars, and he slept.

When he awoke red canyon walls leaned far above him to a gap spanned by blue sky. A song of rushing water murmured near his ears. He looked down; a spring gushed from a crack in the wall; Silvermane cropped green bushes, and Wolf sat on his haunches waiting, but no longer with sad eyes and strange mien. Hare raised himself, looking again and again, and slowly gathered his wits. The crimson blur had gone from his eyes and the burning from his skin, and the painful swelling from his tongue.

He drank long and deeply, and rising with clearing thoughts and thankful heart, he kissed Wolf's white head, and laid his arms round Silvermane's neck. He fed them, and ate himself, not without difficulty, for his lips were puffed and his tongue felt like a piece of rope. When he had eaten, his strength came back.

At a word Wolf, with a wag of his tail, splashed into the gravelly stream bed. Hare followed on foot, leading Silvermane. There were little beds of pebbles and beaches of sand and short steps down which the water babbled. The canyon was narrow and tortuous; Hare could not see ahead or below, for the projecting red cliffs, growing higher as he descended, walled out the view. The blue stream of sky above grew bluer and the light and shade less bright. For an hour he went down steadily without a check, and the farther down the rougher grew the way. Bowlders wedged in narrow places made foaming waterfalls. Silvermane clicked down confidently.

The slender stream of water, swelled by seeping springs and little rills, gained the dignity of a brook; it began to dash merrily and hurriedly downward. The depth of the falls, the height of cliffs, and the size of the bowlders increased in the descent. Wolf splashed on unmindful; there was a new spirit in his movements; and when he looked back for his laboring companions there was friendly protest in his eyes. Silvermane's mien plainly showed that where a dog could go he could follow. Silvermane's blood was heated; the desert was an old story to him; it had only tired him and parched his throat; this canyon of downward steps and falls, with ever-deepening drops, was new to him, and roused his mettle; and from his long training in the wilds he had gained a marvellous sure-footedness.

The canyon narrowed as it deepened; the jutting walls leaned together, shutting out the light; the sky above was now a ribbon of blue, only to be seen when Hare threw back his head and stared straight up.

"It'll be easier climbing up, Silvermane," he panted—"if we ever get the chance."

The sand and gravel and shale had disappeared; all was bare clean-washed rock. In many places the brook failed as a trail, for it leaped down in white sheets over mossy cliffs. Hare faced these walls in despair. But Wolf led on over the ledges and Silvermane followed, nothing daunted. At last Hare shrank back from a hole which defied him utterly. Even Wolf hesitated. The canyon was barely twenty feet wide; the floor ended in a precipice; the stream leaped out and fell into a dark cleft from which no sound arose. On the right there was a shelf of rock; it was scarce half a foot broad at the narrowest and then apparently vanished altogether. Hare stared helplessly up at the slanting shut-in walls.

While he hesitated Wolf pattered out upon the ledge and Silvermane stamped restlessly. With a desperate fear of losing his beloved horse Hare let go the bridle and stepped upon the ledge. He walked rapidly, for a slow step meant uncertainty and a false one meant death. He heard the sharp ring of Silvermane's shoes, and he listened in agonized suspense for the slip, the snort, the crash that he feared must come. But it did not come. Seeing nothing except the narrow ledge, yet feeling the blue abyss beneath him, he bent all his mind to his task, and finally walked out into lighter space upon level rock. To his infinite relief Silvermane appeared rounding a corner out of the dark passage, and was soon beside him.

Hare cried aloud in welcome.

The canyon widened; there was a clear demarcation where the red walls gave place to yellow; the brook showed no outlet from its subterranean channel. Sheer exhaustion made Hare almost forget his mission; the strength of his resolve had gone into mechanical toil; he kept on, conscious only of the smart of bruised hands and feet and the ache of laboring lungs.

Time went on and the sun hung in the midst of the broadening belt of blue sky. A long slant of yellow slope led down to a sage-covered level, which Hare crossed, pleased to see blooming cacti and wondering at their slender lofty green stems shining with gold flowers. He descended into a ravine which became precipitous. Here he made only slow advance. At the bottom he found himself in a wonderful lane with an almost level floor; here flowed a shallow stream bordered by green willows. Wolf took the direction of the flowing water. Hare's thoughts were all of Mescal, and his hopes began to mount, his heart to beat high.

He gazed ahead with straining eyes. Presently there was not a break in the walls. A drowsy hum of falling water came to Hare, strange reminder of the oasis, the dull roar of the Colorado, and of Mescal.

His flagging energies leaped into life with the canyon suddenly opening to bright light and blue sky and beautiful valley, white and gold in blossom, green with grass and cottonwood. On a flower-scented wind rushed that muffled roar again, like distant thunder.

Wolf dashed into the cottonwoods. Silvermane whistled with satisfaction and reached for the long grass.

For Hare the light held something more than beauty, the breeze something more than sweet scent of water and blossom. Both were charged with meaning—with suspense.

Wolf appeared in the open leaping upon a slender brown-garbed form.

"Mescal!" cried Hare.

With a cry she ran to him, her arms outstretched, her hair flying in the wind, her dark eyes wild with joy.

XVI. THUNDER RIVER

FOR an instant Hare's brain reeled, and Mescal's broken murmurings were meaningless. Then his faculties grew steady and acute; he held the girl as if he intended never to let her go. Mescal clung to him with a wildness that gave him anxiety for her reason; there was something almost fierce in the tension of her arms, in the blind groping for his face.

"Mescal! It's Jack, safe and well," he said. "Let me look at you."

At the sound of his voice all her rigid strength changed to a yielding weakness; she leaned back supported by his arms and looked at him. Hare trembled before the dusky level glance he remembered so well, and as tears began to flow he drew her head to his shoulder. He had forgotten to prepare himself for a different Mescal. Despite the quivering smile of happiness, her eyes were strained with pain. The oval contour, the rich bloom of her face had gone; beauty was there still, but it was the ghost of the old beauty.

"Jack—is it—really you?" she asked.

He answered with a kiss.

She slipped out of his arms breathless and scarlet. "Tell me all—"

"There's much to tell, but not before you kiss me. It has been more than a year."

"Only a year! Have I been gone only a year?"

"Yes, a year. But it's past now. Kiss me, Mescal. One kiss will pay for that long year, though it broke my heart."

Shyly she raised her hands to his shoulders and put her lips to his. "Yes, you've found me, Jack, thank God! just in time!"

"Mescal! What's wrong? Aren't you well?"

"Pretty well. But if you had not come soon I should have starved."

"Starved? Let me get my saddle-bags—I have bread and meat."

"Wait. I'm not so hungry now. I mean very soon I should not have had any food at all."

"But your peon—the dumb Indian? Surely he could find something to eat. What of him? Where is he?"

"My peon is dead. He has been dead for months, I don't know how many."

"Dead! What was the matter with him?"

"I never knew. I found him dead one morning and I buried him in the sand."

XVI. THUNDER RIVER

Mescal led Hare under the cottonwoods and pointed to the Indian's grave, now green with grass. Farther on in a circle of trees stood a little hogan skilfully constructed out of brush; the edge of a red blanket peeped from the door; a burnt-out fire smoked on a stone fireplace, and blackened earthen vessels lay near. The white seeds of the cottonwoods were flying light as feathers; plum-trees were pink in blossom; there were vines twining all about; through the openings in the foliage shone the blue of sky and red of cliff. Patches of blossoming Bowers were here and there lit to brilliance by golden shafts of sunlight. The twitter of birds and hum of bees were almost drowned in the soft roar of water.

"Is that the Colorado I hear?" asked Hare.

"No, that's Thunder River. The Colorado is farther down in the Grand Canyon."

"Farther down! Mescal, I must have come a mile from the rim. Where are we?"

"We are almost at the Colorado, and directly under the head of Coconina. We can see the mountain from the break in the valley below."

"Come sit by me here under this tree. Tell me—how did you ever get here?"

Then Mescal told him how the peon had led her on a long trail from Bitter Seeps, how they had camped at desert waterholes, and on the fourth day descended to Thunder River.

"I was quite happy at first. It's always summer down here. There were rabbits, birds, beaver, and fruit—we had enough to eat. I explored the valley with Wolf or rode Noddle up and down the canyon. Then my peon died, and I had to shift for myself. There came a time when the beaver left the valley, and Wolf and I had to make a rabbit serve for days. I knew then I'd have to get across the desert to the Navajos or starve in the canyon. I hesitated about climbing out into the desert, for I wasn't sure of the trail to the waterholes. Noddle wandered off up the canyon and never came back. After he was gone and I knew I couldn't get out I grew homesick. The days weren't so bad because I was always hunting for something to eat, but the nights were lonely. I couldn't sleep. I lay awake listening to the river, and at last I could hear whispering and singing and music, and strange sounds, and low thunder, always low thunder. I wasn't really frightened, only lonely, and the canyon was so black and full of mutterings. Sometimes I'd dream I was back on the plateau with you, Jack, and Bolly and the sheep, and when I'd awake in the loneliness I'd cry right out—"

"Mescal, I heard those cries," said Hare.

"It was strange—the way I felt. I believe if I'd never known and—and loved you, Jack, I'd have forgotten home. After I'd been here a while, I seemed to be drifting, drifting. It was as if I had lived in the canyon long before, and was remembering. The feeling was strong, but always thoughts of you, and of the big world, brought me back to the present with its loneliness and fear of starvation. Then I wanted you, and I'd cry out. I knew I must send Wolf home. How hard it was to make him go! But at last he trotted off, looking backward, and I—waited and waited."

She leaned against him. The hand which had plucked at his sleeve dropped to his fingers and clung there. Hare knew how her story had slighted the perils and privations of that long year. She had grown lonely in the canyon darkness; she had sent Wolf away and had waited—all was said in that. But more than any speech, the look of her, and the story told in the thin brown hands touched his heart. Not for an instant since his arrival had she altogether let loose of his fingers, or coat, or arm. She had lived so long alone in this weird world of silence and moving shadows and murmuring water, that she needed to feel the substance of her hopes, to assure herself of the reality of the man she loved.

"My mustang—Bolly—tell me of her," said Mescal.

"Bolly's fine. Sleek and fat and lazy! She's been in the fields ever since you left. Not a bridle on her. Many times have I seen her poke her black muzzle over the fence and look down the lane. She'd never forget you, Mescal."

"Oh! how I want to see her! Tell me—everything."

"Wait a little. Let me fetch Silvermane and we'll make a fire and eat. Then—"

"Tell me now."

"Well, Mescal, it's soon told." Then came the story of events growing out of her flight. When he told of the shooting at Silver Cup, Mescal rose with heaving bosom and blazing eyes.

"It was nothing—I wasn't hurt much. Only the intention was bad. We saw no more of Snap or Holderness. The worst of it all was that Snap's wife died."

"Oh, I am sorry—sorry. Poor Father Naab! How he must hate me, the cause of it all! But I couldn't stay—I couldn't marry Snap."

"Don't blame yourself, Mescal. What Snap might have done if you had married him is guesswork. He might have left drink alone a while longer. But he was bad clean through. I heard Dave Naab tell him that. Snap would have gone over to Holderness sooner or later. And now he's a rustler, if not worse."

"Then those men think Snap killed you?"

"Yes."

"What's going to happen when you meet Snap, or any of them?"

"Somebody will be surprised," replied Hare, with a laugh.

"Jack, it's no laughing matter." She fastened her hands in the lapels of his coat and her eyes grew sad. "You can never hang up your gun again."

"No. But perhaps I can keep out of their way, especially Snap's. Mescal, you've forgotten Silvermane, and how he can run."

"I haven't forgotten. He can run, but he can't beat Bolly." She said this with a hint of her old spirit. "Jack—you want to take me back home?"

"Of course. What did you expect when you sent Wolf?"

"I didn't expect. I just wanted to see you, or somebody, and I thought of the Navajos. Couldn't I live with them? Why can't we stay here or in a canyon across the Colorado where there's plenty of game?"

"I'm going to take you home and Father Naab shall marry you—to—to me."

Startled, Mescal fell back upon his shoulder and did not stir nor speak for a long time. "Did—did you tell him?"

"Yes."

"What did he say? Was he angry? Tell me."

"He was kind and good as he always is. He said if I found you, then the issue would be between Snap and me, as man to man. You are still pledged to Snap in the Mormon Church and that can't be changed. I don't suppose even if he's outlawed that it could be changed."

"Snap will not let any grass grow in the trails to the oasis," said Mescal. "Once he finds I've come back to life he'll have me. You don't know him, Jack. I'm afraid to go home."

"My dear, there's no other place for us to go. We can't live the life of Indians."

"But Jack, think of me watching you ride out from home! Think of me always looking for Snap! I couldn't endure it. I've grown weak in this year of absence."

"Mescal, look at me." His voice rang as he held her face to face. "We must decide everything. Now—say you love me!"

"Yes—yes."

"Say it."

"I—love you—Jack."

"Say you'll marry me!"

"I will marry you."

"Then listen. I'll get you out of this canyon and take you home. You are mine and I'll keep you." He held her tightly with strong arms; his face paled, his eyes darkened. "I don't want to meet Snap Naab. I shall try to keep out of his way. I hope I can. But Mescal, I'm yours now. Your happiness—perhaps your life—depends on me. That makes a difference. Understand!"

Silvermane walked into the glade with a saddle-girth so tight that his master unbuckled it only by dint of repeated effort. Evidently the rich grass of Thunder River Canyon appealed strongly to the desert stallion.

"Here, Silver, how do you expect to carry us out if you eat and drink like that?" Hare removed the saddle and tethered the gray to one of the cottonwoods. Wolf came trotting into camp proudly carrying a rabbit.

"Mescal, can we get across the Colorado and find a way up over Coconina?" asked Hare.

"Yes, I'm sure we can. My peon never made a mistake about directions. There's no trail, but Navajos have crossed the river at this season, and worked up a canyon."

The shadows had gathered under the cliffs, and the rosy light high up on the ramparts had chilled and waned when Hare and Mescal sat down to their meal. Wolf lay close to the girl and begged for morsels. Then in the twilight they sat together content to be silent, listening to the low thunder of the river. Long after Mescal had retired into her hogan Hare lay awake before her door with his head in his saddle and listened to the low roll, the dull burr, the dreamy hum of the tumbling waters. The place was like the oasis, only infinitely more hidden under the cliffs. A few stars twinkled out of the dark blue, and one hung, beaconlike, on the crest of a noble crag. There were times when he imagined the valley was as silent as the desert night, and other times when he imagined he heard the thundering roll of avalanches and the tramp of armies. Then the voices of Mescal's solitude spoke to him—glorious laughter and low sad wails of woe, sweet songs and whispers and murmurs. His last waking thoughts were of the haunting sound of Thunder River, and that he had come to bear Mescal away from its loneliness.

He bestirred himself at the first glimpse of day, and when the gray mists had lifted to wreathe the crags it was light enough to begin the journey. Mescal shed tears at the grave of the faithful peon. "He loved this canyon," she said, softly. Hare lifted her upon Silvermane. He walked beside the horse and Wolf trotted on before. They travelled awhile under the flowering cottonwoods on a trail bordered with green tufts of grass and great star-shaped lilies. The river was still hidden, but it filled the grove with its soft thunder. Gradually the trees thinned out, hard stony ground encroached upon the sand, bowlders appeared in the way; and presently, when Silvermane stepped out of the shade of the cottonwoods, Hare saw the lower end of the valley with its ragged vent.

"Look back!" said Mescal.

Hare saw the river bursting from the base of the wall in two white streams which soon united below, and leaped down in a continuous cascade. Step by step the stream plunged through the deep gorge, a broken, foaming raceway, and at the lower end of the valley it took its final leap into a blue abyss, and then found its way to the Colorado, hidden underground.

The flower-scented breeze and the rumbling of the river persisted long after the valley lay behind and above, but these failed at length in the close air of the huge abutting walls. The light grew thick, the stones cracked like deep bell-strokes; the voices of man and girl had a hollow sound and echo. Silvermane clattered down the easy trail at a gait which urged Hare now and then from walk to run. Soon the gully opened out upon a plateau through the centre of which, in a black gulf, wound the red Colorado, sullen-voiced, booming, never silent nor restful. Here were distances by which Hare could begin to comprehend the immensity of the canyon, and he felt lost among the great terraces leading up to mesas that dwarfed the Echo Cliffs. All was bare rock of many hues burning under the sun.

"Jack, this is mescal," said the girl, pointing to some towering plants.

All over the sunny slopes cacti lifted slender shafts, unfolding in spiral leaves as they shot upward and bursting at the top into plumes of yellow flowers. The blossoming stalks waved in the wind, and black bees circled round them.

"Mescal, I've always wanted to see the Flower of the Desert from which you're named. It's beautiful."

Hare broke a dead stalk of the cactus and was put to instant flight by a stream of bees pouring with angry buzz from the hollow centre. Two big fellows were so persistent that he had to beat them off with his hat.

"You shouldn't despoil their homes," said Mescal, with a peal of laughter.

"I'll break another stalk and get stung, if you'll laugh again," replied Hare.

They traversed the remaining slope of the plateau, and entering the head of a ravine, descended a steep cleft of flinty rock, rock so hard that Silvermane's iron hoofs not so much as scratched it. Then reaching a level, they passed out to rounded sand and the river.

"It's a little high," said Hare dubiously. "Mescal, I don't like the looks of those rapids."

Only a few hundred rods of the river could be seen. In front of Hare the current was swift but not broken. Above, where the canyon turned, the river sheered out with a majestic roll and falling in a wide smooth curve suddenly narrowed into a leaping crest of reddish waves. Below Hare was a smaller rapid where the broken water turned toward the nearer side of the river, but with an accompaniment of twisting swirls and vicious waves.

"I guess we'd better risk it," said Hare, grimly recalling the hot rock, the sand, and lava of the desert.

"It's safe, if Silvermane is a good swimmer," replied Mescal. "We can take the river above and cut across so the current will help."

"Silvermane loves the water. He'll make this crossing easily. But he can't carry us both, and it's impossible to make two trips. I'll have to swim."

Without wasting more words and time over a task which would only grow more formidable with every look and thought, Hare led Silvermane up the sand-bar to its limit. He removed his coat and strapped it behind the saddle; his belt and revolver and boots he hung over the pommel.

"How about Wolf? I'd forgotten him."

"Never fear for him! He'll stick close to me."

"Now, Mescal, there's the point we want to make, that bar; see it?"

"Surely we can land above that."

"I'll be satisfied if we get even there. You guide him for it. And, Mescal, here's my gun. Try to keep it from getting wet. Balance it on the pommel—so. Come, Silver; come, Wolf."

"Keep up-stream," called Mescal as Hare plunged in. "Don't drift below us."

In two steps Silvermane went in to his saddle, and he rolled with a splash and a snort, sinking Mescal to her hips. His nose level with the water, mane and tail floating, he swam powerfully with the current.

For Hare the water was just cold enough to be delightful after the long hot descent, but its quality was strange. Keeping up-stream of the horse and even with Mescal, he swam with long regular strokes for perhaps one-quarter of the distance. But when they reached the swirling eddies he found that he was tiring. The water was thick and heavy; it compressed his lungs and dragged at his feet. He whirled round and round in the eddies and saw Silvermane doing the same. Only by main force could he breast his way out of these whirlpools. When a wave slapped his face he tasted sand, and then he knew what the strange feeling meant. There was sand here as on the desert. Even in the depths of the canyon he could not escape it. As the current grew rougher he began to feel that he could scarcely spread his arms in the wide stroke. Changing the stroke he discovered that he could not keep up with Silvermane, and he changed back again. Gradually his feet sank lower and lower, the water pressed tighter round him, his arms seemed to grow useless. Then he remembered a saying of August Naab that the Navajos did not attempt to swim the river when it was in flood and full of sand. He ceased to struggle, and drifting with the current, soon was close to Silvermane, and grasped a saddle strap.

"Not there!" called Mescal. "He might strike you. Hang to his tail!"

Hare dropped behind, and catching Silvermane's tail held on firmly. The stallion towed him easily. The waves dashed over him and lapped at Mescal's waist. The current grew stronger, sweeping Silvermane down out of line with the black wall which had frowned closer and closer. Mescal lifted the rifle, and resting the stock on the saddle, held it upright. The roar of the rapids seemed to lose its volume, and presently it died in the splashing and slapping of broken water closer at hand. Mescal turned to him with bright eyes; curving her hand about her lips she shouted:

"Can't make the bar! We've got to go through this side of the rapids. Hang on!"

In the swelling din Hare felt the resistless pull of the current. As he held on with both hands, hard pressed to keep his grasp, Silvermane dipped over a low fall in the river. Then Hare was riding the rushing water of an incline. It ended below in a red-crested wave, and beyond was a chaos of curling breakers. Hare had one glimpse of Mescal crouching low, shoulders narrowed and head bent; then, with one white flash of the stallion's mane against her flying black hair, she went out of sight in leaping waves and spray. Hare was thrown forward into the backlash of the wave. The shock blinded him, stunned him, almost tore his arms from his body, but his hands were so twisted in Silvermane's tail that even this could not loosen them. The current threw him from wave to wave. He was dragged through a caldron, blind from stinging blows, deaf from the tremendous roar. Then the fierce contention of waves lessened, the threshing of crosscurrents straightened, and he could breathe once more. Silvermane dragged him steadily; and, finally, his feet touched the ground. He could scarcely see, so full were his eyes of the sandy water, but he made out Mescal rising from the river on Silvermane, as with loud snorts he climbed to a bar. Hare staggered up and fell on the sand.

"Jack, are you all right?" inquired Mescal.

"All right, only pounded out of breath, and my eyes are full of sand. How about you?"

"I don't think I ever was any wetter," replied Mescal, laughing. "It was hard to stick on holding the rifle. That first wave almost unseated me. I was afraid we might strike the rocks, but the water was deep. Silvermane is grand, Jack. Wolf swam out above the rapids and was waiting for us when we landed."

Hare wiped the sand out of his eyes and rose to his feet, finding himself little the worse for the adventure. Mescal was wringing the water from the long straight braids of her hair. She was smiling, and a tint of color showed in her cheeks. The wet buckskin blouse and short skirt clung tightly to her slender form. She made so pretty a picture and appeared so little affected by the peril they had just passed through that Hare, yielding to a tender rush of pride and possession, kissed the pink cheeks till they flamed.

"All wet," said he, "you and I, clothes, food, guns—everything."

"It's hot and we'll soon dry," returned Mescal. "Here's the canyon and creek we must follow up to Coconina. My peon mapped them in the sand for me one day. It'll probably be a long climb."

Hare poured the water out of his boots, pulled them on, and helping Mescal to mount Silvermane, he took the bridle over his arm and led the way into a black-mouthed canyon, through which flowed a stream of clear water. Wolf splashed and pattered along beside him. Beyond the marble rock this canyon opened out to great breadth and wonderful walls. Hare had eyes only for the gravelly bars and shallow levels of the creek; intent on finding the easy going for his horse he strode on and on thoughtless of time. Nor did he talk to Mescal, for the work was hard, and he needed his breath. Splashing the water, hammering the stones, Silvermane ever kept his nose at Hare's elbow. They climbed little ridges, making short cuts from point to point, they threaded miles of narrow winding creek floor, and passed under ferny cliffs and over grassy banks and through thickets of yellow willow. As they wound along the course of the creek, always up and up, the great walls imperceptibly lowered their rims. The warm sun soared to the zenith. Jumble of bowlders, stretches of white gravel, ridges of sage, blocks of granite, thickets of manzanita, long yellow slopes, crumbling crags, clumps of cedar and lines of pinon—all were passed in the persistent plodding climb. The canon grew narrower toward its source; the creek lost its volume; patches of snow gleamed in sheltered places. At last the yellow-streaked walls edged out upon a grassy hollow and the great dark pines of Coconina shadowed the snow.

"We're up," panted Hare. "What a climb! Five hours! One more day—then home!"

Silvermane's ears shot up and Wolf barked. Two gray deer loped out of a thicket and turned inquisitively. Reaching for his rifle Hare threw back the lever, but the action clogged, it rasped with the sound of crunching sand, and the cartridge could not be pressed into the chamber or ejected. He fumbled about the breach of the gun and his brow clouded.

"Sand! Out of commission!" he exclaimed. "Mescal, I don't like that."

"Use your Colt," suggested Mescal.

The distance was too great. Hare missed, and the deer bounded away into the forest.

Hare built a fire under a sheltering pine where no snow covered the soft mat of needles, and while Mescal dried the blankets and roasted the last portion of meat he made a wind-break of spruce boughs. When they had eaten, not forgetting to give Wolf a portion, Hare fed Silvermane the last few handfuls of grain, and tied him with a long halter on the grassy bank. The daylight failed and darkness came on apace. The old familiar roar of the wind in the pines was disturbing; it might mean only the lull and crash of the breaking night-gusts, and it might mean the north wind, storm, and snow. It whooped down the hollow, scattering the few scrub-oak leaves; it whirled the red embers of the fire away into the dark to sputter in the snow, and blew the burning logs into a white glow. Mescal slept in the shelter of the spruce boughs with Wolf snug and warm beside her. Hare stretched his tired limbs in the heat of the blaze.

When he awakened the fire was low and he was numb with cold. He took care to put on logs enough to last until morning; then he lay down once more, but did not sleep. The dawn came with a gray shade in the forest; it was a cloud, and it rolled over him soft, tangible, moist, and cool, and passed away under the pines. With its vanishing the dawn lightened. "Mescal, if we're on the spur of Coconina, it's only ten miles or so to Silver Cup," said Hare, as he saddled Silvermane. "Mount now and we'll go up out of the hollow and get our bearings."

While ascending the last step to the rim Hare revolved in his mind the probabilities of marking a straight course to Silver Cup.

"Oh! Jack!" exclaimed Mescal, suddenly. "Vermillion Cliffs and home!"

"I've travelled in a circle!" replied Hare.

Mescal was enraptured at the scene. Vermillion Cliffs shone red as a rose. The split in the wall marking the oasis defined its outlines sharply against the sky. Miles of the Colorado River lay in sight. Hare knew he stood on the highest point of Coconina overhanging the Grand Canyon and the Painted Desert, thousands of feet below. He noted the wondrous abyss sleeping in blue mist at his feet, while he gazed across to the desert awakening in the first red rays of the rising sun.

"Mescal, your Thunder River Canyon is only one little crack in the rocks. It is lost in this chasm," said Hare.

"It's lost, surely. I can't even see the tip of the peak that stood so high over the valley."

Once more turning to the left Hare ran his eye over the Vermillion Cliffs, and the strip of red sand shining under them, and so calculating his bearings he headed due north for Silver Cup. What with the snow and the soggy ground the first mile was hard going for Hare, and Silvermane often sank deep. Once off the level spur of the mountain they made better time, for the snow thinned out on the slope and gradually gave way to the brown dry aisles of the forest. Hare mounted in front of Mescal, and put the stallion to an easy trot; after two hours of riding they struck a bridle-trail which Hare recognized as one leading down to the spring. In another hour they reached the steep slope of Coconina, and saw the familiar red wall across the valley, and caught glimpses of gray sage patches down through the pines.

"I smell smoke," said Hare.

"The boys must be at the spring," rejoined Mescal.

"Maybe. I want to be sure who's there. We'll leave the trail and slip down through the woods to the left. I wish we could get down on the home side of the spring. But we can't; we've got to pass it."

With many a pause to peer through openings in the pines Hare traversed a diagonal course down the slope, crossed the line of cedars, and reached the edge of the valley a mile or more above Silver Cup. Then he turned toward it, still cautiously leading Silvermane under cover of the fringe of cedars.

"Mescal, there are too many cattle in the valley," he said, looking at her significantly.

"They can't all be ours, that's sure," she replied. "What do you think?"

"Holderness!" With the word Hare's face grew set and stern. He kept on, cautiously leading the horse under the cedars, careful to avoid breaking brush or rattling stones, occasionally whispering to Wolf; and so worked his way along the curve of the woody slope till further progress was checked by the bulging wall of rock.

"Only cattle in the valley, no horses," he said. "I've a good chance to cut across this curve and reach the trail. If I take time to climb up and see who's at the spring maybe the chance will be gone. I don't believe Dave and the boys are there."

He pondered a moment, then climbed up in front of Mescal, and directed the gray out upon the valley. Soon he was among the grazing cattle. He felt no surprise to see the H brand on their flanks.

"Jack, look at that brand," said Mescal, pointing to a white-flanked steer. "There's an old brand like a cross, Father Naab's cross, and a new brand, a single bar. Together they make an H!"

"Mescal! You've hit it. I remember that steer. He was a very devil to brand. He's the property of August Naab, and Holderness has added the bar, making a clumsy H. What a rustler's trick! It wouldn't deceive a child."

They had reached the cedars and the trail when Wolf began to sniff suspiciously at the wind.

"Look!" whispered Mescal, calling Hare's attention from the dog. "Look! A new corral!"

Bending back to get in line with her pointing finger Hare looked through a network of cedar boughs to see a fence of stripped pines. Farther up were piles of unstripped logs, and close by the spring there was a new cabin with smoke curling from a stone chimney. Hare guided Silvermane off the trail to softer ground and went on. He climbed the slope, passed the old pool, now a mud-puddle, and crossed the dry wash to be brought suddenly to a halt. Wolf had made an uneasy stand with his nose pointing to the left, and Silvermane pricked up his ears. Presently Hare heard the stamping of hoofs off in the cedars, and before he had fully determined the direction from which the sound came three horses and a man stepped from the shade into a sunlit space.

As luck would have it Hare happened to be well screened by a thick cedar; and since there was a possibility that he might remain unseen he chose to take it. Silvermane and Wolf stood still in their tracks. Hare felt Mescal's hands tighten on his coat and he pressed them to reassure her. Peeping out from his covert he saw a man in his shirt-sleeves leading the horses—a slender, clean-faced, dark-haired man—Dene! The blood beat hotly in Hare's temples and he gripped the handle of his Colt. It seemed a fatal chance that sent the outlaw to that trail. He was whistling; he had two halters in one hand and with the other he led his bay horse by the mane. Then Hare saw that he wore no belt; he was unarmed; on the horses were only the halters and clinking hobbles. Hare dropped his Colt back into its holster.

Dene sauntered on, whistling "Dixie." When he reached the trail, instead of crossing it, as Hare had hoped, he turned into it and came down.

Hare swung the switch he had broken from an aspen and struck Silvermane a stinging blow on the flanks. The gray leaped forward. The crash of brush and rattle of hoofs stampeded Dene's horses in a twinkling. But the outlaw paled to a ghastly white and seemed rooted to the trail. It was not fear of a man or a horse that held Dene fixed; in his starting eyes was the terror of the supernatural.

The shoulder of the charging stallion struck Dene and sent him spinning out of the trail. In a backward glance Hare saw the outlaw fall, then rise unhurt to shake his fists wildly and to run yelling toward the cabin.

XVII. THE SWOOP OF THE HAWK

"JACK! the saddle's slipping!" cried Mescal, clinging closer to him. "What luck!" Hare muttered through clinched teeth, and pulled hard on the bridle. But the mouth of the stallion was iron; regardless of the sawing bit, he galloped on. Hare called steadily: "Whoa there, Silver! Whoa—slow now—whoa—easy!" and finally halted him. Hare swung down, and as he lifted Mescal off, the saddle slipped to the ground.

"Lucky not to get a spill! The girth snapped. It was wet, and dried out." Hare hurriedly began to repair the break with buckskin thongs that he found in a saddle-bag.

"Listen! Hear the yells! Oh! hurry!" cried Mescal.

"I've never ridden bareback. Suppose you go ahead with Silver, and I'll hide in the cedars till dark, then walk home!"

"No—No. There's time, but hurry."

"It's got to be strong," muttered Hare, holding the strap over his knee and pulling the laced knot with all his strength, "for we'll have to ride some. If it comes loose—Good-bye!"

Silvermane's broad chest muscles rippled and he stamped restlessly. The dog whined and looked back. Mescal had the blanket smooth on the gray when Hare threw the saddle over him. The yells had ceased, but clattering hoofs on the stony trail were a greater menace. While Hare's brown hands worked swiftly over buckle and strap Mescal climbed to a seat behind the saddle.

"Get into the saddle," said Hare, leaping astride and pressing forward over the pommel. "Slip down—there! and hold to me. Go! Silver!"

The rapid pounding of the stallion's hoofs drowned the clatter coming up the trail. A backward glance relieved Hare, for dust-clouds some few hundred yards in the rear showed the position of the pursuing horsemen. He held in Silvermane to a steady gallop. The trail was up-hill, and steep enough to wind even a desert racer, if put to his limit.

"Look back!" cried Mescal. "Can you see them? Is Snap with them?"

"I can't see for trees," replied Hare, over his shoulder. "There's dust—we're far in the lead—never fear, Mescal. The lead's all we want."

Cedars grew thickly all the way up the steeper part of the divide, and ended abruptly at a pathway of stone, where the ascent became gradual. When Silvermane struck out of the grove upon this slope Hare kept turning keen glances rearward. The dust cloud rolled to the edge of the cedars, and out of it trooped half-a-dozen horsemen who began to shoot as soon as they had reached the open. Bullets zipped along the red stone, cutting little puffs of red dust, and sung through the air.

"Good God!" cried Hare. "They're firing on us! They'd shoot a woman!"

"Has it taken you so long to learn that?"

Hare slashed his steed with the switch. But Silvermane needed no goad or spur; he had been shot at before, and the whistle of one bullet was sufficient to stretch his gallop into a run. Then distance between him and his pursuers grew wider and wider and soon he was out of range. The yells of the rustlers seemed at first to come from baffled rage, but Mescal's startled cry showed their meaning. Other horsemen appeared ahead and to the right of him, tearing down the ridge to the divide. Evidently they had been returning from the western curve of Coconina.

The direction in which Silvermane was stretching was the only possible one for Hare. If he swerved off the trail to the left it would be upon rough rising ground. Not only must he outride this second band to the point where the trail went down on the other side of the divide, but also he must get beyond it before they came within rifle range.

"Now! Silver! Go! Go!" Fast as the noble stallion was speeding he answered to the call. He was in the open now, free of stones and brush, with the spang of rifles in the air. The wind rushed into Hare's ears, filling them with a hollow roar; the ground blurred by in reddish sheets. The horsemen cut down the half mile to a quarter, lessened that, swept closer and closer, till Hare recognized Chance and Culver, and Snap Naab on his cream-colored pinto. Seeing that they could not head the invincible stallion they sheered more to the right. But Silvermane thundered on, crossing the line ahead of them a full three hundred yards, and went over the divide, drawing them in behind him.

Then, at the sharp crack of the rifles, leaden messengers whizzed high in the air over horse and riders, and skipped along the red shale in front of the running dog.

"Oh—Silvermane!" cried Hare. It was just a call, as if the horse were human, and knew what that pace meant to his master. The stern business of the race had ceased to rest on Hare. Silvermane was out to the front! He was like a level-rushing thunderbolt. Hare felt the instantaneous pause between his long low leaps, the gather of mighty muscles, the strain, the tension, then the quivering expulsion of force. It was a perilous ride down that red slope, not so much from the hissing bullets as from the washes and gullies which Silvermane sailed over in magnificent leaps. Hare thrilled with savage delight in the wonderful prowess of his desert king, in the primal instinct of joy at escaping with the woman he loved.

"Outrun!" he cried, with blazing eyes. Mescal's white face was pressed close to his shoulder. "Silver has beaten them. They'll hang on till we reach the sand-strip, hoping the slow-down will let them come up in time. But they'll be far too late."

XVII. THE SWOOP OF THE HAWK

The rustlers continued on the trail, firing desultorily, till Silvermane so far distanced them that even the necessary lapse into a walk in the red sand placed him beyond range when they arrived at the strip.

"They've turned back, Mescal. We're safe. Why, you look as you did the day the bear ran for you."

"I'd rather a bear got me than Snap. Jack, did you see him?"

"See him? Rather! I'll bet he nearly killed his pinto. Mescal, what do you think of Silvermane now? Can he run? Can he outrun Bolly?"

"Yes—yes. Oh! Jack! how I'll love him! Look back again. Are we safe? Will we ever be safe?"

It was still daylight when they rounded the portal of the oasis and entered the lane with the familiar wall on one side, the peeled fence-pickets on the other. Wolf dashed on ahead, and presently a chorus of barks announced that he had been met by the other dogs. Silvermane neighed shrilly, and the horses and mustangs in the corrals trooped noisily to the lower sides and hung inquisitive heads over the top bars.

A Navajo whom Hare remembered stared with axe idle by the woodpile, then Judith Naab dropped a bundle of sticks and with a cry of gladness ran from the house. Before Silvermane had come to a full stop Mescal was off. She put her arms around his neck and kissed him, then she left Judith to dart to the corral where a little black mustang had begun to whistle and stamp and try to climb over the bars.

August Naab, bareheaded, with shaggy locks shaking at every step, strode off the porch and his great hands lifted Hare from the saddle.

"Every day I've watched the river for you," he said. His eyes were warm and his grasp like a vise.

"Mescal—child!" he continued, as she came running to him. "Safe and well. He's brought you back. Thank the Lord!" He took her to his breast and bent his gray head over her.

Then the crowd of big and little Naabs burst from the house and came under the cottonwoods to offer noisy welcome to Mescal and Hare.

"Jack, you look done up," said Dave Naab solicitously, when the first greetings had been spoken, and Mother Ruth had led Mescal indoors. "Silvermane, too—he's wet and winded. He's been running?"

"Yes, a little," replied Hare, as he removed the saddle from the weary horse.

"Ah! What's this?" questioned August Naab, with his hand on Silvermane's flank. He touched a raw groove, and the stallion flinched. "Hare, a bullet made that!"

"Yes."

"Then you didn't ride in by the Navajo crossing?"

"No. I came by Silver Cup."

"Silver Cup? How on earth did you get down there?"

"We climbed out of the canyon up over Coconina, and so made the spring."

Naab whistled in surprise and he flashed another keen glance over Hare and his horse. "Your story can wait. I know about what it is—after you reached Silver Cup. Come in, come in, Dave will look out for the stallion."

But Hare would allow no one else to attend to Silvermane. He rubbed the tired gray, gave him a drink at the trough, led him to the corral, and took leave of him with a caress like Mescal's. Then he went to his room and bathed himself and changed his clothes, afterward presenting himself at the supper-table to eat like one famished. Mescal and he ate alone, as they had been too late for the regular hour. The women-folk waited upon them as if they could not do enough. There were pleasant words and smiles; but in spite of them something sombre attended the meal. There was a shadow in each face, each step was slow, each voice subdued. Naab and his sons were waiting for Hare when he entered the sitting room, and after his entrance the door was closed. They were all quiet and stern, especially the father. "Tell us all," said Naab, simply.

While Hare was telling his adventures not a word or a move interrupted him till he spoke of Silvermane's running Dene down.

"That's the second time!" rolled out Naab. "The stallion will kill him yet!"

Hare finished his story.

"What don't you owe to that whirlwind of a horse!" exclaimed Dave Naab. No other comment on Hare or Silvermane was offered by the Naabs.

"You knew Holderness had taken in Silver Cup?" inquired Hare.

August Naab nodded gloomily.

"I guess we knew it," replied Dave for him. "While I was in White Sage and the boys were here at home, Holderness rode to the spring and took possession. I called to see him on my way back, but he wasn't around. Snap was there, the boss of a bunch of riders. Dene, too, was there."

"Did you go right into camp?" asked Hare.

"Sure. I was looking for Holderness. There were eighteen or twenty riders in the bunch. I talked to several of them, Mormons, good fellows, they used to be. Also I had some words with Dene. He said: 'I shore was sorry Snap got to my spy first. I wanted him bad, an' I'm shore goin' to have his white horse.' Snap and Dene, all of them, thought you were number thirty-one in dad's cemetery."

"Not yet," said Hare. "Dene certainly looked as if he saw a ghost when Silvermane jumped for him. Well, he's at Silver Cup now. They're all there. What's to be done about it? They're openly thieves. The new brand on all your stock proves that."

"Such a trick we never heard of," replied August Naab. "If we had we might have spared ourselves the labor of branding the stock."

"But that new brand of Holderness's upon yours proves his guilt."

"It's not now a question of proof. It's one of possession. Holderness has stolen my water and my stock."

"They are worse than rustlers; firing on Mescal and me proves that."

"Why didn't you unlimber the long rifle?" interposed Dave, curiously.

"I got it full of water and sand. That reminds me I must see about cleaning it. I never thought of shooting back. Silvermane was running too fast."

"Jack, you can see I am in the worst fix of my life," said August Naab. "My sons have persuaded me that I was pushed off my ranges too easily. I've come to believe Martin Cole; certainly his prophecy has come true. Dave brought news from White Sage, and it's almost unbelievable. Holderness has proclaimed himself or has actually got himself elected sheriff. He holds office over the Mormons from whom he steals. Scarcely a day goes by in the village without a killing. The Mormons north of Lund finally banded together, hanged some rustlers, and drove the others out. Many of them have come down into our country, and Holderness now has a strong force. But the Mormons will rise against him. I know it; I see it. I am waiting for it. We are God-fearing, life-loving men, slow to wrath. But—"

The deep rolling burr in his voice showed emotion too deep for words.

"They need a leader," replied Hare, sharply.

August Naab rose with haggard face and his eyes had the look of a man accused.

"Dad figures this way," put in Dave. "On the one hand we lose our water and stock without bloodshed. We have a living in the oasis. There's little here to attract rustlers, so we may live in peace if we give up our rights. On the other hand, suppose Dad gets the Navajos down here and we join them and go after Holderness and his gang. There's going to be an all-fired bloody fight. Of course we'd wipe out the rustlers, but some of us would get killed—and there are the wives and kids. See!"

The force of August Naab's argument for peace, entirely aside from his Christian repugnance to the shedding of blood, was plainly unassailable.

"Remember what Snap said?" asked Hare, suddenly. "One man to kill Dene! Therefore one man to kill Holderness! That would break the power of this band."

"Ah! you've said it," replied Dave, raising a tense arm. "It's a one-man job. D—n Snap! He could have done it, if he hadn't gone to the bad. But it won't be easy. I tried to get Holderness. He was wise, and his men politely said they had enjoyed my call, but I wasn't to come again."

"One man to kill Holderness!" repeated Hare.

August Naab cast at the speaker one of his far-seeing glances; then he shook himself, as if to throw off the grip of something hard and inevitable. "I'm still master here," he said, and his voice showed the conquest of his passions.

"I give up Silver Cup and my stock. Maybe that will content Holderness."

Some days went by pleasantly for Hare, as he rested from his long exertions. Naab's former cheer and that of his family reasserted itself once the decision was made, and the daily life went on as usual. The sons worked in the fields by day, and in the evening played at pitching horseshoes on the bare circle where the children romped. The women went on baking, sewing, and singing. August Naab's prayers were more fervent than ever, and he even prayed for the soul of the man who had robbed him. Mescal's cheeks soon rounded out to their old contour and her eyes shone with a happier light than Hare had ever seen there. The races between Silvermane and Black Bolly were renewed on the long stretch under the wall, and Mescal forgot that she had once acknowledged the superiority of the gray. The cottonwoods showered silken floss till the cabins and grass were white; the birds returned to the oasis; the sun kissed warm color into the cherries, and the distant noise of the river seemed like the humming of a swarm of bees.

"Here, Jack," said August Naab, one morning, "get a spade and come with me. There's a break somewhere in the ditch."

Hare went with him out along the fence by the alfalfa fields, and round the corner of red wall toward the irrigating dam.

"Well, Jack, I suppose you'll be asking me for Mescal one of these days," said Naab.

"Yes," replied Hare.

"There's a little story to tell you about Mescal, when the day comes."

"Tell it now."

"No. Not yet. I'm glad you found her. I never knew her to be so happy, not even when she was a child. But somehow there's a better feeling between her and my womenfolk. The old antagonism is gone. Well, well, life is so. I pray that things may turn out well for you and her. But I fear—I seem to see—Hare, I'm a poor man once more. I can't do for you what I'd like. Still we'll see, we'll hope."

Hare was perfectly happy. The old Mormon's hint did not disturb him; even the thought of Snap Naab did not return to trouble his contentment. The full present was sufficient for Hare, and his joy bubbled over, bringing smiles to August's grave face. Never had a summer afternoon in the oasis been so fair. The green fields, the red walls, the blue sky, all seemed drenched in deeper, richer hues. The wind-song in the crags, the river-murmur from the canyon, filled Hare's ears with music. To be alive, to feel the sun, to see the colors, to hear the sounds, was beautiful; and to know that Mescal awaited him, was enough.

Work on the washed-out bank of the ditch had not gone far when Naab raised his head as if listening.

"Did you hear anything?" he asked.

"No," replied Hare.

"The roar of the river is heavy here. Maybe I was mistaken. I thought I heard shots." Then he went on spading clay into the break, but he stopped every moment or so, uneasily, as if he could not get rid of some disturbing thought. Suddenly he dropped the spade and his eyes flashed.

"Judith! Judith! Here!" he called. Wheeling with a sudden premonition of evil Hare saw the girl running along the wall toward them. Her face was white as death; she wrung her hands and her cries rose above the sound of the river. Naab sprang toward her and Hare ran at his heels.

"Father!— Father!" she panted. "Come—quick—the rustlers!—the rustlers! Snap!—Dene—Oh—hurry! They've killed Dave—they've got Mescal!"

Death itself shuddered through Hare's veins and then a raging flood of fire. He bounded forward to be flung back by Naab's arm.

XVII. THE SWOOP OF THE HAWK

"Fool! Would you throw away your life? Go slowly. We'll slip through the fields, under the trees."

Sick and cold Hare hurried by Naab's side round the wall and into the alfalfa. There were moments when he was weak and trembling; others when he could have leaped like a tiger to rend and kill.

They left the fields and went on more cautiously into the grove. The screaming and wailing of women added certainty to their doubt and dread.

"I see only the women—the children—no—there's a man—Zeke," said Hare, bending low to gaze under the branches.

"Go slow," muttered Naab.

"The rustlers rode off—after Mescal—she's gone!" panted Judith.

Hare, spurred by the possibilities in the half-crazed girl's speech, cast caution to the winds and dashed forward into the glade. Naab's heavy steps thudded behind him.

In the corner of the porch scared and stupefied children huddled in a heap. George and Billy bent over Dave, who sat white-faced against the steps. Blood oozed through the fingers pressed to his breast. Zeke was trying to calm the women.

"My God! Dave!" cried Hare. "You're not hard hit? Don't say it!"

"Hard hit—Jack—old fellow," replied Dave, with a pale smile. His face was white and clammy.

August Naab looked once at him and groaned, "My son! My son!"

"Dad—I got Chance and Culver—there they lie in the road—not bungled, either!"

Hare saw the inert forms of two men lying near the gate; one rested on his face, arm outstretched with a Colt gripped in the stiff hand; the other lay on his back, his spurs deep in the ground, as if driven there in his last convulsion.

August Naab and Zeke carried the injured man into the house. The women and children followed, and Hare, with Billy and George, entered last.

"Dad—I'm shot clean through—low down," said Dave, as they laid him on a couch. "It's just as well I—as any one—somebody had to—start this fight."

Naab got the children and the girls out of the room. The women were silent now, except Dave's wife, who clung to him with low moans. He smiled upon all with a quick intent smile, then he held out a hand to Hare.

"Jack, we got—to be—good friends. Don't forget—that—when you meet—Holderness. He shot me—from behind Chance and Culver—and after I fell—I killed them both—trying to get him. You—won't hang up—your gun—again—will you?"

Hare wrung the cold hand clasping his so feebly. "No! Dave, no!" Then he fled from the room. For an hour he stood on the porch waiting in dumb misery. George and Zeke came noiselessly out, followed by their father.

"It's all over, Hare." Another tragedy had passed by this man of the desert, and left his strength unshaken, but his deadly quiet and the gloom of his iron face were more terrible to see than any grief.

"Father, and you, Hare, come out into the road," said George.

Another motionless form lay beyond Chance and Culver. It was that of a slight man, flat on his back, his arms wide, his long black hair in the dust. Under the white level brow the face had been crushed into a bloody curve.

"Dene!" burst from Hare, in a whisper.

"Killed by a horse!" exclaimed August Naab. "Ah! What horse?"

"Silvermane!" replied George.

"Who rode my horse—tell me—quick!" cried Hare, in a frenzy.

"It was Mescal. Listen. Let me tell you how it all happened. I was out at the forge when I heard a bunch of horses coming up the lane. I wasn't packing my gun, but I ran anyway. When I got to the house there was Dave facing Snap, Dene, and a bunch of rustlers. I saw Chance at first, but not Holderness. There must have been twenty men.

"'I came after Mescal, that's what,' Snap was saying.

"'You can't have her,' Dave answered.

"'We'll shore take her, an' we want Silvermane, too,' said Dene.

"'So you're a horse-thief as well as a rustler?' asked Dave.

"'Naab, I ain't in any mind to fool. Snap wants the girl, an' I want Silvermane, an' that damned spy that come back to life.'

"Then Holderness spoke from the back of the crowd: 'Naab, you'd better hurry, if you don't want the house burned!'

"Dave drew and Holderness fired from behind the men. Dave fell, raised up and shot Chance and Culver, then dropped his gun.

"With that the women in the house began to scream, and Mescal ran out saying she'd go with Snap if they'd do no more harm.

"'All right,' said Snap, 'get a horse, hurry—hurry!'

"Then Dene dismounted and went toward the corral saying, 'I shore want Silvermane.'

"Mescal reached the gate ahead of Dene. 'Let me get Silvermane. He's wild; he doesn't know you; he'll kick you if you go near him.' She dropped the bars and went up to the horse. He was rearing and snorting. She coaxed him down and then stepped up on the fence to untie him. When she had him loose she leaped off the fence to his back, screaming as she hit him with the halter. Silvermane snorted and jumped, and in three jumps he was going like a bullet. Dene tried to stop him, and was knocked twenty feet. He was raising up when the stallion ran over him. He never moved again. Once in the lane Silvermane got going—Lord! how he did run! Mescal hung low over his neck like an Indian. He was gone in a cloud of dust before Snap and the rustlers knew what had happened. Snap came to first and, yelling and waving his gun, spurred down the lane. The rest of the rustlers galloped after him."

August Naab placed a sympathetic hand on Hare's shaking shoulder.

"You see, lad, things are never so bad as they seem at first. Snap might as well try to catch a bird as Silvermane."

XVIII. THE HERITAGE OF THE DESERT

"MESCAL'S far out in front by this time. Depend on it, Hare," went on Naab. "That trick was the cunning Indian of her. She'll ride Silvermane into White Sage to-morrow night. Then she'll hide from Snap. The Bishop will take care of her. She'll be safe for the present in White Sage. Now we must bury these men. To-morrow—my son. Then—"

"What then?" Hare straightened up.

Unutterable pain darkened the flame in the Mormon's gaze. For an instant his face worked spasmodically, only to stiffen into a stony mask. It was the old conflict once more, the never-ending war between flesh and spirit. And now the flesh had prevailed.

"The time has come!" said George Naab.

"Yes," replied his father, harshly.

A great calm settled over Hare; his blood ceased to race, his mind to riot; in August Naab's momentous word he knew the old man had found himself. At last he had learned the lesson of the desert—to strike first and hard.

"Zeke, hitch up a team," said August Naab. "No—wait a moment. Here comes Piute. Let's hear what he has to say."

Piute appeared on the zigzag cliff-trail, driving a burro at dangerous speed.

"He's sighted Silvermane and the rustlers," suggested George, as the shepherd approached.

Naab translated the excited Indian's mingling of Navajo and Piute languages to mean just what George had said. "Snap ahead of riders—Silvermane far, far ahead of Snap—running fast—damn!"

"Mescal's pushing him hard to make the sand-strip," said George.

"Piute—three fires to-night—Lookout Point!" This order meant the execution of August Naab's hurry-signal for the Navajos, and after he had given it, he waved the Indian toward the cliff, and lapsed into a silence which no one dared to break.

Naab consigned the bodies of the rustlers to the famous cemetery under the red wall. He laid Dene in grave thirty-one. It was the grave that the outlaw had promised as the last resting-place of Dene's spy. Chance and Culver he buried together. It was noteworthy that no Mormon rites were conferred on Culver, once a Mormon in good standing, nor were any prayers spoken over the open graves.

What did August Naab intend to do? That was the question in Hare's mind as he left the house. It was a silent day, warm as summer, though the sun was overcast with gray clouds; the birds were quiet in the trees; there was no bray of burro or clarion-call of peacock, even the hum of the river had fallen into silence. Hare wandered over the farm and down the red lane, brooding over the issue. Naab's few words had been full of meaning; the cold gloom so foreign to his nature, had been even more impressive. His had been the revolt of the meek. The gentle, the loving, the administering, the spiritual uses of his life had failed.

Hare recalled what the desert had done to his own nature, how it had bred in him its impulse to fight, to resist, to survive. If he, a stranger of a few years, could be moulded in the flaming furnace of its fiery life, what then must be the cast of August Naab, born on the desert, and sleeping five nights out of seven on the sands for sixty years?

The desert! Hare trembled as he grasped all its meaning. Then he slowly resolved that meaning. There were the measureless distances to narrow the eye and teach restraint; the untrodden trails, the shifting sands, the thorny brakes, the broken lava to pierce the flesh; the heights and depths, unscalable and unplumbed. And over all the sun, red and burning.

The parched plants of the desert fought for life, growing far apart, sending enormous roots deep to pierce the sand and split the rock for moisture, arming every leaf with a barbed thorn or poisoned sap, never thriving and ever thirsting.

The creatures of the desert endured the sun and lived without water, and were at endless war. The hawk had a keener eye than his fellow of more fruitful lands, sharper beak, greater spread of wings, and claws of deeper curve. For him there was little to eat, a rabbit now, a rock-rat then; nature made his swoop like lightning and it never missed its aim. The gaunt wolf never failed in his sure scent, in his silent hunt. The lizard flicked an invisible tongue into the heart of a flower; and the bee he caught stung with a poisoned sting. The battle of life went to the strong.

So the desert trained each of its wild things to survive. No eye of the desert but burned with the flame of the sun. To kill or to escape death—that was the dominant motive. To fight barrenness and heat—that was stern enough, but each creature must fight his fellow.

What then of the men who drifted into the desert and survived? They must of necessity endure the wind and heat, the drouth and famine; they must grow lean and hard, keen-eyed and silent. The weak, the humble, the sacrificing must be winnowed from among them. As each man developed he took on some aspect of the desert—Holderness had the amber clearness of its distances in his eyes, its deceit in his soul; August Naab, the magnificence of the desert-pine in his giant form, its strength in his heart; Snap Naab, the cast of the hawk-beak in his face, its cruelty in his nature. But all shared alike in the common element of survival—ferocity. August Naab had subdued his to the promptings of a Christ-like spirit; yet did not his very energy, his wonderful tirelessness, his will to achieve, his power to resist, partake of that fierceness? Moreover, after many struggles, he too had been overcome by the desert's call for blood. His mystery was no longer a mystery. Always in those moments of revelation which he disclaimed, he had seen himself as faithful to the desert in the end.

Hare's slumbers that night were broken. He dreamed of a great gray horse leaping in the sky from cloud to cloud with the lightning and the thunder under his hoofs, the storm-winds sweeping from his silver mane. He dreamed of Mescal's brooding eyes. They were dark gateways of the desert open only to him, and he entered to chase the alluring stars deep into the purple distance. He dreamed of himself waiting in serene confidence for some unknown thing to pass. He awakened late in the morning and found the house hushed. The day wore on in a repose unstirred by breeze and sound, in accord with the mourning of August Naab. At noon a solemn procession wended its slow course to the shadow of the red cliff, and as solemnly returned.

Then a long-drawn piercing Indian whoop broke the midday hush. It heralded the approach of the Navajos. In single-file they rode up the lane, and when the falcon-eyed Eschtah dismounted before his white friend, the line of his warriors still turned the corner of the red wall. Next to the chieftain rode Scarbreast, the grim war-lord of the Navajos. His followers trailed into the grove. Their sinewy bronze bodies, almost naked, glistened wet from the river. Full a hundred strong were they, a silent, lean-limbed desert troop.

"The White Prophet's fires burned bright," said the chieftain. "Eschtah is here."

"The Navajo is a friend," replied Naab. "The white man needs counsel and help. He has fallen upon evil days."

"Eschtah sees war in the eyes of his friend."

"War, chief, war! Let the Navajo and his warriors rest and eat. Then we shall speak."

A single command from the Navajo broke the waiting files of warriors. Mustangs were turned into the fields, packs were unstrapped from the burros, blankets spread under the cottonwoods. When the afternoon waned and the shade from the western wall crept into the oasis, August Naab came from his cabin clad in buckskins, with a large blue Colt swinging handle outward from his left hip. He ordered his sons to replenish the fire which had been built in the circle, and when the fierce-eyed Indians gathered round the blaze he called to his women to bring meat and drink.

Hare's unnatural calmness had prevailed until he saw Naab stride out to front the waiting Indians. Then a ripple of cold passed over him. He leaned against a tree in the shadow and watched the gray-faced giant stalking to and fro before his Indian friends. A long while he strode in the circle of light to pause at length before the chieftains and to break the impressive silence with his deep voice.

"Eschtah sees before him a friend stung to his heart. Men of his own color have long injured him, yet have lived. The Mormon loved his fellows and forgave. Five sons he laid in their graves, yet his heart was not hardened. His first-born went the trail of the fire-water and is an outcast from his people. Many enemies has he and one is a chief. He has killed the white man's friends, stolen his cattle, and his water. To-day the white man laid another son in his grave. What thinks the chief? Would he not crush the scorpion that stung him?"

The old Navajo answered in speech which, when translated, was as stately as the Mormon's.

"Eschtah respects his friend, but he has not thought him wise. The White Prophet sees visions of things to come, but his blood is cold. He asks too much of the white man's God. He is a chief; he has an eye like the lightning, an arm strong as the pine, yet he has not struck. Eschtah grieves. He does not wish to shed blood for pleasure. But Eschtah's friend has let too many selfish men cross his range and drink at his springs. Only a few can live on the desert. Let him who has found the springs and the trails keep them for his own. Let him who came too late go away to find for himself, to prove himself a warrior, or let his bones whiten in the sand. The Navajo counsels his white friend to kill."

"The great Eschtah speaks wise words," said Naab. "The White Prophet is richer for them. He will lay aside the prayers to his unseeing God, and will seek his foe."

"It is well."

"The white man's foe is strong," went on the Mormon; "he has many men, they will fight. If Eschtah sends his braves with his friend there will be war. Many braves will fall. The White Prophet wishes to save them if he can. He will go forth alone to kill his foe. If the sun sets four times and the white man is not here, then Eschtah will send his great war-chief and his warriors. They will kill whom they find at the white man's springs. And thereafter half of all the white man's cattle that were stolen shall be Eschtah's, so that he watch over the water and range."

"Eschtah greets a chief," answered the Indian. "The White Prophet knows he will kill his enemy, but he is not sure he will return. He is not sure that the little braves of his foe will fly like the winds, yet he hopes. So he holds the Navajo back to the last. Eschtah will watch the sun set four times. If his white friend returns he will rejoice. If he does not return the Navajo will send his warriors on the trail."

August Naab walked swiftly from the circle of light into the darkness; his heavy steps sounded on the porch, and in the hallway. His three sons went toward their cabins with bowed heads and silent tongues. Eschtah folded his blanket about him and stalked off into the gloom of the grove, followed by his warriors.

Hare remained in the shadow of the cottonwood where he had stood unnoticed. He had not moved a muscle since he had heard August Naab's declaration. That one word of Naab's intention, "Alone!" had arrested him. For it had struck into his heart and mind. It had paralyzed him with the revelation it brought; for Hare now knew as he had never known anything before, that he would forestall August Naab, avenge the death of Dave, and kill the rustler Holderness. Through blinding shock he passed slowly into cold acceptance of his heritage from the desert.

The two long years of his desert training were as an open page to Hare's unveiled eyes. The life he owed to August Naab, the strength built up by the old man's knowledge of the healing power of plateau and range—these lay in a long curve between the day Naab had lifted him out of the White Sage trail and this day of the Mormon's extremity. A long curve with Holderness's insulting blow at the beginning, his murder of a beloved friend at the end! For Hare remembered the blow, and never would he forget Dave's last words. Yet unforgetable as these were, it was duty rather than revenge that called him. This was August Naab's hour of need. Hare knew himself to be the tool of inscrutable fate; he was the one to fight the old desert-scarred Mormon's battle. Hare recalled how humbly he had expressed his gratitude to Naab, and the apparent impossibility of ever repaying him, and then Naab's reply: "Lad, you can never tell how one man may repay another." Hare could pay his own debt and that of the many wanderers who had drifted across the sands to find a home with the Mormon. These men stirred in their graves, and from out the shadow of the cliff whispered the voice of Mescal's nameless father: "Is there no one to rise up for this old hero of the desert?"

Softly Hare slipped into his room. Putting on coat and belt and catching up his rifle he stole out again stealthily, like an Indian. In the darkness of the wagon-shed he felt for his saddle, and finding it, he groped with eager hands for the grain-box; raising the lid he filled a measure with grain, and emptied it into his saddle-bag. Then lifting the saddle he carried it out of the yard, through the gate and across the lane to the corrals. The wilder mustangs in the far corral began to kick and snort, and those in the corral where Black Bolly was kept trooped noisily to the bars. Bolly whinnied and thrust her black muzzle over the fence. Hare placed a caressing hand on her while he waited listening and watching. It was not unusual for the mustangs to get restless at any time, and Hare was confident that this would pass without investigation.

Gradually the restless stampings and suspicious snortings ceased, and Hare, letting down the bars, led Bolly out into the lane. It was the work of a moment to saddle her; his bridle hung where he always kept it, on the pommel, and with nimble fingers he shortened the several straps to fit Bolly's head, and slipped the bit between her teeth. Then he put up the bars of the gate.

Before mounting he stood a moment thinking coolly, deliberately numbering the several necessities he must not forget—grain for Bolly, food for himself, his Colt and Winchester, cartridges, canteen, matches, knife. He inserted a hand into one of his saddle-bags expecting to find some strips of meat. The bag was empty. He felt in the other one, and under the grain he found what he sought. The canteen lay in the coil of his lasso tied to the saddle, and its heavy canvas covering was damp to his touch. With that he thrust the long Winchester into its saddle-sheath, and swung his leg over the mustang.

The house of the Naabs was dark and still. The dying council-fire cast flickering shadows under the black cottonwoods where the Navajos slept. The faint breeze that rustled the leaves brought the low sullen roar of the river.

Hare guided Bolly into the thick dust of the lane, laid the bridle loosely on her neck for her to choose the trail, and silently rode out into the lonely desert night.

XIX. UNLEASHED

HARE, listening breathlessly, rode on toward the gateway of the cliffs, and when he had passed the corner of the wall he sighed in relief. Spurring Bolly into a trot he rode forward with a strange elation. He had slipped out of the oasis unheard, and it would be morning before August Naab discovered his absence, perhaps longer before he divined his purpose. Then Hare would have a long start. He thrilled with something akin to fear when he pictured the old man's rage, and wondered what change it would make in his plans. Hare saw in mind Naab and his sons, and the Navajos sweeping in pursuit to save him from the rustlers.

But the future must take care of itself, and he addressed all the faculties at his command to cool consideration of the present. The strip of sand under the Blue Star had to be crossed at night—a feat which even the Navajos did not have to their credit. Yet Hare had no shrinking; he had no doubt; he must go on. As he had been drawn to the Painted Desert by a voiceless call, so now he was urged forward by something nameless.

In the blackness of the night it seemed as if he were riding through a vaulted hall swept by a current of air. The night had turned cold, the stars had brightened icily, the rumble of the river had died away when Bolly's ringing trot suddenly changed to a noiseless floundering walk. She had come upon the sand. Hare saw the Blue Star in the cliff, and once more loosed the rein on Bolly's neck. She stopped and champed her bit, and turned her black head to him as if to intimate that she wanted the guidance of a sure arm. But as it was not forthcoming she stepped onward into the yielding sand.

With hands resting idly on the pommel Hare sat at ease in the saddle. The billowy dunes reflected the pale starlight and fell away from him to darken in obscurity. So long as the Blue Star remained in sight he kept his sense of direction; when it had disappeared he felt himself lost. Bolly's course seemed as crooked as the jagged outline of the cliffs. She climbed straight up little knolls, descended them at an angle, turned sharply at wind-washed gullies, made winding detours, zigzagged levels that shone like a polished floor; and at last (so it seemed to Hare) she doubled back on her trail. The black cliff receded over the waves of sand; the stars changed positions, travelled round in the blue dome, and the few that he knew finally sank below the horizon. Bolly never lagged; she was like the homeward-bound horse, indifferent to direction because sure of it, eager to finish the journey because now it was short. Hare was glad though not surprised when she snorted and cracked her iron-shod hoof on a stone at the edge of the sand. He smiled with tightening lips as he rode into the shadow of a rock which he recognized. Bolly had crossed the treacherous belt of dunes and washes and had struck the trail on the other side.

The long level of wind-carved rocks under the cliffs, the ridges of the desert, the miles of slow ascent up to the rough divide, the gradual descent to the cedars—these stretches of his journey took the night hours and ended with the brightening gray in the east. Within a mile of Silver Cup Spring Hare dismounted, to tie folded pads of buckskin on Bolly's hoofs. When her feet were muffled, he cautiously advanced on the trail for the matter of a hundred rods or more; then sheered off to the right into the cedars. He led Bolly slowly, without rattling a stone or snapping a twig, and stopped every few paces to listen. There was no sound other than the wind in the cedars. Presently, with a gasp, he caught the dull gleam of a burned-out camp-fire. Then his movements became as guarded, as noiseless as those of a scouting Indian. The dawn broke over the red wall as he gained the trail beyond the spring.

He skirted the curve of the valley and led Bolly a little way up the wooded slope to a dense thicket of aspens in a hollow. This thicket encircled a patch of grass. Hare pressed the lithe aspens aside to admit Bolly and left her there free. He drew his rifle from its sheath and, after assuring himself that the mustang could not be seen or heard from below, he bent his steps diagonally up the slope.

Every foot of this ground he knew, and he climbed swiftly until he struck the mountain trail. Then, descending, he entered the cedars. At last he reached a point directly above the cliff-camp where he had spent so many days, and this he knew overhung the cabin built by Holderness. He stole down from tree to tree and slipped from thicket to thicket. The sun, red as blood, raised a bright crescent over the red wall; the soft mists of the valley began to glow and move; cattle were working in toward the spring. Never brushing a branch, never dislodging a stone, Hare descended the slope, his eyes keener, his ears sharper with every step. Soon the edge of the gray stone cliff below shut out the lower level of cedars. While resting he listened. Then he marked his course down the last bit of slanting ground to the cliff bench which faced the valley. This space was open, rough with crumbling rock and dead cedar brush—a difficult place to cross without sound. Deliberate in his choice of steps, very slow in moving, Hare went on with a stealth which satisfied even his intent ear. When the wide gray strip of stone drew slowly into the circle of his downcast gaze he sank to the ground with a slight trembling in all his limbs. There was a thick bush on the edge of the cliff; in three steps he could reach it and, unseen himself, look down upon the camp.

A little cloud or smoke rose lazily and capped a slender column of blue. Sounds were wafted softly upward, the low voices of men in conversation, a merry whistle, and then the humming of a tune. Hare's mouth was dry and his temples throbbed as he asked himself what it was best to do. The answer came instantaneously as though it had lain just below the level of his conscious thought. "I'll watch till Holderness walks out into sight, jump up with a yell when he comes, give him time to see me, to draw his gun—then kill him!"

Hare slipped to the bush, drew in a deep long breath that stilled his agitation, and peered over the cliff. The crude shingles of the cabin first rose into sight; then beyond he saw the corral with a number of shaggy mustangs and a great gray horse. Hare stared blankly. As in a dream he saw the proud arch of a splendid neck, the graceful wave of a white-crested mane.

"Silvermane!... My God!" he gasped, suddenly. "They caught him—after all!"

He fell backward upon the cliff and lay there with hands clinching his rifle, shudderingly conscious of a blow, trying to comprehend its meaning.

"Silvermane!... they caught him—after all!" he kept repeating; then in a flash of agonized understanding he whispered: "Mescal... Mescal!"

He rolled upon his face, shutting out the blue sky; his body stretched stiff as a bent spring released from its compress, and his nails dented the stock of his rifle. Then this rigidity softened to sobs that shook him from head to foot. He sat up, haggard and wild-eyed.

Silvermane had been captured, probably by rustlers waiting at the western edge of the sand-strip. Mescal had fallen into the hands of Snap Naab. But Mescal was surely alive and Snap was there to be killed; his long career of unrestrained cruelty was in its last day—something told Hare that this thing must and should be. The stern deliberation of his intent to kill Holderness, the passion of his purpose to pay his debt to August Naab, were as nothing compared to the gathering might of this new resolve; suddenly he felt free and strong as an untamed lion broken free from his captors.

From the cover of the bush he peered again over the cliff. The cabin with its closed door facing him was scarcely two hundred feet down from his hiding-place. One of the rustlers sang as he bent over the camp-fire and raked the coals around the pots; others lounged on a bench waiting for breakfast; some rolled out of their blankets; they stretched and yawned, and pulling on their boots made for the spring. The last man to rise was Snap Naab, and he had slept with his head on the threshold of the door. Evidently Snap had made Mescal a prisoner in the cabin, and no one could go in or out without stepping upon him. The rustler-foreman of Holderness's company had slept with his belt containing two Colts, nor had he removed his boots. Hare noted these details with grim humor. Now the tall Holderness, face shining, gold-red beard agleam, rounded the cabin whistling. Hare watched the rustlers sit down to breakfast, and here and there caught a loud-spoken word, and marked their leisurely care-free manner. Snap Naab took up a pan of food and a cup of coffee, carried them into the cabin, and came out, shutting the door.

After breakfast most of the rustlers set themselves to their various tasks. Hare watched them with the eyes of a lynx watching deer. Several men were arranging articles for packing, and their actions were slow to the point of laziness; others trooped down toward the corral. Holderness rolled a cigarette and stooped over the campfire to reach a burning stick. Snap Naab stalked to and fro before the door of the cabin. He alone of the rustler's band showed restlessness, and more than once he glanced up the trail that led over the divide toward his father's oasis. Holderness sent expectant glances in the other direction toward Seeping Springs. Once his clear voice rang out:

"I tell you, Naab, there's no hurry. We'll ride in tomorrow."

A thousand thoughts flitted through Hare's mind—a steady stream of questions and answers. Why did Snap look anxiously along the oasis trail? It was not that he feared his father or his brothers alone, but there was always the menace of the Navajos. Why was Holderness in no hurry to leave Silver Cup? Why did he lag at the spring when, if he expected riders from his ranch, he could have gone on to meet them, obviously saving time and putting greater distance between him and the men he had wronged? Was it utter fearlessness or only a deep-played game? Holderness and his rustlers, all except the gloomy Naab, were blind to the peril that lay beyond the divide. How soon would August Naab strike out on the White Sage trail? Would he come alone? Whether he came alone or at the head of his hard-riding Navajos he would arrive too late. Holderness's life was not worth a pinch of the ashes he flecked so carelessly from his cigarette. Snap Naab's gloom, his long stride, his nervous hand always on or near the butt of his Colt, spoke the keenness of his desert instinct. For him the sun had arisen red over the red wall. Had he harmed Mescal? Why did he keep the cabin door shut and guard it so closely?

While Hare watched and thought the hours sped by. Holderness lounged about and Snap kept silent guard. The rustlers smoked, slept, and moved about; the day waned, and the shadow of the cliff crept over the cabin. To Hare the time had been as a moment; he was amazed to find the sun had gone down behind Coconina. If August Naab had left the oasis at dawn he must now be near the divide, unless he had been delayed by a wind-storm at the strip of sand. Hare longed to see the roan charger come up over the crest; he longed to see a file of Navajos, plumes waving, dark mustangs gleaming in the red light, sweep down the stony ridge toward the cedars. "If they come," he whispered, "I'll kill Holderness and Snap and any man who tries to open that cabin door."

So he waited in tense watchfulness, his gaze alternating between the wavy line of the divide and the camp glade. Out in the valley it was still daylight, but under the cliff twilight had fallen. All day Hare had strained his ears to hear the talk of the rustlers, and it now occurred to him that if he climbed down through the split in the cliff to the bench where Dave and George had always hidden to watch the spring he would be just above the camp. This descent involved risk, but since it would enable him to see the cabin door when darkness set in, he decided to venture. The moment was propitious, for the rustlers were bustling around, cooking dinner, unrolling blankets, and moving to and fro from spring and corral. Hare crawled back a few yards and along the cliff until he reached the split. It was a narrow steep crack which he well remembered. Going down was attended with two dangers—losing his hold, and the possible rattling of stones. Face foremost he slipped downward with the gliding, sinuous movement of a snake, and reaching the grassy bench he lay quiet. Jesting voices and loud laughter from below reassured him. He had not been heard. His new position afforded every chance to see and hear, and also gave means of rapid, noiseless retreat along the bench to the cedars. Lying flat he crawled stealthily to the bushy fringe of the bench.

A bright fire blazed under the cliff. Men were moving and laughing. The cabin door was open. Mescal stood leaning back from Snap Naab, struggling to release her hands.

"Let me untie them, I say," growled Snap.

Mescal tore loose from him and stepped back. Her hands were bound before her, and twisting them outward, she warded him off. Her dishevelled hair almost hid her dark eyes. They burned in a level glance of hate and defiance. She was a little lioness, quivering with fiery life, fight in every line of her form.

"All right, don't eat then—starve!" said Snap.

"I'll starve before I eat what you give me."

The rustlers laughed. Holderness blew out a puff of smoke and smiled. Snap glowered upon Mescal and then upon his amiable companions. One of them, a ruddy-faced fellow, walked toward Mescal.

"Cool down, Snap, cool down," he said. "We're not goin' to stand for a girl starvin'. She ain't eat a bite yet. Here, Miss, let me untie your hands—there. . . . Say! Naab, d—n you, her wrists are black an' blue!"

"Look out! Your gun!" yelled Snap.

With a swift movement Mescal snatched the man's Colt from its holster and was raising it when he grasped her arm. She winced and dropped the weapon.

"You little Indian devil!" exclaimed the rustler, in a rapt admiration. "Sorry to hurt you, an' more'n sorry to spoil your aim. Thet wasn't kind to throw my own gun on me, jest after I'd played the gentleman, now, was it?"

"I didn't—intend—to shoot—you," panted Mescal.

"Naab, if this's your Mormon kind of wife—excuse me! Though I ain't denyin' she's the sassiest an' sweetest little cat I ever seen!"

"We Mormons don't talk about our women or hear any talk," returned Snap, a dancing fury in his pale eyes. "You're from Nebraska?"

"Yep, jest a plain Nebraska rustler, cattle-thief, an' all round no-good customer, though I ain't taken to houndin' women yet."

For answer Snap Naab's right hand slowly curved upward before him and stopped taut and inflexible, while his strange eyes seemed to shoot sparks.

"See here, Naab, why do you want to throw a gun on me?" asked the rustler, coolly. "Haven't you shot enough of your friends yet? I reckon I've no right to interfere in your affairs. I was only protestin' friendly like, for the little lady. She's game, an' she's called your hand. An' it's not a straight hand. Thet's all, an' d—n if I care whether you are a Mormon or not. I'll bet a hoss Holderness will back me up."

"Snap, he's right," put in Holderness, smoothly. "You needn't be so touchy about Mescal. She's showed what little use she's got for you. If you must rope her around like you do a mustang, be easy about it. Let's have supper. Now, Mescal, you sit here on the bench and behave yourself. I don't want you shooting up my camp."

Snap turned sullenly aside while Holderness seated Mescal near the door and fetched her food and drink. The rustlers squatted round the camp-fire, and conversation ceased in the business of the meal.

To Hare the scene had brought a storm of emotions. Joy at the sight of Mescal, blessed relief to see her unscathed, pride in her fighting spirit—these came side by side with gratitude to the kind Nebraska rustler, strange deepening insight into Holderness's game, unextinguishable white-hot hatred of Snap Naab. And binding all was the ever-mounting will to rescue Mescal, which was held in check by an inexorable judgment; he must continue to wait. And he did wait with blind faith in the something to be, keeping ever in mind the last resort—the rifle he clutched with eager hands. Meanwhile the darkness descended, the fire sent forth a brighter blaze, and the rustlers finished their supper. Mescal arose and stepped across the threshold of the cabin door.

"Hold on!" ordered Snap, as he approached with swift strides. "Stick out your hands!"

Some of the rustlers grumbled; and one blurted out: "Aw no, Snap, don't tie her up—no!"

"Who says no?" hissed the Mormon, with snapping teeth. As he wheeled upon them his Colt seemed to leap forward, and suddenly quivered at arm's-length, gleaming in the ruddy fire-rays.

Holderness laughed in the muzzle of the weapon. "Go ahead, Snap, tie up your lady love. What a tame little wife she's going to make you! Tie her up, but do it without hurting her."

The rustlers growled or laughed at their leader's order. Snap turned to his task. Mescal stood in the doorway and shrinkingly extended her clasped hands. Holderness whirled to the fire with a look which betrayed his game. Snap bound Mescal's hands securely, thrust her inside the cabin, and after hesitating for a long moment, finally shut the door.

"It's funny about a woman, now, ain't it?" said Nebraska, confidentially, to a companion. "One minnit she'll snatch you bald-headed; the next, she'll melt in your mouth like sugar. An' I'll be darned if the changeablest one ain't the kind to hold a feller longest. But it's h—l. I was married onct. Not any more for mine! A pal I had used to say thet whiskey riled him, thet rattlesnake pisen het up his blood some, but it took a woman to make him plumb bad. D—n if it ain't so. When there's a woman around there's somethin' allus comin' off."

But the strain, instead of relaxing, became portentous. Holderness suddenly showed he was ill at ease; he appeared to be expecting arrivals from the direction of Seeping Springs. Snap Naab leaned against the side of the door, his narrow gaze cunningly studying the rustlers before him. More than any other he had caught a foreshadowing. Like the desert-hawk he could see afar. Suddenly he pressed back against the door, half opening it while he faced the men.

"Stop!" commanded Holderness. The change in his voice was as if it had come from another man. "You don't go in there!"

"I'm going to take the girl and ride to White Sage," replied Naab, in slow deliberation.

"Bah! You say that only for the excuse to get into the cabin with her. You tried it last night and I blocked you. Shut the door, Naab, or something'll happen."

"There's more going to happen than ever you think of, Holderness. Don't interfere now, I'm going."

"Well, go ahead—but you won't take the girl!"

Snap Naab swung off the step, slamming the door behind him.

"So-ho!" he exclaimed, sneeringly. "That's why you've made me foreman, eh?" His claw-like hand moved almost imperceptibly upward while his pale eyes strove to pierce the strength behind Holderness's effrontery. The rustler chief had a trump card to play; one that showed in his sardonic smile.

"Naab, you don't get the girl."

"Maybe you'll get her?" hissed Snap.

"I always intended to."

Surely never before had passion driven Snap's hand to such speed. His Colt gleamed in the camp-fire light. Click! Click! Click! The hammer fell upon empty chambers.

"H—l!" he shrieked.

Holderness laughed sarcastically.

"That's where you're going!" he cried. "Here's to Naab's trick with a gun—Bah!" And he shot his foreman through the heart.

Snap plunged upon his face. His hands beat the ground like the shuffling wings of a wounded partridge. His fingers gripped the dust, spread convulsively, straightened, and sank limp.

Holderness called through the door of the cabin. "Mescal, I've rid you of your would-be husband. Cheer-up!" Then, pointing to the fallen man, he said to the nearest bystanders: "Some of you drag that out for the coyotes."

The first fellow who bent over Snap happened to be the Nebraska rustler, and he curiously opened the breech of the six-shooter he picked up. "No shells!" he said. He pulled Snap's second Colt from his belt, and unbreeched that. "No shells! Well, d—n me!" He surveyed the group of grim men, not one of whom had any reply.

Holderness again laughed harshly, and turning to the cabin, he fastened the door with a lasso.

It was a long time before Hare recovered from the startling revelation of the plot which had put Mescal into Holderness's power. Bad as Snap Naab had been he would have married her, and such a fate was infinitely preferable to the one that now menaced her. Hare changed his position and settled himself to watch and wait out the night. Every hour Holderness and his men tarried at Silver Cup hastened their approaching doom. Hare's strange prescience of the fatality that overshadowed these men had received its first verification in the sudden taking off of Snap Naab. The deep-scheming Holderness, confident that his strong band meant sure protection, sat and smoked and smiled beside the camp-fire. He had not caught even a hint of Snap Naab's suggested warning. Yet somewhere out on the oasis trail rode a man who, once turned from the saving of life to the lust to kill, would be as immutable as death itself. Behind him waited a troop of Navajos, swift as eagles, merciless as wolves, desert warriors with the sunheated blood of generations in their veins. As Hare waited and watched with all his inner being cold, he could almost feel pity for Holderness. His doom was close. Twice, when the rustler chief had sauntered nearer to the cabin door, as if to enter, Hare had covered him with the rifle, waiting, waiting for the step upon the threshold. But Holderness always checked himself in time, and Hare's finger eased its pressure upon the trigger.

The night closed in black; the clouded sky gave forth no starlight; the wind rose and moaned through the cedars. One by one the rustlers rolled in their blankets and all dropped into slumber while the camp-fire slowly burned down. The night hours wore on to the soft wail of the breeze and the wild notes of far-off trailing coyotes.

Hare, watching sleeplessly, saw one of the prone figures stir. The man raised himself very cautiously; he glanced at his companions, and looked long at Holderness, who lay squarely in the dimming light. Then he softly lowered himself. Hare wondered what the rustler meant to do. Presently he again lifted his head and turned it as if listening intently. His companions were motionless in deep-breathing sleep. Gently he slipped aside his blankets and began to rise. He was slow and guarded of movement; it took him long to stand erect. He stepped between the rustlers with stockinged feet which were as noiseless as an Indian's, and he went toward the cabin door.

He softly edged round the sleeping Holderness, showing a glinting six-shooter in his hand. Hare's resolve to kill him before he reached the door was checked. What did it mean, this rustler's stealthy movements, his passing by Holderness with his drawn weapon! Again doom hovered over the rustler chief. If he stirred!—Hare knew instantly that this softly stepping man was a Mormon; he was true to Snap Naab, to the woman pledged in his creed. He meant to free Mescal.

If ever Hare breathed a prayer it was then. What if one of the band awakened! As the rustler turned at the door his dark face gleamed in the flickering light. He unwound the lasso and opened the door without a sound.

Hare whispered: "Heavens! if he goes in she'll scream! that will wake Holderness—then I must shoot—I must!"

But the Mormon rustler added wisdom to his cunning and stealth.

"Hist!" he whispered into the cabin. "Hist!"

Mescal must have been awake; she must have guessed instantly the meaning of that low whisper, for silently she appeared in the doorway, silently she held forth her bound hands. The man untied the bonds and pointed into the cedars toward the corral. Swift and soundless as a flitting shadow Mescal vanished in the gloom. The Mormon stole with wary, unhurried steps back to his bed and rolled in his blankets.

Hare rose unsteadily, wavering in the hot grip of a moment that seemed to have but one issue—the killing of Holderness. Mescal would soon be upon Silvermane, far out on the White Sage trail, and this time there would be no sand-strip to trap her. But Hare could not kill the rustler while he was sleeping; and he could not awaken him without revealing to his men the escape of the girl. Hare stood there on the bench, gazing down on the blanketed Holderness. Why not kill him now, ending forever his power, and trust to chance for the rest? No, no! Hare flung the temptation from him. To ward off pursuit as long as possible, to aid Mescal in every way to some safe hiding-place, and then to seek Holderness—that was the forethought of a man who had learned to wait.

Under the dark projection of the upper cliff Hare felt his way to the cedar slope, and the trail, and then he went swiftly down into the little hollow where he had left Bolly. The darkness of the forest hindered him, but he came at length to the edge of the aspen thicket; he penetrated it, and guided toward Bolly by a suspicious stamp and neigh, he found her and quieted her with a word. He rode down the hollow, out upon the level valley.

The clouds had broken somewhat, letting pale light down through rifts. All about him cattle were lying in a thick gloom. It was penetrable for only a few rods. The ground was like a cushion under Bolly's hoofs, giving forth no sound. The mustang threw up her head, causing Hare to peer into the night-fog. Rapid hoof-beats broke the silence, a vague gray shadow moved into sight. He saw Silvermane and called as loudly as he dared. The stallion melted into the misty curtain, the beating of hoofs softened and ceased. Hare spurred Bolly to her fleetest. He had a long, silent chase, but it was futile, and unnecessarily hard on the mustang; so he pulled her in to a trot.

Hare kept Bolly to this gait the remainder of the night, and when the eastern sky lightened he found the trail and reached Seeping Springs at dawn. Silvermane's tracks were deep in the clay at the drinking-trough. He rested a few moments, gave Bolly sparingly of grain and water, and once more took to the trail.

From the ridge below the spring he saw Silvermane beyond the valley, miles ahead of him. This day seemed shorter than the foregoing one; it passed while he watched Silvermane grow smaller and smaller and disappear on the looming slope of Coconina. Hare's fear that Mescal would run into the riders Holderness expected from his ranch grew less and less after she had reached the cover of the cedars. That she would rest the stallion at the Navajo pool on the mountain he made certain. Late in the night he came to the camping spot and found no trace to prove that she had halted there even to let Silvermane drink. So he tied the tired mustang and slept until daylight.

He crossed the plateau and began the descent. Before he was half-way down the warm bright sun had cleared the valley of vapor and shadow. Far along the winding white trail shone a speck. It was Silvermane almost out of sight.

"Ten miles—fifteen, more maybe," said Hare. "Mescal will soon be in the village."

Again hours of travel flew by like winged moments. Thoughts of time, distance, monotony, fatigue, purpose, were shut out from his mind. A rushing kaleidoscopic dance of images filled his consciousness, but they were all of Mescal. Safety for her had unsealed the fountain of happiness.

It was near sundown when he rode Black Bolly into White Sage, and took the back road, and the pasture lane to Bishop Caldwell's cottage. John, one of the Bishop's sons, was in the barn-yard and ran to open the gate.

"Mescal!" cried Hare.

"Safe," replied the Mormon.

"Have you hidden her?"

"She's in a secret cave, a Mormon hiding-place for women. Only a few men know of its existence. Rest easy, for she's absolutely safe."

"Thank God!... then that's settled." Hare drew a long, deep breath.

"Mescal told us what happened, how she got caught at the sand-strip and escaped from Holderness at Silver Cup. Was Dene hurt?"

"Silvermane killed him."

"Good God! How things come about! I saw you run Dene down that time here in White Sage. It must have been written. Did Holderness shoot Snap Naab?"

"Yes."

"What of old Naab? Won't he come down here now to lead us Mormons against the rustlers?"

"He called the Navajos across the river. He meant to take the trail alone and kill Holderness, keeping the Indians back a few days. If he failed to return then they were to ride out on the rustlers. But his plan must be changed, for I came ahead of him."

"For what? Mescal?"

"No. For Holderness."

"You'll kill him!"

"Yes."

"He'll be coming soon?—When?"

"To-morrow, possibly by daylight. He wants Mescal. There's a chance Naab may have reached Silver Cup before Holderness left, but I doubt it."

"May I know your plan?" The Mormon hesitated while his strong brown face flashed with daring inspiration. "I—I've a good reason."

"Plan?— Yes. Hide Bolly and Silvermane in the little arbor down in the orchard. I'll stay outside to-night, sleep a little—for I'm dead tired—and watch in the morning. Holderness will come here with his men, perhaps not openly at first, to drag Mescal away. He'll mean to use strategy. I'll meet him when he comes—that's all."

"It's well. I ask you not to mention this to my father. Come in, now. You need food and rest. Later I'll hide Bolly and Silvermane in the arbor."

Hare met the Bishop and his family with composure, but his arrival following so closely upon Mescal's, increased their alarm. They seemed repelled yet fascinated by his face. Hare ate in silence. John Caldwell did not come in to supper; his brothers mysteriously left the table before finishing the meal. A subdued murmur of voices floated in at the open window.

Darkness found Hare wrapped in a blanket under the trees. He needed sleep that would loose the strange deadlock of his thoughts, clear the blur from his eyes, ease the pain in his head and weariness of limbs—all these weaknesses of which he had suddenly become conscious. Time and again he had almost wooed slumber to him when soft footsteps on the gravel paths, low voices, the gentle closing of the gate, brought him back to the unreal listening wakefulness. The sounds continued late into the night, and when he did fall asleep he dreamed of them. He awoke to a dawn clearer than the light from the noonday sun. In his ears was the ringing of a bell. He could not stand still, and his movements were subtle and swift. His hands took a peculiar, tenacious, hold of everything he chanced to touch. He paced his hidden walk behind the arbor, at every turn glancing sharply up and down the road. Thoughts came to him clearly, yet one was dominant. The morning was curiously quiet, the sons of the Bishop had strangely disappeared—a sense of imminent catastrophe was in the air.

A band of horsemen closely grouped turned into the road and trotted forward. Some of the men wore black masks. Holderness rode at the front, his red-gold beard shining in the sunlight. The steady clip-clop of hoofs and clinking of iron stirrups broke the morning quiet. Holderness, with two of his men, dismounted before the Bishop's gate; the others of the band trotted on down the road. The ring of Holderness's laugh preceded the snap of the gate-latch.

Hare stood calm and cold behind his green covert watching the three men stroll up the garden path. Holderness took a cigarette from his lips as he neared the porch and blew out circles of white smoke. Bishop Caldwell tottered from the cottage rapping the porch-floor with his cane.

"Good-morning, Bishop," greeted Holderness, blandly, baring his head.

"To you, sir," quavered the old man, with his wavering blue eyes fixed on the spurred and belted rustler. Holderness stepped out in front of his companions, a superb man, courteous, smiling, entirely at his ease.

"I rode in to—"

Hare leaped from his hiding-place.

"Holderness!"

The rustler pivoted on whirling heels.

"Dene's spy!" he exclaimed, aghast. Swift changes swept his mobile features. Fear flickered in his eyes as he faced his foe; then came wonder, a glint of amusement, dark anger, and the terrible instinct of death impending.

"Naab's trick!" hissed Hare, with his hand held high. The suggestion in his words, the meaning in his look, held the three rustlers transfixed. The surprise was his strength.

XIX. UNLEASHED

In Holderness's amber eyes shone his desperate calculation of chances. Hare's fateful glance, impossible to elude, his strung form slightly crouched, his cold deliberate mention of Naab's trick, and more than all the poise of that quivering hand, filled the rustler with a terror that he could not hide.

He had been bidden to draw and he could not summon the force.

"Naab's trick!" repeated Hare, mockingly.

Suddenly Holderness reached for his gun.

Hare's hand leapt like a lightning stroke. Gleam of blue—spurt of red—crash!

Holderness swayed with blond head swinging backward; the amber of his eyes suddenly darkened; the life in them glazed; like a log he fell clutching the weapon he had half drawn.

XX. THE RAGE OF THE OLD LION

"TAKE Holderness away—quick!" ordered Hare. A thin curl of blue smoke floated from the muzzle of his raised weapon.

The rustlers started out of their statue-like immobility, and lifting their dead leader dragged him down the garden path with his spurs clinking on the gravel and ploughing little furrows.

"Bishop, go in now. They may return," said Hare. He hurried up the steps to place his arm round the tottering old man.

"Was that Holderness?"

"Yes," replied Hare.

"The deeds of the wicked return unto them! God's will!"

Hare led the Bishop indoors. The sitting-room was full of wailing women and crying children. None of the young men were present. Again Hare made note of their inexplicable absence. He spoke soothingly to the frightened family. The little boys and girls yielded readily to his persuasion, but the women took no heed of him.

"Where are your sons?" asked Hare.

"I don't know," replied the Bishop. "They should be here to stand by you. It's strange. I don't understand. Last night my sons were visited by many men, coming and going in twos and threes till late. They didn't sleep in their beds. I know not what to think."

Hare remembered John Caldwell's enigmatic face.

"Have the rustlers really come?" asked a young woman, whose eyes were red and cheeks tear-stained.

"They have. Nineteen in all. I counted them," answered Hare.

The young woman burst out weeping afresh, and the wailing of the others answered her. Hare left the cottage. He picked up his rifle and went down through the orchard to the hiding-place of the horses. Silvermane pranced and snorted his gladness at sight of his master. The desert king was fit for a grueling race. Black Bolly quietly cropped the long grass. Hare saddled the stallion to have him in instant readiness, and then returned to the front of the yard.

He heard the sound of a gun down the road, then another, and several shots following in quick succession. A distant angry murmuring and trampling of many feet drew Hare to the gate. Riderless mustangs were galloping down the road;

several frightened boys were fleeing across the square; not a man was in sight. Three more shots cracked, and the low murmur and trampling swelled into a hoarse uproar. Hare had heard that sound before; it was the tumult of mob-violence. A black dense throng of men appeared crowding into the main street, and crossing toward the square. The procession had some order; it was led and flanked by mounted men. But the upflinging of many arms, the craning of necks, and the leaping of men on the outskirts of the mass, the pressure inward and the hideous roar, proclaimed its real character.

"By Heaven!" exclaimed Hare. "The Mormons have risen against the rustlers. I understand now. John Caldwell spent last night in secretly rousing his neighbors. They have surprised the rustlers. Now what?"

Hare vaulted the fence and ran down the road. A compact mob of men, a hundred or more, had halted in the village under the wide-spreading cottonwoods. Hare suddenly grasped the terrible significance of those outstretched branches, and out of the thought grew another which made him run at bursting break-neck speed.

"Open up! Let me in!" he yelled to the thickly thronged circle. Right and left he flung men. "Make way!" His piercing voice stilled the angry murmur. Fierce men with weapons held aloft fell back from his face.

"Dene's spy!" they cried.

The circle opened and closed upon him. He saw bound rustlers under armed guard. Four still forms were on the ground. Holderness lay outstretched, a dark-red blot staining his gray shirt. Flinty-faced Mormons, ruthless now as they had once been mild, surrounded the rustlers. John Caldwell stood foremost, with ashen lips breaking bitterly into speech:

"Mormons, this is Dene's spy, the man who killed Holderness!"

The listeners burst into the short stern shout of men proclaiming a leader in war.

"What's the game?" demanded Hare.

"A fair trial for the rustlers, then a rope," replied John Caldwell. The low ominous murmur swelled through the crowd again.

"There are two men here who have befriended me. I won't see them hanged."

"Pick them out!" A strange ripple of emotion made a fleeting break in John Caldwell's hard face.

Hare eyed the prisoners.

"Nebraska, step out here," said he.

"I reckon you're mistaken," replied the rustler, his blue eyes intently on Hare. "I never seen you before. An' I ain't the kind of a feller to cheat the man you mean."

"I saw you untie the girl's hands."

"You did? Well, d—n me!"

"Nebraska, if I save your life will you quit rustling cattle? You weren't cut out for a thief."

"Will I? D—n me! I'll be straight an' decent. I'll take a job ridin' for you, stranger, an' prove it."

"Cut him loose from the others," said Hare. He scrutinized the line of rustlers. Several were masked in black. "Take off those masks!"

"No! Those men go to their graves masked." Again the strange twinge of pain crossed John Caldwell's face.

"Ah, I see," exclaimed Hare. Then quickly: "I couldn't recognize the other man anyhow; I don't know him. But Mescal can tell. He saved her and I'll save him. But how?"

Every rustler, except the masked ones standing stern and silent, clamored that he was the one to be saved.

"Hurry back home," said Caldwell in Hare's ear. "Tell them to fetch Mescal. Find out and hurry back. Time presses. The Mormons are wavering. You've got only a few minutes."

Hare slipped out of the crowd, sped up the road, jumped the fence on the run, and burst in upon the Bishop and his family.

"No danger—don't be alarmed—all's well," he panted. "The rustlers are captured. I want Mescal. Quick! Where is she? Fetch her, somebody."

One of the women glided from the room. Hare caught the clicking of a latch, the closing of a door, hollow footfalls descending on stone, and dying away under the cottage. They rose again, ending in swiftly pattering footsteps. Like a whirlwind Mescal came through the hall, black hair flying, dark eyes beaming.

"My darling!" Oblivious of the Mormons he swung her up and held her in his arms. "Mescal! Mescal!"

When he raised his face from the tumbling mass of her black hair, the Bishop and his family had left the room.

"Listen, Mescal. Be calm. I'm safe. The rustlers are prisoners. One of them released you from Holderness. Tell me which one?"

"I don't know," replied Mescal. "I've tried to think. I didn't see his face; I can't remember his voice."

"Think! Think! He'll be hanged if you don't recall something to identify him. He deserves a chance. Holderness's crowd are thieves, murderers. But two were not all bad. That showed the night you were at Silver Cup. I saved Nebraska—"

"Were you at Silver Cup? Jack!"

"Hush! don't interrupt me. We must save this man who saved you. Think! Mescal! Think!"

"Oh! I can't. What—how shall I remember?"

"Something about him. Think of his coat, his sleeve. You must remember something. Did you see his hands?"

"Yes, I did—when he was loosing the cords," said Mescal, eagerly. "Long, strong fingers. I felt them too. He has a sharp rough wart on one hand, I don't know which. He wears a leather wristband."

"That's enough!" Hare bounded out upon the garden walk and raced back to the crowded square. The uneasy circle stirred and opened for him to enter. He stumbled over a pile of lassoes which had not been there when he left. The stony Mormons waited; the rustlers coughed and shifted their feet. John Caldwell turned a gray face. Hare bent over the three dead rustlers lying with Holderness, and after a moment of anxious scrutiny he rose to confront the line of prisoners.

"Hold out your hands."

One by one they complied. The sixth rustler in the line, a tall fellow, completely masked, refused to do as he was bidden. Twice Hare spoke. The rustler twisted his bound hands under his coat.

"Let's see them," said Hare, quickly. He grasped the fellow's arm and received a violent push that almost knocked him over. Grappling with the rustler, he pulled up the bound hands, in spite of fierce resistance, and there were the long fingers, the sharp wart, the laced wristband. "Here's my man!" he said.

"No," hoarsely mumbled the rustler. The perspiration ran down his corded neck; his breast heaved convulsively.

"You fool!" cried Hare, dumfounded and resentful. "I recognized you. Would you rather hang than live? What's your secret?"

He snatched off the black mask. The Bishop's eldest son stood revealed.

"Good God!" cried Hare, recoiling from that convulsed face.

"Brother! Oh! I feared this," groaned John Caldwell.

The rustlers broke out into curses and harsh laughter.

"—- —- you Mormons! See him! Paul Caldwell! Son of a Bishop! Thought he was shepherdin' sheep?"

"D—n you, Hare!" shouted the guilty Mormon, in passionate fury and shame. "Why didn't you hang me? Why didn't you bury me unknown?"

"Caldwell! I can't believe it," cried Hare, slowly coming to himself. "But you don't hang. Here, come out of the crowd. Make way, men!"

The silent crowd of Mormons with lowered and averted eyes made passage for Hare and Caldwell. Then cold, stern voices in sharp questions and orders went on with the grim trial. Leading the bowed and stricken Mormon, Hare drew off to the side of the town-hall and turned his back upon the crowd. The constant trampling of many feet, the harsh medley of many voices swelled into one dreadful sound. It passed away, and a long hush followed. But this in turn was suddenly broken by an outcry:

"The Navajos! The Navajos!"

Hare thrilled at that cry and his glance turned to the eastern end of the village road where a column of mounted Indians, four abreast, was riding toward the square.

"Naab and his Indians," shouted Hare. "Naab and his Indians! No fear!" His call was timely, for the aroused Mormons, ignorant of Naab's pursuit, fearful of hostile Navajos, were handling their guns ominously.

But there came a cry of recognition—"August Naab!"

Onward came the band, Naab in the lead on his spotted roan. The mustangs were spent and lashed with foam. Naab reined in his charger and the keen-eyed

Navajos closed in behind him. The old Mormon's eagle glance passed over the dark forms dangling from the cottonwoods to the files of waiting men.

"Where is he?"

"There!" answered John Caldwell, pointing to the body of Holderness.

"Who robbed me of my vengeance? Who killed the rustler?" Naab's stentorian voice rolled over the listening multitude. In it was a hunger of thwarted hate that held men mute. He bent a downward gaze at the dead Holderness as if to make sure of the ghastly reality. Then he seemed to rise in his saddle, and his broad chest to expand. "I know—I saw it all—blind I was not to believe my own eyes! Where is he? Where is Hare?"

Some one pointed Hare out. Naab swung from his saddle and scattered the men before him as if they had been sheep. His shaggy gray head and massive shoulders towered above the tallest there.

Hare felt again a cold sense of fear. He grew weak in all his being. He reeled when the gray shaggy giant laid a huge hand on his shoulder and with one pull dragged him close. Was this his kind Mormon benefactor, this man with the awful eyes?

"You killed Holderness?" roared Naab.

"Yes," whispered Hare.

"You heard me say I'd go alone? You forestalled me? You took upon yourself my work?... Speak."

"I—did."

"By what right?"

"My debt—duty—your family—Dave!"

"Boy! Boy! You've robbed me." Naab waved his arm from the gaping crowd to the swinging rustlers. "You've led these white-livered Mormons to do my work. How can I avenge my sons—seven sons?"

His was the rage of the old desert-lion. He loosed Hare and strode in magnificent wrath over Holderness and raised his brawny fists.

"Eighteen years I prayed for wicked men," he rolled out. "One by one I buried my sons. I gave my springs and my cattle. Then I yielded to the lust for blood. I renounced my religion. I paid my soul to everlasting hell for the life of my foe. But he's dead! Killed by a wild boy! I sold myself to the devil for nothing!"

August Naab raved out his unnatural rage amid awed silence. His revolt was the flood of years undammed at the last. The ferocity of the desert spirit spoke silently in the hanging rustlers, in the ruthlessness of the vigilantes who had destroyed them, but it spoke truest in the sonorous roll of the old Mormon's wrath.

"August, young Hare saved two of the rustlers," spoke up an old friend, hoping to divert the angry flood. "Paul Caldwell there, he was one of them. The other's gone."

Naab loomed over him. "What!" he roared. His friend edged away, repeating his words and jerking his thumb backward toward the Bishop's son.

"Judas Iscariot!" thundered Naab. "False to thyself, thy kin, and thy God! Thrice traitor!... Why didn't you get yourself killed? ... Why are you left? Ah-h! for me—a rustler for me to kill—with my own hands!—A rope there—a rope!"

"I wanted them to hang me," hoarsely cried Caldwell, writhing in Naab's grasp.

Hare threw all his weight and strength upon the Mormon's iron arm. "Naab! Naab! For God's sake, hear! He saved Mescal. This man, thief, traitor, false Mormon—whatever he is—he saved Mescal."

August Naab's eyes were bloodshot. One shake of his great body flung Hare off. He dragged Paul Caldwell across the grass toward the cottonwood as easily as if he were handling an empty grain-sack.

Hare suddenly darted after him. "August! August!—look! look!" he cried. He pointed a shaking finger down the square. The old Bishop came tottering over the grass, leaning on his cane, shading his eyes with his hand. "August. See, the Bishop's coming. Paul's father! Do you hear?"

Hare's appeal pierced Naab's frenzied brain. The Mormon Elder saw his old Bishop pause and stare at the dark shapes suspended from the cottonwoods and hold up his hands in horror.

Naab loosed his hold. His frame seemed wrenched as though by the passing of an evil spirit, and the reaction left his face transfigured.

"Paul, it's your father, the Bishop," he said, brokenly. "Be a man. He must never know." Naab spread wide his arms to the crowd. "Men, listen," he said. "Of all of us Mormons I have lost most, suffered most. Then hear me. Bishop Caldwell must never know of his son's guilt. He would sink under it. Keep the secret. Paul will be a man again. I know. I see. For, Mormons, August Naab has the gift of revelation!"

XXI. MESCAL

SUMMER gleams of golden sunshine swam under the glistening red walls of the oasis. Shadows from white clouds, like sails on a deep-blue sea, darkened the broad fields of alfalfa. Circling columns of smoke were wafted far above the cottonwoods and floated in the still air. The desert-red color of Navajo blankets brightened the grove.

Half-naked bronze Indians lolled in the shade, lounged on the cabin porches and stood about the sunny glade in idle groups. They wore the dress of peace. A single black-tipped white eagle feather waved above the band binding each black head. They watched the merry children tumble round the playground. Silvermane browsed where he listed under the shady trees, and many a sinewy red hand caressed his flowing mane. Black Bolly neighed her jealous displeasure from the corral, and the other mustangs trampled and kicked and whistled defiance across the bars. The peacocks preened their gorgeous plumage and uttered their clarion calls. The belligerent turkey-gobblers sidled about ruffling their feathers. The blackbirds and swallows sang and twittered their happiness to find old nests in the branches and under the eaves. Over all boomed the dull roar of the Colorado in flood.

It was the morning of Mescal's wedding-day.

August Naab, for once without a task, sat astride a peeled log of driftwood in the lane, and Hare stood beside him.

"Five thousand steers, lad! Why do you refuse them? They're worth ten dollars a head to-day in Salt Lake City. A good start for a young man."

"No, I'm still in your debt."

"Then share alike with my sons in work and profit?"

"Yes, I can accept that."

"Good! Jack, I see happiness and prosperity for you. Do you remember that night on the White Sage trail? Ah! Well, the worst is over. We can look forward to better times. It's not likely the rustlers will ride into Utah again. But this desert will never be free from strife."

"Tell me of Mescal," said Hare.

"Ah! Yes, I'm coming to that." Naab bent his head over the log and chipped off little pieces with his knife. "Jack, will you come into the Mormon Church?"

XXI. MESCAL

Long had Hare shrunk from this question which he felt must inevitably come, and now he met it as bravely as he could, knowing he would pain his friend.

"No, August, I can't," he replied. "I feel—differently from Mormons about—about women. If it wasn't for that! I look upon you as a father. I'll do anything for you, except that. No one could pray to be a better man than you. Your work, your religion, your life— Why! I've no words to say what I feel. Teach me what little you can of them, August, but don't ask me—that."

"Well, well," sighed Naab. The gray clearness of his eagle eyes grew shadowed and his worn face was sad. It was the look of a strong wise man who seemed to hear doubt and failure knocking at the gate of his creed. But he loved life too well to be unhappy; he saw it too clearly not to know there was nothing wholly good, wholly perfect, wholly without error. The shade passed from his face like the cloud-shadow from the sunlit lane.

"You ask about Mescal," he mused. "There's little more to tell."

"But her father—can you tell me more of him?"

"Little more than I've already told. He was evidently a man of some rank. I suspected that he ruined his life and became an adventurer. His health was shattered when I brought him here, but he got well after a year or so. He was a splendid, handsome fellow. He spoke very seldom and I don't remember ever seeing him smile. His favorite walk was the river trail. I came upon him there one day, and found him dying. He asked me to have a care of Mescal. And he died muttering a Spanish word, a woman's name, I think."

"I'll cherish Mescal the more," said Hare.

"Cherish her, yes. My Bible will this day give her a name. We know she has the blood of a great chief. Beautiful she is and good. I raised her for the Mormon Church, but God disposes after all, and I—"

A shrill screeching sound split the warm stillness, the long-drawn-out bray of a burro.

"Jack, look down the lane. If it isn't Noddle!"

Under the shady line of the red wall a little gray burro came trotting leisurely along with one long brown ear standing straight up, the other hanging down over his nose.

"By George! it's Noddle!" exclaimed Hare. "He's climbed out of the canyon. Won't this please Mescal?"

"Hey, Mother Mary," called Naab toward the cabin. "Send Mescal out. Here's a wedding-present."

With laughing wonder the women-folk flocked out into the yard. Mescal hung back shy-eyed, roses dyeing the brown of her cheeks.

"Mescal's wedding-present from Thunder River. Just arrived!" called Naab cheerily, yet deep-voiced with the happiness he knew the tidings would give. "A dusty, dirty, shaggy, starved, lop-eared, lazy burro—Noddle!"

Mescal flew out into the lane, and with a strange broken cry of joy that was half a sob she fell upon her knees and clasped the little burro's neck. Noddle wearily flapped his long brown ears, wearily nodded his white nose; then evidently considering the incident closed, he went lazily to sleep.

"Noddle! dear old Noddle!" murmured Mescal, with far-seeing, thought-mirroring eyes. "For you to come back to-day from our canyon! ... Oh! The long dark nights with the thunder of the river and the lonely voices!... they come back to me.... Wolf, Wolf, here's Noddle, the same faithful old Noddle!"

August Naab married Mescal and Hare at noon under the shade of the cottonwoods. Eschtah, magnificent in robes of state, stood up with them. The many members of Naab's family and the grave Navajos formed an attentive circle around them. The ceremony was brief. At its close the Mormon lifted his face and arms in characteristic invocation.

"Almighty God, we entreat Thy blessing upon this marriage. Many and inscrutable are Thy ways; strange are the workings of Thy will; wondrous the purpose with which Thou hast brought this man and this woman together. Watch over them in the new path they are to tread, help them in the trials to come; and in Thy good time, when they have reached the fulness of days, when they have known the joy of life and rendered their service, gather them to Thy bosom in that eternal home where we all pray to meet Thy chosen ones of good; yea, and the evil ones purified in Thy mercy. Amen."

Happy congratulations of the Mormon family, a merry romp of children flinging flowers, marriage-dance of singing Navajos—these, with the feast spread under the cottonwoods, filled the warm noon-hours of the day.

Then the chief Eschtah raised his lofty form, and turned his eyes upon the bride and groom.

THE YOUNG FORESTER

I. CHOOSING A PROFESSION

I loved outdoor life and hunting. Some way a grizzly bear would come in when I tried to explain forestry to my brother.

"Hunting grizzlies!" he cried. "Why, Ken, father says you've been reading dime novels."

"Just wait, Hal, till he comes out here. I'll show him that forestry isn't just bear-hunting."

My brother Hal and I were camping a few days on the Susquehanna River, and we had divided the time between fishing and tramping. Our camp was on the edge of a forest some eight miles from Harrisburg. The property belonged to our father, and he had promised to drive out to see us. But he did not come that day, and I had to content myself with winning Hal over to my side.

"Ken, if the governor lets you go to Arizona can't you ring me in?"

"Not this summer. I'd be afraid to ask him. But in another year I'll do it."

"Won't it be great? But what a long time to wait! It makes me sick to think of you out there riding mustangs and hunting bears and lions."

"You'll have to stand it. You're pretty much of a kid, Hal—not yet fourteen. Besides, I've graduated."

"Kid!" exclaimed Hal, hotly. "You're not such a Methuselah yourself! I'm nearly as big as you. I can ride as well and play ball as well, and I can beat you all—"

"Hold on, Hal! I want you to help me to persuade father, and if you get your temper up you'll like as not go against me. If he lets me go I'll bring you in as soon as I dare. That's a promise. I guess I know how much I'd like to have you."

"All right," replied Hal, resignedly. "I'll have to hold in, I suppose. But I'm crazy to go. And, Ken, the cowboys and lions are not all that interest me. I like what you tell me about forestry. But who ever heard of forestry as a profession?"

"It's just this way, Hal. The natural resources have got to be conserved, and the Government is trying to enlist intelligent young men in the work—particularly in the department of forestry. I'm not exaggerating when I say the prosperity of this country depends upon forestry."

I have to admit that I was repeating what I had read.

"Why does it? Tell me how," demanded Hal.

"Because the lumbermen are wiping out all the timber and never thinking of the future. They are in such a hurry to get rich that they'll leave their grandchildren only a desert. They cut and slash in every direction, and then fires come and the country is ruined. Our rivers depend upon the forests for water. The trees draw the rain; the leaves break it up and let it fall in mists and drippings; it seeps into the ground, and is held by the roots. If the trees are destroyed the rain rushes off on the surface and floods the rivers. The forests store up water, and they do good in other ways."

"We've got to have wood and lumber," said Hal.

"Of course we have. But there won't be any unless we go in for forestry. It's been practiced in Germany for three hundred years."

We spent another hour talking about it, and if Hal's practical sense, which he inherited from father, had not been offset by his real love for the forests I should have been discouraged. Hal was of an industrious turn of mind; he meant to make money, and anything that was good business appealed strongly to him. But, finally, he began to see what I was driving at; he admitted that there was something in the argument.

The late afternoon was the best time for fishing. For the next two hours our thoughts were of quivering rods and leaping bass.

"You'll miss the big bass this August," remarked Hal, laughing. "Guess you won't have all the sport."

"That's so, Hal," I replied, regretfully. "But we're talking as if it were a dead sure thing that I'm going West. Well, I only hope so."

What Hal and I liked best about camping—of course after the fishing—was to sit around the campfire. Tonight it was more pleasant than ever, and when darkness fully settled down it was even thrilling. We talked about bears. Then Hal told of mountain-lions and the habit they have of creeping stealthily after hunters. There was a hoot-owl crying dismally up in the woods, and down by the edge of the river bright-green eyes peered at us from the darkness. When the wind came up and moaned through the trees it was not hard to imagine we were out in the wilderness. This had been a favorite game for Hal and me; only tonight there seemed some reality about it. From the way Hal whispered, and listened, and looked, he might very well have been expecting a visit from lions or, for that matter, even from Indians. Finally we went to bed. But our slumbers were broken. Hal often had nightmares even on ordinary nights, and on this one he moaned so much and thrashed about the tent so desperately that I knew the lions were after him.

I dreamed of forest lands with snow-capped peaks rising in the background; I dreamed of elk standing on the open ridges, of white-tailed deer trooping out of the hollows, of antelope browsing on the sage at the edge of the forests. Here was the broad track of a grizzly in the snow; there on a sunny crag lay a tawny mountain-lion asleep. The bronzed cowboy came in for his share, and the lone bandit played his part in a way to make me shiver. The great pines, the shady, brown trails, the sunlit glades, were as real to me as if I had been among them. Most vivid of all was the lonely forest at night and the campfire. I heard the sputter of the red embers and smelled the wood smoke; I peered into the dark shadows watching and listening for I knew not what.

On the next day early in the afternoon father appeared on the river road.

"There he is," cried Hal. "He's driving Billy. How he's coming."

Billy was father's fastest horse. It pleased me immensely to see the pace, for father would not have been driving fast unless he were in a particularly good humor. And when he stopped on the bank above camp I could have shouted. He wore his corduroys as if he were ready for outdoor life. There was a smile on his face as he tied Billy, and, coming down, he poked into everything in camp and asked innumerable questions. Hal talked about the bass until I was afraid he would want to go fishing and postpone our forestry tramp in the woods. But presently he spoke directly to me.

"Well, Kenneth, are you going to come out with the truth about that Wild-West scheme of yours? Now that you've graduated you want a fling. You want to ride mustangs, to see cowboys, to hunt and shoot—all that sort of thing."

When father spoke in such a way it usually meant the defeat of my schemes. I grew cold all over.

"Yes, father, I'd like all that—But I mean business. I want to be a forest ranger. Let me go to Arizona this summer. And in the fall I'd—I'd like to go to a school of forestry."

There! the truth was out, and my feelings were divided between relief and fear. Before father could reply I launched into a set speech upon forestry, and talked till I was out of breath.

"There's something in what you say," replied my father. "You've been reading up on the subject?"

"Everything I could get, and I've been trying to apply my knowledge in the woods. I love the trees. I'd love an outdoor life. But forestry won't be any picnic. A ranger must be able to ride and pack, make trail and camp, live alone in the woods, fight fire and wild beasts. Oh! It'd be great!"

"I dare say," said father, dryly; "particularly the riding and shooting. Well, I guess you'll make a good-enough doctor to suit me."

"Give me a square deal," I cried, jumping up. "Mayn't I have one word to say about my future? Wouldn't you rather have me happy and successful as a forester, even if there is danger, than just an ordinary, poor doctor? Let's go over our woodland. I'll prove that you are letting your forest run down. You've got sixty acres of hard woods that ought to be bringing a regular income. If I can't prove it, if I can't interest you, I'll agree to study medicine. But if I do you're to let me try forestry."

"Well, Kenneth, that's a fair proposition," returned father, evidently surprised at my earnestness "Come on. We'll go up in the woods. Hal, I suppose he's won you over?"

"Ken's got a big thing in mind," replied Hal, loyally "It's just splendid."

I never saw the long, black-fringed line of trees without joy in the possession of them and a desire to be among them. The sixty acres of timber land covered the whole of a swampy valley, spread over a rolling hill sloping down to the glistening river.

"Now, son? go ahead," said my father, as we clambered over a rail fence and stepped into the edge of shade..

"Well, father—" I began, haltingly, and could not collect my thoughts. Then we were in the cool woods. It was very still, there being only a faint rustling of leaves and the mellow note of a hermit-thrush. The deep shadows were lightened by shafts of sunshine which, here and there, managed to pierce the canopy of foliage. Somehow, the feeling roused by these things loosened my tongue.

"This is an old hard-wood forest," I began. "Much of the white oak, hickory, ash, maple, is virgin timber. These trees have reached maturity; many are dead at the tops; all of them should have been cut long ago. They make too dense a shade for the seedlings to survive. Look at that bunch of sapling maples. See how they reach up, trying to get to the light. They haven't a branch low down and the tops are thin. Yet maple is one of our hardiest trees. Growth has been suppressed. Do you notice there are no small oaks or hickories just here? They can't live in deep shade. Here's the stump of a white oak cut last fall. It was about two feet in diameter. Let's count the rings to find its age—about ninety years. It flourished in its youth and grew rapidly, but it had a hard time after about fifty years. At that time it was either burned, or mutilated by a falling tree, or struck by lightning."

"Now, how do you make that out?" asked father, intensely interested.

"See the free, wide rings from the pith out to about number forty-five. The tree was healthy up to that time. Then it met with an injury of some kind, as is indicated by this black scar. After that the rings grew narrower. The tree struggled to live."

We walked on with me talking as fast as I could get the words out. I showed father a giant, bushy chestnut which was dominating all the trees around it, and told him how it retarded their growth. On the other hand, the other trees were absorbing nutrition from the ground that would have benefited the chestnut.

"There's a sinful waste of wood here," I said, as we climbed over and around the windfalls and rotting tree-trunks. "The old trees die and are blown down. The amount of rotting wood equals the yearly growth. Now, I want to show you the worst enemies of the trees. Here's a big white oak, a hundred and fifty years old. It's almost dead. See the little holes bored in the bark. They were made by a beetle. Look!"

I swung my hatchet and split off a section of bark. Everywhere in the bark and round the tree ran little dust-filled grooves. I pried out a number of tiny brown beetles, somewhat the shape of a pinching-bug, only very much smaller.

"There! You'd hardly think that that great tree was killed by a lot of little bugs, would you? They girdle the trees and prevent the sap from flowing."

I found an old chestnut which contained nests of the deadly white moths, and explained how it laid its eggs, and how the caterpillars that came from them killed the trees by eating the leaves. I showed how mice and squirrels injured the forest by eating the seeds.

"First I'd cut and sell all the matured and dead timber. Then I'd thin out the spreading trees that want all the light, and the saplings that grow too close together. I'd get rid of the beetles, and try to check the spread of caterpillars. For trees grow twice as fast if they are not choked or diseased. Then I'd keep planting seeds and shoots in the open places, taking care to favor the species best adapted to the soil, and cutting those that don't grow well. In this way we'll be keeping our forest while doubling its growth and value, and having a yearly income from it."

"Kenneth, I see you're in dead earnest about this business," said my father, slowly. "Before I came out here today I had been looking up the subject, and I believe, with you, that forestry really means the salvation of our country. I think you are really interested, and I've a mind not to oppose you."

"You'll never regret it. I'll learn; I'll work up. Then it's an outdoor life—healthy, free—why! all the boys I've told take to the idea. There's something fine about it." "Forestry it is, then," replied he. "I like the promise of it, and I like your attitude. If you have learned so much while you were camping out here the past few summers it speaks well for you. But why do you want to go to Arizona?"

"Because the best chances are out West. I'd like to get a line on the National Forests there before I go to college. The work will be different; those Western forests are all pine. I've a friend, Dick Leslie, a fellow I used to fish with, who went West and is now a fire ranger in the new National Forest in Arizona—Penetier is the name of it. He has written me several times to come out and spend a while with him in the woods."

"Penetier? Where is that—near what town?"

"Holston. It's a pretty rough country, Dick says; plenty of deer, bears, and lions on his range. So I could hunt some while studying the forests. I think I'd be safe with Dick, even if it is wild out there."

"All right, I'll let you go. When you return we'll see about the college." Then he surprised me by drawing a letter from his pocket and handing it to me. "My friend, Mr. White, got this letter from the department at Washington. It may be of use to you out there."

So it was settled, and when father drove off homeward Hal and I went back to camp. It would have been hard to say which of us was the more excited. Hal did a war dance round the campfire. I was glad, however, that he did not have the little twinge of remorse which I experienced, for I had not told him or father all that Dick had written about the wilderness of Penetier. I am afraid my mind was as much occupied with rifles and mustangs as with the study of forestry. But, though the adventure called most strongly to me, I knew I was sincere about the forestry end of it, and I resolved that I would never slight my opportunities. So, smothering conscience, I fell to the delight of making plans. I was for breaking camp at once, but Hal persuaded me to stay one more day. We talked for hours. Only one thing bothered me. Hal was jolly and glum by turns. He reveled in the plans for my outfit, but he wanted his own chance. A thousand times I had to repeat my promise, and the last thing he said before we slept was: "Ken, you're going to ring me in next summer!"

II. THE MAN ON THE TRAIN

Travelling was a new experience to me, and on the first night after I left home I lay awake until we reached Altoona. We rolled out of smoky Pittsburg at dawn, and from then on the only bitter drop in my cup of bliss was that the train went so fast I could not see everything out of my window.

Four days to ride! The great Mississippi to cross, the plains, the Rocky Mountains, then the Arizona plateaus-a long, long journey with a wild pine forest at the end! I wondered what more any young fellow could have wished. With my face glued to the car window I watched the level country speed by.

There appeared to be one continuous procession of well-cultivated farms, little hamlets, and prosperous towns. What interested me most, of course, were the farms, for all of them had some kind of wood. We passed a zone of maple forests which looked to be more carefully kept than the others. Then I recognized that they were maple-sugar trees. The farmers had cleaned out the other species, and this primitive method of forestry had produced the finest maples it had ever been my good-fortune to see. Indiana was flatter than Ohio, not so well watered, and therefore less heavily timbered. I saw, with regret, that the woodland was being cut regularly, tree after tree, and stacked in cords for firewood.

At Chicago I was to change for Santa Fe, and finding my train in the station I climbed aboard. My car was a tourist coach. Father had insisted on buying a ticket for the California Limited, but I had argued that a luxurious Pullman was not exactly the thing for a prospective forester. Still I pocketed the extra money which I had assured him he need not spend for the first-class ticket.

The huge station, with its glaring lights and clanging bells, and the outspreading city, soon gave place to prairie land.

That night I slept little, but the very time I wanted to be awake—when we crossed the Mississippi—I was slumbering soundly, and so missed it.

"I'll bet I don't miss it coming back," I vowed.

The sight of the Missouri, however, somewhat repaid me for the loss. What a muddy, wide river! And I thought of the thousands of miles of country it drained, and of the forests there must be at its source. Then came the never-ending Kansas corn-fields. I do not know whether it was their length or their treeless monotony, but I grew tired looking at them.

From then on I began to take some notice of my fellow-travelers. The conductor proved to be an agreeable old fellow; and the train-boy, though I mistrusted his advances because he tried to sell me everything from chewing-gum to mining stock, turned out to be pretty good company. The Negro porter had such a jolly voice and laugh that I talked to him whenever I got the chance. Then occasional passengers occupied the seat opposite me from town to town. They were much alike, all sunburned and loud-voiced, and it looked as though they had all bought their high boots and wide hats at the same shop.

The last traveller to face me was a very heavy man with a great bullet head and a shock of light hair. His blue eyes had a bold flash, his long mustache drooped, and there was something about him that I did not like. He wore a huge diamond in the bosom of his flannel shirt, and a leather watch-chain that was thick and strong enough to have held up a town-clock.

"Hot," he said, as he mopped his moist brow.

"Not so hot as it was," I replied.

"Sure not. We're climbin' a little. He's whistlin' for Dodge City now."

"Dodge City?" I echoed, with interest. The name brought back vivid scenes from certain yellow-backed volumes, and certain uncomfortable memories of my father's displeasure. "Isn't this the old cattle town where there used to be so many fights?"

"Sure. An' not so very long ago. Here, look out the window." He clapped his big hand on my knee; then pointed. "See that hill there. Dead Man's Hill it was once, where they buried the fellers as died with their boots on."

I stared, and even stretched my neck out of the window.

"Yes, old Dodge was sure lively," he continued, as our train passed on. "I seen a little mix-up there myself in the early eighties. Five cow-punchers, friends they was, had been visitin' town. One feller, playful-like, takes another feller's quirt—that's a whip. An' the other feller, playful-like, says, 'Give it back.' Then they tussles for it, an' rolls on the ground. I was laughin', as was everybody, when, suddenly, the owner of the quirt thumps his friend. Both cowboys got up, slow, an' watchin' of each other. Then the first feller, who had started the play, pulls his gun. He'd hardly flashed it when they all pulls guns, an' it was some noisy an' smoky. In about five seconds there was five dead cowpunchers. Killed themselves, as you might say, just for fun. That's what life was worth in old Dodge." After this story I felt more kindly disposed ward my travelling companion, and would have asked for more romances but the conductor came along and engaged him in conversation. Then my neighbor across the aisle, a young fellow not much older than myself, asked me to talk to him.

"Why, yes, if you like," I replied, in surprise. He was pale; there were red spots in his cheeks, and dark lines under his weary eyes.

"You look so strong and eager that it's done me good to watch you," he explained, with a sad smile. "You see—I'm sick."

I told him I was very sorry, and hoped he would get well soon.

II. THE MAN ON THE TRAIN

"I ought to have come West sooner," he replied, "but I couldn't get the money."

He looked up at me and then out of the window at the sun setting red across the plains. I tried to make him think of something beside himself, but I made a mess of it. The meeting with him was a shock to me. Long after dark, when I had stretched out for the night, I kept thinking of him and contrasting what I had to look forward to with his dismal future. Somehow it did not seem fair, and I could not get rid of the idea that I was selfish.

Next day I had my first sight of real mountains. And the Pennsylvania hills, that all my life had appeared so high, dwindled to nothing. At Trinidad, where we stopped for breakfast, I walked out on the platform sniffing at the keen thin air. When we crossed the Raton Mountains into New Mexico the sick boy got off at the first station, and I waved good-bye to him as the train pulled out. Then the mountains and the funny little adobe huts and the Pueblo Indians along the line made me forget everything else.

The big man with the heavy watch-chain was still on the train, and after he had read his newspaper he began to talk to me.

"This road follows the old trail that the goldseekers took in forty-nine," he said. "We're comin' soon to a place, Apache Pass, where the Apaches used to ambush the wagon-trains, It's somewheres along here."

Presently the train wound into a narrow yellow ravine, the walls of which grew higher and higher.

"Them Apaches was the worst redskins ever in the West. They used to hide on top of this pass an' shoot down on the wagon-trains."

Later in the day he drew my attention to a mountain standing all by itself. It was shaped like a cone, green with trees almost to the summit, and ending in a bare stone peak that had a flat top.

"Starvation Peak," he said. "That name's three hundred years old, dates back to the time the Spaniards owned this land. There's a story about it that's likely true enough. Some Spaniards were attacked by Indians an' climbed to the peak, expectin' to be better able to defend themselves up there. The Indians camped below the peak an' starved the Spaniards. Stuck there till they starved to death! That's where it got its name."

"Those times you tell of must have been great," I said, regretfully. "I'd like to have been here then. But isn't the country all settled now? Aren't the Indians dead? There's no more fighting?"

"It's not like it used to be, but there's still warm places in the West. Not that the Indians break out often any more. But bad men are almost as bad, if not so plentiful, as when Billy the Kid run these parts. I saw two men shot an' another knifed jest before I went East to St. Louis."

"Where?"

"In Arizona. Holston is the station where I get off, an' it happened near there."

"Holston is where I'm going."

"You don't say. Well, I'm glad to meet you, young man. My name's Buell, an' I'm some known in Holston. What's your name?"

He eyed me in a sharp but not unfriendly manner, and seemed pleased to learn of my destination.

"Ward. Kenneth Ward. I'm from Pennsylvania."

"You haven't got the bugs. Any one can see that," he said, and as I looked puzzled he went on with a smile, and a sounding rap on his chest: "Most young fellers as come out here have consumption. They call it bugs. I reckon you're seekin' your fortune.'"

"Yes, in a way."

"There's opportunities for husky youngsters out here. What're you goin' to rustle for, if I may ask?"

"I'm going in for forestry."

"Forestry? Do you mean lumberin'?"

"No. Forestry is rather the opposite of lumbering. I'm going in for Government forestry—to save the timber, not cut it."

It seemed to me he gave a little start of surprise; he certainly straightened up and looked at me hard.

"What's Government forestry?"

I told him to the best of my ability. He listened attentively enough, but thereafter he had not another word for me, and presently he went into the next car. I took his manner to be the Western abruptness that I had heard of, and presently forgot him in the scenery along the line. At Albuquerque I got off for a trip to a lunch-counter, and happened to take a seat next to him.

"Know anybody in Holston?" he asked.

As I could not speak because of a mouthful of sandwich I shook my head. For the moment I had forgotten about Dick Leslie, and when it did occur to me some Indians offering to sell me beads straightway drove it out of my mind again.

When I awoke the next day, it was to see the sage ridges and red buttes of Arizona. We were due at Holston at eight o'clock, but owing to a crippled engine the train was hours late. At last I fell asleep to be awakened by a vigorous shake.

"Holston. Your stop. Holston," the conductor was saying.

"All right," I said, sitting up and then making a grab for my grip. "We're pretty late, aren't we?"

"Six hours. It's two o'clock."

"Hope I can get a room," I said, as I followed him out on the platform. He held up his lantern so that the light would shine in my face. "There's a hotel down the street a block or so. Better hurry and look sharp. Holston's not a safe place for a stranger at night."

I stepped off into a windy darkness. A lamp glimmered in the station window. By its light I made out several men, the foremost of whom had a dark, pointed face and glittering eyes. He wore a strange hat, and I knew from pictures I had seen that he was a Mexican. Then the bulky form of Buell loomed up. I called, but evidently he did not hear me. The men took his grips, and they moved away to disappear in the darkness. While I paused, hoping to see some one to direct me, the train puffed out, leaving me alone on the platform.

When I turned the corner I saw two dim lights, one far to the left, the other to the right, and the black outline of buildings under what appeared to be the shadow of a mountain. It was the quietest and darkest town I had ever struck.

I decided to turn toward the right-hand light, for the conductor had said "down the street." I set forth at a brisk pace, but the loneliness and strangeness of the place were rather depressing.

Before I had gone many steps, however, the sound of running water halted me, and just in the nick of time, for I was walking straight into a ditch. By peering hard into the darkness and feeling my way I found a bridge. Then it did not take long to reach the light. But it was a saloon, and not the hotel. One peep into it served to make me face about in double-quick time, and hurry in the opposite direction.

Hearing a soft footfall, I glanced over my shoulder, to see the Mexican that I had noticed at the station. He was coming from across the street. I wondered if he were watching me. He might be. My heart began to beat violently. Turning once again, I discovered that the fellow could not be seen in the pitchy blackness. Then I broke into a run.

III. THE TRAIL

A short dash brought me to the end of the block; the side street was not so dark, and after I had crossed this open space I glanced backward.

Soon I sped into a wan circle of light, and, reaching a door upon which was a hotel sign, I burst in. Chairs were scattered about a bare office; a man stirred on a couch, and then sat up, blinking.

"I'm afraid—I believe some one's chasing me," I said.

He sat there eying me, and then drawled, sleepily:

"Thet ain't no call to wake a feller, is it?"

The man settled himself comfortably again, and closed his eyes.

"Say, isn't this a hotel? I want a room!" I cried.

"Up-stairs; first door." And with that the porter went to sleep in good earnest.

I made for the stairs, and, after a backward look into the street, I ran up. A smelly lamp shed a yellowish glare along a hall. I pushed open the first door, and, entering the room, bolted myself in. Then all the strength went out of my legs. When I sat down on the bed I was in a cold sweat and shaking like a leaf. Soon the weakness passed, and I moved about the room, trying to find a lamp or candle. Evidently the hotel, and, for that matter, the town of Holston, did not concern itself with such trifles as lights. On the instant I got a bad impression of Holston. I had to undress in the dark. When I pulled the window open a little at the top the upper sash slid all the way down. I managed to get it back, and tried raising the lower sash. It was very loose, but it stayed up. Then I crawled into bed.

Though I was tired and sleepy, my mind whirled so that I could not get to sleep. If I had been honest with myself I should have wished myself back home. Pennsylvania seemed a long way off, and the adventures that I had dreamed of did not seem so alluring, now that I was in a lonely room in a lonely, dark town. Buell had seemed friendly and kind—at least, in the beginning. Why had he not answered my call? The incident did not look well to me. Then I fell to wondering if the Mexican had really followed me. The first thing for me in the morning would be to buy a revolver. Then if any Mexicans—

A step on the tin roof outside frightened me stiff. I had noticed a porch, or shed, under my window. Some one must have climbed upon it. I stopped breathing to listen. For what seemed moments there was no sound. I wanted to think that the noise might have been made by a cat, but I couldn't. I was scared—frightened half to death.

If there had been a bolt on the window the matter would not have been so disturbing. I lay there a-quiver, eyes upon the gray window space of my room. Dead silence once more intervened. All I heard was the pound of my heart against my ribs.

Suddenly I froze at the sight of a black figure against the light of my window. I recognized the strange bat, the grotesque outlines. I was about to shout for help when the fellow reached down and softly began to raise the sash.

That made me angry. Jerking up in bed, I caught the heavy pitcher from the wash-stand and flung it with all my might.

Crash!

Had I smashed out the whole side of the room it could scarcely have made more noise. Accompanied by the clinking of glass and the creaking of tin, my visitor rolled off the roof. I waited, expecting an uproar from the other inmates of the hotel. No footstep, no call sounded within hearing. Once again the stillness settled down.

Then, to my relief, the gray gloom lightened, and dawn broke. Never had I been so glad to see the morning. While dressing I cast gratified glances at the ragged hole in the window. With the daylight my courage had returned, and I began to have a sort of pride in my achievement.

"If that fellow had known how I can throw a baseball he'd have been careful," I thought, a little cockily.

I went down-stairs into the office. The sleepy porter was mopping the floor. Behind the desk stood a man so large that he made Buell seem small. He was all shoulders and beard.

"Can I get breakfast?"

"Nobody's got a half-hitch on you, has they?" he replied, jerking a monstrous thumb over his shoulder toward a door.

I knew the words half-hitch had something to do with a lasso, and I was rather taken back by the hotel proprietor's remark. The dining-room was more attractive than anything I had yet seen about the place: the linen was clean, and the ham and eggs and coffee that were being served to several rugged men gave forth a savory odor. But either the waiter was blind or he could not bear, for he paid not the slightest attention to me. I waited, while trying to figure out the situation. Something was wrong, and, whatever it was, I guessed that it must be with me. After about an hour I got my breakfast. Then I went into the office, intending to be brisk, businesslike, and careful about asking questions.

"I'd like to pay my bill, and also for a little damage," I said, telling what had happened.

"Somebody'll kill thet Greaser yet," was all the comment the man made.

I went outside, not knowing whether to be angry or amused with these queer people. In the broad light of day Holston looked as bad as it had made me feel by night. All I could see were the station and freight-sheds, several stores with high, wide signs, glaringly painted, and a long block of saloons. When I had turned a street corner, however, a number of stores came into view with some three-storied brick buildings, and, farther out, many frame houses.

Moreover, this street led my eye to great snowcapped mountains, and I stopped short in my tracks, for I realized they were the Arizona peaks. Up the swelling slopes swept a black fringe that I knew to be timber. The mountains appeared to be close, but I knew that even the foot-bills were miles away. Penetier, I remembered from one of Dick's letters, was on the extreme northern slope, and it must be anywhere from forty to sixty miles off. The sharp, white peaks glistened in the morning sun; the air had a cool touch of snow and a tang of pine. I drew in a full breath, with a sense on being among the pines.

Now I must buy my outfit and take the trail for Penetier. This I resolved to do with as few questions as possible. I never before was troubled by sensitiveness, but the fact had dawned upon me that I did not like being taken for a tenderfoot. So, with this in mind, I entered a general merchandise store.

It was very large, and full of hardware, harness, saddles, blankets—everything that cowboys and ranchmen use. Several men, two in shirt-sleeves, were chatting near the door. They saw me come in, and then, for all that it meant to them, I might as well not have been in existence at all. So I sat down to wait, determined to take Western ways and things as I found them. I sat there fifteen minutes by my watch. This was not so bad; but when a lanky, red-faced, leather-legged individual came in too he at once supplied with his wants, I began to get angry. I waited another five minutes, and still the friendly chatting went on. Finally I could stand it no longer.

"Will somebody wait on me?" I demanded.

One of the shirt-sleeved men leisurely got up and surveyed me.

"Do you want to buy something?" he drawled.

"Yes, I do."

"Why didn't you say so?"

The reply trembling on my lips was cut short by the entrance of Buell.

"Hello!" he said in a loud voice, shaking hands with me. "You've trailed into the right place. Smith, treat this lad right. It's guns an' knives an' lassoes he wants, I'll bet a hoss."

"Yes, I want an outfit," I said, much embarrassed. "I'm going to meet a friend out in Penetier, a ranger—Dick Leslie."

Buell started violently, and his eyes flashed. "Dick—Dick Leslie!" he said, and coughed loudly. "I know Dick.... So you're a friend of his'n? ... Now, let me help you with the outfit."

Anything strange in Buell's manner was forgotten, in the absorbing interest of my outfit. Father had given me plenty of money, so that I had but to choose. I had had sense enough to bring my old corduroys and boots, and I had donned them that morning. One after another I made my purchases—Winchester, revolver, bolsters, ammunition, saddle, bridle, lasso, blanket. When I got so far, Buell said:

"You'll need a mustang an' a pack-pony. I know a feller who's got jest what you want." And with that he led me out of the store.

"Now you take it from me," he went on, in a fatherly voice, "Holston people haven't got any use for Easterners. An' if you mention your business—forestry an' that—why, you wouldn't be safe. There's many in the lumberin' business here as don't take kindly to the Government. See! That's why I'm givin' you advice. Keep it to yourself an' hit the trail today, soon as you can. I'll steer you right."

I was too much excited to answer clearly; indeed, I hardly thanked him. However, he scarcely gave me the chance. He kept up his talk about the townspeople and their attitude toward Easterners until we arrived at a kind of stock-yard full of shaggy little ponies. The sight of them drove every other thought out of my head.

"Mustangs!" I exclaimed.

"Sure. Can you ride?"

"Oh yes. I have a horse at home.... What wiry little fellows! They're so wild-looking."

"You pick out the one as suits you, an' I'll step into Cless's here. He's the man who owns this bunch."

It did not take me long to decide. A black mustang at once took my eye. When he had been curried and brushed he would be a little beauty. I was trying to coax him to me when Buell returned with a man.

"Thet your pick?" he asked, as I pointed. "Well, now, you're not so much of a tenderfoot. Thet's the best mustang in the lot. Cless, how much for him, an' a pack-pony an' pack-saddle?"

"I reckon twenty dollars'll make it square," replied the owner.

This nearly made me drop with amazement. I had only about seventy-five dollars left, and I had been very much afraid that I could not buy the mustang, let alone the pack-pony and saddle.

"Cless, send round to Smith for the lad's outfit, an' saddle up for him at once." Then he turned to me. "Now some grub, an' a pan or two."

Having camped before, I knew how to buy supplies. Buell, however, cut out much that I wanted, saying the thing to think of was a light pack for the pony.

"I'll hurry to the hotel and get my things," I said, "and meet you here. I'll not be a moment."

But Buell said it would be better for him to go with me, though he did not explain. He kept with me, still he remained in the office while I went up-stairs. Somehow this suited me, for I did not want him to see the broken window. I took a few things from my grip and rolled them in a bundle. Then I took a little leather case of odds and ends I had always carried when camping and slipped it into my pocket. Hurrying down-stairs I left my grip with the porter, wrote and mailed a postal card to my father, and followed the impatient Buell.

"You see, it's a smart lick of a ride to Penetier, and I want to get there before dark," he explained, kindly.

I could have shouted for very glee when I saw the black mustang saddled and bridled.

"He's well broke," said Cless. "Keep his bridle down when you ain't in the saddle. An' find a patch of grass fer him at night. The pony'll stick to him."

Cless fell to packing a lean pack-pony.

"Watch me do this," said he; "you'll hev trouble if you don't git the hang of the diamondhitch."

I watched him set the little wooden criss-cross on the pony's back, throw the balance of my outfit (which he had tied up in a canvas) over the saddle, and then pass a long rope in remarkable turns and wonderful loops round pony and pack.

"What's the mustang's name?" I inquired.

"Never had any," replied the former owner.

"Then it's Hal." I thought how that name would please my brother at home.

"Climb up. Let's see if you fit the stirrups," said Cless. "Couldn't be better."

"Now, young feller, you can hit the trail," put in Buell, with his big voice. "An' remember what I told you. This country ain't got much use for a feller as can't look out for himself."

He opened the gate, and led my mustang into the road and quite some distance. The pony jogged along after us. Then Buell stopped with a finger outstretched.

"There, at the end of this street, you'll find a trail. Hit it an' stick to it. All the little trail's leadin' into it needn't bother you."

He swept his hand round to the west of the mountain. The direction did not tally with the idea I had gotten from Dick's letter.

"I thought Penetier was on the north side of the mountains."

"Who said so?" he asked, staring. "Don't I know this country? Take it from me."

I thanked him, and, turning, with a light heart I faced the black mountain and my journey.

It was about ten o'clock when Hal jogged into a broad trail on the outskirts of Holston. A gray flat lay before me, on the other side of which began the slow rise of the slope. I could hardly contain myself. I wanted to run the mustang, but did not for the sake of the burdened pony. That sage-flat was miles wide, though it seemed so narrow. The back of the lower slope began to change to a dark green, which told me I was surely getting closer to the mountains, even if it did not seem so. The trail began to rise, and at last I reached the first pine-trees. They were a disappointment to me, being no larger than many of the white oaks at home, and stunted, with ragged dead tops. They proved to me that trees isolated from their fellows fare as poorly as trees overcrowded. Where pines grow closely, but not too closely, they rise straight and true, cleaning themselves of the low branches, and making good lumber, free of knots. Where they grow far apart, at the mercy of wind and heat and free to spread many branches, they make only gnarled and knotty lumber.

As I rode on the pines became slowly more numerous and loftier. Then, when I had surmounted what I took to be the first foot-hill, I came upon a magnificent forest. A little farther on the trail walled me in with great seamed trunks, six feet in diameter, rising a hundred feet before spreading a single branch.

III. THE TRAIL

Meanwhile my mustang kept steadily up the slow-rising trail, and the time passed. Either the grand old forest had completely bewitched me or the sweet smell of pine had intoxicated me, for as I rode along utterly content I entirely forgot about Dick and the trail and where I was heading. Nor did I come to my senses until Hal snorted and stopped before a tangled windfall.

Then I glanced down to see only the clean, brown pine-needles. There was no trail. Perplexed and somewhat anxious, I rode back a piece, expecting surely to cross the trail. But I did not. I went to the left and to the right, then circled in a wide curve. No trail! The forest about me seemed at once familiar and strange.

It was only when the long shadows began to creep under the trees that I awoke fully to the truth.

I had missed the trail! I was lost in the forest!

IV. LOST IN THE FOREST

For a moment I was dazed. And then came panic. I ran up this ridge and that one, I rushed to and fro over ground which looked, whatever way I turned, exactly the same. And I kept saying, "I'm lost! I'm lost!" Not until I dropped exhausted against a pine-tree did any other thought come to me.

The moment that I stopped running about so aimlessly the panicky feeling left me. I remembered that for a ranger to be lost in the forest was an every-day affair, and the sooner I began that part of my education the better. Then it came to me how foolish I had been to get alarmed, when I knew that the general slope of the forest led down to the open country.

This put an entirely different light upon the matter. I still had some fears that I might not soon find Dick Leslie, but these I dismissed for the present, at least. A suitable place to camp for the night must be found. I led the mustang down into the hollows, keeping my eye sharp for grass. Presently I came to a place that was wet and soggy at the bottom, and, following this up for quite a way, I found plenty of grass and a pool of clear water.

Often as I had made camp back in the woods of Pennsylvania, the doing of it now was new. For this was not play; it was the real thing, and it made the old camping seem tame. I took the saddle off Hal and tied him with my lasso, making as long a halter as possible. Slipping the pack from the pony was an easier task than the getting it back again was likely to prove. Next I broke open a box of cartridges and loaded the Winchester. My revolver was already loaded, and hung on my belt. Remembering Dick's letters about the bears and mountain-lions in Penetier Forest, I got a good deal of comfort out of my weapons. Then I built a fire, and while my supper was cooking I scraped up a mass of pine-needles for a bed. Never had I sat down to a meal with such a sense of strange enjoyment.

But when I had finished and had everything packed away and covered, my mind began to wander in unexpected directions. Why was it that the twilight seemed to move under the giant pines and creep down the hollow? While I gazed the gray shadows deepened to black, and night came suddenly. My campfire seemed to give almost no light, yet close at hand the flickering gleams played hide-and-seek among the pines and chased up the straight tree trunks. The crackling of my fire and the light steps of the grazing mustangs only emphasized the silence of the forest. Then a low moaning from a distance gave me a chill. At first

I had no idea what it was, but presently I thought it must be the wind in the pines. It bore no resemblance to any sound I had ever before heard in the woods. It would murmur from different parts of the forest; sometimes it would cease for a little, and then travel and swell toward me, only to die away again. But it rose steadily, with shorter intervals of silence, until the intermittent gusts swept through the tree-tops with a rushing roar. I had listened to the crash of the ocean surf, and the resemblance was a striking one.

Listening to this mournful wind with all my ears I was the better prepared for any lonesome cries of the forest; nevertheless, a sudden, sharp "Ki-yi-i!" seemingly right at my back, gave me a fright that sent my tongue to the roof of my mouth.

Fumbling at the hammer of my rifle, I peered into the black-streaked gloom of the forest. The crackling of dry twigs brought me to my feet. At the same moment the mustangs snorted. Something was prowling about just beyond the light. I thought of a panther. That was the only beast I could think of which had such an unearthly cry.

Then another bowl, resembling that of a dog, and followed by yelps and barks, told me that I was being visited by a pack of coyotes. I spent the good part of an hour listening to their serenade. The wild, mournful notes sent quivers up my back. By-and-by they went away, and as my fire had burned down to a red glow and the night wind had grown cold I began to think of sleep.

But I was not sleepy. When I had stretched out on the soft bed of pine-needles with my rifle close by, and was all snug and warm under the heavy blanket, it seemed that nothing was so far away from me as sleep. The wonder of my situation kept me wide awake, my eyes on the dim huge pines and the glimmer of stars, and my ears open to the rush and roar of the wind, every sense alert. Hours must have passed as I lay there living over the things that had happened and trying to think out what was to come. At last, however, I rolled over on my side, and with my hand on the rifle and my cheek close to the sweet-smelling pine-needles I dropped asleep.

When I awoke the forest was bright and sunny.

"You'll make a fine forester," I said aloud, in disgust at my tardiness. Then began the stern business of the day. While getting breakfast I turned over in my mind the proper thing for me to do. Evidently I must pack and find the trail. The pony had wandered off into the woods, but was easily caught—a fact which lightened my worry, for I knew how dependent I was upon my mustangs. When I had tried for I do not know how long to get my pack to stay on the pony's back I saw where Mr. Cless had played a joke on me. All memory of the diamond-hitch had faded into utter confusion. First the pack fell over the off-side; next, on top of me; then the saddle slipped awry, and when I did get the pack to remain stationary upon the patient pony, how on earth to tie it there became more and more of a mystery. Finally, in sheer desperation, I ran round the pony, pulled, tugged, and knotted the lasso; more by luck than through sense I had accomplished something in the nature of the diamond-hitch.

I headed Hal up the gentle forest slope, and began the day's journey wherever chance might lead me. As confidence came, my enjoyment increased. I began to believe I could take care of myself. I reasoned out that, as the peaks were snow-capped, I should find water, and very likely game, up higher. Moreover, I might climb a foothill or bluff from which I could get my bearings.

It seemed to me that I passed more pine-trees than I could have imagined there were in the whole world. Miles and miles of pines! And in every mile they grew larger and ruggeder and farther apart, and so high that I could hardly see the tips. After a time I got out of the almost level forest into ground ridged and hollowed, and found it advisable to turn more to the right. On the sunny southern slopes I saw trees that dwarfed the ones on the colder and shady north sides. I also found many small pines and seedlings growing in warm, protected places. This showed me the value of the sun to a forest. Though I kept a lookout for deer or game of any kind, I saw nothing except some black squirrels with white tails. They were beautiful and very tame, and one was nibbling at what I concluded must have been a seed from a pine-cone.

Presently I fancied that I espied a moving speck far down through the forest glades. I stopped Hal, and, watching closely, soon made certain of it. Then it became lost for a time, but reappeared again somewhat closer. It was like a brown blur and scarcely moved. I reined Hal more to the right. Not for quite a while did I see the thing again, and when I did it looked so big and brown that I took up my Winchester. Then it disappeared once more.

I descended into a hollow, and tying Hal, I stole forward on foot, hoping by that means to get close to the strange object without being seen myself.

I waited behind a pine, and suddenly three horsemen rode across a glade not two hundred yards away. The foremost rider was no other than the Mexican whom I had reason to remember.

The huge trunk amply concealed me, but, nevertheless, I crouched down. How strange that I should run into that Mexican again! Where was he going? Had he followed me? Was there a trail?

As long as the three men were in sight I watched them. When the last brown speck had flitted and disappeared far away in the forest I retraced my steps to my mustang, pondering upon this new turn in my affairs.

"Things are bound to happen to me," I concluded, "and I may as well make up my mind to that."

While standing beside Hal, undecided as to my next move, I heard a whistle. It was faint, perhaps miles away, yet unmistakably it was the whistle of an engine. I wondered if the railroad turned round this side of the peaks. Mounting Hal, I rode down the forest to the point where I had seen the men, and there came upon a trail. I proceeded along this in the direction the men had taken. I had come again to the slow-rising level that I had noted earlier in my morning's journey. After several miles a light or opening in the forest ahead caused me to use more caution. As I rode forward I saw a vast area of tree-tops far below, and then I found myself on the edge of a foot-hill.

IV. LOST IN THE FOREST

Right under me was a wide, yellow, bare spot, miles across, a horrible slash in the green forest, and in the middle of it, surrounded by stacks on stacks of lumber, was a great sawmill.

I stared in utter amazement. A sawmill on Penetier! Even as I gazed a train of fresh-cut lumber trailed away into the forest.

V. THE SAWMILL

In my surprise I almost forgot the Mexican. Then I thought that if Dick were there the Mexican would be likely to have troubles of his own. I remembered Dick's reputation as a fighter. But suppose I did not find Dick at the sawmill? This part of the forest was probably owned by private individuals, for I couldn't imagine Government timber being cut in this fashion. So I tied Hal and the pony amidst a thick clump of young pines, and, leaving all my outfit except my revolver, I struck out across the slash.

No second glance was needed to tell that the lumbering here was careless and without thought for the future. It had been a clean cut, and what small saplings had escaped the saw had been crushed by the dropping and hauling of the large pines. The stumps were all about three feet high, and that meant the waste of many thousands of feet of good lumber. Only the straight, unbranched trunks had been used. The tops of the pines had not been lopped, and lay where they had fallen. It was a wilderness of yellow brush, a dry jungle. The smell of pine was so powerful that I could hardly breathe. Fire must inevitably complete this work of ruin; already I was forester enough to see that.

Presently the trail crossed a railroad track which appeared to have been hastily constructed. Swinging along at a rapid step on the ties I soon reached the outskirts of the huge stacks of lumber; I must have walked half a mile between two yellow walls. Then I entered the lumber camp.

It was even worse-looking than the slash. Rows of dirty tents, lines of squatty log-cabins, and many flat-board houses clustered around an immense sawmill. Evidently I had arrived at the noon hour, for the mill was not running, and many rough men were lounging about smoking pipes. At the door of the first shack stood a fat, round-faced Negro wearing a long, dirty apron.

"Is Dick Leslie here?" I asked.

"I dunno if Dick's come in yet, but I 'specks him," he replied. "Be you the young gent Dick's lookin' fer from down East?"

"Yes."

"Come right in, sonny, come right in an' eat. Dick allus eats with me, an' he has spoke often 'bout you." He led me in, and seated me at a bench where several men were eating. They were brawny fellows, clad in overalls and undershirts, and one, who spoke pleasantly to me, had sawdust on his bare arms and even in his hair. The cook set before me a bowl of soup, a plate of beans, potroast, and coffee, all of which I attacked with a good appetite. Presently the men finished their meat and went outside, leaving me alone with the cook.

"Many men on this job?" I asked.

"More'n a thousand. Buell's runnin' two shifts, day an' night."

"Buell? Does he own this land?"

"No. He's only the agent of a 'Frisco lumber company, an' the land belongs to the Government. Buell's sure slashin' the lumber off, though. Two freight-trains of lumber out every day."

"Is this Penetier Forest?" I queried, carelessly, but I had begun to think hard.

"Sure."

I wanted to ask questions, but thought it wiser to wait. I knew enough already to make out that I had come upon the scene of a gigantic lumber steal. Buell's strange manner on the train, at the station, and his eagerness to hurry me out of Holston now needed no more explanation. I began to think the worst of him.

"Did you see a Mexican come into camp?" I inquired of the Negro.

"Sure. Greaser got here this mornin'."

"He tried to rob me in Holston."

"'Tain't nothin' new fer Greaser. He's a thief, but I never heerd of him holdin' anybody up. No nerve 'cept to knife a feller in the back."

"What'll I do if I meet him here?"

"Slam him one! You're a strappin' big lad. Slam him one, an' flash your gun on him. Greaser's a coward. I seen a young feller he'd cheated make him crawl. Anyway, it'll be all day with him when Dick finds out he tried to rob you. An' say, stranger, if a feller stays sober, this camp's safe enough in daytime, but at night, drunk or sober, it's a tough place."

Before I had finished eating a shrill whistle from the sawmill called the hands to work; soon it was followed by the rumble of machinery and the sharp singing of a saw.

I set out to see the lumber-camp, and although I stepped forth boldly, the truth was that with all my love for the Wild West I would have liked to be at home. But here I was, and I determined not to show the white feather.

I passed a row of cook-shacks like the one I had been in, and several stores and saloons. The lumber-camp was a little town. A rambling log cabin attracted me by reason of the shaggy mustangs standing before it and the sounds of mirth within. A peep showed me a room with a long bar, where men and boys were drinking. I heard the rattle of dice and the clink of silver. Seeing the place was crowded, I thought I might find Dick there, so I stepped inside. My entrance was unnoticed, so far as I could tell; in fact, there seemed no reason why it should be otherwise, for, being roughly dressed, I did not look very different from the many young fellows there. I scanned all the faces, but did not see Dick's, nor, for that matter, the Mexican's. Both disappointed and relieved, I turned away, for the picture of low dissipation was not attractive.

The hum of the great sawmill drew me like a magnet. I went out to the lumber-yard at the back of the mill, where a trestle slanted down to a pond full of logs. A train loaded with pines had just pulled in, and dozens of men were rolling logs off the flat-cars into a canal. At stations along the canal stood others pike-poling the logs toward the trestle, where an endless chain caught them with sharp claws and hauled them up. Half-way from, the ground they were washed clean by a circle of water-spouts.

I walked up the trestle and into the mill. The noise almost deafened me. High above all other sounds rose the piercing song of the saw, and the short intervals when it was not cutting were filled with a thunderous crash that jarred the whole building. After a few confused glances I got the working order into my head, and found myself in the most interesting place I had ever seen.

As the stream of logs came up into the mill the first log was shunted off the chain upon a carriage. Two men operated this carriage by levers, one to take the log up to the saw, and the other to run it back for another cut. The run back was very swift. Then a huge black iron head butted up from below and turned the log over as easily as if it had been a straw. This was what made the jar and crash. On the first cut the long strip of bark went to the left and up against five little circular saws. Then the five pieces slipped out of sight down chutes. When the log was trimmed a man stationed near the huge band-saw made signs to those on the carriage, and I saw that they got from him directions whether to cut the log into timbers, planks, or boards. The heavy timbers, after leaving the saw, went straight down the middle of the mill, the planks went to the right, the boards in another direction. Men and boys were everywhere, each with a lever in hand. There was not the slightest cessation of the work. And a log forty feet long and six feet thick, which had taken hundreds of years to grow, was cut up in just four minutes.

The place fascinated me. I had not dreamed that a sawmill could be brought to such a pitch of mechanical perfection, and I wondered how long the timber would last at that rate of cutting. The movement and din tired me, and I went outside upon a long platform. Here workmen caught the planks and boards as they came out, and loaded them upon trucks which were wheeled away. This platform was a world in itself. It sent arms everywhere among the piles of lumber, and once or twice I was as much lost as I had been up in the forest.

While turning into one of these byways I came suddenly upon Buell and another man. They were standing near a little house of weather-strips, evidently an office, and were in their shirt-sleeves. They had not seen or heard me. I dodged behind a pile of planks, intending to slip back the way I had come. Before I could move Buell's voice rooted me to the spot.

"His name's Ward. Tall, well-set lad. I put Greaser after him the other night, hopin' to scare him back East. But nix!"

"Well, he's here now—to study forestry! Ha! ha!" said the other.

"You're sure the boy you mean is the one I mean?"

"Greaser told me so. And this boy is Leslie's friend."

"That's the worst of it," replied Buell, impatiently. "I've got Leslie fixed as far as this lumber deal is concerned, but he won't stand for any more. He was harder to fix than the other rangers, an' I'm afraid of him." he's grouchy now.

"You shouldn't have let the boy get here."

"Stockton, I tried to prevent it. I put Greaser with Bud an' Bill on his trail. They didn't find him, an' now here he turns up."

"Maybe he can be fixed."

"Not if I know my business, he can't; take that from me. This kid is straight. He'll queer my deal in a minute if he gets wise. Mind you, I'm gettin' leary of Washington. We've seen about the last of these lumber deals. If I can pull this one off I'll quit; all I want is a little more time. Then I'll fire the slash, an' that'll cover tracks."

"Buell, I wouldn't want to be near Penetier when you light that fire. This forest will burn like tinder."

"It's a whole lot I care then. Let her burn. Let the Government put out the fire. Now, what's to be done about this boy?"

"I think I'd try to feel him out. Maybe he can be fixed. Boys who want to be foresters can't be rich. Failing that—you say he's a kid who wants to hunt and shoot—get some one to take him up on the mountain."

"See here, Stockton. This young Ward will see the timber is bein' cut clean. If it was only a little patch I wouldn't mind. But this slash an' this mill! He'll know. More'n that, he'll tell Leslie about the Mexican. Dick's no fool. We're up against it."

"It's risky, Buell. You remember the ranger up in Oregon."

"Then we are to fall down on this deal all because of a fresh tenderfoot kid?" demanded Buell.

"Not so loud.... We'll not fall down. But caution—use caution. You made a mistake in trusting so much to the Greaser."

"I know, an' I'm afraid of Leslie. An' that other fire-ranger, Jim Williams, he's a Texan, an' a bad man. The two of them could about trim up this camp. They'll both fight for the boy; take that from me."

"We are sure up against it. Think now, and think quick."

"First, I'll try to fix the boy. If that won't work... we'll kidnap him. Then we'll take no chances with Leslie. There's a cool two hundred an' fifty thousand in this deal for us, an' we're goin' to get it."

With that Buell went into his office and closed the door; the other man, Stockton, walked briskly down the platform. I could not resist peeping from my hiding-place as he passed. He was tall and had a red beard, which would enable me to recognize him if we met.

I waited there for some little time. Then I saw that by squeezing between two plies of lumber could reach the other side of the platform. When I reached the railing I climbed over, and, with the help of braces and posts, soon got to where I could drop down. Once on the ground I ran along under the platform until I saw a lane that led to the street. My one thought was to reach the cabin where the Negro cook stayed and ask him if Dick Leslie had come to camp. If he had not arrived, then I intended to make a bee-line for my mustang.

VI. DICK LESLIE, RANGER

Which end of the street I entered I had no idea. The cabins were all alike, and in my hurry I would have passed the cook's shack had it not been for the sight of a man standing in the door. That stalwart figure I would have known anywhere.

"Dick!" I cried, rushing at him.

What Dick's welcome was I did not hear, but judging from the grip he put on my shoulders and then on my hands, he was glad to see me.

"Ken, blessed if I'd have known you," he said, shoving me back at arm's-length. "Let's have a look at you.... Grown I say, but you're a husky lad!"

While he was looking at me I returned the scrutiny with interest. Dick had always been big, but now he seemed wider and heavier. Among these bronzed Westerners he appeared pale, but that was only on account of his fair skin.

"Ken, didn't you get my letter—the one telling you not to come West yet a while?"

"No," I replied, blankly. "The last one I got was in May—about the middle. I have it with me. You certainly asked me to come then. Dick, don't you want me—now?"

Plain it was that my friend felt uncomfortable; he shifted from one foot to another, and a cloud darkened his brow. But his blue eyes burned with a warm light as he put his hand on my shoulder.

"Ken, I'm glad to see you," he said, earnestly. "It's like getting a glimpse of home. But I wrote you not to come. Conditions have changed—there's something doing here—I'll—"

"You needn't explain, Dick," I replied, gravely. "I know. Buell and—" I waved my hand from the sawmill to the encircling slash.

Dick's face turned a fiery red. I believed that was the only time Dick Leslie ever failed to look a fellow in the eye.

"Ken!... You're on," he said, recovering his composure. "Well, wait till you hear—Hello! here's Jim Williams, my pardner."

A clinking of spurs accompanied a soft step.

"Jim, here's Ken Ward, the kid pardner I used to have back in the States," said Dick. "Ken, you know Jim."

If ever I knew anything by heart it was what Dick had written me about this Texan, Jim Williams.

"Ken, I shore am glad to see you," drawled Jim, giving my hand a squeeze that I thought must break every bone in it.

Though Jim Williams had never been described to me, my first sight of him fitted my own ideas. He was tall and spare; his weather-beaten face seemed set like a dark mask; only his eyes moved, and they had a quivering alertness and a brilliancy that made them hard to look into. He wore a wide sombrero, a blue flannel shirt with a double row of big buttons, overalls, top-boots with very high heels, and long spurs. A heavy revolver swung at his hip, and if I had not already known that Jim Williams had fought Indians and killed bad men, I should still have seen something that awed me in the look of him.

I certainly felt proud to be standing with those two rangers, and for the moment Buell and all his crew could not have daunted me.

"Hello! what's this?" inquired Dick, throwing back my coat; and, catching sight of my revolver, he ejaculated: "Ken Ward!"

"Wal, Ken, if you-all ain't packin' a gun!" said Jim, in his slow, careless drawl. "Dick, he shore is!"

It was now my turn to blush.

"Yes, I've got a gun," I replied, "and I ought to have had it the other night."

"How so?" inquired Dick, quickly.

It did not take me long to relate the incident of the Mexican.

Dick looked like a thunder-cloud, but Jim swayed and shook with laughter.

"You knocked him off the roof? Wal, thet shore is dee-lightful. It shore is!"

"Yes; and, Dick," I went on, breathlessly, "the Greaser followed me, and if I hadn't missed the trail, I don't know what would have happened. Anyway, he got here first."

"The Greaser trailed you?" interrupted Dick, sharply.

When I replied he glanced keenly at me. "How do you know?"

"I suspected it when I saw him with two men in the forest. But now I know it."

"How?"

"I beard Buell tell Stockton he had put the Greaser on my trail."

"Buell—Stockton!" exclaimed Dick. "What'd they have to do with the Greaser?"

"I met Buell on the train. I told him I had come West to study forestry. Buell's afraid I'll find out about this lumber steal, and he wants to shut my mouth."

Dick looked from me to Jim, and Jim slowly straitened his tall form. For a moment neither spoke. Dick's white face caused me to look away from him. Jim put a hand on my arm.

"Ken, you shore was lucky; you shore was."

"I guess he doesn't know how lucky," added Dick, somewhat huskily. "Come on, we'll look up the Mexican."

"It shore is funny how bad I want to see thet Greaser."

Dick's hard look and tone were threatening enough, yet they did not affect me so much as the easy, gay manner of the Texan. Little cold quivers ran over me, and my knees knocked together. For the moment my animosity toward the Mexican vanished, and with it the old hunger to be in the thick of Wild Western life. I was afraid that I was going to see a man killed without being able to lift a hand to prevent it.

The rangers marched me between them down the street and into the corner saloon. Dick held me half behind him with his left hand while Jim sauntered ahead. Strangest of all the things that had happened was the sudden silencing of the noisy crowd.

The Mexican was not there. His companions, Bud and Bill, as Buell had called them, were sitting at a table, and as Jim Williams walked into the center of the room they slowly and gradually rose to their feet. One was a swarthy man with evil eyes and a scar on his cheek; the other had a brick-red face and a sandy mustache with a vicious curl. Neither seemed to be afraid, only cautious.

"We're all lookin' for thet Greaser friend of yourn," drawled Jim. "I shore want to see him bad."

"He's gone, Williams," replied one. "Was in somethin' of a rustle, an' didn't leave no word."

"Wal, I reckon he's all we're lookin' for this pertickler minnit."

Jim spoke in a soft, drawling voice, and his almost expressionless tone seemed to indicate pleasant indifference; still, no one could have been misled by it, for the long, steady gaze he gave the men and his cool presence that held the room quiet meant something vastly different. No reply was offered. Bud and Bill sat down, evidently to resume their card-playing. The uneasy silence broke to a laugh, then to subdued voices, and finally the clatter and hum began again. Dick led me outside, where we were soon joined by Jim.

"He's holed up," suggested Dick.

"Shore. I don't take no stock in his hittin' the trail. He's layin' low."

"Let's look around a bit, anyhow."

Dick took me back to the cook's cabin and, bidding me remain inside, strode away. I beard footsteps so soon after his departure that I made certain he had returned, but the burly form which blocked the light in the cabin door was not Dick's. I was astounded to recognize Buell.

"Hello!" he said, in his blustering voice. "Heard you had reached camp, an' have been huntin' you up."

I greeted him pleasantly enough—more from surprise than from a desire to mislead him. It seemed to me then that a child could have read Buell. He'd an air of suppressed excitement; there was a glow on his face and a kind of daring flash in his eyes. He seemed too eager, too glad to see me.

"I've got a good job for you," he went on, glibly, "jest what you want, an' you're jest what I need. Come into my office an' help me. There'll be plenty of outside work—measurin' lumber, markin' trees, an' such."

"Why, Mr. Buell—I—you see, Dick—he might not—"

I hesitated, not knowing how to proceed. But at my halting speech Buell became even more smiling and voluble.

"Dick? Oh, Dick an' I stand all right; take thet from me. Dick'll agree to what I want. I need a young feller bad. Money's no object. You're a bright youngster. You'll look out for my interests. Here!" He pulled out a large wad of greenbacks, and then spoke in a lower voice. "You understand that money cuts no ice 'round this camp. We've a big deal. We need a smart young feller. There's always some little irregularities about these big timber deals out West. But you'll wear blinkers, an' make some money while you're studyin' forestry. See?"

"Irregularities? What kind of irregularities?"

For the life of me I could not keep a little scorn out of my question. Buell slowly put the bills in his pocket while his eyes searched; I could not control my rising temper.

"You mean you want to fix me?"

He made no answer, and his face stiffened.

"You mean you want to buy my silence, shut my mouth about this lumber steal?"

He drew in his breath audibly, yet still he did not speak. Either he was dull of comprehension or else he was astonished beyond words. I knew I was mad to goad him like that, but I could not help it. I grew hot with anger, and the more clearly I realized that he had believed he could "fix" me with his dirty money the hotter I got.

"You told Stockton you were leary of Washington, and were afraid I'd queer your big deal.... Well, Mr. Buell, that's exactly what I'm going to do—queer it!"

He went black in the face, and, cursing horribly, grasped me by the arm. I struggled, but I could not loose that iron hand. Suddenly I felt a violent wrench that freed me. Then I saw Dick swing back his shoulder and shoot out his arm. He knocked Buell clear across the room, and when the man fell I thought the cabin was coming down in the crash. He appeared stunned, for he groped about with his hands, found a chair, and, using it as a support, rose to his feet, swaying unsteadily.

"Leslie, I'll get you for this—take it from me," he muttered.

Dick's lips were tight, and he watched Buell with flaming eyes. The lumberman lurched out of the door, and we heard him cursing after he had disappeared. Then Dick looked at me with no little disapproval.

"What did you say to make Buell wild like that?"

I told Dick, word for word. First he looked dumfounded, then angry, and he ended up with a grim laugh.

"Ken, you're sure bent on starting something, as Jim would say. You've started it all right. And Jim'll love you for it. But I'm responsible to your mother. Ken, I remember your mother—and you're going back home."

"Dick!"

"You're going back home as fast as I can get you to Holston and put you on a train, that's all."

"I won't go!" I cried.

Without any more words Dick led me down the street to a rude corral; here he rapidly saddled and packed his horses. The only time he spoke was when he asked me where I had tied my mustangs. Soon we were hurrying out through the slash toward the forest. Dick's troubled face kept down my resentment, but my heart grew like lead. What an ending to my long-cherished trip to the West! It had lasted two days. The disappointment seemed more than I could bear.

We found the mustangs as I had left them, and the sight of Hal and the feeling of the saddle made me all the worse. We did not climb the foot-hill by the trail which the Mexican had used, but took a long, slow ascent far round to the left. Dick glanced back often, and when we reached the top he looked again in a way to convince me that he had some apprehensions of being followed.

Twilight of that eventful day found us pitching camp in a thickly timbered hollow. I could not help dwelling on how different my feelings would have been if this night were but the beginning of many nights with Dick. It was the last, and the more I thought about it the more wretched I grew. Dick rolled in his blanket without saying even good-night, and I lay there watching the veils and shadows of firelight flicker on the pines, and listening, to the wind. Gradually the bitterness seemed to go away; my body relaxed and sank into the soft, fragrant pine-needles; the great shadowy trees mixed with the surrounding darkness. When I awoke it was broad daylight, and Dick was shaking my arm.

"Hunt up the horses while I get the grub ready," he said, curtly.

As the hollow was carpeted with thick grass our horses had not strayed. I noticed that here the larger trees had been cut, and the forest resembled a fine park. In the sunny patches seedlings were sprouting, many little bushy pines were growing, and the saplings had sufficient room and light to prosper. I commented to Dick upon the difference between this part of Penetier and the hideous slash we had left.

"There were a couple of Government markers went through here and marked the timber to be cut," said Dick.

"Was the timber cut in the mill I saw?"

"No. Buell's just run up that mill. The old one is out here a ways, nearer Holston."

"Is it possible, Dick, that any of those loggers back there don't know the Government is being defrauded?"

"Ken, hardly any of them know it, and they wouldn't care if they did. You see, this forest-preserve business is new out here. Formerly the lumbermen bought so much land and cut over it—skinned it. Two years ago, when the National Forests were laid out, the lumbering men—that is, the loggers, sawmill hands, and so on—found they did not get as much employment as formerly. So generally they're sore on the National Forest idea."

"But, Dick, if they understand the idea of forestry they'd never oppose it."

"Maybe. I don't understand it too well myself. I can fight fire—that's my business; but this ranger work is new. I doubt if the Westerners will take to forestry. There've been some shady deals all over the West because of it. Buell, now, he's a timber shark. He bought so much timber from the Government, and had the markers come in to mark the cut; then after they were gone, he rushed up a mill and clapped on a thousand hands."

"And the rangers stand for it? Where'll their jobs be when the Government finds out?"

"I was against it from the start. So was Jim, particularly. But the other rangers persuaded us."

It began to dawn upon me that Dick Leslie might, after all, turn out to be good soil in which to plant some seeds of forestry. I said no more then, as we were busy packing for the start, but when we had mounted I began to talk. I told him all I had learned about trees, how I loved them, and how I had determined to devote my life to their study, care, and development. As we rode along under the wide-spreading pines I illustrated my remarks by every example I could possibly use. The more I talked the more interested Dick became, and this spurred me on. Perhaps I exaggerated, but my conscience never pricked me. He began to ask questions.

We reached a spring at midday, and halted for a rest. I kept on pleading, and presently I discovered, to my joy, that I had made a strong impression upon Dick. It seemed a strange thing for me to be trying to explain forestry to a forest ranger, but so it was.

"Ken, it's all news to me. I've been on Penetier about a year, and I never heard a word of what you've been telling me. My duties have been the practical ones that any woodsman knows. Jim and the other rangers—why, they don't know any more than I. It's a great thing, and I've queered my chance with the Government."

"No, you haven't—neither has Jim—not if you'll be straight from now on. You can't keep faith with Buell. He tried to kidnap me. That lets you out. We'll spoil Buell's little deal and save Penetier. A letter to father will do it. He has friends in the Forestry Department at Washington. Dick, what do you say? It's not too late!"

The dark shade lifted from the ranger's face, and he looked at me with the smile of the old fishing days.

"Say? I say yes!" he exclaimed, in ringing voice, "Ken, you've made a man of me!"

VII. BACK TO HOLSTON

Soon we were out of the forest, and riding across the sage-flat with Holston in sight. Both of us avoided the unpleasant subject of my enforced home-going. Evidently Dick felt cut up about it, and it caused me such a pang that I drove it from my mind. Toward the end of our ride Dick began again to talk of forestry.

"Ken, it's mighty interesting—all this you've said about trees. Some of the things are so simple that I wonder I didn't hit on them long ago; in fact, I knew a lot of what you might call forestry, but the scientific ideas—they stump me. Now, what you said about a pine-tree cleaning itself—come back at me with that."

"Why, that's simple enough, Dick," I answered. "Now, say here we have a clump of pine saplings. They stand pretty close—close enough to make dense shade, but not too crowded. The shade has prevented the lower branches from producing leaves. As a consequence these branches die. Then they dry, rot, and fall off, so when the trees mature they are clean-shafted. They have fine, clear trunks. They have cleaned themselves, and so make the best of lumber, free from knots."

So our talk went on. Once in town I was impatient to write to my father, for we had decided that we would not telegraph. Leaving our horses in Cless's corral, we went to the hotel and proceeded to compose the letter. This turned out more of a task than we had bargained for. But we got it finished at last, not forgetting to put in a word for Jim Williams, and then we both signed it.

"There!" I cried. "Dick, something will be doing round Holston before many days."

"That's no joke, you can bet," replied Dick, wiping his face. "Ken, it's made me sweat just to see that letter start East. Buell is a tough sort, and he'll make trouble. Well, he wants to steer clear of Jim and me."

After that we fell silent, and walked slowly back toward Cless's corral. Dick's lips were closed tight, and he did not look at me. Evidently he did not intend to actually put me aboard a train, and the time for parting had come. He watered his horses at the trough, and fussed over his pack and fumbled with his saddle-girths. It looked to me as though he had not the courage to say goodby.

"Ken, it didn't look so bad—so mean till now," he said. "I'm all broken up.... To get you way out here! Oh! what's the use? I'm mighty sorry ....Good-bye—maybe—

He broke off suddenly, and, wringing my hand, he vaulted into the saddle. He growled at his pack-pony, and drove him out of the corral. Then he set off at a steady trot down the street toward the open country.

It came to me in a flash, as I saw him riding farther and farther away, that the reason my heart was not broken was because I did not intend to go home. Dick had taken it for granted that I would board the next train for the East. But I was not going to do anything of the sort. To my amaze I found my mind made up on that score. I had no definite plan, but I was determined to endure almost anything rather than give up my mustang and outfit.

"It's shift for myself now," I thought, soberly. "I guess I can make good. ... I'm going back to Penetier."

Even in the moment of impulse I knew how foolish this would be. But I could not help it. That forest had bewitched me. I meant to go back to it.

"I'll stay away from the sawmill," I meditated, growing lighter of heart every minute. "I'll keep out of sight of the lumbermen. I'll go higher up on the mountain, and hunt, and study the trees.... I'll do it."

Whereupon I marched off at once to a store and bought the supply of provisions that Buell had decided against when he helped me with my outfit. This addition made packing the pony more of a problem than ever, but I contrived to get it all on to my satisfaction. It was nearing sunset when I rode out of Holston this second time. The sage flat was bare and gray. Dick had long since reached the pines, and would probably make camp at the spring where we had stopped for lunch. I certainly did not want to catch up with him, but as there was small chance of that; it caused me no concern.

Shortly after sunset twilight fell, and it was night when I reached the first pine-trees. Still, as the trail was easily to be seen, I kept on, for I did not want to camp without water. The forest was very dark, in some places like a huge black tent, and I had not ridden far when the old fear of night, the fancy of things out there in the darkness, once more possessed me. It made me angry. Why could I not have the same confidence that I had in the daytime? It was impossible. The forest was full of moving shadows. When the wind came up to roar in the pine-tips it was a relief because it broke the silence.

I began to doubt whether I could be sure of locating the spring, and I finally decided to make camp at once. I stopped Hal, and had swung my leg over the pommel when I saw a faint glimmer of light far ahead. It twinkled like a star, but was not white and cold enough for a star.

"That's Dick's campfire," I said. "I'll have to stop here. Maybe I'm too close now."

I pondered the question. The blaze was a long way off, and I concluded I could risk camping on the spot, provided I did not make a fire. Accordingly I dismounted, and was searching for a suitable place when I happened to think that the campfire might not be Dick's, after all. Perhaps Buell had sent the Mexican with Bud and Bill on my trail again. This would not do. But I did not want to go back or turn off the trail.

"I'll slip up and see who it is," I decided.

The idea pleased me; however, I did not yield to it without further consideration. I had a clear sense of responsibility. I knew that from now on I should be called upon to reason out many perplexing things. I did not want to make any mistakes. So I tied Hal and the pack-pony to a bush fringing the trail, and set off through the forest.

It dawned upon me presently that the campfire was much farther away than it appeared. Often it went out of sight behind trees. By degrees it grew larger and larger. Then I slowed down and approached more cautiously. Once when the trees obscured it I traveled some distance without getting a good view of it. Passing down into a little hollow I lost it again. When I climbed out I hauled up short with a sharp catch of my breath. There were several figures moving around the campfire. I had stumbled on a camp that surely was not Dick Leslie's.

The ground was as soft as velvet, and my footsteps gave forth no sound. When the wind lulled I paused behind a tree and waited for another gusty roar. I kept very close to the trail, for that was the only means by which I could return to my horses. I felt the skin tighten on my face. Suddenly, as I paused, I beard angry voices, pitched high. But I could not make out the words.

Curiosity got the better of me. If the men were hired by Buell I wanted to know what they were quarrelling about. I stole stealthily from tree to tree, and another hollow opened beneath me. It was so wide and the pines so overshadowed it that I could not tell how close the opposite side might be to the campfire. I slipped down along the edge of the trail. The blaze disappeared. Only a faint arc of light showed through the gloom.

I peered keenly into the blackness. At length I reached the slope. Here I dropped to my hands and knees.

It was a long crawl to the top. Reaching it, I cautiously peeped over. There were trees hiding the fire. But it was close. I heard the voices of men. I backed down the slope, crossed the trail, and came up on the other side. Pines grew thick on this level, and I stole silently from one to another. Finally I reached the black trunk of a tree close to the campfire.

For a moment I lay low. I did not seem exactly afraid, but I was all tense and hard, and my heart drummed in my ears. There was something ticklish about this scouting. Then I peeped out.

It added little to my excitement to recognize the Mexican. He sat near the fire smoking a cigarette. Near him were several men, one of whom was Bill. Facing them sat a man with his back to a small sapling. He was tied with a lasso.

One glance at his white face made me drop behind the tree, where I lay stunned and bewildered—for that man was Dick Leslie.

VIII. THE LUMBERMEN

For a full moment I just lay still, hugging the ground, and I did not seem to think at all. Voices loud in anger roused me. Raising myself, I guardedly looked from behind the tree.

One of the lumbermen threw brush on the fire, making it blaze brightly. He was tall and had a red beard. I recognized Stockton, Buell's right hand in the lumber deal.

"Leslie, you're a liar!" he said.

Dick's eyes glinted from his pale face.

"Yes, that's your speed, Stockton," he retorted. "You bring your thugs into my camp pretending to be friendly. You grab a fellow behind his back, tie him up, and then call him a liar. Wait, you timber shark!"

"You're lying about that kid, Ward," declared the other. "You sent him back East, that's what. He'll have the whole forest service down here. Buell will be wild. Oh, he won't do a thing when he learns Ward has given us the slip!"

"I tell you, Ken Ward gave me the slip," replied Dick. "I'll admit I meant to see him safe in Holston. But he wouldn't go. He ran off from me right here in this forest."

What could have been Dick's object in telling such a lie? It made me wonder. Perhaps these lumbermen were more dangerous than I had supposed, and Dick did not wish them to believe I had left Penetier. Maybe he was playing for time, and did not want them to get alarmed and escape before the officers came.

"Why did he run off?" asked Stockton.

"Because I meant to send him home, and he didn't want to go. He's crazy to camp out, to hunt and ride."

"If that's true, Leslie, there's been no word sent to Washington."

"How could there be?"

"Well, I've got to hold you anyway till we see Buell. His orders were to keep you and Ward prisoners till this lumber deal is pulled off. We're not going to be stopped now."

Leslie turned crimson, and strained on the lasso that bound him to the sapling. "Somebody is going to pay for this business!" he declared, savagely. "You forget I'm an officer in this forest."

"I'll hold you, Leslie, whatever comes of it," answered the lumberman. "I'd advise you to cool down."

"You and Buell have barked up the wrong tree, mind that, Stockton. Jim Williams, my pardner, is wise. He expects me back tomorrow."

"See hyar, Stockton," put in Bill, "you're new in Arizona, an' I want to give you a hunch. If Jim Williams hits this trail, you ain't goin' to be well enough to care about any old lumber steal."

"Jim hit the trail all right," went on Dick. "He's after Greaser. It'd go hard with you if Jim happened to walk in now."

"I don't want to buck against Williams, that's certain," replied Stockton. "I know his record. But I'll take a chance—anyway, till Buell knows. It's his game."

Dick made no answer, and sat there eyeing his captors. There was little talk after this. Bud threw a log on the fire. Stockton told the Mexican to take a look at the horses. Greaser walked within twenty feet of where I lay, and I held my breath while he passed. The others rolled in their blankets. It was now so dark that I could not distinguish anything outside of the campfire circle. But I heard Greaser's soft, shuffling footsteps as he returned. Then his dark, slim figure made a shadow between me and the light. He sat down before the fire and began to roll a cigarette. He did not seem sleepy.

A daring scheme flashed into my mind. I would crawl into camp and free Dick. Not only would I outwit the lumber thieves, but also make Dick think well of me. What would Jim Williams say of a trick like that? The thought of the Texan banished what little hesitation I felt. Glancing round the bright circle, I made my plan; it was to crawl far back into the darkness, go around to the other side of the camp, and then slip up behind Dick. Already his head was nodding on his breast. It made me furious to see him sitting so uncomfortably, sagging in the lasso.

I tried to beat down my excitement, but there was a tingling all over me that would not subside. But I soon saw that I might have a long wait. The Mexican did not go to sleep, so I had time to cool off.

The campfire gradually burned out, and the white glow changed to red. One of the men snored in a way that sounded like a wheezy whistle. Coyotes howled in the woods, and the longer I listened to the long, strange howls the better I liked them. The roar in the wind had died down to a moaning. I thought of myself lying there, with my skin prickling and my eyes sharp on the darkening forms. I thought of the nights I had spent with Hal in the old woods at home. How full the present seemed! My breast swelled, my hand gripped my revolver, my eyes pierced the darkness, and I would not have been anywhere else for the world.

Greaser smoked out his cigarette, and began to nod. That was the signal for me. I crawled noiselessly from the tree. When I found myself going down into the hollow, I stopped and rose to my feet. The forest was so pitchy black that I could not tell the trees from the darkness. I groped to the left, trying to circle. Once I snapped a twig; it cracked like a pistol-shot, and my heart stopped beating, then began to thump. But Greaser never stirred as he sat in the waning light. At last I had half circled the camp.

After a short rest I started forward, slow and stealthy as a creeping cat. When within fifty feet of the fire I went down on all-fours and began to crawl. Twice I got out of line. But at last Dick's burly shoulders loomed up between me and the light.

Then I halted. My breast seemed bursting, and I panted so hard that I was in a terror lest I should awaken some one. Again I thought of what I was doing, and fought desperately to gain my coolness.

Now the only cover I had was Dick's broad back, for the sapling to which he was tied was small. I drew my hunting-knife. One more wriggle brought me close to Dick, with my face near his hands, which were bound behind him. I slipped the blade under the lasso, and cut it through.

Dick started as if he had received an electric shock. He threw back his head and uttered a sudden exclamation.

Although I was almost paralyzed with fright I put my hand on his shoulder and whispered: "S-s-s-h! It's Ken!"

Greaser uttered a shrill cry. Dick leaped to his feet. Then I grew dizzy, and my sight blurred. I heard hoarse shouts and saw dark forms rising as if out of the earth. All was confusion. I wanted to run, but could not get up. There was a wrestling, whirling mass in front of me.

But this dimness of sight and weakness of body did not last. I saw two men on the ground, with Dick standing over them. Stockton was closing in. Greaser ran around them with something in his hand that glittered in the firelight. Stockton dived for Dick's legs and upset him. They went down together, and the Mexican leaped on them, waving the bright thing high over his head.

I bounded forward, and, grasping his wrist with both hands, I wrenched his arm with all my might. Some one struck me over the head. I saw a million darting points of light—then all went black.

When I opened my eyes the sun was shining. I had a queer, numb feeling all over, and my head hurt terribly. Everything about me was hazy. I did not know where I was. After a little I struggled to sit up, and with great difficulty managed it. My hands were tied. Then it all came back to me. Stockton stood before me holding a tin cup of water toward my lips. My throat was parched, and I drank. Stockton had a great bruise on his forehead; his nostrils were crusted with blood, and his shirt was half torn off.

"You're all right?" he said.

"Sure," I replied, which was not true.

I imagined that a look of relief came over his face. Next I saw Bill nursing his eye, and bathing it with a wet handkerchief. It was swollen shut, puffed out to the size of a goose-egg, and blue as indigo. Dick had certainly landed hard on Bill. Then I turned round to see Dick sitting against the little sapling, bound fast with a lasso. His clean face did not look as if he had been in a fight; he was smiling, yet there was anxiety in his eyes.

"Ken, now you've played hob," he said. It was a reproach, but his look made me proud.

"Oh, Dick, if you hadn't called out!" I exclaimed.

"Darned if you're not right! But it was a slick job, and you'll tickle Jim to death. I was an old woman. But that cold knife-blade made me jump."

I glanced round the camp for the Mexican and Bud and the fifth man, but they were gone. Bill varied his occupation of the moment by kneading biscuit dough in a basin. Then there came such a severe pain in my head that I went blind for a little while. "What's the matter with my head? Who hit me?" I cried.

"Bud slugged you with the butt of his pistol," said Dick. "And, Ken, I think you saved me from being knifed by the Greaser. You twisted his arm half off. He cursed all night.... Ha! there he comes now with your outfit."

Sure enough, the Mexican appeared on the trail, leading my horses. I was so glad to see Hal that I forgot I was a prisoner. But Greaser's sullen face and glittering eyes reminded me of it quickly enough. I read treachery in his glance.

Bud rode into camp from the other direction, and he brought a bunch of horses, two of which I recognized as Dick's. The lumbermen set about getting breakfast, and Stockton helped me to what little I could eat and drink. Now that I was caught he did not appear at all mean or harsh. I did not shrink from him, and had the feeling that he meant well by me.

The horses were saddled and bridled, and Dick and I, still tied, were bundled astride our mounts. The pack-ponies led the way, with Bill following; I came next, Greaser rode behind me, and Dick was between Bud and Stockton. So we traveled, and no time was wasted. I noticed that the men kept a sharp lookout both to the fore and the rear. We branched off the main trail and took a steeper one leading up the slope. We rode for hours. There were moments when I reeled in my saddle, but for the greater while I stood my pain and weariness well enough. Some time in the afternoon a shrill whistle ahead attracted my attention. I made out two horsemen waiting on the trail.

"Huh! about time!" growled Bill. "Hyar's Buell an' Herky-Jerky."

As we approached I saw Buell, and the fellow with the queer name turned out to be no other than the absent man I had been wondering about. He had been dispatched to fetch the lumberman.

Buell was superbly mounted on a sleek bay, and he looked very much the same jovial fellow I had met on the train. He grinned at the disfigured men.

"Take it from me, you fellers wouldn't look any worse bunged up if you'd been jolted by the sawlogs in my mill."

"We can't stand here to crack jokes," said Stockton, sharply. "Some ranger might see us. Now what?"

"You ketched the kid in time. That's all I wanted. Take him an' Leslie up in one of the canyons an' keep them there till further orders. You needn't stay, Stockton, after you get them in a safe place. An' you can send up grub."

Then he turned to me.

"You'll not be hurt if—"

"Don't you speak to me!" I burst out. It was on my lips to tell him of the letter to Washington, but somehow I kept silent.

"Leslie," went on Buell, "I'll overlook your hittin' me an' let you go if you'll give me your word to keep mum about this."

Dick did not speak, but looked at the lumberman with a dark gleam in his eyes.

"There's one thing, Buell," said Stockton. "Jim Williams is wise. You've got to look out for him."

Buell's ruddy face blanched. Then, without another word, he waved his hand toward the slope, and, wheeling his horse, galloped down the trail.

IX. TAKEN INTO THE MOUNTAINS

We climbed to another level bench where we branched off the trail. The forest still kept its open, park-like character. Under the great pines the ground was bare and brown with a thick covering of pine-needles, but in the glades were green grass and blue flowers.

Once across this level we encountered a steeper ascent than any I had yet climbed. Here the character of the forest began to change. There were other trees than pines, and particularly one kind, cone-shaped, symmetrical, and bright, which Dick called a silver spruce. I was glad it belonged to the conifers, or pine-tree family, because it was the most beautiful tree I had ever seen. We climbed ridges and threaded through aspen thickets in hollows till near sunset. Then Stockton ordered a halt for camp.

It came none too soon for me, and I was so exhausted that I had to be helped off my mustang. Stockton arranged my blankets, fed me, and bathed the bruise on my head, but I was too weary and sick to be grateful or to care about anything except sleep. Even the fact that my hands were uncomfortably bound did not keep me awake.

When some one called me next morning my eyes did not want to stay open. I had a lazy feeling and a dull ache in my bones, but the pain had gone from my head. That made everything else seem all right.

Soon we were climbing again, and my interest in my surroundings grew as we went up. For a while we brushed through thickets of scrub oak. The whole slope of the mountain was ridged and hollowed, so that we were always going down and climbing up. The pines and spruces grew smaller, and were more rugged and gnarled.

"Hyar's the canyon!" sang out Bill, presently.

We came out on the edge of a deep hollow. It was half a mile wide. I looked down a long incline of sharp tree-tips. The roar of water rose from below, and in places a white rushing torrent showed. Above loomed the snow-clad peak, glistening in the morning sun. How wonderfully far off and high it still was!

To my regret it was shut off from my sight as we descended into the canyon. However, I soon forgot that. I saw a troop of coyotes, and many black and white squirrels. From time to time huge birds, almost as big as turkeys, crashed out of the thickets and whirred away. They flew swift as pheasants, and I asked Dick what they were.

"Blue grouse," he replied. "Look sharp now, Ken, there are deer ahead of us. See the tracks?"

Looking down I saw little, sharp-pointed, oval tracks. Presently two foxes crossed an open patch not fifty yards from us, but I did not get a glimpse of the deer. Soon we reached the bottom of the canyon, and struck into another trail. The air was full of the low roar of tumbling water. This mountain-torrent was about twenty feet wide, but its swiftness and foam made it impossible to tell its depth. The trail led up-stream, and turned so constantly that half the time Bill, the leader, was not in sight. Once the sharp crack of his rifle halted the train. I heard crashings in the thicket. Dick yelled for me to look up the slope, and there I saw three gray deer with white tails raised. I heard a strange, whistling sound.

On going forward we found that Bill had killed a deer and was roping it on his pack-horse. As we proceeded up the canyon it grew narrower, and soon we entered a veritable gorge. It was short, but the floor was exceedingly rough, and made hard going for the horses. Suddenly I was amazed to see the gorge open out into a kind of amphitheatre several hundred feet across. The walls were steep, and one side shelved out, making a long, shallow cave, In the center of this amphitheatre was a deep hole from which the mountain stream boiled and bubbled.

"Hyar we are," said Bill, and swung out of his saddle. The other men followed suit, and helped Dick and me down. Stockton untied our hands, saying he reckoned we would be more comfortable that way. Indeed we were. My wrists were swollen and blistered. Stockton detailed the Mexican to keep guard over us.

"Ken, I've heard of this place," said Dick. "How's that for a spring? Twenty yards wide, and no telling how deep! This is snow-water straight from the peaks. We're not a thousand feet below the snow-line."

"I can tell that. Look at those Jwari pines," I replied, pointing up over the wall. A rugged slope rose above our camp-site, and it was covered with a tangled mass of stunted pines. Many of them were twisted and misshapen; some were half dead and bleached white at the tops. "It's my first sight of such trees," I went on, "but I've studied about them. Up here it's not lack of moisture that stunts and retards their growth. It's fighting the elements—cold, storm-winds, snowslides. I suppose not one in a thousand seedlings takes root and survives. But the forest fights hard to live."

"Well, Ken, we may as well sit back now and talk forestry till Buell skins all he wants of Penetier," said Dick. "It's really a fine camping-spot. Plenty of deer up here and bear, too."

"Dick, couldn't we escape?" I whispered.

"We're not likely to have a chance. But I say, Ken, how did you happen to turn up? I thought you were going to hop on the first train for home."

"Dick, you had another think coming. I couldn't go home. I'll have a great time yet—I'm having it now."

"Yes, that lump on your head looks like it," replied Dick, with a laugh. "If Bud hadn't put you out we'd have come closer to licking this bunch. Ken, keep your eye on Greaser. He's treacherous. His arm's lame yet."

"We've had two run-ins already," I said. "The third time is the worst, they say. I hope it won't come.... But, Dick, I'm as big—I'm bigger than he is."

"Hear the kid talk! I certainly ought to have put you on that train—"

"What train?" asked Stockton, sharply, from our rear. He took us in with suspicious eyes.

"I was telling Ken I ought to have put him on a train for home," answered Dick.

Stockton let the remark pass without further comment; still, he appeared to be doing some hard thinking. He put Dick at one end of the long cave, me at the other. Our bedding was unpacked and placed at our disposal. We made our beds. After that I kept my eyes open and did not miss anything.

"Leslie, I'm going to treat you and Ward white," said Stockton. "You'll have good grub. Herky-Jerky's the best cook this side of Holston, and you'll be left untied in the daytime. But if either of you attempts to get away it means a leg shot off. Do you get that?"

"All right, Stockton; that's pretty square of you, considering," replied Dick. "You're a decent sort of chap to be mixed up with a thief like Buell. I'm sorry."

Stockton turned away at this rather abruptly. Then Bill appeared on the wall above, and began to throw down firewood. Bud returned from the canyon, where he had driven the horses. Greaser sat on a stone puffing a cigarette. It was the first time I had taken a good look at him. He was smaller than I had fancied; his feet and hands and features resembled those of a woman, but his eyes were live coals of black fire. In the daylight I was not in the least afraid of him.

Herky-Jerky was the most interesting one of our captors. He had a short, stocky figure, and was the most bow-legged man I ever saw. Never on earth could he have stopped a pig in a lane. A stubby beard covered the lower half of his brick-red face. The most striking thing about Herky-Jerky, however, was his perpetual grin. He looked very jolly, yet every time he opened his mouth it was to utter bad language. He cursed the fire, the pans, the coffee, the biscuits, all of which he handled most skillfully. It was disgusting, and yet aside from this I rather liked him.

It grew dark very quickly while we were eating, and the wind that dipped down into the gorge was cold. I kept edging closer and closer to the blazing campfire. I had never tasted venison before, and rather disliked it at first. But I soon cultivated a liking for it.

That night Stockton tied me securely, but in a way which made it easy for me to turn. I slept soundly and awoke late. When I sat up Stockton stood by his saddled horse, and was giving orders to the men. He spoke sharply. He made it clear that they were not to be lax in their vigilance. Then, without a word to Dick or me, he rode down the gorge and disappeared behind a corner of yellow wall.

Bill untied the rope that held Dick's arms, but left his feet bound. I was freed entirely, and it felt so good to have the use of all my limbs once more that I pranced round in a rather lively way. Either my antics annoyed Herky-Jerky or he thought it a good opportunity to show his skill with a lasso, for he shot the loop over me so hard that it stung my back.

"I'm all there as a roper!" he said, pulling the lasso tight round my middle. The men all laughed as I tumbled over in the gravel.

"Better keep a half-hitch on the colt," remarked Bud.

So they left the lasso fast about my waist, and it trailed after me as I walked. Herky-Jerky put me to carrying Dick's breakfast from the campfire up into the cave. This I did with alacrity. Dick and I exchanged commonplace remarks aloud, but we had several little whispers.

"Ken, we may get the drop on them or give them the slip yet," whispered Dick, in one of these interludes.

This put ideas into my head. There might be a chance for me to escape, if not for Dick. I made up my mind to try if a good chance offered, but I did not want to go alone down that canyon without a gun. Stockton had taken my revolver and hunting-knife, but I still had the little leather case which Hal and I had used so often back on the Susquehanna. Besides a pen-knife this case contained salt and pepper, fishing hooks and lines, matches—a host of little things that a boy who had never been lost might imagine he would need in an emergency. While thinking and planning I sat on the edge of the great hole where the spring was. Suddenly I saw a swirl in the water, and then a splendid spotted fish. It broke water twice. It was two feet long.

"Dick, there's fish in this hole!" I yelled, eagerly.

"Shouldn't wonder," replied he. "Sure, kid, thet hole's full of trout—speckled trout," said Herky-Jerky. "But they can't be ketched."

"Why not?" I demanded. I had not caught little trout in the Pennsylvania hills for nothing. "They eat, don't they? That fish I saw was a whale, and he broke water for a bug. Get me a pole and some bugs or worms!"

When I took out my little case and showed the fishing-line, Herky-Jerky said he would find me some bait.

While he was absent I studied that spring with new and awakened eyes. It was round and very deep, and the water bulged up in great greenish swirls. The outlet was a narrow little cleft through which the water flowed slowly, as though it did not want to take its freedom. The rush and roar came from the gorge below.

Herky-Jerky returned with a long, slender pole. It was as pliant as a buggy-whip, and once trimmed and rigged it was far from being a poor tackle. Herky-Jerky watched me with extreme attention, all the time grinning. Then he held out a handful of grubs.

"If you ketch a trout on thet I'll swaller the pole!" he exclaimed.

I stooped low and approached the spring, being careful to keep out of sight.

"You forgot to spit on yer bait, kid," said Bill.

IX. TAKEN INTO THE MOUNTAINS

They all laughed in a way to rouse my ire. But despite it I flipped the bait into the water with the same old thrilling expectancy.

The bait dropped with a little spat. An arrowy shadow, black and gold, flashed up. Splash! The line hissed. Then I jerked hard. The pole bent double, wobbled, and swayed this way and that. The fish was a powerful one; his rushes were like those of a heavy bass. But never had a bass given me such a struggle. Every instant I made sure the tackle would be wrecked. Then, just at the breaking-point, the fish would turn. At last he began to tire. I felt that he was rising to the surface, and I put on more strain. Soon I saw him; then he turned, flashing like a gold bar. I led my captive to the outlet of the spring, where I reached down and got my fingers in his gills. With that I lifted him. Dick whooped when I held up the fish; as for me, I was speechless. The trout was almost two feet long, broad and heavy, with shiny sides flecked with color.

Herky-Jerky celebrated my luck with a generous outburst of enthusiasm, whereupon his comrades reminded him of his offer to swallow my fishing pole.

I put on a fresh bait and instantly hooked another fish, a smaller one, which was not so bard to land. The spring hole was full of trout. They made the water boil when I cast. Several large ones tore the hook loose; I had never dreamed of such fishing. Really it was a strange situation. Here I was a prisoner, with Greaser or Bud taking turns at holding the other end of the lasso. More than once they tethered me up short for no other reason than to torment me. Yet never in my life had I so enjoyed fishing.

By-and-by Bill and Herky-Jerky left the camp. I heard Herky tell Greaser to keep his eye on the stew-pots, and it occurred to me that Greaser had better keep his eye on Ken Ward. When I saw Bud lie down I remembered what Dick had whispered. I pretended to be absorbed in my fishing, but really I was watching Greaser. As usual, he was smoking, and appeared listless, but he still held on to the lasso.

Suddenly I saw a big blue revolver lying on a stone and I could even catch the glint of brass shells in the cylinder. It was not close to Bud nor so very close to Greaser. If he should drop the lasso! A wild idea possessed me—held me in its grip. Just then the stew-pot boiled over. There was a sputter and a cloud of steam, Greaser lazily swore in Mexican; he got up to move the stew-pot and dropped the lasso.

When he reached the fire I bounded up, jerking the lasso far behind me. I ran and grabbed the revolver. Greaser heard me and wheeled with a yell. Bud sat up quickly. I pointed the revolver at him, then at Greaser, and kept moving it from one side to the other.

"Don't move! I'll shoot!" I cried.

"Good boy!" yelled Dick. "You've got the drop. Keep it, Ken, keep it! Don't lose your nerve. Edge round here and cut me loose.... Bud, if you move I'll make him shoot. Come on, Ken."

"Greaser, cut him loose!" I commanded the snarling Mexican.

I trembled so that the revolver wabbled in my hand. Trying to hold it steadied, I squeezed it hard. Bang! It went off with a bellow like a cannon. The bullet scattered the gravel near Greaser. His yellow face turned a dirty white. He jumped straight up in his fright.

"Cut him loose!" I ordered.

Greaser ran toward Dick.

"Look out, Ken! Behind you! Quick!" yelled Dick.

I beard a crunching of gravel. Even as I wheeled I felt a tremendous pull on the lasso and I seemed to be sailing in the air. I got a blurred glimpse of Herky-Jerky leaning back on the taut lasso. Then I plunged down, slid over the rocks, and went souse into the spring.

X. ESCAPE

Down, down I plunged, and the shock of the icy water seemed to petrify me. I should have gone straight to the bottom like a piece of lead but for the lasso. It tightened around my chest, and began to haul me up.

I felt the air and the light, and opened my eyes to see Herky-Jerky hauling away on the rope. When he caught sight of me he looked as if ready to dodge behind the bank.

"Whar's my gun?" he yelled.

I had dropped it in the spring. He let the lasso sag, and I had to swim. Then, seeing that my hands were empty, he began to swear and to drag me round and round in the pool. When he had pulled me across he ran to the other side and jerked me back. I was drawn through the water with a force that I feared would tear me apart. Greaser chattered like a hideous monkey, and ran to and fro in glee. Herky-Jerky soon had me sputtering, gasping, choking. When he finally pulled me out of the hole I was all but drowned.

"You bow-legged beggar!" shouted Dick, "I'll fix you for that."

"Whar's my gun?" yelled Herky, as I fell to the ground.

"I lost—it," I panted.

He began to rave. Then I half swooned, and when sight and hearing fully returned I was lying in the cave on my blankets. A great lassitude weighted me down. The terrible thrashing about in the icy water had quenched my spirit. For a while I was too played out to move, and lay there in my wet clothes. Finally I asked leave to take them off. Bud, who had come back in the meantime, helped me, or I should never have got out of them. Herky brought up my coat, which, fortunately, I had taken off before the ducking. I did not have the heart to speak to Dick or look at him, so I closed my eyes and fell asleep.

It was another day when I awoke. I felt all right except for a soreness under my arms and across my chest where the lasso had chafed and bruised me. Still I did not recover my good spirits. Herky-Jerky kept on grinning and cracking jokes on my failure to escape. He had appropriated my revolver for himself, and he asked me several times if I wanted to borrow it to shoot Greaser.

That day passed quietly, and so did the two that followed. The men would not let me fish nor move about. They had been expecting Stockton, and as he did not come it was decided to send Bud down to the mill; in fact, Bud decided the matter himself. He warned Greaser and Herky to keep close watch over Dick and me. Then he rode away. Dick and I resumed our talk about forestry, and as we were separated by the length of the cave it was necessary to speak loud. So our captors heard every word we said.

"Ken, what's the difference between Government forestry out here and, say, forestry practiced by a farmer back in Pennsylvania?" asked Dick.

"There's a big difference, I imagine. Forestry is established in some parts of the East; it's only an experiment out here."

Then I went on to tell him about the method of the farmer. He usually had a small piece of forest, mostly hard wood. When the snow was on he cut firewood, fence-rails, and lumber for his own use in building. Some seasons lumber brought high prices; then he would select matured logs and haul them to the sawmill. But he would not cut a great deal, and he would use care in the selection. It was his aim to keep the land well covered with forest. He would sow as well as harvest.

"Now the Government policy is to preserve the National Forests for the use of the people. The soil must be kept productive. Agriculture would be impossible without water, and the forests hold water. The West wants people to come to stay. The lumberman who slashes off the timber may get rich himself, but he ruins the land."

"What's that new law Congress is trying to pass?" queried Dick.

I was puzzled, but presently I caught his meaning. Bill and Herky-Jerky were hanging on our words with unconcealed attention. Even the Mexican was listening. Dick's cue was to scare them, or at least to have some fun at their expense.

"They've passed it," I replied. "Fellows like Buell will go to the penitentiary for life. His men'll get twenty years on bread and water. No whiskey! Serves 'em right."

"What'll the President do when he learns these men kidnapped you?"

"Do? He'll have the whole forest service out here and the National Guard. He's a friend of my father's. Why, these kidnappers will be hanged!"

"I wish the Guard would come quick. Too bad you couldn't have sent word! I'd enjoy seeing Greaser swing. Say, he hasn't a ghost of a chance, with the President and Jim Williams after him."

"Dick, I want the rings in Greaser's ears."

"What for? They're only brass."

"Souvenirs. Maybe I'll have watch-charms made of them. Anyway, I can show them to my friends back East."

"It'll be great—what you'll have to tell," went on Dick. "It'll be funny, too."

Greaser had begun to snarl viciously, and Herky and Bill looked glum and thoughtful. The arrival of Bud interrupted the conversation and put an end to our playful mood. We heard a little of what he told his comrades, and gathered that Jim Williams had met Stockton and had asked questions hard to answer. Dick flashed me a significant look, which was as much as to say that Jim was growing suspicious. Bud had brought a store of whiskey, and his companions now kept closer company with him than ever before. But from appearances they did not get all they wanted.

"We've got to move this here camp," said Bud.

Bud and Bill and Herky walked off down the gorge. Perhaps they really went to find another place for the camp, for the present spot was certainly a kind of trap. But from the looks of Greaser I guessed that they were leaving him to keep guard while they went off to drink by themselves. Greaser muttered and snarled. As the moments passed his face grew sullen.

All at once he came toward me. He bound my hands and my feet. Dick was already securely tied, but Greaser put another lasso on him. Then he slouched down the gorge. His high-peaked Mexican sombrero bobbed above the rocks, then disappeared.

"Ken, now's the chance," said Dick, low and quick. "If you can only work loose! There's your rifle and mine, too. We could hold this fort for a month."

"What can I do?" I asked, straining on my ropes.

"You're not fast to the rock, as I am. Rollover here and untie me with your teeth."

I raised my head to get the direction, and then, with a violent twist of my body, I started toward him; but being bound fast I could not guide myself, and I rolled off the ledge. The bank there was pretty steep, and, unable to stop, I kept on like a barrel going down-bill. The thought of rolling into the spring filled me with horror. Suddenly I bumped hard into something that checked me. It was a log of firewood, and in one end stuck the big knife which Herky-Jerky used to cut meat.

Instantly I conceived the idea of cutting my bonds with this knife. But how was I to set about it?

"Dick, here's a knife. How'll I get to it so as to free myself?"

"Easy as pie," replied he, eagerly. "The sharp edge points down. You hitch yourself this way—That's it—good!"

What Dick called easy as pie was the hardest work I ever did. I lay flat on my back, bound hand and foot, and it was necessary to jerk my body along the log till my hands should be under the knife. I lifted my legs and edged along inch by inch.

"Fine work, Ken! Now you're right! Turn on your side! Be careful you don't loosen the knife!"

Not only were my wrists bound, but the lasso had been wrapped round my elbows, holding them close to my body. Turning on my side, I found that I could not reach the knife—not by several inches. This was a bitter disappointment. I strained and heaved. In my effort to lift my body sidewise I pressed my face into the gravel. "Hurry, Ken, hurry!" cried Dick. "Somebody's coming!"

Thus urged, I grew desperate. In my struggle I discovered that it was possible to edge up on the log and stick there. I glued myself to that log. By dint of great exertion I brought the tight cord against the blade. It parted with a little snap, my elbows dropped free. Raising my wrists, I sawed quickly through the bonds. I cut myself, the blood flowed, but that was no matter. Jerking the knife from the log, I severed the ropes round my ankles and leaped up.

"Hurry, boy!" cried Dick, with a sharp note of alarm.

I ran to where he lay, and attacked the heavy halter with which he had been secured. I had cut half through the knots when a shrill cry arrested me. It was the Mexican's voice.

"Head him off! He's after your gun!" yelled Dick.

The sight of Greaser running toward the cave put me into a frenzy. Dropping the knife, I darted to where my rifle leaned across my saddle. But I saw the Mexican would beat me to it. Checking my speed, I grabbed up a round stone and let fly. That was where my ball-playing stood me in good stead, for the stone hit Greaser on the shoulder, knocking him flat. But he got up, and lunged for the rifle just as I reached him.

I kicked the rifle out of his band, grappled with him, and down we went together. We wrestled and thrashed off the ledge, and when we landed in the gravel I was on top.

"Slug him, Ken!" yelled Dick, wildly. "Oh, that's fine! Give it to him! Punch him! Get his wind!"

Either it was a mortal dread of Greaser's knife or some kind of a new-born fury that lent me such strength. He screeched, he snapped like a wolf, he clawed me, he struck me, but he could not shake me off. Several times he had me turning, but a hard rap on his head knocked him back again. Then I began to bang him in the ribs.

"That's the place!" shouted Dick. "Ken, you're going to do him up! Soak him! Oh-h, but this is great!"

I kept the advantage over Greaser, but still he punished me cruelly. Suddenly he got his snaky hands on my throat and began to choke me. With all my might I swung my fist into his stomach.

His hands dropped, his mouth opened in a gasp, his face turned green. The blow had made him horribly sick, and he sank back utterly helpless. I jumped up with a shout of triumph.

"Run! Run for it!" yelled Dick, in piercing tones. "They're coming! Never mind me! Run, I tell you! Not down the gorge! Climb out!"

For a moment I could not move out of my tracks. Then I saw Bill and Herky running up the gorge, and, farther down, Bud staggering and lurching.

This lent me wings. In two jumps I had grabbed my rifle; then, turning, I ran round the pool, and started up the one place in the steep wall where climbing was possible. Above the yells of the men I heard Dick's piercing cry:

"Go-go-go, Ken!"

I sent the loose rocks down in my flight. Here I leaped up; there I ran along a little ledge; in another place I climbed hand and foot. The last few yards was a gravelly incline. I seemed to slide back as much as I gained.

"Come back hyar!" bawled Bill.

X. ESCAPE

Crack! Crack! Crack... The reports rang out in quick succession. A bullet whistled over me, another struck the gravel and sent a shower of dust into my face. I pitched my rifle up over the bank and began to dig my fingers and toes into the loose ground. As I gained the top two more bullets sang past my head so close that I knew Bill was aiming to more than scare me. I dragged myself over the edge and was safe.

The canyon, with its dense thickets and scrubby clumps of trees, lay below in plain sight. Once hidden there, I would be hard to find. Picking up my rifle, I ran swiftly along the base of the slope and soon gained the cover of the woods.

XI. THE OLD HUNTER

I ran till I got a stitch in my side, and then slowed down to a dog-trot. The one thing to do was to get a long way ahead of my pursuers, for surely at the outset they would stick like hounds to my trail.

A mile or more below the gorge I took to the stream and waded. It was slippery, dangerous work, for the current tore about my legs and threatened to upset me. After a little I crossed to the left bank. Here the slope of the canyon was thick with grass that hid my tracks. It was a long climb up to the level. Upon reaching it I dropped, exhausted.

"I've—given them—the slip," I panted, exultantly.... "But—now what?"

It struck me that now I was free, I had only jumped out of the frying-pan into the fire. Hurriedly I examined my Winchester. The magazine contained ten cartridges. What luck that Stockton had neglected to unload it! This made things look better. I had salt and pepper, a knife, and matches—thanks to the little leather case—and so I could live in the woods.

It was too late for regrets. I might have freed Dick somehow or even held the men at bay, but I had thought only of escape. The lack of nerve and judgment stung me. Then I was bitter over losing my mustang and outfit.

But on thinking it all over, I concluded that I ought to be thankful for things as they were. I was free, with a whole skin. That climb out of the gorge had been no small risk. How those bullets had whistled and hissed!

"I'm pretty lucky," I muttered. "Now to get good and clear of this vicinity. They'll ride down the trail after me. Better go over this ridge into the next canyon and strike down that. I must go down. But how far? What must I strike for?"

I took a long look at the canyon. In places the stream showed, also the trail; then there were open patches, but I saw no horses or men. With a grim certainty that I should be lost in a very little while, I turned into the cool, dark forest.

Every stone and log, every bit of hard ground in my path, served to help hide my trail. Herky-Jerky very likely had the cowboy's skill at finding tracks, but I left few traces of my presence on that long slope. Only an Indian or a hound could have trailed me. The timber was small and rough brush grew everywhere. Presently I saw light ahead, and I came to an open space. It was a wide swath in the forest. At once I recognized the path of an avalanche. It sloped up clean and bare to the gray cliffs far above. Below was a great mass of trees and rocks, all tangled in black splintered ruin. I pushed on across the path, into the forest, and up and down the hollows. The sun had gone down behind the mountain, and the shadows were gathering when I came to another large canyon. It looked so much like the first that I feared I had been travelling in a circle. But this one seemed wider, deeper, and there was no roar of rushing water.

It was time to think of making camp, and so I hurried down the slope. At the bottom I found a small brook winding among boulders and ledges of rock. The far side of this canyon was steep and craggy. Soon I discovered a place where I thought it would be safe to build a fire. My clothes were wet, and the air had grown keen and cold. Gathering a store of wood, I made my fire in a niche. For a bed I cut some sweet-scented pine boughs (I thought they must be from a balsam-tree), and these I laid close up in a rocky corner. Thus I had the fire between me and the opening, and with plenty of wood to burn I did not fear visits from bears or lions. At last I lay down, dry and warm indeed, but very tired and hungry.

Darkness closed in upon me. I saw a few stars, heard the cheery crackle of my fire, and then I fell asleep. Twice in the night I awakened cold, but by putting on more firewood I was soon comfortable again.

When I awoke the sun was shining brightly into my rocky bedchamber. The fire had died out completely, there was frost on the stones. To build up another fire and to bathe my face in the ice-water of the brook were my first tasks. The air was sweet; it seemed to freeze as I breathed, and was a bracing tonic. I was tingling all over, and as hungry as a starved wolf.

I set forth on a hunt for game. Even if the sound of a shot betrayed my whereabouts I should have to abide by it, for I had to eat. Stepping softly along, I glanced about me with sharp eyes. Deer trails were thick. The bottom of this canyon was very wide, and grew wider as I proceeded. Then the pines once more became large and thrifty. I judged I had come down the mountain, perhaps a couple of thousand feet below the camp in the gorge. I flushed many of the big blue grouse, and I saw numerous coyotes, a fox, and a large brown beast which moved swiftly into a thicket. It was enough to make my heart rise in my throat. To dream of hunting bears was something vastly different from meeting one in a lonely canyon.

Just after this I saw a herd of deer. They were a good way off. I began to slip from tree to tree, and drew closer. Presently I came to a little hollow with a thick, short patch of underbrush growing on the opposite side. Something crashed in the thicket. Then two beautiful deer ran out. One bounded leisurely up the slope; the other, with long ears erect, stopped to look at me. It was no more than fifty yards away. Trembling with eagerness, I leveled my rifle. I could not get the sight to stay steady on the deer. Even then, with the rifle wobbling in my intense excitement, I thought of how beautiful that wild creature was. Straining every nerve, I drew the sight till it was in line with the gray shape, then fired. The deer leaped down the slope, staggered, and crumpled down in a heap.

I tore through the bushes, and had almost reached the bottom of the hollow when I remembered that a wounded deer was dangerous. So I halted. The gray form was as still as stone. I ventured closer. The deer was dead. My bullet had entered high above the shoulder at the juncture of the neck. Though I had only aimed at him generally, I took a good deal of pride in my first shot at a deer.

Fortunately my pen-knife had a fair-sized blade. With it I decided to cut out part of the deer and carry it back to my camp. Then it occurred to me that I might as well camp where I was. There were several jumbles of rock and a cliff within a stone's-throw of where I stood. Besides, I must get used to making camp wherever I happened to be. Accordingly, I took hold of the deer, and dragged him down the hollow till I came to a leaning slab of rock.

Skinning a deer was, of course, new to me. I haggled the flesh somewhat and cut through the skin often, my knife-blade being much too small for such work. Finally I thought it would be enough for me to cut out the haunches, and then I got down to one haunch. It had bothered me how I was going to sever the joint, but to my great surprise I found there did not seem to be any connection between the bones. The haunch came out easily, and I hung it up on a branch while making a fire.

Herky-Jerky's method of broiling a piece of venison at the end of a stick solved the problem of cooking. Then it was that the little flat flask, full of mixed salt and pepper, rewarded me for the long carrying of it. I was hungry, and I feast-ed.

By this time the sun shone warm, and the canyon was delightful. I roamed around, sat on sunny stones, and lay in the shade of pines. Deer browsed in the glades. When they winded or saw me they would stand erect, shoot up their long cars, and then leisurely lope away. Coyotes trotted out of thickets and watched me suspiciously. I could have shot several, but deemed it wise to be saving of my ammunition. Once I heard a low drumming. I could not imagine what made it. Then a big blue grouse strutted out of a patch of bushes. He spread his wings and tail and neck feathers, after the fashion of a turkey-gobbler. It was a flap or shake of his wings that produced the drumming. I wondered if he intended, by his actions, to frighten me away from his mate's nest. So I went toward him, and got very close before he flew. I caught sight of his mate in the bushes, and, as I had supposed, she was on a nest. Though wanting to see her eggs or young ones, I resisted the temptation, for I was afraid if I went nearer she might abandon her nest, as some mother birds do.

It did not seem to me that I was lost, yet lost I was. The peaks were not in sight. The canyon widened down the slope, and I was pretty sure that it opened out flat into the great pine forest of Penetier. The only thing that bothered me was the loss of my mustang and outfit; I could not reconcile myself to that. So I wandered about with a strange, full sense of freedom such as I had never before known. What was to be the end of my adventure I could not guess, and I wasted no time worrying over it.

The knowledge I had of forestry I tried to apply. I studied the north and south slopes of the canyon, observing how the trees prospered on the sunny side. Certain saplings of a species unknown to me had been gnawed fully ten feet from the ground. This puzzled me. Squirrels could not have done it, nor rabbits, nor birds. Presently I hit upon the solution. The bark and boughs of this particular sapling were food for deer, and to gnaw so high the deer must have stood upon six or seven feet of snow.

I dug into the soft duff under the pines. This covering of the roots was very thick and deep. I made it out to be composed of pine-needles, leaves, and earth. It was like a sponge. No wonder such covering held the water! I pried bark off dead trees and dug into decayed logs to find the insect enemies of the trees. The open places, where little colonies of pine sprouts grew, seemed generally to be downslope from the parent trees. It was easy to tell the places where the wind had blown the seeds.

The hours sped by. The shadows of the pines lengthened, the sun set, and the shade deepened in the hollows. Returning to my camp, I cooked my supper and made my bed. When I had laid up a store of firewood it was nearly dark.

With night came the coyotes. The carcass of the deer attracted them, and they approached from all directions. At first it was fascinating to hear one howl far off in the forest, and then to notice the difference in the sound as he came nearer and nearer. The way they barked and snapped out there in the darkness was as wild a thing to hear as any boy could have wished for. It began to be a little too much for me. I kept up a bright fire, and, though not exactly afraid, I had a perch picked out in the nearest tree. Suddenly the coyotes became silent. Then a low, continuous growling, a snapping of twigs, and the unmistakable drag of a heavy body over the ground made my hair stand on end. Gripping my rifle, I listened. I heard the crunch of teeth on bones, then more sounds of something being dragged down the hollow. The coyotes began to bark again, but now far back in the forest.

Some beast had frightened them. What was it? I did not know whether a bear would eat deer flesh, but I thought not. Perhaps timber-wolves had disturbed the coyotes. But would they run from wolves? It came to me suddenly—a mountain-lion!

I hugged my fire, and sat there, listening with all my ears, imagining every rustle of leaf to be the step of a lion. It was long before the thrills and shivers stopped chasing over me, longer before I could decide to lie down. But after a while the dead quiet of the forest persuaded me that the night was far advanced, and I fell asleep.

The first thing in the morning I took my rifle and went out to where I had left the carcass of the deer. It was gone. It had been dragged away. A dark path on the pine-needles and grass, and small bushes pressed to the ground, plainly marked the trail. But search as I might, I could not find the track of the animal that had dragged off the deer. After following the trail for a few rods, I decided to return to camp and cook breakfast before going any farther. While I was at it I cut many thin slices of venison, and, after roasting them, I stored them away in the capacious pocket of my coat.

My breakfast finished, I again set out to see what had become of the remains of the deer. In two or three places the sharp hoofs had cut lines in the soft earth, and there were tufts of whitish-gray hair elsewhere. A hundred yards or more down the hollow I came to a bare spot where recently there had been a pool of water. Here I found cat tracks as large as my two hands. I had never seen the track of a mountain-lion, but, all the same, I knew that this was the real thing. What an enormous brute he must have been! I cast fearful glances into the surrounding thickets.

It was not needful to travel much farther. Under a bush well hidden in a clump of trees lay what now remained of my deer. A patch of gray hair, a few long bones, a split skull, and two long ears—no more! Even the hide was gone. Perhaps the coyotes had finished the job after the lion had gorged himself, but I did not think so. It seemed to me that coyotes would have scattered the remains. Those two long ears somehow seemed pathetic. I wished for a second that the lion were in range of my rifle.

The lion was driven from my mind when I saw a troop of deer cross a glade below me. I had to fight myself to keep from shooting. The wind blew rather strong in my face, which probably accounted for the deer not winding me.

Then the whip-like crack of a rifle riveted me where I stood. One of the deer fell, and the others bounded away. I saw a tall man stride down the slope and into the glade. He was not like any of the loggers or lumbermen. They were mostly brawny and round-shouldered. This man was lithe, erect; he walked like athletes I had seen. Surely I should find a friend in him, and I lost no time in running down into the glade. He saw me as soon as I was clear of the trees, and stood leaning on his rifle.

"Wal, dog-gone my buttons!" he ejaculated. "Who're you?"

I blurted out all about myself, at the same time taking stock of him. He was not young, but I had never seen a young man so splendid. Hair, beard, and skin were all of a dark gray. His eyes, too, were gray—the keenest and clearest I had ever looked into. They shone with a kindly light, otherwise I might have thought his face hard and stern. His shoulders were very wide, his arms long, his hands enormous. His buckskin shirt attracted my attention to his other clothes, which looked like leather overalls or heavy canvas. A belt carried a huge knife and a number of shells of large caliber; the Winchester he had was exceedingly long and heavy, and of an old pattern. The look of him brought back my old fancy of Wetzel or Kit Carson.

"So I'm lost," I concluded, "and don't know what to do. I daren't try to find the sawmill. I won't go back to Holston just yet."

"An' why not, youngster? 'Pears to me you'd better make tracks from Penetier."

I told him why, at which he laughed.

"Wal, I reckon you can stay with me fer a spell. My camp's in the head of this canyon."

"Oh, thank you, that'll be fine!" I exclaimed. My great good luck filled me with joy. "Do you stay on the mountain?"

"Be'n here goin' on eighteen years, youngster. Mebbe you've heerd my name. Hiram Bent."

XI. THE OLD HUNTER

"Are you a hunter?"

"Wal, I reckon so, though I'm more a trapper. Here, you pack my gun."

With that he drew his knife and set to work on the deer. It was wonderful to see his skill. In a few cuts and strokes, a ripping of the hide and a powerful slash, he had cut out a haunch. It took even less work for the second. Then he hung the rest of the deer on a snag, and wiped his knife and hands on the grass.

"Come on, youngster," he said, starting up the canyon.

I showed him where the carcass of my deer had been devoured.

"Cougar. Thar's a big feller has the run of this canyon."

"Cougar? I thought it was a mountain-lion."

"Cougar, painter, panther, lion—all the same critter. An' if you leave him alone he'll not bother you, but he's bad in a corner."

"He scared away the coyotes."

"Youngster, even a silver-tip—thet's a grizzly bear—will make tracks away from a cougar. I lent my pack of hounds to a pard over near Springer. If I had them we'd put thet cougar up a tree in no time."

"Are there many lions—cougars here?"

"Only a few. Thet's why there's plenty of deer. Other game is plentiful, too. Foxes, wolves, an', up in the mountains, bears are thick."

"Then I may get to see one—get a shot at one?"

"Wal, I reckon."

From that time I trod on air. I found myself wishing for my brother Hal. I became reconciled to the loss of mustang and outfit. For a moment I almost forgot Dick and Buell. Forestry seemed less important than hunting. I had read a thousand books about old hunters and trappers, and here I was in a wild mountain canyon with a hunter who might have stepped out of one of my dreams. So I trudged along beside him, asking a question now and then, and listening always. He certainly knew what would interest me. There was scarcely a thing he said that I would ever forget. After a while, however, the trail became so steep and rough that I, at least, had no breath to spare for talking. We climbed and climbed. The canyon had become a narrow, rocky cleft. Huge stones blocked the way. A ragged growth of underbrush fringed the stream. Dead pines, with branches like spears, lay along the trail.

We came upon a little clearing, where there was a rude log-cabin with a stone chimney. Skins of animals were tacked upon logs. Under the bank was a spring. The mountain overshadowed this wild nook.

"Wal, youngster, here's my shack. Make yourself to home," said Hiram Bent.

I was all eyes as we entered the cabin. Skins, large and small, and of many colors, hung upon the walls. A fire burned in a wide stone grate. A rough table and some pans and cooking utensils showed evidence of recent scouring. A bunch of steel traps lay in a corner. Upon a shelf were tin cans and cloth bags, and against the wall stood a bed of glossy bearskins. To me the cabin was altogether a most satisfactory place.

"I reckon ye're tired?" asked the hunter. "Thet's some pumpkins of a climb unless you're used to it."

I admitted I was pretty tired.

"Wal, rest awhile. You look like you hadn't slept much."

He asked me about my people and home, and was so interested in forestry that he left off his task of the moment to talk about it. I was not long in discovering that what he did not know about trees and forests was hardly worth learning. He called it plain woodcraft. He had never heard of forestry. All the same I hungered for his knowledge. How lucky for me to fall in with him! The things that had puzzled me about the pines he answered easily. Then he volunteered information. From talking of the forest, he drifted to the lumbermen.

"Wal, the lumber-sharks are rippin' holes in Penetier. I reckon they wouldn't stop at nothin'. I've heered some tough stories about thet sawmill gang. I ain't acquainted with Leslie, or any of them fellers you named except Jim Williams. I knowed Jim. He was in Springer fer a while. If Jim's your friend, there'll be somethin' happenin, when he rounds up them kidnappers. I reckon you'd better hang up with me fer a while. You don't want to get ketched again. Your life wasn't much to them fellers. I think they'd held on to you fer money. It's too bad you didn't send word home to your people."

"I sent word home about the big steal of timber. That was before I got kidnapped. By this time the Government knows."

"Wal, you don't say! Thet was pert of you, youngster. An' will the Government round up these sharks?"

"Indeed it will. The Government is in dead earnest about protecting the National Forests."

"So it ought to be. Next to a forest fire, I hate these skinned timber tracts. Wal, old Penetier's going to see somethin' lively before long. Youngster, them lumbermen—leastways, them fellers you call Bud an' Bill, an' such—they're goin' to fight."

The old hunter left me presently, and went outside. I waited awhile for him, but as he did not return I lay down upon the bearskins and dropped to sleep. It seemed I had hardly closed my eyes when I felt a hand on my arm and heard a voice.

"Wake up, youngster. Thar's two old bears an' a cub been foolin' with one of my traps."

In a flash I was wide awake.

"Let's see your gun. Humph! pretty small—38 caliber, ain't it? Wal, it'll do the work if you hold straight. Can you shoot?"

"Fairly well."

He took his heavy Winchester, and threw a coil of thin rope over his shoulder.

"Come on. Stay close to me, an' keep your eyes peeled."

XII. BEARS

The old hunter walked so swiftly that I had to run to keep up with him. The trail led up the creek, now on one side, again on the other, and I was constantly skipping from stone to stone. The grassy slopes grew fewer, and finally gave way altogether to cracked cliffs and weathered rocks. A fringe of pine-trees leaned over the top with here and there a blasted spear standing out white.

"I had my trap set up thet draw," said Hiram Bent, as he pointed toward an intersecting canyon. "Just before I waked you I was comin' along here, an' I heered an all-fired racket up thar, an' so I watched. Soon three black bears come paddlin' down, an' the biggest was draggin' the trap with the chain an' log. Then I hurried to tell you. They can't be far."

"Are they grizzlies?" I asked, trying to speak naturally.

"Nope. Jest plain black bears. But the one with the trap is a whopper. He'll go over four hundred. See the tracks? Looks like somebody'd been plowin' up the stones."

There were deep tracks in the sand, and broad furrows, and stones overturned, and places where a heavy object had crushed the gravel even and smooth.

The old hunter kept striding on, and I wondered bow he could go so fast without running. Presently we came to where the canyon forked. Hiram started up the right-hand fork, then suddenly stopped, and, turning, began to go back, carefully examining the ground.

"They've split on us," he explained. "The ole feller with the trap went up the right-hand draw, an' the mother an' cub took to the left. Now, youngster, can you keep your nerve?"

"I think so."

"Wal, you go after the ole feller. You can't miss him, an' he won't be far. You'll hear him bellerin' long before you git to him, though he might lay low, so you steer clear of big boulders an' thickets. Kill him, an' then run back an' take up this draw. The she bear is cute an' may give me the slip, but if she doesn't climb out soon I'll head her off. Hurry on, now. Keep your eye peeled, an' you'll be safe as if you were to home."

With that he disappeared round the corner of stone wall where the canyon divided. I wheeled and went to the right. This wing of the canyon twisted and turned and was full of stones. A shallow sheet of water gleamed over its colored bed of gravel. The walls were straight up, and, in places, bulged outward. I flinched at every turn in the canyon; but, with rifle cocked and thrust forward, I went on. The cracks in the walls, the boulders and pieces of cliff that obstructed my path, and the occasional thickets—all made me halt with careful step and finger on the trigger. I followed the splashes on the stones, which told me that the bear had passed that way. As I went cautiously on I felt a tightening at my throat. The light above grew dimmer. When I stopped to listen it was so silent that I heard only the pounding of my heart and my own quick breathing. I pressed on and on, going faster all the time not that I felt braver, but I longed to end the suspense. Suddenly the silence was broken by a threatening roar. It swept down on me, swelling as it continued, and it seemed to fill the canyon. It shook my pulses, it urged me to flight, but I could not move. Then as suddenly it ceased.

For a long moment I stood still, with no idea of advancing farther. The clinking of a chain seemed to release my cramped muscles. Very cautiously I peered around a projecting corner of wall. There sat a huge black bear on his haunches holding up a great steel trap which clutched one of his paws. It was such a strange sight that my fear was forgotten. There was something almost human in the way the bear looked at that trap. He touched it gingerly with his free paw, and nosed it. I crept up close to the corner of stone and looked around again. The bear was now close to me. I saw the heavy chain and the log to which it was attached. He looked at trap and log in a grave, pathetic way, as if trying to reason about them. Then he roused into furious action, swinging the trap, dragging the log, and bellowing in such a frightful manner that I dodged back behind the wall.

But this sudden change in the bear, this appalling roar with its note of pain, awakened me to his suffering. When the noise stopped and I looked again, the bear was a sight not to be forgotten. He showed a helpless, terrible fear of the steel-jawed thing on his foot. He dropped down on the sand with a groan, and there was a despairing look in his eyes.

This made me forget my fear, and I had only one thought—to put him out of his misery. When I leveled my rifle it was as steady as the rock beside me. Aiming just below his ear, I pressed the trigger. The dull report re-echoed from wall to wall. The bear lurched slightly, and his head fell upon his outstretched paws. I waited, ready to shoot again upon the slightest movement, but there was none.

With rifle ready I cautiously approached the bear. As I came close he seemed larger and larger, but he showed no signs of life. I looked at the glossy black fur, the flecks of blood on the side of his head where my bullet had entered, the murderous saw-teeth of the heavy trap biting to the bone, and the cruelty of that trap seemed to drive from me all pride of achievement. It was nothing except mercy to kill a trapped crippled bear that could not run or fight. Then and there I gained a dislike for trapping animals.

The crack of the old hunter's rifle made me remember that I was to hurry back up the other canyon, so I began to run. I bounded from stone to stone, dashed over the sand-bars, jumped the brook, and went down that canyon perhaps in far greater danger of bodily harm than when I had gone up.

But when I turned the corner it was another story. The first canyon had been easy climbing compared to this one. It was narrow, steep, and full of dead pines fallen from above. Running was impossible. I clambered upward over the loose stones, under the bridges of pines, round the boulders. Presently I heard a shout. I could not tell where it came from, but I replied. A second call I identified as coming from high up the ragged canyon side, and I started up. It was hard work. Certainly no bears or hunter had climbed out just here. At length, sore, spent, and torn, I fell out of a tangle of brush upon the edge of the canyon. Above me rose the swelling mountain slope thickly covered with dwarf pines.

"This way, youngster!" called the old hunter from my left.

A few more dashes in and out of the brush and trees brought me to a fairly open space with not much slope. Hiram Bent stood under a pine, and at his feet lay a black furry mass.

"Wal, I heerd you shoot. Reckon you got yourn?"

"Yes, I killed him.... Say, Mr. Bent, I don't like traps."

"Nary do I—for bears," replied he, shaking his gray head. "A trapped bear is about the pitifulest thing I ever seen. But it's seldom one ever gits into trap of mine."

"This one you shot must be the old mother bear. Where's the cub? Did it get away?"

"Not yet. Lookup in the tree."

I looked up the black trunk through the network of slender branches, and saw the bear snuggling in a fork. His sharp ears stood up against the sky. He was most anxiously gazing down at us.

"Wal, tumble him out of thar," said Hiram Bent.

With a natural impulse to shoot I raised my rifle, but the cub looked so attractive and so helpless that I hesitated.

"I don't like to do it," I said. "Oh, I wish we could catch him alive!"

"Wal, I reckon we can."

"How?" I inquired, eagerly, and lowered my rifle.

"Are you good on the climb?"

"Climb? This tree? Why, with one hand. Back in Pennsylvania I climbed shellbark hickory-trees with the lowest limb fifty feet from the ground. .. But there weren't any bears up them."

"You must keep out of his way if he comes down on you. He's a sassy little chap. Now take this rope an' go up an' climb round him."

"Climb round him?" I queried, as I gazed dubiously upward. "You mean to slip out on the branches and go up hand-over-hand till I get above him. The branches up there seem pretty close—I might. But suppose he goes higher?"

"I'm lookin' fer him to go clean to the top. But you can beat him to it—mebbe."

"Any danger of his attacking me—up there?"

"Wal, not much. If he hugs the trunk he'll have to hold on fer all he's worth. But if he stands on the branches an' you come up close he might bat you one. Mebbe I'd better go up."

"Oh, I'm going—I only wanted to know what to expect. Now, in case I get above him, what then?"

"Make him back down till he reaches these first branches. When he gets so far I'll tell you what to do." I put my arm through the coil of rope, and, slinging it snugly over my shoulder, began to climb the pine. It was the work of only a moment to reach the first branch.

"Wal, I reckon you're some relation to a squirrel at thet," said Hiram Bent. "Jest as I thought the little cuss is climbin' higher. Thet's goin' to worry us."

It was like stepping up a ladder from the first branch to the fork. The cub had gone up the right-hand trunk some fifteen feet, and was now hugging it. At that short distance he looked alarmingly big. But I saw he would have all he could do to hold on, and if I could climb the left trunk and get above him there would be little to fear. How I did it so quickly was a mystery, but amid the cracking of dead branches and pattering of falling bark and swaying of the tree-top I gained a position above him.

He was so close that I could smell him. His quick little eyes snapped fire and fear at once; he uttered a sound that was between a whine and a growl.

"Hey, youngster!" yelled Hiram, "thet's high enough—'tain't safe—be careful now."

With the words I looked out below me, to see the old hunter standing in the glade waving his arms.

"I'm all right!" I yelled down. "Now, how'll I drive him?"

"Break off a branch an' switch him."

There was not a branch above me that I could break, but a few feet below was a slender, dead limb. I slid down and got it, and, holding on with my left arm and legs, I began to thrash the cub. He growled fiercely. snapped at the stick, and began to back down.

"He's started!" I cried, in glee. "Go on, Cubby—down with you!"

Clumsy as he was, he made swift time. I was hard put to keep close to him. I slipped down the trunk—holding on one instant and sliding down the next. But below the fork it was harder for Cubby and easier for me. The branches rather hindered his backward progress while they aided mine. Growling and whining, with long claws ripping the bark, he went down. All of a sudden I became aware of the old hunter threshing about under the tree.

"Hold on—not so fast!" he yelled.

Still the cub kept going, and stopped with his haunches on the first branch. There, looking down, he saw an enemy below him, and hesitated. But he looked up, and, seeing me, began to back down again. Hiram pounded the tree with a dead branch. Cubby evidently intended to reach the ground, for the noise did not stop him. Then the hunter ran a little way to a windfall, and came back with the upper half of a dead sapling. With this he began to prod the bear. Thereupon, Cubby lost no time in getting up to the first branch again, where he halted.

"Throw the noose on him now—anywhere," ordered the hunter. "An' we've no time to lose. He's gittin' sassier every minnit."

I dropped the wide loop upon Cubby, expecting to catch him first time. The rope went over his bead, but with a dexterous flip of his paw he sent it flying. Then began a duel between us, in which he continually got the better of me. All the while the old hunter prodded Cubby from below.

"You ain't quick enough," said Hiram, impatiently.

Made reckless by this, I stepped down to another branch directly over the bear, and tried again to rope him. It was of no use. He slipped out of the noose with the sinuous movements of an eel. Once it caught over his ears and in his open jaws. He gave a jerk that nearly pulled me from my perch. I could tell he was growing angrier every instant, and also braver. Suddenly the noose, quite by accident, caught his nose. He wagged his head and I pulled. The noose tightened.

"I've got him!" I yelled, and gave the rope a strong pull.

The bear stood up with startling suddenness and reached for me.

"Climb!" shouted Hiram.

I dropped the rope and leaped for the branch above, and, catching it, lifted myself just as the sharp claws of the cub scratched hard over my boot.

Cubby now hugged the tree trunk and started up again.

"We've got him!" yelled Hiram. "Don't move—step on his nose if he gets too close."

Then I saw the halter had come off the bear and had fallen to the ground. Hiram picked it up, arranged the noose, and, holding it in his teeth began to limb after the bear. Cubby was now only a few feet under me, working steadily up, growling, and his little eyes were like points of green fire.

"Stop him! Stand on his head!" mumbled Hiram, with the rope in his teeth.

"What!—not on your life!"

But, reaching up, I grasped a branch, and, swinging clear of the lower one, I began to kick at the bear. This stopped him. Then he squealed, and began to kick on his own account. Hiram was trying to get the noose over a bind foot. After several attempts he succeeded, and then threw the rope over the lowest branch. I gave a wild Indian yell of triumph. The next instant, before I could find a foothold, the branch to which I was hanging snapped like a pistol-shot, and I plunged down with a crash. I struck the bear and the lower branch, and then the ground. The fall half stunned me. I thought every bone in my body was broken. I rose unsteadily, and for a moment everything whirled before my eyes. Then I discovered that the roar in my ears was the old hunter's yell. I saw him hauling on the rope. There was a great ripping of bark and many strange sounds, and then the cub was dangling head downward. Hiram had pulled him from his perch, and hung him over the lowest branch.

"Thar, youngster, git busy now!" yelled the hunter. "Grab the other rope—thar it is—an' rope a front paw while I hold him. Lively now, he's mighty heavy, an' if he ever gits down with only one rope on him we'll think we're fast to chain lightnin'."

The bear swung about five feet from the ground. As I ran at him with the noose he twisted himself, seemed to double up in a knot, then he dropped full-stretched again, and lunged viciously at me. Twice I felt the wind of his paws. He spun around so fast that it kept me dancing. I flung the noose and caught his right paw. Hiram bawled something that made me all the more heedless, and in tightening the noose I ran in too close. The bear gave me a slashing cuff on the side of the head, and I went down like a tenpin.

"Git a hitch thar—to the saplin'!" roared Hiram, as I staggered to my feet. "Rustle now—hurry!"

What with my ringing head, and fingers all thumbs, and Hiram roaring at me, I made a mess of tying the knot. Then Hiram let go his rope, and when the cub dropped to the ground the rope flew up over the branch. Cubby leaped so quickly that he jerked the rope away before Hiram could pick it up, and one hard pull loosened my hitch on the sapling.

The cub bounded through the glade, dragging me with him. For a few long leaps I kept my feet, then down I sprawled.

"Hang on! Hang on!" Hiram yelled from behind.

If I had not been angry clear through at that cub I might have let go. He ploughed my face in the dirt, and almost jerked my arms off. Suddenly the strain lessened. I got up, to see that the old hunter had hold of the other rope.

"Now, stretch him out!" he yelled.

Between us we stretched the cub out, so that all he could do was struggle and paw the air and utter strange cries. Hiram tied his rope to a tree, and then ran back to relieve me. It was high time. He took my rope and fastened it to a stout bush.

"Thar, youngster, I reckon thet'll hold him! Now tie his paws an' muzzle him."

He drew some buckskin thongs from his pocket and handed them to me. We went up to the straining cub, and Hiram, with one pull of his powerful hands, brought the hind legs together.

"Tie 'em," he said.

This done, with the aid of a heavy piece of wood he pressed the cub's head down and wound a thong tightly round the sharp nose. Then he tied the front legs.

"Thar! Now you loosen the ropes an' wind them up."

When I had done this he lifted the cub and swung him over his broad back.

"Come on, you trail behind, an' keep your eye peeled to see he doesn't work thet knot off his jaws.... Say, youngster, now you've got him, what in thunder will you do with him?"

I looked at my torn trousers, at the blood on my skinned and burning hands, and I felt of the bruise on my head, as I said, grimly: "I'll hang to him as long as I can."

XIII. THE CABIN IN THE FOREST

Hiram Bent packed the cub down the canyon as he would have handled a sack of oats. When we reached the cabin he fastened a heavy dog-collar round Cubby's neck and snapped a chain to it. Doubling the halter, he tied one end to the chain and the other to a sturdy branch of a tree. This done, he slipped the thongs off the bear.

"Thar! He'll let you pet him in a few days mebbe," he said.

Our captive did not yet show any signs of becoming tame. No sooner was he free of the buckskin thongs than he leaped away, only to be pulled up by the halter. Then he rolled over and over, clawing at the chain, and squirming to get his head out of the collar.

"He might choke hisself," said Hiram, "but mebbe he'll ease up if we stay away from him. Now we've got to rustle to skin them two bears."

So, after giving me a hunting-knife, and telling me to fetch my rifle, he set off up the canyon. As I trudged along behind him I spoke of Dick Leslie, and asked if there were not some way to get him out of the clutches of the lumber thieves.

"I've been thinkin' about thet," replied the hunter, "an' I reckon we can. Tomorrow we'll cross the ridge high up back of thet spring-hole canyon, an' sneak down. 'Pears to me them fellers will be trailin' you pretty hard, an' mebbe they'll leave only one to guard Leslie. More'n thet, the trail up here to my shack is known, an' I'm thinkin' we'd be smart to go off an' camp somewhere else."

"What'll I do about Cubby?" I asked, quickly.

"Cubby? Oh, thet bear cub. Wal, take him along. Youngster, you don't want to pack thet pesky cub back to Pennsylvania?"

"Yes, I do."

"I reckon it ain't likely you can. He's pretty heavy. Weighs nearly a hundred. An' he'd make a heap of trouble. Mebbe we'll ketch a little cub—one you can carry in your arms."

"That'd be still better," I replied. "But if we don't, I'll try to take him back home."

The old hunter said I made a good shot at the big bear, and that he would give me the skin for a rug. It delighted me to think of that huge glossy bearskin on the floor of my den. I told Hiram how the bear had suffered, and I was glad to see that, although he was a hunter and trapper, he disliked to catch a bear in a trap.

We skinned the animal, and cut out a quantity of meat. He told me that bear meat would make me forget all about venison. By the time we had climbed up the other canyon and skinned the other bear and returned to camp it was dark. As for me, I was so tired I could hardly crawl.

In spite of my aches and pains, that was a night for me to remember. But there was the thought of Dick Leslie. His rescue was the only thing needed to make me happy. Dick was in my mind even when Hiram cooked a supper that almost made me forget my manners. Certainly the broiled bear meat made me forget venison. Then we talked before the burning logs in the stone fire-place. Hiram sat on his home-made chair and smoked a strong-smelling pipe while I lay on a bearskin in blissful ease. Occasionally we heard the cub outside rattling his chain and growling. All of the trappers and Indian fighters I had read of were different from Hiram Bent and Jim Williams. Jim's soft drawl and kind, twinkling eyes were not what any book-reader would expect to find in a dangerous man. And Hiram Bent was so simple and friendly, so glad to have even a boy to talk to, that it seemed he would never stop. If it had not been for his striking appearance and for the strange, wild tales he told of his lonely life, he would have reminded me of the old canal-lock tenders at home.

Once, when he was refilling his pipe and I thought it would be a good time to profit from his knowledge of the forests, I said to him:

"Now, Mr. Bent, let's suppose I'm the President of the United States, and I have just appointed you to the office of Chief Forester of the National Forests. You have full power. The object is to conserve our national resources. What will you do?"

"Wal, Mr. President," he began, slowly and seriously, and with great dignity, "the Government must own the forests an' deal wisely with them. These mountain forests are great sponges to hold the water, an' we must stop fire an' reckless cuttin'. The first thing is to overcome the opposition of the stockmen, an' show them where the benefit will be theirs in the long run. Next the timber must be used, but not all used up. We'll need rangers who're used to rustlin' in the West an' know Western ways. Cabins must be built, trails made, roads cut. We'll need a head forester for every forest. This man must know all that's on his preserve, an' have it mapped. He must teach his rangers what he knows about trees. Penetier will be given over entirely to the growin' of yellow pine. Thet thrives best, an' the parasites must go. All dead an' old timber must be cut, an' much of thet where the trees are crowded. The north slopes must be cut enough to let in the sun an' light. Brush, windfalls rottin' logs must be burned. Thickets of young pine must be thinned. Care oughten be taken not to cut on the north an' west edges of the forests, as the old guard pines will break the wind."

"How will you treat miners and prospectors?"

"They must be as free to take up claims as if there wasn't no National Forest."

"How about the settler, the man seeking a home out West?" I went on.

"We'll encourage him. The more men there are, the better the forester can fight fire. But those home-seekers must want a home, an' not be squattin' for a little, jest to sell out to lumber sharks."

"What's to become of timber and wood?"

"Wal, it's there to be used, an' must be used. We'll give it free to the settler an' prospector. We'll sell it cheap to the lumbermen—big an' little. We'll consider the wants of the local men first."

"Now about the range. Will you keep out the stockmen?"

"Nary. Grazin' for sheep, cattle, an' hosses will go on jest the same. But we must look out for overgrazin'. For instance, too many cattle will stamp down young growth, an' too many sheep leave no grazin' for other stock. The bead forester must know his business, an' not let his range be overstocked. The small local herders an' sheepmen must be considered first, the big stockmen second. Both must be charged a small fee per head for grazin'."

"How will you fight fire?"

"Wal, thet's the hard nut to crack. Fire is the forest's worst enemy. In a dry season like this Penetier would burn like tinder blown by a bellows. Fire would race through here faster 'n a man could run. I'll need special fire rangers, an' all other rangers must be trained to fight fire, an' then any men living in or near the forest will be paid to help. The thing to do is watch for the small fires an' put them out. Campers must be made to put out their fires before leaving camp. Brush piles an' slashes mustn't be burned in dry or windy weather."

Just where we left off talking I could not remember, for I dropped off to sleep. I seemed hardly to have closed my eyes when the hunter called me in the morning. The breakfast was smoking on the red-hot coals, and outside the cabin all was dense gray fog.

When, soon after, we started down the canyon, the fog was lifting and the forest growing lighter. Everything was as white with frost as if it had snowed. A thin, brittle frost crackled under our feet. When we, had gotten below the rocky confines of the canyon we climbed the slope to the level ridge. Here it was impossible not to believe it had snowed. The forest was as still as night, and looked very strange with the white aisles lined by black tree trunks and the gray fog shrouding the tree-tops. Soon we were climbing again, and I saw that Hiram meant to head the canyon where I had left Dick.

The fog split and blew away, and the brilliant sunlight changed the forest. The frost began to melt, and the air was full of mist. We climbed and climbed—out of the stately yellow-pine zone, up among the gnarled and blasted spruces, over and around strips of weathered stone. Once I saw a cold, white snow-peak. It was hard enough for me to carry my rifle and keep up with the hunter without talking. Besides, Hiram had answered me rather shortly, and I thought it best to keep silent. From time to time he stopped to listen. Then when he turned to go down the slope be trod carefully, and cautioned me not to loosen stones, and he went slower and yet slower. From this I made sure we were not far from the springhole.

"Thar's the canyon," he whispered, stopping to point below, where a black, irregular line marked the gorge. "I haven't heerd a thing, an' we're close. Mebbe they're asleep. Mebbe most of them are trallin' you, an' I hope so. Now, don't you put your hand or foot on anythin' thet'll make a noise."

Then he slipped off, and it was wonderful to see how noiselessly he stepped, and how he moved between trees and dead branches without a sound. I managed pretty well, yet more than once a rattling stone or a broken branch stopped Hiram short and made him lift a warning hand.

At last we got down to the narrow bench which separated the canyon-slope from the deep cut. It was level and roughly strewn with boulders. Here we took to all fours and crawled. It was easy to move here without noise, for the ground was rocky and hard, and there was no brush.

Suddenly I fairly bumped into the hunter. Looking up, I saw that he had halted only a few feet from the edge of the gorge where I had climbed out in my escape. He was listening. There was not a sound save the dull roar of rushing water.

Hiram slid forward a little, and rose cautiously to look over. I did the same. When I saw the cave and the spring-hole I felt a catch in my throat.

But there was not a man in sight. Dick's captors had broken camp; they were gone. The only thing left in the gorge to show they had ever been there was a burned-out campfire.

"They're gone," I whispered.

"Wal, it 'pears so," replied Hiram. "An' it's a move I don't like. Youngster, it's you they want. Leslie's no particular use to them. They'll have to let him go sooner or later, if they hain't already."

"What'll we do now?"

"Make tracks. We'll cut back acrost the ridge an' git some blankets an' grub, then light out for the other side of Penetier."

I thought the old hunter had made rapid time on our way up, but now I saw what he really meant by "making tracks." Fortunately, after a short, killing climb, the return was all down-hill. One stride of Hiram's equalled two of mine, and he made his faster, so that I had to trot now and then to catch up. Very soon I was as hot as fire, and every step was an effort. But I kept thinking of Dick, of my mustang and outfit, and I vowed I would stick to Hiram Bent's trail till I dropped. For the matter of that I did drop more than once before we reached the cabin.

A short rest while Hiram was packing a few things put me right again. I strapped my rifle over my shoulder, and then went out to untie my bear cub. It would have cost me a great deal to leave him behind. I knew I ought to, still I could not bring myself to it. All my life I had wanted a bear cub. Here was one that I had helped to lasso and tie up with my own hands. I made up my mind to hold to the cub until the last gasp.

So I walked up to Cubby with a manner more bold than sincere. He had not eaten anything, but he had drunk the water we had left for him. To my surprise he made no fuss when I untied the rope; on the other hand, he seemed to look pleased, and I thought I detected a cunning gleam in his little eyes. He paddled away down the canyon, and, as this was in the direction we wanted to go, I gave him slack rope and followed.

"Wal, you're goin' to have a right pert time, youngster, an' don't you forget it," said Hiram Bent.

The truth of that was very soon in evidence. Cubby would not let well enough alone, and he would not have a slack rope. I think he wanted to choke himself or pull my arms out. When I realized that Cubby was three times as strong as I was I began to see that my work was cut out for me. The more, however, that he jerked me and hauled me along, the more I determined to hang on. I thought I had a genuine love for him up to the time he had almost knocked my head off, but it was funny how easily he roused my anger after that. What would have happened had he taken a notion to go through the brush? Luckily he kept to the trail, which certainly was rough enough. So, with watching the cub and keeping my feet free of roots and rocks, I had no chance to look ahead. Still I had no concern about this, for the old hunter was at my heels, and I knew he would keep a sharp lookout.

Before I was aware of it we had gotten out of the narrow canyon into a valley with well-timbered bottom, and open, slow rising slopes. We were getting down into Penetier. Cubby swerved from the trail and started up the left slope. I did not want to go, but I had to keep with him, and that was the only way. The hunter strode behind without speaking, and so I gathered that the direction suited him. By leaning back on the rope I walked up the slope as easily as if it were a moving stairway. Cubby pulled me up; I had only to move my feet. When we reached a level once more I discovered that the cub was growing stronger and wanted to go faster. We zigzagged across the ridge to the next canyon, which at a glance I saw was deep and steep.

"Thet'll be some work goin' down that!" called Hiram. "Let me pack your gun."

I would have been glad to give it to him, but how was I to manage? I could not let go of the rope, and Hiram, laden as he was, could not catch up with me. Then suddenly it was too late, for Cubby lunged forward and down.

This first downward jump was not vicious—only a playful one perhaps, by way of initiating me; but it upset me, and I was dragged in the pine-needles. I did not leap to my feet; I was jerked up. Then began a wild chase down that steep, bushy slope. Cubby got going, and I could no more have checked him than I could a steam-engine. Very soon I saw that not only was the bear cub running away, but he was running away with me. I slid down yellow places where the earth was exposed, I tore through thickets, I dodged a thousand trees. In some grassy descents it was as if I had seven-league boots. I must have broken all records for jumps. All at once I stumbled just as Cubby made a spurt and flew forward, alighting face downward. I dug up the pine—needles with my outstretched hands, I scraped with my face and ploughed with my nose, I ate the dust; and when I brought up with a jolt against a log a more furious boy than Ken Ward it would be bard to imagine. Leaping up, I strove with every ounce of might to hold in the bear. But though fury lent me new strength, he kept the advantage.

Presently I saw the bottom of the canyon, an open glade, and an old log-cabin. I looked back to see if the hunter was coming. He was not in sight, but I fancied I heard him. Then Cubby, putting on extra steam, took the remaining rods of the slope in another spurt. I had to race, then fly, and at last lost my footing and plunged down into a thicket.

There farther progress stopped for both of us. Cubby had gone down on one side of a sapling and I on the other, with the result that we were brought up short. I crashed through some low bushes and bumped squarely into the cub. Whether it was his frantic effort to escape, or just excitement, or deliberate intention to beat me into a jelly I had no means to tell. The fact was he began to dig at me and paw me and maul me. Never had I been so angry. I began to fight back, to punch and kick him.

Suddenly, with a crashing in the bushes, the cub was hauled away from me, and then I saw Hiram at the rope.

"Wal, wal!" he ejaculated, "your own mother wouldn't own you now!" Then he laughed heartily and chuckled to himself, and gave the cub a couple of jerks that took the mischief out of him. I dragged myself after Hiram into the glade. The cabin was large and very old, and part of the roof was sunken in.

"We'll hang up here an' camp," said Hiram. "This is an old hunters' cabin, an' kinder out of the way. We'll hitch this little fighter inside, where mebbe he won't be so noisy."

The hunter hauled the cub up short, and half pulled, half lifted him into the door. I took off my rifle, emptied my pockets of brush and beat out the dust, and combed the pine-needles from my hair. My hands were puffed and red, and smarted severely. And altogether I was in no amiable frame of mind as regarded my captive bear cub.

When I stepped inside the cabin it was dark, and coming from the bright light I could not for a moment see what the interior looked like. Presently I made out one large room with no opening except the door. There was a tumble-down stone fire-place at one end, and at the other a rude ladder led up to a loft. Hiram had thrown his pack aside, and had tied Cubby to a peg in the log wall.

"Wal, I'll fetch in some fresh venison," said the hunter. "You rest awhile, an' then gather some wood an' make a fire."

The rest I certainly needed, for I was so tired I could scarcely untie the pack to get out the blankets. The bear cub showed signs or weariness, which pleased me. It was not long after Hiram's departure that I sank into a doze.

When my eyes opened I knew I had been awakened by something, but I could not tell what. I listened. Cubby was as quiet as a mouse, and his very quiet and the alert way he held his ears gave me a vague alarm. He had heard something. I thought of the old hunter's return, yet this did not reassure me.

All at once the voices of men made me sit up with a violent start. Who could they be? Had Hiram met a ranger? I began to shake a little, and was about to creep to the door when I heard the clink of stirrups and soft thud of hoofs. Then followed more voices, and last a loud volley of curses.

XIII. THE CABIN IN THE FOREST

"Herky-Jerky!" I gasped, and looked about wildly.

I had no time to dash out of the door. I was caught in a trap, and I felt cold and sick. Suddenly I caught sight of the ladder leading to the loft. Like a monkey I ran up, and crawled as noiselessly as possible upon the rickety flooring of dry pine branches. Then I lay there quivering.

XIV. A PRISONER

It chanced that as I lay on my side my eye caught a gleam of light through a little ragged hole in the matting of pine branches. Part of the interior of the cabin, the doorway, and some space outside were plainly visible. The thud of horses had given place to snorts, and then came a flopping of saddles and packs on the ground. "Any water hyar?" asked a gruff voice I recognized as Bill's. "Spring right thar," replied a voice I knew to be Bud's.

"You onery old cayuse, stand still!"

From that I gathered Herky was taking the saddle off his horse.

"Here, Leslie, I'll untie you—if you'll promise not to bolt."

That voice was Buell's. I would have known it among a thousand. And Dick was still a prisoner.

"Bolt! If you let me loose I'll beat your fat head off!" replied Dick. "Ha! A lot you care about my sore wrists. You're weakening, Buell, and you know it. You've got a yellow streak."

"Shet up!" said Herky, in a low, sharp tone. A silence followed. "Buell, look hyar in the trail. Tracks! Goin' in an' comin' out."

"How old are they?"

"I'll bet a hoss they ain't an hour old."

"Somebody's usin' the cabin, eh?"

The men then fell to whispering, and I could not understand what was said, but I fancied they were thinking only of me. My mind worked fast. Buell and his fellows had surely not run across Hiram Bent. Had the old hunter deserted me? I flouted such a thought. It was next to a certainty that he had seen the lumbermen, and for reasons best known to himself had not returned to the cabin. But he was out there somewhere among the pines, and I did not think any of those ruffians was safe.

Then I heard stealthy footsteps approaching. Soon I saw the Mexican slipping cautiously to the door. He peeped within. Probably the interior was dark to him, as it had been to me. He was not a coward, for he stepped inside.

At that instant there was a clinking sound, a rush and a roar, and a black mass appeared to hurl itself upon the Mexican. He went down with a piercing shriek. Then began a fearful commotion. Screams and roars mingled with the noise of combat. I saw a whirling cloud of dust on the cabin floor. The cub had jumped on the Mexican. What an unmerciful beating he was giving that Greaser! I could have yelled out in my glee. I had to bite my tongue to keep from urging on my docile little pet bear. Greaser surely thought he had fallen in with his evil spirit, for he howled to the saints to save him.

Herky-Jerky was the only one of his companions brave enough to start to help him.

"The cabin's full of b'ars!" he yelled.

At his cry the bear leaped out of the cloud of dust, and shot across the threshold like black lightning. In his onslaught upon Greaser he had broken his halter. Herky-Jerky stood directly in his path. I caught only a glimpse, but it served to show that Herky was badly scared. The cub dove at Herky, under him, straight between his legs like a greased pig, and, spilling him all over the trail, sped on out of sight. Herky raised himself, and then he sat there, red as a lobster, and bawled curses while he made his huge revolver spurt flame on flame.

I could not see the other men, but their uproarious mirth could have been heard half a mile away. When it dawned upon Herky, he was so furious that he spat at them like an angry cat and clicked his empty revolver.

Then Greaser lurched out of the door. I got a glimpse of him, and, for a wonder, was actually sorry for him. He looked as if he had been through a threshing-machine.

"Haw! haw! Ho! ho!" roared the merry lumbermen.

Then they trooped into the cabin. Buell headed the line, and Herky, sullenly reloading his revolver, came last. At first they groped around in the dim light, stumbling over everything. Part of the time they were in the light space near the door, and the rest I could not see them. I scarcely dared to breathe. I felt a creepy chill, and my eyesight grew dim.

"Who does this stuff belong to, anyhow?" Buell was saying. "An' what was thet bear doin' in here?"

"He was roped up—hyar's the hitch," answered Bud.

"An' hyar's a rifle—Winchester—ain't been used much. Buell, it's thet kid's!"

I heard rapid footsteps and smothered exclamations.

"Take it from me, you're right!" ejaculated Buell. "We jest missed him. Herky, them tracks out there? Somebody's with this boy—who?"

"It's Jim Williams," put in Dick Leslie, cool-voiced and threatening.

The little stillness that followed his words was broken by Buell.

"Naw! 'Twasn't Williams. You can't bluff this bunch, Leslie. By your own words Williams is lookin' for us, an' if he's lookin' for anybody I know he's lookin' for 'em. See!"

"Buell, the kid's fell in with old Bent, the b'ar hunter," said Bill. "Thet accounts fer the cub. Bent's allus got cubs, an' kittens, an' sich. An' I'll tell you, he ain't no better friend of ourn than Jim Williams."

"I'd about as soon tackle Williams as Bent," put in Bud.

Buell shook his fist. "What luck the kid has! But I'll get him, take it from me! Now, what's best to do?"

"Buell, the game's going against you," said Dick Leslie. "The penitentiary is where you'll finish. You'd better let me loose. Old Bent will find Jim Williams, and then you fellows will be up against it. There's going to be somebody killed. The best thing for you to do is to let me go and then cut out yourself."

Buell breathed as heavily as a porpoise, and his footsteps pounded hard.

"Leslie, I'm seein' this out—understand? When Bud rode down to the mill an' told me the kid had got away I made up my mind to ketch him an' shet his mouth—one way or another. An' I'll do it. Take thet from me!"

"Bah!" sneered Dick. "You're sca'red into the middle of next week right now.... Besides, if you do ketch Ken it won't do you any good-now!"

"What?"

But Dick shut up like a clam, and not another word could be gotten from him. Buell fumed and stamped.

"Bud, you're the only one in this bunch of loggerheads thet has any sense. What d'you say?"

"Quiet down an' wait here," replied Bud. "Mebbe old Bent didn't hear them shots of Herky's. He may come back. Let's wait awhile, an', if he doesn't come, put Herky on the trail."

"Good! Greaser, go out an' hide the hosses—drive them up the canyon."

The Mexican shuffled out, and all the others settled down to quiet. I heard some of them light their pipes. Bud leaned against the left of the door, Buell sat on the other side, and beyond them I saw as much of Herky as his boots. I knew him by his bow-legs.

The stillness that set in began to be hard on me'. When the men were moving about and talking I had been so interested that my predicament did not occupy my mind. But now, with those ruffians waiting silently below, I was beset with a thousand fears. The very consciousness that I must be quiet made it almost impossible. Then I became aware that my one position cramped my arm and side. A million prickling needles were at my elbow. A band as of steel tightened about my breast. I grew hot and cold, and trembled. I knew the slightest move would be fatal, so I bent all my mind to lying quiet as a stone.

Greaser came limping back into the cabin, and found a seat without any one speaking. It was so still that I heard the silken rustle of paper as he rolled a cigarette. Moments that seemed long as years passed, with my muscles clamped as in a vise. If only I had lain down upon my back! But there I was, half raised on my elbow, in a most awkward and uncomfortable position. I tried not to mind the tingling in my arm, but to think of Hiram, of Jim, of my mustang. But presently I could not think of anything except the certainty that I would soon lose control of my muscles and fall over.

The tingling changed to a painful vibration, and perspiration stung my face. The strain became unbearable. All of a sudden something seemed to break within me, and my muscles began to ripple and shake. I had no power to stop it. More than that, the feeling was so terrible that I knew I would welcome discovery as a relief.

"Sh-s-s-h!" whispered some one below.

I turned my eyes down to the peep-hole. Bud had moved over squarely into the light of the door. He was bending over something. Then he extended his hand, back uppermost, toward Buell. On the back of that broad brown hand were pieces of leaf and bits of pine-needles. The trembling of my body had shaken these from the brush on the rickety loft. More than that, in the yellow bar of sunlight which streamed in at the door there floated particles of dust.

Bud silently looked upward. There was a gleam in his black eyes, and his mouth was agape. Buell's gaze followed Bud's, and his face grew curious, intent, then fixed in a cunning, bold smile of satisfaction. He rose to his feet.

"Come down out o' thet!" he ordered, harshly. "Come down!"

The sound of his voice stilled my trembling. I did not move nor breathe. I saw Buell loom up hugely and Bud slowly rise. Herky-Jerky's boots suddenly stood on end, and I knew then he had also risen. The silence which followed Buell's order was so dense that it oppressed me.

"Come down!" repeated Buell.

There was no hint of doubt in his deep voice, but a cold certainty and a brutal note. I had feared the man before, but that gave me new terror.

"Bud, climb the ladder," commanded Buell.

"I ain't stuck on thet job," rejoined Bud.

As his heavy boots thumped on the ladder they jarred the whole cabin. My very desperation filled me with the fierceness of a cornered animal. I caught sight of a short branch of the thickness of a man's arm, and, grasping it, I slowly raised myself. When Bud's black, round head appeared above the loft I hit it with all my might.

Bud bawled like a wounded animal, and fell to the ground with the noise of a load of bricks. Through my peep-hole I saw him writhing, with both hands pressed to his head. Then, lying flat on his back, he whipped out his revolver. I saw the red spurt, the puff of smoke. Bang!

A bullet zipped through the brush, and tore a hole through the roof.

Bang! Bang!

I felt a hot, tearing pain in my arm.

"Stop, you black idiot!" yelled Buell. He kicked the revolver out of Bud's hand. "What d'you mean by thet?"

In the momentary silence that followed I listened intently, even while I held tightly to my arm. From its feeling my arm seemed to be shot off, but it was only a flesh-wound. After the first instant of shock I was not scared. But blood flowed fast. Warm, oily, slippery, it ran down inside my shirt sleeve and dripped off my fingers.

"Bud," hoarsely spoke up Bill, breaking the stillness, "mebbe you killed him!"

Buell coughed, as if choking.

"What's thet?" For once his deep voice was pitched low. "Listen."

Drip! drip! drip! It was like the sound of water dripping from a leak in a roof. It was directly under me, and, quick as thought, I knew the sound was made by my own dripping blood.

"Find thet, somebody," ordered Buell.

Drip! drip! drip!

One of the men stepped noisily.

"Hyar it is—thar," said Bill. "Look on my hand.... Blood! I knowed it. Bud got him, all right."

There was a sudden rustling such as might come from a quick, strained movement.

"Buell," cried Dick Leslie, in piercing tones, "Heaven help you murdering thieves if that boy's killed! I'll see you strung up right in this forest. Ken, speak! Speak!"

It seemed then, in my pain and bitterness, that I would rather let Buell think me dead. Dick's voice went straight to my heart, but I made no answer.

"Leslie, I didn't kill him, an' I didn't order it," said Buell, in a voice strangely shrunk and shaken. "I meant no harm to the lad.... Go up, Bud, an' get him."

Bud made no move, nor did Greaser when he was ordered. "Go up, somebody, an' see what's up there!" shouted Buell. "Strikes me you might go yourself," said Bill, coolly.

With a growl Buell mounted the ladder. When his great shock head hove in sight I was seized by a mad desire to give him a little of his own medicine. With both hands I lifted the piece of pine branch and brought it down with every ounce of strength in me.

Like a pistol it cracked on Buell's head and snapped into bits. The lumberman gave a smothered groan, then clattered down the ladder and rolled on the floor. There he lay quiet.

"All-fired dead—thet kid—now, ain't he?" said Bud, sarcastically. "How'd you like thet crack on the knob? You'll need a larger size hat, mebbe. Herky-Jerky, you go up an' see what's up there."

"I've a picture of myself goin'," replied Herky, without moving.

"Whar's the water? Get some water, Greaser," chimed in Bill.

From the way they worked over Buell, I concluded he had been pretty badly stunned. But he came to presently.

"What struck me?" he asked.

"Oh, nothin'," replied Bud, derisively. "The loft up thar's full of air, an' it blowed on you, thet's all."

Buell got up, and began walking around.

"Bill, go out an' fetch in some long poles," he said.

When Bill returned with a number of sharp, bayonet-like pikes I knew the game was all up for me. Several of the men began to prod through the thin covering of dry brush. One of them reached me, and struck so hard that I lurched violently.

XIV. A PRISONER

That was too much for the rickety loft floor. It was only a bit of brush laid on a netting of slender poles. It creaked, rasped, and went down with a crash. I alighted upon somebody, and knocked him to the floor. Whoever it was, seized me with iron hands. I was buried, almost smothered, in the dusty mass. My captor began to curse cheerfully, and I knew then that Herky-Jerky had made me a prisoner.

XV. THE FIGHT

Herky hauled me out of the brush, and held me in the light. The others scrambled from under the remains of the loft, and all viewed me curiously.

"Kid, you ain't hurt much?" queried Buell, with concern.

I would have snapped out a reply, but I caught sight of Dick's pale face and anxious eyes.

"Ken," he called, with both gladness and doubt in his voice, "you look pretty good—but that blood.... Tell me, quick!"

"It's nothing, Dick, only a little cut. The bullet just ticked my arm."

Whatever Dick's reply was it got drowned in Herky-Jerky's long explosion of strange language. Herky was plainly glad I had not been badly hurt. I had already heard mirth, anger, disgust, and fear in his outbreaks, and now relief was added. He stripped off my coat, cut off the bloody sleeve of my shirt, and washed the wound. It was painful and bled freely, but it was not much worse than cuts from spikes when playing ball. Herky bound it tightly with a strip of my shirt-sleeve, and over that my handkerchief.

"Thar, kid, thet'll stiffen up an' be sore fer a day or two, but it ain't nothin'. You'll soon be bouncin' clubs offen our heads."

It was plain that Herky—and the others, for that matter, except Buell—thought more of me because I had wielded a club so vigorously.

"Look at thet lump, kid," said Bud, bending his head. "Now, ain't thet a nice way to treat a feller? It made me plumb mad, it did."

"I'm likely to hurt somebody yet," I declared.

They looked at me curiously. Buell raised his face with a queer smile. Bud broke into a laugh.

"Oh, you're goin' to? Mebbe you think you need an axe," said he.

They made no offer to tie me up then. Bud went to the door and sat in it, and I heard him half whisper to Buell: "What 'd I tell you? Thet's a game kid. If he ever wakes up right we'll have a wildcat on our hands. He'll do fer one of us yet." These men all took pleasure in saying things like this to Buell. This time Buell had no answer ready, and sat nursing his head. "Wal, I hev a little headache myself, an' the crack I got wasn't nothin' to yourn," concluded Bud. Then Bill began packing the supplies indoors, and Herky started a fire. Bud kept a sharp eye on me; still, he made no objection when I walked over and lay down upon the blankets near Dick.

"Dick, I shot a bear and helped to tie up a cub," I said. And then I told him all that had happened from the time I scrambled out of the spring-hole till I was discovered up in the loft. Dick shook his head, as if he did not know what to make of me, and all he said was that he would give a year's pay to have me safe back in Pennsylvania.

Herky-Jerky announced supper in his usual manner—a challenge to find as good a cook as he was, and a cheerful call to "grub." I did not know what to think of his kindness to me. Remembering how he had nearly drowned me in the spring, I resented his sudden change. He could not do enough for me. I asked the reason for my sudden popularity.

Herky scratched his head and grinned. "Yep, kid, you sure hev riz in my estimashun."

"Hey, you rummy cow-puncher," broke in Bud, scornfully. "Mebbe you'd like the kid more'n you do if you'd got one of them wollops."

"Bud, I ain't sayin'," replied Herky, with his mouth full of meat. "Considerin' all points, howsoever, I'm thinkin' them wallops was distributed very proper."

They bandied such talk between them, and occasionally Bill chimed in with a joke. Greaser ate in morose silence. There must have been something on his mind. Buell took very little dinner, and appeared to be in pain. It was dark when the meal ended. Bud bound me up for the night, and he made a good job of it. My arm burned and throbbed, but not badly enough to prevent sleep. Twice I had nearly dropped off when loud laughs or voices roused me. My eyes closed with a picture of those rough, dark men sitting before the fire.

A noise like muffled thunder burst into my slumber. I awakened with my body cramped and stiff. It was daylight, and something had happened. Buell ran in and out of the cabin yelling at his men. All of them except Herky were wildly excited. Buell was abusing Bud for something, and Bud was blaming Buell.

"Thet's no way to talk to me!" said Bud, angrily. "He didn't break loose in my watch!'

"You an' Greaser had the job. Both of you—went to sleep—take thet from me!"

"Wal, he's gone, an' he took the kid's gun with him," said Bill, coolly. "Now we'll be dodgin' bullets."

Dick Leslie had escaped! I could hardly keep down a cry of triumph. I did ask if it was true, but none of them paid any attention to me. Buell then ordered Herky-Jerky to trail Dick and see where he had gone. Herky refused point-blank. "Nope. Not fer me," he said. "Leslie has a rifle. So has Bent, an' we haven't one among us. An', Buell, if Leslie falls in with Bent, it's goin' to git hot fer us round here."

This silenced Buell, but did not stop his restless pacings. His face was like a thunder-cloud, and he was plainly worried and harassed. Once Bud deliberately asked what he intended to do with me, and Buell snarled a reply which no one understood. His gloom extended to the others, except Herky, who whistled and sang as he busied himself about the campfire. Greaser appeared to be particularly cast down.

"Buell, what are you going to do with me?" I demanded. But he made no answer.

"Well, anyway," I went on, "somebody cut these ropes. I'm mighty sore and uncomfortable."

Herky-Jerky did not wait for permission; he untied me, and helped me to my feet. I was rather unsteady on my legs at first, and my injured arm felt like a board. It seemed dead; but after I had moved it a little the pain came back, and it had apparently come to stay. We ate breakfast, and then settled down to do nothing, or to wait for something to turn up. Buell sat in the doorway, moodily watching the trail. Once he spoke, ordering the Mexican to drive in the horses. I fancied from this that Buell might have decided to break camp, but there was no move to pack.

The morning quiet was suddenly split by the stinging crack of a rifle and a yell of agony.

Buell leaped to his feet, his ruddy face white.

"Greaser!" he exclaimed.

"Thet was about where Greaser cashed," relied Bill, coolly knocking the ashes from his pipe.

"No, Bill, you're wrong. Here comes Greaser, runnin' like an Indian."

"Look at the blood! He's been plugged, all right!" exclaimed Herky-Jerky.

The sound of running feet drew nearer, and suddenly the group at the door broke to admit the Mexican. One side of his terrified face was covered with blood. His eyes were staring, his hands raised, he staggered as if about to fall.

"Senyor William! Senyor William!" he cried, and then called on Saint Somebody.

"Jim Williams! I said so," muttered Bud.

Bill caught hold of the excited Mexican, and pulled him nearer the light.

"Thet ain't a bad hurt. Jest cut his ear off!" aid Bill. "Hyar, stand still, you wild man! you're not goin' to die. Git some water, Herky. Fellers, Greaser has been oneasy ever since he knew Jim Williams was lookin' fer him. He thinks Jim did this. But Jim Williams don't use a rifle, an', what's more, when he shoots he don't miss. You all heerd the rifle-shot."

"Then it was old Bent or Leslie?" questioned Buell.

"Leslie it were. Bent uses a 45-90 caliber. Thet shot we heerd was from the little 38—the kid's gun."

"Wal, it was a narrer escape fer Greaser," said Bud. "Leslie's sore, an' he'll shoot fer keeps. Buell, you've started somethin'."

When Bill had washed the blood off the Mexican it was found that the ball had carried away the lower part of the ear, and with it, of course, the gold earring. The wound must have been extremely painful; it certainly took all the starch out of

Greaser. He kept mumbling in his own language, and rolling his wicked black eyes and twisting his thin, yellow hands.

"What's to be done?" asked Buell, sharply.

"Thet's fer you to say," replied Bill, with his exasperating calmness.

"Must we hang up here to be shot at? Leslie's takin' a long chance on thet kid's life if he comes slingin' lead round this cabin."

Herky-Jerky spat tobacco-juice across the room and grunted. Then, with his beady little eyes as keen and cold as flint, he said: "Buell, Leslie knows you daren't harm the kid; an' as fer bullets, he'll take good care where he stings 'em. This deal of ours begins to look like a wild-goose stunt. It never was safe, an' now it's worse."

Here was even Herky-Jerky harping on Buell's situation. To me it did not appear much more serious than before. But evidently they thought Buell seemed on the verge of losing control of himself. He glared at Herky, and rammed his fists in his pockets and paced the long room. Presently he stepped out of the door.

A rifle cracked clear and sharp, another bellowed out heavy and hollow. A bullet struck the door-post, a second hummed through the door and budded into the log wall. Buell jumped back into the room. His face worked, his breath hissed between his teeth, as with trembling hand he examined the front of his coat. A big bullet had torn through both lapels.

Bill stuck his pudgy finger in the hole. "The second bullet made thet. It was from old Hiram's gun—a 45-90!"

"Bent an' Leslie! My God! They're shootin' to kill!" cried Buell.

"I should smile," replied Herky-Jerky.

Bud was peeping out through a chink between the logs. "I got their smoke," he said; "look, Bill, up the slope. They're too fur off, but we may as well send up respects." With that he aimed his revolver through the narrow crack and deliberately shot six times. The reports clapped like thunder, the smoke from burnt powder and the smell of brimstone filled the room. By way of reply old Hiram's rifle boomed out twice, and two heavy slugs crashed through the roof, sending down a shower of dust and bits of decayed wood.

"Thet's jist to show what a 45-90 can do," remarked Bill.

Bud reloaded his weapon while Bill shot several times. Herky-Jerky had his gun in hand, but contented himself with peering from different chinks between the logs. I hid behind the wide stone fireplace, and though I felt pretty safe from flying bullets, I began to feel the icy grip of fear. I had seen too much of these men in excitement, and knew if circumstances so brought it about there might come a moment when my life would not be worth a pin. They were all sober now, and deadly quiet. Buell showed the greatest alarm, though he had begun to settle down to what looked like fight. Herky was more fearless than any of them, and cooler even than Bill. All at once I missed the Mexican. If he had not slipped out of the room he had hidden under the brush of the fallen loft or in a pile of blankets. But the room was smoky, and it was hard for me to be certain.

Some time passed with no shots and with no movement inside the cabin. Slowly the blue smoke wafted out of the door. The sunlight danced in gleams through the holes in the ragged roof. There was a pleasant swish of pine branches against the cabin.

"Listen," whispered Bud, hoarsely. "I heerd a pony snort."

Then the rapid beat of hard hoofs on the trail was followed by several shots from the hillside. Soon the clatter of hoofs died away in the distance.

"Who was thet?" asked three of Buell's men in unison.

"Take it from me, Greaser's sneaked," replied Buell.

"How'd he git out?"

With that Bud and Bill began kicking in the piles of brush.

"Aha! Hyar's the place," sang out Bud.

In one corner of the back wall a rotten log had crumbled, and here it was plain to all eyes that Greaser had slipped out. I remembered that on this side of the cabin there was quite a thick growth of young pine. Greaser had been able to conceal himself as he crawled toward the horses, and had probably been seen at the last moment. Herky-Jerky was the only one to make comment.

"I ain't wishin' Greaser any hard luck, but hope he carried away a couple Of 45-90 slugs somewheres in his yaller carcass."

"It'd be worth a lot to the feller who can show me a way out of this mess," said Buell, mopping the beads of sweat from his face.

I got up—it seemed to me my mind was made up for me—and walked into the light of the room.

"Buell, I can show you the way," I said, quietly.

"What!" His mouth opened in astonishment. "Speak up, then."

The other men stepped forward, and I felt their eyes upon me.

"Let me go free. Let me out of here to find Dick Leslie! Then when you go to jail in Holston for stealing lumber I'll say a good word for you and your men. There won't be any charge of kidnapping or violence."

After a long pause, during which Buell bored me with gimlet eyes, he said, in a queer voice: "Say thet again."

I repeated it, and added that he could not gain anything now by holding me a prisoner. I think he saw what I meant, but hated to believe it.

"It's too late," I said, as he hesitated.

"You mean Leslie lied an' you fooled me—you did get to Holston?" he shouted. He was quivering with rage, and the red flamed in his neck and face.

"Buell, I did get to Holston and I did send word to Washington," I went on, hurriedly for I had begun to lose my calmness. "I wrote to my father. He knows a friend of the Chief Forester who is close to the Department at Washington. By this time Holston is full of officers of the forest service. Perhaps they're already at your mill. Anyway, the game's up, and you'd better let me go."

Buell's face lost all its ruddy color, slowly blanched, and changed terribly. The boldness fled, leaving it craven, almost ghastly. Realizing he had more to fear from the law than conviction of his latest lumber steal, he made at me in blind anger.

"Hold on!" Herky-Jerky yelled, as he jumped between Buell and me.

Buell's breath was a hiss, and the words he bit between his clinched teeth were unintelligible. In that moment he would have killed me.

Herky-Jerky met his onslaught, and flung him back. Then, with his hand on the butt of his revolver, he spoke:

"Buell, hyar's where you an' me split. You've bungled your big deal. The kid stacked the deck on you. But I ain't a-goin' to see you do him harm fer it."

"Herky's right, boss," put in Bill, "thar's no sense in addin' murder to this mess. Strikes me you're in bad enough."

"So thet's your game? You're double-crossin' me now—all on a chance at kidnappin' for ransom money. Well, I'm through with the kid an' all of you. Take thet from me!"

"You skunk!" exclaimed Herky-Jerky, with the utmost cheerfulness.

"Wal, Buell," said Bill, in cool disdain, "comsiderin' my fondness fer fresh air an' open country, I can't say I'm sorry to dissolve future relashuns. I was only in jail onct, an' I couldn't breathe free."

It was then Buell went beside himself with rage. He raised his huge fists, and shook himself, and plunged about the room, cursing. Suddenly he picked up an axe, and began chopping at the rotten log above the hole where Greaser had slipped out. Bud yelled at him, so did Bill; Herky-Jerky said unpleasant things. But Buell did not hear them. He hacked and dug away like one possessed. The dull, sodden blows fell fast, scattering pieces of wood about the floor. The madness that was in Buell was the madness to get out, to escape the consequences of his acts. His grunts and pants as he worked showed his desperate energy. Then he slammed the axe against the wall, and, going down flat, began to crawl through the opening. Buell was a thick man, and the hole appeared too small. He stuck in it, but he squeezed and flattened himself, finally worked through, and disappeared.

A sudden quiet fell upon his departure.

"Hands up!"

Jim Williams's voice! It was strange to see Herky and Bud flash up their arms without turning. But I wheeled quickly. Bill, too, had his hands high in the air.

In the sunlight of the doorway stood Jim Williams. Low down, carelessly, it seemed, he held two long revolvers. He looked the same easy, slow Texan I remembered. But the smile was not now in his eyes, and his lips were set in a thin, hard line.

XVI. THE FOREST'S GREATEST FOE

Jim Williams sent out a sharp call. From the canyon-slope came answering shouts. There were sounds of heavy bodies breaking through brush, followed by the thudding of feet. Then men could be plainly heard running up the trail. Jim leaned against the door-post, and the three fellows before him stood rigid as stone.

Suddenly a form leaped past Jim. It was Dick Leslie, bareheaded, his hair standing like a lion's mane, and he had a cocked rifle in his hands. Close behind him came old Hiram Bent, slower, more cautious, but no less formidable. As these men glanced around with fiery eyes the quick look of relief that shot across their faces told of ungrounded fears.

"Where's Buell?" sharply queried Dick.

Jim Williams did not reply, and a momentary silence ensued.

"Buell lit out after the Greaser," said Bill, finally.

"Cut and run, did he? That's his speed," grimly said Dick. "Here, Bent, find some rope. We've got to tie up these jacks."

"Hands back, an' be graceful like. Quick!" sang out Jim Williams.

It seemed to me human beings could not have more eagerly and swiftly obeyed an order. Herky and Bill and Bud jerked their arms down and extended their hands out behind. After that quick action they again turned into statues. There was a breathless suspense in every act. And there was something about Jim Williams then that I did not like. I was in a cold perspiration for fear one of the men would make some kind of a move. As the very mention of the Texan had always caused a little silence, so his presence changed the atmosphere of that cabin room. Before his coming there had been the element of chance—a feeling of danger, to be sure, but a healthy spirit of give and take. That had all changed with Jim Williams's words "Hands up!" There was now something terrible hanging in the balance. I had but to look at Jim's eyes, narrow slits of blue fire, at the hard jaw and tight lips, to see a glimpse of the man who thought nothing of life. It turned me sick, and I was all in a tremor till Dick and Hiram had the men bound fast.

Then Jim dropped the long, blue guns into the holsters on his belt.

"Ken, I shore am glad to see you," said he.

The soft, drawling voice, the sleepy smile, the careless good-will all came back, utterly transforming the man. This was the Jim Williams I had come to love. With a wrench I recovered myself.

XVI. THE FOREST'S GREATEST FOE

"Are you all right, Ken?" asked Dick. And old Hiram questioned me with a worried look. This anxiety marked the difference between these men and Williams. I hastened to assure my friends that I was none the worse for my captivity.

"Ken, your little gun doesn't shoot where it points," said Jim. "I shore had a bead on the Greaser an' missed him. First Greaser I ever missed."

"You shot his ear off," I replied. "He came running back covered with blood. I never saw a man so scared."

"Wal, I shore am glad," drawled Jim.

"He made off with your mustang," said Dick.

This information lessened my gladness at Greaser's escape. Still, I would rather have had him get away on my horse than stay to be shot by Jim.

Dick called me to go outside with him. My pack was lying under one of the pines near the cabin, and examination proved that nothing had been disturbed. We found the horses grazing up the canyon. Buell had taken the horse of one of his men, and had left his own superb bay. Most likely he had jumped astride the first animal he saw. Dick said I could have Buell's splendid horse. I had some trouble in catching him, as he was restive and spirited, but I succeeded eventually, and we drove the other horses and ponies into the glade. My comrades then fell to arguing about what to do with the prisoners. Dick was for packing them off to Holston. Bent talked against this, saying it was no easy matter to drive bound men over rough trails, and Jim sided with him.

Once, while they were talking, I happened to catch Herky-Jerky's eye. He was lying on his back in the light from the door. Herky winked at me, screwed up his face in the most astonishing manner, all of which I presently made out to mean that he wanted to speak to me. So I went over to him.

"Kid, you ain't a-goin' to fergit I stalled off Buell?" whispered Herky. "He'd hev done fer you, an' thet's no lie. You won't fergit when we're rustled down to Holston?"

"I'll remember, Herky," I promised, and I meant to put in a good word for him. Because, whether or not his reasons had to do with kidnapping and ransom, he had saved me from terrible violence, perhaps death.

It was decided that we would leave the prisoners in the cabin and ride down to the sawmill. Hiram was to return at once with officers. If none could be found at the mill he was to guard the prisoners and take care of them till Dick could send officers to relieve him. Thereupon we cooked a meal, and I was put to feeding Herky and his companions. Dick ordered me especially to make them drink water, as it might be a day or longer before Hiram could get back. I made Bill drink, and easily filled up Herky; but Bud, who never drank anything save whiskey, gave me a job. He refused with a growl, and I insisted with what I felt sure was Christian patience. Still he would not drink, so I put the cup to his lips and tipped it. Bud promptly spat the water all over me. And I as promptly got another cupful and dashed it all over him.

"Bud, you'll drink or I'll drown you," I declared.

So while Bill cracked hoarse jokes and Herky swore his pleasure, I made Bud drink all he could hold. Jim got a good deal of fun out of it, but Dick and Hiram never cracked a smile. Possibly the latter two saw something far from funny in the outlook; at any rate, they were silent, almost moody, and in a hurry to be off.

Dick was so anxious to be on the trail that he helped me pack my pony, and saddled Buell's horse. It was one thing to admire the big bay from the ground, and it was another to be astride him. Target—that was his name—had a spirited temper, an iron mouth, and he had been used to a sterner hand than mine. He danced all over the glade before he decided to behave himself. Riding him, however, was such a great pleasure that a more timid boy than I would have taken the risk. He would not let any horse stay near him; he pulled on the bridle, and leaped whenever a branch brushed him. I had been on some good horses, but never on one with a swing like his, and I grew more and more possessed with the desire to let him run.

"Like as not he'll bolt with you. Hold him in, Ken!" called Dick, as he mounted. Then he shouted a final word to the prisoners, saying they would be looked after, and drove the pack-ponies into the trail. As we rode out we passed several of the horses that we had decided to leave behind, and as they wanted to follow us it was necessary to drive them back.

I had my hands full with the big, steel-jawed steed I was trying to hold in. It was the hardest work of the kind that I had ever undertaken. I had never worn spurs, but now I began to wish for them. We traveled at a good clip, as fast as the pack-ponies could go, and covered a long distance by camping-time. I was surprised that we did not get out of the canyon. The place where we camped was a bare, rocky opening, with a big pool in the center. While we were making camp it suddenly came over me that I was completely bewildered as to our whereabouts. I could not see the mountain peaks and did not know one direction from another. Even when Jim struck out of our trail and went off alone toward Holston I could not form an idea of where I was. All this, however, added to my feeling of the bigness of Penetier.

Dick was taciturn, and old Hiram, when I tried to engage him in conversation, cut me off with the remark that I would need my breath on the morrow. This somewhat offended me. So I made my bed and rolled into it. Not till I had lain quiet for a little did I realize that every bone and muscle felt utterly worn out. I seemed to deaden and stiffen more each moment. Presently Dick breathed heavily and Hiram snored. The red glow of fire paled and died. I heard the clinking of the hobbles on Target, and a step, now and then, of the other horses. The sky grew ever bluer and colder, the stars brighter and larger, and the night wind moaned in the pines. I heard a coyote bark, a trout splash in the pool, and the hoot of an owl. Then the sounds and the clear, cold night seemed to fade away.

When Dick roused me the forest was shrouded in gray, cold fog. No time was lost in getting breakfast, driving in the horses, and packing. Hardly any words were exchanged. My comrades appeared even soberer than on the day before. The fog lifted quickly that morning, and soon the sun was shining.

XVI. THE FOREST'S GREATEST FOE

We got under way at once, and took to the trail at a jog-trot. I knew my horse better and he was more used to me, which made it at least bearable to both of us. Before long the canyon widened out into the level forest land thickly studded with magnificent pines. I had again the feeling of awe and littleness. Everything was solemn and still. The morning air was cool, and dry as toast; the smell of pitch-pine choked my nostrils. We rode briskly down the broad brown aisles, across the sunny glades, under the murmuring pines.

The old hunter was leading our train, and evidently knew perfectly what he was about. Unexpectedly he halted, bringing us up short. The pack-ponies lined up behind us. Hiram looked at Dick.

"I smell smoke," he said, sniffing at the fragrant air.

Dick stared at the old hunter and likewise sniffed. I followed their lead, but all I could smell was the thick, piney odor of the forest.

"I don't catch it," replied Dick.

We continued on our journey perhaps for a quarter of a mile, and then Hiram Bent stopped again. This time he looked significantly at Dick without speaking a word.

"Ah!" exclaimed Dick. I thought his tone sounded queer, but it did not at the moment strike me forcibly. We rode on. The forest became lighter, glimpses of sky showed low down through the trees, we were nearing a slope.

For the third time the old hunter brought us to a stop, this time on the edge of a slope that led down to the rolling foot-hills. I could only stand and gaze. Those open stretches, sloping down, all green and brown and beautiful, robbed me of thought.

"Look thar!" cried Hiram Bent.

His tone startled me. I faced about, to see his powerful arm outstretched and his finger pointing. His stern face added to my sudden concern. Something was wrong with my friends. I glanced in the direction he indicated. There were two rolling slopes or steps below us, and they were like gigantic swells of a green ocean. Beyond the second one rose a long, billowy, bluish cloud. It was smoke. All at once I smelled smoke, too. It came on the fresh, strong wind.

"Forest fire!" exclaimed Dick.

"Wal, I reckon," replied Hiram, tersely. "An' look thar, an' thar!"

Far to the right and far to the left, over the green, swelling foot-hills, rose that rounded, changing line of blue cloud.

"The slash! the slash! Buell's fired the slash!" cried Dick, as one suddenly awakened. "Penetier will go!"

"Wal, I reckon. But thet's not the worst."

"You mean—"

"Mebbe we can't get out. The forest's dry as powder, an' thet's the worst wind we could have. These canyon-draws suck in the wind, an' fire will race up them fast as a hoss can run."

"Good God, man! What'll we do?"

"Wait. Mebbe it ain't so bad—yet. Now let's all listen."

The faces of my friends, more than words, terrified me. I listened with all my ears while watching with all my eyes. The line of rolling cloud expanded, seemed to burst and roll upward, to bulge and mushroom. In a few short moments it covered the second slope as far to the right and left as we could see. The under surface was a bluish white. It shot up swiftly, to spread out into immense, slow-moving clouds of creamy yellow.

"Hear thet?" Hiram Bent shook his gray head as one who listened to dire tidings.

The wind, sweeping up the slope of Penetier, carried a strong, pungent odor of burning pitch. It brought also a low roar, not like the wind in the trees or rapid-rushing water. It might have been my imagination, but I fancied it was like the sound of flames blowing through the wood of a campfire.

"Fire! Fire!" exclaimed Hiram, with another ominous shake of his head. "We must be up an' doin'."

"The forest's greatest foe! Old Penetier is doomed!" cried Dick Leslie. "That line of fire is miles long, and is spreading fast. It'll shoot up the canyons and crisscross the forest in no time. Bent, what'll we do?"

"Mebbe we can get around the line. We must, or we'll have to make tracks for the mountain, an' thet's a long chance. You take to the left an' I'll go to the right, an' we'll see how the fire's runnin'."

"What will Ken do?"

"Wal, let him stay here—no, thet won't do! We might get driven back a little an' have to circle. The safest place in this forest is where we camped. Thet's not far. Let him drive the ponies back thar an' wait."

"All right. Ken, you hustle the pack-team back to our last night's camp. Wait there for us. We won't be long."

Dick galloped off through the forest, and Hiram went down the slope in almost the opposite direction. Left alone, I turned my horse and drove the pack-ponies along our back-trail. Thus engaged, I began to recover somewhat from the terror that had stupefied me. Still, I kept looking back. I found the mouth of the canyon and the trail, and in what I thought a very short time I reached the bare, rocky spot where we had last camped. The horses all drank thirstily, and I discovered that I was hot and dry.

Then I waited. At every glance I expected to see Dick and Hiram riding up the canyon. But moments dragged by, and they did not come. Here there was no sign of smoke, nor even the faintest hint of the roar of the fire. The wind blew strongly up the canyon, and I kept turning my ear to it. In spite of the fact that my friends did not come quickly I had begun to calm my fears. They would return presently with knowledge of the course of the fire and the way to avoid it. My thoughts were mostly occupied with sorrow for beautiful Penetier. What a fiend Buell was! I had heard him say he would fire the slash, and he had kept his word.

Half an hour passed. I saw a flash of gray down the canyon, and shouted in joy. But what I thought Dick and Hiram was a herd of deer. They were running wildly. They clicked on the stones, and scarcely swerved for the pack-ponies. It took no second glance to see that they were fleeing from the fire. This brought back all my alarms, and every moment that I waited thereafter added to them. I watched the trail and under the trees for my friends, and I scanned the sky for signs of the blue-white clouds of smoke. But I saw neither.

"Dick told me to wait here; but how long shall I wait?" I muttered. "Something's happened to him. If only I could see what that fire is doing!"

The camping-place was low down between two slopes, one of which was high and had a rocky cliff standing bare in the sunlight. I conceived the idea of climbing to it. I could not sit quietly waiting any longer. So, mounting Target, I put him up the slope. It was not a steep climb, still it was long and took considerable time. Before I reached the gray cliff I looked down over the forest to see the rolling, smoky clouds. We climbed higher and still higher, till Target reached the cliff and could go no farther. Leaping off, I tied him securely and bent my efforts to getting around on top of the cliff. If I had known what a climb it was I should not have attempted it, but I could not back out with the summit looming over me. It ran up to a ragged crag. Hot, exhausted, and out of breath, I at last got there.

As I looked I shouted in surprise. It seemed that the whole of Penetier was under my feet. The green slope disappeared in murky clouds of smoke. There were great pillars and huge banks of yellow and long streaks of black, and here and there, underneath, moving splashes of red. The thing did not stay still one instant. It changed so that I could not tell what it did look like. Them were life and movement in it, and something terribly sinister. I tried to calculate how far distant the fire was and how fast it was coming, but that, in my state of mind, I could not do. The whole sweep of forest below me was burning. I felt the strong breeze and smelled the burnt wood. Puffs of white smoke ran out ahead of the main clouds, and I saw three of them widely separated. What they meant puzzled me. But all of a sudden I saw in front of the nearest a flickering gleam of red. Then I knew those white streams of smoke rose where the fire was being sucked up the canyons. They leaped along with amazing speed. It was then that I realized that Dick and Hiram had been caught by one of these offshoots of the fire, and had been compelled to turn away to save their lives. Perhaps they would both be lost. For a moment I felt faint, but I fought it off. I had to think of myself. It was every one for himself, and perhaps there was many a man caught on Penetier with only a slender chance for life.

"Oh! oh!" I cried, suddenly. "Herky, Bud, and Bill tied helpless in that cabin! Dick forgot them. They'll be burned to death!"

As I stood there, trembling at the thought of Herky and his comrades bound hand and foot, the first roar of the forest fire reached my ears. It threatened, but it roused my courage. I jumped as if I had been shot, and clattered down that crag with wings guiding my long leaps. No crevice or jumble of loose stones or steep descent daunted me. I reached the horse, and, grasping the bridle, I started to lead him. We had zigzagged up, we went straight down. Target was too spirited to balk, but he did everything else. More than once he reared with his hoofs high in the air, and, snorting, crashed down. He pulled me off my feet, he pawed at me with his great iron shoes. When we got clear of the roughest and most thickly overgrown part of the descent I mounted him. Then I needed no longer to urge him. The fire had entered the canyon, the hollow roar swept up and filled Target with the same fright that possessed me. He plunged down, slid on his haunches, jumped the logs, crashed through brush. I had continually to rein him toward the camp. He wanted to turn from that hot wind and strange roar.

We reached a level, the open, stony ground, then the pool. The pack-ponies were standing patiently with drooping heads. The sun was obscured in thin blue haze. Smoke and dust and ashes blew by with the wind. I put Target's nose down to the water, so that he would drink. Then I cut packs off the ponies, spilled the contents, and filled my pockets with whatever I could lay my hands on in the way of eatables. I hung a canteen on the pommel, and threw a bag of biscuits over the saddle and tied it fast. My fingers worked swiftly. There was a fluttering in my throat, and my sight was dim. All the time the roar of the forest fire grew louder and more ominous.

The ponies would be safe. I would be safe in the lee of the big rocks near the pool. But I did not mean to stay. I could not stay with those men lying tied up in the cabin. Herky had saved me. Still it was not that which spurred me on.

Target snorted shrilly and started back from the water, ready to stampede. Slipping the bridle into place, I snapped the bit between his teeth. I had to swing off my feet to pull his head down.

Even as I did this I felt the force of the wind. It was hard to breathe. A white tumbling column of smoke hid sky and sun. All about me it was like a blue twilight.

The appalling roar held me spellbound with my foot in the stirrup. It drew my glance even in that moment of flight.

Under the shifting cloud flashes of red followed by waves of fire raced through the tree-tops. That the forest fire traveled through the tree-tops was as new to me as it was terrible. The fire seemed to make and drive the wind. Lower down along the ground was a dull furnace-glow, now dark, now bright. It all brought into my mind a picture I had seen of the end of the world.

Target broke the spell by swinging me up into the saddle as he leaped forward with a furious snort. I struck him with the bridle, and yelled:

"You iron-jawed brute! You've been crazy to run—now run!"

XVII. THE BACK-FIRE

Target pounded over the scaly ground and thundered into the hard trail. Then he stretched out. As we cleared the last obstructing pile of rocks I looked back. There was a vast wave of fire rolling up the canyon and spreading up the slopes. It was so close that I nearly fainted. With both hands knotted and stiff I clung to the pommel in a cold horror, and I looked back no more to see the flames reaching out for me. But I could not keep the dreadful roar from filling my ears, and it weakened me so that I all but dropped from the saddle. Only an unconscious instinct to fight for life made me hold on.

Blue and white puffs of smoke swept by me. The trail was a dim, twisting line. The slopes and pines, merged in a mass, flew backward in brown sheets. Above the roar of the pursuing fire I heard the thunder of Target's hoofs. I scarcely felt him or the saddle, only a motion and the splitting of the wind.

The fear of death by fire, which had almost robbed me of strength, passed from me. My brain cleared. Still I had no kind of hope, only a desperate resolve not to give up.

The great bay horse was running to save his life and to save mine. It was a race with fire. When I thought of the horse, and saw how fast he was going, and realized that I must do my part, I was myself again.

The trail was a winding, hard-packed thread of white ground. It had been made for leisurely travel. Many turns were sudden and sharp. I loosened the reins, and cried out to Target. Evidently I had unknowingly held him in, for he lengthened out, and went on in quicker, longer leaps. In that moment riding seemed easy. I listened to the roar behind me, now a little less deafening, and began to thrill. We were running away from the fire.

Hope made the race seem different. Something stirred and beat warm within me, driving out the chill in my marrow. I leaned over the neck of the great bay horse, and called to him and cheered him on. Then I saw he was deaf and blind to me, for he was wild. He had the bit between his teeth, and was running away.

The roar behind us relentlessly pursuing, only a little less appalling, was now not my only source of peril. Target could no more be guided nor stopped than could the forest fire. The trail grew more winding and overhung more thickly by pine branches. The horse did not swerve an inch for tree or thicket, but ran as if free, and the saving of my life began to be a matter of dodging. Once a crashing blow from a branch almost knocked me from the saddle. The wind in my ears half drowned the roar behind me. With hands twisted in Target's mane I bent low, watching with keen eyes for the trees and branches ahead. I drew up my knees and bent my body, and dodged and went down flat over the pommel like a wild-riding Indian. Target kept that straining run for a longer distance than I could judge. With the same breakneck speed he thundered on over logs and little washes, through the thick, bordering bushes, and around the sudden turns. His foam moistened my face and flecked my sleeves. The wind came stinging into my face, the heavy roar followed at my back with its menace.

Swift and terrible as the forest fire was, Target was winning the race. I knew it. Steadily the roar softened, but it did not die away. Pound! pound! pound! The big bay charged up the trail. How long could he stand that killing pace? I began to talk soothingly to him, to pull on the bridle; but he might have been an avalanche for all he heeded. Still I kept at him, fighting him every moment that I was free from low branches. Gradually the strain began to tell.

The sight of a cabin brought back to my mind the meaning of the wild race with fire. I had forgotten the prisoners. I had reached the forest glade and the cabin, but Target was still going hard. What if I could not stop him! Summoning all my strength, I quickly threw weight and muscle back on the reins and snapped the bit out of his teeth. Then coaxing, commanding, I pulled him back. In the glade were four horses, standing bunched with heads and ears up, uneasy, and beginning to be frightened. Perhaps the sight of them helped me to stop Target; at any rate, he slackened his pace and halted. He was spotted with foam, dripping wet, and his broad sides heaved.

I jumped off, stiff and cramped. I could scarcely walk. The air was clear, though the fog of smoke overspread the sun. The wind blew strong with a scent of pitch. Now that I was not riding, the roar of the fire sounded close. I caught the same strange growl, the note of on-sweeping fury. Again the creepy cold went over me. I felt my face blanch, and the skin tighten over my cheeks. I dashed into the cabin, crying: "Fire! Fire! Fire!"

"Whoop! It's the kid!" yelled Herky-Jerky.

He was lying near the door, red as a brick in the face, and panting hard. In one cut I severed the rope on his feet; in another, that round his raw and bloody wrists. Herky had torn his flesh trying to release his hands.

"Kid, how'd you git back hyar?" he questioned, with his sharp little eyes glinting on me. "Did the fire chase you? Whar's Leslie?"

"Buell fired the slash. Penetier is burning. Dick and Hiram sent me back to the pool below, and then didn't come. They got caught—oh!... I'm afraid—lost!... Then I remembered you fellows. The fire's coming—it's awful—we must fly!"

"You thought of us?" Herky's voice sounded queer and strangled. "Bud! Bill! Did you hear thet? Wal, wal!"

While he muttered on I cut Bill's bonds. He rose without a word. Bud was almost unconscious. He had struggled terribly. His heels had dug a hole in the hard clay floor; his wrists were skinned; his mouth and chin covered with earth, probably from his having bitten the ground in his agony. Herky helped him up and gave him a drink from a little pocket-flask.

"Herky, if you think you've rid some in your day, look at thet hoss," said Bill, coolly, from the door. He eyed me coolly; in fact, he was as cool as if there were no fire on Penetier. But Bud was white and sick, and Herky flaming with excitement.

"We hain't got a chance. Listen! Thet roar! She's hummin'."

"It's runnin' up the draw. We don't stand no showdown in hyar. Grab a hoss now, an' we'll try to head acrost the ridge."

I remounted Target, and the three men caught horses and climbed up bareback. Bill led the way across the glade, up the slope, into the level forest. There we broke into a gallop. The air upon this higher ground was dark and thick, but not so hard to breathe as that lower down. We pressed on. For a while the roar receded, and almost deadened. Then it grew clearer again' filled out, and swelled. Bud wanted to sheer off to the left. Herky swore we were being surrounded. Bill turned a deaf ear to them. From my own sense of direction I fancied we were going wrong, but Bill was so cool he gave me courage. Soon a blue, windy haze, shrouding the giant pines ahead, caused Bill to change his course.

"Do you know whar you're headin'?" yelled Herky, high above the roar.

"I hain't got the least idee, Herky," shouted Bill, as cool as could be, "but I guess somewhar whar it'll be hot!"

We were lost in the forest and almost surrounded by fire, if the roar was anything to tell by. We galloped on, always governed by the roar, always avoiding the slope up the mountain. If we once started up that with the fire in our rear we were doomed. Perhaps there were times when the wind deceived us. It was hard to tell. Anyway, we kept on, growing more bewildered. Bud looked like a dead man already and reeled in his saddle. The horses were getting hard to manage, and the wind was strengthening and puffed at us from all quarters. Bill still looked cool, but the last vestige of color had faded from his face. These things boded ill. Herky had grown strangely silent, which fact was the worst of all for me. For that tough, scarred, reckless little wretch to hold his tongue was the last straw.

The air freshened somewhat, and the forest lightened. Almost abruptly we rode out to the edge of a great, wide canyon. It must have crossed the forest at right angles to the canyon we had left. It was twice as wide and deep as any I had yet seen. In the bottom wound a broad brook.

"Which way now?" asked Herky.

Bill shook his head. Far to our right a pall of smoke moved over the tree-tops, to our left was foggy gloom, behind rolled the unceasing roar. We all looked straight across. Probably each of us harbored the same thought. Before that wind the fire would leap the canyon in flaming bounds, and on the opposite level was the thick pitch-pine forest of Penetier proper. So far we had been among the foothills. We dared not enter the real forest with that wild-fire back of us. Momentarily we stood irresolute. It was a pause full of hopelessness, such as might have come to tired deer, close harried by hounds.

The winding brook and the brown slope, comparatively bare of trees, brought me a sudden inspiration.

"Back-fire! Back-fire!" I cried to my companions, in wild appeal. "We must back-fire. It's our chance! Here's the place!"

Bud scowled and Herky grumbled, but Bill grasped at the idea.

"I've heerd of back-firin'. The rangers do it. But how? How?"

They caught his hope, and their haggard faces lightened.

"Kid, we ain't forest rangers," said Herky. "Do you know what you're talkin' about?"

"Yes, yes! Come on! We'll back-fire!"

I led the way down the slope, and they came close at my heels. I rode into the shallow brook, and dismounted about the middle between the banks. I hung my coat on the pommel of my saddle.

"Bud, you and Bill hold the horses here!" I shouted, intensely excited. "Herky, have you matches?"

"Nary a match."

"Hyar's a box," said Bill, tossing it.

"Come on, Herky! You run up the brook. Light a match, and drop it every hundred feet. Be sure it catches. Lucky there's little wind down here. Go as far as you can. I'll run down!"

We splashed out of the brook and leaped up the bank. The grass was long and dry. There was brush near by, and the pine-needle mats almost bordered the bank. I struck a match and dropped it.

Sis-s-s! Flare! It was almost like dropping a spark into gunpowder. The flame ran quickly, reached the pine-needles, then sputtered and fizzed into a big blaze. The first pine-tree exploded and went off like a rocket. We were startled by the sound and the red, up-leaping pillar of fire. Sudden heat shot back at us as if from a furnace. Great sparks began to fall.

"It's goin'!" yelled Herky-Jerky, his voice ringing strong. He clapped his hat down on my bare head. Then he started running up-stream.

I darted in the opposite direction. I heard Bud and Bill yelling, and the angry crack and hiss of the fire. A few rods down I stopped, struck another match, and lit the grass. There was a sputter and flash. Then the flame flared up, spread like running quicksilver, and, meeting the pine-needles, changed to red. I ran on. There was a loud flutter behind me, then a crack almost like a shot, then a seething roar. Another pine had gone off. As I stopped to strike the third match there came three distinct reports, and then others that seemed dulled in a windy roar. I raced onward, daring only once to look back. A fearful sight met my gaze. The slope was a red wave. The pines were tufts of flame. The air was filled with steaming clouds of whirling smoke. Then I fled onward again.

Match after match I struck, and when the box was empty I must have been a mile, two miles, maybe more, from the starting-point. I was wringing-wet, and there was a piercing pain in my side. I plunged across the brook, and in as deep water as I could find knelt down to cover all but my face. Then, with laboring breaths that bubbled the water near my mouth, I kept still and watched.

The back-fire which I had started swept up over the slope and down the brook like a charge of red lancers. Spears of flame led the advance. The flame licked up the dry surface-grass and brush, and, meeting the pines, circled them in a whirlwind of fire, like lightning flashing upward. Then came prolonged reports, and after that a long, blistering roar in the tree-tops. Even as I gazed, appalled in the certainty of a horrible fate, I thrilled at the grand spectacle. Fire had always fascinated me. The clang of the engines and the call of "Fire!" would tear me from any task or play. But I had never known what fire was. I knew now. Storms of air and sea were nothing compared to this. It was the greatest force in nature. It was fire. On one hand, I seemed cool and calculated the chances; on the other, I had flashes in my brain, and kept crying out crazily, in a voice like a whisper: "Fire! Fire! Fire!"

But presently the wall of fire rolled by and took the roar with it. Dense billows of smoke followed, and hid everything in opaque darkness. I heard the hiss of failing sparks and the crackle of burning wood, and occasionally the crash of a failing branch. It was intolerably hot, but I could stand the heat better than the air. I coughed and strangled. I could not get my breath. My eyes smarted and burned. Crawling close under the bank, I leaned against it and waited.

Some hours must have passed. I suffered, not exactly pain, but a discomfort that was almost worse. By-and-by the air cleared a little. Rifts in the smoke drifted over me, always toward the far side of the canyon. Twice I crawled out upon the bank, but the heat drove me back into the water. The snow-water from the mountain-peaks had changed from cold to warm; still, it gave a relief from the hot blast of air. More time dragged by. Weary to the point of collapse, I grew not to care about anything.

Then the yellow fog lightened, and blew across the brook and lifted and split. The parts of the canyon-slope that I could see were seared and blackened. The pines were columns of living coals. The fire was eating into their hearts. Presently they would snap at the trunk, crash down, and burn to ashes. Wreathes of murky smoke circled them, and drifted aloft to join the overhanging clouds.

I floundered out on the bank, and began to walk up-stream. After all, it was not so very hot, but I felt queer. I did not seem to be able to step where I looked or see where I stepped. Still, that caused me no worry. The main thing was that the fire had not yet crossed the brook. I wanted to feel overjoyed at that, but I was too tired. Anyway I was sure the fire had crossed below or above. It would be tearing down on this side presently, and then I would have to crawl into the brook or burn up. It did not matter much which I had to do. Then I grew dizzy, my legs trembled, my feet lost all sense of touching the ground. I could not go much farther. Just then I heard a shout. It was close by. I answered, and heard heavy steps. I peered through the smoky haze. Something dark moved up in the gloom.

"Ho, kid! Thar you are!" I felt a strong arm go round my waist. "Wal, wal!" That was Herky. His voice sounded glad. It roused a strange eagerness in me; his rough greeting seemed to bring me back from a distance.

"All wet, but not burned none, I see. We kinder was afeared.... Say, kid, thet back-fire, now. It was a dandy. It did the biz. Our whiskers was singed, but we're safe. An' kid, it was your game, played like a man."

After that his voice grew faint, and I felt as if I were walking in a dream.

XVIII. CONCLUSION

That dreadful feeling of motion went away, and I became unconscious of everything. When I awoke the sun was gleaming dimly through thin films of smoke. I was lying in a pleasant little ravine with stunted pines fringing its slopes. The brook bowled merrily over stones.

Bud snored in the shade of a big boulder. Herky whistled as he broke dead branches into fagots for a campfire. Bill was nowhere in sight. I saw several of the horses browsing along the edge of the water.

My drowsy eyelids fell back again. When I awoke a long time seemed to have passed. The air was clearer, the sky darker, and the sun had gone behind the peaks. I saw Bill and Herky skinning a deer.

"Where are we?" I asked, sitting up.

"Hello, kid!" replied Herky, cheerily. "We come up to the head of the canyon, thet's all. How're you feelin'?"

"I'm all right, only tired. Where's the forest fire?"

"It's most burned out by now. It didn't jump the canyon into the big forest. Thet back-fire did the biz. Say, kid, wasn't settin' off them pines an' runnin' fer your life jest like bein' in a battle?"

"It certainly was. Herky, how long will we be penned up here?"

"Only a day or two. I reckon we'd better not risk takin' you back to Holston till we're sure about the fire. Anyways, kid, you need rest. You're all played out."

Indeed, I was so weary that it took an effort to lift my hand. A strange lassitude made me indifferent. But Herky's calm mention of taking me back to Holston changed the color of my mood. I began to feel more cheerful. The meal we ate was scant enough—biscuits and steaks of broiled venison with a pinch of salt; but, starved as we were, it was more than satisfactory. Herky and Bill were absurdly eager to serve me. Even Bud was kind to me, though he still wore conspicuously over his forehead the big bruise I had given him. After I had eaten I began to gain strength. But my face was puffed from the heat, my injured arm was stiff and sore, and my legs seemed never to have been used before.

Darkness came on quickly. The dew fell heavily, and the air grew chilly. Our blazing campfire was a comfort. Bud and Bill carried in logs for firewood, while Herky made me a bed of dry pine needles.

"It'll be some cold tonight," he said, "an' we'll hev to hug the fire. Now if we was down in the foot-hills we'd be warmer, hey? Look thar!"

He pointed down the ravine, and I saw a great white arc of light extending up into the steely sky.

"The forest fire?"

"Yep, she's burnin' some. But you oughter seen it last night. Not thet it ain't worth seein' jest now. Come along with me."

He led me where the ravine opened wide. I felt, rather than saw, a steep slope beneath. Far down was a great patch of fire. It was like a crazy quilt, here dark, there light, with streaks and stars and streams of fire shining out of the blackness. Masses of slow-moving smoke overhung the brighter areas. The night robbed the forest fire of its fierceness and lent it a kind of glory. The fire had ceased to move; it had spent its force, run its race, and was now dying. But I could not forget what it had been, what it had done. Thousands of acres of magnificent pines had perished. The shade and color and beauty of that part of the forest had gone. The heart of the great trees was now slowly rolling away in those dark, weird clouds of smoke. I was sad for the loss and sick with fear for Dick and Hiram.

Herky must have known my mind.

"You needn't feel bad, kid. Thet's only a foothill or so of Penetier gone up in smoke. An' Buell's sawmill went, too. It's almost a sure thing thet Leslie an' old Bent got out safe, though they must be doin' some tall worryin' about you. I wonder how they feel about me an' Bud an' Bill? A little prematoore roastin' for us, eh? Wal, wal!"

We went back to the camp. I lay down near the fire and fell asleep. Some time in the night I awoke. The fire was still burning brightly. Bud and Bill were lying with their backs to it almost close enough to scorch. Herky sat in his shirtsleeves. The smoke of his pipe and the smoke of the campfire wafted up together. Then I saw and felt that he had covered me with his coat and vest.

I slept far into the next day. Herky was in camp alone. The others had gone, Herky said, and he would not tell me where. He did not appear as cheerful as usual. I suspected he had quarreled with his companions, very likely about what was to be done with me. The day passed, and again I slept. Herky awakened me before it was light.

"Come, kid, we'll rustle in to Holston today."

We cooked our breakfast of venison, and then Herky went in search of the horses. They had browsed far up the ravine, and the dawn had broken by the time he returned. Target stood well to be saddled, nor did he bolt when I climbed up. Perhaps that ride I gave him had chastened and subdued his spirit. Well, it had nearly killed me. Herky mounted the one horse left, a sorry-looking pack-pony, and we started down the ravine.

An hour of steady descent passed by before we caught sight of any burned forest land. Then as we descended into the big canyon we turned a curve and saw, far ahead to the left, a black, smoky, hideous slope. We kept to the right side of the brook and sheered off just as we reached a point opposite, where the burned line began. Fire had run up that side till checked by bare weathered slopes and cliffs. As far down the brook as eye could see through the smoky haze there stretched that black line of charred, spear-pointed pines, some glowing, some blazing, all smoking.

From time to time, as we climbed up the slope, I looked back. The higher I got the more hideous became the outlook over the burned district. I was glad when Herky led the way into the deep shade of level forest, shutting out the view. It would take a hundred years to reforest those acres denuded of their timber by the fire of a few days. But as hour after hour went by, with our trail leading through miles and miles of the same old forest that had bewitched me, I began to feel a little less grief at the thought of what the fire had destroyed. It was a loss, yet only a small part of vast Penetier. If only my friends had gotten out alive!

Herky was as relentless in his travelling as I had found him in some other ways. He kept his pony at a trot. The trail was open, we made fast time, and when the sun had begun to cast a shadow before us we were going down-hill. Busy with the thought of my friends, I scarcely noted the passing of time. It was a surprise to me when we rode down the last little foot-hill, out into the scattered pines, and saw Holston only a few miles across the sage-flat.

"Wal, kid, we've come to the partin' of the ways," said Herky, with a strange smile on his smug face.

"Herky, won't you ride in with me?"

"Naw, I reckon it'd not be healthy fer me."

"But you haven't even a saddle or blanket or any grub."

"I've a friend across hyar a ways, a rancher, an' he'll fix me up. But, kid, I'd like to hev thet hoss. He was Buell's, an' Buell owed me money. Now I calkilate you can't take Target back East with you, an' you might as well let me have him."

"Sure, Herky." I jumped off at once, led the horse over, and held out the bridle. Herky dismounted, and began fumbling with the stirrup straps.

"Your legs are longer'n mine," he explained.

"Oh yes, Herky, I almost forgot to return your hat," I said, removing the wide sombrero. It had a wonderful band made of horsehair and a buckle of silver with a strange device.

"Wal, you keep the hat," he replied, with his back turned. "Greaser stole your hoss an' your outfit's lost, an' you might want somethin' to remember your—your friends in Arizony.... Thet hat ain't much, but, say, the buckle was an Injun's I shot, an' I made the band when I was in jail in Yuma."

"Thank you, Herky. I'll keep it, though I'd never need anything to make me remember Arizona—or you."

Herky swung his bow-legs over Target and I got astride the lean-backed pony. There did not seem to be any more to say, yet we both lingered.

"Good-bye, Herky, I'm glad I met you," I said, offering my hand.

He gave it a squeeze that nearly crushed my fingers. His keen little eyes gleamed, but he turned away without another word, and, slapping Target on the flank, rode off under the trees.

I put the hat back on my head and watched Herky for a moment. His silence and abrupt manner were unlike him, but what struck me most was the fact that in our last talk every word had been clean and sincere. Somehow it pleased me. Then I started the pony toward Holston.

He was tired and I was ready to drop, and those last few miles were long. We reached the outskirts of the town perhaps a couple of hours before sundown. A bank of clouds had spread out of the west and threatened rain.

The first person I met was Cless, and he put the pony in his corral and hurried me round to the hotel. On the way he talked so fast and said so much that I was bewildered before we got there. The office was full of men, and Cless shouted to them. There was the sound of a chair scraping hard on the floor, then I felt myself clasped by brawny arms. After that all was rather hazy in my mind. I saw Dick and Jim and old Hiram, though, I could not see them distinctly, and I heard them all talking, all questioning at once. Then I was talking in a somewhat silly way, I thought, and after that some one gave me a hot, nasty drink, and I felt the cool sheets of a bed.

The next morning all was clear. Dick came to my room and tried to keep me in bed, but I refused to stay. We went down to breakfast, and sat at a table with Jim and Hiram. It seemed to me that I could not answer any questions till I had asked a thousand.

What news had they for me? Buell had escaped, after firing the slash. His sawmill and lumber-camp and fifty thousand acres of timber had been burned. The fire had in some way been confined to the foot-hills. It had rained all night, so the danger of spreading was now over. My letter had brought the officers of the forest service; even the Chief, who had been travelling west over the Santa Fe, had stopped off and was in Holston then. There had been no arrests, nor would there be, unless Buell or Stockton could be found. A new sawmill was to be built by the service. Buell's lumbermen would have employment in the mill and as rangers in the forest.

But I was more interested in matters which Dick seemed to wish to avoid.

"How did you get out of the burning forest?" I asked, for the second time.

"We didn't get out. We went back to the pool where we sent you. The pack-ponies were there, but you were gone. By George! I was mad, and then I was just broken up. I was... afraid you'd been burned. We weathered the fire all right, and then rode in to Holston. Now the mystery is where were you?"

"Then you saved all the ponies?"

"Yes, and brought your outfit in. But, Ken, we—that was awful of us to forget those poor fellows tied fast in the cabin." Dick looked haggard, there was a dark gloom in his eyes, and he gulped. Then I knew why he avoided certain references to the fire. "To be burned alive... horrible! I'll never get over it. It'll haunt me always. Of course we had to save our own lives; we had no time to go to them. Yet—"

"Don't let it worry you, Dick," I interrupted.

"What do you mean?" he asked, slowly.

XVIII. CONCLUSION

"Why, I beat the fire up to the cabin, that's all. Buell's horse can run some. I cut the men loose, and we made up across the ridge, got lost, surrounded by fire, and then I got Herky to help me start a back-fire in that big canyon."

"Back-fire!" exclaimed Dick, slamming the table with his big fist. Then he settled down and looked at me. Hiram looked at me. Jim looked at me, and not one of them said a word for what seemed a long time. It brought the blood to my face. But for all my embarrassment it was sweet praise. At last Dick broke the silence.

"Ken Ward, this stumps me I... Tell us about it."

So I related my adventures from the moment they had left me till we met again.

"It was a wild boy's trick, Ken—that ride in the very face of fire in a dry forest. But, thank God, you saved the lives of those fellows." "Amen!" exclaimed old Hiram, fervently. "My lad, you saved Penetier, too; thar's no doubt on it. The fire was sweepin' up the canyon, an' it would have crossed the brook somewhars in thet stretch you back-fired."

"Ken, you shore was born in Texas," drawl Jim Williams.

His remark was unrelated to our talk, I did not know what he meant by it; nevertheless it pleased me more than anything that had ever been said me in my life.

Then came the reading of letters that had a rived for me. In Hal's letter, first and last harped on having been left behind. Father sent me a check, and wrote that in the event of a trouble in the lumber district he trusted me to take the first train for Harrisburg. That, I knew, meant that I must get out of my ragged clothes. That I did, and packed them up—all except Herky sombrero, which I wore. Then I went to the railroad station to see the schedule, and I compromised with father by deciding to take the limited. The fast east-bound train had gone a little before, and the next one did not leave until six o'clock. They would give me half a day with my friends.

When I returned to the hotel Dick was looking for me. He carried me off upstairs to a hall full of men. At one end were tables littered with papers, and here men were signing their name Dick explained that forest rangers were being paid and new ones hired. Then he introduced me officers of the service and the Chief. I knew by the way they looked at me that Dick had been talking. It made me so tongue-tied that I could not find my voice when the Chief spoke to me and shook my hand warmly. He was a tall man, with a fine face and kind eyes and hair just touched with gray.

"Kenneth Ward," he went on, pleasantly, "I hope that letter of introduction I dictated for you some time ago has been of some service."

"I haven't had a chance to use it yet," I blurted out, and I dived into my pocket to bring forth the letter. It was wrinkled, soiled, and had been soaked with water. I began to apologize for its disreputable appearance when he interrupted me.

"I've heard about the ducking you got and all the rest of it," he said, smiling. Then his manner changed to one of business and hurry.

"You are studying forestry?"

"Yes, sir. I'm going to college this fall."

"My friend in Harrisburg wrote me of your ambition and, I may say, aptness for the forest service. I'm very much pleased. We need a host of bright young fellows. Here, look at this map."

He drew my attention to a map lying on the table, and made crosses and tracings with a pencil while he talked.

"This is Penetier. Here are the Arizona Peaks. The heavy shading represents timbered land. All these are canyons. Here's Oak Creek Canyon, the one the fire bordered. Now I want you to tell me how you worked that back-fire, and, if you can, mark the line you fired."

This appeared to me an easy task, and certainly one I was enthusiastic over. I told him just how I had come to the canyon, and how I saw that the fire would surely cross there, and that a back-fire was the only chance. Then, carefully studying the map, I marked off the three miles Herky and I had fired.

"Very good. You had help in this?"

"Yes. A fellow called Herky-Jerky. He was one of Buell's men who kept me a prisoner."

"But he turned out a pretty good sort, didn't he?"

"Indeed, yes, sir."

"Well, I'll try to locate him, and offer him a job in the service. Now, Mr. Ward, you've had special opportunities; you have an eye in your head, and you are interested in forestry. Perhaps you can help us. Personally I shall be most pleased to hear what you think might be done in Penetier."

I gasped and stared, and could scarcely believe my ears. But he was not joking; he was as serious as if he had addressed himself to one of his officers. I looked at them all, standing interested and expectant. Dick was as grave and erect as a deacon. Jim seemed much impressed. But old Hiram Bent, standing somewhat back of the others, deliberately winked at me.

But for that wink I never could have seized my opportunity. It made me remember my talks with Hiram. So I boiled down all that I had learned and launched it on the Chief. Whether I was brief or not, I was out of breath when I stopped. He appeared much surprised.

"Thank you," he said, finally. "You certainly have been observant." Then he turned to his officers. "Gentlemen, here's a new point of view from first-hand observation. I call it splendid conservation. It's in the line of my policy. It considers the settler and lumberman instead of combating him."

He shook hands with me again. "You may be sure I'll not lose sight of you. Of course you will be coming West next summer, after your term at college?"

"Yes, sir, I want to—if Dick—"

He smiled as I hesitated. That man read my mind like an open book.

"Mr. Leslie goes to the Coconina Forest as head forest ranger. Mr. Williams goes as his assistant. And I have appointed Mr. Bent game warden in the same forest. You may spend next summer with them."

I stammered some kind of thanks, and found myself going out and down-stairs with my friends.

XVIII. CONCLUSION

"Oh, Dick! Wasn't he fine?... Say, where's Coconina Forest?"

"It's over across the desert and beyond the Grand Canyon of Arizona. Penetier is tame compared to Coconina. I'm afraid to let you come out there."

"I don't have to ask you, Mr. Dick," I replied.

"Lad, I'll need a young fellar bad next summer," said old Hiram, with twinkling eyes. "One as can handle a rope, an' help tie up lions an' sich."

"Oh! my bear cub! I'd forgotten him. I wanted to take him home."

"Wal, thar weren't no sense in thet, youngster, fer you couldn't do it. He was a husky cub."

"I hate to give up my mustang, too. Dick, have you heard of the Greaser?"

"Not yet, but he'll be trailing into Holston before long."

Jim Williams removed his pipe, and puffed a cloud of white smoke.

"Ken, I shore ain't fergot Greaser," he drawled with his slow smile. "Hev you any pertickler thing you want did to him?"

"Jim, don't kill him!" I burst out, impetuously, and then paused, frightened out of speech. Why I was afraid of him I did not know, he seemed so easy-going, so careless—almost sweet, like a woman; but then I had seen his face once with a look that I could never forget.

"Wal, Ken, I'll dodge Greaser if he ever crosses my trail again."

That promise was a relief. I knew Greaser would come to a bad end, and certainly would get his just deserts; but I did not want him punished any more for what he had done to me.

Those last few hours sped like winged moments. We talked and planned a little, I divided my outfit among my friends, and then it was time for the train. That limited train had been late, so they said, every day for a week, and this day it was on time to the minute. I had no luck.

My friends bade me good-bye as if they expected to see me next day, and I said good-bye calmly. I had my part to play. My short stay with them had made me somehow different. But my coolness was deceitful. Dick helped me on the train and wrung my hand again.

"Good-bye, Ken. It's been great to have you out.... Next year you'll be back in the forests!"

He had to hurry to get off. The train started as I looked out of my window. There stood the powerful hunter, his white head bare, and he was waving his hat. Jim leaned against a railing with his sleepy, careless smile. I caught a gleam of the blue gun swinging at his hip. Dick's eyes shone warm and blue; he was shouting something. Then they all passed back out of sight. So my gaze wandered to the indistinct black line of Penetier, to the purple slopes, and up to the cold, white mountain-peaks, and Dick's voice rang in my ears like a prophecy: "You'll be back in the forests."

RIDERS OF THE PURPLE SAGE

CHAPTER I. LASSITER

A sharp clip-crop of iron-shod hoofs deadened and died away, and clouds of yellow dust drifted from under the cottonwoods out over the sage.

Jane Withersteen gazed down the wide purple slope with dreamy and troubled eyes. A rider had just left her and it was his message that held her thoughtful and almost sad, awaiting the churchmen who were coming to resent and attack her right to befriend a Gentile.

She wondered if the unrest and strife that had lately come to the little village of Cottonwoods was to involve her. And then she sighed, remembering that her father had founded this remotest border settlement of southern Utah and that he had left it to her. She owned all the ground and many of the cottages. Withersteen House was hers, and the great ranch, with its thousands of cattle, and the swiftest horses of the sage. To her belonged Amber Spring, the water which gave verdure and beauty to the village and made living possible on that wild purple upland waste. She could not escape being involved by whatever befell Cottonwoods.

That year, 1871, had marked a change which had been gradually coming in the lives of the peace-loving Mormons of the border. Glaze—Stone Bridge—Sterling, villages to the north, had risen against the invasion of Gentile settlers and the forays of rustlers. There had been opposition to the one and fighting with the other. And now Cottonwoods had begun to wake and bestir itself and grown hard.

Jane prayed that the tranquillity and sweetness of her life would not be permanently disrupted. She meant to do so much more for her people than she had done. She wanted the sleepy quiet pastoral days to last always. Trouble between the Mormons and the Gentiles of the community would make her unhappy. She was Mormon-born, and she was a friend to poor and unfortunate Gentiles. She wished only to go on doing good and being happy. And she thought of what that great ranch meant to her. She loved it all—the grove of cottonwoods, the old stone house, the amber-tinted water, and the droves of shaggy, dusty horses and mustangs, the sleek, clean-limbed, blooded racers, and the browsing herds of cattle and the lean, sun-browned riders of the sage.

While she waited there she forgot the prospect of untoward change. The bray of a lazy burro broke the afternoon quiet, and it was comfortingly suggestive of the drowsy farmyard, and the open corrals, and the green alfalfa fields. Her clear sight intensified the purple sage-slope as it rolled before her. Low swells of prairie-like ground sloped up to the west. Dark, lonely cedar-trees, few and far between, stood out strikingly, and at long distances ruins of red rocks. Farther on, up the gradual slope, rose a broken wall, a huge monument, looming dark purple and stretching its solitary, mystic way, a wavering line that faded in the north. Here to the westward was the light and color and beauty. Northward the slope descended to a dim line of canyons from which rose an up-flinging of the earth, not mountainous, but a vast heave of purple uplands, with ribbed and fan-shaped walls, castle-crowned cliffs, and gray escarpments. Over it all crept the lengthening, waning afternoon shadows.

The rapid beat of hoofs recalled Jane Withersteen to the question at hand. A group of riders cantered up the lane, dismounted, and threw their bridles. They were seven in number, and Tull, the leader, a tall, dark man, was an elder of Jane's church.

"Did you get my message?" he asked, curtly.

"Yes," replied Jane.

"I sent word I'd give that rider Venters half an hour to come down to the village. He didn't come."

"He knows nothing of it;" said Jane. "I didn't tell him. I've been waiting here for you."

"Where is Venters?"

"I left him in the courtyard."

"Here, Jerry," called Tull, turning to his men, "take the gang and fetch Venters out here if you have to rope him."

The dusty-booted and long-spurred riders clanked noisily into the grove of cottonwoods and disappeared in the shade.

"Elder Tull, what do you mean by this?" demanded Jane. "If you must arrest Venters you might have the courtesy to wait till he leaves my home. And if you do arrest him it will be adding insult to injury. It's absurd to accuse Venters of being mixed up in that shooting fray in the village last night. He was with me at the time. Besides, he let me take charge of his guns. You're only using this as a pretext. What do you mean to do to Venters?"

"I'll tell you presently," replied Tull. "But first tell me why you defend this worthless rider?"

"Worthless!" exclaimed Jane, indignantly. "He's nothing of the kind. He was the best rider I ever had. There's not a reason why I shouldn't champion him and every reason why I should. It's no little shame to me, Elder Tull, that through my friendship he has roused the enmity of my people and become an outcast. Besides I owe him eternal gratitude for saving the life of little Fay."

"I've heard of your love for Fay Larkin and that you intend to adopt her. But—Jane Withersteen, the child is a Gentile!"

"Yes. But, Elder, I don't love the Mormon children any less because I love a Gentile child. I shall adopt Fay if her mother will give her to me."

"I'm not so much against that. You can give the child Mormon teaching," said Tull. "But I'm sick of seeing this fellow Venters hang around you. I'm going to put a stop to it. You've so much love to throw away on these beggars of Gentiles that I've an idea you might love Venters."

Tull spoke with the arrogance of a Mormon whose power could not be brooked and with the passion of a man in whom jealousy had kindled a consuming fire.

"Maybe I do love him," said Jane. She felt both fear and anger stir her heart. "I'd never thought of that. Poor fellow! he certainly needs some one to love him."

"This'll be a bad day for Venters unless you deny that," returned Tull, grimly.

Tull's men appeared under the cottonwoods and led a young man out into the lane. His ragged clothes were those of an outcast. But he stood tall and straight, his wide shoulders flung back, with the muscles of his bound arms rippling and a blue flame of defiance in the gaze he bent on Tull.

For the first time Jane Withersteen felt Venters's real spirit. She wondered if she would love this splendid youth. Then her emotion cooled to the sobering sense of the issue at stake.

"Venters, will you leave Cottonwoods at once and forever?" asked Tull, tensely.

"Why?" rejoined the rider.

"Because I order it."

Venters laughed in cool disdain.

The red leaped to Tull's dark cheek.

"If you don't go it means your ruin," he said, sharply.

"Ruin!" exclaimed Venters, passionately. "Haven't you already ruined me? What do you call ruin? A year ago I was a rider. I had horses and cattle of my own. I had a good name in Cottonwoods. And now when I come into the village to see this woman you set your men on me. You hound me. You trail me as if I were a rustler. I've no more to lose—except my life."

"Will you leave Utah?"

"Oh! I know," went on Venters, tauntingly, "it galls you, the idea of beautiful Jane Withersteen being friendly to a poor Gentile. You want her all yourself. You're a wiving Mormon. You have use for her—and Withersteen House and Amber Spring and seven thousand head of cattle!"

Tull's hard jaw protruded, and rioting blood corded the veins of his neck.

"Once more. Will you go?"

"NO!"

"Then I'll have you whipped within an inch of your life," replied Tull, harshly. "I'll turn you out in the sage. And if you ever come back you'll get worse."

Venters's agitated face grew coldly set and the bronze changed

Jane impulsively stepped forward. "Oh! Elder Tull!" she cried. "You won't do that!"

Tull lifted a shaking finger toward her.

"That'll do from you. Understand, you'll not be allowed to hold this boy to a friendship that's offensive to your Bishop. Jane Withersteen, your father left you wealth and power. It has turned your head. You haven't yet come to see the place of Mormon women. We've reasoned with you, borne with you. We've patiently waited. We've let you have your fling, which is more than I ever saw granted to a Mormon woman. But you haven't come to your senses. Now, once for all, you can't have any further friendship with Venters. He's going to be whipped, and he's got to leave Utah!"

"Oh! Don't whip him! It would be dastardly!" implored Jane, with slow certainty of her failing courage.

Tull always blunted her spirit, and she grew conscious that she had feigned a boldness which she did not possess. He loomed up now in different guise, not as a jealous suitor, but embodying the mysterious despotism she had known from childhood—the power of her creed.

"Venters, will you take your whipping here or would you rather go out in the sage?" asked Tull. He smiled a flinty smile that was more than inhuman, yet seemed to give out of its dark aloofness a gleam of righteousness.

"I'll take it here—if I must," said Venters. "But by God!—Tull you'd better kill me outright. That'll be a dear whipping for you and your praying Mormons. You'll make me another Lassiter!"

The strange glow, the austere light which radiated from Tull's face, might have been a holy joy at the spiritual conception of exalted duty. But there was something more in him, barely hidden, a something personal and sinister, a deep of himself, an engulfing abyss. As his religious mood was fanatical and inexorable, so would his physical hate be merciless.

"Elder, I—I repent my words," Jane faltered. The religion in her, the long habit of obedience, of humility, as well as agony of fear, spoke in her voice. "Spare the boy!" she whispered.

"You can't save him now," replied Tull stridently.

Her head was bowing to the inevitable. She was grasping the truth, when suddenly there came, in inward constriction, a hardening of gentle forces within her breast. Like a steel bar it was stiffening all that had been soft and weak in her. She felt a birth in her of something new and unintelligible. Once more her strained gaze sought the sage-slopes. Jane Withersteen loved that wild and purple wilderness. In times of sorrow it had been her strength, in happiness its beauty was her continual delight. In her extremity she found herself murmuring, "Whence cometh my help!" It was a prayer, as if forth from those lonely purple reaches and walls of red and clefts of blue might ride a fearless man, neither creed-bound nor creed-mad, who would hold up a restraining hand in the faces of her ruthless people.

The restless movements of Tull's men suddenly quieted down. Then followed a low whisper, a rustle, a sharp exclamation.

"Look!" said one, pointing to the west.

"A rider!"

Jane Withersteen wheeled and saw a horseman, silhouetted against the western sky, coming riding out of the sage. He had ridden down from the left, in the golden glare of the sun, and had been unobserved till close at hand. An answer to her prayer!

"Do you know him? Does any one know him?" questioned Tull, hurriedly.

His men looked and looked, and one by one shook their heads.

"He's come from far," said one.

"Thet's a fine hoss," said another.

"A strange rider."

"Huh! he wears black leather," added a fourth.

With a wave of his hand, enjoining silence, Tull stepped forward in such a way that he concealed Venters.

The rider reined in his mount, and with a lithe forward-slipping action appeared to reach the ground in one long step. It was a peculiar movement in its quickness and inasmuch that while performing it the rider did not swerve in the slightest from a square front to the group before him.

"Look!" hoarsely whispered one of Tull's companions. "He packs two black-butted guns—low down—they're hard to see—black akin them black chaps."

"A gun-man!" whispered another. "Fellers, careful now about movin' your hands."

The stranger's slow approach might have been a mere leisurely manner of gait or the cramped short steps of a rider unused to walking; yet, as well, it could have been the guarded advance of one who took no chances with men.

"Hello, stranger!" called Tull. No welcome was in this greeting only a gruff curiosity.

The rider responded with a curt nod. The wide brim of a black sombrero cast a dark shade over his face. For a moment he closely regarded Tull and his comrades, and then, halting in his slow walk, he seemed to relax.

"Evenin', ma'am," he said to Jane, and removed his sombrero with quaint grace.

Jane, greeting him, looked up into a face that she trusted instinctively and which riveted her attention. It had all the characteristics of the range rider's—the leanness, the red burn of the sun, and the set changelessness that came from years of silence and solitude. But it was not these which held her, rather the intensity of his gaze, a strained weariness, a piercing wistfulness of keen, gray sight, as if the man was forever looking for that which he never found. Jane's subtle woman's intuition, even in that brief instant, felt a sadness, a hungering, a secret.

"Jane Withersteen, ma'am?" he inquired.

"Yes," she replied.

"The water here is yours?"

"Yes."

"May I water my horse?"

"Certainly. There's the trough."

"But mebbe if you knew who I was—" He hesitated, with his glance on the listening men. "Mebbe you wouldn't let me water him—though I ain't askin' none for myself."

"Stranger, it doesn't matter who you are. Water your horse. And if you are thirsty and hungry come into my house."

"Thanks, ma'am. I can't accept for myself—but for my tired horse—"

Trampling of hoofs interrupted the rider. More restless movements on the part of Tull's men broke up the little circle, exposing the prisoner Venters.

"Mebbe I've kind of hindered somethin'—for a few moments, perhaps?" inquired the rider.

"Yes," replied Jane Withersteen, with a throb in her voice.

She felt the drawing power of his eyes; and then she saw him look at the bound Venters, and at the men who held him, and their leader.

"In this here country all the rustlers an' thieves an' cut-throats an' gun-throwers an' all-round no-good men jest happen to be Gentiles. Ma'am, which of the no-good class does that young feller belong to?"

"He belongs to none of them. He's an honest boy."

"You KNOW that, ma'am?"

"Yes—yes."

"Then what has he done to get tied up that way?"

His clear and distinct question, meant for Tull as well as for Jane Withersteen, stilled the restlessness and brought a momentary silence.

"Ask him," replied Jane, her voice rising high.

The rider stepped away from her, moving out with the same slow, measured stride in which he had approached, and the fact that his action placed her wholly to one side, and him no nearer to Tull and his men, had a penetrating significance.

"Young feller, speak up," he said to Venters.

"Here stranger, this's none of your mix," began Tull. "Don't try any interference. You've been asked to drink and eat. That's more than you'd have got in any other village of the Utah border. Water your horse and be on your way."

"Easy—easy—I ain't interferin' yet," replied the rider. The tone of his voice had undergone a change. A different man had spoken. Where, in addressing Jane, he had been mild and gentle, now, with his first speech to Tull, he was dry, cool, biting. "I've lest stumbled onto a queer deal. Seven Mormons all packin' guns, an' a Gentile tied with a rope, an' a woman who swears by his honesty! Queer, ain't that?"

"Queer or not, it's none of your business," retorted Tull.

"Where I was raised a woman's word was law. I ain't quite outgrowed that yet."

Tull fumed between amaze and anger.

"Meddler, we have a law here something different from woman's whim—Mormon law!... Take care you don't transgress it."

"To hell with your Mormon law!"

The deliberate speech marked the rider's further change, this time from kindly interest to an awakening menace. It produced a transformation in Tull and his companions. The leader gasped and staggered backward at a blasphemous affront to an institution he held most sacred. The man Jerry, holding the horses, dropped the bridles and froze in his tracks. Like posts the other men stood watchful-eyed, arms hanging rigid, all waiting.

"Speak up now, young man. What have you done to be roped that way?"

"It's a damned outrage!" burst out Venters. "I've done no wrong. I've offended this Mormon Elder by being a friend to that woman."

"Ma'am, is it true—what he says?" asked the rider of Jane, but his quiveringly alert eyes never left the little knot of quiet men.

"True? Yes, perfectly true," she answered.

"Well, young man, it seems to me that bein' a friend to such a woman would be what you wouldn't want to help an' couldn't help.... What's to be done to you for it?"

"They intend to whip me. You know what that means—in Utah!"

"I reckon," replied the rider, slowly.

With his gray glance cold on the Mormons, with the restive bit-champing of the horses, with Jane failing to repress her mounting agitations, with Venters standing pale and still, the tension of the moment tightened. Tull broke the spell with a laugh, a laugh without mirth, a laugh that was only a sound betraying fear.

"Come on, men!" he called.

Jane Withersteen turned again to the rider.

"Stranger, can you do nothing to save Venters?"

"Ma'am, you ask me to save him—from your own people?"

"Ask you? I beg of you!"

"But you don't dream who you're askin'."

"Oh, sir, I pray you—save him!"

"These are Mormons, an' I..."

"At—at any cost—save him. For I—I care for him!"

Tull snarled. "You love-sick fool! Tell your secrets. There'll be a way to teach you what you've never learned.... Come men out of here!"

"Mormon, the young man stays," said the rider.

Like a shot his voice halted Tull.

"What!"

"Who'll keep him? He's my prisoner!" cried Tull, hotly. "Stranger, again I tell you—don't mix here. You've meddled enough. Go your way now or—"

"Listen!... He stays."

Absolute certainty, beyond any shadow of doubt, breathed in the rider's low voice.

"Who are you? We are seven here."

The rider dropped his sombrero and made a rapid movement, singular in that it left him somewhat crouched, arms bent and stiff, with the big black gun-sheaths swung round to the fore.

"LASSITER!"

It was Venters's wondering, thrilling cry that bridged the fateful connection between the rider's singular position and the dreaded name.

Tull put out a groping hand. The life of his eyes dulled to the gloom with which men of his fear saw the approach of death. But death, while it hovered over him, did not descend, for the rider waited for the twitching fingers, the downward flash of hand that did not come. Tull, gathering himself together, turned to the horses, attended by his pale comrades.

CHAPTER II. COTTONWOODS

Venters appeared too deeply moved to speak the gratitude his face expressed. And Jane turned upon the rescuer and gripped his hands. Her smiles and tears seemingly dazed him. Presently as something like calmness returned, she went to Lassiter's weary horse.

"I will water him myself," she said, and she led the horse to a trough under a huge old cottonwood. With nimble fingers she loosened the bridle and removed the bit. The horse snorted and bent his head. The trough was of solid stone, hollowed out, moss-covered and green and wet and cool, and the clear brown water that fed it spouted and splashed from a wooden pipe.

"He has brought you far to-day?"

"Yes, ma'am, a matter of over sixty miles, mebbe seventy."

"A long ride—a ride that—Ah, he is blind!"

"Yes, ma'am," replied Lassiter.

"What blinded him?"

"Some men once roped an' tied him, an' then held white-iron close to his eyes."

"Oh! Men? You mean devils.... Were they your enemies—Mormons?"

"Yes, ma'am."

"To take revenge on a horse! Lassiter, the men of my creed are unnaturally cruel. To my everlasting sorrow I confess it. They have been driven, hated, scourged till their hearts have hardened. But we women hope and pray for the time when our men will soften."

"Beggin' your pardon, ma'am—that time will never come."

"Oh, it will!... Lassiter, do you think Mormon women wicked? Has your hand been against them, too?"

"No. I believe Mormon women are the best and noblest, the most long-sufferin', and the blindest, unhappiest women on earth."

"Ah!" She gave him a grave, thoughtful look. "Then you will break bread with me?"

Lassiter had no ready response, and he uneasily shifted his weight from one leg to another, and turned his sombrero round and round in his hands. "Ma'am," he began, presently, "I reckon your kindness of heart makes you overlook things. Perhaps I ain't well known hereabouts, but back up North there's Mormons who'd rest uneasy in their graves at the idea of me sittin' to table with you."

"I dare say. But—will you do it, anyway?" she asked.

"Mebbe you have a brother or relative who might drop in an' be offended, an' I wouldn't want to—"

"I've not a relative in Utah that I know of. There's no one with a right to question my actions." She turned smilingly to Venters. "You will come in, Bern, and Lassiter will come in. We'll eat and be merry while we may."

"I'm only wonderin' if Tull an' his men'll raise a storm down in the village," said Lassiter, in his last weakening stand.

"Yes, he'll raise the storm—after he has prayed," replied Jane. "Come."

She led the way, with the bridle of Lassiter's horse over her arm. They entered a grove and walked down a wide path shaded by great low-branching cottonwoods. The last rays of the setting sun sent golden bars through the leaves. The grass was deep and rich, welcome contrast to sage-tired eyes. Twittering quail darted across the path, and from a tree-top somewhere a robin sang its evening song, and on the still air floated the freshness and murmur of flowing water.

The home of Jane Withersteen stood in a circle of cottonwoods, and was a flat, long, red-stone structure with a covered court in the center through which flowed a lively stream of amber-colored water. In the massive blocks of stone and heavy timbers and solid doors and shutters showed the hand of a man who had builded against pillage and time; and in the flowers and mosses lining the stone-bedded stream, in the bright colors of rugs and blankets on the court floor, and the cozy corner with hammock and books and the clean-linened table, showed the grace of a daughter who lived for happiness and the day at hand.

Jane turned Lassiter's horse loose in the thick grass. "You will want him to be near you," she said, "or I'd have him taken to the alfalfa fields." At her call appeared women who began at once to bustle about, hurrying to and fro, setting the table. Then Jane, excusing herself, went within.

She passed through a huge low ceiled chamber, like the inside of a fort, and into a smaller one where a bright wood-fire blazed in an old open fireplace, and from this into her own room. It had the same comfort as was manifested in the home-like outer court; moreover, it was warm and rich in soft hues.

Seldom did Jane Withersteen enter her room without looking into her mirror. She knew she loved the reflection of that beauty which since early childhood she had never been allowed to forget. Her relatives and friends, and later a horde of Mormon and Gentile suitors, had fanned the flame of natural vanity in her. So that at twenty-eight she scarcely thought at all of her wonderful influence for good in the little community where her father had left her practically its beneficent landlord, but cared most for the dream and the assurance and the allurement of her beauty. This time, however, she gazed into her glass with more than the usual happy motive, without the usual slight conscious smile. For she was thinking of more than the desire to be fair in her own eyes, in those of her friend; she wondered if she were to seem fair in the eyes of this Lassiter, this man whose name had crossed the long, wild brakes of stone and plains of sage, this gentle-voiced, sad-faced man who was a hater and a killer of Mormons. It was not now her usual half-conscious vain obsession that actuated her as she hurriedly changed her riding-dress to one of white, and then looked long at the stately form with its gracious contours, at the fair face with its strong chin and full firm lips, at the dark-blue, proud, and passionate eyes.

"If by some means I can keep him here a few days, a week—he will never kill another Mormon," she mused. "Lassiter!... I shudder when I think of that name, of him. But when I look at the man I forget who he is—I almost like him. I remember only that he saved Bern. He has suffered. I wonder what it was—did he love a Mormon woman once? How splendidly he championed us poor misunderstood souls! Somehow he knows—much."

Jane Withersteen joined her guests and bade them to her board. Dismissing her woman, she waited upon them with her own hands. It was a bountiful supper and a strange company. On her right sat the ragged and half-starved Venters; and though blind eyes could have seen what he counted for in the sum of her happiness, yet he looked the gloomy outcast his allegiance had made him, and about him there was the shadow of the ruin presaged by Tull. On her left sat black-leather-garbed Lassiter looking like a man in a dream. Hunger was not with him, nor composure, nor speech, and when he twisted in frequent unquiet movements the heavy guns that he had not removed knocked against the table-legs. If it had been otherwise possible to forget the presence of Lassiter those telling little jars would have rendered it unlikely. And Jane Withersteen talked and smiled and laughed with all the dazzling play of lips and eyes that a beautiful, daring woman could summon to her purpose.

When the meal ended, and the men pushed back their chairs, she leaned closer to Lassiter and looked square into his eyes.

"Why did you come to Cottonwoods?"

Her question seemed to break a spell. The rider arose as if he had just remembered himself and had tarried longer than his wont.

"Ma'am, I have hunted all over the southern Utah and Nevada for—somethin'. An' through your name I learned where to find it—here in Cottonwoods."

"My name! Oh, I remember. You did know my name when you spoke first. Well, tell me where you heard it and from whom?"

"At the little village—Glaze, I think it's called—some fifty miles or more west of here. An' I heard it from a Gentile, a rider who said you'd know where to tell me to find—"

"What?" she demanded, imperiously, as Lassiter broke off.

"Milly Erne's grave," he answered low, and the words came with a wrench.

Venters wheeled in his chair to regard Lassiter in amazement, and Jane slowly raised herself in white, still wonder.

"Milly Erne's grave?" she echoed, in a whisper. "What do you know of Milly Erne, my best-beloved friend—who died in my arms? What were you to her?"

"Did I claim to be anythin'?" he inquired. "I know people—relatives—who have long wanted to know where she's buried, that's all."

"Relatives? She never spoke of relatives, except a brother who was shot in Texas. Lassiter, Milly Erne's grave is in a secret burying-ground on my property."

"Will you take me there?... You'll be offendin' Mormons worse than by breakin' bread with me."

"Indeed yes, but I'll do it. Only we must go unseen. To-morrow, perhaps."

"Thank you, Jane Withersteen," replied the rider, and he bowed to her and stepped backward out of the court.

"Will you not stay—sleep under my roof?" she asked.

"No, ma'am, an' thanks again. I never sleep indoors. An' even if I did there's that gatherin' storm in the village below. No, no. I'll go to the sage. I hope you won't suffer none for your kindness to me."

"Lassiter," said Venters, with a half-bitter laugh, "my bed too, is the sage. Perhaps we may meet out there."

"Mebbe so. But the sage is wide an' I won't be near. Good night."

At Lassiter's low whistle the black horse whinnied, and carefully picked his blind way out of the grove. The rider did not bridle him, but walked beside him, leading him by touch of hand and together they passed slowly into the shade of the cottonwoods.

"Jane, I must be off soon," said Venters. "Give me my guns. If I'd had my guns—"

"Either my friend or the Elder of my church would be lying dead," she interposed.

"Tull would be—surely."

"Oh, you fierce-blooded, savage youth! Can't I teach you forebearance, mercy? Bern, it's divine to forgive your enemies. 'Let not the sun go down upon thy wrath.'"

"Hush! Talk to me no more of mercy or religion—after to-day. To-day this strange coming of Lassiter left me still a man, and now I'll die a man!... Give me my guns."

Silently she went into the house, to return with a heavy cartridge-belt and gun-filled sheath and a long rifle; these she handed to him, and as he buckled on the belt she stood before him in silent eloquence.

"Jane," he said, in gentler voice, "don't look so. I'm not going out to murder your churchman. I'll try to avoid him and all his men. But can't you see I've reached the end of my rope? Jane, you're a wonderful woman. Never was there a woman so unselfish and good. Only you're blind in one way.... Listen!"

From behind the grove came the clicking sound of horses in a rapid trot.

"Some of your riders," he continued. "It's getting time for the night shift. Let us go out to the bench in the grove and talk there."

It was still daylight in the open, but under the spreading cottonwoods shadows were obscuring the lanes. Venters drew Jane off from one of these into a shrub-lined trail, just wide enough for the two to walk abreast, and in a roundabout way led her far from the house to a knoll on the edge of the grove. Here in a secluded nook was a bench from which, through an opening in the tree-tops, could be seen the sage-slope and the wall of rock and the dim lines of canyons. Jane had not spoken since Venters had shocked her with his first harsh speech; but all the way she had clung to his arm, and now, as he stopped and laid his rifle against the bench, she still clung to him.

"Jane, I'm afraid I must leave you."

"Bern!" she cried.

"Yes, it looks that way. My position is not a happy one—I can't feel right—I've lost all—"

"I'll give you anything you—"

"Listen, please. When I say loss I don't mean what you think. I mean loss of good-will, good name—that which would have enabled me to stand up in this village without bitterness. Well, it's too late.... Now, as to the future, I think you'd do best to give me up. Tull is implacable. You ought to see from his intention to-day that—But you can't see. Your blindness—your damned religion!... Jane, forgive me—I'm sore within and something rankles. Well, I fear that invisible hand will turn its hidden work to your ruin."

"Invisible hand? Bern!"

"I mean your Bishop." Venters said it deliberately and would not release her as she started back. "He's the law. The edict went forth to ruin me. Well, look at me! It'll now go forth to compel you to the will of the Church."

"You wrong Bishop Dyer. Tull is hard, I know. But then he has been in love with me for years."

"Oh, your faith and your excuses! You can't see what I know—and if you did see it you'd not admit it to save your life. That's the Mormon of you. These elders and bishops will do absolutely any deed to go on building up the power and wealth of their church, their empire. Think of what they've done to the Gentiles here, to me—think of Milly Erne's fate!"

"What do you know of her story?"

"I know enough—all, perhaps, except the name of the Mormon who brought her here. But I must stop this kind of talk."

She pressed his hand in response. He helped her to a seat beside him on the bench. And he respected a silence that he divined was full of woman's deep emotion beyond his understanding.

It was the moment when the last ruddy rays of the sunset brightened momentarily before yielding to twilight. And for Venters the outlook before him was in some sense similar to a feeling of his future, and with searching eyes he studied the beautiful purple, barren waste of sage. Here was the unknown and the perilous. The whole scene impressed Venters as a wild, austere, and mighty manifestation of nature. And as it somehow reminded him of his prospect in life, so it suddenly resembled the woman near him, only in her there were greater beauty and peril, a mystery more unsolvable, and something nameless that numbed his heart and dimmed his eye.

"Look! A rider!" exclaimed Jane, breaking the silence. "Can that be Lassiter?"

Venters moved his glance once more to the west. A horseman showed dark on the sky-line, then merged into the color of the sage.

"It might be. But I think not—that fellow was coming in. One of your riders, more likely. Yes, I see him clearly now. And there's another."

"I see them, too."

"Jane, your riders seem as many as the bunches of sage. I ran into five yesterday 'way down near the trail to Deception Pass. They were with the white herd."

"You still go to that canyon? Bern, I wish you wouldn't. Oldring and his rustlers live somewhere down there."

"Well, what of that?"

"Tull has already hinted to your frequent trips into Deception Pass."

"I know." Venters uttered a short laugh. "He'll make a rustler of me next. But, Jane, there's no water for fifty miles after I leave here, and the nearest is in the canyon. I must drink and water my horse. There! I see more riders. They are going out."

"The red herd is on the slope, toward the Pass."

Twilight was fast falling. A group of horsemen crossed the dark line of low ground to become more distinct as they climbed the slope. The silence broke to a clear call from an incoming rider, and, almost like the peal of a hunting-horn, floated back the answer. The outgoing riders moved swiftly, came sharply into sight as they topped a ridge to show wild and black above the horizon, and then passed down, dimming into the purple of the sage.

"I hope they don't meet Lassiter," said Jane.

"So do I," replied Venters. "By this time the riders of the night shift know what happened to-day. But Lassiter will likely keep out of their way."

"Bern, who is Lassiter? He's only a name to me—a terrible name."

"Who is he? I don't know, Jane. Nobody I ever met knows him. He talks a little like a Texan, like Milly Erne. Did you note that?"

"Yes. How strange of him to know of her! And she lived here ten years and has been dead two. Bern, what do you know of Lassiter? Tell me what he has done—why you spoke of him to Tull—threatening to become another Lassiter yourself?"

"Jane, I only heard things, rumors, stories, most of which I disbelieved. At Glaze his name was known, but none of the riders or ranchers I knew there ever met him. At Stone Bridge I never heard him mentioned. But at Sterling and villages north of there he was spoken of often. I've never been in a village which he had been known to visit. There were many conflicting stories about him and his doings. Some said he had shot up this and that Mormon village, and others denied it. I'm inclined to believe he has, and you know how Mormons hide the truth. But there was one feature about Lassiter upon which all agree—that he was what riders in this country call a gun-man. He's a man with a marvelous quickness and accuracy in the use of a Colt. And now that I've seen him I know more. Lassiter was born without fear. I watched him with eyes which saw him my friend. I'll never forget the moment I recognized him from what had been told me of his crouch before the draw. It was then I yelled his name. I believe that yell saved Tull's life. At any rate, I know this, between Tull and death then there was not the breadth of the littlest hair. If he or any of his men had moved a finger downward—"

Venters left his meaning unspoken, but at the suggestion Jane shuddered.

The pale afterglow in the west darkened with the merging of twilight into night. The sage now spread out black and gloomy. One dim star glimmered in the southwest sky. The sound of trotting horses had ceased, and there was silence broken only by a faint, dry pattering of cottonwood leaves in the soft night wind.

Into this peace and calm suddenly broke the high-keyed yelp of a coyote, and from far off in the darkness came the faint answering note of a trailing mate.

"Hello! the sage-dogs are barking," said Venters.

"I don't like to hear them," replied Jane. "At night, sometimes when I lie awake, listening to the long mourn or breaking bark or wild howl, I think of you asleep somewhere in the sage, and my heart aches."

"Jane, you couldn't listen to sweeter music, nor could I have a better bed."

"Just think! Men like Lassiter and you have no home, no comfort, no rest, no place to lay your weary heads. Well!... Let us be patient. Tull's anger may cool, and time may help us. You might do some service to the village—who can tell? Suppose you discovered the long-unknown hiding-place of Oldring and his band, and told it to my riders? That would disarm Tull's ugly hints and put you in favor. For years my riders have trailed the tracks of stolen cattle. You know as well as I how dearly we've paid for our ranges in this wild country. Oldring drives our cattle down into the network of deceiving canyons, and somewhere far to the north or east he drives them up and out to Utah markets. If you will spend time in Deception Pass try to find the trails."

"Jane, I've thought of that. I'll try."

"I must go now. And it hurts, for now I'll never be sure of seeing you again. But to-morrow, Bern?"

"To-morrow surely. I'll watch for Lassiter and ride in with him."

"Good night."

Then she left him and moved away, a white, gliding shape that soon vanished in the shadows.

Venters waited until the faint slam of a door assured him she had reached the house, and then, taking up his rifle, he noiselessly slipped through the bushes, down the knoll, and on under the dark trees to the edge of the grove. The sky was now turning from gray to blue; stars had begun to lighten the earlier blackness; and from the wide flat sweep before him blew a cool wind, fragrant with the breath of sage. Keeping close to the edge of the cottonwoods, he went swiftly and silently westward. The grove was long, and he had not reached the end when he heard something that brought him to a halt. Low padded thuds told him horses were coming this way. He sank down in the gloom, waiting, listening. Much before he had expected, judging from sound, to his amazement he descried horsemen near at hand. They were riding along the border of the sage, and instantly he knew the hoofs of the horses were muffled. Then the pale starlight afforded him indistinct sight of the riders. But his eyes were keen and used to the dark, and by peering closely he recognized the huge bulk and black-bearded visage of Oldring and the lithe, supple form of the rustler's lieutenant, a masked rider. They passed on; the darkness swallowed them. Then, farther out on the sage, a dark, compact body of horsemen went by, almost without sound, almost like specters, and they, too, melted into the night.

CHAPTER III. AMBER SPRING

No unusual circumstances was it for Oldring and some of his men to visit Cottonwoods in the broad light of day, but for him to prowl about in the dark with the hoofs of his horses muffled meant that mischief was brewing. Moreover, to Venters the presence of the masked rider with Oldring seemed especially ominous. For about this man there was mystery, he seldom rode through the village, and when he did ride through it was swiftly; riders seldom met by day on the sage, but wherever he rode there always followed deeds as dark and mysterious as the mask he wore. Oldring's band did not confine themselves to the rustling of cattle.

Venters lay low in the shade of the cottonwoods, pondering this chance meeting, and not for many moments did he consider it safe to move on. Then, with sudden impulse, he turned the other way and went back along the grove. When he reached the path leading to Jane's home he decided to go down to the village. So he hurried onward, with quick soft steps. Once beyond the grove he entered the one and only street. It was wide, lined with tall poplars, and under each row of trees, inside the foot-path, were ditches where ran the water from Jane Withersteen's spring.

Between the trees twinkled lights of cottage candles, and far down flared bright windows of the village stores. When Venters got closer to these he saw knots of men standing together in earnest conversation. The usual lounging on the corners and benches and steps was not in evidence. Keeping in the shadow Venters went closer and closer until he could hear voices. But he could not distinguish what was said. He recognized many Mormons, and looked hard for Tull and his men, but looked in vain. Venters concluded that the rustlers had not passed along the village street. No doubt these earnest men were discussing Lassiter's coming. But Venters felt positive that Tull's intention toward himself that day had not been and would not be revealed.

So Venters, seeing there was little for him to learn, began retracing his steps. The church was dark, Bishop Dyer's home next to it was also dark, and likewise Tull's cottage. Upon almost any night at this hour there would be lights here, and Venters marked the unusual omission.

As he was about to pass out of the street to skirt the grove, he once more slunk down at the sound of trotting horses. Presently he descried two mounted men riding toward him. He hugged the shadow of a tree. Again the starlight, brighter now, aided him, and he made out Tull's stalwart figure, and beside him the short, froglike shape of the rider Jerry. They were silent, and they rode on to disappear.

Venters went his way with busy, gloomy mind, revolving events of the day, trying to reckon those brooding in the night. His thoughts overwhelmed him. Up in that dark grove dwelt a woman who had been his friend. And he skulked about her home, gripping a gun stealthily as an Indian, a man without place or people or purpose. Above her hovered the shadow of grim, hidden, secret power. No queen could have given more royally out of a bounteous store than Jane Withersteen gave her people, and likewise to those unfortunates whom her people hated. She asked only the divine right of all women—freedom; to love and to live as her heart willed. And yet prayer and her hope were vain.

"For years I've seen a storm clouding over her and the village of Cottonwoods," muttered Venters, as he strode on. "Soon it'll burst. I don't like the prospects." That night the villagers whispered in the street—and night-riding rustlers muffled horses—and Tull was at work in secret—and out there in the sage hid a man who meant something terrible—Lassiter!

Venters passed the black cottonwoods, and, entering the sage, climbed the gradual slope. He kept his direction in line with a western star. From time to time he stopped to listen and heard only the usual familiar bark of coyote and sweep of wind and rustle of sage. Presently a low jumble of rocks loomed up darkly somewhat to his right, and, turning that way, he whistled softly. Out of the rocks glided a dog that leaped and whined about him. He climbed over rough, broken rock, picking his way carefully, and then went down. Here it was darker, and sheltered from the wind. A white object guided him. It was another dog, and this one was asleep, curled up between a saddle and a pack. The animal awoke and thumped his tail in greeting. Venters placed the saddle for a pillow, rolled in his blankets, with his face upward to the stars. The white dog snuggled close to him. The other whined and pattered a few yards to the rise of ground and there crouched on guard. And in that wild covert Venters shut his eyes under the great white stars and intense vaulted blue, bitterly comparing their loneliness to his own, and fell asleep.

When he awoke, day had dawned and all about him was bright steel-gray. The air had a cold tang. Arising, he greeted the fawning dogs and stretched his cramped body, and then, gathering together bunches of dead sage sticks, he lighted a fire. Strips of dried beef held to the blaze for a moment served him and the dogs. He drank from a canteen. There was nothing else in his outfit; he had grown used to a scant fire. Then he sat over the fire, palms outspread, and waited. Waiting had been his chief occupation for months, and he scarcely knew what he waited for unless it was the passing of the hours. But now he sensed action in the immediate present; the day promised another meeting with Lassiter and Jane, perhaps news of the rustlers; on the morrow he meant to take the trail to Deception Pass.

And while he waited he talked to his dogs. He called them Ring and Whitie; they were sheep-dogs, half collie, half deerhound, superb in build, perfectly trained. It seemed that in his fallen fortunes these dogs understood the nature of their value to him, and governed their affection and faithfulness accordingly. Whitie watched him with somber eyes of love, and Ring, crouched on the little rise of ground above, kept tireless guard. When the sun rose, the white dog took the place of the other, and Ring went to sleep at his master's feet.

By and by Venters rolled up his blankets and tied them and his meager pack together, then climbed out to look for his horse. He saw him, presently, a little way off in the sage, and went to fetch him. In that country, where every rider boasted of a fine mount and was eager for a race, where thoroughbreds dotted the wonderful grazing ranges, Venters rode a horse that was sad proof of his misfortunes.

Then, with his back against a stone, Venters faced the east, and, stick in hand and idle blade, he waited. The glorious sunlight filled the valley with purple fire. Before him, to left, to right, waving, rolling, sinking, rising, like low swells of a purple sea, stretched the sage. Out of the grove of cottonwoods, a green patch on the purple, gleamed the dull red of Jane Withersteen's old stone house. And from there extended the wide green of the village gardens and orchards marked by the graceful poplars; and farther down shone the deep, dark richness of the alfalfa fields. Numberless red and black and white dots speckled the sage, and these were cattle and horses.

So, watching and waiting, Venters let the time wear away. At length he saw a horse rise above a ridge, and he knew it to be Lassiter's black. Climbing to the highest rock, so that he would show against the sky-line, he stood and waved his hat. The almost instant turning of Lassiter's horse attested to the quickness of that rider's eye. Then Venters climbed down, saddled his horse, tied on his pack, and, with a word to his dogs, was about to ride out to meet Lassiter, when he concluded to wait for him there, on higher ground, where the outlook was commanding.

It had been long since Venters had experienced friendly greeting from a man. Lassiter's warmed in him something that had grown cold from neglect. And when he had returned it, with a strong grip of the iron hand that held his, and met the gray eyes, he knew that Lassiter and he were to be friends.

"Venters, let's talk awhile before we go down there," said Lassiter, slipping his bridle. "I ain't in no hurry. Them's sure fine dogs you've got." With a rider's eye he took in the points of Venter's horse, but did not speak his thought. "Well, did anythin' come off after I left you last night?"

Venters told him about the rustlers.

"I was snug hid in the sage," replied Lassiter, "an' didn't see or hear no one. Oldrin's got a high hand here, I reckon. It's no news up in Utah how he holes in canyons an' leaves no track." Lassiter was silent a moment. "Me an' Oldrin' wasn't exactly strangers some years back when he drove cattle into Bostil's Ford, at the head of the Rio Virgin. But he got harassed there an' now he drives some place else."

"Lassiter, you knew him? Tell me, is he Mormon or Gentile?"

"I can't say. I've knowed Mormons who pretended to be Gentiles."

"No Mormon ever pretended that unless he was a rustler," declared Venters.

"Mebbe so."

"It's a hard country for any one, but hardest for Gentiles. Did you ever know or hear of a Gentile prospering in a Mormon community?"

"I never did."

"Well, I want to get out of Utah. I've a mother living in Illinois. I want to go home. It's eight years now."

The older man's sympathy moved Venters to tell his story. He had left Quincy, run off to seek his fortune in the gold fields had never gotten any farther than Salt Lake City, wandered here and there as helper, teamster, shepherd, and drifted southward over the divide and across the barrens and up the rugged plateau through the passes to the last border settlements. Here he became a rider of the sage, had stock of his own, and for a time prospered, until chance threw him in the employ of Jane Withersteen.

"Lassiter, I needn't tell you the rest."

"Well, it'd be no news to me. I know Mormons. I've seen their women's strange love en' patience en' sacrifice an' silence en' whet I call madness for their idea of God. An' over against that I've seen the tricks of men. They work hand in hand, all together, an' in the dark. No man can hold out against them, unless he takes to packin' guns. For Mormons are slow to kill. That's the only good I ever seen in their religion. Venters, take this from me, these Mormons ain't just right in their minds. Else could a Mormon marry one woman when he already has a wife, an' call it duty?"

"Lassiter, you think as I think," returned Venters.

"How'd it come then that you never throwed a gun on Tull or some of them?" inquired the rider, curiously.

"Jane pleaded with me, begged me to be patient, to overlook. She even took my guns from me. I lost all before I knew it," replied Venters, with the red color in his face. "But, Lassiter, listen. Out of the wreck I saved a Winchester, two Colts, and plenty of shells. I packed these down into Deception Pass. There, almost every day for six months, I have practiced with my rifle till the barrel burnt my hands. Practised the draw—the firing of a Colt, hour after hour!"

"Now that's interestin' to me," said Lassiter, with a quick uplift of his head and a concentration of his gray gaze on Venters. "Could you throw a gun before you began that practisin'?"

"Yes. And now..." Venters made a lightning-swift movement.

Lassiter smiled, and then his bronzed eyelids narrowed till his eyes seemed mere gray slits. "You'll kill Tull!" He did not question; he affirmed.

"I promised Jane Withersteen I'd try to avoid Tull. I'll keep my word. But sooner or later Tull and I will meet. As I feel now, if he even looks at me I'll draw!"

"I reckon so. There'll be hell down there, presently." He paused a moment and flicked a sage-brush with his quirt. "Venters, seein' as you're considerable worked up, tell me Milly Erne's story."

CHAPTER III. AMBER SPRING

Venters's agitation stilled to the trace of suppressed eagerness in Lassiter's query.

"Milly Erne's story? Well, Lassiter, I'll tell you what I know. Milly Erne had been in Cottonwoods years when I first arrived there, and most of what I tell you happened before my arrival. I got to know her pretty well. She was a slip of a woman, and crazy on religion. I conceived an idea that I never mentioned—I thought she was at heart more Gentile than Mormon. But she passed as a Mormon, and certainly she had the Mormon woman's locked lips. You know, in every Mormon village there are women who seem mysterious to us, but about Milly there was more than the ordinary mystery. When she came to Cottonwoods she had a beautiful little girl whom she loved passionately. Milly was not known openly in Cottonwoods as a Mormon wife. That she really was a Mormon wife I have no doubt. Perhaps the Mormon's other wife or wives would not acknowledge Milly. Such things happen in these villages. Mormon wives wear yokes, but they get jealous. Well, whatever had brought Milly to this country—love or madness of religion—she repented of it. She gave up teaching the village school. She quit the church. And she began to fight Mormon upbringing for her baby girl. Then the Mormons put on the screws—slowly, as is their way. At last the child disappeared. 'Lost' was the report. The child was stolen, I know that. So do you. That wrecked Milly Erne. But she lived on in hope. She became a slave. She worked her heart and soul and life out to get back her child. She never heard of it again. Then she sank.... I can see her now, a frail thing, so transparent you could almost look through her—white like ashes—and her eyes!... Her eyes have always haunted me. She had one real friend—Jane Withersteen. But Jane couldn't mend a broken heart, and Milly died."

For moments Lassiter did not speak, or turn his head.

"The man!" he exclaimed, presently, in husky accents.

"I haven't the slightest idea who the Mormon was," replied Venters; "nor has any Gentile in Cottonwoods."

"Does Jane Withersteen know?"

"Yes. But a red-hot running-iron couldn't burn that name out of her!"

Without further speech Lassiter started off, walking his horse and Venters followed with his dogs. Half a mile down the slope they entered a luxuriant growth of willows, and soon came into an open space carpeted with grass like deep green velvet. The rushing of water and singing of birds filled their ears. Venters led his comrade to a shady bower and showed him Amber Spring. It was a magnificent outburst of clear, amber water pouring from a dark, stone-lined hole. Lassiter knelt and drank, lingered there to drink again. He made no comment, but Venters did not need words. Next to his horse a rider of the sage loved a spring. And this spring was the most beautiful and remarkable known to the upland riders of southern Utah. It was the spring that made old Withersteen a feudal lord and now enabled his daughter to return the toll which her father had exacted from the toilers of the sage.

The spring gushed forth in a swirling torrent, and leaped down joyously to make its swift way along a willow-skirted channel. Moss and ferns and lilies overhung its green banks. Except for the rough-hewn stones that held and directed the water, this willow thicket and glade had been left as nature had made it.

Below were artificial lakes, three in number, one above the other in banks of raised earth, and round about them rose the lofty green-foliaged shafts of poplar trees. Ducks dotted the glassy surface of the lakes; a blue heron stood motionless on a water-gate; kingfishers darted with shrieking flight along the shady banks; a white hawk sailed above; and from the trees and shrubs came the song of robins and cat-birds. It was all in strange contrast to the endless slopes of lonely sage and the wild rock environs beyond. Venters thought of the woman who loved the birds and the green of the leaves and the murmur of the water.

Next on the slope, just below the third and largest lake, were corrals and a wide stone barn and open sheds and coops and pens. Here were clouds of dust, and cracking sounds of hoofs, and romping colts and heehawing burros. Neighing horses trampled to the corral fences. And on the little windows of the barn projected bobbing heads of bays and blacks and sorrels. When the two men entered the immense barnyard, from all around the din increased. This welcome, however, was not seconded by the several men and boys who vanished on sight.

Venters and Lassiter were turning toward the house when Jane appeared in the lane leading a horse. In riding-skirt and blouse she seemed to have lost some of her statuesque proportions, and looked more like a girl rider than the mistress of Withersteen. She was brightly smiling, and her greeting was warmly cordial.

"Good news," she announced. "I've been to the village. All is quiet. I expected—I don't know what. But there's no excitement. And Tull has ridden out on his way to Glaze."

"Tull gone?" inquired Venters, with surprise. He was wondering what could have taken Tull away. Was it to avoid another meeting with Lassiter that he went? Could it have any connection with the probable nearness of Oldring and his gang?

"Gone, yes, thank goodness," replied Jane. "Now I'll have peace for a while. Lassiter, I want you to see my horses. You are a rider, and you must be a judge of horseflesh. Some of mine have Arabian blood. My father got his best strain in Nevada from Indians who claimed their horses were bred down from the original stock left by the Spaniards."

"Well, ma'am, the one you've been ridin' takes my eye," said Lassiter, as he walked round the racy, clean-limbed, and fine-pointed roan.

"Where are the boys?" she asked, looking about. "Jerd, Paul, where are you? Here, bring out the horses."

The sound of dropping bars inside the barn was the signal for the horses to jerk their heads in the windows, to snort and stamp. Then they came pounding out of the door, a file of thoroughbreds, to plunge about the barnyard, heads and tails up, manes flying. They halted afar off, squared away to look, came slowly forward with whinnies for their mistress, and doubtful snorts for the strangers and their horses.

CHAPTER III. AMBER SPRING

"Come—come—come," called Jane, holding out her hands. "Why, Bells—Wrangle, where are your manners? Come, Black Star—come, Night. Ah, you beauties! My racers of the sage!"

Only two came up to her; those she called Night and Black Star. Venters never looked at them without delight. The first was soft dead black, the other glittering black, and they were perfectly matched in size, both being high and long-bodied, wide through the shoulders, with lithe, powerful legs. That they were a woman's pets showed in the gloss of skin, the fineness of mane. It showed, too, in the light of big eyes and the gentle reach of eagerness.

"I never seen their like," was Lassiter's encomium, "an' in my day I've seen a sight of horses. Now, ma'am, if you was wantin' to make a long an' fast ride across the sage—say to elope—"

Lassiter ended there with dry humor, yet behind that was meaning. Jane blushed and made arch eyes at him.

"Take care, Lassiter, I might think that a proposal," she replied, gaily. "It's dangerous to propose elopement to a Mormon woman. Well, I was expecting you. Now will be a good hour to show you Milly Erne's grave. The day-riders have gone, and the night-riders haven't come in. Bern, what do you make of that? Need I worry? You know I have to be made to worry."

"Well, it's not usual for the night shift to ride in so late," replied Venters, slowly, and his glance sought Lassiter's. "Cattle are usually quiet after dark. Still, I've known even a coyote to stampede your white herd."

"I refuse to borrow trouble. Come," said Jane.

They mounted, and, with Jane in the lead, rode down the lane, and, turning off into a cattle trail, proceeded westward. Venters's dogs trotted behind them. On this side of the ranch the outlook was different from that on the other; the immediate foreground was rough and the sage more rugged and less colorful; there were no dark-blue lines of canyons to hold the eye, nor any uprearing rock walls. It was a long roll and slope into gray obscurity. Soon Jane left the trail and rode into the sage, and presently she dismounted and threw her bridle. The men did likewise. Then, on foot, they followed her, coming out at length on the rim of a low escarpment. She passed by several little ridges of earth to halt before a faintly defined mound. It lay in the shade of a sweeping sage-brush close to the edge of the promontory; and a rider could have jumped his horse over it without recognizing a grave.

"Here!"

She looked sad as she spoke, but she offered no explanation for the neglect of an unmarked, uncared-for grave. There was a little bunch of pale, sweet lavender daisies, doubtless planted there by Jane.

"I only come here to remember and to pray," she said. "But I leave no trail!"

A grave in the sage! How lonely this resting-place of Milly Erne! The cottonwoods or the alfalfa fields were not in sight, nor was there any rock or ridge or cedar to lend contrast to the monotony. Gray slopes, tinging the purple, barren and wild, with the wind waving the sage, swept away to the dim horizon.

Lassiter looked at the grave and then out into space. At that moment he seemed a figure of bronze.

Jane touched Venters's arm and led him back to the horses.

"Bern!" cried Jane, when they were out of hearing. "Suppose Lassiter were Milly's husband—the father of that little girl lost so long ago!"

"It might be, Jane. Let us ride on. If he wants to see us again he'll come."

So they mounted and rode out to the cattle trail and began to climb. From the height of the ridge, where they had started down, Venters looked back. He did not see Lassiter, but his glance, drawn irresistibly farther out on the gradual slope, caught sight of a moving cloud of dust.

"Hello, a rider!"

"Yes, I see," said Jane.

"That fellow's riding hard. Jane, there's something wrong."

"Oh yes, there must be.... How he rides!"

The horse disappeared in the sage, and then puffs of dust marked his course.

"He's short-cut on us—he's making straight for the corrals."

Venters and Jane galloped their steeds and reined in at the turning of the lane. This lane led down to the right of the grove. Suddenly into its lower entrance flashed a bay horse. Then Venters caught the fast rhythmic beat of pounding hoofs. Soon his keen eye recognized the swing of the rider in his saddle.

"It's Judkins, your Gentile rider!" he cried. "Jane, when Judkins rides like that it means hell!"

CHAPTER IV. DECEPTION PASS

The rider thundered up and almost threw his foam-flecked horse in the sudden stop. He was a giant form, and with fearless eyes.

"Judkins, you're all bloody!" cried Jane, in affright. "Oh, you've been shot!"

"Nothin' much Miss Withersteen. I got a nick in the shoulder. I'm some wet an' the hoss's been throwin' lather, so all this ain't blood."

"What's up?" queried Venters, sharply.

"Rustlers sloped off with the red herd."

"Where are my riders?" demanded Jane.

"Miss Withersteen, I was alone all night with the herd. At daylight this mornin' the rustlers rode down. They began to shoot at me on sight. They chased me hard an' far, burnin' powder all the time, but I got away."

"Jud, they meant to kill you," declared Venters.

"Now I wonder," returned Judkins. "They wanted me bad. An' it ain't regular for rustlers to waste time chasin' one rider."

"Thank heaven you got away," said Jane. "But my riders—where are they?"

"I don't know. The night-riders weren't there last night when I rode down, en' this mornin' I met no day-riders."

"Judkins! Bern, they've been set upon—killed by Oldring's men!"

"I don't think so," replied Venters, decidedly. "Jane, your riders haven't gone out in the sage."

"Bern, what do you mean?" Jane Withersteen turned deathly pale.

"You remember what I said about the unseen hand?"

"Oh!... Impossible!"

"I hope so. But I fear—" Venters finished, with a shake of his head.

"Bern, you're bitter; but that's only natural. We'll wait to see what's happened to my riders. Judkins, come to the house with me. Your wound must be attended to."

"Jane, I'll find out where Oldring drives the herd," vowed Venters.

"No, no! Bern, don't risk it now—when the rustlers are in such shooting mood."

"I'm going. Jud, how many cattle in that red herd?"

"Twenty-five hundred head."

"Whew! What on earth can Oldring do with so many cattle? Why, a hundred head is a big steal. I've got to find out."

"Don't go," implored Jane.

"Bern, you want a hoss thet can run. Miss Withersteen, if it's not too bold of me to advise, make him take a fast hoss or don't let him go."

"Yes, yes, Judkins. He must ride a horse that can't be caught. Which one—Black Star—Night?"

"Jane, I won't take either," said Venters, emphatically. "I wouldn't risk losing one of your favorites."

"Wrangle, then?"

"Thet's the hoss," replied Judkins. "Wrangle can outrun Black Star an' Night. You'd never believe it, Miss Withersteen, but I know. Wrangle's the biggest en' fastest hoss on the sage."

"Oh no, Wrangle can't beat Black Star. But, Bern, take Wrangle if you will go. Ask Jerd for anything you need. Oh, be watchful, careful.... God speed you."

She clasped his hand, turned quickly away, and went down a lane with the rider.

Venters rode to the barn, and, leaping off, shouted for Jerd. The boy came running. Venters sent him for meat, bread, and dried fruits, to be packed in saddlebags. His own horse he turned loose into the nearest corral. Then he went for Wrangle. The giant sorrel had earned his name for a trait the opposite of amiability. He came readily out of the barn, but once in the yard he broke from Venters, and plunged about with ears laid back. Venters had to rope him, and then he kicked down a section of fence, stood on his hind legs, crashed down and fought the rope. Jerd returned to lend a hand.

"Wrangle don't git enough work," said Jerd, as the big saddle went on. "He's unruly when he's corralled, an' wants to run. Wait till he smells the sage!"

"Jerd, this horse is an iron-jawed devil. I never straddled him but once. Run? Say, he's swift as wind!"

When Venters's boot touched the stirrup the sorrel bolted, giving him the rider's flying mount. The swing of this fiery horse recalled to Venters days that were not really long past, when he rode into the sage as the leader of Jane Withersteen's riders. Wrangle pulled hard on a tight rein. He galloped out of the lane, down the shady border of the grove, and hauled up at the watering-trough, where he pranced and champed his bit. Venters got off and filled his canteen while the horse drank. The dogs, Ring and Whitie, came trotting up for their drink. Then Venters remounted and turned Wrangle toward the sage.

A wide, white trail wound away down the slope. One keen, sweeping glance told Venters that there was neither man nor horse nor steer within the limit of his vision, unless they were lying down in the sage. Ring loped in the lead and Whitie loped in the rear. Wrangle settled gradually into an easy swinging canter, and Venters's thoughts, now that the rush and flurry of the start were past, and the long miles stretched before him, reverted to a calm reckoning of late singular coincidences.

CHAPTER IV. DECEPTION PASS

There was the night ride of Tull's, which, viewed in the light of subsequent events, had a look of his covert machinations; Oldring and his Masked Rider and his rustlers riding muffled horses; the report that Tull had ridden out that morning with his man Jerry on the trail to Glaze, the strange disappearance of Jane Withersteen's riders, the unusually determined attempt to kill the one Gentile still in her employ, an intention frustrated, no doubt, only by Judkin's magnificent riding of her racer, and lastly the driving of the red herd. These events, to Venters's color of mind, had a dark relationship. Remembering Jane's accusation of bitterness, he tried hard to put aside his rancor in judging Tull. But it was bitter knowledge that made him see the truth. He had felt the shadow of an unseen hand; he had watched till he saw its dim outline, and then he had traced it to a man's hate, to the rivalry of a Mormon Elder, to the power of a Bishop, to the long, far-reaching arm of a terrible creed. That unseen hand had made its first move against Jane Withersteen. Her riders had been called in, leaving her without help to drive seven thousand head of cattle. But to Venters it seemed extraordinary that the power which had called in these riders had left so many cattle to be driven by rustlers and harried by wolves. For hand in glove with that power was an insatiate greed; they were one and the same.

"What can Oldring do with twenty-five hundred head of cattle?" muttered Venters. "Is he a Mormon? Did he meet Tull last night? It looks like a black plot to me. But Tull and his churchmen wouldn't ruin Jane Withersteen unless the Church was to profit by that ruin. Where does Oldring come in? I'm going to find out about these things."

Wrangle did the twenty-five miles in three hours and walked little of the way. When he had gotten warmed up he had been allowed to choose his own gait. The afternoon had well advanced when Venters struck the trail of the red herd and found where it had grazed the night before. Then Venters rested the horse and used his eyes. Near at hand were a cow and a calf and several yearlings, and farther out in the sage some straggling steers. He caught a glimpse of coyotes skulking near the cattle. The slow sweeping gaze of the rider failed to find other living things within the field of sight. The sage about him was breast-high to his horse, oversweet with its warm, fragrant breath, gray where it waved to the light, darker where the wind left it still, and beyond the wonderful haze-purple lent by distance. Far across that wide waste began the slow lift of uplands through which Deception Pass cut its tortuous many-canyoned way.

Venters raised the bridle of his horse and followed the broad cattle trail. The crushed sage resembled the path of a monster snake. In a few miles of travel he passed several cows and calves that had escaped the drive. Then he stood on the last high bench of the slope with the floor of the valley beneath. The opening of the canyon showed in a break of the sage, and the cattle trail paralleled it as far as he could see. That trail led to an undiscovered point where Oldring drove cattle into the pass, and many a rider who had followed it had never returned. Venters satisfied himself that the rustlers had not deviated from their usual course, and then he turned at right angles off the cattle trail and made for the head of the pass.

The sun lost its heat and wore down to the western horizon, where it changed from white to gold and rested like a huge ball about to roll on its golden shadows down the slope. Venters watched the lengthening of the rays and bars, and marveled at his own league-long shadow. The sun sank. There was instant shading of brightness about him, and he saw a kind of cold purple bloom creep ahead of him to cross the canyon, to mount the opposite slope and chase and darken and bury the last golden flare of sunlight.

Venters rode into a trail that he always took to get down into the canyon. He dismounted and found no tracks but his own made days previous. Nevertheless he sent the dog Ring ahead and waited. In a little while Ring returned. Whereupon Venters led his horse on to the break in the ground.

The opening into Deception Pass was one of the remarkable natural phenomena in a country remarkable for vast slopes of sage, uplands insulated by gigantic red walls, and deep canyons of mysterious source and outlet. Here the valley floor was level, and here opened a narrow chasm, a ragged vent in yellow walls of stone. The trail down the five hundred feet of sheer depth always tested Venters's nerve. It was bad going for even a burro. But Wrangle, as Venters led him, snorted defiance or disgust rather than fear, and, like a hobbled horse on the jump, lifted his ponderous iron-shod fore hoofs and crashed down over the first rough step. Venters warmed to greater admiration of the sorrel; and, giving him a loose bridle, he stepped down foot by foot. Oftentimes the stones and shale started by Wrangle buried Venters to his knees; again he was hard put to it to dodge a rolling boulder, there were times when he could not see Wrangle for dust, and once he and the horse rode a sliding shelf of yellow, weathered cliff. It was a trail on which there could be no stops, and, therefore, if perilous, it was at least one that did not take long in the descent.

Venters breathed lighter when that was over, and felt a sudden assurance in the success of his enterprise. For at first it had been a reckless determination to achieve something at any cost, and now it resolved itself into an adventure worthy of all his reason and cunning, and keenness of eye and ear.

Pinyon pines clustered in little clumps along the level floor of the pass. Twilight had gathered under the walls. Venters rode into the trail and up the canyon. Gradually the trees and caves and objects low down turned black, and this blackness moved up the walls till night enfolded the pass, while day still lingered above. The sky darkened; and stars began to show, at first pale and then bright. Sharp notches of the rim-wall, biting like teeth into the blue, were landmarks by which Venters knew where his camping site lay. He had to feel his way through a thicket of slender oaks to a spring where he watered Wrangle and drank himself. Here he unsaddled and turned Wrangle loose, having no fear that the horse would leave the thick, cool grass adjacent to the spring. Next he satisfied his own hunger, fed Ring and Whitie and, with them curled beside him, composed himself to await sleep.

There had been a time when night in the high altitude of these Utah uplands had been satisfying to Venters. But that was before the oppression of enemies had made the change in his mind. As a rider guarding the herd he had never thought of the night's wildness and loneliness; as an outcast, now when the full silence set in, and the deep darkness, and trains of radiant stars shone cold and calm, he lay with an ache in his heart. For a year he had lived as a black fox, driven from his kind. He longed for the sound of a voice, the touch of a hand. In the daytime there was riding from place to place, and the gun practice to which something drove him, and other tasks that at least necessitated action, at night, before he won sleep, there was strife in his soul. He yearned to leave the endless sage slopes, the wilderness of canyons, and it was in the lonely night that this yearning grew unbearable. It was then that he reached forth to feel Ring or Whitie, immeasurably grateful for the love and companionship of two dogs.

On this night the same old loneliness beset Venters, the old habit of sad thought and burning unquiet had its way. But from it evolved a conviction that his useless life had undergone a subtle change. He had sensed it first when Wrangle swung him up to the high saddle, he knew it now when he lay in the gateway of Deception Pass. He had no thrill of adventure, rather a gloomy perception of great hazard, perhaps death. He meant to find Oldring's retreat. The rustlers had fast horses, but none that could catch Wrangle. Venters knew no rustler could creep upon him at night when Ring and Whitie guarded his hiding-place. For the rest, he had eyes and ears, and a long rifle and an unerring aim, which he meant to use. Strangely his foreshadowing of change did not hold a thought of the killing of Tull. It related only to what was to happen to him in Deception Pass; and he could no more lift the veil of that mystery than tell where the trails led to in that unexplored canyon. Moreover, he did not care. And at length, tired out by stress of thought, he fell asleep.

When his eyes unclosed, day had come again, and he saw the rim of the opposite wall tipped with the gold of sunrise. A few moments sufficed for the morning's simple camp duties. Near at hand he found Wrangle, and to his surprise the horse came to him. Wrangle was one of the horses that left his viciousness in the home corral. What he wanted was to be free of mules and burros and steers, to roll in dust-patches, and then to run down the wide, open, windy sage-plains, and at night browse and sleep in the cool wet grass of a springhole. Jerd knew the sorrel when he said of him, "Wait till he smells the sage!"

Venters saddled and led him out of the oak thicket, and, leaping astride, rode up the canyon, with Ring and Whitie trotting behind. An old grass-grown trail followed the course of a shallow wash where flowed a thin stream of water. The canyon was a hundred rods wide, its yellow walls were perpendicular; it had abundant sage and a scant growth of oak and pinon. For five miles it held to a comparatively straight bearing, and then began a heightening of rugged walls and a deepening of the floor. Beyond this point of sudden change in the character of the canyon Venters had never explored, and here was the real door to the intricacies of Deception Pass.

He reined Wrangle to a walk, halted now and then to listen, and then proceeded cautiously with shifting and alert gaze. The canyon assumed proportions that dwarfed those of its first ten miles. Venters rode on and on, not losing in the interest of his wide surroundings any of his caution or keen search for tracks or sight of living thing. If there ever had been a trail here, he could not find it. He rode through sage and clumps of pinon trees and grassy plots where long-petaled purple lilies bloomed. He rode through a dark constriction of the pass no wider than the lane in the grove at Cottonwoods. And he came out into a great amphitheater into which jutted huge towering corners of a confluence of intersecting canyons.

Venters sat his horse, and, with a rider's eye, studied this wild cross-cut of huge stone gullies. Then he went on, guided by the course of running water. If it had not been for the main stream of water flowing north he would never have been able to tell which of those many openings was a continuation of the pass. In crossing this amphitheater he went by the mouths of five canyons, fording little streams that flowed into the larger one. Gaining the outlet which he took to be the pass, he rode on again under over hanging walls. One side was dark in shade, the other light in sun. This narrow passageway turned and twisted and opened into a valley that amazed Venters.

Here again was a sweep of purple sage, richer than upon the higher levels. The valley was miles long, several wide, and inclosed by unscalable walls. But it was the background of this valley that so forcibly struck him. Across the sage-flat rose a strange up-flinging of yellow rocks. He could not tell which were close and which were distant. Scrawled mounds of stone, like mountain waves, seemed to roll up to steep bare slopes and towers.

In this plain of sage Venters flushed birds and rabbits, and when he had proceeded about a mile he caught sight of the bobbing white tails of a herd of running antelope. He rode along the edge of the stream which wound toward the western end of the slowly looming mounds of stone. The high slope retreated out of sight behind the nearer protection. To Venters the valley appeared to have been filled in by a mountain of melted stone that had hardened in strange shapes of rounded outline. He followed the stream till he lost it in a deep cut. Therefore Venters quit the dark slit which baffled further search in that direction, and rode out along the curved edge of stone where it met the sage. It was not long before he came to a low place, and here Wrangle readily climbed up.

All about him was ridgy roll of wind-smoothed, rain-washed rock. Not a tuft of grass or a bunch of sage colored the dull rust-yellow. He saw where, to the right, this uneven flow of stone ended in a blunt wall. Leftward, from the hollow that lay at his feet, mounted a gradual slow-swelling slope to a great height topped by leaning, cracked, and ruined crags. Not for some time did he grasp the wonder of that acclivity. It was no less than a mountain-side, glistening in the sun like polished granite, with cedar-trees springing as if by magic out of the denuded surface. Winds had swept it clear of weathered shale, and rains had washed it free of dust. Far up the curved slope its beautiful lines broke to meet the vertical rim-wall, to lose its grace in a different order and color of rock, a stained yellow cliff of cracks and caves and seamed crags. And straight before Venters was a scene less striking but more significant to his keen survey. For beyond a mile of the bare, hummocky rock began the valley of sage, and the mouths of canyons, one of which surely was another gateway into the pass.

He got off his horse, and, giving the bridle to Ring to hold, he commenced a search for the cleft where the stream ran. He was not successful and concluded the water dropped into an underground passage. Then he returned to where he had left Wrangle, and led him down off the stone to the sage. It was a short ride to the opening canyons. There was no reason for a choice of which one to enter. The one he rode into was a clear, sharp shaft in yellow stone a thousand feet deep, with wonderful wind-worn caves low down and high above buttressed and turreted ramparts. Farther on Venters came into a region where deep indentations marked the line of canyon walls. These were huge, cove-like blind pockets extending back to a sharp corner with a dense growth of underbrush and trees.

Venters penetrated into one of these offshoots, and, as he had hoped, he found abundant grass. He had to bend the oak saplings to get his horse through. Deciding to make this a hiding-place if he could find water, he worked back to the limit of the shelving walls. In a little cluster of silver spruces he found a spring. This inclosed nook seemed an ideal place to leave his horse and to camp at night, and from which to make stealthy trips on foot. The thick grass hid his trail; the dense growth of oaks in the opening would serve as a barrier to keep Wrangle in, if, indeed, the luxuriant browse would not suffice for that. So Venters, leaving Whitie with the horse, called Ring to his side, and, rifle in hand, worked his way out to the open. A careful photographing in mind of the formation of the bold outlines of rimrock assured him he would be able to return to his retreat even in the dark.

Bunches of scattered sage covered the center of the canyon, and among these Venters threaded his way with the step of an Indian. At intervals he put his hand on the dog and stopped to listen. There was a drowsy hum of insects, but no other sound disturbed the warm midday stillness. Venters saw ahead a turn, more abrupt than any yet. Warily he rounded this corner, once again to halt bewildered.

The canyon opened fan-shaped into a great oval of green and gray growths. It was the hub of an oblong wheel, and from it, at regular distances, like spokes, ran the outgoing canyons. Here a dull red color predominated over the fading yellow. The corners of wall bluntly rose, scarred and scrawled, to taper into towers and serrated peaks and pinnacled domes.

Venters pushed on more heedfully than ever. Toward the center of this circle the sage-brush grew smaller and farther apart He was about to sheer off to the right, where thickets and jumbles of fallen rock would afford him cover, when he ran right upon a broad cattle trail. Like a road it was, more than a trail, and the cattle tracks were fresh. What surprised him more, they were wet! He pondered over this feature. It had not rained. The only solution to this puzzle was that the cattle had been driven through water, and water deep enough to wet their legs.

Suddenly Ring growled low. Venters rose cautiously and looked over the sage. A band of straggling horsemen were riding across the oval. He sank down, startled and trembling. "Rustlers!" he muttered. Hurriedly he glanced about for a place to hide. Near at hand there was nothing but sage-brush. He dared not risk crossing the open patches to reach the rocks. Again he peeped over the sage. The rustlers—four—five—seven—eight in all, were approaching, but not directly in line with him. That was relief for a cold deadness which seemed to be creeping inward along his veins. He crouched down with bated breath and held the bristling dog.

He heard the click of iron-shod hoofs on stone, the coarse laughter of men, and then voices gradually dying away. Long moments passed. Then he rose. The rustlers were riding into a canyon. Their horses were tired, and they had several pack animals; evidently they had traveled far. Venters doubted that they were the rustlers who had driven the red herd. Olding's band had split. Venters watched these horsemen disappear under a bold canyon wall.

The rustlers had come from the northwest side of the oval. Venters kept a steady gaze in that direction, hoping, if there were more, to see from what canyon they rode. A quarter of an hour went by. Reward for his vigilance came when he descried three more mounted men, far over to the north. But out of what canyon they had ridden it was too late to tell. He watched the three ride across the oval and round the jutting red corner where the others had gone.

"Up that canyon!" exclaimed Venters. "Oldring's den! I've found it!"

A knotty point for Venters was the fact that the cattle tracks all pointed west. The broad trail came from the direction of the canyon into which the rustlers had ridden, and undoubtedly the cattle had been driven out of it across the oval. There were no tracks pointing the other way. It had been in his mind that Oldring had driven the red herd toward the rendezvous, and not from it. Where did that broad trail come down into the pass, and where did it lead? Venters knew he wasted time in pondering the question, but it held a fascination not easily dispelled. For many years Oldring's mysterious entrance and exit to Deception Pass had been all-absorbing topics to sage-riders.

All at once the dog put an end to Venters's pondering. Ring sniffed the air, turned slowly in his tracks with a whine, and then growled. Venters wheeled. Two horsemen were within a hundred yards, coming straight at him. One, lagging behind the other, was Oldring's Masked Rider.

Venters cunningly sank, slowly trying to merge into sage-brush. But, guarded as his action was, the first horse detected it. He stopped short, snorted, and shot up his ears. The rustler bent forward, as if keenly peering ahead. Then, with a swift sweep, he jerked a gun from its sheath and fired.

The bullet zipped through the sage-brush. Flying bits of wood struck Venters, and the hot, stinging pain seemed to lift him in one leap. Like a flash the blue barrel of his rifle gleamed level and he shot once—twice.

The foremost rustler dropped his weapon and toppled from his saddle, to fall with his foot catching in a stirrup. The horse snorted wildly and plunged away, dragging the rustler through the sage.

The Masked Rider huddled over his pommel slowly swaying to one side, and then, with a faint, strange cry, slipped out of the saddle.

CHAPTER V. THE MASKED RIDER

Venters looked quickly from the fallen rustlers to the canyon where the others had disappeared. He calculated on the time needed for running horses to return to the open, if their riders heard shots. He waited breathlessly. But the estimated time dragged by and no riders appeared. Venters began presently to believe that the rifle reports had not penetrated into the recesses of the canyon, and felt safe for the immediate present.

He hurried to the spot where the first rustler had been dragged by his horse. The man lay in deep grass, dead, jaw fallen, eyes protruding—a sight that sickened Venters. The first man at whom he had ever aimed a weapon he had shot through the heart. With the clammy sweat oozing from every pore Venters dragged the rustler in among some boulders and covered him with slabs of rock. Then he smoothed out the crushed trail in grass and sage. The rustler's horse had stopped a quarter of a mile off and was grazing.

When Venters rapidly strode toward the Masked Rider not even the cold nausea that gripped him could wholly banish curiosity. For he had shot Oldring's infamous lieutenant, whose face had never been seen. Venters experienced a grim pride in the feat. What would Tull say to this achievement of the outcast who rode too often to Deception Pass?

Venters's curious eagerness and expectation had not prepared him for the shock he received when he stood over a slight, dark figure. The rustler wore the black mask that had given him his name, but he had no weapons. Venters glanced at the drooping horse, there were no gun-sheaths on the saddle.

"A rustler who didn't pack guns!" muttered Venters. "He wears no belt. He couldn't pack guns in that rig.... Strange!"

A low, gasping intake of breath and a sudden twitching of body told Venters the rider still lived.

"He's alive!... I've got to stand here and watch him die. And I shot an unarmed man."

Shrinkingly Venters removed the rider's wide sombrero and the black cloth mask. This action disclosed bright chestnut hair, inclined to curl, and a white, youthful face. Along the lower line of cheek and jaw was a clear demarcation, where the brown of tanned skin met the white that had been hidden from the sun.

"Oh, he's only a boy!... What! Can he be Oldring's Masked Rider?"

The boy showed signs of returning consciousness. He stirred; his lips moved; a small brown hand clenched in his blouse.

Venters knelt with a gathering horror of his deed. His bullet had entered the rider's right breast, high up to the shoulder. With hands that shook, Venters untied a black scarf and ripped open the blood-wet blouse.

First he saw a gaping hole, dark red against a whiteness of skin, from which welled a slender red stream. Then the graceful, beautiful swell of a woman's breast!

"A woman!" he cried. "A girl!... I've killed a girl!"

She suddenly opened eyes that transfixed Venters. They were fathomless blue. Consciousness of death was there, a blended terror and pain, but no consciousness of sight. She did not see Venters. She stared into the unknown.

Then came a spasm of vitality. She writhed in a torture of reviving strength, and in her convulsions she almost tore from Ventner's grasp. Slowly she relaxed and sank partly back. The ungloved hand sought the wound, and pressed so hard that her wrist half buried itself in her bosom. Blood trickled between her spread fingers. And she looked at Venters with eyes that saw him.

He cursed himself and the unerring aim of which he had been so proud. He had seen that look in the eyes of a crippled antelope which he was about to finish with his knife. But in her it had infinitely more—a revelation of mortal spirit. The instinctive bringing to life was there, and the divining helplessness and the terrible accusation of the stricken.

"Forgive me! I didn't know!" burst out Venters.

"You shot me—you've killed me!" she whispered, in panting gasps. Upon her lips appeared a fluttering, bloody froth. By that Venters knew the air in her lungs was mixing with blood. "Oh, I knew—it would—come—some day!... Oh, the burn!... Hold me—I'm sinking—it's all dark.... Ah, God!... Mercy—"

Her rigidity loosened in one long quiver and she lay back limp, still, white as snow, with closed eyes.

Venters thought then that she died. But the faint pulsation of her breast assured him that life yet lingered. Death seemed only a matter of moments, for the bullet had gone clear through her. Nevertheless, he tore sageleaves from a bush, and, pressing them tightly over her wounds, he bound the black scarf round her shoulder, tying it securely under her arm. Then he closed the blouse, hiding from his sight that blood-stained, accusing breast.

"What—now?" he questioned, with flying mind. "I must get out of here. She's dying—but I can't leave her."

He rapidly surveyed the sage to the north and made out no animate object. Then he picked up the girl's sombrero and the mask. This time the mask gave him as great a shock as when he first removed it from her face. For in the woman he had forgotten the rustler, and this black strip of felt-cloth established the identity of Oldring's Masked Rider. Venters had solved the mystery. He slipped his rifle under her, and, lifting her carefully upon it, he began to retrace his steps. The dog trailed in his shadow. And the horse, that had stood drooping by, followed without a call. Venters chose the deepest tufts of grass and clumps of sage on his return. From time to time he glanced over his shoulder. He did not rest. His concern was to avoid jarring the girl and to hide his trail. Gaining the narrow canyon, he turned and held close to the wall till he reached his hiding-place. When he entered the dense thicket of oaks he was hard put to it to force a way through. But he held his burden almost upright, and by slipping side wise and bending the saplings he got in. Through sage and grass he hurried to the grove of silver spruces.

He laid the girl down, almost fearing to look at her. Though marble pale and cold, she was living. Venters then appreciated the tax that long carry had been to his strength. He sat down to rest. Whitie sniffed at the pale girl and whined and crept to Venters's feet. Ring lapped the water in the runway of the spring.

Presently Venters went out to the opening, caught the horse and, leading him through the thicket, unsaddled him and tied him with a long halter. Wrangle left his browsing long enough to whinny and toss his head. Venters felt that he could not rest easily till he had secured the other rustler's horse; so, taking his rifle and calling for Ring, he set out. Swiftly yet watchfully he made his way through the canyon to the oval and out to the cattle trail. What few tracks might have betrayed him he obliterated, so only an expert tracker could have trailed him. Then, with many a wary backward glance across the sage, he started to round up the rustler's horse. This was unexpectedly easy. He led the horse to lower ground, out of sight from the opposite side of the oval along the shadowy western wall, and so on into his canyon and secluded camp.

The girl's eyes were open; a feverish spot burned in her cheeks she moaned something unintelligible to Venters, but he took the movement of her lips to mean that she wanted water. Lifting her head, he tipped the canteen to her lips. After that she again lapsed into unconsciousness or a weakness which was its counterpart. Venters noted, however, that the burning flush had faded into the former pallor.

The sun set behind the high canyon rim, and a cool shade darkened the walls. Venters fed the dogs and put a halter on the dead rustlers horse. He allowed Wrangle to browse free. This done, he cut spruce boughs and made a lean-to for the girl. Then, gently lifting her upon a blanket, he folded the sides over her. The other blanket he wrapped about his shoulders and found a comfortable seat against a spruce-tree that upheld the little shack. Ring and Whitie lay near at hand, one asleep, the other watchful.

Venters dreaded the night's vigil. At night his mind was active, and this time he had to watch and think and feel beside a dying girl whom he had all but murdered. A thousand excuses he invented for himself, yet not one made any difference in his act or his self-reproach.

It seemed to him that when night fell black he could see her white face so much more plainly.

"She'll go, presently," he said, "and be out of agony—thank God!"

Every little while certainty of her death came to him with a shock; and then he would bend over and lay his ear on her breast. Her heart still beat.

The early night blackness cleared to the cold starlight. The horses were not moving, and no sound disturbed the deathly silence of the canyon.

"I'll bury her here," thought Venters, "and let her grave be as much a mystery as her life was."

For the girl's few words, the look of her eyes, the prayer, had strangely touched Venters.

"She was only a girl," he soliloquized. "What was she to Oldring? Rustlers don't have wives nor sisters nor daughters. She was bad—that's all. But somehow... well, she may not have willingly become the companion of rustlers. That prayer of hers to God for mercy!... Life is strange and cruel. I wonder if other members of Oldring's gang are women? Likely enough. But what was his game? Oldring's Mask Rider! A name to make villagers hide and lock their doors. A name credited with a dozen murders, a hundred forays, and a thousand stealings of cattle. What part did the girl have in this? It may have served Oldring to create mystery."

Hours passed. The white stars moved across the narrow strip of dark-blue sky above. The silence awoke to the low hum of insects. Venters watched the immovable white face, and as he watched, hour by hour waiting for death, the infamy of her passed from his mind. He thought only of the sadness, the truth of the moment. Whoever she was—whatever she had done—she was young and she was dying.

The after-part of the night wore on interminably. The starlight failed and the gloom blackened to the darkest hour. "She'll die at the gray of dawn," muttered Venters, remembering some old woman's fancy. The blackness paled to gray, and the gray lightened and day peeped over the eastern rim. Venters listened at the breast of the girl. She still lived. Did he only imagine that her heart beat stronger, ever so slightly, but stronger? He pressed his ear closer to her breast. And he rose with his own pulse quickening.

"If she doesn't die soon—she's got a chance—the barest chance to live," he said.

He wondered if the internal bleeding had ceased. There was no more film of blood upon her lips. But no corpse could have been whiter. Opening her blouse, he untied the scarf, and carefully picked away the sage leaves from the wound in her shoulder. It had closed. Lifting her lightly, he ascertained that the same was true of the hole where the bullet had come out. He reflected on the fact that clean wounds closed quickly in the healing upland air. He recalled instances of riders who had been cut and shot apparently to fatal issues; yet the blood had clotted, the wounds closed, and they had recovered. He had no way to tell if internal hemorrhage still went on, but he believed that it had stopped. Otherwise she would surely not have lived so long. He marked the entrance of the bullet, and concluded that it had just touched the upper lobe of her lung. Perhaps the wound in the lung had also closed. As he began to wash the blood stains from her breast and carefully rebandage the wound, he was vaguely conscious of a strange, grave happiness in the thought that she might live.

CHAPTER V. THE MASKED RIDER

Broad daylight and a hint of sunshine high on the cliff-rim to the west brought him to consideration of what he had better do. And while busy with his few camp tasks he revolved the thing in his mind. It would not be wise for him to remain long in his present hiding-place. And if he intended to follow the cattle trail and try to find the rustlers he had better make a move at once. For he knew that rustlers, being riders, would not make much of a day's or night's absence from camp for one or two of their number; but when the missing ones failed to show up in reasonable time there would be a search. And Venters was afraid of that.

"A good tracker could trail me," he muttered. "And I'd be cornered here. Let's see. Rustlers are a lazy set when they're not on the ride. I'll risk it. Then I'll change my hiding-place."

He carefully cleaned and reloaded his guns. When he rose to go he bent a long glance down upon the unconscious girl. Then ordering Whitie and Ring to keep guard, he left the camp.

The safest cover lay close under the wall of the canyon, and here through the dense thickets Venters made his slow, listening advance toward the oval. Upon gaining the wide opening he decided to cross it and follow the left wall till he came to the cattle trail. He scanned the oval as keenly as if hunting for antelope. Then, stooping, he stole from one cover to another, taking advantage of rocks and bunches of sage, until he had reached the thickets under the opposite wall. Once there, he exercised extreme caution in his surveys of the ground ahead, but increased his speed when moving. Dodging from bush to bush, he passed the mouths of two canyons, and in the entrance of a third canyon he crossed a wash of swift clear water, to come abruptly upon the cattle trail.

It followed the low bank of the wash, and, keeping it in sight, Venters hugged the line of sage and thicket. Like the curves of a serpent the canyon wound for a mile or more and then opened into a valley. Patches of red showed clear against the purple of sage, and farther out on the level dotted strings of red led away to the wall of rock.

"Ha, the red herd!" exclaimed Venters.

Then dots of white and black told him there were cattle of other colors in this inclosed valley. Oldring, the rustler, was also a rancher. Venters's calculating eye took count of stock that outnumbered the red herd.

"What a range!" went on Venters. "Water and grass enough for fifty thousand head, and no riders needed!"

After his first burst of surprise and rapid calculation Venters lost no time there, but slunk again into the sage on his back trail. With the discovery of Oldring's hidden cattle-range had come enlightenment on several problems. Here the rustler kept his stock, here was Jane Withersteen's red herd; here were the few cattle that had disappeared from the Cottonwoods slopes during the last two years. Until Oldring had driven the red herd his thefts of cattle for that time had not been more than enough to supply meat for his men. Of late no drives had been reported from Sterling or the villages north. And Venters knew that the riders had wondered at Oldring's inactivity in that particular field. He and his band had been active enough in their visits to Glaze and Cottonwoods; they always had gold; but of late the amount gambled away and drunk and thrown away in the villages had given rise to much conjecture. Oldring's more frequent visits had resulted in new saloons, and where there had formerly been one raid or shooting fray in the little hamlets there were now many. Perhaps Oldring had another range farther on up the pass, and from there drove the cattle to distant Utah towns where he was little known But Venters came finally to doubt this. And, from what he had learned in the last few days, a belief began to form in Venters's mind that Oldring's intimidations of the villages and the mystery of the Masked Rider, with his alleged evil deeds, and the fierce resistance offered any trailing riders, and the rustling of cattle—these things were only the craft of the rustler-chief to conceal his real life and purpose and work in Deception Pass.

And like a scouting Indian Venters crawled through the sage of the oval valley, crossed trail after trail on the north side, and at last entered the canyon out of which headed the cattle trail, and into which he had watched the rustlers disappear.

If he had used caution before, now he strained every nerve to force himself to creeping stealth and to sensitiveness of ear. He crawled along so hidden that he could not use his eyes except to aid himself in the toilsome progress through the brakes and ruins of cliff-wall. Yet from time to time, as he rested, he saw the massive red walls growing higher and wilder, more looming and broken. He made note of the fact that he was turning and climbing. The sage and thickets of oak and brakes of alder gave place to pinyon pine growing out of rocky soil. Suddenly a low, dull murmur assailed his ears. At first he thought it was thunder, then the slipping of a weathered slope of rock. But it was incessant, and as he progressed it filled out deeper and from a murmur changed into a soft roar.

"Falling water," he said. "There's volume to that. I wonder if it's the stream I lost."

The roar bothered him, for he could hear nothing else. Likewise, however, no rustlers could hear him. Emboldened by this and sure that nothing but a bird could see him, he arose from his hands and knees to hurry on. An opening in the pinyons warned him that he was nearing the height of slope.

He gained it, and dropped low with a burst of astonishment. Before him stretched a short canyon with rounded stone floor bare of grass or sage or tree, and with curved, shelving walls. A broad rippling stream flowed toward him, and at the back of the canyon waterfall burst from a wide rent in the cliff, and, bounding down in two green steps, spread into a long white sheet.

If Venters had not been indubitably certain that he had entered the right canyon his astonishment would not have been so great. There had been no breaks in the walls, no side canyons entering this one where the rustlers' tracks and the cattle trail had guided him, and, therefore, he could not be wrong. But here the canyon ended, and presumably the trails also.

"That cattle trail headed out of here," Venters kept saying to himself. "It headed out. Now what I want to know is how on earth did cattle ever get in here?"

CHAPTER V. THE MASKED RIDER

If he could be sure of anything it was of the careful scrutiny he had given that cattle track, every hoofmark of which headed straight west. He was now looking east at an immense round boxed corner of canyon down which tumbled a thin, white veil of water, scarcely twenty yards wide. Somehow, somewhere, his calculations had gone wrong. For the first time in years he found himself doubting his rider's skill in finding tracks, and his memory of what he had actually seen. In his anxiety to keep under cover he must have lost himself in this offshoot of Deception Pass, and thereby in some unaccountable manner, missed the canyon with the trails. There was nothing else for him to think. Rustlers could not fly, nor cattle jump down thousand-foot precipices. He was only proving what the sage-riders had long said of this labyrinthine system of deceitful canyons and valleys—trails led down into Deception Pass, but no rider had ever followed them.

On a sudden he heard above the soft roar of the waterfall an unusual sound that he could not define. He dropped flat behind a stone and listened. From the direction he had come swelled something that resembled a strange muffled pounding and splashing and ringing. Despite his nerve the chill sweat began to dampen his forehead. What might not be possible in this stonewalled maze of mystery? The unnatural sound passed beyond him as he lay gripping his rifle and fighting for coolness. Then from the open came the sound, now distinct and different. Venters recognized a hobble-bell of a horse, and the cracking of iron on submerged stones, and the hollow splash of hoofs in water.

Relief surged over him. His mind caught again at realities, and curiosity prompted him to peep from behind the rock.

In the middle of the stream waded a long string of packed burros driven by three superbly mounted men. Had Venters met these dark-clothed, dark-visaged, heavily armed men anywhere in Utah, let alone in this robbers' retreat, he would have recognized them as rustlers. The discerning eye of a rider saw the signs of a long, arduous trip. These men were packing in supplies from one of the northern villages. They were tired, and their horses were almost played out, and the burros plodded on, after the manner of their kind when exhausted, faithful and patient, but as if every weary, splashing, slipping step would be their last.

All this Venters noted in one glance. After that he watched with a thrilling eagerness. Straight at the waterfall the rustlers drove the burros, and straight through the middle, where the water spread into a fleecy, thin film like dissolving smoke. Following closely, the rustlers rode into this white mist, showing in bold black relief for an instant, and then they vanished.

Venters drew a full breath that rushed out in brief and sudden utterance.

"Good Heaven! Of all the holes for a rustler!... There's a cavern under that waterfall, and a passageway leading out to a canyon beyond. Oldring hides in there. He needs only to guard a trail leading down from the sage-flat above. Little danger of this outlet to the pass being discovered. I stumbled on it by luck, after I had given up. And now I know the truth of what puzzled me most—why that cattle trail was wet!"

He wheeled and ran down the slope, and out to the level of the sage-brush. Returning, he had no time to spare, only now and then, between dashes, a moment when he stopped to cast sharp eyes ahead. The abundant grass left no trace of his trail. Short work he made of the distance to the circle of canyons. He doubted that he would ever see it again; he knew he never wanted to; yet he looked at the red corners and towers with the eyes of a rider picturing landmarks never to be forgotten.

Here he spent a panting moment in a slow-circling gaze of the sage-oval and the gaps between the bluffs. Nothing stirred except the gentle wave of the tips of the brush. Then he pressed on past the mouths of several canyons and over ground new to him, now close under the eastern wall. This latter part proved to be easy traveling, well screened from possible observation from the north and west, and he soon covered it and felt safer in the deepening shade of his own canyon. Then the huge, notched bulge of red rim loomed over him, a mark by which he knew again the deep cove where his camp lay hidden. As he penetrated the thicket, safe again for the present, his thoughts reverted to the girl he had left there. The afternoon had far advanced. How would he find her? He ran into camp, frightening the dogs.

The girl lay with wide-open, dark eyes, and they dilated when he knelt beside her. The flush of fever shone in her cheeks. He lifted her and held water to her dry lips, and felt an inexplicable sense of lightness as he saw her swallow in a slow, choking gulp. Gently he laid her back.

"Who—are—you?" she whispered, haltingly.

"I'm the man who shot you," he replied.

"You'll—not—kill me—now?"

"No, no."

"What—will—you—do—with me?"

"When you get better—strong enough—I'll take you back to the canyon where the rustlers ride through the waterfall."

As with a faint shadow from a flitting wing overhead, the marble whiteness of her face seemed to change.

"Don't—take—me—back—there!"

CHAPTER VI. THE MILL-WHEEL OF STEERS

Meantime, at the ranch, when Judkins's news had sent Venters on the trail of the rustlers, Jane Withersteen led the injured man to her house and with skilled fingers dressed the gunshot wound in his arm.

"Judkins, what do you think happened to my riders?"

"I—I d rather not say," he replied.

"Tell me. Whatever you'll tell me I'll keep to myself. I'm beginning to worry about more than the loss of a herd of cattle. Venters hinted of—but tell me, Judkins."

"Well, Miss Withersteen, I think as Venters thinks—your riders have been called in."

"Judkins!... By whom?"

"You know who handles the reins of your Mormon riders."

"Do you dare insinuate that my churchmen have ordered in my riders?"

"I ain't insinuatin' nothin', Miss Withersteen," answered Judkins, with spirit. "I know what I'm talking about. I didn't want to tell you."

"Oh, I can't believe that! I'll not believe it! Would Tull leave my herds at the mercy of rustlers and wolves just because—because—? No, no! It's unbelievable."

"Yes, thet particular thing's onheard of around Cottonwoods But, beggin' pardon, Miss Withersteen, there never was any other rich Mormon woman here on the border, let alone one thet's taken the bit between her teeth."

That was a bold thing for the reserved Judkins to say, but it did not anger her. This rider's crude hint of her spirit gave her a glimpse of what others might think. Humility and obedience had been hers always. But had she taken the bit between her teeth? Still she wavered. And then, with quick spurt of warm blood along her veins, she thought of Black Star when he got the bit fast between his iron jaws and ran wild in the sage. If she ever started to run! Jane smothered the glow and burn within her, ashamed of a passion for freedom that opposed her duty.

"Judkins, go to the village," she said, "and when you have learned anything definite about my riders please come to me at once."

When he had gone Jane resolutely applied her mind to a number of tasks that of late had been neglected. Her father had trained her in the management of a hundred employees and the working of gardens and fields; and to keep record of the movements of cattle and riders. And beside the many duties she had added to this work was one of extreme delicacy, such as required all her tact and ingenuity. It was an unobtrusive, almost secret aid which she rendered to the Gentile families of the village. Though Jane Withersteen never admitted so to herself, it amounted to no less than a system of charity. But for her invention of numberless kinds of employment, for which there was no actual need, these families of Gentiles, who had failed in a Mormon community, would have starved.

In aiding these poor people Jane thought she deceived her keen churchmen, but it was a kind of deceit for which she did not pray to be forgiven. Equally as difficult was the task of deceiving the Gentiles, for they were as proud as they were poor. It had been a great grief to her to discover how these people hated her people; and it had been a source of great joy that through her they had come to soften in hatred. At any time this work called for a clearness of mind that precluded anxiety and worry; but under the present circumstances it required all her vigor and obstinate tenacity to pin her attention upon her task.

Sunset came, bringing with the end of her labor a patient calmness and power to wait that had not been hers earlier in the day. She expected Judkins, but he did not appear. Her house was always quiet; to-night, however, it seemed unusually so. At supper her women served her with a silent assiduity; it spoke what their sealed lips could not utter—the sympathy of Mormon women. Jerd came to her with the key of the great door of the stone stable, and to make his daily report about the horses. One of his daily duties was to give Black Star and Night and the other racers a ten-mile run. This day it had been omitted, and the boy grew confused in explanations that she had not asked for. She did inquire if he would return on the morrow, and Jerd, in mingled surprise and relief, assured her he would always work for her. Jane missed the rattle and trot, canter and gallop of the incoming riders on the hard trails. Dusk shaded the grove where she walked; the birds ceased singing; the wind sighed through the leaves of the cottonwoods, and the running water murmured down its stone-bedded channel. The glimmering of the first star was like the peace and beauty of the night. Her faith welled up in her heart and said that all would soon be right in her little world. She pictured Venters about his lonely camp-fire sitting between his faithful dogs. She prayed for his safety, for the success of his undertaking.

Early the next morning one of Jane's women brought in word that Judkins wished to speak to her. She hurried out, and in her surprise to see him armed with rifle and revolver, she forgot her intention to inquire about his wound.

"Judkins! Those guns? You never carried guns."

"It's high time, Miss Withersteen," he replied. "Will you come into the grove? It ain't jest exactly safe for me to be seen here."

She walked with him into the shade of the cottonwoods.

"What do you mean?"

"Miss Withersteen, I went to my mother's house last night. While there, some one knocked, an' a man asked for me. I went to the door. He wore a mask. He said

I'd better not ride any more for Jane Withersteen. His voice was hoarse an' strange, disguised I reckon, like his face. He said no more, an' ran off in the dark."

"Did you know who he was?" asked Jane, in a low voice.

"Yes."

Jane did not ask to know; she did not want to know; she feared to know. All her calmness fled at a single thought.

"Thet's why I'm packin' guns," went on Judkins. "For I'll never quit ridin' for you, Miss Withersteen, till you let me go."

"Judkins, do you want to leave me?"

"Do I look thet way? Give me a hoss—a fast hoss, an' send me out on the sage."

"Oh, thank you, Judkins! You're more faithful than my own people. I ought not accept your loyalty—you might suffer more through it. But what in the world can I do? My head whirls. The wrong to Venters—the stolen herd—these masks, threats, this coil in the dark! I can't understand! But I feel something dark and terrible closing in around me."

"Miss Withersteen, it's all simple enough," said Judkins, earnestly. "Now please listen—an' beggin' your pardon—jest turn thet deaf Mormon ear aside, an' let me talk clear an' plain in the other. I went around to the saloons an' the stores an' the loafin' places yesterday. All your riders are in. There's talk of a vigilance band organized to hunt down rustlers. They call themselves 'The Riders.' Thet's the report—thet's the reason given for your riders leavin' you. Strange thet only a few riders of other ranchers joined the band! An' Tull's man, Jerry Card—he's the leader. I seen him en' his hoss. He 'ain't been to Glaze. I'm not easy to fool on the looks of a hoss thet's traveled the sage. Tull an' Jerry didn't ride to Glaze!... Well, I met Blake en' Dorn, both good friends of mine, usually, as far as their Mormon lights will let 'em go. But these fellers couldn't fool me, an' they didn't try very hard. I asked them, straight out like a man, why they left you like thet. I didn't forget to mention how you nursed Blake's poor old mother when she was sick, an' how good you was to Dorn's kids. They looked ashamed, Miss Withersteen. An' they jest froze up—thet dark set look thet makes them strange an' different to me. But I could tell the difference between thet first natural twinge of conscience an' the later look of some secret thing. An' the difference I caught was thet they couldn't help themselves. They hadn't no say in the matter. They looked as if their bein' unfaithful to you was bein' faithful to a higher duty. An' there's the secret. Why it's as plain as—as sight of my gun here."

"Plain!... My herds to wander in the sage—to be stolen! Jane Withersteen a poor woman! Her head to be brought low and her spirit broken!... Why, Judkins, it's plain enough."

"Miss Withersteen, let me get what boys I can gather, an' hold the white herd. It's on the slope now, not ten miles out—three thousand head, an' all steers. They're wild, an' likely to stampede at the pop of a jack-rabbit's ears. We'll camp right with them, en' try to hold them."

"Judkins, I'll reward you some day for your service, unless all is taken from me. Get the boys and tell Jerd to give you pick of my horses, except Black Star and Night. But—do not shed blood for my cattle nor heedlessly risk your lives."

Jane Withersteen rushed to the silence and seclusion of her room, and there could not longer hold back the bursting of her wrath. She went stone-blind in the fury of a passion that had never before showed its power. Lying upon her bed, sightless, voiceless, she was a writhing, living flame. And she tossed there while her fury burned and burned, and finally burned itself out.

Then, weak and spent, she lay thinking, not of the oppression that would break her, but of this new revelation of self. Until the last few days there had been little in her life to rouse passions. Her forefathers had been Vikings, savage chieftains who bore no cross and brooked no hindrance to their will. Her father had inherited that temper; and at times, like antelope fleeing before fire on the slope, his people fled from his red rages. Jane Withersteen realized that the spirit of wrath and war had lain dormant in her. She shrank from black depths hitherto unsuspected. The one thing in man or woman that she scorned above all scorn, and which she could not forgive, was hate. Hate headed a flaming pathway straight to hell. All in a flash, beyond her control there had been in her a birth of fiery hate. And the man who had dragged her peaceful and loving spirit to this degradation was a minister of God's word, an Elder of her church, the counselor of her beloved Bishop.

The loss of herds and ranges, even of Amber Spring and the Old Stone House, no longer concerned Jane Withersteen, she faced the foremost thought of her life, what she now considered the mightiest problem—the salvation of her soul.

She knelt by her bedside and prayed; she prayed as she had never prayed in all her life—prayed to be forgiven for her sin to be immune from that dark, hot hate; to love Tull as her minister, though she could not love him as a man; to do her duty by her church and people and those dependent upon her bounty; to hold reverence of God and womanhood inviolate.

When Jane Withersteen rose from that storm of wrath and prayer for help she was serene, calm, sure—a changed woman. She would do her duty as she saw it, live her life as her own truth guided her. She might never be able to marry a man of her choice, but she certainly never would become the wife of Tull. Her churchmen might take her cattle and horses, ranges and fields, her corrals and stables, the house of Withersteen and the water that nourished the village of Cottonwoods; but they could not force her to marry Tull, they could not change her decision or break her spirit. Once resigned to further loss, and sure of herself, Jane Withersteen attained a peace of mind that had not been hers for a year. She forgave Tull, and felt a melancholy regret over what she knew he considered duty, irrespective of his personal feeling for her. First of all, Tull, as he was a man, wanted her for himself; and secondly, he hoped to save her and her riches for his church. She did not believe that Tull had been actuated solely by his minister's zeal to save her soul. She doubted her interpretation of one of his dark sayings—that if she were lost to him she might as well be lost to heaven. Jane Withersteen's common sense took arms against the binding limits of her religion; and she doubted that her Bishop, whom she had been taught had direct communication with God—would damn her soul for refusing to marry a Mormon. As for Tull and his churchmen, when they had harassed her, perhaps made her poor, they would find her unchangeable, and then she would get back most of what she had lost. So she reasoned, true at last to her faith in all men, and in their ultimate goodness.

The clank of iron hoofs upon the stone courtyard drew her hurriedly from her retirement. There, beside his horse, stood Lassiter, his dark apparel and the great black gun-sheaths contrasting singularly with his gentle smile. Jane's active mind took up her interest in him and her half-determined desire to use what charm she had to foil his evident design in visiting Cottonwoods. If she could mitigate his hatred of Mormons, or at least keep him from killing more of them, not only would she be saving her people, but also be leading back this bloodspiller to some semblance of the human.

"Mornin', ma'am," he said, black sombrero in hand.

"Lassiter I'm not an old woman, or even a madam," she replied, with her bright smile. "If you can't say Miss Withersteen—call me Jane."

"I reckon Jane would be easier. First names are always handy for me."

"Well, use mine, then. Lassiter, I'm glad to see you. I'm in trouble."

Then she told him of Judkins's return, of the driving of the red herd, of Venters's departure on Wrangle, and the calling-in of her riders.

"'Pears to me you're some smilin' an' pretty for a woman with so much trouble," he remarked.

"Lassiter! Are you paying me compliments? But, seriously I've made up my mind not to be miserable. I've lost much, and I'll lose more. Nevertheless, I won't be sour, and I hope I'll never be unhappy—again."

Lassiter twisted his hat round and round, as was his way, and took his time in replying.

"Women are strange to me. I got to back-trailin' myself from them long ago. But I'd like a game woman. Might I ask, seein' as how you take this trouble, if you're goin' to fight?"

"Fight! How? Even if I would, I haven't a friend except that boy who doesn't dare stay in the village."

"I make bold to say, ma'am—Jane—that there's another, if you want him."

"Lassiter!... Thank you. But how can I accept you as a friend? Think! Why, you'd ride down into the village with those terrible guns and kill my enemies—who are also my churchmen."

"I reckon I might be riled up to jest about that," he replied, dryly.

She held out both hands to him.

"Lassiter! I'll accept your friendship—be proud of it—return it—if I may keep you from killing another Mormon."

"I'll tell you one thing," he said, bluntly, as the gray lightning formed in his eyes. "You're too good a woman to be sacrificed as you're goin' to be.... No, I reckon you an' me can't be friends on such terms."

In her earnestness she stepped closer to him, repelled yet fascinated by the sudden transition of his moods. That he would fight for her was at once horrible and wonderful.

"You came here to kill a man—the man whom Milly Erne—"

"The man who dragged Milly Erne to hell—put it that way!... Jane Withersteen, yes, that's why I came here. I'd tell so much to no other livin' soul.... There're things such a woman as you'd never dream of—so don't mention her again. Not till you tell me the name of the man!"

"Tell you! I? Never!"

"I reckon you will. An' I'll never ask you. I'm a man of strange beliefs an' ways of thinkin', an' I seem to see into the future an' feel things hard to explain. The trail I've been followin' for so many years was twisted en' tangled, but it's straightenin' out now. An', Jane Withersteen, you crossed it long ago to ease poor Milly's agony. That, whether you want or not, makes Lassiter your friend. But you cross it now strangely to mean somethin to me—God knows what!—unless by your noble blindness to incite me to greater hatred of Mormon men."

Jane felt swayed by a strength that far exceeded her own. In a clash of wills with this man she would go to the wall. If she were to influence him it must be wholly through womanly allurement. There was that about Lassiter which commanded her respect. She had abhorred his name; face to face with him, she found she feared only his deeds. His mystic suggestion, his foreshadowing of something that she was to mean to him, pierced deep into her mind. She believed fate had thrown in her way the lover or husband of Milly Erne. She believed that through her an evil man might be reclaimed. His allusion to what he called her blindness terrified her. Such a mistaken idea of his might unleash the bitter, fatal mood she sensed in him. At any cost she must placate this man; she knew the die was cast, and that if Lassiter did not soften to a woman's grace and beauty and wiles, then it would be because she could not make him.

"I reckon you'll hear no more such talk from me," Lassiter went on, presently. "Now, Miss Jane, I rode in to tell you that your herd of white steers is down on the slope behind them big ridges. An' I seen somethin' goin' on that'd be mighty interestin' to you, if you could see it. Have you a field-glass?"

"Yes, I have two glasses. I'll get them and ride out with you. Wait, Lassiter, please," she said, and hurried within. Sending word to Jerd to saddle Black Star and fetch him to the court, she then went to her room and changed to the riding-clothes she always donned when going into the sage. In this male attire her mirror showed her a jaunty, handsome rider. If she expected some little need of admiration from Lassiter, she had no cause for disappointment. The gentle smile that she liked, which made of him another person, slowly overspread his face.

"If I didn't take you for a boy!" he exclaimed. "It's powerful queer what difference clothes make. Now I've been some scared of your dignity, like when the other night you was all in white but in this rig—"

CHAPTER VI. THE MILL-WHEEL OF STEERS

Black Star came pounding into the court, dragging Jerd half off his feet, and he whistled at Lassiter's black. But at sight of Jane all his defiant lines seemed to soften, and with tosses of his beautiful head he whipped his bridle.

"Down, Black Star, down," said Jane.

He dropped his head, and, slowly lengthening, he bent one foreleg, then the other, and sank to his knees. Jane slipped her left foot in the stirrup, swung lightly into the saddle, and Black Star rose with a ringing stamp. It was not easy for Jane to hold him to a canter through the grove, and like the wind he broke when he saw the sage. Jane let him have a couple of miles of free running on the open trail, and then she coaxed him in and waited for her companion. Lassiter was not long in catching up, and presently they were riding side by side. It reminded her how she used to ride with Venters. Where was he now? She gazed far down the slope to the curved purple lines of Deception Pass and involuntarily shut her eyes with a trembling stir of nameless fear.

"We'll turn off here," Lassiter said, "en' take to the sage a mile or so. The white herd is behind them big ridges."

"What are you going to show me?" asked Jane. "I'm prepared—don't be afraid."

He smiled as if he meant that bad news came swiftly enough without being presaged by speech.

When they reached the lee of a rolling ridge Lassiter dismounted, motioning to her to do likewise. They left the horses standing, bridles down. Then Lassiter, carrying the field-glasses began to lead the way up the slow rise of ground. Upon nearing the summit he halted her with a gesture.

"I reckon we'd see more if we didn't show ourselves against the sky," he said. "I was here less than an hour ago. Then the herd was seven or eight miles south, an' if they ain't bolted yet—"

"Lassiter!... Bolted?"

"That's what I said. Now let's see."

Jane climbed a few more paces behind him and then peeped over the ridge. Just beyond began a shallow swale that deepened and widened into a valley and then swung to the left. Following the undulating sweep of sage, Jane saw the straggling lines and then the great body of the white herd. She knew enough about steers, even at a distance of four or five miles, to realize that something was in the wind. Bringing her field-glass into use, she moved it slowly from left to right, which action swept the whole herd into range. The stragglers were restless; the more compactly massed steers were browsing. Jane brought the glass back to the big sentinels of the herd, and she saw them trot with quick steps, stop short and toss wide horns, look everywhere, and then trot in another direction.

"Judkins hasn't been able to get his boys together yet," said Jane. "But he'll be there soon. I hope not too late. Lassiter, what's frightening those big leaders?"

"Nothin' jest on the minute," replied Lassiter. "Them steers are quietin' down. They've been scared, but not bad yet. I reckon the whole herd has moved a few miles this way since I was here."

"They didn't browse that distance—not in less than an hour. Cattle aren't sheep."

"No, they jest run it, en' that looks bad."

"Lassiter, what frightened them?" repeated Jane, impatiently.

"Put down your glass. You'll see at first better with a naked eye. Now look along them ridges on the other side of the herd, the ridges where the sun shines bright on the sage.... That's right. Now look en' look hard en' wait."

Long-drawn moments of straining sight rewarded Jane with nothing save the low, purple rim of ridge and the shimmering sage.

"It's begun again!" whispered Lassiter, and he gripped her arm. "Watch.... There, did you see that?"

"No, no. Tell me what to look for?"

"A white flash—a kind of pin-point of quick light—a gleam as from sun shinin' on somethin' white."

Suddenly Jane's concentrated gaze caught a fleeting glint. Quickly she brought her glass to bear on the spot. Again the purple sage, magnified in color and size and wave, for long moments irritated her with its monotony. Then from out of the sage on the ridge flew up a broad, white object, flashed in the sunlight and vanished. Like magic it was, and bewildered Jane.

"What on earth is that?"

"I reckon there's some one behind that ridge throwin' up a sheet or a white blanket to reflect the sunshine."

"Why?" queried Jane, more bewildered than ever.

"To stampede the herd," replied Lassiter, and his teeth clicked.

"Ah!" She made a fierce, passionate movement, clutched the glass tightly, shook as with the passing of a spasm, and then dropped her head. Presently she raised it to greet Lassiter with something like a smile. "My righteous brethren are at work again," she said, in scorn. She had stifled the leap of her wrath, but for perhaps the first time in her life a bitter derision curled her lips. Lassiter's cool gray eyes seemed to pierce her. "I said I was prepared for anything; but that was hardly true. But why would they—anybody stampede my cattle?"

"That's a Mormon's godly way of bringin' a woman to her knees."

"Lassiter, I'll die before I ever bend my knees. I might be led I won't be driven. Do you expect the herd to bolt?"

"I don't like the looks of them big steers. But you can never tell. Cattle sometimes stampede as easily as buffalo. Any little flash or move will start them. A rider gettin' down an' walkin' toward them sometimes will make them jump an' fly. Then again nothin' seems to scare them. But I reckon that white flare will do the biz. It's a new one on me, an' I've seen some ridin' an' rustlin'. It jest takes one of them God-fearin' Mormons to think of devilish tricks."

"Lassiter, might not this trick be done by Oldring's men?" asked Jane, ever grasping at straws.

"It might be, but it ain't," replied Lassiter. "Oldring's an honest thief. He don't skulk behind ridges to scatter your cattle to the four winds. He rides down on you, an' if you don't like it you can throw a gun."

Jane bit her tongue to refrain from championing men who at the very moment were proving to her that they were little and mean compared even with rustlers.

"Look!... Jane, them leadin' steers have bolted. They're drawin' the stragglers, an' that'll pull the whole herd."

Jane was not quick enough to catch the details called out by Lassiter, but she saw the line of cattle lengthening. Then, like a stream of white bees pouring from a huge swarm, the steers stretched out from the main body. In a few moments, with astonishing rapidity, the whole herd got into motion. A faint roar of trampling hoofs came to Jane's ears, and gradually swelled; low, rolling clouds of dust began to rise above the sage.

"It's a stampede, an' a hummer," said Lassiter.

"Oh, Lassiter! The herd's running with the valley! It leads into the canyon! There's a straight jump-off!"

"I reckon they'll run into it, too. But that's a good many miles yet. An', Jane, this valley swings round almost north before it goes east. That stampede will pass within a mile of us."

The long, white, bobbing line of steers streaked swiftly through the sage, and a funnel-shaped dust-cloud arose at a low angle. A dull rumbling filled Jane's ears.

"I'm thinkin' of millin' that herd," said Lassiter. His gray glance swept up the slope to the west. "There's some specks an' dust way off toward the village. Mebbe that's Judkins an' his boys. It ain't likely he'll get here in time to help. You'd better hold Black Star here on this high ridge."

He ran to his horse and, throwing off saddle-bags and tightening the cinches, he leaped astride and galloped straight down across the valley.

Jane went for Black Star and, leading him to the summit of the ridge, she mounted and faced the valley with excitement and expectancy. She had heard of milling stampeded cattle, and knew it was a feat accomplished by only the most daring riders.

The white herd was now strung out in a line two miles long. The dull rumble of thousands of hoofs deepened into continuous low thunder, and as the steers swept swiftly closer the thunder became a heavy roll. Lassiter crossed in a few moments the level of the valley to the eastern rise of ground and there waited the coming of the herd. Presently, as the head of the white line reached a point opposite to where Jane stood, Lassiter spurred his black into a run.

Jane saw him take a position on the off side of the leaders of the stampede, and there he rode. It was like a race. They swept on down the valley, and when the end of the white line neared Lassiter's first stand the head had begun to swing round to the west. It swung slowly and stubbornly, yet surely, and gradually assumed a long, beautiful curve of moving white. To Jane's amaze she saw the leaders swinging, turning till they headed back toward her and up the valley. Out to the right of these wild plunging steers ran Lassiter's black, and Jane's keen eye appreciated the fleet stride and sure-footedness of the blind horse. Then it seemed that the herd moved in a great curve, a huge half-moon with the points of head and tail almost opposite, and a mile apart But Lassiter relentlessly crowded the leaders, sheering them to the left, turning them little by little. And the dust-blinded wild followers plunged on madly in the tracks of their leaders. This ever-moving, ever-changing curve of steers rolled toward Jane and when below her, scarce half a mile, it began to narrow and close into a circle. Lassiter had ridden parallel with her position, turned toward her, then aside, and now he was riding directly away from her, all the time pushing the head of that bobbing line inward.

It was then that Jane, suddenly understanding Lassiter's feat stared and gasped at the riding of this intrepid man. His horse was fleet and tireless, but blind. He had pushed the leaders around and around till they were about to turn in on the inner side of the end of that line of steers. The leaders were already running in a circle; the end of the herd was still running almost straight. But soon they would be wheeling. Then, when Lassiter had the circle formed, how would he escape? With Jane Withersteen prayer was as ready as praise; and she prayed for this man's safety. A circle of dust began to collect. Dimly, as through a yellow veil, Jane saw Lassiter press the leaders inward to close the gap in the sage. She lost sight of him in the dust, again she thought she saw the black, riderless now, rear and drag himself and fall. Lassiter had been thrown—lost! Then he reappeared running out of the dust into the sage. He had escaped, and she breathed again.

Spellbound, Jane Withersteen watched this stupendous millwheel of steers. Here was the milling of the herd. The white running circle closed in upon the open space of sage. And the dust circles closed above into a pall. The ground quaked and the incessant thunder of pounding hoofs rolled on. Jane felt deafened, yet she thrilled to a new sound. As the circle of sage lessened the steers began to bawl, and when it closed entirely there came a great upheaval in the center, and a terrible thumping of heads and clicking of horns. Bawling, climbing, goring, the great mass of steers on the inside wrestled in a crashing din, heaved and groaned under the pressure. Then came a deadlock. The inner strife ceased, and the hideous roar and crash. Movement went on in the outer circle, and that, too, gradually stilled. The white herd had come to a stop, and the pall of yellow dust began to drift away on the wind.

Jane Withersteen waited on the ridge with full and grateful heart. Lassiter appeared, making his weary way toward her through the sage. And up on the slope Judkins rode into sight with his troop of boys. For the present, at least, the white herd would be looked after.

When Lassiter reached her and laid his hand on Black Star's mane, Jane could not find speech.

"Killed—my—hoss," he panted.

"Oh! I'm sorry," cried Jane. "Lassiter! I know you can't replace him, but I'll give you any one of my racers—Bells, or Night, even Black Star."

"I'll take a fast hoss, Jane, but not one of your favorites," he replied. "Only—will you let me have Black Star now an' ride him over there an' head off them fellers who stampeded the herd?"

He pointed to several moving specks of black and puffs of dust in the purple sage.

"I can head them off with this hoss, an' then—"

"Then, Lassiter?"

"They'll never stampede no more cattle."

"Oh! No! No!... Lassiter, I won't let you go!"

But a flush of fire flamed in her cheeks, and her trembling hands shook Black Star's bridle, and her eyes fell before Lassiter's.

CHAPTER VII. THE DAUGHTER OF WITHERSTEEN

"Lassiter, will you be my rider?" Jane had asked him.

"I reckon so," he had replied.

Few as the words were, Jane knew how infinitely much they implied. She wanted him to take charge of her cattle and horse and ranges, and save them if that were possible. Yet, though she could not have spoken aloud all she meant, she was perfectly honest with herself. Whatever the price to be paid, she must keep Lassiter close to her; she must shield from him the man who had led Milly Erne to Cottonwoods. In her fear she so controlled her mind that she did not whisper this Mormon's name to her own soul, she did not even think it. Besides, beyond this thing she regarded as a sacred obligation thrust upon her, was the need of a helper, of a friend, of a champion in this critical time. If she could rule this gun-man, as Venters had called him, if she could even keep him from shedding blood, what strategy to play his flame and his presence against the game of oppression her churchmen were waging against her? Never would she forget the effect on Tull and his men when Venters shouted Lassiter's name. If she could not wholly control Lassiter, then what she could do might put off the fatal day.

One of her safe racers was a dark bay, and she called him Bells because of the way he struck his iron shoes on the stones. When Jerd led out this slender, beautifully built horse Lassiter suddenly became all eyes. A rider's love of a thoroughbred shone in them. Round and round Bells he walked, plainly weakening all the time in his determination not to take one of Jane's favorite racers.

"Lassiter, you're half horse, and Bells sees it already," said Jane, laughing. "Look at his eyes. He likes you. He'll love you, too. How can you resist him? Oh, Lassiter, but Bells can run! It's nip and tuck between him and Wrangle, and only Black Star can beat him. He's too spirited a horse for a woman. Take him. He's yours."

"I jest am weak where a hoss's concerned," said Lassiter. "I'll take him, an' I'll take your orders, ma'am."

"Well, I'm glad, but never mind the ma'am. Let it still be Jane."

From that hour, it seemed, Lassiter was always in the saddle, riding early and late, and coincident with his part in Jane's affairs the days assumed their old tranquillity. Her intelligence told her this was only the lull before the storm, but her faith would not have it so.

She resumed her visits to the village, and upon one of these she encountered Tull. He greeted her as he had before any trouble came between them, and she, responsive to peace if not quick to forget, met him halfway with manner almost cheerful. He regretted the loss of her cattle; he assured her that the vigilantes which had been organized would soon rout the rustlers; when that had been accomplished her riders would likely return to her.

"You've done a headstrong thing to hire this man Lassiter," Tull went on, severely. "He came to Cottonwoods with evil intent."

"I had to have somebody. And perhaps making him my rider may turn out best in the end for the Mormons of Cottonwoods."

"You mean to stay his hand?"

"I do—if I can."

"A woman like you can do anything with a man. That would be well, and would atone in some measure for the errors you have made."

He bowed and passed on. Jane resumed her walk with conflicting thoughts. She resented Elder Tull's cold, impassive manner that looked down upon her as one who had incurred his just displeasure. Otherwise he would have been the same calm, dark-browed, impenetrable man she had known for ten years. In fact, except when he had revealed his passion in the matter of the seizing of Venters, she had never dreamed he could be other than the grave, reproving preacher. He stood out now a strange, secretive man. She would have thought better of him if he had picked up the threads of their quarrel where they had parted. Was Tull what he appeared to be? The question flung itself in-voluntarily over Jane Withersteen's inhibitive habit of faith without question. And she refused to answer it. Tull could not fight in the open. Venters had said, Lassiter had said, that her Elder shirked fight and worked in the dark. Just now in this meeting Tull had ignored the fact that he had sued, exhorted, demanded that she marry him. He made no mention of Venters. His manner was that of the minister who had been outraged, but who overlooked the frailties of a woman. Beyond question he seemed unutterably aloof from all knowledge of pressure being brought to bear upon her, absolutely guiltless of any connection with secret power over riders, with night journeys, with rustlers and stampedes of cattle. And that convinced her again of unjust suspicions. But it was convincement through an obstinate faith. She shuddered as she accepted it, and that shudder was the nucleus of a terrible revolt.

Jane turned into one of the wide lanes leading from the main street and entered a huge, shady yard. Here were sweet-smelling clover, alfalfa, flowers, and vegetables, all growing in happy confusion. And like these fresh green things were the dozens of babies, tots, toddlers, noisy urchins, laughing girls, a whole multitude of children of one family. For Collier Brandt, the father of all this numerous progeny, was a Mormon with four wives.

The big house where they lived was old, solid, picturesque the lower part built of logs, the upper of rough clapboards, with vines growing up the outside stone chimneys. There were many wooden-shuttered windows, and one pretentious window of glass proudly curtained in white. As this house had four mistresses, it likewise had four separate sections, not one of which communicated with another, and all had to be entered from the outside.

In the shade of a wide, low, vine-roofed porch Jane found Brandt's wives entertaining Bishop Dyer. They were motherly women, of comparatively similar ages, and plain-featured, and just at this moment anything but grave. The Bishop was rather tall, of stout build, with iron-gray hair and beard, and eyes of light blue. They were merry now; but Jane had seen them when they were not, and then she feared him as she had feared her father.

The women flocked around her in welcome.

"Daughter of Withersteen," said the Bishop, gaily, as he took her hand, "you have not been prodigal of your gracious self of late. A Sabbath without you at service! I shall reprove Elder Tull."

"Bishop, the guilt is mine. I'll come to you and confess," Jane replied, lightly; but she felt the undercurrent of her words.

"Mormon love-making!" exclaimed the Bishop, rubbing his hands. "Tull keeps you all to himself."

"No. He is not courting me."

"What? The laggard! If he does not make haste I'll go a-courting myself up to Withersteen House."

There was laughter and further bantering by the Bishop, and then mild talk of village affairs, after which he took his leave, and Jane was left with her friend, Mary Brandt.

"Jane, you're not yourself. Are you sad about the rustling of the cattle? But you have so many, you are so rich."

Then Jane confided in her, telling much, yet holding back her doubts of fear.

"Oh, why don't you marry Tull and be one of us?

"But, Mary, I don't love Tull," said Jane, stubbornly.

"I don't blame you for that. But, Jane Withersteen, you've got to choose between the love of man and love of God. Often we Mormon women have to do that. It's not easy. The kind of happiness you want I wanted once. I never got it, nor will you, unless you throw away your soul. We've all watched your affair with Venters in fear and trembling. Some dreadful thing will come of it. You don't want him hanged or shot—or treated worse, as that Gentile boy was treated in Glaze for fooling round a Mormon woman. Marry Tull. It's your duty as a Mormon. You'll feel no rapture as his wife—but think of Heaven! Mormon women don't marry for what they expect on earth. Take up the cross, Jane. Remember your father found Amber Spring, built these old houses, brought Mormons here, and fathered them. You are the daughter of Withersteen!"

Jane left Mary Brandt and went to call upon other friends. They received her with the same glad welcome as had Mary, lavished upon her the pent-up affection of Mormon women, and let her go with her ears ringing of Tull, Venters, Lassiter, of duty to God and glory in Heaven.

"Verily," murmured Jane, "I don't know myself when, through all this, I remain unchanged—nay, more fixed of purpose."

She returned to the main street and bent her thoughtful steps toward the center of the village. A string of wagons drawn by oxen was lumbering along. These "sage-freighters," as they were called, hauled grain and flour and merchandise from Sterling, and Jane laughed suddenly in the midst of her humility at the thought that they were her property, as was one of the three stores for which they freighted goods. The water that flowed along the path at her feet, and turned into each cottage-yard to nourish garden and orchard, also was hers, no less her private property because she chose to give it free. Yet in this village of Cottonwoods, which her father had founded and which she maintained she was not her own mistress; she was not able to abide by her own choice of a husband. She was the daughter of Withersteen. Suppose she proved it, imperiously! But she quelled that proud temptation at its birth.

Nothing could have replaced the affection which the village people had for her; no power could have made her happy as the pleasure her presence gave. As she went on down the street past the stores with their rude platform entrances, and the saloons where tired horses stood with bridles dragging, she was again assured of what was the bread and wine of life to her—that she was loved. Dirty boys playing in the ditch, clerks, teamsters, riders, loungers on the corners, ranchers on dusty horses, little girls running errands, and women hurrying to the stores all looked up at her coming with glad eyes.

Jane's various calls and wandering steps at length led her to the Gentile quarter of the village. This was at the extreme southern end, and here some thirty Gentile families lived in huts and shacks and log-cabins and several dilapidated cottages. The fortunes of these inhabitants of Cottonwoods could be read in their abodes. Water they had in abundance, and therefore grass and fruit-trees and patches of alfalfa and vegetable gardens. Some of the men and boys had a few stray cattle, others obtained such intermittent employment as the Mormons reluctantly tendered them. But none of the families was prosperous, many were very poor, and some lived only by Jane Withersteen's beneficence.

As it made Jane happy to go among her own people, so it saddened her to come in contact with these Gentiles. Yet that was not because she was unwelcome; here she was gratefully received by the women, passionately by the children. But poverty and idleness, with their attendant wretchedness and sorrow, always hurt her. That she could alleviate this distress more now than ever before proved the adage that it was an ill wind that blew nobody good. While her Mormon riders were in her employ she had found few Gentiles who would stay with her, and now she was able to find employment for all the men and boys. No little shock was it to have man after man tell her that he dare not accept her kind offer.

"It won't do," said one Carson, an intelligent man who had seen better days. "We've had our warning. Plain and to the point! Now there's Judkins, he packs guns, and he can use them, and so can the daredevil boys he's hired. But they've little responsibility. Can we risk having our homes burned in our absence?"

Jane felt the stretching and chilling of the skin of her face as the blood left it.

"Carson, you and the others rent these houses?" she asked.

"You ought to know, Miss Withersteen. Some of them are yours."

"I know?... Carson, I never in my life took a day's labor for rent or a yearling calf or a bunch of grass, let alone gold."

"Bivens, your store-keeper, sees to that."

"Look here, Carson," went on Jane, hurriedly, and now her cheeks were burning. "You and Black and Willet pack your goods and move your families up to my cabins in the grove. They're far more comfortable than these. Then go to work for me. And if aught happens to you there I'll give you money—gold enough to leave Utah!"

The man choked and stammered, and then, as tears welled into his eyes, he found the use of his tongue and cursed. No gentle speech could ever have equaled that curse in eloquent expression of what he felt for Jane Withersteen. How strangely his look and tone reminded her of Lassiter!

"No, it won't do," he said, when he had somewhat recovered himself. "Miss Withersteen, there are things that you don't know, and there's not a soul among us who can tell you."

"I seem to be learning many things, Carson. Well, then, will you let me aid you—say till better times?"

"Yes, I will," he replied, with his face lighting up. "I see what it means to you, and you know what it means to me. Thank you! And if better times ever come, I'll be only too happy to work for you."

"Better times will come. I trust God and have faith in man. Good day, Carson."

The lane opened out upon the sage-inclosed alfalfa fields, and the last habitation, at the end of that lane of hovels, was the meanest. Formerly it had been a shed; now it was a home. The broad leaves of a wide-spreading cottonwood sheltered the sunken roof of weathered boards. Like an Indian hut, it had one floor. Round about it were a few scanty rows of vegetables, such as the hand of a weak woman had time and strength to cultivate. This little dwelling-place was just outside the village limits, and the widow who lived there had to carry her water from the nearest irrigation ditch. As Jane Withersteen entered the unfenced yard a child saw her, shrieked with joy, and came tearing toward her with curls flying. This child was a little girl of four called Fay. Her name suited her, for she was an elf, a sprite, a creature so fairy-like and beautiful that she seemed unearthly.

"Muvver sended for oo," cried Fay, as Jane kissed her, "an' oo never tome."

"I didn't know, Fay; but I've come now."

Fay was a child of outdoors, of the garden and ditch and field, and she was dirty and ragged. But rags and dirt did not hide her beauty. The one thin little bedraggled garment she wore half covered her fine, slim body. Red as cherries were her cheeks and lips; her eyes were violet blue, and the crown of her childish loveliness was the curling golden hair. All the children of Cottonwoods were Jane Withersteen's friends, she loved them all. But Fay was dearest to her. Fay had few playmates, for among the Gentile children there were none near her age, and the

Mormon children were forbidden to play with her. So she was a shy, wild, lonely child.

"Muvver's sick," said Fay, leading Jane toward the door of the hut.

Jane went in. There was only one room, rather dark and bare, but it was clean and neat. A woman lay upon a bed.

"Mrs. Larkin, how are you?" asked Jane, anxiously.

"I've been pretty bad for a week, but I'm better now."

"You haven't been here all alone—with no one to wait on you?"

"Oh no! My women neighbors are kind. They take turns coming in."

"Did you send for me?"

"Yes, several times."

"But I had no word—no messages ever got to me."

"I sent the boys, and they left word with your women that I was ill and would you please come."

A sudden deadly sickness seized Jane. She fought the weakness, as she fought to be above suspicious thoughts, and it passed, leaving her conscious of her utter impotence. That, too, passed as her spirit rebounded. But she had again caught a glimpse of dark underhand domination, running its secret lines this time into her own household. Like a spider in the blackness of night an unseen hand had begun to run these dark lines, to turn and twist them about her life, to plait and weave a web. Jane Withersteen knew it now, and in the realization further coolness and sureness came to her, and the fighting courage of her ancestors.

"Mrs. Larkin, you're better, and I'm so glad," said Jane. "But may I not do something for you—a turn at nursing, or send you things, or take care of Fay?"

"You're so good. Since my husband's been gone what would have become of Fay and me but for you? It was about Fay that I wanted to speak to you. This time I thought surely I'd die, and I was worried about Fay. Well, I'll be around all right shortly, but my strength's gone and I won't live long. So I may as well speak now. You remember you've been asking me to let you take Fay and bring her up as your daughter?"

"Indeed yes, I remember. I'll be happy to have her. But I hope the day—"

"Never mind that. The day'll come—sooner or later. I refused your offer, and now I'll tell you why."

"I know why," interposed Jane. "It's because you don't want her brought up as a Mormon."

"No, it wasn't altogether that." Mrs. Larkin raised her thin hand and laid it appealingly on Jane's. "I don't like to tell you. But—it's this: I told all my friends what you wanted. They know you, care for you, and they said for me to trust Fay to you. Women will talk, you know. It got to the ears of Mormons—gossip of your love for Fay and your wanting her. And it came straight back to me, in jealousy, perhaps, that you wouldn't take Fay as much for love of her as because of your religious duty to bring up another girl for some Mormon to marry."

"That's a damnable lie!" cried Jane Withersteen.

"It was what made me hesitate," went on Mrs. Larkin, "but I never believed it at heart. And now I guess I'll let you—"

"Wait! Mrs. Larkin, I may have told little white lies in my life, but never a lie that mattered, that hurt any one. Now believe me. I love little Fay. If I had her near me I'd grow to worship her. When I asked for her I thought only of that love.... Let me prove this. You and Fay come to live with me. I've such a big house, and I'm so lonely. I'll help nurse you, take care of you. When you're better you can work for me. I'll keep little Fay and bring her up—without Mormon teaching. When she's grown, if she should want to leave me, I'll send her, and not empty-handed, back to Illinois where you came from. I promise you."

"I knew it was a lie," replied the mother, and she sank back upon her pillow with something of peace in her white, worn face. "Jane Withersteen, may Heaven bless you! I've been deeply grateful to you. But because you're a Mormon I never felt close to you till now. I don't know much about religion as religion, but your God and my God are the same."

CHAPTER VIII. SURPRISE VALLEY

Back in that strange canyon, which Venters had found indeed a valley of surprises, the wounded girl's whispered appeal, almost a prayer, not to take her back to the rustlers crowned the events of the last few days with a confounding climax. That she should not want to return to them staggered Venters. Presently, as logical thought returned, her appeal confirmed his first impression—that she was more unfortunate than bad—and he experienced a sensation of gladness. If he had known before that Oldring's Masked Rider was a woman his opinion would have been formed and he would have considered her abandoned. But his first knowledge had come when he lifted a white face quivering in a convulsion of agony; he had heard God's name whispered by blood-stained lips; through her solemn and awful eyes he had caught a glimpse of her soul. And just now had come the entreaty to him, "Don't—take—me—back—there!"

Once for all Venters's quick mind formed a permanent conception of this poor girl. He based it, not upon what the chances of life had made her, but upon the revelation of dark eyes that pierced the infinite, upon a few pitiful, halting words that betrayed failure and wrong and misery, yet breathed the truth of a tragic fate rather than a natural leaning to evil.

"What's your name?" he inquired.

"Bess," she answered.

"Bess what?"

"That's enough—just Bess."

The red that deepened in her cheeks was not all the flush of fever. Venters marveled anew, and this time at the tint of shame in her face, at the momentary drooping of long lashes. She might be a rustler's girl, but she was still capable of shame, she might be dying, but she still clung to some little remnant of honor.

"Very well, Bess. It doesn't matter," he said. "But this matters—what shall I do with you?"

"Are—you—a rider?" she whispered.

"Not now. I was once. I drove the Withersteen herds. But I lost my place—lost all I owned—and now I'm—I'm a sort of outcast. My name's Bern Venters."

"You won't—take me—to Cottonwoods—or Glaze? I'd be—hanged."

"No, indeed. But I must do something with you. For it's not safe for me here. I shot that rustler who was with you. Sooner or later he'll be found, and then my tracks. I must find a safer hiding-place where I can't be trailed."

"Leave me—here."

"Alone—to die!"

"Yes."

"I will not." Venters spoke shortly with a kind of ring in his voice.

"What—do you want—to do—with me?" Her whispering grew difficult, so low and faint that Venters had to stoop to hear her.

"Why, let's see," he replied, slowly. "I'd like to take you some place where I could watch by you, nurse you, till you're all right."

"And—then?"

"Well, it'll be time to think of that when you're cured of your wound. It's a bad one. And—Bess, if you don't want to live—if you don't fight for life—you'll never—"

"Oh! I want—to live! I'm afraid—to die. But I'd rather—die—than go back—to—to—"

"To Oldring?" asked Venters, interrupting her in turn.

Her lips moved in an affirmative.

"I promise not to take you back to him or to Cottonwoods or to Glaze."

The mournful earnestness of her gaze suddenly shone with unutterable gratitude and wonder. And as suddenly Venters found her eyes beautiful as he had never seen or felt beauty. They were as dark blue as the sky at night. Then the flashing changed to a long, thoughtful look, in which there was a wistful, unconscious searching of his face, a look that trembled on the verge of hope and trust.

"I'll try—to live," she said. The broken whisper just reached his ears. "Do what—you want—with me."

"Rest then—don't worry—sleep," he replied.

Abruptly he arose, as if words had been decision for him, and with a sharp command to the dogs he strode from the camp. Venters was conscious of an indefinite conflict of change within him. It seemed to be a vague passing of old moods, a dim coalescing of new forces, a moment of inexplicable transition. He was both cast down and uplifted. He wanted to think and think of the meaning, but he resolutely dispelled emotion. His imperative need at present was to find a safe retreat, and this called for action.

So he set out. It still wanted several hours before dark. This trip he turned to the left and wended his skulking way southward a mile or more to the opening of the valley, where lay the strange scrawled rocks. He did not, however, venture boldly out into the open sage, but clung to the right-hand wall and went along that till its perpendicular line broke into the long incline of bare stone.

Before proceeding farther he halted, studying the strange character of this slope and realizing that a moving black object could be seen far against such background. Before him ascended a gradual swell of smooth stone. It was hard, polished, and full of pockets worn by centuries of eddying rain-water. A hundred yards up began a line of grotesque cedar-trees, and they extended along the slope clear to its most southerly end. Beyond that end Venters wanted to get, and he concluded the cedars, few as they were, would afford some cover.

Therefore he climbed swiftly. The trees were farther up than he had estimated, though he had from long habit made allowance for the deceiving nature of distances in that country. When he gained the cover of cedars he paused to rest and look, and it was then he saw how the trees sprang from holes in the bare rock. Ages of rain had run down the slope, circling, eddying in depressions, wearing deep round holes. There had been dry seasons, accumulations of dust, wind-blown seeds, and cedars rose wonderfully out of solid rock. But these were not beautiful cedars. They were gnarled, twisted into weird contortions, as if growth were torture, dead at the tops, shrunken, gray, and old. Theirs had been a bitter fight, and Venters felt a strange sympathy for them. This country was hard on trees—and men.

He slipped from cedar to cedar, keeping them between him and the open valley. As he progressed, the belt of trees widened and he kept to its upper margin. He passed shady pockets half full of water, and, as he marked the location for possible future need, he reflected that there had been no rain since the winter snows. From one of these shady holes a rabbit hopped out and squatted down, laying its ears flat.

Venters wanted fresh meat now more than when he had only himself to think of. But it would not do to fire his rifle there. So he broke off a cedar branch and threw it. He crippled the rabbit, which started to flounder up the slope. Venters did not wish to lose the meat, and he never allowed crippled game to escape, to die lingeringly in some covert. So after a careful glance below, and back toward the canyon, he began to chase the rabbit.

The fact that rabbits generally ran uphill was not new to him. But it presently seemed singular why this rabbit, that might have escaped downward, chose to ascend the slope. Venters knew then that it had a burrow higher up. More than once he jerked over to seize it, only in vain, for the rabbit by renewed effort eluded his grasp. Thus the chase continued on up the bare slope. The farther Venters climbed the more determined he grew to catch his quarry. At last, panting and sweating, he captured the rabbit at the foot of a steeper grade. Laying his rifle on the bulge of rising stone, he killed the animal and slung it from his belt.

Before starting down he waited to catch his breath. He had climbed far up that wonderful smooth slope, and had almost reached the base of yellow cliff that rose skyward, a huge scarred and cracked bulk. It frowned down upon him as if to forbid further ascent. Venters bent over for his rifle, and, as he picked it up from where it leaned against the steeper grade, he saw several little nicks cut in the solid stone.

They were only a few inches deep and about a foot apart. Venters began to count them—one—two—three—four—on up to sixteen. That number carried his glance to the top of his first bulging bench of cliff-base. Above, after a more level offset, was still steeper slope, and the line of nicks kept on, to wind round a projecting corner of wall.

A casual glance would have passed by these little dents; if Venters had not known what they signified he would never have bestowed upon them the second glance. But he knew they had been cut there by hand, and, though age-worn, he recognized them as steps cut in the rock by the cliff-dwellers. With a pulse beginning to beat and hammer away his calmness, he eyed that indistinct line of steps, up to where the buttress of wall hid further sight of them. He knew that behind the corner of stone would be a cave or a crack which could never be suspected from below. Chance, that had sported with him of late, now directed him to a probable hiding-place. Again he laid aside his rifle, and, removing boots and belt, he began to walk up the steps. Like a mountain goat, he was agile, sure-footed, and he mounted the first bench without bending to use his hands. The next ascent took grip of fingers as well as toes, but he climbed steadily, swiftly, to reach the projecting corner, and slipped around it. Here he faced a notch in the cliff. At the apex he turned abruptly into a ragged vent that split the ponderous wall clear to the top, showing a narrow streak of blue sky.

At the base this vent was dark, cool, and smelled of dry, musty dust. It zigzagged so that he could not see ahead more than a few yards at a time. He noticed tracks of wildcats and rabbits in the dusty floor. At every turn he expected to come upon a huge cavern full of little square stone houses, each with a small aperture like a staring dark eye. The passage lightened and widened, and opened at the foot of a narrow, steep, ascending chute.

Venters had a moment's notice of the rock, which was of the same smoothness and hardness as the slope below, before his gaze went irresistibly upward to the precipitous walls of this wide ladder of granite. These were ruined walls of yellow sandstone, and so split and splintered, so overhanging with great sections of balancing rim, so impending with tremendous crumbling crags, that Venters caught his breath sharply, and, appalled, he instinctively recoiled as if a step upward might jar the ponderous cliffs from their foundation. Indeed, it seemed that these ruined cliffs were but awaiting a breath of wind to collapse and come tumbling down. Venters hesitated. It would be a foolhardy man who risked his life under the leaning, waiting avalanches of rock in that gigantic split. Yet how many years had they leaned there without falling! At the bottom of the incline was an immense heap of weathered sandstone all crumbling to dust, but there were no huge rocks as large as houses, such as rested so lightly and frightfully above, waiting patiently and inevitably to crash down. Slowly split from the parent rock by the weathering process, and carved and sculptured by ages of wind and rain, they waited their moment. Venters felt how foolish it was for him to fear these broken walls; to fear that, after they had endured for thousands of years, the moment of his passing should be the one for them to slip. Yet he feared it.

"What a place to hide!" muttered Venters. "I'll climb—I'll see where this thing goes. If only I can find water!"

CHAPTER VIII. SURPRISE VALLEY

With teeth tight shut he essayed the incline. And as he climbed he bent his eyes downward. This, however, after a little grew impossible; he had to look to obey his eager, curious mind. He raised his glance and saw light between row on row of shafts and pinnacles and crags that stood out from the main wall. Some leaned against the cliff, others against each other; many stood sheer and alone; all were crumbling, cracked, rotten. It was a place of yellow, ragged ruin. The passage narrowed as he went up; it became a slant, hard for him to stick on; it was smooth as marble. Finally he surmounted it, surprised to find the walls still several hundred feet high, and a narrow gorge leading down on the other side. This was a divide between two inclines, about twenty yards wide. At one side stood an enormous rock. Venters gave it a second glance, because it rested on a pedestal. It attracted closer attention. It was like a colossal pear of stone standing on its stem. Around the bottom were thousands of little nicks just distinguishable to the eye. They were marks of stone hatchets. The cliff-dwellers had chipped and chipped away at this boulder till it rested its tremendous bulk upon a mere pin-point of its surface. Venters pondered. Why had the little stone-men hacked away at that big boulder? It bore no semblance to a statue or an idol or a godhead or a sphinx. Instinctively he put his hands on it and pushed; then his shoulder and heaved. The stone seemed to groan, to stir, to grate, and then to move. It tipped a little downward and hung balancing for a long instant, slowly returned, rocked slightly, groaned, and settled back to its former position.

Venters divined its significance. It had been meant for defense. The cliff-dwellers, driven by dreaded enemies to this last stand, had cunningly cut the rock until it balanced perfectly, ready to be dislodged by strong hands. Just below it leaned a tottering crag that would have toppled, starting an avalanche on an acclivity where no sliding mass could stop. Crags and pinnacles, splintered cliffs, and leaning shafts and monuments, would have thundered down to block forever the outlet to Deception Pass.

"That was a narrow shave for me," said Venters, soberly. "A balancing rock! The cliff-dwellers never had to roll it. They died, vanished, and here the rock stands, probably little changed.... But it might serve another lonely dweller of the cliffs. I'll hide up here somewhere, if I can only find water."

He descended the gorge on the other side. The slope was gradual, the space narrow, the course straight for many rods. A gloom hung between the upsweeping walls. In a turn the passage narrowed to scarce a dozen feet, and here was darkness of night. But light shone ahead; another abrupt turn brought day again, and then wide open space.

Above Venters loomed a wonderful arch of stone bridging the canyon rims, and through the enormous round portal gleamed and glistened a beautiful valley shining under sunset gold reflected by surrounding cliffs. He gave a start of surprise. The valley was a cove a mile long, half that wide, and its enclosing walls were smooth and stained, and curved inward, forming great caves. He decided that its floor was far higher than the level of Deception Pass and the intersecting canyons. No purple sage colored this valley floor. Instead there were the white of aspens, streaks of branch and slender trunk glistening from the green of leaves, and the darker green of oaks, and through the middle of this forest, from wall to wall, ran a winding line of brilliant green which marked the course of cottonwoods and willows.

"There's water here—and this is the place for me," said Venters. "Only birds can peep over those walls, I've gone Oldring one better."

Venters waited no longer, and turned swiftly to retrace his steps. He named the canyon Surprise Valley and the huge boulder that guarded the outlet Balancing Rock. Going down he did not find himself attended by such fears as had beset him in the climb; still, he was not easy in mind and could not occupy himself with plans of moving the girl and his outfit until he had descended to the notch. There he rested a moment and looked about him. The pass was darkening with the approach of night. At the corner of the wall, where the stone steps turned, he saw a spur of rock that would serve to hold the noose of a lasso. He needed no more aid to scale that place. As he intended to make the move under cover of darkness, he wanted most to be able to tell where to climb up. So, taking several small stones with him, he stepped and slid down to the edge of the slope where he had left his rifle and boots. He placed the stones some yards apart. He left the rabbit lying upon the bench where the steps began. Then he addressed a keen-sighted, remembering gaze to the rim-wall above. It was serrated, and between two spears of rock, directly in line with his position, showed a zigzag crack that at night would let through the gleam of sky. This settled, he put on his belt and boots and prepared to descend. Some consideration was necessary to decide whether or not to leave his rifle there. On the return, carrying the girl and a pack, it would be added encumbrance; and after debating the matter he left the rifle leaning against the bench. As he went straight down the slope he halted every few rods to look up at his mark on the rim. It changed, but he fixed each change in his memory. When he reached the first cedar-tree, he tied his scarf upon a dead branch, and then hurried toward camp, having no more concern about finding his trail upon the return trip.

Darkness soon emboldened and lent him greater speed. It occurred to him, as he glided into the grassy glade near camp and head the whinny of a horse, that he had forgotten Wrangle. The big sorrel could not be gotten into Surprise Valley. He would have to be left here.

Venters determined at once to lead the other horses out through the thicket and turn them loose. The farther they wandered from this canyon the better it would suit him. He easily descried Wrangle through the gloom, but the others were not in sight. Venters whistled low for the dogs, and when they came trotting to him he sent them out to search for the horses, and followed. It soon developed that they were not in the glade nor the thicket. Venters grew cold and rigid at the thought of rustlers having entered his retreat. But the thought passed, for the demeanor of Ring and Whitie reassured him. The horses had wandered away.

Under the clump of silver spruces a denser mantle of darkness, yet not so thick that Venter's night-practiced eyes could not catch the white oval of a still face. He bent over it with a slight suspension of breath that was both caution lest he frighten her and chill uncertainty of feeling lest he find her dead. But she slept, and he arose to renewed activity.

He packed his saddle-bags. The dogs were hungry, they whined about him and nosed his busy hands; but he took no time to feed them nor to satisfy his own hunger. He slung the saddlebags over his shoulders and made them secure with his lasso. Then he wrapped the blankets closer about the girl and lifted her in his arms. Wrangle whinnied and thumped the ground as Venters passed him with the dogs. The sorrel knew he was being left behind, and was not sure whether he liked it or not. Venters went on and entered the thicket. Here he had to feel his way in pitch blackness and to wedge his progress between the close saplings. Time meant little to him now that he had started, and he edged along with slow side movement till he got clear of the thicket. Ring and Whitie stood waiting for him. Taking to the open aisles and patches of the sage, he walked guardedly, careful not to stumble or step in dust or strike against spreading sage-branches.

If he were burdened he did not feel it. From time to time, when he passed out of the black lines of shade into the wan starlight, he glanced at the white face of the girl lying in his arms. She had not awakened from her sleep or stupor. He did not rest until he cleared the black gate of the canyon. Then he leaned against a stone breast-high to him and gently released the girl from his hold. His brow and hair and the palms of his hands were wet, and there was a kind of nervous contraction of his muscles. They seemed to ripple and string tense. He had a desire to hurry and no sense of fatigue. A wind blew the scent of sage in his face. The first early blackness of night passed with the brightening of the stars. Somewhere back on his trail a coyote yelped, splitting the dead silence. Venters's faculties seemed singularly acute.

He lifted the girl again and pressed on. The valley better traveling than the canyon. It was lighter, freer of sage, and there were no rocks. Soon, out of the pale gloom shone a still paler thing, and that was the low swell of slope. Venters mounted it and his dogs walked beside him. Once upon the stone he slowed to snail pace, straining his sight to avoid the pockets and holes. Foot by foot he went up. The weird cedars, like great demons and witches chained to the rock and writhing in silent anguish, loomed up with wide and twisting naked arms. Venters crossed this belt of cedars, skirted the upper border, and recognized the tree he had marked, even before he saw his waving scarf.

Here he knelt and deposited the girl gently, feet first and slowly laid her out full length. What he feared was to reopen one of her wounds. If he gave her a violent jar, or slipped and fell! But the supreme confidence so strangely felt that night admitted no such blunders.

The slope before him seemed to swell into obscurity to lose its definite outline in a misty, opaque cloud that shaded into the over-shadowing wall. He scanned the rim where the serrated points speared the sky, and he found the zigzag crack. It was dim, only a shade lighter than the dark ramparts, but he distinguished it, and that served.

Lifting the girl, he stepped upward, closely attending to the nature of the path under his feet. After a few steps he stopped to mark his line with the crack in the rim. The dogs clung closer to him. While chasing the rabbit this slope had appeared interminable to him; now, burdened as he was, he did not think of length or height or toil. He remembered only to avoid a misstep and to keep his direction. He climbed on, with frequent stops to watch the rim, and before he dreamed of gaining the bench he bumped his knees into it, and saw, in the dim gray light, his rifle and the rabbit. He had come straight up without mishap or swerving off his course, and his shut teeth unlocked.

As he laid the girl down in the shallow hollow of the little ridge with her white face upturned, she opened her eyes. Wide, staring black, at once like both the night and the stars, they made her face seem still whiter.

"Is—it—you?" she asked, faintly.

"Yes," replied Venters.

"Oh! Where—are we?"

"I'm taking you to a safe place where no one will ever find you. I must climb a little here and call the dogs. Don't be afraid. I'll soon come for you."

She said no more. Her eyes watched him steadily for a moment and then closed. Venters pulled off his boots and then felt for the little steps in the rock. The shade of the cliff above obscured the point he wanted to gain, but he could see dimly a few feet before him. What he had attempted with care he now went at with surpassing lightness. Buoyant, rapid, sure, he attained the corner of wall and slipped around it. Here he could not see a hand before his face, so he groped along, found a little flat space, and there removed the saddle-bags. The lasso he took back with him to the corner and looped the noose over the spur of rock.

"Ring—Whitie—come," he called, softly.

Low whines came up from below.

"Here! Come, Whitie—Ring," he repeated, this time sharply.

Then followed scraping of claws and pattering of feet; and out of the gray gloom below him swiftly climbed the dogs to reach his side and pass beyond.

Venters descended, holding to the lasso. He tested its strength by throwing all his weight upon it. Then he gathered the girl up, and, holding her securely in his left arm, he began to climb, at every few steps jerking his right hand upward along the lasso. It sagged at each forward movement he made, but he balanced himself lightly during the interval when he lacked the support of a taut rope. He climbed as if he had wings, the strength of a giant, and knew not the sense of fear. The sharp corner of cliff seemed to cut out of the darkness. He reached it and the protruding shelf, and then, entering the black shade of the notch, he moved blindly but surely to the place where he had left the saddle-bags. He heard the dogs, though he could not see them. Once more he carefully placed the girl at his feet. Then, on hands and knees, he went over the little flat space, feeling for stones. He removed a number, and, scraping the deep dust into a heap, he unfolded the outer blanket from around the girl and laid her upon this bed. Then he went down the slope again for his boots, rifle, and the rabbit, and, bringing also his lasso with him, he made short work of that trip.

"Are—you—there?" The girl's voice came low from the blackness.

"Yes," he replied, and was conscious that his laboring breast made speech difficult.

"Are we—in a cave?"

"Yes."

"Oh, listen!... The waterfall!... I hear it! You've brought me back!"

Venters heard a murmuring moan that one moment swelled to a pitch almost softly shrill and the next lulled to a low, almost inaudible sigh.

"That's—wind blowing—in the—cliffs," he panted. "You're far from Oldring's—canyon."

The effort it cost him to speak made him conscious of extreme lassitude following upon great exertion. It seemed that when he lay down and drew his blanket over him the action was the last before utter prostration. He stretched inert, wet, hot, his body one great strife of throbbing, stinging nerves and bursting veins. And there he lay for a long while before he felt that he had begun to rest.

Rest came to him that night, but no sleep. Sleep he did not want. The hours of strained effort were now as if they had never been, and he wanted to think. Earlier in the day he had dismissed an inexplicable feeling of change; but now, when there was no longer demand on his cunning and strength and he had time to think, he could not catch the illusive thing that had sadly perplexed as well as elevated his spirit.

Above him, through a V-shaped cleft in the dark rim of the cliff, shone the lustrous stars that had been his lonely accusers for a long, long year. To-night they were different. He studied them. Larger, whiter, more radiant they seemed; but that was not the difference he meant. Gradually it came to him that the distinction was not one he saw, but one he felt. In this he divined as much of the baffling change as he thought would be revealed to him then. And as he lay there, with the singing of the cliff-winds in his ears, the white stars above the dark, bold vent, the difference which he felt was that he was no longer alone.

CHAPTER IX. SILVER SPRUCE AND ASPENS

The rest of that night seemed to Venters only a few moments of starlight, a dark overcasting of sky, an hour or so of gray gloom, and then the lighting of dawn.

When he had bestirred himself, feeding the hungry dogs and breaking his long fast, and had repacked his saddle-bags, it was clear daylight, though the sun had not tipped the yellow wall in the east. He concluded to make the climb and descent into Surprise Valley in one trip. To that end he tied his blanket upon Ring and gave Whitie the extra lasso and the rabbit to carry. Then, with the rifle and saddle-bags slung upon his back, he took up the girl. She did not awaken from heavy slumber.

That climb up under the rugged, menacing brows of the broken cliffs, in the face of a grim, leaning boulder that seemed to be weary of its age-long wavering, was a tax on strength and nerve that Venters felt equally with something sweet and strangely exulting in its accomplishment. He did not pause until he gained the narrow divide and there he rested. Balancing Rock loomed huge, cold in the gray light of dawn, a thing without life, yet it spoke silently to Venters: "I am waiting to plunge down, to shatter and crash, roar and boom, to bury your trail, and close forever the outlet to Deception Pass!"

On the descent of the other side Venters had easy going, but was somewhat concerned because Whitie appeared to have succumbed to temptation, and while carrying the rabbit was also chewing on it. And Ring evidently regarded this as an injury to himself, especially as he had carried the heavier load. Presently he snapped at one end of the rabbit and refused to let go. But his action prevented Whitie from further misdoing, and then the two dogs pattered down, carrying the rabbit between them.

Venters turned out of the gorge, and suddenly paused stock-still, astounded at the scene before him. The curve of the great stone bridge had caught the sunrise, and through the magnificent arch burst a glorious stream of gold that shone with a long slant down into the center of Surprise Valley. Only through the arch did any sunlight pass, so that all the rest of the valley lay still asleep, dark green, mysterious, shadowy, merging its level into walls as misty and soft as morning clouds.

Venters then descended, passing through the arch, looking up at its tremendous height and sweep. It spanned the opening to Surprise Valley, stretching in almost perfect curve from rim to rim. Even in his hurry and concern Venters could not but feel its majesty, and the thought came to him that the cliff-dwellers must have regarded it as an object of worship.

Down, down, down Venters strode, more and more feeling the weight of his burden as he descended, and still the valley lay below him. As all other canyons and coves and valleys had deceived him, so had this deep, nestling oval. At length he passed beyond the slope of weathered stone that spread fan-shape from the arch, and encountered a grassy terrace running to the right and about on a level with the tips of the oaks and cottonwoods below. Scattered here and there upon this shelf were clumps of aspens, and he walked through them into a glade that surpassed in beauty and adaptability for a wild home, any place he had ever seen. Silver spruces bordered the base of a precipitous wall that rose loftily. Caves indented its surface, and there were no detached ledges or weathered sections that might dislodge a stone. The level ground, beyond the spruces, dropped down into a little ravine. This was one dense line of slender aspens from which came the low splashing of water. And the terrace, lying open to the west, afforded unobstructed view of the valley of green treetops.

For his camp Venters chose a shady, grassy plot between the silver spruces and the cliff. Here, in the stone wall, had been wonderfully carved by wind or washed by water several deep caves above the level of the terrace. They were clean, dry, roomy.

He cut spruce boughs and made a bed in the largest cave and laid the girl there. The first intimation that he had of her being aroused from sleep or lethargy was a low call for water.

He hurried down into the ravine with his canteen. It was a shallow, grass-green place with aspens growing up everywhere. To his delight he found a tiny brook of swift-running water. Its faint tinge of amber reminded him of the spring at Cottonwoods, and the thought gave him a little shock. The water was so cold it made his fingers tingle as he dipped the canteen. Having returned to the cave, he was glad to see the girl drink thirstily. This time he noted that she could raise her head slightly without his help.

"You were thirsty," he said. "It's good water. I've found a fine place. Tell me—how do you feel?"

"There's pain—here," she replied, and moved her hand to her left side.

"Why, that's strange! Your wounds are on your right side. I believe you're hungry. Is the pain a kind of dull ache—a gnawing?"

"It's like—that."

"Then it's hunger." Venters laughed, and suddenly caught himself with a quick breath and felt again the little shock. When had he laughed? "It's hunger," he went on. "I've had that gnaw many a time. I've got it now. But you mustn't eat. You can have all the water you want, but no food just yet."

"Won't I—starve?"

"No, people don't starve easily. I've discovered that. You must lie perfectly still and rest and sleep—for days."

"My hands—are dirty; my face feels—so hot and sticky; my boots hurt." It was her longest speech as yet, and it trailed off in a whisper.

"Well, I'm a fine nurse!"

It annoyed him that he had never thought of these things. But then, awaiting her death and thinking of her comfort were vastly different matters. He unwrapped the blanket which covered her. What a slender girl she was! No wonder he had been able to carry her miles and pack her up that slippery ladder of stone. Her boots were of soft, fine leather, reaching clear to her knees. He recognized the make as one of a boot-maker in Sterling. Her spurs, that he had stupidly neglected to remove, consisted of silver frames and gold chains, and the rowels, large as silver dollars, were fancifully engraved. The boots slipped off rather hard. She wore heavy woollen rider's stockings, half length, and these were pulled up over the ends of her short trousers. Venters took off the stockings to note her little feet were red and swollen. He bathed them. Then he removed his scarf and bathed her face and hands.

"I must see your wounds now," he said, gently.

She made no reply, but watched him steadily as he opened her blouse and untied the bandage. His strong fingers trembled a little as he removed it. If the wounds had reopened! A chill struck him as he saw the angry red bullet-mark, and a tiny stream of blood winding from it down her white breast. Very carefully he lifted her to see that the wound in her back had closed perfectly. Then he washed the blood from her breast, bathed the wound, and left it unbandaged, open to the air.

Her eyes thanked him.

"Listen," he said, earnestly. "I've had some wounds, and I've seen many. I know a little about them. The hole in your back has closed. If you lie still three days the one in your breast will close and you'll be safe. The danger from hemorrhage will be over."

He had spoken with earnest sincerity, almost eagerness.

"Why—do you—want me—to get well?" she asked, wonderingly.

The simple question seemed unanswerable except on grounds of humanity. But the circumstances under which he had shot this strange girl, the shock and realization, the waiting for death, the hope, had resulted in a condition of mind wherein Venters wanted her to live more than he had ever wanted anything. Yet he could not tell why. He believed the killing of the rustler and the subsequent excitement had disturbed him. For how else could he explain the throbbing of his brain, the heat of his blood, the undefined sense of full hours, charged, vibrant with pulsating mystery where once they had dragged in loneliness?

"I shot you," he said, slowly, "and I want you to get well so I shall not have killed a woman. But—for your own sake, too—"

A terrible bitterness darkened her eyes, and her lips quivered.

"Hush," said Venters. "You've talked too much already."

In her unutterable bitterness he saw a darkness of mood that could not have been caused by her present weak and feverish state. She hated the life she had led, that she probably had been compelled to lead. She had suffered some unforgivable wrong at the hands of Oldring. With that conviction Venters felt a shame throughout his body, and it marked the rekindling of fierce anger and ruthlessness. In the past long year he had nursed resentment. He had hated the wilderness—the loneliness of the uplands. He had waited for something to come to pass. It had come. Like an Indian stealing horses he had skulked into the recesses of the canyons. He had found Oldring's retreat; he had killed a rustler; he had shot an unfortunate girl, then had saved her from this unwitting act, and he meant to save her from the consequent wasting of blood, from fever and weakness. Starvation he had to fight for her and for himself. Where he had been sick at the letting of blood, now he remembered it in grim, cold calm. And as he lost that softness of nature, so he lost his fear of men. He would watch for Oldring, biding his time, and he would kill this great black-bearded rustler who had held a girl in bondage, who had used her to his infamous ends.

Venters surmised this much of the change in him—idleness had passed; keen, fierce vigor flooded his mind and body; all that had happened to him at Cottonwoods seemed remote and hard to recall; the difficulties and perils of the present absorbed him, held him in a kind of spell.

First, then, he fitted up the little cave adjoining the girl's room for his own comfort and use. His next work was to build a fireplace of stones and to gather a store of wood. That done, he spilled the contents of his saddle-bags upon the grass and took stock. His outfit consisted of a small-handled axe, a hunting-knife, a large number of cartridges for rifle or revolver, a tin plate, a cup, and a fork and spoon, a quantity of dried beef and dried fruits, and small canvas bags containing tea, sugar, salt, and pepper. For him alone this supply would have been bountiful to begin a sojourn in the wilderness, but he was no longer alone. Starvation in the uplands was not an unheard-of thing; he did not, however, worry at all on that score, and feared only his possible inability to supply the needs of a woman in a weakened and extremely delicate condition.

If there was no game in the valley—a contingency he doubted—it would not be a great task for him to go by night to Oldring's herd and pack out a calf. The exigency of the moment was to ascertain if there were game in Surprise Valley. Whitie still guarded the dilapidated rabbit, and Ring slept near by under a spruce. Venters called Ring and went to the edge of the terrace, and there halted to survey the valley.

He was prepared to find it larger than his unstudied glances had made it appear; for more than a casual idea of dimensions and a hasty conception of oval shape and singular beauty he had not had time. Again the felicity of the name he had given the valley struck him forcibly. Around the red perpendicular walls, except under the great arc of stone, ran a terrace fringed at the cliff-base by silver spruces; below that first terrace sloped another wider one densely overgrown with aspens, and the center of the valley was a level circle of oaks and alders, with the glittering green line of willows and cottonwood dividing it in half. Venters saw a number and variety of birds flitting among the trees. To his left, facing the stone bridge, an enormous cavern opened in the wall; and low down, just above the tree-tops, he made out a long shelf of cliff-dwellings, with little black, staring windows or doors. Like eyes they were, and seemed to watch him. The few cliff-dwellings he had seen—all ruins—had left him with haunting memory of age and solitude and of something past. He had come, in a way, to be a cliff-dweller himself, and those silent eyes would look down upon him, as if in surprise that after thousands of years a man had invaded the valley. Venters felt sure that he was the only white man who had ever walked under the shadow of the wonderful stone bridge, down into that wonderful valley with its circle of caves and its terraced rings of silver spruce and aspens.

The dog growled below and rushed into the forest. Venters ran down the declivity to enter a zone of light shade streaked with sunshine. The oak-trees were slender, none more than half a foot thick, and they grew close together, intermingling their branches. Ring came running back with a rabbit in his mouth. Venters took the rabbit and, holding the dog near him, stole softly on. There were fluttering of wings among the branches and quick bird-notes, and rustling of dead leaves and rapid patterings. Venters crossed well-worn trails marked with fresh tracks; and when he had stolen on a little farther he saw many birds and running quail, and more rabbits than he could count. He had not penetrated the forest of oaks for a hundred yards, had not approached anywhere near the line of willows and cottonwoods which he knew grew along a stream. But he had seen enough to know that Surprise Valley was the home of many wild creatures.

Venters returned to camp. He skinned the rabbits, and gave the dogs the one they had quarreled over, and the skin of this he dressed and hung up to dry, feeling that he would like to keep it. It was a particularly rich, furry pelt with a beautiful white tail. Venters remembered that but for the bobbing of that white tail catching his eye he would not have espied the rabbit, and he would never have discovered Surprise Valley. Little incidents of chance like this had turned him here and there in Deception Pass; and now they had assumed to him the significance and direction of destiny.

His good fortune in the matter of game at hand brought to his mind the necessity of keeping it in the valley. Therefore he took the axe and cut bundles of aspens and willows, and packed them up under the bridge to the narrow outlet of the gorge. Here he began fashioning a fence, by driving aspens into the ground and lacing them fast with willows. Trip after trip he made down for more building material, and the afternoon had passed when he finished the work to his satisfaction. Wildcats might scale the fence, but no coyote could come in to search for prey, and no rabbits or other small game could escape from the valley.

Upon returning to camp he set about getting his supper at ease, around a fine fire, without hurry or fear of discovery. After hard work that had definite purpose, this freedom and comfort gave him peculiar satisfaction. He caught himself often, as he kept busy round the camp-fire, stopping to glance at the quiet form in the cave, and at the dogs stretched cozily near him, and then out across the beautiful valley. The present was not yet real to him.

CHAPTER IX. SILVER SPRUCE AND ASPENS

While he ate, the sun set beyond a dip in the rim of the curved wall. As the morning sun burst wondrously through a grand arch into this valley, in a golden, slanting shaft, so the evening sun, at the moment of setting, shone through a gap of cliffs, sending down a broad red burst to brighten the oval with a blaze of fire. To Venters both sunrise and sunset were unreal.

A cool wind blew across the oval, waving the tips of oaks, and while the light lasted, fluttering the aspen leaves into millions of facets of red, and sweeping the graceful spruces. Then with the wind soon came a shade and a darkening, and suddenly the valley was gray. Night came there quickly after the sinking of the sun. Venters went softly to look at the girl. She slept, and her breathing was quiet and slow. He lifted Ring into the cave, with stern whisper for him to stay there on guard. Then he drew the blanket carefully over her and returned to the camp-fire.

Though exceedingly tired, he was yet loath to yield to lassitude, but this night it was not from listening, watchful vigilance; it was from a desire to realize his position. The details of his wild environment seemed the only substance of a strange dream. He saw the darkening rims, the gray oval turning black, the undulating surface of forest, like a rippling lake, and the spear-pointed spruces. He heard the flutter of aspen leaves and the soft, continuous splash of falling water. The melancholy note of a canyon bird broke clear and lonely from the high cliffs. Venters had no name for this night singer, and he had never seen one, but the few notes, always pealing out just at darkness, were as familiar to him as the canyon silence. Then they ceased, and the rustle of leaves and the murmur of water hushed in a growing sound that Venters fancied was not of earth. Neither had he a name for this, only it was inexpressibly wild and sweet. The thought came that it might be a moan of the girl in her last outcry of life, and he felt a tremor shake him. But no! This sound was not human, though it was like despair. He began to doubt his sensitive perceptions, to believe that he half-dreamed what he thought he heard. Then the sound swelled with the strengthening of the breeze, and he realized it was the singing of the wind in the cliffs.

By and by a drowsiness overcame him, and Venters began to nod, half asleep, with his back against a spruce. Rousing himself and calling Whitie, he went to the cave. The girl lay barely visible in the dimness. Ring crouched beside her, and the patting of his tail on the stone assured Venters that the dog was awake and faithful to his duty. Venters sought his own bed of fragrant boughs; and as he lay back, somehow grateful for the comfort and safety, the night seemed to steal away from him and he sank softly into intangible space and rest and slumber.

Venters awakened to the sound of melody that he imagined was only the haunting echo of dream music. He opened his eyes to another surprise of this valley of beautiful surprises. Out of his cave he saw the exquisitely fine foliage of the silver spruces crossing a round space of blue morning sky; and in this lacy leafage fluttered a number of gray birds with black and white stripes and long tails. They were mocking-birds, and they were singing as if they wanted to burst their throats. Venters listened. One long, silver-tipped branch dropped almost to his cave, and upon it, within a few yards of him, sat one of the graceful birds.

Venters saw the swelling and quivering of its throat in song. He arose, and when he slid down out of his cave the birds fluttered and flew farther away.

Venters stepped before the opening of the other cave and looked in. The girl was awake, with wide eyes and listening look, and she had a hand on Ring's neck.

"Mocking-birds!" she said.

"Yes," replied Venters, "and I believe they like our company."

"Where are we?"

"Never mind now. After a little I'll tell you."

"The birds woke me. When I heard them—and saw the shiny trees—and the blue sky—and then a blaze of gold dropping down—I wondered—"

She did not complete her fancy, but Venters imagined he understood her meaning. She appeared to be wandering in mind. Venters felt her face and hands and found them burning with fever. He went for water, and was glad to find it almost as cold as if flowing from ice. That water was the only medicine he had, and he put faith in it. She did not want to drink, but he made her swallow, and then he bathed her face and head and cooled her wrists.

The day began with the heightening of the fever. Venters spent the time reducing her temperature, cooling her hot cheeks and temples. He kept close watch over her, and at the least indication of restlessness, that he knew led to tossing and rolling of the body, he held her tightly, so no violent move could reopen her wounds. Hour after hour she babbled and laughed and cried and moaned in delirium; but whatever her secret was she did not reveal it. Attended by something somber for Venters, the day passed. At night in the cool winds the fever abated and she slept.

The second day was a repetition of the first. On the third he seemed to see her wither and waste away before his eyes. That day he scarcely went from her side for a moment, except to run for fresh, cool water; and he did not eat. The fever broke on the fourth day and left her spent and shrunken, a slip of a girl with life only in her eyes. They hung upon Venters with a mute observance, and he found hope in that.

To rekindle the spark that had nearly flickered out, to nourish the little life and vitality that remained in her, was Venters's problem. But he had little resource other than the meat of the rabbits and quail; and from these he made broths and soups as best he could, and fed her with a spoon. It came to him that the human body, like the human soul, was a strange thing and capable of recovering from terrible shocks. For almost immediately she showed faint signs of gathering strength. There was one more waiting day, in which he doubted, and spent long hours by her side as she slept, and watched the gentle swell of her breast rise and fall in breathing, and the wind stir the tangled chestnut curls. On the next day he knew that she would live.

Upon realizing it he abruptly left the cave and sought his accustomed seat against the trunk of a big spruce, where once more he let his glance stray along the sloping terraces. She would live, and the somber gloom lifted out of the valley, and he felt relief that was pain. Then he roused to the call of action, to the many things he needed to do in the way of making camp fixtures and utensils, to the necessity of hunting food, and the desire to explore the valley.

But he decided to wait a few more days before going far from camp, because he fancied that the girl rested easier when she could see him near at hand. And on the first day her languor appeared to leave her in a renewed grip of life. She awoke stronger from each short slumber; she ate greedily, and she moved about in her bed of boughs; and always, it seemed to Venters, her eyes followed him. He knew now that her recovery would be rapid. She talked about the dogs, about the caves, the valley, about how hungry she was, till Venters silenced her, asking her to put off further talk till another time. She obeyed, but she sat up in her bed, and her eyes roved to and fro, and always back to him.

Upon the second morning she sat up when he awakened her, and would not permit him to bathe her face and feed her, which actions she performed for herself. She spoke little, however, and Venters was quick to catch in her the first intimations of thoughtfulness and curiosity and appreciation of her situation. He left camp and took Whitie out to hunt for rabbits. Upon his return he was amazed and somewhat anxiously concerned to see his invalid sitting with her back to a corner of the cave and her bare feet swinging out. Hurriedly he approached, intending to advise her to lie down again, to tell her that perhaps she might overtax her strength. The sun shone upon her, glinting on the little head with its tangle of bright hair and the small, oval face with its pallor, and dark-blue eyes underlined by dark-blue circles. She looked at him and he looked at her. In that exchange of glances he imagined each saw the other in some different guise. It seemed impossible to Venters that this frail girl could be Oldring's Masked Rider. It flashed over him that he had made a mistake which presently she would explain.

"Help me down," she said.

"But—are you well enough?" he protested. "Wait—a little longer."

"I'm weak—dizzy. But I want to get down."

He lifted her—what a light burden now!—and stood her upright beside him, and supported her as she essayed to walk with halting steps. She was like a stripling of a boy; the bright, small head scarcely reached his shoulder. But now, as she clung to his arm, the rider's costume she wore did not contradict, as it had done at first, his feeling of her femininity. She might be the famous Masked Rider of the uplands, she might resemble a boy; but her outline, her little hands and feet, her hair, her big eyes and tremulous lips, and especially a something that Venters felt as a subtle essence rather than what he saw, proclaimed her sex.

She soon tired. He arranged a comfortable seat for her under the spruce that overspread the camp-fire.

"Now tell me—everything," she said.

He recounted all that had happened from the time of his discovery of the rustlers in the canyon up to the present moment.

"You shot me—and now you've saved my life?"

"Yes. After almost killing you I've pulled you through."

"Are you glad?"

"I should say so!"

Her eyes were unusually expressive, and they regarded him steadily; she was unconscious of that mirroring of her emotions and they shone with gratefulness and interest and wonder and sadness.

"Tell me—about yourself?" she asked.

He made this a briefer story, telling of his coming to Utah, his various occupations till he became a rider, and then how the Mormons had practically driven him out of Cottonwoods, an outcast.

Then, no longer able to withstand his own burning curiosity, he questioned her in turn.

"Are you Oldring's Masked Rider?"

"Yes," she replied, and dropped her eyes.

"I knew it—I recognized your figure—and mask, for I saw you once. Yet I can't believe it!... But you never were really that rustler, as we riders knew him? A thief—a marauder—a kidnapper of women—a murderer of sleeping riders!"

"No! I never stole—or harmed any one—in all my life. I only rode and rode—"

"But why—why?" he burst out. "Why the name? I understand Oldring made you ride. But the black mask—the mystery—the things laid to your hands—the threats in your infamous name—the night-riding credited to you—the evil deeds deliberately blamed on you and acknowledged by rustlers—even Oldring himself! Why? Tell me why?"

"I never knew that," she answered low. Her drooping head straightened, and the large eyes, larger now and darker, met Venters's with a clear, steadfast gaze in which he read truth. It verified his own conviction.

"Never knew? That's strange! Are you a Mormon?"

"No."

"Is Oldring a Mormon?"

"No."

"Do you—care for him?"

"Yes. I hate his men—his life—sometimes I almost hate him!"

Venters paused in his rapid-fire questioning, as if to brace him self to ask for a truth that would be abhorrent for him to confirm, but which he seemed driven to hear.

"What are—what were you to Oldring?"

Like some delicate thing suddenly exposed to blasting heat, the girl wilted; her head dropped, and into her white, wasted cheeks crept the red of shame.

Venters would have given anything to recall that question. It seemed so different—his thought when spoken. Yet her shame established in his mind something akin to the respect he had strangely been hungering to feel for her.

"D—n that question!—forget it!" he cried, in a passion of pain for her and anger at himself. "But once and for all—tell me—I know it, yet I want to hear you say so—you couldn't help yourself?"

"Oh no."

"Well, that makes it all right with me," he went on, honestly. "I—I want you to feel that... you see—we've been thrown together—and—and I want to help you—not hurt you. I thought life had been cruel to me, but when I think of yours I feel mean and little for my complaining. Anyway, I was a lonely outcast. And now!... I don't see very clearly what it all means. Only we are here—together. We've got to stay here, for long, surely till you are well. But you'll never go back to Oldring. And I'm sure helping you will help me, for I was sick in mind. There's something now for me to do. And if I can win back your strength—then get you away, out of this wild country—help you somehow to a happier life—just think how good that'll be for me!"

CHAPTER X. LOVE

During all these waiting days Venters, with the exception of the afternoon when he had built the gate in the gorge, had scarcely gone out of sight of camp and never out of hearing. His desire to explore Surprise Valley was keen, and on the morning after his long talk with the girl he took his rifle and, calling Ring, made a move to start. The girl lay back in a rude chair of boughs he had put together for her. She had been watching him, and when he picked up the gun and called the dog Venters thought she gave a nervous start.

"I'm only going to look over the valley," he said.

"Will you be gone long?"

"No," he replied, and started off. The incident set him thinking of his former impression that, after her recovery from fever, she did not seem at ease unless he was close at hand. It was fear of being alone, due, he concluded, most likely to her weakened condition. He must not leave her much alone.

As he strode down the sloping terrace, rabbits scampered before him, and the beautiful valley quail, as purple in color as the sage on the uplands, ran fleetly along the ground into the forest. It was pleasant under the trees, in the gold-flecked shade, with the whistle of quail and twittering of birds everywhere. Soon he had passed the limit of his former excursions and entered new territory. Here the woods began to show open glades and brooks running down from the slope, and presently he emerged from shade into the sunshine of a meadow. The shaking of the high grass told him of the running of animals, what species he could not tell, but from Ring's manifest desire to have a chase they were evidently some kind wilder than rabbits. Venters approached the willow and cottonwood belt that he had observed from the height of slope. He penetrated it to find a considerable stream of water and great half-submerged mounds of brush and sticks, and all about him were old and new gnawed circles at the base of the cottonwoods.

"Beaver!" he exclaimed. "By all that's lucky! The meadow's full of beaver! How did they ever get here?"

Beaver had not found a way into the valley by the trail of the cliff-dwellers, of that he was certain; and he began to have more than curiosity as to the outlet or inlet of the stream. When he passed some dead water, which he noted was held by a beaver dam, there was a current in the stream, and it flowed west. Following its course, he soon entered the oak forest again, and passed through to find himself before massed and jumbled ruins of cliff wall. There were tangled thickets of wild plum-trees and other thorny growths that made passage extremely laborsome. He found innumerable tracks of wildcats and foxes. Rustlings in the thick undergrowth told him of stealthy movements of these animals. At length his further advance appeared futile, for the reason that the stream disappeared in a split at the base of immense rocks over which he could not climb. To his relief he concluded that though beaver might work their way up the narrow chasm where the water rushed, it would be impossible for men to enter the valley there.

This western curve was the only part of the valley where the walls had been split asunder, and it was a wildly rough and inaccessible corner. Going back a little way, he leaped the stream and headed toward the southern wall. Once out of the oaks he found again the low terrace of aspens, and above that the wide, open terrace fringed by silver spruces. This side of the valley contained the wind or water worn caves. As he pressed on, keeping to the upper terrace, cave after cave opened out of the cliff; now a large one, now a small one. Then yawned, quite suddenly and wonderfully above him, the great cavern of the cliff-dwellers.

It was still a goodly distance, and he tried to imagine, if it appeared so huge from where he stood, what it would be when he got there. He climbed the terrace and then faced a long, gradual ascent of weathered rock and dust, which made climbing too difficult for attention to anything else. At length he entered a zone of shade, and looked up. He stood just within the hollow of a cavern so immense that he had no conception of its real dimensions. The curved roof, stained by ages of leakage, with buff and black and rust-colored streaks, swept up and loomed higher and seemed to soar to the rim of the cliff. Here again was a magnificent arch, such as formed the grand gateway to the valley, only in this instance it formed the dome of a cave instead of the span of a bridge.

Venters passed onward and upward. The stones he dislodged rolled down with strange, hollow crack and roar. He had climbed a hundred rods inward, and yet he had not reached the base of the shelf where the cliff-dwellings rested, a long half-circle of connected stone house, with little dark holes that he had fancied were eyes. At length he gained the base of the shelf, and here found steps cut in the rock. These facilitated climbing, and as he went up he thought how easily this vanished race of men might once have held that stronghold against an army. There was only one possible place to ascend, and this was narrow and steep.

Venters had visited cliff-dwellings before, and they had been in ruins, and of no great character or size but this place was of proportions that stunned him, and it had not been desecrated by the hand of man, nor had it been crumbled by the hand of time. It was a stupendous tomb. It had been a city. It was just as it had been left by its builders. The little houses were there, the smoke-blackened stains of fires, the pieces of pottery scattered about cold hearths, the stone hatchets; and stone pestles and mealing-stones lay beside round holes polished by years of grinding maize—lay there as if they had been carelessly dropped yesterday. But the cliff-dwellers were gone!

Dust! They were dust on the floor or at the foot of the shelf, and their habitations and utensils endured. Venters felt the sublimity of that marvelous vaulted arch, and it seemed to gleam with a glory of something that was gone. How many years had passed since the cliff-dwellers gazed out across the beautiful valley as he was gazing now? How long had it been since women ground grain in those polished holes? What time had rolled by since men of an unknown race lived, loved, fought, and died there? Had an enemy destroyed them? Had disease destroyed them, or only that greatest destroyer—time? Venters saw a long line of blood-red hands painted low down upon the yellow roof of stone. Here was strange portent, if not an answer to his queries. The place oppressed him. It was light, but full of a transparent gloom. It smelled of dust and musty stone, of age and disuse. It was sad. It was solemn. It had the look of a place where silence had become master and was now irrevocable and terrible and could not be broken. Yet, at the moment, from high up in the carved crevices of the arch, floated down the low, strange wail of wind—a knell indeed for all that had gone.

Venters, sighing, gathered up an armful of pottery, such pieces as he thought strong enough and suitable for his own use, and bent his steps toward camp. He mounted the terrace at an opposite point to which he had left. He saw the girl looking in the direction he had gone. His footsteps made no sound in the deep grass, and he approached close without her being aware of his presence. Whitie lay on the ground near where she sat, and he manifested the usual actions of welcome, but the girl did not notice them. She seemed to be oblivious to everything near at hand. She made a pathetic figure drooping there, with her sunny hair contrasting so markedly with her white, wasted cheeks and her hands listlessly clasped and her little bare feet propped in the framework of the rude seat. Venters could have sworn and laughed in one breath at the idea of the connection between this girl and Oldring's Masked Rider. She was the victim of more than accident of fate—a victim to some deep plot the mystery of which burned him. As he stepped forward with a half-formed thought that she was absorbed in watching for his return, she turned her head and saw him. A swift start, a change rather than rush of blood under her white cheeks, a flashing of big eyes that fixed their glance upon him, transformed her face in that single instant of turning, and he knew she had been watching for him, that his return was the one thing in her mind. She did not smile; she did not flush; she did not look glad. All these would have meant little compared to her indefinite expression. Venters grasped the peculiar, vivid, vital something that leaped from her face. It was as if she had been in a dead, hopeless clamp of inaction and feeling, and had been suddenly shot through and through with quivering animation. Almost it was as if she had returned to life.

And Venters thought with lightning swiftness, "I've saved her—I've unlinked her from that old life—she was watching as if I were all she had left on earth—she belongs to me!" The thought was startlingly new. Like a blow it was in an unprepared moment. The cheery salutation he had ready for her died unborn and he tumbled the pieces of pottery awkwardly on the grass while some unfamiliar, deep-seated emotion, mixed with pity and glad assurance of his power to succor her, held him dumb.

"What a load you had!" she said. "Why, they're pots and crocks! Where did you get them?"

Venters laid down his rifle, and, filling one of the pots from his canteen, he placed it on the smoldering campfire.

"Hope it'll hold water," he said, presently. "Why, there's an enormous cliff-dwelling just across here. I got the pottery there. Don't you think we needed something? That tin cup of mine has served to make tea, broth, soup—everything."

"I noticed we hadn't a great deal to cook in."

She laughed. It was the first time. He liked that laugh, and though he was tempted to look at her, he did not want to show his surprise or his pleasure.

"Will you take me over there, and all around in the valley—pretty soon, when I'm well?" she added.

"Indeed I shall. It's a wonderful place. Rabbits so thick you can't step without kicking one out. And quail, beaver, foxes, wildcats. We're in a regular den. But—haven't you ever seen a cliff-dwelling?"

"No. I've heard about them, though. The—the men say the Pass is full of old houses and ruins."

"Why, I should think you'd have run across one in all your riding around," said Venters. He spoke slowly, choosing his words carefully, and he essayed a perfectly casual manner, and pretended to be busy assorting pieces of pottery. She must have no cause again to suffer shame for curiosity of his. Yet never in all his days had he been so eager to hear the details of anyone's life.

"When I rode—I rode like the wind," she replied, "and never had time to stop for anything."

"I remember that day I—I met you in the Pass—how dusty you were, how tired your horse looked. Were you always riding?"

"Oh, no. Sometimes not for months, when I was shut up in the cabin."

Venters tried to subdue a hot tingling.

"You were shut up, then?" he asked, carelessly.

"When Oldring went away on his long trips—he was gone for months sometimes—he shut me up in the cabin."

"What for?"

"Perhaps to keep me from running away. I always threatened that. Mostly, though, because the men got drunk at the villages. But they were always good to me. I wasn't afraid."

"A prisoner! That must have been hard on you?"

"I liked that. As long as I can remember I've been locked up there at times, and those times were the only happy ones I ever had. It's a big cabin, high up on a cliff, and I could look out. Then I had dogs and pets I had tamed, and books. There was a spring inside, and food stored, and the men brought me fresh meat. Once I was there one whole winter."

It now required deliberation on Venters's part to persist in his unconcern and to keep at work. He wanted to look at her, to volley questions at her.

"As long as you can remember—you've lived in Deception Pass?" he went on.

"I've a dim memory of some other place, and women and children; but I can't make anything of it. Sometimes I think till I'm weary."

"Then you can read—you have books?"

"Oh yes, I can read, and write, too, pretty well. Oldring is educated. He taught me, and years ago an old rustler lived with us, and he had been something different once. He was always teaching me."

"So Oldring takes long trips," mused Venters. "Do you know where he goes?"

"No. Every year he drives cattle north of Sterling—then does not return for months. I heard him accused once of living two lives—and he killed the man. That was at Stone Bridge."

Venters dropped his apparent task and looked up with an eagerness he no longer strove to hide.

"Bess," he said, using her name for the first time, "I suspected Oldring was something besides a rustler. Tell me, what's his purpose here in the Pass? I believe much that he has done was to hide his real work here."

"You're right. He's more than a rustler. In fact, as the men say, his rustling cattle is now only a bluff. There's gold in the canyons!"

"Ah!"

"Yes, there's gold, not in great quantities, but gold enough for him and his men. They wash for gold week in and week out. Then they drive a few cattle and go into the villages to drink and shoot and kill—to bluff the riders."

"Drive a few cattle! But, Bess, the Withersteen herd, the red herd—twenty-five hundred head! That's not a few. And I tracked them into a valley near here."

"Oldring never stole the red herd. He made a deal with Mormons. The riders were to be called in, and Oldring was to drive the herd and keep it till a certain time—I won't know when—then drive it back to the range. What his share was I didn't hear."

"Did you hear why that deal was made?" queried Venters.

"No. But it was a trick of Mormons. They're full of tricks. I've heard Oldring's men tell about Mormons. Maybe the Withersteen woman wasn't minding her halter! I saw the man who made the deal. He was a little, queer-shaped man, all humped up. He sat his horse well. I heard one of our men say afterward there was no better rider on the sage than this fellow. What was the name? I forget."

"Jerry Card?" suggested Venters.

"That's it. I remember—it's a name easy to remember—and Jerry Card appeared to be on fair terms with Oldring's men."

"I shouldn't wonder," replied Venters, thoughtfully. Verification of his suspicions in regard to Tull's underhand work—for the deal with Oldring made by Jerry Card assuredly had its inception in the Mormon Elder's brain, and had been accomplished through his orders—revived in Venters a memory of hatred that had been smothered by press of other emotions. Only a few days had elapsed since the hour of his encounter with Tull, yet they had been forgotten and now seemed far off, and the interval one that now appeared large and profound with incalculable change in his feelings. Hatred of Tull still existed in his heart, but it had lost its white heat. His affection for Jane Withersteen had not changed in the least; nevertheless, he seemed to view it from another angle and see it as another thing—what, he could not exactly define. The recalling of these two feelings was to Venters like getting glimpses into a self that was gone; and the wonder of them—perhaps the change which was too illusive for him—was the fact that a strange irritation accompanied the memory and a desire to dismiss it from mind. And straightway he did dismiss it, to return to thoughts of his significant present.

"Bess, tell me one more thing," he said. "Haven't you known any women—any young people?"

"Sometimes there were women with the men; but Oldring never let me know them. And all the young people I ever saw in my life was when I rode fast through the villages."

Perhaps that was the most puzzling and thought-provoking thing she had yet said to Venters. He pondered, more curious the more he learned, but he curbed his inquisitive desires, for he saw her shrinking on the verge of that shame, the causing of which had occasioned him such self-reproach. He would ask no more. Still he had to think, and he found it difficult to think clearly. This sad-eyed girl was so utterly different from what it would have been reason to believe such a remarkable life would have made her. On this day he had found her simple and frank, as natural as any girl he had ever known. About her there was something sweet. Her voice was low and well modulated. He could not look into her face, meet her steady, unabashed, yet wistful eyes, and think of her as the woman she had confessed herself. Oldring's Masked Rider sat before him, a girl dressed as a man. She had been made to ride at the head of infamous forays and drives. She had been imprisoned for many months of her life in an obscure cabin. At times the most vicious of men had been her companions; and the vilest of women, if they had not been permitted to approach her, had, at least, cast their shadows over her. But—but in spite of all this—there thundered at Venters some truth that lifted its voice higher than the clamoring facts of dishonor, some truth that was the very life of her beautiful eyes; and it was innocence.

In the days that followed, Venters balanced perpetually in mind this haunting conception of innocence over against the cold and sickening fact of an unintentional yet actual gift. How could it be possible for the two things to be true? He believed the latter to be true, and he would not relinquish his conviction of the former; and these conflicting thoughts augmented the mystery that appeared to be a part of Bess. In those ensuing days, however, it became clear as clearest light that Bess was rapidly regaining strength; that, unless reminded of her long association with Oldring, she seemed to have forgotten it; that, like an Indian who lives solely from moment to moment, she was utterly absorbed in the present.

Day by day Venters watched the white of her face slowly change to brown, and the wasted cheeks fill out by imperceptible degrees. There came a time when he could just trace the line of demarcation between the part of her face once hidden by a mask and that left exposed to wind and sun. When that line disappeared in clear bronze tan it was as if she had been washed clean of the stigma of Oldring's Masked Rider. The suggestion of the mask always made Venters remember; now that it was gone he seldom thought of her past. Occasionally he tried to piece together the several stages of strange experience and to make a whole. He had shot a masked outlaw the very sight of whom had been ill omen to riders; he had carried off a wounded woman whose bloody lips quivered in prayer; he had nursed what seemed a frail, shrunken boy; and now he watched a girl whose face had become strangely sweet, whose dark-blue eyes were ever upon him without boldness, without shyness, but with a steady, grave, and growing light. Many times Venters found the clear gaze embarrassing to him, yet, like wine, it had an exhilarating effect. What did she think when she looked at him so? Almost he believed she had no thought at all. All about her and the present there in Surprise Valley, and the dim yet subtly impending future, fascinated Venters and made him thoughtful as all his lonely vigils in the sage had not.

Chiefly it was the present that he wished to dwell upon; but it was the call of the future which stirred him to action. No idea had he of what that future had in store for Bess and him. He began to think of improving Surprise Valley as a place to live in, for there was no telling how long they would be compelled to stay there. Venters stubbornly resisted the entering into his mind of an insistent thought that, clearly realized, might have made it plain to him that he did not want to leave Surprise Valley at all. But it was imperative that he consider practical matters; and whether or not he was destined to stay long there, he felt the immediate need of a change of diet. It would be necessary for him to go farther afield for a variety of meat, and also that he soon visit Cottonwoods for a supply of food.

It occurred again to Venters that he could go to the canyon where Oldring kept his cattle, and at little risk he could pack out some beef. He wished to do this, however, without letting Bess know of it till after he had made the trip. Presently he hit upon the plan of going while she was asleep.

That very night he stole out of camp, climbed up under the stone bridge, and entered the outlet to the Pass. The gorge was full of luminous gloom. Balancing Rock loomed dark and leaned over the pale descent. Transformed in the shadowy light, it took shape and dimensions of a spectral god waiting—waiting for the moment to hurl himself down upon the tottering walls and close forever the outlet to Deception Pass. At night more than by day Venters felt something fearful and fateful in that rock, and that it had leaned and waited through a thousand years to have somehow to deal with his destiny.

"Old man, if you must roll, wait till I get back to the girl, and then roll!" he said, aloud, as if the stones were indeed a god.

And those spoken words, in their grim note to his ear, as well as contents to his mind, told Venters that he was all but drifting on a current which he had not power nor wish to stem.

Venters exercised his usual care in the matter of hiding tracks from the outlet, yet it took him scarcely an hour to reach Oldring's cattle. Here sight of many calves changed his original intention, and instead of packing out meat he decided to take a calf out alive. He roped one, securely tied its feet, and swung it over his shoulder. Here was an exceedingly heavy burden, but Venters was powerful—he could take up a sack of grain and with ease pitch it over a pack-saddle—and he made long distance without resting. The hardest work came in the climb up to the outlet and on through to the valley. When he had accomplished it, he became fired with another idea that again changed his intention. He would not kill the calf, but keep it alive. He would go back to Oldring's herd and pack out more calves. Thereupon he secured the calf in the best available spot for the moment and turned to make a second trip.

When Venters got back to the valley with another calf, it was close upon day-break. He crawled into his cave and slept late. Bess had no inkling that he had been absent from camp nearly all night, and only remarked solicitously that he appeared to be more tired than usual, and more in the need of sleep. In the after-noon Venters built a gate across a small ravine near camp, and here corralled the calves; and he succeeded in completing his task without Bess being any the wiser.

That night he made two more trips to Oldring's range, and again on the follow-ing night, and yet another on the next. With eight calves in his corral, he concluded that he had enough; but it dawned upon him then that he did not want to kill one. "I've rustled Oldring's cattle," he said, and laughed. He noted then that all the calves were red. "Red!" he exclaimed. "From the red herd. I've stolen Jane Withersteen's cattle!... That's about the strangest thing yet."

One more trip he undertook to Oldring's valley, and this time he roped a year-ling steer and killed it and cut out a small quarter of beef. The howling of coyotes told him he need have no apprehension that the work of his knife would be dis-covered. He packed the beef back to camp and hung it upon a spruce-tree. Then he sought his bed.

On the morrow he was up bright and early, glad that he had a surprise for Bess. He could hardly wait for her to come out. Presently she appeared and walked under the spruce. Then she approached the camp-fire. There was a tinge of healthy red in the bronze of her cheeks, and her slender form had begun to round out in graceful lines.

"Bess, didn't you say you were tired of rabbit?" inquired Venters. "And quail and beaver?"

"Indeed I did."

"What would you like?"

"I'm tired of meat, but if we have to live on it I'd like some beef."

"Well, how does that strike you?" Venters pointed to the quarter hanging from the spruce-tree. "We'll have fresh beef for a few days, then we'll cut the rest into strips and dry it."

"Where did you get that?" asked Bess, slowly.

"I stole that from Oldring."

"You went back to the canyon—you risked—" While she hesitated the tinge of bloom faded out of her cheeks.

"It wasn't any risk, but it was hard work."

"I'm sorry I said I was tired of rabbit. Why! How—When did you get that beef?"

"Last night."

"While I was asleep?"

"Yes."

"I woke last night sometime—but I didn't know."

Her eyes were widening, darkening with thought, and whenever they did so the steady, watchful, seeing gaze gave place to the wistful light. In the former she saw as the primitive woman without thought; in the latter she looked inward, and her gaze was the reflection of a troubled mind. For long Venters had not seen that dark change, that deepening of blue, which he thought was beautiful and sad. But now he wanted to make her think.

"I've done more than pack in that beef," he said. "For five nights I've been working while you slept. I've got eight calves corralled near a ravine. Eight calves, all alive and doing fine!"

"You went five nights!"

All that Venters could make of the dilation of her eyes, her slow pallor, and her exclamation, was fear—fear for herself or for him.

"Yes. I didn't tell you, because I knew you were afraid to be left alone."

"Alone?" She echoed his word, but the meaning of it was nothing to her. She had not even thought of being left alone. It was not, then, fear for herself, but for him. This girl, always slow of speech and action, now seemed almost stupid. She put forth a hand that might have indicated the groping of her mind. Suddenly she stepped swiftly to him, with a look and touch that drove from him any doubt of her quick intelligence or feeling.

"Oldring has men watch the herds—they would kill you. You must never go again!"

When she had spoken, the strength and the blaze of her died, and she swayed toward Venters.

"Bess, I'll not go again," he said, catching her.

She leaned against him, and her body was limp and vibrated to a long, wavering tremble. Her face was upturned to his. Woman's face, woman's eyes, woman's lips—all acutely and blindly and sweetly and terribly truthful in their betrayal! But as her fear was instinctive, so was her clinging to this one and only friend.

Venters gently put her from him and steadied her upon her feet; and all the while his blood raced wild, and a thrilling tingle unsteadied his nerve, and something—that he had seen and felt in her—that he could not understand—seemed very close to him, warm and rich as a fragrant breath, sweet as nothing had ever before been sweet to him.

With all his will Venters strove for calmness and thought and judgment unbiased by pity, and reality unswayed by sentiment. Bess's eyes were still fixed upon him with all her soul bright in that wistful light. Swiftly, resolutely he put out of mind all of her life except what had been spent with him. He scorned himself for the intelligence that made him still doubt. He meant to judge her as she had judged him. He was face to face with the inevitableness of life itself. He saw destiny in the dark, straight path of her wonderful eyes. Here was the simplicity, the sweetness of a girl contending with new and strange and enthralling emotions here the living truth of innocence; here the blind terror of a woman confronted with the thought of death to her savior and protector. All this Venters saw, but, besides, there was in Bess's eyes a slow-dawning consciousness that seemed about to break out in glorious radiance.

"Bess, are you thinking?" he asked.

"Yes—oh yes!"

"Do you realize we are here alone—man and woman?"

"Yes."

"Have you thought that we may make our way out to civilization, or we may have to stay here—alone—hidden from the world all our lives?"

"I never thought—till now."

"Well, what's your choice—to go—or to stay here—alone with me?"

"Stay!" New-born thought of self, ringing vibrantly in her voice, gave her answer singular power.

Venters trembled, and then swiftly turned his gaze from her face—from her eyes. He knew what she had only half divined—that she loved him.

CHAPTER XI. FAITH AND UNFAITH

At Jane Withersteen's home the promise made to Mrs. Larkin to care for little Fay had begun to be fulfilled. Like a gleam of sunlight through the cottonwoods was the coming of the child to the gloomy house of Withersteen. The big, silent halls echoed with childish laughter. In the shady court, where Jane spent many of the hot July days, Fay's tiny feet pattered over the stone flags and splashed in the amber stream. She prattled incessantly. What difference, Jane thought, a child made in her home! It had never been a real home, she discovered. Even the tidiness and neatness she had so observed, and upon which she had insisted to her women, became, in the light of Fay's smile, habits that now lost their importance. Fay littered the court with Jane's books and papers, and other toys her fancy improvised, and many a strange craft went floating down the little brook.

And it was owing to Fay's presence that Jane Withersteen came to see more of Lassiter. The rider had for the most part kept to the sage. He rode for her, but he did not seek her except on business; and Jane had to acknowledge in pique that her overtures had been made in vain. Fay, however, captured Lassiter the moment he first laid eyes on her.

Jane was present at the meeting, and there was something about it which dimmed her sight and softened her toward this foe of her people. The rider had clanked into the court, a tired yet wary man, always looking for the attack upon him that was inevitable and might come from any quarter; and he had walked right upon little Fay. The child had been beautiful even in her rags and amid the surroundings of the hovel in the sage, but now, in a pretty white dress, with her shining curls brushed and her face clean and rosy, she was lovely. She left her play and looked up at Lassiter.

If there was not an instinct for all three of them in that meeting, an unreasoning tendency toward a closer intimacy, then Jane Withersteen believed she had been subject to a queer fancy. She imagined any child would have feared Lassiter. And Fay Larkin had been a lonely, a solitary elf of the sage, not at all an ordinary child, and exquisitely shy with strangers. She watched Lassiter with great, round, grave eyes, but showed no fear. The rider gave Jane a favorable report of cattle and horses; and as he took the seat to which she invited him, little Fay edged as much as half an inch nearer. Jane replied to his look of inquiry and told Fay's story. The rider's gray, earnest gaze troubled her. Then he turned to Fay and smiled in a way that made Jane doubt her sense of the true relation of things. How could Lassiter smile so at a child when he had made so many children fatherless? But he did smile, and to the gentleness she had seen a few times he added something that was infinitely sad and sweet. Jane's intuition told her that Lassiter had never been a father, but if life ever so blessed him he would be a good one. Fay, also, must have found that smile singularly winning. For she edged closer and closer, and then, by way of feminine capitulation, went to Jane, from whose side she bent a beautiful glance upon the rider.

Lassiter only smiled at her.

Jane watched them, and realized that now was the moment she should seize, if she was ever to win this man from his hatred. But the step was not easy to take. The more she saw of Lassiter the more she respected him, and the greater her respect the harder it became to lend herself to mere coquetry. Yet as she thought of her great motive, of Tull, and of that other whose name she had schooled herself never to think of in connection with Milly Erne's avenger, she suddenly found she had no choice. And her creed gave her boldness far beyond the limit to which vanity would have led her.

"Lassiter, I see so little of you now," she said, and was conscious of heat in her cheeks.

"I've been riding hard," he replied.

"But you can't live in the saddle. You come in sometimes. Won't you come here to see me—oftener?"

"Is that an order?"

"Nonsense! I simply ask you to come to see me when you find time."

"Why?"

The query once heard was not so embarrassing to Jane as she might have imagined. Moreover, it established in her mind a fact that there existed actually other than selfish reasons for her wanting to see him. And as she had been bold, so she determined to be both honest and brave.

"I've reasons—only one of which I need mention," she answered. "If it's possible I want to change you toward my people. And on the moment I can conceive of little I wouldn't do to gain that end."

How much better and freer Jane felt after that confession! She meant to show him that there was one Mormon who could play a game or wage a fight in the open.

"I reckon," said Lassiter, and he laughed.

It was the best in her, if the most irritating, that Lassiter always aroused.

"Will you come?" She looked into his eyes, and for the life of her could not quite subdue an imperiousness that rose with her spirit. "I never asked so much of any man—except Bern Venters."

"'Pears to me that you'd run no risk, or Venters, either. But mebbe that doesn't hold good for me."

"You mean it wouldn't be safe for you to be often here? You look for ambush in the cottonwoods?"

"Not that so much."

At this juncture little Fay sidled over to Lassiter.

"Has oo a little dirl?" she inquired.

"No, lassie," replied the rider.

Whatever Fay seemed to be searching for in Lassiter's sun-reddened face and quiet eyes she evidently found. "Oo tan tom to see me," she added, and with that, shyness gave place to friendly curiosity. First his sombrero with its leather band and silver ornaments commanded her attention; next his quirt, and then the clinking, silver spurs. These held her for some time, but presently, true to childish fickleness, she left off playing with them to look for something else. She laughed in glee as she ran her little hands down the slippery, shiny surface of Lassiter's leather chaps. Soon she discovered one of the hanging gun—sheaths, and she dragged it up and began tugging at the huge black handle of the gun. Jane Withersteen repressed an exclamation. What significance there was to her in the little girl's efforts to dislodge that heavy weapon! Jane Withersteen saw Fay's play and her beauty and her love as most powerful allies to her own woman's part in a game that suddenly had acquired a strange zest and a hint of danger. And as for the rider, he appeared to have forgotten Jane in the wonder of this lovely child playing about him. At first he was much the shyer of the two. Gradually her confidence overcame his backwardness, and he had the temerity to stroke her golden curls with a great hand. Fay rewarded his boldness with a smile, and when he had gone to the extreme of closing that great hand over her little brown one, she said, simply, "I like oo!"

Sight of his face then made Jane oblivious for the time to his character as a hater of Mormons. Out of the mother longing that swelled her breast she divined the child hunger in Lassiter.

He returned the next day, and the next; and upon the following he came both at morning and at night. Upon the evening of this fourth day Jane seemed to feel the breaking of a brooding struggle in Lassiter. During all these visits he had scarcely a word to say, though he watched her and played absent-mindedly with Fay. Jane had contented herself with silence. Soon little Fay substituted for the expression of regard, "I like oo," a warmer and more generous one, "I love oo."

Thereafter Lassiter came oftener to see Jane and her little protegee. Daily he grew more gentle and kind, and gradually developed a quaintly merry mood. In the morning he lifted Fay upon his horse and let her ride as he walked beside her to the edge of the sage. In the evening he played with the child at an infinite variety of games she invented, and then, oftener than not, he accepted Jane's invitation to supper. No other visitor came to Withersteen House during those days. So that in spite of watchfulness he never forgot, Lassiter began to show he felt at home there. After the meal they walked into the grove of cottonwoods or up by the lakes, and little Fay held Lassiter's hand as much as she held Jane's. Thus a strange relationship was established, and Jane liked it. At twilight they always returned to the house, where Fay kissed them and went in to her mother. Lassiter and Jane were left alone.

CHAPTER XI. FAITH AND UNFAITH

Then, if there were anything that a good woman could do to win a man and still preserve her self-respect, it was something which escaped the natural subtlety of a woman determined to allure. Jane's vanity, that after all was not great, was soon satisfied with Lassiter's silent admiration. And her honest desire to lead him from his dark, blood-stained path would never have blinded her to what she owed herself. But the driving passion of her religion, and its call to save Mormons' lives, one life in particular, bore Jane Withersteen close to an infringement of her womanhood. In the beginning she had reasoned that her appeal to Lassiter must be through the senses. With whatever means she possessed in the way of adornment she enhanced her beauty. And she stooped to artifices that she knew were unworthy of her, but which she deliberately chose to employ. She made of herself a girl in every variable mood wherein a girl might be desirable. In those moods she was not above the methods of an inexperienced though natural flirt. She kept close to him whenever opportunity afforded; and she was forever playfully, yet passionately underneath the surface, fighting him for possession of the great black guns. These he would never yield to her. And so in that manner their hands were often and long in contact. The more of simplicity that she sensed in him the greater the advantage she took.

She had a trick of changing—and it was not altogether voluntary—from this gay, thoughtless, girlish coquettishness to the silence and the brooding, burning mystery of a woman's mood. The strength and passion and fire of her were in her eyes, and she so used them that Lassiter had to see this depth in her, this haunting promise more fitted to her years than to the flaunting guise of a wilful girl.

The July days flew by. Jane reasoned that if it were possible for her to be happy during such a time, then she was happy. Little Fay completely filled a long aching void in her heart. In fettering the hands of this Lassiter she was accomplishing the greatest good of her life, and to do good even in a small way rendered happiness to Jane Withersteen. She had attended the regular Sunday services of her church; otherwise she had not gone to the village for weeks. It was unusual that none of her churchmen or friends had called upon her of late; but it was neglect for which she was glad. Judkins and his boy riders had experienced no difficulty in driving the white herd. So these warm July days were free of worry, and soon Jane hoped she had passed the crisis; and for her to hope was presently to trust, and then to believe. She thought often of Venters, but in a dreamy, abstract way. She spent hours teaching and playing with little Fay. And the activity of her mind centered around Lassiter. The direction she had given her will seemed to blunt any branching off of thought from that straight line. The mood came to obsess her.

In the end, when her awakening came, she learned that she had builded better than she knew. Lassiter, though kinder and gentler than ever, had parted with his quaint humor and his coldness and his tranquillity to become a restless and unhappy man. Whatever the power of his deadly intent toward Mormons, that passion now had a rival, the one equally burning and consuming. Jane Withersteen had one moment of exultation before the dawn of a strange uneasiness.

What if she had made of herself a lure, at tremendous cost to him and to her, and all in vain!

That night in the moonlit grove she summoned all her courage and, turning suddenly in the path, she faced Lassiter and leaned close to him, so that she touched him and her eyes looked up to his.

"Lassiter!... Will you do anything for me?"

In the moonlight she saw his dark, worn face change, and by that change she seemed to feel him immovable as a wall of stone.

Jane slipped her hands down to the swinging gun-sheaths, and when she had locked her fingers around the huge, cold handles of the guns, she trembled as with a chilling ripple over all her body.

"May I take your guns?"

"Why?" he asked, and for the first time to her his voice carried a harsh note. Jane felt his hard, strong hands close round her wrists. It was not wholly with intent that she leaned toward him, for the look of his eyes and the feel of his hands made her weak.

"It's no trifle—no woman's whim—it's deep—as my heart. Let me take them?"

"Why?"

"I want to keep you from killing more men—Mormons. You must let me save you from more wickedness—more wanton bloodshed—" Then the truth forced itself falteringly from her lips. "You must—let—help me to keep my vow to Milly Erne. I swore to her—as she lay dying—that if ever any one came here to avenge her—I swore I would stay his hand. Perhaps I—I alone can save the—the man who—who—Oh, Lassiter!... I feel that I can't change you—then soon you'll be out to kill—and you'll kill by instinct—and among the Mormons you kill will be the one—who... Lassiter, if you care a little for me—let me—for my sake—let me take your guns!"

As if her hands had been those of a child, he unclasped their clinging grip from the handles of his guns, and, pushing her away, he turned his gray face to her in one look of terrible realization and then strode off into the shadows of the cottonwoods.

When the first shock of her futile appeal to Lassiter had passed, Jane took his cold, silent condemnation and abrupt departure not so much as a refusal to her entreaty as a hurt and stunned bitterness for her attempt at his betrayal. Upon further thought and slow consideration of Lassiter's past actions, she believed he would return and forgive her. The man could not be hard to a woman, and she doubted that he could stay away from her. But at the point where she had hoped to find him vulnerable she now began to fear he was proof against all persuasion. The iron and stone quality that she had early suspected in him had actually cropped out as an impregnable barrier. Nevertheless, if Lassiter remained in Cottonwoods she would never give up her hope and desire to change him. She would change him if she had to sacrifice everything dear to her except hope of heaven. Passionately devoted as she was to her religion, she had yet refused to marry a Mormon. But a situation had developed wherein self paled in the great white light of religious duty of the highest order. That was the leading motive, the divinely spiritual one; but there were other motives, which, like tentacles, aided in drawing her will to the acceptance of a possible abnegation. And through the watches of that sleepless night Jane Withersteen, in fear and sorrow and doubt, came finally to believe that if she must throw herself into Lassiter's arms to make him abide by "Thou shalt not kill!" she would yet do well.

In the morning she expected Lassiter at the usual hour, but she was not able to go at once to the court, so she sent little Fay. Mrs. Larkin was ill and required attention. It appeared that the mother, from the time of her arrival at Withersteen House, had relaxed and was slowly losing her hold on life. Jane had believed that absence of worry and responsibility coupled with good nursing and comfort would mend Mrs. Larkin's broken health. Such, however, was not the case.

When Jane did get out to the court, Fay was there alone, and at the moment embarking on a dubious voyage down the stone-lined amber stream upon a craft of two brooms and a pillow. Fay was as delightfully wet as she could possibly wish to get.

Clatter of hoofs distracted Fay and interrupted the scolding she was gleefully receiving from Jane. The sound was not the light-spirited trot that Bells made when Lassiter rode him into the outer court. This was slower and heavier, and Jane did not recognize in it any of her other horses. The appearance of Bishop Dyer startled Jane. He dismounted with his rapid, jerky motion flung the bridle, and, as he turned toward the inner court and stalked up on the stone flags, his boots rang. In his authoritative front, and in the red anger unmistakably flaming in his face, he reminded Jane of her father.

"Is that the Larkin pauper?" he asked, bruskly, without any greeting to Jane.

"It's Mrs. Larkin's little girl," replied Jane, slowly.

"I hear you intend to raise the child?"

"Yes."

"Of course you mean to give her Mormon bringing-up?"

"No."

His questions had been swift. She was amazed at a feeling that some one else was replying for her.

"I've come to say a few things to you." He stopped to measure her with stern, speculative eye.

Jane Withersteen loved this man. From earliest childhood she had been taught to revere and love bishops of her church. And for ten years Bishop Dyer had been the closest friend and counselor of her father, and for the greater part of that period her own friend and Scriptural teacher. Her interpretation of her creed and her religious activity in fidelity to it, her acceptance of mysterious and holy Mormon truths, were all invested in this Bishop. Bishop Dyer as an entity was next to God. He was God's mouthpiece to the little Mormon community at Cottonwoods. God revealed himself in secret to this mortal.

And Jane Withersteen suddenly suffered a paralyzing affront to her consciousness of reverence by some strange, irresistible twist of thought wherein she saw this Bishop as a man. And the train of thought hurdled the rising, crying protests of that other self whose poise she had lost. It was not her Bishop who eyed her in curious measurement. It was a man who tramped into her presence without removing his hat, who had no greeting for her, who had no semblance of courtesy. In looks, as in action, he made her think of a bull stamping cross-grained into a corral. She had heard of Bishop Dyer forgetting the minister in the fury of a common man, and now she was to feel it. The glance by which she measured him in turn momentarily veiled the divine in the ordinary. He looked a rancher; he was booted, spurred, and covered with dust; he carried a gun at his hip, and she remembered that he had been known to use it. But during the long moment while he watched her there was nothing commonplace in the slow-gathering might of his wrath.

"Brother Tull has talked to me," he began. "It was your father's wish that you marry Tull, and my order. You refused him?"

"Yes."

"You would not give up your friendship with that tramp Venters?"

"No."

"But you'll do as *I* order!" he thundered. "Why, Jane Withersteen, you are in danger of becoming a heretic! You can thank your Gentile friends for that. You face the damning of your soul to perdition."

In the flux and reflux of the whirling torture of Jane's mind, that new, daring spirit of hers vanished in the old habitual order of her life. She was a Mormon, and the Bishop regained ascendance.

"It's well I got you in time, Jane Withersteen. What would your father have said to these goings-on of yours? He would have put you in a stone cage on bread and water. He would have taught you something about Mormonism. Remember, you're a born Mormon. There have been Mormons who turned heretic—damn their souls!—but no born Mormon ever left us yet. Ah, I see your shame. Your faith is not shaken. You are only a wild girl." The Bishop's tone softened. "Well, it's enough that I got to you in time.... Now tell me about this Lassiter. I hear strange things."

"What do you wish to know?" queried Jane.

"About this man. You hired him?"

"Yes, he's riding for me. When my riders left me I had to have any one I could get."

"Is it true what I hear—that he's a gun-man, a Mormon-hater, steeped in blood?"

"True—terribly true, I fear."

"But what's he doing here in Cottonwoods? This place isn't notorious enough for such a man. Sterling and the villages north, where there's universal gun-packing and fights every day—where there are more men like him, it seems to me they would attract him most. We're only a wild, lonely border settlement. It's only recently that the rustlers have made killings here. Nor have there been saloons till lately, nor the drifting in of outcasts. Has not this gun-man some special mission here?"

Jane maintained silence.

"Tell me," ordered Bishop Dyer, sharply.

"Yes," she replied.

"Do you know what it is?"

"Yes."

"Tell me that."

"Bishop Dyer, I don't want to tell."

He waved his hand in an imperative gesture of command. The red once more leaped to his face, and in his steel-blue eyes glinted a pin-point of curiosity.

"That first day," whispered Jane, "Lassiter said he came here to find—Milly Erne's grave!"

With downcast eyes Jane watched the swift flow of the amber water. She saw it and tried to think of it, of the stones, of the ferns; but, like her body, her mind was in a leaden vise. Only the Bishop's voice could release her. Seemingly there was silence of longer duration than all her former life.

"For what—else?" When Bishop Dyer's voice did cleave the silence it was high, curiously shrill, and on the point of breaking. It released Jane's tongue, but she could not lift her eyes.

"To kill the man who persuaded Milly Erne to abandon her home and her husband—and her God!"

With wonderful distinctness Jane Withersteen heard her own clear voice. She heard the water murmur at her feet and flow on to the sea; she heard the rushing of all the waters in the world. They filled her ears with low, unreal murmurings—these sounds that deadened her brain and yet could not break the long and terrible silence. Then, from somewhere—from an immeasurable distance—came a slow, guarded, clinking, clanking step. Into her it shot electrifying life. It released the weight upon her numbed eyelids. Lifting her eyes she saw—ashen, shaken, stricken—not the Bishop but the man! And beyond him, from round the corner came that soft, silvery step. A long black boot with a gleaming spur swept into sight—and then Lassiter! Bishop Dyer did not see, did not hear: he stared at Jane in the throes of sudden revelation.

"Ah, I understand!" he cried, in hoarse accents. "That's why you made love to this Lassiter—to bind his hands!"

It was Jane's gaze riveted upon the rider that made Bishop Dyer turn. Then clear sight failed her. Dizzily, in a blur, she saw the Bishop's hand jerk to his hip. She saw gleam of blue and spout of red. In her ears burst a thundering report. The court floated in darkening circles around her, and she fell into utter blackness.

The darkness lightened, turned to slow-drifting haze, and lifted. Through a thin film of blue smoke she saw the rough-hewn timbers of the court roof. A cool, damp touch moved across her brow. She smelled powder, and it was that which galvanized her suspended thought. She moved, to see that she lay prone upon the stone flags with her head on Lassiter's knee, and he was bathing her brow with water from the stream. The same swift glance, shifting low, brought into range of her sight a smoking gun and splashes of blood.

"Ah-h!" she moaned, and was drifting, sinking again into darkness, when Lassiter's voice arrested her.

"It's all right, Jane. It's all right."

"Did—you—kill—him?" she whispered.

"Who? That fat party who was here? No. I didn't kill him."

"Oh!... Lassiter!"

"Say! It was queer for you to faint. I thought you were such a strong woman, not faintish like that. You're all right now—only some pale. I thought you'd never come to. But I'm awkward round women folks. I couldn't think of anythin'."

"Lassiter!... the gun there!... the blood!"

"So that's troublin' you. I reckon it needn't. You see it was this way. I come round the house an' seen that fat party an' heard him talkin' loud. Then he seen me, an' very impolite goes straight for his gun. He oughtn't have tried to throw a gun on me—whatever his reason was. For that's meetin' me on my own grounds. I've seen runnin' molasses that was quicker 'n him. Now I didn't know who he was, visitor or friend or relation of yours, though I seen he was a Mormon all over, an' I couldn't get serious about shootin'. So I winged him—put a bullet through his arm as he was pullin' at his gun. An' he dropped the gun there, an' a little blood. I told him he'd introduced himself sufficient, an' to please move out of my vicinity. An' he went."

Lassiter spoke with slow, cool, soothing voice, in which there was a hint of levity, and his touch, as he continued to bathe her brow, was gentle and steady. His impassive face, and the kind gray eyes, further stilled her agitation.

"He drew on you first, and you deliberately shot to cripple him—you wouldn't kill him—you—Lassiter?"

"That's about the size of it."

Jane kissed his hand.

All that was calm and cool about Lassiter instantly vanished.

"Don't do that! I won't stand it! An' I don't care a damn who that fat party was."

He helped Jane to her feet and to a chair. Then with the wet scarf he had used to bathe her face he wiped the blood from the stone flags and, picking up the gun, he threw it upon a couch. With that he began to pace the court, and his silver spurs jangled musically, and the great gun-sheaths softly brushed against his leather chaps.

"So—it's true—what I heard him say?" Lassiter asked, presently halting before her. "You made love to me—to bind my hands?"

"Yes," confessed Jane. It took all her woman's courage to meet the gray storm of his glance.

"All these days that you've been so friendly an' like a pardner—all these evenin's that have been so bewilderin' to me—your beauty—an'—an' the way you looked an' came close to me—they were woman's tricks to bind my hands?"

"Yes."

"An' your sweetness that seemed so natural, an' your throwin' little Fay an' me so much together—to make me love the child—all that was for the same reason?"

"Yes."

Lassiter flung his arms—a strange gesture for him.

"Mebbe it wasn't much in your Mormon thinkin', for you to play that game. But to ring the child in—that was hellish!"

Jane's passionate, unheeding zeal began to loom darkly.

"Lassiter, whatever my intention in the beginning, Fay loves you dearly—and I—I've grown to—to like you."

"That's powerful kind of you, now," he said. Sarcasm and scorn made his voice that of a stranger. "An' you sit there an' look me straight in the eyes! You're a wonderful strange woman, Jane Withersteen."

"I'm not ashamed, Lassiter. I told you I'd try to change you."

"Would you mind tellin' me just what you tried?"

"I tried to make you see beauty in me and be softened by it. I wanted you to care for me so that I could influence you. It wasn't easy. At first you were stone-blind. Then I hoped you'd love little Fay, and through that come to feel the horror of making children fatherless."

"Jane Withersteen, either you're a fool or noble beyond my understandin'. Mebbe you're both. I know you're blind. What you meant is one thing—what you did was to make me love you."

"Lassiter!"

"I reckon I'm a human bein', though I never loved any one but my sister, Milly Erne. That was long—"

"Oh, are you Milly's brother?"

"Yes, I was, an' I loved her. There never was any one but her in my life till now. Didn't I tell you that long ago I back-trailed myself from women? I was a Texas ranger till—till Milly left home, an' then I became somethin' else—Lassiter! For years I've been a lonely man set on one thing. I came here an' met you. An' now I'm not the man I was. The change was gradual, an' I took no notice of it. I understand now that never-satisfied longin' to see you, listen to you, watch you, feel you near me. It's plain now why you were never out of my thoughts. I've had no thoughts but of you. I've lived an' breathed for you. An' now when I know what it means—what you've done—I'm burnin' up with hell's fire!"

"Oh, Lassiter—no—no—you don't love me that way!" Jane cased.

"If that's what love is, then I do."

"Forgive me! I didn't mean to make you love me like that. Oh, what a tangle of our lives! You—Milly Erne's brother! And I—heedless, mad to melt your heart toward Mormons. Lassiter, I may be wicked but not wicked enough to hate. If I couldn't hate Tull, could I hate you?"

"After all, Jane, mebbe you're only blind—Mormon blind. That only can explain what's close to selfishness—"

"I'm not selfish. I despise the very word. If I were free—"

"But you're not free. Not free of Mormonism. An' in playin' this game with me you've been unfaithful."

"Un-faithful!" faltered Jane.

"Yes, I said unfaithful. You're faithful to your Bishop an' unfaithful to yourself. You're false to your womanhood an' true to your religion. But for a savin' innocence you'd have made yourself low an' vile—betrayin' yourself, betrayin' me—all to bind my hands an' keep me from snuffin' out Mormon life. It's your damned Mormon blindness."

"Is it vile—is it blind—is it only Mormonism to save human life? No, Lassiter, that's God's law, divine, universal for all Christians."

"The blindness I mean is blindness that keeps you from seein' the truth. I've known many good Mormons. But some are blacker than hell. You won't see that even when you know it. Else, why all this blind passion to save the life of that—that...."

Jane shut out the light, and the hands she held over her eyes trembled and quivered against her face.

"Blind—yes, en' let me make it clear en' simple to you," Lassiter went on, his voice losing its tone of anger. "Take, for instance, that idea of yours last night when you wanted my guns. It was good an' beautiful, an' showed your heart—but—why, Jane, it was crazy. Mind I'm assumin' that life to me is as sweet as to any other man. An' to preserve that life is each man's first an' closest thought. Where would any man be on this border without guns? Where, especially, would Lassiter be? Well, I'd be under the sage with thousands of other men now livin' an' sure better men than me. Gun-packin' in the West since the Civil War has growed into a kind of moral law. An' out here on this border it's the difference between a man an' somethin' not a man. Look what your takin' Venters's guns from him all but made him! Why, your churchmen carry guns. Tull has killed a man an' drawed on others. Your Bishop has shot a half dozen men, an' it wasn't through prayers of his that they recovered. An' to-day he'd have shot me if he'd been quick enough on the draw. Could I walk or ride down into Cottonwoods without my guns? This is a wild time, Jane Withersteen, this year of our Lord eighteen seventy-one."

"No time—for a woman!" exclaimed Jane, brokenly. "Oh, Lassiter, I feel helpless—lost—and don't know where to turn. If I am blind—then—I need some one—a friend—you, Lassiter—more than ever!"

"Well, I didn't say nothin' about goin' back on you, did I?"

CHAPTER XII. THE INVISIBLE HAND

Jane received a letter from Bishop Dyer, not in his own handwriting, which stated that the abrupt termination of their interview had left him in some doubt as to her future conduct. A slight injury had incapacitated him from seeking another meeting at present, the letter went on to say, and ended with a request which was virtually a command, that she call upon him at once.

The reading of the letter acquainted Jane Withersteen with the fact that something within her had all but changed. She sent no reply to Bishop Dyer nor did she go to see him. On Sunday she remained absent from the service—for the second time in years—and though she did not actually suffer there was a dead-lock of feelings deep within her, and the waiting for a balance to fall on either side was almost as bad as suffering. She had a gloomy expectancy of untoward circumstances, and with it a keen-edged curiosity to watch developments. She had a half-formed conviction that her future conduct—as related to her churchmen—was beyond her control and would be governed by their attitude toward her. Something was changing in her, forming, waiting for decision to make it a real and fixed thing. She had told Lassiter that she felt helpless and lost in the fateful tangle of their lives; and now she feared that she was approaching the same chaotic condition of mind in regard to her religion. It appalled her to find that she questioned phases of that religion. Absolute faith had been her serenity. Though leaving her faith unshaken, her serenity had been disturbed, and now it was broken by open war between her and her ministers. That something within her—a whisper—which she had tried in vain to hush had become a ringing voice, and it called to her to wait. She had transgressed no laws of God. Her churchmen, however invested with the power and the glory of a wonderful creed, however they sat in inexorable judgment of her, must now practice toward her the simple, common, Christian virtue they professed to preach, "Do unto others as you would have others do unto you!"

Jane Withersteen, waiting in darkness of mind, remained faithful still. But it was darkness that must soon be pierced by light. If her faith were justified, if her churchmen were trying only to intimidate her, the fact would soon be manifest, as would their failure, and then she would redouble her zeal toward them and toward what had been the best work of her life—work for the welfare and happiness of those among whom she lived, Mormon and Gentile alike. If that secret, intangible power closed its coils round her again, if that great invisible hand moved here and there and everywhere, slowly paralyzing her with its mystery and its inconceivable sway over her affairs, then she would know beyond doubt that it was not chance, nor jealousy, nor intimidation, nor ministerial wrath at her revolt, but a cold and calculating policy thought out long before she was born, a dark, immutable will of whose empire she and all that was hers was but an atom.

Then might come her ruin. Then might come her fall into black storm. Yet she would rise again, and to the light. God would be merciful to a driven woman who had lost her way.

A week passed. Little Fay played and prattled and pulled at Lassiter's big black guns. The rider came to Withersteen House oftener than ever. Jane saw a change in him, though it did not relate to his kindness and gentleness. He was quieter and more thoughtful. While playing with Fay or conversing with Jane he seemed to be possessed of another self that watched with cool, roving eyes, that listened, listened always as if the murmuring amber stream brought messages, and the moving leaves whispered something. Lassiter never rode Bells into the court any more, nor did he come by the lane or the paths. When he appeared it was suddenly and noiselessly out of the dark shadow of the grove.

"I left Bells out in the sage," he said, one day at the end of that week. "I must carry water to him."

"Why not let him drink at the trough or here?" asked Jane, quickly.

"I reckon it'll be safer for me to slip through the grove. I've been watched when I rode in from the sage."

"Watched? By whom?"

"By a man who thought he was well hid. But my eyes are pretty sharp. An', Jane," he went on, almost in a whisper, "I reckon it'd be a good idea for us to talk low. You're spied on here by your women."

"Lassiter!" she whispered in turn. "That's hard to believe. My women love me."

"What of that?" he asked. "Of course they love you. But they're Mormon women."

Jane's old, rebellious loyalty clashed with her doubt.

"I won't believe it," she replied, stubbornly.

"Well then, just act natural an' talk natural, an' pretty soon—give them time to hear us—pretend to go over there to the table, en' then quick-like make a move for the door en' open it."

"I will," said Jane, with heightened color. Lassiter was right; he never made mistakes; he would not have told her unless he positively knew. Yet Jane was so tenacious of faith that she had to see with her own eyes, and so constituted that to employ even such small deceit toward her women made her ashamed, and angry for her shame as well as theirs. Then a singular thought confronted her that made her hold up this simple ruse—which hurt her, though it was well justified—against the deceit she had wittingly and eagerly used toward Lassiter. The difference was staggering in its suggestion of that blindness of which he had accused her. Fairness and justice and mercy, that she had imagined were anchor-cables to hold fast her soul to righteousness had not been hers in the strange, biased duty that had so exalted and confounded her.

Presently Jane began to act her little part, to laugh and play with Fay, to talk of horses and cattle to Lassiter. Then she made deliberate mention of a book in which she kept records of all pertaining to her stock, and she walked slowly toward the table, and when near the door she suddenly whirled and thrust it open. Her sharp action nearly knocked down a woman who had undoubtedly been listening.

"Hester," said Jane, sternly, "you may go home, and you need not come back."

Jane shut the door and returned to Lassiter. Standing unsteadily, she put her hand on his arm. She let him see that doubt had gone, and how this stab of disloyalty pained her.

"Spies! My own women!... Oh, miserable!" she cried, with flashing, tearful eyes.

"I hate to tell you," he replied. By that she knew he had long spared her. "It's begun again—that work in the dark."

"Nay, Lassiter—it never stopped!"

So bitter certainty claimed her at last, and trust fled Withersteen House and fled forever. The women who owed much to Jane Withersteen changed not in love for her, nor in devotion to their household work, but they poisoned both by a thousand acts of stealth and cunning and duplicity. Jane broke out once and caught them in strange, stone-faced, unhesitating falsehood. Thereafter she broke out no more. She forgave them because they were driven. Poor, fettered, and sealed Hagars, how she pitied them! What terrible thing bound them and locked their lips, when they showed neither consciousness of guilt toward their benefactress nor distress at the slow wearing apart of long-established and dear ties?

"The blindness again!" cried Jane Withersteen. "In my sisters as in me!... O God!"

There came a time when no words passed between Jane and her women. Silently they went about their household duties, and secretly they went about the underhand work to which they had been bidden. The gloom of the house and the gloom of its mistress, which darkened even the bright spirit of little Fay, did not pervade these women. Happiness was not among them, but they were aloof from gloom. They spied and listened; they received and sent secret messengers; and they stole Jane's books and records, and finally the papers that were deeds of her possessions. Through it all they were silent, rapt in a kind of trance. Then one by one, without leave or explanation or farewell, they left Withersteen House, and never returned.

Coincident with this disappearance Jane's gardeners and workers in the alfalfa fields and stable men quit her, not even asking for their wages. Of all her Mormon employees about the great ranch only Jerd remained. He went on with his duty, but talked no more of the change than if it had never occurred.

"Jerd," said Jane, "what stock you can't take care of turn out in the sage. Let your first thought be for Black Star and Night. Keep them in perfect condition. Run them every day and watch them always."

Though Jane Withersteen gave them such liberality, she loved her possessions. She loved the rich, green stretches of alfalfa, and the farms, and the grove, and the old stone house, and the beautiful, ever-faithful amber spring, and every one of a myriad of horses and colts and burros and fowls down to the smallest rabbit that nipped her vegetables; but she loved best her noble Arabian steeds. In common with all riders of the upland sage Jane cherished two material things—the cold, sweet, brown water that made life possible in the wilderness and the horses which were a part of that life. When Lassiter asked her what Lassiter would be without his guns he was assuming that his horse was part of himself. So Jane loved Black Star and Night because it was her nature to love all beautiful creatures—perhaps all living things; and then she loved them because she herself was of the sage and in her had been born and bred the rider's instinct to rely on his four-footed brother. And when Jane gave Jerd the order to keep her favorites trained down to the day it was a half-conscious admission that presaged a time when she would need her fleet horses.

Jane had now, however, no leisure to brood over the coils that were closing round her. Mrs. Larkin grew weaker as the August days began; she required constant care; there was little Fay to look after; and such household work as was imperative. Lassiter put Bells in the stable with the other racers, and directed his efforts to a closer attendance upon Jane. She welcomed the change. He was always at hand to help, and it was her fortune to learn that his boast of being awkward around women had its root in humility and was not true.

His great, brown hands were skilled in a multiplicity of ways which a woman might have envied. He shared Jane's work, and was of especial help to her in nursing Mrs. Larkin. The woman suffered most at night, and this often broke Jane's rest. So it came about that Lassiter would stay by Mrs. Larkin during the day, when she needed care, and Jane would make up the sleep she lost in night-watches. Mrs. Larkin at once took kindly to the gentle Lassiter, and, without ever asking who or what he was, praised him to Jane. "He's a good man and loves children," she said. How sad to hear this truth spoken of a man whom Jane thought lost beyond all redemption! Yet ever and ever Lassiter towered above her, and behind or through his black, sinister figure shone something luminous that strangely affected Jane. Good and evil began to seem incomprehensibly blended in her judgment. It was her belief that evil could not come forth from good; yet here was a murderer who dwarfed in gentleness, patience, and love any man she had ever known.

She had almost lost track of her more outside concerns when early one morning Judkins presented himself before her in the courtyard.

Thin, hard, burnt, bearded, with the dust and sage thick on him, with his leather wrist-bands shining from use, and his boots worn through on the stirrup side, he looked the rider of riders. He wore two guns and carried a Winchester.

Jane greeted him with surprise and warmth, set meat and bread and drink before him; and called Lassiter out to see him. The men exchanged glances, and the meaning of Lassiter's keen inquiry and Judkins's bold reply, both unspoken, was not lost upon Jane.

"Where's your hoss?" asked Lassiter, aloud.

"Left him down the slope," answered Judkins. "I footed it in a ways, an' slept last night in the sage. I went to the place you told me you 'moss always slept, but didn't strike you."

"I moved up some, near the spring, an' now I go there nights."

"Judkins—the white herd?" queried Jane, hurriedly.

"Miss Withersteen, I make proud to say I've not lost a steer. Fer a good while after thet stampede Lassiter milled we hed no trouble. Why, even the sage dogs left us. But it's begun agin—thet flashin' of lights over ridge tips, an' queer puffin' of smoke, en' then at night strange whistles en' noises. But the herd's acted magnificent. An' my boys, say, Miss Withersteen, they're only kids, but I ask no better riders. I got the laugh in the village fer takin' them out. They're a wild lot, an' you know boys hev more nerve than grown men, because they don't know what danger is. I'm not denyin' there's danger. But they glory in it, an' mebbe I like it myself—anyway, we'll stick. We're goin' to drive the herd on the far side of the first break of Deception Pass. There's a great round valley over there, an' no ridges or piles of rocks to aid these stampeders. The rains are due. We'll hev plenty of water fer a while. An' we can hold thet herd from anybody except Oldrin'. I come in fer supplies. I'll pack a couple of burros an' drive out after dark to-night."

"Judkins, take what you want from the store-room. Lassiter will help you. I—I can't thank you enough... but—wait."

Jane went to the room that had once been her father's, and from a secret chamber in the thick stone wall she took a bag of gold, and, carrying it back to the court, she gave it to the rider.

"There, Judkins, and understand that I regard it as little for your loyalty. Give what is fair to your boys, and keep the rest. Hide it. Perhaps that would be wisest."

"Oh... Miss Withersteen!" ejaculated the rider. "I couldn't earn so much in—in ten years. It's not right—I oughtn't take it."

"Judkins, you know I'm a rich woman. I tell you I've few faithful friends. I've fallen upon evil days. God only knows what will become of me and mine! So take the gold."

She smiled in understanding of his speechless gratitude, and left him with Lassiter. Presently she heard him speaking low at first, then in louder accents emphasized by the thumping of his rifle on the stones. "As infernal a job as even you, Lassiter, ever heerd of."

"Why, son," was Lassiter's reply, "this breakin' of Miss Withersteen may seem bad to you, but it ain't bad—yet. Some of these wall-eyed fellers who look jest as if they was walkin' in the shadow of Christ himself, right down the sunny road, now they can think of things en' do things that are really hell-bent."

Jane covered her ears and ran to her own room, and there like caged lioness she paced to and fro till the coming of little Fay reversed her dark thoughts.

The following day, a warm and muggy one threatening rain awhile Jane was resting in the court, a horseman clattered through the grove and up to the hitching-rack. He leaped off and approached Jane with the manner of a man determined to execute difficult mission, yet fearful of its reception. In the gaunt, wiry figure and the lean, brown face Jane recognized one of her Mormon riders, Blake. It was he of whom Judkins had long since spoken. Of all the riders ever in her employ Blake owed her the most, and as he stepped before her, removing his hat and making manly efforts to subdue his emotion, he showed that he remembered.

"Miss Withersteen, mother's dead," he said.

"Oh—Blake!" exclaimed Jane, and she could say no more.

"She died free from pain in the end, and she's buried—resting at last, thank God!... I've come to ride for you again, if you'll have me. Don't think I mentioned mother to get your sympathy. When she was living and your riders quit, I had to also. I was afraid of what might be done—said to her.... Miss Withersteen, we can't talk of—of what's going on now—"

"Blake, do you know?"

"I know a great deal. You understand, my lips are shut. But without explanation or excuse I offer my services. I'm a Mormon—I hope a good one. But—there are some things!... It's no use, Miss Withersteen, I can't say any more—what I'd like to. But will you take me back?"

"Blake!... You know what it means?"

"I don't care. I'm sick of—of—I'll show you a Mormon who'll be true to you!"

"But, Blake—how terribly you might suffer for that!"

"Maybe. Aren't you suffering now?"

"God knows indeed I am!"

"Miss Withersteen, it's a liberty on my part to speak so, but I know you pretty well—know you'll never give in. I wouldn't if I were you. And I—I must—Something makes me tell you the worst is yet to come. That's all. I absolutely can't say more. Will you take me back—let me ride for you—show everybody what I mean?"

"Blake, it makes me happy to hear you. How my riders hurt me when they quit!" Jane felt the hot tears well to her eyes and splash down upon her hands. "I thought so much of them—tried so hard to be good to them. And not one was true. You've made it easy to forgive. Perhaps many of them really feel as you do, but dare not return to me. Still, Blake, I hesitate to take you back. Yet I want you so much."

"Do it, then. If you're going to make your life a lesson to Mormon women, let me make mine a lesson to the men. Right is right. I believe in you, and here's my life to prove it."

"You hint it may mean your life!" said Jane, breathless and low.

"We won't speak of that. I want to come back. I want to do what every rider aches in his secret heart to do for you.... Miss Withersteen, I hoped it'd not be necessary to tell you that my mother on her deathbed told me to have courage. She knew how the thing galled me—she told me to come back.... Will you take me?"

"God bless you, Blake! Yes, I'll take you back. And will you—will you accept gold from me?"

"Miss Withersteen!"

"I just gave Judkins a bag of gold. I'll give you one. If you will not take it you must not come back. You might ride for me a few months—weeks—days till the storm breaks. Then you'd have nothing, and be in disgrace with your people. We'll forearm you against poverty, and me against endless regret. I'll give you gold which you can hide—till some future time."

"Well, if it pleases you," replied Blake. "But you know I never thought of pay. Now, Miss Withersteen, one thing more. I want to see this man Lassiter. Is he here?"

"Yes, but, Blake—what—Need you see him? Why?" asked Jane, instantly worried. "I can speak to him—tell him about you."

"That won't do. I want to—I've got to tell him myself. Where is he?"

"Lassiter is with Mrs. Larkin. She is ill. I'll call him," answered Jane, and going to the door she softly called for the rider. A faint, musical jingle preceded his step—then his tall form crossed the threshold.

"Lassiter, here's Blake, an old rider of mine. He has come back to me and he wishes to speak to you."

Blake's brown face turned exceedingly pale.

"Yes, I had to speak to you," he said, swiftly. "My name's Blake. I'm a Mormon and a rider. Lately I quit Miss Withersteen. I've come to beg her to take me back. Now I don't know you; but I know—what you are. So I've this to say to your face. It would never occur to this woman to imagine—let alone suspect me to be a spy. She couldn't think it might just be a low plot to come here and shoot you in the back. Jane Withersteen hasn't that kind of a mind.... Well, I've not come for that. I want to help her—to pull a bridle along with Judkins and—and you. The thing is—do you believe me?"

"I reckon I do," replied Lassiter. How this slow, cool speech contrasted with Blake's hot, impulsive words! "You might have saved some of your breath. See here, Blake, cinch this in your mind. Lassiter has met some square Mormons! An' mebbe—"

"Blake," interrupted Jane, nervously anxious to terminate a colloquy that she perceived was an ordeal for him. "Go at once and fetch me a report of my horses."

"Miss Withersteen!... You mean the big drove—down in the sage-cleared fields?"

"Of course," replied Jane. "My horses are all there, except the blooded stock I keep here."

"Haven't you heard—then?"

"Heard? No! What's happened to them?"

"They're gone, Miss Withersteen, gone these ten days past. Dorn told me, and I rode down to see for myself."

"Lassiter—did you know?" asked Jane, whirling to him.

"I reckon so.... But what was the use to tell you?"

It was Lassiter turning away his face and Blake studying the stone flags at his feet that brought Jane to the understanding of what she betrayed. She strove desperately, but she could not rise immediately from such a blow.

"My horses! My horses! What's become of them?"

"Dorn said the riders report another drive by Oldring.... And I trailed the horses miles down the slope toward Deception Pass."

"My red herd's gone! My horses gone! The white herd will go next. I can stand that. But if I lost Black Star and Night, it would be like parting with my own flesh and blood. Lassiter—Blake—am I in danger of losing my racers?"

"A rustler—or—or anybody stealin' hosses of yours would most of all want the blacks," said Lassiter. His evasive reply was affirmative enough. The other rider nodded gloomy acquiescence.

"Oh! Oh!" Jane Withersteen choked, with violent utterance.

"Let me take charge of the blacks?" asked Blake. "One more rider won't be any great help to Judkins. But I might hold Black Star and Night, if you put such store on their value."

"Value! Blake, I love my racers. Besides, there's another reason why I mustn't lose them. You go to the stables. Go with Jerd every day when he runs the horses, and don't let them out of your sight. If you would please me—win my gratitude, guard my black racers."

When Blake had mounted and ridden out of the court Lassiter regarded Jane with the smile that was becoming rarer as the days sped by.

"'Pears to me, as Blake says, you do put some store on them hosses. Now I ain't gainsayin' that the Arabians are the handsomest hosses I ever seen. But Bells can beat Night, an' run neck en' neck with Black Star."

"Lassiter, don't tease me now. I'm miserable—sick. Bells is fast, but he can't stay with the blacks, and you know it. Only Wrangle can do that."

"I'll bet that big raw-boned brute can more'n show his heels to your black racers. Jane, out there in the sage, on a long chase, Wrangle could kill your favorites."

"No, no," replied Jane, impatiently. "Lassiter, why do you say that so often? I know you've teased me at times, and I believe it's only kindness. You're always trying to keep my mind off worry. But you mean more by this repeated mention of my racers?"

"I reckon so." Lassiter paused, and for the thousandth time in her presence moved his black sombrero round and round, as if counting the silver pieces on the band. "Well, Jane, I've sort of read a little that's passin' in your mind."

"You think I might fly from my home—from Cottonwoods—from the Utah border?"

"I reckon. An' if you ever do an' get away with the blacks I wouldn't like to see Wrangle left here on the sage. Wrangle could catch you. I know Venters had him. But you can never tell. Mebbe he hasn't got him now.... Besides—things are happenin', an' somethin' of the same queer nature might have happened to Venters."

"God knows you're right!... Poor Bern, how long he's gone! In my trouble I've been forgetting him. But, Lassiter, I've little fear for him. I've heard my riders say he's as keen as a wolf.... As to your reading my thoughts—well, your suggestion makes an actual thought of what was only one of my dreams. I believe I dreamed of flying from this wild borderland, Lassiter. I've strange dreams. I'm not always practical and thinking of my many duties, as you said once. For instance—if I dared—if I dared I'd ask you to saddle the blacks and ride away with me—and hide me."

"Jane!"

The rider's sunburnt face turned white. A few times Jane had seen Lassiter's cool calm broken—when he had met little Fay, when he had learned how and why he had come to love both child and mistress, when he had stood beside Milly Erne's grave. But one and all they could not be considered in the light of his present agitation. Not only did Lassiter turn white—not only did he grow tense, not only did he lose his coolness, but also he suddenly, violently, hungrily took her into his arms and crushed her to his breast.

"Lassiter!" cried Jane, trembling. It was an action for which she took sole blame. Instantly, as if dazed, weakened, he released her. "Forgive me!" went on Jane. "I'm always forgetting your—your feelings. I thought of you as my faithful friend. I'm always making you out more than human... only, let me say—I meant that—about riding away. I'm wretched, sick of this—this—Oh, something bitter and black grows on my heart!"

"Jane, the hell—of it," he replied, with deep intake of breath, "is you can't ride away. Mebbe realizin' it accounts for my grabbin' you—that way, as much as the crazy boy's rapture your words gave me. I don't understand myself.... But the hell of this game is—you can't ride away."

"Lassiter!... What on earth do you mean? I'm an absolutely free woman."

"You ain't absolutely anythin' of the kind.... I reckon I've got to tell you!"

"Tell me all. It's uncertainty that makes me a coward. It's faith and hope—blind love, if you will, that makes me miserable. Every day I awake believing—still believing. The day grows, and with it doubts, fears, and that black bat hate that bites hotter and hotter into my heart. Then comes night—I pray—I pray for all, and for myself—I sleep—and I awake free once more, trustful, faithful, to believe—to hope! Then, O my God! I grow and live a thousand years till night again!... But if you want to see me a woman, tell me why I can't ride away—tell me what more I'm to lose—tell me the worst."

"Jane, you're watched. There's no single move of yours, except when you're hid in your house, that ain't seen by sharp eyes. The cottonwood grove's full of creepin', crawlin' men. Like Indians in the grass. When you rode, which wasn't often lately, the sage was full of sneakin' men. At night they crawl under your windows into the court, an' I reckon into the house. Jane Withersteen, you know, never locked a door! This here grove's a hummin' bee-hive of mysterious happenin's. Jane, it ain't so much that these soles keep out of my way as me keepin' out of theirs. They're goin' to try to kill me. That's plain. But mebbe I'm as hard to shoot in the back as in the face. So far I've seen fit to watch only. This all means, Jane, that you're a marked woman. You can't get away—not now. Mebbe later, when you're broken, you might. But that's sure doubtful. Jane, you're to lose the cattle that's left—your home an' ranch—an' Amber Spring. You can't even hide a sack of gold! For it couldn't be slipped out of the house, day or night, an' hid or buried, let alone be rid off with. You may lose all. I'm tellin' you, Jane, hopin' to prepare you, if the worst does come. I told you once before about that strange power I've got to feel things."

"Lassiter, what can I do?"

"Nothin', I reckon, except know what's comin' an' wait an' be game. If you'd let me make a call on Tull, an' a long-deferred call on—"

"Hush!... Hush!" she whispered.

"Well, even that wouldn't help you any in the end."

"What does it mean? Oh, what does it mean? I am my father's daughter—a Mormon, yet I can't see! I've not failed in religion—in duty. For years I've given with a free and full heart. When my father died I was rich. If I'm still rich it's because I couldn't find enough ways to become poor. What am I, what are my possessions to set in motion such intensity of secret oppression?"

"Jane, the mind behind it all is an empire builder."

"But, Lassiter, I would give freely—all I own to avert this—this wretched thing. If I gave—that would leave me with faith still. Surely my—my churchmen think of my soul? If I lose my trust in them—"

"Child, be still!" said Lassiter, with a dark dignity that had in it something of pity. "You are a woman, fine en' big an' strong, an' your heart matches your size. But in mind you're a child. I'll say a little more—then I'm done. I'll never mention this again. Among many thousands of women you're one who has bucked against your churchmen. They tried you out, an' failed of persuasion, an' finally of threats. You meet now the cold steel of a will as far from Christlike as the universe is wide. You're to be broken. Your body's to be held, given to some man, made, if possible, to bring children into the world. But your soul?... What do they care for your soul?"

CHAPTER XIII. SOLITUDE AND STORM

In his hidden valley Venters awakened from sleep, and his ears rang with innumerable melodies from full-throated mockingbirds, and his eyes opened wide upon the glorious golden shaft of sunlight shining through the great stone bridge. The circle of cliffs surrounding Surprise Valley lay shrouded in morning mist, a dim blue low down along the terraces, a creamy, moving cloud along the ramparts. The oak forest in the center was a plumed and tufted oval of gold.

He saw Bess under the spruces. Upon her complete recovery of strength she always rose with the dawn. At the moment she was feeding the quail she had tamed. And she had begun to tame the mocking-birds. They fluttered among the branches overhead and some left off their songs to flit down and shyly hop near the twittering quail. Little gray and white rabbits crouched in the grass, now nibbling, now laying long ears flat and watching the dogs.

Venters's swift glance took in the brightening valley, and Bess and her pets, and Ring and Whitie. It swept over all to return again and rest upon the girl. She had changed. To the dark trousers and blouse she had added moccasins of her own make, but she no longer resembled a boy. No eye could have failed to mark the rounded contours of a woman. The change had been to grace and beauty. A glint of warm gold gleamed from her hair, and a tint of red shone in the clear dark brown of cheeks. The haunting sweetness of her lips and eyes, that earlier had been illusive, a promise, had become a living fact. She fitted harmoniously into that wonderful setting; she was like Surprise Valley—wild and beautiful.

Venters leaped out of his cave to begin the day.

He had postponed his journey to Cottonwoods until after the passing of the summer rains. The rains were due soon. But until their arrival and the necessity for his trip to the village he sequestered in a far corner of mind all thought of peril, of his past life, and almost that of the present. It was enough to live. He did not want to know what lay hidden in the dim and distant future. Surprise Valley had enchanted him. In this home of the cliff-dwellers there were peace and quiet and solitude, and another thing, wondrous as the golden morning shaft of sunlight, that he dared not ponder over long enough to understand.

The solitude he had hated when alone he had now come to love. He was assimilating something from this valley of gleams and shadows. From this strange girl he was assimilating more.

The day at hand resembled many days gone before. As Venters had no tools with which to build, or to till the terraces, he remained idle. Beyond the cooking of the simple fare there were no tasks. And as there were no tasks, there was no system. He and Bess began one thing, to leave it; to begin another, to leave that; and then do nothing but lie under the spruces and watch the great cloud-sails majestically move along the ramparts, and dream and dream. The valley was a golden, sunlit world. It was silent. The sighing wind and the twittering quail and the singing birds, even the rare and seldom-occurring hollow crack of a sliding weathered stone, only thickened and deepened that insulated silence.

Venters and Bess had vagrant minds.

"Bess, did I tell you about my horse Wrangle?" inquired Venters.

"A hundred times," she replied.

"Oh, have I? I'd forgotten. I want you to see him. He'll carry us both."

"I'd like to ride him. Can he run?"

"Run? He's a demon. Swiftest horse on the sage! I hope he'll stay in that canyon.

"He'll stay."

They left camp to wander along the terraces, into the aspen ravines, under the gleaming walls. Ring and Whitie wandered in the fore, often turning, often trotting back, open-mouthed and solemn-eyed and happy. Venters lifted his gaze to the grand archway over the entrance to the valley, and Bess lifted hers to follow his, and both were silent. Sometimes the bridge held their attention for a long time. To-day a soaring eagle attracted them.

"How he sails!" exclaimed Bess. "I wonder where his mate is?"

"She's at the nest. It's on the bridge in a crack near the top. I see her often. She's almost white."

They wandered on down the terrace, into the shady, sun-flecked forest. A brown bird fluttered crying from a bush. Bess peeped into the leaves. "Look! A nest and four little birds. They're not afraid of us. See how they open their mouths. They're hungry."

Rabbits rustled the dead brush and pattered away. The forest was full of a drowsy hum of insects. Little darts of purple, that were running quail, crossed the glades. And a plaintive, sweet peeping came from the coverts. Bess's soft step disturbed a sleeping lizard that scampered away over the leaves. She gave chase and caught it, a slim creature of nameless color but of exquisite beauty.

"Jewel eyes," she said. "It's like a rabbit—afraid. We won't eat you. There—go."

Murmuring water drew their steps down into a shallow shaded ravine where a brown brook brawled softly over mossy stones. Multitudes of strange, gray frogs with white spots and black eyes lined the rocky bank and leaped only at close approach. Then Venters's eye descried a very thin, very long green snake coiled round a sapling. They drew closer and closer till they could have touched it. The snake had no fear and watched them with scintillating eyes.

"It's pretty," said Bess. "How tame! I thought snakes always ran."

"No. Even the rabbits didn't run here till the dogs chased them."

On and on they wandered to the wild jumble of massed and broken fragments of cliff at the west end of the valley. The roar of the disappearing stream dinned in their ears. Into this maze of rocks they threaded a tortuous way, climbing, descending, halting to gather wild plums and great lavender lilies, and going on at the will of fancy. Idle and keen perceptions guided them equally.

"Oh, let us climb there!" cried Bess, pointing upward to a small space of terrace left green and shady between huge abutments of broken cliff. And they climbed to the nook and rested and looked out across the valley to the curling column of blue smoke from their campfire. But the cool shade and the rich grass and the fine view were not what they had climbed for. They could not have told, although whatever had drawn them was well-satisfying. Light, sure-footed as a mountain goat, Bess pattered down at Venters's heels; and they went on, calling the dogs, eyes dreamy and wide, listening to the wind and the bees and the crickets and the birds.

Part of the time Ring and Whitie led the way, then Venters, then Bess; and the direction was not an object. They left the sun-streaked shade of the oaks, brushed the long grass of the meadows, entered the green and fragrant swaying willows, to stop, at length, under the huge old cottonwoods where the beavers were busy.

Here they rested and watched. A dam of brush and logs and mud and stones backed the stream into a little lake. The round, rough beaver houses projected from the water. Like the rabbits, the beavers had become shy. Gradually, however, as Venters and Bess knelt low, holding the dogs, the beavers emerged to swim with logs and gnaw at cottonwoods and pat mud walls with their paddle-like tails, and, glossy and shiny in the sun, to go on with their strange, persistent industry. They were the builders. The lake was a mud-hole, and the immediate environment a scarred and dead region, but it was a wonderful home of wonderful animals.

"Look at that one—he puddles in the mud," said Bess. "And there! See him dive! Hear them gnawing! I'd think they'd break their teeth. How's it they can stay out of the water and under the water?"

And she laughed.

Then Venters and Bess wandered farther, and, perhaps not all unconsciously this time, wended their slow steps to the cave of the cliff-dwellers, where she liked best to go.

The tangled thicket and the long slant of dust and little chips of weathered rock and the steep bench of stone and the worn steps all were arduous work for Bess in the climbing. But she gained the shelf, gasping, hot of cheek, glad of eye, with her hand in Venters's. Here they rested. The beautiful valley glittered below with its millions of wind-turned leaves bright-faced in the sun, and the mighty bridge towered heavenward, crowned with blue sky. Bess, however, never rested for long. Soon she was exploring, and Venters followed; she dragged forth from corners and shelves a multitude of crudely fashioned and painted pieces of pottery, and he carried them. They peeped down into the dark holes of the kivas, and Bess gleefully dropped a stone and waited for the long-coming hollow sound to rise.

They peeped into the little globular houses, like mud-wasp nests, and wondered if these had been store-places for grain, or baby cribs, or what; and they crawled into the larger houses and laughed when they bumped their heads on the low roofs, and they dug in the dust of the floors. And they brought from dust and darkness armloads of treasure which they carried to the light. Flints and stones and strange curved sticks and pottery they found; and twisted grass rope that crumbled in their hands, and bits of whitish stone which crushed to powder at a touch and seemed to vanish in the air.

"That white stuff was bone," said Venters, slowly. "Bones of a cliff-dweller."

"No!" exclaimed Bess.

"Here's another piece. Look!... Whew! dry, powdery smoke! That's bone."

Then it was that Venters's primitive, childlike mood, like a savage's, seeing, yet unthinking, gave way to the encroachment of civilized thought. The world had not been made for a single day's play or fancy or idle watching. The world was old. Nowhere could be gotten a better idea of its age than in this gigantic silent tomb. The gray ashes in Venters's hand had once been bone of a human being like himself. The pale gloom of the cave had shadowed people long ago. He saw that Bess had received the same shock—could not in moments such as this escape her feeling living, thinking destiny.

"Bern, people have lived here," she said, with wide, thoughtful eyes.

"Yes," he replied.

"How long ago?"

"A thousand years and more."

"What were they?"

"Cliff-dwellers. Men who had enemies and made their homes high out of reach."

"They had to fight?"

"Yes."

"They fought for—what?"

"For life. For their homes, food, children, parents—for their women!"

"Has the world changed any in a thousand years?"

"I don't know—perhaps a little."

"Have men?"

"I hope so—I think so."

"Things crowd into my mind," she went on, and the wistful light in her eyes told Venters the truth of her thoughts. "I've ridden the border of Utah. I've seen people—know how they live—but they must be few of all who are living. I had my books and I studied them. But all that doesn't help me any more. I want to go out into the big world and see it. Yet I want to stay here more. What's to become of us? Are we cliff-dwellers? We're alone here. I'm happy when I don't think. These—these bones that fly into dust—they make me sick and a little afraid. Did the people who lived here once have the same feelings as we have? What was the good of their living at all? They're gone! What's the meaning of it all—of us?"

"Bess, you ask more than I can tell. It's beyond me. Only there was laughter here once—and now there's silence. There was life—and now there's death. Men cut these little steps, made these arrow-heads and mealing-stones, plaited the ropes we found, and left their bones to crumble in our fingers. As far as time is concerned it might all have been yesterday. We're here to-day. Maybe we're higher in the scale of human beings—in intelligence. But who knows? We can't be any higher in the things for which life is lived at all."

"What are they?"

"Why—I suppose relationship, friendship—love."

"Love!"

"Yes. Love of man for woman—love of woman for man. That's the nature, the meaning, the best of life itself."

She said no more. Wistfulness of glance deepened into sadness.

"Come, let us go," said Venters.

Action brightened her. Beside him, holding his hand she slipped down the shelf, ran down the long, steep slant of sliding stones, out of the cloud of dust, and likewise out of the pale gloom.

"We beat the slide," she cried.

The miniature avalanche cracked and roared, and rattled itself into an inert mass at the base of the incline. Yellow dust like the gloom of the cave, but not so changeless, drifted away on the wind; the roar clapped in echo from the cliff, returned, went back, and came again to die in the hollowness. Down on the sunny terrace there was a different atmosphere. Ring and Whitie leaped around Bess. Once more she was smiling, gay, and thoughtless, with the dream-mood in the shadow of her eyes.

"Bess, I haven't seen that since last summer. Look!" said Venters, pointing to the scalloped edge of rolling purple clouds that peeped over the western wall. "We're in for a storm."

"Oh, I hope not. I'm afraid of storms."

"Are you? Why?"

"Have you ever been down in one of these walled-up pockets in a bad storm?"

"No, now I think of it, I haven't."

"Well, it's terrible. Every summer I get scared to death and hide somewhere in the dark. Storms up on the sage are bad, but nothing to what they are down here in the canyons. And in this little valley—why, echoes can rap back and forth so quick they'll split our ears."

"We're perfectly safe here, Bess."

"I know. But that hasn't anything to do with it. The truth is I'm afraid of lightning and thunder, and thunder-claps hurt my head. If we have a bad storm, will you stay close to me?"

"Yes."

When they got back to camp the afternoon was closing, and it was exceedingly sultry. Not a breath of air stirred the aspen leaves, and when these did not quiver the air was indeed still. The dark-purple clouds moved almost imperceptibly out of the west.

"What have we for supper?" asked Bess.

"Rabbit."

"Bern, can't you think of another new way to cook rabbit?" went on Bess, with earnestness.

"What do you think I am—a magician?" retorted Venters.

"I wouldn't dare tell you. But, Bern, do you want me to turn into a rabbit?"

There was a dark-blue, merry flashing of eyes and a parting of lips; then she laughed. In that moment she was naive and wholesome.

"Rabbit seems to agree with you," replied Venters. "You are well and strong—and growing very pretty."

Anything in the nature of compliment he had never before said to her, and just now he responded to a sudden curiosity to see its effect. Bess stared as if she had not heard aright, slowly blushed, and completely lost her poise in happy confusion.

"I'd better go right away," he continued, "and fetch supplies from Cottonwoods."

A startlingly swift change in the nature of her agitation made him reproach himself for his abruptness.

"No, no, don't go!" she said. "I didn't mean—that about the rabbit. I—I was only trying to be—funny. Don't leave me all alone!"

"Bess, I must go sometime."

"Wait then. Wait till after the storms."

The purple cloud-bank darkened the lower edge of the setting sun, crept up and up, obscuring its fiery red heart, and finally passed over the last ruddy crescent of its upper rim.

The intense dead silence awakened to a long, low, rumbling roll of thunder.

"Oh!" cried Bess, nervously.

"We've had big black clouds before this without rain," said Venters. "But there's no doubt about that thunder. The storms are coming. I'm glad. Every rider on the sage will hear that thunder with glad ears."

Venters and Bess finished their simple meal and the few tasks around the camp, then faced the open terrace, the valley, and the west, to watch and await the approaching storm.

It required keen vision to see any movement whatever in the purple clouds. By infinitesimal degrees the dark cloud-line merged upward into the golden-red haze of the afterglow of sunset. A shadow lengthened from under the western wall across the valley. As straight and rigid as steel rose the delicate spear-pointed silver spruces; the aspen leaves, by nature pendant and quivering, hung limp and heavy; no slender blade of grass moved. A gentle splashing of water came from the ravine. Then again from out of the west sounded the low, dull, and rumbling roll of thunder.

CHAPTER XIII. SOLITUDE AND STORM

A wave, a ripple of light, a trembling and turning of the aspen leaves, like the approach of a breeze on the water, crossed the valley from the west; and the lull and the deadly stillness and the sultry air passed away on a cool wind.

The night bird of the canyon, with clear and melancholy notes announced the twilight. And from all along the cliffs rose the faint murmur and moan and mourn of the wind singing in the caves. The bank of clouds now swept hugely out of the western sky. Its front was purple and black, with gray between, a bulging, mushrooming, vast thing instinct with storm. It had a dark, angry, threatening aspect. As if all the power of the winds were pushing and piling behind, it rolled ponderously across the sky. A red flare burned out instantaneously, flashed from the west to east, and died. Then from the deepest black of the purple cloud burst a boom. It was like the bowling of a huge boulder along the crags and ramparts, and seemed to roll on and fall into the valley to bound and bang and boom from cliff to cliff.

"Oh!" cried Bess, with her hands over her ears. "What did I tell you?"

"Why, Bess, be reasonable!" said Venters.

"I'm a coward."

"Not quite that, I hope. It's strange you're afraid. I love a storm."

"I tell you a storm down in these canyons is an awful thing. I know Oldring hated storms. His men were afraid of them. There was one who went deaf in a bad storm, and never could hear again."

"Maybe I've lots to learn, Bess. I'll lose my guess if this storm isn't bad enough. We're going to have heavy wind first, then lightning and thunder, then the rain. Let's stay out as long as we can."

The tips of the cottonwoods and the oaks waved to the east, and the rings of aspens along the terraces twinkled their myriad of bright faces in fleet and glancing gleam. A low roar rose from the leaves of the forest, and the spruces swished in the rising wind. It came in gusts, with light breezes between. As it increased in strength the lulls shortened in length till there was a strong and steady blow all the time, and violent puffs at intervals, and sudden whirling currents. The clouds spread over the valley, rolling swiftly and low, and twilight faded into a sweeping darkness. Then the singing of the wind in the caves drowned the swift roar of rustling leaves; then the song swelled to a mourning, moaning wail; then with the gathering power of the wind the wail changed to a shriek. Steadily the wind strengthened and constantly the strange sound changed.

The last bit of blue sky yielded to the on-sweep of clouds. Like angry surf the pale gleams of gray, amid the purple of that scudding front, swept beyond the eastern rampart of the valley. The purple deepened to black. Broad sheets of lightning flared over the western wall. There were not yet any ropes or zigzag streaks darting down through the gathering darkness. The storm center was still beyond Surprise Valley.

"Listen!... Listen!" cried Bess, with her lips close to Venters's ear. "You'll hear Oldring's knell!"

"What's that?"

"Oldring's knell. When the wind blows a gale in the caves it makes what the rustlers call Oldring's knell. They believe it bodes his death. I think he believes so, too. It's not like any sound on earth.... It's beginning. Listen!"

The gale swooped down with a hollow unearthly howl. It yelled and pealed and shrilled and shrieked. It was made up of a thousand piercing cries. It was a rising and a moving sound. Beginning at the western break of the valley, it rushed along each gigantic cliff, whistling into the caves and cracks, to mount in power, to bellow a blast through the great stone bridge. Gone, as into an engulfing roar of surging waters, it seemed to shoot back and begin all over again.

It was only wind, thought Venters. Here sped and shrieked the sculptor that carved out the wonderful caves in the cliffs. It was only a gale, but as Venters listened, as his ears became accustomed to the fury and strife, out of it all or through it or above it pealed low and perfectly clear and persistently uniform a strange sound that had no counterpart in all the sounds of the elements. It was not of earth or of life. It was the grief and agony of the gale. A knell of all upon which it blew!

Black night enfolded the valley. Venters could not see his companion, and knew of her presence only through the tightening hold of her hand on his arm. He felt the dogs huddle closer to him. Suddenly the dense, black vault overhead split asunder to a blue-white, dazzling streak of lightning. The whole valley lay vividly clear and luminously bright in his sight. Upreared, vast and magnificent, the stone bridge glimmered like some grand god of storm in the lightning's fire. Then all flashed black again—blacker than pitch—a thick, impenetrable coal-blackness. And there came a ripping, crashing report. Instantly an echo resounded with clapping crash. The initial report was nothing to the echo. It was a terrible, living, reverberating, detonating crash. The wall threw the sound across, and could have made no greater roar if it had slipped in avalanche. From cliff to cliff the echo went in crashing retort and banged in lessening power, and boomed in thinner volume, and clapped weaker and weaker till a final clap could not reach across the waiting cliff.

In the pitchy darkness Venters led Bess, and, groping his way, by feel of hand found the entrance to her cave and lifted her up. On the instant a blinding flash of lightning illumined the cave and all about him. He saw Bess's face white now with dark, frightened eyes. He saw the dogs leap up, and he followed suit. The golden glare vanished; all was black; then came the splitting crack and the infernal din of echoes.

Bess shrank closer to him and closer, found his hands, and pressed them tightly over her ears, and dropped her face upon his shoulder, and hid her eyes.

Then the storm burst with a succession of ropes and streaks and shafts of lightning, playing continuously, filling the valley with a broken radiance; and the cracking shots followed each other swiftly till the echoes blended in one fearful, deafening crash.

Venters looked out upon the beautiful valley—beautiful now as never before—mystic in its transparent, luminous gloom, weird in the quivering, golden haze of lightning. The dark spruces were tipped with glimmering lights; the aspens bent low in the winds, as waves in a tempest at sea; the forest of oaks tossed wildly and shone with gleams of fire. Across the valley the huge cavern of the cliff-dwellers yawned in the glare, every little black window as clear as at noon-day; but the night and the storm added to their tragedy. Flung arching to the black clouds, the great stone bridge seemed to bear the brunt of the storm. It caught the full fury of the rushing wind. It lifted its noble crown to meet the lightnings. Venters thought of the eagles and their lofty nest in a niche under the arch. A driving pall of rain, black as the clouds, came sweeping on to obscure the bridge and the gleaming walls and the shining valley. The lightning played incessantly, streaking down through opaque darkness of rain. The roar of the wind, with its strange knell and the re-crashing echoes, mingled with the roar of the flooding rain, and all seemingly were deadened and drowned in a world of sound.

In the dimming pale light Venters looked down upon the girl. She had sunk into his arms, upon his breast, burying her face. She clung to him. He felt the softness of her, and the warmth, and the quick heave of her breast. He saw the dark, slender, graceful outline of her form. A woman lay in his arms! And he held her closer. He who had been alone in the sad, silent watches of the night was not now and never must be again alone. He who had yearned for the touch of a hand felt the long tremble and the heart-beat of a woman. By what strange chance had she come to love him! By what change—by what marvel had she grown into a treasure!

No more did he listen to the rush and roar of the thunder-storm. For with the touch of clinging hands and the throbbing bosom he grew conscious of an inward storm—the tingling of new chords of thought, strange music of unheard, joyous bells sad dreams dawning to wakeful delight, dissolving doubt, resurging hope, force, fire, and freedom, unutterable sweetness of desire. A storm in his breast—a storm of real love.

CHAPTER XIV. WEST WIND

When the storm abated Venters sought his own cave, and late in the night, as his blood cooled and the stir and throb and thrill subsided, he fell asleep.

With the breaking of dawn his eyes unclosed. The valley lay drenched and bathed, a burnished oval of glittering green. The rain-washed walls glistened in the morning light. Waterfalls of many forms poured over the rims. One, a broad, lacy sheet, thin as smoke, slid over the western notch and struck a ledge in its downward fall, to bound into broader leap, to burst far below into white and gold and rosy mist.

Venters prepared for the day, knowing himself a different man.

"It's a glorious morning," said Bess, in greeting.

"Yes. After the storm the west wind," he replied.

"Last night was I—very much of a baby?" she asked, watching him.

"Pretty much."

"Oh, I couldn't help it!"

"I'm glad you were afraid."

"Why?" she asked, in slow surprise.

"I'll tell you some day," he answered, soberly. Then around the camp-fire and through the morning meal he was silent; afterward he strolled thoughtfully off alone along the terrace. He climbed a great yellow rock raising its crest among the spruces, and there he sat down to face the valley and the west.

"I love her!"

Aloud he spoke—unburdened his heart—confessed his secret. For an instant the golden valley swam before his eyes, and the walls waved, and all about him whirled with tumult within.

"I love her!... I understand now."

Reviving memory of Jane Withersteen and thought of the complications of the present amazed him with proof of how far he had drifted from his old life. He discovered that he hated to take up the broken threads, to delve into dark problems and difficulties. In this beautiful valley he had been living a beautiful dream. Tranquillity had come to him, and the joy of solitude, and interest in all the wild creatures and crannies of this incomparable valley—and love. Under the shadow of the great stone bridge God had revealed Himself to Venters.

"The world seems very far away," he muttered, "but it's there—and I'm not yet done with it. Perhaps I never shall be.... Only—how glorious it would be to live here always and never think again!"

Whereupon the resurging reality of the present, as if in irony of his wish, steeped him instantly in contending thought. Out of it all he presently evolved these things: he must go to Cottonwoods; he must bring supplies back to Surprise Valley; he must cultivate the soil and raise corn and stock, and, most imperative of all, he must decide the future of the girl who loved him and whom he loved. The first of these things required tremendous effort, the last one, concerning Bess, seemed simply and naturally easy of accomplishment. He would marry her. Suddenly, as from roots of poisonous fire, flamed up the forgotten truth concerning her. It seemed to wither and shrivel up all his joy on its hot, tearing way to his heart. She had been Oldring's Masked Rider. To Venters's question, "What were you to Oldring?" she had answered with scarlet shame and drooping head.

"What do I care who she is or what she was!" he cried, passionately. And he knew it was not his old self speaking. It was this softer, gentler man who had awakened to new thoughts in the quiet valley. Tenderness, masterful in him now, matched the absence of joy and blunted the knife-edge of entering jealousy. Strong and passionate effort of will, surprising to him, held back the poison from piercing his soul.

"Wait!... Wait!" he cried, as if calling. His hand pressed his breast, and he might have called to the pang there. "Wait! It's all so strange—so wonderful. Anything can happen. Who am I to judge her? I'll glory in my love for her. But I can't tell it—can't give up to it."

Certainly he could not then decide her future. Marrying her was impossible in Surprise Valley and in any village south of Sterling. Even without the mask she had once worn she would easily have been recognized as Oldring's Rider. No man who had ever seen her would forget her, regardless of his ignorance as to her sex. Then more poignant than all other argument was the fact that he did not want to take her away from Surprise Valley. He resisted all thought of that. He had brought her to the most beautiful and wildest place of the uplands; he had saved her, nursed her back to strength, watched her bloom as one of the valley lilies; he knew her life there to be pure and sweet—she belonged to him, and he loved her. Still these were not all the reasons why he did not want to take her away. Where could they go? He feared the rustlers—he feared the riders—he feared the Mormons. And if he should ever succeed in getting Bess safely away from these immediate perils, he feared the sharp eyes of women and their tongues, the big outside world with its problems of existence. He must wait to decide her future, which, after all, was deciding his own. But between her future and his something hung impending. Like Balancing Rock, which waited darkly over the steep gorge, ready to close forever the outlet to Deception Pass, that nameless thing, as certain yet intangible as fate, must fall and close forever all doubts and fears of the future.

"I've dreamed," muttered Venters, as he rose. "Well, why not?... To dream is happiness! But let me just once see this clearly wholly; then I can go on dreaming till the thing falls. I've got to tell Jane Withersteen. I've dangerous trips to take. I've work here to make comfort for this girl. She's mine. I'll fight to keep her safe from that old life. I've already seen her forget it. I love her. And if a beast ever rises in me I'll burn my hand off before I lay it on her with shameful intent. And, by God! sooner or later I'll kill the man who hid her and kept her in Deception Pass!"

As he spoke the west wind softly blew in his face. It seemed to soothe his passion. That west wind was fresh, cool, fragrant, and it carried a sweet, strange burden of far-off things—tidings of life in other climes, of sunshine asleep on other walls—of other places where reigned peace. It carried, too, sad truth of human hearts and mystery—of promise and hope unquenchable. Surprise Valley was only a little niche in the wide world whence blew that burdened wind. Bess was only one of millions at the mercy of unknown motive in nature and life. Content had come to Venters in the valley; happiness had breathed in the slow, warm air; love as bright as light had hovered over the walls and descended to him; and now on the west wind came a whisper of the eternal triumph of faith over doubt.

"How much better I am for what has come to me!" he exclaimed. "I'll let the future take care of itself. Whatever falls, I'll be ready."

Venters retraced his steps along the terrace back to camp, and found Bess in the old familiar seat, waiting and watching for his return.

"I went off by myself to think a little," he explained.

"You never looked that way before. What—what is it? Won't you tell me?"

"Well, Bess, the fact is I've been dreaming a lot. This valley makes a fellow dream. So I forced myself to think. We can't live this way much longer. Soon I'll simply have to go to Cottonwoods. We need a whole pack train of supplies. I can get—"

"Can you go safely?" she interrupted.

"Why, I'm sure of it. I'll ride through the Pass at night. I haven't any fear that Wrangle isn't where I left him. And once on him—Bess, just wait till you see that horse!"

"Oh, I want to see him—to ride him. But—but, Bern, this is what troubles me," she said. "Will—will you come back?"

"Give me four days. If I'm not back in four days you'll know I'm dead. For that only shall keep me."

"Oh!"

"Bess, I'll come back. There's danger—I wouldn't lie to you—but I can take care of myself."

"Bern, I'm sure—oh, I'm sure of it! All my life I've watched hunted men. I can tell what's in them. And I believe you can ride and shoot and see with any rider of the sage. It's not—not that I—fear."

"Well, what is it, then?"

"Why—why—why should you come back at all?"

"I couldn't leave you here alone."

"You might change your mind when you get to the village—among old friends—"

"I won't change my mind. As for old friends—" He uttered a short, expressive laugh.

"Then—there—there must be a—a woman!" Dark red mantled the clear tan of temple and cheek and neck. Her eyes were eyes of shame, upheld a long moment by intense, straining search for the verification of her fear. Suddenly they drooped, her head fell to her knees, her hands flew to her hot cheeks.

"Bess—look here," said Venters, with a sharpness due to the violence with which he checked his quick, surging emotion.

As if compelled against her will—answering to an irresistible voice—Bess raised her head, looked at him with sad, dark eyes, and tried to whisper with tremulous lips.

"There's no woman," went on Venters, deliberately holding her glance with his. "Nothing on earth, barring the chances of life, can keep me away."

Her face flashed and flushed with the glow of a leaping joy; but like the vanishing of a gleam it disappeared to leave her as he had never beheld her.

"I am nothing—I am lost—I am nameless!"

"Do you want me to come back?" he asked, with sudden stern coldness. "Maybe you want to go back to Oldring!"

That brought her erect, trembling and ashy pale, with dark, proud eyes and mute lips refuting his insinuation.

"Bess, I beg your pardon. I shouldn't have said that. But you angered me. I intend to work—to make a home for you here—to be a—a brother to you as long as ever you need me. And you must forget what you are—were—I mean, and be happy. When you remember that old life you are bitter, and it hurts me."

"I was happy—I shall be very happy. Oh, you're so good that—that it kills me! If I think, I can't believe it. I grow sick with wondering why. I'm only a let me say it—only a lost, nameless—girl of the rustlers. Oldring's Girl, they called me. That you should save me—be so good and kind—want to make me happy—why, it's beyond belief. No wonder I'm wretched at the thought of your leaving me. But I'll be wretched and bitter no more. I promise you. If only I could repay you even a little—"

"You've repaid me a hundredfold. Will you believe me?"

"Believe you! I couldn't do else."

"Then listen!... Saving you, I saved myself. Living here in this valley with you, I've found myself. I've learned to think while I was dreaming. I never troubled myself about God. But God, or some wonderful spirit, has whispered to me here. I absolutely deny the truth of what you say about yourself. I can't explain it. There are things too deep to tell. Whatever the terrible wrongs you've suffered, God holds you blameless. I see that—feel that in you every moment you are near me. I've a mother and a sister 'way back in Illinois. If I could I'd take you to them—tomorrow."

"If it were true! Oh, I might—I might lift my head!" she cried.

"Lift it then—you child. For I swear it's true."

She did lift her head with the singular wild grace always a part of her actions, with that old unconscious intimation of innocence which always tortured Venters, but now with something more—a spirit rising from the depths that linked itself to his brave words.

"I've been thinking—too," she cried, with quivering smile and swelling breast. "I've discovered myself—too. I'm young—I'm alive—I'm so full—oh! I'm a woman!"

"Bess, I believe I can claim credit of that last discovery—before you," Venters said, and laughed.

"Oh, there's more—there's something I must tell you."

"Tell it, then."

"When will you go to Cottonwoods?"

"As soon as the storms are past, or the worst of them."

"I'll tell you before you go. I can't now. I don't know how I shall then. But it must be told. I'd never let you leave me without knowing. For in spite of what you say there's a chance you mightn't come back."

Day after day the west wind blew across the valley. Day after day the clouds clustered gray and purple and black. The cliffs sang and the caves rang with Oldring's knell, and the lightning flashed, the thunder rolled, the echoes crashed and crashed, and the rains flooded the valley. Wild flowers sprang up everywhere, swaying with the lengthening grass on the terraces, smiling wanly from shady nooks, peeping wondrously from year-dry crevices of the walls. The valley bloomed into a paradise. Every single moment, from the breaking of the gold bar through the bridge at dawn on to the reddening of rays over the western wall, was one of colorful change. The valley swam in thick, transparent haze, golden at dawn, warm and white at noon, purple in the twilight. At the end of every storm a rainbow curved down into the leaf-bright forest to shine and fade and leave lingeringly some faint essence of its rosy iris in the air.

Venters walked with Bess, once more in a dream, and watched the lights change on the walls, and faced the wind from out of the west.

Always it brought softly to him strange, sweet tidings of far-off things. It blew from a place that was old and whispered of youth. It blew down the grooves of time. It brought a story of the passing hours. It breathed low of fighting men and praying women. It sang clearly the song of love. That ever was the burden of its tidings—youth in the shady woods, waders through the wet meadows, boy and girl at the hedgerow stile, bathers in the booming surf, sweet, idle hours on grassy, windy hills, long strolls down moonlit lanes—everywhere in far-off lands, fingers locked and bursting hearts and longing lips—from all the world tidings of unquenchable love.

Often, in these hours of dreams he watched the girl, and asked himself of what was she dreaming? For the changing light of the valley reflected its gleam and its color and its meaning in the changing light of her eyes. He saw in them infinitely more than he saw in his dreams. He saw thought and soul and nature—strong vision of life. All tidings the west wind blew from distance and age he found deep in those dark-blue depths, and found them mysteries solved. Under their wistful shadow he softened, and in the softening felt himself grow a sadder, a wiser, and a better man.

While the west wind blew its tidings, filling his heart full, teaching him a man's part, the days passed, the purple clouds changed to white, and the storms were over for that summer.

"I must go now," he said.

"When?" she asked.

"At once—to-night."

"I'm glad the time has come. It dragged at me. Go—for you'll come back the sooner."

Late in the afternoon, as the ruddy sun split its last flame in the ragged notch of the western wall, Bess walked with Venters along the eastern terrace, up the long, weathered slope, under the great stone bridge. They entered the narrow gorge to climb around the fence long before built there by Venters. Farther than this she had never been. Twilight had already fallen in the gorge. It brightened to waning shadow in the wider ascent. He showed her Balancing Rock, of which he had often told her, and explained its sinister leaning over the outlet. Shuddering, she looked down the long, pale incline with its closed-in, toppling walls.

"What an awful trail! Did you carry me up here?"

"I did, surely," replied he.

"It frightens me, somehow. Yet I never was afraid of trails. I'd ride anywhere a horse could go, and climb where he couldn't. But there's something fearful here. I feel as—as if the place was watching me."

"Look at this rock. It's balanced here—balanced perfectly. You know I told you the cliff-dwellers cut the rock, and why. But they're gone and the rock waits. Can't you see—feel how it waits here? I moved it once, and I'll never dare again. A strong heave would start it. Then it would fall and bang, and smash that crag, and jar the walls, and close forever the outlet to Deception Pass!"

"Ah! When you come back I'll steal up here and push and push with all my might to roll the rock and close forever the outlet to the Pass!" She said it lightly, but in the undercurrent of her voice was a heavier note, a ring deeper than any ever given mere play of words.

"Bess!... You can't dare me! Wait till I come back with supplies—then roll the stone."

"I—was—in—fun." Her voice now throbbed low. "Always you must be free to go when you will. Go now... this place presses on me—stifles me."

"I'm going—but you had something to tell me?"

"Yes.... Will you—come back?"

"I'll come if I live."

"But—but you mightn't come?"

"That's possible, of course. It'll take a good deal to kill me. A man couldn't have a faster horse or keener dog. And, Bess, I've guns, and I'll use them if I'm pushed. But don't worry."

"I've faith in you. I'll not worry until after four days. Only—because you mightn't come—I must tell you—"

She lost her voice. Her pale face, her great, glowing, earnest eyes, seemed to stand alone out of the gloom of the gorge. The dog whined, breaking the silence.

"I must tell you—because you mightn't come back," she whispered. "You must know what—what I think of your goodness—of you. Always I've been tongue-tied. I seemed not to be grateful. It was deep in my heart. Even now—if I were other than I am—I couldn't tell you. But I'm nothing—only a rustler's girl—nameless—infamous. You've saved me—and I'm—I'm yours to do with as you like.... With all my heart and soul—I love you!"

CHAPTER XV. SHADOWS ON THE SAGE-SLOPE

In the cloudy, threatening, waning summer days shadows lengthened down the sage-slope, and Jane Withersteen likened them to the shadows gathering and closing in around her life.

Mrs. Larkin died, and little Fay was left an orphan with no known relative. Jane's love redoubled. It was the saving brightness of a darkening hour. Fay turned now to Jane in childish worship. And Jane at last found full expression for the mother-longing in her heart. Upon Lassiter, too, Mrs. Larkin's death had some subtle reaction. Before, he had often, without explanation, advised Jane to send Fay back to any Gentile family that would take her in. Passionately and reproachfully and wonderingly Jane had refused even to entertain such an idea. And now Lassiter never advised it again, grew sadder and quieter in his contemplation of the child, and infinitely more gentle and loving. Sometimes Jane had a cold, inexplicable sensation of dread when she saw Lassiter watching Fay. What did the rider see in the future? Why did he, day by day, grow more silent, calmer, cooler, yet sadder in prophetic assurance of something to be?

No doubt, Jane thought, the rider, in his almost superhuman power of foresight, saw behind the horizon the dark, lengthening shadows that were soon to crowd and gloom over him and her and little Fay. Jane Withersteen awaited the long-deferred breaking of the storm with a courage and embittered calm that had come to her in her extremity. Hope had not died. Doubt and fear, subservient to her will, no longer gave her sleepless nights and tortured days. Love remained. All that she had loved she now loved the more. She seemed to feel that she was defiantly flinging the wealth of her love in the face of misfortune and of hate. No day passed but she prayed for all—and most fervently for her enemies. It troubled her that she had lost, or had never gained, the whole control of her mind. In some measure reason and wisdom and decision were locked in a chamber of her brain, awaiting a key. Power to think of some things was taken from her. Meanwhile, abiding a day of judgment, she fought ceaselessly to deny the bitter drops in her cup, to tear back the slow, the intangibly slow growth of a hot, corrosive lichen eating into her heart.

On the morning of August 10th, Jane, while waiting in the court for Lassiter, heard a clear, ringing report of a rifle. It came from the grove, somewhere toward the corrals. Jane glanced out in alarm. The day was dull, windless, soundless. The leaves of the cottonwoods drooped, as if they had foretold the doom of Withersteen House and were now ready to die and drop and decay. Never had Jane seen such shade. She pondered on the meaning of the report. Revolver shots had of late cracked from different parts of the grove—spies taking snap-shots at Lassiter from a cowardly distance! But a rifle report meant more. Riders seldom used rifles. Judkins and Venters were the exceptions she called to mind. Had the men who hounded her hidden in her grove, taken to the rifle to rid her of Lassiter, her last friend? It was probable—it was likely. And she did not share his cool assumption that his death would never come at the hands of a Mormon. Long had she expected it. His constancy to her, his singular reluctance to use the fatal skill for which he was famed—both now plain to all Mormons—laid him open to inevitable assassination. Yet what charm against ambush and aim and enemy he seemed to bear about him! No, Jane reflected, it was not charm; only a wonderful training of eye and ear, and sense of impending peril. Nevertheless that could not forever avail against secret attack.

That moment a rustling of leaves attracted her attention; then the familiar clinking accompaniment of a slow, soft, measured step, and Lassiter walked into the court.

"Jane, there's a fellow out there with a long gun," he said, and, removing his sombrero, showed his head bound in a bloody scarf.

"I heard the shot; I knew it was meant for you. Let me see—you can't be badly injured?"

"I reckon not. But mebbe it wasn't a close call!... I'll sit here in this corner where nobody can see me from the grove." He untied the scarf and removed it to show a long, bleeding furrow above his left temple.

"It's only a cut," said Jane. "But how it bleeds! Hold your scarf over it just a moment till I come back."

She ran into the house and returned with bandages; and while she bathed and dressed the wound Lassiter talked.

"That fellow had a good chance to get me. But he must have flinched when he pulled the trigger. As I dodged down I saw him run through the trees. He had a rifle. I've been expectin' that kind of gun play. I reckon now I'll have to keep a little closer hid myself. These fellers all seem to get chilly or shaky when they draw a bead on me, but one of them might jest happen to hit me."

"Won't you go away—leave Cottonwoods as I've begged you to—before some one does happen to hit you?" she appealed to him.

"I reckon I'll stay."

"But, oh, Lassiter—your blood will be on my hands!"

"See here, lady, look at your hands now, right now. Aren't they fine, firm, white hands? Aren't they bloody now? Lassiter's blood! That's a queer thing to stain your beautiful hands. But if you could only see deeper you'd find a redder color of blood. Heart color, Jane!"

"Oh!... My friend!"

"No, Jane, I'm not one to quit when the game grows hot, no more than you. This game, though, is new to me, an' I don't know the moves yet, else I wouldn't have stepped in front of that bullet."

"Have you no desire to hunt the man who fired at you—to find him—and—and kill him?"

"Well, I reckon I haven't any great hankerin' for that."

"Oh, the wonder of it!... I knew—I prayed—I trusted. Lassiter, I almost gave—all myself to soften you to Mormons. Thank God, and thank you, my friend.... But, selfish woman that I am, this is no great test. What's the life of one of those sneaking cowards to such a man as you? I think of your great hate toward him who—I think of your life's implacable purpose. Can it be—"

"Wait!... Listen!" he whispered. "I hear a hoss."

He rose noiselessly, with his ear to the breeze. Suddenly he pulled his sombrero down over his bandaged head and, swinging his gun-sheaths round in front, he stepped into the alcove.

"It's a hoss—comin' fast," he added.

Jane's listening ear soon caught a faint, rapid, rhythmic beat of hoofs. It came from the sage. It gave her a thrill that she was at a loss to understand. The sound rose stronger, louder. Then came a clear, sharp difference when the horse passed from the sage trail to the hard-packed ground of the grove. It became a ringing run—swift in its bell-like clatterings, yet singular in longer pause than usual between the hoofbeats of a horse.

"It's Wrangle!... It's Wrangle!" cried Jane Withersteen. "I'd know him from a million horses!"

Excitement and thrilling expectancy flooded out all Jane Withersteen's calm. A tight band closed round her breast as she saw the giant sorrel flit in reddish-brown flashes across the openings in the green. Then he was pounding down the lane—thundering into the court—crashing his great iron-shod hoofs on the stone flags. Wrangle it was surely, but shaggy and wild-eyed, and sage-streaked, with dust-caked lather staining his flanks. He reared and crashed down and plunged. The rider leaped off, threw the bridle, and held hard on a lasso looped round Wrangle's head and neck. Janet's heart sank as she tried to recognize Venters in the rider. Something familiar struck her in the lofty stature in the sweep of powerful shoulders. But this bearded, longhaired, unkempt man, who wore ragged clothes patched with pieces of skin, and boots that showed bare legs and feet—this dusty, dark, and wild rider could not possibly be Venters.

"Whoa, Wrangle, old boy! Come down. Easy now. So—so—so. You're home, old boy, and presently you can have a drink of water you'll remember."

In the voice Jane knew the rider to be Venters. He tied Wrangle to the hitching-rack and turned to the court.

"Oh, Bern!... You wild man!" she exclaimed.

"Jane—Jane, it's good to see you! Hello, Lassiter! Yes, it's Venters."

Like rough iron his hard hand crushed Jane's. In it she felt the difference she saw in him. Wild, rugged, unshorn—yet how splendid! He had gone away a boy—he had returned a man. He appeared taller, wider of shoulder, deeper-chested, more powerfully built. But was that only her fancy—he had always been a young giant—was the change one of spirit? He might have been absent for years, proven by fire and steel, grown like Lassiter, strong and cool and sure. His eyes—were they keener, more flashing than before?—met hers with clear, frank, warm regard, in which perplexity was not, nor discontent, nor pain.

"Look at me long as you like," he said, with a laugh. "I'm not much to look at. And, Jane, neither you nor Lassiter, can brag. You're paler than I ever saw you. Lassiter, here, he wears a bloody bandage under his hat. That reminds me. Some one took a flying shot at me down in the sage. It made Wrangle run some.... Well, perhaps you've more to tell me than I've got to tell you."

Briefly, in few words, Jane outlined the circumstances of her undoing in the weeks of his absence.

Under his beard and bronze she saw his face whiten in terrible wrath.

"Lassiter—what held you back?"

No time in the long period of fiery moments and sudden shocks had Jane Withersteen ever beheld Lassiter as calm and serene and cool as then.

"Jane had gloom enough without my addin' to it by shootin' up the village," he said.

As strange as Lassiter's coolness was Venters's curious, intent scrutiny of them both, and under it Jane felt a flaming tide wave from bosom to temples.

"Well—you're right," he said, with slow pause. "It surprises me a little, that's all."

Jane sensed then a slight alteration in Venters, and what it was, in her own confusion, she could not tell. It had always been her intention to acquaint him with the deceit she had fallen to in her zeal to move Lassiter. She did not mean to spare herself. Yet now, at the moment, before these riders, it was an impossibility to explain.

Venters was speaking somewhat haltingly, without his former frankness. "I found Oldring's hiding-place and your red herd. I learned—I know—I'm sure there was a deal between Tull and Oldring." He paused and shifted his position and his gaze. He looked as if he wanted to say something that he found beyond him. Sorrow and pity and shame seemed to contend for mastery over him. Then he raised himself and spoke with effort. "Jane I've cost you too much. You've almost ruined yourself for me. It was wrong, for I'm not worth it. I never deserved such friendship. Well, maybe it's not too late. You must give me up. Mind, I haven't changed. I am just the same as ever. I'll see Tull while I'm here, and tell him to his face."

"Bern, it's too late," said Jane.

"I'll make him believe!" cried Venters, violently.

"You ask me to break our friendship?"

"Yes. If you don't, I shall."

"Forever?"

"Forever!"

Jane sighed. Another shadow had lengthened down the sage slope to cast further darkness upon her. A melancholy sweetness pervaded her resignation. The boy who had left her had returned a man, nobler, stronger, one in whom she divined something unbending as steel. There might come a moment later when she would wonder why she had not fought against his will, but just now she yielded to it. She liked him as well—nay, more, she thought, only her emotions were deadened by the long, menacing wait for the bursting storm.

Once before she had held out her hand to him—when she gave it; now she stretched it tremblingly forth in acceptance of the decree circumstance had laid upon them. Venters bowed over it kissed it, pressed it hard, and half stifled a sound very like a sob. Certain it was that when he raised his head tears glistened in his eyes.

"Some—women—have a hard lot," he said, huskily. Then he shook his powerful form, and his rags lashed about him. "I'll say a few things to Tull—when I meet him."

"Bern—you'll not draw on Tull? Oh, that must not be! Promise me—"

"I promise you this," he interrupted, in stern passion that thrilled while it terrorized her. "If you say one more word for that plotter I'll kill him as I would a mad coyote!"

Jane clasped her hands. Was this fire-eyed man the one whom she had once made as wax to her touch? Had Venters become Lassiter and Lassiter Venters?

"I'll—say no more," she faltered.

"Jane, Lassiter once called you blind," said Venters. "It must be true. But I won't upbraid you. Only don't rouse the devil in me by praying for Tull! I'll try to keep cool when I meet him. That's all. Now there's one more thing I want to ask of you—the last. I've found a valley down in the Pass. It's a wonderful place. I intend to stay there. It's so hidden I believe no one can find it. There's good water, and browse, and game. I want to raise corn and stock. I need to take in supplies. Will you give them to me?"

"Assuredly. The more you take the better you'll please me—and perhaps the less my—my enemies will get."

"Venters, I reckon you'll have trouble packin' anythin' away," put in Lassiter.

"I'll go at night."

"Mebbe that wouldn't be best. You'd sure be stopped. You'd better go early in the mornin'—say, just after dawn. That's the safest time to move round here."

"Lassiter, I'll be hard to stop," returned Venters, darkly.

"I reckon so."

"Bern," said Jane, "go first to the riders' quarters and get yourself a complete outfit. You're a—a sight. Then help yourself to whatever else you need—burros, packs, grain, dried fruits, and meat. You must take coffee and sugar and flour—all kinds of supplies. Don't forget corn and seeds. I remember how you used to starve. Please—please take all you can pack away from here. I'll make a bundle for you, which you mustn't open till you're in your valley. How I'd like to see it! To judge by you and Wrangle, how wild it must be!"

Jane walked down into the outer court and approached the sorrel. Upstarting, he laid back his ears and eyed her.

"Wrangle—dear old Wrangle," she said, and put a caressing hand on his matted mane. "Oh, he's wild, but he knows me! Bern, can he run as fast as ever?"

"Run? Jane, he's done sixty miles since last night at dark, and I could make him kill Black Star right now in a ten-mile race."

"He never could," protested Jane. "He couldn't even if he was fresh."

"I reckon mebbe the best hoss'll prove himself yet," said Lassiter, "an', Jane, if it ever comes to that race I'd like you to be on Wrangle."

"I'd like that, too," rejoined Venters. "But, Jane, maybe Lassiter's hint is extreme. Bad as your prospects are, you'll surely never come to the running point."

"Who knows!" she replied, with mournful smile.

"No, no, Jane, it can't be so bad as all that. Soon as I see Tull there'll be a change in your fortunes. I'll hurry down to the village.... Now don't worry."

Jane retired to the seclusion of her room. Lassiter's subtle forecasting of disaster, Venters's forced optimism, neither remained in mind. Material loss weighed nothing in the balance with other losses she was sustaining. She wondered dully at her sitting there, hands folded listlessly, with a kind of numb deadness to the passing of time and the passing of her riches. She thought of Venters's friendship. She had not lost that, but she had lost him. Lassiter's friendship—that was more than love—it would endure, but soon he, too, would be gone. Little Fay slept dreamlessly upon the bed, her golden curls streaming over the pillow. Jane had the child's worship. Would she lose that, too? And if she did, what then would be left? Conscience thundered at her that there was left her religion. Conscience thundered that she should be grateful on her knees for this baptism of fire; that through misfortune, sacrifice, and suffering her soul might be fused pure gold. But the old, spontaneous, rapturous spirit no more exalted her. She wanted to be a woman—not a martyr. Like the saint of old who mortified his flesh, Jane Withersteen had in her the temper for heroic martyrdom, if by sacrificing herself she could save the souls of others. But here the damnable verdict blistered her that the more she sacrificed herself the blacker grew the souls of her churchmen. There was something terribly wrong with her soul, something terribly wrong with her churchmen and her religion. In the whirling gulf of her thought there was yet one shining light to guide her, to sustain her in her hope; and it was that, despite her errors and her frailties and her blindness, she had one absolute and unfaltering hold on ultimate and supreme justice. That was love. "Love your enemies as yourself!" was a divine word, entirely free from any church or creed.

Jane's meditations were disturbed by Lassiter's soft, tinkling step in the court. Always he wore the clinking spurs. Always he was in readiness to ride. She passed out and called him into the huge, dim hall.

"I think you'll be safer here. The court is too open," she said.

"I reckon," replied Lassiter. "An' it's cooler here. The day's sure muggy. Well, I went down to the village with Venters."

"Already! Where is he?" queried Jane, in quick amaze.

"He's at the corrals. Blake's helpin' him get the burros an' packs ready. That Blake is a good fellow."

"Did—did Bern meet Tull?"

"I guess he did," answered Lassiter, and he laughed dryly.

"Tell me! Oh, you exasperate me! You're so cool, so calm! For Heaven's sake, tell me what happened!"

"First time I've been in the village for weeks," went on Lassiter, mildly. "I reckon there 'ain't been more of a show for a long time. Me an' Venters walkin' down the road! It was funny. I ain't sayin' anybody was particular glad to see us. I'm not much thought of hereabouts, an' Venters he sure looks like what you called him, a wild man. Well, there was some runnin' of folks before we got to the stores. Then everybody vamoosed except some surprised rustlers in front of a saloon. Venters went right in the stores an' saloons, an' of course I went along. I don't know which tickled me the most—the actions of many fellers we met, or Venters's nerve. Jane, I was downright glad to be along. You see that sort of thing is my element, an' I've been away from it for a spell. But we didn't find Tull in one of them places. Some Gentile feller at last told Venters he'd find Tull in that long buildin' next to Parsons's store. It's a kind of meetin'-room; and sure enough, when we peeped in, it was half full of men.

"Venters yelled: 'Don't anybody pull guns! We ain't come for that!' Then he tramped in, an' I was some put to keep alongside him. There was a hard, scrapin' sound of feet, a loud cry, an' then some whisperin', an' after that stillness you could cut with a knife. Tull was there, an' that fat party who once tried to throw a gun on me, an' other important-lookin' men, en' that little frog-legged feller who was with Tull the day I rode in here. I wish you could have seen their faces, 'specially Tull's an' the fat party's. But there ain't no use of me tryin' to tell you how they looked.

"Well, Venters an' I stood there in the middle of the room with that batch of men all in front of us, en' not a blamed one of them winked an eyelash or moved a finger. It was natural, of course, for me to notice many of them packed guns. That's a way of mine, first noticin' them things. Venters spoke up, an' his voice sort of chilled an' cut, en' he told Tull he had a few things to say."

Here Lassiter paused while he turned his sombrero round and round, in his familiar habit, and his eyes had the look of a man seeing over again some thrilling spectacle, and under his red bronze there was strange animation.

"Like a shot, then, Venters told Tull that the friendship between you an' him was all over, an' he was leaving your place. He said you'd both of you broken off in the hope of propitiatin' your people, but you hadn't changed your mind otherwise, an' never would.

"Next he spoke up for you. I ain't goin' to tell you what he said. Only—no other woman who ever lived ever had such tribute! You had a champion, Jane, an' never fear that those thick-skulled men don't know you now. It couldn't be otherwise. He spoke the ringin', lightnin' truth.... Then he accused Tull of the underhand, miserable robbery of a helpless woman. He told Tull where the red herd was, of a deal made with Oldrin', that Jerry Card had made the deal. I thought Tull was goin' to drop, an' that little frog-legged cuss, he looked some limp an' white. But Venters's voice would have kept anybody's legs from bucklin'. I was stiff myself. He went on an' called Tull—called him every bad name ever known to a rider, an' then some. He cursed Tull. I never hear a man get such a cursin'. He laughed in scorn at the idea of Tull bein' a minister. He said Tull an' a few more dogs of hell builded their empire out of the hearts of such innocent an' God-fearin' women as Jane Withersteen. He called Tull a binder of women, a callous beast who hid behind a mock mantle of righteousness—an' the last an' lowest coward on the face of the earth. To prey on weak women through their religion—that was the last unspeakable crime!

"Then he finished, an' by this time he'd almost lost his voice. But his whisper was enough. 'Tull,' he said, 'she begged me not to draw on you to-day. She would pray for you if you burned her at the stake.... But listen!... I swear if you and I ever come face to face again, I'll kill you!'

"We backed out of the door then, an' up the road. But nobody follered us."

Jane found herself weeping passionately. She had not been conscious of it till Lassiter ended his story, and she experienced exquisite pain and relief in shedding tears. Long had her eyes been dry, her grief deep; long had her emotions been dumb. Lassiter's story put her on the rack; the appalling nature of Venters's act and speech had no parallel as an outrage; it was worse than bloodshed. Men like Tull had been shot, but had one ever been so terribly denounced in public? Overmounting her horror, an uncontrollable, quivering passion shook her very soul. It was sheer human glory in the deed of a fearless man. It was hot, primitive instinct to live—to fight. It was a kind of mad joy in Venters's chivalry. It was close to the wrath that had first shaken her in the beginning of this war waged upon her.

"Well, well, Jane, don't take it that way," said Lassiter, in evident distress. "I had to tell you. There's some things a feller jest can't keep. It's strange you give up on hearin' that, when all this long time you've been the gamest woman I ever seen. But I don't know women. Mebbe there's reason for you to cry. I know this—nothin' ever rang in my soul an' so filled it as what Venters did. I'd like to have done it, but—I'm only good for throwin' a gun, en' it seems you hate that.... Well, I'll be goin' now."

"Where?"

"Venters took Wrangle to the stable. The sorrel's shy a shoe, an' I've got to help hold the big devil an' put on another."

"Tell Bern to come for the pack I want to give him—and—and to say good-by," called Jane, as Lassiter went out.

Jane passed the rest of that day in a vain endeavor to decide what and what not to put in the pack for Venters. This task was the last she would ever perform for him, and the gifts were the last she would ever make him. So she picked and chose and rejected, and chose again, and often paused in sad revery, and began again, till at length she filled the pack.

It was about sunset, and she and Fay had finished supper and were sitting in the court, when Venters's quick steps rang on the stones. She scarcely knew him, for he had changed the tattered garments, and she missed the dark beard and long hair. Still he was not the Venters of old. As he came up the steps she felt herself pointing to the pack, and heard herself speaking words that were meaningless to her. He said good-by; he kissed her, released her, and turned away. His tall figure blurred in her sight, grew dim through dark, streaked vision, and then he vanished.

Twilight fell around Withersteen House, and dusk and night. Little Fay slept; but Jane lay with strained, aching eyes. She heard the wind moaning in the cottonwoods and mice squeaking in the walls. The night was interminably long, yet she prayed to hold back the dawn. What would another day bring forth? The blackness of her room seemed blacker for the sad, entering gray of morning light. She heard the chirp of awakening birds, and fancied she caught a faint clatter of hoofs. Then low, dull distant, throbbed a heavy gunshot. She had expected it, was waiting for it; nevertheless, an electric shock checked her heart, froze the very living fiber of her bones. That vise-like hold on her faculties apparently did not relax for a long time, and it was a voice under her window that released her.

"Jane!... Jane!" softly called Lassiter.

She answered somehow.

"It's all right. Venters got away. I thought mebbe you'd heard that shot, en' I was worried some."

"What was it—who fired?"

"Well—some fool feller tried to stop Venters out there in the sage—an' he only stopped lead!... I think it'll be all right. I haven't seen or heard of any other fellers round. Venters'll go through safe. An', Jane, I've got Bells saddled, an' I'm going to trail Venters. Mind, I won't show myself unless he falls foul of somebody an' needs me. I want to see if this place where he's goin' is safe for him. He says nobody can track him there. I never seen the place yet I couldn't track a man to. Now, Jane, you stay indoors while I'm gone, an' keep close watch on Fay. Will you?"

"Yes! Oh yes!"

"An' another thing, Jane," he continued, then paused for long—"another thing—if you ain't here when I come back—if you're gone—don't fear, I'll trail you—I'll find you out."

"My dear Lassiter, where could I be gone—as you put it?" asked Jane, in curious surprise.

"I reckon you might be somewhere. Mebbe tied in an old barn—or corralled in some gulch—or chained in a cave! Milly Erne was—till she give in! Mebbe that's news to you.... Well, if you're gone I'll hunt for you."

"No, Lassiter," she replied, sadly and low. "If I'm gone just forget the unhappy woman whose blinded selfish deceit you repaid with kindness and love."

She heard a deep, muttering curse, under his breath, and then the silvery tinkling of his spurs as he moved away.

Jane entered upon the duties of that day with a settled, gloomy calm. Disaster hung in the dark clouds, in the shade, in the humid west wind. Blake, when he reported, appeared without his usual cheer; and Jerd wore a harassed look of a worn and worried man. And when Judkins put in appearance, riding a lame horse, and dismounted with the cramp of a rider, his dust-covered figure and his darkly grim, almost dazed expression told Jane of dire calamity. She had no need of words.

"Miss Withersteen, I have to report—loss of the—white herd," said Judkins, hoarsely.

"Come, sit down, you look played out," replied Jane, solicitously. She brought him brandy and food, and while he partook of refreshments, of which he appeared badly in need, she asked no questions.

"No one rider—could hev done more—Miss Withersteen," he went on, presently.

"Judkins, don't be distressed. You've done more than any other rider. I've long expected to lose the white herd. It's no surprise. It's in line with other things that are happening. I'm grateful for your service."

"Miss Withersteen, I knew how you'd take it. But if anythin', that makes it harder to tell. You see, a feller wants to do so much fer you, an' I'd got fond of my job. We led the herd a ways off to the north of the break in the valley. There was a big level an' pools of water an' tip-top browse. But the cattle was in a high nervous condition. Wild—as wild as antelope! You see, they'd been so scared they never slept. I ain't a-goin' to tell you of the many tricks that were pulled off out there in the sage. But there wasn't a day for weeks thet the herd didn't get started to run. We allus managed to ride 'em close an' drive 'em back an' keep 'em bunched. Honest, Miss Withersteen, them steers was thin. They was thin when water and grass was everywhere. Thin at this season—thet'll tell you how your steers was pestered. Fer instance, one night a strange runnin' streak of fire run right through the herd. That streak was a coyote—with an oiled an' blazin' tail! Fer I shot it an' found out. We had hell with the herd that night, an' if the sage an' grass hadn't been wet—we, hosses, steers, an' all would hev burned up. But I said I wasn't goin' to tell you any of the tricks.... Strange now, Miss Withersteen, when the stampede did come it was from natural cause—jest a whirlin' devil of dust. You've seen the like often. An' this wasn't no big whirl, fer the dust was mostly settled. It had dried out in a little swale, an' ordinarily no steer would ever hev run fer it. But the herd was nervous en' wild. An' jest as Lassiter said, when that bunch of white steers got to movin' they was as bad as buffalo. I've seen some buffalo stampedes back in Nebraska, an' this bolt of the steers was the same kind.

"I tried to mill the herd jest as Lassiter did. But I wasn't equal to it, Miss Withersteen. I don't believe the rider lives who could hev turned thet herd. We kept along of the herd fer miles, an' more 'n one of my boys tried to get the steers a-millin'. It wasn't no use. We got off level ground, goin' down, an' then the steers ran somethin' fierce. We left the little gullies an' washes level-full of dead steers. Finally I saw the herd was makin' to pass a kind of low pocket between ridges. There was a hog-back—as we used to call 'em—a pile of rocks stickin' up, and I saw the herd was goin' to split round it, or swing out to the left. An' I wanted 'em to go to the right so mebbe we'd be able to drive 'em into the pocket. So, with all my boys except three, I rode hard to turn the herd a little to the right. We couldn't budge 'em. They went on en' split round the rocks, en' the most of 'em was turned sharp to the left by a deep wash we hedn't seen—hed no chance to see.

"The other three boys—Jimmy Vail, Joe Willis, an' thet little Cairns boy—a nervy kid! they, with Cairns leadin', tried to buck thet herd round to the pocket. It was a wild, fool idee. I couldn't do nothin'. The boys got hemmed in between the steers an' the wash—thet they hedn't no chance to see, either. Vail an' Willis was run down right before our eyes. An' Cairns, who rode a fine hoss, he did some ridin'. I never seen equaled, en' would hev beat the steers if there'd been any room to run in. I was high up an' could see how the steers kept spillin' by twos an' threes over into the wash. Cairns put his hoss to a place thet was too wide fer any hoss, an' broke his neck an' the hoss's too. We found that out after, an' as fer Vail an' Willis—two thousand steers ran over the poor boys. There wasn't much left to pack home fer burying!... An', Miss Withersteen, thet all happened yesterday, en' I believe, if the white herd didn't run over the wall of the Pass, it's runnin' yet."

On the morning of the second day after Judkins's recital, during which time Jane remained indoors a prey to regret and sorrow for the boy riders, and a new and now strangely insistent fear for her own person, she again heard what she had missed more than she dared honestly confess—the soft, jingling step of Lassiter. Almost overwhelming relief surged through her, a feeling as akin to joy as any she could have been capable of in those gloomy hours of shadow, and one that suddenly stunned her with the significance of what Lassiter had come to mean to her. She had begged him, for his own sake, to leave Cottonwoods. She might yet beg that, if her weakening courage permitted her to dare absolute loneliness and helplessness, but she realized now that if she were left alone her life would become one long, hideous nightmare.

When his soft steps clinked into the hall, in answer to her greeting, and his tall, black-garbed form filled the door, she felt an inexpressible sense of immediate safety. In his presence she lost her fear of the dim passageways of Withersteen House and of every sound. Always it had been that, when he entered the court or the hall, she had experienced a distinctly sickening but gradually lessening shock at sight of the huge black guns swinging at his sides. This time the sickening shock again visited her, it was, however, because a revealing flash of thought told her that it was not alone Lassiter who was thrillingly welcome, but also his fatal weapons. They meant so much. How she had fallen—how broken and spiritless must she be—to have still the same old horror of Lassiter's guns and his name, yet feel somehow a cold, shrinking protection in their law and might and use.

"Did you trail Venters—find his wonderful valley?" she asked, eagerly.

"Yes, an' I reckon it's sure a wonderful place."

"Is he safe there?"

"That's been botherin' me some. I tracked him an' part of the trail was the hardest I ever tackled. Mebbe there's a rustler or somebody in this country who's as good at trackin' as I am. If that's so Venters ain't safe."

"Well—tell me all about Bern and his valley."

To Jane's surprise Lassiter showed disinclination for further talk about his trip. He appeared to be extremely fatigued. Jane reflected that one hundred and twenty miles, with probably a great deal of climbing on foot, all in three days, was enough to tire any rider. Moreover, it presently developed that Lassiter had re-turned in a mood of singular sadness and preoccupation. She put it down to a moodiness over the loss of her white herd and the now precarious condition of her fortune.

Several days passed, and as nothing happened, Jane's spirits began to brighten. Once in her musings she thought that this tendency of hers to rebound was as sad as it was futile. Meanwhile, she had resumed her walks through the grove with little Fay.

One morning she went as far as the sage. She had not seen the slope since the beginning of the rains, and now it bloomed a rich deep purple. There was a high wind blowing, and the sage tossed and waved and colored beautifully from light to dark. Clouds scudded across the sky and their shadows sailed darkly down the sunny slope.

Upon her return toward the house she went by the lane to the stables, and she had scarcely entered the great open space with its corrals and sheds when she saw Lassiter hurriedly approaching. Fay broke from her and, running to a corral fence, began to pat and pull the long, hanging ears of a drowsy burro.

One look at Lassiter armed her for a blow.

Without a word he led her across the wide yard to the rise of the ground upon which the stable stood.

"Jane—look!" he said, and pointed to the ground.

Jane glanced down, and again, and upon steadier vision made out splotches of blood on the stones, and broad, smooth marks in the dust, leading out toward the sage.

"What made these?" she asked.

"I reckon somebody has dragged dead or wounded men out to where there was hosses in the sage."

"Dead—or—wounded—men!"

"I reckon—Jane, are you strong? Can you bear up?"

His hands were gently holding hers, and his eyes—suddenly she could no longer look into them. "Strong?" she echoed, trembling. "I—I will be."

Up on the stone-flag drive, nicked with the marks made by the iron-shod hoofs of her racers, Lassiter led her, his grasp ever growing firmer.

"Where's Blake—and—and Jerb?" she asked, haltingly.

"I don't know where Jerb is. Bolted, most likely," replied Lassiter, as he took her through the stone door. "But Blake—poor Blake! He's gone forever!... Be prepared, Jane."

With a cold prickling of her skin, with a queer thrumming in her ears, with fixed and staring eyes, Jane saw a gun lying at her feet with chamber swung and empty, and discharged shells scattered near.

Outstretched upon the stable floor lay Blake, ghastly white—dead—one hand clutching a gun and the other twisted in his bloody blouse.

"Whoever the thieves were, whether your people or rustlers—Blake killed some of them!" said Lassiter.

"Thieves?" whispered Jane.

"I reckon. Hoss-thieves!... Look!" Lassiter waved his hand toward the stalls.

The first stall—Bells's stall—was empty. All the stalls were empty. No racer whinnied and stamped greeting to her. Night was gone! Black Star was gone!

CHAPTER XVI. GOLD

As Lassiter had reported to Jane, Venters "went through" safely, and after a toilsome journey reached the peaceful shelter of Surprise Valley. When finally he lay wearily down under the silver spruces, resting from the strain of dragging packs and burros up the slope and through the entrance to Surprise Valley, he had leisure to think, and a great deal of the time went in regretting that he had not been frank with his loyal friend, Jane Withersteen.

But, he kept continually recalling, when he had stood once more face to face with her and had been shocked at the change in her and had heard the details of her adversity, he had not had the heart to tell her of the closer interest which had entered his life. He had not lied; yet he had kept silence.

Bess was in transports over the stores of supplies and the outfit he had packed from Cottonwoods. He had certainly brought a hundred times more than he had gone for; enough, surely, for years, perhaps to make permanent home in the valley. He saw no reason why he need ever leave there again.

After a day of rest he recovered his strength and shared Bess's pleasure in rummaging over the endless packs, and began to plan for the future. And in this planning, his trip to Cottonwoods, with its revived hate of Tull and consequent unleashing of fierce passions, soon faded out of mind. By slower degrees his friendship for Jane Withersteen and his contrition drifted from the active preoccupation of his present thought to a place in memory, with more and more infrequent recalls.

And as far as the state of his mind was concerned, upon the second day after his return, the valley, with its golden hues and purple shades, the speaking west wind and the cool, silent night, and Bess's watching eyes with their wonderful light, so wrought upon Venters that he might never have left them at all.

That very afternoon he set to work. Only one thing hindered him upon beginning, though it in no wise checked his delight, and that in the multiplicity of tasks planned to make a paradise out of the valley he could not choose the one with which to begin. He had to grow into the habit of passing from one dreamy pleasure to another, like a bee going from flower to flower in the valley, and he found this wandering habit likely to extend to his labors. Nevertheless, he made a start.

At the outset he discovered Bess to be both a considerable help in some ways and a very great hindrance in others. Her excitement and joy were spurs, inspirations; but she was utterly impracticable in her ideas, and she flitted from one plan to another with bewildering vacillation. Moreover, he fancied that she grew more eager, youthful, and sweet; and he marked that it was far easier to watch her and listen to her than it was to work. Therefore he gave her tasks that necessitated her going often to the cave where he had stored his packs.

Upon the last of these trips, when he was some distance down the terrace and out of sight of camp, he heard a scream, and then the sharp barking of the dogs.

For an instant he straightened up, amazed. Danger for her had been absolutely out of his mind. She had seen a rattlesnake—or a wildcat. Still she would not have been likely to scream at sight of either; and the barking of the dogs was ominous. Dropping his work, he dashed back along the terrace. Upon breaking through a clump of aspens he saw the dark form of a man in the camp. Cold, then hot, Venters burst into frenzied speed to reach his guns. He was cursing himself for a thoughtless fool when the man's tall form became familiar and he recognized Lassiter. Then the reversal of emotions changed his run to a walk; he tried to call out, but his voice refused to carry; when he reached camp there was Lassiter staring at the white-faced girl. By that time Ring and Whitie had recognized him.

"Hello, Venters! I'm makin' you a visit," said Lassiter, slowly. "An' I'm some surprised to see you've a—a young feller for company."

One glance had sufficed for the keen rider to read Bess's real sex, and for once his cool calm had deserted him. He stared till the white of Bess's cheeks flared into crimson. That, if it were needed, was the concluding evidence of her femininity, for it went fittingly with her sun-tinted hair and darkened, dilated eyes, the sweetness of her mouth, and the striking symmetry of her slender shape.

"Heavens! Lassiter!" panted Venters, when he caught his breath. "What relief—it's only you! How—in the name of all that's wonderful—did you ever get here?"

"I trailed you. We—I wanted to know where you was, if you had a safe place. So I trailed you."

"Trailed me," cried Venters, bluntly.

"I reckon. It was some of a job after I got to them smooth rocks. I was all day trackin' you up to them little cut steps in the rock. The rest was easy."

"Where's your hoss? I hope you hid him."

"I tied him in them queer cedars down on the slope. He can't be seen from the valley."

"That's good. Well, well! I'm completely dumfounded. It was my idea that no man could track me in here."

"I reckon. But if there's a tracker in these uplands as good as me he can find you."

"That's bad. That'll worry me. But, Lassiter, now you're here I'm glad to see you. And—and my companion here is not a young fellow!... Bess, this is a friend of mine. He saved my life once."

The embarrassment of the moment did not extend to Lassiter. Almost at once his manner, as he shook hands with Bess, relieved Venters and put the girl at ease.

After Venters's words and one quick look at Lassiter, her agitation stilled, and, though she was shy, if she were conscious of anything out of the ordinary in the situation, certainly she did not show it.

"I reckon I'll only stay a little while," Lassiter was saying. "An' if you don't mind troublin', I'm hungry. I fetched some biscuits along, but they're gone. Venters, this place is sure the wonderfullest ever seen. Them cut steps on the slope! That outlet into the gorge! An' it's like climbin' up through hell into heaven to climb through that gorge into this valley! There's a queer-lookin' rock at the top of the passage. I didn't have time to stop. I'm wonderin' how you ever found this place. It's sure interestin'."

During the preparation and eating of dinner Lassiter listened mostly, as was his wont, and occasionally he spoke in his quaint and dry way. Venters noted, however, that the rider showed an increasing interest in Bess. He asked her no questions, and only directed his attention to her while she was occupied and had no opportunity to observe his scrutiny. It seemed to Venters that Lassiter grew more and more absorbed in his study of Bess, and that he lost his coolness in some strange, softening sympathy. Then, quite abruptly, he arose and announced the necessity for his early departure. He said good-by to Bess in a voice gentle and somewhat broken, and turned hurriedly away. Venters accompanied him, and they had traversed the terrace, climbed the weathered slope, and passed under the stone bridge before either spoke again.

Then Lassiter put a great hand on Venters's shoulder and wheeled him to meet a smoldering fire of gray eyes.

"Lassiter, I couldn't tell Jane! I couldn't," burst out Venters, reading his friend's mind. "I tried. But I couldn't. She wouldn't understand, and she has troubles enough. And I love the girl!"

"Venters, I reckon this beats me. I've seen some queer things in my time, too. This girl—who is she?"

"I don't know."

"Don't know! What is she, then?"

"I don't know that, either. Oh, it's the strangest story you ever heard. I must tell you. But you'll never believe."

"Venters, women were always puzzles to me. But for all that, if this girl ain't a child, an' as innocent, I'm no fit person to think of virtue an' goodness in anybody. Are you goin' to be square with her?"

"I am—so help me God!"

"I reckoned so. Mebbe my temper oughtn't led me to make sure. But, man, she's a woman in all but years. She's sweeter 'n the sage."

"Lassiter, I know, I know. And the hell of it is that in spite of her innocence and charm she's—she's not what she seems!"

"I wouldn't want to—of course, I couldn't call you a liar, Venters," said the older man.

"What's more, she was Oldring's Masked Rider!"

Venters expected to floor his friend with that statement, but he was not in any way prepared for the shock his words gave. For an instant he was astounded to see Lassiter stunned; then his own passionate eagerness to unbosom himself, to tell the wonderful story, precluded any other thought.

"Son, tell me all about this," presently said Lassiter as he seated himself on a stone and wiped his moist brow.

Thereupon Venters began his narrative at the point where he had shot the rustler and Oldring's Masked Rider, and he rushed through it, telling all, not holding back even Bess's unreserved avowal of her love or his deepest emotions.

"That's the story," he said, concluding. "I love her, though I've never told her. If I did tell her I'd be ready to marry her, and that seems impossible in this country. I'd be afraid to risk taking her anywhere. So I intend to do the best I can for her here."

"The longer I live the stranger life is," mused Lassiter, with downcast eyes. "I'm reminded of somethin' you once said to Jane about hands in her game of life. There's that unseen hand of power, an' Tull's black hand, an' my red one, an' your indifferent one, an' the girl's little brown, helpless one. An', Venters there's another one that's all-wise an' all-wonderful. That's the hand guidin' Jane Withersteen's game of life!... Your story's one to daze a far clearer head than mine. I can't offer no advice, even if you asked for it. Mebbe I can help you. Anyway, I'll hold Oldrin' up when he comes to the village an' find out about this girl. I knew the rustler years ago. He'll remember me."

"Lassiter, if I ever meet Oldring I'll kill him!" cried Venters, with sudden intensity.

"I reckon that'd be perfectly natural," replied the rider.

"Make him think Bess is dead—as she is to him and that old life."

"Sure, sure, son. Cool down now. If you're goin' to begin pullin' guns on Tull an' Oldin' you want to be cool. I reckon, though, you'd better keep hid here. Well, I must be leavin'."

"One thing, Lassiter. You'll not tell Jane about Bess? Please don't!"

"I reckon not. But I wouldn't be afraid to bet that after she'd got over anger at your secrecy—Venters, she'd be furious once in her life!—she'd think more of you. I don't mind sayin' for myself that I think you're a good deal of a man."

In the further ascent Venters halted several times with the intention of saying good-by, yet he changed his mind and kept on climbing till they reached Balancing Rock. Lassiter examined the huge rock, listened to Venters's idea of its position and suggestion, and curiously placed a strong hand upon it.

"Hold on!" cried Venters. "I heaved at it once and have never gotten over my scare."

"Well, you do seem uncommon nervous," replied Lassiter, much amused. "Now, as for me, why I always had the funniest notion to roll stones! When I was a kid I did it, an' the bigger I got the bigger stones I'd roll. Ain't that funny? Honest—even now I often get off my hoss just to tumble a big stone over a precipice, en' watch it drop, en' listen to it bang an' boom. I've started some slides in my time, an' don't you forget it. I never seen a rock I wanted to roll as bad as this one! Wouldn't there jest be roarin', crashin' hell down that trail?"

"You'd close the outlet forever!" exclaimed Venters. "Well, good-by, Lassiter. Keep my secret and don't forget me. And be mighty careful how you get out of the valley below. The rustlers' canyon isn't more than three miles up the Pass. Now you've tracked me here, I'll never feel safe again."

In his descent to the valley, Venters's emotion, roused to stirring pitch by the recital of his love story, quieted gradually, and in its place came a sober, thoughtful mood. All at once he saw that he was serious, because he would never more regain his sense of security while in the valley. What Lassiter could do another skilful tracker might duplicate. Among the many riders with whom Venters had ridden he recalled no one who could have taken his trail at Cottonwoods and have followed it to the edge of the bare slope in the pass, let alone up that glistening smooth stone. Lassiter, however, was not an ordinary rider. Instead of hunting cattle tracks he had likely spent a goodly portion of his life tracking men. It was not improbable that among Oldring's rustlers there was one who shared Lassiter's gift for trailing. And the more Venters dwelt on this possibility the more perturbed he grew.

Lassiter's visit, moreover, had a disquieting effect upon Bess, and Venters fancied that she entertained the same thought as to future seclusion. The breaking of their solitude, though by a well-meaning friend, had not only dispelled all its dream and much of its charm, but had instilled a canker of fear. Both had seen the footprint in the sand.

Venters did no more work that day. Sunset and twilight gave way to night, and the canyon bird whistled its melancholy notes, and the wind sang softly in the cliffs, and the camp-fire blazed and burned down to red embers. To Venters a subtle difference was apparent in all of these, or else the shadowy change had been in him. He hoped that on the morrow this slight depression would have passed away.

In that measure, however, he was doomed to disappointment. Furthermore, Bess reverted to a wistful sadness that he had not observed in her since her recovery. His attempt to cheer her out of it resulted in dismal failure, and consequently in a darkening of his own mood. Hard work relieved him; still, when the day had passed, his unrest returned. Then he set to deliberate thinking, and there came to him the startling conviction that he must leave Surprise Valley and take Bess with him. As a rider he had taken many chances, and as an adventurer in Deception Pass he had unhesitatingly risked his life, but now he would run no preventable hazard of Bess's safety and happiness, and he was too keen not to see that hazard. It gave him a pang to think of leaving the beautiful valley just when he had the means to establish a permanent and delightful home there. One flashing thought tore in hot temptation through his mind—why not climb up into the gorge, roll Balancing Rock down the trail, and close forever the outlet to Deception Pass? "That was the beast in me—showing his teeth!" muttered Venters, scornfully. "I'll just kill him good and quick! I'll be fair to this girl, if it's the last thing I do on earth!"

Another day went by, in which he worked less and pondered more and all the time covertly watched Bess. Her wistfulness had deepened into downright unhappiness, and that made his task to tell her all the harder. He kept the secret another day, hoping by some chance she might grow less moody, and to his exceeding anxiety she fell into far deeper gloom. Out of his own secret and the torment of it he divined that she, too, had a secret and the keeping of it was torturing her. As yet he had no plan thought out in regard to how or when to leave the valley, but he decided to tell her the necessity of it and to persuade her to go. Furthermore, he hoped his speaking out would induce her to unburden her own mind.

"Bess, what's wrong with you?" he asked.

"Nothing," she answered, with averted face.

Venters took hold of her gently, though masterfully, forced her to meet his eyes.

"You can't look at me and lie," he said. "Now—what's wrong with you? You're keeping something from me. Well, I've got a secret, too, and I intend to tell it presently."

"Oh—I have a secret. I was crazy to tell you when you came back. That's why I was so silly about everything. I kept holding my secret back—gloating over it. But when Lassiter came I got an idea—that changed my mind. Then I hated to tell you."

"Are you going to now?"

"Yes—yes. I was coming to it. I tried yesterday, but you were so cold. I was afraid. I couldn't keep it much longer."

"Very well, most mysterious lady, tell your wonderful secret."

"You needn't laugh," she retorted, with a first glimpse of reviving spirit. "I can take the laugh out of you in one second."

"It's a go."

She ran through the spruces to the cave, and returned carrying something which was manifestly heavy. Upon nearer view he saw that whatever she held with such evident importance had been bound up in a black scarf he well remembered. That alone was sufficient to make him tingle with curiosity.

"Have you any idea what I did in your absence?" she asked.

"I imagine you lounged about, waiting and watching for me," he replied, smiling. "I've my share of conceit, you know."

"You're wrong. I worked. Look at my hands." She dropped on her knees close to where he sat, and, carefully depositing the black bundle, she held out her hands. The palms and inside of her fingers were white, puckered, and worn.

"Why, Bess, you've been fooling in the water," he said.

"Fooling? Look here!" With deft fingers she spread open the black scarf, and the bright sun shone upon a dull, glittering heap of gold.

"Gold!" he ejaculated.

"Yes, gold! See, pounds of gold! I found it—washed it out of the stream—picked it out grain by grain, nugget by nugget!"

"Gold!" he cried.

"Yes. Now—now laugh at my secret!"

For a long minute Venters gazed. Then he stretched forth a hand to feel if the gold was real.

"Gold!" he almost shouted. "Bess, there are hundreds—thousands of dollars' worth here!"

He leaned over to her, and put his hand, strong and clenching now, on hers.

"Is there more where this came from?" he whispered.

"Plenty of it, all the way up the stream to the cliff. You know I've often washed for gold. Then I've heard the men talk. I think there's no great quantity of gold here, but enough for—for a fortune for you."

"That—was—your—secret!"

"Yes. I hate gold. For it makes men mad. I've seen them drunk with joy and dance and fling themselves around. I've seen them curse and rave. I've seen them fight like dogs and roll in the dust. I've seen them kill each other for gold."

"Is that why you hated to tell me?"

"Not—not altogether." Bess lowered her head. "It was because I knew you'd never stay here long after you found gold."

"You were afraid I'd leave you?"

"Yes.

"Listen!... You great, simple child! Listen... You sweet, wonderful, wild, blue-eyed girl! I was tortured by my secret. It was that I knew we—we must leave the valley. We can't stay here much longer. I couldn't think how we'd get away—out of the country—or how we'd live, if we ever got out. I'm a beggar. That's why I kept my secret. I'm poor. It takes money to make way beyond Sterling. We couldn't ride horses or burros or walk forever. So while I knew we must go, I was distracted over how to go and what to do. Now! We've gold! Once beyond Sterling, we'll be safe from rustlers. We've no others to fear.

"Oh! Listen! Bess!" Venters now heard his voice ringing high and sweet, and he felt Bess's cold hands in his crushing grasp as she leaned toward him pale, breathless. "This is how much I'd leave you! You made me live again! I'll take you away—far away from this wild country. You'll begin a new life. You'll be happy. You shall see cities, ships, people. You shall have anything your heart craves. All the shame and sorrow of your life shall be forgotten—as if they had never been. This is how much I'd leave you here alone—you sad-eyed girl. I love you! Didn't you know it? How could you fail to know it? I love you! I'm free! I'm a man—a man you've made—no more a beggar!... Kiss me! This is how much I'd leave you here alone—you beautiful, strange, unhappy girl. But I'll make you happy. What—what do I care for—your past! I love you! I'll take you home to Illinois—to my mother. Then I'll take you to far places. I'll make up all you've lost. Oh, I know you love me—knew it before you told me. And it changed my life. And you'll go with me, not as my companion as you are here, nor my sister, but, Bess, darling!... As my wife!"

CHAPTER XVII. WRANGLE'S RACE RUN

The plan eventually decided upon by the lovers was for Venters to go to the village, secure a horse and some kind of a disguise for Bess, or at least less striking apparel than her present garb, and to return post-haste to the valley. Meanwhile, she would add to their store of gold. Then they would strike the long and perilous trail to ride out of Utah. In the event of his inability to fetch back a horse for her, they intended to make the giant sorrel carry double. The gold, a little food, saddle blankets, and Venters's guns were to compose the light outfit with which they would make the start.

"I love this beautiful place," said Bess. "It's hard to think of leaving it."

"Hard! Well, I should think so," replied Venters. "Maybe—in years—" But he did not complete in words his thought that might be possible to return after many years of absence and change.

Once again Bess bade Venters farewell under the shadow of Balancing Rock, and this time it was with whispered hope and tenderness and passionate trust. Long after he had left her, all down through the outlet to the Pass, the clinging clasp of her arms, the sweetness of her lips, and the sense of a new and exquisite birth of character in her remained hauntingly and thrillingly in his mind. The girl who had sadly called herself nameless and nothing had been marvelously transformed in the moment of his avowal of love. It was something to think over, something to warm his heart, but for the present it had absolutely to be forgotten so that all his mind could be addressed to the trip so fraught with danger.

He carried only his rifle, revolver, and a small quantity of bread and meat, and thus lightly burdened, he made swift progress down the slope and out into the valley. Darkness was coming on, and he welcomed it. Stars were blinking when he reached his old hiding-place in the split of canyon wall, and by their aid he slipped through the dense thickets to the grassy enclosure. Wrangle stood in the center of it with his head up, and he appeared black and of gigantic proportions in the dim light. Venters whistled softly, began a slow approach, and then called. The horse snorted and, plunging away with dull, heavy sound of hoofs, he disappeared in the gloom. "Wilder than ever!" muttered Venters. He followed the sorrel into the narrowing split between the walls, and presently had to desist because he could not see a foot in advance. As he went back toward the open Wrangle jumped out of an ebony shadow of cliff and like a thunderbolt shot huge and black past him down into the starlit glade. Deciding that all attempts to catch Wrangle at night would be useless, Venters repaired to the shelving rock where he had hidden saddle and blanket, and there went to sleep.

The first peep of day found him stirring, and as soon as it was light enough to distinguish objects, he took his lasso off his saddle and went out to rope the sorrel. He espied Wrangle at the lower end of the cove and approached him in a perfectly natural manner. When he got near enough, Wrangle evidently recognized him, but was too wild to stand. He ran up the glade and on into the narrow lane between the walls. This favored Venters's speedy capture of the horse, so, coiling his noose ready to throw, he hurried on. Wrangle let Venters get to within a hundred feet and then he broke. But as he plunged by, rapidly getting into his stride, Venters made a perfect throw with the rope. He had time to brace himself for the shock; nevertheless, Wrangle threw him and dragged him several yards before halting.

"You wild devil," said Venters, as he slowly pulled Wrangle up. "Don't you know me? Come now—old fellow—so—so—"

Wrangle yielded to the lasso and then to Venters's strong hand. He was as straggly and wild-looking as a horse left to roam free in the sage. He dropped his long ears and stood readily to be saddled and bridled. But he was exceedingly sensitive, and quivered at every touch and sound. Venters led him to the thicket, and, bending the close saplings to let him squeeze through, at length reached the open. Sharp survey in each direction assured him of the usual lonely nature of the canyon, then he was in the saddle, riding south.

Wrangle's long, swinging canter was a wonderful ground-gainer. His stride was almost twice that of an ordinary horse; and his endurance was equally remarkable. Venters pulled him in occasionally, and walked him up the stretches of rising ground and along the soft washes. Wrangle had never yet shown any indication of distress while Venters rode him. Nevertheless, there was now reason to save the horse, therefore Venters did not resort to the hurry that had characterized his former trip. He camped at the last water in the Pass. What distance that was to Cottonwoods he did not know; he calculated, however, that it was in the neighborhood of fifty miles.

Early in the morning he proceeded on his way, and about the middle of the forenoon reached the constricted gap that marked the southerly end of the Pass, and through which led the trail up to the sage-level. He spied out Lassiter's tracks in the dust, but no others, and dismounting, he straightened out Wrangle's bridle and began to lead him up the trail. The short climb, more severe on beast than on man, necessitated a rest on the level above, and during this he scanned the wide purple reaches of slope.

Wrangle whistled his pleasure at the smell of the sage. Remounting, Venters headed up the white trail with the fragrant wind in his face. He had proceeded for perhaps a couple of miles when Wrangle stopped with a suddenness that threw Venters heavily against the pommel.

"What's wrong, old boy?" called Venters, looking down for a loose shoe or a snake or a foot lamed by a picked-up stone. Unrewarded, he raised himself from his scrutiny. Wrangle stood stiff head high, with his long ears erect. Thus guided, Venters swiftly gazed ahead to make out a dust-clouded, dark group of horsemen riding down the slope. If they had seen him, it apparently made no difference in their speed or direction.

"Wonder who they are!" exclaimed Venters. He was not disposed to run. His cool mood tightened under grip of excitement as he reflected that, whoever the approaching riders were, they could not be friends. He slipped out of the saddle and led Wrangle behind the tallest sage-brush. It might serve to conceal them until the riders were close enough for him to see who they were; after that he would be indifferent to how soon they discovered him.

After looking to his rifle and ascertaining that it was in working order, he watched, and as he watched, slowly the force of a bitter fierceness, long dormant, gathered ready to flame into life. If those riders were not rustlers he had forgotten how rustlers looked and rode. On they came, a small group, so compact and dark that he could not tell their number. How unusual that their horses did not see Wrangle! But such failure, Venters decided, was owing to the speed with which they were traveling. They moved at a swift canter affected more by rustlers than by riders. Venters grew concerned over the possibility that these horsemen would actually ride down on him before he had a chance to tell what to expect. When they were within three hundred yards he deliberately led Wrangle out into the trail.

Then he heard shouts, and the hard scrape of sliding hoofs, and saw horses rear and plunge back with up-flung heads and flying manes. Several little white puffs of smoke appeared sharply against the black background of riders and horses, and shots rang out. Bullets struck far in front of Venters, and whipped up the dust and then hummed low into the sage. The range was great for revolvers, but whether the shots were meant to kill or merely to check advance, they were enough to fire that waiting ferocity in Venters. Slipping his arm through the bridle, so that Wrangle could not get away, Venters lifted his rifle and pulled the trigger twice.

He saw the first horseman lean sideways and fall. He saw another lurch in his saddle and heard a cry of pain. Then Wrangle, plunging in fright, lifted Venters and nearly threw him. He jerked the horse down with a powerful hand and leaped into the saddle. Wrangle plunged again, dragging his bridle, that Venters had not had time to throw in place. Bending over with a swift movement, he secured it and dropped the loop over the pommel. Then, with grinding teeth, he looked to see what the issue would be.

The band had scattered so as not to afford such a broad mark for bullets. The riders faced Venters, some with red-belching guns. He heard a sharper report, and just as Wrangle plunged again he caught the whim of a leaden missile that would have hit him but for Wrangle's sudden jump. A swift, hot wave, turning cold, passed over Venters. Deliberately he picked out the one rider with a carbine, and killed him. Wrangle snorted shrilly and bolted into the sage. Venters let him run a few rods, then with iron arm checked him.

Five riders, surely rustlers, were left. One leaped out of the saddle to secure his fallen comrade's carbine. A shot from Venters, which missed the man but sent the dust flying over him made him run back to his horse. Then they separated. The crippled rider went one way; the one frustrated in his attempt to get the carbine rode another, Venters thought he made out a third rider, carrying a strange-appearing bundle and disappearing in the sage. But in the rapidity of action and vision he could not discern what it was. Two riders with three horses swung out to the right. Afraid of the long rifle—a burdensome weapon seldom carried by rustlers or riders—they had been put to rout.

Suddenly Venters discovered that one of the two men last noted was riding Jane Withersteen's horse Bells—the beautiful bay racer she had given to Lassiter. Venters uttered a savage outcry. Then the small, wiry, frog-like shape of the second rider, and the ease and grace of his seat in the saddle—things so strikingly incongruous—grew more and more familiar in Venters's sight.

"Jerry Card!" cried Venters.

It was indeed Tull's right-hand man. Such a white hot wrath inflamed Venters that he fought himself to see with clearer gaze.

"It's Jerry Card!" he exclaimed, instantly. "And he's riding Black Star and leading Night!"

The long-kindling, stormy fire in Venters's heart burst into flame. He spurred Wrangle, and as the horse lengthened his stride Venters slipped cartridges into the magazine of his rifle till it was once again full. Card and his companion were now half a mile or more in advance, riding easily down the slope. Venters marked the smooth gait, and understood it when Wrangle galloped out of the sage into the broad cattle trail, down which Venters had once tracked Jane Withersteen's red herd. This hard-packed trail, from years of use, was as clean and smooth as a road. Venters saw Jerry Card look back over his shoulder, the other rider did likewise. Then the three racers lengthened their stride to the point where the swinging canter was ready to break into a gallop.

"Wrangle, the race's on," said Venters, grimly. "We'll canter with them and gallop with them and run with them. We'll let them set the pace."

Venters knew he bestrode the strongest, swiftest, most tireless horse ever ridden by any rider across the Utah uplands. Recalling Jane Withersteen's devoted assurance that Night could run neck and neck with Wrangle, and Black Star could show his heels to him, Venters wished that Jane were there to see the race to recover her blacks and in the unqualified superiority of the giant sorrel. Then Venters found himself thankful that she was absent, for he meant that race to end in Jerry Card's death. The first flush, the raging of Venters's wrath, passed, to leave him in sullen, almost cold possession of his will. It was a deadly mood, utterly foreign to his nature, engendered, fostered, and released by the wild passions of wild men in a wild country. The strength in him then—the thing rife in him that was not hate, but something as remorseless—might have been the fiery fruition of a whole lifetime of vengeful quest. Nothing could have stopped him.

Venters thought out the race shrewdly. The rider on Bells would probably drop behind and take to the sage. What he did was of little moment to Venters. To stop Jerry Card, his evil hidden career as well as his present flight, and then to catch the blacks—that was all that concerned Venters. The cattle trail wound for miles and miles down the slope. Venters saw with a rider's keen vision ten, fifteen, twenty miles of clear purple sage. There were no on-coming riders or rustlers to aid Card. His only chance to escape lay in abandoning the stolen horses and creeping away in the sage to hide. In ten miles Wrangle could run Black Star and Night off their feet, and in fifteen he could kill them outright. So Venters held the sorrel in, letting Card make the running. It was a long race that would save the blacks.

In a few miles of that swinging canter Wrangle had crept appreciably closer to the three horses. Jerry Card turned again, and when he saw how the sorrel had gained, he put Black Star to a gallop. Night and Bells, on either side of him, swept into his stride.

Venters loosened the rein on Wrangle and let him break into a gallop. The sorrel saw the horses ahead and wanted to run. But Venters restrained him. And in the gallop he gained more than in the canter. Bells was fast in that gait, but Black Star and Night had been trained to run. Slowly Wrangle closed the gap down to a quarter of a mile, and crept closer and closer.

Jerry Card wheeled once more. Venters distinctly saw the red flash of his red face. This time he looked long. Venters laughed. He knew what passed in Card's mind. The rider was trying to make out what horse it happened to be that thus gained on Jane Withersteen's peerless racers. Wrangle had so long been away from the village that not improbably Jerry had forgotten. Besides, whatever Jerry's qualifications for his fame as the greatest rider of the sage, certain it was that his best point was not far-sightedness. He had not recognized Wrangle. After what must have been a searching gaze he got his comrade to face about. This action gave Venters amusement. It spoke so surely of the facts that neither Card nor the rustler actually knew their danger. Yet if they kept to the trail—and the last thing such men would do would be to leave it—they were both doomed.

This comrade of Card's whirled far around in his saddle, and he even shaded his eyes from the sun. He, too, looked long. Then, all at once, he faced ahead again and, bending lower in the saddle, began to fling his right arm up and down. That flinging Venters knew to be the lashing of Bells. Jerry also became active. And the three racers lengthened out into a run.

"Now, Wrangle!" cried Venters. "Run, you big devil! Run!"

Venters laid the reins on Wrangle's neck and dropped the loop over the pommel. The sorrel needed no guiding on that smooth trail. He was surer-footed in a run than at any other fast gait, and his running gave the impression of something devilish. He might now have been actuated by Venters's spirit; undoubtedly his savage running fitted the mood of his rider. Venters bent forward swinging with the horse, and gripped his rifle. His eye measured the distance between him and Jerry Card.

CHAPTER XVII. WRANGLE'S RACE RUN

In less than two miles of running Bells began to drop behind the blacks, and Wrangle began to overhaul him. Venters anticipated that the rustler would soon take to the sage. Yet he did not. Not improbably he reasoned that the powerful sorrel could more easily overtake Bells in the heavier going outside of the trail. Soon only a few hundred yards lay between Bells and Wrangle. Turning in his saddle, the rustler began to shoot, and the bullets beat up little whiffs of dust. Venters raised his rifle, ready to take snap shots, and waited for favorable opportunity when Bells was out of line with the forward horses. Venters had it in him to kill these men as if they were skunk-bitten coyotes, but also he had restraint enough to keep from shooting one of Jane's beloved Arabians.

No great distance was covered, however, before Bells swerved to the left, out of line with Black Star and Night. Then Venters, aiming high and waiting for the pause between Wrangle's great strides, began to take snap shots at the rustler. The fleeing rider presented a broad target for a rifle, but he was moving swiftly forward and bobbing up and down. Moreover, shooting from Wrangle's back was shooting from a thunderbolt. And added to that was the danger of a low-placed bullet taking effect on Bells. Yet, despite these considerations, making the shot exceedingly difficult, Venters's confidence, like his implacability, saw a speedy and fatal termination of that rustler's race. On the sixth shot the rustler threw up his arms and took a flying tumble off his horse. He rolled over and over, hunched himself to a half-erect position, fell, and then dragged himself into the sage. As Venters went thundering by he peered keenly into the sage, but caught no sign of the man. Bells ran a few hundred yards, slowed up, and had stopped when Wrangle passed him.

Again Venters began slipping fresh cartridges into the magazine of his rifle, and his hand was so sure and steady that he did not drop a single cartridge. With the eye of a rider and the judgment of a marksman he once more measured the distance between him and Jerry Card. Wrangle had gained, bringing him into rifle range. Venters was hard put to it now not to shoot, but thought it better to withhold his fire. Jerry, who, in anticipation of a running fusillade, had huddled himself into a little twisted ball on Black Star's neck, now surmising that this pursuer would make sure of not wounding one of the blacks, rose to his natural seat in the saddle.

In his mind perhaps, as certainly as in Venters's, this moment was the beginning of the real race.

Venters leaned forward to put his hand on Wrangle's neck, then backward to put it on his flank. Under the shaggy, dusty hair trembled and vibrated and rippled a wonderful muscular activity. But Wrangle's flesh was still cold. What a cold-blooded brute thought Venters, and felt in him a love for the horse he had never given to any other. It would not have been humanly possible for any rider, even though clutched by hate or revenge or a passion to save a loved one or fear of his own life, to be astride the sorrel to swing with his swing, to see his magnificent stride and hear the rapid thunder of his hoofs, to ride him in that race and not glory in the ride.

So, with his passion to kill still keen and unabated, Venters lived out that ride, and drank a rider's sage-sweet cup of wildness to the dregs.

When Wrangle's long mane, lashing in the wind, stung Venters in the cheek, the sting added a beat to his flying pulse. He bent a downward glance to try to see Wrangle's actual stride, and saw only twinkling, darting streaks and the white rush of the trail. He watched the sorrel's savage head, pointed level, his mouth still closed and dry, but his nostrils distended as if he were snorting unseen fire. Wrangle was the horse for a race with death. Upon each side Venters saw the sage merged into a sailing, colorless wall. In front sloped the lay of ground with its purple breadth split by the white trail. The wind, blowing with heavy, steady blast into his face, sickened him with enduring, sweet odor, and filled his ears with a hollow, rushing roar.

Then for the hundredth time he measured the width of space separating him from Jerry Card. Wrangle had ceased to gain. The blacks were proving their fleetness. Venters watched Jerry Card, admiring the little rider's horsemanship. He had the incomparable seat of the upland rider, born in the saddle. It struck Venters that Card had changed his position, or the position of the horses. Presently Venters remembered positively that Jerry had been leading Night on the right-hand side of the trail. The racer was now on the side to the left. No—it was Black Star. But, Venters argued in amaze, Jerry had been mounted on Black Star. Another clearer, keener gaze assured Venters that Black Star was really riderless. Night now carried Jerry Card.

"He's changed from one to the other!" ejaculated Venters, realizing the astounding feat with unstinted admiration. "Changed at full speed! Jerry Card, that's what you've done unless I'm drunk on the smell of sage. But I've got to see the trick before I believe it."

Thenceforth, while Wrangle sped on, Venters glued his eyes to the little rider. Jerry Card rode as only he could ride. Of all the daring horsemen of the uplands, Jerry was the one rider fitted to bring out the greatness of the blacks in that long race. He had them on a dead run, but not yet at the last strained and killing pace. From time to time he glanced backward, as a wise general in retreat calculating his chances and the power and speed of pursuers, and the moment for the last desperate burst. No doubt, Card, with his life at stake, gloried in that race, perhaps more wildly than Venters. For he had been born to the sage and the saddle and the wild. He was more than half horse. Not until the last call—the sudden up-flashing instinct of self-preservation—would he lose his skill and judgment and nerve and the spirit of that race. Venters seemed to read Jerry's mind. That little crime-stained rider was actually thinking of his horses, husbanding their speed, handling them with knowledge of years, glorying in their beautiful, swift, racing stride, and wanting them to win the race when his own life hung suspended in quivering balance. Again Jerry whirled in his saddle and the sun flashed red on his face. Turning, he drew Black Star closer and closer toward Night, till they ran side by side, as one horse. Then Card raised himself in the saddle, slipped out of the stirrups, and, somehow twisting himself, leaped upon Black Star. He did not even lose the swing of the horse. Like a leech he was there in the other saddle, and as the horses separated, his right foot, that had been apparently doubled under him, shot down to catch the stirrup. The grace and dexterity and daring of that rider's act won something more than admiration from Venters.

For the distance of a mile Jerry rode Black Star and then changed back to Night. But all Jerry's skill and the running of the blacks could avail little more against the sorrel.

Venters peered far ahead, studying the lay of the land. Straightaway for five miles the trail stretched, and then it disappeared in hummocky ground. To the right, some few rods, Venters saw a break in the sage, and this was the rim of Deception Pass. Across the dark cleft gleamed the red of the opposite wall. Venters imagined that the trail went down into the Pass somewhere north of those ridges. And he realized that he must and would overtake Jerry Card in this straight course of five miles.

Cruelly he struck his spurs into Wrangle's flanks. A light touch of spur was sufficient to make Wrangle plunge. And now, with a ringing, wild snort, he seemed to double up in muscular convulsions and to shoot forward with an impetus that almost unseated Venters. The sage blurred by, the trail flashed by, and the wind robbed him of breath and hearing. Jerry Card turned once more. And the way he shifted to Black Star showed he had to make his last desperate running. Venters aimed to the side of the trail and sent a bullet puffing the dust beyond Jerry. Venters hoped to frighten the rider and get him to take to the sage. But Jerry returned the shot, and his ball struck dangerously close in the dust at Wrangle's flying feet. Venters held his fire then, while the rider emptied his revolver. For a mile, with Black Star leaving Night behind and doing his utmost, Wrangle did not gain; for another mile he gained little, if at all. In the third he caught up with the now galloping Night and began to gain rapidly on the other black.

Only a hundred yards now stretched between Black Star and Wrangle. The giant sorrel thundered on—and on—and on. In every yard he gained a foot. He was whistling through his nostrils, wringing wet, flying lather, and as hot as fire. Savage as ever, strong as ever, fast as ever, but each tremendous stride jarred Venters out of the saddle! Wrangle's power and spirit and momentum had begun to run him off his legs. Wrangle's great race was nearly won—and run. Venters seemed to see the expanse before him as a vast, sheeted, purple plain sliding under him. Black Star moved in it as a blur. The rider, Jerry Card, appeared a mere dot bobbing dimly. Wrangle thundered on—on—on! Venters felt the increase in quivering, straining shock after every leap. Flecks of foam flew into Venters's eyes, burning him, making him see all the sage as red. But in that red haze he saw, or seemed to see, Black Star suddenly riderless and with broken gait. Wrangle thundered on to change his pace with a violent break. Then Venters pulled him hard. From run to gallop, gallop to canter, canter to trot, trot to walk, and walk to stop, the great sorrel ended his race.

Venters looked back. Black Star stood riderless in the trail. Jerry Card had taken to the sage. Far up the white trail Night came trotting faithfully down. Venters leaped off, still half blind, reeling dizzily. In a moment he had recovered sufficiently to have a care for Wrangle. Rapidly he took off the saddle and bridle. The sorrel was reeking, heaving, whistling, shaking. But he had still the strength to stand, and for him Venters had no fears.

As Venters ran back to Black Star he saw the horse stagger on shaking legs into the sage and go down in a heap. Upon reaching him Venters removed the saddle and bridle. Black Star had been killed on his legs, Venters thought. He had no hope for the stricken horse. Black Star lay flat, covered with bloody froth, mouth wide, tongue hanging, eyes glaring, and all his beautiful body in convulsions.

Unable to stay there to see Jane's favorite racer die, Venters hurried up the trail to meet the other black. On the way he kept a sharp lookout for Jerry Card. Venters imagined the rider would keep well out of range of the rifle, but, as he would be lost on the sage without a horse, not improbably he would linger in the vicinity on the chance of getting back one of the blacks. Night soon came trotting up, hot and wet and run out. Venters led him down near the others, and unsaddling him, let him loose to rest. Night wearily lay down in the dust and rolled, proving himself not yet spent.

Then Venters sat down to rest and think. Whatever the risk, he was compelled to stay where he was, or comparatively near, for the night. The horses must rest and drink. He must find water. He was now seventy miles from Cottonwoods, and, he believed, close to the canyon where the cattle trail must surely turn off and go down into the Pass. After a while he rose to survey the valley.

He was very near to the ragged edge of a deep canyon into which the trail turned. The ground lay in uneven ridges divided by washes, and these sloped into the canyon. Following the canyon line, he saw where its rim was broken by other intersecting canyons, and farther down red walls and yellow cliffs leading toward a deep blue cleft that he made sure was Deception Pass. Walking out a few rods to a promontory, he found where the trail went down. The descent was gradual, along a stone-walled trail, and Venters felt sure that this was the place where Oldring drove cattle into the Pass. There was, however, no indication at all that he ever had driven cattle out at this point. Oldring had many holes to his burrow.

In searching round in the little hollows Venters, much to his relief, found water. He composed himself to rest and eat some bread and meat, while he waited for a sufficient time to elapse so that he could safely give the horses a drink. He judged the hour to be somewhere around noon. Wrangle lay down to rest and Night followed suit. So long as they were down Venters intended to make no move. The longer they rested the better, and the safer it would be to give them water. By and by he forced himself to go over to where Black Star lay, expecting to find him dead. Instead he found the racer partially if not wholly recovered. There was recognition, even fire, in his big black eyes. Venters was overjoyed. He sat by the black for a long time. Black Star presently labored to his feet with a heave and a groan, shook himself, and snorted for water. Venters repaired to the little pool he had found, filled his sombrero, and gave the racer a drink. Black Star gulped it at one draught, as if it were but a drop, and pushed his nose into the hat and snorted for more. Venters now led Night down to drink, and after a further time Black Star also. Then the blacks began to graze.

The sorrel had wandered off down the sage between the trail and the canyon. Once or twice he disappeared in little swales. Finally Venters concluded Wrangle had grazed far enough, and, taking his lasso, he went to fetch him back. In crossing from one ridge to another he saw where the horse had made muddy a pool of water. It occurred to Venters then that Wrangle had drunk his fill, and did not seem the worse for it, and might be anything but easy to catch. And, true enough, he could not come within roping reach of the sorrel. He tried for an hour, and gave up in disgust. Wrangle did not seem so wild as simply perverse. In a quandary Venters returned to the other horses, hoping much, yet doubting more, that when Wrangle had grazed to suit himself he might be caught.

As the afternoon wore away Venters's concern diminished, yet he kept close watch on the blacks and the trail and the sage. There was no telling of what Jerry Card might be capable. Venters sullenly acquiesced to the idea that the rider had been too quick and too shrewd for him. Strangely and doggedly, however, Venters clung to his foreboding of Card's downfall.

The wind died away; the red sun topped the far distant western rise of slope; and the long, creeping purple shadows lengthened. The rims of the canyons gleamed crimson and the deep clefts appeared to belch forth blue smoke. Silence enfolded the scene.

It was broken by a horrid, long-drawn scream of a horse and the thudding of heavy hoofs. Venters sprang erect and wheeled south. Along the canyon rim, near the edge, came Wrangle, once more in thundering flight.

Venters gasped in amazement. Had the wild sorrel gone mad? His head was high and twisted, in a most singular position for a running horse. Suddenly Venters descried a frog-like shape clinging to Wrangle's neck. Jerry Card! Somehow he had straddled Wrangle and now stuck like a huge burr. But it was his strange position and the sorrel's wild scream that shook Venters's nerves. Wrangle was pounding toward the turn where the trail went down. He plunged onward like a blind horse. More than one of his leaps took him to the very edge of the precipice.

Jerry Card was bent forward with his teeth fast in the front of Wrangle's nose! Venters saw it, and there flashed over him a memory of this trick of a few desperate riders. He even thought of one rider who had worn off his teeth in this terrible hold to break or control desperate horses. Wrangle had indeed gone mad. The marvel was what guided him. Was it the half-brute, the more than half-horse instinct of Jerry Card? Whatever the mystery, it was true. And in a few more rods Jerry would have the sorrel turning into the trail leading down into the canyon.

"No—Jerry!" whispered Venters, stepping forward and throwing up the rifle. He tried to catch the little humped, frog-like shape over the sights. It was moving too fast; it was too small. Yet Venters shot once... twice... the third time... four times... five! all wasted shots and precious seconds!

With a deep-muttered curse Venters caught Wrangle through the sights and pulled the trigger. Plainly he heard the bullet thud. Wrangle uttered a horrible strangling sound. In swift death action he whirled, and with one last splendid leap he cleared the canyon rim. And he whirled downward with the little frog-like shape clinging to his neck!

There was a pause which seemed never ending, a shock, and an instant's silence.

Then up rolled a heavy crash, a long roar of sliding rocks dying away in distant echo, then silence unbroken.

Wrangle's race was run.

CHAPTER XVIII. OLDRING'S KNELL

Some forty hours or more later Venters created a commotion in Cottonwoods by riding down the main street on Black Star and leading Bells and Night. He had come upon Bells grazing near the body of a dead rustler, the only incident of his quick ride into the village.

Nothing was farther from Venters's mind than bravado. No thought came to him of the defiance and boldness of riding Jane Withersteen's racers straight into the arch-plotter's stronghold. He wanted men to see the famous Arabians; he wanted men to see them dirty and dusty, bearing all the signs of having been driven to their limit; he wanted men to see and to know that the thieves who had ridden them out into the sage had not ridden them back. Venters had come for that and for more—he wanted to meet Tull face to face; if not Tull, then Dyer; if not Dyer, then anyone in the secret of these master conspirators. Such was Venters's passion. The meeting with the rustlers, the unprovoked attack upon him, the spilling of blood, the recognition of Jerry Card and the horses, the race, and that last plunge of mad Wrangle—all these things, fuel on fuel to the smoldering fire, had kindled and swelled and leaped into living flame. He could have shot Dyer in the midst of his religious services at the altar; he could have killed Tull in front of wives and babes.

He walked the three racers down the broad, green-bordered village road. He heard the murmur of running water from Amber Spring. Bitter waters for Jane Withersteen! Men and women stopped to gaze at him and the horses. All knew him; all knew the blacks and the bay. As well as if it had been spoken, Venters read in the faces of men the intelligence that Jane Withersteen's Arabians had been known to have been stolen. Venters reined in and halted before Dyer's residence. It was a low, long, stone structure resembling Withersteen House. The spacious front yard was green and luxuriant with grass and flowers; gravel walks led to the huge porch; a well-trimmed hedge of purple sage separated the yard from the church grounds; birds sang in the trees; water flowed musically along the walks; and there were glad, careless shouts of children. For Venters the beauty of this home, and the serenity and its apparent happiness, all turned red and black. For Venters a shade overspread the lawn, the flowers, the old vine-clad stone house. In the music of the singing birds, in the murmur of the running water, he heard an ominous sound. Quiet beauty—sweet music—innocent laughter! By what monstrous abortion of fate did these abide in the shadow of Dyer?

Venters rode on and stopped before Tull's cottage. Women stared at him with white faces and then flew from the porch. Tull himself appeared at the door, bent low, craning his neck. His dark face flashed out of sight; the door banged; a heavy bar dropped with a hollow sound.

Then Venters shook Black Star's bridle, and, sharply trotting, led the other horses to the center of the village. Here at the intersecting streets and in front of the stores he halted once more. The usual lounging atmosphere of that prominent corner was not now in evidence. Riders and ranchers and villagers broke up what must have been absorbing conversation. There was a rush of many feet, and then the walk was lined with faces.

Venters's glance swept down the line of silent stone-faced men. He recognized many riders and villagers, but none of those he had hoped to meet. There was no expression in the faces turned toward him. All of them knew him, most were inimical, but there were few who were not burning with curiosity and wonder in regard to the return of Jane Withersteen's racers. Yet all were silent. Here were the familiar characteristics—masked feeling—strange secretiveness—expressionless expression of mystery and hidden power.

"Has anybody here seen Jerry Card?" queried Venters, in a loud voice.

In reply there came not a word, not a nod or shake of head, not so much as dropping eye or twitching lip—nothing but a quiet, stony stare.

"Been under the knife? You've a fine knife-wielder here—one Tull, I believe!... Maybe you've all had your tongues cut out?"

This passionate sarcasm of Venters brought no response, and the stony calm was as oil on the fire within him.

"I see some of you pack guns, too!" he added, in biting scorn. In the long, tense pause, strung keenly as a tight wire, he sat motionless on Black Star. "All right," he went on. "Then let some of you take this message to Tull. Tell him I've seen Jerry Card! ... Tell him Jerry Card will never return!"

Thereupon, in the same dead calm, Venters backed Black Star away from the curb, into the street, and out of range. He was ready now to ride up to Withersteen House and turn the racers over to Jane.

"Hello, Venters!" a familiar voice cried, hoarsely, and he saw a man running toward him. It was the rider Judkins who came up and gripped Venters's hand. "Venters, I could hev dropped when I seen them hosses. But thet sight ain't a marker to the looks of you. What's wrong? Hev you gone crazy? You must be crazy to ride in here this way—with them hosses—talkie' thet way about Tull en' Jerry Card."

"Jud, I'm not crazy—only mad clean through," replied Venters.

"Mad, now, Bern, I'm glad to hear some of your old self in your voice. Fer when you come up you looked like the corpse of a dead rider with fire fer eyes. You hed thet crowd too stiff fer throwin' guns. Come, we've got to hev a talk. Let's go up the lane. We ain't much safe here."

Judkins mounted Bells and rode with Venters up to the cottonwood grove. Here they dismounted and went among the trees.

"Let's hear from you first," said Judkins. "You fetched back them hosses. Thet is the trick. An', of course, you got Jerry the same as you got Horne."

"Horne!"

"Sure. He was found dead yesterday all chewed by coyotes, en' he'd been shot plumb center."

"Where was he found?"

"At the split down the trail—you know where Oldring's cattle trail runs off north from the trail to the pass."

"That's where I met Jerry and the rustlers. What was Horne doing with them? I thought Horne was an honest cattle-man."

"Lord—Bern, don't ask me thet! I'm all muddled now tryin' to figure things."

Venters told of the fight and the race with Jerry Card and its tragic conclusion.

"I knowed it! I knowed all along that Wrangle was the best hoss!" exclaimed Judkins, with his lean face working and his eyes lighting. "Thet was a race! Lord, I'd like to hev seen Wrangle jump the cliff with Jerry. An' thet was good-by to the grandest hoss an' rider ever on the sage!... But, Bern, after you got the hosses why'd you want to bolt right in Tull's face?"

"I want him to know. An' if I can get to him I'll—"

"You can't get near Tull," interrupted Judkins. "Thet vigilante bunch hev taken to bein' bodyguard for Tull an' Dyer, too."

"Hasn't Lassiter made a break yet?" inquired Venters, curiously.

"Naw!" replied Judkins, scornfully. "Jane turned his head. He's mad in love over her—follers her like a dog. He ain't no more Lassiter! He's lost his nerve, he doesn't look like the same feller. It's village talk. Everybody knows it. He hasn't thrown a gun, an' he won't!"

"Jud, I'll bet he does," replied Venters, earnestly. "Remember what I say. This Lassiter is something more than a gun-man. Jud, he's big—he's great!... I feel that in him. God help Tull and Dyer when Lassiter does go after them. For horses and riders and stone walls won't save them."

"Wal, hev it your way, Bern. I hope you're right. Nat'rully I've been some sore on Lassiter fer gittin' soft. But I ain't denyin' his nerve, or whatever's great in him thet sort of paralyzes people. No later 'n this mornin' I seen him saunterin' down the lane, quiet an' slow. An' like his guns he comes black—black, thet's Lassiter. Wal, the crowd on the corner never batted an eye, en' I'll gamble my hoss thet there wasn't one who hed a heartbeat till Lassiter got by. He went in Snell's saloon, an' as there wasn't no gun play I had to go in, too. An' there, darn my pictures, if Lassiter wasn't standin' to the bar, drinking en' talkin' with Oldrin'."

"Oldring!" whispered Venters. His voice, as all fire and pulse within him, seemed to freeze.

"Let go my arm!" exclaimed Judkins. "Thet's my bad arm. Sure it was Oldrin'. What the hell's wrong with you, anyway? Venters, I tell you somethin's wrong. You're whiter 'n a sheet. You can't be scared of the rustler. I don't believe you've got a scare in you. Wal, now, jest let me talk. You know I like to talk, an' if I'm slow I allus git there sometime. As I said, Lassiter was talkie' chummy with Oldrin'. There wasn't no hard feelin's. An' the gang wasn't payin' no pertic'lar attention. But like a cat watchin' a mouse I hed my eyes on them two fellers. It was strange to me, thet confab. I'm gittin' to think a lot, fer a feller who doesn't know much. There's been some queer deals lately an' this seemed to me the queerest. These men stood to the bar alone, an' so close their big gun-hilts butted together. I seen Oldrin' was some surprised at first, an' Lassiter was cool as ice. They talked, an' presently at somethin' Lassiter said the rustler bawled out a curse, an' then he jest fell up against the bar, an' sagged there. The gang in the saloon looked around an' laughed, an' thet's about all. Finally Oldrin' turned, and it was easy to see somethin' hed shook him. Yes, sir, thet big rustler—you know he's as broad as he is long, an' the powerfulest build of a man—yes, sir, the nerve had been taken out of him. Then, after a little, he began to talk an' said a lot to Lassiter, an' by an' by it didn't take much of an eye to see thet Lassiter was gittin' hit hard. I never seen him anyway but cooler 'n ice—till then. He seemed to be hit harder 'n Oldrin', only he didn't roar out thet way. He jest kind of sunk in, an' looked an' looked, an' he didn't see a livin' soul in thet saloon. Then he sort of come to, an' shakin' hands—mind you, shakin' hands with Oldrin'—he went out. I couldn't help thinkin' how easy even a boy could hev dropped the great gun-man then!... Wal, the rustler stood at the bar fer a long time, en' he was seein' things far off, too; then he come to an' roared fer whisky, an' gulped a drink thet was big enough to drown me."

"Is Oldring here now?" whispered Venters. He could not speak above a whisper. Judkins's story had been meaningless to him.

"He's at Snell's yet. Bern, I hevn't told you yet thet the rustlers hev been raisin' hell. They shot up Stone Bridge an' Glaze, an' fer three days they've been here drinkin' an' gamblin' an' throwin' of gold. These rustlers hev a pile of gold. If it was gold dust or nugget gold I'd hev reason to think, but it's new coin gold, as if it had jest come from the United States treasury. An' the coin's genuine. Thet's all been proved. The truth is Oldrin's on a rampage. A while back he lost his Masked Rider, an' they say he's wild about thet. I'm wonderin' if Lassiter could hev told the rustler anythin' about thet little masked, hard-ridin' devil. Ride! He was most as good as Jerry Card. An', Bern, I've been wonderin' if you know—"

"Judkins, you're a good fellow," interrupted Venters. "Some day I'll tell you a story. I've no time now. Take the horses to Jane."

Judkins stared, and then, muttering to himself, he mounted Bells, and stared again at Venters, and then, leading the other horses, he rode into the grove and disappeared.

Once, long before, on the night Venters had carried Bess through the canyon and up into Surprise Valley, he had experienced the strangeness of faculties singularly, tinglingly acute. And now the same sensation recurred. But it was different in that he felt cold, frozen, mechanical incapable of free thought, and all about him seemed unreal, aloof, remote. He hid his rifle in the sage, marking its exact location with extreme care. Then he faced down the lane and strode toward the center of the village. Perceptions flashed upon him, the faint, cold touch of the breeze, a cold, silvery tinkle of flowing water, a cold sun shining out of a cold sky, song of birds and laugh of children, coldly distant. Cold and intangible were all things in earth and heaven. Colder and tighter stretched the skin over his face; colder and harder grew the polished butts of his guns; colder and steadier became his hands as he wiped the clammy sweat from his face or reached low to his gun-sheaths. Men meeting him in the walk gave him wide berth. In front of Bevin's store a crowd melted apart for his passage, and their faces and whispers were faces and whispers of a dream. He turned a corner to meet Tull face to face, eye to eye. As once before he had seen this man pale to a ghastly, livid white so again he saw the change. Tull stopped in his tracks, with right hand raised and shaking. Suddenly it dropped, and he seemed to glide aside, to pass out of Venters's sight. Next he saw many horses with bridles down—all clean-limbed, dark bays or blacks—rustlers' horses! Loud voices and boisterous laughter, rattle of dice and scrape of chair and clink of gold, burst in mingled din from an open doorway. He stepped inside.

With the sight of smoke-hazed room and drinking, cursing, gambling, dark-visaged men, reality once more dawned upon Venters.

His entrance had been unnoticed, and he bent his gaze upon the drinkers at the bar. Dark-clothed, dark-faced men they all were, burned by the sun, bow-legged as were most riders of the sage, but neither lean nor gaunt. Then Venters's gaze passed to the tables, and swiftly it swept over the hard-featured gamesters, to alight upon the huge, shaggy, black head of the rustler chief.

"Oldring!" he cried, and to him his voice seemed to split a bell in his ears.

It stilled the din.

That silence suddenly broke to the scrape and crash of Oldring's chair as he rose; and then, while he passed, a great gloomy figure, again the thronged room stilled in silence yet deeper.

"Oldring, a word with you!" continued Venters.

"Ho! What's this?" boomed Oldring, in frowning scrutiny.

"Come outside, alone. A word for you—from your Masked Rider!"

Oldring kicked a chair out of his way and lunged forward with a stamp of heavy boot that jarred the floor. He waved down his muttering, rising men.

Venters backed out of the door and waited, hearing, as no sound had ever before struck into his soul, the rapid, heavy steps of the rustler.

Oldring appeared, and Venters had one glimpse of his great breadth and bulk, his gold-buckled belt with hanging guns, his high-top boots with gold spurs. In that moment Venters had a strange, unintelligible curiosity to see Oldring alive. The rustler's broad brow, his large black eyes, his sweeping beard, as dark as the wing of a raven, his enormous width of shoulder and depth of chest, his whole splendid presence so wonderfully charged with vitality and force and strength, seemed to afford Venters an unutterable fiendish joy because for that magnificent manhood and life he meant cold and sudden death.

"Oldring, Bess is alive! But she's dead to you—dead to the life you made her lead—dead as you will be in one second!"

Swift as lightning Venters's glance dropped from Oldring's rolling eyes to his hands. One of them, the right, swept out, then toward his gun—and Venters shot him through the heart.

Slowly Oldring sank to his knees, and the hand, dragging at the gun, fell away. Venters's strangely acute faculties grasped the meaning of that limp arm, of the swaying hulk, of the gasp and heave, of the quivering beard. But was that awful spirit in the black eyes only one of vitality?

"Man—why—didn't—you—wait? Bess—was—" Oldring's whisper died under his beard, and with a heavy lurch he fell forward.

Bounding swiftly away, Venters fled around the corner, across the street, and, leaping a hedge, he ran through yard, orchard, and garden to the sage. Here, under cover of the tall brush, he turned west and ran on to the place where he had hidden his rifle. Securing that, he again set out into a run, and, circling through the sage, came up behind Jane Withersteen's stable and corrals. With laboring, dripping chest, and pain as of a knife thrust in his side, he stopped to regain his breath, and while resting his eyes roved around in search of a horse. Doors and windows of the stable were open wide and had a deserted look. One dejected, lonely burro stood in the near corral. Strange indeed was the silence brooding over the once happy, noisy home of Jane Withersteen's pets.

He went into the corral, exercising care to leave no tracks, and led the burro to the watering-trough. Venters, though not thirsty, drank till he could drink no more. Then, leading the burro over hard ground, he struck into the sage and down the slope.

He strode swiftly, turning from time to time to scan the slope for riders. His head just topped the level of sage-brush, and the burro could not have been seen at all. Slowly the green of Cottonwoods sank behind the slope, and at last a wavering line of purple sage met the blue of sky.

To avoid being seen, to get away, to hide his trail—these were the sole ideas in his mind as he headed for Deception Pass, and he directed all his acuteness of eye and ear, and the keenness of a rider's judgment for distance and ground, to stern accomplishment of the task. He kept to the sage far to the left of the trail leading into the Pass. He walked ten miles and looked back a thousand times. Always the graceful, purple wave of sage remained wide and lonely, a clear, undotted waste. Coming to a stretch of rocky ground, he took advantage of it to cross the trail and then continued down on the right. At length he persuaded himself that he would be able to see riders mounted on horses before they could see him on the little burro, and he rode bareback.

Hour by hour the tireless burro kept to his faithful, steady trot. The sun sank and the long shadows lengthened down the slope. Moving veils of purple twilight crept out of the hollows and, mustering and forming on the levels, soon merged and shaded into night. Venters guided the burro nearer to the trail, so that he could see its white line from the ridges, and rode on through the hours.

CHAPTER XVIII. OLDRING'S KNELL

Once down in the Pass without leaving a trail, he would hold himself safe for the time being. When late in the night he reached the break in the sage, he sent the burro down ahead of him, and started an avalanche that all but buried the animal at the bottom of the trail. Bruised and battered as he was, he had a moment's elation, for he had hidden his tracks. Once more he mounted the burro and rode on. The hour was the blackest of the night when he made the thicket which inclosed his old camp. Here he turned the burro loose in the grass near the spring, and then lay down on his old bed of leaves.

He felt only vaguely, as outside things, the ache and burn and throb of the muscles of his body. But a dammed-up torrent of emotion at last burst its bounds, and the hour that saw his release from immediate action was one that confounded him in the reaction of his spirit. He suffered without understanding why. He caught glimpses into himself, into unlit darkness of soul. The fire that had blistered him and the cold which had frozen him now united in one torturing possession of his mind and heart, and like a fiery steed with ice-shod feet, ranged his being, ran rioting through his blood, trampling the resurging good, dragging ever at the evil.

Out of the subsiding chaos came a clear question. What had happened? He had left the valley to go to Cottonwoods. Why? It seemed that he had gone to kill a man—Oldring! The name riveted his consciousness upon the one man of all men upon earth whom he had wanted to meet. He had met the rustler. Venters recalled the smoky haze of the saloon, the dark-visaged men, the huge Oldring. He saw him step out of the door, a splendid specimen of manhood, a handsome giant with purple-black and sweeping beard. He remembered inquisitive gaze of falcon eyes. He heard himself repeating: "OLDRING, BESS IS ALIVE! BUT SHE'S DEAD TO YOU," and he felt himself jerk, and his ears throbbed to the thunder of a gun, and he saw the giant sink slowly to his knees. Was that only the vitality of him—that awful light in the eyes—only the hard-dying life of a tremendously powerful brute? A broken whisper, strange as death: "MAN—WHY—DIDN'T—YOU WAIT! BESS—WAS—" And Oldring plunged face forward, dead.

"I killed him," cried Venters, in remembering shock. "But it wasn't THAT. Ah, the look in his eyes and his whisper!"

Herein lay the secret that had clamored to him through all the tumult and stress of his emotions. What a look in the eyes of a man shot through the heart! It had been neither hate nor ferocity nor fear of men nor fear of death. It had been no passionate glinting spirit of a fearless foe, willing shot for shot, life for life, but lacking physical power. Distinctly recalled now, never to be forgotten, Venters saw in Oldring's magnificent eyes the rolling of great, glad surprise—softness—love! Then came a shadow and the terrible superhuman striving of his spirit to speak. Oldring shot through the heart, had fought and forced back death, not for a moment in which to shoot or curse, but to whisper strange words.

What words for a dying man to whisper! Why had not Venters waited? For what? That was no plea for life. It was regret that there was not a moment of life left in which to speak. Bess was—Herein lay renewed torture for Venters. What had Bess been to Oldring? The old question, like a specter, stalked from its grave to haunt him. He had overlooked, he had forgiven, he had loved and he had forgotten; and now, out of the mystery of a dying man's whisper rose again that perperverse, unsatisfied, jealous uncertainty. Bess had loved that splendid, black-crowned giant—by her own confession she had loved him; and in Venters's soul again flamed up the jealous hell. Then into the clamoring hell burst the shot that had killed Oldring, and it rang in a wild fiendish gladness, a hateful, vengeful joy. That passed to the memory of the love and light in Oldring's eyes and the mystery in his whisper. So the changing, swaying emotions fluctuated in Venters's heart.

This was the climax of his year of suffering and the crucial struggle of his life. And when the gray dawn came he rose, a gloomy, almost heartbroken man, but victor over evil passions. He could not change the past; and, even if he had not loved Bess with all his soul, he had grown into a man who would not change the future he had planned for her. Only, and once for all, he must know the truth, know the worst, stifle all these insistent doubts and subtle hopes and jealous fancies, and kill the past by knowing truly what Bess had been to Oldring. For that matter he knew—he had always known, but he must hear it spoken. Then, when they had safely gotten out of that wild country to take up a new and an absorbing life, she would forget, she would be happy, and through that, in the years to come, he could not but find life worth living.

All day he rode slowly and cautiously up the Pass, taking time to peer around corners, to pick out hard ground and grassy patches, and to make sure there was no one in pursuit. In the night sometime he came to the smooth, scrawled rocks dividing the valley, and here set the burro at liberty. He walked beyond, climbed the slope and the dim, starlit gorge. Then, weary to the point of exhaustion, he crept into a shallow cave and fell asleep.

In the morning, when he descended the trail, he found the sun was pouring a golden stream of light through the arch of the great stone bridge. Surprise Valley, like a valley of dreams, lay mystically soft and beautiful, awakening to the golden flood which was rolling away its slumberous bands of mist, brightening its walled faces.

While yet far off he discerned Bess moving under the silver spruces, and soon the barking of the dogs told him that they had seen him. He heard the mocking-birds singing in the trees, and then the twittering of the quail. Ring and Whitie came bounding toward him, and behind them ran Bess, her hands outstretched.

"Bern! You're back! You're back!" she cried, in joy that rang of her loneliness.

"Yes, I'm back," he said, as she rushed to meet him.

She had reached out for him when suddenly, as she saw him closely, something checked her, and as quickly all her joy fled, and with it her color, leaving her pale and trembling.

"Oh! What's happened?"

"A good deal has happened, Bess. I don't need to tell you what. And I'm played out. Worn out in mind more than body."

"Dear—you look strange to me!" faltered Bess.

"Never mind that. I'm all right. There's nothing for you to be scared about. Things are going to turn out just as we have planned. As soon as I'm rested we'll make a break to get out of the country. Only now, right now, I must know the truth about you."

"Truth about me?" echoed Bess, shrinkingly. She seemed to be casting back into her mind for a forgotten key. Venters himself, as he saw her, received a pang.

"Yes—the truth. Bess, don't misunderstand. I haven't changed that way. I love you still. I'll love you more afterward. Life will be just as sweet—sweeter to us. We'll be—be married as soon as ever we can. We'll be happy—but there's a devil in me. A perverse, jealous devil! Then I've queer fancies. I forgot for a long time. Now all those fiendish little whispers of doubt and faith and fear and hope come torturing me again. I've got to kill them with the truth."

"I'll tell you anything you want to know," she replied, frankly.

"Then by Heaven! we'll have it over and done with!... Bess—did Oldring love you?"

"Certainly he did."

"Did—did you love him?"

"Of course. I told you so."

"How can you tell it so lightly?" cried Venters, passionately. "Haven't you any sense of—of—" He choked back speech. He felt the rush of pain and passion. He seized her in rude, strong hands and drew her close. He looked straight into her dark-blue eyes. They were shadowing with the old wistful light, but they were as clear as the limpid water of the spring. They were earnest, solemn in unutterable love and faith and abnegation. Venters shivered. He knew he was looking into her soul. He knew she could not lie in that moment; but that she might tell the truth, looking at him with those eyes, almost killed his belief in purity.

"What are—what were you to—to Oldring?" he panted, fiercely.

"I am his daughter," she replied, instantly.

Venters slowly let go of her. There was a violent break in the force of his feeling—then creeping blankness.

"What—was it—you said?" he asked, in a kind of dull wonder.

"I am his daughter."

"Oldring's daughter?" queried Venters, with life gathering in his voice.

"Yes."

With a passionately awakening start he grasped her hands and drew her close.

"All the time—you've been Oldring's daughter?"

"Yes, of course all the time—always."

"But Bess, you told me—you let me think—I made out you were—a—so—so ashamed."

"It is my shame," she said, with voice deep and full, and now the scarlet fired her cheek. "I told you—I'm nothing—nameless—just Bess, Oldring's girl!"

"I know—I remember. But I never thought—" he went on, hurriedly, huskily. "That time—when you lay dying—you prayed—you—somehow I got the idea you were bad."

"Bad?" she asked, with a little laugh.

She looked up with a faint smile of bewilderment and the absolute unconsciousness of a child. Venters gasped in the gathering might of the truth. She did not understand his meaning.

"Bess! Bess!" He clasped her in his arms, hiding her eyes against his breast. She must not see his face in that moment. And he held her while he looked out across the valley. In his dim and blinded sight, in the blur of golden light and moving mist, he saw Oldring. She was the rustler's nameless daughter. Oldring had loved her. He had so guarded her, so kept her from women and men and knowledge of life that her mind was as a child's. That was part of the secret—part of the mystery. That was the wonderful truth. Not only was she not bad, but good, pure, innocent above all innocence in the world—the innocence of lonely girlhood.

He saw Oldring's magnificent eyes, inquisitive, searching, softening. He saw them flare in amaze, in gladness, with love, then suddenly strain in terrible effort of will. He heard Oldring whisper and saw him sway like a log and fall. Then a million bellowing, thundering voices—gunshots of conscience, thunderbolts of remorse—dinned horribly in his ears. He had killed Bess's father. Then a rushing wind filled his ears like a moan of wind in the cliffs, a knell indeed—Oldring's knell.

He dropped to his knees and hid his face against Bess, and grasped her with the hands of a drowning man.

"My God!... My God!... Oh, Bess!... Forgive me! Never mind what I've done—what I've thought. But forgive me. I'll give you my life. I'll live for you. I'll love you. Oh, I do love you as no man ever loved a woman. I want you to know—to remember that I fought a fight for you—however blind I was. I thought—I thought—never mind what I thought—but I loved you—I asked you to marry me. Let that—let me have that to hug to my heart. Oh, Bess, I was driven! And I might have known! I could not rest nor sleep till I had this mystery solved. God! how things work out!"

"Bern, you're weak—trembling—you talk wildly," cried Bess. "You've overdone your strength. There's nothing to forgive. There's no mystery except your love for me. You have come back to me!"

And she clasped his head tenderly in her arms and pressed it closely to her throbbing breast.

CHAPTER XIX. FAY

At the home of Jane Withersteen Little Fay was climbing Lassiter's knee.

"Does oo love me?" she asked.

Lassiter, who was as serious with Fay as he was gentle and loving, assured her in earnest and elaborate speech that he was her devoted subject. Fay looked thoughtful and appeared to be debating the duplicity of men or searching for a supreme test to prove this cavalier.

"Does oo love my new muvver?" she asked, with bewildering suddenness.

Jane Withersteen laughed, and for the first time in many a day she felt a stir of her pulse and warmth in her cheek.

It was a still drowsy summer of afternoon, and the three were sitting in the shade of the wooded knoll that faced the sage-slope. Little Fay's brief spell of unhappy longing for her mother—the childish, mystic gloom—had passed, and now where Fay was there were prattle and laughter and glee. She had emerged from sorrow to be the incarnation of joy and loveliness. She had grown supernaturally sweet and beautiful. For Jane Withersteen the child was an answer to prayer, a blessing, a possession infinitely more precious than all she had lost. For Lassiter, Jane divined that little Fay had become a religion.

"Does oo love my new muvver?" repeated Fay.

Lassiter's answer to this was a modest and sincere affirmative.

"Why don't oo marry my new muvver an' be my favver?"

Of the thousands of questions put by little Fay to Lassiter this was the first he had been unable to answer.

"Fay—Fay, don't ask questions like that," said Jane.

"Why?"

"Because," replied Jane. And she found it strangely embarrassing to meet the child's gaze. It seemed to her that Fay's violet eyes looked through her with piercing wisdom.

"Oo love him, don't oo?"

"Dear child—run and play," said Jane, "but don't go too far. Don't go from this little hill."

Fay pranced off wildly, joyous over freedom that had not been granted her for weeks.

"Jane, why are children more sincere than grown-up persons?" asked Lassiter.

"Are they?"

"I reckon so. Little Fay there—she sees things as they appear on the face. An Indian does that. So does a dog. An' an Indian an' a dog are most of the time right in what they see. Mebbe a child is always right."

"Well, what does Fay see?" asked Jane.

"I reckon you know. I wonder what goes on in Fay's mind when she sees part of the truth with the wise eyes of a child, an' wantin' to know more, meets with strange falseness from you? Wait! You are false in a way, though you're the best woman I ever knew. What I want to say is this. Fay has taken you're pretendin' to—to care for me for the thing it looks on the face. An' her little formin' mind asks questions. An' the answers she gets are different from the looks of things. So she'll grow up gradually takin' on that falseness, an' be like the rest of the women, an' men, too. An' the truth of this falseness to life is proved by your appearin' to love me when you don't. Things aren't what they seem."

"Lassiter, you're right. A child should be told the absolute truth. But—is that possible? I haven't been able to do it, and all my life I've loved the truth, and I've prided myself upon being truthful. Maybe that was only egotism. I'm learning much, my friend. Some of those blinding scales have fallen from my eyes. And—and as to caring for you, I think I care a great deal. How much, how little, I couldn't say. My heart is almost broken, Lassiter. So now is not a good time to judge of affection. I can still play and be merry with Fay. I can still dream. But when I attempt serious thought I'm dazed. I don't think. I don't care any more. I don't pray!... Think of that, my friend! But in spite of my numb feeling I believe I'll rise out of all this dark agony a better woman, with greater love of man and God. I'm on the rack now; I'm senseless to all but pain, and growing dead to that. Sooner or later I shall rise out of this stupor. I'm waiting the hour."

"It'll soon come, Jane," replied Lassiter, soberly. "Then I'm afraid for you. Years are terrible things, an' for years you've been bound. Habit of years is strong as life itself. Somehow, though, I believe as you—that you'll come out of it all a finer woman. I'm waitin', too. An' I'm wonderin'—I reckon, Jane, that marriage between us is out of all human reason?"

"Lassiter!... My dear friend!... It's impossible for us to marry!"

"Why—as Fay says?" inquired Lassiter, with gentle persistence.

"Why! I never thought why. But it's not possible. I am Jane, daughter of Withersteen. My father would rise out of his grave. I'm of Mormon birth. I'm being broken. But I'm still a Mormon woman. And you—you are Lassiter!"

"Mebbe I'm not so much Lassiter as I used to be."

"What was it you said? Habit of years is strong as life itself! You can't change the one habit—the purpose of your life. For you still pack those black guns! You still nurse your passion for blood."

A smile, like a shadow, flickered across his face.

"No."

"Lassiter, I lied to you. But I beg of you—don't you lie to me. I've great respect for you. I believe you're softened toward most, perhaps all, my people except—But when I speak of your purpose, your hate, your guns, I have only him in mind. I don't believe you've changed."

For answer he unbuckled the heavy cartridge-belt, and laid it with the heavy, swing gun-sheaths in her lap.

"Lassiter!" Jane whispered, as she gazed from him to the black, cold guns. Without them he appeared shorn of strength, defenseless, a smaller man. Was she Delilah? Swiftly, conscious of only one motive—refusal to see this man called craven by his enemies—she rose, and with blundering fingers buckled the belt round his waist where it belonged.

"Lassiter, I am a coward."

"Come with me out of Utah—where I can put away my guns an' be a man," he said. "I reckon I'll prove it to you then! Come! You've got Black Star back, an' Night an' Bells. Let's take the racers an' little Fay, en' race out of Utah. The hosses an' the child are all you have left. Come!"

"No, no, Lassiter. I'll never leave Utah. What would I do in the world with my broken fortunes and my broken heart? I'll never leave these purple slopes I love so well."

"I reckon I ought to 've knowed that. Presently you'll be livin' down here in a hovel, en' presently Jane Withersteen will be a memory. I only wanted to have a chance to show you how a man—any man—can be better 'n he was. If we left Utah I could prove—I reckon I could prove this thing you call love. It's strange, an' hell an' heaven at once, Jane Withersteen. 'Pears to me that you've thrown away your big heart on love—love of religion an' duty an' churchmen, an' riders an' poor families an' poor children! Yet you can't see what love is—how it changes a person!... Listen, an' in tellin' you Milly Erne's story I'll show you how love changed her.

"Milly an' me was children when our family moved from Missouri to Texas, an' we growed up in Texas ways same as if we'd been born there. We had been poor, an' there we prospered. In time the little village where we went became a town, an' strangers an' new families kept movin' in. Milly was the belle them days. I can see her now, a little girl no bigger 'n a bird, an' as pretty. She had the finest eyes, dark blue-black when she was excited, an' beautiful all the time. You remember Milly's eyes! An' she had light-brown hair with streaks of gold, an' a mouth that every feller wanted to kiss.

"An' about the time Milly was the prettiest an' the sweetest, along came a young minister who began to ride some of a race with the other fellers for Milly. An' he won. Milly had always been strong on religion, an' when she met Frank Erne she went in heart an' soul for the salvation of souls. Fact was, Milly, through study of the Bible an' attendin' church an' revivals, went a little out of her head. It didn't worry the old folks none, an' the only worry to me was Milly's everlastin' prayin' an' workin' to save my soul. She never converted me, but we was the best of comrades, an' I reckon no brother an' sister ever loved each other better. Well, Frank Erne an me hit up a great friendship. He was a strappin' feller, good to look at, an' had the most pleasin' ways. His religion never bothered me, for he could hunt an' fish an' ride an' be a good feller. After buffalo once, he come pretty near to savin' my life. We got to be thick as brothers, an' he was the only man I ever seen who I thought was good enough for Milly. An' the day they were married I got drunk for the only time in my life.

"Soon after that I left home—it seems Milly was the only one who could keep me home—an' I went to the bad, as to prosperin' I saw some pretty hard life in the Pan Handle, an' then I went North. In them days Kansas an' Nebraska was as bad, come to think of it, as these days right here on the border of Utah. I got to be pretty handy with guns. An' there wasn't many riders as could beat me ridin'. An' I can say all modest-like that I never seen the white man who could track a hoss or a steer or a man with me. Afore I knowed it two years slipped by, an' all at once I got homesick, en' purled a bridle south.

"Things at home had changed. I never got over that homecomin'. Mother was dead an' in her grave. Father was a silent, broken man, killed already on his feet. Frank Erne was a ghost of his old self, through with workin', through with preachin', almost through with livin', an' Milly was gone!... It was a long time before I got the story. Father had no mind left, an' Frank Erne was afraid to talk. So I had to pick up whet 'd happened from different people.

"It 'pears that soon after I left home another preacher come to the little town. An' he an' Frank become rivals. This feller was different from Frank. He preached some other kind of religion, and he was quick an' passionate, where Frank was slow an' mild. He went after people, women specially. In looks he couldn't compare to Frank Erne, but he had power over women. He had a voice, an' he talked an' talked an' preached an' preached. Milly fell under his influence.. She became mightily interested in his religion. Frank had patience with her, as was his way, an' let her be as interested as she liked. All religions were devoted to one God, he said, an' it wouldn't hurt Milly none to study a different point of view. So the new preacher often called on Milly, an' sometimes in Frank's absence. Frank was a cattle-man between Sundays.

"Along about this time an incident come off that I couldn't get much light on. A stranger come to town, an' was seen with the preacher. This stranger was a big man with an eye like blue ice, an' a beard of gold. He had money, an' he 'peered a man of mystery, an' the town went to buzzin' when he disappeared about the same time as a young woman known to be mightily interested in the new preacher's religion. Then, presently, along comes a man from somewheres in Illinois, en' he up an' spots this preacher as a famous Mormon proselyter. That riled Frank Erne as nothin' ever before, an' from rivals they come to be bitter enemies. An' it ended in Frank goin' to the meetin'-house where Milly was listenin', en' before her en' everybody else he called that preacher—called him, well, almost as hard as Venters called Tull here sometime back. An' Frank followed up that call with a hosswhippin', en' he drove the proselyter out of town.

"People noticed, so 'twas said, that Milly's sweet disposition changed. Some said it was because she would soon become a mother, en' others said she was pinin' after the new religion. An' there was women who said right out that she was pinin' after the Mormon. Anyway, one mornin' Frank rode in from one of his trips, to find Milly gone. He had no real near neighbors—livin' a little out of town—but those who was nearest said a wagon had gone by in the night, an' they thought it stopped at her door. Well, tracks always tell, an' there was the wagon tracks an' hoss tracks an' man tracks. The news spread like wildfire that Milly had run off from her husband. Everybody but Frank believed it an' wasn't slow in tellin' why she run off. Mother had always hated that strange streak of Milly's, takin' up with the new religion as she had, an' she believed Milly ran off with the Mormon. That hastened mother's death, an' she died unforgivin'. Father wasn't the kind to bow down under disgrace or misfortune but he had surpassin' love for Milly, an' the loss of her broke him.

"From the minute I heard of Milly's disappearance I never believed she went off of her own free will. I knew Milly, an' I knew she couldn't have done that. I stayed at home awhile, tryin' to make Frank Erne talk. But if he knowed anythin' then he wouldn't tell it. So I set out to find Milly. An' I tried to get on the trail of that proselyter. I knew if I ever struck a town he'd visited that I'd get a trail. I knew, too, that nothin' short of hell would stop his proselytin'. An' I rode from town to town. I had a blind faith that somethin' was guidin' me. An' as the weeks an' months went by I growed into a strange sort of a man, I guess. Anyway, people were afraid of me. Two years after that, way over in a corner of Texas, I struck a town where my man had been. He'd jest left. People said he came to that town without a woman. I back-trailed my man through Arkansas an' Mississippi, an' the old trail got hot again in Texas. I found the town where he first went after leavin' home. An' here I got track of Milly. I found a cabin where she had given birth to her baby. There was no way to tell whether she'd been kept a prisoner or not. The feller who owned the place was a mean, silent sort of a skunk, an' as I was leavin' I jest took a chance an' left my mark on him. Then I went home again.

"It was to find I hadn't any home, no more. Father had been dead a year. Frank Erne still lived in the house where Milly had left him. I stayed with him awhile, an' I grew old watchin' him. His farm had gone to weed, his cattle had strayed or been rustled, his house weathered till it wouldn't keep out rain nor wind. An' Frank set on the porch and whittled sticks, an' day by day wasted away. There was times when he ranted about like a crazy man, but mostly he was always sittin' an' starin' with eyes that made a man curse. I figured Frank had a secret fear that I needed to know. An' when I told him I'd trailed Milly for near three years an' had got trace of her, an' saw where she'd had her baby, I thought he would drop dead at my feet. An' when he'd come round more natural-like he begged me to give up the trail. But he wouldn't explain. So I let him alone, an' watched him day en' night.

"An' I found there was one thing still precious to him, an' it was a little drawer where he kept his papers. This was in the room where he slept. An' it 'peered he seldom slept. But after bein' patient I got the contents of that drawer an' found two letters from Milly. One was a long letter written a few months after her disappearance. She had been bound an' gagged an' dragged away from her home by three men, an' she named them—Hurd, Metzger, Slack. They was strangers to her. She was taken to the little town where I found trace of her two years after. But she didn't send the letter from that town. There she was penned in. 'Peared that the proselytes, who had, of course, come on the scene, was not runnin' any risks of losin' her. She went on to say that for a time she was out of her head, an' when she got right again all that kept her alive was the baby. It was a beautiful baby, she said, an' all she thought an' dreamed of was somehow to get baby back to its father, an' then she'd thankfully lay down and die. An' the letter ended abrupt, in the middle of a sentence, en' it wasn't signed.

"The second letter was written more than two years after the first. It was from Salt Lake City. It simply said that Milly had heard her brother was on her trail. She asked Frank to tell her brother to give up the search because if he didn't she would suffer in a way too horrible to tell. She didn't beg. She just stated a fact an' made the simple request. An' she ended that letter by sayin' she would soon leave Salt Lake City with the man she had come to love, en' would never be heard of again.

"I recognized Milly's handwritin', an' I recognized her way of puttin' things. But that second letter told me of some great change in her. Ponderin' over it, I felt at last she'd either come to love that feller an' his religion, or some terrible fear made her lie an' say so. I couldn't be sure which. But, of course, I meant to find out. I'll say here, if I'd known Mormons then as I do now I'd left Milly to her fate. For mebbe she was right about what she'd suffer if I kept on her trail. But I was young an' wild them days. First I went to the town where she'd first been taken, an' I went to the place where she'd been kept. I got that skunk who owned the place, an' took him out in the woods, an' made him tell all he knowed. That wasn't much as to length, but it was pure hell's-fire in substance. This time I left him some incapacitated for any more skunk work short of hell. Then I hit the trail for Utah.

"That was fourteen years ago. I saw the incomin' of most of the Mormons. It was a wild country an' a wild time. I rode from town to town, village to village, ranch to ranch, camp to camp. I never stayed long in one place. I never had but one idea. I never rested. Four years went by, an' I knowed every trail in northern Utah. I kept on an' as time went by, an' I'd begun to grow old in my search, I had firmer, blinder faith in whatever was guidin' me. Once I read about a feller who sailed the seven seas an' traveled the world, an' he had a story to tell, an' whenever he seen the man to whom he must tell that story he knowed him on sight. I was like that, only I had a question to ask. An' always I knew the man of whom I must ask. So I never really lost the trail, though for many years it was the dimmest trail ever followed by any man.

"Then come a change in my luck. Along in Central Utah I rounded up Hurd, an' I whispered somethin' in his ear, an' watched his face, an' then throwed a gun against his bowels. An' he died with his teeth so tight shut I couldn't have pried them open with a knife. Slack an' Metzger that same year both heard me whisper the same question, an' neither would they speak a word when they lay dyin'. Long before I'd learned no man of this breed or class—or God knows what—would give up any secrets! I had to see in a man's fear of death the connections with Milly Erne's fate. An' as the years passed at long intervals I would find such a man.

"So as I drifted on the long trail down into southern Utah my name preceded me, an' I had to meet a people prepared for me, an' ready with guns. They made me a gun-man. An' that suited me. In all this time signs of the proselyter an' the giant with the blue-ice eyes an' the gold beard seemed to fade dimmer out of the trail. Only twice in ten years did I find a trace of that mysterious man who had visited the proselyter at my home village. What he had to do with Milly's fate was beyond all hope for me to learn, unless my guidin' spirit led me to him! As for the other man, I knew, as sure as I breathed en' the stars shone en' the wind blew, that I'd meet him some day.

"Eighteen years I've been on the trail. An' it led me to the last lonely villages of the Utah border. Eighteen years!... I feel pretty old now. I was only twenty when I hit that trail. Well, as I told you, back here a ways a Gentile said Jane Withersteen could tell me about Milly Erne an' show me her grave!"

The low voice ceased, and Lassiter slowly turned his sombrero round and round, and appeared to be counting the silver ornaments on the band. Jane, leaning toward him, sat as if petrified, listening intently, waiting to hear more. She could have shrieked, but power of tongue and lips were denied her. She saw only this sad, gray, passion-worn man, and she heard only the faint rustling of the leaves.

"Well, I came to Cottonwoods," went on Lassiter, "an' you showed me Milly's grave. An' though your teeth have been shut tighter 'n them of all the dead men lyin' back along that trail, jest the same you told me the secret I've lived these eighteen years to hear! Jane, I said you'd tell me without ever me askin'. I didn't need to ask my question here. The day, you remember, when that fat party throwed a gun on me in your court, an'—"

"Oh! Hush!" whispered Jane, blindly holding up her hands.

"I seen in your face that Dyer, now a bishop, was the proselyter who ruined Milly Erne."

For an instant Jane Withersteen's brain was a whirling chaos and she recovered to find herself grasping at Lassiter like one drowning. And as if by a lightning stroke she sprang from her dull apathy into exquisite torture.

"It's a lie! Lassiter! No, no!" she moaned. "I swear—you're wrong!"

"Stop! You'd perjure yourself! But I'll spare you that. You poor woman! Still blind! Still faithful!... Listen. I know. Let that settle it. An' I give up my purpose!"

"What is it—you say?"

"I give up my purpose. I've come to see an' feel differently. I can't help poor Milly. An' I've outgrowed revenge. I've come to see I can be no judge for men. I can't kill a man jest for hate. Hate ain't the same with me since I loved you and little Fay."

"Lassiter! You mean you won't kill him?" Jane whispered.

"No."

"For my sake?"

"I reckon. I can't understand, but I'll respect your feelin's."

"Because you—oh, because you love me?... Eighteen years! You were that terrible Lassiter! And now—because you love me?"

"That's it, Jane."

"Oh, you'll make me love you! How can I help but love you? My heart must be stone. But—oh, Lassiter, wait, wait! Give me time. I'm not what I was. Once it was so easy to love. Now it's easy to hate. Wait! My faith in God—some God—still lives. By it I see happier times for you, poor passion-swayed wanderer! For me—a miserable, broken woman. I loved your sister Milly. I will love you. I can't have fallen so low—I can't be so abandoned by God—that I've no love left to give you. Wait! Let us forget Milly's sad life. Ah, I knew it as no one else on earth! There's one thing I shall tell you—if you are at my death-bed, but I can't speak now."

"I reckon I don't want to hear no more," said Lassiter.

Jane leaned against him, as if some pent-up force had rent its way out, she fell into a paroxysm of weeping. Lassiter held her in silent sympathy. By degrees she regained composure, and she was rising, sensible of being relieved of a weighty burden, when a sudden start on Lassiter's part alarmed her.

"I heard hosses—hosses with muffled hoofs!" he said; and he got up guardedly.

"Where's Fay?" asked Jane, hurriedly glancing round the shady knoll. The bright-haired child, who had appeared to be close all the time, was not in sight.

"Fay!" called Jane.

No answering shout of glee. No patter of flying feet. Jane saw Lassiter stiffen.

"Fay—oh—Fay!" Jane almost screamed.

The leaves quivered and rustled; a lonesome cricket chirped in the grass, a bee hummed by. The silence of the waning afternoon breathed hateful portent. It terrified Jane. When had silence been so infernal?

"She's—only—strayed—out—of earshot," faltered Jane, looking at Lassiter.

Pale, rigid as a statue, the rider stood, not in listening, searching posture, but in one of doomed certainty. Suddenly he grasped Jane with an iron hand, and, turning his face from her gaze, he strode with her from the knoll.

"See—Fay played here last—a house of stones an' sticks.... An' here's a corral of pebbles with leaves for hosses," said Lassiter, stridently, and pointed to the ground. "Back an' forth she trailed here.... See, she's buried somethin'—a dead grasshopper—there's a tombstone... here she went, chasin' a lizard—see the tiny streaked trail... she pulled bark off this cottonwood... look in the dust of the path—the letters you taught her—she's drawn pictures of birds en' hosses an' people.... Look, a cross! Oh, Jane, your cross!"

Lassiter dragged Jane on, and as if from a book read the meaning of little Fay's trail. All the way down the knoll, through the shrubbery, round and round a cottonwood, Fay's vagrant fancy left records of her sweet musings and innocent play.

CHAPTER XIX. FAY

Long had she lingered round a bird-nest to leave therein the gaudy wing of a butterfly. Long had she played beside the running stream sending adrift vessels freighted with pebbly cargo. Then she had wandered through the deep grass, her tiny feet scarcely turning a fragile blade, and she had dreamed beside some old faded flowers. Thus her steps led her into the broad lane. The little dimpled imprints of her bare feet showed clean-cut in the dust they went a little way down the lane; and then, at a point where they stopped, the great tracks of a man led out from the shrubbery and returned.

CHAPTER XX. LASSITER'S WAY

Footprints told the story of little Fay's abduction. In anguish Jane Withersteen turned speechlessly to Lassiter, and, confirming her fears, she saw him gray-faced, aged all in a moment, stricken as if by a mortal blow.

Then all her life seemed to fall about her in wreck and ruin.

"It's all over," she heard her voice whisper. "It's ended. I'm going—I'm going—"

"Where?" demanded Lassiter, suddenly looming darkly over her.

"To—to those cruel men—"

"Speak names!" thundered Lassiter.

"To Bishop Dyer—to Tull," went on Jane, shocked into obedience.

"Well—what for?"

"I want little Fay. I can't live without her. They've stolen her as they stole Milly Erne's child. I must have little Fay. I want only her. I give up. I'll go and tell Bishop Dyer—I'm broken. I'll tell him I'm ready for the yoke—only give me back Fay—and—and I'll marry Tull!"

"Never!" hissed Lassiter.

His long arm leaped at her. Almost running, he dragged her under the cottonwoods, across the court, into the huge hall of Withersteen House, and he shut the door with a force that jarred the heavy walls. Black Star and Night and Bells, since their return, had been locked in this hall, and now they stamped on the stone floor.

Lassiter released Jane and like a dizzy man swayed from her with a hoarse cry and leaned shaking against a table where he kept his rider's accoutrements. He began to fumble in his saddlebags. His action brought a clinking, metallic sound—the rattling of gun-cartridges. His fingers trembled as he slipped cartridges into an extra belt. But as he buckled it over the one he habitually wore his hands became steady. This second belt contained two guns, smaller than the black ones swinging low, and he slipped them round so that his coat hid them. Then he fell to swift action. Jane Withersteen watched him, fascinated but uncomprehending and she saw him rapidly saddle Black Star and Night. Then he drew her into the light of the huge windows, standing over her, gripping her arm with fingers like cold steel.

"Yes, Jane, it's ended—but you're not goin' to Dyer!... I'm goin' instead!"

Looking at him—he was so terrible of aspect—she could not comprehend his words. Who was this man with the face gray as death, with eyes that would have made her shriek had she the strength, with the strange, ruthlessly bitter lips? Where was the gentle Lassiter? What was this presence in the hall, about him, about her—this cold, invisible presence?

"Yes, it's ended, Jane," he was saying, so awfully quiet and cool and implacable, "an' I'm goin' to make a little call. I'll lock you in here, an' when I get back have the saddle-bags full of meat an bread. An' be ready to ride!"

"Lassiter!" cried Jane.

Desperately she tried to meet his gray eyes, in vain, desperately she tried again, fought herself as feeling and thought resurged in torment, and she succeeded, and then she knew.

"No—no—no!" she wailed. "You said you'd foregone your vengeance. You promised not to kill Bishop Dyer."

"If you want to talk to me about him—leave off the Bishop. I don't understand that name, or its use."

"Oh, hadn't you foregone your vengeance on—on Dyer?

"Yes."

"But—your actions—your words—your guns—your terrible looks!... They don't seem foregoing vengeance?"

"Jane, now it's justice."

"You'll—kill him?"

"If God lets me live another hour! If not God—then the devil who drives me!"

"You'll kill him—for yourself—for your vengeful hate?"

"No!"

"For Milly Erne's sake?"

"No."

"For little Fay's?"

"No!"

"Oh—for whose?"

"For yours!"

"His blood on my soul!" whispered Jane, and she fell to her knees. This was the long-pending hour of fruition. And the habit of years—the religious passion of her life—leaped from lethargy, and the long months of gradual drifting to doubt were as if they had never been. "If you spill his blood it'll be on my soul—and on my father's. Listen." And she clasped his knees, and clung there as he tried to raise her. "Listen. Am I nothing to you?"

"Woman—don't trifle at words! I love you! An' I'll soon prove it."

"I'll give myself to you—I'll ride away with you—marry you, if only you'll spare him?"

His answer was a cold, ringing, terrible laugh.

"Lassiter—I'll love you. Spare him!"

"No."

She sprang up in despairing, breaking spirit, and encircled his neck with her arms, and held him in an embrace that he strove vainly to loosen. "Lassiter, would you kill me? I'm fighting my last fight for the principles of my youth—love of religion, love of father. You don't know—you can't guess the truth, and I can't speak ill. I'm losing all. I'm changing. All I've gone through is nothing to this hour. Pity me—help me in my weakness. You're strong again—oh, so cruelly, coldly strong! You're killing me. I see you—feel you as some other Lassiter! My master, be merciful—spare him!"

His answer was a ruthless smile.

She clung the closer to him, and leaned her panting breast on him, and lifted her face to his. "Lassiter, I do love you! It's leaped out of my agony. It comes suddenly with a terrible blow of truth. You are a man! I never knew it till now. Some wonderful change came to me when you buckled on these guns and showed that gray, awful face. I loved you then. All my life I've loved, but never as now. No woman can love like a broken woman. If it were not for one thing—just one thing—and yet! I can't speak it—I'd glory in your manhood—the lion in you that means to slay for me. Believe me—and spare Dyer. Be merciful—great as it's in you to be great.... Oh, listen and believe—I have nothing, but I'm a woman—a beautiful woman, Lassiter—a passionate, loving woman—and I love you! Take me—hide me in some wild place—and love me and mend my broken heart. Spare him and take me away."

She lifted her face closer and closer to his, until their lips nearly touched, and she hung upon his neck, and with strength almost spent pressed and still pressed her palpitating body to his.

"Kiss me!" she whispered, blindly.

"No—not at your price!" he answered. His voice had changed or she had lost clearness of hearing.

"Kiss me!... Are you a man? Kiss me and save me!"

"Jane, you never played fair with me. But now you're blisterin' your lips—blackenin' your soul with lies!"

"By the memory of my mother—by my Bible—no! No, I have no Bible! But by my hope of heaven I swear I love you!"

Lassiter's gray lips formed soundless words that meant even her love could not avail to bend his will. As if the hold of her arms was that of a child's he loosened it and stepped away.

"Wait! Don't go! Oh, hear a last word!... May a more just and merciful God than the God I was taught to worship judge me—forgive me—save me! For I can no longer keep silent!... Lassiter, in pleading for Dyer I've been pleading more for my father. My father was a Mormon master, close to the leaders of the church. It was my father who sent Dyer out to proselyte. It was my father who had the blue-ice eye and the beard of gold. It was my father you got trace of in the past years. Truly, Dyer ruined Milly Erne—dragged her from her home—to Utah—to Cottonwoods. But it was for my father! If Milly Erne was ever wife of a Mormon that Mormon was my father! I never knew—never will know whether or not she was a wife. Blind I may be, Lassiter—fanatically faithful to a false religion I may have been but I know justice, and my father is beyond human justice. Surely he is meeting just punishment—somewhere. Always it has appalled me—the thought of your killing Dyer for my father's sins. So I have prayed!"

"Jane, the past is dead. In my love for you I forgot the past. This thing I'm about to do ain't for myself or Milly or Fay. It's not because of anythin' that ever happened in the past, but for what is happenin' right now. It's for you!... An' listen. Since I was a boy I've never thanked God for anythin'. If there is a God—an' I've come to believe it—I thank Him now for the years that made me Lassiter!... I can reach down en' feel these big guns, en' know what I can do with them. An', Jane, only one of the miracles Dyer professes to believe in can save him!"

Again for Jane Withersteen came the spinning of her brain in darkness, and as she whirled in endless chaos she seemed to be falling at the feet of a luminous figure—a man—Lassiter—who had saved her from herself, who could not be changed, who would slay rightfully. Then she slipped into utter blackness.

When she recovered from her faint she became aware that she was lying on a couch near the window in her sitting-room. Her brow felt damp and cold and wet, some one was chafing her hands; she recognized Judkins, and then saw that his lean, hard face wore the hue and look of excessive agitation.

"Judkins!" Her voice broke weakly.

"Aw, Miss Withersteen, you're comin' round fine. Now jest lay still a little. You're all right; everythin's all right."

"Where is—he?"

"Who?"

"Lassiter!"

"You needn't worry none about him."

"Where is he? Tell me—instantly."

"Wal, he's in the other room patchin' up a few triflin' bullet holes."

"Ah!... Bishop' Dyer?"

"When I seen him last—a matter of half an hour ago, he was on his knees. He was some busy, but he wasn't prayin'!"

"How strangely you talk! I'll sit up. I'm—well, strong again. Tell me. Dyer on his knees! What was he doing?"

"Wal, beggin' your pardon fer blunt talk, Miss Withersteen, Dyer was on his knees an' not prayin'. You remember his big, broad hands? You've seen 'em raised in blessin' over old gray men an' little curly-headed children like—like Fay Larkin! Come to think of thet, I disremember ever hearin' of his liftin' his big hands in blessin' over a woman. Wal, when I seen him last—jest a little while ago—he was on his knees, not prayin', as I remarked—an' he was pressin' his big hands over some bigger wounds."

"Man, you drive me mad! Did Lassiter kill Dyer?"

"Yes."

"Did he kill Tull?"

"No. Tull's out of the village with most of his riders. He's expected back before evenin'. Lassiter will hev to git away before Tull en' his riders come in. It's sure death fer him here. An' wuss fer you, too, Miss Withersteen. There'll be some of an uprisin' when Tull gits back."

"I shall ride away with Lassiter. Judkins, tell me all you saw—all you know about this killing." She realized, without wonder or amaze, how Judkins's one word, affirming the death of Dyer—that the catastrophe had fallen—had completed the change whereby she had been molded or beaten or broken into another woman. She felt calm, slightly cold, strong as she had not been strong since the first shadow fell upon her.

"I jest saw about all of it, Miss Withersteen, an' I'll be glad to tell you if you'll only hev patience with me," said Judkins, earnestly. "You see, I've been pecooliarly interested, an' nat'rully I'm some excited. An' I talk a lot thet mebbe ain't necessary, but I can't help thet.

"I was at the meetin'-house where Dyer was holdin' court. You know he allus acts as magistrate an' judge when Tull's away. An' the trial was fer tryin' what's left of my boy riders—thet helped me hold your cattle—fer a lot of hatched-up things the boys never did. We're used to thet, an' the boys wouldn't hev minded bein' locked up fer a while, or hevin' to dig ditches, or whatever the judge laid down. You see, I divided the gold you give me among all my boys, an' they all hid it, en' they all feel rich. Howsomever, court was adjourned before the judge passed sentence. Yes, ma'm, court was adjourned some strange an' quick, much as if lightnin' hed struck the meetin'-house.

"I hed trouble attendin' the trial, but I got in. There was a good many people there, all my boys, an' Judge Dyer with his several clerks. Also he hed with him the five riders who've been guardin' him pretty close of late. They was Carter, Wright, Jengessen, an' two new riders from Stone Bridge. I didn't hear their names, but I heard they was handy men with guns an' they looked more like rustlers than riders. Anyway, there they was, the five all in a row.

"Judge Dyer was tellin' Willie Kern, one of my best an' steadiest boys—Dyer was tellin' him how there was a ditch opened near Willie's home lettin' water through his lot, where it hadn't ought to go. An' Willie was tryin' to git a word in to prove he wasn't at home all the day it happened—which was true, as I know—but Willie couldn't git a word in, an' then Judge Dyer went on layin' down the law. An' all to onct he happened to look down the long room. An' if ever any man turned to stone he was thet man.

"Nat'rully I looked back to see what hed acted so powerful strange on the judge. An' there, half-way up the room, in the middle of the wide aisle, stood Lassiter! All white an' black he looked, an' I can't think of anythin' he resembled, onless it's death. Venters made thet same room some still an' chilly when he called Tull; but this was different. I give my word, Miss Withersteen, thet I went cold to my very marrow. I don't know why. But Lassiter had a way about him thet's awful. He spoke a word—a name—I couldn't understand it, though he spoke clear as a bell. I was too excited, mebbe. Judge Dyer must hev understood it, an' a lot more thet was mystery to me, for he pitched forrard out of his chair right onto the platform.

"Then them five riders, Dyer's bodyguards, they jumped up, an' two of them thet I found out afterward were the strangers from Stone Bridge, they piled right out of a winder, so quick you couldn't catch your breath. It was plain they wasn't Mormons.

"Jengessen, Carter, an' Wright eyed Lassiter, for what must hev been a second an' seemed like an hour, an' they went white en' strung. But they didn't weaken nor lose their nerve.

"I hed a good look at Lassiter. He stood sort of stiff, bendin' a little, an' both his arms were crooked an' his hands looked like a hawk's claws. But there ain't no tellin' how his eyes looked. I know this, though, an' thet is his eyes could read the mind of any man about to throw a gun. An' in watchin' him, of course, I couldn't see the three men go fer their guns. An' though I was lookin' right at Lassiter—lookin' hard—I couldn't see how he drawed. He was quicker 'n eyesight—thet's all. But I seen the red spurtin' of his guns, en' heard his shots jest the very littlest instant before I heard the shots of the riders. An' when I turned, Wright an' Carter was down, en' Jengessen, who's tough like a steer, was pullin' the trigger of a wabblin' gun. But it was plain he was shot through, plumb center. An' sudden he fell with a crash, an' his gun clattered on the floor.

"Then there was a hell of a silence. Nobody breathed. Sartin I didn't, anyway. I saw Lassiter slip a smokin' gun back in a belt. But he hadn't throwed either of the big black guns, an' I thought thet strange. An' all this was happenin' quick—you can't imagine how quick.

"There come a scrapin' on the floor an' Dyer got up, his face like lead. I wanted to watch Lassiter, but Dyer's face, onct I seen it like thet, glued my eyes. I seen him go fer his gun—why, I could hev done better, quicker—an' then there was a thunderin' shot from Lassiter, an' it hit Dyer's right arm, an' his gun went off as it dropped. He looked at Lassiter like a cornered sage-wolf, an' sort of howled, an' reached down fer his gun. He'd jest picked it off the floor an' was raisin' it when another thunderin' shot almost tore thet arm off—so it seemed to me. The gun dropped again an' he went down on his knees, kind of flounderin' after it. It was some strange an' terrible to see his awful earnestness. Why would such a man cling so to life? Anyway, he got the gun with left hand an' was raisin' it, pullin' trigger in his madness, when the third thunderin' shot hit his left arm, an' he dropped the gun again. But thet left arm wasn't useless yet, fer he grabbed up the gun, an' with a shakin' aim thet would hev been pitiful to me—in any other man—he began to shoot. One wild bullet struck a man twenty feet from Lassiter. An' it killed thet man, as I seen afterward. Then come a bunch of thunderin' shots—nine I calkilated after, fer they come so quick I couldn't count them—an' I knew Lassiter hed turned the black guns loose on Dyer.

"I'm tellin' you straight, Miss Withersteen, fer I want you to know. Afterward you'll git over it. I've seen some soul-rackin' scenes on this Utah border, but this was the awfulest. I remember I closed my eyes, an' fer a minute I thought of the strangest things, out of place there, such as you'd never dream would come to mind. I saw the sage, an' runnin' hosses—an' thet's the beautfulest sight to me—an' I saw dim things in the dark, an' there was a kind of hummin' in my ears. An' I remember distinctly—fer it was what made all these things whirl out of my mind an' opened my eyes—I remember distinctly it was the smell of gunpowder.

"The court had about adjourned fer thet judge. He was on his knees, en' he wasn't prayin'. He was gaspin' an' tryin' to press his big, floppin', crippled hands over his body. Lassiter had sent all those last thunderin' shots through his body. Thet was Lassiter's way.

"An' Lassiter spoke, en' if I ever forgit his words I'll never forgit the sound of his voice.

"'Proselyter, I reckon you'd better call quick on thet God who reveals Hisself to you on earth, because He won't be visitin' the place you're goin' to!"

"An' then I seen Dyer look at his big, hangin' hands thet wasn't big enough fer the last work he set them to. An' he looked up at Lassiter. An' then he stared horrible at somethin' thet wasn't Lassiter, nor anyone there, nor the room, nor the branches of purple sage peepin' into the winder. Whatever he seen, it was with the look of a man who discovers somethin' too late. Thet's a terrible look!... An' with a horrible understandin' cry he slid forrard on his face."

Judkins paused in his narrative, breathing heavily while he wiped his perspiring brow.

"Thet's about all," he concluded. "Lassiter left the meetin'-house an' I hurried to catch up with him. He was bleedin' from three gunshots, none of them much to bother him. An' we come right up here. I found you layin' in the hall, an' I hed to work some over you."

Jane Withersteen offered up no prayer for Dyer's soul.

Lassiter's step sounded in the hall—the familiar soft, silver-clinking step—and she heard it with thrilling new emotions in which was a vague joy in her very fear of him. The door opened, and she saw him, the old Lassiter, slow, easy, gentle, cool, yet not exactly the same Lassiter. She rose, and for a moment her eyes blurred and swam in tears.

"Are you—all—all right?" she asked, tremulously.

"I reckon."

"Lassiter, I'll ride away with you. Hide me till danger is past—till we are forgotten—then take me where you will. Your people shall be my people, and your God my God!"

He kissed her hand with the quaint grace and courtesy that came to him in rare moments.

"Black Star an' Night are ready," he said, simply.

His quiet mention of the black racers spurred Jane to action. Hurrying to her room, she changed to her rider's suit, packed her jewelry, and the gold that was left, and all the woman's apparel for which there was space in the saddle-bags, and then returned to the hall. Black Star stamped his iron-shod hoofs and tossed his beautiful head, and eyed her with knowing eyes.

"Judkins, I give Bells to you," said Jane. "I hope you will always keep him and be good to him."

Judkins mumbled thanks that he could not speak fluently, and his eyes flashed.

Lassiter strapped Jane's saddle-bags upon Black Star, and led the racers out into the court.

"Judkins, you ride with Jane out into the sage. If you see any riders comin' shout quick twice. An', Jane, don't look back! I'll catch up soon. We'll get to the break into the Pass before midnight, an' then wait until mornin' to go down."

Black Star bent his graceful neck and bowed his noble head, and his broad shoulders yielded as he knelt for Jane to mount.

She rode out of the court beside Judkins, through the grove, across the wide lane into the sage, and she realized that she was leaving Withersteen House forever, and she did not look back. A strange, dreamy, calm peace pervaded her soul. Her doom had fallen upon her, but, instead of finding life no longer worth living she found it doubly significant, full of sweetness as the western breeze, beautiful and unknown as the sage-slope stretching its purple sunset shadows before her. She became aware of Judkins's hand touching hers; she heard him speak a husky good-by; then into the place of Bells shot the dead-black, keen, racy nose of Night, and she knew Lassiter rode beside her.

"Don't—look—back!" he said, and his voice, too, was not clear.

Facing straight ahead, seeing only the waving, shadowy sage, Jane held out her gauntleted hand, to feel it enclosed in strong clasp. So she rode on without a backward glance at the beautiful grove of Cottonwoods. She did not seem to think of the past of what she left forever, but of the color and mystery and wildness of the sage-slope leading down to Deception Pass, and of the future. She watched the shadows lengthen down the slope; she felt the cool west wind sweeping by from the rear; and she wondered at low, yellow clouds sailing swiftly over her and beyond.

"Don't look—back!" said Lassiter.

Thick-driving belts of smoke traveled by on the wind, and with it came a strong, pungent odor of burning wood.

Lassiter had fired Withersteen House! But Jane did not look back.

A misty veil obscured the clear, searching gaze she had kept steadfastly upon the purple slope and the dim lines of canyons. It passed, as passed the rolling clouds of smoke, and she saw the valley deepening into the shades of twilight. Night came on, swift as the fleet racers, and stars peeped out to brighten and grow, and the huge, windy, eastern heave of sage-level paled under a rising moon and turned to silver. Blanched in moonlight, the sage yet seemed to hold its hue of purple and was infinitely more wild and lonely. So the night hours wore on, and Jane Withersteen never once looked back.

CHAPTER XXI. BLACK STAR AND NIGHT

The time had come for Venters and Bess to leave their retreat. They were at great pains to choose the few things they would be able to carry with them on the journey out of Utah.

"Bern, whatever kind of a pack's this, anyhow?" questioned Bess, rising from her work with reddened face.

Venters, absorbed in his own task, did not look up at all, and in reply said he had brought so much from Cottonwoods that he did not recollect the half of it.

"A woman packed this!" Bess exclaimed.

He scarcely caught her meaning, but the peculiar tone of her voice caused him instantly to rise, and he saw Bess on her knees before an open pack which he recognized as the one given him by Jane.

"By George!" he ejaculated, guiltily, and then at sight of Bess's face he laughed outright.

"A woman packed this," she repeated, fixing woeful, tragic eyes on him.

"Well, is that a crime?'

"There—there is a woman, after all!"

"Now Bess—"

"You've lied to me!"

Then and there Venters found it imperative to postpone work for the present. All her life Bess had been isolated, but she had inherited certain elements of the eternal feminine.

"But there was a woman and you did lie to me," she kept repeating, after he had explained.

"What of that? Bess, I'll get angry at you in a moment. Remember you've been pent up all your life. I venture to say that if you'd been out in the world you'd have had a dozen sweethearts and have told many a lie before this."

"I wouldn't anything of the kind," declared Bess, indignantly.

"Well—perhaps not lie. But you'd have had the sweethearts—You couldn't have helped that—being so pretty."

This remark appeared to be a very clever and fortunate one; and the work of selecting and then of stowing all the packs in the cave went on without further interruption.

CHAPTER XXI. BLACK STAR AND NIGHT

Venters closed up the opening of the cave with a thatch of willows and aspens, so that not even a bird or a rat could get in to the sacks of grain. And this work was in order with the precaution habitually observed by him. He might not be able to get out of Utah, and have to return to the valley. But he owed it to Bess to make the attempt, and in case they were compelled to turn back he wanted to find that fine store of food and grain intact. The outfit of implements and utensils he packed away in another cave.

"Bess, we have enough to live here all our lives," he said once, dreamily.

"Shall I go roll Balancing Rock?" she asked, in light speech, but with deep-blue fire in her eyes.

"No—no."

"Ah, you don't forget the gold and the world," she sighed.

"Child, you forget the beautiful dresses and the travel—and everything."

"Oh, I want to go. But I want to stay!"

"I feel the same way."

They let the eight calves out of the corral, and kept only two of the burros Venters had brought from Cottonwoods. These they intended to ride. Bess freed all her pets—the quail and rabbits and foxes.

The last sunset and twilight and night were both the sweetest and saddest they had ever spent in Surprise Valley. Morning brought keen exhilaration and excitement. When Venters had saddled the two burros, strapped on the light packs and the two canteens, the sunlight was dispersing the lazy shadows from the valley. Taking a last look at the caves and the silver spruces, Venters and Bess made a reluctant start, leading the burros. Ring and Whitie looked keen and knowing. Something seemed to drag at Venters's feet and he noticed Bess lagged behind. Never had the climb from terrace to bridge appeared so long.

Not till they reached the opening of the gorge did they stop to rest and take one last look at the valley. The tremendous arch of stone curved clear and sharp in outline against the morning sky. And through it streaked the golden shaft. The valley seemed an enchanted circle of glorious veils of gold and wraiths of white and silver haze and dim, blue, moving shade—beautiful and wild and unreal as a dream.

"We—we can—th—think of it—always—re—remember," sobbed Bess.

"Hush! Don't cry. Our valley has only fitted us for a better life somewhere. Come!"

They entered the gorge and he closed the willow gate. From rosy, golden morning light they passed into cool, dense gloom. The burros pattered up the trail with little hollow-cracking steps. And the gorge widened to narrow outlet and the gloom lightened to gray. At the divide they halted for another rest. Venters's keen, remembering gaze searched Balancing Rock, and the long incline, and the cracked toppling walls, but failed to note the slightest change.

The dogs led the descent; then came Bess leading her burro; then Venters leading his. Bess kept her eyes bent downward. Venters, however, had an irresistible desire to look upward at Balancing Rock. It had always haunted him, and now he wondered if he were really to get through the outlet before the huge stone thundered down. He fancied that would be a miracle. Every few steps he answered to the strange, nervous fear and turned to make sure the rock still stood like a giant statue. And, as he descended, it grew dimmer in his sight. It changed form; it swayed it nodded darkly; and at last, in his heightened fancy, he saw it heave and roll. As in a dream when he felt himself falling yet knew he would never fall, so he saw this long-standing thunderbolt of the little stone-men plunge down to close forever the outlet to Deception Pass.

And while he was giving way to unaccountable dread imaginations the descent was accomplished without mishap.

"I'm glad that's over," he said, breathing more freely. "I hope I'm by that hanging rock for good and all. Since almost the moment I first saw it I've had an idea that it was waiting for me. Now, when it does fall, if I'm thousands of miles away, I'll hear it."

With the first glimpses of the smooth slope leading down to the grotesque cedars and out to the Pass, Venters's cool nerve returned. One long survey to the left, then one to the right, satisfied his caution. Leading the burros down to the spur of rock, he halted at the steep incline.

"Bess, here's the bad place, the place I told you about, with the cut steps. You start down, leading your burro. Take your time and hold on to him if you slip. I've got a rope on him and a half-hitch on this point of rock, so I can let him down safely. Coming up here was a killing job. But it'll be easy going down."

Both burros passed down the difficult stairs cut by the cliff-dwellers, and did it without a misstep. After that the descent down the slope and over the mile of scrawled, ripped, and ridged rock required only careful guidance, and Venters got the burros to level ground in a condition that caused him to congratulate himself.

"Oh, if we only had Wrangle!" exclaimed Venters. "But we're lucky. That's the worst of our trail passed. We've only men to fear now. If we get up in the sage we can hide and slip along like coyotes."

They mounted and rode west through the valley and entered the canyon. From time to time Venters walked, leading his burro. When they got by all the canyons and gullies opening into the Pass they went faster and with fewer halts. Venters did not confide in Bess the alarming fact that he had seen horses and smoke less than a mile up one of the intersecting canyons. He did not talk at all. And long after he had passed this canyon and felt secure once more in the certainty that they had been unobserved he never relaxed his watchfulness. But he did not walk any more, and he kept the burros at a steady trot. Night fell before they reached the last water in the Pass and they made camp by starlight. Venters did not want the burros to stray, so he tied them with long halters in the grass near the spring. Bess, tired out and silent, laid her head in a saddle and went to sleep between the two dogs. Venters did not close his eyes. The canyon silence appeared full of the low, continuous hum of insects. He listened until the hum grew into a roar, and then, breaking the spell, once more he heard it low and clear. He watched the stars and the moving shadows, and always his glance returned to the girl's dimly pale face.

And he remembered how white and still it had once looked in the starlight. And again stern thought fought his strange fancies. Would all his labor and his love be for naught? Would he lose her, after all? What did the dark shadow around her portend? Did calamity lurk on that long upland trail through the sage? Why should his heart swell and throb with nameless fear? He listened to the silence and told himself that in the broad light of day he could dispel this leaden-weighted dread.

At the first hint of gray over the eastern rim he awoke Bess, saddled the burros, and began the day's travel. He wanted to get out of the Pass before there was any chance of riders coming down. They gained the break as the first red rays of the rising sun colored the rim.

For once, so eager was he to get up to level ground, he did not send Ring or Whitie in advance. Encouraging Bess to hurry pulling at his patient, plodding burro, he climbed the soft, steep trail.

Brighter and brighter grew the light. He mounted the last broken edge of rim to have the sun-fired, purple sage-slope burst upon him as a glory. Bess panted up to his side, tugging on the halter of her burro.

"We're up!" he cried, joyously. "There's not a dot on the sage. We're safe. We'll not be seen! Oh, Bess—"

Ring growled and sniffed the keen air and bristled. Venters clutched at his rifle. Whitie sometimes made a mistake, but Ring never. The dull thud of hoofs almost deprived Venters of power to turn and see from where disaster threatened. He felt his eyes dilate as he stared at Lassiter leading Black Star and Night out of the sage, with Jane Withersteen, in rider's costume, close beside them.

For an instant Venters felt himself whirl dizzily in the center of vast circles of sage. He recovered partially, enough to see Lassiter standing with a glad smile and Jane riveted in astonishment.

"Why, Bern!" she exclaimed. "How good it is to see you! We're riding away, you see. The storm burst—and I'm a ruined woman!... I thought you were alone."

Venters, unable to speak for consternation, and bewildered out of all sense of what he ought or ought not to do, simply stared at Jane.

"Son, where are you bound for?" asked Lassiter.

"Not safe—where I was. I'm—we're going out of Utah—back East," he found tongue to say.

"I reckon this meetin's the luckiest thing that ever happened to you an' to me—an' to Jane—an' to Bess," said Lassiter, coolly.

"Bess!" cried Jane, with a sudden leap of blood to her pale cheek.

It was entirely beyond Venters to see any luck in that meeting.

Jane Withersteen took one flashing, woman's glance at Bess's scarlet face, at her slender, shapely form.

"Venters! is this a girl—a woman?" she questioned, in a voice that stung.

"Yes."

"Did you have her in that wonderful valley?"

"Yes, but Jane—"

"All the time you were gone?"

"Yes, but I couldn't tell—"

"Was it for her you asked me to give you supplies? Was it for her that you wanted to make your valley a paradise?"

"Oh—Jane—"

"Answer me."

"Yes."

"Oh, you liar!" And with these passionate words Jane Withersteen succumbed to fury. For the second time in her life she fell into the ungovernable rage that had been her father's weakness. And it was worse than his, for she was a jealous woman—jealous even of her friends.

As best he could, he bore the brunt of her anger. It was not only his deceit to her that she visited upon him, but her betrayal by religion, by life itself.

Her passion, like fire at white heat, consumed itself in little time. Her physical strength failed, and still her spirit attempted to go on in magnificent denunciation of those who had wronged her. Like a tree cut deep into its roots, she began to quiver and shake, and her anger weakened into despair. And her ringing voice sank into a broken, husky whisper. Then, spent and pitiable, upheld by Lassiter's arm, she turned and hid her face in Black Star's mane.

Numb as Venters was when at length Jane Withersteen lifted her head and looked at him, he yet suffered a pang.

"Jane, the girl is innocent!" he cried.

"Can you expect me to believe that?" she asked, with weary, bitter eyes.

"I'm not that kind of a liar. And you know it. If I lied—if I kept silent when honor should have made me speak, it was to spare you. I came to Cottonwoods to tell you. But I couldn't add to your pain. I intended to tell you I had come to love this girl. But, Jane I hadn't forgotten how good you were to me. I haven't changed at all toward you. I prize your friendship as I always have. But, however it may look to you—don't be unjust. The girl is innocent. Ask Lassiter."

"Jane, she's jest as sweet an' innocent as little Fay," said Lassiter. There was a faint smile upon his face and a beautiful light.

Venters saw, and knew that Lassiter saw, how Jane Withersteen's tortured soul wrestled with hate and threw it—with scorn doubt, suspicion, and overcame all.

"Bern, if in my misery I accused you unjustly, I crave forgiveness," she said. "I'm not what I once was. Tell me—who is this girl?"

"Jane, she is Oldring's daughter, and his Masked Rider. Lassiter will tell you how I shot her for a rustler, saved her life—all the story. It's a strange story, Jane, as wild as the sage. But it's true—true as her innocence. That you must believe."

"Oldring's Masked Rider! Oldring's daughter!" exclaimed Jane "And she's innocent! You ask me to believe much. If this girl is—is what you say, how could she be going away with the man who killed her father?"

"Why did you tell that?" cried Venters, passionately.

CHAPTER XXI. BLACK STAR AND NIGHT

Jane's question had roused Bess out of stupefaction. Her eyes suddenly darkened and dilated. She stepped toward Venters and held up both hands as if to ward off a blow.

"Did—did you kill Oldring?"

"I did, Bess, and I hate myself for it. But you know I never dreamed he was your father. I thought he'd wronged you. I killed him when I was madly jealous."

For a moment Bess was shocked into silence.

"But he was my father!" she broke out, at last. "And now I must go back—I can't go with you. It's all over—that beautiful dream. Oh, I knew it couldn't come true. You can't take me now."

"If you forgive me, Bess, it'll all come right in the end!" implored Venters.

"It can't be right. I'll go back. After all, I loved him. He was good to me. I can't forget that."

"If you go back to Oldring's men I'll follow you, and then they'll kill me," said Venters, hoarsely.

"Oh no, Bern, you'll not come. Let me go. It's best for you to forget me. I've brought you only pain and dishonor."

She did not weep. But the sweet bloom and life died out of her face. She looked haggard and sad, all at once stunted; and her hands dropped listlessly; and her head drooped in slow, final acceptance of a hopeless fate.

"Jane, look there!" cried Venters, in despairing grief. "Need you have told her? Where was all your kindness of heart? This girl has had a wretched, lonely life. And I'd found a way to make her happy. You've killed it. You've killed something sweet and pure and hopeful, just as sure as you breathe."

"Oh, Bern! It was a slip. I never thought—I never thought!" replied Jane. "How could I tell she didn't know?"

Lassiter suddenly moved forward, and with the beautiful light on his face now strangely luminous, he looked at Jane and Venters and then let his soft, bright gaze rest on Bess.

"Well, I reckon you've all had your say, an' now it's Lassiter's turn. Why, I was jest praying for this meetin'. Bess, jest look here."

Gently he touched her arm and turned her to face the others, and then outspread his great hand to disclose a shiny, battered gold locket.

"Open it," he said, with a singularly rich voice.

Bess complied, but listlessly.

"Jane—Venters—come closer," went on Lassiter. "Take a look at the picture. Don't you know the woman?"

Jane, after one glance, drew back.

"Milly Erne!" she cried, wonderingly.

Venters, with tingling pulse, with something growing on him, recognized in the faded miniature portrait the eyes of Milly Erne.

"Yes, that's Milly," said Lassiter, softly. "Bess, did you ever see her face—look hard—with all your heart an' soul?"

"The eyes seem to haunt me," whispered Bess. "Oh, I can't remember—they're eyes of my dreams—but—but—"

Lassiter's strong arm went round her and he bent his head.

"Child, I thought you'd remember her eyes. They're the same beautiful eyes you'd see if you looked in a mirror or a clear spring. They're your mother's eyes. You are Milly Erne's child. Your name is Elizabeth Erne. You're not Oldring's daughter. You're the daughter of Frank Erne, a man once my best friend. Look! Here's his picture beside Milly's. He was handsome, an' as fine an' gallant a Southern gentleman as I ever seen. Frank came of an old family. You come of the best of blood, lass, and blood tells."

Bess slipped through his arm to her knees and hugged the locket to her bosom, and lifted wonderful, yearning eyes.

"It—can't—be—true!"

"Thank God, lass, it is true," replied Lassiter. "Jane an' Bern here—they both recognize Milly. They see Milly in you. They're so knocked out they can't tell you, that's all."

"Who are you?" whispered Bess.

"I reckon I'm Milly's brother an' your uncle!... Uncle Jim! Ain't that fine?"

"Oh, I can't believe—Don't raise me! Bern, let me kneel. I see truth in your face—in Miss Withersteen's. But let me hear it all—all on my knees. Tell me how it's true!"

"Well, Elizabeth, listen," said Lassiter. "Before you was born your father made a mortal enemy of a Mormon named Dyer. They was both ministers an' come to be rivals. Dyer stole your mother away from her home. She gave birth to you in Texas eighteen years ago. Then she was taken to Utah, from place to place, an' finally to the last border settlement—Cottonwoods. You was about three years old when you was taken away from Milly. She never knew what had become of you. But she lived a good while hopin' and prayin' to have you again. Then she gave up an' died. An' I may as well put in here your father died ten years ago. Well, I spent my time tracin' Milly, an' some months back I landed in Cottonwoods. An' jest lately I learned all about you. I had a talk with Oldrin' an' told him you was dead, an' he told me what I had so long been wantin' to know. It was Dyer, of course, who stole you from Milly. Part reason he was sore because Milly refused to give you Mormon teachin', but mostly he still hated Frank Erne so infernally that he made a deal with Oldrin' to take you an' bring you up as an infamous rustler an' rustler's girl. The idea was to break Frank Erne's heart if he ever came to Utah—to show him his daughter with a band of low rustlers. Well—Oldrin' took you, brought you up from childhood, an' then made you his Masked Rider. He made you infamous. He kept that part of the contract, but he learned to love you as a daughter an' never let any but his own men know you was a girl. I heard him say that with my own ears, an' I saw his big eyes grow dim. He told me how he had guarded you always, kept you locked up in his absence, was always at your side or near you on those rides that made you famous on the sage. He said he an' an old rustler whom he trusted had taught you how to read an' write. They selected the books for you. Dyer had wanted you brought up the vilest of the vile! An' Oldrin' brought you up the innocentest of the innocent. He said you didn't know what vileness was. I can hear his big voice tremble now as he said it. He told me how the men—rustlers an' outlaws—who from time to time tried to approach you familiarly—he told me how he shot them dead. I'm tellin' you this 'specially because you've showed such shame—sayin' you was nameless an' all that. Nothin' on earth can be wronger than that idea of yours. An' the truth of it is here. Oldrin' swore to me that if Dyer died, releasin' the contract, he intended to hunt up your father an' give you back to him. It seems Oldrin' wasn't all bad, en' he sure loved you."

Venters leaned forward in passionate remorse.

"Oh, Bess! I know Lassiter speaks the truth. For when I shot Oldring he dropped to his knees and fought with unearthly power to speak. And he said: 'Man—why—didn't—you—wait? Bess was—' Then he fell dead. And I've been haunted by his look and words. Oh, Bess, what a strange, splendid thing for Oldring to do! It all seems impossible. But, dear, you really are not what you thought."

"Elizabeth Erne!" cried Jane Withersteen. "I loved your mother and I see her in you!"

What had been incredible from the lips of men became, in the tone, look, and gesture of a woman, a wonderful truth for Bess. With little tremblings of all her slender body she rocked to and fro on her knees. The yearning wistfulness of her eyes changed to solemn splendor of joy. She believed. She was realizing happiness. And as the process of thought was slow, so were the variations of her expression. Her eyes reflected the transformation of her soul. Dark, brooding, hopeless belief—clouds of gloom—drifted, paled, vanished in glorious light. An exquisite rose flush—a glow—shone from her face as she slowly began to rise from her knees. A spirit uplifted her. All that she had held as base dropped from her.

Venters watched her in joy too deep for words. By it he divined something of what Lassiter's revelation meant to Bess, but he knew he could only faintly understand. That moment when she seemed to be lifted by some spiritual transfiguration was the most beautiful moment of his life. She stood with parted, quivering lips, with hands tightly clasping the locket to her heaving breast. A new conscious pride of worth dignified the old wild, free grace and poise.

"Uncle Jim!" she said, tremulously, with a different smile from any Venters had ever seen on her face.

Lassiter took her into his arms.

"I reckon. It's powerful fine to hear that," replied Lassiter, unsteadily.

Venters, feeling his eyes grow hot and wet, turned away, and found himself looking at Jane Withersteen. He had almost forgotten her presence. Tenderness and sympathy were fast hiding traces of her agitation. Venters read her mind—felt the reaction of her noble heart—saw the joy she was beginning to feel at the happiness of others. And suddenly blinded, choked by his emotions, he turned from her also. He knew what she would do presently; she would make some magnificent amend for her anger; she would give some manifestation of her love; probably all in a moment, as she had loved Milly Erne, so would she love Elizabeth Erne.

"'Pears to me, folks, that we'd better talk a little serious now," remarked Lassiter, at length. "Time flies."

"You're right," replied Venters, instantly. "I'd forgotten time—place—danger. Lassiter, you're riding away. Jane's leaving Withersteen House?"

"Forever," replied Jane.

"I fired Withersteen House," said Lassiter.

"Dyer?" questioned Venters, sharply.

"I reckon where Dyer's gone there won't be any kidnappin' of girls."

"Ah! I knew it. I told Judkins—And Tull?" went on Venters, passionately.

"Tull wasn't around when I broke loose. By now he's likely on our trail with his riders."

"Lassiter, you're going into the Pass to hide till all this storm blows over?"

"I reckon that's Jane's idea. I'm thinkin' the storm'll be a powerful long time blowin' over. I was comin' to join you in Surprise Valley. You'll go back now with me?"

"No. I want to take Bess out of Utah. Lassiter, Bess found gold in the valley. We've a saddle-bag full of gold. If we can reach Sterling—"

"Man! how're you ever goin' to do that? Sterlin' is a hundred miles."

"My plan is to ride on, keeping sharp lookout. Somewhere up the trail we'll take to the sage and go round Cottonwoods and then hit the trail again."

"It's a bad plan. You'll kill the burros in two days."

"Then we'll walk."

"That's more bad an' worse. Better go back down the Pass with me."

"Lassiter, this girl has been hidden all her life in that lonely place," went on Venters. "Oldring's men are hunting me. We'd not be safe there any longer. Even if we would be I'd take this chance to get her out. I want to marry her. She shall have some of the pleasures of life—see cities and people. We've gold—we'll be rich. Why, life opens sweet for both of us. And, by Heaven! I'll get her out or lose my life in the attempt!"

"I reckon if you go on with them burros you'll lose your life all right. Tull will have riders all over this sage. You can't get out on them burros. It's a fool idea. That's not doin' best by the girl. Come with me en' take chances on the rustlers."

Lassiter's cool argument made Venters waver, not in determination to go, but in hope of success.

"Bess, I want you to know. Lassiter says the trip's almost useless now. I'm afraid he's right. We've got about one chance in a hundred to go through. Shall we take it? Shall we go on?"

"We'll go on," replied Bess.

"That settles it, Lassiter."

Lassiter spread wide his hands, as if to signify he could do no more, and his face clouded.

Venters felt a touch on his elbow. Jane stood beside him with a hand on his arm. She was smiling. Something radiated from her, and like an electric current accelerated the motion of his blood.

"Bern, you'd be right to die rather than not take Elizabeth out of Utah—out of this wild country. You must do it. You'll show her the great world, with all its wonders. Think how little she has seen! Think what delight is in store for her! You have gold, You will be free; you will make her happy. What a glorious prospect! I share it with you. I'll think of you—dream of you—pray for you."

"Thank you, Jane," replied Venters, trying to steady his voice. "It does look bright. Oh, if we were only across that wide, open waste of sage!"

"Bern, the trip's as good as made. It'll be safe—easy. It'll be a glorious ride," she said, softly.

Venters stared. Had Jane's troubles made her insane? Lassiter, too, acted queerly, all at once beginning to turn his sombrero round in hands that actually shook.

"You are a rider. She is a rider. This will be the ride of your lives," added Jane, in that same soft undertone, almost as if she were musing to herself.

"Jane!" he cried.

"I give you Black Star and Night!"

"Black Star and Night!" he echoed.

"It's done. Lassiter, put our saddle-bags on the burros."

Only when Lassiter moved swiftly to execute her bidding did Venters's clogged brain grasp at literal meanings. He leaped to catch Lassiter's busy hands.

"No, no! What are you doing?" he demanded, in a kind of fury. "I won't take her racers. What do you think I am? It'd be monstrous. Lassiter! stop it, I say!... You've got her to save. You've miles and miles to go. Tull is trailing you. There are rustlers in the Pass. Give me back that saddle-bag!"

"Son—cool down," returned Lassiter, in a voice he might have used to a child. But the grip with which he tore away Venters's grasping hands was that of a giant. "Listen—you fool boy! Jane's sized up the situation. The burros'll do for us. We'll sneak along an' hide. I'll take your dogs an' your rifle. Why, it's the trick. The blacks are yours, an' sure as I can throw a gun you're goin' to ride safe out of the sage."

"Jane—stop him—please stop him," gasped Venters. "I've lost my strength. I can't do—anything. This is hell for me! Can't you see that? I've ruined you—it was through me you lost all. You've only Black Star and Night left. You love these horses. Oh! I know how you must love them now! And—you're trying to give them to me. To help me out of Utah! To save the girl I love!"

"That will be my glory."

Then in the white, rapt face, in the unfathomable eyes, Venters saw Jane Withersteen in a supreme moment. This moment was one wherein she reached up to the height for which her noble soul had ever yearned. He, after disrupting the calm tenor of her peace, after bringing down on her head the implacable hostility of her churchmen, after teaching her a bitter lesson of life—he was to be her salvation. And he turned away again, this time shaken to the core of his soul. Jane Withersteen was the incarnation of selflessness. He experienced wonder and terror, exquisite pain and rapture. What were all the shocks life had dealt him compared to the thought of such loyal and generous friendship?

And instantly, as if by some divine insight, he knew himself in the remaking—tried, found wanting; but stronger, better, surer—and he wheeled to Jane Withersteen, eager, joyous, passionate, wild, exalted. He bent to her; he left tears and kisses on her hands.

"Jane, I—I can't find words—now," he said. "I'm beyond words. Only—I understand. And I'll take the blacks."

"Don't be losin' no more time," cut in Lassiter. "I ain't certain, but I think I seen a speck up the sage-slope. Mebbe I was mistaken. But, anyway, we must all be movin'. I've shortened the stirrups on Black Star. Put Bess on him."

Jane Withersteen held out her arms.

"Elizabeth Erne!" she cried, and Bess flew to her.

How inconceivably strange and beautiful it was for Venters to see Bess clasped to Jane Withersteen's breast!

Then he leaped astride Night.

"Venters, ride straight on up the slope," Lassiter was saying, "'an if you don't meet any riders keep on till you're a few miles from the village, then cut off in the sage an' go round to the trail. But you'll most likely meet riders with Tull. Jest keep right on till you're jest out of gunshot an' then make your cut-off into the sage. They'll ride after you, but it won't be no use. You can ride, an' Bess can ride. When you're out of reach turn on round to the west, an' hit the trail somewhere. Save the hosses all you can, but don't be afraid. Black Star and Night are good for a hundred miles before sundown, if you have to push them. You can get to Sterlin' by night if you want. But better make it along about to-morrow mornin'. When you get through the notch on the Glaze trail, swing to the right. You'll be able to see both Glaze an' Stone Bridge. Keep away from them villages. You won't run no risk of meetin' any of Oldrin's rustlers from Sterlin' on. You'll find water in them deep hollows north of the Notch. There's an old trail there, not much used, en' it leads to Sterlin'. That's your trail. An' one thing more. If Tull pushes you—or keeps on persistent-like, for a few miles—jest let the blacks out an' lose him an' his riders."

"Lassiter, may we meet again!" said Venters, in a deep voice.

"Son, it ain't likely—it ain't likely. Well, Bess Oldrin'—Masked Rider—Elizabeth Erne—now you climb on Black Star. I've heard you could ride. Well, every rider loves a good horse. An', lass, there never was but one that could beat Black Star."

"Ah, Lassiter, there never was any horse that could beat Black Star," said Jane, with the old pride.

"I often wondered—mebbe Venters rode out that race when he brought back the blacks. Son, was Wrangle the best hoss?"

"No, Lassiter," replied Venters. For this lie he had his reward in Jane's quick smile.

"Well, well, my hoss-sense ain't always right. An' here I'm talkin' a lot, wastin' time. It ain't so easy to find an' lose a pretty niece all in one hour! Elizabeth—good-by!"

"Oh, Uncle Jim!... Good-by!"

"Elizabeth Erne, be happy! Good-by," said Jane.

"Good-by—oh—good-by!" In lithe, supple action Bess swung up to Black Star's saddle.

"Jane Withersteen!... Good-by!" called Venters hoarsely.

"Bern—Bess—riders of the purple sage—good-by!"

CHAPTER XXII. RIDERS OF THE PURPLE SAGE

Black Star and Night, answering to spur, swept swiftly westward along the white, slow-rising, sage-bordered trail. Venters heard a mournful howl from Ring, but Whitie was silent. The blacks settled into their fleet, long-striding gallop. The wind sweetly fanned Venters's hot face. From the summit of the first low-swelling ridge he looked back. Lassiter waved his hand; Jane waved her scarf. Venters replied by standing in his stirrups and holding high his sombrero. Then the dip of the ridge hid them. From the height of the next he turned once more. Lassiter, Jane, and the burros had disappeared. They had gone down into the Pass. Venters felt a sensation of irreparable loss.

"Bern—look!" called Bess, pointing up the long slope.

A small, dark, moving dot split the line where purple sage met blue sky. That dot was a band of riders.

"Pull the black, Bess."

They slowed from gallop to canter, then to trot. The fresh and eager horses did not like the check.

"Bern, Black Star has great eyesight."

"I wonder if they're Tull's riders. They might be rustlers. But it's all the same to us."

The black dot grew to a dark patch moving under low dust clouds. It grew all the time, though very slowly. There were long periods when it was in plain sight, and intervals when it dropped behind the sage. The blacks trotted for half an hour, for another half-hour, and still the moving patch appeared to stay on the horizon line. Gradually, however, as time passed, it began to enlarge, to creep down the slope, to encroach upon the intervening distance.

"Bess, what do you make them out?" asked Venters. "I don't think they're rustlers."

"They're sage-riders," replied Bess. "I see a white horse and several grays. Rustlers seldom ride any horses but bays and blacks."

"That white horse is Tull's. Pull the black, Bess. I'll get down and cinch up. We're in for some riding. Are you afraid?"

"Not now," answered the girl, smiling.

"You needn't be. Bess, you don't weigh enough to make Black Star know you're on him. I won't be able to stay with you. You'll leave Tull and his riders as if they were standing still."

"How about you?"

"Never fear. If I can't stay with you I can still laugh at Tull."

"Look, Bern! They've stopped on that ridge. They see us."

"Yes. But we're too far yet for them to make out who we are. They'll recognize the blacks first. We've passed most of the ridges and the thickest sage. Now, when I give the word, let Black Star go and ride!"

Venters calculated that a mile or more still intervened between them and the riders. They were approaching at a swift canter. Soon Venters recognized Tull's white horse, and concluded that the riders had likewise recognized Black Star and Night. But it would be impossible for Tull yet to see that the blacks were not ridden by Lassiter and Jane. Venters noted that Tull and the line of horsemen, perhaps ten or twelve in number, stopped several times and evidently looked hard down the slope. It must have been a puzzling circumstance for Tull. Venters laughed grimly at the thought of what Tull's rage would be when he finally discovered the trick. Venters meant to sheer out into the sage before Tull could possibly be sure who rode the blacks.

The gap closed to a distance of half a mile. Tull halted. His riders came up and formed a dark group around him. Venters thought he saw him wave his arms and was certain of it when the riders dashed into the sage, to right and left of the trail. Tull had anticipated just the move held in mind by Venters.

"Now Bess!" shouted Venters. "Strike north. Go round those riders and turn west."

Black Star sailed over the low sage, and in a few leaps got into his stride and was running. Venters spurred Night after him. It was hard going in the sage. The horses could run as well there, but keen eyesight and judgment must constantly be used by the riders in choosing ground. And continuous swerving from aisle to aisle between the brush, and leaping little washes and mounds of the pack-rats, and breaking through sage, made rough riding. When Venters had turned into a long aisle he had time to look up at Tull's riders. They were now strung out into an extended line riding northeast. And, as Venters and Bess were holding due north, this meant, if the horses of Tull and his riders had the speed and the staying power, they would head the blacks and turn them back down the slope. Tull's men were not saving their mounts; they were driving them desperately. Venters feared only an accident to Black Star or Night, and skilful riding would mitigate possibility of that. One glance ahead served to show him that Bess could pick a course through the sage as well as he. She looked neither back nor at the running riders, and bent forward over Black Star's neck and studied the ground ahead.

It struck Venters, presently, after he had glanced up from time to time, that Bess was drawing away from him as he had expected. He had, however, only thought of the light weight Black Star was carrying and of his superior speed; he saw now that the black was being ridden as never before, except when Jerry Card lost the race to Wrangle. How easily, gracefully, naturally, Bess sat her saddle! She could ride! Suddenly Venters remembered she had said she could ride. But he had not dreamed she was capable of such superb horsemanship. Then all at once, flashing over him, thrilling him, came the recollection that Bess was Oldring's Masked Rider.

He forgot Tull—the running riders—the race. He let Night have a free rein and felt him lengthen out to suit himself, knowing he would keep to Black Star's course, knowing that he had been chosen by the best rider now on the upland sage. For Jerry Card was dead. And fame had rivaled him with only one rider, and that was the slender girl who now swung so easily with Black Star's stride. Venters had abhorred her notoriety, but now he took passionate pride in her skill, her daring, her power over a horse. And he delved into his memory, recalling famous rides which he had heard related in the villages and round the camp-fires. Oldring's Masked Rider! Many times this strange rider, at once well known and unknown, had escaped pursuers by matchless riding. He had to run the gantlet of vigilantes down the main street of Stone Bridge, leaving dead horses and dead rustlers behind. He had jumped his horse over the Gerber Wash, a deep, wide ravine separating the fields of Glaze from the wild sage. He had been surrounded north of Sterling; and he had broken through the line. How often had been told the story of day stampedes, of night raids, of pursuit, and then how the Masked Rider, swift as the wind, was gone in the sage! A fleet, dark horse—a slender, dark form—a black mask—a driving run down the slope—a dot on the purple sage—a shadowy, muffled steed disappearing in the night!

And this Masked Rider of the uplands had been Elizabeth Erne!

The sweet sage wind rushed in Venters's face and sang a song in his ears. He heard the dull, rapid beat of Night's hoofs; he saw Black Star drawing away, farther and farther. He realized both horses were swinging to the west. Then gunshots in the rear reminded him of Tull. Venters looked back. Far to the side, dropping behind, trooped the riders. They were shooting. Venters saw no puffs or dust, heard no whistling bullets. He was out of range. When he looked back again Tull's riders had given up pursuit. The best they could do, no doubt, had been to get near enough to recognize who really rode the blacks. Venters saw Tull drooping in his saddle.

Then Venters pulled Night out of his running stride. Those few miles had scarcely warmed the black, but Venters wished to save him. Bess turned, and, though she was far away, Venters caught the white glint of her waving hand. He held Night to a trot and rode on, seeing Bess and Black Star, and the sloping upward stretch of sage, and from time to time the receding black riders behind. Soon they disappeared behind a ridge, and he turned no more. They would go back to Lassiter's trail and follow it, and follow in vain. So Venters rode on, with the wind growing sweeter to taste and smell, and the purple sage richer and the sky bluer in his sight; and the song in his ears ringing. By and by Bess halted to wait for him, and he knew she had come to the trail. When he reached her it was to smile at sight of her standing with arms round Black Star's neck.

"Oh, Bern! I love him!" she cried. "He's beautiful; he knows; and how he can run! I've had fast horses. But Black Star!... Wrangle never beat him!"

"I'm wondering if I didn't dream that. Bess, the blacks are grand. What it must have cost Jane—ah!—well, when we get out of this wild country with Star and Night, back to my old home in Illinois, we'll buy a beautiful farm with meadows and springs and cool shade. There we'll turn the horses free—free to roam and browse and drink—never to feel a spur again—never to be ridden!"

"I would like that," said Bess.

They rested. Then, mounting, they rode side by side up the white trail. The sun rose higher behind them. Far to the left a low line of green marked the site of Cottonwoods. Venters looked once and looked no more. Bess gazed only straight ahead. They put the blacks to the long, swinging rider's canter, and at times pulled them to a trot, and occasionally to a walk. The hours passed, the miles slipped behind, and the wall of rock loomed in the fore. The Notch opened wide. It was a rugged, stony pass, but with level and open trail, and Venters and Bess ran the blacks through it. An old trail led off to the right, taking the line of the wall, and this Venters knew to be the trail mentioned by Lassiter.

The little hamlet, Glaze, a white and green patch in the vast waste of purple, lay miles down a slope much like the Cottonwoods slope, only this descended to the west. And miles farther west a faint green spot marked the location of Stone Bridge. All the rest of that world was seemingly smooth, undulating sage, with no ragged lines of canyons to accentuate its wildness.

"Bess, we're safe—we're free!" said Venters. "We're alone on the sage. We're half way to Sterling."

"Ah! I wonder how it is with Lassiter and Miss Withersteen."

"Never fear, Bess. He'll outwit Tull. He'll get away and hide her safely. He might climb into Surprise Valley, but I don't think he'll go so far."

"Bern, will we ever find any place like our beautiful valley?"

"No. But, dear, listen. Well go back some day, after years—ten years. Then we'll be forgotten. And our valley will be just as we left it."

"What if Balancing Rock falls and closes the outlet to the Pass?"

"I've thought of that. I'll pack in ropes and ropes. And if the outlet's closed we'll climb up the cliffs and over them to the valley and go down on rope ladders. It could be done. I know just where to make the climb, and I'll never forget."

"Oh yes, let us go back!"

"It's something sweet to look forward to. Bess, it's like all the future looks to me."

"Call me—Elizabeth," she said, shyly.

"Elizabeth Erne! It's a beautiful name. But I'll never forget Bess. Do you know—have you thought that very soon—by this time to-morrow—you will be Elizabeth Venters?"

So they rode on down the old trail. And the sun sloped to the west, and a golden sheen lay on the sage. The hours sped now; the afternoon waned. Often they rested the horses. The glisten of a pool of water in a hollow caught Venters's eye, and here he unsaddled the blacks and let them roll and drink and browse. When he and Bess rode up out of the hollow the sun was low, a crimson ball, and the valley seemed veiled in purple fire and smoke. It was that short time when the sun appeared to rest before setting, and silence, like a cloak of invisible life, lay heavy on all that shimmering world of sage.

They watched the sun begin to bury its red curve under the dark horizon.

"We'll ride on till late," he said. "Then you can sleep a little, while I watch and graze the horses. And we'll ride into Sterling early to-morrow. We'll be married!... We'll be in time to catch the stage. We'll tie Black Star and Night behind—and then—for a country not wild and terrible like this!"

"Oh, Bern!... But look! The sun is setting on the sage—the last time for us till we dare come again to the Utah border. Ten years! Oh, Bern, look, so you will never forget!"

Slumbering, fading purple fire burned over the undulating sage ridges. Long streaks and bars and shafts and spears fringed the far western slope. Drifting, golden veils mingled with low, purple shadows. Colors and shades changed in slow, wondrous transformation.

Suddenly Venters was startled by a low, rumbling roar—so low that it was like the roar in a sea-shell.

"Bess, did you hear anything?" he whispered.

"No."

"Listen!... Maybe I only imagined—Ah!"

Out of the east or north from remote distance, breathed an infinitely low, continuously long sound—deep, weird, detonating, thundering, deadening—dying.

CHAPTER XXIII. THE FALL OF BALANCING ROCK

Through tear-blurred sight Jane Withersteen watched Venters and Elizabeth Erne and the black racers disappear over the ridge of sage.

"They're gone!" said Lassiter. "An' they're safe now. An' there'll never be a day of their comin' happy lives but what they'll remember Jane Withersteen an'—an' Uncle Jim!... I reckon, Jane, we'd better be on our way."

The burros obediently wheeled and started down the break with little cautious steps, but Lassiter had to leash the whining dogs and lead them. Jane felt herself bound in a feeling that was neither listlessness nor indifference, yet which rendered her incapable of interest. She was still strong in body, but emotionally tired. That hour at the entrance to Deception Pass had been the climax of her suffering—the flood of her wrath—the last of her sacrifice—the supremity of her love—and the attainment of peace. She thought that if she had little Fay she would not ask any more of life.

Like an automaton she followed Lassiter down the steep trail of dust and bits of weathered stone; and when the little slides moved with her or piled around her knees she experienced no alarm. Vague relief came to her in the sense of being enclosed between dark stone walls, deep hidden from the glare of sun, from the glistening sage. Lassiter lengthened the stirrup straps on one of the burros and bade her mount and ride close to him. She was to keep the burro from cracking his little hard hoofs on stones. Then she was riding on between dark, gleaming walls. There were quiet and rest and coolness in this canyon. She noted indifferently that they passed close under shady, bulging shelves of cliff, through patches of grass and sage and thicket and groves of slender trees, and over white, pebbly washes, and around masses of broken rock. The burros trotted tirelessly; the dogs, once more free, pattered tirelessly; and Lassiter led on with never a stop, and at every open place he looked back. The shade under the walls gave place to sunlight. And presently they came to a dense thicket of slender trees, through which they passed to rich, green grass and water. Here Lassiter rested the burros for a little while, but he was restless, uneasy, silent, always listening, peering under the trees. She dully reflected that enemies were behind them—before them; still the thought awakened no dread or concern or interest.

At his bidding she mounted and rode on close to the heels of his burro. The canyon narrowed; the walls lifted their rugged rims higher; and the sun shone down hot from the center of the blue stream of sky above. Lassiter traveled slower, with more exceeding care as to the ground he chose, and he kept speaking low to the dogs. They were now hunting-dogs—keen, alert, suspicious, sniffing the warm breeze. The monotony of the yellow walls broke in change of color and smooth surface, and the rugged outline of rims grew craggy. Splits appeared in deep breaks, and gorges running at right angles, and then the Pass opened wide at a junction of intersecting canyons.

Lassiter dismounted, led his burro, called the dogs close, and proceeded at snail pace through dark masses of rock and dense thickets under the left wall. Long he watched and listened before venturing to cross the mouths of side canyons. At length he halted, fled his burro, lifted a warning hand to Jane, and then slipped away among the boulders, and, followed by the stealthy dogs, disappeared from sight. The time he remained absent was neither short nor long to Jane Withersteen.

When he reached her side again he was pale, and his lips were set in a hard line, and his gray eyes glittered coldly. Bidding her dismount, he led the burros into a covert of stones and cedars, and tied them.

"Jane, I've run into the fellers I've been lookin' for, an' I'm goin' after them," he said.

"Why?" she asked.

"I reckon I won't take time to tell you."

"Couldn't we slip by without being seen?"

"Likely enough. But that ain't my game. An' I'd like to know, in case I don't come back, what you'll do."

"What can I do?"

"I reckon you can go back to Tull. Or stay in the Pass an' be taken off by rustlers. Which'll you do?"

"I don't know. I can't think very well. But I believe I'd rather be taken off by rustlers."

Lassiter sat down, put his head in his hands, and remained for a few moments in what appeared to be deep and painful thought. When he lifted his face it was haggard, lined, cold as sculptured marble.

"I'll go. I only mentioned that chance of my not comin' back. I'm pretty sure to come."

"Need you risk so much? Must you fight more? Haven't you shed enough blood?"

"I'd like to tell you why I'm goin'," he continued, in coldness he had seldom used to her. She remarked it, but it was the same to her as if he had spoken with his old gentle warmth. "But I reckon I won't. Only, I'll say that mercy an' goodness, such as is in you, though they're the grand things in human nature, can't be lived up to on this Utah border. Life's hell out here. You think—or you used to think—that your religion made this life heaven. Mebbe them scales on your eyes has dropped now. Jane, I wouldn't have you no different, an' that's why I'm going to try to hide you somewhere in this Pass. I'd like to hide many more women, for I've come to see there are more like you among your people. An' I'd like you to see jest how hard an' cruel this border life is. It's bloody. You'd think churches an' churchmen would make it better. They make it worse. You give names to things—bishops, elders, ministers, Mormonism, duty, faith, glory. You dream—or you're driven mad. I'm a man, an' I know. I name fanatics, followers, blind women, oppressors, thieves, ranchers, rustlers, riders. An' we have—what you've lived through these last months. It can't be helped. But it can't last always. An' remember this—some day the border'll be better, cleaner, for the ways of ten like Lassiter!"

She saw him shake his tall form erect, look at her strangely and steadfastly, and then, noiselessly, stealthily slip away amid the rocks and trees. Ring and Whitie, not being bidden to follow, remained with Jane. She felt extreme weariness, yet somehow it did not seem to be of her body. And she sat down in the shade and tried to think. She saw a creeping lizard, cactus flowers, the drooping burros, the resting dogs, an eagle high over a yellow crag. Once the meanest flower, a color, the flight of the bee, or any living thing had given her deepest joy. Lassiter had gone off, yielding to his incurable blood lust, probably to his own death; and she was sorry, but there was no feeling in her sorrow.

Suddenly from the mouth of the canyon just beyond her rang out a clear, sharp report of a rifle. Echoes clapped. Then followed a piercingly high yell of anguish, quickly breaking. Again echoes clapped, in grim imitation. Dull revolver shots—hoarse yells—pound of hoofs—shrill neighs of horses—commingling of echoes—and again silence! Lassiter must be busily engaged, thought Jane, and no chill trembled over her, no blanching tightened her skin. Yes, the border was a bloody place. But life had always been bloody. Men were blood-spillers. Phases of the history of the world flashed through her mind—Greek and Roman wars, dark, mediaeval times, the crimes in the name of religion. On sea, on land, everywhere—shooting, stabbing, cursing, clashing, fighting men! Greed, power, oppression, fanaticism, love, hate, revenge, justice, freedom—for these, men killed one another.

She lay there under the cedars, gazing up through the delicate lacelike foliage at the blue sky, and she thought and wondered and did not care.

More rattling shots disturbed the noonday quiet. She heard a sliding of weathered rock, a hoarse shout of warning, a yell of alarm, again the clear, sharp crack of the rifle, and another cry that was a cry of death. Then rifle reports pierced a dull volley of revolver shots. Bullets whizzed over Jane's hiding-place; one struck a stone and whined away in the air. After that, for a time, succeeded desultory shots; and then they ceased under long, thundering fire from heavier guns.

Sooner or later, then, Jane heard the cracking of horses' hoofs on the stones, and the sound came nearer and nearer. Silence intervened until Lassiter's soft, jingling step assured her of his approach. When he appeared he was covered with blood.

"All right, Jane," he said. "I come back. An' don't worry."

With water from a canteen he washed the blood from his face and hands.

"Jane, hurry now. Tear my scarf in two, en' tie up these places. That hole through my hand is some inconvenient, worse 'n this at over my ear. There—you're doin' fine! Not a bit nervous—no tremblin'. I reckon I ain't done your courage justice. I'm glad you're brave jest now—you'll need to be. Well, I was hid pretty good, enough to keep them from shootin' me deep, but they was slingin' lead close all the time. I used up all the rifle shells, an' en I went after them. Mebbe you heard. It was then I got hit. Had to use up every shell in my own gun, an' they did, too, as I seen. Rustlers an' Mormons, Jane! An' now I'm packin' five bullet holes in my carcass, an' guns without shells. Hurry, now."

He unstrapped the saddle-bags from the burros, slipped the saddles and let them lie, turned the burros loose, and, calling the dogs, led the way through stones and cedars to an open where two horses stood.

"Jane, are you strong?" he asked.

"I think so. I'm not tired," Jane replied.

"I don't mean that way. Can you bear up?"

"I think I can bear anything."

"I reckon you look a little cold an' thick. So I'm preparin' you."

"For what?"

"I didn't tell you why I jest had to go after them fellers. I couldn't tell you. I believe you'd have died. But I can tell you now—if you'll bear up under a shock?"

"Go on, my friend."

"I've got little Fay! Alive—bad hurt—but she'll live!"

Jane Withersteen's dead-locked feeling, rent by Lassiter's deep, quivering voice, leaped into an agony of sensitive life.

"Here," he added, and showed her where little Fay lay on the grass.

Unable to speak, unable to stand, Jane dropped on her knees. By that long, beautiful golden hair Jane recognized the beloved Fay. But Fay's loveliness was gone. Her face was drawn and looked old with grief. But she was not dead—her heart beat—and Jane Withersteen gathered strength and lived again.

"You see I jest had to go after Fay," Lassiter was saying, as he knelt to bathe her little pale face. "But I reckon I don't want no more choices like the one I had to make. There was a crippled feller in that bunch, Jane. Mebbe Venters crippled him. Anyway, that's why they were holding up here. I seen little Fay first thing, en' was hard put to it to figure out a way to get her. An' I wanted hosses, too. I had to take chances. So I crawled close to their camp. One feller jumped a hoss with little Fay, an' when I shot him, of course she dropped. She's stunned an' bruised—she fell right on her head. Jane, she's comin' to! She ain't bad hurt!"

Fay's long lashes fluttered; her eyes opened. At first they seemed glazed over. They looked dazed by pain. Then they quickened, darkened, to shine with intelligence—bewilderment—memory—and sudden wonderful joy.

"Muvver—Jane!" she whispered.

"Oh, little Fay, little Fay!" cried Jane, lifting, clasping the child to her.

CHAPTER XXIII. THE FALL OF BALANCING ROCK

"Now, we've got to rustle!" said Lassiter, in grim coolness. "Jane, look down the Pass!"

Across the mounds of rock and sage Jane caught sight of a band of riders filing out of the narrow neck of the Pass; and in the lead was a white horse, which, even at a distance of a mile or more, she knew.

"Tull!" she almost screamed.

"I reckon. But, Jane, we've still got the game in our hands. They're ridin' tired hosses. Venters likely give them a chase. He wouldn't forget that. An' we've fresh hosses."

Hurriedly he strapped on the saddle-bags, gave quick glance to girths and cinches and stirrups, then leaped astride.

"Lift little Fay up," he said.

With shaking arms Jane complied.

"Get back your nerve, woman! This's life or death now. Mind that. Climb up! Keep your wits. Stick close to me. Watch where your hoss's goin' en' ride!"

Somehow Jane mounted; somehow found strength to hold the reins, to spur, to cling on, to ride. A horrible quaking, craven fear possessed her soul. Lassiter led the swift flight across the wide space, over washes, through sage, into a narrow canyon where the rapid clatter of hoofs rapped sharply from the walls. The wind roared in her ears; the gleaming cliffs swept by; trail and sage and grass moved under her. Lassiter's bandaged, blood-stained face turned to her; he shouted encouragement; he looked back down the Pass; he spurred his horse. Jane clung on, spurring likewise. And the horses settled from hard, furious gallop into a long-striding, driving run. She had never ridden at anything like that pace; desperately she tried to get the swing of the horse, to be of some help to him in that race, to see the best of the ground and guide him into it. But she failed of everything except to keep her seat the saddle, and to spur and spur. At times she closed her eyes unable to bear sight of Fay's golden curls streaming in the wind. She could not pray; she could not rail; she no longer cared for herself. All of life, of good, of use in the world, of hope in heaven entered in Lassiter's ride with little Fay to safety. She would have tried to turn the iron-jawed brute she rode, she would have given herself to that relentless, dark-browed Tull. But she knew Lassiter would turn with her, so she rode on and on.

Whether that run was of moments or hours Jane Withersteen could not tell. Lassiter's horse covered her with froth that blew back in white streams. Both horses ran their limit, were allowed slow down in time to save them, and went on dripping, heaving, staggering.

"Oh, Lassiter, we must run—we must run!"

He looked back, saying nothing. The bandage had blown from his head, and blood trickled down his face. He was bowing under the strain of injuries, of the ride, of his burden. Yet how cool and gay he looked—how intrepid!

The horses walked, trotted, galloped, ran, to fall again to walk. Hours sped or dragged. Time was an instant—an eternity. Jane Withersteen felt hell pursuing her, and dared not look back for fear she would fall from her horse.

"Oh, Lassiter! Is he coming?"

The grim rider looked over his shoulder, but said no word. Fay's golden hair floated on the breeze. The sun shone; the walls gleamed; the sage glistened. And then it seemed the sun vanished, the walls shaded, the sage paled. The horses walked—trotted—galloped—ran—to fall again to walk. Shadows gathered under shelving cliffs. The canyon turned, brightened, opened into a long, wide, wall-enclosed valley. Again the sun, lowering in the west, reddened the sage. Far ahead round, scrawled stone appeared to block the Pass.

"Bear up, Jane, bear up!" called Lassiter. "It's our game, if you don't weaken."

"Lassiter! Go on—alone! Save little Fay!"

"Only with you!"

"Oh!—I'm a coward—a miserable coward! I can't fight or think or hope or pray! I'm lost! Oh, Lassiter, look back! Is he coming? I'll not—hold out—"

"Keep your breath, woman, an' ride not for yourself or for me, but for Fay!"

A last breaking run across the sage brought Lassiter's horse to a walk.

"He's done," said the rider.

"Oh, no—no!" moaned Jane.

"Look back, Jane, look back. Three—four miles we've come across this valley, en' no Tull yet in sight. Only a few more miles!"

Jane looked back over the long stretch of sage, and found the narrow gap in the wall, out of which came a file of dark horses with a white horse in the lead. Sight of the riders acted upon Jane as a stimulant. The weight of cold, horrible terror lessened. And, gazing forward at the dogs, at Lassiter's limping horse, at the blood on his face, at the rocks growing nearer, last at Fay's golden hair, the ice left her veins, and slowly, strangely, she gained hold of strength that she believed would see her to the safety Lassiter promised. And, as she gazed, Lassiter's horse stumbled and fell.

He swung his leg and slipped from the saddle.

"Jane, take the child," he said, and lifted Fay up. Jane clasped her arms suddenly strong. "They're gainin'," went on Lassiter, as he watched the pursuing riders. "But we'll beat 'em yet."

Turning with Jane's bridle in his hand, he was about to start when he saw the saddle-bag on the fallen horse.

"I've jest about got time," he muttered, and with swift fingers that did not blunder or fumble he loosened the bag and threw it over his shoulder. Then he started to run, leading Jane's horse, and he ran, and trotted, and walked, and ran again. Close ahead now Jane saw a rise of bare rock. Lassiter reached it, searched along the base, and, finding a low place, dragged the weary horse up and over round, smooth stone. Looking backward, Jane saw Tull's white horse not a mile distant, with riders strung out in a long line behind him. Looking forward, she saw more valley to the right, and to the left a towering cliff. Lassiter pulled the horse and kept on.

Little Fay lay in her arms with wide-open eyes—eyes which were still shadowed by pain, but no longer fixed, glazed in terror. The golden curls blew across

Jane's lips; the little hands feebly clasped her arm; a ghost of a troubled, trustful smile hovered round the sweet lips. And Jane Withersteen awoke to the spirit of a lioness.

Lassiter was leading the horse up a smooth slope toward cedar trees of twisted and bleached appearance. Among these he halted.

"Jane, give me the girl en' get down," he said. As if it wrenched him he unbuckled the empty black guns with a strange air of finality. He then received Fay in his arms and stood a moment looking backward. Tull's white horse mounted the ridge of round stone, and several bays or blacks followed. "I wonder what he'll think when he sees them empty guns. Jane, bring your saddle-bag and climb after me."

A glistening, wonderful bare slope, with little holes, swelled up and up to lose itself in a frowning yellow cliff. Jane closely watched her steps and climbed behind Lassiter. He moved slowly. Perhaps he was only husbanding his strength. But she saw drops of blood on the stone, and then she knew. They climbed and climbed without looking back. Her breast labored; she began to feel as if little points of fiery steel were penetrating her side into her lungs. She heard the panting of Lassiter and the quicker panting of the dogs.

"Wait—here," he said.

Before her rose a bulge of stone, nicked with little cut steps, and above that a corner of yellow wall, and overhanging that a vast, ponderous cliff.

The dogs pattered up, disappeared round the corner. Lassiter mounted the steps with Fay, and he swayed like a drunken man, and he too disappeared. But instantly he returned alone, and half ran, half slipped down to her.

Then from below pealed up hoarse shouts of angry men. Tull and several of his riders had reached the spot where Lassiter had parted with his guns.

"You'll need that breath—mebbe!" said Lassiter, facing downward, with glittering eyes.

"Now, Jane, the last pull," he went on. "Walk up them little steps. I'll follow an' steady you. Don't think. Jest go. Little Fay's above. Her eyes are open. She jest said to me, 'Where's muvver Jane?'"

Without a fear or a tremor or a slip or a touch of Lassiter's hand Jane Withersteen walked up that ladder of cut steps.

He pushed her round the corner of the wall. Fay lay, with wide staring eyes, in the shade of a gloomy wall. The dogs waited. Lassiter picked up the child and turned into a dark cleft. It zigzagged. It widened. It opened. Jane was amazed at a wonderfully smooth and steep incline leading up between ruined, splintered, toppling walls. A red haze from the setting sun filled this passage. Lassiter climbed with slow, measured steps, and blood dripped from him to make splotches on the white stone. Jane tried not to step in his blood, but was compelled, for she found no other footing. The saddle-bag began to drag her down; she gasped for breath, she thought her heart was bursting. Slower, slower yet the rider climbed, whistling as he breathed. The incline widened. Huge pinnacles and monuments of stone stood alone, leaning fearfully. Red sunset haze shone through cracks where the wall had split. Jane did not look high, but she felt the overshadowing of broken rims above. She felt that it was a fearful, menacing place. And she climbed on in heartrending effort. And she fell beside Lassiter and Fay at the top of the incline in a narrow, smooth divide.

He staggered to his feet—staggered to a huge, leaning rock that rested on a small pedestal. He put his hand on it—the hand that had been shot through—and Jane saw blood drip from the ragged hole. Then he fell.

"Jane—I—can't—do—it!" he whispered.

"What?"

"Roll the—stone!... All my—life I've loved—to roll stones—en' now I—can't!"

"What of it? You talk strangely. Why roll that stone?"

"I planned to—fetch you here—to roll this stone. See! It'll smash the crags—loosen the walls—close the outlet!"

As Jane Withersteen gazed down that long incline, walled in by crumbling cliffs, awaiting only the slightest jar to make them fall asunder, she saw Tull appear at the bottom and begin to climb. A rider followed him—another—and another.

"See! Tull! The riders!"

"Yes—they'll get us—now."

"Why? Haven't you strength left to roll the stone?"

"Jane—it ain't that—I've lost my nerve!"

"You!... Lassiter!"

"I wanted to roll it—meant to—but I—can't. Venters's valley is down behind here. We could—live there. But if I roll the stone—we're shut in for always. I don't dare. I'm thinkin' of you!"

"Lassiter! Roll the stone!" she cried.

He arose, tottering, but with set face, and again he placed the bloody hand on the Balancing Rock. Jane Withersteen gazed from him down the passageway. Tull was climbing. Almost, she thought, she saw his dark, relentless face. Behind him more riders climbed. What did they mean for Fay—for Lassiter—for herself?

"Roll the stone!... Lassiter, I love you!"

Under all his deathly pallor, and the blood, and the iron of seared cheek and lined brow, worked a great change. He placed both hands on the rock and then leaned his shoulder there and braced his powerful body.

ROLL THE STONE!

It stirred, it groaned, it grated, it moved, and with a slow grinding, as of wrathful relief, began to lean. It had waited ages to fall, and now was slow in starting. Then, as if suddenly instinct with life, it leaped hurtlingly down to alight on the steep incline, to bound more swiftly into the air, to gather momentum, to plunge into the lofty leaning crag below. The crag thundered into atoms. A wave of air—a splitting shock! Dust shrouded the sunset red of shaking rims; dust shrouded Tull as he fell on his knees with uplifted arms. Shafts and monuments and sections of wall fell majestically.

From the depths there rose a long-drawn rumbling roar. The outlet to Deception Pass closed forever.

KEN WARD IN THE JUNGLE

I THE PRIZE

"What a change from the Arizona desert!"

The words broke from the lips of Ken Ward as he leaned from the window of the train which was bearing his brother and himself over the plateau to Tampico in Tamaulipas, the southeastern state of Mexico. He had caught sight of a river leaping out between heavily wooded slopes and plunging down in the most beautiful waterfall he had ever seen.

"Look, Hal," he cried.

The first fall was a long white streak, ending in a dark pool; below came cascade after cascade, fall after fall, some wide, others narrow, and all white and green against the yellow rock. Then the train curved round a spur of the mountain, descended to a level, to be lost in a luxuriance of jungle growth.

It was indeed a change for Ken Ward, young forester, pitcher of the varsity nine at school, and hunter of lions in the Arizona cañons. Here he was entering the jungle of the tropics. The rifles and the camp outfit on the seat beside his brother Hal and himself spoke of coming adventures. Before them lay an unknown wilderness--the semi-tropical jungle. And the future was to show that the mystery of the jungle was stranger even than their imaginings.

It was not love of adventure alone or interest in the strange new forest growths that had drawn Ken to the jungle. His uncle, the one who had gotten Ken letters from the Forestry Department at Washington, had been proud of Ken's Arizona achievements. This uncle was a member of the American Geographical Society and a fellow of the New York Museum of Natural History. He wanted Ken to try his hand at field work in the jungle of Mexico, and if that was successful, then to explore the ruined cities of wild Yucatan. If Ken made good as an explorer his reward was to be a trip to Equatorial Africa after big game. And of course that trip meant opportunity to see England and France, and, what meant more to Ken, a chance to see the great forests of Germany, where forestry had been carried on for three hundred years.

In spite of the fact that the inducement was irresistible, and that Ken's father was as proud and eager as Ken's uncle to have him make a name for himself, and that Hal would be allowed to go with him, Ken had hesitated. There was the responsibility for Hal and the absolute certainty that Hal could not keep out of mischief. Still Ken simply could not have gone to Mexico leaving his brother at home broken-hearted.

At last the thing had been decided. It was Hal's ambition to be a naturalist and to collect specimens, and the uncle had held out possible recognition from the Smithsonian Institution at Washington. Perhaps he might find a new variety of some animal to which the scientists would attach his name. Then the lad was passionately eager to see Ken win that trip to Africa. There had been much study of maps and books of travel, science, and natural history. There had been the most careful instruction and equipment for semi-tropical camp life. The uncle had given Ken valuable lessons in map-drawing, in estimating distance and topography, and he had indicated any one of several rivers in the jungle belt of Mexico. Traversing one hundred miles of unknown jungle river, with intelligent observation and accurate reports, would win the prize for Ken Ward. Now the race was on. Would Ken win?

Presently the train crossed a bridge. Ken Ward had a brief glance at clear green water, at great cypress-trees, gray and graceful with long, silvery, waving moss, and at the tangled, colorful banks. A water-fowl black as coal, with white-crested wings, skimmed the water in swift wild flight, to disappear up the shady river-lane. Then the train clattered on, and, a mile or more beyond the bridge, stopped at a station called Valles. In the distance could be seen the thatched palm-leaf huts and red-tiled roofs of a hamlet.

The boys got out to stretch their legs. The warm, sweet, balmy air was a new and novel thing to them. They strolled up and down the gravel walk, watching the natives. Hal said he rather liked the looks of their brown bare feet and the thin cotton trousers and shirts, but he fancied the enormous sombreros were too heavy and unwieldy. Ken spoke to several pleasant-faced Mexicans, each of whom replied: "No sabe, Señor."

The ticket agent at the station was an American, and from the way he smiled and spoke Ken knew he was more than glad to see one of his own kind. So, after Ken had replied to many questions about the States, he began to ask some of his own.

"What's the name of the waterfall we passed?"

"Micas Falls," replied the agent.

"And the river?"

"It's called the Santa Rosa."

"Where does it go?"

The agent did not know, except that it disappeared in the jungle. Southward the country was wild. The villages were few and all along the railroad; and at Valles the river swung away to the southwest.

"But it must flow into the Panuco River," said Ken. He had studied maps of Mexico and had learned all that it was possible to learn before he undertook the journey.

"Why, yes, it must find the Panuco somewhere down over the mountain," answered the agent.

"Then there are rapids in this little river?" asked Ken, in growing interest.

"Well, I guess. It's all rapids."

"How far to Tampico by rail?" went on Ken.

"Something over a hundred miles."

"Any game in the jungle hereabouts--or along the Santa Rosa?" continued Ken.

The man laughed, and laughed in such a way that Ken did not need his assertion that it was not safe to go into the jungle.

Whereupon Ken Ward became so thoughtful that he did not hear the talk that followed between the agent and Hal. The engine bell roused him into action, and with Hal he hurried back to their seats. And then the train sped on. But the beauty of Micas Falls and the wildness of the Santa Rosa remained with Ken. Where did that river go? How many waterfalls and rapids did it have? What teeming life must be along its rich banks! It haunted Ken. He wanted to learn the mystery of the jungle. There was the same longing which had gotten him into the wild adventures in Penetier Forest and the Grand Cañon country of Arizona. And all at once flashed over him the thought that here was the jungle river for him to explore.

"Why, that's the very thing," he said, thinking aloud.

"What's wrong with you," asked Hal, "talking to yourself that way?"

Ken did not explain. The train clattered between green walls of jungle, and occasionally stopped at a station. But the thought of the jungle haunted him until the train arrived at Tampico.

Ken had the name of an American hotel, and that was all he knew about Tampico. The station was crowded with natives. Man after man accosted the boys, jabbering excitedly in Mexican. Some of these showed brass badges bearing a number and the word *Cargodore*.

"Hal, I believe these fellows are porters or baggage-men," said Ken. And he showed his trunk check to one of them. The fellow jerked it out of Ken's hand and ran off. The boys ran after him. They were relieved to see him enter a shed full of baggage. And they were amazed to see him kneel down and take their trunk on his back. It was a big trunk and heavy. The man was small and light.

"It 'll smash him!" cried Hal.

But the little *cargodore* walked off with the trunk on his back. Then Ken and Hal saw other *cargodores* packing trunks. The boys kept close to their man and used their eyes with exceeding interest. The sun was setting, and the square, colored buildings looked as if they were in a picture of Spain.

"Look at the boats--canoes!" cried Hal, as they crossed a canal.

Ken saw long narrow canoes that had been hollowed out from straight tree-trunks. They were of every size, and some of the paddles were enormous. Crowds of natives were jabbering and jostling each other at a rude wharf.

"Look back," called Hal, who seemed to have a hundred eyes.

Ken saw a wide, beautiful river, shining red in the sunset. Palm-trees on the distant shore showed black against the horizon.

"Hal, that's the Panuco. What a river!"

"Makes the Susquehanna look like a creek," was Hal's comment.

The *cargodore* led the boys through a plaza, down a narrow street to the hotel. Here they were made to feel at home. The proprietor was a kindly American. The hotel was crowded, and many of the guests were Englishmen there for the tarpon-fishing, with sportsmen from the States, and settlers coming in to take up new lands. It was pleasant for Ken and Hal to hear their own language once more. After dinner they sallied forth to see the town. But the narrow dark streets and the blanketed natives stealing silently along were not particularly inviting. The boys got no farther than the plaza, where they sat down on a bench. It was wholly different from any American town. Ken suspected that Hal was getting homesick, for the boy was quiet and inactive.

"I don't like this place," said Hal. "What 'd you ever want to drag me way down here for?"

"Humph! drag you? Say, you pestered the life out of me, and bothered Dad till he was mad, and worried mother sick to let you come on this trip."

Hal hung his head.

"Now, you're not going to show a streak of yellow?" asked Ken. He knew how to stir his brother.

Hal rose to the attack and scornfully repudiated the insinuation. Ken replied that they were in a new country and must not reach conclusions too hastily.

"I liked it back up there at the little village where we saw the green river and the big trees with the gray streamers on them," said Hal.

"Well, I liked that myself," rejoined Ken. "I'd like to go back there and put a boat in the river and come all the way here."

Ken had almost unconsciously expressed the thought that had been forming in his mind. Hal turned slowly and looked at his brother.

"Ken, that 'd be great--that's what we came for!"

"I should say so," replied Ken.

"Well?" asked Hal, simply.

That question annoyed Ken. Had he not come south to go into the jungle? Had he come with any intention of shirking the danger of a wild trip? There was a subtle flattery in Hal's question.

"That Santa Rosa River runs through the jungle," went on Hal. "It flows into the Panuco somewhere. You know we figured out on the map that the Panuco's the only big river in this jungle. That's all we want to know. And, Ken, you know you're a born boatman. Why, look at the rapids we've shot on the Susquehanna. Remember that trip we came down the Juniata? The water was high, too. Ken, you can take a boat down that Santa Rosa!"

"By George! I believe I can," exclaimed Ken, and he thrilled at the thought.

"Ken, let's go. You'll win the prize, and I'll get specimens. Think what we'd have to tell Jim Williams and Dick Leslie when we go West next summer!"

"Oh, Hal, I know--but this idea of a trip seems too wild."

"Maybe it wouldn't be so wild."

In all fairness Ken could not deny this, so he kept silent.

"Ken, listen," went on Hal, and now he was quite cool. "If we'd promised the Governor not to take a wild trip I wouldn't say another word. But we're absolutely free."

"That's why we ought to be more careful. Dad trusts me."

"He trusts you because he knows you can take care of yourself, and me, too. You're a wonder, Ken. Why, if you once made up your mind, you'd make that Santa Rosa River look like a canal."

Ken began to fear that he would not be proof against the haunting call of that jungle river and the flattering persuasion of his brother and the ever-present ambition to show his uncle what he could do.

"Hal, if I didn't have you with me I'd already have made up my mind to tackle this river."

That appeared to insult Hal.

"All I've got to say is I'd be a help to you--not a drag," he said, with some warmth.

"You're always a help, Hal. I can't say anything against your willingness. But you know your weakness. By George! you made trouble enough for me in Arizona. On a trip such as this you'd drive me crazy."

"Ken, I won't make any rash promises. I don't want to queer myself with you. But I'm all right."

"Look here, Hal; let's wait. We've only got to Tampico. Maybe such a trip is impracticable--impossible. Let's find out more about the country."

Hal appeared to take this in good spirit. The boys returned to the hotel and went to bed. Hal promptly fell asleep. But Ken Ward lay awake a long time thinking of the green Santa Rosa, with its magnificent moss-festooned cypresses. And when he did go to sleep it was to dream of the beautiful waterfowl with the white-crested wings, and he was following it on its wild flight down the dark, mysterious river-trail into the jungle.

II THE HOME OF THE TARPON

Hal's homesickness might never have been in evidence at all, to judge from the way the boy, awakening at dawn, began to talk about the Santa Rosa trip.

"Well," said Ken, as he rolled out of bed, "I guess we're in for it."

"Ken, will we go?" asked Hal, eagerly.

"I'm on the fence."

"But you're leaning on the jungle side?"

"Yes, kid--I'm slipping."

Hal opened his lips to let out a regular Hiram Bent yell, when Ken clapped a hand over his mouth.

"Hold on--we're in the hotel yet."

It took the brothers long to dress, because they could not keep away from the window. The sun was rising in rosy glory over misty lagoons. Clouds of creamy mist rolled above the broad Panuco. Wild ducks were flying low. The tiled roofs of the stone houses gleamed brightly, and the palm-trees glistened with dew. The soft breeze that blew in was warm, sweet, and fragrant.

After breakfast the boys went out to the front and found the hotel lobby full of fishermen and their native boatmen. It was an interesting sight, as well as a surprise, for Ken and Hal did not know that Tampico was as famous for fishing as it was for hunting. The huge rods and reels amazed them.

"What kind of fish do these fellows fish for?" asked Hal.

Ken was well enough acquainted with sport to know something about tarpon, but he had never seen one of the great silver fish. And he was speechless when Hal led him into a room upon the walls of which were mounted specimens of tarpon from six to seven feet in length and half as wide as a door.

"Say, Ken! We've come to the right place. Those fishermen are all going out to fish for such whales as these here."

"Hal, we never saw a big fish before," said Ken. "And before we leave Tampico we'll know what it means to hook tarpon."

"I'm with you," replied Hal, gazing doubtfully and wonderingly at a fish almost twice as big as himself.

Then Ken, being a practical student of fishing, as of other kinds of sport, began to stroll round the lobby with an intent to learn. He closely scrutinized the tackle. And he found that the bait used was a white mullet six to ten inches long, a little fish which resembled the chub. Ken did not like the long, cruel gaff which seemed a necessary adjunct to each outfit of tackle, and he vowed that in his fishing for tarpon he would dispense with it.

Ken was not backward about asking questions, and he learned that Tampico, during the winter months, was a rendezvous for sportsmen from all over the world. For the most part, they came to catch the leaping tarpon; the shooting along the Panuco, however, was as well worth while as the fishing. But Ken could not learn anything about the Santa Rosa River. The *tierra caliente*, or hot belt, along the curve of the Gulf was intersected by small streams, many of them unknown and unnamed. The Panuco swung round to the west and had its source somewhere up in the mountains. Ken decided that the Santa Rosa was one of its headwaters. Valles lay up on the first swell of higher ground, and was distant from Tampico some six hours by train. So, reckoning with the meandering course of jungle streams, Ken calculated he would have something like one hundred and seventy-five miles to travel by water from Valles to Tampico. There were Indian huts strung along the Panuco River, and fifty miles inland a village named Panuco. What lay between Panuco and Valles, up over the wild steppes of that jungle, Ken Ward could only conjecture.

Presently he came upon Hal in conversation with an American boy, who at once volunteered to show them around. So they set out, and were soon becoming well acquainted. Their guide said he was from Kansas; had been working in the railroad offices for two years; and was now taking a vacation. His name was George Alling. Under his guidance the boys spent several interesting hours going about the city. During this walk Hal showed his first tendency to revert to his natural bent of mind. Not for long could Hal Ward exist without making trouble for something. In this case it was buzzards, of which the streets of Tampico were full. In fact, George explained, the buzzards were the only street-cleaning department in the town. They were as tame as tame turkeys, and Hal could not resist the desire to chase them. And he could be made to stop only after a white-helmeted officer had threatened him. George explained further that although Tampico had no game-laws it protected these buzzard-scavengers of the streets.

The market-house at the canal wharf was one place where Ken thought Hal would forget himself in the bustle and din and color. All was so strange and new. Indeed, for a time Hal appeared to be absorbed in his surroundings, but when he came to a stall where a man had parrots and racoons and small deer, and three little yellow, black-spotted tiger-cats, as George called them, then once more Ken had to take Hal in tow. Outside along the wharf were moored a hundred or more canoes of manifold variety. All had been hewn from solid tree-trunks. Some were long, slender, graceful, pretty to look at, and easy to handle in shallow lagoons, but Ken thought them too heavy and cumbersome for fast water. Happening just then to remember Micas Falls, Ken had a momentary chill and a check to his enthusiasm for the jungle trip. What if he encountered, in coming down the Santa Rosa, some such series of cascades as those which made Micas Falls!

It was about noon when George led the boys out to the banks of the broad Panuco. Both Hal and Ken were suffering from the heat. They had removed their coats, and were now very glad to rest in the shade.

"This is a nice cool day," said George, and he looked cool.

"We've got on our heavy clothes, and this tropic sun is new to us," replied Ken. "Say, Hal--"

A crash in the water near the shore interrupted Ken.

"Was that a rhinoceros?" inquired Hal.

"Savalo," said George.

"What's that?"

"Silver king. A tarpon. Look around and you'll see one break water. There are some fishermen trolling down-stream. Watch. Maybe one will hook a fish presently. Then you'll see some jumping."

It was cool in the shade, as the brothers soon discovered, and they spent a delightful hour watching the river and the wild fowl and the tarpon. Ken and Hal were always lucky. Things happened for their benefit and pleasure. Not only did they see many tarpon swirl like bars of silver on the water, but a fisherman hooked one of the great fish not fifty yards from where the boys sat. And they held their breath, and with starting eyes watched the marvelous leaps and dashes of the tarpon till, as he shot up in a last mighty effort, wagging his head, slapping his huge gills, and flinging the hook like a bullet, he plunged back free.

"Nine out of ten get away," remarked George.

"Did you ever catch one?" asked Hal.

"Sure."

"Hal, I've got to have some of this fishing," said Ken. "But if we start at it now--would we ever get that jungle trip?"

"Oh, Ken, you've made up your mind to go!" exclaimed Hal, in glee.

"No, I haven't," protested Ken.

"Yes, you have," declared Hal. "I know you." And the whoop that he had suppressed in the hotel he now let out with good measure.

Naturally George was interested, and at his inquiry Ken told him the idea for the Santa Rosa trip.

"Take me along," said George. There was a note of American spirit in his voice, a laugh on his lips, and a flash in his eyes that made Ken look at him attentively. He was a slim youth, not much Hal's senior, and Ken thought if ever a boy had been fashioned to be a boon comrade of Hal Ward this George Alling was the boy.

"What do you think of the trip?" inquired Ken, curiously.

"Fine. We'll have some fun. We'll get a boat and a mozo--"

"What's a mozo?"

"A native boatman."

"That's a good idea. I hadn't thought of a boatman to help row. But the boat is the particular thing. I wouldn't risk a trip in one of those canoes."

"Come on, I'll find a boat," said George.

II THE HOME OF THE TARPON

And before he knew it George and Hal were leading him back from the river. George led him down narrow lanes, between painted stone houses and iron-barred windows, till they reached the canal. They entered a yard where buzzards, goats, and razor-back pigs were contesting over the scavenger rights. George went into a boat-house and pointed out a long, light, wide skiff with a flat bottom. Ken did not need George's praise, or the shining light in Hal's eyes, or the boat-keeper's importunities to make him eager to try this particular boat. Ken Ward knew a boat when he saw one. He jumped in, shoved it out, rowed up the canal, pulled and turned, backed water, and tried every stroke he knew. Then he rested on the oars and whistled. Hal's shout of delight made him stop whistling. Those two boys would have him started on the trip if he did not look sharp.

"It's a dandy boat," said Ken.

"Only a peso a day, Ken," went on Hal. "One dollar Mex--fifty cents in our money. Quick, Ken, hire it before somebody else gets it."

"Sure I'll hire the boat," replied Ken; "but Hal, it's not for that Santa Rosa trip. We'll have to forget that."

"Forget your grandmother!" cried Hal. And then it was plain that he tried valiantly to control himself, to hide his joy, to pretend to agree with Ken's ultimatum.

Ken had a feeling that his brother knew him perfectly, and he was divided between anger and amusement. They returned to the hotel and lounged in the lobby. The proprietor was talking with some Americans, and as he now appeared to be at leisure he introduced the brothers and made himself agreeable. Moreover, he knew George Alling well. They began to chat, and Ken was considerably annoyed to hear George calmly state that he and his new-found friends intended to send a boat up to Valles and come down an unknown jungle river.

The proprietor laughed, and, though the laugh was not unpleasant, somehow it nettled Ken Ward.

"Why not go?" he asked, quietly, and he looked at the hotel man.

"My boy, you can't undertake any trip like that."

"Why not?" persisted Ken. "Is there any law here to prevent our going into the jungle?"

"There's no law. No one could stop you. But, my lad, what's the sense of taking such a fool trip? The river here is full of tarpon right now. There are millions of ducks and geese on the lagoons. You can shoot deer and wild turkey right on the edge of town. If you want tiger and javelin, go out to one of the ranches where they have dogs to hunt with, where you'll have a chance for your life. These tigers and boars will kill a man. There's all the sport any one wants right close to Tampico."

"I don't see how all that makes a reason why we shouldn't come down the Santa Rosa," replied Ken. "We want to explore--map the river."

The hotel man seemed nettled in return.

"You're only kids. It 'd be crazy to start out on that wild trip."

It was on Ken's lips to mention a few of the adventures which he believed justly gave him a right to have pride and confidence in his ability. But he forbore.

"It's a fool trip," continued the proprietor. "You don't know this river. You don't know where you'll come out. It's wild up in that jungle. I've hunted up at Valles, and no native I ever met would go a mile from the village. If you take a mozo he'll get soaked with canya. He'll stick a knife in you or run off and leave you when you most need help. Nobody ever explored that river. It 'll likely be full of swamps, sandbars, bogs. You'd get fever. Then the crocodiles, the boars, the bats, the snakes, the tigers! Why, if you could face these you'd still have the ticks--the worst of all. The ticks would drive men crazy, let alone boys. It's no undertaking for a boy."

The mention of all these dangers would have tipped the balance for Ken in favor of the Santa Rosa trip, even if the hint of his callowness had not roused his spirit.

"Thank you. I'm sure you mean kindly," said Ken. "But I'm going to Valles and I'll come down that jungle river."

III AN INDIAN BOATMAN

The moment the decision was made Ken felt both sorry and glad. He got the excited boys outside away from the critical and anxious proprietor. And Ken decided it was incumbent upon him to adopt a serious and responsible manner, which he was far from feeling. So he tried to be as cool as Hiram Bent, with a fatherly interest in the two wild boys who were to accompany him down the Santa Rosa.

"Now, George, steer us around till we find a mozo," said Ken. "Then we'll buy an outfit and get started on this trip before you can say Jack Robinson."

All the mozos the boys interviewed were eager to get work; however, when made acquainted with the nature of the trip they refused point blank.

"Tigre!" exclaimed one.

"Javelin!" exclaimed another.

The big spotted jaguar of the jungle and the wild boar, or peccary, were held in much dread by the natives.

"These natives will climb a tree at sight of a tiger or pig," said George. "For my part I'm afraid of the garrapatoes and the pinilius."

"What 're they?" asked Hal.

"Ticks--jungle ticks. Just wait till you make their acquaintance."

Finally the boys met a *mozo* named Pepe, who had often rowed a boat for George. Pepe looked sadly in need of a job; still he did not ask for it. George said that Pepe had been one of the best boatmen on the river until *canya*, the fiery white liquor to which the natives were addicted, had ruined his reputation. Pepe wore an old sombrero, a cotton, shirt and sash, and ragged trousers. He was barefooted. Ken noted the set of his muscular neck, his brawny shoulders and arms, and appreciated the years of rowing that had developed them. But Pepe's haggard face, deadened eyes, and listless manner gave Ken pause. Still, Ken reflected, there was never any telling what a man might do, if approached right. Pepe's dejection excited Ken's sympathy. So Ken clapped him on the shoulder, and, with George acting as interpreter, offered Pepe work for several weeks at three pesos a day. That was more than treble the *mozo's* wage. Pepe nearly fell off the canal bridge, where he was sitting, and a light as warm and bright as sunshine flashed into his face.

"Si, Señor--Si, Señor," he began to jabber, and waved his brown hands.

Ken suspected that Pepe needed a job and a little kind treatment. He was sure of it when George said Pepe's wife and children were in want. Somehow Ken conceived a liking for Pepe, and believed he could trust him. He thought he knew how to deal with poor Pepe. So he gave him money, told him to get a change of clothes and a pair of shoes, and come to the hotel next day.

"He'll spend the money for canya, and not show up to-morrow," said George.

"I don't know anything about your natives, but that fellow will come," declared Ken.

It appeared that the whole American colony in Tampico had been acquainted with Ken Ward's project, and made a business to waylay the boys at each corner. They called the trip a wild-goose chase. They declared it was a dime-novel idea, and could hardly take Ken seriously. They mingled astonishment with amusement and concern. They advised Ken not to go, and declared they would not let him go. Over and over again the boys were assured of the peril from ticks, bats, boars, crocodiles, snakes, tigers, and fevers.

"That's what I'm taking the trip for," snapped Ken, driven to desperation by all this nagging.

"Well, young man, I admire your nerve," concluded the hotel man. "If you're determined to go, we can't stop you. And there's some things we would like you to find out for us. How far do tarpon run up the Panuco River? Do they spawn up there? How big are the new-born fish? I'll furnish you with tackle and preserved mullet, for bait. We've always wondered about how far tarpon go up into fresh water. Keep your eye open for signs of oil. Also look at the timber. And be sure to make a map of the river."

When it came to getting the boat shipped the boys met with more obstacles. But for the friendly offices of a Texan, an employee of the railroad, they would never have been able to convince the native shipping agent that a boat was merchandise. The Texan arranged the matter and got Ken a freight bill. He took an entirely different view of Ken's enterprise, compared with that of other Americans, and in a cool, drawling voice, which somehow reminded Ken of Jim Williams, he said:

"Shore you-all will have the time of your lives. I worked at Valles for a year. That jungle is full of game. I killed three big tigers. You-all want to look out for those big yellow devils. One in every three will jump for a man. There's nothing but shoot, then. And the wild pigs are bad. They put me up a tree more than once. I don't know much about the Santa Rosa. Its source is above Micas Falls. Never heard where it goes. I know it's full of crocodiles and rapids. Never saw a boat or a canoe at Valles. And say--there are big black snakes in the jungle. Look out for them, too. Shore you-all have sport a-comin'."

Ken thanked the Texan, and as he went on up-street, for all his sober thoughtfulness, he was as eager as Hal or George. However, his position as their guardian would not permit any show of extravagant enthusiasm.

III AN INDIAN BOATMAN

Ken bought blankets, cooking utensils, and supplies for three weeks. There was not such a thing as a tent in Tampico. The best the boys could get for a shelter was a long strip of canvas nine feet wide.

"That 'll keep off the wet," said Ken, "but it won't keep out the mosquitoes and things."

"Couldn't keep 'em out if we had six tents," replied George.

The remainder of that day the boys were busy packing the outfit.

Pepe presented himself at the hotel next morning an entirely different person. He was clean-shaven, and no longer disheveled. He wore a new sombrero, a white cotton shirt, a red sash, and blue trousers. He earned a small bundle, a pair of shoes, and a long *machete*. The dignity with which he approached before all the other *mozos* was not lost upon Ken Ward. A sharp scrutiny satisfied him that Pepe had not been drinking. Ken gave him several errands to do. Then he ordered the outfit taken to the station in Pepe's charge.

The boys went down early in the afternoon. It was the time when the *mozos* were returning from the day's tarpon-fishing on the river, and they, with the *cargodores*, streamed to and fro on the platform. Pepe was there standing guard over Ken's outfit. He had lost his fame among his old associates, and for long had been an outsider. Here he was in charge of a pile of fine guns, fishing-tackle, baggage, and supplies--a collection representing a fortune to him and his simple class. He had been trusted with it. It was under his eye. All his old associates passed by to see him there. That was a great time for Pepe. He looked bright, alert, and supremely happy. It would have fared ill with thieves or loafers who would have made themselves free with any of the articles under his watchful eye.

The train pulled out of Tampico at five o'clock, and Hal's "We're off!" was expressive.

The railroad lay along the river-bank, and the broad Panuco was rippling with the incoming tide. If Ken and Hal had not already found George to be invaluable as a companion in this strange country they would have discovered it then. For George could translate Pepe's talk, and explain much that otherwise would have been dark to the brothers. Wild ducks dotted the green surface, and spurts showed where playful *ravalo* were breaking water. Great green-backed tarpon rolled their silver sides against the little waves. White cranes and blue herons stood like statues upon the reedy bars. Low down over the opposite bank of the river a long line of wild geese winged its way toward a shimmering lagoon. And against the gold and crimson of the sunset sky a flight of wild fowl stood out in bold black relief. The train crossed the Tamesi River and began to draw away from the Panuco. On the right, wide marshes, gleaming purple in the darkening light, led the eye far beyond to endless pale lagoons. Birds of many kinds skimmed the weedy flats. George pointed out a flock of aigrets, the beautiful wild fowl with the priceless plumes. Then there was a string of pink flamingoes, tall, grotesque, wading along with waddling stride, feeding with heads under water.

"Great!" exclaimed Ken Ward.

"It's all so different from Arizona," said Hal.

At Tamos, twelve miles out of Tampico, the train entered the jungle. Thereafter the boys could see nothing but the impenetrable green walls that lined the track. At dusk the train reached a station called Las Palmas, and then began to ascend the first step of the mountain. The ascent was steep, and, when it was accomplished, Ken looked down and decided that step of the mountain was between two and three thousand feet high. The moon was in its first quarter, and Ken, studying this tropical moon, found it large, radiant, and a wonderful green-gold. It shed a soft luminous glow down upon the sleeping, tangled web of jungle. It was new and strange to Ken, so vastly different from barren desert or iron-ribbed cañon, and it thrilled him with nameless charm.

The train once more entered jungle walls, and as the boys could not see anything out of the windows they lay back in their seats and waited for the ride to end. They were due at Valles at ten o'clock, and the impatient Hal complained that they would never get there. At length a sharp whistle from the engine caused Pepe to turn to the boys with a smile.

"Valles," he said.

With rattle and clank the train came to a halt. Ken sent George and Pepe out, and he and Hal hurriedly handed the luggage through the open window. When the last piece had been passed into Pepe's big hands the boys made a rush for the door, and jumped off as the train started.

"Say, but it's dark," said Hal.

As the train with its lights passed out of sight Ken found himself in what seemed a pitchy blackness. He could not see the boys. And he felt a little cold sinking of his heart at the thought of such black nights on an unknown jungle river.

IV AT THE JUNGLE RIVER

Presently, as Ken's eyes became accustomed to the change, the darkness gave place to pale moonlight. A crowd of chattering natives, with wide sombreros on their heads and blankets over their shoulders, moved round the little stone station. Visitors were rare in Valles, as was manifested by the curiosity aroused by the boys and the pile of luggage.

"Ask Pepe to find some kind of lodging for the night," said Ken to George.

Pepe began to question the natives, and soon was lost in the crowd. Awhile after, as Ken was making up his mind they might have to camp on the station platform, a queer low 'bus drawn by six little mules creaked up. Pepe jumped off the seat beside the driver, and began to stow the luggage away in the 'bus. Then the boys piled in behind, and were soon bowling along a white moonlit road. The soft voices of natives greeted their passing.

Valles appeared to be about a mile from the station, and as they entered the village Ken made out rows of thatched huts, and here and there a more pretentious habitation of stone. At length the driver halted before a rambling house, partly stone and partly thatch. There were no lights; in fact, Ken did not see a light in the village. George told the boys to take what luggage each could carry and follow the guide. Inside the house it was as dark as a dungeon. The boys bumped into things and fell over each other trying to keep close to the barefooted and mysterious guide. Finally they climbed to a kind of loft, where the moonlight streamed in at the open sides.

"What do you think of this?" panted Hal, who had struggled with a heavy load of luggage. Pepe and the guide went down to fetch up the remainder of the outfit. Ken thought it best to stand still until he knew just where he was. But Hal and George began moving about in the loft. It was very large and gloomy, and seemed open, yet full of objects. Hal jostled into something which creaked and fell with a crash. Then followed a yell, a jabbering of a frightened native, and a scuffling about.

"Hal, what 'd you do?" called Ken, severely.

"You can search me," replied Hal Ward. "One thing--I busted my shin."

"He knocked over a bed with some one sleeping in it," said George.

Pepe arrived in the loft then and soon soothed the injured feelings of the native who had been so rudely disturbed. He then led the boys to their cots, which were no more than heavy strips of canvas stretched over tall frameworks. They appeared to be enormously high for beds. Ken's was as high as his head, and Ken was tall for his age.

"Say, I'll never get up into this thing," burst out Hal. "These people must be afraid to sleep near the floor. George, why are these cots so high?"

"I reckon to keep the pigs and dogs and all that from sleeping with the natives," answered George. "Besides, the higher you sleep in Mexico the farther you get from creeping, crawling things."

Ken had been of half a mind to sleep on the floor, but George's remark had persuaded him to risk the lofty cot. It was most awkward to climb into. Ken tried several times without success, and once he just escaped a fall. By dint of muscle and a good vault he finally landed in the center of his canvas. From there he listened to his more

IV AT THE JUNGLE RIVER

Presently, as Ken's eyes became accustomed to the change, the darkness gave place to pale moonlight. A crowd of chattering natives, with wide sombreros on their heads and blankets over their shoulders, moved round the little stone station. Visitors were rare in Valles, as was manifested by the curiosity aroused by the boys and the pile of luggage.

"Ask Pepe to find some kind of lodging for the night," said Ken to George.

Pepe began to question the natives, and soon was lost in the crowd. Awhile after, as Ken was making up his mind they might have to camp on the station platform, a queer low 'bus drawn by six little mules creaked up. Pepe jumped off the seat beside the driver, and began to stow the luggage away in the 'bus. Then the boys piled in behind, and were soon bowling along a white moonlit road. The soft voices of natives greeted their passing.

Valles appeared to be about a mile from the station, and as they entered the village Ken made out rows of thatched huts, and here and there a more pretentious habitation of stone. At length the driver halted before a rambling house, partly stone and partly thatch. There were no lights; in fact, Ken did not see a light in the village. George told the boys to take what luggage each could carry and follow the guide. Inside the house it was as dark as a dungeon. The boys bumped into things and fell over each other trying to keep close to the barefooted and mysterious guide. Finally they climbed to a kind of loft, where the moonlight streamed in at the open sides.

"What do you think of this?" panted Hal, who had struggled with a heavy load of luggage. Pepe and the guide went down to fetch up the remainder of the outfit. Ken thought it best to stand still until he knew just where he was. But Hal and George began moving about in the loft. It was very large and gloomy, and seemed open, yet full of objects. Hal jostled into something which creaked and fell with a crash. Then followed a yell, a jabbering of a frightened native, and a scuffling about.

"Hal, what 'd you do?" called Ken, severely.

"You can search me," replied Hal Ward. "One thing--I busted my shin."

"He knocked over a bed with some one sleeping in it," said George.

Pepe arrived in the loft then and soon soothed the injured feelings of the native who had been so rudely disturbed. He then led the boys to their cots, which were no more than heavy strips of canvas stretched over tall frameworks. They appeared to be enormously high for beds. Ken's was as high as his head, and Ken was tall for his age.

"Say, I'll never get up into this thing," burst out Hal. "These people must be afraid to sleep near the floor. George, why are these cots so high?"

"I reckon to keep the pigs and dogs and all that from sleeping with the natives," answered George. "Besides, the higher you sleep in Mexico the farther you get from creeping, crawling things."

Ken had been of half a mind to sleep on the floor, but George's remark had persuaded him to risk the lofty cot. It was most awkward to climb into. Ken tried several times without success, and once he just escaped a fall. By dint of muscle and a good vault he finally landed in the center of his canvas. From there he listened to his more unfortunate comrades. Pepe got into his without much difficulty. George, however, in climbing up, on about the fifth attempt swung over too hard and rolled off on the other side. The thump he made when he dropped jarred the whole loft. From the various growls out of the darkness it developed that the loft was full of sleepers, who were not pleased at this invasion. Then Hal's cot collapsed, and went down with a crash. And Hal sat on the flattened thing and laughed.

"Mucho malo," Pepe said, and he laughed, too. Then he had to get out and put up Hal's trestle bed. Hal once again went to climbing up the framework, and this time, with Pepe's aid, managed to surmount it.

"George, what does Pepe mean by *mucho malo*?" asked Hal.

"Bad--very much bad," replied George.

"Nix--tell him nix. This is fine," said Hal.

"Boys, if you don't want to sleep yourselves, shut up so the rest of us can," ordered Ken.

He liked the sense of humor and the good fighting spirit of the boys, and fancied they were the best attributes in comrades on a wild trip. For a long time he heard a kind of shuddering sound, which he imagined was Hal's cot quivering as the boy laughed. Then absolute quiet prevailed, the boys slept, and Ken felt himself drifting.

When he awakened the sun was shining through the holes in the thatched roof. Pepe was up, and the other native sleepers were gone. Ken and the boys descended from their perches without any tumbles, had a breakfast that was palatable--although even George could not name what they ate--and then were ready for the day.

Valles consisted of a few stone houses and many thatched huts of bamboo and palm. There was only one street, and it was full of pigs, dogs, and buzzards. The inhabitants manifested a kindly interest and curiosity, which changed to consternation when they learned of the boys' project. Pepe questioned many natives, and all he could learn about the Santa Rosa was that there was an impassable waterfall some few kilometers below Valles. Ken gritted his teeth and said they would have to get past it. Pepe did not encounter a man who had ever heard of the headwaters of the Panuco River. There were only a few fields under cultivation around Valles, and they were inclosed by impenetrable jungle. It seemed useless to try to find out anything about the river. But Pepe's advisers in the village told enough about *tigre* and *javelin* to make Hal's hair stand on end, and George turn pale, and Ken himself wish they had not come. It all gave Ken both a thrill and a shock.

There was not much conversation among the boys on the drive back to the station. However, sight of the boat, which had come by freight, stirred Ken with renewed spirit, and through him that was communicated to the others.

The hardest task, so far, developed in the matter of transporting boat and supplies out to the river. Ken had hoped to get a handcar and haul the outfit on the track down to where the bridge crossed the Santa Rosa. But there was no handcar. Then came the staggering information that there was no wagon which would carry the boat, and then worse still in the fact that there was no road. This discouraged Ken; nevertheless he had not the least idea of giving up. He sent Pepe out to tell the natives there must be some way to get the outfit to the river.

Finally Pepe found a fellow who had a cart. This fellow claimed he knew a trail that went to a point from which it would be easy to carry the boat to the river. Ken had Pepe hire the man at once.

"Bring on your old cart," said the irrepressible Hal.

That cart turned out to be a remarkable vehicle. It consisted of a narrow body between enormously high wheels. A trio of little mules was hitched to it. The driver willingly agreed to haul the boat and outfit for one *peso*, but when he drove up to the platform to be surrounded by neighbors, he suddenly discovered that he could not possibly accommodate the boys. Patiently Pepe tried to persuade him. No, the thing was impossible. He made no excuses, but he looked mysterious.

"George, tell Pepe to offer him five pesos," said Ken.

Pepe came out bluntly with the inducement, and the driver began to sweat. From the look of his eyes Ken fancied he had not earned so much money in a year. Still he was cunning, and his whispering neighbors lent him support. He had the only cart in the village, and evidently it seemed that fortune had come to knock at least once at his door. He shook his head.

Ken held up both hands with fingers spread. "Ten pesos," he said.

The driver, like a crazy man, began to jabber his consent.

The boys lifted the boat upon the cart, and tied it fast in front so that the stern would not sag. Then they packed the rest of the outfit inside.

Ken was surprised to see how easily the little mules trotted off with such a big load. At the edge of the jungle he looked back toward the station. The motley crowd of natives were watching, making excited gestures, and all talking at once. The driver drove into a narrow trail, which closed behind him. Pepe led on foot, brushing aside the thick foliage. Ken drew a breath of relief as he passed into the cool shade. The sun was very hot. Hal and George brought up the rear, talking fast.

IV AT THE JUNGLE RIVER

The trail was lined and overgrown with slender trees, standing very close, making dense shade. Many birds, some of beautiful coloring, flitted in the branches. In about an hour the driver entered a little clearing where there were several thatched huts. Ken heard the puffing of an engine, and, looking through the trees, he saw the railroad and knew they had arrived at the pumping-station and the bridge over the Santa Rosa.

Pepe lost no time in rounding up six natives to carry the boat. They did not seem anxious to oblige Pepe, although they plainly wanted the money he offered. The trouble was the boat, at which they looked askance. As in the case with the driver, however, the weight and clinking of added silver overcame their reluctance. They easily lifted the boat upon their shoulders. And as they entered the trail, making a strange procession in the close-bordering foliage, they encountered two natives, who jumped and ran, yelling: "La diable! La diable!"

"What ails those gazabos?" asked Hal.

"They're scared," replied George. "They thought the boat was the devil."

If Ken needed any more than had already come to him about the wildness of the Santa Rosa, he had it in the frightened cries and bewilderment of these natives. They had never seen a boat. The Santa Rosa was a beautiful wild river upon which boats were unknown. Ken had not hoped for so much. And now that the die was cast he faced the trip with tingling gladness.

"George and Hal, you stay behind to watch the outfit. Pepe and I will carry what we can and follow the boat. I'll send back after you," said Ken.

Then as he followed Pepe and the natives down the trail there was a deep satisfaction within him. He heard the soft rush of water over stones and the mourning of turtledoves. He rounded a little hill to come abruptly upon the dense green mass of river foliage. Giant cypress-trees, bearded with gray moss, fringed the banks. Through the dark green of leaves Ken caught sight of light-green water. Birds rose all about him. There were rustlings in the thick underbrush and the whir of ducks. The natives penetrated the dark shade and came out to an open, grassy point.

The Santa Rosa, glistening, green, swift, murmured at Ken's feet. The natives dropped the boat into the water, and with Pepe went back for the rest of the outfit. Ken looked up the shady lane of the river and thought of the moment when he had crossed the bridge in the train. Then, as much as he had longed to be there, he had not dared to hope it. And here he was! How strange it was, just then, to see a large black duck with white-crested wings sweep by as swift as the wind! Ken had seen that wild fowl, or one of his kind, and it had haunted him.

V THE FIRST CAMP

In less than an hour all the outfit had been carried down to the river, and the boys sat in the shade, cooling off, happily conscious that they had made an auspicious start.

It took Ken only a moment to decide to make camp there and the next day try to reach Micas Falls. The mountains appeared close at hand, and were so lofty that, early in the afternoon as it was, the westering sun hung over the blue summits. The notch where the Santa Rosa cut through the range stood out clear, and at most it was not more than eighteen miles distant. So Ken planned to spend a day pulling up the river, and then to turn for the down-stream trip.

"Come, boys, let's make camp," said Ken.

He sent Pepe with his long *machete* into the brush to cut fire-wood. Hal he set to making a stone fireplace, which work the boy rather prided himself upon doing well. Ken got George to help him to put up the strip of canvas. They stretched a rope between two trees, threw the canvas over it, and pegged down the ends.

"Say, how 're we going to sleep?" inquired Hal, suddenly.

"Sleep? Why, on our backs, of course," retorted Ken, who could read Hal's mind.

"If we don't have some hot old times keeping things out of this tent, I'm a lobster," said George, dubiously. "I'm going to sleep in the middle."

"You're a brave boy, George," replied Ken.

"Me for between Ken and Pepe," added Hal.

"And you're twice as brave," said Ken. "I dare say Pepe and I will be able to keep things from getting at you."

Just as Pepe came into camp staggering under a load of wood, a flock of russet-colored ducks swung round the bend. They alighted near the shore at a point opposite the camp. The way George and Hal made headers into the pile of luggage for their guns gave Ken an inkling of what he might expect from these lads. He groaned, and then he laughed. George came up out of the luggage first, and he had a .22-caliber rifle, which he quickly loaded and fired into the flock. He crippled one; the others flew up-stream. Then George began to waste shells trying to kill the crippled duck. Hal got into action with his .22. They bounced bullets off the water all around the duck, but they could not hit it.

V THE FIRST CAMP

Pepe grew as excited as the boys, and he jumped into the boat and with a long stick began to pole out into the stream. Ken had to caution George and Hal to lower their guns and not shoot Pepe. Below camp and just under the bridge the water ran into a shallow rift. The duck got onto the current and went round the bend, with Pepe poling in pursuit and George and Hal yelling along the shore. When they returned a little later, they had the duck, which was of an unknown species to Ken. Pepe had fallen overboard; George was wet to his knees; and, though Hal did not show any marks of undue exertion, his eyes would have enlightened any beholder. The fact was that they were glowing with the excitement of the chase. It amused Ken. He felt that he had to try to stifle his own enthusiasm. There had to be one old head in the party. But if he did have qualms over the possibilities of the boys to worry him with their probable escapades, he still felt happy at their boundless life and spirit.

It was about the middle of the afternoon, and the heat had become intense. Ken realized it doubly when he saw Pepe favoring the shade. George and Hal were hot, but they appeared to be too supremely satisfied with their surroundings to care about that.

During this hot spell, which lasted from three o'clock until five, there was a quiet and a lack of life around camp that surprised Ken. It was slumberland; even the insects seemed drowsy. Not a duck and scarcely a bird passed by. Ken heard the mourning of turtle-doves, and was at once struck with the singular deep, full tone. Several trains crossed the bridge, and at intervals the engine at the pumping-tank puffed and chugged. From time to time a native walked out upon the bridge to stare long and curiously at the camp.

When the sun set behind the mountain a hard breeze swept down the river. Ken did not know what to make of it, and at first thought there was going to be a storm. Pepe explained that the wind blew that way every day after sunset. For a while it tossed the willows, and waved the Spaniard's-beard upon the cypresses. Then as suddenly as it had come it died away, taking the heat with it.

Whereupon the boys began to get supper.

"George, do you know anything about this water?" asked Ken. "Is it safe?"

George supposed it was all right, but he did not know. The matter of water had bothered Ken more than any other thing in consideration of the trip. This river-water was cool and clear; it apparently was safe. But Ken decided not to take any chances, and to boil all the water used. All at once George yelled, "Canvas-backs!" and made a dive for his gun. Ken saw a flock of ducks swiftly winging flight up-stream.

"Hold on, George; don't shoot," called Ken. "Let's go a little slow at the start."

George appeared to be disappointed, though he promptly obeyed.

Then the boys had supper, finding the russet duck much to their taste. Ken made a note of Pepe's capacity, and was glad there were prospects of plenty of meat. While they were eating, a group of natives gathered on the bridge. Ken would not have liked to interpret their opinion of his party from their actions.

Night came on almost before the boys were ready for it. They replenished the camp-fire, and sat around it, looking into the red blaze and then out into the flickering shadows. Ken thought the time propitious for a little lecture he had to give the boys, and he remembered how old Hiram Bent had talked to him and Hal that first night down under the great black rim-wall of the Grand Cañon.

"Well, fellows," began Ken, "we're started, we're here, and the trip looks great to me. Now, as I am responsible, I intend to be boss. I want you boys to do what I tell you. I may make mistakes, but if I do I'll take them on my shoulders. Let's try to make the trip a great success. Let's be careful. We're not game-hogs. We'll not kill any more than we can eat. I want you boys to be careful with your guns. Think all the time where you're pointing them. And as to thinking, we'd do well to use our heads all the time. We've no idea what we're going up against in this jungle."

Both boys listened to Ken with attention and respect, but they did not bind themselves by any promises.

Ken had got out the mosquito-netting, expecting any moment to find it very serviceable; however, to his surprise it was not needed. When it came time to go to bed, Hal and George did not forget to slip in between Pepe and Ken. The open-sided tent might keep off rain or dew, but for all the other protection it afforded, the boys might as well have slept outside. Nevertheless they were soon fast asleep. Ken awoke a couple of times during the night and rolled over to find a softer spot in the hard bed. These times he heard only the incessant hum of insects.

When he opened his eyes in the gray morning light, he did hear something that made him sit up with a start. It was a deep booming sound, different from anything that he had ever heard. Ken called Pepe, and that roused the boys.

"Listen," said Ken.

In a little while the sound was repeated, a heavy "boo-oom! ... boo-oom!" There was a resemblance to the first strong beats of a drumming grouse, only infinitely wilder.

Pepe called it something like "*faisan real*."

"What's that?" asked Hal.

The name was as new to Ken as the noise itself. Pepe explained through George that it was made by a huge black bird not unlike a turkey. It had a golden plume, and could run as fast as a deer. The boys rolled out, all having conceived a desire to see such a strange bird. The sound was not repeated. Almost immediately, however, the thicket across the river awoke to another sound, as much a contrast to the boom as could be imagined. It was a bird medley. At first Ken thought of magpies, but Pepe dispelled this illusion with another name hard to pronounce.

"Chicalocki," he said.

And that seemed just like what they were singing. It was a sharp, clear song--"Chic-a-lock-i ... chic-a-lock-i," and to judge from the full chorus there must have been many birds.

"They're a land of pheasant," added George, "and make fine pot-stews."

The *chicalocki* ceased their salute to the morning, and then, as the river mist melted away under the rising sun, other birds took it up. Notes new to Ken burst upon the air. And familiar old songs thrilled him, made him think of summer days on the Susquehanna--the sweet carol of the meadow-lark, the whistle of the quail, the mellow, sad call of the swamp-blackbird. The songs blended in an exquisite harmony.

"Why, some of them are our own birds come south for the winter," declared Hal.

"It's music," said Ken.

"Just wait," laughed George.

It dawned upon Ken then that George was a fellow who had the mysterious airs of a prophet hinting dire things.

Ken did not know what to wait for, but he enjoyed the suggestion and anticipated much. Ducks began to whir by; flocks of blackbirds alighted in the trees across the river. Suddenly Hal jumped up, and Ken was astounded at a great discordant screeching and a sweeping rush of myriads of wings. Ken looked up to see the largest flock of birds he had ever seen.

"Parrots," he yelled.

Indeed they were, and they let the boys know it. They flew across the river, wheeled to come back, all the time screeching, and then they swooped down into the tops of the cypress-trees.

"Red-heads," said George. "Just wait till you see the yellow-heads!"

At the moment the red-heads were quite sufficient for Ken. They broke out into a chattering, screaming, cackling discordance. It was plainly directed at the boys. These intelligent birds were curious and resentful. As Pepe put it, they were scolding. Ken enjoyed it for a full half-hour and reveled in the din. That morning serenade was worth the trip. Presently the parrots flew away, and Ken was surprised to find that most of the other birds had ceased singing. They had set about the business of the day--something it was nigh time for Ken to consider.

Breakfast over, the boys broke camp, eager for the adventures that they felt to be before them.

VI WILDERNESS LIFE

"Now for the big job, boys," called Ken. "Any ideas will be welcome, but don't all talk at once."

And this job was the packing of the outfit in the boat. It was a study for Ken, and he found himself thanking his lucky stars that he had packed boats for trips on rapid rivers. George and Hal came to the fore with remarkable advice which Ken was at the pains of rejecting. And as fast as one wonderful idea emanated from the fertile minds another one came in. At last Ken lost patience.

"Kids, it's going to take brains to pack this boat," he said, with some scorn.

And when Hal remarked that in that case he did not see how they ever were going to pack the boat, Ken drove both boys away and engaged Pepe to help.

The boat had to be packed for a long trip, with many things taken into consideration. The very best way to pack it must be decided upon and thereafter held to strictly. Balance was all-important; comfort and elbow-room were not to be overlooked; a flat surface easy to crawl and jump over was absolutely necessary. Fortunately, the boat was large and roomy, although not heavy. The first thing Ken did was to cut out the narrow bow-seat. Here he packed a small bucket of preserved mullet, some bottles of kerosene and *canya*, and a lantern. The small, flat trunk, full of supplies, went in next. Two boxes with the rest of the supplies filled up the space between the trunk and the rowing-seat. By slipping an extra pair of oars, coils of rope, the ax, and a few other articles between the gunwales and the trunk and boxes Ken made them fit snugly. He cut off a piece of the canvas, and, folding it, he laid it with the blankets lengthwise over the top. This made a level surface, one that could be gotten over quickly, or a place to sleep, for that matter, and effectually disposed of the bow half of the boat. Of course the boat sank deep at the bow, but Ken calculated when they were all aboard their weight would effect an even balance.

The bags with clothing Ken put under the second seat. Then he arranged the other piece of canvas so that it projected up back of the stern of the boat. He was thinking of the waves to be buffeted in going stern first down-stream through the rapids. The fishing-tackle and guns he laid flat from seat to seat. Last of all he placed the ammunition on one side next the gunwale, and the suit-case carrying camera, films, medicines, on the other.

"Come now, fellows," called Ken. "Hal, you and George take the second seat. Pepe will take the oars. I'll sit in the stern."

Pepe pushed off, jumped to his place, and grasped the oars. Ken was delighted to find the boat trim, and more buoyant than he had dared to hope.

"We're off," cried Hal, and he whooped. And George exercised his already well-developed faculty of imitating Hal.

Pepe bent to the oars, and under his powerful strokes the boat glided up-stream. Soon the bridge disappeared. Ken had expected a long, shady ride, but it did not turn out so. Shallow water and gravelly rapids made rowing impossible.

"Pile out, boys, and pull," said Ken.

The boys had dressed for wading and rough work, and went overboard with a will. Pulling, at first, was not hard work. They were fresh and eager, and hauled the boat up swift, shallow channels, making nearly as good time as when rowing in smooth water. Then, as the sun began to get hot, splashing in the cool river was pleasant. They passed little islands green with willows and came to high clay-banks gradually wearing away, and then met with rocky restrictions in the stream-bed. From round a bend came a hollow roar of a deeper rapid. Ken found it a swift-rushing incline, very narrow, and hard to pull along. The margin of the river was hidden and obstructed by willows so that the boys could see very little ahead.

When they got above this fall the water was deep and still. Entering the boat again, they turned a curve into a long, beautiful stretch of river.

"Ah! this 's something like," said Hal.

The green, shady lane was alive with birds and water-fowl. Ducks of various kinds rose before the boat. White, blue, gray, and speckled herons, some six feet tall, lined the low bars, and flew only at near approach. There were many varieties of bitterns, one kind with a purple back and white breast. They were very tame and sat on the overhanging branches, uttering dismal croaks. Everywhere was the flash and glitter and gleam of birds in flight, up and down and across the river.

Hal took his camera and tried to get pictures.

The strangeness, beauty, and life of this jungle stream absorbed Ken. He did not take his guns from their cases. The water was bright green and very deep; here and there were the swirls of playing fish. The banks were high and densely covered with a luxuriant foliage. Huge cypress-trees, moss-covered, leaned half-way across the river. Giant gray-barked ceibas spread long branches thickly tufted with aloes, orchids, and other jungle parasites. Palm-trees lifted slender stems and graceful broad-leaved heads. Clumps of bamboo spread an enormous green arch out over the banks. These bamboo-trees were particularly beautiful to Ken. A hundred yellow, black-circled stems grew out of the ground close together, and as they rose high they gracefully leaned their bodies and drooped their tips. The leaves were arrowy, exquisite in their fineness.

He looked up the long river-lane, bright in the sun, dark and still under the moss-veiled cypresses, at the turning vines and blossoming creepers, at the changeful web of moving birds, and indulged to the fullest that haunting sense for wild places.

"Chicalocki," said Pepe, suddenly.

A flock of long-tailed birds, resembling the pheasant in body, was sailing across the river. Again George made a dive for a gun. This one was a sixteen-gage and worn out. He shot twice at the birds on the wing. Then Pepe rowed under the overhanging branches, and George killed three *chicalocki* with his rifle. They were olive green in color, and the long tail had a brownish cast. Heavy and plump, they promised fine eating.

"Pato real!" yelled Pepe, pointing excitedly up the river.

Several black fowl, as large as geese, hove in sight, flying pretty low. Ken caught a glimpse of wide, white-crested wings, and knew then that these were the birds he had seen.

"Load up and get ready," he said to George. "They're coming fast--shoot ahead of them."

How swift and powerful they were on the wing! They swooped up when they saw the boat, and offered a splendid target. The little sixteen-gage rang out. Ken heard the shot strike. The leader stopped in midair, dipped, and plunged with a sounding splash. Ken picked him up and found him to be most beautiful, and as large and heavy as a goose. His black feathers shone with the latent green luster of an opal, and the pure white of the shoulder of the wings made a remarkable contrast.

"George, we've got enough meat for to-day, more than we can use. Don't shoot any more," said Ken.

Pepe resumed rowing, and Ken told him to keep under the overhanging branches and to row without splashing. He was skilled in the use of the oars, so the boat glided along silently. Ken felt he was rewarded for this stealth. Birds of rare and brilliant plumage flitted among the branches. There was one, a long, slender bird, gold and black with a white ring round its neck. There were little yellow-breasted kingfishers no larger than a wren, and great red-breasted kingfishers with blue backs and tufted heads. The boat passed under a leaning ceiba-tree that was covered with orchids. Ken saw the slim, sharp head of a snake dart from among the leaves. His neck was as thick as Ken's wrist.

"What kind of a snake, Pepe?" whispered Ken, as he fingered the trigger of George's gun. But Pepe did not see the snake, and then Ken thought better of disturbing the silence with a gunshot. He was reminded, however, that the Texan had told him of snakes in this jungle, some of which measured more than fifteen feet and were as large as a man's leg.

Most of the way the bank was too high and steep and overgrown for any animal to get down to the water. Still there were dry gullies, or arroyos, every few hundred yards, and these showed the tracks of animals, but Pepe could not tell what species from the boat. Often Ken heard the pattering of hard feet, and then he would see a little cloud of dust in one of these drinking-places. So he cautioned Pepe to row slower and closer in to the bank.

"Look there! lemme out!" whispered Hal, and he seemed to be on the point of jumping overboard.

"Coons," said George. "Oh, a lot of them. There--some young ones."

Ken saw that they had come abruptly upon a band of racoons, not less than thirty in number, some big, some little, and a few like tiny balls of fur, and all had long white-ringed tails. What a scampering the big ones set up! The little ones were frightened, and the smallest so tame they scarcely made any effort to escape. Pepe swung the boat in to the bank, and reaching out he caught a baby racoon and handed it to Hal.

"Whoop! We'll catch things and tame them," exclaimed Hal, much delighted, and he proceeded to tie the little racoon under the seat.

"Sure, we'll get a whole menagerie," said George.

So they went on up-stream. Often Ken motioned Pepe to stop in dark, cool places under the golden-green canopy of bamboos. He was as much fascinated by the beautiful foliage and tree growths as by the wild life. Hal appeared more taken up with the fluttering of birds in the thick jungle, rustlings, and soft, stealthy steps. Then as they moved on Ken whispered and pointed out a black animal vanishing in the thicket. Three times he caught sight of a spotted form slipping away in the shade. George saw it the last time, and whispered: "Tiger-cat! Let's get him."

"What's that, Ken, a kind of a wildcat?" asked Hal.

"Yes." Ken took George's .32-caliber and tried to find a way up the bank. There was no place to climb up unless he dragged himself up branches of trees or drooping bamboos, and this he did not care to attempt encumbered with a rifle. Only here and there could he see over the matted roots and creepers. Then the sound of rapids put hunting out of his mind.

"Boys, we've got Micas Falls to reach," he said, and told Pepe to row on.

The long stretch of deep river ended in a wide, shallow, noisy rapid. Fir-trees lined the banks. The palms, cypresses, bamboos, and the flowery, mossy growths were not here in evidence. Thickly wooded hills rose on each side. The jungle looked sear and yellow.

The boys began to wade up the rapid, and before they had reached the head of it Pepe yelled and jumped back from where he was wading at the bow. He took an oar and began to punch at something in the water, at the same time calling out.

"Crocodile!" cried George, and he climbed in the boat. Hal was not slow in following suit. Then Ken saw Pepe hitting a small crocodile, which lashed out with its tail and disappeared.

"Come out of there," called Ken to the boys. "We can't pull you up-stream."

"Say, I don't want to step on one of those ugly brutes," protested Hal.

"Look sharp, then. Come out."

Above the rapid extended a quarter-mile stretch where Pepe could row, and beyond that another long rapid. When the boys had waded up that it was only to come to another. It began to be hard work. But Ken kept the boys buckled down, and they made fair progress. They pulled up through eighteen rapids, and covered distance that Ken estimated to be about ten miles. The blue mountain loomed closer and higher, yet Ken began to have doubts of reaching Micas Falls that day.

Moreover, as they ascended the stream, the rapids grew rougher.

"It 'll be great coming down," panted Hal.

Finally they reached a rapid which had long dinned in Ken's ears. All the water in the river rushed down on the right-hand side through a channel scarcely twenty feet wide. It was deep and swift. With the aid of ropes, and by dint of much hard wading and pulling, the boys got the boat up. A little farther on was another bothersome rapid. At last they came to a succession of falls, steps in the river, that barred farther advance up-stream.

Here Ken climbed up on the bank, to find the country hilly and open, with patches of jungle and palm groves leading up to the mountains. Then he caught a glint of Micas Falls, and decided that it would be impossible to get there. He made what observations he could, and returned to camp.

"Boys, here's where we stop," said Ken. "It 'll be all down-stream now, and I'm glad."

There was no doubt that the boys were equally glad. They made camp on a grassy bench above a foam-flecked pool. Ken left the others to get things in shape for supper, and, taking his camera, he hurried off to try to get a picture of Micas Falls. He found open places and by-paths through the brushy forest. He saw evidences of forest fire, and then knew what had ruined that part of the jungle. There were no birds. It was farther than he had estimated to the foothill he had marked, but, loath to give up, he kept on and finally reached a steep, thorny ascent. Going up he nearly suffocated with heat. He felt rewarded for his exertions when he saw Micas Falls glistening in the distance. It was like a string of green fans connected by silver ribbons. He remained there watching it while the sun set in the golden notch between the mountains.

On the way back to camp he waded through a flat overgrown with coarse grass and bushes. Here he jumped a herd of deer, eight in number. These small, sleek, gray deer appeared tame, and if there had been sufficient light, Ken would have photographed them. It cost him an effort to decide not to fetch his rifle, but as he had meat enough in camp there was nothing to do except let the deer go.

When he got back to the river Pepe grinned at him, and, pointing to little red specks on his shirt, he said:

"Pinilius."

"Aha! the ticks!" exclaimed Ken.

They were exceedingly small, not to be seen without close scrutiny. They could not be brushed off, so Ken began laboriously to pick them off. Pepe and George laughed, and Hal appeared to derive some sort of enjoyment from the incident.

"Say, these ticks don't bother me any," declared Ken.

Pepe grunted; and George called out, "Just wait till you get the big fellows--the garrapatoes."

It developed presently that the grass and bushes on the camp-site contained millions of the ticks. Ken found several of the larger ticks--almost the size of his little finger-nail--but he did not get bitten. Pepe and George, however, had no such good luck, as was manifested at different times. By the time they had cut down the bushes and carried in a stock of fire-wood, both were covered with the little pests. Hal found a spot where there appeared to be none, and here he stayed.

Pepe and George had the bad habit of smoking, and Ken saw them burning the ticks off shirt-sleeves and trousers-legs, using the fiery end of their cigarettes. This feat did not puzzle Ken anything like the one where they held the red point of the cigarettes close to their naked flesh. Ken, and Hal, too, had to see that performance at close range.

"Why do you do that?" asked Ken.

"Popping ticks," replied George. He and Pepe were as sober as judges.

The fact of the matter was soon clear to Ken. The ticks stuck on as if glued. When the hot end of the burning cigarette was held within a quarter of an inch of them they simply blew up, exploded with a pop. Ken could easily distinguish between the tiny pop of an exploding *pinilius* and the heavier pop of a *garrapato.*

"But, boy, while you're taking time to do that, half a dozen other ticks can bite you!" exclaimed Ken.

"Sure they can," replied George. "But if they get on me I'll kill 'em. I don't mind the little ones--it's the big boys I hate."

On the other hand, Pepe seemed to mind most the *pinilius.*

"Say, from now on you fellows will be Garrapato George and Pinilius Pepe."

"Pretty soon you'll laugh on the other side of your face," said George. "In three days you'll be popping ticks yourself."

Just then Hal let out a yell and began to hunt for a tick that had bit him. If there was anything that could bother Hal Ward it was a crawling bug of some kind.

"I'll have to christen you too, brother," said Ken, gurgling with mirth. "A very felicitous name--Hollering Hal!"

Despite the humor of the thing, Ken really saw its serious side. When he found the grass under his feet alive with ticks he cast about in his mind for some way to get rid of them. And he hit upon a remedy. On the ridge above the bench was a palm-tree, and under it were many dead palm leaves. These were large in size, had long stems, and were as dry as tinder. Ken lighted one, and it made a flaming hot torch. It did not take him long to scorch all the ticks near that camp.

The boys had supper and enjoyed it hugely. The scene went well with the camp-fire and game-dinner. They gazed out over the foaming pool, the brawling rapids, to the tufted palm-trees, and above them the dark-blue mountain. At dusk Hal and George were so tired they went to bed and at once dropped into slumber. Pepe sat smoking before the slumbering fire.

And Ken chose that quiet hour to begin the map of the river, and to set down in his note-book his observations on the mountains and in the valley, and what he had seen that day of bird, animal, and plant life in the jungle.

VII RUNNING THE RAPIDS

Some time in the night a yell awakened Ken. He sat up, clutching his revolver. The white moonlight made all as clear as day. Hal lay deep in slumber. George was raising himself, half aroused. But Pepe was gone.

Ken heard a thrashing about outside. Leaping up he ran out, and was frightened to see Pepe beating and clawing and tearing at himself like a man possessed of demons.

"Pepe, what's wrong?" shouted Ken.

It seemed that Pepe only grew more violent in his wrestling about. Then Ken was sure Pepe had been stung by a scorpion or bitten by a snake.

But he was dumfounded to see George bound like an apparition out of the tent and begin evolutions that made Pepe's look slow.

"Hey, what's wrong with you jumping-jacks?" yelled Ken.

George was as grimly silent as an Indian running the gantlet, but Ken thought it doubtful if any Indian ever slapped and tore at his body in George's frantic manner. To add to the mystery Hal suddenly popped out of the tent. He was yelling in a way to do justice to the name Ken had lately given him, and, as for wild and whirling antics, his were simply marvelous.

"Good land!" ejaculated Ken. Had the boys all gone mad? Despite his alarm, Ken had to roar with laughter at those three dancing figures in the moonlight. A rush of ideas went through Ken's confused mind. And the last prompted him to look in the tent.

He saw a wide bar of black crossing the moonlit ground, the grass, and the blankets. This bar moved. It was alive. Bending low Ken descried that it was made by ants. An army of jungle ants on a march! They had come in a straight line along the base of the little hill and their passageway led under the canvas. Pepe happened to be the first in line, and they had surged over him. As he had awakened, and jumped up of course, the ants had begun to bite. The same in turn happened to George and then Hal.

Ken was immensely relieved, and had his laugh out. The stream of ants moved steadily and quite rapidly, and soon passed from sight. By this time Pepe and the boys had threshed themselves free of ants and into some degree of composure.

"Say, you nightmare fellows! Come back to bed," said Ken. "Any one would think something had really happened to you."

Pepe snorted, which made Ken think the native understood something of English. And the boys grumbled loudly.

"Ants! Ants as big as wasps! They bit worse than helgramites," declared Hal. "Oh, they missed you. You always are lucky. I'm not afraid of all the old jaguars in this jungle. But I can't stand biting, crawling bugs. I wish you hadn't made me come on this darn trip."

"Ha! Ha!" laughed Ken.

"Just wait, Hal," put in George, grimly. "Just wait. It's coming to him!"

The boys slept well the remainder of the night and, owing to the break in their rest, did not awaken early. The sun shone hot when Ken rolled out; a creamy mist was dissolving over the curve of the mountain-range; parrots were screeching in the near-by trees.

After breakfast Ken set about packing the boat as it had been done the day before.

"I think we'll do well to leave the trunk in the boat after this, unless we find a place where we want to make a permanent camp for a while," said Ken.

Before departing he carefully looked over the ground to see that nothing was left, and espied a heavy fish-line which George had baited, set, and forgotten.

"Hey, George, pull up your trot-line. It looks pretty much stretched to me. Maybe you've got a fish."

Ken happened to be busy at the boat when George started to take in the line. An exclamation from Pepe, George's yell, and a loud splash made Ken jump up in double-quick time. Hal also came running.

George was staggering on the bank, leaning back hard on the heavy line. A long, angry swirl in the pool told of a powerful fish. It was likely to pull George in.

"Let go the line!" yelled Ken.

But George was not letting go of any fish-lines. He yelled for Pepe, and went down on his knees before Pepe got to him. Both then pulled on the line. The fish, or whatever it was at the other end, gave a mighty jerk that almost dragged the two off the bank.

"Play him, play him!" shouted Ken. "You've got plenty of line. Give him some."

Hal now added his weight and strength, and the three of them, unmindful of Ken's advice, hauled back with might and main. The line parted and they sprawled on the grass.

"What a sockdologer!" exclaimed Hal.

"I had that hook baited with a big piece of duck meat," said George. "We must have been hooked to a crocodile. Things are happening to us."

"Yes, so I've noticed," replied Ken, dryly. "But if you fellows hadn't pulled so hard you might have landed that thing, whatever it was. All aboard now. We must be on the move--we don't know what we have before us."

When they got into the boat Ken took the oars, much to Pepe's surprise. It was necessary to explain to him that Ken would handle the boat in swift water. They shoved off, and Ken sent one regretful glance up the river, at the shady aisle between the green banks, at the white rapids, and the great colored dome of the mountain. He almost hesitated, for he desired to see more of that jungle-covered mountain. But something already warned Ken to lose no time in the trip down the Santa Rosa. There did not seem to be any reason for hurry, yet he felt it necessary. But he asked Pepe many questions and kept George busy interpreting names of trees and flowers and wild creatures.

Going down-stream on any river, mostly, would have been pleasure, but drifting on the swift current of the Santa Rosa and rowing under the wonderful moss-bearded cypresses was almost like a dream. It was too beautiful to seem real. The smooth stretch before the first rapid was short, however, and then all Ken's attention had to be given to the handling of the boat. He saw that George and Pepe both expected to get out and wade down the rapids as they had waded up. He had a surprise in store for them. The rapids that he could not shoot would have to be pretty bad.

"You're getting close," shouted George, warningly.

With two sweeps of the oars Ken turned the boat stern first down-stream, then dipped on the low green incline, and sailed down toward the waves. They struck the first wave with a shock, and the water flew all over the boys. Pepe was tremendously excited; he yelled and made wild motions with his hands; George looked a little frightened. Hal enjoyed it. Whatever the rapid appeared to them, it was magnificent to Ken; and it was play to manage the boat in such water. A little pull on one oar and then on the other kept the stern straight down-stream. The channel he could make out a long way ahead. He amused himself by watching George and Pepe. There were stones in the channel, and the water rose angrily about them. A glance was enough to tell that he could float over these without striking. But the boys thought they were going to hit every stone, and were uneasy all the time. Twice he had to work to pass ledges and sunken trees upon which the current bore down hard. When Ken neared one of these he dipped the oars and pulled back to stop or lessen the momentum; then a stroke turned the boat half broadside to the current. That would force it to one side, and another stroke would turn the boat straight. At the bottom of this rapid they encountered a long triangle of choppy waves that they bumped and splashed over. They came through with nothing wet but the raised flap of canvas in the stern.

Pepe regarded Ken with admiring eyes, and called him *grande mozo*.

"Shooting rapids is great sport," proclaimed George.

They drifted through several little rifts, and then stopped at the head of the narrow chute that had been such a stumbling-block on the way up. Looked at from above, this long, narrow channel, with several S curves, was a fascinating bit of water for a canoeist. It tempted Ken to shoot it even with the boat. But he remembered the four-foot waves at the bottom, and besides he resented the importunity of the spirit of daring so early in the game. Risk, and perhaps peril, would come soon enough. So he decided to walk along the shore and float the boat through with a rope.

The thing looked a good deal easier than it turned out to be. Half-way through, at the narrowest point and most abrupt curve, Pepe misunderstood directions and pulled hard on the bow-rope, when he should have let it slack.

The boat swung in, nearly smashing Ken against the bank, and the sweeping current began to swell dangerously near the gunwale.

"Let go! Let go!" yelled Ken. "George, make him let go!"

But George, who was trying to get the rope out of Pepe's muscular hands, suddenly made a dive for his rifle.

"Deer! deer!" he cried, hurriedly throwing a shell into the chamber. He shot downstream, and Ken, looking that way, saw several deer under the firs on a rocky flat. George shot three more times, and the bullets went "spinging" into the trees. The deer bounded out of sight.

When Ken turned again, water was roaring into the boat. He was being pressed harder into the bank, and he saw disaster ahead.

"Loosen the rope--tell him, George," yelled Ken.

Pepe only pulled the harder.

"Quick, or we're ruined," cried Ken.

George shouted in Spanish, and Pepe promptly dropped the rope in the water. That was the worst thing he could have done.

"Grab the rope!" ordered Ken, wildly. "Grab the bow! Don't let it swing out! Hal!"

Before either boy could reach it the bow swung out into the current. Ken was not only helpless, but in a dangerous position. He struggled to get out from where the swinging stern was wedging him into the bank, but could not budge. Fearing that all the outfit would be lost in the river, he held on to the boat and called for some one to catch the rope.

George pushed Pepe head first into the swift current. Pepe came up, caught the rope, and then went under again. The boat swung round and, now half full of water, got away from Ken. It gathered headway. Ken leaped out on the ledge and ran along with the boat. It careened round the bad curve and shot down-stream. Pepe was still under water.

"He's drowned! He's drowned!" cried George.

Hal took a header right off the ledge, came up, and swam with a few sharp strokes to the drifting boat. He gained the bow, grasped it, and then pulled on the rope.

Ken had a sickening feeling that Pepe might be drowned. Suddenly Pepe appeared like a brown porpoise. He was touching bottom in places and holding back on the rope. Then the current rolled him over and over. The boat drifted back of a rocky point into shallow water. Hal gave a haul that helped to swing it out of the dangerous current. Then Pepe came up, and he, too, pulled hard. Just as Ken plunged in the boat sank in two feet of water. Ken's grip, containing camera, films, and other perishable goods, was on top, and he got it just in time. He threw it out on the rocks. Then together the boys lifted the boat and hauled the bow well up on the shore.

"Pretty lucky!" exclaimed Ken, as he flopped down.

"Doggone it!" yelled Hal, suddenly. And he dove for the boat, and splashed round in the water under his seat, to bring forth a very limp and drenched little racoon.

"Good! he's all right," said Ken.

Pepe said "Mucho malo," and pointed to his shins, which bore several large bumps from contact with the rocks in the channel.

"I should say mucha malo," growled George.

He jerked open his grip, and, throwing out articles of wet clothing--for which he had no concern--he gazed in dismay at his whole store of cigarettes wet by the water.

"So that's all you care for," said Ken, severely. "Young man, I'll have something to say to you presently. All hands now to unpack the boat."

Fortunately nothing had been carried away. That part of the supplies which would have been affected by water was packed in tin cases, and so suffered no damage. The ammunition was waterproof. Ken's Parker hammerless and his 351 automatic rifle were full of water, and so were George's guns and Hal's. While they took their weapons apart, wiped them, and laid them in the sun, Pepe spread out the rest of the things and then baled out the boat. The sun was so hot that everything dried quickly and was not any the worse for the wetting. The boys lost scarcely an hour by the accident. Before the start Ken took George and Pepe to task, and when he finished they were both very sober and quiet.

Ken observed, however, that by the time they had run the next rapid they were enjoying themselves again. Then came a long succession of rapids which Ken shot without anything approaching a mishap. When they drifted into the level stretch Pepe relieved him at the oars. They glided down-stream under the drooping bamboo, under the silken streamers of silvery moss, under the dark, cool bowers of matted vine and blossoming creepers. And as they passed this time the jungle silence awoke to the crack of George's .22 and the discordant cry of river fowl. Ken's guns were both at hand, and the rifle was loaded, but he did not use either. He contented himself with snapping a picture here and there and watching the bamboo thickets and the mouths of the little dry ravines.

That ride was again so interesting, so full of sound and action and color, that it seemed a very short one. The murmur of the water on the rocks told Ken that it was time to change seats with Pepe. They drifted down two short rapids, and then came to the gravelly channels between the islands noted on the way up. The water was shallow down these rippling channels; and, fearing they might strike a stone, Ken tumbled out over the bow and, wading slowly, let the boat down to still water again. He was about to get in when he espied what he thought was an alligator lying along a log near the river. He pointed it out to Pepe.

That worthy yelled gleefully in Mexican, and reached for his *machete*.

"Iguana!" exclaimed George. "I've heard it's good to eat."

The reptile had a body about four feet long and a very long tail. Its color was a steely blue-black on top, and it had a blunt, rounded head.

Pepe slipped out of the boat and began to wade ashore. When the iguana raised itself on short, stumpy legs George shot at it, and missed, as usual. But he effectually frightened the reptile, which started to climb the bank with much nimbleness. Pepe began to run, brandishing his long *machete*. George plunged into the water in hot pursuit, and then Hal yielded to the call of the chase. Pepe reached the iguana before it got up the bank, aimed a mighty blow with his *machete*, and would surely have cut the reptile in two pieces if the blade had not caught on an overhanging branch. Then Pepe fell up the bank and barely grasped the tail of the iguana. Pepe hauled back, and Pepe was powerful. The frantic creature dug its feet in the clay-bank and held on for dear life. But Pepe was too strong. He jerked the iguana down and flung it square upon George, who had begun to climb the bank.

George uttered an awful yell, as if he expected to be torn asunder, and rolled down, with the reptile on top of him. Ken saw that it was as badly frightened as George. But Hal did not see this. And he happened to have gained a little sandbar below the bank, in which direction the iguana started with wonderful celerity. Then Hal made a jump that Ken believed was a record.

Remarkably awkward as that iguana was, he could surely cover ground with his stumpy legs. Again he dashed up the bank. Pepe got close enough once more, and again he swung the *machete*. The blow cut off a piece of the long tail, but the only effect this produced was to make the iguana run all the faster. It disappeared over the bank, with Pepe scrambling close behind. Then followed a tremendous crashing in the dry thickets, after which the iguana could be heard rattling and tearing away through the jungle. Pepe returned to the boat with the crestfallen boys, and he was much concerned over the failure to catch the big lizard, which he said made fine eating.

"What next?" asked George, ruefully, and at that the boys all laughed.

"The fun is we don't have any idea what's coming off," said Hal.

"Boys, if you brave hunters had thought to throw a little salt on that lizard's tail you might have caught him," added Ken.

Presently Pepe espied another iguana in the forks of a tree, and he rowed ashore. This lizard was only a small one, not over two feet in length, but he created some excitement among the boys. George wanted him to eat, and Hal wanted the skin for a specimen, and Ken wanted to see what the lizard looked like close at hand. So they all clamored for Pepe to use caution and to be quick.

When Pepe started up the tree the iguana came down on the other side, quick as a squirrel. Then they had a race round the trunk until Pepe ended it with a well-directed blow from his *machete*.

Hal began to skin the iguana.

"Ken, I'm going to have trouble preserving specimens in this hot place," he said.

"Salt and alum will do the trick. Remember what old Hiram used to say," replied Ken.

Shortly after that the boat passed the scene of the first camp, and then drifted under the railroad bridge.

Hal and George, and Pepe too, looked as if they were occupied with the same thought troubling Ken--that once beyond the bridge they would plunge into the jungle wilderness from which there could be no turning back.

VIII THE FIRST TIGER-CAT

The Santa Rosa opened out wide, and ran swiftly over smooth rock. Deep cracks, a foot or so wide, crossed the river diagonally, and fish darted in and out.

The boys had about half a mile of this, when, after turning a hilly bend, they entered a long rapid. It was a wonderful stretch of river to look down.

"By George!" said Ken, as he stood up to survey it. "This is great!"

"It's all right *now*," added George, with his peculiar implication as to the future.

"What gets me is the feeling of what might be round the next bend," said Hal.

This indeed, Ken thought, made the fascination of such travel. The water was swift and smooth and shallow. There was scarcely a wave or ripple. At times the boat stuck fast on the flat rock, and the boys would have to get out to shove off. As far ahead as Ken could see extended this wide slant of water. On the left rose a thick line of huge cypresses all festooned with gray moss that drooped to the water; on the right rose a bare bluff of crumbling rock. It looked like blue clay baked and cracked by the sun. A few palms fringed the top.

"Say, we can beat this," said Ken, as for the twentieth time the boys had to step out and shove off a flat, shallow place. "Two of you in the bow and Pepe with me in the stern, feet overboard."

The little channels ran every way, making it necessary often to turn the boat. Ken's idea was to drift along and keep the boat from grounding by an occasional kick.

"Ken manages to think of something once in a while," observed Hal.

Then the boat drifted down-stream, whirling round and round. Here Pepe would drop his brown foot in and kick his end clear of a shallow ledge; there George would make a great splash when his turn came to ward off from a rock; and again Hal would give a greater kick than was necessary to the righting of the boat. Probably Hal was much influenced by the fact that when he kicked hard he destroyed the lazy equilibrium of his companions.

It dawned upon Ken that here was a new and unique way to travel down a river. It was different from anything he had ever tried before. The water was swift and seldom more than a foot deep, except in diagonal cracks that ribbed the river-bed. This long, shut-in stretch appeared to be endless. But for the quick, gliding movement of the boat, which made a little breeze, the heat would have been intolerable. When one of Hal's kicks made Ken lurch overboard to sit down ludicrously, the cool water sent thrills over him. Instead of retaliating on Hal, he was glad to be wet. And the others, soon discovering the reason for Ken's remarkable good-nature, went overboard and lay flat in the cool ripples. Then little clouds of steam began to rise from their soaked clothes.

Ken began to have an idea that he had been wise in boiling the water which they drank. They all suffered from a parching thirst. Pepe scooped up water in his hand; George did likewise, and then Hal.

"You've all got to stop that," ordered Ken, sharply. "No drinking this water unless it's boiled."

The boys obeyed, for the hour, but they soon forgot, or deliberately allayed their thirst despite Ken's command. Ken himself found his thirst unbearable. He squeezed the juice of a wild lime into a cup of water and drank that. Then he insisted on giving the boys doses of quinine and anti-malaria pills, which treatment he meant to continue daily.

Toward the lower part of that rapid, where the water grew deeper, fish began to be so numerous that the boys kicked at many as they darted under the boat. There were thousands of small fish and some large ones. Occasionally, as a big fellow lunged for a crack in the rock, he would make the water roar. There was a fish that resembled a mullet, and another that Hal said was some kind of bass with a blue tail. Pepe chopped at them with his *machete*; George whacked with an oar; Hal stood up in the boat and shot at them with his .22 rifle.

"Say, I've got to see what that blue-tailed bass looks like," said Ken. "You fellows will never get one."

Whereupon Ken jointed up a small rod and, putting on a spinner, began to cast it about. He felt two light fish hit it. Then came a heavy shock that momentarily checked the boat. The water foamed as the line cut through, and Ken was just about to jump off the boat to wade and follow the fish, when it broke the leader.

"That was a fine exhibition," remarked the critical Hal.

"What's the matter with you?" retorted Ken, who was sensitive as to his fishing abilities. "It was a big fish. He broke things."

"Haven't you got a reel on that rod and fifty yards of line?" queried Hal.

Ken did not have another spinner, and he tried an artificial minnow, but could not get a strike on it. He took Hal's gun and shot at several of the blue-tailed fish, but though he made them jump out of the water like a real northern black-bass, it was all of no avail.

Then Hal caught one with a swoop of the landing net. It was a beautiful fish, and it did have a blue tail. Pepe could not name it, nor could Ken classify it, so Hal was sure he had secured a rare specimen.

When the boat drifted round a bend to enter another long, wide, shallow rapid, the boys demurred a little at the sameness of things. The bare blue bluffs persisted, and the line of gray-veiled cypresses and the strange formation of stream-bed. Five more miles of drifting under the glaring sun made George and Hal lie back in the boat, under an improvised sun-shade. The ride was novel and strange to Ken

Ward, and did not pall upon him, though he suffered from the heat and glare. He sat on the bow, occasionally kicking the boat off a rock.

All at once a tense whisper from Pepe brought Ken round with a jerk. Pepe was pointing down along the right-hand shore. George heard, and, raising himself, called excitedly: "Buck! buck!"

Ken saw a fine deer leap back from the water and start to climb the side of a gully that indented the bluff. Snatching up the .351 rifle, he shoved in the safety catch. The distance was far--perhaps two hundred yards--but without elevating the sights he let drive. A cloud of dust puffed up under the nose of the climbing deer.

"Wow!" yelled George, and Pepe began to jabber. Hal sprang up, nearly falling overboard, and he shouted: "Give it to him, Ken!"

The deer bounded up a steep, winding trail, his white flag standing, his reddish coat glistening. Ken fired again. The bullet sent up a white puff of dust, this time nearer still. That shot gave Ken the range, and he pulled the automatic again--and again. Each bullet hit closer. The boys were now holding their breath, watching, waiting. Ken aimed a little firmer and finer at the space ahead of the deer--for in that instant he remembered what the old hunter on Penetier had told him--and he pulled the trigger twice.

The buck plunged down, slipped off the trail, and, raising a cloud of dust, rolled over and over. Then it fell sheer into space, and whirled down to strike the rock with a sodden crash.

It was Ken's first shooting on this trip, and he could not help adding a cry of exultation to the yells of his admiring comrades.

"Guess you didn't plug him!" exclaimed Hal Ward, with flashing eyes.

Wading, the boys pulled the boat ashore. Pepe pronounced the buck to be very large, but to Ken, remembering the deer in Coconino Forest, it appeared small. If there was an unbroken bone left in that deer, Ken greatly missed his guess. He and Pepe cut out the haunch least crushed by the fail.

"There's no need to carry along more meat than we can use," said George. "It spoils overnight. That's the worst of this jungle, I've heard hunters say."

Hal screwed up his face in the manner he affected when he tried to imitate old Hiram Bent. "Wal, youngster, I reckon I'm right an' down proud of thet shootin'. You air comin' along."

Ken was as pleased as Hal, but he replied, soberly: "Well, kid, I hope I can hold as straight as that when we run up against a jaguar."

"Do you think we'll see one?" asked Hal.

"Just you wait!" exclaimed George, replying for Ken. "Pepe says we'll have to sleep in the boat, and anchor the boat in the middle of the river."

"What for?"

"To keep those big yellow tigers from eating us up."

"How nice!" replied Hal, with a rather forced laugh.

So, talking and laughing, the boys resumed their down-stream journey. Ken, who was always watching with sharp eyes, saw buzzards appear, as if by magic.

Before the boat was half a mile down the river buzzards were circling over the remains of the deer. These birds of prey did not fly from the jungle on either side of the stream. They sailed, dropped down from the clear blue sky where they had been invisible. How wonderful that was to Ken! Nature had endowed these vulture-like birds with wonderful scent or instinct or sight, or all combined. But Ken believed that it was power of sight which brought the buzzards so quickly to the scene of the killing. He watched them circling, sweeping down till a curve in the river hid them from view.

And with this bend came a welcome change. The bluff played out in a rocky slope below which the green jungle was relief to aching eyes. As the boys made this point, the evening breeze began to blow. They beached the boat and unloaded to make camp.

"We haven't had any work to-day, but we're all tired just the same," observed Ken.

"The heat makes a fellow tired," said George.

They were fortunate in finding a grassy plot where there appeared to be but few ticks and other creeping things. That evening it was a little surprise to Ken to realize how sensitive he had begun to feel about these jungle vermin.

Pepe went up the bank for fire-wood. Ken heard him slashing away with his *machete*. Then this sound ceased, and Pepe yelled in fright. Ken and George caught up guns as they bounded into the thicket; Hal started to follow, likewise armed. Ken led the way through a thorny brake to come suddenly upon Pepe. At the same instant Ken caught a glimpse of gray, black-striped forms slipping away in the jungle. Pepe shouted out something.

"Tiger-cats!" exclaimed George.

Ken held up his finger to enjoin silence. With that he stole cautiously forward, the others noiselessly at his heels. The thicket was lined with well-beaten trails, and by following these and stooping low it was possible to go ahead without rustling the brush. Owing to the gathering twilight Ken could not see very far. When he stopped to listen he heard the faint crackling of dead brush and soft, quick steps. He had not proceeded far when pattering footsteps halted him. Ken dropped to his knee. The boys knelt behind him, and Pepe whispered. Peering along the trail Ken saw what he took for a wildcat. Its boldness amazed him. Surely it had heard him, but instead of bounding into the thicket it crouched not more than twenty-five feet away. Ken took a quick shot at the gray huddled form. It jerked, stretched out, and lay still. Then a crashing in the brush, and gray streaks down the trail told Ken of more game.

"There they go. Peg away at them," called Ken.

George and Hal burned a good deal of powder and sent much lead whistling through the dry branches, but the gray forms vanished in the jungle.

"We got one, anyway," said Ken.

He advanced to find his quarry quite dead. It was bigger than any wildcat Ken had ever seen. The color was a grayish yellow, almost white, lined and spotted with black. Ken lifted it and found it heavy enough to make a good load.

"He's a beauty," said Hal.

"Pepe says it's a tiger-cat," remarked George. "There are two or three kinds besides the big tiger. We may run into a lot of them and get some skins."

It was almost dark when they reached camp. While Pepe and Hal skinned the tiger-cat and stretched the pelt over a framework of sticks the other boys got supper. They were all very hungry and tired, and pleased with the events of the day. As they sat round the camp-fire there was a constant whirring of water-fowl over their heads and an incessant hum of insects from the jungle.

"Ken, does it feel as wild to you here as on Buckskin Mountain?" asked Hal.

"Oh yes, much wilder, Hal," replied his brother. "And it's different, somehow. Out in Arizona there was always the glorious expectancy of to-morrow's fun or sport. Here I have a kind of worry--a feeling--"

But he concluded it wiser to keep to himself that strange feeling of dread which came over him at odd moments.

"It suits me," said Hal. "I want to get a lot of things and keep them alive. Of course, I want specimens. I'd like some skins for my den, too. But I don't care so much about killing things."

"Just wait!" retorted George, who evidently took Hal's remark as a reflection upon his weakness. "Just wait! You'll be shooting pretty soon for your life."

"Now, George, what do you mean by that?" questioned Ken, determined to pin George down to facts. "You said you didn't really know anything about this jungle. Why are you always predicting disaster for us?"

"Why? Because I've heard things about the jungle," retorted George. "And Pepe says wait till we get down off the mountain. He doesn't *know* anything, either. But it's his instinct--Pepe's half Indian. So I say, too, wait till we get down in the jungle!"

"Confound you! Where are we now?" queried Ken.

"The real jungle is the lowland. There we'll find the tigers and the crocodiles and the wild cattle and wild pigs."

"Bring on your old pigs and things," replied Hal.

But Ken looked into the glowing embers of the camp-fire and was silent. When he got out his note-book and began his drawing, he forgot the worry and dread in the interest of his task. He was astonished at his memory, to see how he could remember every turn in the river and yet not lose his sense of direction. He could tell almost perfectly the distance traveled, because he knew so well just how much a boat would cover in swift or slow waters in a given time. He thought he could give a fairly correct estimate of the drop of the river. And, as for descriptions of the jungle life along the shores, that was a delight, all except trying to understand and remember and spell the names given to him by Pepe. Ken imagined Pepe spoke a mixture of Toltec, Aztec, Indian, Spanish, and English.

IX IN THE WHITE WATER

Upon awakening next morning Ken found the sun an hour high. He was stiff and sore and thirsty. Pepe and the boys slept so soundly it seemed selfish to wake them.

All around camp there was a melodious concourse of birds. But the parrots did not make a visit that morning. While Ken was washing in the river a troop of deer came down to the bar on the opposite side. Ken ran for his rifle, and by mistake took up George's .32. He had a splendid shot at less than one hundred yards. But the bullet dropped fifteen feet in front of the leading buck. The deer ran into the deep, bushy willows.

"That gun's leaded," muttered Ken. "It didn't shoot where I aimed."

Pepe jumped up; George rolled out of his blanket with one eye still glued shut; and Hal stretched and yawned and groaned.

"Do I have to get up?" he asked.

"Shore, lad," said Ken, mimicking Jim Williams, "or I'll hev to be reconsiderin' that idee of mine about you bein' pards with me."

Such mention of Hal's ranger friend brought the boy out of his lazy bed with amusing alacrity.

"Rustle breakfast, now, you fellows," said Ken, and, taking his rifle, he started off to climb the high river bluff.

It was his idea to establish firmly in mind the trend of the mountain-range, and the relation of the river to it. The difficulty in mapping the river would come after it left the mountains to wind away into the wide lowlands. The matter of climbing the bluff would have been easy but for the fact that he wished to avoid contact with grass, brush, trees, even dead branches, as all were covered with ticks. The upper half of the bluff was bare, and when he reached that part he soon surmounted it. Ken faced south with something of eagerness. Fortunately the mist had dissolved under the warm rays of the sun, affording an unobstructed view. That scene was wild and haunting, yet different from what his fancy had pictured. The great expanse of jungle was gray, the green line of cypress, palm, and bamboo following the southward course of the river. The mountain-range some ten miles distant sloped to the south and faded away in the haze. The river disappeared in rich dark verdure, and but for it, which afforded a water-road back to civilization, Ken would have been lost in a dense gray-green overgrowth of tropical wilderness. Once or twice he thought he caught the faint roar of a waterfall on the morning breeze, yet could not be sure, and he returned toward camp with a sober appreciation of the difficulty of his enterprise and a more thrilling sense of its hazard and charm.

"Didn't see anything to peg at, eh?" greeted Hal. "Well, get your teeth in some of this venison before it's all gone."

Soon they were under way again, Pepe strong and willing at the oars. This time Ken had his rifle and shotgun close at hand, ready for use. Half a mile below, the river, running still and deep, entered a shaded waterway so narrow that in places the branches of wide-spreading and leaning cypresses met and intertwined their moss-fringed foliage. This lane was a paradise for birds, that ranged from huge speckled cranes, six feet high, to little yellow birds almost too small to see.

Black squirrels were numerous and very tame. In fact, all the creatures along this shaded stream were so fearless that it was easy to see they had never heard a shot. Ken awoke sleepy cranes with his fishing-rod and once pushed a blue heron off a log. He heard animals of some species running back from the bank, out could not see them. All at once a soft breeze coming up-stream bore a deep roar of tumbling rapids. The sensation of dread which had bothered Ken occasionally now returned and fixed itself in his mind. He was in the jungle of Mexico, and knew not what lay ahead of him. But if he had been in the wilds of unexplored Brazil and had heard that roar, it would have been familiar to him. In his canoe experience on the swift streams of Pennsylvania Ken Ward had learned, long before he came to rapids, to judge what they were from the sound. His attention wandered from the beautiful birds, the moss-shaded bowers, and the overhanging jungle. He listened to the heavy, sullen roar of the rapids.

"That water sounds different," remarked George.

"Grande," said Pepe, with a smile.

"Pretty heavy, Ken, eh?" asked Hal, looking quickly at his brother.

But Ken Ward made his face a mask, and betrayed nothing of the grim nature of his thought. Pepe and the boys had little idea of danger, and they had now a blind faith in Ken.

"I dare say we'll get used to that roar," replied Ken, easily, and he began to pack his guns away in their cases.

Hal forgot his momentary anxiety; Pepe rowed on, leisurely; and George lounged in his seat. There was no menace for them in that dull, continuous roar.

But Ken knew they would soon be in fast water and before long would drop down into the real wilderness. It was not now too late to go back up the river, but soon that would be impossible. Keeping a sharp lookout ahead, Ken revolved in mind the necessity for caution and skilful handling of the boat. But he realized, too, that overzealousness on the side of caution was a worse thing for such a trip than sheer recklessness. Good judgment in looking over rapids, a quick eye to pick the best channel, then a daring spirit--that was the ideal to be striven for in going down swift rivers.

Presently Ken saw a break in the level surface of the water. He took Pepe's place at the oars, and, as usual, turned the boat stern first down-stream. The banks were low and shelved out in rocky points. This relieved Ken, for he saw that he could land just above the falls. What he feared was a narrow gorge impossible to portage round or go through. As the boat approached the break the roar seemed to divide itself, hollow and shallow near at hand, rushing and heavy farther on.

Ken rowed close to the bank and landed on the first strip of rock. He got out and, walking along this ledge, soon reached the fall. It was a straight drop of some twelve or fifteen feet. The water was shallow all the way across.

"Boys, this is easy," said Ken. "We'll pack the outfit round the fall, and slide the boat over."

But Ken did not say anything about the white water extending below the fall as far as he could see. From here came the sullen roar that had worried him.

Portaging the supplies around that place turned out to be far from easy. The portage was not long nor rugged, but the cracked, water-worn, rock made going very difficult. The boys often stumbled. Pepe fell and broke open a box, and almost broke his leg. Ken had a hard knock. Then, when it came to carrying the trunk, one at each corner, progress was laborious and annoying. Full two hours were lost in transporting the outfit around the fall.

Below there was a wide, shelving apron, over which the water ran a foot or so in depth. Ken stationed Pepe and the boys there, and went up to get the boat. He waded out with it. Ken saw that his end of this business was going to be simple enough, but he had doubts as to what would happen to the boys.

"Brace yourselves, now," he yelled. "When I drop her over she'll come a-humming. Hang on if she drags you a mile!"

Wading out deeper Ken let the boat swing down with the current till the stern projected over the fall. He had trouble in keeping his footing, for the rock was slippery. Then with a yell he ran the stern far out over the drop, bore down hard on the bow, and shoved off.

The boat shot out and down, to alight with a heavy souse. Then it leaped into the swift current. George got his hands on it first, and went down like a ninepin. The boat floated over him. The bow struck Hal, and would have dragged him away had not Pepe laid powerful hands on the stern. They waded to the lower ledge.

"Didn't ship a bucketful," said Hal. "Fine work, Ken."

"I got all the water," added the drenched and dripping George.

"Bail out, boys, and repack, while I look below," said Ken.

He went down-stream a little way to take a survey of the rapids. If those rapids had been back in Pennsylvania, Ken felt that he could have gone at them in delight. If the jungle country had been such that damage to boat or supplies could have been remedied or replaced, these rapids would not have appeared so bad. Ken walked up and down looking over the long white inclines more than was wise, and he hesitated about going into them. But it had to be done. So he went back to the boys. Then he took the oars with gripping fingers.

"George, can you swim?" he asked.

"I'm a second cousin to a fish," replied George.

"All right. We're off. Now, if we upset, hang to the boat, if you can, and hold up your legs. George, tell Pepe."

Ken backed the boat out from the shore. To his right in the middle of the narrow river was a racy current that he kept out of as long as possible. But presently he was drawn into it, and the boat shot forward, headed into the first incline, and went racing smoothly down toward the white waves of the rapids.

This was a trying moment for Ken. Grip as hard as he might, the oar-handles slipped in his sweaty hands.

The boys were yelling, but Ken could not hear for the din of roaring waters. The boat sailed down with swift, gliding motion. When it thumped into the backlash of the first big waves the water threshed around and over the boys. Then they were in the thick of rush and roar. Ken knew he was not handling the boat well. It grazed stones that should have been easy to avoid, and bumped on hidden ones, and got half broadside to the current. Pepe, by quick action with an oar, pushed the stern aside from collision with more than one rock. Several times Ken missed a stroke when a powerful one was needed. He passed between stones so close together that he had to ship the oars. It was all rapid water, this stretch, but the bad places, with sunken rocks, falls, and big waves, were strung out at such distances apart that Ken had time to get the boat going right before entering them.

Ken saw scarcely anything of the banks of the river. They blurred in his sight. Sometimes they were near, sometimes far. The boat turned corners where rocky ledges pointed out, constricting the stream and making a curved channel. What lay around the curve was always a question and a cause for suspense. Often the boat raced down a chute and straight toward a rocky wall. Ken would pull back with all his might, and Pepe would break the shock by striking the wall with his oar.

More than once Pepe had a narrow escape from being knocked overboard. George tried to keep him from standing up. Finally at the end of a long rapid, Pepe, who had the stern-seat, jumped up and yelled. Ken saw a stone directly in the path of the boat, and he pulled back on the oars with a quick, strong jerk. Pepe shot out of the stern as if he had been flung from a catapult. He swam with the current while the boat drifted. He reached smooth water and the shore before Ken could pick him up.

It was fun for everybody but Ken. There were three inches of water in the boat. The canvas, however, had been arranged to protect guns, grips, and supplies. George had been wet before he entered the rapids, so a little additional water did not matter to him. Hal was almost as wet as Pepe.

"I'm glad that's past," said Ken.

With that long rapid behind him he felt different. It was what he had needed. His nervousness disappeared and he had no dread of the next fall. While the boys bailed out the boat Ken rested and thought. He had made mistakes in that rapid just passed. Luck had favored him. He went over the mistakes and saw where he had been wrong, and how he could have avoided them if he had felt right. Ken realized now that this was a daredevil trip. And the daredevil in him had been shut up in dread. It took just that nervous dread, and the hard work, blunders and accidents, the danger and luck, to liberate the spirit that would make the trip a success. Pepe and George were loud in their praises of Ken. But they did not appreciate the real hazard of the undertaking, and if Hal did he was too much of a wild boy to care.

"All aboard," called George.

Then they were on their way again. Ken found himself listening for rapids. It was no surprise to hear a dull roar round the next bend. His hair rose stiffly under his hat. But this time he did not feel the chill, the uncertainty, the lack of confidence that had before weakened him.

At the head of a long, shallow incline the boys tumbled overboard, Ken and Hal at the bow, Pepe and George at the stern. They waded with the bow upstream. The water tore around their legs, rising higher and higher. Soon Pepe and George had to climb in the boat, for the water became so deep and swift they could not wade.

"Jump in, Hal," called Ken.

Then he held to the bow an instant longer, wading a little farther down. This was ticklish business, and all depended upon Ken. He got the stern of the boat straight in line with the channel he wanted to run, then he leaped aboard and made for the oars. The boat sped down. At the bottom of this incline was a mass of leaping green and white waves. The blunt stern of the boat made a great splash and the water flew over the boys. They came through the roar and hiss and spray to glide into a mill-race current.

"Never saw such swift water!" exclaimed Ken.

This incline ended in a sullen plunge between two huge rocks. Ken saw the danger long before it became evident to his companions. There was no other way to shoot the rapid. He could not reach the shore. He must pass between the rocks. Ken pushed on one oar, then on the other, till he got the boat in line, and then he pushed with both oars. The boat flew down that incline. It went so swiftly that if it had hit one of the rocks it would have been smashed to kindling wood. Hal crouched low. George's face was white. And Pepe leaned forward with his big arms outstretched, ready to try to prevent a collision.

Down! down with the speed of the wind! The boat flashed between the black stones. Then it was raised aloft, light as a feather, to crash into the back-lashers. The din deafened Ken; the spray blinded him. The boat seemed to split a white pall of water, then, with many a bounce, drifted out of that rapid into little choppy waves, and from them into another long, smooth runway.

Ken rested, and had nothing to say. Pepe shook his black head. Hal looked at his brother. George had forgotten his rifle. No one spoke.

IX IN THE WHITE WATER

Soon Ken had more work on hand. For round another corner lay more fast water. The boat dipped on a low fall, and went down into the midst of green waves with here and there ugly rocks splitting the current. The stream-bed was continually new and strange to Ken, and he had never seen such queer formation of rocks. This rapid, however, was easy to navigate. A slanting channel of swift water connected it with another rapid. Ken backed into that one, passed through, only to face another. And so it went for a long succession of shallow rapids.

A turn in the winding lane of cypresses revealed walls of gray, between which the river disappeared.

"Aha!" muttered Ken.

"Ken, I'll bet this is the place you've been looking for," said Hal.

The absence of any roar of water emboldened Ken. Nearing the head of the ravine, he stood upon the seat and looked ahead. But Ken could not see many rods ahead. The ravine turned, and it was the deceiving turns in the river that he had feared. What a strange sensation Ken had when he backed the boat into the mouth of that gorge! He was forced against his will. Yet there seemed to be a kind of blood-tingling pleasure in the prospect.

The current caught the boat and drew it between the gray-green walls of rock.

"It's coming to us," said the doubtful George.

The current ran all of six miles an hour. This was not half as fast as the boys had traveled in rapids, but it appeared swift enough because of the nearness of the overshadowing walls. In the shade the water took on a different coloring. It was brown and oily. It slid along silently. It was deep, and the swirling current suggested power. Here and there long, creeping ferns covered the steep stone sides, and above ran a stream of blue sky fringed by leaning palms. Once Hal put his hands to his lips and yelled: "Hel-lo!" The yell seemed to rip the silence and began to clap from wall to wall. It gathered quickness until it clapped in one fiendish rattle. Then it wound away from the passage, growing fainter and fainter, and at last died in a hollow echo.

"Don't do that again," ordered Ken.

He began to wish he could see the end of that gorge. But it grew narrower, and the shade changed to twilight, and there were no long, straight stretches. The river kept turning corners. Quick to note the slightest change in conditions, Ken felt a breeze, merely a zephyr, fan his hot face. The current had almost imperceptibly quickened. Yet it was still silent. Then on the gentle wind came a low murmur. Ken's pulse beat fast. Turning his ear down-stream, he strained his hearing. The low murmur ceased. Perhaps he had imagined it. Still he kept listening. There! Again it came, low, far away, strange. It might have been the wind in the palms. But no, he could not possibly persuade himself it was wind. And as that faint breeze stopped he lost the sound once more. The river was silent, and the boat, and the boys--it was a silent ride. Ken divined that his companions were enraptured. But this ride had no beauty, no charm for him.

There! Another faint puff of wind, and again the low murmur! He fancied it was louder. He was beginning to feel an icy dread when all was still once more.

So the boat drifted swiftly on with never a gurgle of water about her gunwales. The river gleamed in brown shadows. Ken saw bubbles rise and break on the surface, and there was a slight rise or swell of the water toward the center of the channel. This bothered him. He could not understand it. But then there had been many other queer formations of rock and freaks of current along this river.

The boat glided on and turned another corner, the sharpest one yet. A long, shadowy water-lane, walled in to the very sides, opened up to Ken's keen gaze. The water here began to race onward, still wonderfully silent. And now the breeze carried a low roar. It was changeable yet persistent. It deepened.

Once more Ken felt his hair rise under his hat. Cold sweat wet his skin. Despite the pounding of his heart and the throb of his veins, his blood seemed to clog, to freeze, to stand still.

That roar was the roar of rapids. Impossible to go back! If there had been four sets of oars, Ken and his comrades could not row the heavy boat back up that swift, sliding river.

They must go on.

X LOST!

"Ken, old man, do you hear that?" questioned Hal, waking from his trance.

George likewise rose out of his lazy contentment. "Must be rapids," he muttered. "If we strike rapids in this gorge it's all day with us. What did I tell you!"

Pepe's dark, searching eyes rested on Ken.

But Ken had no word for any of them. He was fighting an icy numbness, and the weakness of muscle and the whirl of his mind. It was thought of responsibility that saved him from collapse.

"It's up to you, old man," said Hal, quietly.

In a moment like this the boy could not wholly be deceived.

Ken got a grip upon himself. He looked down the long, narrow lane of glancing water. Some hundred yards on, it made another turn round a corner, and from this dim curve came the roar. The current was hurrying the boat toward it, but not fast enough to suit Ken. He wanted to see the worst, to get into the thick of it, to overcome it. So he helped the boat along. A few moments sufficed to cover that gliding stretch of river, yet to Ken it seemed never to have an end. The roar steadily increased. The current became still stronger. Ken saw eruptions of water rising as from an explosion beneath the surface. Whirlpools raced along with the boat. The dim, high walls re-echoed the roaring of the water.

The first thing Ken saw when he sailed round that corner was a widening of the chasm and bright sunlight ahead. Perhaps an eighth of a mile below the steep walls ended abruptly. Next in quick glance he saw a narrow channel of leaping, tossing, curling white-crested waves under sunlighted mist and spray.

Pulling powerfully back and to the left Ken brought the boat alongside the cliff. Then he shipped his oars.

"Hold hard," he yelled, and he grasped the stone. The boys complied, and thus stopped the boat. Ken stood up on the seat. It was a bad place he looked down into, but he could not see any rocks. And rocks were what he feared most.

"Hold tight, boys," he said. Then he got Pepe to come to him and sit on the seat. Ken stepped up on Pepe's shoulders and, by holding to the rock, was able to get a good view of the rapid. It was not a rapid at all, but a constriction of the channel, and also a steep slant. The water rushed down so swiftly to get through that it swelled in the center in a long frothy ridge of waves. The water was deep. Ken could not see any bumps or splits or white-wreathed rocks, such as were conspicuous in a rapid. The peril here for Ken was to let the boat hit the wall or turn broadside or get out of that long swelling ridge.

He stepped down and turned to the white-faced boys. He had to yell close to them to make them hear him in the roar.

"I--can--run--this--place. But--you've got--to help. Pull--the canvas--up higher in the stern--and hold it."

Then he directed Pepe to kneel in the bow of the boat with an oar and be ready to push off from the walls.

If Ken had looked again or hesitated a moment he would have lost his nerve. He recognized that fact. And he shoved off instantly. Once the boat had begun to glide down, gathering momentum, he felt his teeth grind hard and his muscles grow tense. He had to bend his head from side to side to see beyond the canvas George and Hal were holding round their shoulders. He believed with that acting as a buffer in the stern he could go pounding through those waves. Then he was in the middle of the channel, and the boat fairly sailed along. Ken kept his oars poised, ready to drop either one for a stroke. All he wanted was to enter those foaming, tumultuous waves with his boat pointed right. He knew he could not hope to see anything low down after he entered the race. He calculated that the last instant would give him an opportunity to get his direction in line with some object.

Then, even as he planned it, the boat dipped on a beautiful glassy incline, and glided down toward the engulfing, roaring waves. Above them, just in the center, Ken caught sight of the tufted top of a palm-tree. That was his landmark!

The boat shot into a great, curling, back-lashing wave. There was a heavy shock, a pause, and then Ken felt himself lifted high, while a huge sheet of water rose fan-shape behind the buffer in the stern. Walls and sky and tree faded under a watery curtain. Then the boat shot on again; the light came, the sky shone, and Ken saw his palm-tree. He pulled hard on the right oar to get the stern back in line. Another heavy shock, a pause, a blinding shower of water, and then the downward rush! Ken got a fleeting glimpse of his guiding mark, and sunk the left oar deep for a strong stroke. The beating of the waves upon the upraised oars almost threw him out of the boat. The wrestling waters hissed and bellowed. Down the boat shot and up, to pound and pound, and then again shoot down. Through the pall of mist and spray Ken always got a glimpse, quick as lightning, of the palm-tree, and like a demon he plunged in his oars to keep the boat in line. He was only dimly conscious of the awfulness of the place. But he was not afraid. He felt his action as being inspirited by something grim and determined. He was fighting the river.

All at once a grating jar behind told him the bow had hit a stone or a wall. He did not dare look back. The most fleeting instant of time might be the one for him to see his guiding mark. Then the boat lurched under him, lifted high with bow up, and lightened. He knew Pepe had been pitched overboard.

In spite of the horror of the moment, Ken realized that the lightening of the boat made it more buoyant, easier to handle. That weight in the bow had given him an unbalanced craft. But now one stroke here and one there kept the stern straight. The palm-tree loomed higher and closer through the brightening mist. Ken no longer felt the presence of the walls. The thunderous roar had begun to lose some of its volume. Then with a crash through a lashing wave the boat raced out into the open light. Ken saw a beautiful foam-covered pool, down toward which the boat kept bumping over a succession of diminishing waves.

He gave a start of joy to see Pepe's black head bobbing in the choppy channel. Pepe had beat the boat to the outlet. He was swimming easily, and evidently he had not been injured.

Ken turned the bow toward him. But Pepe did not need any help, and a few more strokes put him in shallow water. Ken discovered that the boat, once out of the current, was exceedingly loggy and hard to row. It was half full of water. Ken's remaining strength went to pull ashore, and there he staggered out and dropped on the rocky bank.

The blue sky was very beautiful and sweet to look at just then. But Ken had to close his eyes. He did not have strength left to keep them open. For a while all seemed dim and obscure to him. Then he felt a dizziness, which in turn succeeded to a racing riot of his nerves and veins. His heart gradually resumed a normal beat, and his bursting lungs seemed to heal. A sickening languor lay upon him. He could not hold little stones which he felt under his fingers. He could not raise his hands. The life appeared to have gone from his legs.

All this passed, at length, and, hearing Hal's voice, Ken sat up. The outfit was drying in the sun; Pepe was bailing out the boat; George was wiping his guns; and Hal was nursing a very disheveled little racoon.

"You can bring on any old thing now, for all I care," said Hal. "I'd shoot Lachine Rapids with Ken at the oars."

"He's a fine boatman," replied George. "Weren't you scared when we were in the middle of that darned place?"

"Me? Naw!"

"Well, I was scared, and don't you forget it," said Ken to them.

"You were all in, Ken," replied Hal. "Never saw you so tuckered out. The day you and Prince went after the cougar along that cañon precipice--you were all in that time. George, it took Ken six hours to climb out of that hole."

"Tell me about it," said George, all eyes.

"No stories now," put in Ken. "The sun is still high. We've got to be on our way. Let's look over the lay of the land."

Below the pool was a bold, rocky bluff, round which the river split. What branch to take was a matter of doubt and anxiety to Ken. Evidently this bluff was an island. It had a yellow front and long bare ledges leading into the river.

Ken climbed the bluff, accompanied by the boys, and found it covered with palm-trees. Up there everything was so dry and hot that it did not seem to be jungle at all. Even the palms were yellow and parched. Pepe stood the heat, but the others could not endure it. Ken took one long look at the surrounding country, so wild and dry and still, and then led the way down the loose, dusty shelves.

Thereupon he surveyed the right branch of the river and followed it a little distance. The stream here foamed and swirled among jagged rocks. At the foot of this rapid stretched the first dead water Ken had encountered for miles. A flock of wild geese rose from under his feet and flew down-stream.

"Geese!" exclaimed Ken. "I wonder if that means we are getting down near lagoons or big waters. George, wild geese don't frequent little streams, do they?"

"There's no telling where you'll find them in this country," answered George. "I've chased them right in our orange groves."

They returned to look at the left branch of the river. It was open and one continuous succession of low steps. That would have decided Ken even if the greater volume of water had not gone down on this left side. As far as he could see was a wide, open river running over little ledges. It looked to be the easiest and swiftest navigation he had come upon, and so indeed it proved. The water was swift, and always dropped over some ledge in a rounded fall that was safe for him to shoot. It was great fun going over these places. The boys hung their feet over the gunwales most of the time, sliding them along the slippery ledge or giving a kick to help the momentum. When they came to a fall, Ken would drop off the bow, hold the boat back and swing it straight, then jump in, and over it would go--souse!

There were so many of these ledges, and they were so close together, that going over them grew to be a habit. It induced carelessness. The boat drifted to a brow of a fall full four feet high. Ken, who was at the bow. leaped off just in time to save the boat. He held on while the swift water surged about his knees. He yelled for the boys to jump. As the stern where they sat was already over the fall it was somewhat difficult to make the boys vacate quickly enough.

"Tumble out! Quick!" bawled Ken. "Do you think I'm Samson?"

Over they went, up to their necks in the boiling foam, and not a second too soon, for Ken could hold the boat no longer. It went over smoothly, just dipping the stern under water. If the boys had remained aboard, the boat would have swamped. As it was, Pepe managed to catch the rope, which Ken had wisely thrown out, and he drifted down to the next ledge. Ken found this nearly as high as the last one. So he sent the boys below to catch the boat. This worked all right. The shelves slanted slightly, with the shallow part of the water just at the break of the ledge. They passed half a dozen of these, making good time, and before they knew it were again in a deep, smooth jungle lane with bamboo and streamers of moss waving over them.

The shade was cool, and Ken settled down in the stern-seat, grateful for a rest. To his surprise, he did not see a bird. The jungle was asleep. Once or twice Ken fancied he heard the tinkle and gurgle of water running over rocks. The boat glided along silently, with Pepe rowing leisurely, George asleep, Hal dreaming.

Ken watched the beautiful green banks. They were high, a mass of big-leafed vines, flowering and fragrant, above which towered the jungle giants. Ken wanted to get out and study those forest trees. But he made no effort to act upon his good intentions, and felt that he must take the most of his forestry study at long range. He was reveling in the cool recesses under the leaning cypresses, in the soft swish of bearded moss, and the strange rustle of palms, in the dreamy hum of the resting jungle, when his pleasure was brought to an abrupt end.

"Santa Maria!" yelled Pepe.

George woke up with a start. Hal had been jarred out of his day-dream, and looked resentful. Ken gazed about him with the feeling of a man going into a trance, instead of coming out of one.

The boat was fast on a mud-bank. That branch of the river ended right there. The boys had come all those miles to run into a blind pocket.

Ken's glance at the high yellow bank, here crumbling and bare, told him there was no outlet. He had a sensation of blank dismay.

"Gee!" exclaimed Hal, softly.

George rubbed his eyes; and, searching for a cigarette, he muttered: "We're lost! I said it was coming to us. We've got to go back!"

XI AN ARMY OF SNAKES

For a moment Ken Ward was utterly crushed under the weight of this sudden blow. It was so sudden that he had no time to think; or his mind was clamped on the idea of attempting to haul the boat up that long, insurmountable series of falls.

"It 'll be an awful job," burst out Hal.

No doubt in the mind of each boy was the same idea--the long haul, wading over slippery rocks; the weariness of pushing legs against the swift current; the packing of supplies uphill; and then the toil of lifting the heavy boat up over a fall.

"Mucho malo," said Pepe, and he groaned. That was significant, coming from a *mozo*, who thought nothing of rowing forty miles in a day.

"Oh, but it's tough luck," cried Ken. "Why didn't I choose the right branch of this pesky river?"

"I think you used your head at that," said Hal. "Most of the water came down on this side. Where did it go?"

Hal had hit the vital question, and it cleared Ken's brain.

"Hal, you're talking sense. Where did that water go? It couldn't all have sunk into the earth. We'll find out. We won't try to go back. We *can't* go back."

Pepe shoved off the oozy mud, and, reluctantly, as if he appreciated the dilemma, he turned the boat and rowed along the shore. As soon as Ken had recovered somewhat he decided there must be an outlet which he had missed. This reminded him that at a point not far back he had heard the tinkle and gurgle of unseen water flowing over rocks.

He directed Pepe to row slowly along the bank that he thought was the island side. As they glided under the drooping bamboos and silky curtains of moss George began to call out: "Low bridge! Low bridge!" For a boy who was forever voicing ill-omened suggestions as to what might soon happen he was extraordinarily cheerful.

There were places where all had to lie flat and others where Pepe had to use his *machete*. This disturbed the *siesta* of many aquatic birds, most of which flew swiftly away. But there were many of the gray-breasted, blue-backed bitterns that did not take to flight. These croaked dismally, and looked down upon the boys with strange, protruding eyes.

XI AN ARMY OF SNAKES

"Those darn birds 'll give me the willies," declared Hal. "George, you just look like them when you croak about what's coming to us."

"Just wait!" retorted George. "It 'll come, all right. Then I'll have the fun of seeing you scared silly."

"What! You'll not do anything of the kind!" cried Hal, hotly. "I've been in places where such--such a skinny little sap-head as you--"

"Here, you kids stop wrangling," ordered Ken, who sensed hostilities in the air. "We've got trouble enough."

Suddenly Ken signaled Pepe to stop rowing.

"Boys, I hear running water. Aha! Here's a current. See--it's making right under this bank."

Before them was a high wall of broad-leaved vines, so thick that nothing could be seen through them. Apparently this luxuriant canopy concealed the bank. Pepe poked an oar into it, but found nothing solid.

"Pepe, cut a way through. We've got to see where this water runs."

It was then that Ken came to a full appreciation of a *machete*. He had often fancied it a much less serviceable tool than an ax. Pepe flashed the long, bright blade up, down, and around, and presently the boat was its own length in a green tunnel. Pepe kept on slashing while Ken poled the boat in and the other boys dumped the cut foliage overboard. Soon they got through this mass of hanging vine and creeper. Much to Ken's surprise and delight, he found no high bank, but low, flat ground, densely wooded, through which ran a narrow, deep outlet of the river.

"By all that's lucky!" ejaculated Ken.

George and Hal whooped their pleasure, and Pepe rubbed his muscular hands. Then all fell silent. The deep, penetrating silence of that jungle was not provocative of speech. The shade was so black that when a ray of sunlight did manage to pierce the dense canopy overhead it resembled a brilliant golden spear. A few lofty palms and a few clumps of bamboo rather emphasized the lack of these particular species in this forest. Nor was there any of the familiar streaming moss hanging from the trees. This glen was green, cool, dark. It did not smell exactly swampy, but rank, like a place where many water plants were growing.

The outlet was so narrow that Ken was not able to use the oars. Still, as the current was swift, the boat went along rapidly. He saw a light ahead and heard the babble of water. The current quickened, and the boat drifted suddenly upon the edge of an oval glade, where the hot sun beat down. A series of abrupt mossy benches, over which the stream slid almost noiselessly, blocked further progress.

The first thing about this glade that Ken noted particularly, after the difficulties presented by the steep steps, was the multitude of snakes sunning themselves along the line of further progress.

"Boys, it 'll be great wading down there, hey?" he queried.

Pepe grumbled for the first time on the trip. Ken gathered from the native's looks and speech that he did not like snakes.

"Watch me peg 'em!" yelled Hal, and he began to throw stones with remarkable accuracy. "Hike, you brown sons-of-guns!"

George, not to be outdone, made a dive for his .22 and began to pop as if he had no love for snakes. Ken had doubts about this species. The snakes were short, thick, dull brown in color, and the way they slipped into the stream proved they were water-snakes. Ken had never read of a brown water-moccasin, so he doubted that these belonged to that poisonous family. Anyway, snakes were the least of his troubles.

"Boys, you're doing fine," he said. "There are about a thousand snakes there, and you've hit about six."

He walked down through the glade into the forest, and was overjoyed to hear once more the heavy roar of rapids. He went on. The timber grew thinner, and light penetrated the jungle. Presently he saw the gleam of water through the trees. Then he hurried back.

"All right, boys," he shouted. "Here's the river."

The boys were so immensely relieved that packing the outfit round the waterfalls was work they set about with alacrity. Ken, who had on his boots, broke a trail through the ferns and deep moss. Pepe, being barefoot, wasted time looking for snakes. George teased him. But Pepe was deadly serious. And the way he stepped and looked made Ken thoughtful. He had made his last trip with supplies, and was about to start back to solve the problem of getting the boat down, when a hoarse yell resounded through the sleeping jungle. Parrots screeched, and other birds set up a cackling.

Ken bounded up the slope.

"Santa Maria!" cried Pepe.

Ken followed the direction indicated by Pepe's staring eyes and trembling finger. Hanging from a limb of a tree was a huge black-snake. It was as thick as Ken's leg. The branch upon which it poised its neck so gracefully was ten feet high, and the tail curled into the ferns on the ground.

"Boys, it's one of the big fellows," cried Ken.

"Didn't I tell you!" yelled George, running down for his gun.

Hal seemed rooted to the spot. Pepe began to jabber. Ken watched the snake, and felt instinctively from its sinister looks that it was dangerous. George came running back with his .32 and waved it in the air as he shot. He was so frightened that he forgot to aim. Ken took the rifle from him.

"You can't hit him with this. Run after your shotgun. Quick!"

But the sixteen-gage was clogged with a shell that would not eject. Ken's guns were in their cases.

"Holy smoke!" cried George. "He's coming down."

The black-snake moved his body and began to slide toward the tree-trunk.

Ken shot twice at the head of the snake. It was a slow-swaying mark hard to hit. The reptile stopped and poised wonderfully on the limb. He was not coiled about it, but lay over it with about four feet of neck waving, swaying to and fro.

He watched the boys, and his tongue, like a thin, black streak, darted out viciously.

Ken could not hit the head, so he sent a bullet through the thick part of the body. Swift as a gleam the snake darted from the limb.

"Santa Maria!" yelled Pepe, and he ran off.

"Look out, boys," shouted Ken. He picked up Pepe's *machete* and took to his heels. George and Hal scrambled before him. They ran a hundred yards or more, and Ken halted in an open rocky spot. He was angry, and a little ashamed that he had run. The snake did not pursue, and probably was as badly frightened as the boys had been. Pepe stopped some distance away, and Hal and George came cautiously back.

"I don't see anything of him," said Ken. "I'm going back."

He walked slowly, keeping a sharp outlook, and, returning to the glade, found blood-stains under the tree. The snake had disappeared without leaving a trail.

"If I'd had my shotgun ready!" exclaimed Ken, in disgust. And he made a note that in the future he would be prepared to shoot.

"Wasn't he a whopper, Ken?" said Hal. "We ought to have got his hide. What a fine specimen!"

"Boys, you drive away those few little snakes while I figure on a way to get the boat down."

"Not on your life!" replied Hal.

George ably sustained Hal's objection.

"Mucho malo," said Pepe, and then added a loud "No" in English.

"All right, my brave comrades," rejoined Ken, scornfully. "As I've not done any work yet or taken any risks, I'll drive the snakes away."

With Pepe's *machete* he cut a long forked pole, trimmed it, and, armed with this weapon, he assaulted the rolls and bands and balls of brown snakes. He stalked boldly down upon them, pushed and poled, and even kicked them off the mossy banks. Hal could not stand that, and presently he got a pole and went to Ken's assistance.

"Who's hollering now?" he yelled to George.

Whereupon George cut a long branch and joined the battle. They whacked and threshed and pounded, keeping time with yells. Everywhere along the wet benches slipped and splashed the snakes. But after they were driven into the water they did not swim away. They dove under the banks and then stretched out their pointed heads from the dripping edge of moss.

"Say, fellows, we're making it worse for us," declared Ken. "See, the brown devils won't swim off. We'd better have left them on the bank. Let's catch one and see if he'll bite."

He tried to pick up one on his pole, but it slipped off. George fished after another. Hal put the end of his stick down inside the coil of still another and pitched it. The brown, wriggling, wet snake shot straight at the unsuspecting George, and struck him and momentarily wound about him.

"Augrrh!" bawled George, flinging off the reptile and leaping back. "What 'd you do that for? I'll punch you!"

"George, he didn't mean it," said Ken. "It was an accident. Come on, let's tease that fellow and see if he'll bite."

The snake coiled and raised his flat head and darted a wicked tongue out and watched with bright, beady eyes, but he did not strike. Ken went as close as he thought safe and studied the snake.

"Boys, his head isn't a triangle, and there are no little pits under his eyes. Those are two signs of a poisonous snake. I don't believe this fellow's one."

"He'll be a dead snake, b' gosh," replied George, and he fell to pounding it with his pole.

"Don't smash him. I want the skin," yelled Hal.

Ken pondered on the situation before him.

"Come, the sooner we get at this the better," he said.

There was a succession of benches through which the stream zigzagged and tumbled. These benches were rock ledges over which moss had grown fully a foot thick, and they were so oozy and slippery that it was no easy task to walk upon them. Then they were steep, so steep that it was remarkable how the water ran over them so smoothly, with very little noise or break. It was altogether a new kind of waterfall to Ken. But if the snakes had not been hidden there, navigation would have presented an easier problem.

"Come on boys, alongside now, and hold back," he ordered, gripping the bow.

Exactly what happened the next few seconds was not clear in his mind. There was a rush, and all were being dragged by the boat. The glade seemed to whizz past. There were some sodden thumps, a great splashing, a check--and lo! they were over several benches. It was the quickest and easiest descent he had ever made down a steep waterfall.

"Fine!" ejaculated George, wiping the ooze from his face.

"Yes, it was fine," Ken replied. "But unless this boat has wings something 'll happen soon."

Below was a long, swift curve of water, very narrow and steep, with a moss-covered rock dividing the lower end. Ken imagined if there was a repetition of the first descent the boat would be smashed on that rock. He ordered Pepe, who was of course the strongest, to go below and jump to the rock. There he might prevent a collision.

Pepe obeyed, but as he went he yelled and doubled up in contortions as he leaped over snakes in the moss.

Then gently, gingerly the boys started the boat off the bench, where it had lodged. George was at the stern, Ken and Hal at the bow. Suddenly Hal shrieked and jumped straight up, to land in the boat.

"Snakes!" he howled.

"Give us a rest!" cried Ken, in disgust.

The boat moved as if instinct with life. It dipped, then--*wheeze!* it dove over the bench. Hal was thrown off his feet, fell back on the gunwale, and thence into the snaky moss. George went sprawling face downward into the slimy ooze, and Ken was jerked clear off the bench into the stream. He got his footing and stood firm in water to his waist, and he had the bow-rope coiled round his hands.

"Help! Help!" he yelled, as he felt the dragging weight too much for him.

If Ken retarded the progress of the boat at all, it was not much. George saw his distress and the danger menacing the boat, and he leaped valiantly forward. As he dashed down a slippery slant his feet flew up higher than where his head had been; he actually turned over in the air, and fell with a great sop.

Hal had been trying to reach Ken, but here he stopped and roared with laughter.

Despite Ken's anger and fear of snakes, and his greater fear for the boat, he likewise had to let out a peal of laughter. That tumble of George's was great. Then Ken's footing gave way and he went down. His mouth filled with nasty water, nearly strangling him. He was almost blinded, too. His arms seemed to be wrenched out of their sockets, and he felt himself bumping over moss-covered rocks as soft as cushions. Slimy ropes or roots of vegetation, that felt like snakes, brushed his face and made him cold and sick. It was impossible to hold the boat any longer. He lodged against a stone, and the swift water forced him upon it. Blinking and coughing, he stuck fast.

Ken saw the boat headed like a dart for the rock where Pepe stood.

"Let 'er go!" yelled Ken. "Don't try to stop her. Pepe, you'll be smashed!"

Pepe acted like a man determined to make up for past cowardice. He made a great show of brave intentions. He was not afraid of a boat. He braced himself and reached out with his brawny arms. Ken feared for the obstinate native's life, for the boat moved with remarkable velocity.

At the last second Pepe's courage vanished. He turned tail to get out of the way. But he slipped. The boat shot toward him and the blunt stern struck him with a dull thud. Pepe sailed into the air, over the rock, and went down cleaving the water.

The boat slipped over the stone as easily as if it had been a wave and, gliding into still water below, lodged on the bank.

Ken crawled out of the stream, and when he ascertained that no one was injured he stretched himself on the ground and gave up to mirth. Pepe resembled a drowned rat; Hal was an object to wonder at; and George, in his coating of slime and with strings of moss in his hair, was the funniest thing Ken had ever seen. It was somewhat of a surprise to him to discover, presently, that the boys were convulsed with fiendish glee over the way he himself looked.

By and by they recovered, and, with many a merry jest and chuckle of satisfaction, they repacked the boat and proceeded on their way. No further obstacle hindered them. They drifted out of the shady jungle into the sunlit river.

In half a mile of drifting the heat of the sun dried the boys' clothes. The water was so hot that it fairly steamed. Once more the boat entered a placid aisle over which the magnificent gray-wreathed cypresses bowed, and the west wind waved long ribbons of moss, and wild fowl winged reluctant flight.

Ken took advantage of this tranquil stretch of river to work on his map. He realized that he must use every spare moment and put down his drawings and notes as often as time and travel permitted. It had dawned on Ken that rapids and snakes, and all the dangers along the river, made his task of observation and study one apt to be put into eclipse at times. Once or twice he landed on shore to climb a bluff, and was pleased each time to see that he had lined a comparatively true course on his map. He had doubts of its absolute accuracy, yet he could not help having pride in his work. So far so good, he thought, and hoped for good-fortune farther down the river.

XII CATCHING STRANGE FISH

Beyond a bend in the river the boys came upon an island with a narrow, shaded channel on one side, a wide shoal on the other, and a group of huge cypresses at the up-stream end.

"Looks good to me," said Hal.

The instant Ken saw the island he knew it was the place he had long been seeking to make a permanent camp for a few days. They landed, to find an ideal camping site. The ground under the cypresses was flat, dry, and covered with short grass. Not a ray of sunlight penetrated the foliage. A pile of driftwood had lodged against one of the trees, and this made easy the question of fire-wood.

"Great!" exclaimed Ken. "Come on, let's look over the ground."

The island was about two hundred yards long, and the lower end was hidden by a growth of willows. Bursting through this, the boys saw a weedy flat leading into a wide, shallow back-eddy. Great numbers of ducks were sporting and feeding. The stones of the rocky shore were lined with sleeping ducks. Herons of all colors and sizes waded about, or slept on one leg. Snipe ran everywhere. There was a great squawking and flapping of wings. But at least half the number of waterfowl were too tame or too lazy to fly.

Ken returned to camp with his comrades, all highly elated over the prospects. The best feature about this beautiful island was the absence of ticks and snakes.

"Boys, this is the place," said Ken. "We'll hang up here for a while. Maybe we won't strike another such nice place to stay."

So they unloaded the boat, taking everything out, and proceeded to pitch a camp that was a delight. They were all loud in expressions of satisfaction. Then Pepe set about leisurely peeling potatoes; George took his gun and slipped off toward the lower end of the island; Hal made a pen for his racoon, and then more pens, as if he meant to capture a menagerie; and Ken made a comfortable lounging-bed under a cypress. He wanted to forget that nagging worry as to farther descent of the river, and to enjoy this place.

"Bang!" went George's sixteen-gage. A loud whirring of wings followed, and the air was full of ducks.

"Never touched one!" yelled Hal, in taunting voice.

A flock of teal skimmed the water and disappeared up-stream. The shot awakened parrots in the trees, where for a while there was clamor. Ken saw George wade out into the shoal and pick up three ducks.

"Pot-shot!" exclaimed Hal, disgustedly. "Why couldn't he be a sport and shoot them on the fly?"

George crossed to the opposite shore and, climbing a bare place, stood looking before him.

"Hey, George, don't go far," called Ken.

"Fine place over here," replied George, and, waving his hand, he passed into the bushes out of sight.

Ken lay back upon his blanket with a blissful sense of rest and contentment. Many a time he had lain so, looking up through the broad leaves of a sycamore or the lacy foliage of a birch or the delicate crisscross of millions of pine needles. This overhead canopy, however, was different. Only here and there could he catch little slivers of blue sky. The graceful streamers of exquisite moss hung like tassels of silver. In the dead stillness of noonday they seemed to float curved in the shape in which the last soft breeze had left them. High upon a branch he saw a red-headed parrot hanging back downward, after the fashion of a monkey. Then there were two parrots asleep in the fork of a branch. It was the middle of the day, and all things seemed tired and sleepy. The deep channel murmured drowsily, and the wide expanse of river on the other side lapped lazily at the shore. The only other sound was the mourning of turtle-doves, one near and another far away. Again the full richness, the mellow sweetness of this song struck Ken forcibly. He remembered that all the way down the river he had heard that mournful note. It was beautiful but melancholy. Somehow it made him think that it had broken the dreamy stillness of the jungle noonday long, long ago. It was sweet but sad and old. He did not like to hear it.

Ken yielded to the soothing influence of the hour and fell asleep. When he awoke there was George, standing partially undressed and very soberly popping ticks. He had enlisted the services of Pepe, and, to judge from the remarks of both, they needed still more assistance.

"Say, Garrapato George, many ticks over there?"

"Ticks!" shouted George, wildly, waving his cigarette. "Millions of 'em! And there's--ouch! Kill that one, Pepe. Wow! he's as big as a penny. There's game over there. It's a flat with some kind of berry bush. There's lots of trails. I saw cat-tracks, and I scared up wild turkeys--"

"Turkeys!" Ken exclaimed, eagerly.

"You bet. I saw a dozen. How they can run! I didn't flush them. Then I saw a flock of those black and white ducks, like the big fellow I shot. They were feeding. I believe they're Muscovy ducks."

"I'm sure I don't know, but we can call them that."

"Well, I'd got a shot, too, but I saw some gray things sneaking in the bushes. I thought they were pigs, so I got out of there quick."

"You mean javelin?"

"Yep, I mean wild pigs. Oh! We've struck the place for game. I'll bet it's coming to us."

When George anticipated pleasurable events he was the most happy of companions. It was good to look forward. He was continually expecting things to happen; he was always looking ahead with great eagerness. But unfortunately he had a twist of mind toward the unfavorable side of events, and so always had the boys fearful.

"Well, pigs or no pigs, ticks or no ticks, we'll hunt and fish, and see all there is to see," declared Ken, and he went back to his lounging.

When he came out of that lazy spell, George and Hal were fishing. George had Ken's rod, and it happened to be the one Ken thought most of.

"Do you know how to fish?" he asked.

"I've caught tarpon bigger'n you," retorted George.

That fact was indeed too much for Ken, and he had nothing to do but risk his beloved rod in George's hands. And the way George swung it about, slashed branches with it, dropped the tip in the water, was exceedingly alarming to Ken. The boy would break the tip in a minute. Yet Ken could not take his rod away from a boy who had caught tarpon.

There were fish breaking water. Where a little while before the river had been smooth, now it was ruffled by *ravalo*, gar, and other fish Pepe could not name. But George and Hal did not get a bite. They tried all their artificial flies and spoons and minnows, then the preserved mullet, and finally several kinds of meat.

"Bah! they want pie," said Hal.

For Ken Ward to see little and big fish capering around under his very nose and not be able to hook one was exasperating. He shot a small fish, not unlike a pickerel, and had the boys bait with that. Still no strike was forthcoming.

This put Ken on his mettle. He rigged up a minnow tackle, and, going to the lower end of the island, he tried to catch some minnows. There were plenty of them in the shallow water, but they would not bite. Finally Ken waded in the shoal and turned over stones. He found some snails almost as large as mussels, and with these he hurried back to the boys.

"Here, if you don't get a bite on one of these I'm no fisherman," said Ken. "Try one."

George got his hands on the new bait in advance of Hal and so threw his hook into the water first. No sooner had the bait sunk than he got a strong pull.

"There! Careful now," said Ken.

George jerked up, hooking a fish that made the rod look like a buggy-whip.

"Give me the rod," yelled Ken, trying to take it.

"It's my fish," yelled back George.

He held on and hauled with all his might. A long, finely built fish, green as emerald, split the water and churned it into foam. Then, sweeping out in strong dash, it broke Ken's rod square in the middle. Ken eyed the wreck with sorrow, and George with no little disapproval.

"You said you knew how to fish," protested Ken.

"Those split-bamboo rods are no good," replied George. "They won't hold a fish."

"George, you're a grand fisherman!" observed Hal, with a chuckle. "Why, you only dreamed you've caught tarpon."

Just then Hal had a tremendous strike. He was nearly hauled off the bank. But he recovered his balance and clung to his nodding rod. Hal's rod was heavy cane, and his line was thick enough to suit. So nothing broke. The little brass reel buzzed and rattled.

"I've got a whale!" yelled Hal.

"It's a big gar--alligator-gar," said George. "You haven't got him. He's got you."

The fish broke water, showing long, open jaws with teeth like saw-teeth. It threshed about and broke away. Hal reeled in to find the hook straightened out. Then George kindly commented upon the very skilful manner in which Hal had handled the gar. For a wonder Hal did not reply.

By four o'clock, when Ken sat down to supper, he was so thirsty that his mouth puckered as dry as if he had been eating green persimmons. This matter of thirst had become serious. Twice each day Ken had boiled a pot of water, into which he mixed cocoa, sugar, and condensed milk, and begged the boys to drink that and nothing else. Nevertheless Pepe and George, and occasionally Hal, would drink unboiled water. For this meal the boys had venison and duck, and canned vegetables and fruit, so they fared sumptuously.

Pepe pointed to a string of Muscovy ducks sailing up the river. George had a good shot at the tail end of the flock, and did not even loosen a feather. Then a line of cranes and herons passed over the island. When a small bunch of teal flew by, to be followed by several canvasbacks, Ken ran for his shotgun. It was a fine hammerless, a hard-shooting gun, and one Ken used for grouse-hunting. In his hurry he grasped a handful of the first shells he came to and, when he ran to the river-bank, found they were loads of small shot. He decided to try them anyhow.

While Pepe leisurely finished the supper Ken and George and Hal sat on the bank watching for ducks. Just before the sun went down a hard wind blew, making difficult shooting. Every few moments ducks would whir by. George's gun missed fire often, and when it did work all right, he missed the ducks. To Ken's surprise he found the load of small shot very deadly. He could sometimes reach a duck at eighty yards. The little brown ducks and teal he stopped as if they had hit a stone wall. He dropped a canvasback with the sheer dead plunge that he liked. Ken thought a crippled duck enough to make a hunter quit shooting. With six ducks killed, he decided to lay aside his gun for that time, when Pepe pointed down the river.

"Pato real," he said.

Ken looked eagerly and saw three of the big black ducks flying as high as the treetops and coming fast. Snapping a couple of shells in the gun, Ken stood ready. At the end of the island two of the ducks wheeled to the left, but the big leader came on like a thunderbolt. To Ken he made a canvasback seem slow.

Ken caught him over the sights of the gun, followed him up till he was abreast and beyond; then, sweeping a little ahead of him, Ken pulled both triggers. The Muscovy swooped up and almost stopped in his flight while a cloud of black feathers puffed away on the wind. He sagged a little, recovered, and flew on as strong as ever. The small shot were not heavy enough to stop him.

"We'll need big loads for the Muscovies and the turkeys," said George.

"We've all sizes up to BB's," replied Ken. "George, let's take a walk over there where you saw the turkeys. It's early yet."

Then Pepe told George if they wanted to see game at that hour the thing to do was to sit still in camp and watch the game come down to the river to drink. And he pointed down-stream to a herd of small deer quietly walking out on the bar.

"After all the noise we made!" exclaimed Ken. "Well, this beats me. George, we'll stay right here and not shoot again to-night. I've an idea we'll see something worth while."

It was Pepe's idea, but Ken instantly saw its possibilities. There were no tributaries to the river or springs in that dry jungle, and, as manifestly the whole country abounded in game, it must troop down to the river in the cool of the evening to allay the hot day's thirst. The boys were perfectly situated for watching the dark bank on the channel side of the island as well as the open bars on the other. The huge cypresses cast shadows that even in daylight effectually concealed them. They put out the camp-fire and, taking comfortable seats in the folds of the great gnarled roots, began to watch and listen.

The vanguard of thirsty deer had prepared Ken for something remarkable, and he was in no wise disappointed. The trooping of deer down to the water's edge and the flight of wild fowl up-stream increased in proportion to the gathering shadows of twilight. The deer must have got a scent, for they raised their long ears and stood still as statues, gazing across toward the upper end of the island. But they showed no fear. It was only when they had drunk their fill and wheeled about to go up the narrow trails over the bank that they showed uneasiness and haste. This made Ken wonder if they were fearful of being ambushed by jaguars. Soon the dark line of deer along the shore shaded into the darkness of night. Then Ken heard soft splashes and an occasional patter of hard hoofs. The whir of wings had ceased.

A low exclamation from Pepe brought attention to interesting developments closer at hand.

"Javelin!" he whispered.

On the channel side of the island was impenetrable pitchy blackness. Ken tried to pierce it with straining eyes, but he could not even make out the shore-line that he knew was only ten yards distant. Still he could hear, and that was thrilling enough. Everywhere on this side, along the edge of the water and up the steep bank, were faint tickings of twigs and soft rustlings of leaves. Then there was a continuous sound, so low as to be almost inaudible, that resembled nothing Ken could think of so much as a long line of softly dripping water. It swelled in volume to a tiny roll, and ended in a sharp clicking on rocks and a gentle splashing in the water. A drove of *javelin* had come down to drink. Occasionally the glint of green eyes made the darkness all the more weird. Suddenly a long, piercing wail, a keen cry almost human, quivered into the silence.

"Panther!" Ken whispered, instantly, to the boys. It was a different cry from that of the lion of the cañon, but there was a strange wild note that betrayed the species. A stillness fell, dead as that of a subterranean cavern. Strain his ears as he might, Ken could not detect the slightest sound. It was as if no *javelin* or any other animals had come down to drink. That listening, palpitating moment seemed endless. What mystery of wild life it meant, that silence following the cry of the panther! Then the jungle sounds recommenced--the swishing of water, the brushing in the thicket, stealthy padded footsteps, the faint snapping of twigs. Some kind of a cat uttered an unearthly squall. Close upon this the clattering of deer up the bank on the other side rang out sharply. The deer were running, and the striking of the little hoofs ceased in short order. Ken listened intently. From far over the bank came a sound not unlike a cough--deep, hoarse, inexpressibly wild and menacing.

"Tigre!" cried Pepe, gripping Ken hard with both hands. He could feel him trembling. It showed how the native of the jungle-belt feared the jaguar.

Again the cough rasped out, nearer and louder this time. It was not a courage-provoking sound, and seemed on second thought more of a growl than a cough. Ken felt safe on the island; nevertheless, he took up his rifle.

"That's a tiger," whispered George. "I heard one once from the porch of the Alamitas hacienda."

A third time the jaguar told of his arrival upon the night scene. Ken was excited, and had a thrill of fear. He made up his mind to listen with clearer ears, but the cough or growl was not repeated.

Then a silence set in, so unbroken that it seemed haunted by the echoes of those wild jungle cries. Perhaps Ken had the haunting echoes in mind. He knew what had sent the deer away and stilled the splashings and creepings. It was the hoarse voice of the lord of the jungle.

Pepe and the boys, too, fell under the spell of the hour. They did not break the charm by talking. Giant fireflies accentuated the ebony blackness and a low hum of insects riveted the attention on the stillness. Ken could not understand why he was more thoughtful on this trip than he had ever been before. Somehow he felt immeasurably older. Probably that was because it had seemed necessary for him to act like a man, even if he was only a boy.

The black mantle of night lifted from under the cypresses, leaving a gloom that slowly paled. Through the dark foliage, low down over the bank, appeared the white tropical moon. Shimmering gleams chased the shadows across the ripples, and slowly the river brightened to a silver sheen.

A great peace fell upon the jungle world. How white, how wild, how wonderful! It only made the island more beautiful and lonely. The thought of leaving it gave Ken Ward a pang. Almost he wished he were a savage.

XII CATCHING STRANGE FISH

And he lay there thinking of the wild places that he could never see, where the sun shone, the wind blew, the twilight shadowed, the rain fell; where the colors and beauties changed with the passing hours; where a myriad of wild creatures preyed upon each other and night never darkened but upon strife and death.

XIII A TURKEY-HUNT

Upon awakening in the early morning Ken found his state one of huge enjoyment. He was still lazily tired, but the dead drag and ache had gone from his bones. A cool breeze wafted the mist from the river, breaking it up into clouds, between which streamed rosy shafts of sunlight. Wood-smoke from the fire Pepe was starting blew fragrantly over him. A hundred thousand birds seemed to be trying to burst their throats. The air was full of music. He lay still, listening to this melodious herald of the day till it ceased.

Then a flock of parrots approached and circled over the island, screeching like a band of flying imps. Presently they alighted in the cypresses, bending the branches to a breaking-point and giving the trees a spotted appearance of green and red. Pepe waved his hand toward another flock sweeping over.

"Parrakeets," he said.

These birds were a solid green, much smaller than the red-heads, with longer tails. They appeared wilder than the red-heads, and flew higher, circling the same way and screeching, but they did not alight. Other flocks sailed presently from all directions. The last one was a cloud of parrots, a shining green and yellow mass several acres in extent. They flew still higher than the parrakeets.

"Yellow-heads!" shouted George. "They're the big fellows, the talkers. If there ain't a million of 'em!"

The boys ate breakfast in a din that made conversation useless. The red-heads swooped down upon the island, and the two unfriendly species flew back and forth, manifestly trying to drive the boys off. The mist had blown away, the sun was shining bright, when the myriad of parrots, in large and small flocks, departed to other jungle haunts.

Pepe rowed across the wide shoal to the sand-bars. There in the soft ooze, among the hundreds of deer-tracks, Ken found a jaguar-track larger than his spread hand. It was different from a lion-track, yet he could not distinguish just what the difference was. Pepe, who had accompanied the boys to carry the rifles and game, pointed to the track and said, vehemently:

"Tigre!" He pronounced it "tee-gray." And he added, "Grande!"

"Big he certainly is," Ken replied. "Boys, we'll kill this jaguar. We'll bait this drinking-trail with a deer carcass and watch to-night."

XIII A TURKEY-HUNT

Once upon the bank, Ken was surprised to see a wide stretch of comparatively flat land. It was covered with a low vegetation, with here and there palm-trees on the little ridges and bamboo clumps down in the swales. Beyond the flat rose the dark line of dense jungle. It was not clear to Ken why that low piece of ground was not overgrown with the matted thickets and vines and big trees characteristic of other parts of the jungle. They struck into one of the trails, and had not gone a hundred paces when they espied a herd of deer. The grass and low bushes almost covered them. George handed his shotgun to Pepe and took his rifle.

"Shoot low," said Ken.

George pulled the trigger, and with the report a deer went down, but it was not the one Ken was looking at, nor the one at which he believed George had aimed. The rest of the herd bounded away, to disappear in a swale. Wading through bushes and grass, they found George's quarry, a small deer weighing perhaps sixty pounds. Pepe carried it over to the trail. Ken noted that he was exceedingly happy to carry the rifles. They went on at random, somehow feeling that, no matter in what direction, they would run into something to shoot at.

The first bamboo swale was alive with *chicalocki*. Up to this time Ken had not seen this beautiful pheasant fly in the open, and he was astonished at its speed. It would burst out of the thick bamboo, whir its wings swiftly, then sail. That sail was a most graceful thing to see. George pulled his 16-gage twice, and missed both times. He had the beginner's fault--shooting too soon. Presently Pepe beat a big cock *chicalocki* out of the bush. He made such a fine target, he sailed so evenly, that Ken simply looked at him over the gun-sights and followed him till he was out of sight. The next one he dropped like a plummet. Shooting *chicalocki* was too easy, he decided; they presented so fair a mark that it was unfair to pull on them.

George was an impetuous hunter. Ken could not keep near him, nor coax or command him to stay near. He would wander off by himself. That was one mark in his favor: at least he had no fear. Pepe hung close to Ken and Hal, with his dark eyes roving everywhere. Ken climbed out on one side of the swale, George on the other. Catching his whistle, Ken turned to look after him. He waved, and, pointing ahead, began to stoop and slip along from bush to bush. Presently a flock of Muscovy ducks rose before him, sailed a few rods, and alighted. Then from right under his feet labored up great gray birds. Wild geese! Ken recognized them as George's gun went *bang*! One tumbled over, the others wheeled toward the river. Ken started down into the swale to cross to where George was, when Pepe touched his arm.

"Turkeys!" he whispered.

That changed Ken's mind. Pepe pointed into the low bushes ahead and slowly led Ken forward. He heard a peculiar low thumping. Trails led everywhere, and here and there were open patches covered with a scant growth of grass. Across one of these flashed a bronze streak, then another and another.

"Shoot! Shoot!" said Pepe, tensely.

Those bronze streaks were running turkeys! The thumpings were made by their rapidly moving feet!

"Don't they flush--fly?" Ken queried of Pepe.

"No--no--shoot!" exclaimed he, as another streak of brown crossed an open spot. Ken hurriedly unbreached his gun and changed the light shells for others loaded with heavy shot. He reached the edge of a bare spot across which a turkey ran with incredible swiftness. He did not get the gun in line with it at all. Then two more broke out of the bushes. Run! They were as swift as flying quail. Ken took two snap-shots, and missed both times. If any one had told him that he would miss a running turkey at fifty feet, he would have been insulted. But he did not loosen a feather. Loading again, he yelled for George.

"Hey, George--turkeys!"

He whooped, and started across on the run.

"Gee!" said Hal. "Ken, I couldn't do any worse shooting than you. Let me take a few pegs."

Ken handed over the heavy gun and fell back a little, giving Hal the lead. They walked on, peering closely into the bushes. Suddenly a beautiful big gobbler ran out of a thicket, and then stopped to stretch out his long neck and look.

"Shoot--hurry!" whispered Ken. "What a chance!"

"That's a tame turkey," said Hal.

"Tame! Why, you tenderfoot! He's as wild as wild. Can't you see that?"

Ken's excitement and Pepe's intense eagerness all at once seemed communicated to Hal. He hauled up the gun, fingered the triggers awkwardly, then shot both barrels. He tore a tremendous hole in the brush some few feet to one side of the turkey. Then the great bird ran swiftly out of sight.

"Didn't want to kill him sitting, anyhow," said Hal, handing the gun back to Ken.

"We want to eat some wild turkey, don't we? Well, we'd better take any chance. These birds are game, Hal, and don't you forget that!"

"What's all the shooting?" panted George, as he joined the march.

Just then there was a roar in the bushes, and a brown blur rose and whizzed ahead like a huge bullet. That turkey had flushed. Ken watched him fly till he went down out of sight into a distant swale.

"Pretty nifty flier, eh?" said George. "He was too quick for me."

"Great!" replied Ken.

There was another roar, and a huge bronze cannon-ball sped straight ahead. Ken shot both barrels, then George shot one, all clean misses. Ken watched this turkey fly, and saw him clearer. He had to admit that the wild turkey of the Tamaulipas jungle had a swifter and more beautiful flight than his favorite bird, the ruffled grouse.

"Walk faster," said George. "They'll flush better. I don't see how I'm to hit one. This goose I'm carrying weighs about a ton."

The hunters hurried along, crashing through the bushes. They saw turkey after turkey. *Bang!* went George's gun.

Then a beautiful sight made Ken cry out and forget to shoot. Six turkeys darted across an open patch--how swiftly they ran!--then rose in a bunch. The roar they made, the wonderfully rapid action of their powerful wings, and then the size of them, their wildness and noble gameness made them the royal game for Ken.

At the next threshing in the bushes his gun was leveled; he covered the whistling bronze thing that shot up. The turkey went down with a crash. Pepe yelled, and as he ran forward the air all about him was full of fine bronze feathers. Ken hurried forward to see his bird. Its strength and symmetry, and especially the beautiful shades of bronze, captivated his eye.

"Come on, boys--this is the greatest game I ever hunted," he called.

Again Pepe yelled, and this time he pointed. From where Ken stood he could not see anything except low, green bushes. In great excitement George threw up his gun and shot. Ken heard a squealing.

"Javelin! Javelin!" yelled Pepe, in piercing alarm.

George jerked a rifle from him and began to shoot. Hal pumped his .22 into the bushes. The trampling of hard little hoofs and a cloud of dust warned Ken where the javelin were. Suddenly Pepe broke and fled for the river.

"Hyar, Pepe, fetch back my rifle," shouted Ken, angrily.

Pepe ran all the faster.

George turned and dashed away yelling: "Wild pigs! Wild pigs!"

"Look out, Ken! Run! Run!" added Hal; and he likewise took to his heels.

It looked as if there was nothing else for Ken to do but to make tracks from that vicinity. Never before had he run from a danger which he had not seen; but the flight of the boys was irresistibly contagious, and this, coupled with the many stories he had heard of the *javelin*, made Ken execute a sprint that would have been a record but for the hampering weight of gun and turkey. He vowed he would hold on to both, pigs or no pigs; nevertheless he listened as he ran and nervously looked back often. It may have been excited imagination that the dust-cloud appeared to be traveling in his wake. Fortunately, the distance to the river did not exceed a short quarter of a mile. Hot, winded, and thoroughly disgusted with himself, Ken halted on the bank. Pepe was already in the boat, and George was scrambling aboard.

"A fine--chase--you've given--me," Ken panted. "There's nothing--after us."

"Don't you fool yourself," returned George, quickly. "I saw those pigs, and, like the ass I am, I blazed away at one with my shotgun."

"Did he run at you? That's what I want to know?" demanded Ken.

George said he was not certain about that, but declared there always was danger if a wounded *javelin* squealed. Pepe had little to say; he refused to go back after the deer left in the trail. So they rowed across the shoal, and on the way passed within a rod of a big crocodile.

"Look at that fellow," cried George. "Wish I had my rifle loaded. He's fifteen feet long."

"Oh no, George, he's not more than ten feet," said Ken.

"You don't see his tail. He's a whopper. Pepe told me there was one in this pool. We'll get him, all right."

They reached camp tired out, and all a little ruffled in temper, which certainly was not eased by the discovery that they were covered with ticks. Following the cue of his companions, Ken hurriedly stripped off his clothes and hung them where they could singe over the camp-fire. There were broad red bands of *pinilius* round both ankles, and reddish patches on the skin of his arms. Here and there were black spots about the size of his little finger-nail, and these were *garrapatoes*. He picked these off one by one, rather surprised to find them come off so easily. Suddenly he jumped straight up with a pain as fierce as if it had been a puncture from a red-hot wire.

Pepe grinned; and George cried:

"Aha! that was a garrapato bite, that was! You just wait!"

George had a hundred or more of the big black ticks upon him, and he was remorselessly popping them with his cigarette. Some of them were biting him, too, judging from the way he flinched. Pepe had attracted to himself a million or more of the *pinilius*, but very few of the larger pests. He generously came to Ken's assistance. Ken was trying to pull off the *garrapato* that had bitten a hole in him. Pepe said it had embedded its head, and if pulled would come apart, leaving the head buried in the flesh, which would cause inflammation. Pepe held the glowing end of his cigarette close over the tick, and it began to squirm and pull out its head. When it was free of the flesh Pepe suddenly touched it with the cigarette, and it exploded with a pop. A difficult question was: Which hurt Ken the most, the burn from the cigarette or the bite of the tick? Pepe scraped off as many *pinilius* as would come, and then rubbed Ken with *canya*, the native alcohol. If this was not some kind of vitriol, Ken missed his guess. It smarted so keenly he thought his skin was peeling off. Presently, however, the smarting subsided, and so did the ticks.

Hal, who by far was the most sensitive one in regard to the crawling and biting of the jungle pests, had been remarkably fortunate in escaping them. So he made good use of his opportunity to poke fun at the others, particularly Ken.

George snapped out: "Just wait, Hollering Hal!"

"Don't you call me that!" said Hal, belligerently.

Ken eyed his brother in silence, but with a dark, meaning glance. It had occurred to Ken that here in this jungle was the only place in the world where he could hope to pay off old scores on Hal. And plots began to form in his mind.

They lounged about camp, resting in the shade during the hot midday hours. For supper they had a superfluity of meat, the waste of which Ken deplored, and he assuaged his conscience by deciding to have a taste of each kind. The wild turkey he found the most toothsome, delicious meat it had ever been his pleasure to eat. What struck him at once was the flavor, and he could not understand it until Pepe explained that the jungle turkey lived upon a red pepper. So the Tamaulipas wild turkey turned out to be doubly the finest game he had ever shot.

All afternoon the big crocodile sunned himself on the surface of the shoal.

Ken wanted a crocodile-skin, and this was a chance to get one; but he thought it as well to wait, and kept the boys from wasting ammunition.

Before sundown Pepe went across the river and fetched the deer carcass down to the sandbar, where the jaguar-trail led to the water.

At twilight Ken stationed the boys at the lower end of the island, ambushed behind stones. He placed George and Pepe some rods below his own position. They had George's .32 rifle, and the 16-gage loaded with a solid ball. Ken put Hal, with the double-barreled shotgun, also loaded with ball, some little distance above. And Ken, armed with his automatic, hid just opposite the deer-trails.

"Be careful where you shoot," Ken warned repeatedly. "Be cool--think quick--and aim."

Ken settled down for a long wait, some fifty yards from the deer carcass. A wonderful procession of wild fowl winged swift flight over his head. They flew very low. It was strange to note the difference in the sound of their flying. The cranes and herons softly swished the air, the teal and canvasbacks whirred by, and the great Muscovies whizzed like bullets.

When the first deer came down to drink it was almost dark, and when they left the moon was up, though obscured by clouds. Faint sounds rose from the other side of the island. Ken listened until his ears ached, but he could hear nothing. Heavier clouds drifted over the moon. The deer carcass became indistinct, and then faded entirely, and the bar itself grew vague. He was about to give up watching for that night when he heard a faint rustling below. Following it came a grating or crunching of gravel.

Bright flares split the darkness--*crack! crack!* rang out George's rifle, then the heavy *boom! boom!* of the shotgun.

"There he is!" yelled George. "He's down--we got him--there's two! Look out!"

Boom! Boom! roared the heavy shotgun from Hal's covert.

"George missed him! I got him!" yelled Hal. "No, there he goes--Ken! Ken!"

Ken caught the flash of a long gray body in the hazy gloom of the bar and took a quick shot at it. The steel-jacketed bullet scattered the gravel and then hummed over the bank. The gray body moved fast up the bank. Ken could just see it. He turned loose the little automatic and made the welkin ring.

XIV A FIGHT WITH A JAGUAR

When the echoes of the shots died away the stillness seemed all the deeper. No rustle in the brush or scuffle on the sand gave evidence of a wounded or dying jaguar. George and Hal and Pepe declared there were two tigers, and that they had hit one. Ken walked out upon the stones till he could see the opposite bar, but was not rewarded by a sight of dead game. Thereupon they returned to camp, somewhat discouraged at their ill luck, but planning another night-watch.

In the morning George complained that he did not feel well. Ken told him he had been eating too much fresh meat, and that he had better be careful. Then Ken set off alone, crossed the river, and found that the deer carcass was gone. In the sand near where it had lain were plenty of cat-tracks, but none of the big jaguar. Upon closer scrutiny he found the cat-tracks to be those of a panther. He had half dragged, half carried the carcass up one of the steep trails, but from that point there was no further trace.

Ken struck out across the fiat, intending to go as far as the jungle. Turtle-doves fluttered before him in numberless flocks. Far to one side he saw Muscovy ducks rising, sailing a few rods, then alighting. This occurred several times before he understood what it meant. There was probably a large flock feeding on the flat, and the ones in the rear were continually flying to get ahead of those to the fore.

Several turkeys ran through the bushes before Ken, but as he was carrying a rifle he paid little heed to them. He kept a keen lookout for *javelin.* Two or three times he was tempted to turn off the trail into little bamboo hollows; this, however, owing to a repugnance to ticks, he did not do. Finally, as he neared the high moss-decked wall of the jungle, he came upon a runway leading through the bottom of a deep swale, and here he found tiger-tracks.

Farther down the swale, under a great cluster of bamboo, he saw the scattered bones of several deer. Ken was sure that in this spot the lord of the jungle had feasted more than once. It was an open hollow, with the ground bare under the bamboos. The runway led on into dense, leafy jungle. Ken planned to bait that lair with a deer carcass and watch it during the late afternoon.

First, it was necessary to get the deer. This might prove bothersome, for Ken's hands and wrists were already sprinkled with *pinilius*, and he certainly did not want to stay very long in the brush. Ken imagined he felt an itching all the time, and writhed inside his clothes.

"Say, blame you! bite!" he exclaimed, resignedly, and stepped into the low bushes. He went up and out of the swale. Scarcely had he reached a level when he saw a troop of deer within easy range. Before they winded danger Ken shot, and the one he had singled out took a few bounds, then fell over sideways. The others ran off into the brush. Ken remembered that the old hunter on Penetier had told him how seldom a deer dropped at once. When he saw the work of the soft-nose .351 bullet, he no longer wondered at this deer falling almost in his tracks.

"If I ever hit a jaguar like that it will be all day with him," was Ken's comment.

There were two things about hunting the jaguar that Ken had been bidden to keep in mind--fierce aggressiveness and remarkable tenacity of life.

Ken dragged the deer down into the bamboo swale and skinned out a haunch. Next to wild-turkey meat, he liked venison best. He was glad to have that as an excuse, for killing these tame tropical deer seemed like murder to Ken. He left the carcass in a favorable place and then hurried back to camp.

To Ken's relief, he managed to escape bringing any *garrapatoes* with him, but it took a half-hour to rid himself of the collection of *pinilius*.

"George, ask Pepe what's the difference between a garrapato and a pinilius," said Ken.

"The big tick is the little one's mother," replied Pepe.

"Gee! you fellows fuss a lot about ticks," said Hal, looking up from his task. He was building more pens to accommodate the turtles, snakes, snails, mice, and young birds that he had captured during the morning.

Pepe said there were few ticks there in the uplands compared to the number down along the Panuco River. In the lowlands where the cattle roamed there were millions in every square rod. The under side of every leaf and blade of grass was red with ticks. The size of these pests depended on whether or not they got a chance to stick to a steer or any beast. They appeared to live indefinitely, but if they could not suck blood they could not grow. The *pinilius* grew into a *garrapato*, and a *garrapato* bred a hundred thousand *pinilius* in her body. Two singular things concerning these ticks were that they always crawled upward, and they vanished from the earth during the wet season.

Ken soaked his Duxbax hunting-suit in kerosene in the hope that this method would enable him to spend a reasonable time hunting. Then, while the other boys fished and played around, he waited for the long, hot hours to pass. It was cool in the shade, but the sunlight resembled the heat of fire. At last five o'clock came, and Ken put on the damp suit. Soaked with the oil, it was heavier and hotter than sealskin, and before he got across the river he was nearly roasted. The evening wind sprang up, and the gusts were like blasts from a furnace. Ken's body was bathed in perspiration; it ran down his wrists, over his hands, and wet the gun. This cure for ticks--if it were one--was worse than their bites. When he reached the shade of the bamboo swale it was none too soon for him. He threw off the coat, noticing there were more ticks upon it than at anytime before. The bottom of his trousers, too, had gathered an exceeding quantity. He brushed them off, muttering the while that he believed they liked kerosene, and looked as if they were drinking it. Ken found it easy, however, to brush them off the wet Duxbax, and soon composed himself to rest and watch.

The position chosen afforded Ken a clear view of the bare space under the bamboos and of the hollow where the runway disappeared in the jungle. The deer carcass, which lay as he had left it, was about a hundred feet from him. This seemed rather close, but he had to accept it, for if he had moved farther away he could not have commanded both points.

Ken sat with his back against a clump of bamboos, the little rifle across his knees and an extra clip of cartridges on the ground at his left. After taking that position he determined not to move a yard when the tiger came, and to kill him.

Ken went over in mind the lessons he had learned hunting bear in Penetier Forest with old Hiram Bent and lassoing lions on the wild north-rim of the Grand Cañon. Ken knew that the thing for a hunter to do, when his quarry was dangerous, was to make up his mind beforehand. Ken had twelve powerful shells that he could shoot in the half of twelve seconds. He would have been willing to face two jaguars.

The sun set and the wind died down. What a relief was the cooling shade! The little breeze that was left fortunately blew at right angles to the swale, so that there did not seem much danger of the tiger winding Ken down the jungle runway.

For long moments he was tense and alert. He listened till he thought he had almost lost the sense of hearing. The jungle leaves were whispering; the insects were humming. He had expected to hear myriad birds and see processions of deer, and perhaps a drove of *javelin.* But if any living creatures ventured near him it was without his knowledge. The hour between sunset and twilight passed--a long wait; still he did not lose the feeling that something would happen. Ken's faculties of alertness tired, however, and needed distraction. So he took stock of the big clump of bamboos under which lay the deer carcass.

It was a remarkable growth, that gracefully drooping cluster of slender bamboo poles. He remembered how, as a youngster, not many years back, he had wondered where the fishing-poles came from. Here Ken counted one hundred and sixty-nine in a clump no larger than a barrel. They were yellow in color with black bands, and they rose straight for a few yards, then began to lean out, to bend slightly, at last to droop with their abundance of spiked leaves. Ken was getting down to a real, interested study of this species of jungle growth when a noise startled him.

He straightened out of his lounging position and looked around. The sound puzzled him. He could not place its direction or name what it was. The jungle seemed strangely quiet. He listened. After a moment of waiting he again heard the sound. Instantly Ken was as tense and vibrating as a violin string. The thing he had heard was from the lungs of some jungle beast. He was almost ready to pronounce it a cough. Warily he glanced around, craning his neck. Then a deep, hoarse growl made him whirl.

There stood a jaguar with head up and paw on the deer carcass. Ken imagined he felt perfectly cool, but he knew he was astounded. And even as he cautiously edged the rifle over his knee he took in the beautiful points of the jaguar. He was yellow, almost white, with black spots. He was short and stocky, with powerful stumpy bow-legs. But his head most amazed Ken. It was enormous. And the expression of his face was so singularly savage and wild that Ken seemed to realize instantly the difference between a mountain-lion and this fierce tropical brute.

The jaguar opened his jaws threateningly. He had an enormous stretch of jaw. His long, yellow fangs gleamed. He growled again.

Not hurriedly, nor yet slowly, Ken fired.

He heard the bullet strike him as plainly as if he had hit him with a board. He saw dust fly from his hide. Ken expected to see the jaguar roll over. Instead of that he leaped straight up with a terrible roar. Something within Ken shook. He felt cold and sick.

When the jaguar came down, sprawled on all fours, Ken pulled the automatic again, and he saw the fur fly. Then the jaguar leaped forward with a strange, hoarse cry. Ken shot again, and knocked the beast flat. He tumbled and wrestled about, scattering the dust and brush. Three times more Ken fired, too hastily, and inflicted only slight wounds.

In reloading Ken tried to be deliberate in snapping in the second clip and pushing down the rod that threw the shell into the barrel. But his hands shook. His fingers were all thumbs, and he fumbled at the breech of the rifle.

In that interval, if the jaguar could have kept his sense of direction, he would have reached Ken. But the beast zigzagged; he had lost his equilibrium; he was hard hit.

Then he leaped magnificently. He landed within twenty-five feet of Ken, and when he plunged down he rolled clear over. Ken shot him through and through. Yet he got up, wheezing blood, uttering a hoarse bellow, and made again at Ken.

Ken had been cold, sick. Now panic almost overpowered him. The rifle wabbled. The bamboo glade blurred in his sight. A terrible dizziness and numbness almost paralyzed him. He was weakening, sinking, when thought of life at stake lent him a momentary grim and desperate spirit.

Once while the jaguar was in the air Ken pulled, twice while he was down. Then the jaguar stood up pawing the air with great spread claws, coughing, bleeding, roaring. He was horrible.

Ken shot him straight between the wide-spread paws.

With twisted body, staggering, and blowing bloody froth all over Ken, the big tiger blindly lunged forward and crashed to earth.

Then began a furious wrestling. Ken imagined it was the death-throes of the jaguar. Ken could not see him down among the leaves and vines; nevertheless, he shot into the commotion. The struggles ceased. Then a movement of the weeds showed Ken that the jaguar was creeping toward the jungle.

Ken fell rather than sat down. He found he was wringing wet with cold sweat. He was panting hard.

"Say, but--that--was--awful!" he gasped. "What--was--wrong--with me?"

He began to reload the clips. They were difficult to load for even a calm person, and now, in the reaction, Ken was the farthest removed from calm. The jaguar crept steadily away, as Ken could tell by the swaying weeds and shaking vines.

"What--a hard-lived beast!" muttered Ken. "I--must have shot--him all to pieces. Yet he's getting away from me."

At last Ken's trembling fingers pushed some shells in the two clips, and once more he reloaded the rifle. Then he stood up, drew a deep, full breath, and made a strong effort at composure.

"I've shot at bear--and deer--and lions out West," said Ken. "But this was different. I'll never get over it."

How close that jaguar came to reaching Ken was proved by the blood coughed into his face. He recalled that he had felt the wind of one great sweeping paw.

Ken regained his courage and determination. He meant to have that beautiful spotted skin for his den. So he hurried along the runway and entered the jungle. Beyond the edge, where the bushes made a dense thicket, it was dry forest, with little green low down. The hollow gave place to a dry wash. He could not see the jaguar, but he could hear him dragging himself through the brush, cracking sticks, shaking saplings.

Presently Ken ran across a bloody trail and followed it. Every little while he would stop to listen. When the wounded jaguar was still, he waited until he started to move again. It was hard going. The brush was thick, and had to be broken and crawled under or through. As Ken had left his coat behind, his shirt was soon torn to rags. He peered ahead with sharp eyes, expecting every minute to come in sight of the poor, crippled beast. He wanted to put him out of agony. So he kept on doggedly for what must have been a long time.

The first premonition he had of carelessness was to note that the shadows were gathering in the jungle. It would soon be night. He must turn back while there was light enough to follow his back track out to the open. The second came in shape of a hot pain in his arm, as keen as if he had jagged it with a thorn. Holding it out, he discovered to his dismay that it was spotted with *garrapatoes*.

XV THE VICIOUS GARRAPATOES

At once Ken turned back, and if he thought again of the jaguar it was that he could come after him the next day or send Pepe. Another vicious bite, this time on his leg, confirmed his suspicions that many of the ticks had been on him long enough to get their heads in. Then he was bitten in several places.

Those bites were as hot as the touch of a live coal, yet they made Ken break out in dripping cold sweat. It was imperative that he get back to camp without losing a moment which could be saved. From a rapid walk he fell into a trot. He got off his back trail and had to hunt for it. Every time a tick bit he jumped as if stung. The worst of it was that he knew he was collecting more *garrapatoes* with almost every step. When he grasped a dead branch to push it out of the way he could feel the ticks cling to his hand. Then he would whip his arm in the air, flinging some of them off to patter on the dry ground. Impossible as it was to run through that matted jungle, Ken almost accomplished it. When he got out into the open he did run, not even stopping for his coat, and he crossed the flat at top speed.

It was almost dark when Ken reached the river-bank and dashed down to frighten a herd of drinking deer. He waded the narrowest part of the shoal. Running up the island he burst into the bright circle of camp-fire. Pepe dropped a stew-pan and began to jabber. George dove for a gun.

"What's after you?" shouted Hal, in alarm.

Ken was so choked up and breathless that at first he could not speak. His fierce aspect and actions, as he tore off his sleeveless and ragged shirt and threw it into the fire, added to the boys' fright.

"Good Lord! are you bug-house, Ken?" shrieked Hal.

"*Bug-house! Yes!*" roared Ken, swiftly undressing. "Look at me!"

In the bright glare he showed his arms black with *garrapatoes* and a sprinkling of black dots over the rest of his body.

"Is that all?" demanded Hal, in real or simulated scorn. "Gee! but you're a brave hunter. I thought not less than six tigers were after you."

"I'd rather have six tigers after me," yelled Ken. "You little freckle-faced red-head!"

It was seldom indeed that Ken called his brother that name. Hal was proof against any epithets except that one relating to his freckles and his hair. But just now Ken felt that he was being eaten alive. He was in an agony, and he lost his temper. And therefore he laid himself open to Hal's scathing humor.

"Never mind the kid," said Ken to Pepe and George. "Hurry now, and get busy with these devils on me."

It was well for Ken that he had a native like Pepe with him. For Pepe knew just what to do. First he dashed a bucket of cold water over Ken. How welcome that was!

"Pepe says for you to point out the ticks that 're biting the hardest," said George.

In spite of his pain Ken stared in mute surprise.

"Pepe wants you to point out the ticks that are digging in the deepest," explained George. "Get a move on, now."

"What!" roared Ken, glaring at Pepe and George. He thought even the native might be having fun with him. And for Ken this was not a funny time.

But Pepe was in dead earnest.

"Say, it's impossible to tell *where* I'm being bitten most! It's all over!" protested Ken.

Still he discovered that by absolute concentration on the pain he was enduring he was able to locate the severest points. And that showed him the soundness of Pepe's advice.

"Here--this one--here--there.... Oh! here," began Ken, indicating certain ticks.

"Not so fast, now," interrupted the imperturbable George, as he and Pepe set to work upon Ken.

Then the red-hot cigarette-tips scorched Ken's skin. Ken kept pointing and accompanying his directions with wild gestures and exclamations.

"Here.... Oo-oo! Here.... Wow! Here.... Ouch!--that one stung! Here.... *Augh*! Say, can't you hurry? Here! ... Oh! that one was in a mile! Here.... *Hold on*! You're burning a hole in me! ... George, you're having fun out of this. Pepe gets two to your one."

"He's been popping ticks all his life," was George's reasonable protest.

"Hurry!" cried Ken, in desperation. "George, if you monkey round--fool over this job--I'll--I'll punch you good."

All this trying time Hal Ward sat on a log and watched the proceedings with great interest and humor. Sometimes he smiled, at others he laughed, and yet again he burst out into uproarious mirth.

"George, he wouldn't punch anybody," said Hal. "I tell you he's all in. He hasn't any nerve left. It's a chance of your life. You'll never get another. He's been bossing you around. Pay him up. Make him holler. Why, what's a few little ticks? Wouldn't phase me! But Ken Ward's such a delicate, fine-skinned, sensitive, girly kind of a boy! He's too nice to be bitten by bugs. Oh dear, yes, yes! ... Ken, why don't you show courage?"

Ken shook his fist at Hal.

"All right," said Ken, grimly. "Have all the fun you can. Because I'll get even with you."

XV THE VICIOUS GARRAPATOES

Hal relapsed into silence, and Ken began to believe he had intimidated his brother. But he soon realized how foolish it was to suppose such a thing. Hal had only been working his fertile brain.

"George, here's a little verse for the occasion," said Hal.

"There was a brave hunter named Ken,
And he loved to get skins for his den,
Not afraid was he of tigers or pigs,
Or snakes or cats or any such things,
But one day in the jungle he left his clothes,
And came hollering back with *garrapatoes*."

"Gre-at-t-t!" sputtered Ken. "Oh, brother mine, we're a long way from home, I'll make you crawl."

Pepe smoked, and wore out three cigarettes, and George two, before they had popped all the biting ticks. Then Ken was still covered with them. Pepe bathed him in *canya*, which was like a bath of fire, and soon removed them all. Ken felt flayed alive, peeled of his skin, and sprinkled with fiery sparks. When he lay down he was as weak as a sick cat. Pepe said the *canya* would very soon take the sting away, but it was some time before Ken was resting easily.

It would not have been fair to ask Ken just then whether the prize for which he worked was worth his present gain. *Garrapatoes* may not seem important to one who simply reads about them, but such pests are a formidable feature of tropical life.

However, Ken presently felt that he was himself again.

Then he put his mind to the serious problem of his note-book and the plotting of the island. As far as his trip was concerned, Cypress Island was an important point. When he had completed his map down to the island, he went on to his notes. He believed that what he had found out from his knowledge of forestry was really worth something. He had seen a gradual increase in the size and number of trees as he had proceeded down the river, a difference in the density and color of the jungle, a flattening-out of the mountain range, and a gradual change from rocky to clayey soil. And on the whole his note-book began to assume such a character that he was beginning to feel willing to submit it to his uncle.

XVI FIELD WORK OF A NATURALIST

That night Ken talked natural history to the boys and read extracts from a small copy of Sclater he had brought with him.

They were all particularly interested in the cat tribe.

The fore feet of all cats have five toes, the hind feet only four. Their claws are curved and sharp, and, except in case of one species of leopard, can be retracted in their sheaths. The claws of the great cat species are kept sharp by pulling them down through bark of trees. All cats walk on their toes. And the stealthy walk is due to hairy pads or cushions. The claws of a cat do not show in its track as do those of a dog. The tongues of all cats are furnished with large papillæ. They are like files, and the use is to lick bones and clean their fur. Their long whiskers are delicate organs of perception to aid them in finding their way on their night quests. The eyes of all cats are large and full, and can be altered by contraction or expansion of iris, according to the amount of light they receive. The usual color is gray or tawny with dark spots or stripes. The uniform tawny color of the lion and the panther is perhaps an acquired color, probably from the habit of these animals of living in desert countries. It is likely that in primitive times cats were all spotted or striped.

Naturally the boys were most interested in the jaguar, which is the largest of the cat tribe in the New World. The jaguar ranges from northern Mexico to northern Patagonia. Its spots are larger than those of the leopard. Their ground color is a rich tan or yellow, sometimes almost gold. Large specimens have been known nearly seven feet from nose to end of tail.

The jaguar is an expert climber and swimmer. Humboldt says that where the South American forests are subject to floods the jaguar sometimes takes to tree life, living on monkeys. All naturalists agree on the ferocious nature of jaguars, and on the loudness and frequency of their cries. There is no record of their attacking human beings without provocation. Their favorite haunts are the banks of jungle rivers, and they often prey upon fish and turtles.

The attack of a jaguar is terrible. It leaps on the back of its prey and breaks its neck. In some places there are well-known scratching trees where jaguars sharpen their claws. The bark is worn smooth in front from contact with the breasts of the animals as they stand up, and there is a deep groove on each side. When new scars appear on these trees it is known that jaguars are in the vicinity. The cry of the jaguar is loud, deep, hoarse, something like *pu, pu, pu*. There is much enmity between the panther, or mountain-lion, and the jaguar, and it is very strange that generally the jaguar fears the lion, although he is larger and more powerful.

Pepe had interesting things to say about jaguars, or *tigres*, as he called them. But Ken, of course, could not tell how much Pepe said was truth and how much just native talk. At any rate, Pepe told of one Mexican who had a blind and deaf jaguar that he had tamed. Ken knew that naturalists claimed the jaguar could not be tamed, but in this instance Ken was inclined to believe Pepe. This blind jaguar was enormous in size, terrible of aspect, and had been trained to trail anything his master set him to. And Tigre, as he was called, never slept or stopped till he had killed the thing he was trailing. As he was blind and deaf, his power of scent had been abnormally developed.

Pepe told of a fight between a huge crocodile and a jaguar in which both were killed. He said jaguars stalked natives and had absolutely no fear. He knew natives who said that jaguars had made off with children and eaten them. Lastly, Pepe told of an incident that had happened in Tampico the year before. There was a ship at dock below Tampico, just on the outskirts where the jungle began, and one day at noon two big jaguars leaped on the deck. They frightened the crew out of their wits. George verified this story, and added that the jaguars had been chased by dogs, had boarded the ship, where they climbed into the rigging, and stayed there till they were shot.

"Well," said Ken, thoughtfully, "from my experience I believe a jaguar would do anything."

The following day promised to be a busy one for Hal, without any time for tricks. George went hunting before breakfast--in fact, before the others were up--and just as the boys were sitting down to eat he appeared on the nearer bank and yelled for Pepe. It developed that for once George had bagged game.

He had a black squirrel, a small striped wildcat, a peccary, a three-foot crocodile, and a duck of rare plumage.

After breakfast Hal straightway got busy, and his skill and knowledge earned praise from George and Pepe. They volunteered to help, which offer Hal gratefully accepted. He had brought along a folding canvas tank, forceps, knives, scissors, several packages of preservatives, and tin boxes in which to pack small skins.

His first task was to mix a salt solution in the canvas tank. This was for immersing skins. Then he made a paste of salt and alum, and after that a mixture of two-thirds glycerin and one-third water and carbolic acid, which was for preserving small skins and to keep them soft.

And as he worked he gave George directions on how to proceed with the wildcat and squirrel skins.

"Skin carefully and tack up the pelts fur side down. Scrape off all the fat and oil, but don't scrape through. To-morrow when the skins are dry soak them in cold water till soft. Then take them out and squeeze dry. I'll make a solution of three quarts water, one-half pint salt, and one ounce oil of vitriol. Put the skins in that for half an hour. Squeeze dry again, and hang in shade. That 'll tan the skin, and the moths will never hurt them."

When Hal came to take up the duck he was sorry that some of the beautiful plumage had been stained.

"I want only a few water-fowl," he said. "And particularly one of the big Muscovies. And you must keep the feathers from getting soiled."

It was interesting to watch Hal handle that specimen. First he took full measurements. Then, separating the feathers along the breast, he made an incision with a sharp knife, beginning high up on breast-bone and ending at tail. He exercised care so as not to cut through the abdomen. Raising the skin carefully along the cut as far as the muscles of the leg, he pushed out the knee joint and cut it off. Then he loosened the skin from the legs and the back, and bent the tail down to cut through the tail joint. Next he removed the skin from the body and cut off the wings at the shoulder joint. Then he proceeded down the neck, being careful not to pull or stretch the skin. Extreme care was necessary in cutting round the eyes. Then, when he had loosened the skin from the skull, he severed the head and cleaned out the skull. He coated all with the paste, filled the skull with cotton, and then immersed them in the glycerin bath.

The skinning of the crocodile was an easy matter compared with that of the duck. Hal made an incision at the throat, cut along the middle of the abdomen all the way to the tip of the tail, and then cut the skin away all around the carcass. Then he set George and Pepe to scraping the skin, after which he immersed it in the tank.

About that time Ken, who was lazily fishing in the shade of the cypresses, caught one of the blue-tailed fish. Hal was delighted. He had made a failure of the other specimen of this unknown fish. This one was larger and exquisitely marked, being dark gold on the back, white along the belly, and its tail had a faint bluish tinge. Hal promptly killed the fish, and then made a dive for his suitcase. He produced several sheets of stiff cardboard and a small box of water-colors and brushes. He laid the fish down on a piece of paper and outlined its exact size. Then, placing it carefully in an upright position on a box, he began to paint it in the actual colors of the moment. Ken laughed and teased him. George also was inclined to be amused. But Pepe was amazed and delighted. Hal worked on unmindful of his audience, and, though he did not paint a very artistic picture, he produced the vivid colors of the fish before they faded.

His next move was to cover the fish with strips of thin cloth, which adhered to the scales and kept them from being damaged. Then he cut along the middle line of the belly, divided the pelvic arch where the ventral fins joined, cut through the spines, and severed the fins from the bones. Then he skinned down to the tail, up to the back, and cut through caudal processes. The vertebral column he severed at the base of the skull. He cleaned and scraped the entire inside of the skin, and then put it to soak.

"Hal, you're much more likely to make good with Uncle Jim than I am," said Ken. "You've really got skill, and you know what to do. Now, my job is different.

So far I've done fairly well with my map of the river. But as soon as we get on level ground I'll be stumped."

"We'll cover a hundred miles before we get to low land," replied Hal, cheerily. "That's enough, even if we do get lost for the rest of the way. You'll win that trip abroad, Ken, never fear, and little Willie is going to be with you."

XVII A MIXED-UP TIGER-HUNT

Next morning Hal arose bright as a lark, but silent, mysterious, and with far-seeing eyes. It made Ken groan in spirit to look at the boy. Yes, indeed, they were far from home, and the person did not live on the earth who could play a trick on Hal Ward and escape vengeance.

After breakfast Hal went off with a long-handled landing-net, obviously to capture birds or fish or mice or something.

George said he did not feel very well, and he looked grouchy. He growled around camp in a way that might have nettled Ken, but Ken, having had ten hours of undisturbed sleep, could not have found fault with anybody.

"Garrapato George, come out of it. Cheer up," said Ken. "Why don't you take Pinilius Pepe as gun-bearer and go out to shoot something? You haven't used up much ammunition yet."

Ken's sarcasm was not lost upon George.

"Well, if I do go, I'll not come running back to camp without some game."

"My son," replied Ken, genially, "if you should happen to meet a jaguar you'd--you'd just let out one squawk and then never touch even the high places of the jungle. You'd take that crazy .32 rifle for a golf-stick."

"Would I?" returned George. "All right."

Ken watched George awhile that morning. The lad performed a lot of weird things around camp. Then he bounced bullets off the water in vain effort to locate the basking crocodile. Then he tried his hand at fishing once more. He could get more bites than any fisherman Ken ever saw, but he could not catch anything.

By and by the heat made Ken drowsy, and, stretching himself in the shade, he thought of a scheme to rid the camp of the noisy George.

"Say, George, take my hammerless and get Pepe to row you up along the shady bank of the river," suggested Ken. "Go sneaking along and you'll have some sport."

George was delighted with that idea. He had often cast longing eyes at the hammerless gun. Pepe, too, looked exceedingly pleased. They got in the boat and were in the act of starting when George jumped ashore. He reached for his .32 and threw the lever down to see if there was a shell in the chamber. Then he proceeded to fill his pockets with ammunition.

"Might need a rifle," he said. "You can't tell what you're going to see in this unholy jungle."

Whereupon he went aboard again and Pepe rowed leisurely up-stream.

"Be careful, boys," Ken called, and composed himself for a nap. He promptly fell asleep. How long he slept he had no idea, and when he awoke he lay with languor, not knowing at the moment what had awakened him. Presently he heard a shout, then a rifle-shot. Sitting up, he saw the boat some two hundred yards above, drifting along about the edge of the shade. Pepe was in it alone. He appeared to be excited, for Ken observed him lay down an oar and pick up a gun, and then reverse the performance. Also he was jabbering to George, who evidently was out on the bank, but invisible to Ken.

"Hey, Pepe!" Ken yelled. "What 're you doing?"

Strange to note, Pepe did not reply or even turn.

"Now where in the deuce is George?" Ken said, impatiently.

The hollow crack of George's .32 was a reply to the question. Ken heard the singing of a bullet. Suddenly, *spou!* it twanged on a branch not twenty feet over his head, and then went whining away. He heard it tick a few leaves or twigs. There was not any languor in the alacrity with which Ken put the big cypress-tree between him and up-stream. Then he ventured to peep forth.

"Look out where you're slinging lead!" he yelled. He doubted not that George had treed a black squirrel or was pegging away at parrots. Yet Pepe's motions appeared to carry a good deal of feeling, too much, he thought presently, for small game. So Ken began to wake up thoroughly. He lost sight of Pepe behind a low branch of a tree that leaned some fifty yards above the island. Then he caught sight of him again. He was poling with an oar, evidently trying to go up or down--Ken could not tell which.

Spang! *Spang*! George's .32 spoke twice more, and the bullets both struck in the middle of the stream and ricochetted into the far bank with little thuds.

Something prompted Ken to reach for his automatic, snap the clip in tight, and push in the safety. At the same time he muttered George's words: "You can never tell what's coming off in this unholy jungle."

Then, peeping out from behind the cypress, Ken watched the boat drift downstream. Pepe had stopped poling and was looking closely into the thick grass and vines of the bank. Ken heard his voice, but could not tell what he said. He watched keenly for some sight of George. The moments passed, the boat drifted, and Ken began to think there was nothing unusual afoot. In this interval Pepe drifted within seventy-five yards of camp. Again Ken called to ask him what George was stalking, and this time Pepe yelled; but Ken did not know what he said. Hard upon this came George's sharp voice:

"Look out, there, on the island. Get behind something. I've got him between the river and the flat. He's in this strip of shore brush. There!"

Spang! *Spang*! *Spang*! Bullets hummed and whistled all about the island. Ken was afraid to peep out with even one eye. He began to fancy that George was playing Indian.

"Fine, Georgie! You're doing great!" he shouted. "You couldn't come any closer to me if you were aiming at me. What is it?"

Then a crashing of brush and a flash of yellow low down along the bank changed the aspect of the situation.

"Panther! or jaguar!" Ken ejaculated, in amaze. In a second he was tight-muscled, cold, and clear-witted. At that instant he saw George's white shirt about the top of the brush.

"Go back! Get out in the open!" Ken ordered. "Do you hear me?"

"Where is he?" shouted George, paying not the slightest attention to Ken. Ken jumped from behind the tree, and, running to the head of the island, he knelt low near the water with rifle ready.

"Tigre! Tigre! Tigre!" screamed Pepe, waving his arms, then pointing.

George crashed into the brush. Ken saw the leaves move, then a long yellow shape. With the quickness of thought and the aim of the wing-shot, Ken fired. From the brush rose a strange wild scream. George aimed at a shaking mass of grass and vines, but, before he could fire, a long, lean, ugly beast leaped straight out from the bank to drop into the water with a heavy splash.

Like a man half scared to death Pepe waved Ken's double-barreled gun. Then a yellow head emerged from the water. It was in line with the boat. Ken dared not shoot.

"Kill him, George," yelled Ken. "Tell Pepe to kill him."

George seemed unaccountably silent. But Ken had no time to look for him, for his eyes were riveted on Pepe. The native did not know how to hold a gun properly, let alone aim it. He had, however, sense enough to try. He got the stock under his chin, and, pointing the gun, he evidently tried to fire. But the hammerless did not go off. Then Pepe fumbled at the safety-catch, which he evidently remembered seeing Ken use.

The jaguar, swimming with difficulty, perhaps badly wounded, made right for the boat. Pepe was standing on the seat. Awkwardly he aimed.

Boom! He had pulled both triggers. The recoil knocked him backward. The hammerless fell in the boat, and Pepe's broad back hit the water; his bare, muscular legs clung to the gunwale, and slipped loose.

He had missed the jaguar, for it kept on toward the boat. Still Ken dared not shoot.

"George, what on earth is the matter with you?" shouted Ken.

Then Ken saw him standing in the brush on the bank, fussing over the crazy .32. Of course at the critical moment something had gone wrong with the old rifle.

Pepe's head bobbed up just on the other side of the boat. The jaguar was scarcely twenty feet distant and now in line with both boat and man. At that instant a heavy swirl in the water toward the middle of the river drew Ken's attention. He saw the big crocodile, and the great creature did not seem at all lazy at that moment.

XVII A MIXED-UP TIGER-HUNT

George began to scream in Spanish. Ken felt his hair stiffen and his face blanch. Pepe, who had been solely occupied with the jaguar, caught George's meaning and turned to see the peril in his rear.

He bawled his familiar appeal to the saints. Then he grasped the gunwale of the boat just as it swung against the branches of the low-leaning tree. He vaulted rather than climbed aboard.

Ken forgot that Pepe could understand little English, and he yelled: "Grab an oar, Pepe. Keep the jaguar in the water. Don't let him in the boat."

But Pepe, even if he had understood, had a better idea. Nimble, he ran over the boat and grasped the branches of the tree just as the jaguar flopped paws and head over the stern gunwale.

Ken had only a fleeting instant to get a bead on that yellow body, and before he could be sure of an aim the branch weighted with Pepe sank down to hide both boat and jaguar. The chill of fear for Pepe changed to hot rage at this new difficulty.

Then George began to shoot.

Spang!

Ken heard the bullet hit the boat.

"George--wait!" shouted Ken. "Don't shoot holes in the boat. You'll sink it."

Spang! *Spang*! *Spang*! *Spang*!

That was as much as George cared about such a possibility. He stood on the bank and worked the lever of his .32 with wild haste. Ken plainly heard the spat of the bullets, and the sound was that of lead in contact with wood. So he knew George was not hitting the jaguar.

"You'll ruin the boat!" roared Ken.

Pepe had worked up from the lower end of the branch, and as soon as he straddled it and hunched himself nearer shore the foliage rose out of the water, exposing the boat. George kept on shooting till his magazine was empty. Ken's position was too low for him to see the jaguar.

Then the boat swung loose from the branch and, drifting down, gradually approached the shore.

"Pull yourself together, George," called Ken. "Keep cool. Make sure of your aim. We've got him now."

"He's mine! He's mine! He's mine! Don't you dare shoot!" howled George. "I got him!"

"All right. But steady up, can't you? Hit him once, anyway."

Apparently without aim George fired. Then, jerking the lever, he fired again. The boat drifted into overhanging vines. Once more Ken saw a yellow and black object, then a trembling trail of leaves.

"He's coming out below you. Look out," yelled Ken.

George disappeared. Ken saw no sign of the jaguar and heard no shot or shout from George. Pepe dropped from his branch to the bank and caught the boat. Ken called, and while Pepe rowed over to the island, he got into some clothes fit to hunt in. Then they hurried back across the channel to the bank.

Ken found the trail of the jaguar, followed it up to the edge of the brush, and lost it in the weedy flat. George came out of a patch of bamboos. He looked white and shaky and wild with disappointment.

"Oh, I had a dandy shot as he came out, but the blamed gun jammed again. Come on, we'll get him. He's all shot up. I bet I hit him ten times. He won't get away."

Ken finally got George back to camp. The boat was half full of water, making it necessary to pull it out on the bank and turn it over. There were ten bullet-holes in it.

"George, you hit the boat, anyway," Ken said; "now we've a job on our hands."

Hal came puffing into camp. He was red of face, and the sweat stood out on his forehead. He had a small animal of some kind in a sack, and his legs were wet to his knees.

"What was--all the--pegging about?" he asked, breathlessly. "I expected to find camp surrounded by Indians."

"Kid, it's been pretty hot round here for a little. George and Pepe rounded up a tiger. Tell us about it, George," said Ken.

So while Ken began to whittle pegs to pound into the bullet-holes, George wiped his flushed, sweaty face and talked.

"We were up there a piece, round the bend. I saw a black squirrel and went ashore to get him. But I couldn't find him, and in kicking round in the brush I came into a kind of trail or runway. Then I ran plumb into that darned jaguar. I was so scared I couldn't remember my gun. But the cat turned and ran. It was lucky he didn't make at me. When I saw him run I got back my courage. I called for Pepe to row down-stream and keep a lookout. Then I got into the flat. I must have come down a good ways before I saw him. I shot, and he dodged back into the brush again. I fired into the moving bushes where he was. And pretty soon I ventured to get in on the bank, where I had a better chance. I guess it was about that time that I heard you yell. Then it all happened. You hit him! Didn't you hear him scream? What a jump he made! If it hadn't been so terrible when your hammerless kicked Pepe overboard, I would have died laughing. Then I was paralyzed when the jaguar swam for the boat. He was hurt, for the water was bloody. Things came off quick, I tell you. Like a monkey Pepe scrambled into the tree. When I got my gun loaded the jaguar was crouched down in the bottom of the boat watching Pepe. Then I began to shoot. I can't realize he got away from us. What was the reason you didn't knock him?"

"Well, you see, George, there were two good reasons," Ken replied. "The first was that at that time I was busy dodging bullets from your rifle. And the second was that you threatened my life if I killed your jaguar."

"Did I get as nutty as that? But it was pretty warm there for a little.... Say, was he a big one? My eyes were so hazy I didn't see him clear."

"He wasn't big, not half as big as the one I lost yesterday. Yours was a long, wiry beast, like a panther, and mean-looking."

XVII A MIXED-UP TIGER-HUNT

Pepe sat on the bank, and while he nursed his bruises he smoked. Once he made a speech that was untranslatable, but Hal gave it an interpretation which was probably near correct.

"That's right, Pepe. Pretty punk tiger-hunters--mucho punk!"

XVIII WATCHING A RUNWAY

"I'll tell you what, fellows," said Hal. "I know where we *can* get a tiger."

"We'll get one in the neck if we don't watch out," replied George.

Ken thought that Hal looked very frank and earnest, and honest and eager, but there was never any telling about him.

"Where?" he asked, skeptically.

"Down along the river. You know I've been setting traps all along. There's a flat sand-bar for a good piece down. I came to a little gully full of big tracks, big as my two hands. And fresh!"

"Honest Injun, kid?" queried Ken.

"Hope to die if I'm lyin'," replied Hal. "I want to see somebody kill a tiger. Now let's go down there in the boat and wait for one to come to drink. There's a big log with driftwood lodged on it. We can hide behind that."

"Great idea, Hal," said Ken. "We'd be pretty safe in the boat. I want to say that tigers have sort of got on my nerves. I ought to go over in the jungle to look for the one I crippled. He's dead by now. But the longer I put it off the harder it is to go. I'll back out yet.... Come, we'll have an early dinner. Then to watch for Hal's tiger."

The sun had just set, and the hot breeze began to swirl up the river when Ken slid the boat into the water. He was pleased to find that it did not leak.

"We'll take only two guns," said Ken, "my .351 and the hammerless, with some ball-cartridges. We want to be quiet to-night, and if you fellows take your guns you'll be pegging at ducks and things. That won't do."

Pepe sat at the oars with instructions to row easily. George and Hal occupied the stern-seats, and Ken took his place in the bow, with both guns at hand.

The hot wind roared in the cypresses, and the river whipped up little waves with white crests. Long streamers of gray moss waved out over the water and branches tossed and swayed. The blow did not last for many minutes. Trees and river once more grew quiet. And suddenly the heat was gone.

As Pepe rowed on down the river, Cypress Island began to disappear round a bend, and presently was out of sight. Ducks were already in flight. They flew low over the boat, so low that Ken could almost have reached them with the barrel of his gun. The river here widened. It was full of huge snags. A high, wooded bluff shadowed the western shore. On the left, towering cypresses, all laced together in dense vine and moss webs, leaned out.

Under Hal's direction Pepe rowed to a pile of driftwood, and here the boat was moored. The gully mentioned by Hal was some sixty yards distant. It opened like the mouth of a cave. Beyond the cypresses thick, intertwining bamboos covered it.

"I wish we'd gone in to see the tracks," said Ken. "But I'll take your word, Hal."

"Oh, they're there, all right."

"I don't doubt it. Looks great to me! That's a runway, Hal.... Now, boys, get a comfortable seat, and settle down to wait. Don't talk. Just listen and watch. Remember, soon we'll be out of the jungle, back home. So make hay while the sun shines. Watch and listen! Whoever sees or hears anything first is the best man."

For once the boys were as obedient as lambs. But then, Ken thought, the surroundings were so beautiful and wild and silent that any boys would have been watchful.

There was absolutely no sound but the intermittent whir of wings. The water-fowl flew by in companies--ducks, cranes, herons, snipe, and the great Muscovies. Ken never would have tired of that procession. It passed all too soon, and then only an occasional water-fowl swept swiftly by, as if belated.

Slowly the wide river-lane shaded. But it was still daylight, and the bank and the runway were clearly distinguishable. There was a moment--Ken could not tell just how he knew--when the jungle awakened. It was not only the faint hum of insects; it was a sense as if life stirred with the coming of twilight.

Pepe was the first to earn honors at the listening game. He held up a warning forefinger. Then he pointed under the bluff. Ken saw a doe stepping out of a fringe of willows.

"Don't move--don't make a noise," whispered Ken.

The doe shot up long ears and watched the boat. Then a little fawn trotted out and splashed in the water. Both deer drank, then seemed in no hurry to leave the river.

Next moment Hal heard something downstream and George saw something up-stream. Pepe again whispered. As for Ken, he saw little dark shapes moving out of the shadow of the runway. He heard a faint trampling of hard little hoofs. But if these animals were *javelin*--of which he was sure--they did not come out into the open runway. Ken tried to catch Pepe's attention without making a noise; however, Pepe was absorbed in his side of the river. Ken then forgot he had companions. All along the shores were faint splashings and rustlings and crackings.

A loud, trampling roar rose in the runway and seemed to move backward toward the jungle, diminishing in violence.

"Pigs running--something scared 'em," said George.

"S-s-s-sh!" whispered Ken.

All the sounds ceased. The jungle seemed to sleep in deep silence.

Ken's eyes were glued to the light patch of sand-bank where it merged in the dark of the runway. Then Ken heard a sound--what, he could not have told. But it made his heart beat fast.

There came a few pattering thuds, soft as velvet; and a shadow, paler than the dark background, moved out of the runway.

With that a huge jaguar loped into the open. He did not look around. He took a long, easy bound down to the water and began to lap.

Either Pepe or George jerked so violently as to make the boat lurch. They seemed to be stifling.

"Oh, Ken, don't miss!" whispered Hal.

Ken had the automatic over the log and in line. His teeth were shut tight, and he was cold and steady. He meant not to hurry.

The jaguar was a heavy, squat, muscular figure, not graceful and beautiful like the one Ken had crippled. Suddenly he raised his head and looked about. He had caught a scent.

It was then that Ken lowered the rifle till the sight covered the beast--lower yet to his huge paws, then still lower to the edge of the water. Ken meant to shoot low enough this time. Holding the rifle there, and holding it with all his strength, he pressed the trigger once--twice. The two shots rang out almost simultaneously. Ken expected to see this jaguar leap, but the beast crumpled up and sank in his tracks.

Then the boys yelled, and Ken echoed them. Pepe was wildly excited, and began to fumble with the oars.

"Wait! Wait, I tell you!" ordered Ken.

"Oh, Ken, you pegged him!" cried Hal. "He doesn't move. Let's go ashore. What did I tell you? It took me to find the tiger."

Ken watched with sharp eyes and held his rifle ready, but the huddled form on the sand never so much as twitched.

"I guess I plugged him," said Ken, with unconscious pride.

Pepe rowed the boat ashore, and when near the sand-bar he reached out with an oar to touch the jaguar. There was no doubt about his being dead. The boys leaped ashore and straightened out the beast. He was huge, dirty, spotted, bloody, and fiercely savage even in death. Ken's bullets had torn through the chest, making fearful wounds. Pepe jabbered, and the boys all talked at once. When it came to lifting the jaguar into the boat they had no slight task. The short, thick-set body was very heavy. But at last they loaded it in the bow, and Pepe rowed back to the island. It was still a harder task to get the jaguar up the high bank. Pepe kindled a fire so they would have plenty of light, and then they set to work at the skinning.

What with enthusiasm over the stalk, and talk of the success of the trip, and compliments to Ken's shooting, and care of the skinning, the boys were three hours at the job. Ken, remembering Hiram Bent's teachings, skinned out the great claws himself. They salted the pelt and nailed it up on the big cypress.

"You'd never have got one but for me," said Hal. "That's how I pay you for the tricks you've played me!"

"By George, Hal, it's a noble revenge!" cried Ken, who, in the warmth and glow of happiness of the time, quite believed his brother.

Pepe went to bed first. George turned in next. Ken took a last look at the great pelt stretched on the cypress, and then he sought his blankets. Hal, however, remained up. Ken heard him pounding stakes in the ground.

"Hal, what 're you doing?"

"I'm settin' my trot-lines," replied Hal, cheerfully.

"Well, come to bed."

"Keep your shirt on, Ken, old boy. I'll be along presently."

Ken fell asleep. He did not have peaceful slumbers. He had been too excited to rest well. He would wake up out of a nightmare, then go to sleep again. He seemed to wake suddenly out of one of these black spells, and he was conscious of pain. Something tugged at his leg.

"What the dickens!" he said, and raised on his elbow. Hal was asleep between George and Pepe, who were snoring.

Just then Ken felt a violent jerk. The blankets flew up at his feet, and his left leg went out across his brother's body. There was a string--a rope--something fast round his ankle, and it was pulling hard. It hurt.

"Jiminy!" shouted Ken, reaching for his foot. But before he could reach it another tug, more violent, pulled his leg straight out. Ken began to slide.

"What on earth?" yelled Ken. "Say! Something's got me!"

The yells and Ken's rude exertions aroused the boys. And they were frightened. Ken got an arm around Hal and the other around George and held on for dear life. He was more frightened than they. Pepe leaped up, jabbering, and, tripping, he fell all in a heap.

"Oh! my leg!" howled Ken. "It's being pulled off. Say, I can't be dreaming!"

Most assuredly Ken was wide awake. The moonlight showed his bare leg sticking out and round his ankle a heavy trot-line. It was stretched tight. It ran down over the bank. And out there in the river a tremendous fish or a crocodile was surging about, making the water roar.

Pepe was trying to loosen the line or break it. George, who was always stupid when first aroused, probably imagined he was being mauled by a jaguar, for he loudly bellowed. Ken had a strangle-hold on Hal.

"Oh! *Oh*! *Oh-h-h*!" bawled Ken. Not only was he scared out of a year's growth; he was in terrible pain. Then his cries grew unintelligible. He was being dragged out of the tent. Still he clung desperately to the howling George and the fighting Hal.

All at once something snapped. The tension relaxed. Ken fell back upon Hal.

"Git off me, will you?" shouted Hal. "Are you c-c-cr-azy?"

But Hal's voice had not the usual note when he was angry or impatient. He was laughing so he could not speak naturally.

"Uh-huh!" said Ken, and sat up. "I guess here was where I got it. Is my leg broken? What came off?"

Pepe was staggering about on the bank, going through strange motions. He had the line in his hands, and at the other end was a monster of some land threshing about in the water. It was moonlight and Ken could see plainly. Around the ankle that felt broken was a twisted loop of trot-line. Hal had baited a hook and slipped the end of the trot-line over Ken's foot. During the night the crocodile or an enormous fish had taken the bait. Then Ken had nearly been hauled off the island.

Pepe was doing battle with the hooked thing, whatever it was, and Ken was about to go to his assistance when again the line broke.

"Great! Hal, you have a nice disposition," exclaimed Ken. "You have a wonderful affection for your brother. You care a lot about his legs or his life. Idiot! Can't you play a safe trick? If I hadn't grabbed you and George, I'd been pulled into the river. Eaten up, maybe! And my ankle is sprained. It won't be any good for a week. You are a bright boy!"

And in spite of his laughter Hal began to look ashamed.

XIX ADVENTURES WITH CROCODILES

The rest of that night Ken had more dreams; and they were not pleasant. He awoke from one in a cold fright.

It must have been late, for the moon was low. His ankle pained and throbbed, and to that he attributed his nightmare. He was falling asleep again when the clink of tin pans made him sit up with a start. Some animal was prowling about camp. He peered into the moonlit shadows, but could make out no unfamiliar object. Still he was not satisfied; so he awoke Pepe.

Certainly it was not Ken's intention to let Pepe get out ahead; nevertheless he was lame and slow, and before he started Pepe rolled out of the tent.

"Santa Maria!" shrieked Pepe.

Ken fumbled under his pillow for a gun. Hal raised up so quickly that he bumped Ken's head, making him see a million stars. George rolled over, nearly knocking down the tent.

From outside came a sliddery, rustling noise, then another yell that was deadened by a sounding splash. Ken leaped out with his gun, George at his elbow. Pepe stood just back of the tent, his arms upraised, and he appeared stunned. The water near the bank was boiling and bubbling; waves were dashing on the shore and ripples spreading in a circle.

George shouted in Spanish.

"Crocodile!" cried Ken.

"Si, si, Señor," replied Pepe. Then he said that when he stepped out of the tent the crocodile was right in camp, not ten feet from where the boys lay. Pepe also said that these brutes were man-eaters, and that he had better watch for the rest of the night. Ken thought him, like all the natives, inclined to exaggerate; however, he made no objection to Pepe's holding watch over the crocodile.

"What'd I tell you?" growled George. "Why didn't you let me shoot him? Let's go back to bed."

In the morning when Ken got up he viewed his body with great curiosity. The ticks and the cigarette burns had left him a beautifully tattoed specimen of aborigine. His body, especially his arms, bore hundreds of little reddish scars--bites and burns together. There was not, however, any itching or irritation, for which he made sure he had to thank Pepe's skill and the *canya*.

George did not get up when Ken called him. Thinking his sleep might have been broken, Ken let him alone a while longer, but when breakfast was smoking he gave him a prod. George rolled over, looking haggard and glum.

"I'm sick," he said.

Ken's cheerfulness left him, for he knew what sickness or injury did to a camping trip. George complained of aching bones, headache and cramps, and showed a tongue with a yellow coating. Ken said he had eaten too much fresh meat, but Pepe, after looking George over, called it a name that sounded like *calentura*.

"What's that?" Ken inquired.

"Tropic fever," replied George. "I've had it before."

For a while he was a very sick boy. Ken had a little medicine-case, and from it he administered what he thought was best, and George grew easier presently. Then Ken sat down to deliberate on the situation.

Whatever way he viewed it, he always came back to the same thing--they must get out of the jungle; and as they could not go back, they must go on down the river. That was a bad enough proposition without being hampered by a sick boy. It was then Ken had a subtle change of feeling; a shade of gloom seemed to pervade his spirit.

By nine o'clock they were packed, and, turning into the shady channel, soon were out in the sunlight saying good-by to Cypress Island. At the moment Ken did not feel sorry to go, yet he knew that feeling would come by and by, and that Cypress Island would take its place in his memory as one more haunting, calling wild place.

They turned a curve to run under a rocky bluff from which came a muffled roar of rapids. A long, projecting point of rock extended across the river, allowing the water to rush through only at a narrow mill-race channel close to the shore. It was an obstacle to get around. There was no possibility of lifting the boat over the bridge of rock, and the alternative was shooting the channel. Ken got out upon the rocks, only to find that drifting the boat round the sharp point was out of the question, owing to a dangerously swift current. Ken tried the depth of the water--about four feet. Then he dragged the boat back a little distance and stepped into the river.

"Look! Look!" cried Pepe, pointing to the bank.

About ten yards away was a bare shelf of mud glistening with water and showing the deep tracks of a crocodile. It was a slide, and manifestly had just been vacated. The crocodile-tracks resembled the imprints of a giant's hand.

"Come out!" yelled George, and Pepe jabbered to his saints.

"We've got to go down this river," Ken replied, and he kept on wading till he got the boat in the current. He was frightened, of course, but he kept on despite that. The boat lurched into the channel, stern first, and he leaped up on the bow. It shot down with the speed of a toboggan, and the boat whirled before he could scramble to the oars. What was worse, an overhanging tree with dead snags left scarce room to pass beneath. Ken ducked to prevent being swept overboard, and one of the snags that brushed and scraped him ran under his belt and lifted him into the air. He grasped at the first thing he could lay hands on, which happened to be a box, but he could not hold to it because the boat threatened to go on, leaving him kicking in midair and holding up a box of potatoes. Ken clutched a gunwale, only to see the water swell dangerously over the edge. In angry helplessness he loosened his hold. Then the snag broke, just in the nick of time, for in a second more the boat would have been swept away. Ken fell across the bow, held on, and soon drifted from under the threshing branches, and seized the oars.

Pepe and George and Hal walked round the ledge and, even when they reached Ken, had not stopped laughing.

"Boys, it wasn't funny," declared Ken, soberly.

"I said it was coming to us," replied George.

There were rapids below, and Ken went at them with stern eyes and set lips. It was the look of men who face obstacles in getting out of the wilderness. More than one high wave circled spitefully round Pepe's broad shoulders.

They came to a fall where the river dropped a few feet straight down. Ken sent the boys below. Hal and George made a detour. But Pepe jumped off the ledge into shallow water.

"*Ah-h!*" yelled Pepe.

Ken was becoming accustomed to Pepe's wild yell, but there was a note in this which sent a shiver over him. Before looking, Ken snatched his rifle from the boat.

Pepe appeared to be sailing out into the pool. But his feet were not moving.

Ken had only an instant, but in that he saw under Pepe a long, yellow, swimming shape, leaving a wake in the water. Pepe had jumped upon the back of a crocodile. He seemed paralyzed, or else he was wisely trusting himself there rather than in the water. Ken was too shocked to offer advice. Indeed, he would not have known how to meet this situation.

Suddenly Pepe leaped for a dry stone, and the energy of his leap carried him into the river beyond. Like a flash he was out again, spouting water.

Ken turned loose the automatic on the crocodile and shot a magazine of shells. The crocodile made a tremendous surge, churning up a slimy foam, then vanished in a pool.

"Guess this 'll be crocodile day," said Ken, changing the clip in his rifle. "I'll bet I made a hole in that one. Boys, look out below."

Ken shoved the boat over the ledge in line with Pepe, and it floated to him, while Ken picked his way round the rocky shore. The boys piled aboard again. The day began to get hot. Ken cautioned the boys to avoid wading, if possible, and to be extremely careful where they stepped. Pepe pointed now and then to huge bubbles breaking on the surface of the water and said they were made by crocodiles.

From then on Ken's hands were full. He struck swift water, where rapid after rapid, fall on fall, took the boat downhill at a rate to afford him satisfaction. The current had a five or six mile speed, and, as Ken had no portages to make and the corrugated rapids of big waves gave him speed, he made by far the best time of the voyage.

The hot hours passed--cool for the boys because they were always wet. The sun sank behind a hill. The wind ceased to whip the streamers of moss. At last, in a gathering twilight, Ken halted at a wide, flat rock to make camp.

"Forty miles to-day if we made an inch!" exclaimed Ken.

The boys said more.

They built a fire, cooked supper, and then, weary and silent, Hal and George and Pepe rolled into their blankets. But Ken doggedly worked an hour at his map and notes. That hard forty miles meant a long way toward the success of his trip.

Next morning the mists had not lifted from the river when they shoved off, determined to beat the record of yesterday. Difficulties beset them from the start--the highest waterfall of the trip, a leak in the boat, deep, short rapids, narrows with choppy waves, and a whirlpool where they turned round and round, unable to row out. Nor did they get free till Pepe lassoed a snag and pulled them out.

About noon they came to another narrow chute brawling down into a deep, foamy pool. Again Ken sent the boys around, and he backed the boat into the chute; and just as the current caught it he leaped aboard. He was either tired or careless, for he drifted too close to a half-submerged rock, and, try as he might, at the last moment he could not avoid a collision.

As the stern went hard on the rock Ken expected to break something, but was surprised at the soft thud with which he struck. It flashed into his mind that the rock was moss-covered.

Quick as the thought there came a rumble under the boat, the stern heaved up, there was a great sheet-like splash, and then a blow that splintered the gunwale. Then the boat shunted off, affording the astounded Ken a good view of a very angry crocodile. He had been sleeping on the rock.

The boys were yelling and crowding down to the shore where Ken was drifting in. Pepe waded in to catch the boat.

"What was it hit you, Ken?" asked Hal.

"Mucho malo," cried Pepe.

"The boat's half full of water--the gunwale's all split!" ejaculated George.

"Only an accident of river travel," replied Ken, with mock nonchalance. "Say, Garrapato, *when*, about *when* is it coming to me?"

"Well, if he didn't get slammed by a crocodile!" continued George.

They unloaded, turned out the water, broke up a box to use for repairs, and mended the damaged gunwale--work that lost more than a good hour. Once again under way, Ken made some interesting observations. The river ceased to stand on end in places; crocodiles slipped off every muddy promontory, and wide trails ridged the steep clay-banks.

"Cattle-trails, Pepe says," said George. "Wild cattle roam all through the jungle along the Panuco."

It was a well-known fact that the rancheros of Tamaulipas State had no idea how many cattle they owned. Ken was so eager to see if Pepe had been correct that he went ashore, to find the trails were, indeed, those of cattle.

"Then, Pepe, we must be somewhere near the Panuco River," he said.

"Quien sabe?" rejoined he, quietly.

When they rounded the curve they came upon a herd of cattle that clattered up the bank, raising a cloud of dust.

"Wilder than deer!" Ken exclaimed.

From that point conditions along the river changed. The banks were no longer green; the beautiful cypresses gave place to other trees, as huge, as moss-wound, but more rugged and of gaunt outline; the flowers and vines and shady nooks disappeared. Everywhere wide-horned steers and cows plunged up the banks. Everywhere buzzards rose from gruesome feasts. The shore was lined with dead cattle, and the stench of putrefying flesh was almost unbearable. They passed cattle mired in the mud, being slowly tortured to death by flies and hunger; they passed cattle that had slipped off steep banks and could not get back and were bellowing dismally; and also strangely acting cattle that Pepe said had gone crazy from ticks in their ears. Ken would have put these miserable beasts out of their misery had not George restrained him with a few words about Mexican law.

A sense of sickness came to Ken, and though he drove the feeling from him, it continually returned. George and Hal lay flat on the canvas, shaded with a couple of palm leaves; Pepe rowed on and on, growing more and more serious and quiet. His quick, responsive smile was wanting now.

By way of diversion, and also in the hope of securing a specimen, Ken began to shoot at the crocodiles. George came out of his lethargy and took up his rifle. He would have had to be ill indeed, to forswear any possible shooting; and, now that Ken had removed the bar, he forgot he had fever. Every hundred yards or so they would come upon a crocodile measuring somewhere from about six feet upward, and occasionally they would see a great yellow one, as large as a log. Seldom did they get within good range of these huge fellows, and shooting from a moving boat was not easy. The smaller ones, however, allowed the boat to approach quite close. George bounced many a .32 bullet off the bank, but he never hit a crocodile. Ken allowed him to have the shots for the fun of it, and, besides, he was watching for a big one.

"George, that rifle of yours is leaded. It doesn't shoot where you aim."

When they got unusually close to a small crocodile George verified Ken's statement by missing his game some yards. He promptly threw the worn-out rifle overboard, an act that caused Pepe much concern.

Whereupon Ken proceeded to try his luck. Instructing Pepe to row about in the middle of the stream, he kept eye on one shore while George watched the other. He shot half a dozen small crocodiles, but they slipped off the bank before Pepe could get ashore. This did not appear to be the fault of the rifle, for some of the reptiles were shot almost in two pieces. But Ken had yet to learn more about the tenacity of life of these water-brutes. Several held still long enough for Ken to shoot them through, then with a plunge they went into the water, sinking at once in a bloody foam. He knew he had shot them through, for he saw large holes in the mud-banks lined with bits of bloody skin and bone.

"There's one," said George, pointing. "Let's get closer, so we can grab him. He's got a good piece to go before he reaches the water."

Pepe rowed slowly along, guiding the boat a little nearer the shore. At forty feet the crocodile raised up, standing on short legs, so that all but his tail was free of the ground. He opened his huge jaws either in astonishment or to intimidate them, and then Ken shot him straight down the throat. He flopped convulsively and started to slide and roll. When he reached the water he turned over on his back, with his feet sticking up, resembling a huge frog. Pepe rowed hard to the shore, just as the crocodile with one last convulsion rolled off into deeper water. Ken reached over, grasped his foot, and was drawing it up when a sight of cold, glassy eyes and open-fanged jaws made him let go. Then the crocodile sank in water where Pepe could not touch bottom with an oar.

"Let's get one if it takes a week," declared George. The lad might be sick, but there was nothing wrong with his spirit. "Look there!" he exclaimed. "Oh, I guess it's a log. Too big!"

They had been unable to tell the difference between a crocodile and a log of driftwood until it was too late. In this instance a long, dirty-gray object lay upon a low bank. Despite its immense size, which certainly made the chances in favor of its being a log, Ken determined this time to be fooled on the right side. He had seen a dozen logs--as he thought--suddenly become animated and slip into the river.

"Hold steady, Pepe. I'll take a crack at that just for luck."

The distance was about a hundred yards, a fine range for the little rifle. Resting on his knee, he sighted low, under the gray object, and pulled the trigger twice. There were two spats so close together as to be barely distinguishable. The log of driftwood leaped into life.

"Whoop!" shouted Hal.

"It's a crocodile!" yelled George. "You hit--you hit! Will you listen to that?"

"Row hard, Pepe--pull!"

He bent to the oars, and the boat flew shoreward.

The huge crocodile, opening yard-long jaws, snapped them shut with loud cracks. Then he beat the bank with his tail. It was as limber as a willow, but he seemed unable to move his central parts, his thick bulk, where Ken had sent the two mushroom bullets. *Whack*! *Whack*! *Whack*! The sodden blows jarred pieces from the clay-bank above him. Each blow was powerful enough to have staved in the planking of a ship. All at once he lunged upward and, falling over backward, slid down his runway into a few inches of water, where he stuck.

"Go in above him, Pepe," Ken shouted. "Here-- Heavens! What a monster!"

Deliberately, at scarce twenty feet, Ken shot the remaining four shells into the crocodile. The bullets tore through his horny hide, and blood and muddy water spouted up. George and Pepe and Hal yelled, and Ken kept time with them. The terrible lashing tail swung back and forth almost too swiftly for the eye to catch. A deluge of mud and water descended upon the boys, bespattering, blinding them and weighing down the boat. They jumped out upon the bank to escape it. They ran to and fro in aimless excitement. Ken still clutched the rifle, but he had no shells for it. George was absurd enough to fling a stone into the blood-tinged cloud of muddy froth and spray that hid the threshing leviathan. Presently the commotion subsided enough for them to see the great crocodile lying half on his back, with belly all torn and bloody and huge claw-like hands pawing the air. He was edging, slipping off into deeper water.

"He'll get away--he'll get away!" cried Hal. "What 'll we do?"

Ken racked his brains.

"Pepe, get your lasso--rope him--rope him! Hurry! he's slipping!" yelled George.

Pepe snatched up his lariat, and, without waiting to coil it, cast the loop. He caught one of the flippers and hauled tight on it just as the crocodile slipped out of sight off the muddy ledge. The others ran to the boat, and, grasping hold of the lasso with Pepe, squared away and began to pull. Plain it was that the crocodile was not coming up so easily. They could not budge him.

"Hang on, boys!" Ken shouted. "It's a tug-of-war."

The lasso was suddenly jerked out with a kind of twang. Crash! went Pepe and Hal into the bottom of the boat. Ken went sprawling into the mud, and George, who had the last hold, went to his knees, but valiantly clung to the slipping rope. Bounding up, Ken grasped it from him and wound it round the sharp nose of the bowsprit.

"Get in--hustle!" he called, falling aboard. "You're always saying it's coming to us. Here's where!"

George had hardly got into the boat when the crocodile pulled it off shore, and away it went, sailing down-stream.

"Whoop! All aboard for Panuco!" yelled Hal.

"Now, Pepe, you don't need to row any more--we've a water-horse," Ken added.

But Pepe did not enter into the spirit of the occasion. He kept calling on the saints and crying, "Mucho malo." George and Ken and Hal, however, were hilarious. They had not yet had experience enough to know crocodiles.

Faster and faster they went. The water began to surge away from the bow and leave a gurgling wake behind the stern. Soon the boat reached the middle of the river where the water was deepest, and the lasso went almost straight down.

Ken felt the stern of the boat gradually lifted, and then, in alarm, he saw the front end sinking in the water. The crocodile was hauling the bow under.

"Pepe--your machete--cut the lasso!" he ordered, sharply. George had to repeat the order.

Wildly Pepe searched under the seat and along the gunwales. He could not find the *machete*.

"Cut the rope!" Ken thundered. "Use a knife, the ax--anything--only cut it--and cut it quick!"

Pepe could find nothing. Knife in hand, Ken leaped over his head, sprawled headlong over the trunk, and slashed the taut lasso just as the water began to roar into the boat. The bow bobbed up as a cork that had been under. But the boat had shipped six inches of water.

"Row ashore, Pepe. Steady, there. Trim the boat, George."

They beached at a hard clay-bank and rested a little before unloading to turn out the water.

"Grande!" observed Pepe.

"Yes; he was big," assented George.

"I wonder what's going to happen to us next," added Hal.

Ken Ward looked at these companions of his and he laughed outright. "Well, if you all don't take the cake for nerve!"

XX TREED BY WILD PIGS

Pepe's long years of *mozo* work, rowing for tarpon fishermen, now stood the boys in good stead. All the hot hours of the day he bent steadily to the oars. Occasionally they came to rifts, but these were not difficult to pass, being mere swift, shallow channels over sandy bottom. The rocks and the rapids were things of the past.

George lay in a kind of stupor, and Hal lolled in his seat. Ken, however, kept alert, and as the afternoon wore on began to be annoyed at the scarcity of camp-sites.

The muddy margins of the river, the steep banks, and the tick-infested forests offered few places where it was possible to rest, to say nothing of sleep. Every turn in the widening river gave Ken hope, which resulted in disappointment. He found consolation, however, in the fact that every turn and every hour put him so much farther on the way.

About five o'clock Ken had unexpected good luck in shape of a small sand-bar cut off from the mainland, and therefore free of cattle-tracks. It was clean and dry, with a pile of driftwood at one end.

"Tumble out, boys," called Ken, as Pepe beached the boat. "We'll pitch camp here."

Neither Hal nor George showed any alacrity. Ken watched his brother; he feared to see some of the symptoms of George's sickness. Both lads, however, seemed cheerful, though too tired to be of much use in the pitching of camp.

Ken could not recover his former good spirits. There was a sense of foreboding in his mind that all was not well, that he must hurry, hurry. And although George appeared to be holding his own, Hal healthy enough, and Pepe's brooding quiet at least no worse, Ken could not rid himself of gloom. If he had answered the question that knocked at his mind he would have admitted a certainty of disaster. So he kept active, and when there were no more tasks for that day he worked on his note-book, and then watched the flight of wild fowl.

The farther down the river the boys traveled the more numerous were the herons and cranes and ducks. But they saw no more of the beautiful *pato real*, as Pepe called them, or the little russet-colored ducks, or the dismal-voiced bitterns. On the other hand, wild geese were common, and there were flocks and flocks of teal and canvasbacks.

Pepe, as usual, cooked duck. And he had to eat it. George had lost his appetite altogether. Hal had lost his taste for meat, at least. And Ken made a frugal meal of rice.

"Boys," he said, "the less you eat from now on the better for you."

It took resolution to drink the cocoa, for Ken could not shut out remembrance of the green water and the shore-line of dead and decaying cattle. Still, he was parched with thirst; he had to drink. That night he slept ten hours without turning over. Next morning he had to shake Pepe to rouse him.

Ken took turns at the oars with Pepe. It was not only that he fancied Pepe was weakening and in need of an occasional rest, but the fact that he wanted to be occupied, and especially to keep in good condition. They made thirty miles by four o'clock, and most of it against a breeze. Not in the whole distance did they pass half a dozen places fit for a camp. Toward evening the river narrowed again, resembling somewhat the Santa Rosa of earlier acquaintance. The magnificent dark forests crowded high on the banks, always screened and curtained by gray moss, as if to keep their secrets.

The sun was just tipping with gold the mossy crests of a grove of giant ceibas, when the boys rounded a bend to come upon the first ledge of rocks for two days. A low, grassy promontory invited the eyes searching for camping-ground. This spot appeared ideal; it certainly was beautiful. The ledge jutted into the river almost to the opposite shore, forcing the water to rush through a rocky trough into a great foam-spotted pool below.

They could not pitch the tent, since the stony ground would not admit stakes, so they laid the canvas flat. Pepe went up the bank with his *machete* in search of firewood. To Ken's utmost delight he found a little spring of sweet water trickling from the ledge, and by digging a hole was enabled to get a drink, the first one in more than a week.

A little later, as he was spreading the blankets, George called his attention to shouts up in the woods.

"Pepe's treed something," Ken said. "Take your gun and hunt him up."

Ken went on making a bed and busying himself about camp, with little heed to George's departure. Presently, however, he was startled by unmistakable sounds of alarm. George and Pepe were yelling in unison, and, from the sound, appeared to be quite a distance away.

"What the deuce!" Ken ejaculated, snatching up his rifle. He snapped a clip in the magazine and dropped several loaded clips and a box of extra shells into his coat pocket. After his adventure with the jaguar he decided never again to find himself short of ammunition. Running up the sloping bank, he entered the forest, shouting for his companions. Answering cries came from in front and a little to the left. He could not make out what was said.

Save for drooping moss the forest was comparatively open, and at a hundred paces from the river-bank were glades covered with thickets and long grass and short palm-trees. The ground sloped upward quite perceptibly.

"Hey, boys, where are you?" called Ken.

XX TREED BY WILD PIGS

Pepe's shrill yells mingled with George's shouts. At first their meaning was unintelligible, but after calling twice Ken understood.

"Javelin! Go back! Javelin! We're treed! Wild pigs! Santa Maria! Run for your life!"

This was certainly enlightening and rather embarrassing. Ken remembered the other time the boys had made him run, and he grew hot with anger.

"I'll be blessed if I'll run!" he said, in the pride of conceit and wounded vanity. Whereupon he began to climb the slope, stopping every few steps to listen and look. Ken wondered what had made Pepe go so far for fire-wood; still, there was nothing but green wood all about. Walking round a clump of seared and yellow palms that rustled in the breeze, Ken suddenly espied George's white shirt. He was in a scrubby sapling not fifteen feet from the ground. Then Ken espied Pepe, perched in the forks of a ceiba, high above the thickets and low shrubbery. Ken was scarcely more than a dozen rods from them down the gradual slope. Both saw him at once.

"Run, you Indian! Run!" bawled George, waving his hands.

George implored Ken to fly to save his precious life.

"What for? you fools! I don't see anything to run from," Ken shouted back. His temper had soured a little during the last few days.

"You'd better run, or you'll have to climb," replied George. "Wild pigs--a thousand of 'em!"

"Where?"

"Right under us. There! Oh, if they see you! Listen to this." He broke off a branch, trimmed it of leaves, and flung it down. Ken heard a low, trampling roar of many hard little feet, brushings in the thicket, and cracking of twigs. As close as he was, however, he could not see a moving object. The dead grass and brush were several feet high, up to his waist in spots, and, though he changed position several times, no *javelin* did he see.

"You want to look out. Say, man, these are wild pigs--boars, I tell you! They'll kill you!" bellowed George.

"Are you going to stay up there all night?" Ken asked, sarcastically.

"We'll stay till they go away."

"All right, I'll scare them away," Ken replied, and, suiting action to word, he worked the automatic as fast as it would shoot, aiming into the thicket under George.

Of all the foolish things a nettled hunter ever did that was the worst. A roar answered the echoes of the rifle, and the roar rose from every side of the trees the victims were in. Nervously Ken clamped a fresh clip of shells into the rifle. Clouds of dust arose, and strange little squeals and grunts seemed to come from every quarter. Then the grass and bushes were suddenly torn apart by swift gray forms with glittering eyes. They were everywhere.

"*Run*! *Run*!" shrieked George, high above the tumult.

For a thrilling instant Ken stood his ground and fired at the bobbing gray backs. But every break made in the ranks by the powerful shells filled in a flash. Before that vicious charge he wavered, then ran as if pursued by demons.

The way was downhill. Ken tripped, fell, rolled over and over, then, still clutching the rifle, rose with a bound and fled. The javelin had gained. They were at his heels. He ran like a deer. Then, seeing a low branch, he leaped for it, grasped it with one hand, and, crooking an elbow round it, swung with the old giant swing.

Before Ken knew how it had happened he was astride a dangerously swaying branch directly over a troop of brownish-gray, sharp-snouted, fiendish-eyed little peccaries.

Some were young and sleek, others were old and rough; some had little yellow teeth or tusks, and all pointed their sharp noses upward, as if expecting him to fall into their very mouths. Feeling safe, once more Ken loaded the rifle and began to kill the biggest, most vicious *javelin*. When he had killed twelve in twelve shots, he saw that shooting a few would be of no avail. There were hundreds, it seemed, and he had scarcely fifty shells left. Moreover, the rifle-barrel grew so hot that it burnt his hands. Hearing George's yell, he replied, somewhat to his disgust:

"I'm all right, George--only treed. How 're you?"

"Pigs all gone--they chased you--Pepe thinks we can risk running."

"Don't take any chances," Ken yelled, in answer.

"Hi! Hi! What's wrong with you gazabos?" came Hal's yell from down the slope.

"Go back to the boat," shouted Ken.

"What for?"

"We're all treed by javelin--wild pigs."

"I've got to see that," was Hal's reply.

Ken called a sharp, angry order for Hal to keep away. But Hal did not obey. Ken heard him coming, and presently saw him enter one of the little glades. He had Ken's shotgun, and was peering cautiously about.

"Ken, where are you?"

"Here! Didn't I tell you to keep away? The pigs heard you--some of them are edging out there. Look out! Run, kid, run!"

A troop of *javelin* flashed into the glade. Hal saw them and raised the shotgun.

Boom! He shot both barrels.

The shot tore through the brush all around Ken, but fortunately beneath him. Neither the noise nor the lead stopped the pugnacious little peccaries.

Hal dropped Ken's hammerless and fled.

"Run faster!" yelled George, who evidently enjoyed Hal's plight. "They'll get you! Run hard!"

The lad was running close to the record when he disappeared.

In trying to find a more comfortable posture, so he could apply himself to an interesting study of his captors, Ken made the startling discovery that the branch which upheld him was splitting from the tree-trunk. His heart began to pound in his breast; then it went up into his throat. Every move he made--for he had started to edge toward the tree--widened the little white split.

"Boys, my branch is breaking!" he called, piercingly.

"Can't you get another?" returned George.

"No; I daren't move! Hurry, boys! If you don't scare these brutes off I'm a goner!"

Ken's eyes were riveted upon the gap where the branch was slowly separating from the tree-trunk. He glanced about to see if he could not leap to another branch. There was nothing near that would hold him. In desperation he resolved to drop the rifle, cautiously get to his feet upon the branch, and with one spring try to reach the tree. When about to act upon this last chance he heard Pepe's shrill yell and a crashing in the brush. Then followed the unmistakable roar and crackling of fire. Pepe had fired the brush--no, he was making his way toward Ken, armed with a huge torch.

"Pepe, you'll fire the jungle!" cried Ken, forgetting what was at stake and that Pepe could not understand much English. But Ken had been in one forest-fire and remembered it with horror.

The *javelin* stirred uneasily, and ran around under Ken, tumbling over one another.

When Pepe burst through the brush, holding before him long-stemmed palm leaves flaring in hissing flames, the whole pack of pigs bowled away into the forest at breakneck speed.

Ken leaped down, and the branch came with him. George came running up, his face white, his eyes big. Behind him rose a roar that Ken thought might be another drove of pigs till he saw smoke and flame.

"Boys, the jungle's on fire. Run for the river!"

In their hurry they miscalculated the location of camp and dashed out of the jungle over a steep bank, and they all had a tumble. It was necessary to wade to reach the rocky ledge.

Ken shook hands with Pepe.

"George, tell him that was a nervy thing to do. He saved my life, I do believe."

"You fellows did a lot of hollering," said Hal, from his perch in the boat.

"Say, young man, you've got to go back after my gun. Why didn't you do what I told you? Foolish, to run into danger that way!" declared Ken, severely.

"You don't suppose I was going to overlook a chance to see Ken Ward treed, do you?"

"Well, you saw him, and that was no joke. But I wish Pepe could have scared those pigs off without firing the jungle."

"Pepe says it 'll give the ticks a good roasting," said George.

"We'll have roast pig, anyway," added Ken.

He kept watching the jungle back of the camp as if he expected it to blow up like a powder-mine. But this Tamaulipas jungle was not Penetier Forest. A cloud of smoke rolled up; there was a frequent roaring of dry palms; but the green growths did not burn. It was not much of a forest-fire, and Ken concluded that it would soon burn out.

So he took advantage of the waning daylight to spread out his map and plot in the day's travel. This time Hal watched him with a quiet attention that was both flattering and stimulating; and at the conclusion of the task he said:

"Well, Ken, we're having sport, but we're doing something more--something worth while."

XXI THE LEAPING TARPON

Just before dark, when the boys were at supper, a swarm of black mosquitoes swooped down upon camp.

Pepe could not have shown more fear at angry snakes, and he began to pile green wood and leaves on the fire to make a heavy smoke.

These mosquitoes were very large, black-bodied, with white-barred wings. Their bite was as painful as the sting of a bee. After threshing about until tired out the boys went to bed. But it was only to get up again, for the mosquitoes could bite through two thicknesses of blanket.

For a wonder every one was quiet. Even George did not grumble. The only thing to do was to sit or stand in the smoke of the campfire. The boys wore their gloves and wrapped blankets round heads and shoulders. They crouched over the fire until tired of that position, then stood up till they could stand no longer. It was a wretched, sleepless night with the bloodthirsty mosquitoes humming about like a swarm of bees. They did not go away until dawn.

"That's what I get for losing the mosquito-netting," said Ken, wearily.

Breakfast was not a cheerful meal, despite the fact that the boys all tried to brace up.

George's condition showed Ken the necessity for renewed efforts to get out of the jungle. Pepe appeared heavy and slow, and, what was more alarming, he had lost his appetite. Hal was cross, but seemed to keep well. It was hard enough for Ken to persuade George and Pepe to take the bitter doses of quinine, and Hal positively refused.

"It makes me sick, I tell you," said Hal, impatiently.

"But Hal, you ought to be guided by my judgment now," replied Ken, gently.

"I don't care. I've had enough of bitter pills."

"I ask you--as a favor?" persisted Ken, quietly.

"No!"

"Well, then, I'll have to make you take them."

"Wha-at?" roared Hal.

"If necessary, I'll throw you down and pry open your mouth and get Pepe to stuff these pills down your throat. There!" went on Ken, and now he did not recognize his own voice.

Hal looked quickly at his brother, and was amazed and all at once shaken.

"Why, Ken--" he faltered.

"I ought to have made you take them before," interrupted Ken. "But I've been too easy. Now, Hal, listen--and you, too, George. I've made a bad mess of this trip. I got you into this jungle, and I ought to have taken better care of you, whether you would or not. George has fever. Pepe is getting it. I'm afraid you won't escape. You all *would* drink unboiled water."

"Ken, that's all right, but you can get fever from the bites of the ticks," said George.

"I dare say. But just the same you could have been careful about the water. Not only that--look how careless we have been. Think of the things that have happened! We've gotten almost wild on this trip. We don't realize. But wait till we get home. Then we'll hardly be able to believe we ever had these adventures. But our foolishness, our carelessness, must stop right here. If we can't profit by our lucky escapes yesterday--from that lassoed crocodile and the wild pigs--we are simply no good. I love fun and sport. But there's a limit. Hal, remember what old Hiram told you about being foolhardily brave. I think we have been wonderfully lucky. Now let's deserve our good luck. Let's not prove what that Tampico hotel-man said. Let's show we are not just wild-goose-chasing boys. I put it to you straight. I think the real test is yet to come, and I want you to help me. No more tricks. No more drinking unboiled water. No more shooting except in self-defense. We must not eat any more meat. No more careless wandering up the banks. No chances. See? And fight the fever. Don't give up. Then when we get out of this awful jungle we can look back at our adventures--and, better, we can be sure we've learned a lot. We shall have accomplished something, and that's learning. Now, how about it? Will you help me?"

"You can just bet your life," replied George, and he held out his hand.

"Ken, I'm with you," was Hal's quiet promise; and Ken knew from the way the lad spoke that he was in dead earnest. When it came to the last ditch Hal Ward was as true as steel. He took the raw, bitter quinine Ken offered and swallowed it without a grimace.

"Good!" exclaimed Ken. "Now, boys, let's pack. Hal, you let your menagerie go. There's no use keeping your pets any longer. George, you make yourself a bed on the trunk, and fix a palm-leaf sun-shelter. Then lie down."

When the boat had been packed and all was in readiness for the start, George was sound asleep. They shoved off into the current. Pepe and Ken took turns at the oars, making five miles an hour.

As on the day before, they glided under the shadows of the great moss-twined cypresses, along the muddy banks where crocodiles basked in the sun and gaunt cattle came down to drink. Once the boat turned a bushy point to startle a large flock of wild turkeys, perhaps thirty-five in number. They had been resting in the cool sand along the river. Some ran up the bank, some half-dozen flew right over the boat, and most of them squatted down as if to evade detection. Thereafter turkeys and ducks and geese became so common as to be monotonous.

XXI THE LEAPING TARPON

About one o'clock Ken sighted a thatched bamboo and palm-leaf hut on the bank.

"Oh, boys, look! look!" cried Ken, joyfully.

Hal was as pleased as Ken, and George roused out of his slumber. Pepe grinned and nodded his head.

Some naked little children ran like quail. A disheveled black head peeped out of a door, then swiftly vanished.

"Indians," said George.

"I don't care," replied Ken, "they're human beings--people. We're getting somewhere."

From there on the little bamboo huts were frequently sighted. And soon Ken saw a large one situated upon a high bluff. Ken was wondering if these natives would be hospitable.

Upon rounding the next bend the boys came unexpectedly upon a connecting river. It was twice as wide as the Santa Rosa, and quite swift.

"Tamaulipas," said Pepe.

"Hooray! boys, this is the source of the Panuco, sure as you're born," cried Ken. "I told you we were getting somewhere."

He was overcome with the discovery. This meant success.

"Savalo! Savalo!" exclaimed Pepe, pointing.

"Tarpon! Tarpon! What do you think of that? 'Way up here! We must be a long distance from tide-water," said George.

Ken looked around over the broad pool below the junction of the two rivers. And here and there he saw swirls, and big splashes, and then the silver sides of rolling tarpon.

"Boys, seeing we've packed that can of preserved mullet all the way, and those thundering heavy tackles, let's try for tarpon," suggested Ken.

It was wonderful to see how the boys responded. Pepe was no longer slow and heavy. George forgot he was sick. Hal, who loved to fish better than to hunt, was as enthusiastic as on the first day.

"Ken, let me boss this job," said George, as he began to rig the tackles. "Pepe will row; you and Hal sit back here and troll. I'll make myself useful. Open the can. See, I hook the mullet just back of the head, letting the bar come out free. There! Now run out about forty feet of line. Steady the butt of the rod under your leg. Put your left hand above the reel. Hold the handle of the reel in your right, and hold it hard. The drag is in the handle. Now when a tarpon takes the bait, jerk with all your might. Their mouths are like iron, and it's hard to get a hook to stick."

Pepe rowed at a smooth, even stroke and made for the great curve of the pool where tarpon were breaking water.

"If they're on the feed, we'll have more sport than we've had yet," said George.

Ken was fascinated, and saw that Hal was going to have the best time of the trip. Also Ken was very curious to have a tarpon strike. He had no idea what it would be like. Presently, when the boat glided among the rolling fish and there was prospect of one striking at any moment, Ken could not subdue a mounting excitement.

"Steady now--be ready," warned George.

Suddenly Hal's line straightened. The lad yelled and jerked at the same instant. There came a roar of splitting waters, and a beautiful silver fish, longer than Hal himself, shot up into the air. The tarpon shook himself and dropped back into the water with a crash.

Hal was speechless. He wound in his line to find the bait gone.

"Threw the hook," said George, as he reached into the can for another bait. "He wasn't so big. You'll get used to losing 'em. There! try again."

Ken had felt several gentle tugs at his line, as if tarpon were rolling across it. And indeed he saw several fish swim right over where his line disappeared in the water. There were splashes all around the boat, some gentle swishes and others hard, cutting rushes. Then his line straightened with a heavy jerk. He forgot to try to hook the fish; indeed, he had no time. The tarpon came half out of the water, wagged his head, and plumped back. Ken had not hooked the fish, nor had the fish got the bait. So Ken again let out his line.

The next thing which happened was that the boys both had strikes at the same instant. Hal stood up, and as his tarpon leaped it pulled him forward, and he fell into the stern-seat. His reel-handle rattled on the gunwale. The line hissed. Ken leaned back and jerked. His fish did not break water, but he was wonderfully active under the surface. Pepe was jabbering. George was yelling. Hal's fish was tearing the water to shreds. He crossed Ken's fish; the lines fouled, and then slacked. Ken began to wind in. Hal rose to do likewise.

"Gee!" he whispered, with round eyes.

Both lines had been broken. George made light of this incident, and tied on two more leaders and hooks and baited afresh.

"The fish are on the feed, boys. It's a cinch you'll each catch one. Better troll one at a time, unless you can stand for crossed lines."

But Ken and Hal were too eager to catch a tarpon to troll one at a time, so once more they let their lines out. A tarpon took Hal's bait right under the stern of the boat. Hal struck with all his might. This fish came up with a tremendous splash, drenching the boys. His great, gleaming silver sides glistened in the sun. He curved his body and straightened out with a snap like the breaking of a board, and he threw the hook whistling into the air.

Before Hal had baited up, Ken got another strike. This fish made five leaps, one after the other, and upon the last threw the hook like a bullet. As he plunged down, a beautiful rainbow appeared in the misty spray.

"Hal, do you see that rainbow?" cried Ken, quickly. "There's a sight for a fisherman!"

This time in turn, before Ken started to troll, Hal hooked another tarpon. This one was not so large, but he was active. His first rush was a long surge on the surface. He sent the spray in two streaks like a motor-boat. Then he sounded.

"Hang on, Hal!" yelled George and Ken in unison.

XXI THE LEAPING TARPON

Hal was bent almost double and his head was bobbing under the strain. He could not hold the drag. The line was whizzing out.

"You got that one hooked," shouted George. "Let go the reel--drop the handle. Let him run."

He complied, and then his fish began a marvelous exhibition of lofty tumbling. He seemed never to stay down at all. Now he shot up, mouth wide, gills spread, eyes wild, and he shook himself like a wet dog. Then he dropped back, and before the boys had time to think where he might be he came up several rods to the right and cracked his gills like pistol-shots. He skittered on his tail and stood on his head and dropped flat with a heavy smack. Then he stayed under and began to tug.

"Hang on, now," cried George. "Wind in. Hold him tight. Don't give him an inch unless he jumps."

This was heartbreaking work for Hal. He toiled to keep the line in. He grew red in the face. He dripped with sweat. He panted for breath. But he hung on.

Ken saw how skilfully Pepe managed the boat. The *mozo* seemed to know just which way the fish headed, and always kept the boat straight. Sometimes he rowed back and lent his help to Hal. But this appeared to anger the tarpon, for the line told he was coming to the surface. Then, as Pepe ceased to let him feel the weight of the boat, the tarpon sank again. So the battle went on round and round the great pool. After an hour of it Hal looked ready to drop.

"Land him alone if you can," said Ken. "He's tiring, Hal."

"I'll--land him--or--or bust!" panted Hal.

"Look out, now!" warned George again. "He's coming up. See the line. Be ready to trim the boat if he drops aboard. *Wow!*"

The tarpon slipped smoothly out of the water and shot right over the bow of the boat. Quick-witted George flung out his hand and threw Hal's rod round in time to save the line from catching. The fish went down, came up wagging his head, and then fell with sullen splash.

"He's done," yelled George. "Now, Hal, hold him for all you're worth. Not an inch of line!"

Pepe headed the boat for a sandy beach; and Hal, looking as if about to have a stroke of apoplexy, clung desperately to the bending rod. The tarpon rolled and lashed his tail, but his power was mostly gone. Gradually he ceased to roll, until by the time Pepe reached shore he was sliding wearily through the water, his silvery side glittering in the light.

The boat grated on the sand. Pepe leaped out. Then he grasped Hal's line, slipped his hands down to the long wire leader, and with a quick, powerful pull slid the tarpon out upon the beach.

"Oh-h!" gasped Hal, with glistening eyes. "Oh-h! Ken, just look!"

"I'm looking, son, and don't you forget it."

The tarpon lay inert, a beautiful silver-scaled creature that looked as if he had just come from a bath of melted opals. The great dark eyes were fixed and staring, the tail moved feebly, the long dorsal fin quivered.

He measured five feet six inches in length, which was one inch more than Hal's height.

"Ken, the boys back home will never believe I caught him," said Hal, in distress.

"Take his picture to prove it," replied Ken.

Hal photographed his catch. Pepe took out the hook, showing, as he did so, the great iron-like plates in the mouth of the fish.

"No wonder it's hard to hook them," said Ken.

Hal certainly wanted his beautiful fish to go back, free and little hurt, to the river. But also he wanted him for a specimen. Hal deliberated. Evidently he was considering the labor of skinning such a huge fish and the difficulty of preserving and packing the hide.

"Say, Hal, wouldn't you like to see me hook one?" queried Ken, patiently.

That brought Hal to his senses.

"Sure, Ken, old man, I want you to catch one--a big one--bigger than mine," replied Hal, and restored the fish to the water.

They all watched the liberated tarpon swim wearily off and slip down under the water.

"He'll have something to tell the rest, won't he?" said George.

In a few minutes the boat was again in the center of the great pool among the rolling tarpon. Ken had a strike immediately. He missed. Then he tried again. And in a short space of time he saw five tarpon in the air, one after the other, and not one did he hook securely. He got six leaps out of one, however, and that was almost as good as landing him.

"There 're some whales here," said George.

"Grande savalo," added Pepe, and he rowed over to where a huge fish was rolling.

"Oh, I don't want to hook the biggest one first," protested Ken.

Pepe rowed to and fro. The boys were busy trying to see the rolling tarpon. There would be a souse on one side, then a splash on the other, then a thump behind. What with trying to locate all these fish and still keep an eye on Ken's line the boys almost dislocated their necks.

Then, quick as a flash, Ken had a strike that pulled him out of his seat to his knees. He could not jerk. His line was like a wire. It began to rise. With all his strength he held on. The water broke in a hollow, slow roar, and a huge hump-backed tarpon seemed to be climbing into the air. But he did not get all the way out, and he plunged back with a thunderous crash. He made as much noise as if a horse had fallen off a bridge.

The handle of the reel slipped out of Ken's grasp, and it was well. The tarpon made a long, wonderful run and showed on the surface a hundred yards from the boat. He was irresistibly powerful. Ken was astounded and thrilled at his strength and speed. There, far away from the boat, the tarpon leaped magnificently, clearing the water, and then went down. He did not come up again.

"Ken, he's a whale," said George. "I believe he's well hooked. He won't jump any more. And you've got a job on your hands."

"I want him to jump."

"The big ones seldom break water after the first rush or so."

"Ken, it's coming to you with that fellow," said Hal. "My left arm is paralyzed. Honestly, I can pinch it and not feel the pain."

Pepe worked the boat closer and Ken reeled in yard after yard of line. The tarpon was headed down-stream, and he kept up a steady, strong strain.

"Let him tow the boat," said George. "Hold the drag, Ken. Let him tow the boat."

"What!" exclaimed Ken, in amaze.

"Oh, he'll do it, all right."

And so it proved. Ken's tarpon, once headed with the current, did not turn, and he towed the boat.

"This is a new way for me to tire out a fish," said Ken. "What do you think of it, Hal?"

Hal's eyes glistened.

"This is fishing. Ken, did you see him when he came up?"

"Not very clearly. I had buck-fever. You know how a grouse looks when he flushes right under your feet--a kind of brown blur. Well, this was the same, only silver."

At the end of what Ken judged to be a mile the tarpon was still going. At the end of the second mile he was tired. And three miles down the river from where the fish was hooked Pepe beached the boat on a sandbar and hauled ashore a tarpon six feet ten inches long.

Here Ken echoed Hal's panting gasp of wonder and exultation. As he sat down on the boat to rest he had no feeling in his left arm, and little in his right. His knuckles were skinned and bloody. No game of baseball he had ever pitched had taken his strength like the conquest of this magnificent fish.

"Hal, we'll have some more of this fishing when we get to Tampico," said Ken. "Why, this beats hunting. You have the sport, and you needn't kill anything. This tarpon isn't hurt."

So Ken photographed his prize and measured him, and, taking a last lingering glance at the great green back, the silver-bronze sides, the foot-wide flukes of the tail, at the whole quivering fire-tinted length, he slid the tarpon back into the river.

XXII STRICKEN DOWN

Much as Ken would have liked to go back to that pool, he did not think of it twice. And as soon as the excitement had subsided and the journey was resumed, George and Hal, and Pepe, too, settled down into a silent weariness that made Ken anxious.

During the afternoon Ken saw Pepe slowly droop lower and lower at the oars till the time came when he could scarcely lift them to make a stroke. And when Ken relieved him of them, Pepe fell like a log in the boat.

George slept. Hal seemed to be fighting stupor. Pepe lay motionless on his seat. They were all going down with the fever, that Ken knew, and it took all his courage to face the situation. It warmed his heart to see how Hal was trying to bear up under a languor that must have been well-nigh impossible to resist. At last Hal said:

"Ken, let me row." He would not admit that he was sick.

Ken thought it would do Hal no harm to work. But Ken did not want to lose time. So he hit upon a plan that pleased him. There was an extra pair of oars in the boat. Ken fashioned rude pegs from a stick and drove these down into the cleat inside the gunwales. With stout rope he tied the oars to the pegs, which answered fairly well as oarlocks. Then they had a double set of oars going, and made much better time.

George woke and declared that he must take a turn at the oars. So Ken let him row, too, and rested himself. He had a grim foreboding that he would need all his strength.

The succeeding few hours before sunset George and Hal more than made up for all their delinquencies of the past. At first it was not very hard for them to row; but soon they began to weary, then weaken. Neither one, however, would give up. Ken let them row, knowing that it was good for them. Slower and slower grew George's strokes, there were times when he jerked up spasmodically and made an effort, only to weaken again. At last, with a groan he dropped the oars. Ken had to lift him back into the bow.

Hal was not so sick as George, and therefore not so weak. He lasted longer. Ken had seen the lad stick to many a hard job, but never as he did to this one. Hal was making good his promise. There were times when his breath came in whistles. He would stop and pant awhile, then row on. Ken pretended he did not notice. But he had never been so proud of his brother nor loved him so well.

"Ken, old man," said Hal, presently. "I was--wrong--about the water. I ought to have obeyed you. I--I'm pretty sick."

What a confession for Hal Ward!

Ken turned in time to see Hal vomit over the gunwale.

"It's pretty tough, Hal," said Ken, as he reached out to hold his brother's head; "but you're game. I'm so glad to see that."

Whereupon Hal went back to his oars and stayed till he dropped. Ken lifted him and laid him beside George.

Ken rowed on with his eyes ever in search of a camping-site. But there was no place to camp. The muddy banks were too narrow at the bottom, too marshy and filthy. And they were too steep to climb to the top.

The sun set. Twilight fell. Darkness came on, and still Ken rowed down the river. At last he decided to make a night of it at the oars. He preferred to risk the dangers of the river at night rather than spend miserable hours in the mud. Rousing the boys, he forced them to swallow a little cold rice and some more quinine. Then he covered them with blankets, and had scarce completed the task when they were deep in slumber.

Then the strange, dense tropical night settled down upon Ken. The oars were almost noiseless, and the water gurgled softly from the bow. Overhead the expanse was dark blue, with a few palpitating stars. The river was shrouded in gray gloom, and the banks were lost in black obscurity. Great fireflies emphasized the darkness. He trusted a good deal to luck in the matter of going right; yet he kept his ear keen for the sound of quickening current, and turned every few strokes to peer sharply into the gloom. He seemed to have little sense of peril, for, though he hit submerged logs and stranded on bars, he kept on unmindful, and by and by lost what anxiety he had felt. The strange wildness of the river at night, the gray, veiled space into which he rowed unheeding began to work upon his mind.

That was a night to remember--a night of sounds and smells, of the feeling of the cool mist, the sight of long, dark forest-line and a golden moon half hidden by clouds. Prominent among these was the trill of river frogs. The trill of a northern frog was music, but that of these great, silver-throated jungle frogs was more than music. Close at hand one would thrill Ken with mellow, rich notes; and then from far would come the answer, a sweet, high tenor, wilder than any other wilderness sound, long sustained, dying away till he held his breath to listen.

So the hours passed; and the moon went down into the weird shadows, and the Southern Cross rose pale and wonderful.

Gradually the stars vanished in a kind of brightening gray, and dawn was at hand. Ken felt weary for sleep, and his arms and back ached. Morning came, with its steely light on the river, the rolling and melting of vapors, the flight of ducks and call of birds. The rosy sun brought no cheer.

Ken beached the boat on a sand-bar. While he was building a fire George raised his head and groaned. But neither Pepe nor Hal moved. Ken cooked rice and boiled cocoa, which he choked down. He opened a can of fruit and found that most welcome. Then he lifted George's head, shook him, roused him, and held him, and made him eat and drink. Nor did he neglect to put a liberal dose of quinine in the food. Pepe was easily managed, but poor Hal was almost unable to swallow. Something terribly grim mingled with a strong, passionate thrill as Ken looked at Hal's haggard face. Then Ken Ward knew how much he could stand, what work he could do to get his brother out of the jungle.

He covered the boys again and pushed out the boat. At the moment he felt a strength that he had never felt before. There was a good, swift current in the river, and Ken was at great pains to keep in it. The channel ran from one side of the river to the other. Many times Ken stranded on sandy shoals and had to stand up and pole the boat into deeper water. This was work that required all his attention. It required more than patience. But as he rowed and poled and drifted he studied the shallow ripples and learned to avoid the places where the boat would not float.

There were stretches of river where the water was comparatively deep, and along these he rested and watched the shores as he drifted by. He saw no Indian huts that morning. The jungle loomed high and dark, a matted gray wall. The heat made the river glare and smoke. Then where the current quickened he rowed steadily and easily, husbanding his strength.

More than all else, even the ravings of Hal in fever, the thing that wore on Ken and made him gloomy was the mourning of turtle-doves. As there had been thousands of these beautiful birds along the Santa Rosa River, so there were millions along the Panuco. Trees were blue with doves. There was an incessant soft, sad moaning. He fought his nervous, sensitive imaginings. And for a time he would conquer the sense of some sad omen sung by the doves. Then the monotony, the endless sweet "coo-ooo-ooo," seemed to drown him in melancholy sound. There were three distinct tones--a moan, swelling to full ring, and dying away: "Coo-*ooo*-ooo--coo-*ooo*-ooo."

All the afternoon the mourning, haunting song filled Ken Ward's ears. And when the sun set and night came, with relief to his tortured ear but not to mind, Ken kept on without a stop.

The day had slipped behind Ken with the miles, and now it was again dark. It seemed that he had little sense of time. But his faculties of sight and hearing were singularly acute. Otherwise his mind was like the weird gloom into which he was drifting.

Before the stars came out the blackness was as thick as pitch. He could not see a yard ahead. He backed the boat stern first down-stream and listened for the soft murmur of ripples on shoals. He avoided these by hearing alone. Occasionally a huge, dark pile of driftwood barred his passage, and he would have to go round it. Snags loomed up specter-like in his path, seemingly to reach for him with long, gaunt arms. Sometimes he drifted upon sand-bars, from which he would patiently pole the boat.

XXII STRICKEN DOWN

When the heavy dew began to fall he put on his waterproof coat. The night grew chill. Then the stars shone out. This lightened the river. Yet everywhere were shadows. Besides, clouds of mist hung low, in places obscuring the stars.

Ken turned the boat bow first downstream and rowed with slow, even stroke. He no longer felt tired. He seemed to have the strength of a giant. He fancied that with one great heave he could lift the boat out of the water or break the oars. From time to time he ceased to row, and, turning his head, he looked and listened. The river had numerous bends, and it was difficult for Ken to keep in the middle channel. He managed pretty well to keep right by watching the dark shore-line where it met the deep-blue sky. In the bends the deepest water ran close to the shore of the outside curve. And under these high banks and the leaning cypresses shadows were thicker and blacker than in the earlier night. There was mystery in them that Ken felt.

The sounds he heard when he stopped during these cautious resting intervals were the splashes of fish breaking water, the low hum of insects, and the trill of frogs. The mourning of the doves during daylight had haunted him, and now he felt the same sensation at this long-sustained, exquisitely sweet trill. It pierced him, racked him, and at last, from sheer exhaustion of his sensibilities, he seemed not to hear it any more, but to have it in his brain.

The moon rose behind the left-hand jungle wall, silvered half of the river and the opposite line of cypresses, then hid under clouds.

Suddenly, near or far away, down the river Ken saw a wavering light. It was too large for a firefly, and too steady. He took it for a Jack-o'-lantern. And for a while it enhanced the unreality, the ghostliness of the river. But it was the means of bringing Ken out of his dreamy gloom. It made him think. The light was moving. It was too wavering for a Jack-o'-lantern. It was coming up-stream. It grew larger.

Then, as suddenly as it had appeared, it vanished. Ken lost sight of it under a deep shadow of overhanging shore. As he reached a point opposite to where it disappeared he thought he heard a voice. But he could not be sure. He did not trust his ears. The incident, however, gave him a chill. What a lonesome ride! He was alone on that unknown river with three sick boys in the boat. Their lives depended upon his care, his strength, his skill, his sight and hearing. And the realization, striking him afresh, steeled his arms again and his spirit.

The night wore on. The moon disappeared entirely. The mists hung low like dim sheets along the water. Ken was wringing-wet with dew. Long periods of rowing he broke with short intervals of drifting, when he rested at the oars.

Then drowsiness attacked him. For hours it seemed he fought it off. But at length it grew overpowering. Only hard rowing would keep him awake. And, as he wanted to reserve his strength, he did not dare exert himself violently. He could not keep his eyes open. Time after time he found himself rowing when he was half asleep. The boat drifted against a log and stopped. Ken drooped over his oars and slept, and yet he seemed not altogether to lose consciousness. He roused again to row on.

It occurred to him presently that he might let the boat drift and take naps between whiles. When he drifted against a log or a sand-bar the jar would awaken him. The current was sluggish. There seemed to be no danger whatever. He must try to keep his strength. A little sleep would refresh him. So he reasoned, and fell asleep over the oars.

Sooner or later--he never knew how long after he had fallen asleep--a little jar awakened him. Then the gurgle and murmur of water near him and the rush and roar of a swift current farther off made him look up with a violent start. All about him was wide, gray gloom. Yet he could see the dark, glancing gleam of the water. Movement of the oars told him the boat was fast on a sand-bar. That relieved him, for he was not drifting at the moment into the swift current he heard. Ken peered keenly into the gloom. Gradually he made out a long, dark line running diagonally ahead of him and toward the right-hand shore. It could not be an island or a sand-bar or a shore-line. It could not be piles of driftwood. There was a strange regularity in the dark upheavals of this looming object. Ken studied it. He studied the black, glancing water. Whatever the line was, it appeared to shunt the current over to the right, whence came the low rush and roar.

Altogether it was a wild, strange place. Ken felt a fear of something he could not name. It was the river--the night--the loneliness--the unknown about him and before him.

Suddenly he saw a dull, red light far down the river. He stiffened in his seat. Then he saw another red light. They were like two red eyes. Ken shook himself to see if he had nightmare. No; the boat was there; the current was there; the boys were there, dark and silent under their blankets. This was no dream. Ken's fancy conjured up some red-eyed river demon come to destroy him and his charges. He scorned the fancy, laughed at it. But, all the same, in that dark, weird place, with the murmuring of notes in his ears and with those strange red eyes glowing in the distance, he could not help what his emotions made the truth. He was freezing to the marrow, writhing in a clammy sweat when a low "chug-chug-chug" enlightened him. The red eyes were those of a steamboat.

A steamboat on the wild Panuco! Ken scarcely believed his own judgment. Then he remembered that George said there were a couple of boats plying up and down the lower Panuco, mostly transporting timber and cattle. Besides, he had proof of his judgment in the long, dark line that had so puzzled him--it was a breakwater. It turned the current to the left, where there evidently was a channel.

The great, red eyes gleamed closer, the "chug-chug-chug" sounded louder. Then another sound amazed Ken--a man's voice crying out steadily and monotonously.

Ken wanted to rouse the boys and Pepe, but he refrained. It was best for them to sleep. How surprised they would be when he told them about the boat that passed in the night! Ken now clearly heard the splashing of paddles, the chug of machinery, and the man's voice. He was singsonging: "Dos y media, dos y media, dos y media."

XXII STRICKEN DOWN

Ken understood a little Mexican, and this strange cry became clear to him. The man was taking soundings with a lead and crying out to the pilot. *Dos y media* meant two and a half feet of water. Then the steam-boat loomed black in the gray gloom. It was pushing a low, flat barge. Ken could not see the man taking soundings, but he heard him and knew he was on the front end of the barge. The boat passed at fair speed, and it cheered Ken. For he certainly ought to be able to take a rowboat where a steamboat had passed. And, besides, he must be getting somewhere near the little village of Panuco.

He poled off the bar and along the breakwater to the channel. It was narrow and swift. He wondered how the pilot of the steamboat had navigated in the gloom. He slipped down-stream, presently to find himself once more in a wide river. Refreshed by his sleep and encouraged by the meeting with the steamboat, Ken settled down to steady rowing.

The stars paled, the mist thickened, fog obscured the water and shore; then all turned gray, lightened, and dawn broke. The sun burst out. Ken saw thatched huts high on the banks and occasionally natives. This encouraged him all the more.

He was not hungry, but he was sick for a drink. He had to fight himself to keep from drinking the dirty river-water. How different it was here from the clear green of the upper Santa Rosa! Ken would have given his best gun for one juicy orange. George was restless and rolling about, calling for water; Hal lay in slumber or stupor; and Pepe sat up. He was a sick-looking fellow, but he was better; and that cheered Ken as nothing yet had.

Ken beached the boat on a sandy shore, and once again forced down a little rice and cocoa. Pepe would not eat, yet he drank a little. George was burning up with fever, and drank a full cup. Hal did not stir, and Ken thought it best to let him lie.

As Ken resumed the journey the next thing to attract his attention was a long canoe moored below one of the thatched huts. This afforded him great satisfaction. At least he had passed the jungle wilderness, where there was nothing that even suggested civilization. In the next few miles he noticed several canoes and as many natives. Then he passed a canoe that was paddled by two half-naked bronze Indians. Pepe hailed them, but either they were too unfriendly to reply or they did not understand him.

Some distance below Pepe espied a banana grove, and he motioned Ken to row ashore. Ken did so with pleasure at the thought of getting some fresh fruit. There was a canoe moored to the roots of a tree and a path leading up the steep bank. Pepe got out and laboriously toiled up the bare path. He was gone a good while.

Presently Ken heard shouts, then the bang of a lightly loaded gun, then yells from Pepe.

"What on earth!" cried Ken, looking up in affright.

Pepe appeared with his arms full of red bananas. He jumped and staggered down the path and almost fell into the boat. But he hung on to the bananas.

"Santa Maria!" gasped Pepe, pointing to little bloody spots on the calf of his leg.

"Pepe, you've been shot!" ejaculated Ken. "You stole the fruit--somebody shot you!"

Pepe howled his affirmative. Ken was angry at himself, angrier at Pepe, and angriest at the native who had done the shooting. With a strong shove Ken put the boat out and then rowed hard down-stream. As he rounded a bend a hundred yards below he saw three natives come tumbling down the path. They had a gun. They leaped into the canoe. They meant pursuit.

"Say, but this is a pretty kettle of fish!" muttered Ken, and he bent to the oars.

Of course Pepe had been in the wrong. He should have paid for the bananas or asked for them. All the same, Ken was not in any humor to be fooled with by excitable natives. He had a sick brother in the boat and meant to get that lad out of the jungle as quickly as will and strength could do it. He certainly did not intend to be stopped by a few miserable Indians angry over the loss of a few bananas. If it had not been for the gun, Ken would have stopped long enough to pay for the fruit. But he could not risk it now. So he pulled a strong stroke down-stream.

The worst of the matter developed when Pepe peeled one of the bananas. It was too green to eat.

Presently the native canoe hove in sight round the bend. All three men were paddling. They made the long craft fly through the water. Ken saw instantly that they would overhaul him in a long race, and this added to his resentment. Pepe looked back and jabbered and shook his brawny fists at the natives. Ken was glad to see that the long stretch of river below did not show a canoe or hut along the banks. He preferred to be overhauled, if he had to be, in a rather lonely spot.

It was wonderful how those natives propelled that log canoe. And when one of the three dropped his paddle to pick up the gun, the speed of the canoe seemed not to diminish. They knew the channels, and so gained on Ken. He had to pick the best he could choose at short notice, and sometimes he chose poorly.

Two miles or more below the bend the natives with the gun deliberately fired, presumably at Pepe. The shot scattered and skipped along the water and did not come near the boat. Nevertheless, as the canoe was gaining and the crazy native was reloading, Ken saw he would soon be within range. Something had to be done.

Ken wondered if he could not frighten those natives. They had probably never heard the quick reports of a repeating rifle, let alone the stinging cracks of an automatic. Ken decided it would be worth trying. But he must have a chance to get the gun out of its case and load it.

That chance came presently. The natives, in paddling diagonally across a narrow channel, ran aground in the sand. They were fast for only a few moments, but in that time Ken had got out the little rifle and loaded it.

Pepe's dark face turned a dirty white, and his eyes dilated. He imagined Ken was going to kill some of his countrymen. But Pepe never murmured. He rubbed the place in his leg where he had been shot, and looked back.

XXII STRICKEN DOWN

Ken rowed on, now leisurely. There was a hot anger within him, but he had it in control. He knew what he was about. Again the native fired, and again his range was short. The distance was perhaps two hundred yards.

Ken waited until the canoe, in crossing one of the many narrow places, was broadside toward him. Then he raised the automatic. There were at least ten feet in the middle of the canoe where it was safe for him to hit without harm to the natives. And there he aimed. The motion of his boat made it rather hard to keep the sights right. He was cool, careful; he aimed low, between gunwale and the water, and steadily he pulled the trigger--once, twice, three times, four, five.

The steel-jacketed bullets "spoued" on the water and "cracked" into the canoe. They evidently split both gunwales low down at the water-line. The yelling, terror-stricken natives plunged about, and what with their actions and the great split in the middle the canoe filled and sank. The natives were not over their depth; that was plainly evident. Moreover, it was equally evident that they dared not wade in the quicksand. So they swam to the shallower water, and there, like huge turtles, floundered toward the shore.

XXIII OUT OF THE JUNGLE

Before the natives had reached the shore they were hidden from Ken's sight by leaning cypress-trees. Ken, however, had no fear for their safety. He was sorry to cause the Indians' loss of a gun and a canoe; nevertheless, he was not far from echoing Pepe's repeated: "Bueno! Bueno! Bueno!"

Upon examination Ken found two little bloody holes in the muscles of Pepe's leg. A single shot had passed through. Ken bathed the wounds with an antiseptic lotion and bound them with clean bandages.

Pepe appeared to be pretty weak, so Ken did not ask him to take the oars. Then, pulling with long, steady stroke, Ken set out to put a long stretch between him and the angry natives. The current was swift, and Ken made five miles or more an hour. He kept that pace for three hours without a rest. And then he gave out. It seemed that all at once he weakened. His back bore an immense burden. His arms were lead, and his hands were useless. There was an occasional mist or veil before his sight. He was wet, hot, breathless, numb. But he knew he was safe from pursuit. So he rested and let the boat drift.

George sat up, green in the face, a most miserable-looking boy. But that he could sit up at all was hopeful.

"Oh, my head!" he moaned. "Is there anything I can drink? My mouth is dry--pasted shut."

Ken had two lemons he had been saving. He cut one in halves and divided it between Pepe and George. The relief the sour lemon afforded both showed Ken how wise he had been to save the lemons. Then he roused Hal, and, lifting the lad's head, made him drink a little of the juice. Hal was a sick boy, too weak to sit up without help.

"Don't--you worry--Ken," he said. "I'm going--to be--all right."

Hal was still fighting.

Ken readjusted the palm-leaf shelter over the boys so as to shade them effectually from the hot sun, and then he went back to the oars.

As he tried once more to row, Ken was reminded of the terrible lassitude that had overtaken him the day he had made the six-hour climb out of the Grand Cañon. The sensation now was worse, but Ken had others depending upon his exertions, and that spurred him to the effort which otherwise would have been impossible.

XXIII OUT OF THE JUNGLE

It was really not rowing that Ken accomplished. It was a weary puttering with oars he could not lift, handles he could not hold. At best he managed to guide the boat into the swiftest channels. Whenever he felt that he was just about to collapse, then he would look at Hal's pale face. That would revive him. So the hot hours dragged by.

They came, after several miles, upon more huts and natives. And farther down they met canoes on the river. Pepe interrogated the natives. According to George, who listened, Panuco was far, far away, many kilometers. This was most disheartening. Another native said the village was just round the next bend. This was most nappy information. But it turned out to be a lie. There was no village around any particular bend--nothing save bare banks for miles. The stretches of the river were long, and bends far apart.

Ken fell asleep. When he awoke he found Pepe at the oars. Watching him, Ken fancied he was recovering, and was overjoyed.

About four o'clock in the afternoon Pepe rowed ashore and beached the boat at the foot of a trail leading up to a large bamboo and thatch hut. This time Ken thought it well to accompany Pepe. And as he climbed the path he found his legs stiffer and shakier than ever before.

Ken saw a cleared space in which were several commodious huts, gardens, and flowers. There was a grassy yard in which little naked children were playing with tame deer and tiger-cats. Parrots were screeching, and other tame birds fluttered about. It appeared a real paradise to Ken.

Two very kindly disposed and wondering native women made them welcome. Then Ken and Pepe went down to the boat and carried Hal up, and went back for George.

It developed that the native women knew just what to do for the fever-stricken boys. They made some kind of a native drink for them, and after that gave them hot milk and chicken and rice soup. George improved rapidly, and Hal brightened a little and showed signs of gathering strength.

Ken could not eat until he had something to quench his thirst. Upon inquiring, Pepe found that the natives used the river-water. Ken could not drink that. Then Pepe pointed out an orange-tree, and Ken made a dive for it. The ground was littered with oranges. Collecting an armful, Ken sat under the tree and with wild haste began to squeeze the juice into his mouth. Never had anything before tasted so cool, so sweet, so life-giving! He felt a cool, wet sensation steal all through his body. He never knew till that moment how really wonderful and precious an orange could be. He thought that as he would hate mourning turtle-doves all the rest of his life, so he would love the sight and smell and taste of oranges. And he demolished twenty-two before he satisfied his almost insatiable thirst. After that the chicken and rice made him feel like a new boy.

Then Ken made beds under a kind of porch, and he lay down in one, stretched out languidly and gratefully, as if he never intended to move again, and his eyes seemed to be glued shut.

When he awoke the sun was shining in his face. When he had gone to bed it had been shining at his back. He consulted his watch. He had slept seventeen hours.

When he got up and found Pepe as well as before he had been taken with the fever and George on his feet and Hal awake and actually smiling, Ken experienced a sensation of unutterable thankfulness. A terrible burden slipped from his shoulders. For a moment he felt a dimming of his eyes and a lump in his throat.

"How about you, Ken, old man?" inquired Hal, with a hint of his usual spirit.

"Wal, youngster, I reckon fer a man who's been through some right pert happenin's, I'm in tol'able shape," drawled Ken.

"I'll bet two dollars you've been up against it," declared Hal, solemnly.

Then, as they sat to an appetizing breakfast, Ken gave them a brief account of the incidents of the two days and two nights when they were too ill to know anything.

It was a question whether George's voluble eulogy of Ken's feat or Hal's silent, bright-eyed pride in his brother was the greater compliment.

Finally Hal said: "Won't that tickle Jim Williams when we tell him how you split up the Indians' canoe and spilled them into the river?"

Then Ken conceived the idea of climbing into the giant ceiba that stood high on the edge of the bluff. It was hard work, but he accomplished it, and from a fork in the top-most branches he looked out. That was a warm, rich, wonderful scene. Ken felt that he would never forget it. His interest now, however, was not so much in its beauty and wildness. His keen eye followed the river as it wound away into the jungle, and when he could no longer see the bright ribbon of water he followed its course by the line of magnificent trees. It was possible to trace the meandering course of the river clear to the rise of the mountains, dim and blue in the distance. And from here Ken made more observations and notes.

As he went over in his mind the map and notes and report he had prepared he felt that he had made good. He had explored and mapped more than a hundred miles of wild jungle river. He felt confident that he had earned the trip to England and the German forests. He might win a hunting trip on the vast uplands of British East Africa. But he felt also that the reward of his uncle's and his father's pride would be more to him. That was a great moment for Ken Ward. And there was yet much more that he could do to make this exploring trip a success.

When he joined the others he found that Pepe had learned that the village of Panuco was distant a day or a night by canoe. How many miles or kilometers Pepe could not learn. Ken decided it would be best to go on at once. It was not easy to leave that pleasant place, with its music of parrots and other birds, and the tiger-cats that played like kittens, and the deer that ate from the hand. The women would accept no pay, so Ken made them presents.

Once more embarked, Ken found his mood reverting to that of the last forty-eight hours. He could not keep cheerful. The river was dirty and the smell sickening. The sun was like the open door of a furnace. And Ken soon discovered he was tired, utterly tired.

XXIII OUT OF THE JUNGLE

That day was a repetition of the one before, hotter, wearier, and the stretches of river were longer, and the natives met in canoes were stolidly ignorant of distance. The mourning of turtle-doves almost drove Ken wild. There were miles and miles of willows, and every tree was full of melancholy doves. At dusk the boys halted on a sand-bar, too tired to cook a dinner, and sprawled in the warm sand to sleep like logs.

In the morning they brightened up a little, for surely just around the bend they would come to Panuco. Pepe rowed faithfully on, and bend after bend lured Ken with deceit. He was filled with weariness and disgust, so tired he could hardly lift his hand, so sleepy he could scarcely keep his eyes open. He hated the wide, glassy stretches of river and the muddy banks and dusty cattle.

At noon they came unexpectedly upon a cluster of thatched huts, to find that they made up the village of Panuco. Ken was sick, for he had expected a little town where they could get some drinking-water and hire a launch to speed them down to Tampico. This appeared little more than the other places he had passed, and he climbed up the bank wearily, thinking of the long fifty miles still to go.

But Panuco was bigger and better than it looked from the river. The boys found a clean, comfortable inn, where they dined well, and learned to their joy that a coach left in an hour for Tamos to meet the five-o'clock train to Tampico.

They hired a *mozo* to row the boat to Tampico and, carrying the lighter things, boarded the coach, and, behind six mules, were soon bowling over a good level road.

It was here that the spirit of Ken's mood again changed, and somehow seemed subtly conveyed to the others. The gloom faded away as Ken had seen the mist-clouds dissolve in the morning sunlight. It was the end of another wild trip. Hal was ill, but a rest and proper care would soon bring him around. Ken had some trophies and pictures, but he also had memories. And he believed he had acquired an accurate knowledge of the jungle and its wild nature, and he had mapped the river from Micas Falls to Panuco.

"Well, it certainly *did come* to us, didn't it?" asked George, naïvely, for the hundredth time. "Didn't I tell you? By gosh, I can't remember what did come off. But we had a dandy time."

"Great!" replied Ken. "I had more than I wanted. I'll never spring another stunt like this one!"

Hal gazed smilingly at his brother.

"Bah! Ken Ward, bring on your next old trip!"

Which proved decidedly that Hal was getting better and that he alone understood his brother.

Pepe listened and rubbed his big hands, and there was a light in his dark eyes.

Ken laughed. It was good to feel happy just then; it was enough to feel safe and glad in the present, with responsibility removed, without a thought of the future.

Yet, when some miles across country he saw the little town of Tamos shining red-roofed against the sky, he came into his own again. The old calling, haunting love of wild places and wild nature returned, and with dreamy eyes he looked out. He saw the same beauty and life and wildness. Beyond the glimmering lagoons stretched the dim, dark jungle. A flock of flamingoes showed pink across the water. Ducks dotted the weedy marshes. And low down on the rosy horizon a long curved line of wild geese sailed into the sunset.

When the boys arrived at Tampico and George had secured comfortable lodgings for them, the first thing Ken did was to put Hal to bed. It required main strength to do this. Ken was not taking any chances with tropical fever, and he sent for a doctor.

It was not clear whether the faces Hal made were at the little dried-up doctor or at the medicine he administered. However, it was very clear that Hal made fun of him and grew bolder the more he believed the man could not understand English.

Ken liked the silent, kindly physician, and remonstrated with Hal, and often, just to keep Hal's mind occupied, he would talk of the university and baseball, topics that were absorbing to the boy.

And one day, as the doctor was leaving, he turned to Ken with a twinkle in his eyes and said in perfect English: "I won't need to come any more."

Hal's jaw began to drop.

"Your brother is all right," went on the doctor. "But he's a fresh kid, and he'll never make the Wayne Varsity--or a good explorer, either--till he gets over that freshness. I'm a Wayne man myself. Class of '82. Good day, boys."

Ken Ward was astounded. "By George! What do you think of that? He's a Wayne med. I'll have to look him up. And, Hal, he was just right about you."

Hal looked extremely crestfallen and remorseful.

"I'm always getting jars."

It took a whole day for him to recover his usual spirits.

Ken had promptly sent the specimens and his notes to his uncle, and as the days passed the boys began to look anxiously for some news. In ten days Hal was as well as ever, and then the boys had such sport with the tarpon and big sharks and alligator-gars that they almost forgot about the rewards they had striven so hard for and hoped to win. But finally, when the mail arrived from home, they were at once happy and fearful. George was with them that evening, and shared their excitement and suspense. Hal's letters were from his mother and his sister, and they were read first. Judge Ward's letter to Ken was fatherly and solicitous, but brief. He gave the boys six more weeks, cautioned them to be sensible and to profit by their opportunity, and he inclosed a bank-draft. Not a word about rewards!

Ken's fingers trembled a little as he tore open the uncle's letter. He read it aloud:

DEAR KEN,--Congratulations! You've done well. You win the trip to Africa. Hal's work also was good--several specimens accepted by the Smithsonian. I'll back you for the Yucatan trip. Will send letters to the American consul at Progreso, and arrange for you to meet the Austrian archæologist Maler, who I hope will take you in hand.

I want you to make a study of some of the ruins of Yucatan, which I believe are as wonderful as any in Egypt. I advise you to make this trip short and to the point, for there are indications of coming revolution throughout Mexico.

With best wishes,
UNCLE G.

The old varsity cheer rang out from Ken, and Hal began a war-dance. Then both boys pounced upon George, and for a few moments made life miserable for him.

"And I can't go with you!" he exclaimed, sorrowfully.

Both Ken and Hal shared his disappointment. But presently. George brightened up. The smile came back which he always wore when prophesying the uncertain adventures of the future.

"Well, anyway, I'll be safe home. And you fellows! You'll be getting yours when you're lost in the wilderness of Yucatan!"

DESERT GOLD

A ROMANCE OF THE BORDER

PROLOGUE

I

A FACE haunted Cameron—a woman's face. It was there in the white heart of the dying campfire; it hung in the shadows that hovered over the flickering light; it drifted in the darkness beyond.

This hour, when the day had closed and the lonely desert night set in with its dead silence, was one in which Cameron's mind was thronged with memories of a time long past—of a home back in Peoria, of a woman he had wronged and lost, and loved too late. He was a prospector for gold, a hunter of solitude, a lover of the drear, rock-ribbed infinitude, because he wanted to be alone to remember.

A sound disturbed Cameron's reflections. He bent his head listening. A soft wind fanned the paling embers, blew sparks and white ashes and thin smoke away into the enshrouding circle of blackness. His burro did not appear to be moving about. The quiet split to the cry of a coyote. It rose strange, wild, mournful—not the howl of a prowling upland beast baying the campfire or barking at a lonely prospector, but the wail of a wolf, full-voiced, crying out the meaning of the desert and the night. Hunger throbbed in it—hunger for a mate, for offspring, for life. When it ceased, the terrible desert silence smote Cameron, and the cry echoed in his soul. He and that wandering wolf were brothers.

Then a sharp clink of metal on stone and soft pads of hoofs in sand prompted Cameron to reach for his gun, and to move out of the light of the waning campfire. He was somewhere along the wild border line between Sonora and Arizona; and the prospector who dared the heat and barrenness of that region risked other dangers sometimes as menacing.

Figures darker than the gloom approached and took shape, and in the light turned out to be those of a white man and a heavily packed burro.

"Hello there," the man called, as he came to a halt and gazed about him. "I saw your fire. May I make camp here?"

Cameron came forth out of the shadow and greeted his visitor, whom he took for a prospector like himself. Cameron resented the breaking of his lonely campfire vigil, but he respected the law of the desert.

The stranger thanked him, and then slipped the pack from his burro. Then he rolled out his pack and began preparations for a meal. His movements were slow and methodical.

Cameron watched him, still with resentment, yet with a curious and growing interest. The campfire burst into a bright blaze, and by its light Cameron saw a man whose gray hair somehow did not seem to make him old, and whose stooped shoulders did not detract from an impression of rugged strength.

"Find any mineral?" asked Cameron, presently.

His visitor looked up quickly, as if startled by the sound of a human voice. He replied, and then the two men talked a little. But the stranger evidently preferred silence. Cameron understood that. He laughed grimly and bent a keener gaze upon the furrowed, shadowy face. Another of those strange desert prospectors in whom there was some relentless driving power besides the lust for gold! Cameron felt that between this man and himself there was a subtle affinity, vague and undefined, perhaps born of the divination that here was a desert wanderer like himself, perhaps born of a deeper, an unintelligible relation having its roots back in the past. A long-forgotten sensation stirred in Cameron's breast, one so long forgotten that he could not recognize it. But it was akin to pain.

II

When he awakened he found, to his surprise, that his companion had departed. A trail in the sand led off to the north. There was no water in that direction. Cameron shrugged his shoulders; it was not his affair; he had his own problems. And straightway he forgot his strange visitor.

Cameron began his day, grateful for the solitude that was now unbroken, for the canyon-furrowed and cactus-spired scene that now showed no sign of life. He traveled southwest, never straying far from the dry stream bed; and in a desultory way, without eagerness, he hunted for signs of gold.

The work was toilsome, yet the periods of rest in which he indulged were not taken because of fatigue. He rested to look, to listen, to feel. What the vast silent world meant to him had always been a mystical thing, which he felt in all its incalculable power, but never understood.

That day, while it was yet light, and he was digging in a moist white-bordered wash for water, he was brought sharply up by hearing the crack of hard hoofs on stone. There down the canyon came a man and a burro. Cameron recognized them.

"Hello, friend," called the man, halting. "Our trails crossed again. That's good."

"Hello," replied Cameron, slowly. "Any mineral sign to-day?"

"No."

They made camp together, ate their frugal meal, smoked a pipe, and rolled in their blankets without exchanging many words. In the morning the same reticence, the same aloofness characterized the manner of both. But Cameron's companion, when he had packed his burro and was ready to start, faced about and said: "We might stay together, if it's all right with you."

"I never take a partner," replied Cameron.

"You're alone; I'm alone," said the other, mildly. "It's a big place. If we find gold there'll be enough for two."

"I don't go down into the desert for gold alone," rejoined Cameron, with a chill note in his swift reply.

His companion's deep-set, luminous eyes emitted a singular flash. It moved Cameron to say that in the years of his wandering he had met no man who could endure equally with him the blasting heat, the blinding dust storms, the wilderness of sand and rock and lava and cactus, the terrible silence and desolation of the desert. Cameron waved a hand toward the wide, shimmering, shadowy descent of plain and range. "I may strike through the Sonora Desert. I may head for Pinacate or north for the Colorado Basin. You are an old man."

"I don't know the country, but to me one place is the same as another," replied his companion. For moments he seemed to forget himself, and swept his far-reaching gaze out over the colored gulf of stone and sand. Then with gentle slaps he drove his burro in behind Cameron. "Yes, I'm old. I'm lonely, too. It's come to me just lately. But, friend, I can still travel, and for a few days my company won't hurt you."

"Have it your way," said Cameron.

They began a slow march down into the desert. At sunset they camped under the lee of a low mesa. Cameron was glad his comrade had the Indian habit of silence. Another day's travel found the prospectors deep in the wilderness. Then there came a breaking of reserve, noticeable in the elder man, almost imperceptibly gradual in Cameron. Beside the meager mesquite campfire this gray-faced, thoughtful old prospector would remove his black pipe from his mouth to talk a little; and Cameron would listen, and sometimes unlock his lips to speak a word. And so, as Cameron began to respond to the influence of a desert less lonely than habitual, he began to take keener note of his comrade, and found him different from any other he had ever encountered in the wilderness. This man never grumbled at the heat, the glare, the driving sand, the sour water, the scant fare. During the daylight hours he was seldom idle. At night he sat dreaming before the fire or paced to and fro in the gloom. He slept but little, and that long after Cameron had had his own rest. He was tireless, patient, brooding.

Cameron's awakened interest brought home to him the realization that for years he had shunned companionship. In those years only three men had wandered into the desert with him, and these had left their bones to bleach in the shifting sands. Cameron had not cared to know their secrets. But the more he studied this latest comrade the more he began to suspect that he might have missed something in the others. In his own driving passion to take his secret into the limitless abode of silence and desolation, where he could be alone with it, he had forgotten that life dealt shocks to other men. Somehow this silent comrade reminded him.

One afternoon late, after they had toiled up a white, winding wash of sand and gravel, they came upon a dry waterhole. Cameron dug deep into the sand, but without avail. He was turning to retrace weary steps back to the last water when his comrade asked him to wait. Cameron watched him search in his pack and bring forth what appeared to be a small, forked branch of a peach tree. He grasped the prongs of the fork and held them before him with the end standing straight out, and then he began to walk along the stream bed. Cameron, at first amused, then amazed, then pitying, and at last curious, kept pace with the prospector. He saw a strong tension of his comrade's wrists, as if he was holding hard against a considerable force. The end of the peach branch began to quiver and turn. Cameron reached out a hand to touch it, and was astounded at feeling a powerful vibrant force pulling the branch downward. He felt it as a magnetic shock. The branch kept turning, and at length pointed to the ground.

"Dig here," said the prospector.

"What!" ejaculated Cameron. Had the man lost his mind?

Then Cameron stood by while his comrade dug in the sand. Three feet he dug—four—five, and the sand grew dark, then moist. At six feet water began to seep through.

"Get the little basket in my pack," he said.

Cameron complied, and saw his comrade drop the basket into the deep hole, where it kept the sides from caving in and allowed the water to seep through. While Cameron watched, the basket filled. Of all the strange incidents of his desert career this was the strangest. Curiously he picked up the peach branch and held it as he had seen it held. The thing, however, was dead in his hands.

"I see you haven't got it," remarked his comrade. "Few men have."

"Got what?" demanded Cameron.

"A power to find water that way. Back in Illinois an old German used to do that to locate wells. He showed me I had the same power. I can't explain. But you needn't look so dumfounded. There's nothing supernatural about it."

"You mean it's a simple fact—that some men have a magnetism, a force or power to find water as you did?"

"Yes. It's not unusual on the farms back in Illinois, Ohio, Pennsylvania. The old German I spoke of made money traveling round with his peach fork."

"What a gift for a man in the desert!"

Cameron's comrade smiled—the second time in all those days.

They entered a region where mineral abounded, and their march became slower. Generally they took the course of a wash, one on each side, and let the burros travel leisurely along nipping at the bleached blades of scant grass, or at sage or cactus, while they searched in the canyons and under the ledges for signs of gold. When they found any rock that hinted of gold they picked off a piece and gave it a chemical test. The search was fascinating. They interspersed the work with long, restful moments when they looked afar down the vast reaches and smoky shingles to the line of dim mountains. Some impelling desire, not all the lure of gold, took them to the top of mesas and escarpments; and here, when they had dug and picked, they rested and gazed out at the wide prospect. Then, as the sun lost its heat and sank lowering to dent its red disk behind far-distant spurs, they halted in a shady canyon or likely spot in a dry wash and tried for water. When they found it they unpacked, gave drink to the tired burros, and turned them loose. Dead mesquite served for the campfire. While the strange twilight deepened into weird night they sat propped against stones, with eyes on the dying embers of the fire, and soon they lay on the sand with the light of white stars on their dark faces.

Each succeeding day and night Cameron felt himself more and more drawn to this strange man. He found that after hours of burning toil he had insensibly grown nearer to his comrade. He reflected that after a few weeks in the desert he had always become a different man. In civilization, in the rough mining camps, he had been a prey to unrest and gloom. But once down on the great billowing sweep of this lonely world, he could look into his unquiet soul without bitterness. Did not the desert magnify men? Cameron believed that wild men in wild places, fighting cold, heat, starvation, thirst, barrenness, facing the elements in all their ferocity, usually retrograded, descended to the savage, lost all heart and soul and became mere brutes. Likewise he believed that men wandering or lost in the wilderness often reversed that brutal order of life and became noble, wonderful, super-human. So now he did not marvel at a slow stir stealing warmer along his veins, and at the premonition that perhaps he and this man, alone on the desert, driven there by life's mysterious and remorseless motive, were to see each other through God's eyes.

His companion was one who thought of himself last. It humiliated Cameron that in spite of growing keenness he could not hinder him from doing more than an equal share of the day's work. The man was mild, gentle, quiet, mostly silent, yet under all his softness he seemed to be made of the fiber of steel. Cameron could not thwart him. Moreover, he appeared to want to find gold for Cameron, not for himself. Cameron's hands always trembled at the turning of rock that promised gold; he had enough of the prospector's passion for fortune to thrill at the chance of a strike. But the other never showed the least trace of excitement.

One night they were encamped at the head of a canyon. The day had been exceedingly hot, and long after sundown the radiation of heat from the rocks persisted. A desert bird whistled a wild, melancholy note from a dark cliff, and a distant coyote wailed mournfully. The stars shone white until the huge moon rose to burn out all their whiteness. And on this night Cameron watched his comrade, and yielded to interest he had not heretofore voiced.

"Pardner, what drives you into the desert?"

"Do I seem to be a driven man?"

"No. But I feel it. Do you come to forget?"

"Yes."

"Ah!" softly exclaimed Cameron. Always he seemed to have known that. He said no more. He watched the old man rise and begin his nightly pace to and fro, up and down. With slow, soft tread, forward and back, tirelessly and ceaselessly, he paced that beat. He did not look up at the stars or follow the radiant track of the moon along the canyon ramparts. He hung his head. He was lost in another world. It was a world which the lonely desert made real. He looked a dark, sad, plodding figure, and somehow impressed Cameron with the helplessness of men.

Cameron grew acutely conscious of the pang in his own breast, of the fire in his heart, the strife and torment of his passion-driven soul. He had come into the desert to remember a woman. She appeared to him then as she had looked when first she entered his life—a golden-haired girl, blue-eyed, white-skinned, red-lipped, tall and slender and beautiful. He had never forgotten, and an old, sickening remorse knocked at his heart. He rose and climbed out of the canyon and to the top of a mesa, where he paced to and fro and looked down into the weird and mystic shadows, like the darkness of his passion, and farther on down the moon track and the glittering stretches that vanished in the cold, blue horizon. The moon soared radiant and calm, the white stars shone serene. The vault of heaven seemed illimitable and divine. The desert surrounded him, silver-streaked and black-mantled, a chaos of rock and sand, silent, austere, ancient, always waiting. It spoke to Cameron. It was a naked corpse, but it had a soul. In that wild solitude the white stars looked down upon him pitilessly and pityingly. They had shone upon a desert that might once have been alive and was now dead, and might again throb with life, only to die. It was a terrible ordeal for him to stand alone and realize that he was only a man facing eternity. But that was what gave him strength to endure. Somehow he was a part of it all, some atom in that vastness, somehow necessary to an inscrutable purpose, something indestructible in that desolate world of ruin and death and decay, something perishable and changeable and growing under all the fixity of heaven. In that endless, silent hall of desert there was a spirit; and Cameron felt hovering near him what he imagined to be phantoms of peace.

He returned to camp and sought his comrade.

"I reckon we're two of a kind," he said. "It was a woman who drove me into the desert. But I come to remember. The desert's the only place I can do that."

"Was she your wife?" asked the elder man.

"No."

A long silence ensued. A cool wind blew up the canyon, sifting the sand through the dry sage, driving away the last of the lingering heat. The campfire wore down to a ruddy ashen heap.

"I had a daughter," said Cameron's comrade. "She lost her mother at birth. And I—I didn't know how to bring up a girl. She was pretty and gay. It was the—the old story."

His words were peculiarly significant to Cameron. They distressed him. He had been wrapped up in his remorse. If ever in the past he had thought of any one connected with the girl he had wronged he had long forgotten. But the consequences of such wrong were far-reaching. They struck at the roots of a home. Here in the desert he was confronted by the spectacle of a splendid man, a father, wasting his life because he could not forget—because there was nothing left to live for. Cameron understood better now why his comrade was drawn by the desert.

"Well, tell me more?" asked Cameron, earnestly.

"It was the old, old story. My girl was pretty and free. The young bucks ran after her. I guess she did not run away from them. And I was away a good deal—working in another town. She was in love with a wild fellow. I knew nothing of it till too late. He was engaged to marry her. But he didn't come back. And when the disgrace became plain to all, my girl left home. She went West. After a while I heard from her. She was well—working—living for her baby. A long time passed. I had no ties. I drifted West. Her lover had also gone West. In those days everybody went West. I trailed him, intending to kill him. But I lost his trail. Neither could I find any trace of her. She had moved on, driven, no doubt, by the hound of her past. Since then I have taken to the wilds, hunting gold on the desert."

"Yes, it's the old, old story, only sadder, I think," said Cameron; and his voice was strained and unnatural. "Pardner, what Illinois town was it you hailed from?"

"Peoria."

"And your—your name?" went on Cameron huskily.

"Warren—Jonas Warren."

That name might as well have been a bullet. Cameron stood erect, motionless, as men sometimes stand momentarily when shot straight through the heart. In an instant, when thoughts resurged like blinding flashes of lightning through his mind, he was a swaying, quivering, terror-stricken man. He mumbled something hoarsely and backed into the shadow. But he need not have feared discovery, however surely his agitation might have betrayed him. Warren sat brooding over the campfire, oblivious of his comrade, absorbed in the past.

Cameron swiftly walked away in the gloom, with the blood thrumming thick in his ears, whispering over and over:

"Merciful God! Nell was his daughter!"

III

As thought and feeling multiplied, Cameron was overwhelmed. Beyond belief, indeed, was it that out of the millions of men in the world two who had never seen each other could have been driven into the desert by memory of the same woman. It brought the past so close. It showed Cameron how inevitably all his spiritual life was governed by what had happened long ago. That which made life significant to him was a wandering in silent places where no eye could see him with his secret. Some fateful chance had thrown him with the father of the girl he had wrecked. It was incomprehensible; it was terrible. It was the one thing of all possible happenings in the world of chance that both father and lover would have found unendurable.

Cameron's pain reached to despair when he felt this relation between Warren and himself. Something within him cried out to him to reveal his identity. Warren would kill him; but it was not fear of death that put Cameron on the rack. He had faced death too often to be afraid. It was the thought of adding torture to this long-suffering man. All at once Cameron swore that he would not augment Warren's trouble, or let him stain his hands with blood. He would tell the truth of Nell's sad story and his own, and make what amends he could.

Then Cameron's thought shifted from father to daughter. She was somewhere beyond the dim horizon line. In those past lonely hours by the campfire his fancy had tortured him with pictures of Nell. But his remorseful and cruel fancy had lied to him. Nell had struggled upward out of menacing depths. She had reconstructed a broken life. And now she was fighting for the name and happiness of her child. Little Nell! Cameron experienced a shuddering ripple in all his being—the physical rack of an emotion born of a new and strange consciousness.

As Cameron gazed out over the blood-red, darkening desert suddenly the strife in his soul ceased. The moment was one of incalculable change, in which his eyes seemed to pierce the vastness of cloud and range, and mystery of gloom and shadow—to see with strong vision the illimitable space before him. He felt the grandeur of the desert, its simplicity, its truth. He had learned at last the lesson it taught. No longer strange was his meeting and wandering with Warren. Each had marched in the steps of destiny; and as the lines of their fates had been inextricably tangled in the years that were gone, so now their steps had crossed and turned them toward one common goal. For years they had been two men marching alone, answering to an inward driving search, and the desert had brought them together. For years they had wandered alone in silence and solitude, where the sun burned white all day and the stars burned white all night, blindly following the whisper of a spirit. But now Cameron knew that he was no longer blind, and in this flash of revelation he felt that it had been given him to help Warren with his burden.

He returned to camp trying to evolve a plan. As always at that long hour when the afterglow of sunset lingered in the west, Warren plodded to and fro in the gloom. All night Cameron lay awake thinking.

In the morning, when Warren brought the burros to camp and began preparations for the usual packing, Cameron broke silence.

"Pardner, your story last night made me think. I want to tell you something about myself. It's hard enough to be driven by sorrow for one you've loved, as you've been driven; but to suffer sleepless and eternal remorse for the ruin of one you've loved as I have suffered—that is hell.... Listen. In my younger days—it seems long now, yet it's not so many years—I was wild. I wronged the sweetest and loveliest girl I ever knew. I went away not dreaming that any disgrace might come to her. Along about that time I fell into terrible moods—I changed—I learned I really loved her. Then came a letter I should have gotten months before. It told of her trouble—importuned me to hurry to save her. Half frantic with shame and fear, I got a marriage certificate and rushed back to her town. She was gone—had been gone for weeks, and her disgrace was known. Friends warned me to keep out of reach of her father. I trailed her—found her. I married her. But too late!... She would not live with me. She left me—I followed her west, but never found her."

Warren leaned forward a little and looked into Cameron's eyes, as if searching there for the repentance that might make him less deserving of a man's scorn.

Cameron met the gaze unflinchingly, and again began to speak:

"You know, of course, how men out here somehow lose old names, old identities. It won't surprise you much to learn my name really isn't Cameron, as I once told you."

Warren stiffened upright. It seemed that there might have been a blank, a suspension, between his grave interest and some strange mood to come.

Cameron felt his heart bulge and contract in his breast; all his body grew cold; and it took tremendous effort for him to make his lips form words.

"Warren, I'm the man you're hunting. I'm Burton. I was Nell's lover!"

The old man rose and towered over Cameron, and then plunged down upon him, and clutched at his throat with terrible stifling hands. The harsh contact, the pain awakened Cameron to his peril before it was too late. Desperate fighting saved him from being hurled to the ground and stamped and crushed. Warren seemed a maddened giant. There was a reeling, swaying, wrestling struggle before the elder man began to weaken. The Cameron, buffeted, bloody, half-stunned, panted for speech.

"Warren—hold on! Give me—a minute. I married Nell. Didn't you know that?... I saved the child!"

Cameron felt the shock that vibrated through Warren. He repeated the words again and again. As if compelled by some resistless power, Warren released Cameron, and, staggering back, stood with uplifted, shaking hands. In his face was a horrible darkness.

"Warren! Wait—listen!" panted Cameron. "I've got that marriage certificate—I've had it by me all these years. I kept it—to prove to myself I did right."

The old man uttered a broken cry.

Cameron stole off among the rocks. How long he absented himself or what he did he had no idea. When he returned Warren was sitting before the campfire, and once more he appeared composed. He spoke, and his voice had a deeper note; but otherwise he seemed as usual.

They packed the burros and faced the north together.

Cameron experienced a singular exaltation. He had lightened his comrade's burden. Wonderfully it came to him that he had also lightened his own. From that hour it was not torment to think of Nell. Walking with his comrade through the silent places, lying beside him under the serene luminous light of the stars, Cameron began to feel the haunting presence of invisible things that were real to him—phantoms whispering peace. In the moan of the cool wind, in the silken seep of sifting sand, in the distant rumble of a slipping ledge, in the faint rush of a shooting star he heard these phantoms of peace coming with whispers of the long pain of men at the last made endurable. Even in the white noonday, under the burning sun, these phantoms came to be real to him. In the dead silence of the midnight hours he heard them breathing nearer on the desert wind—nature's voices of motherhood, whispers of God, peace in the solitude.

IV

There came a morning when the sun shone angry and red through a dull, smoky haze.

"We're in for sandstorms," said Cameron.

They had scarcely covered a mile when a desert-wide, moaning, yellow wall of flying sand swooped down upon them. Seeking shelter in the lee of a rock, they waited, hoping the storm was only a squall, such as frequently whipped across the open places. The moan increased to a roar, and the dull red slowly dimmed, to disappear in the yellow pall, and the air grew thick and dark. Warren slipped the packs from the burros. Cameron feared the sandstorms had arrived some weeks ahead of their usual season.

The men covered their heads and patiently waited. The long hours dragged, and the storm increased in fury. Cameron and Warren wet scarfs with water from their canteens, and bound them round their faces, and then covered their heads. The steady, hollow bellow of flying sand went on. It flew so thickly that enough sifted down under the shelving rock to weight the blankets and almost bury the men. They were frequently compelled to shake off the sand to keep from being borne to the ground. And it was necessary to keep digging out the packs. The floor of their shelter gradually rose higher and higher. They tried to eat, and seemed to be grinding only sand between their teeth. They lost the count of time. They dared not sleep, for that would have meant being buried alive. The could only crouch close to the leaning rock, shake off the sand, blindly dig out their packs, and every moment gasp and cough and choke to fight suffocation.

The storm finally blew itself out. It left the prospectors heavy and stupid for want of sleep. Their burros had wandered away, or had been buried in the sand. Far as eye could reach the desert had marvelously changed; it was now a rippling sea of sand dunes. Away to the north rose the peak that was their only guiding mark. They headed toward it, carrying a shovel and part of their packs.

At noon the peak vanished in the shimmering glare of the desert. The prospectors pushed on, guided by the sun. In every wash they tried for water. With the forked peach branch in his hands Warren always succeeded in locating water. They dug, but it lay too deep. At length, spent and sore, they fell and slept through that night and part of the next day. Then they succeeded in getting water, and quenched their thirst, and filled the canteens, and cooked a meal.

The burning day found them in an interminably wide plain, where there was no shelter from the fierce sun. The men were exceedingly careful with their water, though there was absolute necessity of drinking a little every hour. Late in the afternoon they came to a canyon that they believed was the lower end of the one in which they had last found water. For hours they traveled toward its head, and, long after night had set, found what they sought. Yielding to exhaustion, they slept, and next day were loath to leave the waterhole. Cool night spurred them on with canteens full and renewed strength.

Morning told Cameron that they had turned back miles into the desert, and it was desert new to him. The red sun, the increasing heat, and especially the variety and large size of the cactus plants warned Cameron that he had descended to a lower level. Mountain peaks loomed on all sides, some near, others distant; and one, a blue spur, splitting the glaring sky far to the north, Cameron thought he recognized as a landmark. The ascent toward it was heartbreaking, not in steepness, but in its league-and-league-long monotonous rise. Cameron knew there was only one hope—to make the water hold out and never stop to rest. Warren began to weaken. Often he had to halt. The burning white day passed, and likewise the night, with its white stars shining so pitilessly cold and bright.

Cameron measured the water in his canteen by its weight. Evaporation by heat consumed as much as he drank. During one of the rests, when he had wetted his parched mouth and throat, he found opportunity to pour a little water from his canteen into Warren's.

At first Cameron had curbed his restless activity to accommodate the pace of his elder comrade. But now he felt that he was losing something of his instinctive and passionate zeal to get out of the desert. The thought of water came to occupy his mind. He began to imagine that his last little store of water did not appreciably diminish. He knew he was not quite right in his mind regarding water; nevertheless, he felt this to be more of fact than fancy, and he began to ponder.

When next they rested he pretended to be in a kind of stupor; but he covertly watched Warren. The man appeared far gone, yet he had cunning. He cautiously took up Cameron's canteen and poured water into it from his own.

This troubled Cameron. The old irritation at not being able to thwart Warren returned to him. Cameron reflected, and concluded that he had been unwise not to expect this very thing. Then, as his comrade dropped into weary rest, he lifted both canteens. If there were any water in Warren's, it was only very little. Both men had been enduring the terrible desert thirst, concealing it, each giving his water to the other, and the sacrifice had been useless.

Instead of ministering to the parched throats of one or both, the water had evaporated. When Cameron made sure of this, he took one more drink, the last, and poured the little water left into Warren's canteen. He threw his own away.

Soon afterward Warren discovered the loss.

"Where's your canteen?" he asked.

"The heat was getting my water, so I drank what was left."

"My son!" said Warren.

The day opened for them in a red and green hell of rock and cactus. Like a flame the sun scorched and peeled their faces. Warren went blind from the glare, and Cameron had to lead him. At last Warren plunged down, exhausted, in the shade of a ledge.

Cameron rested and waited, hopeless, with hot, weary eyes gazing down from the height where he sat. The ledge was the top step of a ragged gigantic stairway.

Below stretched a sad, austere, and lonely valley. A dim, wide streak, lighter than the bordering gray, wound down the valley floor. Once a river had flowed there, leaving only a forlorn trace down the winding floor of this forlorn valley.

Movement on the part of Warren attracted Cameron's attention. Evidently the old prospector had recovered his sight and some of his strength, for he had arisen, and now began to walk along the arroyo bed with his forked peach branch held before him. He had clung to the precious bit of wood. Cameron considered the prospect for water hopeless, because he saw that the arroyo had once been a canyon, and had been filled with sands by desert winds. Warren, however, stopped in a deep pit, and, cutting his canteen in half, began to use one side of it as a scoop. He scooped out a wide hollow, so wide that Cameron was certain he had gone crazy. Cameron gently urged him to stop, and then forcibly tried to make him. But these efforts were futile. Warren worked with slow, ceaseless, methodical movement. He toiled for what seemed hours. Cameron, seeing the darkening, dampening sand, realized a wonderful possibility of water, and he plunged into the pit with the other half of the canteen. Then both men toiled, round and round the wide hole, down deeper and deeper. The sand grew moist, then wet. At the bottom of the deep pit the sand coarsened, gave place to gravel. Finally water welled in, a stronger volume than Cameron ever remembered finding on the desert. It would soon fill the hole and run over. He marveled at the circumstance. The time was near the end of the dry season. Perhaps an underground stream flowed from the range behind down to the valley floor, and at this point came near to the surface. Cameron had heard of such desert miracles.

The finding of water revived Cameron's flagging hopes. But they were short-lived. Warren had spend himself utterly.

"I'm done. Don't linger," he whispered. "My son, go—go!"

Then he fell. Cameron dragged him out of the sand pit to a sheltered place under the ledge. While sitting beside the failing man Cameron discovered painted images on the wall. Often in the desert he had found these evidences of a prehistoric people. Then, from long habit, he picked up a piece of rock and examined it. Its weight made him closely scrutinize it. The color was a peculiar black. He scraped through the black rust to find a piece of gold. Around him lay scattered heaps of black pebbles and bits of black, weathered rock and pieces of broken ledge, and they showed gold.

"Warren! Look! See it! Feel it! Gold!"

But Warren had never cared, and now he was too blind to see.

"Go—go!" he whispered.

Cameron gazed down the gray reaches of the forlorn valley, and something within him that was neither intelligence nor emotion—something inscrutably strange—impelled him to promise.

Then Cameron built up stone monuments to mark his gold strike. That done, he tarried beside the unconscious Warren. Moments passed—grew into hours. Cameron still had strength left to make an effort to get out of the desert. But that same inscrutable something which had ordered his strange involuntary promise to

Warren held him beside his fallen comrade. He watched the white sun turn to gold, and then to red and sink behind mountains in the west. Twilight stole into the arroyo. It lingered, slowly turning to gloom. The vault of blue black lightened to the blinking of stars. Then fell the serene, silent, luminous desert night.

Cameron kept his vigil. As the long hours wore on he felt creep over him the comforting sense that he need not forever fight sleep. A wan glow flared behind the dark, uneven horizon, and a melancholy misshapen moon rose to make the white night one of shadows. Absolute silence claimed the desert. It was mute. Then that inscrutable something breathed to him, telling him when he was alone. He need not have looked at the dark, still face beside him.

Another face haunted Cameron's—a woman's face. It was there in the white moonlit shadows; it drifted in the darkness beyond; it softened, changed to that of a young girl, sweet, with the same dark, haunting eyes of her mother. Cameron prayed to that nameless thing within him, the spirit of something deep and mystical as life. He prayed to that nameless thing outside, of which the rocks and the sand, the spiked cactus and the ragged lava, the endless waste, with its vast star-fired mantle, were but atoms. He prayed for mercy to a woman—for happiness to her child. Both mother and daughter were close to him then. Time and distance were annihilated. He had faith—he saw into the future. The fateful threads of the past, so inextricably woven with his error, wound out their tragic length here in this forlorn desert.

Cameron then took a little tin box from his pocket, and, opening it, removed a folded certificate. He had kept a pen, and now he wrote something upon the paper, and in lieu of ink he wrote with blood. The moon afforded him enough light to see; and, having replaced the paper, he laid the little box upon a shelf of rock. It would remain there unaffected by dust, moisture, heat, time. How long had those painted images been there clear and sharp on the dry stone walls? There were no trails in that desert, and always there were incalculable changes. Cameron saw this mutable mood of nature—the sands would fly and seep and carve and bury; the floods would dig and cut; the ledges would weather in the heat and rain; the avalanches would slide; the cactus seeds would roll in the wind to catch in a niche and split the soil with thirsty roots. Years would pass. Cameron seemed to see them, too; and likewise destiny leading a child down into this forlorn waste, where she would find love and fortune, and the grave of her father.

Cameron covered the dark, still face of his comrade from the light of the waning moon.

That action was the severing of his hold on realities. They fell away from him in final separation. Vaguely, dreamily he seemed to behold his soul. Night merged into gray day; and night came again, weird and dark. Then up out of the vast void of the desert, from the silence and illimitableness, trooped his phantoms of peace. Majestically they formed around him, marshalling and mustering in ceremonious state, and moved to lay upon him their passionless serenity.

I OLD FRIENDS

RICHARD GALE reflected that his sojourn in the West had been what his disgusted father had predicted—idling here and there, with no objective point or purpose.

It was reflection such as this, only more serious and perhaps somewhat desperate, that had brought Gale down to the border. For some time the newspapers had been printing news of Mexican revolution, guerrilla warfare, United States cavalry patrolling the international line, American cowboys fighting with the rebels, and wild stories of bold raiders and bandits. But as opportunity, and adventure, too, had apparently given him a wide berth in Montana, Wyoming, Colorado, he had struck southwest for the Arizona border, where he hoped to see some stirring life. He did not care very much what happened. Months of futile wandering in the hope of finding a place where he fitted had inclined Richard to his father's opinion.

It was after dark one evening in early October when Richard arrived in Casita. He was surprised to find that it was evidently a town of importance. There was a jostling, jabbering, sombreroed crowd of Mexicans around the railroad station. He felt as if he were in a foreign country. After a while he saw several men of his nationality, one of whom he engaged to carry his luggage to a hotel. They walked up a wide, well-lighted street lined with buildings in which were bright windows. Of the many people encountered by Gale most were Mexicans. His guide explained that the smaller half of Casita lay in Arizona, the other half in Mexico, and of several thousand inhabitants the majority belonged on the southern side of the street, which was the boundary line. He also said that rebels had entered the town that day, causing a good deal of excitement.

Gale was almost at the end of his financial resources, which fact occasioned him to turn away from a pretentious hotel and to ask his guide for a cheaper lodging-house. When this was found, a sight of the loungers in the office, and also a desire for comfort, persuaded Gale to change his traveling-clothes for rough outing garb and boots.

"Well, I'm almost broke," he soliloquized, thoughtfully. "The governor said I wouldn't make any money. He's right—so far. And he said I'd be coming home beaten. There he's wrong. I've got a hunch that something 'll happen to me in this Greaser town."

He went out into a wide, whitewashed, high-ceiled corridor, and from that into an immense room which, but for pool tables, bar, benches, would have been like a courtyard. The floor was cobblestoned, the walls were of adobe, and the large windows opened like doors. A blue cloud of smoke filled the place. Gale heard the click of pool balls and the clink of glasses along the crowded bar. Barelegged, sandal-footed Mexicans in white rubbed shoulders with Mexicans mantled in black and red. There were others in tight-fitting blue uniforms with gold fringe or tassels at the shoulders. These men wore belts with heavy, bone-handled guns, and evidently were the rurales, or native policemen. There were black-bearded, coarse-visaged Americans, some gambling round the little tables, others drinking. The pool tables were the center of a noisy crowd of younger men, several of whom were unsteady on their feet. There were khaki-clad cavalrymen strutting in and out.

At one end of the room, somewhat apart from the general meelee, was a group of six men round a little table, four of whom were seated, the other two standing. These last two drew a second glance from Gale. The sharp-featured, bronzed faces and piercing eyes, the tall, slender, loosely jointed bodies, the quiet, easy, reckless air that seemed to be a part of the men—these things would plainly have stamped them as cowboys without the buckled sombreros, the colored scarfs, the high-topped, high-heeled boots with great silver-roweled spurs. Gale did not fail to note, also, that these cowboys wore guns, and this fact was rather a shock to his idea of the modern West. It caused him to give some credence to the rumors of fighting along the border, and he felt a thrill.

He satisfied his hunger in a restaurant adjoining, and as he stepped back into the saloon a man wearing a military cape jostled him. Apologies from both were instant. Gale was moving on when the other stopped short as if startled, and, leaning forward, exclaimed:

"Dick Gale?"

"You've got me," replied Gale, in surprise. "But I don't know you."

He could not see the stranger's face, because it was wholly shaded by a wide-brimmed hat pulled well down.

"By Jove! It's Dick! If this isn't great! Don't you know me?"

"I've heard your voice somewhere," replied Gale. "Maybe I'll recognize you if you come out from under that bonnet."

For answer the man, suddenly manifesting thought of himself, hurriedly drew Gale into the restaurant, where he thrust back his hat to disclose a handsome, sunburned face.

"George Thorne! So help me—"

"'S-s-ssh. You needn't yell," interrupted the other, as he met Gale's outstretched hand. There was a close, hard, straining grip. "I must not be recognized here. There are reasons. I'll explain in a minute. Say, but it's fine to see you! Five years, Dick, five years since I saw you run down University Field and spread-eagle the whole Wisconsin football team."

"Don't recollect that," replied Dick, laughing. "George, I'll bet you I'm gladder to see you than you are to see me. It seems so long. You went into the army, didn't you?"

"I did. I'm here now with the Ninth Cavalry. But—never mind me. What're you doing way down here? Say, I just noticed your togs. Dick, you can't be going in for mining or ranching, not in this God-forsaken desert?"

"On the square, George, I don't know any more why I'm here than—than you know."

"Well, that beats me!" ejaculated Thorne, sitting back in his chair, amaze and concern in his expression. "What the devil's wrong? Your old man's got too much money for you ever to be up against it. Dick, you couldn't have gone to the bad?"

A tide of emotion surged over Gale. How good it was to meet a friend—some one to whom to talk! He had never appreciated his loneliness until that moment.

"George, how I ever drifted down here I don't know. I didn't exactly quarrel with the governor. But—damn it, Dad hurt me—shamed me, and I dug out for the West. It was this way. After leaving college I tried to please him by tackling one thing after another that he set me to do. On the square, I had no head for business. I made a mess of everything. The governor got sore. He kept ramming the harpoon into me till I just couldn't stand it. What little ability I possessed deserted me when I got my back up, and there you are. Dad and I had a rather uncomfortable half hour. When I quit—when I told him straight out that I was going West to fare for myself, why, it wouldn't have been so tough if he hadn't laughed at me. He called me a rich man's son—an idle, easy-going spineless swell. He said I didn't even have character enough to be out and out bad. He said I didn't have sense enough to marry one of the nice girls in my sister's crowd. He said I couldn't get back home unless I sent to him for money. He said he didn't believe I could fight—could really make a fight for anything under the sun. Oh—he—he shot it into me, all right."

Dick dropped his head upon his hands, somewhat ashamed of the smarting dimness in his eyes. He had not meant to say so much. Yet what a relief to let out that long-congested burden!

"Fight!" cried Thorne, hotly. "What's ailing him? Didn't they call you Biff Gale in college? Dick, you were one of the best men Stagg ever developed. I heard him say so—that you were the fastest, one-hundred-and-seventy-five-pound man he'd ever trained, the hardest to stop."

"The governor didn't count football," said Dick. "He didn't mean that kind of fight. When I left home I don't think I had an idea what was wrong with me. But, George, I think I know now. I was a rich man's son—spoiled, dependent, absolutely ignorant of the value of money. I haven't yet discovered any earning capacity in me. I seem to be unable to do anything with my hands. That's the trouble. But I'm at the end of my tether now. And I'm going to punch cattle or be a miner, or do some real stunt—like joining the rebels."

"Aha! I thought you'd spring that last one on me," declared Thorne, wagging his head. "Well, you just forget it. Say, old boy, there's something doing in Mexico. The United States in general doesn't realize it. But across that line there are crazy revolutionists, ill-paid soldiers, guerrilla leaders, raiders, robbers, outlaws, bandits galore, starving peons by the thousand, girls and women in terror. Mexico is like some of her volcanoes—ready to erupt fire and hell! Don't make the awful mistake of joining rebel forces. Americans are hated by Mexicans of the lower class—the fighting class, both rebel and federal. Half the time these crazy Greasers are on one side, then on the other. If you didn't starve or get shot in ambush, or die of thirst, some Greaser would knife you in the back for you belt buckle or boots. There are a good many Americans with the rebels eastward toward Agua, Prieta and Juarez. Orozco is operating in Chihuahua, and I guess he has some idea of warfare. But this is Sonora, a mountainous desert, the home of the slave and the Yaqui. There's unorganized revolt everywhere. The American miners and ranchers, those who could get away, have fled across into the States, leaving property. Those who couldn't or wouldn't come must fight for their lives, are fighting now."

"That's bad," said Gale. "It's news to me. Why doesn't the government take action, do something?"

"Afraid of international complications. Don't want to offend the Maderists, or be criticized by jealous foreign nations. It's a delicate situation, Dick. The Washington officials know the gravity of it, you can bet. But the United States in general is in the dark, and the army—well, you ought to hear the inside talk back at San Antonio. We're patrolling the boundary line. We're making a grand bluff. I could tell you of a dozen instances where cavalry should have pursued raiders on the other side of the line. But we won't do it. The officers are a grouchy lot these days. You see, of course, what significance would attach to United States cavalry going into Mexican territory. There would simply be hell. My own colonel is the sorest man on the job. We're all sore. It's like sitting on a powder magazine. We can't keep the rebels and raiders from crossing the line. Yet we don't fight. My commission expires soon. I'll be discharged in three months. You can bet I'm glad for more reasons than I've mentioned."

Thorne was evidently laboring under strong, suppressed excitement. His face showed pale under the tan, and his eyes gleamed with a dark fire. Occasionally his delight at meeting, talking with Gale, dominated the other emotions, but not for long. He had seated himself at a table near one of the doorlike windows leading into the street, and every little while he would glance sharply out. Also he kept consulting his watch.

These details gradually grew upon Gale as Thorne talked.

"George, it strikes me that you're upset," said Dick, presently. "I seem to remember you as a cool-headed fellow whom nothing could disturb. Has the army changed you?"

Thorne laughed. It was a laugh with a strange, high note. It was reckless—it hinted of exaltation. He rose abruptly; he gave the waiter money to go for drinks; he looked into the saloon, and then into the street. On this side of the house there was a porch opening on a plaza with trees and shrubbery and branches. Thorne peered out one window, then another. His actions were rapid. Returning to the table, he put his hands upon it and leaned over to look closely into Gale's face.

"I'm away from camp without leave," he said.

"Isn't that a serious offense?" asked Dick.

"Serious? For me, if I'm discovered, it means ruin. There are rebels in town. Any moment we might have trouble. I ought to be ready for duty—within call. If I'm discovered it means arrest. That means delay—the failure of my plans—ruin."

Gale was silenced by his friend's intensity. Thorne bent over closer with his dark eyes searching bright.

"We were old pals—once?"

"Surely," replied Dick.

"What would you say, Dick Gale, if I told you that you're the one man I'd rather have had come along than any other at this crisis of my life?"

The earnest gaze, the passionate voice with its deep tremor drew Dick upright, thrilling and eager, conscious of strange, unfamiliar impetuosity.

"Thorne, I should say I was glad to be the fellow," replied Dick.

Their hands locked for a moment, and they sat down again with heads close over the table.

"Listen," began Thorne, in low, swift whisper, "a few days, a week ago—it seems like a year!—I was of some assistance to refugees fleeing from Mexico into the States. They were all women, and one of them was dressed as a nun. Quite by accident I saw her face. It was that of a beautiful girl. I observed she kept aloof from the others. I suspected a disguise, and, when opportunity afforded, spoke to her, offered my services. She replied to my poor efforts at Spanish in fluent English. She had fled in terror from her home, some place down in Sinaloa. Rebels are active there. Her father was captured and held for ransom. When the ransom was paid the rebels killed him. The leader of these rebels was a bandit named Rojas. Long before the revolution began he had been feared by people of class—loved by the peons. Bandits are worshiped by the peons. All of the famous bandits have robbed the rich and given to the poor. Rojas saw the daughter, made off with her. But she contrived to bribe her guards, and escaped almost immediately before any harm befell her. She hid among friends. Rojas nearly tore down the town in his efforts to find her. Then she disguised herself, and traveled by horseback, stage, and train to Casita.

"Her story fascinated me, and that one fleeting glimpse I had of her face I couldn't forget. She had no friends here, no money. She knew Rojas was trailing her. This talk I had with her was at the railroad station, where all was bustle and confusion. No one noticed us, so I thought. I advised her to remove the disguise of a nun before she left the waiting-room. And I got a boy to guide her. But he fetched her to his house. I had promised to come in the evening to talk over the situation with her.

"I found her, Dick, and when I saw her—I went stark, staring, raving mad over her. She is the most beautiful, wonderful girl I ever saw. Her name is Mercedes Castaneda, and she belongs to one of the old wealthy Spanish families. She has lived abroad and in Havana. She speaks French as well as English. She is—but I must be brief.

"Dick, think, think! With Mercedes also it was love at first sight. My plan is to marry her and get her farther to the interior, away from the border. It may not be easy. She's watched. So am I. It was impossible to see her without the women of this house knowing. At first, perhaps, they had only curiosity—an itch to gossip. But the last two days there has been a change. Since last night there's some powerful influence at work. Oh, these Mexicans are subtle, mysterious! After all, they are Spaniards. They work in secret, in the dark. They are dominated first by religion, then by gold, then by passion for a woman. Rojas must have got word to his friends here; yesterday his gang of cutthroat rebels arrived, and to-day he came. When I learned that, I took my chance and left camp. I hunted up a priest. He promised to come here. It's time he's due. But I'm afraid he'll be stopped."

"Thorne, why don't you take the girl and get married without waiting, without running these risks?" said Dick.

"I fear it's too late now. I should have done that last night. You see, we're over the line—"

"Are we in Mexican territory now?" queried Gale, sharply.

"I guess yes, old boy. That's what complicates it. Rojas and his rebels have Casita in their hands. But Rojas without his rebels would be able to stop me, get the girl, and make for his mountain haunts. If Mercedes is really watched—if her identity is known, which I am sure is the case—we couldn't get far from this house before I'd be knifed and she seized."

"Good Heavens! Thorne, can that sort of thing happen less than a stone's throw from the United States line?" asked Gale, incredulously.

"It can happen, and don't you forget it. You don't seem to realize the power these guerrilla leaders, these rebel captains, and particularly these bandits, exercise over the mass of Mexicans. A bandit is a man of honor in Mexico. He is feared, envied, loved. In the hearts of the people he stands next to the national idol—the bull-fighter, the matador. The race has a wild, barbarian, bloody strain. Take Quinteros, for instance. He was a peon, a slave. He became a famous bandit. At the outbreak of the revolution he proclaimed himself a leader, and with a band of followers he devastated whole counties. The opposition to federal forces was only a blind to rob and riot and carry off women. The motto of this man and his followers was: 'Let us enjoy ourselves while we may!'

"There are other bandits besides Quinteros, not so famous or such great leaders, but just as bloodthirsty. I've seen Rojas. He's a handsome, bold sneering devil, vainer than any peacock. He decks himself in gold lace and sliver trappings, in all the finery he can steal. He was one of the rebels who helped sack Sinaloa and carry off half a million in money and valuables. Rojas spends gold like he spills blood. But he is chiefly famous for abducting women. The peon girls consider it an honor to be ridden off with. Rojas has shown a penchant for girls of the better class."

I OLD FRIENDS

Thorne wiped the perspiration from his pale face and bent a dark gaze out of the window before he resumed his talk.

"Consider what the position of Mercedes really is. I can't get any help from our side of the line. If so, I don't know where. The population on that side is mostly Mexican, absolutely in sympathy with whatever actuates those on this side. The whole caboodle of Greasers on both sides belong to the class in sympathy with the rebels, the class that secretly respects men like Rojas, and hates an aristocrat like Mercedes. They would conspire to throw her into his power. Rojas can turn all the hidden underground influences to his ends. Unless I thwart him he'll get Mercedes as easily as he can light a cigarette. But I'll kill him or some of his gang or her before I let him get her.... This is the situation, old friend. I've little time to spare. I face arrest for desertion. Rojas is in town. I think I was followed to this hotel. The priest has betrayed me or has been stopped. Mercedes is here alone, waiting, absolutely dependent upon me to save her from—from.... She's the sweetest, loveliest girl!... In a few moments—sooner or later there'll be hell here! Dick, are you with me?"

Dick Gale drew a long, deep breath. A coldness, a lethargy, an indifference that had weighed upon him for months had passed out of his being. On the instant he could not speak, but his hand closed powerfully upon his friend's. Thorne's face changed wonderfully, the distress, the fear, the appeal all vanishing in a smile of passionate gratefulness.

Then Dick's gaze, attracted by some slight sound, shot over his friend's shoulder to see a face at the window—a handsome, bold, sneering face, with glittering dark eyes that flashed in sinister intentness.

Dick stiffened in his seat. Thorne, with sudden clenching of hands, wheeled toward the window.

"Rojas!" he whispered.

II MERCEDES CASTANEDA

THE dark face vanished. Dick Gale heard footsteps and the tinkle of spurs. He strode to the window, and was in time to see a Mexican swagger into the front door of the saloon. Dick had only a glimpse; but in that he saw a huge black sombrero with a gaudy band, the back of a short, tight-fitting jacket, a heavy pearl-handled gun swinging with a fringe of sash, and close-fitting trousers spreading wide at the bottom. There were men passing in the street, also several Mexicans lounging against the hitching-rail at the curb.

"Did you see him? Where did he go?" whispered Thorne, as he joined Gale. "Those Greasers out there with the cartridge belts crossed over their breasts—they are rebels."

"I think he went into the saloon," replied Dick. "He had a gun, but for all I can see the Greasers out there are unarmed."

"Never believe it! There! Look, Dick! That fellow's a guard, though he seems so unconcerned. See, he has a short carbine, almost concealed.... There's another Greaser farther down the path. I'm afraid Rojas has the house spotted."

"If we could only be sure."

"I'm sure, Dick. Let's cross the hall; I want to see how it looks from the other side of the house."

Gale followed Thorne out of the restaurant into the high-ceiled corridor which evidently divided the hotel, opening into the street and running back to a patio. A few dim, yellow lamps flickered. A Mexican with a blanket round his shoulders stood in the front entrance. Back toward the patio there were sounds of boots on the stone floor. Shadows flitted across that end of the corridor. Thorne entered a huge chamber which was even more poorly lighted than the hall. It contained a table littered with papers, a few high-backed chairs, a couple of couches, and was evidently a parlor.

"Mercedes has been meeting me here," said Thorne. "At this hour she comes every moment or so to the head of the stairs there, and if I am here she comes down. Mostly there are people in this room a little later. We go out into the plaza. It faces the dark side of the house, and that's the place I must slip out with her if there's any chance at all to get away."

They peered out of the open window. The plaza was gloomy, and at first glance apparently deserted. In a moment, however, Gale made out a slow-pacing dark form on the path. Farther down there was another. No particular keenness was required to see in these forms a sentinel-like stealthiness.

Gripping Gale's arm, Thorne pulled back from the window.

"You saw them," he whispered. "It's just as I feared. Rojas has the place surrounded. I should have taken Mercedes away. But I had no time—no chance! I'm bound!... There's Mercedes now! My God!... Dick, think—think if there's a way to get her out of this trap!"

Gale turned as his friend went down the room. In the dim light at the head of the stairs stood the slim, muffled figure of a woman. When she saw Thorne she flew noiselessly down the stairway to him. He caught her in his arms. Then she spoke softly, brokenly, in a low, swift voice. It was a mingling of incoherent Spanish and English; but to Gale it was mellow, deep, unutterably tender, a voice full of joy, fear, passion, hope, and love. Upon Gale it had an unaccountable effect. He found himself thrilling, wondering.

Thorne led the girl to the center of the room, under the light where Gale stood. She had raised a white hand, holding a black-laced mantilla half aside. Dick saw a small, dark head, proudly held, an oval face half hidden, white as a flower, and magnificent black eyes.

Then Thorne spoke.

"Mercedes—Dick Gale, an old friend—the best friend I ever had."

She swept the mantilla back over her head, disclosing a lovely face, strange and striking to Gale in its pride and fire, its intensity.

"Senor Gale—ah! I cannot speak my happiness. His friend!"

"Yes, Mercedes; my friend and yours," said Thorne, speaking rapidly. "We'll have need of him. Dear, there's bad news and no time to break it gently. The priest did not come. He must have been detained. And listen—be brave, dear Mercedes—Rojas is here!"

She uttered an inarticulate cry, the poignant terror of which shook Gale's nerve, and swayed as if she would faint. Thorne caught her, and in husky voice importuned her to bear up.

"My darling! For God's sake don't faint—don't go to pieces! We'd be lost! We've got a chance. We'll think of something. Be strong! Fight!"

It was plain to Gale that Thorne was distracted. He scarcely knew what he was saying. Pale and shaking, he clasped Mercedes to him. Her terror had struck him helpless. It was so intense—it was so full of horrible certainty of what fate awaited her.

She cried out in Spanish, beseeching him; and as he shook his head, she changed to English:

"Senor, my lover, I will be strong—I will fight—I will obey. But swear by my Virgin, if need be to save me from Rojas—you will kill me!"

"Mercedes! Yes, I'll swear," he replied hoarsely. "I know—I'd rather have you dead than— But don't give up. Rojas can't be sure of you, or he wouldn't wait. He's in there. He's got his men there—all around us. But he hesitates. A beast like Rojas doesn't stand idle for nothing. I tell you we've a chance. Dick, here, will think of something. We'll slip away. Then he'll take you somewhere. Only—speak to him—show him you won't weaken. Mercedes, this is more than love and happiness for us. It's life or death."

She became quiet, and slowly recovered control of herself.

Suddenly she wheeled to face Gale with proud dark eyes, tragic sweetness of appeal, and exquisite grace.

"Senor, you are an American. You cannot know the Spanish blood—the peon bandit's hate and cruelty. I wish to die before Rojas's hand touches me. If he takes me alive, then the hour, the little day that my life lasts afterward will be tortured—torture of hell. If I live two days his brutal men will have me. If I live three, the dogs of his camp... Senor, have you a sister whom you love? Help Senor Thorne to save me. He is a soldier. He is bound. He must not betray his honor, his duty, for me.... Ah, you two splendid Americans—so big, so strong, so fierce! What is that little black half-breed slave Rojas to such men? Rojas is a coward. Now, let me waste no more precious time. I am ready. I will be brave."

She came close to Gale, holding out her white hands, a woman all fire and soul and passion. To Gale she was wonderful. His heart leaped. As he bent over her hands and kissed them he seemed to feel himself renewed, remade.

"Senorita," he said, "I am happy to be your servant. I can conceive of no greater pleasure than giving the service you require."

"And what is that?" inquired Thorne, hurriedly.

"That of incapacitating Senor Rojas for to-night, and perhaps several nights to come," replied Gale.

"Dick, what will you do?" asked Thorne, now in alarm.

"I'll make a row in that saloon," returned Dick, bluntly. "I'll start something. I'll rush Rojas and his crowd. I'll—"

"Lord, no; you mustn't, Dick—you'll be knifed!" cried Thorne. He was in distress, yet his eyes were shining.

"I'll take a chance. Maybe I can surprise that slow Greaser bunch and get away before they know what's happened.... You be ready watching at the window. When the row starts those fellows out there in the plaza will run into the saloon. Then you slip out, go straight through the plaza down the street. It's a dark street, I remember. I'll catch up with you before you get far."

Thorne gasped, but did not say a word. Mercedes leaned against him, her white hands now at her breast, her great eyes watching Gale as he went out.

In the corridor Gale stopped long enough to pull on a pair of heavy gloves, to muss his hair, and disarrange his collar. Then he stepped into the restaurant, went through, and halted in the door leading into the saloon. His five feet eleven inches and one hundred and eighty pounds were more noticeable there, and it was part of his plan to attract attention to himself. No one, however, appeared to notice him. The pool-players were noisily intent on their game, the same crowd of motley-robed Mexicans hung over the reeking bar. Gale's roving glance soon fixed upon the man he took to be Rojas. He recognized the huge, high-peaked, black sombrero with its ornamented band. The Mexican's face was turned aside. He was in earnest, excited colloquy with a dozen or more comrades, most of whom were sitting round a table. They were listening, talking, drinking. The fact that they wore cartridge belts crossed over their breasts satisfied that these were the rebels. He had noted the belts of the Mexicans outside, who were apparently guards. A waiter brought more drinks to this group at the table, and this caused the leader to turn so Gale could see his face. It was indeed the sinister, sneering face of the bandit Rojas. Gale gazed at the man with curiosity. He was under medium height, and striking in appearance only because of his dandified dress and evil visage. He wore a lace scarf, a tight, bright-buttoned jacket, a buckskin vest embroidered in red, a sash and belt joined by an enormous silver clasp. Gale saw again the pearl-handled gun swinging at the bandit's hip. Jewels flashed in his scarf. There were gold rings in his ears and diamonds on his fingers.

Gale became conscious of an inward fire that threatened to overrun his coolness. Other emotions harried his self-control. It seemed as if sight of the man liberated or created a devil in Gale. And at the bottom of his feelings there seemed to be a wonder at himself, a strange satisfaction for the something that had come to him.

He stepped out of the doorway, down the couple of steps to the floor of the saloon, and he staggered a little, simulating drunkenness. He fell over the pool tables, jostled Mexicans at the bar, laughed like a maudlin fool, and, with his hat slouched down, crowded here and there. Presently his eye caught sight of the group of cowboys whom he had before noticed with such interest.

They were still in a corner somewhat isolated. With fertile mind working, Gale lurched over to them. He remembered his many unsuccessful attempts to get acquainted with cowboys. If he were to get any help from these silent aloof rangers it must be by striking fire from them in one swift stroke. Planting himself squarely before the two tall cowboys who were standing, he looked straight into their lean, bronzed faces. He spared a full moment for that keen cool gaze before he spoke.

"I'm not drunk. I'm throwing a bluff, and I mean to start a rough house. I'm going to rush that damned bandit Rojas. It's to save a girl—to give her lover, who is my friend, a chance to escape with her. When I start a row my friend will try to slip out with her. Every door and window is watched. I've got to raise hell to draw the guards in.... Well, you're my countrymen. We're in Mexico. A beautiful girl's honor and life are at stake. Now, gentlemen, watch me!"

One cowboy's eyes narrowed, blinking a little, and his lean jaw dropped; the other's hard face rippled with a fleeting smile.

Gale backed away, and his pulse leaped when he saw the two cowboys, as if with one purpose, slowly stride after him. Then Gale swerved, staggering along, brushed against the tables, kicked over the empty chairs. He passed Rojas and his gang, and out of the tail of his eye saw that the bandit was watching him, waving his hands and talking fiercely. The hum of the many voices grew louder, and when Dick lurched against a table, overturning it and spilling glasses into the laps of several Mexicans, there arose a shrill cry. He had succeeded in attracting attention; almost every face turned his way. One of the insulted men, a little tawny fellow, leaped up to confront Gale, and in a frenzy screamed a volley of Spanish, of which Gale distinguished "Gringo!" The Mexican stamped and made a threatening move with his right hand. Dick swung his leg and with a swift side kick knocked the fellows feet from under him, whirling him down with a thud.

The action was performed so suddenly, so adroitly, it made the Mexican such a weakling, so like a tumbled tenpin, that the shrill jabbering hushed. Gale knew this to be the significant moment.

Wheeling, he rushed at Rojas. It was his old line-breaking plunge. Neither Rojas nor his men had time to move. The black-skinned bandit's face turned a dirty white; his jaw dropped; he would have shrieked if Gale had not hit him. The blow swept him backward against his men. Then Gale's heavy body, swiftly following with the momentum of that rush, struck the little group of rebels. They went down with table and chairs in a sliding crash.

Gale carried by his plunge, went with them. Like a cat he landed on top. As he rose his powerful hands fastened on Rojas. He jerked the little bandit off the tangled pile of struggling, yelling men, and, swinging him with terrific force, let go his hold. Rojas slid along the floor, knocking over tables and chairs. Gale bounded back, dragged Rojas up, handling him as if he were a limp sack.

A shot rang out above the yells. Gale heard the jingle of breaking glass. The room darkened perceptibly. He flashed a glance backward. The two cowboys were between him and the crowd of frantic rebels. One cowboy held two guns low down, level in front of him. The other had his gun raised and aimed. On the instant it spouted red and white. With the crack came the crashing of glass, another darkening shade over the room. With a cry Gale slung the bleeding Rojas from him. The bandit struck a table, toppled over it, fell, and lay prone.

Another shot made the room full of moving shadows, with light only back of the bar. A white-clad figure rushed at Gale. He tripped the man, but had to kick hard to disengage himself from grasping hands. Another figure closed in on Gale. This one was dark, swift. A blade glinted—described a circle aloft. Simultaneously with a close, red flash the knife wavered; the man wielding it stumbled backward. In the din Gale did not hear a report, but the Mexican's fall was significant. Then pandemonium broke loose. The din became a roar. Gale heard shots that sounded like dull spats in the distance. The big lamp behind the bar seemingly split, then sputtered and went out, leaving the room in darkness.

Gale leaped toward the restaurant door, which was outlined faintly by the yellow light within. Right and left he pushed the groping men who jostled with him. He vaulted a pool table, sent tables and chairs flying, and gained the door, to be the first of a wedging mob to squeeze through. One sweep of his arm knocked the restaurant lamp from its stand; and he ran out, leaving darkness behind him. A few bounds took him into the parlor. It was deserted. Thorne had gotten away with Mercedes.

It was then Gale slowed up. For the space of perhaps sixty seconds he had been moving with startling velocity. He peered cautiously out into the plaza. The paths, the benches, the shady places under the trees contained no skulking men. He ran out, keeping to the shade, and did not go into the path till he was halfway through the plaza. Under a street lamp at the far end of the path he thought he saw two dark figures. He ran faster, and soon reached the street. The uproar back in the hotel began to diminish, or else he was getting out of hearing. The few people he saw close at hand were all coming his way, and only the foremost showed any excitement. Gale walked swiftly, peering ahead for two figures. Presently he saw them—one tall, wearing a cape; the other slight, mantled. Gale drew a sharp breath of relief. Thorne and Mercedes were not far ahead.

From time to time Thorne looked back. He strode swiftly, almost carrying Mercedes, who clung closely to him. She, too, looked back. Once Gale saw her white face flash in the light of a street lamp. He began to overhaul them; and soon, when the last lamp had been passed and the street was dark, he ventured a whistle. Thorne heard it, for he turned, whistled a low reply, and went on. Not for some distance beyond, where the street ended in open country, did they halt to wait. The desert began here. Gale felt the soft sand under his feet and saw the grotesque forms of cactus. Then he came up with the fugitives.

"Dick! Are you—all right?" panted Thorne, grasping Gale.

"I'm—out of breath—but—O.K.," replied Gale.

"Good! Good!" choked Thorne. "I was scared—helpless.... Dick, it worked splendidly. We had no trouble. What on earth did you do?"

"I made the row, all right," said Dick.

"Good Heavens! It was like a row I once heard made by a mob. But the shots, Dick—were they at you? They paralyzed me. Then the yells. What happened? Those guards of Rojas ran round in front at the first shot. Tell me what happened."

"While I was rushing Rojas a couple of cowboys shot out the lamplights. A Mexican who pulled a knife on me got hurt, I guess. Then I think there was some shooting from the rebels after the room was dark."

"Rushing Rojas?" queried Thorne, leaning close to Dick. His voice was thrilling, exultant, deep with a joy that yet needed confirmation. "What did you do to him?"

"I handed him one off side, tackled, then tried a forward pass," replied Dick, lightly speaking the football vernacular so familiar to Thorne.

Thorne leaned closer, his fine face showing fierce and corded in the starlight. "Tell me straight," he demanded, in thick voice.

Gale then divined something of the suffering Thorne had undergone—something of the hot, wild, vengeful passion of a lover who must have brutal truth.

It stilled Dick's lighter mood, and he was about to reply when Mercedes pressed close to him, touched his hands, looked up into his face with wonderful eyes. He thought he would not soon forget their beauty—the shadow of pain that had been, the hope dawning so fugitively.

"Dear lady," said Gale, with voice not wholly steady, "Rojas himself will hound you no more to-night, nor for many nights."

She seemed to shake, to thrill, to rise with the intelligence. She pressed his hand close over her heaving breast. Gale felt the quick throb of her heart.

"Senor! Senor Dick!" she cried. Then her voice failed. But her hands flew up; quick as a flash she raised her face—kissed him. Then she turned and with a sob fell into Thorne's arms.

There ensued a silence broken only by Mercedes' sobbing. Gale walked some paces away. If he were not stunned, he certainly was agitated. The strange, sweet fire of that girl's lips remained with him. On the spur of the moment he imagined he had a jealousy of Thorne. But presently this passed. It was only that he had been deeply moved—stirred to the depths during the last hour—had become conscious of the awakening of a spirit. What remained with him now was the splendid glow of gladness that he had been of service to Thorne. And by the intensity of Mercedes' abandon of relief and gratitude he measured her agony of terror and the fate he had spared her.

"Dick, Dick, come here!" called Thorne softly. "Let's pull ourselves together now. We've got a problem yet. What to do? Where to go? How to get any place? We don't dare risk the station—the corrals where Mexicans hire out horses. We're on good old U.S. ground this minute, but we're not out of danger."

As he paused, evidently hoping for a suggestion from Gale, the silence was broken by the clear, ringing peal of a bugle. Thorne gave a violent start. Then he bent over, listening. The beautiful notes of the bugle floated out of the darkness, clearer, sharper, faster.

"It's a call, Dick! It's a call!" he cried.

Gale had no answer to make. Mercedes stood as if stricken. The bugle call ended. From a distance another faintly pealed. There were other sounds too remote to recognize. Then scattering shots rattled out.

"Dick, the rebels are fighting somebody," burst out Thorne, excitedly. "The little federal garrison still holds its stand. Perhaps it is attacked again. Anyway, there's something doing over the line. Maybe the crazy Greasers are firing on our camp. We've feared it—in the dark.... And here I am, away without leave—practically a deserter!"

"Go back! Go back, before you're too late!" cried Mercedes.

"Better make tracks, Thorne," added Gale. "It can't help our predicament for you to be arrested. I'll take care of Mercedes."

"No, no, no," replied Thorne. "I can get away—avoid arrest."

"That'd be all right for the immediate present. But it's not best for the future. George, a deserter is a deserter!... Better hurry. Leave the girl to me till tomorrow."

Mercedes embraced her lover, begged him to go. Thorne wavered.

"Dick, I'm up against it," he said. "You're right. If only I can get back in time. But, oh, I hate to leave her! Old fellow, you've saved her! I already owe you everlasting gratitude. Keep out of Casita, Dick. The U.S. side might be safe, but

I'm afraid to trust it at night. Go out in the desert, up in the mountains, in some safe place. Then come to me in camp. We'll plan. I'll have to confide in Colonel Weede. Maybe he'll help us. Hide her from the rebels—that's all."

He wrung Dick's hand, clasped Mercedes tightly in his arms, kissed her, and murmured low over her, then released her to rush off into the darkness. He disappeared in the gloom. The sound of his dull footfalls gradually died away.

For a moment the desert silence oppressed Gale. He was unaccustomed to such strange stillness. There was a low stir of sand, a rustle of stiff leaves in the wind. How white the stars burned! Then a coyote barked, to be bayed by a dog. Gale realized that he was between the edge of an unknown desert and the edge of a hostile town. He had to choose the desert, because, though he had no doubt that in Casita there were many Americans who might befriend him, he could not chance the risks of seeking them at night.

He felt a slight touch on his arm, felt it move down, felt Mercedes slip a trembling cold little hand into his. Dick looked at her. She seemed a white-faced girl now, with staring, frightened black eyes that flashed up at him. If the loneliness, the silence, the desert, the unknown dangers of the night affected him, what must they be to this hunted, driven girl? Gale's heart swelled. He was alone with her. He had no weapon, no money, no food, no drink, no covering, nothing except his two hands. He had absolutely no knowledge of the desert, of the direction or whereabouts of the boundary line between the republics; he did not know where to find the railroad, or any road or trail, or whether or not there were towns near or far. It was a critical, desperate situation. He thought first of the girl, and groaned in spirit, prayed that it would be given him to save her. When he remembered himself it was with the stunning consciousness that he could conceive of no situation which he would have exchanged for this one—where fortune had set him a perilous task of loyalty to a friend, to a helpless girl.

"Senor, senor!" suddenly whispered Mercedes, clinging to him. "Listen! I hear horses coming!"

III A FLIGHT INTO THE DESERT

UNEASY and startled, Gale listened and, hearing nothing, wondered if Mercedes's fears had not worked upon her imagination. He felt a trembling seize her, and he held her hands tightly.

"You were mistaken, I guess," he whispered.

"No, no, senor."

Dick turned his ear to the soft wind. Presently he heard, or imagined he heard, low beats. Like the first faint, far-off beats of a drumming grouse, they recalled to him the Illinois forests of his boyhood. In a moment he was certain the sounds were the padlike steps of hoofs in yielding sand. The regular tramp was not that of grazing horses.

On the instant, made cautious and stealthy by alarm, Gale drew Mercedes deeper into the gloom of the shrubbery. Sharp pricks from thorns warned him that he was pressing into a cactus growth, and he protected Mercedes as best he could. She was shaking as one with a severe chill. She breathed with little hurried pants and leaned upon him almost in collapse. Gale ground his teeth in helpless rage at the girl's fate. If she had not been beautiful she might still have been free and happy in her home. What a strange world to live in—how unfair was fate!

The sounds of hoofbeats grew louder. Gale made out a dark moving mass against a background of dull gray. There was a line of horses. He could not discern whether or not all the horses carried riders. The murmur of a voice struck his ear—then a low laugh. It made him tingle, for it sounded American. Eagerly he listened. There was an interval when only the hoofbeats could be heard.

"It shore was, Laddy, it shore was," came a voice out of the darkness. "Rough house! Laddy, since wire fences drove us out of Texas we ain't seen the like of that. An' we never had such a call."

"Call? It was a burnin' roast," replied another voice. "I felt low down. He vamoosed some sudden, an' I hope he an' his friends shook the dust of Casita. That's a rotten town Jim."

Gale jumped up in joy. What luck! The speakers were none other than the two cowboys whom he had accosted in the Mexican hotel.

"Hold on, fellows," he called out, and strode into the road.

The horses snorted and stamped. Then followed swift rustling sounds—a clinking of spurs, then silence. The figures loomed clearer in the gloom.. Gale saw five or six horses, two with riders, and one other, at least, carrying a pack. When Gale got within fifteen feet of the group the foremost horseman said:

"I reckon that's close enough, stranger."

Something in the cowboy's hand glinted darkly bright in the starlight.

"You'd recognize me, if it wasn't so dark," replied Gale, halting. "I spoke to you a little while ago—in the saloon back there."

"Come over an' let's see you," said the cowboy curtly.

Gale advanced till he was close to the horse. The cowboy leaned over the saddle and peered into Gale's face. Then, without a word, he sheathed the gun and held out his hand. Gale met a grip of steel that warmed his blood. The other cowboy got off his nervous, spirited horse and threw the bridle. He, too, peered closely into Gale's face.

"My name's Ladd," he said. "Reckon I'm some glad to meet you again."

Gale felt another grip as hard and strong as the other had been. He realized he had found friends who belonged to a class of men whom he had despaired of ever knowing.

"Gale—Dick Gale is my name," he began, swiftly. "I dropped into Casita to-night hardly knowing where I was. A boy took me to that hotel. There I met an old friend whom I had not seen for years. He belongs to the cavalry stationed here. He had befriended a Spanish girl—fallen in love with her. Rojas had killed this girl's father—tried to abduct her.... You know what took place at the hotel. Gentlemen, if it's ever possible, I'll show you how I appreciate what you did for me there. I got away, found my friend with the girl. We hurried out here beyond the edge of town. Then Thorne had to make a break for camp. We heard bugle calls, shots, and he was away without leave. That left the girl with me. I don't know what to do. Thorne swears Casita is no place for Mercedes at night."

"The girl ain't no peon, no common Greaser?" interrupted Ladd.

"No. Her name is Castaneda. She belongs to an old Spanish family, once rich and influential."

"Reckoned as much," replied the cowboy. "There's more than Rojas's wantin' to kidnap a pretty girl. Shore he does that every day or so. Must be somethin' political or feelin' against class. Well, Casita ain't no place for your friend's girl at night or day, or any time. Shore, there's Americans who'd take her in an' fight for her, if necessary. But it ain't wise to risk that. Lash, what do you say?"

"It's been gettin' hotter round this Greaser corral for some weeks," replied the other cowboy. "If that two-bit of a garrison surrenders, there's no tellin' what'll happen. Orozco is headin' west from Agua Prieta with his guerrillas. Campo is burnin' bridges an' tearin' up the railroad south of Nogales. Then there's all these bandits callin' themselves revolutionists just for an excuse to steal, burn, kill, an' ride off with women. It's plain facts, Laddy, an' bein' across the U.S. line a few inches or so don't make no hell of a difference. My advice is, don't let Miss Castaneda ever set foot in Casita again."

"Looks like you've shore spoke sense," said Ladd. "I reckon, Gale, you an' the girl ought to come with us. Casita shore would be a little warm for us to-morrow.

We didn't kill anybody, but I shot a Greaser's arm off, an' Lash strained friendly relations by destroyin' property. We know people who'll take care of the senorita till your friend can come for her."

Dick warmly spoke his gratefulness, and, inexpressibly relieved and happy for Mercedes, he went toward the clump of cactus where he had left her. She stood erect, waiting, and, dark as it was, he could tell she had lost the terror that had so shaken her.

"Senor Gale, you are my good angel," she said, tremulously.

"I've been lucky to fall in with these men, and I'm glad with all my heart," he replied. "Come."

He led her into the road up to the cowboys, who now stood bareheaded in the starlight. They seemed shy, and Lash was silent while Ladd made embarrassed, unintelligible reply to Mercedes's thanks.

There were five horses—two saddled, two packed, and the remaining one carried only a blanket. Ladd shortened the stirrups on his mount, and helped Mercedes up into the saddle. From the way she settled herself and took the few restive prances of the mettlesome horse Gale judged that she could ride. Lash urged Gale to take his horse. But this Gale refused to do.

"I'll walk," he said. "I'm used to walking. I know cowboys are not."

They tried again to persuade him, without avail. Then Ladd started off, riding bareback. Mercedes fell in behind, with Gale walking beside her. The two pack animals came next, and Lash brought up the rear.

Once started with protection assured for the girl and a real objective point in view, Gale relaxed from the tense strain he had been laboring under. How glad he would have been to acquaint Thorne with their good fortune! Later, of course, there would be some way to get word to the cavalryman. But till then what torments his friend would suffer!

It seemed to Dick that a very long time had elapsed since he stepped off the train; and one by one he went over every detail of incident which had occurred between that arrival and the present moment. Strange as the facts were, he had no doubts. He realized that before that night he had never known the deeps of wrath undisturbed in him; he had never conceived even a passing idea that it was possible for him to try to kill a man. His right hand was swollen stiff, so sore that he could scarcely close it. His knuckles were bruised and bleeding, and ached with a sharp pain. Considering the thickness of his heavy glove, Gale was of the opinion that so to bruise his hand he must have struck Rojas a powerful blow. He remembered that for him to give or take a blow had been nothing. This blow to Rojas, however, had been a different matter. The hot wrath which had been his motive was not puzzling; but the effect on him after he had cooled off, a subtle difference, something puzzled and eluded him. The more it baffled him the more he pondered. All those wandering months of his had been filled with dissatisfaction, yet he had been too apathetic to understand himself. So he had not been much of a person to try. Perhaps it had not been the blow to Rojas any more than other things that had wrought some change in him.

III A FLIGHT INTO THE DESERT

His meeting with Thorne; the wonderful black eyes of a Spanish girl; her appeal to him; the hate inspired by Rojas, and the rush, the blow, the action; sight of Thorne and Mercedes hurrying safely away; the girl's hand pressing his to her heaving breast; the sweet fire of her kiss; the fact of her being alone with him, dependent upon him—all these things Gale turned over and over in his mind, only to fail of any definite conclusion as to which had affected him so remarkably, or to tell what had really happened to him.

Had he fallen in love with Thorne's sweetheart? The idea came in a flash. Was he, all in an instant, and by one of those incomprehensible reversals of character, jealous of his friend? Dick was almost afraid to look up at Mercedes. Still he forced himself to do so, and as it chanced Mercedes was looking down at him. Somehow the light was better, and he clearly saw her white face, her black and starry eyes, her perfect mouth. With a quick, graceful impulsiveness she put her hand upon his shoulder. Like her appearance, the action was new, strange, striking to Gale; but it brought home suddenly to him the nature of gratitude and affection in a girl of her blood. It was sweet and sisterly. He knew then that he had not fallen in love with her. The feeling that was akin to jealousy seemed to be of the beautiful something for which Mercedes stood in Thorne's life. Gale then grasped the bewildering possibilities, the infinite wonder of what a girl could mean to a man.

The other haunting intimations of change seemed to be elusively blended with sensations—the heat and thrill of action, the sense of something done and more to do, the utter vanishing of an old weary hunt for he knew not what. Maybe it had been a hunt for work, for energy, for spirit, for love, for his real self. Whatever it might be, there appeared to be now some hope of finding it.

The desert began to lighten. Gray openings in the border of shrubby growths changed to paler hue. The road could be seen some rods ahead, and it had become a stony descent down, steadily down. Dark, ridged backs of mountains bounded the horizon, and all seemed near at hand, hemming in the plain. In the east a white glow grew brighter and brighter, reaching up to a line of cloud, defined sharply below by a rugged notched range. Presently a silver circle rose behind the black mountain, and the gloom of the desert underwent a transformation. From a gray mantle it changed to a transparent haze. The moon was rising.

"Senor I am cold," said Mercedes.

Dick had been carrying his coat upon his arm. He had felt warm, even hot, and had imagined that the steady walk had occasioned it. But his skin was cool. The heat came from an inward burning. He stopped the horse and raised the coat up, and helped Mercedes put it on.

"I should have thought of you," he said. "But I seemed to feel warm... The coat's a little large; we might wrap it round you twice."

Mercedes smiled and lightly thanked him in Spanish. The flash of mood was in direct contrast to the appealing, passionate, and tragic states in which he had successively viewed her; and it gave him a vivid impression of what vivacity and charm she might possess under happy conditions. He was about to start when he observed that Ladd had halted and was peering ahead in evident caution. Mercedes' horse began to stamp impatiently, raised his ears and head, and acted as if he was about to neigh.

A warning "hist!" from Ladd bade Dick to put a quieting hand on the horse. Lash came noiselessly forward to join his companion. The two then listened and watched.

An uneasy yet thrilling stir ran through Gale's veins. This scene was not fancy. These men of the ranges had heard or seen or scented danger. It was all real, as tangible and sure as the touch of Mercedes's hand upon his arm. Probably for her the night had terrors beyond Gale's power to comprehend. He looked down into the desert, and would have felt no surprise at anything hidden away among the bristling cactus, the dark, winding arroyos, the shadowed rocks with their moonlit tips, the ragged plain leading to the black bold mountains. The wind appeared to blow softly, with an almost imperceptible moan, over the desert. That was a new sound to Gale. But he heard nothing more.

Presently Lash went to the rear and Ladd started ahead. The progress now, however, was considerably slower, not owing to a road—for that became better—but probably owing to caution exercised by the cowboy guide. At the end of a half hour this marked deliberation changed, and the horses followed Ladd's at a gait that put Gale to his best walking-paces.

Meanwhile the moon soared high above the black corrugated peaks. The gray, the gloom, the shadow whitened. The clearing of the dark foreground appeared to lift a distant veil and show endless aisles of desert reaching down between dim horizon-bounding ranges.

Gale gazed abroad, knowing that as this night was the first time for him to awake to consciousness of a vague, wonderful other self, so it was one wherein he began to be aware of an encroaching presence of physical things—the immensity of the star-studded sky, the soaring moon, the bleak, mysterious mountains, and limitless slope, and plain, and ridge, and valley. These things in all their magnificence had not been unnoticed by him before; only now they spoke a different meaning. A voice that he had never heard called him to see, to feel the vast hard externals of heaven and earth, all that represented the open, the free, silence and solitude and space.

Once more his thoughts, like his steps, were halted by Ladd's actions. The cowboy reined in his horse, listened a moment, then swung down out of the saddle. He raised a cautioning hand to the others, then slipped into the gloom and disappeared. Gale marked that the halt had been made in a ridged and cut-up pass between low mesas. He could see the columns of cactus standing out black against the moon-white sky. The horses were evidently tiring, for they showed no impatience. Gale heard their panting breaths, and also the bark of some animal—a dog or a coyote. It sounded like a dog, and this led Gale to wonder if there was any house near at hand. To the right, up under the ledges some distance away, stood two square black objects, too uniform, he thought, to be rocks. While he was peering at them, uncertain what to think, the shrill whistle of a horse pealed out, to be followed by the rattling of hoofs on hard stone. Then a dog barked. At the same moment that Ladd hurriedly appeared in the road a light shone out and danced before one of the square black objects.

"Keep close an' don't make no noise," he whispered, and led his horse at right angles off the road.

Gale followed, leading Mercedes's horse. As he turned he observed that Lash also had dismounted.

To keep closely at Ladd's heels without brushing the cactus or stumbling over rocks and depressions was a task Gale found impossible. After he had been stabbed several times by the bayonetlike spikes, which seemed invisible, the matter of caution became equally one of self-preservation. Both the cowboys, Dick had observed, wore leather chaps. It was no easy matter to lead a spirited horse through the dark, winding lanes walled by thorns. Mercedes horse often balked and had to be coaxed and carefully guided. Dick concluded that Ladd was making a wide detour. The position of certain stars grown familiar during the march veered round from one side to another. Dick saw that the travel was fast, but by no means noiseless. The pack animals at times crashed and ripped through the narrow places. It seemed to Gale that any one within a mile could have heard these sounds. From the tops of knolls or ridges he looked back, trying to locate the mesas where the light had danced and the dog had barked alarm. He could not distinguish these two rocky eminences from among many rising in the background.

Presently Ladd let out into a wider lane that appeared to run straight. The cowboy mounted his horse, and this fact convinced Gale that they had circled back to the road. The march proceeded then once more at a good, steady, silent walk. When Dick consulted his watch he was amazed to see that the hour was still early. How much had happened in little time! He now began to be aware that the night was growing colder; and, strange to him, he felt something damp that in a country he knew he would have recognized as dew. He had not been aware there was dew on the desert. The wind blew stronger, the stars shone whiter, the sky grew darker, and the moon climbed toward the zenith. The road stretched level for miles, then crossed arroyos and ridges, wound between mounds of broken ruined rock, found a level again, and then began a long ascent. Dick asked Mercedes if she was cold, and she answered that she was, speaking especially of her feet, which were growing numb. Then she asked to be helped down to walk awhile. At first she was cold and lame, and accepted the helping hand Dick proffered. After a little, however, she recovered and went on without assistance. Dick could scarcely believe his eyes, as from time to time he stole a sidelong glance at this silent girl, who walked with lithe and rapid stride. She was wrapped in his long coat, yet it did not hide her slender grace. He could not see her face, which was concealed by the black mantle.

A low-spoken word from Ladd recalled Gale to the question of surroundings and of possible dangers. Ladd had halted a few yards ahead. They had reached the summit of what was evidently a high ridge which sloped with much greater steepness on the far side. It was only after a few more forward steps, however, that Dick could see down the slope. Then full in view flashed a bright campfire around which clustered a group of dark figures. They were encamped in a wide arroyo, where horses could be seen grazing in black patches of grass between clusters of trees. A second look at the campers told Gale they were Mexicans. At this moment Lash came forward to join Ladd, and the two spent a long, uninterrupted moment studying the arroyo. A hoarse laugh, faint yet distinct, floated up on the cool wind.

"Well, Laddy, what're you makin' of that outfit?" inquired Lash, speaking softly.

"Same as any of them raider outfits," replied Ladd. "They're across the line for beef. But they'll run off any good stock. As hoss thieves these rebels have got 'em all beat. That outfit is waitin' till it's late. There's a ranch up the arroyo."

Gale heard the first speaker curse under his breath.

"Sure, I feel the same," said Ladd. "But we've got a girl an' the young man to look after, not to mention our pack outfit. An' we're huntin' for a job, not a fight, old hoss. Keep on your chaps!"

"Nothin' to it but head south for the Rio Forlorn."

"You're talkin' sense now, Jim. I wish we'd headed that way long ago. But it ain't strange I'd want to travel away from the border, thinkin' of the girl. Jim, we can't go round this Greaser outfit an' strike the road again. Too rough. So we'll have to give up gettin' to San Felipe."

"Perhaps it's just as well, Laddy. Rio Forlorn is on the border line, but it's country where these rebels ain't been yet."

"Wait till they learn of the oasis an' Beldin's hosses!" exclaimed Laddy. "I'm not anticipatin' peace anywhere along the border, Jim. But we can't go ahead; we can't go back."

"What'll we do, Laddy? It's a hike to Beldin's ranch. An' if we get there in daylight some Greaser will see the girl before Beldin' can hide her. It'll get talked about. The news'll travel to Casita like sage balls before the wind."

"Shore we won't ride into Rio Forlorn in the daytime. Let's slip the packs, Jim. We can hid them off in the cactus an' come back after them. With the young man ridin' we—"

The whispering was interrupted by a loud ringing neigh that whistled up from the arroyo. One of the horses had scented the travelers on the ridge top. The indifference of the Mexicans changed to attention.

Ladd and Lash turned back and led the horses into the first opening on the south side of the road. There was nothing more said at the moment, and manifestly the cowboys were in a hurry. Gale had to run in the open places to keep up. When they did stop it was welcome to Gale, for he had begun to fall behind.

The packs were slipped, securely tied and hidden in a mesquite clump. Ladd strapped a blanket around one of the horses. His next move was to take off his chaps.

"Gale, you're wearin' boots, an' by liftin' your feet you can beat the cactus," he whispered. "But the—the—Miss Castaneda, she'll be torn all to pieces unless she puts these on. Please tell her—an' hurry."

Dick took the caps, and, going up to Mercedes, he explained the situation. She laughed, evidently at his embarrassed earnestness, and slipped out of the saddle.

"Senor, chapparejos and I are not strangers," she said.

Deftly and promptly she equipped herself, and then Gale helped her into the saddle, called to her horse, and started off. Lash directed Gale to mount the other saddled horse and go next.

Dick had not ridden a hundred yards behind the trotting leaders before he had sundry painful encounters with reaching cactus arms. The horse missed these by a narrow margin. Dick's knees appeared to be in line, and it became necessary for him to lift them high and let his boots take the onslaught of the spikes. He was at home in the saddle, and the accomplishment was about the only one he possessed that had been of any advantage during his sojourn in the West.

Ladd pursued a zigzag course southward across the desert, trotting down the aisles, cantering in wide, bare patches, walking through the clumps of cacti. The desert seemed all of a sameness to Dick—a wilderness of rocks and jagged growths hemmed in by lowering ranges, always looking close, yet never growing any nearer. The moon slanted back toward the west, losing its white radiance, and the gloom of the earlier evening began to creep into the washes and to darken under the mesas. By and by Ladd entered an arroyo, and here the travelers turned and twisted with the meanderings of a dry stream bed. At the head of a canyon they had to take once more to the rougher ground. Always it led down, always it grew rougher, more rolling, with wider bare spaces, always the black ranges loomed close.

Gale became chilled to the bone, and his clothes were damp and cold. His knees smarted from the wounds of the poisoned thorns, and his right hand was either swollen stiff or too numb to move. Moreover, he was tiring. The excitement, the long walk, the miles on miles of jolting trot—these had wearied him. Mercedes must be made of steel, he thought, to stand all that she had been subjected to and yet, when the stars were paling and dawn perhaps not far away, stay in the saddle.

So Dick Gale rode on, drowsier for each mile, and more and more giving the horse a choice of ground. Sometimes a prod from a murderous spine roused Dick. A grayness had blotted out the waning moon in the west and the clear, dark, starry sky overhead. Once when Gale, thinking to fight his weariness, raised his head, he saw that one of the horses in the lead was riderless. Ladd was carrying Mercedes. Dick marveled that her collapse had not come sooner. Another time, rousing himself again, he imagined they were now on a good hard road.

It seemed that hours passed, though he knew only little time had elapsed, when once more he threw off the spell of weariness. He heard a dog bark. Tall trees lined the open lane down which he was riding. Presently in the gray gloom he saw low, square houses with flat roofs. Ladd turned off to the left down another lane, gloomy between trees. Every few rods there was one of the squat houses. This lane opened into wider, lighter space. The cold air bore a sweet perfume—whether of flowers or fruit Dick could not tell. Ladd rode on for perhaps a quarter of a mile, though it seemed interminably long to Dick. A grove of trees loomed dark in the gray morning. Ladd entered it and was lost in the shade. Dick rode on among trees. Presently he heard voices, and soon another house, low and flat like the others, but so long he could not see the farther end, stood up blacker than the trees. As he dismounted, cramped and sore, he could scarcely stand. Lash came alongside. He spoke, and some one with a big, hearty voice replied to him. Then it seemed to Dick that he was led into blackness like pitch, where, presently, he felt blankets thrown on him and then his drowsy faculties faded.

IV FORLORN RIVER

WHEN Dick opened his eyes a flood of golden sunshine streamed in at the open window under which he lay. His first thought was one of blank wonder as to where in the world he happened to be. The room was large, square, adobe-walled. It was littered with saddles, harness, blankets. Upon the floor was a bed spread out upon a tarpaulin. Probably this was where some one had slept. The sight of huge dusty spurs, a gun belt with sheath and gun, and a pair of leather chaps bristling with broken cactus thorns recalled to Dick the cowboys, the ride, Mercedes, and the whole strange adventure that had brought him there.

He did not recollect having removed his boots; indeed, upon second thought, he knew he had not done so. But there they stood upon the floor. Ladd and Lash must have taken them off when he was so exhausted and sleepy that he could not tell what was happening. He felt a dead weight of complete lassitude, and he did not want to move. A sudden pain in his hand caused him to hold it up. It was black and blue, swollen to almost twice its normal size, and stiff as a board. The knuckles were skinned and crusted with dry blood. Dick soliloquized that it was the worst-looking hand he had seen since football days, and that it would inconvenience him for some time.

A warm, dry, fragrant breeze came through the window. Dick caught again the sweet smell of flowers or fruit. He heard the fluttering of leaves, the murmur of running water, the twittering of birds, then the sound of approaching footsteps and voices. The door at the far end of the room was open. Through it he saw poles of peeled wood upholding a porch roof, a bench, rose bushes in bloom, grass, and beyond these bright-green foliage of trees.

"He shore was sleepin' when I looked in an hour ago," said a voice that Dick recognized as Ladd's.

"Let him sleep," came the reply in deep, good-natured tones. "Mrs. B. says the girl's never moved. Must have been a tough ride for them both. Forty miles through cactus!"

"Young Gale hoofed darn near half the way," replied Ladd. "We tried to make him ride one of our hosses. If we had, we'd never got here. A walk like that'd killed me an' Jim."

"Well, Laddy, I'm right down glad to see you boys, and I'll do all I can for the young couple," said the other. "But I'm doing some worry here; don't mistake me."

"About your stock?"

"I've got only a few head of cattle at the oasis now, I'm worrying some, mostly about my horses. The U. S. is doing some worrying, too, don't mistake me. The rebels have worked west and north as far as Casita. There are no cavalrymen along the line beyond Casita, and there can't be. It's practically waterless desert. But these rebels are desert men. They could cross the line beyond the Rio Forlorn and smuggle arms into Mexico. Of course, my job is to keep tab on Chinese and Japs trying to get into the U.S. from Magdalena Bay. But I'm supposed to patrol the border line. I'm going to hire some rangers. Now, I'm not so afraid of being shot up, though out in this lonely place there's danger of it; what I'm afraid of most is losing that bunch of horses. If any rebels come this far, or if they ever hear of my horses, they're going to raid me. You know what those guerrilla Mexicans will do for horses. They're crazy on horse flesh. They know fine horses. They breed the finest in the world. So I don't sleep nights any more."

"Reckon me an' Jim might as well tie up with your for a spell, Beldin'. We've been ridin' up an' down Arizona tryin' to keep out of sight of wire fences."

"Laddy, it's open enough around Forlorn River to satisfy even an old-time cowpuncher like you," laughed Belding. "I'd take your staying on as some favor, don't mistake me. Perhaps I can persuade the young man Gale to take a job with me."

"That's shore likely. He said he had no money, no friends. An' if a scrapper's all you're lookin' for he'll do," replied Ladd, with a dry chuckle.

"Mrs. B. will throw some broncho capers round this ranch when she hears I'm going to hire a stranger."

"Why?"

"Well, there's Nell— And you said this Gale was a young American. My wife will be scared to death for fear Nell will fall in love with him."

Laddy choked off a laugh, then evidently slapped his knee or Belding's, for there was a resounding smack.

"He's a fine-spoken, good-looking chap, you said?" went on Belding.

"Shore he is," said Laddy, warmly. "What do you say, Jim?"

By this time Dick Gale's ears began to burn and he was trying to make himself deaf when he wanted to hear every little word.

"Husky young fellow, nice voice, steady, clear eyes, kinda proud, I thought, an' some handsome, he was," replied Jim Lash.

"Maybe I ought to think twice before taking a stranger into my family," said Belding, seriously. "Well, I guess he's all right, Laddy, being the cavalryman's friend. No bum or lunger? He must be all right?"

"Bum? Lunger? Say, didn't I tell you I shook hands with this boy an' was plumb glad to meet him?" demanded Laddy, with considerable heat. Manifestly he had been affronted. "Tom Beldin', he's a gentleman, an' he could lick you in—in half a second. How about that, Jim?"

"Less time," replied Lash. "Tom, here's my stand. Young Gale can have my hoss, my gun, anythin' of mine."

"Aw, I didn't mean to insult you, boys, don't mistake me," said Belding. "Course he's all right."

The object of this conversation lay quiet upon his bed, thrilling and amazed at being so championed by the cowboys, delighted with Belding's idea of employing him, and much amused with the quaint seriousness of the three.

"How's the young man?" called a woman's voice. It was kind and mellow and earnest.

Gale heard footsteps on flagstones.

"He's asleep yet, wife," replied Belding. "Guess he was pretty much knocked out.... I'll close the door there so we won't wake him."

There were slow, soft steps, then the door softly closed. But the fact scarcely made a perceptible difference in the sound of the voices outside.

"Laddy and Jim are going to stay," went on Belding. "It'll be like the old Panhandle days a little. I'm powerful glad to have the boys, Nellie. You know I meant to sent to Casita to ask them. We'll see some trouble before the revolution is ended. I think I'll make this young man Gale an offer."

"He isn't a cowboy?" asked Mrs. Belding, quickly.

"No."

"Shore he'd make a darn good one," put in Laddy.

"What is he? Who is he? Where did he come from? Surely you must be—"

"Laddy swears he's all right," interrupted the husband. "That's enough reference for me. Isn't it enough for you?"

"Humph! Laddy knows a lot about young men, now doesn't he, especially strangers from the East?... Tom, you must be careful!"

"Wife, I'm only too glad to have a nervy young chap come along. What sense is there in your objection, if Jim and Laddy stick up for him?"

"But, Tom—he'll fall in love with Nell!" protested Mrs. Belding.

"Well, wouldn't that be regular? Doesn't every man who comes along fall in love with Nell? Hasn't it always happened? When she was a schoolgirl in Kansas didn't it happen? Didn't she have a hundred moon-eyed ninnies after her in Texas? I've had some peace out here in the desert, except when a Greaser or a prospector or a Yaqui would come along. Then same old story—in love with Nell!"

"But, Tom, Nell might fall in love with this young man!" exclaimed the wife, in distress.

"Laddy, Jim, didn't I tell you?" cried Belding. "I knew she'd say that.... My dear wife, I would be simply overcome with joy if Nell did fall in love once. Real good and hard! She's wilder than any antelope out there on the desert. Nell's nearly twenty now, and so far as we know she's never cared a rap for any fellow. And she's just as gay and full of the devil as she was at fourteen. Nell's as good and lovable as she is pretty, but I'm afraid she'll never grow into a woman while we live out in this lonely land. And you've always hated towns where there was a chance for the girl—just because you were afraid she'd fall in love. You've always been strange, even silly, about that. I've done my best for Nell—loved her as if she were my own daughter. I've changed many business plans to suit your whims. There are rough times ahead, maybe. I need men. I'll hire this chap Gale if he'll stay. Let Nell take her chance with him, just as she'll have to take chances with men when we get out of the desert. She'll be all the better for it."

"I hope Laddy's not mistaken in his opinion of this newcomer," replied Mrs. Belding, with a sigh of resignation.

"Shore I never made a mistake in my life figger'n' people," said Laddy, stoutly.

"Yes, you have, Laddy," replied Mrs. Belding. "You're wrong about Tom.... Well, supper is to be got. That young man and the girl will be starved. I'll go in now. If Nell happens around don't—don't flatter her, Laddy, like you did at dinner. Don't make her think of her looks."

Dick heard Mrs. Belding walk away.

"Shore she's powerful particular about that girl," observed Laddy. "Say, Tom, Nell knows she's pretty, doesn't she?"

"She's liable to find it out unless you shut up, Laddy. When you visited us out here some weeks ago, you kept paying cowboy compliments to her."

"An' it's your idea that cowboy compliments are plumb bad for girls?"

"Downright bad, Laddy, so my wife says."

"I'll be darned if I believe any girl can be hurt by a little sweet talk. It pleases 'em.... But say, Beldin', speaking of looks, have you got a peek yet at the Spanish girl?"

"Not in the light."

"Well, neither have I in daytime. I had enough by moonlight. Nell is some on looks, but I'm regretful passin' the ribbon to the lady from Mex. Jim, where are you?"

"My money's on Nell," replied Lash. "Gimme a girl with flesh an' color, an' blue eyes a-laughin'. Miss Castaneda is some peach, I'll not gainsay. But her face seemed too white. An' when she flashed those eyes on me, I thought I was shot! When she stood up there at first, thankin' us, I felt as if a—a princess was round somewhere. Now, Nell is kiddish an' sweet an'—"

"Chop it," interrupted Belding. "Here comes Nell now."

Dick's tingling ears took in the pattering of light footsteps, the rush of some one running.

"Here you are," cried a sweet, happy voice. "Dad, the Senorita is perfectly lovely. I've been peeping at her. She sleeps like—like death. She's so white. Oh, I hope she won't be ill."

"Shore she's only played out," said Laddy. "But she had spunk while it lasted.... I was just arguin' with Jim an' Tom about Miss Castaneda."

"Gracious! Why, she's beautiful. I never saw any one so beautiful.... How strange and sad, that about her! Tell me more, Laddy. You promised. I'm dying to know. I never hear anything in this awful place. Didn't you say the Senorita had a sweetheart?"

"Shore I did."

"And he's a cavalryman?"

"Yes."

"Is he the young man who came with you?"

"Nope. That fellow's the one who saved the girl from Rojas."

"Ah! Where is he, Laddy?"

"He's in there asleep."

"Is he hurt?"

"I reckon not. He walked about fifteen miles."

"Is he—nice, Laddy?"

"Shore."

"What is he like?"

"Well, I'm not long acquainted, never saw him by day, but I was some tolerable took with him. An' Jim here, Jim says the young man can have his gun an' his hoss."

"Wonderful! Laddy, what on earth did this stranger do to win you cowboys in just one night?"

"I'll shore have to tell you. Me an' Jim were watchin' a game of cards in the Del Sol saloon in Casita. That's across the line. We had acquaintances—four fellows from the Cross Bar outfit, where we worked a while back. This Del Sol is a billiard hall, saloon, restaurant, an' the like. An' it was full of Greasers. Some of Camp's rebels were there drinkin' an' playin' games. Then pretty soon in come Rojas with some of his outfit. They were packin' guns an' kept to themselves off to one side. I didn't give them a second look till Jim said he reckoned there was somethin' in the wind. Then, careless-like, I began to peek at Rojas. They call Rojas the 'dandy rebel,' an' he shore looked the part. It made me sick to see him in all that lace an' glitter, knowin' him to be the cutthroat robber he is. It's no oncommon sight to see excited Greasers. They're all crazy. But this bandit was shore some agitated. He kept his men in a tight bunch round a table. He talked an' waved his hands. He was actually shakin'. His eyes had a wild glare. Now I figgered that trouble was brewin', most likely for the little Casita garrison. People seemed to think Campo an' Rojas would join forces to oust the federals. Jim thought Rojas's excitement was at the hatchin' of some plot. Anyway, we didn't join no card games, an' without pretendin' to, we was some watchful.

"A little while afterward I seen a fellow standin' in the restaurant door. He was a young American dressed in corduroys and boots, like a prospector. You know it's no onusual fact to see prospectors in these parts. What made me think twice about this one was how big he seemed, how he filled up that door. He looked round the saloon, an' when he spotted Rojas he sorta jerked up. Then he pulled his slouch hat lopsided an' began to stagger down, down the steps. First off I made shore he was drunk. But I remembered he didn't seem drunk before. It was some queer. So I watched that young man.

"He reeled around the room like a fellow who was drunker'n a lord. Nobody but me seemed to notice him. Then he began to stumble over pool-players an' get his feet tangled up in chairs an' bump against tables. He got some pretty hard looks. He came round our way, an' all of a sudden he seen us cowboys. He gave another start, like the one when he first seen Rojas, then he made for us. I tipped Jim off that somethin' was doin'.

"When he got close he straightened up, put back his slouch hat, an' looked at us. Then I saw his face. It sorta electrified yours truly. It was white, with veins standin' out an' eyes flamin'—a face of fury. I was plumb amazed, didn't know what to think. Then this queer young man shot some cool, polite words at me an' Jim.

"He was only bluffin' at bein' drunk—he meant to rush Rojas, to start a rough house. The bandit was after a girl. This girl was in the hotel, an' she was the sweetheart of a soldier, the young fellow's friend. The hotel was watched by Rojas's guards, an' the plan was to make a fuss an' get the girl away in the excitement. Well, Jim an' me got a hint of our bein' Americans—that cowboys generally had a name for loyalty to women. Then this amazin' chap—you can't imagine how scornful—said for me an' Jim to watch him.

"Before I could catch my breath an' figger out what he meant by 'rush' an' 'rough house' he had knocked over a table an' crowded some Greaser half off the map. One little funny man leaped up like a wild monkey an' began to screech. An' in another second he was in the air upside down. When he lit, he laid there. Then, quicker'n I can tell you, the young man dove at Rojas. Like a mad steer on the rampage he charged Rojas an' his men. The whole outfit went down—smash! I figgered then what 'rush' meant. The young fellow came up out of the pile with Rojas, an' just like I'd sling an empty sack along the floor he sent the bandit. But swift as that went he was on top of Rojas before the chairs an' tables had stopped rollin'.

"I woke up then, an' made for the center of the room. Jim with me. I began to shoot out the lamps. Jim throwed his guns on the crazy rebels, an' I was afraid there'd be blood spilled before I could get the room dark. Bein's shore busy, I lost sight of the young fellow for a second or so, an' when I got an eye free for him I seen a Greaser about to knife him. Think I was some considerate of the Greaser by only shootin' his arm off. Then I cracked the last lamp, an' in the hullabaloo me an' Jim vamoosed.

"We made tracks for our hosses an' packs, an' was hittin' the San Felipe road when we run right plumb into the young man. Well, he said his name was Gale—Dick Gale. The girl was with him safe an' well; but her sweetheart, the soldier, bein' away without leave, had to go back sudden. There shore was some trouble, for Jim an' me heard shootin'. Gale said he had no money, no friends, was a stranger in a desert country; an' he was distracted to know how to help the girl. So me an' Jim started off with them for San Felipe, got switched, and' then we headed for the Rio Forlorn."

"Oh, I think he was perfectly splendid!" exclaimed the girl.

"Shore he was. Only, Nell, you can't lay no claim to bein' the original discoverer of that fact."

"But, Laddy, you haven't told me what he looks like."

At this juncture Dick Gale felt it absolutely impossible for him to play the eavesdropper any longer. Quietly he rolled out of bed. The voices still sounded close outside, and it was only by effort that he kept from further listening. Belding's kindly interest, Laddy's blunt and sincere cowboy eulogy, the girl's sweet eagerness and praise—these warmed Gale's heart. He had fallen among simple people, into whose lives the advent of an unknown man was welcome. He found himself in a singularly agitated mood. The excitement, the thrill, the difference felt in himself, experienced the preceding night, had extended on into his present. And the possibilities suggested by the conversation he had unwittingly overheard added sufficiently to the other feelings to put him into a peculiarly receptive state of mind. He was wild to be one of the Belding rangers. The idea of riding a horse in the open desert, with a dangerous duty to perform, seemed to strike him with an appealing force. Something within him went out to the cowboys, to this blunt and kind Belding. He was afraid to meet the girl. If every man who came along fell in love with this sweet-voiced Nell, then what hope had he to escape—now, when his whole inner awakening betokened a change of spirit, hope, a finding of real worth, real good, real power in himself? He did not understand wholly, yet he felt ready to ride, to fight, to love the desert, to love these outdoor men, to love a woman. That beautiful Spanish girl had spoken to something dead in him and it had quickened to life. The sweet voice of an audacious, unseen girl warned him that presently a still more wonderful thing would happen to him.

Gale imagined he made noise enough as he clumsily pulled on his boots, yet the voices, split by a merry laugh, kept on murmuring outside the door. It was awkward for him, having only one hand available to lace up his boots. He looked out of the window. Evidently this was at the end of the house. There was a flagstone walk, beside which ran a ditch full of swift, muddy water. It made a pleasant sound. There were trees strange of form and color to to him. He heard bees, birds, chickens, saw the red of roses and green of grass. Then he saw, close to the wall, a tub full of water, and a bench upon which lay basin, soap, towel, comb, and brush. The window was also a door, for under it there was a step.

Gale hesitated a moment, then went out. He stepped naturally, hoping and expecting that the cowboys would hear him. But nobody came. Awkwardly, with left hand, he washed his face. Upon a nail in the wall hung a little mirror, by the aid of which Dick combed and brushed his hair. He imagined he looked a most haggard wretch. With that he faced forward, meaning to go round the corner of the house to greet the cowboys and these new-found friends.

Dick had taken but one step when he was halted by laugher and the patter of light feet.

From close around the corner pealed out that sweet voice. "Dad, you'll have your wish, and mama will be wild!"

Dick saw a little foot sweep into view, a white dress, then the swiftly moving form of a girl. She was looking backward.

"Dad, I shall fall in love with your new ranger. I will—I have—"

Then she plumped squarely into Dick's arms.

She started back violently.

Dick saw a fair face and dark-blue, audaciously flashing eyes. Swift as lightning their expression changed to surprise, fear, wonder. For an instant they were level with Dick's grave questioning. Suddenly, sweetly, she blushed.

"Oh-h!" she faltered.

Then the blush turned to a scarlet fire. She whirled past him, and like a white gleam was gone.

Dick became conscious of the quickened beating of his heart. He experienced a singular exhilaration. That moment had been the one for which he had been ripe, the event upon which strange circumstances had been rushing him.

With a couple of strides he turned the corner. Laddy and Lash were there talking to a man of burly form. Seen by day, both cowboys were gray-haired, red-skinned, and weather-beaten, with lean, sharp features, and gray eyes so much alike that they might have been brothers.

"Hello, there's the young fellow," spoke up the burly man. "Mr. Gale, I'm glad to meet you. My name's Belding."

His greeting was as warm as his handclasp was long and hard. Gale saw a heavy man of medium height. His head was large and covered with grizzled locks. He wore a short-cropped mustache and chin beard. His skin was brown, and his dark eyes beamed with a genial light.

The cowboys were as cordial as if Dick had been their friend for years.

"Young man, did you run into anything as you came out?" asked Belding, with twinkling eyes.

"Why, yes, I met something white and swift flying by," replied Dick.

"Did she see you?" asked Laddy.

"I think so; but she didn't wait for me to introduce myself."

"That was Nell Burton, my girl—step-daughter, I should say," said Belding. "She's sure some whirlwind, as Laddy calls her. Come, let's go in and meet the wife."

The house was long, like a barracks, with porch extending all the way, and doors every dozen paces. When Dick was ushered into a sitting-room, he was amazed at the light and comfort. This room had two big windows and a door opening into a patio, where there were luxuriant grass, roses in bloom, and flowering trees. He heard a slow splashing of water.

In Mrs. Belding, Gale found a woman of noble proportions and striking appearance. Her hair was white. She had a strong, serious, well-lined face that bore haunting evidences of past beauty. The gaze she bent upon him was almost piercing in its intensity. Her greeting, which seemed to Dick rather slow in coming, was kind though not cordial. Gale's first thought, after he had thanked these good people for their hospitality, was to inquire about Mercedes. He was informed that the Spanish girl had awakened with a considerable fever and nervousness. When, however, her anxiety had been allayed and her thirst relieved, she had fallen asleep again. Mrs. Belding said the girl had suffered no great hardship, other than mental, and would very soon be rested and well.

"Now, Gale," said Belding, when his wife had excused herself to get supper, "the boys, Jim and Laddy, told me about you and the mix-up at Casita. I'll be glad to take care of the girl till it's safe for your soldier friend to get her out of the country. That won't be very soon, don't mistake me.... I don't want to seem over-curious about you—Laddy has interested me in you—and straight out I'd like to know what you propose to do now."

"I haven't any plans," replied Dick; and, taking the moment as propitious, he decided to speak frankly concerning himself. "I just drifted down here. My home is in Chicago. When I left school some years ago—I'm twenty-five now—I went to work for my father. He's—he has business interests there. I tried all kinds of inside jobs. I couldn't please my father. I guess I put no real heart in my work. The fact was I didn't know how to work. The governor and I didn't exactly quarrel; but he hurt my feelings, and I quit. Six months or more ago I came West, and have knocked about from Wyoming southwest to the border. I tried to find congenial work, but nothing came my way. To tell you frankly, Mr. Belding, I suppose I didn't much care. I believe, though, that all the time I didn't know what I wanted. I've learned—well, just lately—"

"What do you want to do?" interposed Belding.

"I want a man's job. I want to do things with my hands. I want action. I want to be outdoors."

Belding nodded his head as if he understood that, and he began to speak again, cut something short, then went on, hesitatingly:

"Gale—you could go home again—to the old man—it'd be all right?"

"Mr. Belding, there's nothing shady in my past. The governor would be glad to have me home. That's the only consolation I've got. But I'm not going. I'm broke. I won't be a tramp. And it's up to me to do something."

"How'd you like to be a border ranger?" asked Belding, laying a hand on Dick's knee. "Part of my job here is United States Inspector of Immigration. I've got that boundary line to patrol—to keep out Chinks and Japs. This revolution has added complications, and I'm looking for smugglers and raiders here any day. You'll not be hired by the U. S. You'll simply be my ranger, same as Laddy and Jim, who have promised to work for me. I'll pay you well, give you a room here, furnish everything down to guns, and the finest horse you ever saw in your life. Your job won't be safe and healthy, sometimes, but it'll be a man's job—don't mistake me! You can gamble on having things to do outdoors. Now, what do you say?"

"I accept, and I thank you—I can't say how much," replied Gale, earnestly.

"Good! That's settled. Let's go out and tell Laddy and Jim."

Both boys expressed satisfaction at the turn of affairs, and then with Belding they set out to take Gale around the ranch. The house and several outbuildings were constructed of adobe, which, according to Belding, retained the summer heat on into winter, and the winter cold on into summer. These gray-red mud habitations were hideous to look at, and this fact, perhaps, made their really comfortable interiors more vividly a contrast. The wide grounds were covered with luxuriant grass and flowers and different kinds of trees. Gale's interest led him to ask about fig trees and pomegranates, and especially about a beautiful specimen that Belding called palo verde.

Belding explained that the luxuriance of this desert place was owing to a few springs and the dammed-up waters of the Rio Forlorn. Before he had come to the oasis it had been inhabited by a Papago Indian tribe and a few peon families. The oasis lay in an arroyo a mile wide, and sloped southwest for some ten miles or more. The river went dry most of the year; but enough water was stored in flood season to irrigate the gardens and alfalfa fields.

"I've got one never-failing spring on my place," said Belding. "Fine, sweet water! You know what that means in the desert. I like this oasis. The longer I live here the better I like it. There's not a spot in southern Arizona that'll compare with this valley for water or grass or wood. It's beautiful and healthy. Forlorn and lonely, yes, especially for women like my wife and Nell; but I like it.... And between you and me, boys, I've got something up my sleeve. There's gold dust in the arroyos, and there's mineral up in the mountains. If we only had water! This hamlet has steadily grown since I took up a station here. Why, Casita is no place beside Forlorn River. Pretty soon the Southern Pacific will shoot a railroad branch out here. There are possibilities, and I want you boys to stay with me and get in on the ground floor. I wish this rebel war was over.... Well, here are the corrals and the fields. Gale, take a look at that bunch of horses!"

Belding's last remark was made as he led his companions out of shady gardens into the open. Gale saw an adobe shed and a huge pen fenced by strangely twisted and contorted branches or trunks of mesquite, and, beyond these, wide, flat fields, green—a dark, rich green—and dotted with beautiful horses. There were whites and blacks, and bays and grays. In his admiration Gale searched his memory to see if he could remember the like of these magnificent animals, and had to admit that the only ones he could compare with them were the Arabian steeds.

"Every ranch loves his horses," said Belding. "When I was in the Panhandle I had some fine stock. But these are Mexican. They came from Durango, where they were bred. Mexican horses are the finest in the world, bar none."

"Shore I reckon I savvy why you don't sleep nights," drawled Laddy. "I see a Greaser out there—no, it's an Indian."

"That's my Papago herdsman. I keep watch over the horses now day and night. Lord, how I'd hate to have Rojas or Salazar—any of those bandit rebels—find my horses!... Gale, can you ride?"

Dick modestly replied that he could, according to the Eastern idea of horsemanship.

"You don't need to be half horse to ride one of that bunch. But over there in the other field I've iron-jawed broncos I wouldn't want you to tackle—except to see the fun. I've an outlaw I'll gamble even Laddy can't ride."

"So. How much'll you gamble?" asked Laddy, instantly.

The ringing of a bell, which Belding said was a call to supper, turned the men back toward the house. Facing that way, Gale saw dark, beetling ridges rising from the oasis and leading up to bare, black mountains. He had heard Belding call them No Name Mountains, and somehow the appellation suited those lofty, mysterious, frowning peaks.

It was not until they reached the house and were about to go in that Belding chanced to discover Gale's crippled hand.

"What an awful hand!" he exclaimed. "Where the devil did you get that?"

"I stove in my knuckles on Rojas," replied Dick.

"You did that in one punch? Say, I'm glad it wasn't me you hit! Why didn't you tell me? That's a bad hand. Those cuts are full of dirt and sand. Inflammation's setting in. It's got to be dressed. Nell!" he called.

There was no answer. He called again, louder.

"Mother, where's the girl?"

"She's there in the dining-room," replied Mrs. Belding.

"Did she hear me?" he inquired, impatiently.

"Of course."

"Nell!" roared Belding.

This brought results. Dick saw a glimpse of golden hair and a white dress in the door. But they were not visible longer than a second.

"Dad, what's the matter?" asked a voice that was still as sweet as formerly, but now rather small and constrained.

"Bring the antiseptics, cotton, bandages—and things out here. Hurry now."

Belding fetched a pail of water and a basin from the kitchen. His wife followed him out, and, upon seeing Dick's hand, was all solicitude. Then Dick heard light, quick footsteps, but he did not look up.

"Nell, this is Mr. Gale—Dick Gale, who came with the boys last last night," said Belding. "He's got an awful hand. Got it punching that greaser Rojas. I want you to dress it.... Gale, this is my step-daughter, Nell Burton, of whom I spoke. She's some good when there's somebody sick or hurt. Shove out your fist, my boy, and let her get at it. Supper's nearly ready."

Dick felt that same strange, quickening heart throb, yet he had never been cooler in his life. More than anything else in the world he wanted to look at Nell Burton; however, divining that the situation might be embarrassing to her, he refrained from looking up. She began to bathe his injured knuckles. He noted the softness, the deftness of her touch, and then it seemed her fingers were not quite as steady as they might have been. Still, in a moment they appeared to become surer in their work. She had beautiful hands, not too large, though certainly not small, and they were strong, brown, supple. He observed next, with stealthy, upward-stealing glance, that she had rolled up her sleeves, exposing fine, round arms graceful in line. Her skin was brown—no, it was more gold than brown. It had a wonderful clear tint. Dick stoically lowered his eyes then, putting off as long as possible the alluring moment when he was to look into her face. That would be a fateful moment. He played with a certain strange joy of anticipation. When, however, she sat down beside him and rested his injured hand in her lap as she cut bandages, she was so thrillingly near that he yielded to an irrepressible desire to look up. She had a sweet, fair face warmly tinted with that same healthy golden-brown sunburn. Her hair was light gold and abundant, a waving mass. Her eyes were shaded by long, downcast lashes, yet through them he caught a gleam of blue.

Despite the stir within him, Gale, seeing she was now absorbed in her task, critically studied her with a second closer gaze. She was a sweet, wholesome, joyous, pretty girl.

"Shore it musta hurt?" replied Laddy, who sat an interested spectator.

"Yes, I confess it did," replied Dick, slowly, with his eyes on Nell's face. "But I didn't mind."

The girl's lashes swept up swiftly in surprise. She had taken his words literally. But the dark-blue eyes met his for only a fleeting second. Then the warm tint in her cheeks turned as red as her lips. Hurriedly she finished tying the bandage and rose to her feet.

"I thank you," said Gale, also rising.

With that Belding appeared in the doorway, and finding the operation concluded, called them in to supper. Dick had the use of only one arm, and he certainly was keenly aware of the shy, silent girl across the table; but in spite of these considerable handicaps he eclipsed both hungry cowboys in the assault upon Mrs. Belding's bounteous supper. Belding talked, the cowboys talked more or less. Mrs. Belding put in a word now and then, and Dick managed to find brief intervals when it was possible for him to say yes or no. He observed gratefully that no one round the table seemed to be aware of his enormous appetite.

After supper, having a favorable opportunity when for a moment no one was at hand, Dick went out through the yard, past the gardens and fields, and climbed the first knoll. From that vantage point he looked out over the little hamlet, somewhat to his right, and was surprised at its extent, its considerable number of adobe houses. The overhanging mountains, ragged and darkening, a great heave of splintered rock, rather chilled and affronted him.

Westward the setting sun gilded a spiked, frost-colored, limitless expanse of desert. It awed Gale. Everywhere rose blunt, broken ranges or isolated groups of mountains. Yet the desert stretched away down between and beyond them. When the sun set and Gale could not see so far, he felt a relief.

That grand and austere attraction of distance gone, he saw the desert nearer at hand—the valley at his feet. What a strange gray, somber place! There was a lighter strip of gray winding down between darker hues. This he realized presently was the river bed, and he saw how the pools of water narrowed and diminished in size till they lost themselves in gray sand. This was the rainy season, near its end, and here a little river struggled hopelessly, forlornly to live in the desert. He received a potent impression of the nature of that blasted age-worn waste which he had divined was to give him strength and work and love.

V A DESERT ROSE

BELDING assigned Dick to a little room which had no windows but two doors, one opening into the patio, the other into the yard on the west side of the house. It contained only the barest necessities for comfort. Dick mentioned the baggage he had left in the hotel at Casita, and it was Belding's opinion that to try to recover his property would be rather risky; on the moment Richard Gale was probably not popular with the Mexicans at Casita. So Dick bade good-by to fine suits of clothes and linen with a feeling that, as he had said farewell to an idle and useless past, it was just as well not to have any old luxuries as reminders. As he possessed, however, not a thing save the clothes on his back, and not even a handkerchief, he expressed regret that he had come to Forlorn River a beggar.

"Beggar hell!" exploded Belding, with his eyes snapping in the lamplight. "Money's the last thing we think of out here. All the same, Gale, if you stick you'll be rich."

"It wouldn't surprise me," replied Dick, thoughtfully. But he was not thinking of material wealth. Then, as he viewed his stained and torn shirt, he laughed and said "Belding, while I'm getting rich I'd like to have some respectable clothes."

"We've a little Mex store in town, and what you can't get there the women folks will make for you."

When Dick lay down he was dully conscious of pain and headache, that he did not feel well. Despite this, and a mind thronging with memories and anticipations, he succumbed to weariness and soon fell asleep.

It was light when he awoke, but a strange brightness seen through what seemed blurred eyes. A moment passed before his mind worked clearly, and then he had to make an effort to think. He was dizzy. When he essayed to lift his right arm, an excruciating pain made him desist. Then he discovered that his arm was badly swollen, and the hand had burst its bandages. The injured member was red, angry, inflamed, and twice its normal size. He felt hot all over, and a raging headache consumed him.

Belding came stamping into the room.

"Hello, Dick. Do you know it's late? How's the busted fist this morning?"

Dick tried to sit up, but his effort was a failure. He got about half up, then felt himself weakly sliding back.

"I guess—I'm pretty sick," he said.

He saw Belding lean over him, feel his face, and speak, and then everything seemed to drift, not into darkness, but into some region where he had dim perceptions of gray moving things, and of voices that were remote. Then there came an interval when all was blank. He knew not whether it was one of minutes or hours, but after it he had a clearer mind. He slept, awakened during night-time, and slept again. When he again unclosed his eyes the room was sunny, and cool with a fragrant breeze that blew through the open door. Dick felt better; but he had no particular desire to move or talk or eat. He had, however, a burning thirst. Mrs. Belding visited him often; her husband came in several times, and once Nell slipped in noiselessly. Even this last event aroused no interest in Dick.

On the next day he was very much improved.

"We've been afraid of blood poisoning," said Belding. "But my wife thinks the danger's past. You'll have to rest that arm for a while."

Ladd and Jim came peeping in at the door.

"Come in, boys. He can have company—the more the better—if it'll keep him content. He mustn't move, that's all."

The cowboys entered, slow, easy, cool, kind-voiced.

"Shore it's tough," said Ladd, after he had greeted Dick. "You look used up."

Jim Lash wagged his half-bald, sunburned head, "Musta been more'n tough for Rojas."

"Gale, Laddy tells me one of our neighbors, fellow named Carter, is going to Casita," put in Belding. "Here's a chance to get word to your friend the soldier."

"Oh, that will be fine!" exclaimed Dick. "I declare I'd forgotten Thorne.... How is Miss Castaneda? I hope—"

"She's all right, Gale. Been up and around the patio for two days. Like all the Spanish—the real thing—she's made of Damascus steel. We've been getting acquainted. She and Nell made friends at once. I'll call them in."

He closed the door leading out into the yard, explaining that he did not want to take chances of Mercedes's presence becoming known to neighbors. Then he went to the patio and called.

Both girls came in, Mercedes leading. Like Nell, she wore white, and she had a red rose in her hand. Dick would scarcely have recognized anything about her except her eyes and the way she carried her little head, and her beauty burst upon him strange and anew. She was swift, impulsive in her movements to reach his side.

"Senor, I am so sorry you were ill—so happy you are better."

Dick greeted her, offering his left hand, gravely apologizing for the fact that, owing to a late infirmity, he could not offer the right. Her smile exquisitely combined sympathy, gratitude, admiration. Then Dick spoke to Nell, likewise offering his hand, which she took shyly. Her reply was a murmured, unintelligible one; but her eyes were glad, and the tint in her cheeks threatened to rival the hue of the rose she carried.

Everybody chatted then, except Nell, who had apparently lost her voice. Presently Dick remembered to speak of the matter of getting news to Thorne.

"Senor, may I write to him? Will some one take a letter?... I shall hear from him!" she said; and her white hands emphasized her words.

"Assuredly. I guess poor Thorne is almost crazy. I'll write to him.... No, I can't with this crippled hand."

"That'll be all right, Gale," said Belding. "Nell will write for you. She writes all my letters."

So Belding arranged it; and Mercedes flew away to her room to write, while Nell fetched pen and paper and seated herself beside Gale's bed to take his dictation.

What with watching Nell and trying to catch her glance, and listening to Belding's talk with the cowboys, Dick was hard put to it to dictate any kind of a creditable letter. Nell met his gaze once, then no more. The color came and went in her cheeks, and sometimes, when he told her to write so and so, there was a demure smile on her lips. She was laughing at him. And Belding was talking over the risks involved in a trip to Casita.

"Shore I'll ride in with the letters," Ladd said.

"No you won't," replied Belding. "That bandit outfit will be laying for you."

"Well, I reckon if they was I wouldn't be oncommon grieved."

"I'll tell you, boys, I'll ride in myself with Carter. There's business I can see to, and I'm curious to know what the rebels are doing. Laddy, keep one eye open while I'm gone. See the horses are locked up.... Gale, I'm going to Casita myself. Ought to get back tomorrow some time. I'll be ready to start in an hour. Have your letter ready. And say—if you want to write home it's a chance. Sometimes we don't go to the P. O. in a month."

He tramped out, followed by the tall cowboys, and then Dick was enabled to bring his letter to a close. Mercedes came back, and her eyes were shining. Dick imagined a letter received from her would be something of an event for a fellow. Then, remembering Belding's suggestion, he decided to profit by it.

"May I trouble you to write another for me?" asked Dick, as he received the letter from Nell.

"It's no trouble, I'm sure—I'd be pleased," she replied.

That was altogether a wonderful speech of hers, Dick thought, because the words were the first coherent ones she had spoken to him.

"May I stay?" asked Mercedes, smiling.

"By all means," he answered, and then he settled back and began.

Presently Gale paused, partly because of genuine emotion, and stole a look from under his hand at Nell. She wrote swiftly, and her downcast face seemed to be softer in its expression of sweetness. If she had in the very least been drawn to him— But that was absurd—impossible!

When Dick finished dictating, his eyes were upon Mercedes, who sat smiling curious and sympathetic. How responsive she was! He heard the hasty scratch of Nell's pen. He looked at Nell. Presently she rose, holding out his letter. He was just in time to see a wave of red recede from her face. She gave him one swift gaze, unconscious, searching, then averted it and turned away. She left the room with Mercedes before he could express his thanks.

But that strange, speaking flash of eyes remained to haunt and torment Gale. It was indescribably sweet, and provocative of thoughts that he believed were wild without warrant. Something within him danced for very joy, and the next instant he was conscious of wistful doubt, a gravity that he could not understand. It dawned upon him that for the brief instant when Nell had met his gaze she had lost her shyness. It was a woman's questioning eyes that had pierced through him.

During the rest of the day Gale was content to lie still on his bed thinking and dreaming, dozing at intervals, and watching the lights change upon the mountain peaks, feeling the warm, fragrant desert wind that blew in upon him. He seemed to have lost the faculty of estimating time. A long while, strong in its effect upon him, appeared to have passed since he had met Thorne. He accepted things as he felt them, and repudiated his intelligence. His old inquisitive habit of mind returned. Did he love Nell? Was he only attracted for the moment? What was the use of worrying about her or himself? He refused to answer, and deliberately gave himself up to dreams of her sweet face and of that last dark-blue glance.

Next day he believed he was well enough to leave his room; but Mrs. Belding would not permit him to do so. She was kind, soft-handed, motherly, and she was always coming in to minister to his comfort. This attention was sincere, not in the least forced; yet Gale felt that the friendliness so manifest in the others of the household did not extend to her. He was conscious of something that a little thought persuaded him was antagonism. It surprised and hurt him. He had never been much of a success with girls and young married women, but their mothers and old people had generally been fond of him. Still, though Mrs. Belding's hair was snow-white, she did not impress him as being old. He reflected that there might come a time when it would be desirable, far beyond any ground of everyday friendly kindliness, to have Mrs. Belding be well disposed toward him. So he thought about her, and pondered how to make her like him. It did not take very long for Dick to discover that he liked her. Her face, except when she smiled, was thoughtful and sad. It was a face to make one serious. Like a haunting shadow, like a phantom of happier years, the sweetness of Nell's face was there, and infinitely more of beauty than had been transmitted to the daughter. Dick believed Mrs. Belding's friendship and motherly love were worth striving to win, entirely aside from any more selfish motive. He decided both would be hard to get. Often he felt her deep, penetrating gaze upon him; and, though this in no wise embarrassed him—for he had no shameful secrets of past or present—it showed him how useless it would be to try to conceal anything from her. Naturally, on first impulse, he wanted to hide his interest in the daughter; but he resolved to be absolutely frank and true, and through that win or lose. Moreover, if Mrs. Belding asked him any questions about his home, his family, his connections, he would not avoid direct and truthful answers.

Toward evening Gale heard the tramp of horses and Belding's hearty voice. Presently the rancher strode in upon Gale, shaking the gray dust from his broad shoulders and waving a letter.

"Hello, Dick! Good news and bad!" he said, putting the letter in Dick's hand. "Had no trouble finding your friend Thorne. Looked like he'd been drunk for a week! Say, he nearly threw a fit. I never saw a fellow so wild with joy. He made sure you and Mercedes were lost in the desert. He wrote two letters which I brought. Don't mistake me, boy, it was some fun with Mercedes just now. I teased her, wouldn't give her the letter. You ought to have seen her eyes. If ever you see a black-and-white desert hawk swoop down upon a quail, then you'll know how Mercedes pounced upon her letter... Well, Casita is one hell of a place these days. I tried to get your baggage, and I think I made a mistake. We're going to see travel toward Forlorn River. The federal garrison got reinforcements from somewhere, and is holding out. There's been fighting for three days. The rebels have a string of flat railroad cars, all iron, and they ran this up within range of the barricades. They've got some machine guns, and they're going to lick the federals sure. There are dead soldiers in the ditches, Mexican non-combatants lying dead in the streets—and buzzards everywhere! It's reported that Campo, the rebel leader, is on the way up from Sinaloa, and Huerta, a federal general, is coming to relieve the garrison. I don't take much stock in reports. But there's hell in Casita, all right."

"Do you think we'll have trouble out here?" asked Dick, excitedly.

"Sure. Some kind of trouble sooner or later," replied Belding, gloomily. "Why, you can stand on my ranch and step over into Mexico. Laddy says we'll lose horses and other stock in night raids. Jim Lash doesn't look for any worse. But Jim isn't as well acquainted with Greasers as I am. Anyway, my boy, as soon as you can hold a bridle and a gun you'll be on the job, don't mistake me."

"With Laddy and Jim?" asked Dick, trying to be cool.

"Sure. With them and me, and by yourself."

Dick drew a deep breath, and even after Belding had departed he forgot for a moment about the letter in his hand. Then he unfolded the paper and read:

> Dear Dick,—You've more than saved my life. To the end of my days you'll be the one man to whom I owe everything. Words fail to express my feelings.
>
> This must be a brief note. Belding is waiting, and I used up most of the time writing to Mercedes. I like Belding. He was not unknown to me, though I never met or saw him before. You'll be interested to learn that he's the unadulterated article, the real Western goods. I've heard of some of his stunts, and they made my hair curl. Dick, your luck is staggering. The way Belding spoke of you was great. But you deserve it, old man.
>
> I'm leaving Mercedes in your charge, subject, of course, to advice from Belding. Take care of her, Dick, for my life is wrapped up in her. By all means keep her from being seen by Mexicans. We are

sitting tight here—nothing doing. If some action doesn't come soon, it'll be darned strange. Things are centering this way. There's scrapping right along, and people have begun to move. We're still patrol-patrolling the line eastward of Casita. It'll be impossible to keep any tab on the line west of Casita, for it's too rough. That cactus desert is awful. Cowboys or rangers with desert-bred horses might keep raiders and smugglers from crossing. But if cavalrymen could stand that waterless wilderness, which I doubt much, their horses would drop under them.

If things do quiet down before my commission expires, I'll get leave of absence, run out to Forlorn River, marry my beautiful Spanish princess, and take her to a civilized country, where, I opine, every son of a gun who sees her will lose his head, and drive me mad. It's my great luck, old pal, that you are a fellow who never seemed to care about pretty girls. So you won't give me the double cross and run off with Mercedes—carry her off, like the villain in the play, I mean.

That reminds me of Rojas. Oh, Dick, it was glorious! You didn't do anything to the Dandy Rebel! Not at all! You merely caressed him—gently moved him to one side. Dick, harken to these glad words: Rojas is in the hospital. I was interested to inquire. He had a smashed finger, a dislocated collar bone, three broken ribs, and a fearful gash on his face. He'll be in the hospital for a month. Dick, when I meet that pig-headed dad of yours I'm going to give him the surprise of his life.

Send me a line whenever any one comes in from F. R., and inclose Mercedes's letter in yours. Take care of her, Dick, and may the future hold in store for you some of the sweetness I know now!

Faithfully yours, Thorne.

Dick reread the letter, then folded it and placed it under his pillow.

"Never cared for pretty girls, huh?" he soliloquized. "George, I never saw any till I struck Southern Arizona! Guess I'd better make up for lost time."

While he was eating his supper, with appetite rapidly returning to normal, Ladd and Jim came in, bowing their tall heads to enter the door. Their friendly advances were singularly welcome to Gale, but he was still backward. He allowed himself to show that he was glad to see them, and he listened. Jim Lash had heard from Belding the result of the mauling given to Rojas by Dick. And Jim talked about what a grand thing that was. Ladd had a good deal to say about Belding's horses. It took no keen judge of human nature to see that horses constituted Ladd's ruling passion.

"I've had wimmen go back on me, but never no hoss!" declared Ladd, and manifestly that was a controlling truth with him.

"Shore it's a cinch Beldin' is agoin' to lose some of them hosses," he said. "You can search me if I don't think there'll be more doin' on the border here than along the Rio Grande. We're just the same as on Greaser soil. Mebbe we don't stand no such chance of bein' shot up as we would across the line. But who's goin' to give up his hosses without a fight? Half the time when Beldin's stock is out of the alfalfa it's grazin' over the line. He thinks he's careful about them hosses, but he ain't."

"Look a-here, Laddy; you cain't believe all you hear," replied Jim, seriously. "I reckon we mightn't have any trouble."

"Back up, Jim. Shore you're standin' on your bridle. I ain't goin' much on reports. Remember that American we met in Casita, the prospector who'd just gotten out of Sonora? He had some story, he had. Swore he'd killed seventeen Greasers breakin' through the rebel line round the mine where he an' other Americans were corralled. The next day when I met him again, he was drunk, an' then he told me he'd shot thirty Greasers. The chances are he did kill some. But reports are exaggerated. There are miners fightin' for life down in Sonora, you can gamble on that. An' the truth is bad enough. Take Rojas's harryin' of the Senorita, for instance. Can you beat that? Shore, Jim, there's more doin' than the raidin' of a few hosses. An' Forlorn River is goin' to get hers!"

Another dawn found Gale so much recovered that he arose and looked after himself, not, however, without considerable difficulty and rather disheartening twinges of pain.

Some time during the morning he heard the girls in the patio and called to ask if he might join them. He received one response, a mellow, "Si, Senor." It was not as much as he wanted, but considering that it was enough, he went out. He had not as yet visited the patio, and surprise and delight were in store for him. He found himself lost in a labyrinth of green and rose-bordered walks. He strolled around, discovering that the patio was a courtyard, open at an end; but he failed to discover the young ladies. So he called again. The answer came from the center of the square. After stooping to get under shrubs and wading through bushes he entered an open sandy circle, full of magnificent and murderous cactus plants, strange to him. On the other side, in the shade of a beautiful tree, he found the girls. Mercedes sitting in a hammock, Nell upon a blanket.

"What a beautiful tree!" he exclaimed. "I never saw one like that. What is it?"

"Palo verde," replied Nell.

"Senor, palo verde means 'green tree,'" added Mercedes.

This desert tree, which had struck Dick as so new and strange and beautiful, was not striking on account of size, for it was small, scarcely reaching higher than the roof; but rather because of its exquisite color of green, trunk and branch alike, and owing to the odd fact that it seemed not to possess leaves. All the tree from ground to tiny flat twigs was a soft polished green. It bore no thorns.

Right then and there began Dick's education in desert growths; and he felt that even if he had not had such charming teachers he would still have been absorbed. For the patio was full of desert wonders. A twisting-trunked tree with full foliage of small gray leaves Nell called a mesquite. Then Dick remembered the name, and now he saw where the desert got its pale-gray color. A huge, lofty, fluted column of green was a saguaro, or giant cactus. Another oddshaped cactus, resembling the legs of an inverted devil-fish, bore the name ocatillo. Each branch rose high and symmetrical, furnished with sharp blades that seemed to be at once leaves and thorns. Yet another cactus interested Gale, and it looked like a huge, low barrel covered with green-ribbed cloth and long thorns. This was the bisnaga, or barrel cactus. According to Nell and Mercedes, this plant was a happy exception to its desert neighbors, for it secreted water which had many times saved the lives of men. Last of the cacti to attract Gale, and the one to make him shiver, was a low plant, consisting of stem and many rounded protuberances of a frosty, steely white, and covered with long murderous spikes. From this plant the desert got its frosty glitter. It was as stiff, as unyielding as steel, and bore the name *choya.*

Dick's enthusiasm was contagious, and his earnest desire to learn was flattering to his teachers. When it came to assimilating Spanish, however, he did not appear to be so apt a pupil. He managed, after many trials, to acquire "buenos dias" and "buenos tardes," and "senorita" and "gracias," and a few other short terms. Dick was indeed eager to get a little smattering of Spanish, and perhaps he was not really quite so stupid as he pretended to be. It was delightful to be taught by a beautiful Spaniard who was so gracious and intense and magnetic of personality, and by a sweet American girl who moment by moment forgot her shyness. Gale wished to prolong the lessons.

So that was the beginning of many afternoons in which he learned desert lore and Spanish verbs, and something else that he dared not name.

Nell Burton had never shown to Gale that daring side of her character which had been so suggestively defined in Belding's terse description and Ladd's encomiums, and in her own audacious speech and merry laugh and flashing eye of that never-to-be-forgotten first meeting. She might have been an entirely different girl. But Gale remembered; and when the ice had been somewhat broken between them, he was always trying to surprise her into her real self. There were moments that fairly made him tingle with expectation. Yet he saw little more than a ghost of her vivacity, and never a gleam of that individuality which Belding had called a devil. On the few occasions that Dick had been left alone with her in the patio Nell had grown suddenly unresponsive and restrained, or she had left him on some transparent pretext. On the last occasion Mercedes returned to find Dick staring disconsolately at the rose-bordered path, where Nell had evidently vanished. The Spanish girl was wonderful in her divination.

"Senor Dick!" she cried.

Dick looked at her, soberly nodded his head, and then he laughed. Mercedes had seen through him in one swift glance. Her white hand touched his in wordless sympathy and thrilled him. This Spanish girl was all fire and passion and love. She understood him, she was his friend, she pledged him what he felt would be the most subtle and powerful influence.

Little by little he learned details of Nell's varied life. She had lived in many places. As a child she remembered moving from town to town, of going to school among schoolmates whom she never had time to know. Lawrence, Kansas, where she studied for several years, was the later exception to this changeful nature of her schooling. Then she moved to Stillwater, Oklahoma, from there to Austin, Texas, and on to Waco, where her mother met and married Belding. They lived in New Mexico awhile, in Tucson, Arizona, in Douglas, and finally had come to lonely Forlorn River.

"Mother could never live in one place any length of time," said Nell. "And since we've been in the Southwest she has never ceased trying to find some trace of her father. He was last heard of in Nogales fourteen years ago. She thinks grandfather was lost in the Sonora Desert.... And every place we go is worse. Oh, I love the desert. But I'd like to go back to Lawrence—or to see Chicago or New York—some of the places Mr. Gale speaks of.... I remember the college at Lawrence, though I was only twelve. I saw races—and once real football. Since then I've read magazines and papers about big football games, and I was always fascinated .... Mr. Gale, of course, you've seen games?

"Yes, a few," replied Dick; and he laughed a little. It was on his lips then to tell her about some of the famous games in which he had participated. But he refrained from exploiting himself. There was little, however, of the color and sound and cheer, of the violent action and rush and battle incidental to a big college football game that he did not succeed in making Mercedes and Nell feel just as if they had been there. They hung breathless and wide-eyed upon his words.

Some one else was present at the latter part of Dick's narrative. The moment he became aware of Mrs. Belding's presence he remembered fancying he had heard her call, and now he was certain she had done so. Mercedes and Nell, however, had been and still were oblivious to everything except Dick's recital. He saw Mrs. Belding cast a strange, intent glance upon Nell, then turn and go silently through the patio. Dick concluded his talk, but the brilliant beginning was not sustained.

Dick was haunted by the strange expression he had caught on Mrs. Belding's face, especially the look in her eyes. It had been one of repressed pain liberated in a flash of certainty. The mother had seen just as quickly as Mercedes how far he had gone on the road of love. Perhaps she had seen more—even more than he dared hope. The incident roused Gale. He could not understand Mrs. Belding, nor why that look of hers, that seeming baffled, hopeless look of a woman who saw the inevitable forces of life and could not thwart them, should cause him perplexity and distress. He wanted to go to her and tell her how he felt about Nell, but fear of absolute destruction of his hopes held him back. He would wait. Nevertheless, an instinct that was perhaps akin to self-preservation prompted him to want to let Nell know the state of his mind. Words crowded his brain seeking utterance. Who and what he was, how he loved her, the work he expected to take up soon, his longings, hopes, and plans—there was all this and more. But something checked him. And the repression made him so thoughtful and quiet, even melancholy, that he went outdoors to try to throw off the mood. The sun was yet high, and a dazzling white light enveloped valleys and peaks. He felt that the wonderful sunshine was the dominant feature of that arid region. It was like white gold. It had burned its color in a face he knew. It was going to warm his blood and brown his skin. A hot, languid breeze, so dry that he felt his lips shrink with its contact, came from the desert; and it seemed to smell of wide-open, untainted places where sand blew and strange, pungent plants gave a bitter-sweet tang to the air.

When he returned to the house, some hours later, his room had been put in order. In the middle of the white coverlet on his table lay a fresh red rose. Nell had dropped it there. Dick picked it up, feeling a throb in his breast. It was a bud just beginning to open, to show between its petals a dark-red, unfolding heart. How fragrant it was, how exquisitely delicate, how beautiful its inner hue of red, deep and dark, the crimson of life blood!

Had Nell left it there by accident or by intent? Was it merely kindness or a girl's subtlety? Was it a message couched elusively, a symbol, a hope in a half-blown desert rose?

VI THE YAQUI

TOWARD evening of a lowering December day, some fifty miles west of Forlorn River, a horseman rode along an old, dimly defined trail. From time to time he halted to study the lay of the land ahead. It was bare, somber, ridgy desert, covered with dun-colored greasewood and stunted prickly pear. Distant mountains hemmed in the valley, raising black spurs above the round lomas and the square-walled mesas.

This lonely horseman bestrode a steed of magnificent build, perfectly white except for a dark bar of color running down the noble head from ears to nose. Sweatcaked dust stained the long flanks. The horse had been running. His mane and tail were laced and knotted to keep their length out of reach of grasping cactus and brush. Clumsy home-made leather shields covered the front of his forelegs and ran up well to his wide breast. What otherwise would have been muscular symmetry of limb was marred by many a scar and many a lump. He was lean, gaunt, worn, a huge machine of muscle and bone, beautiful only in head and mane, a weight-carrier, a horse strong and fierce like the desert that had bred him.

The rider fitted the horse as he fitted the saddle. He was a young man of exceedingly powerful physique, wide-shouldered, long-armed, big-legged. His lean face, where it was not red, blistered and peeling, was the hue of bronze. He had a dark eye, a falcon gaze, roving and keen. His jaw was prominent and set, mastiff-like; his lips were stern. It was youth with its softness not yet quite burned and hardened away that kept the whole cast of his face from being ruthless.

This young man was Dick Gale, but not the listless traveler, nor the lounging wanderer who, two months before, had by chance dropped into Casita. Friendship, chivalry, love—the deep-seated, unplumbed emotions that had been stirred into being with all their incalculable power for spiritual change, had rendered different the meaning of life. In the moment almost of their realization the desert had claimed Gale, and had drawn him into its crucible. The desert had multiplied weeks into years. Heat, thirst, hunger, loneliness, toil, fear, ferocity, pain—he knew them all. He had felt them all—the white sun, with its glazed, coalescing, lurid fire; the caked split lips and rasping, dry-puffed tongue; the sickening ache in the pit of his stomach; the insupportable silence, the empty space, the utter desolation, the contempt of life; the weary ride, the long climb, the plod in sand, the search, search, search for water; the sleepless night alone, the watch and wait, the dread of ambush, the swift flight; the fierce pursuit of men wild as Bedouins and as fleet, the willingness to deal sudden death, the pain of poison thorn, the stinging tear of lead through flesh; and that strange paradox of the burning desert, the cold at night, the piercing icy wind, the dew that penetrated to the marrow, the numbing desert cold of the dawn.

Beyond any dream of adventure he had ever had, beyond any wild story he had ever read, had been his experience with those hard-riding rangers, Ladd and Lash. Then he had traveled alone the hundred miles of desert between Forlorn River and the Sonoyta Oasis. Ladd's prophecy of trouble on the border had been mild compared to what had become the actuality. With rebel occupancy of the garrison at Casita, outlaws, bandits, raiders in rioting bands had spread westward. Like troops of Arabs, magnificently mounted, they were here, there, everywhere along the line; and if murder and worse were confined to the Mexican side, pillage and raiding were perpetrated across the border. Many a dark-skinned raider bestrode one of Belding's fast horses, and indeed all except his selected white thoroughbreds had been stolen. So the job of the rangers had become more than a patrolling of the boundary line to keep Japanese and Chinese from being smuggled into the United States. Belding kept close at home to protect his family and to hold his property. But the three rangers, in fulfilling their duty had incurred risks on their own side of the line, had been outraged, robbed, pursued, and injured on the other. Some of the few waterholes that had to be reached lay far across the border in Mexican territory. Horses had to drink, men had to drink; and Ladd and Lash were not of the stripe that forsook a task because of danger. Slow to wrath at first, as became men who had long lived peaceful lives, they had at length revolted; and desert vultures could have told a gruesome story. Made a comrade and ally of these bordermen, Dick Gale had leaped at the desert action and strife with an intensity of heart and a rare physical ability which accounted for the remarkable fact that he had not yet fallen by the way.

On this December afternoon the three rangers, as often, were separated. Lash was far to the westward of Sonoyta, somewhere along Camino del Diablo, that terrible Devil's Road, where many desert wayfarers had perished. Ladd had long been overdue in a prearranged meeting with Gale. The fact that Ladd had not shown up miles west of the Papago Well was significant.

The sun had hidden behind clouds all the latter part of that day, an unusual occurrence for that region even in winter. And now, as the light waned suddenly, telling of the hidden sunset, a cold dry, penetrating wind sprang up and blew in Gale's face. Not at first, but by imperceptible degrees it chilled him. He untied his coat from the back of the saddle and put it on. A few cold drops of rain touched his cheek.

He halted upon the edge of a low escarpment. Below him the narrowing valley showed bare, black ribs of rock, long, winding gray lines leading down to a central floor where mesquite and cactus dotted the barren landscape. Moving objects, diminutive in size, gray and white in color, arrested Gale's roving sight.

They bobbed away for a while, then stopped. They were antelope, and they had seen his horse. When he rode on they started once more, keeping to the lowest level. These wary animals were often desert watchdogs for the ranger, they would betray the proximity of horse or man. With them trotting forward, he made better time for some miles across the valley. When he lost them, caution once more slowed his advance.

The valley sloped up and narrowed, to head into an arroyo where grass began to show gray between the clumps of mesquite. Shadows formed ahead in the hollows, along the walls of the arroyo, under the trees, and they seemed to creep, to rise, to float into a veil cast by the background of bold mountains, at last to claim the skyline. Night was not close at hand, but it was there in the east, lifting upward, drooping downward, encroaching upon the west.

Gale dismounted to lead his horse, to go forward more slowly. He had ridden sixty miles since morning, and he was tired, and a not entirely healed wound in his hip made one leg drag a little. A mile up the arroyo, near its head, lay the Papago Well. The need of water for his horse entailed a risk that otherwise he could have avoided. The well was on Mexican soil. Gale distinguished a faint light flickering through the thin, sharp foliage. Campers were at the well, and, whoever they were, no doubt they had prevented Ladd from meeting Gale. Ladd had gone back to the next waterhole, or maybe he was hiding in an arroyo to the eastward, awaiting developments.

Gale turned his horse, not without urge of iron arm and persuasive speech, for the desert steed scented water, and plodded back to the edge of the arroyo, where in a secluded circle of mesquite he halted. The horse snorted his relief at the removal of the heavy, burdened saddle and accoutrements, and sagging, bent his knees, lowered himself with slow heave, and plunged down to roll in the sand. Gale poured the contents of his larger canteen into his hat and held it to the horse's nose.

"Drink, Sol," he said.

It was but a drop for a thirsty horse. However, Blanco Sol rubbed a wet muzzle against Gale's hand in appreciation. Gale loved the horse, and was loved in return. They had saved each other's lives, and had spent long days and nights of desert solitude together. Sol had known other masters, though none so kind as this new one; but it was certain that Gale had never before known a horse.

The spot of secluded ground was covered with bunches of galleta grass upon which Sol began to graze. Gale made a long halter of his lariat to keep the horse from wandering in search of water. Next Gale kicked off the cumbersome chapparejos, with their flapping, tripping folds of leather over his feet, and drawing a long rifle from its leather sheath, he slipped away into the shadows.

The coyotes were howling, not here and there, but in concerted volume at the head of the arroyo. To Dick this was no more reassuring than had been the flickering light of the campfire. The wild desert dogs, with their characteristic insolent curiosity, were baying men round a campfire. Gale proceeded slowly, halting every few steps, careful not to brush against the stiff greasewood. In the soft sand his steps made no sound. The twinkling light vanished occasionally, like a Jack-o'lantern, and when it did show it seemed still a long way off. Gale was not seeking trouble or inviting danger. Water was the thing that drove him. He must see who these campers were, and then decide how to give Blanco Sol a drink.

A rabbit rustled out of brush at Gale's feet and thumped away over the sand. The wind pattered among dry, broken stalks of dead ocatilla. Every little sound brought Gale to a listening pause. The gloom was thickening fast into darkness. It would be a night without starlight. He moved forward up the pale, zigzag aisles between the mesquite. He lost the light for a while, but the coyotes' chorus told him he was approaching the campfire. Presently the light danced through the black branches, and soon grew into a flame. Stooping low, with bushy mesquites between him and the fire, Gale advanced. The coyotes were in full cry. Gale heard the tramping, stamping thumps of many hoofs. The sound worried him. Foot by foot he advanced, and finally began to crawl. The wind favored his position, so that neither coyotes nor horses could scent him. The nearer he approached the head of the arroyo, where the well was located, the thicker grew the desert vegetation. At length a dead palo verde, with huge black clumps of its parasite mistletoe thick in the branches, marked a distance from the well that Gale considered close enough. Noiselessly he crawled here and there until he secured a favorable position, and then rose to peep from behind his covert.

He saw a bright fire, not a cooking-fire, for that would have been low and red, but a crackling blaze of mesquite. Three men were in sight, all close to the burning sticks. They were Mexicans and of the coarse type of raiders, rebels, bandits that Gale expected to see. One stood up, his back to the fire; another sat with shoulders enveloped in a blanket, and the third lounged in the sand, his feet almost in the blaze. They had cast off belts and weapons. A glint of steel caught Gale's eye. Three short, shiny carbines leaned against a rock. A little to the left, within the circle of light, stood a square house made of adobe bricks. Several untrimmed poles upheld a roof of brush, which was partly fallen in. This house was a Papago Indian habitation, and a month before had been occupied by a family that had been murdered or driven off by a roving band of outlaws. A rude corral showed dimly in the edge of firelight, and from a black mass within came the snort and stamp and whinney of horses.

Gale took in the scene in one quick glance, then sank down at the foot of the mesquite. He had naturally expected to see more men. But the situation was by no means new. This was one, or part of one, of the raider bands harrying the border. They were stealing horses, or driving a herd already stolen. These bands were more numerous than the waterholes of northern Sonora; they never camped long at one place; like Arabs, they roamed over the desert all the way from Nogales to Casita. If Gale had gone peaceably up to this campfire there were a hundred chances that the raiders would kill and rob him to one chance that they might not. If they recognized him as a ranger comrade of Ladd and Lash, if they got a glimpse of Blanco Sol, then Gale would have no chance.

These Mexicans had evidently been at the well some time. Their horses being in the corral meant that grazing had been done by day. Gale revolved questions in mind. Had this trio of outlaws run across Ladd? It was not likely, for in that event they might not have been so comfortable and care-free in camp. Were they waiting for more members of their gang? That was very probable. With Gale, however, the most important consideration was how to get his horse to water. Sol must have a drink if it cost a fight. There was stern reason for Gale to hurry eastward along the trail. He thought it best to go back to where he had left his horse and not make any decisive move until daylight.

With the same noiseless care he had exercised in the advance, Gale retreated until it was safe for him to rise and walk on down the arroyo. He found Blanco Sol contentedly grazing. A heavy dew was falling, and, as the grass was abundant, the horse did not show the usual restlessness and distress after a dry and exhausting day. Gale carried his saddle blankets and bags into the lee of a little greasewood-covered mound, from around which the wind had cut the soil, and here, in a wash, he risked building a small fire. By this time the wind was piercingly cold. Gale's hands were numb and he moved them to and fro in the little blaze. Then he made coffee in a cup, cooked some slices of bacon on the end of a stick, and took a couple of hard biscuits from a saddlebag. Of these his meal consisted. After that he removed the halter from Blanco Sol, intending to leave him free to graze for a while.

Then Gale returned to his little fire, replenished it with short sticks of dead greasewood and mesquite, and, wrapping his blanket round his shoulders he sat down to warm himself and to wait till it was time to bring in the horse and tie him up.

The fire was inadequate and Gale was cold and wet with dew. Hunger and thirst were with him. His bones ached, and there was a dull, deep-seated pain throbbing in his unhealed wound. For days unshaven, his beard seemed like a million pricking needles in his blistered skin. He was so tired that once having settled himself, he did not move hand or foot. The night was dark, dismal, cloudy, windy, growing colder. A moan of wind in the mesquite was occasionally pierced by the high-keyed yelp of a coyote. There were lulls in which the silence seemed to be a thing of stifling, encroaching substance—a thing that enveloped, buried the desert.

Judged by the great average of ideals and conventional standards of life, Dick Gale was a starved, lonely, suffering, miserable wretch. But in his case the judgment would have hit only externals, would have missed the vital inner truth. For Gale was happy with a kind of strange, wild glory in the privations, the pains, the perils, and the silence and solitude to be endured on this desert land. In the past he had not been of any use to himself or others; and he had never know what it meant to be hungry, cold, tired, lonely. He had never worked for anything. The needs of the day had been provided, and to-morrow and the future looked the same. Danger, peril, toil—these had been words read in books and papers.

In the present he used his hands, his senses, and his wits. He had a duty to a man who relied on his services. He was a comrade, a friend, a valuable ally to riding, fighting rangers. He had spent endless days, weeks that seemed years, alone with a horse, trailing over, climbing over, hunting over a desert that was harsh and hostile by nature, and perilous by the invasion of savage men. That horse had become human to Gale. And with him Gale had learned to know the simple needs of existence. Like dead scales the superficialities, the falsities, the habits that had once meant all of life dropped off, useless things in this stern waste of rock and sand.

Gale's happiness, as far as it concerned the toil and strife, was perhaps a grim and stoical one. But love abided with him, and it had engendered and fostered other undeveloped traits—romance and a feeling for beauty, and a keen observation of nature. He felt pain, but he was never miserable. He felt the solitude, but he was never lonely.

As he rode across the desert, even though keen eyes searched for the moving black dots, the rising puffs of white dust that were warnings, he saw Nell's face in every cloud. The clean-cut mesas took on the shape of her straight profile, with its strong chin and lips, its fine nose and forehead. There was always a glint of gold or touch of red or graceful line or gleam of blue to remind him of her. Then at night her face shone warm and glowing, flushing and paling, in the campfire.

To-night, as usual, with a keen ear to the wind, Gale listened as one on guard; yet he watched the changing phantom of a sweet face in the embers, and as he watched he thought. The desert developed and multiplied thought. A thousand sweet faces glowed in the pink and white ashes of his campfire, the faces of other sweethearts or wives that had gleamed for other men. Gale was happy in his thought of Nell, for Nell, for something, when he was alone this way in the wilderness, told him she was near him, she thought of him, she loved him. But there were many men alone on that vast southwestern plateau, and when they saw dream faces, surely for some it was a fleeting flash, a gleam soon gone, like the hope and the name and the happiness that had been and was now no more. Often Gale thought of those hundreds of desert travelers, prospectors, wanderers who had ventured down the Camino del Diablo, never to be heard of again. Belding had told him of that most terrible of all desert trails—a trail of shifting sands. Lash had traversed it, and brought back stories of buried waterholes, of bones bleaching white in the sun, of gold mines as lost as were the prospectors who had sought them, of the merciless Yaqui and his hatred for the Mexican. Gale thought of this trail and the men who had camped along it. For many there had been one night, one campfire that had been the last. This idea seemed to creep in out of the darkness, the loneliness, the silence, and to find a place in Gale's mind, so that it had strange fascination for him. He knew now as he had never dreamed before how men drifted into the desert, leaving behind graves, wrecked homes, ruined lives, lost wives and sweethearts. And for every wanderer every campfire had a phantom face. Gale measured the agony of these men at their last campfire by the joy and promise he traced in the ruddy heart of his own.

By and by Gale remembered what he was waiting for; and, getting up, he took the halter and went out to find Blanco Sol. It was pitch-dark now, and Gale could not see a rod ahead. He felt his way, and presently as he rounded a mesquite he saw Sol's white shape outlined against the blackness. The horse jumped and wheeled, ready to run. It was doubtful if any one unknown to Sol could ever have caught him. Gale's low call reassured him, and he went on grazing. Gale haltered him in the likeliest patch of grass and returned to his camp. There he lifted his saddle into a protected spot under a low wall of the mound, and, laying one blanket on the sand, he covered himself with the other and stretched himself for the night.

Here he was out of reach of the wind; but he heard its melancholy moan in the mesquite. There was no other sound. The coyotes had ceased their hungry cries. Gale dropped to sleep, and slept soundly during the first half of the night; and after that he seemed always to be partially awake, aware of increasing cold and damp. The dark mantle turned gray, and then daylight came quickly. The morning was clear and nipping cold. He threw off the wet blanket and got up cramped and half frozen. A little brisk action was all that was necessary to warm his blood and loosen his muscles, and then he was fresh, tingling, eager. The sun rose in a golden blaze, and the descending valley took on wondrous changing hues. Then he fetched up Blanco Sol, saddled him, and tied him to the thickest clump of mesquite.

"Sol, we'll have a drink pretty soon," he said, patting the splendid neck.

Gale meant it. He would not eat till he had watered his horse. Sol had gone nearly forty-eight hours without a sufficient drink, and that was long enough, even for a desert-bred beast. No three raiders could keep Gale away from that well. Taking his rifle in hand, he faced up the arroyo. Rabbits were frisking in the short willows, and some were so tame he could have kicked them. Gale walked swiftly for a goodly part of the distance, and then, when he saw blue smoke curling up above the trees, he proceeded slowly, with alert eye and ear. From the lay of the land and position of trees seen by daylight, he found an easier and safer course that the one he had taken in the dark. And by careful work he was enabled to get closer to the well, and somewhat above it.

The Mexicans were leisurely cooking their morning meal. They had two fires, one for warmth, the other to cook over. Gale had an idea these raiders were familiar to him. It seemed all these border hawks resembled one another—being mostly small of build, wiry, angular, swarthy-faced, and black-haired, and they wore the oddly styled Mexican clothes and sombreros. A slow wrath stirred in Gale as he watched the trio. They showed not the slightest indication of breaking camp. One fellow, evidently the leader, packed a gun at his hip, the only weapon in sight. Gale noted this with speculative eyes. The raiders had slept inside the little adobe house, and had not yet brought out the carbines. Next Gale swept his gaze to the corral, in which he saw more than a dozen horses, some of them fine animals. They were stamping and whistling, fighting one another, and pawing the dirt. This was entirely natural behavior for desert horses penned in when they wanted to get at water and grass.

But suddenly one of the blacks, a big, shaggy fellow, shot up his ears and pointed his nose over the top of the fence. He whistled. Other horses looked in the same direction, and their ears went up, and they, too, whistled. Gale knew that other horses or men, very likely both, were approaching. But the Mexicans did not hear the alarm, or show any interest if they did. These mescal-drinking raiders were not scouts. It was notorious how easily they could be surprised or ambushed. Mostly they were ignorant, thick-skulled peons. They were wonderful horsemen, and could go long without food or water; but they had not other accomplishments or attributes calculated to help them in desert warfare. They had poor sight, poor hearing, poor judgment, and when excited they resembled crazed ants running wild.

Gale saw two Indians on burros come riding up the other side of the knoll upon which the adobe house stood; and apparently they were not aware of the presence of the Mexicans, for they came on up the path. One Indian was a Papago. The other, striking in appearance for other reasons than that he seemed to be about to fall from the burro, Gale took to be a Yaqui. These travelers had absolutely nothing for an outfit except a blanket and a half-empty bag. They came over the knoll and down the path toward the well, turned a corner of the house, and completely surprised the raiders.

Gale heard a short, shrill cry, strangely high and wild, and this came from one of the Indians. It was answered by hoarse shouts. Then the leader of the trio, the Mexican who packed a gun, pulled it and fired point-blank. He missed once—and again. At the third shot the Papago shrieked and tumbled off his burro to fall in a heap. The other Indian swayed, as if the taking away of the support lent by his comrade had brought collapse, and with the fourth shot he, too, slipped to the ground.

The reports had frightened the horses in the corral; and the vicious black, crowding the rickety bars, broke them down. He came plunging out. Two of the Mexicans ran for him, catching him by nose and mane, and the third ran to block the gateway.

Then, with a splendid vaulting mount, the Mexican with the gun leaped to the back of the horse. He yelled and waved his gun, and urged the black forward. The manner of all three was savagely jocose. They were having sport. The two on the ground began to dance and jabber. The mounted leader shot again, and then stuck like a leech upon the bare back of the rearing black. It was a vain show of horsemanship. Then this Mexican, by some strange grip, brought the horse down, plunging almost upon the body of the Indian that had fallen last.

Gale stood aghast with his rifle clutched tight. He could not divine the intention of the raider, but suspected something brutal. The horse answered to that cruel, guiding hand, yet he swerved and bucked. He reared aloft, pawing the air, wildly snorting, then he plunged down upon the prostrate Indian. Even in the act the intelligent animal tried to keep from striking the body with his hoofs. But that was not possible. A yell, hideous in its passion, signaled this feat of horsemanship.

The Mexican made no move to trample the body of the Papago. He turned the black to ride again over the other Indian. That brought into Gale's mind what he had heard of a Mexican's hate for a Yaqui. It recalled the barbarism of these savage peons, and the war of extermination being waged upon the Yaquis.

Suddenly Gale was horrified to see the Yaqui writhe and raise a feeble hand. The action brought renewed and more savage cries from the Mexicans. The horse snorted in terror.

Gale could bear no more. He took a quick shot at the rider. He missed the moving figure, but hit the horse. There was a bound, a horrid scream, a mighty plunge, then the horse went down, giving the Mexican a stunning fall. Both beast and man lay still.

Gale rushed from his cover to intercept the other raiders before they could reach the house and their weapons. One fellow yelled and ran wildly in the opposite direction; the other stood stricken in his tracks. Gale ran in close and picked up the gun that had dropped from the raider leader's hand. This fellow had begun to stir, to come out of his stunned condition. Then the frightened horses burst the corral bars, and in a thundering, dust-mantled stream fled up the arroyo.

The fallen raider sat up, mumbling to his saints in one breath, cursing in his next. The other Mexican kept his stand, intimidated by the threatening rifle.

"Go, Greasers! Run!" yelled Gale. Then he yelled it in Spanish. At the point of his rifle he drove the two raiders out of the camp. His next move was to run into the house and fetch out the carbines. With a heavy stone he dismantled each weapon. That done, he set out on a run for his horse. He took the shortest cut down the arroyo, with no concern as to whether or not he would encounter the raiders. Probably such a meeting would be all the worse for them, and they knew it. Blanco Sol heard him coming and whistled a welcome, and when Gale ran up the horse was snorting war. Mounting, Gale rode rapidly back to the scene of the action, and his first thought, when he arrived at the well, was to give Sol a drink and to fill his canteens.

Then Gale led his horse up out of the waterhole, and decided before remounting to have a look at the Indians. The Papago had been shot through the heart, but the Yaqui was still alive. Moreover, he was conscious and staring up at Gale with great, strange, somber eyes, black as volcanic slag.

"Gringo good—no kill," he said, in husky whisper.

His speech was not affirmative so much as questioning.

"Yaqui, you're done for," said Gale, and his words were positive. He was simply speaking aloud his mind.

"Yaqui—no hurt—much," replied the Indian, and then he spoke a strange word—repeated it again and again.

An instinct of Gale's, or perhaps some suggestion in the husky, thick whisper or dark face, told Gale to reach for his canteen. He lifted the Indian and gave him a drink, and if ever in all his life he saw gratitude in human eyes he saw it then.

Then he examined the injured Yaqui, not forgetting for an instant to send wary, fugitive glances on all sides. Gale was not surprised. The Indian had three wounds—a bullet hole in his shoulder, a crushed arm, and a badly lacerated leg. What had been the matter with him before being set upon by the raider Gale could not be certain.

The ranger thought rapidly. This Yaqui would live unless left there to die or be murdered by the Mexicans when they found courage to sneak back to the well. It never occurred to Gale to abandon the poor fellow. That was where his old training, the higher order of human feeling, made impossible the following of any elemental instinct of self-preservation. All the same, Gale knew he multiplied his perils a hundredfold by burdening himself with a crippled Indian. Swiftly he set to work, and with rifle ever under his hand, and shifting glance spared from his task, he bound up the Yaqui's wounds. At the same time he kept keen watch.

The Indians' burros and the horses of the raiders were all out of sight. Time was too valuable for Gale to use any in what might be a vain search. Therefore, he lifted the Yaqui upon Sol's broad shoulders and climbed into the saddle. At a word Sol dropped his head and started eastward up the trail, walking swiftly, without resentment for his double burden.

Far ahead, between two huge mesas where the trail mounted over a pass, a long line of dust clouds marked the position of the horses that had escaped from the corral. Those that had been stolen would travel straight and true for home, and perhaps would lead the others with them. The raiders were left on the desert without guns or mounts.

Blanco Sol walked or jog-trotted six miles to the hour. At that gait fifty miles would not have wet or turned a hair of his dazzling white coat. Gale, bearing in mind the ever-present possibility of encountering more raiders and of being pursued, saved the strength of the horse. Once out of sight of Papago Well, Gale dismounted and walked beside the horse, steadying with one firm hand the helpless, dangling Yaqui.

The sun cleared the eastern ramparts, and the coolness of morning fled as if before a magic foe. The whole desert changed. The grays wore bright; the mesquites glistened; the cactus took the silver hue of frost, and the rocks gleamed gold and red. Then, as the heat increased, a wind rushed up out of the valley behind Gale, and the hotter the sun blazed down the swifter rushed the wind. The wonderful transparent haze of distance lost its bluish hue for one with tinge of yellow. Flying sand made the peaks dimly outlined.

Gale kept pace with his horse. He bore the twinge of pain that darted through his injured hip at every stride. His eye roved over the wide, smoky prospect seeking the landmarks he knew. When the wild and bold spurs of No Name Mountains loomed through a rent in flying clouds of sand he felt nearer home. Another hour brought him abreast of a dark, straight shaft rising clear from a beetling escarpment. This was a monument marking the international boundary line. When he had passed it he had his own country under foot. In the heat of midday he halted in the shade of a rock, and, lifting the Yaqui down, gave him a drink. Then, after a long, sweeping survey of the surrounding desert, he removed Sol's saddle and let him roll, and took for himself a welcome rest and a bite to eat.

The Yaqui was tenacious of life. He was still holding his own. For the first time Gale really looked at the Indian to study him. He had a large head nobly cast, and a face that resembled a shrunken mask. It seemed chiseled in the dark-red, volcanic lava of his Sooner wilderness. The Indian's eyes were always black and mystic, but this Yaqui's encompassed all the tragic desolation of the desert. They were fixed on Gale, moved only when he moved. The Indian was short and broad, and his body showed unusual muscular development, although he seemed greatly emaciated from starvation or illness.

Gale resumed his homeward journey. When he got through the pass he faced a great depression, as rough as if millions of gigantic spikes had been driven by the hammer of Thor into a seamed and cracked floor. This was Altar Valley. It was a chaos of arroyo's, canyons, rocks, and ridges all mantled with cactus, and at its eastern end it claimed the dry bed of Forlorn River and water when there was any.

With a wounded, helpless man across the saddle, this stretch of thorny and contorted desert was practically impassable. Yet Gale headed into it unflinchingly. He would carry the Yaqui as far as possible, or until death make the burden no longer a duty. Blanco Sol plodded on over the dragging sand, up and down the steep, loose banks of washes, out on the rocks, and through the rows of white-toothed *choyas*.

The sun sloped westward, bending fiercer heat in vengeful, parting reluctance. The wind slackened. The dust settled. And the bold, forbidding front of No Name Mountains changed to red and gold. Gale held grimly by the side of the tireless, implacable horse, holding the Yaqui on the saddle, taking the brunt of the merciless thorns. In the end it became heartrending toil. His heavy chaps dragged him down; but he dared not go on without them, for, thick and stiff as they were, the terrible, steel-bayoneted spikes of the *choyas* pierced through to sting his legs.

To the last mile Gale held to Blanco Sol's gait and kept ever-watchful gaze ahead on the trail. Then, with the low, flat houses of Forlorn River shining red in the sunset, Gale flagged and rapidly weakened. The Yaqui slipped out of the saddle and dropped limp in the sand. Gale could not mount his horse. He clutched Sol's long tail and twisted his hand in it and staggered on.

Blanco Sol whistled a piercing blast. He scented cool water and sweet alfalfa hay. Twinkling lights ahead meant rest. The melancholy desert twilight rapidly succeeded the sunset. It accentuated the forlorn loneliness of the gray, winding river of sand and its grayer shores. Night shadows trooped down from the black and looming mountains.

VII WHITE HORSES

"A CRIPPLED Yaqui! Why the hell did you saddle yourself with him?" roared Belding, as he laid Gale upon the bed.

Belding had grown hard these late, violent weeks.

"Because I chose," whispered Gale, in reply. "Go after him—he dropped in the trail—across the river—near the first big saguaro."

Belding began to swear as he fumbled with matches and the lamp; but as the light flared up he stopped short in the middle of a word.

"You said you weren't hurt?" he demanded, in sharp anxiety, as he bent over Gale.

"I'm only—all in.... Will you go—or send some one—for the Yaqui?"

"Sure, Dick, sure," Belding replied, in softer tones. Then he stalked out; his heels rang on the flagstones; he opened a door and called: "Mother—girls, here's Dick back. He's done up.... Now—no, no, he's not hurt or in bad shape. You women!... Do what you can to make him comfortable. I've got a little job on hand."

There were quick replies that Gale's dulling ears did not distinguish. Then it seemed Mrs. Belding was beside his bed, her presence so cool and soothing and helpful, and Mercedes and Nell, wide-eyed and white-faced, were fluttering around him. He drank thirstily, but refused food. He wanted rest. And with their faces drifting away in a kind of haze, with the feeling of gentle hands about him, he lost consciousness.

He slept twenty hours. Then he arose, thirsty, hungry, lame, overworn, and presently went in search of Belding and the business of the day.

"Your Yaqui was near dead, but guess we'll pull him through," said Belding. "Dick, the other day that Indian came here by rail and foot and Lord only knows how else, all the way from New Orleans! He spoke English better than most Indians, and I know a little Yaqui. I got some of his story and guessed the rest. The Mexican government is trying to root out the Yaquis. A year ago his tribe was taken in chains to a Mexican port on the Gulf. The fathers, mothers, children, were separated and put in ships bound for Yucatan. There they were made slaves on the great henequen plantations. They were driven, beaten, starved. Each slave had for a day's rations a hunk of sour dough, no more. Yucatan is low, marshy, damp, hot. The Yaquis were bred on the high, dry Sonoran plateau, where the air is like a knife. They dropped dead in the henequen fields, and their places were taken by more. You see, the Mexicans won't kill outright in their war of extermination of the Yaquis. They get use out of them. It's a horrible thing.... Well, this Yaqui you brought in escaped from his captors, got aboard ship, and eventually reached New Orleans. Somehow he traveled way out here. I gave him a bag of food, and he went off with a Papago Indian. He was a sick man then. And he must have fallen foul of some Greasers."

Gale told of his experience at Papago Well.

"That raider who tried to grind the Yaqui under a horse's hoofs—he was a hyena!" concluded Gale, shuddering. "I've seen some blood spilled and some hard sights, but that inhuman devil took my nerve. Why, as I told you, Belding, I missed a shot at him—not twenty paces!"

"Dick, in cases like that the sooner you clean up the bunch the better," said Belding, grimly. "As for hard sights—wait till you've seen a Yaqui do up a Mexican. Bar none, that is the limit! It's blood lust, a racial hate, deep as life, and terrible. The Spaniards crushed the Aztecs four or five hundred years ago. That hate has had time to grow as deep as a cactus root. The Yaquis are mountain Aztecs. Personally, I think they are noble and intelligent, and if let alone would be peaceable and industrious. I like the few I've known. But they are a doomed race. Have you any idea what ailed this Yaqui before the raider got in his work?"

"No, I haven't. I noticed the Indian seemed in bad shape; but I couldn't tell what was the matter with him."

"Well, my idea is another personal one. Maybe it's off color. I think that Yaqui was, or is, for that matter, dying of a broken heart. All he wanted was to get back to his mountains and die. There are no Yaquis left in that part of Sonora he was bound for."

"He had a strange look in his eyes," said Gale, thoughtfully.

"Yes, I noticed that. But all Yaquis have a wild look. Dick, if I'm not mistaken, this fellow was a chief. It was a waste of strength, a needless risk for you to save him, pack him back here. But, damn the whole Greaser outfit generally, I'm glad you did!"

Gale remembered then to speak of his concern for Ladd.

"Laddy didn't go out to meet you," replied Belding. "I knew you were due in any day, and, as there's been trouble between here and Casita, I sent him that way. Since you've been out our friend Carter lost a bunch of horses and a few steers. Did you get a good look at the horses those raiders had at Papago Well?"

Dick had learned, since he had become a ranger, to see everything with keen, sure, photographic eye; and, being put to the test so often required of him, he described the horses as a dark-colored drove, mostly bays and blacks, with one spotted sorrel.

"Some of Carter's—sure as you're born!" exclaimed Belding. "His bunch has been split up, divided among several bands of raiders. He has a grass ranch up here in Three Mile Arroyo. It's a good long ride in U. S. territory from the border."

"Those horses I saw will go home, don't you think?" asked Dick.

"Sure. They can't be caught or stopped."

"Well, what shall I do now?"

"Stay here and rest," bluntly replied Belding. "You need it. Let the women fuss over you—doctor you a little. When Jim gets back from Sonoyta I'll know more about what we ought to do. By Lord! it seems our job now isn't keeping Japs and Chinks out of the U. S. It's keeping our property from going into Mexico."

"Are there any letters for me?" asked Gale.

"Letters! Say, my boy, it'd take something pretty important to get me or any man here back Casita way. If the town is safe these days the road isn't. It's a month now since any one went to Casita."

Gale had received several letters from his sister Elsie, the last of which he had not answered. There had not been much opportunity for writing on his infrequent returns to Forlorn River; and, besides, Elsie had written that her father had stormed over what he considered Dick's falling into wild and evil ways.

"Time flies," said Dick. "George Thorne will be free before long, and he'll be coming out. I wonder if he'll stay here or try to take Mercedes away?"

"Well, he'll stay right here in Forlorn River, if I have any say," replied Belding. "I'd like to know how he'd ever get that Spanish girl out of the country now, with all the trails overrun by rebels and raiders. It'd be hard to disguise her. Say, Dick, maybe we can get Thorne to stay here. You know, since you've discovered the possibility of a big water supply, I've had dreams of a future for Forlorn River.... If only this war was over! Dick, that's what it is—war—scattered war along the northern border of Mexico from gulf to gulf. What if it isn't our war? We're on the fringe. No, we can't develop Forlorn River until there's peace."

The discovery that Belding alluded to was one that might very well lead to the making of a wonderful and agricultural district of Altar Valley. While in college Dick Gale had studied engineering, but he had not set the scientific world afire with his brilliance. Nor after leaving college had he been able to satisfy his father that he could hold a job. Nevertheless, his smattering of engineering skill bore fruit in the last place on earth where anything might have been expected of it—in the desert. Gale had always wondered about the source of Forlorn River. No white man or Mexican, or, so far as known, no Indian, had climbed those mighty broken steps of rock called No Name Mountains, from which Forlorn River was supposed to come. Gale had discovered a long, narrow, rock-bottomed and rock-walled gulch that could be dammed at the lower end by the dynamiting of leaning cliffs above. An inexhaustible supply of water could be stored there. Furthermore, he had worked out an irrigation plan to bring the water down for mining uses, and to make a paradise out of that part of Altar Valley which lay in the United States. Belding claimed there was gold in the arroyos, gold in the gulches, not in quantities to make a prospector rejoice, but enough to work for. And the soil on the higher levels of Altar Valley needed only water to make it grow anything the year round. Gale, too, had come to have dreams of a future for Forlorn River.

On the afternoon of the following day Ladd unexpectedly appeared leading a lame and lathered horse into the yard. Belding and Gale, who were at work at the forge, looked up and were surprised out of speech. The legs of the horse were raw and red, and he seemed about to drop. Ladd's sombrero was missing; he wore a bloody scarf round his head; sweat and blood and dust had formed a crust on his face; little streams of powdery dust slid from him; and the lower half of his scarred chaps were full of broken white thorns.

"Howdy, boys," he drawled. "I shore am glad to see you all."

"Where'n hell's your hat?" demanded Belding, furiously. It was a ridiculous greeting. But Belding's words signified little. The dark shade of worry and solicitude crossing his face told more than his black amaze.

The ranger stopped unbuckling the saddle girths, and, looking at Belding, broke into his slow, cool laugh.

"Tom, you recollect that whopper of a saguaro up here where Carter's trail branches off the main trail to Casita? Well, I climbed it an' left my hat on top for a woodpecker's nest."

"You've been running—fighting?" queried Belding, as if Ladd had not spoken at all.

"I reckon it'll dawn on you after a while," replied Ladd, slipping the saddle.

"Laddy, go in the house to the women," said Belding. "I'll tend to your horse."

"Shore, Tom, in a minute. I've been down the road. An' I found hoss tracks an' steer tracks goin' across the line. But I seen no sign of raiders till this mornin'. Slept at Carter's last night. That raid the other day cleaned him out. He's shootin' mad. Well, this mornin' I rode plumb into a bunch of Carter's hosses, runnin' wild for home. Some Greasers were tryin' to head them round an' chase them back across the line. I rode in between an' made matters embarrassin'. Carter's hosses got away. Then me an' the Greasers had a little game of hide an' seek in the cactus. I was on the wrong side, an' had to break through their line to head toward home. We run some. But I had a closer call than I'm stuck on havin'."

"Laddy, you wouldn't have any such close calls if you'd ride one of my horses," expostulated Belding. "This broncho of yours can run, and Lord knows he's game. But you want a big, strong horse, Mexican bred, with cactus in his blood. Take one of the bunch—Bull, White Woman, Blanco Jose."

"I had a big, fast horse a while back, but I lost him," said Ladd. "This bronch ain't so bad. Shore Bull an' that white devil with his Greaser name—they could run down my bronch, kill him in a mile of cactus. But, somehow, Tom, I can't make up my mind to take one of them grand white hosses. Shore I reckon I'm kinda soft. An' mebbe I'd better take one before the raiders clean up Forlorn River."

Belding cursed low and deep in his throat, and the sound resembled muttering thunder. The shade of anxiety on his face changed to one of dark gloom and passion. Next to his wife and daughter there was nothing so dear to him as those white horses. His father and grandfather—all his progenitors of whom he had trace—had been lovers of horses. It was in Belding's blood.

"Laddy, before it's too late can't I get the whites away from the border?"

"Mebbe it ain't too late; but where can we take them?"

"To San Felipe?"

"No. We've more chance to hold them here."

"To Casita and the railroad?"

"Afraid to risk gettin' there. An' the town's full of rebels who need hosses."

"Then straight north?"

"Shore man, you're crazy. Ther's no water, no grass for a hundred miles. I'll tell you, Tom, the safest plan would be to take the white bunch south into Sonora, into some wild mountain valley. Keep them there till the raiders have traveled on back east. Pretty soon there won't be any rich pickin' left for these Greasers. An' then they'll ride on to new ranges."

"Laddy, I don't know the trails into Sonora. An' I can't trust a Mexican or a Papago. Between you and me, I'm afraid of this Indian who herds for me."

"I reckon we'd better stick here, Tom.... Dick, it's some good to see you again. But you seem kinda quiet. Shore you get quieter all the time. Did you see any sign of Jim out Sonoyta way?"

Then Belding led the lame horse toward the watering-trough, while the two rangers went toward the house, Dick was telling Ladd about the affair at Papago Well when they turned the corner under the porch. Nell was sitting in the door. She rose with a little scream and came flying toward them.

"Now I'll get it," whispered Ladd. "The women'll make a baby of me. An' shore I can't help myself."

"Oh, Laddy, you've been hurt!" cried Nell, as with white cheeks and dilating eyes she ran to him and caught his arm.

"Nell, I only run a thorn in my ear."

"Oh, Laddy, don't lie! You've lied before. I know you're hurt. Come in to mother."

"Shore, Nell, it's only a scratch. My bronch throwed me."

"Laddy, no horse every threw you." The girl's words and accusing eyes only hurried the ranger on to further duplicity.

"Mebbe I got it when I was ridin' hard under a mesquite, an' a sharp snag—"

"You've been shot!... Mama, here's Laddy, and he's been shot!.... Oh, these dreadful days we're having! I can't bear them! Forlorn River used to be so safe and quiet. Nothing happened. But now! Jim comes home with a bloody hole in him—then Dick—then Laddy!.... Oh, I'm afraid some day they'll never come home."

The morning was bright, still, and clear as crystal. The heat waves had not yet begun to rise from the desert.

A soft gray, white, and green tint perfectly blended lay like a mantle over mesquite and sand and cactus. The canyons of distant mountain showed deep and full of lilac haze.

Nell sat perched high upon the topmost bar of the corral gate. Dick leaned beside her, now with his eyes on her face, now gazing out into the alfalfa field where Belding's thoroughbreds grazed and pranced and romped and whistled. Nell watched the horses. She loved them, never tired of watching them. But her gaze was too consciously averted from the yearning eyes that tried to meet hers to be altogether natural.

A great fenced field of dark velvety green alfalfa furnished a rich background for the drove of about twenty white horses. Even without the horses the field would have presented a striking contrast to the surrounding hot, glaring blaze of rock and sand. Belding had bred a hundred or more horses from the original stock he had brought up from Durango. His particular interest was in the almost unblemished whites, and these he had given especial care. He made a good deal of money selling this strain to friends among the ranchers back in Texas. No mercenary consideration, however, could have made him part with the great, rangy white horses he had gotten from the Durango breeder. He called them Blanco Diablo (White Devil), Blanco Sol (White Sun), Blanca Reina (White Queen), Blanca Mujer (White Woman), and El Gran Toro Blanco (The Big White Bull). Belding had been laughed at by ranchers for preserving the sentimental Durango names, and he had been unmercifully ridiculed by cowboys. But the names had never been changed.

Blanco Diablo was the only horse in the field that was not free to roam and graze where he listed. A stake and a halter held him to one corner, where he was severely let alone by the other horses. He did not like this isolation. Blanco Diablo was not happy unless he was running, or fighting a rival. Of the two he would rather fight. If anything white could resemble a devil, this horse surely did. He had nothing beautiful about him, yet he drew the gaze and held it. The look of him suggested discontent, anger, revolt, viciousness. When he was not grazing or prancing, he held his long, lean head level, pointing his nose and showing his teeth. Belding's favorite was almost all the world to him, and he swore Diablo could stand more heat and thirst and cactus than any other horse he owned, and could run down and kill any horse in the Southwest. The fact that Ladd did not agree with Belding on these salient points was a great disappointment, and also a perpetual source for argument. Ladd and Lash both hated Diablo; and Dick Gale, after one or two narrow escapes from being brained, had inclined to the cowboys' side of the question.

El Gran Toro Blanco upheld his name. He was a huge, massive, thick-flanked stallion, a kingly mate for his full-bodied, glossy consort, Blanca Reina. The other mare, Blanca Mujer, was dazzling white, without a spot, perfectly pointed, racy, graceful, elegant, yet carrying weight and brawn and range that suggested her relation to her forebears.

The cowboys admitted some of Belding's claims for Diablo, but they gave loyal and unshakable allegiance to Blanco Sol. As for Dick, he had to fight himself to keep out of arguments, for he sometimes imagined he was unreasonable about the horse. Though he could not understand himself, he knew he loved Sol as a man loved a friend, a brother. Free of heavy saddle and the clumsy leg shields, Blanco Sol was somehow all-satisfying to the eyes of the rangers. As long and big as Diablo was, Sol was longer and bigger. Also, he was higher, more powerful. He looked more a thing for action—speedier. At a distance the honorable scars and lumps that marred his muscular legs were not visible. He grazed aloof from the others, and did not cavort nor prance; but when he lifted his head to whistle, how wild he appeared, and proud and splendid! The dazzling whiteness of the desert sun shone from his coat; he had the fire and spirit of the desert in his noble head, its strength and power in his gigantic frame.

"Belding swears Sol never beat Diablo," Dick was saying.

"He believes it," replied Nell. "Dad is queer about that horse."

"But Laddy rode Sol once—made him beat Diablo. Jim saw the race."

Nell laughed. "I saw it, too. For that matter, even I have made Sol put his nose before Dad's favorite."

"I'd like to have seen that. Nell, aren't you ever going to ride with me?"

"Some day—when it's safe."

"Safe!"

"I—I mean when the raiders have left the border."

"Oh, I'm glad you mean that," said Dick, laughing. "Well, I've often wondered how Belding ever came to give Blanco Sol to me."

"He was jealous. I think he wanted to get rid of Sol."

"No? Why, Nell, he'd give Laddy or Jim one of the whites any day."

"Would he? Not Devil or Queen or White Woman. Never in this world! But Dad has lots of fast horses the boys could pick from. Dick, I tell you Dad wants Blanco Sol to run himself out—lose his speed on the desert. Dad is just jealous for Diablo."

"Maybe. He surely has strange passion for horses. I think I understand better than I used to. I owned a couple of racers once. They were just animals to me, I guess. But Blanco Sol!"

"Do you love him?" asked Nell; and now a warm, blue flash of eyes swept his face.

"Do I? Well, rather."

"I'm glad. Sol has been finer, a better horse since you owned him. He loves you, Dick. He's always watching for you. See him raise his head. That's for you. I know as much about horses as Dad or Laddy any day. Sol always hated Diablo, and he never had much use for Dad."

Dick looked up at her.

"It'll be—be pretty hard to leave Sol—when I go away."

Nell sat perfectly still.

"Go away?" she asked, presently, with just the faintest tremor in her voice.

"Yes. Sometimes when I get blue—as I am to-day—I think I'll go. But, in sober truth, Nell, it's not likely that I'll spend all my life here."

There was no answer to this. Dick put his hand softly over hers; and, despite her half-hearted struggle to free it, he held on.

"Nell!"

Her color fled. He saw her lips part. Then a heavy step on the gravel, a cheerful, complaining voice interrupted him, and made him release Nell and draw back. Belding strode into view round the adobe shed.

"Hey, Dick, that darned Yaqui Indian can't be driven or hired or coaxed to leave Forlorn River. He's well enough to travel. I offered him horse, gun, blanket, grub. But no go."

"That's funny," replied Gale, with a smile. "Let him stay—put him to work."

"It doesn't strike me funny. But I'll tell you what I think. That poor, homeless, heartbroken Indian has taken a liking to you, Dick. These desert Yaquis are strange folk. I've heard strange stories about them. I'd believe 'most anything. And that's how I figure his case. You saved his life. That sort of thing counts big with any Indian, even with an Apache. With a Yaqui maybe it's of deep significance. I've heard a Yaqui say that with his tribe no debt to friend or foe ever went unpaid. Perhaps that's what ails this fellow."

"Dick, don't laugh," said Nell. "I've noticed the Yaqui. It's pathetic the way his great gloomy eyes follow you."

"You've made a friend," continued Belding. "A Yaqui could be a real friend on this desert. If he gets his strength back he'll be of service to you, don't mistake me. He's welcome here. But you're responsible for him, and you'll have trouble keeping him from massacring all the Greasers in Forlorn River."

The probability of a visit from the raiders, and a dash bolder than usual on the outskirts of a ranch, led Belding to build a new corral. It was not sightly to the eye, but it was high and exceedingly strong. The gate was a massive affair, swinging on huge hinges and fastening with heavy chains and padlocks. On the outside it had been completely covered with barb wire, which would make it a troublesome thing to work on in the dark.

At night Belding locked his white horses in this corral. The Papago herdsman slept in the adobe shed adjoining. Belding did not imagine that any wooden fence, however substantially built, could keep determined raiders from breaking it down. They would have to take time, however, and make considerable noise; and Belding relied on these facts. Belding did not believe a band of night raiders would hold out against a hot rifle fire. So he began to make up some of the sleep he had lost. It was noteworthy, however, that Ladd did not share Belding's sanguine hopes.

Jim Lash rode in, reporting that all was well out along the line toward the Sonoyta Oasis. Days passed, and Belding kept his rangers home. Nothing was heard of raiders at hand. Many of the newcomers, both American and Mexican, who came with wagons and pack trains from Casita stated that property and life were cheap back in that rebel-infested town.

One January morning Dick Gale was awakened by a shrill, menacing cry. He leaped up bewildered and frightened. He heard Belding's booming voice answering shouts, and rapid steps on flagstones. But these had not awakened him. Heavy breaths, almost sobs, seemed at his very door. In the cold and gray dawn

Dick saw something white. Gun in hand, he bounded across the room. Just outside his door stood Blanco Sol.

It was not unusual for Sol to come poking his head in at Dick's door during daylight. But now in the early dawn, when he had been locked in the corral, it meant raiders—no less. Dick called softly to the snorting horse; and, hurriedly getting into clothes and boots, he went out with a gun in each hand. Sol was quivering in every muscle. Like a dog he followed Dick around the house. Hearing shouts in the direction of the corrals, Gale bent swift steps that way.

He caught up with Jim Lash, who was also leading a white horse.

"Hello, Jim! Guess it's all over but the fireworks," said Dick.

"I cain't say just what has come off," replied Lash. "I've got the Bull. Found him runnin' in the yard."

They reached the corral to find Belding shaking, roaring like a madman. The gate was open, the corral was empty. Ladd stooped over the ground, evidently trying to find tracks.

"I reckon we might jest as well cool off an' wait for daylight," suggested Jim.

"Shore. They've flown the coop, you can gamble on that. Tom, where's the Papago?" said Ladd.

"He's gone, Laddy—gone!"

"Double-crossed us, eh? I see here's a crowbar lyin' by the gatepost. That Indian fetched it from the forge. It was used to pry out the bolts an' steeples. Tom, I reckon there wasn't much time lost forcin' that gate."

Belding, in shirt sleeves and barefooted, roared with rage. He said he had heard the horses running as he leaped out of bed.

"What woke you?" asked Laddy.

"Sol. He came whistling for Dick. Didn't you hear him before I called you?"

"Hear him! He came thunderin' right under my window. I jumped up in bed, an' when he let out that blast Jim lit square in the middle of the floor, an' I was scared stiff. Dick, seein' it was your room he blew into, what did you think?"

"I couldn't think. I'm shaking yet, Laddy."

"Boys, I'll bet Sol spilled a few raiders if any got hands on him," said Jim. "Now, let's sit down an' wait for daylight. It's my idea we'll find some of the hosses runnin' loose. Tom, you go an' get some clothes on. It's freezin' cold. An' don't forget to tell the women folks we're all right."

Daylight made clear some details of the raid. The cowboys found tracks of eight raiders coming up from the river bed where their horses had been left. Evidently the Papago had been false to his trust. His few personal belongings were gone. Lash was correct in his idea of finding more horses loose in the fields. The men soon rounded up eleven of the whites, all more or less frightened, and among the number were Queen and Blanca Mujer. The raiders had been unable to handle more than one horse for each man. It was bitter irony of fate that Belding should lose his favorite, the one horse more dear to him than all the others. Somewhere out on the trail a raider was fighting the iron-jawed savage Blanco Diablo.

"I reckon we're some lucky," observed Jim Lash.

"Lucky ain't enough word," replied Ladd. "You see, it was this way. Some of the raiders piled over the fence while the others worked on the gate. Mebbe the Papago went inside to pick out the best hosses. But it didn't work except with Diablo, an' how they ever got him I don't know. I'd have gambled it'd take all of eight men to steal him. But Greasers have got us skinned on handlin' hosses."

Belding was unconsolable. He cursed and railed, and finally declared he was going to trail the raiders.

"Tom, you just ain't agoin' to do nothin' of the kind," said Ladd coolly.

Belding groaned and bowed his head.

"Laddy, you're right," he replied, presently. "I've got to stand it. I can't leave the women and my property. But it's sure tough. I'm sore way down deep, and nothin' but blood would ever satisfy me."

"Leave that to me an' Jim," said Ladd.

"What do you mean to do?" demanded Belding, starting up.

"Shore I don't know yet.... Give me a light for my pipe. An' Dick, go fetch out your Yaqui."

VIII THE RUNNING OF BLANCO SOL

THE Yaqui's strange dark glance roved over the corral, the swinging gate with its broken fastenings, the tracks in the road, and then rested upon Belding.

"Malo," he said, and his Spanish was clear.

"Shore Yaqui, about eight bad men, an' a traitor Indian," said Ladd.

"I think he means my herder," added Belding. "If he does, that settles any doubt it might be decent to have—Yaqui—malo Papago—Si?"

The Yaqui spread wide his hands. Then he bent over the tracks in the road. They led everywhither, but gradually he worked out of the thick net to take the trail that the cowboys had followed down to the river. Belding and the rangers kept close at his heels. Occasionally Dick lent a helping hand to the still feeble Indian. He found a trampled spot where the raiders had left their horses. From this point a deeply defined narrow trail led across the dry river bed.

Belding asked the Yaqui where the raiders would head for in the Sonora Desert. For answer the Indian followed the trail across the stream of sand, through willows and mesquite, up to the level of rock and cactus. At this point he halted. A sand-filled, almost obliterated trail led off to the left, and evidently went round to the east of No Name Mountains. To the right stretched the road toward Papago Well and the Sonoyta Oasis. The trail of the raiders took a southeasterly course over untrodden desert. The Yaqui spoke in his own tongue, then in Spanish.

"Think he means slow march," said Belding. "Laddy, from the looks of that trail the Greasers are having trouble with the horses."

"Tom, shore a boy could see that," replied Laddy. "Ask Yaqui to tell us where the raiders are headin', an' if there's water."

It was wonderful to see the Yaqui point. His dark hand stretched, he sighted over his stretched finger at a low white escarpment in the distance. Then with a stick he traced a line in the sand, and then at the end of that another line at right angles. He made crosses and marks and holes, and as he drew the rude map he talked in Yaqui, in Spanish; with a word here and there in English. Belding translated as best he could. The raiders were heading southeast toward the railroad that ran from Nogales down into Sonora. It was four days' travel, bad trail, good sure waterhole one day out; then water not sure for two days. Raiders traveling slow; bothered by too many horses, not looking for pursuit; were never pursued, could be headed and ambushed that night at the first waterhole, a natural trap in a valley.

The men returned to the ranch. The rangers ate and drank while making hurried preparations for travel. Blanco Sol and the cowboys' horses were fed, watered, and saddled. Ladd again refused to ride one of Belding's whites. He was quick and cold.

"Get me a long-range rifle an' lots of shells. Rustle now," he said.

"Laddy, you don't want to be weighted down?" protested Belding.

"Shore I want a gun that'll outshoot the dinky little carbines an' muskets used by the rebels. Trot one out an' be quick."

"I've got a .405, a long-barreled heavy rifle that'll shoot a mile. I use it for mountain sheep. But Laddy, it'll break that bronch's back."

"His back won't break so easy.... Dick, take plenty of shells for your Remington. An' don't forget your field glass."

In less than an hour after the time of the raid the three rangers, heavily armed and superbly mounted on fresh horses, rode out on the trail. As Gale turned to look back from the far bank of Forlorn River, he saw Nell waving a white scarf. He stood high in his stirrups and waved his sombrero. Then the mesquites hid the girl's slight figure, and Gale wheeled grim-faced to follow the rangers.

They rode in single file with Ladd in the lead. He did not keep to the trail of the raiders all the time. He made short cuts. The raiders were traveling leisurely, and they evinced a liking for the most level and least cactus-covered stretches of ground. But the cowboy took a bee-line course for the white escarpment pointed out by the Yaqui; and nothing save deep washes and impassable patches of cactus or rocks made him swerve from it. He kept the broncho at a steady walk over the rougher places and at a swinging Indian canter over the hard and level ground. The sun grew hot and the wind began to blow. Dust clouds rolled along the blue horizon. Whirling columns of sand, like water spouts at sea, circled up out of white arid basins, and swept away and spread aloft before the wind. The escarpment began to rise, to change color, to show breaks upon its rocky face.

Whenever the rangers rode out on the brow of a knoll or ridge or an eminence, before starting to descend, Ladd required of Gale a long, careful, sweeping survey of the desert ahead through the field glass. There were streams of white dust to be seen, streaks of yellow dust, trailing low clouds of sand over the glistening dunes, but no steadily rising, uniformly shaped puffs that would tell a tale of moving horses on the desert.

At noon the rangers got out of the thick cactus. Moreover, the gravel-bottomed washes, the low weathering, rotting ledges of yellow rock gave place to hard sandy rolls and bare clay knolls. The desert resembled a rounded hummocky sea of color. All light shades of blue and pink and yellow and mauve were there dominated by the glaring white sun. Mirages glistened, wavered, faded in the shimmering waves of heat. Dust as fine as powder whiffed up from under the tireless hoofs.

The rangers rode on and the escarpment began to loom. The desert floor inclined perceptibly upward. When Gale got an unobstructed view of the slope of the escarpment he located the raiders and horses. In another hour's travel the rangers could see with naked eyes a long, faint moving streak of black and white dots.

"They're headin' for that yellow pass," said Ladd, pointing to a break in the eastern end of the escarpment. "When they get out of sight we'll rustle. I'm thinkin' that waterhole the Yaqui spoke of lays in the pass."

The rangers traveled swiftly over the remaining miles of level desert leading to the ascent of the escarpment. When they achieved the gateway of the pass the sun was low in the west. Dwarfed mesquite and greasewood appeared among the rocks. Ladd gave the word to tie up horses and go forward on foot.

The narrow neck of the pass opened and descended into a valley half a mile wide, perhaps twice that in length. It had apparently unscalable slopes of weathered rock leading up to beetling walls. With floor bare and hard and white, except for a patch of green mesquite near the far end it was a lurid and desolate spot, the barren bottom of a desert bowl.

"Keep down, boys" said Ladd. "There's the waterhole an' hosses have sharp eyes. Shore the Yaqui figgered this place. I never seen its like for a trap."

Both white and black horses showed against the green, and a thin curling column of blue smoke rose lazily from amid the mesquites.

"I reckon we'd better wait till dark, or mebbe daylight," said Jim Lash.

"Let me figger some. Dick, what do you make of the outlet to this hole? Looks rough to me."

With his glass Gale studied the narrow construction of walls and roughened rising floor.

"Laddy, it's harder to get out at that end than here," he replied.

"Shore that's hard enough. Let me have a look.... Well, boys, it don't take no figgerin' for this job. Jim, I'll want you at the other end blockin' the pass when we're ready to start."

"When'll that be?" inquired Jim.

"Soon as it's light enough in the mornin'. That Greaser outfit will hang till tomorrow. There's no sure water ahead for two days, you remember."

"I reckon I can slip through to the other end after dark," said Lash, thoughtfully. "It might get me in bad to go round."

The rangers stole back from the vantage point and returned to their horses, which they untied and left farther round among broken sections of cliff. For the horses it was a dry, hungry camp, but the rangers built a fire and had their short though strengthening meal.

The location was high, and through a break in the jumble of rocks the great colored void of desert could be seen rolling away endlessly to the west. The sun set, and after it had gone down the golden tips of mountains dulled, their lower shadows creeping upward.

Jim Lash rolled in his saddle blanket, his feet near the fire, and went to sleep. Ladd told Gale to do likewise while he kept the fire up and waited until it was late enough for Jim to undertake circling round the raiders. When Gale awakened the night was dark, cold, windy. The stars shone with white brilliance. Jim was up saddling his horse, and Ladd was talking low. When Gale rose to accompany them both rangers said he need not go. But Gale wanted to go because that was the thing Ladd or Jim would have done.

With Ladd leading, they moved away into the gloom. Advance was exceedingly slow, careful, silent. Under the walls the blackness seemed impenetrable. The horse was as cautious as his master. Ladd did not lose his way, nevertheless he wound between blocks of stone and clumps of mesquite, and often tried a passage to abandon it. Finally the trail showed pale in the gloom, and eastern stars twinkled between the lofty ramparts of the pass.

The advance here was still as stealthily made as before, but not so difficult or slow. When the dense gloom of the pass lightened, and there was a wide space of sky and stars overhead, Ladd halted and stood silent a moment.

"Luck again!" he whispered. "The wind's in your face, Jim. The horses won't scent you. Go slow. Don't crack a stone. Keep close under the wall. Try to get up as high as this at the other end. Wait till daylight before riskin' a loose slope. I'll be ridin' the job early. That's all."

Ladd's cool, easy speech was scarcely significant of the perilous undertaking. Lash moved very slowly away, leading his horse. The soft pads of hoofs ceased to sound about the time the gray shape merged into the black shadows. Then Ladd touched Dick's arm, and turned back up the trail.

But Dick tarried a moment. He wanted a fuller sense of that ebony-bottomed abyss, with its pale encircling walls reaching up to the dusky blue sky and the brilliant stars. There was absolutely no sound.

He retraced his steps down, soon coming up with Ladd; and together they picked a way back through the winding recesses of cliff. The campfire was smoldering. Ladd replenished it and lay down to get a few hours' sleep, while Gale kept watch. The after part of the night wore on till the paling of stars, the thickening of gloom indicated the dark hour before dawn. The spot was secluded from wind, but the air grew cold as ice. Gale spent the time stripping wood from a dead mesquite, in pacing to and fro, in listening. Blanco Sol stamped occasionally, which sound was all that broke the stilliness. Ladd awoke before the faintest gray appeared. The rangers ate and drank. When the black did lighten to gray they saddled the horses and led them out to the pass and down to the point where they had parted with Lash. Here they awaited daylight.

To Gale it seemed long in coming. Such a delay always aggravated the slow fire within him. He had nothing of Ladd's patience. He wanted action. The gray shadow below thinned out, and the patch of mesquite made a blot upon the pale valley. The day dawned.

Still Ladd waited. He grew more silent, grimmer as the time of action approached. Gale wondered what the plan of attack would be. Yet he did not ask. He waited ready for orders.

The valley grew clear of gray shadow except under leaning walls on the eastern side. Then a straight column of smoke rose from among the mesquites. Manifestly this was what Ladd had been awaiting. He took the long .405 from its sheath and tried the lever. Then he lifted a cartridge belt from the pommel of his saddle. Every ring held a shell and these shells were four inches long. He buckled the belt round him.

"Come on, Dick."

Ladd led the way down the slope until he reached a position that commanded the rising of the trail from a level. It was the only place a man or horse could leave the valley for the pass.

"Dick, here's your stand. If any raider rides in range take a crack at him.... Now I want the lend of your hoss."

"Blanco Sol!" exclaimed Gale, more in amazement that Ladd should ask for the horse than in reluctance to lend him.

"Will you let me have him?" Ladd repeated, almost curtly.

"Certainly, Laddy."

A smile momentarily chased the dark cold gloom that had set upon the ranger's lean face.

"Shore I appreciate it, Dick. I know how you care for that hoss. I guess mebbe Charlie Ladd has loved a hoss! An' one not so good as Sol. I was only tryin' your nerve, Dick, askin' you without tellin' my plan. Sol won't get a scratch, you can gamble on that! I'll ride him down into the valley an' pull the greasers out in the open. They've got short-ranged carbines. They can't keep out of range of the .405, an' I'll be takin' the dust of their lead. Sabe, senor?"

"Laddy! You'll run Sol away from the raiders when they chase you? Run him after them when they try to get away?"

"Shore. I'll run all the time. They can't gain on Sol, an' he'll run them down when I want. Can you beat it?"

"No. It's great!... But suppose a raider comes out on Blanco Diablo?"

"I reckon that's the one weak place in my plan. I'm figgerin' they'll never think of that till it's too late. But if they do, well, Sol can outrun Diablo. An' I can always kill the white devil!"

Ladd's strange hate of the horse showed in the passion of his last words, in his hardening jaw and grim set lips.

Gale's hand went swiftly to the ranger's shoulder.

"Laddy. Don't kill Diablo unless it's to save your life."

"All right. But, by God, if I get a chance I'll make Blanco Sol run him off his legs!"

He spoke no more and set about changing the length of Sol's stirrups. When he had them adjusted to suit he mounted and rode down the trail and out upon the level. He rode leisurely as if merely going to water his horse. The long black rifle lying across his saddle, however, was ominous.

Gale securely tied the other horse to a mesquite at hand, and took a position behind a low rock over which he could easily see and shoot when necessary. He imagined Jim Lash in a similar position at the far end of the valley blocking the outlet. Gale had grown accustomed to danger and the hard and fierce feelings peculiar to it. But the coming drama was so peculiarly different in promise from all he had experienced, that he waited the moment of action with thrilling intensity. In him stirred long, brooding wrath at these border raiders—affection for Belding, and keen desire to avenge the outrages he had suffered—warm admiration for the cold, implacable Ladd and his absolute fearlessness, and a curious throbbing interest in the old, much-discussed and never-decided argument as to whether Blanco Sol was fleeter, stronger horse than Blanco Diablo. Gale felt that he was to see a race between these great rivals—the kind of race that made men and horses terrible.

Ladd rode a quarter of a mile out upon the flat before anything happened. Then a whistle rent the still, cold air. A horse had seen or scented Blanco Sol. The whistle was prolonged, faint, but clear. It made the blood thrum in Gale's ears. Sol halted. His head shot up with the old, wild, spirited sweep. Gale leveled his glass at the patch of mesquites. He saw the raiders running to an open place, pointing, gesticulating. The glass brought them so close that he saw the dark faces. Suddenly they broke and fled back among the trees. Then he got only white and dark gleams of moving bodies. Evidently that moment was one of boots, guns, and saddles for the raiders.

Lowering the glass, Gale saw that Blanco Sol had started forward again. His gait was now a canter, and he had covered another quarter of a mile before horses and raiders appeared upon the outskirts of the mesquites. Then Blanco Sol stopped. His shrill, ringing whistle came distinctly to Gale's ears. The raiders were mounted on dark horses, and they stood abreast in a motionless line. Gale chuckled as he appreciated what a puzzle the situation presented for them. A lone horseman in the middle of the valley did not perhaps seem so menacing himself as the possibilities his presence suggested.

Then Gale saw a raider gallop swiftly from the group toward the farther outlet of the valley. This might have been owing to characteristic cowardice; but it was more likely a move of the raiders to make sure of retreat. Undoubtedly Ladd saw this galloping horseman. A few waiting moments ensued. The galloping horseman reached the slope, began to climb. With naked eyes Gale saw a puff of white smoke spring out of the rocks. Then the raider wheeled his plunging horse back to the level, and went racing wildly down the valley.

The compact bunch of bays and blacks seemed to break apart and spread rapidly from the edge of the mesquites. Puffs of white smoke indicated firing, and showed the nature of the raiders' excitement. They were far out of ordinary range, but they spurred toward Ladd, shooting as they rode. Ladd held his ground; the big white horse stood like a rock in his tracks. Gale saw little spouts of dust rise in front of Blanco Sol and spread swift as sight to his rear. The raiders' bullets, striking low, were skipping along the hard, bare floor of the valley. Then Ladd raised the long rifle. There was no smoke, but three high, spanging reports rang out. A gap opened in the dark line of advancing horsemen; then a riderless steed sheered off to the right. Blanco Sol seemed to turn as on a pivot and charged back toward the lower end of the valley. He circled over to Gale's right and stretched out into his run. There were now five raiders in pursuit, and they came sweeping down, yelling and shooting, evidently sure of their quarry. Ladd reserved his fire. He kept turning from back to front in his saddle.

Gale saw how the space widened between pursuers and pursued, saw distinctly when Ladd eased up Sol's running. Manifestly Ladd intended to try to lead the raiders round in front of Gale's position, and, presently, Gale saw he was going to succeed. The raiders, riding like vaqueros, swept on in a curve, cutting off what distance they could. One fellow, a small, wiry rider, high on his mount's neck like a jockey, led his companions by many yards. He seemed to be getting the range of Ladd, or else he shot high, for his bullets did not strike up the dust behind Sol. Gale was ready to shoot. Blanco Sol pounded by, his rapid, rhythmic hoofbeats plainly to be heard. He was running easily.

Gale tried to still the jump of heart and pulse, and turned his eye again on the nearest pursuer. This raider was crossing in, his carbine held muzzle up in his right hand, and he was coming swiftly. It was a long shot, upward of five hundred yards. Gale had not time to adjust the sights of the Remington, but he knew the gun and, holding coarsely upon the swiftly moving blot, he began to shoot. The first bullet sent up a great splash of dust beneath the horse's nose, making him leap as if to hurdle a fence. The rifle was automatic; Gale needed only to pull the trigger. He saw now that the raiders behind were in line. Swiftly he worked the trigger. Suddenly the leading horse leaped convulsively, not up nor aside, but straight ahead, and then he crashed to the ground throwing his rider like a catapult, and then slid and rolled. He half got up, fell back, and kicked; but his rider never moved.

The other raiders sawed the reins of plunging steeds and whirled to escape the unseen battery. Gale slipped a fresh clip into the magazine of his rifle. He restrained himself from useless firing and gave eager eye to the duel below. Ladd began to shoot while Sol was running. The .405 rang out sharply—then again. The heavy bullets streaked the dust all the way across the valley. Ladd aimed deliberately and pulled slowly, unmindful of the kicking dust-puffs behind Sol, and to the side. The raiders spurred madly in pursuit, loading and firing. They shot ten times while Ladd shot once, and all in vain; and on Ladd's sixth shot a raider topped backward, threw his carbine and fell with his foot catching in a stirrup. The frightened horse plunged away, dragging him in a path of dust.

Gale had set himself to miss nothing of that fighting race, yet the action passed too swiftly for clear sight of all. Ladd had emptied a magazine, and now Blanco Sol quickened and lengthened his running stride. He ran away from his pursuers. Then it was that the ranger's ruse was divined by the raiders. They hauled sharply up and seemed to be conferring. But that was a fatal mistake. Blanco Sol was seen to break his gait and slow down in several jumps, then square away and stand stockstill. Ladd fired at the closely grouped raiders. An instant passed. Then Gale heard the spat of a bullet out in front, saw a puff of dust, then heard the lead strike the rocks and go whining away. And it was after this that one of the raiders fell prone from his saddle. The steel-jacketed .405 had gone through him on its uninterrupted way to hum past Gale's position.

The remaining two raiders frantically spurred their horses and fled up the valley. Ladd sent Sol after them. It seemed to Gale, even though he realized his excitement, that Blanco Sol made those horses seem like snails. The raiders split, one making for the eastern outlet, the other circling back of the mesquites. Ladd kept on after the latter. Then puffs of white smoke and rifle shots faintly crackling told Jim Lash's hand in the game. However, he succeeded only in driving the raider back into the valley. But Ladd had turned the other horseman, and now it appeared the two raiders were between Lash above on the stony slope and Ladd below on the level. There was desperate riding on part of the raiders to keep from being hemmed in closer. Only one of them got away, and he came riding for life down under the eastern wall. Blanco Sol settled into his graceful, beautiful swing. He gained steadily, though he was far from extending himself. By Gale's actual count the raider fired eight times in that race down the valley, and all his bullets went low and wide. He pitched the carbine away and lost all control in headlong flight.

Some few hundred rods to the left of Gale the raider put his horse to the weathered slope. He began to climb. The horse was superb, infinitely more courageous than his rider. Zigzag they went up and up, and when Ladd reached the edge of the slope they were high along the cracked and guttered rampart. Once—twice Ladd raised the long rifle, but each time he lowered it. Gale divined that the ranger's restraint was not on account of the Mexican, but for that valiant and faithful horse. Up and up he went, and the yellow dust clouds rose, and an avalanche rolled rattling and cracking down the slope. It was beyond belief that a horse, burdened or unburdened, could find footing and hold it upon that wall of narrow ledges and inverted, slanting gullies. But he climbed on, sure-footed as a mountain goat, and, surmounting the last rough steps, he stood a moment silhouetted against the white sky. Then he disappeared. Ladd sat astride Blanco Sol gazing upward. How the cowboy must have honored that raider's brave steed!

Gale, who had been too dumb to shout the admiration he felt, suddenly leaped up, and his voice came with a shriek:

"LOOK OUT, LADDY!"

A big horse, like a white streak, was bearing down to the right of the ranger. Blanco Diablo! A matchless rider swung with the horse's motion. Gale was stunned. Then he remembered the first raider, the one Lash had shot at and driven away from the outlet. This fellow had made for the mesquite and had put a saddle on Belding's favorite. In the heat of the excitement, while Ladd had been intent upon the climbing horse, this last raider had come down with the speed of the wind straight for the western outlet. Perhaps, very probably, he did not know Gale was there to block it; and certainly he hoped to pass Ladd and Blanco Sol.

A touch of the spur made Sol lunge forward to head off the raider. Diablo was in his stride, but the distance and angle favored Sol. The raider had no carbine. He held aloft a gun ready to level it and fire. He sat the saddle as if it were a stationary seat. Gale saw Ladd lean down and drop the .405 in the sand. He would take no chances of wounding Belding's best-loved horse.

Then Gale sat transfixed with suspended breath watching the horses thundering toward him. Blanco Diablo was speeding low, fleet as an antelope, fierce and terrible in his devilish action, a horse for war and blood and death. He seemed unbeatable. Yet to see the magnificently running Blanco Sol was but to court a doubt. Gale stood spellbound. He might have shot the raider; but he never thought of such a thing. The distance swiftly lessened. Plain it was the raider could not make the opening ahead of Ladd. He saw it and swerved to the left, emptying his six-shooter as he turned. His dark face gleamed as he flashed by Gale.

Blanco Sol thundered across. Then the race became straight away up the valley. Diablo was cold and Sol was hot; therein lay the only handicap and vantage. It was a fleet, beautiful, magnificent race. Gale thrilled and exulted and yelled as his horse settled into a steadily swifter run and began to gain. The dust rolled in a funnel-shaped cloud from the flying hoofs. The raider wheeled with gun puffing white, and Ladd ducked low over the neck of his horse.

The gap between Diablo and Sol narrowed yard by yard. At first it had been a wide one. The raider beat his mount and spurred, beat and spurred, wheeled round to shoot, then bent forward again. In his circle at the upper end of the valley he turned far short of the jumble of rocks.

All the devil that was in Blanco Diablo had its running on the downward stretch. The strange, cruel urge of bit and spur, the crazed rider who stuck like a burr upon him, the shots and smoke added terror to his natural violent temper. He ran himself off his feet. But he could not elude that relentless horse behind him. The running of Blanco Sol was that of a sure, remorseless driving power—steadier—stronger—swifter with every long and wonderful stride.

The raider tried to sheer Diablo off closer under the wall, to make the slope where his companion had escaped. But Diablo was uncontrollable. He was running wild, with breaking gait. Closer and closer crept that white, smoothly gliding, beautiful machine of speed.

Then, like one white flash following another, the two horses gleamed down the bank of a wash and disappeared in clouds of dust.

Gale watched with strained and smarting eyes. The thick throb in his ears was pierced by faint sounds of gunshots. Then he waited in almost unendurable suspense.

Suddenly something whiter than the background of dust appeared above the low roll of valley floor. Gale leveled his glass. In the clear circle shone Blanco

Sol's noble head with its long black bar from ears to nose. Sol's head was drooping now. Another second showed Ladd still in the saddle.

The ranger was leading Blanco Diable—spent—broken—dragging—riderless.

IX AN INTERRUPTED SIESTA

NO man ever had a more eloquent and beautiful pleader for his cause than had Dick Gale in Mercedes Castaneda. He peeped through the green, shining twigs of the palo verde that shaded his door. The hour was high noon, and the patio was sultry. The only sounds were the hum of bees in the flowers and the low murmur of the Spanish girl's melodious voice. Nell lay in the hammock, her hands behind her head, with rosy cheeks and arch eyes. Indeed, she looked rebellious. Certain it was, Dick reflected, that the young lady had fully recovered the wilful personality which had lain dormant for a while. Equally certain it seemed that Mercedes's earnestness was not apparently having the effect it should have had.

Dick was inclined to be rebellious himself. Belding had kept the rangers in off the line, and therefore Dick had been idle most of the time, and, though he tried hard, he had been unable to stay far from Nell's vicinity. He believed she cared for him; but he could not catch her alone long enough to verify his tormenting hope. When alone she was as illusive as a shadow, as quick as a flash, as mysterious as a Yaqui. When he tried to catch her in the garden or fields, or corner her in the patio, she eluded him, and left behind a memory of dark-blue, haunting eyes. It was that look in her eyes which lent him hope. At other times, when it might have been possible for Dick to speak, Nell clung closely to Mercedes. He had long before enlisted the loyal Mercedes in his cause; but in spite of this Nell had been more than a match for them both.

Gale pondered over an idea he had long revolved in mind, and which now suddenly gave place to a decision that made his heart swell and his cheek burn. He peeped again through the green branches to see Nell laughing at the fiery Mercedes.

"Qui'en sabe," he called, mockingly, and was delighted with Nell's quick, amazed start.

Then he went in search of Mrs. Belding, and found her busy in the kitchen. The relation between Gale and Mrs. Belding had subtly and incomprehensively changed. He understood her less than when at first he divined an antagonism in her. If such a thing were possible she had retained the antagonism while seeming to yield to some influence that must have been fondness for him. Gale was in no wise sure of her affection, and he had long imagined she was afraid of him, or of something that he represented. He had gone on, openly and fairly, though discreetly, with his rather one-sided love affair; and as time passed he had grown less conscious of what had seemed her unspoken opposition. Gale had come to care greatly for Nell's mother. Not only was she the comfort and strength of her home, but also of the inhabitants of Forlorn River. Indian, Mexican, American were all the same to her in trouble or illness; and then she was nurse, doctor, peacemaker, helper. She was good and noble, and there was not a child or grownup in Forlorn River who did not love and bless her. But Mrs. Belding did not seem happy. She was brooding, intense, deep, strong, eager for the happiness and welfare of others; and she was dominated by a worship of her daughter that was as strange as it was pathetic. Mrs. Belding seldom smiled, and never laughed. There was always a soft, sad, hurt look in her eyes. Gale often wondered if there had been other tragedy in her life than the supposed loss of her father in the desert. Perhaps it was the very unsolved nature of that loss which made it haunting.

Mrs. Belding heard Dick's step as he entered the kitchen, and, looking up, greeted him.

"Mother," began Dick, earnestly. Belding called her that, and so did Ladd and Lash, but it was the first time for Dick. "Mother—I want to speak to you."

The only indication Mrs. Belding gave of being started was in her eyes, which darkened, shadowed with multiplying thought.

"I love Nell," went on Dick, simply, "and I want you to let me ask her to be my wife."

Mrs. Belding's face blanched to a deathly white. Gale, thinking with surprise and concern that she was going to faint, moved quickly toward her, took her arm.

"Forgive me. I was blunt.... But I thought you knew."

"I've known for a long time," replied Mrs. Belding. Her voice was steady, and there was no evidence of agitation except in her pallor. "Then you—you haven't spoken to Nell?"

Dick laughed. "I've been trying to get a chance to tell her. I haven't had it yet. But she knows. There are other ways besides speech. And Mercedes has told her. I hope, I almost believe Nell cares a little for me."

"I've known that, too, for a long time," said Mrs. Belding, low almost as a whisper.

"You know!" cried Dick, with a glow and rush of feeling.

"Dick, you must be very blind not to see what has been plain to all of us.... I guess—it couldn't have been helped. You're a splendid fellow. No wonder she loves you."

"Mother! You'll give her to me?"

She drew him to the light and looked with strange, piercing intentness into his face. Gale had never dreamed a woman's eyes could hold such a world of thought and feeling. It seemed all the sweetness of life was there, and all the pain.

"Do you love her?" she asked.

"With all my heart."

"You want to marry her?"

"Ah, I want to! As much as I want to live and work for her."

"When would you marry her?"

"Why!... Just as soon as she will do it. To-morrow!" Dick gave a wild, exultant little laugh.

"Dick Gale, you want my Nell? You love her just as she is—her sweetness—her goodness? Just herself, body and soul?... There's nothing could change you—nothing?"

"Dear Mrs. Belding, I love Nell for herself. If she loves me I'll be the happiest of men. There's absolutely nothing that could make any difference in me."

"But your people? Oh, Dick, you come of a proud family. I can tell. I—I once knew a young man like you. A few months can't change pride—blood. Years can't change them. You've become a ranger. You love the adventure—the wild life. That won't last. Perhaps you'll settle down to ranching. I know you love the West. But, Dick, there's your family—"

"If you want to know anything about my family, I'll tell you," interrupted Dick, with strong feeling. "I've not secrets about them or myself. My future and happiness are Nell's to make. No one else shall count with me."

"Then, Dick—you may have her. God—bless—you—both."

Mrs. Belding's strained face underwent a swift and mobile relaxation, and suddenly she was weeping in strangely mingled happiness and bitterness.

"Why, mother!" Gale could say no more. He did not comprehend a mood seemingly so utterly at variance with Mrs. Belding's habitual temperament. But he put his arm around her. In another moment she had gained command over herself, and, kissing him, she pushed him out of the door.

"There! Go tell her, Dick... And have some spunk about it!"

Gale went thoughtfully back to his room. He vowed that he would answer for Nell's happiness, if he had the wonderful good fortune to win her. Then remembering the hope Mrs. Belding had given him, Dick lost his gravity in a flash, and something began to dance and ring within him. He simply could not keep his steps turned from the patio. Every path led there. His blood was throbbing, his hopes mounting, his spirit soaring. He knew he had never before entered the patio with that inspirited presence.

"Now for some spunk!" he said, under his breath.

Plainly he meant his merry whistle and his buoyant step to interrupt this first languorous stage of the siesta which the girls always took during the hot hours. Nell had acquired the habit long before Mercedes came to show how fixed a thing it was in the life of the tropics. But neither girl heard him. Mercedes lay under the palo verde, her beautiful head dark and still upon a cushion. Nell was asleep in the hammock. There was an abandonment in her deep repose, and a faint smile upon her face. Her sweet, red lips, with the soft, perfect curve, had always fascinated Dick, and now drew him irresistibly. He had always been consumed with a desire to kiss her, and now he was overwhelmed with his opportunity. It would be a terrible thing to do, but if she did not awaken at once— No, he would fight the temptation. That would be more than spunk. It would— Suddenly an ugly green fly sailed low over Nell, appeared about to alight on her. Noiselessly Dick stepped close to the hammock bent under the tree, and with a sweep of his hand chased the intruding fly away. But he found himself powerless to straighten up. He was close to her—bending over her face—near the sweet lips. The insolent, dreaming smile just parted them. Then he thought he was lost. But she stirred—he feared she would awaken.

He had stepped back erect when she opened her eyes. They were sleepy, yet surprised until she saw him. Then she was wide awake in a second, bewildered, uncertain.

"Why—you here?" she asked, slowly.

"Large as life!" replied Dick, with unusual gayety.

"How long have you been here?"

"Just got here this fraction of a second," he replied, lying shamelessly.

It was evident that she did not know whether or not to believe him, and as she studied him a slow blush dyed her cheek.

"You are absolutely truthful when you say you just stepped there?"

"Why, of course," answered Dick, right glad he did not have to lie about that.

"I thought—I was—dreaming," she said, and evidently the sound of her voice reassured her.

"Yes, you looked as if you were having pleasant dreams," replied Dick. "So sorry to wake you. I can't see how I came to do it, I was so quiet. Mercedes didn't wake. Well, I'll go and let you have your siesta and dreams."

But he did not move to go. Nell regarded him with curious, speculative eyes.

"Isn't it a lovely day?" queried Dick.

"I think it's hot."

"Only ninety in the shade. And you've told me the mercury goes to one hundred and thirty in midsummer. This is just a glorious golden day."

"Yesterday was finer, but you didn't notice it."

"Oh, yesterday was somewhere back in the past—the inconsequential past."

Nell's sleepy blue eyes opened a little wider. She did not know what to make of this changed young man. Dick felt gleeful and tried hard to keep the fact from becoming manifest.

"What's the inconsequential past? You seem remarkably happy to-day."

"I certainly am happy. Adios. Pleasant dreams."

Dick turned away then and left the patio by the opening into the yard. Nell was really sleepy, and when she had fallen asleep again he would return. He walked around for a while. Belding and the rangers were shoeing a broncho. Yaqui was in the field with the horses. Blanco Sol grazed contently, and now and then lifted his head to watch. His long ears went up at sight of his master, and he whistled. Presently Dick, as if magnet-drawn, retraced his steps to the patio and entered noiselessly.

Nell was now deep in her siesta. She was inert, relaxed, untroubled by dreams. Her hair was damp on her brow.

Again Nell stirred, and gradually awakened. Her eyes unclosed, humid, shadowy, unconscious. They rested upon Dick for a moment before they became clear and comprehensive. He stood back fully ten feet from her, and to all outside appearances regarded her calmly.

"I've interrupted your siesta again," he said. "Please forgive me. I'll take myself off."

He wandered away, and when it became impossible for him to stay away any longer he returned to the patio.

The instant his glance rested upon Nell's face he divined she was feigning sleep. The faint rose-blush had paled. The warm, rich, golden tint of her skin had fled. Dick dropped upon his knees and bent over her. Though his blood was churning in his veins, his breast laboring, his mind whirling with the wonder of that moment and its promise, he made himself deliberate. He wanted more than anything he had ever wanted in his life to see if she would keep up that pretense of sleep and let him kiss her. She must have felt his breath, for her hair waved off her brow. Her cheeks were now white. Her breast swelled and sank. He bent down closer—closer. But he must have been maddeningly slow, for as he bent still closer Nell's eyes opened, and he caught a swift purple gaze of eyes as she whirled her head. Then, with a little cry, she rose and fled.

X ROJAS

NO word from George Thorne had come to Forlorn River in weeks. Gale grew concerned over the fact, and began to wonder if anything serious could have happened to him. Mercedes showed a slow, wearing strain.

Thorne's commission expired the end of January, and if he could not get his discharge immediately, he surely could obtain leave of absence. Therefore, Gale waited, not without growing anxiety, and did his best to cheer Mercedes. The first of February came bringing news of rebel activities and bandit operations in and around Casita, but not a word from the cavalryman.

Mercedes became silent, mournful. Her eyes were great black windows of tragedy. Nell devoted herself entirely to the unfortunate girl; Dick exerted himself to persuade her that all would yet come well; in fact, the whole household could not have been kinder to a sister or a daughter. But their united efforts were unavailing. Mercedes seemed to accept with fatalistic hopelessness a last and crowning misfortune.

A dozen times Gale declared he would ride in to Casita and find out why they did not hear from Thorne; however, older and wiser heads prevailed over his impetuosity. Belding was not sanguine over the safety of the Casita trail. Refugees from there arrived every day in Forlorn River, and if tales they told were true, real war would have been preferable to what was going on along the border. Belding and the rangers and the Yaqui held a consultation. Not only had the Indian become a faithful servant to Gale, but he was also of value to Belding. Yaqui had all the craft of his class, and superior intelligence. His knowledge of Mexicans was second only to his hate of them. And Yaqui, who had been scouting on all the trails, gave information that made Belding decide to wait some days before sending any one to Casita. He required promises from his rangers, particularly Gale, not to leave without his consent.

It was upon Gale's coming from this conference that he encountered Nell. Since the interrupted siesta episode she had been more than ordinarily elusive, and about all he had received from her was a tantalizing smile from a distance. He got the impression now, however, that she had awaited him. When he drew close to her he was certain of it, and he experienced more than surprise.

"Dick," she began, hurriedly. "Dad's not going to send any one to see about Thorne?"

"No, not yet. He thinks it best not to. We all think so. I'm sorry. Poor Mercedes!"

"I knew it. I tried to coax him to send Laddy or even Yaqui. He wouldn't listen to me. Dick, Mercedes is dying by inches. Can't you see what ails her? It's more than love or fear. It's uncertainty—suspense. Oh, can't we find out for her?"

"Nell, I feel as badly as you about her. I wanted to ride in to Casita. Belding shut me up quick, the last time."

Nell came close to Gale, clasped his arm. There was no color in her face. Her eyes held a dark, eager excitement.

"Dick, will you slip off without Dad's consent? Risk it! Go to Casita and find out what's happened to Thorne—at least if he ever started for Forlorn River?"

"No, Nell, I won't do that."

She drew away from him with passionate suddenness.

"Are you afraid?"

This certainly was not the Nell Burton that Gale knew.

"No, I'm not afraid," Gale replied, a little nettled.

"Will you go—for my sake?" Like lightning her mood changed and she was close to him again, hands on his, her face white, her whole presence sweetly alluring.

"Nell, I won't disobey Belding," protested Gale. "I won't break my word."

"Dick, it'll not be so bad as that. But—what if it is?... Go, Dick, if not for poor Mercedes's sake, then for mine—to please me. I'll—I'll... you won't lose anything by going. I think I know how Mercedes feels. Just a word from Thorne or about him would save her. Take Blanco Sol and go, Dick. What rebel outfit could ever ride you down on that horse? Why, Dick, if I was up on Sol I wouldn't be afraid of the whole rebel army."

"My dear girl, it's not a question of being afraid. It's my word—my duty to Belding."

"You said you loved me. If you love me you will go... You don't love me!"

Gale could only stare at this transformed girl.

"Dick, listen!... If you go—if you fetch some word of Thorne to comfort Mercedes, you—well, you will have your reward."

"Nell!"

Her dangerous sweetness was as amazing as this newly revealed character.

"Dick, will you go?"

"No-no!" cried Gale, in violence, struggling with himself. "Nell Burton, I'll tell you this. To have the reward I want would mean pretty near heaven for me. But not even for that will I break my word to your father."

She seemed the incarnation of girlish scorn and wilful passion.

"Gracias, senor," she replied, mockingly. "Adios." Then she flashed out of his sight.

Gale went to his room at once, disturbed and thrilling, and did not soon recover from that encounter.

The following morning at the breakfast table Nell was not present. Mrs. Belding evidently considered the fact somewhat unusual, for she called out into the patio and then into the yard. Then she went to Mercedes's room. But Nell was not there, either.

"She's in one of her tantrums lately," said Belding. "Wouldn't speak to me this morning. Let her alone, mother. She's spoiled enough, without running after her. She's always hungry. She'll be on hand presently, don't mistake me."

Notwithstanding Belding's conviction, which Gale shared, Nell did not appear at all during the hour. When Belding and the rangers went outside, Yaqui was eating his meal on the bench where he always sat.

"Yaqui—Lluvia d' oro, si?" asked Belding, waving his hand toward the corrals. The Indian's beautiful name for Nell meant "shower of gold," and Belding used it in asking Yaqui if he had seen her. He received a negative reply.

Perhaps half an hour afterward, as Gale was leaving his room, he saw the Yaqui running up the path from the fields. It was markedly out of the ordinary to see the Indian run. Gale wondered what was the matter. Yaqui ran straight to Belding, who was at work at his bench under the wagon shed. In less than a moment Belding was bellowing for his rangers. Gale got to him first, but Ladd and Lash were not far behind.

"Blanco Sol gone!" yelled Belding, in a rage.

"Gone? In broad daylight, with the Indian a-watch-in?" queried Ladd.

"It happened while Yaqui was at breakfast. That's sure. He'd just watered Sol."

"Raiders!" exclaimed Jim Lash.

"Lord only knows. Yaqui says it wasn't raiders."

"Mebbe Sol's just walked off somewheres."

"He was haltered in the corral."

"Send Yaqui to find the hoss's trail, an' let's figger," said Ladd. "Shore this 's no raider job."

In the swift search that ensued Gale did not have anything to say; but his mind was forming a conclusion. When he found his old saddle and bridle missing from the peg in the barn his conclusion became a positive conviction, and it made him, for the moment, cold and sick and speechless.

"Hey, Dick, don't take it so much to heart," said Belding. "We'll likely find Sol, and if we don't, there's other good horses."

"I'm not thinking of Sol," replied Gale.

Ladd cast a sharp glance at Gale, snapped his fingers, and said:

"Damn me if I ain't guessed it, too!"

"What's wrong with you locoed gents?" bluntly demanded Belding.

"Nell has slipped away on Sol," answered Dick.

There was a blank pause, which presently Belding broke.

"Well, that's all right, if Nell's on him. I was afraid we'd lost the horse."

"Belding, you're trackin' bad," said Ladd, wagging his head.

"Nell has started for Casita," burst out Gale. "She has gone to fetch Mercedes some word about Thorne. Oh, Belding, you needn't shake your head. I know she's gone. She tried to persuade me to go, and was furious when I wouldn't."

"I don't believe it," replied Belding, hoarsely. "Nell may have her temper. She's a little devil at times, but she always had good sense."

"Tom, you can gamble she's gone," said Ladd.

"Aw, hell, no! Jim, what do you think?" implored Belding.

"I reckon Sol's white head is pointed level an' straight down the Casita trail. An' Nell can ride. We're losing' time."

That roused Belding to action.

"I say you're all wrong," he yelled, starting for the corrals. "She's only taking a little ride, same as she's done often. But rustle now. Find out. Dick, you ride cross the valley. Jim, you hunt up and down the river. I'll head up San Felipe way. And you, Laddy, take Diablo and hit the Casita trail. If she really has gone after Thorne you can catch her in an hour or so."

"Shore I'll go," replied Ladd. "But, Beldin', if you're not plumb crazy you're close to it. That big white devil can't catch Sol. Not in an hour or a day or a week! What's more, at the end of any runnin' time, with an even start, Sol will be farther in the lead. An' now Sol's got an hour's start."

"Laddy, you mean to say Sol is a faster horse than Diablo?" thundered Belding, his face purple.

"Shore. I mean to tell you just that there," replied the ranger.

"I'll—I'll bet a—"

"We're wastin' time," curtly interrupted Ladd. "You can gamble on this if you want to. I'll ride your Blanco Devil as he never was rid before, 'cept once when a damn sight better hossman than I am couldn't make him outrun Sol."

Without more words the men saddled and were off, not waiting for the Yaqui to come in with possible information as to what trail Blanco Sol had taken. It certainly did not show in the clear sand of the level valley where Gale rode to and fro. When Gale returned to the house he found Belding and Lash awaiting him. They did not mention their own search, but stated that Yaqui had found Blanco Sol's tracks in the Casita trail. After some consultation Belding decided to send Lash along after Ladd.

The interminable time that followed contained for Gale about as much suspense as he could well bear. What astonished him and helped him greatly to fight off actual distress was the endurance of Nell's mother.

Early on the morning of the second day, Gale, who had acquired an unbreakable habit of watching, saw three white horses and a bay come wearily stepping down the road. He heard Blanco Sol's familiar whistle, and he leaped up wild with joy. The horse was riderless. Gale's sudden joy received a violent check, then resurged when he saw a limp white form in Jim Lash's arms. Ladd was supporting a horseman who wore a military uniform.

Gale shouted with joy and ran into the house to tell the good news. It was the ever-thoughtful Mrs. Belding who prevented him from rushing in to tell Mercedes. Then he hurried out into the yard, closely followed by the Beldings.

Lash handed down a ragged, travel-stained, wan girl into Belding's arms.

"Dad! Mama!"

It was indeed a repentant Nell, but there was spirit yet in the tired blue eyes. Then she caught sight of Gale and gave him a faint smile.

"Hello—Dick."

"Nell!" Gale reached for her hand, held it tightly, and found speech difficult.

"You needn't worry—about your old horse," she said, as Belding carried her toward the door. "Oh, Dick! Blanco Sol is—glorious!"

Gale turned to greet his friend. Indeed, it was but a haggard ghost of the cavalryman. Thorne looked ill or wounded. Gale's greeting was also a question full of fear.

Thorne's answer was a faint smile. He seemed ready to drop from the saddle. Gale helped Ladd hold Thorne upon the horse until they reached the house. Belding came out again. His welcome was checked as he saw the condition of the cavalryman. Thorne reeled into Dick's arms. But he was able to stand and walk.

"I'm not—hurt. Only weak—starved," he said. "Is Mercedes— Take me to her."

"She'll be well the minute she sees him," averred Belding, as he and Gale led the cavalryman to Mercedes's room. There they left him; and Gale, at least, felt his ears ringing with the girl's broken cry of joy.

When Belding and Gale hurried forth again the rangers were tending the tired horses. Upon returning to the house Jim Lash calmly lit his pipe, and Ladd declared that, hungry as he was, he had to tell his story.

"Shore, Beldin'," began Ladd, "that was funny about Diablo catchin' Blanco Sol. Funny ain't the word. I nearly laughed myself to death. Well, I rode in Sol's tracks all the way to Casita. Never seen a rebel or a raider till I got to town. Figgered Nell made the trip in five hours. I went straight to the camp of the cavalrymen, an' found them just coolin' off an' dressin' down their hosses after what looked to me like a big ride. I got there too late for the fireworks.

"Some soldier took me to an officer's tent. Nell was there, some white an' all in. She just said, 'Laddy!' Thorne was there, too, an' he was bein' worked over by the camp doctor. I didn't ask no questions, because I seen quiet was needed round that tent. After satisfying myself that Nell was all right, an' Thorne in no danger, I went out.

"Shore there was so darn many fellers who wanted to an' tried to tell me what'd come off, I thought I'd never find out. But I got the story piece by piece. An' here's what happened.

"Nell rode Blanco Sol a-tearin' into camp, an' had a crowd round her in a jiffy. She told who she was, where she'd come from, an' what she wanted. Well, it seemed a day or so before Nell got there the cavalrymen had heard word of Thorne. You see, Thorne had left camp on leave of absence some time before.

He was shore mysterious, they said, an' told nobody where he was goin'. A week or so after he left camp some Greaser give it away that Rojas had a prisoner in a dobe shack near his camp. Nobody paid much attention to what the Greaser said. He wanted money for mescal. An' it was usual for Rojas to have prisoners. But in a few more days it turned out pretty sure that for some reason Rojas was holdin' Thorne.

"Now it happened when this news came Colonel Weede was in Nogales with his staff, an' the officer left in charge didn't know how to proceed. Rojas's camp was across the line in Mexico, an' ridin' over there was serious business. It meant a whole lot more than just scatterin' one Greaser camp. It was what had been botherin' more'n one colonel along the line. Thorne's feller soldiers was anxious to get him out of a bad fix, but they had to wait for orders.

"When Nell found out Thorne was bein' starved an' beat in a dobe shack no more'n two mile across the line, she shore stirred up that cavalry camp. Shore! She told them soldiers Rojas was holdin' Thorne—torturin' him to make him tell where Mercedes was. She told about Mercedes—how sweet an' beautiful she was—how her father had been murdered by Rojas—how she had been hounded by the bandit—how ill an' miserable she was, waitin' for her lover. An' she begged the cavalrymen to rescue Thorne.

"From the way it was told to me I reckon them cavalrymen went up in the air. Fine, fiery lot of young bloods, I thought, achin' for a scrap. But the officer in charge, bein' in a ticklish place, still held out for higher orders.

"Then Nell broke loose. You-all know Nell's tongue is sometimes like a *choya* thorn. I'd have give somethin' to see her work up that soldier outfit. Nell's never so pretty as when she's mad. An' this last stunt of hers was no girly tantrum, as Beldin' calls it. She musta been ragin' with all the hell there's in a woman.... Can't you fellers see her on Blanco Sol with her eyes turnin' black?"

Ladd mopped his sweaty face with his dusty scarf. He was beaming. He was growing excited, hurried in his narrative.

"Right out then Nell swore she'd go after Thorne. If them cavalrymen couldn't ride with a Western girl to save a brother American—let them hang back! One feller, under orders, tried to stop Blanco Sol. An' that feller invited himself to the hospital. Then the cavalrymen went flyin' for their hosses. Mebbe Nell's move was just foxy—woman's cunnin'. But I'm thinkin' as she felt then she'd have sent Blanco Sol straight into Rojas's camp, which, I'd forgot to say, was in plain sight.

"It didn't take long for every cavalryman in that camp to get wind of what was comin' off. Shore they musta been wild. They strung out after Nell in a thunderin' troop.

"Say, I wish you fellers could see the lane that bunch of hosses left in the greasewood an' cactus. Looks like there'd been a cattle stampede on the desert.... Blanco Sol stayed out in front, you can gamble on that. Right into Rojas's camp! Sabe, you senors? Gawd Almighty! I never had grief that 'd hold a candle to this one of bein' too late to see Nell an' Sol in their one best race.

"Rojas an' his men vamoosed without a shot. That ain't surprisin'. There wasn't a shot fired by anybody. The cavalrymen soon found Thorne an' hurried with him back on Uncle Sam's land. Thorne was half naked, black an' blue all over, thin as a rail. He looked mighty sick when I seen him first. That was a little after midday. He was given food an' drink. Shore he seemed a starved man. But he picked up wonderful, an' by the time Jim came along he was wantin' to start for Forlorn River. So was Nell. By main strength as much as persuasion we kept the two of them quiet till next evenin' at dark.

"Well, we made as sneaky a start in the dark as Jim an' me could manage, an' never hit the trail till we was miles from town. Thorne's nerve held him up for a while. Then all at once he tumbled out of his saddle. We got him back, an' Lash held him on. Nell didn't give out till daybreak."

As Ladd paused in his story Belding began to stutter, and finally he exploded. His mighty utterances were incoherent. But plainly the wrath he had felt toward the wilful girl was forgotten. Gale remained gripped by silence.

"I reckon you'll all be some surprised when you see Casita," went on Ladd. "It's half burned an' half tore down. An' the rebels are livin' fat. There was rumors of another federal force on the road from Casa Grandes. I seen a good many Americans from interior Mexico, an' the stories they told would make your hair stand up. They all packed guns, was fightin' mad at Greasers, an' sore on the good old U. S. But shore glad to get over the line! Some were waitin' for trains, which don't run reg'lar no more, an' others were ready to hit the trails north."

"Laddy, what knocks me is Rojas holding Thorne prisoner, trying to make him tell where Mercedes had been hidden," said Belding.

"Shore. It 'd knock anybody."

"The bandit's crazy over her. That's the Spanish of it," replied Belding, his voice rolling. "Rojas is a peon. He's been a slave to the proud Castilian. He loves Mercedes as he hates her. When I was down in Durango I saw something of these peons' insane passions. Rojas wants this girl only to have her, then kill her. It's damn strange, boys, and even with Thorne here our troubles have just begun."

"Tom, you spoke correct," said Jim Ladd, in his cool drawl.

"Shore I'm not sayin' what I think," added Ladd. But the look of him was not indicative of a tranquil optimism.

Thorne was put to bed in Gale's room. He was very weak, yet he would keep Mercedes's hand and gaze at her with unbelieving eyes. Mercedes's failing hold on hope and strength seemed to have been a fantasy; she was again vivid, magnetic, beautiful, shot through and through with intense and throbbing life. She induced him to take food and drink. Then, fighting sleep with what little strength he had left, at last he succumbed.

For all Dick could ascertain his friend never stirred an eyelash nor a finger for twenty-seven hours. When he awoke he was pale, weak, but the old Thorne.

"Hello, Dick; I didn't dream it then," he said. "There you are, and my darling with the proud, dark eyes—she's here?"

"Why, yes, you locoed cavalryman."

"Say, what's happened to you? It can't be those clothes and a little bronze on your face.... Dick, you're older—you've changed. You're not so thickly built. By Gad, if you don't look fine!"

"Thanks. I'm sorry I can't return the compliment. You're about the seediest, hungriest-looking fellow I ever saw.... Say, old man, you must have had a tough time."

A dark and somber fire burned out the happiness in Thorne's eyes.

"Dick, don't make me—don't let me think of that fiend Rojas!.... I'm here now. I'll be well in a day or two. Then!..."

Mercedes came in, radiant and soft-voiced. She fell upon her knees beside Thorne's bed, and neither of them appeared to see Nell enter with a tray. Then Gale and Nell made a good deal of unnecessary bustle in moving a small table close to the bed. Mercedes had forgotten for the moment that her lover had been a starving man. If Thorne remembered it he did not care. They held hands and looked at each other without speaking.

"Nell, I thought I had it bad," whispered Dick. "But I'm not—"

"Hush. It's beautiful," replied Nell, softly; and she tried to coax Dick from the room.

Dick, however, thought he ought to remain at least long enough to tell Thorne that a man in his condition could not exist solely upon love.

Mercedes sprang up blushing with pretty, penitent manner and moving white hands eloquent of her condition.

"Oh, Mercedes—don't go!" cried Thorne, as she stepped to the door.

"Senor Dick will stay. He is not mucha malo for you—as I am."

Then she smiled and went out.

"Good Lord!" exclaimed Thorne. "How I love her. Dick, isn't she the most beautiful, the loveliest, the finest—"

"George, I share your enthusiasm," said Dick, dryly, "but Mercedes isn't the only girl on earth."

Manifestly this was a startling piece of information, and struck Thorne in more than one way.

"George," went on Dick, "did you happen to observe the girl who saved your life—who incidentally just fetched in your breakfast?"

"Nell Burton! Why, of course. She's brave, a wonderful girl, and really nice-looking."

"You long, lean, hungry beggar! That was the young lady who might answer the raving eulogy you just got out of your system.... I—well, you haven't cornered the love market!"

Thorne uttered some kind of a sound that his weakened condition would not allow to be a whoop.

"Dick! Do you mean it?"

"I shore do, as Laddy says."

"I'm glad, Dick, with all my heart. I wondered at the changed look you wear. Why, boy, you've got a different front.... Call the lady in, and you bet I'll look her over right. I can see better now."

"Eat your breakfast. There's plenty of time to dazzle you afterward."

Thorne fell to upon his breakfast and made it vanish with magic speed. Meanwhile Dick told him something of a ranger's life along the border.

"You needn't waste your breath," said Thorne. "I guess I can see. Belding and those rangers have made you the real thing—the real Western goods.... What I want to know is all about the girl."

"Well, Laddy swears she's got your girl roped in the corral for looks."

"That's not possible. I'll have to talk to Laddy.... But she must be a wonder, or Dick Gale would never have fallen for her.... Isn't it great, Dick? I'm here! Mercedes is well—safe! You've got a girl! Oh!.... But say, I haven't a dollar to my name. I had a lot of money, Dick, and those robbers stole it, my watch—everything. Damn that little black Greaser! He got Mercedes's letters. I wish you could have seen him trying to read them. He's simply nutty over her, Dick. I could have borne the loss of money and valuables—but those beautiful, wonderful letters—they're gone!"

"Cheer up. You have the girl. Belding will make you a proposition presently. The future smiles, old friend. If this rebel business was only ended!"

"Dick, you're going to be my savior twice over.... Well, now, listen to me." His gay excitement changed to earnest gravity. "I want to marry Mercedes at once. Is there a padre here?"

"Yes. But are you wise in letting any Mexican, even a priest, know Mercedes is hidden in Forlorn River?"

"It couldn't be kept much longer."

Gale was compelled to acknowledge the truth of this statement.

"I'll marry her first, then I'll face my problem. Fetch the padre, Dick. And ask our kind friends to be witnesses at the ceremony."

Much to Gale's surprise neither Belding nor Ladd objected to the idea of bringing a padre into the household, and thereby making known to at least one Mexican the whereabouts of Mercedes Castaneda. Belding's caution was wearing out in wrath at the persistent unsettled condition of the border, and Ladd grew only the cooler and more silent as possibilities of trouble multiplied.

Gale fetched the padre, a little, weazened, timid man who was old and without interest or penetration. Apparently he married Mercedes and Thorne as he told his beads or mumbled a prayer. It was Mrs. Belding who kept the occasion from being a merry one, and she insisted on not exciting Thorne. Gale marked her unusual pallor and the singular depth and sweetness of her voice.

"Mother, what's the use of making a funeral out of a marriage?" protested Belding. "A chance for some fun doesn't often come to Forlorn River. You're a fine doctor. Can't you see the girl is what Thorne needed? He'll be well tomorrow, don't mistake me."

"George, when you're all right again we'll add something to present congratulations," said Gale.

"We shore will," put in Ladd.

So with parting jests and smiles they left the couple to themselves.

Belding enjoyed a laugh at his good wife's expense, for Thorne could not be kept in bed, and all in a day, it seemed, he grew so well and so hungry that his friends were delighted, and Mercedes was radiant. In a few days his weakness disappeared and he was going the round of the fields and looking over the ground marked out in Gale's plan of water development. Thorne was highly enthusiastic, and at once staked out his claim for one hundred and sixty acres of land adjoining that of Belding and the rangers. These five tracts took in all the ground necessary for their operations, but in case of the success of the irrigation project the idea was to increase their squatter holdings by purchase of more land down the valley. A hundred families had lately moved to Forlorn River; more were coming all the time; and Belding vowed he could see a vision of the whole Altar Valley green with farms.

Meanwhile everybody in Belding's household, except the quiet Ladd and the watchful Yaqui, in the absence of disturbance of any kind along the border, grew freer and more unrestrained, as if anxiety was slowly fading in the peace of the present. Jim Lash made a trip to the Sonoyta Oasis, and Ladd patrolled fifty miles of the line eastward without incident or sight of raiders. Evidently all the border hawks were in at the picking of Casita.

The February nights were cold, with a dry, icy, penetrating coldness that made a warm fire most comfortable. Belding's household usually congregated in the sitting-room, where burning mesquite logs crackled in the open fireplace. Belding's one passion besides horses was the game of checkers, and he was always wanting to play. On this night he sat playing with Ladd, who never won a game and never could give up trying. Mrs. Belding worked with her needle, stopping from time to time to gaze with thoughtful eyes into the fire. Jim Lash smoked his pipe by the hearth and played with the cat on his knee. Thorne and Mercedes were at the table with pencil and paper; and he was trying his best to keep his attention from his wife's beautiful, animated face long enough to read and write a little Spanish. Gale and Nell sat in a corner watching the bright fire.

There came a low knock on the door. It may have been an ordinary knock, for it did not disturb the women; but to Belding and his rangers it had a subtle meaning.

"Who's that?" asked Belding, as he slowly pushed back his chair and looked at Ladd.

"Yaqui," replied the ranger.

"Come in," called Belding.

The door opened, and the short, square, powerfully built Indian entered. He had a magnificent head, strangely staring, somber black eyes, and very darkly bronzed face. He carried a rifle and strode with impressive dignity.

"Yaqui, what do you want?" asked Belding, and repeated his question in Spanish.

"Senor Dick," replied the Indian.

Gale jumped up, stifling an exclamation, and he went outdoors with Yaqui. He felt his arm gripped, and allowed himself to be led away without asking a question. Yaqui's presence was always one of gloom, and now his stern action boded catastrophe. Once clear of trees he pointed to the level desert across the river, where a row of campfires shone bright out of the darkness.

"Raiders!" ejaculated Gale.

Then he cautioned Yaqui to keep sharp lookout, and, hurriedly returning to the house, he called the men out and told them there were rebels or raiders camping just across the line.

Ladd did not say a word. Belding, with an oath, slammed down his cigar.

"I knew it was too good to last.... Dick, you and Jim stay here while Laddy and I look around."

Dick returned to the sitting-room. The women were nervous and not to be deceived. So Dick merely said Yaqui had sighted some lights off in the desert, and they probably were campfires. Belding did not soon return, and when he did he was alone, and, saying he wanted to consult with the men, he sent Mrs. Belding and the girls to their rooms. His gloomy anxiety had returned.

"Laddy's gone over to scout around and try to find out who the outfit belongs to and how many are in it," said Belding.

"I reckon if they're raiders with bad intentions we wouldn't see no fires," remarked Jim, calmly.

"It 'd be useless, I suppose, to send for the cavalry," said Gale. "Whatever's coming off would be over before the soldiers could be notified, let alone reach here."

"Hell, fellows! I don't look for an attack on Forlorn River," burst out Belding. "I can't believe that possible. These rebel-raiders have a little sense. They wouldn't spoil their game by pulling U. S. soldiers across the line from Yuma to El Paso. But, as Jim says, if they wanted to steal a few horses or cattle they wouldn't build fires. I'm afraid it's—"

Belding hesitated and looked with grim concern at the cavalryman.

"What?" queried Thorne.

"I'm afraid it's Rojas."

Thorne turned pale but did not lose his nerve.

"I thought of that at once. If true, it'll be terrible for Mercedes and me. But Rojas will never get his hands on my wife. If I can't kill him, I'll kill her!... Belding, this is tough on you—this risk we put upon your family. I regret—"

"Cut that kind of talk," replied Belding, bluntly. "Well, if it is Rojas he's acting damn strange for a raider. That's what worries me. We can't do anything but wait. With Laddy and Yaqui out there we won't be surprised. Let's take the best possible view of the situation until we know more. That'll not likely be before tomorrow."

X ROJAS

The women of the house might have gotten some sleep that night, but it was certain the men did not get any. Morning broke cold and gray, the 19th of February. Breakfast was prepared earlier than usual, and an air of suppressed waiting excitement pervaded the place. Otherwise the ordinary details of the morning's work continued as on any other day. Ladd came in hungry and cold, and said the Mexicans were not breaking camp. He reported a good-sized force of rebels, and was taciturn as to his idea of forthcoming events.

About an hour after sunrise Yaqui ran in with the information that part of the rebels were crossing the river.

"That can't mean a fight yet," declared Belding. "But get in the house, boys, and make ready anyway. I'll meet them."

"Drive them off the place same as if you had a company of soldiers backin' you," said Ladd. "Don't give them an inch. We're in bad, and the bigger bluff we put up the more likely our chance."

"Belding, you're an officer of the United States. Mexicans are much impressed by show of authority. I've seen that often in camp," said Thorne.

"Oh, I know the white-livered Greasers better than any of you, don't mistake me," replied Belding. He was pale with rage, but kept command over himself.

The rangers, with Yaqui and Thorne, stationed themselves at the several windows of the sitting-room. Rifles and smaller arms and boxes of shells littered the tables and window seats. No small force of besiegers could overcome a resistance such as Belding and his men were capable of making.

"Here they come, boys," called Gale, from his window.

"Rebel-raiders I should say, Laddy."

"Shore. An' a fine outfit of buzzards!"

"Reckon there's about a dozen in the bunch," observed the calm Lash. "Some hosses they're ridin'. Where 'n the hell do they get such hosses, anyhow?"

"Shore, Jim, they work hard an' buy 'em with real silver pesos," replied Ladd, sarcastically.

"Do any of you see Rojas?" whispered Thorne.

"Nix. No dandy bandit in that outfit."

"It's too far to see," said Gale.

The horsemen halted at the corrals. They were orderly and showed no evidence of hostility. They were, however, fully armed. Belding stalked out to meet them. Apparently a leader wanted to parley with him, but Belding would hear nothing. He shook his head, waved his arms, stamped to and fro, and his loud, angry voice could be heard clear back at the house. Whereupon the detachment of rebels retired to the bank of the river, beyond the white post that marked the boundary line, and there they once more drew rein. Belding remained by the corrals watching them, evidently still in threatening mood. Presently a single rider left the troop and trotted his horse back down the road. When he reached the corrals he was seen to halt and pass something to Belding. Then he galloped away to join his comrades.

Belding looked at whatever it was he held in his hand, shook his burley head, and started swiftly for the house. He came striding into the room holding a piece of soiled paper.

"Can't read it and don't know as I want to," he said, savagely.

"Beldin', shore we'd better read it," replied Ladd. "What we want is a line on them Greasers. Whether they're Campo's men or Salazar's, or just a wanderin' bunch of rebels—or Rojas's bandits. Sabe, senor?"

Not one of the men was able to translate the garbled scrawl.

"Shore Mercedes can read it," said Ladd.

Thorne opened a door and called her. She came into the room followed by Nell and Mrs. Belding. Evidently all three divined a critical situation.

"My dear, we want you to read what's written on this paper," said Thorne, as he led her to the table. "It was sent in by rebels, and—and we fear contains bad news for us."

Mercedes gave the writing one swift glance, then fainted in Thorne's arms. He carried her to a couch, and with Nell and Mrs. Belding began to work over her.

Belding looked at his rangers. It was characteristic of the man that, now when catastrophe appeared inevitable, all the gloom and care and angry agitation passed from him.

"Laddy, it's Rojas all right. How many men has he out there?"

"Mebbe twenty. Not more."

"We can lick twice that many Greasers."

"Shore."

Jim Lash removed his pipe long enough to speak.

"I reckon. But it ain't sense to start a fight when mebbe we can avoid it."

"What's your idea?"

"Let's stave the Greaser off till dark. Then Laddy an' me an' Thorne will take Mercedes an' hit the trail for Yuma."

"Camino del Diablo! That awful trail with a woman! Jim, do you forget how many hundreds of men have perished on the Devil's Road?"

"I reckon I ain't forgettin' nothin'," replied Jim. "The waterholes are full now. There's grass, an' we can do the job in six days."

"It's three hundred miles to Yuma."

"Beldin', Jim's idea hits me pretty reasonable," interposed Ladd. "Lord knows that's about the only chance we've got except fightin'."

"But suppose we do stave Rojas off, and you get safely away with Mercedes. Isn't Rojas going to find it out quick? Then what'll he try to do to us who're left here?"

"I reckon he'd find out by daylight," replied Jim. "But, Tom, he ain't agoin' to start a scrap then. He'd want time an' hosses an' men to chase us out on the trail. You see, I'm figgerin' on the crazy Greaser wantin' the girl. I reckon he'll try to clean up here to get her. But he's too smart to fight you for nothin'. Rojas may be nutty about women, but he's afraid of the U. S. Take my word for it he'd discover the trail in the mornin' an' light out on it. I reckon with ten hours' start we could travel comfortable."

Belding paced up and down the room. Jim and Ladd whispered together. Gale walked to the window and looked out at the distant group of bandits, and then turned his gaze to rest upon Mercedes. She was conscious now, and her eyes seemed all the larger and blacker for the whiteness of her face. Thorne held her hands, and the other women were trying to still her tremblings.

No one but Gale saw the Yaqui in the background looking down upon the Spanish girl. All of Yaqui's looks were strange; but this singularly so. Gale marked it, and felt he would never forget. Mercedes's beauty had never before struck him as being so exquisite, so alluring as now when she lay stricken. Gale wondered if the Indian was affected by her loveliness, her helplessness, or her terror. Yaqui had seen Mercedes only a few times, and upon each of these he had appeared to be fascinated. Could the strange Indian, because his hate for Mexicans was so great, be gloating over her misery? Something about Yaqui—a noble austerity of countenance—made Gale feel his suspicion unjust.

Presently Belding called his rangers to him, and then Thorne.

"Listen to this," he said, earnestly. "I'll go out and have a talk with Rojas. I'll try to reason with him; tell him to think a long time before he sheds blood on Uncle Sam's soil. That he's now after an American's wife! I'll not commit myself, nor will I refuse outright to consider his demands, nor will I show the least fear of him. I'll play for time. If my bluff goes through... well and good.... After dark the four of you, Laddy, Jim, Dick, and Thorne, will take Mercedes and my best white horses, and, with Yaqui as guide, circle round through Altar Valley to the trail, and head for Yuma.... Wait now, Laddy. Let me finish. I want you to take the white horses for two reasons—to save them and to save you. Savvy? If Rojas should follow on my horses he'd be likely to catch you. Also, you can pack a great deal more than on the bronchs. Also, the big horses can travel faster and farther on little grass and water. I want you to take the Indian, because in a case of this kind he'll be a godsend. If you get headed or lost or have to circle off the trail, think what it 'd mean to have Yaqui with you. He knows Sonora as no Greaser knows it. He could hide you, find water and grass, when you would absolutely believe it impossible. The Indian is loyal. He has his debt to pay, and he'll pay it, don't mistake me. When you're gone I'll hide Nell so Rojas won't see her if he searches the place. Then I think I could sit down and wait without any particular worry."

The rangers approved of Belding's plan, and Thorne choked in his effort to express his gratitude.

"All right, we'll chance it," concluded Belding. "I'll go out now and call Rojas and his outfit over... Say, it might be as well for me to know just what he said in that paper."

Thorne went to the side of his wife.

"Mercedes, we've planned to outwit Rojas. Will you tell us just what he wrote?"

The girl sat up, her eyes dilating, and with her hands clasping Thorne's. She said:

"Rojas swore—by his saints and his virgin—that if I wasn't given—to him—in twenty-four hours—he would set fire to the village—kill the men—carry off the women—hang the children on cactus thorns!"

A moment's silence followed her last halting whisper.

"By his saints an' his virgin!" echoed Ladd. He laughed—a cold, cutting, deadly laugh—significant and terrible.

Then the Yaqui uttered a singular cry. Gale had heard this once before, and now he remembered it was at the Papago Well.

"Look at the Indian," whispered Belding, hoarsely. "Damn if I don't believe he understood every word Mercedes said. And, gentlemen, don't mistake me, if he ever gets near Senor Rojas there'll be some gory Aztec knife work."

Yaqui had moved close to Mercedes, and stood beside her as she leaned against her husband. She seemed impelled to meet the Indian's gaze, and evidently it was so powerful or hypnotic that it wrought irresistibly upon her. But she must have seen or divined what was beyond the others, for she offered him her trembling hand. Yaqui took it and laid it against his body in a strange motion, and bowed his head. Then he stepped back into the shadow of the room.

Belding went outdoors while the rangers took up their former position at the west window. Each had his own somber thoughts, Gale imagined, and knew his own were dark enough. A slow fire crept along his veins. He saw Belding halt at the corrals and wave his hand. Then the rebels mounted and came briskly up the road, this time to rein in abreast.

Wherever Rojas had kept himself upon the former advance was not clear; but he certainly was prominently in sight now. He made a gaudy, almost a dashing figure. Gale did not recognize the white sombrero, the crimson scarf, the velvet jacket, nor any feature of the dandy's costume; but their general effect, the whole ensemble, recalled vividly to mind his first sight of the bandit. Rojas dismounted and seemed to be listening. He betrayed none of the excitement Gale had seen in him that night at the Del Sol. Evidently this composure struck Ladd and Lash as unusual in a Mexican supposed to be laboring under stress of feeling. Belding made gestures, vehemently bobbed his big head, appeared to talk with his body as much as with his tongue. Then Rojas was seen to reply, and after that it was clear that the talk became painful and difficult. It ended finally in what appeared to be mutual understanding. Rojas mounted and rode away with his men, while Belding came tramping back to the house.

As he entered the door his eyes were shining, his big hands were clenched, and he was breathing audibly.

"You can rope me if I'm not locoed!" he burst out. "I went out to conciliate a red-handed little murderer, and damn me if I didn't meet a—a—well, I've not suitable name handy. I started my bluff and got along pretty well, but I forgot to mention that Mercedes was Thorne's wife. And what do you think? Rojas swore he loved Mercedes—swore he'd marry her right here in Forlorn River—swore he would give up robbing and killing people, and take her away from Mexico. He has gold—jewels. He swore if he didn't get her nothing mattered. He'd die anyway without her.... And here's the strange thing. I believe him! He was cold as ice, and all hell inside. Never saw a Greaser like him. Well, I pretended to be greatly impressed. We got to talking friendly, I suppose, though I didn't understand half he said, and I imagine he gathered less what I said. Anyway, without my asking he said for me to think it over for a day and then we'd talk again."

"Shore we're born lucky!" ejaculated Ladd.

"I reckon Rojas'll be smart enough to string his outfit across the few trails leadin' out of Forlorn River," remarked Jim.

"That needn't worry us. All we want is dark to come," replied Belding. "Yaqui will slip through. If we thank any lucky stars let it be for the Indian.... Now, boys, put on your thinking caps. You'll take eight horses, the pick of my bunch. You must pack all that's needed for a possible long trip. Mind, Yaqui may lead you down into some wild Sonora valley and give Rojas the slip. You may get to Yuma in six days, and maybe in six weeks. Yet you've got to pack light—a small pack in saddles—larger ones on the two free horses. You may have a big fight. Laddy, take the .405. Dick will pack his Remington. All of you go gunned heavy. But the main thing is a pack that 'll be light enough for swift travel, yet one that 'll keep you from starving on the desert."

The rest of that day passed swiftly. Dick had scarcely a word with Nell, and all the time, as he chose and deliberated and worked over his little pack, there was a dull pain in his heart.

The sun set, twilight fell, then night closed down fortunately a night slightly overcast. Gale saw the white horses pass his door like silent ghosts. Even Blanco Diablo made no sound, and that fact was indeed a tribute to the Yaqui. Gale went out to put his saddle on Blanco Sol. The horse rubbed a soft nose against his shoulder. Then Gale returned to the sitting-room. There was nothing more to do but wait and say good-by. Mercedes came clad in leather chaps and coat, a slim stripling of a cowboy, her dark eyes flashing. Her beauty could not be hidden, and now hope and courage had fired her blood.

Gale drew Nell off into the shadow of the room. She was trembling, and as she leaned toward him she was very different from the coy girl who had so long held him aloof. He took her into his arms.

"Dearest, I'm going—soon.... And maybe I'll never—"

"Dick, do—don't say it," sobbed Nell, with her head on his breast.

"I might never come back," he went on, steadily. "I love you—I've loved you ever since the first moment I saw you. Do you care for me—a little?"

"Dear Dick—de-dear Dick, my heart is breaking," faltered Nell, as she clung to him.

"It might be breaking for Mercedes—for Laddy and Jim. I want to hear something for myself. Something to have on long marches—round lonely campfires. Something to keep my spirit alive. Oh, Nell, you can't imagine that silence out there—that terrible world of sand and stone!... Do you love me?"

"Yes, yes. Oh, I love you so! I never knew it till now. I love you so. Dick, I'll be safe and I'll wait—and hope and pray for your return."

"If I come back—no—when I come back, will you marry me?"

"I—I—oh yes!" she whispered, and returned his kiss.

Belding was in the room speaking softly.

"Nell, darling, I must go," said Dick.

"I'm a selfish little coward," cried Nell. "It's so splendid of you all. I ought to glory in it, but I can't. ... Fight if you must, Dick. Fight for that lovely persecuted girl. I'll love you—the more.... Oh! Good-by! Good-by!"

With a wrench that shook him Gale let her go. He heard Belding's soft voice.

"Yaqui says the early hour's best. Trust him, Laddy. Remember what I say—Yaqui's a godsend."

Then they were all outside in the pale gloom under the trees. Yaqui mounted Blanco Diablo; Mercedes was lifted upon White Woman; Thorne climbed astride Queen; Jim Lash was already upon his horse, which was as white as the others but bore no name; Ladd mounted the stallion Blanco Torres, and gathered up the long halters of the two pack horses; Gale came last with Blanco Sol.

As he toed the stirrup, hand on mane and pommel, Gale took one more look in at the door. Nell stood in the gleam of light, her hair shining, face like ashes, her eyes dark, her lips parted, her arms outstretched. That sweet and tragic picture etched its cruel outlines into Gale's heart. He waved his hand and then fiercely leaped into the saddle.

Blanco Sol stepped out.

Before Gale stretched a line of moving horses, white against dark shadows. He could not see the head of that column; he scarcely heard a soft hoofbeat. A single star shone out of a rift in thin clouds. There was no wind. The air was cold. The dark space of desert seemed to yawn. To the left across the river flickered a few campfires. The chill night, silent and mystical, seemed to close in upon Gale; and he faced the wide, quivering, black level with keen eyes and grim intent, and an awakening of that wild rapture which came like a spell to him in the open desert.

XI ACROSS CACTUS AND LAVA

BLANCO SOL showed no inclination to bend his head to the alfalfa which swished softly about his legs. Gale felt the horse's sensitive, almost human alertness. Sol knew as well as his master the nature of that flight.

At the far corner of the field Yaqui halted, and slowly the line of white horses merged into a compact mass. There was a trail here leading down to the river. The campfires were so close that the bright blazes could be seen in movement, and dark forms crossed in front of them. Yaqui slipped out of his saddle. He ran his hand over Diablo's nose and spoke low, and repeated this action for each of the other horses. Gale had long ceased to question the strange Indian's behavior. There was no explaining or understanding many of his manoeuvers. But the results of them were always thought-provoking. Gale had never seen horse stand so silently as in this instance; no stamp—no champ of bit—no toss of head—no shake of saddle or pack—no heave or snort! It seemed they had become imbued with the spirit of the Indian.

Yaqui moved away into the shadows as noiselessly as if he were one of them. The darkness swallowed him. He had taken a parallel with the trail. Gale wondered if Yaqui meant to try to lead his string of horses by the rebel sentinels. Ladd had his head bent low, his ear toward the trail. Jim's long neck had the arch of a listening deer. Gale listened, too, and as the slow, silent moments went by his faculty of hearing grew more acute from strain. He heard Blanco Sol breathe; he heard the pound of his own heart; he heard the silken rustle of the alfalfa; he heard a faint, far-off sound of voice, like a lost echo. Then his ear seemed to register a movement of air, a disturbance so soft as to be nameless. Then followed long, silent moments.

Yaqui appeared as he had vanished. He might have been part of the shadows. But he was there. He started off down the trail leading Diablo. Again the white line stretched slowly out. Gale fell in behind. A bench of ground, covered with sparse greasewood, sloped gently down to the deep, wide arroyo of Forlorn River. Blanco Sol shied a few feet out of the trail. Peering low with keen eyes, Gale made out three objects—a white sombrero, a blanket, and a Mexican lying face down. The Yaqui had stolen upon this sentinel like a silent wind of death. Just then a desert coyote wailed, and the wild cry fitted the darkness and the Yaqui's deed.

Once under the dark lee of the river bank Yaqui caused another halt, and he disappeared as before. It seemed to Gale that the Indian started to cross the pale level sandbed of the river, where stones stood out gray, and the darker line of opposite shore was visible. But he vanished, and it was impossible to tell whether he went one way or another. Moments passed. The horses held heads up, looked toward the glimmering campfires and listened. Gale thrilled with the meaning of it all—the night—the silence—the flight—and the wonderful Indian stealing with the slow inevitableness of doom upon another sentinel. An hour passed and Gale seemed to have become deadened to all sense of hearing. There were no more sounds in the world. The desert was as silent as it was black. Yet again came that strange change in the tensity of Gale's ear-strain, a check, a break, a vibration—and this time the sound did not go nameless. It might have been moan of wind or wail of far-distant wolf, but Gale imagined it was the strangling death-cry of another guard, or that strange, involuntary utterance of the Yaqui. Blanco Sol trembled in all his great frame, and then Gale was certain the sound was not imagination.

That certainty, once for all, fixed in Gale's mind the mood of his flight. The Yaqui dominated the horses and the rangers. Thorne and Mercedes were as persons under a spell. The Indian's strange silence, the feeling of mystery and power he seemed to create, all that was incomprehensible about him were emphasized in the light of his slow, sure, and ruthless action. If he dominated the others, surely he did more for Gale—colored his thoughts—presage the wild and terrible future of that flight. If Rojas embodied all the hatred and passion of the peon—scourged slave for a thousand years—then Yaqui embodied all the darkness, the cruelty, the white, sun-heated blood, the ferocity, the tragedy of the desert.

Suddenly the Indian stalked out of the gloom. He mounted Diablo and headed across the river. Once more the line of moving white shadows stretched out. The soft sand gave forth no sound at all. The glimmering campfires sank behind the western bank. Yaqui led the way into the willows, and there was faint swishing of leaves; then into the mesquite, and there was faint rustling of branches. The glimmering lights appeared again, and grotesque forms of saguaros loomed darkly. Gale peered sharply along the trail, and, presently, on the pale sand under a cactus, there lay a blanketed form, prone, outstretched, a carbine clutched in one hand, a cigarette, still burning, in the other.

The cavalcade of white horses passed within five hundred yards of campfires, around which dark forms moved in plain sight. Soft pads in sand, faint metallic tickings of steel on thorns, low, regular breathing of horses—these were all the sounds the fugitives made, and they could not have been heard at one-fifth the distance. The lights disappeared from time to time, grew dimmer, more flickering, and at last they vanished altogether. Belding's fleet and tireless steeds were out in front; the desert opened ahead wide, dark, vast. Rojas and his rebels were behind, eating, drinking, careless. The somber shadow lifted from Gale's heart. He held now an unquenchable faith in the Yaqui. Belding would be listening back there along the river. He would know of the escape. He would tell Nell, and then hide her safely. As Gale accepted a strange and fatalistic foreshadowing of toil, blood, and agony in this desert journey, so he believed in Mercedes's ultimate freedom and happiness, and his own return to the girl who had grown dearer than life.

A cold, gray dawn was fleeing before a rosy sun when Yaqui halted the march at Papago Well. The horses were taken to water, then led down the arroyo into the grass. Here packs were slipped, saddles removed. Mercedes was cold, lame, tired, but happy. It warmed Gale's blood to look at her. The shadow of fear still lay in her eyes, but it was passing. Hope and courage shone there, and affection for her ranger protectors and the Yaqui, and unutterable love for the cavalryman. Jim Lash remarked how cleverly they had fooled the rebels.

"Shore they'll be comin' along," replied Ladd.

They built a fire, cooked and ate. The Yaqui spoke only one word: "Sleep." Blankets were spread. Mercedes dropped into a deep slumber, her head on Thorne's shoulder. Excitement kept Thorne awake. The two rangers dozed beside the fire. Gale shared the Yaqui's watch. The sun began to climb and the icy edge of dawn to wear away. Rabbits bobbed their cotton tails under the mesquite. Gale climbed a rocky wall above the arroyo bank, and there, with command over the miles of the back-trail, he watched.

It was a sweeping, rolling, wrinkled, and streaked range of desert that he saw, ruddy in the morning sunlight, with patches of cactus and mesquite rough-etched in shimmering gloom. No Name Mountains split the eastern sky, towering high, gloomy, grand, with purple veils upon their slopes. They were forty miles away and looked five. Gale thought of the girl who was there under their shadow.

Yaqui kept the horses bunched, and he led them from one little park of galleta grass to another. At the end of three hours he took them to water. Upon his return Gale clambered down from his outlook, the rangers grew active. Mercedes was awakened; and soon the party faced westward, their long shadows moving before them. Yaqui led with Blanco Diablo in a long, easy lope. The arroyo washed itself out into flat desert, and the greens began to shade into gray, and then the gray into red. Only sparse cactus and weathered ledges dotted the great low roll of a rising escarpment. Yaqui suited the gait of his horse to the lay of the land, and his followers accepted his pace. There were canter and trot, and swift walk and slow climb, and long swing—miles up and down and forward. The sun soared hot. The heated air lifted, and incoming currents from the west swept low and hard over the barren earth. In the distance, all around the horizon, accumulations of dust seemed like ranging, mushrooming yellow clouds.

Yaqui was the only one of the fugitives who never looked back. Mercedes did it the most. Gale felt what compelled her, he could not resist it himself. But it was a vain search. For a thousand puffs of white and yellow dust rose from that backward sweep of desert, and any one of them might have been blown from under horses' hoofs. Gale had a conviction that when Yaqui gazed back toward the well and the shining plain beyond, there would be reason for it. But when the sun lost its heat and the wind died down Yaqui took long and careful surveys westward from the high points on the trail. Sunset was not far off, and there in a bare, spotted valley lay Coyote Tanks, the only waterhole between Papago Well and the Sonoyta Oasis. Gale used his glass, told Yaqui there was no smoke, no sign of life; still the Indian fixed his falcon eyes on distant spots looked long. It was as if his vision could not detect what reason or cunning or intuition, perhaps an instinct, told him was there. Presently in a sheltered spot, where blown sand had not obliterated the trail, Yaqui found the tracks of horses. The curve of the iron shoes pointed westward. An intersecting trail from the north came in here. Gale thought the tracks either one or two days old. Ladd said they were one day. The Indian shook his head.

No farther advance was undertaken. The Yaqui headed south and traveled slowly, climbing to the brow of a bold height of weathered mesa. There he sat his horse and waited. No one questioned him. The rangers dismounted to stretch their legs, and Mercedes was lifted to a rock, where she rested. Thorne had gradually yielded to the desert's influence for silence. He spoke once or twice to Gale, and occasionally whispered to Mercedes. Gale fancied his friend would soon learn that necessary speech in desert travel meant a few greetings, a few words to make real the fact of human companionship, a few short, terse terms for the business of day or night, and perhaps a stern order or a soft call to a horse.

The sun went down, and the golden, rosy veils turned to blue and shaded darker till twilight was there in the valley. Only the spurs of mountains, spiring the near and far horizon, retained their clear outline. Darkness approached, and the clear peaks faded. The horses stamped to be on the move.

"Malo!" exclaimed the Yaqui.

He did not point with arm, but his falcon head was outstretched, and his piercing eyes gazed at the blurring spot which marked the location of Coyote Tanks.

"Jim, can you see anything?" asked Ladd.

"Nope, but I reckon he can."

Darkness increased momentarily till night shaded the deepest part of the valley.

Then Ladd suddenly straightened up, turned to his horse, and muttered low under his breath.

"I reckon so," said Lash, and for once his easy, good-natured tone was not in evidence. His voice was harsh.

Gale's eyes, keen as they were, were last of the rangers to see tiny, needlepoints of light just faintly perceptible in the blackness.

"Laddy! Campfires?" he asked, quickly.

"Shore's you're born, my boy."

"How many?"

Ladd did not reply; but Yaqui held up his hand, his fingers wide. Five campfires! A strong force of rebels or raiders or some other desert troop was camping at Coyote Tanks.

Yaqui sat his horse for a moment, motionless as stone, his dark face immutable and impassive. Then he stretched wide his right arm in the direction of No Name Mountains, now losing their last faint traces of the afterglow, and he shook his head. He made the same impressive gesture toward the Sonoyta Oasis with the same somber negation.

Thereupon he turned Diablo's head to the south and started down the slope. His manner had been decisive, even stern. Lash did not question it, nor did Ladd. Both rangers hesitated, however, and showed a strange, almost sullen reluctance which Gale had never seen in them before. Raiders were one thing, Rojas was another; Camino del Diablo still another; but that vast and desolate and unwatered waste of cactus and lava, the Sonora Desert, might appall the stoutest heart. Gale felt his own sink—felt himself flinch.

"Oh, where is he going?" cried Mercedes. Her poignant voice seemed to break a spell.

"Shore, lady, Yaqui's goin' home," replied Ladd, gently. "An' considerin' our troubles I reckon we ought to thank God he knows the way."

They mounted and rode down the slope toward the darkening south.

Not until night travel was obstructed by a wall of cactus did the Indian halt to make a dry camp. Water and grass for the horses and fire to cook by were not to be had. Mercedes bore up surprisingly; but she fell asleep almost the instant her thirst had been allayed. Thorne laid her upon a blanket and covered her. The men ate and drank. Diablo was the only horse that showed impatience; but he was angry, and not in distress. Blanco Sol licked Gale's hand and stood patiently. Many a time had he taken his rest at night without a drink. Yaqui again bade the men sleep. Ladd said he would take the early watch; but from the way the Indian shook his head and settled himself against a stone, it appeared if Ladd remained awake he would have company. Gale lay down weary of limb and eye. He heard the soft thump of hoofs, the sough of wind in the cactus—then no more.

When he awoke there was bustle and stir about him. Day had not yet dawned, and the air was freezing cold. Yaqui had found a scant bundle of greasewood which served to warm them and to cook breakfast. Mercedes was not aroused till the last moment.

Day dawned with the fugitives in the saddle. A picketed wall of cactus hedged them in, yet the Yaqui made a tortuous path, that, zigzag as it might, in the main always headed south. It was wonderful how he slipped Diablo through the narrow aisles of thorns, saving the horse and saving himself. The others were torn and clutched and held and stung. The way was a flat, sandy pass between low mountain ranges. There were open spots and aisles and squares of sand; and hedging rows of prickly pear and the huge spider-legged ocatillo and hummocky masses of clustered bisnagi. The day grew dry and hot. A fragrant wind blew through the pass. Cactus flowers bloomed, red and yellow and magenta. The sweet, pale Ajo lily gleamed in shady corners.

Ten miles of travel covered the length of the pass. It opened wide upon a wonderful scene, an arboreal desert, dominated by its pure light green, yet lined by many merging colors. And it rose slowly to a low dim and dark-red zone of lava, spurred, peaked, domed by volcano cones, a wild and ragged region, illimitable as the horizon.

The Yaqui, if not at fault, was yet uncertain. His falcon eyes searched and roved, and became fixed at length at the southwest, and toward this he turned his horse. The great, fluted saguaros, fifty, sixty feet high, raised columnal forms, and their branching limbs and curving lines added a grace to the desert. It was the low-bushed cactus that made the toil and pain of travel. Yet these thorny forms were beautiful.

In the basins between the ridges, to right and left along the floor of low plains the mirage glistened, wavered, faded, vanished—lakes and trees and clouds. Inverted mountains hung suspended in the lilac air and faint tracery of white-walled cities.

At noon Yaqui halted the cavalcade. He had selected a field of bisnagi cactus for the place of rest. Presently his reason became obvious. With long, heavy knife he cut off the tops of these barrel-shaped plants. He scooped out soft pulp, and with stone and hand then began to pound the deeper pulp into a juicy mass. When he threw this out there was a little water left, sweet, cool water which man and horse shared eagerly. Thus he made even the desert's fiercest growths minister to their needs.

But he did not halt long. Miles of gray-green spiked walls lay between him and that line of ragged, red lava which manifestly he must reach before dark. The travel became faster, straighter. And the glistening thorns clutched and clung to leather and cloth and flesh. The horses reared, snorted, balked, leaped—but they were sent on. Only Blanco Sol, the patient, the plodding, the indomitable, needed no goad or spur. Waves and scarfs and wreaths of heat smoked up from the sand. Mercedes reeled in her saddle. Thorne bade her drink, bathed her face, supported her, and then gave way to Ladd, who took the girl with him on Torre's broad back. Yaqui's unflagging purpose and iron arm were bitter and hateful to the proud and haughty spirit of Blanco Diablo. For once Belding's great white devil had met his master. He fought rider, bit, bridle, cactus, sand—and yet he went on and on, zigzagging, turning, winding, crashing through the barbed growths. The middle of the afternoon saw Thorne reeling in his saddle, and then, wherever possible, Gale's powerful arm lent him strength to hold his seat.

The giant cactus came to be only so in name. These saguaros were thinning out, growing stunted, and most of them were single columns. Gradually other cactus forms showed a harder struggle for existence, and the spaces of sand between were wider. But now the dreaded, glistening *choya* began to show pale and gray and white upon the rising slope. Round-topped hills, sunset-colored above, blue-black below, intervened to hide the distant spurs and peaks. Mile and mile long tongues of red lava streamed out between the hills and wound down to stop abruptly upon the slope.

The fugitives were entering a desolate, burned-out world. It rose above them in limitless, gradual ascent and spread wide to east and west. Then the waste of sand began to yield to cinders. The horses sank to their fetlocks as they toiled on. A fine, choking dust blew back from the leaders, and men coughed and horses snorted. The huge, round hills rose smooth, symmetrical, colored as if the setting sun was shining on bare, blue-black surfaces. But the sun was now behind the hills. In between ran the streams of lava. The horsemen skirted the edge between slope of hill and perpendicular ragged wall. This red lava seemed to have flowed and hardened there only yesterday. It was broken sharp, dull rust color, full of cracks and caves and crevices, and everywhere upon its jagged surface grew the white-thorned *choya*.

Again twilight encompassed the travelers. But there was still light enough for Gale to see the constricted passage open into a wide, deep space where the dull color was relieved by the gray of gnarled and dwarfed mesquite. Blanco Sol, keenest of scent, whistled his welcome herald of water. The other horses answered, quickened their gait. Gale smelled it, too, sweet, cool, damp on the dry air.

Yaqui turned the corner of a pocket in the lava wall. The file of white horses rounded the corner after him. And Gale, coming last, saw the pale, glancing gleam of a pool of water beautiful in the twilight.

Next day the Yaqui's relentless driving demand on the horses was no longer in evidence. He lost no time, but he did not hasten. His course wound between low cinder dunes which limited their view of the surrounding country. These dunes finally sank down to a black floor as hard as flint with tongues of lava to the left, and to the right the slow descent into the cactus plain. Yaqui was now traveling due west. It was Gale's idea that the Indian was skirting the first sharp-toothed slope of a vast volcanic plateau which formed the western half of the Sonora Desert and extended to the Gulf of California. Travel was slow, but not exhausting for rider or beast. A little sand and meager grass gave a grayish tinge to the strip of black ground between lava and plain.

That day, as the manner rather than the purpose of the Yaqui changed, so there seemed to be subtle differences in the others of the party. Gale himself lost a certain sickening dread, which had not been for himself, but for Mercedes and Nell, and Thorne and the rangers. Jim, good-natured again, might have been patrolling the boundary line. Ladd lost his taciturnity and his gloom changed to a cool, careless air. A mood that was almost defiance began to be manifested in Thorne. It was in Mercedes, however, that Gale marked the most significant change. Her collapse the preceding day might never have been. She was lame and sore; she rode her saddle sidewise, and often she had to be rested and helped; but she had found a reserve fund of strength, and her mental condition was not the same that it had been. Her burden of fear had been lifted. Gale saw in her the difference he always felt in himself after a few days in the desert. Already Mercedes and he, and all of them, had begun to respond to the desert spirit. Moreover, Yaqui's strange influence must have been a call to the primitive.

Thirty miles of easy stages brought the fugitives to another waterhole, a little round pocket under the heaved-up edge of lava. There was spare, short, bleached grass for the horses, but no wood for a fire. This night there was question and reply, conjecture, doubt, opinion, and conviction expressed by the men of the party. But the Indian, who alone could have told where they were, where they were going, what chance they had to escape, maintained his stoical silence. Gale took the early watch, Ladd the midnight one, and Lash that of the morning.

The day broke rosy, glorious, cold as ice. Action was necessary to make useful benumbed hands and feet. Mercedes was fed while yet wrapped in blankets. Then, while the packs were being put on and horses saddled, she walked up and down, slapping her hands, warming her ears. The rose color of the dawn was in her cheeks, and the wonderful clearness of desert light in her eyes. Thorne's eyes sought her constantly. The rangers watched her. The Yaqui bent his glance upon her only seldom; but when he did look it seemed that his strange, fixed, and inscrutable face was about to break into a smile. Yet that never happened. Gale himself was surprised to find how often his own glance found the slender, dark, beautiful Spaniard. Was this because of her beauty? he wondered. He thought not altogether. Mercedes was a woman. She represented something in life that men of all races for thousands of years had loved to see and own, to revere and debase, to fight and die for.

It was a significant index to the day's travel that Yaqui should keep a blanket from the pack and tear it into strips to bind the legs of the horses. It meant the dreaded *choya* and the knife-edged lava. That Yaqui did not mount Diablo was still more significant. Mercedes must ride; but the others must walk.

The Indian led off into one of the gray notches between the tumbled streams of lava. These streams were about thirty feet high, a rotting mass of splintered lava, rougher than any other kind of roughness in the world. At the apex of the notch, where two streams met, a narrow gully wound and ascended. Gale caught sight of the dim, pale shadow of a one-time trail. Near at hand it was invisible; he had to look far ahead to catch the faint tracery. Yaqui led Diablo into it, and then began the most laborious and vexatious and painful of all slow travel.

Once up on top of that lava bed, Gale saw stretching away, breaking into millions of crests and ruts, a vast, red-black field sweeping onward and upward, with ragged, low ridges and mounds and spurs leading higher and higher to a great, split escarpment wall, above which dim peaks shone hazily blue in the distance.

He looked no more in that direction. To keep his foothold, to save his horse, cost him all energy and attention. The course was marked out for him in the tracks of the other horses. He had only to follow. But nothing could have been more difficult. The disintegrating surface of a lava bed was at once the roughest, the hardest, the meanest, the cruelest, the most deceitful kind of ground to travel.

It was rotten, yet it had corners as hard and sharp as pikes. It was rough, yet as slippery as ice. If there was a foot of level surface, that space would be one to break through under a horse's hoofs. It was seamed, lined, cracked, ridged, knotted iron. This lava bed resembled a tremendously magnified clinker. It had been a running sea of molten flint, boiling, bubbling, spouting, and it had burst its surface into a million sharp facets as it hardened. The color was dull, dark, angry red, like no other red, inflaming to the eye. The millions of minute crevices were dominated by deep fissures and holes, ragged and rough beyond all comparison.

XI ACROSS CACTUS AND LAVA

The fugitives made slow progress. They picked a cautious, winding way to and fro in little steps here and there along the many twists of the trail, up and down the unavoidable depressions, round and round the holes. At noon, so winding back upon itself had been their course, they appeared to have come only a short distance up the lava slope.

It was rough work for them; it was terrible work for the horses. Blanco Diablo refused to answer to the power of the Yaqui. He balked, he plunged, he bit and kicked. He had to be pulled and beaten over many places. Mercedes's horse almost threw her, and she was put upon Blanco Sol. The white charger snorted a protest, then, obedient to Gale's stern call, patiently lowered his noble head and pawed the lava for a footing that would hold.

The lava caused Gale toil and worry and pain, but he hated the *choyas*. As the travel progressed this species of cactus increased in number of plants and in size. Everywhere the red lava was spotted with little round patches of glistening frosty white. And under every bunch of *choya*, along and in the trail, were the discarded joints, like little frosty pine cones covered with spines. It was utterly impossible always to be on the lookout for these, and when Gale stepped on one, often as not the steel-like thorns pierced leather and flesh. Gale came almost to believe what he had heard claimed by desert travelers—that the *choya* was alive and leaped at man or beast. Certain it was when Gale passed one, if he did not put all attention to avoiding it, he was hooked through his chaps and held by barbed thorns. The pain was almost unendurable. It was like no other. It burned, stung, beat—almost seemed to freeze. It made useless arm or leg. It made him bite his tongue to keep from crying out. It made the sweat roll off him. It made him sick.

Moreover, bad as the *choya* was for man, it was infinitely worse for beast. A jagged stab from this poisoned cactus was the only thing Blanco Sol could not stand. Many times that day, before he carried Mercedes, he had wildly snorted, and then stood trembling while Gale picked broken thorns from the muscular legs. But after Mercedes had been put upon Sol Gale made sure no *choya* touched him.

The afternoon passed like the morning, in ceaseless winding and twisting and climbing along this abandoned trail. Gale saw many waterholes, mostly dry, some containing water, all of them catch-basins, full only after rainy season. Little ugly bunched bushes, that Gale scarcely recognized as mesquites, grew near these holes; also stunted greasewood and prickly pear. There was no grass, and the *choya* alone flourished in that hard soil.

Darkness overtook the party as they unpacked beside a pool of water deep under an overhanging shelf of lava. It had been a hard day. The horses drank their fill, and then stood patiently with drooping heads. Hunger and thirst appeased, and a warm fire cheered the weary and foot-sore fugitives. Yaqui said, "Sleep." And so another night passed.

Upon the following morning, ten miles or more up the slow-ascending lava slope, Gale's attention was called from his somber search for the less rough places in the trail.

"Dick, why does Yaqui look back?" asked Mercedes.

Gale was startled.

"Does he?"

"Every little while," replied Mercedes.

Gale was in the rear of all the other horses, so as to take, for Mercedes's sake, the advantage of the broken trail. Yaqui was leading Diablo, winding around a break. His head was bent as he stepped slowly and unevenly upon the lava. Gale turned to look back, the first time in several days. The mighty hollow of the desert below seemed wide strip of red—wide strip of green—wide strip of gray—streaking to purple peaks. It was all too vast, too mighty to grasp any little details. He thought, of course, of Rojas in certain pursuit; but it seemed absurded to look for him.

Yaqui led on, and Gale often glanced up from his task to watch the Indian. Presently he saw him stop, turn, and look back. Ladd did likewise, and then Jim and Thorne. Gale found the desire irresistible. Thereafter he often rested Blanco Sol, and looked back the while. He had his field-glass, but did not choose to use it.

"Rojas will follow," said Mercedes.

Gale regarded her in amaze. The tone of her voice had been indefinable. If there were fear then he failed to detect it. She was gazing back down the colored slope, and something about her, perhaps the steady, falcon gaze of her magnificent eyes, reminded him of Yaqui.

Many times during the ensuing hour the Indian faced about, and always his followers did likewise. It was high noon, with the sun beating hot and the lava radiating heat, when Yaqui halted for a rest. The place selected was a ridge of lava, almost a promontory, considering its outlook. The horses bunched here and drooped their heads. The rangers were about to slip the packs and remove saddles when Yaqui restrained them.

He fixed a changeless, gleaming gaze on the slow descent; but did not seem to look afar.

Suddenly he uttered his strange cry—the one Gale considered involuntary, or else significant of some tribal trait or feeling. It was incomprehensible, but no one could have doubted its potency. Yaqui pointed down the lava slope, pointed with finger and arm and neck and head—his whole body was instinct with direction. His whole being seemed to have been animated and then frozen. His posture could not have been misunderstood, yet his expression had not altered. Gale had never seen the Indian's face change its hard, red-bronze calm. It was the color and the flintiness and the character of the lava at his feet.

"Shore he sees somethin'," said Ladd. "But my eyes are not good."

"I reckon I ain't sure of mine," replied Jim. "I'm bothered by a dim movin' streak down there."

Thorne gazed eagerly down as he stood beside Mercedes, who sat motionless facing the slope. Gale looked and looked till he hurt his eyes. Then he took his glass out of its case on Sol's saddle.

XI ACROSS CACTUS AND LAVA

There appeared to be nothing upon the lava but the innumerable dots of *choya* shining in the sun. Gale swept his glass slowly forward and back. Then into a nearer field of vision crept a long white-and-black line of horses and men. Without a word he handed the glass to Ladd. The ranger used it, muttering to himself.

"They're on the lava fifteen miles down in an air line," he said, presently. "Jim, shore they're twice that an' more accordin' to the trail."

Jim had his look and replied: "I reckon we're a day an' a night in the lead."

"Is it Rojas?" burst out Thorne, with set jaw.

"Yes, Thorne. It's Rojas and a dozen men or more," replied Gale, and he looked up at Mercedes.

She was transformed. She might have been a medieval princess embodying all the Spanish power and passion of that time, breathing revenge, hate, unquenchable spirit of fire. If her beauty had been wonderful in her helpless and appealing moments, now, when she looked back white-faced and flame-eyed, it was transcendant.

Gale drew a long, deep breath. The mood which had presaged pursuit, strife, blood on this somber desert, returned to him tenfold. He saw Thorne's face corded by black veins, and his teeth exposed like those of a snarling wolf. These rangers, who had coolly risked death many times, and had dealt it often, were white as no fear or pain could have made them. Then, on the moment, Yaqui raised his hand, not clenched or doubled tight, but curled rigid like an eagle's claw; and he shook it in a strange, slow gesture which was menacing and terrible.

It was the woman that called to the depths of these men. And their passion to kill and to save was surpassed only by the wild hate which was yet love, the unfathomable emotion of a peon slave. Gale marveled at it, while he felt his whole being cold and tense, as he turned once more to follow in the tracks of his leaders. The fight predicted by Belding was at hand. What a fight that must be! Rojas was traveling light and fast. He was gaining. He had bought his men with gold, with extravagant promises, perhaps with offers of the body and blood of an aristocrat hateful to their kind. Lastly, there was the wild, desolate environment, a tortured wilderness of jagged lava and poisoned *choya*, a lonely, fierce, and repellant world, a red stage most somberly and fittingly colored for a supreme struggle between men.

Yaqui looked back no more. Mercedes looked back no more. But the others looked, and the time came when Gale saw the creeping line of pursuers with naked eyes.

A level line above marked the rim of the plateau. Sand began to show in the little lava pits. On and upward toiled the cavalcade, still very slowly advancing. At last Yaqui reached the rim. He stood with his hand on Blanco Diablo; and both were silhouetted against the sky. That was the outlook for a Yaqui. And his great horse, dazzlingly white in the sunlight, with head wildly and proudly erect, mane and tail flying in the wind, made a magnificent picture. The others toiled on and upward, and at last Gale led Blanco Sol over the rim. Then all looked down the red slope.

But shadows were gathering there and no moving line could be seen.

Yaqui mounted and wheeled Diablo away. The others followed. Gale saw that the plateau was no more than a vast field of low, ragged circles, levels, mounds, cones, and whirls of lava. The lava was of a darker red than that down upon the slope, and it was harder than flint. In places fine sand and cinders covered the uneven floor. Strange varieties of cactus vied with the omnipresent *choya*. Yaqui, however, found ground that his horse covered at a swift walk.

But there was only an hour, perhaps, of this comparatively easy going. Then the Yaqui led them into a zone of craters. The top of the earth seemed to have been blown out in holes from a few rods in width to large craters, some shallow, others deep, and all red as fire. Yaqui circled close to abysses which yawned sheer from a level surface, and he appeared always to be turning upon his course to avoid them.

The plateau had now a considerable dip to the west. Gale marked the slow heave and ripple of the ocean of lava to the south, where high, rounded peaks marked the center of this volcanic region. The uneven nature of the slope westward prevented any extended view, until suddenly the fugitives emerged from a rugged break to come upon a sublime and awe-inspiring spectacle.

They were upon a high point of the western slope of the plateau. It was a slope, but so many leagues long in its descent that only from a height could any slant have been perceptible. Yaqui and his white horse stood upon the brink of a crater miles in circumference, a thousand feet deep, with its red walls patched in frost-colored spots by the silvery *choya*. The giant tracery of lava streams waved down the slope to disappear in undulating sand dunes. And these bordered a seemingly endless arm of blue sea. This was the Gulf of California. Beyond the Gulf rose dim, bold mountains, and above them hung the setting sun, dusky red, flooding all that barren empire with a sinister light.

It was strange to Gale then, and perhaps to the others, to see their guide lead Diablo into a smooth and well-worn trail along the rim of the awful crater. Gale looked down into that red chasm. It resembled an inferno. The dark cliffs upon the opposite side were veiled in blue haze that seemed like smoke. Here Yaqui was at home. He moved and looked about him as a man coming at last into his own. Gale saw him stop and gaze out over that red-ribbed void to the Gulf.

Gale devined that somewhere along this crater of hell the Yaqui would make his final stand; and one look into his strange, inscrutable eyes made imagination picture a fitting doom for the pursuing Rojas.

XII THE CRATER OF HELL

THE trail led along a gigantic fissure in the side of the crater, and then down and down into a red-walled, blue hazed labyrinth.

Presently Gale, upon turning a sharp corner, was utterly amazed to see that the split in the lava sloped out and widened into an arroyo. It was so green and soft and beautiful in all the angry, contorted red surrounding that Gale could scarcely credit his sight. Blanco Sol whistled his welcome to the scent of water. Then Gale saw a great hole, a pit in the shiny lava, a dark, cool, shady well. There was evidence of the fact that at flood seasons the water had an outlet into the arroyo. The soil appeared to be a fine sand, in which a reddish tinge predominated; and it was abundantly covered with a long grass, still partly green. Mesquites and palo verdes dotted the arroyo and gradually closed in thickets that obstructed the view.

"Shore it all beats me," exclaimed Ladd. "What a place to hole-up in! We could have hid here for a long time. Boys, I saw mountain sheep, the real old genuine Rocky Mountain bighorn. What do you think of that?"

"I reckon it's a Yaqui hunting-ground," replied Lash. "That trail we hit must be hundreds of years old. It's worn deep and smooth in iron lava."

"Well, all I got to say is—Beldin' was shore right about the Indian. An' I can see Rojas's finish somewhere up along that awful hell-hole."

Camp was made on a level spot. Yaqui took the horses to water, and then turned them loose in the arroyo. It was a tired and somber group that sat down to eat. The strain of suspense equaled the wearing effects of the long ride. Mercedes was calm, but her great dark eyes burned in her white face. Yaqui watched her. The others looked at her with unspoken pride. Presently Thorne wrapped her in his blankets, and she seemed to fall asleep at once. Twilight deepened. The campfire blazed brighter. A cool wind played with Mercedes's black hair, waving strands across her brow.

Little of Yaqui's purpose or plan could be elicited from him. But the look of him was enough to satisfy even Thorne. He leaned against a pile of wood, which he had collected, and his gloomy gaze pierced the campfire, and at long intervals strayed over the motionless form of the Spanish girl.

The rangers and Thorne, however, talked in low tones. It was absolutely impossible for Rojas and his men to reach the waterhole before noon of the next day. And long before that time the fugitives would have decided on a plan of defense.

What that defense would be, and where it would be made, were matters over which the men considered gravely. Ladd averred the Yaqui would put them into an impregnable position, that at the same time would prove a death-trap for their pursuers. They exhausted every possibility, and then, tired as they were, still kept on talking.

"What stuns me is that Rojas stuck to our trail," said Thorne, his lined and haggard face expressive of dark passion. "He has followed us into this fearful desert. He'll lose men, horses, perhaps his life. He's only a bandit, and he stands to win no gold. If he ever gets out of here it 'll be by herculean labor and by terrible hardship. All for a poor little helpless woman—just a woman! My God, I can't understand it."

"Shore—just a woman," replied Ladd, solemnly nodding his head.

Then there was a long silence during which the men gazed into the fire. Each, perhaps, had some vague conception of the enormity of Rojas's love or hate—some faint and amazing glimpse of the gulf of human passion. Those were cold, hard, grim faces upon which the light flickered.

"Sleep," said the Yaqui.

Thorne rolled in his blanket close beside Mercedes. Then one by one the rangers stretched out, feet to the fire. Gale found that he could not sleep. His eyes were weary, but they would not stay shut; his body ached for rest, yet he could not lie still. The night was so somber, so gloomy, and the lava-encompassed arroyo full of shadows. The dark velvet sky, fretted with white fire, seemed to be close. There was an absolute silence, as of death. Nothing moved—nothing outside of Gale's body appeared to live. The Yaqui sat like an image carved out of lava. The others lay prone and quiet. Would another night see any of them lie that way, quiet forever? Gale felt a ripple pass over him that was at once a shudder and a contraction of muscles. Used as he was to the desert and its oppression, why should he feel to-night as if the weight of its lava and the burden of its mystery were bearing him down?

He sat up after a while and again watched the fire. Nell's sweet face floated like a wraith in the pale smoke—glowed and flushed and smiled in the embers. Other faces shone there—his sister's—that of his mother. Gale shook off the tender memories. This desolate wilderness with its forbidding silence and its dark promise of hell on the morrow—this was not the place to unnerve oneself with thoughts of love and home. But the torturing paradox of the thing was that this was just the place and just the night for a man to be haunted.

By and by Gale rose and walked down a shadowy aisle between the mesquites. On his way back the Yaqui joined him. Gale was not surprised. He had become used to the Indian's strange guardianship. But now, perhaps because of Gale's poignancy of thought, the contending tides of love and regret, the deep, burning premonition of deadly strife, he was moved to keener scrutiny of the Yaqui. That, of course, was futile. The Indian was impenetrable, silent, strange. But suddenly, inexplicably, Gale felt Yaqui's human quality. It was aloof, as was everything about this Indian; but it was there. This savage walked silently beside him, without glance or touch or word. His thought was as inscrutable as if mind had never awakened in his race. Yet Gale was conscious of greatness, and, somehow, he was reminded of the Indian's story. His home had been desolated, his people carried off to slavery, his wife and children separated from him to die. What had life meant to the Yaqui? What had been in his heart? What was now in his mind? Gale could not answer these questions. But the difference between himself and Yaqui, which he had vaguely felt as that between savage and civilized men, faded out of his mind forever. Yaqui might have considered he owed Gale a debt, and, with a Yaqui's austere and noble fidelity to honor, he meant to pay it. Nevertheless, this was not the thing Gale found in the Indian's silent presence. Accepting the desert with its subtle and inconceivable influence, Gale felt that the savage and the white man had been bound in a tie which was no less brotherly because it could not be comprehended.

Toward dawn Gale managed to get some sleep. Then the morning broke with the sun hidden back of the uplift of the plateau. The horses trooped up the arroyo and snorted for water. After a hurried breakfast the packs were hidden in holes in the lava. The saddles were left where they were, and the horses allowed to graze and wander at will. Canteens were filled, a small bag of food was packed, and blankets made into a bundle. Then Yaqui faced the steep ascent of the lava slope.

The trail he followed led up on the right side of the fissure, opposite to the one he had come down. It was a steep climb, and encumbered as the men were they made but slow progress. Mercedes had to be lifted up smooth steps and across crevices. They passed places where the rims of the fissure were but a few yards apart. At length the rims widened out and the red, smoky crater yawned beneath. Yaqui left the trail and began clambering down over the rough and twisted convolutions of lava which formed the rim. Sometimes he hung sheer over the precipice. It was with extreme difficulty that the party followed him. Mercedes had to be held on narrow, foot-wide ledges. The *choya* was there to hinder passage. Finally the Indian halted upon a narrow bench of flat, smooth lava, and his followers worked with exceeding care and effort down to his position.

At the back of this bench, between bunches of *choya*, was a niche, a shallow cave with floor lined apparently with mold. Ladd said the place was a refuge which had been inhabited by mountain sheep for many years. Yaqui spread blankets inside, left the canteen and the sack of food, and with a gesture at once humble, yet that of a chief, he invited Mercedes to enter. A few more gestures and fewer words disclosed his plan. In this inaccessible nook Mercedes was to be hidden. The men were to go around upon the opposite rim, and block the trail leading down to the waterhole.

Gale marked the nature of this eyrie. It was the wildest and most rugged place he had ever stepped upon. Only a sheep could have climbed up the wall above or along the slanting shelf of lava beyond. Below glistened a whole bank of *choya*, frosty in the sunlight, and it overhung an apparently bottomless abyss.

Ladd chose the smallest gun in the party and gave it to Mercedes.

"Shore it's best to go the limit on bein' ready," he said, simply. "The chances are you'll never need it. But if you do—"

He left off there, and his break was significant. Mercedes answered him with a fearless and indomitable flash of eyes. Thorne was the only one who showed any shaken nerve. His leave-taking of his wife was affecting and hurried. Then he and the rangers carefully stepped in the tracks of the Yaqui.

They climbed up to the level of the rim and went along the edge. When they reached the fissure and came upon its narrowest point, Yaqui showed in his actions that he meant to leap it. Ladd restrained the Indian. They then continued along the rim till they reached several bridges of lava which crossed it. The fissures was deep in some parts, choked in others. Evidently the crater had no direct outlet into the arroyo below. Its bottom, however, must have been far beneath the level of the waterhole.

After the fissure was crossed the trail was soon found. Here it ran back from the rim. Yaqui waved his hand to the right, where along the corrugated slope of the crater there were holes and crevices and coverts for a hundred men. Yaqui strode on up the trail toward a higher point, where presently his dark figure stood motionless against the sky. The rangers and Thorne selected a deep depression, out of which led several ruts deep enough for cover. According to Ladd it was as good a place as any, perhaps not so hidden as others, but freer from the dreaded *choya*. Here the men laid down rifles and guns, and, removing their heavy cartridge belts, settled down to wait.

Their location was close to the rim wall and probably five hundred yards from the opposite rim, which was now seen to be considerably below them. The glaring red cliff presented a deceitful and baffling appearance. It had a thousand ledges and holes in its surfaces, and one moment it looked perpendicular and the next there seemed to be a long slant. Thorne pointed out where he thought Mercedes was hidden; Ladd selected another place, and Lash still another. Gale searched for the bank of *choya* he had seen under the bench where Mercedes's retreat lay, and when he found it the others disputed his opinion. Then Gale brought his field glass into requisition, proving that he was right. Once located and fixed in sight, the white patch of *choya*, the bench, and the sheep eyrie stood out from the other features of that rugged wall. But all the men were agreed that Yaqui had hidden Mercedes where only the eyes of a vulture could have found her.

Jim Lash crawled into a little strip of shade and bided the time tranquilly. Ladd was restless and impatient and watchful, every little while rising to look up the far-reaching slope, and then to the right, where Yaqui's dark figure stood out from a high point of the rim. Thorne grew silent, and seemed consumed by a slow, sullen rage. Gale was neither calm nor free of a gnawing suspense nor of a waiting wrath. But as best he could he put the pending action out of mind.

It came over him all of a sudden that he had not grasped the stupendous nature of this desert setting. There was the measureless red slope, its lower ridges finally sinking into white sand dunes toward the blue sea. The cold, sparkling light, the white sun, the deep azure of sky, the feeling of boundless expanse all around him—these meant high altitude. Southward the barren red simply merged into distance. The field of craters rose in high, dark wheels toward the dominating peaks. When Gale withdrew his gaze from the magnitude of these spaces and heights the crater beneath him seemed dwarfed. Yet while he gazed it spread and deepened and multiplied its ragged lines. No, he could not grasp the meaning of size or distance here. There was too much to stun the sight. But the mood in which nature had created this convulsed world of lava seized hold upon him.

Meanwhile the hours passed. As the sun climbed the clear, steely lights vanished, the blue hazes deepened, and slowly the glistening surfaces of lava turned redder. Ladd was concerned to discover that Yaqui was missing from his outlook upon the high point. Jim Lash came out of the shady crevice, and stood up to buckle on his cartridge belt. His narrow, gray glance slowly roved from the height of lava down along the slope, paused in doubt, and then swept on to resurvey the whole vast eastern dip of the plateau.

"I reckon my eyes are pore," he said. "Mebbe it's this damn red glare. Anyway, what's them creepin' spots up there?"

"Shore I seen them. Mountain sheep," replied Ladd.

"Guess again, Laddy. Dick, I reckon you'd better flash the glass up the slope."

Gale adjusted the field glass and began to search the lava, beginning close at hand and working away from him. Presently the glass became stationary.

"I see half a dozen small animals, brown in color. They look like sheep. But I couldn't distinguish mountain sheep from antelope."

"Shore they're bighorn," said Laddy.

"I reckon if you'll pull around to the east an' search under that long wall of lava—there—you'll see what I see," added Jim.

The glass climbed and circled, wavered an instant, then fixed steady as a rock. There was a breathless silence.

"Fourteen horses—two packed—some mounted—others without riders, and lame," said Gale, slowly.

Yaqui appeared far up the trail, coming swiftly. Presently he saw the rangers and halted to wave his arms and point. Then he vanished as if the lava had opened beneath him.

"Lemme that glass," suddenly said Jim Lash. "I'm seein' red, I tell you.... Well, pore as my eyes are they had it right. Rojas an' his outfit have left the trail."

"Jim, you ain't meanin' they've taken to that awful slope?" queried Ladd.

"I sure do. There they are—still comin', but goin' down, too."

"Mebbe Rojas is crazy, but it begins to look like he—"

"Laddy, I'll be danged if the Greaser bunch hasn't vamoosed. Gone out of sight! Right there not a half mile away, the whole caboodle—gone!"

"Shore they're behind a crust or have gone down into a rut," suggested Ladd. "They'll show again in a minute. Look sharp, boys, for I'm figgerin' Rojas 'll spread his men."

Minutes passed, but nothing moved upon the slope. Each man crawled up to a vantage point along the crest of rotting lava. The watchers were careful to peer through little notches or from behind a spur, and the constricted nature of their hiding-place kept them close together. Ladd's muttering grew into a growl, then lapsed into the silence that marked his companions. From time to time the rangers looked inquiringly at Gale. The field glass, however, like the naked sight, could not catch the slightest moving object out there upon the lava. A long hour of slow, mounting suspense wore on.

"Shore it's all goin' to be as queer as the Yaqui," said Ladd.

Indeed, the strange mien, the silent action, the somber character of the Indian had not been without effect upon the minds of the men. Then the weird, desolate, tragic scene added to the vague sense of mystery. And now the disappearance of Rojas's band, the long wait in the silence, the boding certainty of invisible foes crawling, circling closer and closer, lent to the situation a final touch that made it unreal.

"I'm reckonin' there's a mind behind them Greasers," replied Jim. "Or mebbe we ain't done Rojas credit... If somethin' would only come off!"

That Lash, the coolest, most provokingly nonchalant of men in times of peril, should begin to show a nervous strain was all the more indicative of a subtle pervading unreality.

"Boys, look sharp!" suddenly called Lash. "Low down to the left—mebbe three hundred yards. See, along by them seams of lava—behind the *choyas*. First off I thought it was a sheep. But it's the Yaqui!... Crawlin' swift as a lizard! Can't you see him?"

It was a full moment before Jim's companions could locate the Indian. Flat as a snake Yaqui wound himself along with incredible rapidity. His advance was all the more remarkable for the fact that he appeared to pass directly under the dreaded *choyas*. Sometimes he paused to lift his head and look. He was directly in line with a huge whorl of lava that rose higher than any point on the slope. This spur was a quarter of a mile from the position of the rangers.

"Shore he's headin' for that high place," said Ladd. "He's goin' slow now. There, he's stopped behind some *choyas*. He's gettin' up—no, he's kneelin'.... Now what the hell!"

"Laddy, take a peek at the side of that lava ridge," sharply called Jim. "I guess mebbe somethin' ain't comin' off. See! There's Rojas an' his outfit climbin'. Don't make out no hosses.... Dick, use your glass an' tell us what's doin'. I'll watch Yaqui an' tell you what his move means."

Clearly and distinctly, almost as if he could have touched them, Gale had Rojas and his followers in sight. They were toiling up the rough lava on foot. They were heavily armed. Spurs, chaps, jackets, scarfs were not in evidence. Gale saw the lean, swarthy faces, the black, straggly hair, the ragged, soiled garments which had once been white.

"They're almost up now," Gale was saying. "There! They halt on top. I see Rojas. He looks wild. By ——! fellows, an Indian!... It's a Papago. Belding's old herder!... The Indian points—this way—then down. He's showing Rojas the lay of the trail."

"Boys, Yaqui's in range of that bunch," said Jim, swiftly. "He's raisin' his rifle slow—Lord, how slow he is!... He's covered some one. Which one I can't say. But I think he'll pick Rojas."

"The Yaqui can shoot. He'll pick Rojas," added Gale, grimly.

"Rojas—yes—yes!" cried Thorne, in passion of suspense.

"Not on your life!" Ladd's voice cut in with scorn. "Gentlemen, you can gamble Yaqui 'll kill the Papago. That traitor Indian knows these sheep haunts. He's tellin' Rojas—"

A sharp rifle shot rang out.

"Laddy's right," called Gale. "The Papago's hit—his arm falls—There, he tumbles!"

More shots rang out. Yaqui was seen standing erect firing rapidly at the darting Mexicans. For all Gale could make out no second bullet took effect. Rojas and his men vanished behind the bulge of lava. Then Yaqui deliberately backed away from his position. He made no effort to run or hide. Evidently he watched cautiously for signs of pursuers in the ruts and behind the *choyas*. Presently he turned and came straight toward the position of the rangers, sheered off perhaps a hundred paces below it, and disappeared in a crevice. Plainly his intention was to draw pursuers within rifle shot.

"Shore, Jim, you had your wish. Somethin' come off," said Ladd. "An' I'm sayin' thank God for the Yaqui! That Papago 'd have ruined us. Even so, mebbe he's told Rojas more'n enough to make us sweat blood."

"He had a chance to kill Rojas," cried out the drawn-faced, passionate Thorne. "He didn't take it!... He didn't take it!"

Only Ladd appeared to be able to answer the cavalryman's poignant cry.

"Listen, son," he said, and his voice rang. "We-all know how you feel. An' if I'd had that one shot never in the world could I have picked the Papago guide. I'd have had to kill Rojas. That's the white man of it. But Yaqui was right. Only an Indian could have done it. You can gamble the Papago alive meant slim chance for us. Because he'd led straight to where Mercedes is hidden, an' then we'd have left cover to fight it out... When you come to think of the Yaqui's hate for Greasers, when you just seen him pass up a shot at one—well, I don't know how to say what I mean, but damn me, my som-brer-ro is off to the Indian!"

"I reckon so, an' I reckon the ball's opened," rejoined Lash, and now that former nervous impatience so unnatural to him was as if it had never been. He was smilingly cool, and his voice had almost a caressing note. He tapped the breech of his Winchester with a sinewy brown hand, and he did not appear to be addressing any one in particular. "Yaqui's opened the ball. Look up your pardners there, gents, an' get ready to dance."

Another wait set in then, and judging by the more direct rays of the sun and a receding of the little shadows cast by the *choyas*, Gale was of the opinion that it was a long wait. But it seemed short. The four men were lying under the bank of a half circular hole in the lava. It was notched and cracked, and its rim was fringed by *choyas*. It sloped down and opened to an unobstructed view of the crater. Gale had the upper position, fartherest to the right, and therefore was best shielded from possible fire from the higher ridges of the rim, some three hundred yards distant. Jim came next, well hidden in a crack. The positions of Thorne and Ladd were most exposed. They kept sharp lookout over the uneven rampart of their hiding-place.

The sun passed the zenith, began to slope westward, and to grow hotter as it sloped. The men waited and waited. Gale saw no impatience even in Thorne. The sultry air seemed to be laden with some burden or quality that was at once composed of heat, menace, color, and silence. Even the light glancing up from the lava seemed red and the silence had substance. Sometimes Gale felt that it was unbearable. Yet he made no effort to break it.

Suddenly this dead stillness was rent by a shot, clear and stinging, close at hand. It was from a rifle, not a carbine. With startling quickness a cry followed—a cry that pierced Gale—it was so thin, so high-keyed, so different from all other cries. It was the involuntary human shriek at death.

"Yaqui's called out another pardner," said Jim Lash, laconically.

Carbines began to crack. The reports were quick, light, like sharp spats without any ring. Gale peered from behind the edge of his covert. Above the ragged wave of lava floated faint whitish clouds, all that was visible of smokeless powder. Then Gale made out round spots, dark against the background of red, and in front of them leaped out small tongues of fire. Ladd's .405 began to "spang" with its beautiful sound of power. Thorne was firing, somewhat wildly Gale thought. Then Jim Lash pushed his Winchester over the rim under a *choya*, and between shots Gale could hear him singing: "Turn the lady, turn—turn the lady, turn!... Alaman left!... Swing your pardners!... Forward an' back!... Turn the lady, turn!" Gale got into the fight himself, not so sure that he hit any of the round, bobbing objects he aimed at, but growing sure of himself as action liberated something forced and congested within his breast.

Then over the position of the rangers came a hail of steel bullets. Those that struck the lava hissed away into the crater; those that came biting through the *choyas* made a sound which resembled a sharp ripping of silk. Bits of cactus stung Gale's face, and he dreaded the flying thorns more than he did the flying bullets.

"Hold on, boys," called Ladd, as he crouched down to reload his rifle. "Save your shells. The greasers are spreadin' on us, some goin' down below Yaqui, others movin' up for that high ridge. When they get up there I'm damned if it won't be hot for us. There ain't room for all of us to hide here."

Ladd raised himself to peep over the rim. Shots were now scattering, and all appeared to come from below. Emboldened by this he rose higher. A shot from in front, a rip of bullet through the *choya*, a spat of something hitting Ladd's face, a steel missle hissing onward—these inseparably blended sounds were all registered by Gale's sensitive ear.

With a curse Ladd tumbled down into the hole. His face showed a great gray blotch, and starting blood. Gale felt a sickening assurance of desperate injury to the ranger. He ran to him calling: "Laddy! Laddy!"

"Shore I ain't plugged. It's a damn *choya* burr. The bullet knocked it in my face. Pull it out!"

The oval, long-spiked cone was firmly imbedded in Ladd's cheek. Blood streamed down his face and neck. Carefully, yet with no thought of pain to himself, Gale tried to pull the cactus joint away. It was as firm as if it had been nailed there. That was the damnable feature of the barbed thorns: once set, they held on as that strange plant held to its desert life. Ladd began to writhe, and sweat mingled with the blood on his face. He cursed and raved, and his movements made it almost impossible for Gale to do anything.

"Put your knife-blade under an' tear it out!" shouted Ladd, hoarsely.

Thus ordered, Gale slipped a long blade in between the imbedded thorns, and with a powerful jerk literally tore the *choya* out of Ladd's quivering flesh. Then, where the ranger's face was not red and raw, it certainly was white.

A volley of shots from a different angle was followed by the quick ring of steel bullets striking the lava all around Gale. His first idea, as he heard the projectiles sing and hum and whine away into the air, was that they were coming from above him. He looked up to see a number of low, white and dark knobs upon the high point of lava. They had not been there before. Then he saw little, pale, leaping tongues of fire. As he dodged down he distinctly heard a bullet strike Ladd. At the same instant he seemed to hear Thorne cry out and fall, and Lash's boots scrape rapidly away.

Ladd fell backward still holding the .405. Gale dragged him into the shelter of his own position, and dreading to look at him, took up the heavy weapon. It was with a kind of savage strength that he gripped the rifle; and it was with a cold and deadly intent that he aimed and fired. The first Greaser huddled low, let his carbine go clattering down, and then crawled behind the rim. The second and third jerked back. The fourth seemed to flop up over the crest of lava. A dark arm reached for him, clutched his leg, tried to drag him up. It was in vain. Wildly grasping at the air the bandit fell, slid down a steep shelf, rolled over the rim, to go hurtling down out of sight.

Fingering the hot rifle with close-pressed hands, Gale watched the sky line along the high point of lava. It remained unbroken. As his passion left him he feared to look back at his companions, and the cold chill returned to his breast.

"Shore—I'm damn glad—them Greasers ain't usin' soft-nose bullets," drawled a calm voice.

Swift as lightning Gale whirled.

"Laddy! I thought you were done for," cried Gale, with a break in his voice.

"I ain't a-mindin' the bullet much. But that *choya* joint took my nerve, an' you can gamble on it. Dick, this hole's pretty high up, ain't it?"

The ranger's blouse was open at the neck, and on his right shoulder under the collar bone was a small hole just beginning to bleed.

"Sure it's high, Laddy," replied Gale, gladly. "Went clear through, clean as a whistle!"

He tore a handkerchief into two parts, made wads, and pressing them close over the wounds he bound them there with Ladd's scarf.

"Shore it's funny how a bullet can floor a man an' then not do any damage," said Ladd. "I felt a zip of wind an' somethin' like a pat on my chest an' down I went. Well, so much for the small caliber with their steel bullets. Supposin' I'd connected with a .405!"

"Laddy, I—I'm afraid Thorne's done for," whispered Gale. "He's lying over there in that crack. I can see part of him. He doesn't move."

"I was wonderin' if I'd have to tell you that. Dick, he went down hard hit, fall-in', you know, limp an' soggy. It was a moral cinch one of us would get it in this fight; but God! I'm sorry Thorne had to be the man."

"Laddy, maybe he's not dead," replied Gale. He called aloud to his friend. There was no answer.

Ladd got up, and, after peering keenly at the height of lava, he strode swiftly across the space. It was only a dozen steps to the crack in the lava where Thorne had fallen head first. Ladd bent over, went to his knees, so that Gale saw only his head. Then he appeared rising with arms round the cavalryman. He dragged him across the hole to the sheltered corner that alone afforded protection. He had scarcely reached it when a carbine cracked and a bullet struck the flinty lava, striking sparks, then singing away into the air.

Thorne was either dead or unconscious, and Gale, with a contracting throat and numb heart, decided for the former. Not so Ladd, who probed the bloody gash on Thorne's temple, and then felt his breast.

"He's alive an' not bad hurt. That bullet hit him glancin'. Shore them steel bul-lets are some lucky for us. Dick, you needn't look so glum. I tell you he ain't bad hurt. I felt his skull with my finger. There's no hole in it. Wash him off an' tie—Wow! did you get the wind of that one? An' mebbe it didn't sing off the lava!... Dick, look after Thorne now while I—"

The completion of his speech was the stirring ring of the .405, and then he ut-tered a laugh that was unpleasant.

"Shore, Greaser, there's a man's size bullet for you. No slim, sharp-pointed, steel-jacket nail! I'm takin' it on me to believe you're appreciatin' of the .405, see-in' as you don't make no fuss."

It was indeed a joy to Gale to find that Thorne had not received a wound nec-essarily fatal, though it was serious enough. Gale bathed and bound it, and laid the cavalryman against the slant of the bank, his head high to lessen the probabil-ity of bleeding.

As Gale straightened up Ladd muttered low and deep, and swung the heavy ri-fle around to the left. Far along the slope a figure moved. Ladd began to work the lever of the Winchester and to shoot. At every shot the heavy firearm sprang up, and the recoil made Ladd's shoulder give back. Gale saw the bullets strike the lava behind, beside, before the fleeing Mexican, sending up dull puffs of dust. On the sixth shot he plunged down out of sight, either hit or frightened into seeking cover.

"Dick, mebbe there's one or two left above; but we needn't figure much on it," said Ladd, as, loading the rifle, he jerked his fingers quickly from the hot breech. "Listen! Jim an' Yaqui are hittin' it up lively down below. I'll sneak down there. You stay here an' keep about half an eye peeled up yonder, an' keep the rest my way."

Ladd crossed the hole, climbed down into the deep crack where Thorne had fallen, and then went stooping along with only his head above the level. Presently he disappeared. Gale, having little to fear from the high ridge, directed most of his attention toward the point beyond which Ladd had gone. The firing had become desultory, and the light carbine shots outnumbered the sharp rifle shots five to one. Gale made a note of the fact that for some little time he had not heard the unmistakable report of Jim Lash's automatic. Then ensued a long interval in which the desert silence seemed to recover its grip. The .405 ripped it asunder—spang—spang—spang. Gale fancied he heard yells. There were a few pattering shots still farther down the trail. Gale had an uneasy conviction that Rojas and some of his band might go straight to the waterhole. It would be hard to dislodge even a few men from that retreat.

There seemed a lull in the battle. Gale ventured to stand high, and screened behind *choyas*, he swept the three-quarter circle of lava with his glass. In the distance he saw horses, but no riders. Below him, down the slope along the crater rim and the trail, the lava was bare of all except tufts of *choya*. Gale gathered assurance. It looked as if the day was favoring his side. Then Thorne, coming partly to consciousness, engaged Gale's care. The cavalryman stirred and moaned, called for water, and then for Mercedes. Gale held him back with a strong hand, and presently he was once more quiet.

For the first time in hours, as it seemed, Gale took note of the physical aspect of his surroundings. He began to look upon them without keen gaze strained for crouching form, or bobbing head, or spouting carbine. Either Gale's sense of color and proportion had become deranged during the fight, or the encompassing air and the desert had changed. Even the sun had changed. It seemed lowering, oval in shape, magenta in hue, and it had a surface that gleamed like oil on water. Its red rays shone through red haze. Distances that had formerly been clearly outlined were now dim, obscured. The yawning chasm was not the same. It circled wider, redder, deeper. It was a weird, ghastly mouth of hell. Gale stood fascinated, unable to tell how much he saw was real, how much exaggeration of overwrought emotions. There was no beauty here, but an unparalleled grandeur, a sublime scene of devastation and desolation which might have had its counterpart upon the burned-out moon. The mood that gripped Gale now added to its somber portent an unshakable foreboding of calamity.

He wrestled with the spell as if it were a physical foe. Reason and intelligence had their voices in his mind; but the moment was not one wherein these things could wholly control. He felt life strong within his breast, yet there, a step away, was death, yawning, glaring, smoky, red. It was a moment—an hour for a savage, born, bred, developed in this scarred and blasted place of jagged depths and red distances and silences never meant to be broken. Since Gale was not a savage he fought that call of the red gods which sent him back down the long ages toward his primitive day. His mind combated his sense of sight and the hearing that seemed useless; and his mind did not win all the victory. Something fatal was here, hanging in the balance, as the red haze hung along the vast walls of that crater of hell.

Suddenly harsh, prolonged yells brought him to his feet, and the unrealities vanished. Far down the trails where the crater rims closed in the deep fissure he saw moving forms. They were three in number. Two of them ran nimbly across the lava bridge. The third staggered far behind. It was Ladd. He appeared hard hit. He dragged at the heavy rifle which he seemed unable to raise. The yells came from him. He was calling the Yaqui.

Gale's heart stood still momentarily. Here, then, was the catastrophe! He hardly dared sweep that fissure with his glass. The two fleeing figures halted—turned to fire at Ladd. Gale recognized the foremost one—small, compact, gaudy. Rojas! The bandit's arm was outstretched. Puffs of white smoke rose, and shots rapped out. When Ladd went down Rojas threw his gun aside and with a wild yell bounded over the lava. His companion followed.

A tide of passion, first hot as fire, then cold as ice, rushed over Gale when he saw Rojas take the trail toward Mercedes's hiding-place. The little bandit appeared to have the sure-footedness of a mountain sheep. The Mexican following was not so sure or fast. He turned back. Gale heard the trenchant bark of the .405. Ladd was kneeling. He shot again—again. The retreating bandit seemed to run full into an invisible obstacle, then fell lax, inert, lifeless. Rojas sped on unmindful of the spurts of dust about him. Yaqui, high above Ladd, was also firing at the bandit. Then both rifles were emptied. Rojas turned at a high break in the trail. He shook a defiant hand, and his exulting yell pealed faintly to Gale's ears. About him there was something desperate, magnificent. Then he clambered down the trail.

Ladd dropped the .405, and rising, gun in hand, he staggered toward the bridge of lava. Before he had crossed it Yaqui came bounding down the slope, and in one splendid leap he cleared the fissure. He ran beyond the trail and disappeared on the lava above. Rojas had not seen this sudden, darting move of the Indian.

Gale felt himself bitterly powerless to aid in that pursuit. He could only watch. He wondered, fearfully, what had become of Lash. Presently, when Rojas came out of the cracks and ruts of lava there might be a chance of disabling him by a long shot. His progress was now slow. But he was making straight for Mercedes's hiding-place. What was it leading him there—an eagle eye, or hate, or instinct? Why did he go on when there could be no turning back for him on that trail? Ladd was slow, heavy, staggering on the trail; but he was relentless. Only death could stop the ranger now. Surely Rojas must have known that when he chose the trail. From time to time Gale caught glimpses of Yaqui's dark figure stealing along the higher rim of the crater. He was making for a point above the bandit.

Moments—endless moments dragged by. The lowering sun colored only the upper half of the crater walls. Far down the depths were murky blue. Again Gale felt the insupportable silence. The red haze became a transparent veil before his eyes. Sinister, evil, brooding, waiting, seemed that yawning abyss. Ladd staggered along the trail, at times he crawled. The Yaqui gained; he might have had wings; he leaped from jagged crust to jagged crust; his sure-footedness was a wonderful thing.

But for Gale the marvel of that endless period of watching was the purpose of the bandit Rojas. He had now no weapon. Gale's glass made this fact plain. There was death behind him, death below him, death before him, and though he could not have known it, death above him. He never faltered—never made a misstep upon the narrow, flinty trail. When he reached the lower end of the level ledge Gale's poignant doubt became a certainty. Rojas had seen Mercedes. It was incredible, yet Gale believed it. Then, his heart clamped as in an icy vise, Gale threw forward the Remington, and sinking on one knee, began to shoot. He emptied the magazine. Puffs of dust near Rojas did not even make him turn.

As Gale began to reload he was horror-stricken by a low cry from Thorne. The cavalryman had recovered consciousness. He was half raised, pointing with shaking hand at the opposite ledge. His distended eyes were riveted upon Rojas. He was trying to utter speech that would not come.

Gale wheeled, rigid now, steeling himself to one last forlorn hope—that Mercedes could defend herself. She had a gun. He doubted not at all that she would use it. But, remembering her terror of this savage, he feared for her.

Rojas reached the level of the ledge. He halted. He crouched. It was the act of a panther. Manifestly he saw Mercedes within the cave. Then faint shots patted the air, broke in quick echo. Rojas went down as if struck a heavy blow. He was hit. But even as Gale yelled in sheer madness the bandit leaped erect. He seemed too quick, too supple to be badly wounded. A slight, dark figure flashed out of the cave. Mercedes! She backed against the wall. Gale saw a puff of white—heard a report. But the bandit lunged at her. Mercedes ran, not to try to pass him, but straight for the precipice. Her intention was plain. But Rojas outstripped her, even as she reached the verge. Then a piercing scream pealed across the crater—a scream of despair.

Gale closed his eyes. He could not bear to see more.

Thorne echoed Mercedes's scream. Gale looked round just in time to leap and catch the cavalryman as he staggered, apparently for the steep slope. And then, as Gale dragged him back, both fell. Gale saved his friend, but he plunged into a *choya*. He drew his hands away full of the great glistening cones of thorns.

"For God's sake, Gale, shoot! Shoot! Kill her! Kill her!... Can't—you—see—Rojas—"

Thorne fainted.

Gale, stunned for the instant, stood with uplifted hands, and gazed from Thorne across the crater. Rojas had not killed Mercedes. He was overpowering her. His actions seemed slow, wearing, purposeful. Hers were violent. Like a trapped she-wolf, Mercedes was fighting. She tore, struggled, flung herself.

Rojas's intention was terribly plain.

In agony now, both mental and physical, cold and sick and weak, Gale gripped his rifle and aimed at the struggling forms on the ledge. He pulled the trigger. The bullet struck up a cloud of red dust close to the struggling couple. Again Gale fired, hoping to hit Rojas, praying to kill Mercedes. The bullet struck high. A third—fourth—fifth time the Remington spoke—in vain! The rifle fell from Gale's racked hands.

How horribly plain that fiend's intention! Gale tried to close his eyes, but could not. He prayed wildly for a sudden blindness—to faint as Thorne had fainted. But he was transfixed to the spot with eyes that pierced the red light.

Mercedes was growing weaker, seemed about to collapse.

"Oh, Jim Lash, are you dead?" cried Gale. "Oh, Laddy!... Oh, Yaqui!"

Suddenly a dark form literally fell down the wall behind the ledge where Rojas fought the girl. It sank in a heap, then bounded erect.

"Yaqui!" screamed Gale, and he waved his bleeding hands till the blood bespattered his face. Then he choked. Utterance became impossible.

The Indian bent over Rojas and flung him against the wall. Mercedes, sinking back, lay still. When Rojas got up the Indian stood between him and escape from the ledge. Rojas backed the other way along the narrowing shelf of lava. His manner was abject, stupefied. Slowly he stepped backward.

It was then that Gale caught the white gleam of a knife in Yaqui's hand. Rojas turned and ran. He rounded a corner of wall where the footing was precarious. Yaqui followed slowly. His figure was dark and menacing. But he was not in a hurry. When he passed off the ledge Rojas was edging farther and farther along the wall. He was clinging now to the lava, creeping inch by inch. Perhaps he had thought to work around the buttress or climb over it. Evidently he went as far as possible, and there he clung, an unscalable wall above, the abyss beneath.

The approach of the Yaqui was like a slow dark shadow of gloom. If it seemed so to the stricken Gale what must it have been to Rojas? He appeared to sink against the wall. The Yaqui stole closer and closer. He was the savage now, and for him the moment must have been glorified. Gale saw him gaze up at the great circling walls of the crater, then down into the depths. Perhaps the red haze hanging above him, or the purple haze below, or the deep caverns in the lava, held for Yaqui spirits of the desert, his gods to whom he called. Perhaps he invoked shadows of his loved ones and his race, calling them in this moment of vengeance.

Gale heard—or imagined he heard—that wild, strange Yaqui cry.

Then the Indian stepped close to Rojas, and bent low, keeping out of reach. How slow were his motions! Would Yaqui never—never end it?... A wail drifted across the crater to Gale's ears.

Rojas fell backward and plunged sheer. The bank of white *choyas* caught him, held him upon their steel spikes. How long did the dazed Gale sit there watching Rojas wrestling and writhing in convulsive frenzy? The bandit now seemed mad to win the delayed death.

When he broke free he was a white patched object no longer human, a ball of *choya* burrs, and he slipped off the bank to shoot down and down into the purple depths of the crater.

XIII CHANGES AT FORLORN RIVER

THE first of March saw the federal occupation of the garrison at Casita. After a short, decisive engagement the rebels were dispersed into small bands and driven eastward along the boundary line toward Nogales.

It was the destiny of Forlorn River, however, never to return to the slow, sleepy tenor of its former existence. Belding's predictions came true. That straggling line of home-seekers was but a forerunner of the real invasion of Altar Valley. Refugees from Mexico and from Casita spread the word that water and wood and grass and land were to be had at Forlorn River; and as if by magic the white tents and red adobe houses sprang up to glisten in the sun.

Belding was happier than he had been for a long time. He believed that evil days for Forlorn River, along with the apathy and lack of enterprise, were in the past. He hired a couple of trustworthy Mexicans to ride the boundary line, and he settled down to think of ranching and irrigation and mining projects. Every morning he expected to receive some word form Sonoyta or Yuma, telling him that Yaqui had guided his party safely across the desert.

Belding was simple-minded, a man more inclined to action than reflection. When the complexities of life hemmed him in, he groped his way out, never quite understanding. His wife had always been a mystery to him. Nell was sunshine most of the time, but, like the sun-dominated desert, she was subject to strange changes, wilful, stormy, sudden. It was enough for Belding now to find his wife in a lighter, happier mood, and to see Nell dreamily turning a ring round and round the third finger of her left hand and watching the west. Every day both mother and daughter appeared farther removed from the past darkly threatening days. Belding was hearty in his affections, but undemonstrative. If there was any sentiment in his make-up it had an outlet in his memory of Blanco Diablo and a longing to see him. Often Belding stopped his work to gaze out over the desert toward the west. When he thought of his rangers and Thorne and Mercedes he certainly never forgot his horse. He wondered if Diablo was running, walking, resting; if Yaqui was finding water and grass.

In March, with the short desert winter over, the days began to grow warm. The noon hours were hot, and seemed to give promise of the white summer blaze and blasting furnace wind soon to come. No word was received from the rangers.

But this caused Belding no concern, and it seemed to him that his women folk considered no news good news.

Among the many changes coming to pass in Forlorn River were the installing of post-office service and the building of a mescal drinking-house. Belding had worked hard for the post office, but he did not like the idea of a saloon for Forlorn River. Still, that was an inevitable evil. The Mexicans would have mescal. Belding had kept the little border hamlet free of an establishment for distillation of the fiery cactus drink. A good many Americans drifted into Forlorn River—miners, cowboys, prospectors, outlaws, and others of nondescript character; and these men, of course, made the saloon, which was also an inn, their headquarters. Belding, with Carter and other old residents, saw the need of a sheriff for Forlorn River.

One morning early in this spring month, while Belding was on his way from the house to the corrals, he saw Nell running Blanco Jose down the road at a gait that amazed him. She did not take the turn of the road to come in by the gate. She put Jose at a four-foot wire fence, and came clattering into the yard.

"Nell must have another tantrum," said Belding. "She's long past due."

Blanco Jose, like the other white horses, was big of frame and heavy, and thunder rolled from under his great hoofs. Nell pulled him up, and as he pounded and slid to a halt in a cloud of dust she swung lightly down.

It did not take more than half an eye for Belding to see that she was furious.

"Nell, what's come off now?" asked Belding.

"I'm not going to tell you," she replied, and started away, leading Jose toward the corral.

Belding leisurely followed. She went into the corral, removed Jose's bridle, and led him to the watering-trough. Belding came up, and without saying anything began to unbuckle Jose's saddle girths. But he ventured a look at Nell. The red had gone from her face, and he was surprised to see her eyes brimming with tears. Most assuredly this was not one of Nell's tantrums. While taking off Jose's saddle and hanging it in the shed Belding pondered in his slow way. When he came back to the corral Nell had her face against the bars, and she was crying. He slipped a big arm around her and waited. Although it was not often expressed, there was a strong attachment between them.

"Dad, I don't want you to think me a—a baby any more," she said. "I've been insulted."

With a specific fact to make clear thought in Belding's mind he was never slow.

"I knew something unusual had come off. I guess you'd better tell me."

"Dad, I will, if you promise."

"What?"

"Not to mention it to mother, not to pack a gun down there, and never, never tell Dick."

Belding was silent. Seldom did he make promises readily.

"Nell, sure something must have come off, for you to ask all that."

"If you don't promise I'll never tell, that's all," she declared, firmly.

Belding deliberated a little longer. He knew the girl.

"Well, I promise not to tell mother," he said, presently; "and seeing you're here safe and well, I guess I won't go packing a gun down there, wherever that is. But I won't promise to keep anything from Dick that perhaps he ought to know."

"Dad, what would Dick do if—if he were here and I were to tell him I'd—I'd been horribly insulted?"

"I guess that 'd depend. Mostly, you know, Dick does what you want. But you couldn't stop him—nobody could—if there was reason, a man's reason, to get started. Remember what he did to Rojas!... Nell, tell me what's happened."

Nell, regaining her composure, wiped her eyes and smoothed back her hair.

"The other day, Wednesday," she began, "I was coming home, and in front of that mescal drinking-place there was a crowd. It was a noisy crowd. I didn't want to walk out into the street or seem afraid. But I had to do both. There were several young men, and if they weren't drunk they certainly were rude. I never saw them before, but I think they must belong to the mining company that was run out of Sonora by rebels. Mrs. Carter was telling me. Anyway, these young fellows were Americans. They stretched themselves across the walk and smiled at me. I had to go out in the road. One of them, the rudest, followed me. He was a big fellow, red-faced, with prominent eyes and a bold look. He came up beside me and spoke to me. I ran home. And as I ran I heard his companions jeering.

"Well, to-day, just now, when I was riding up the valley road I came upon the same fellows. They had instruments and were surveying. Remembering Dick, and how he always wished for an instrument to help work out his plan for irrigation, I was certainly surprised to see these strangers surveying—and surveying upon Laddy's plot of land. It was a sandy road there, and Jose happened to be walking. So I reined in and asked these engineers what they were doing. The leader, who was that same bold fellow who had followed me, seemed much pleased at being addressed. He was swaggering—too friendly; not my idea of a gentleman at all. He said he was glad to tell me he was going to run water all over Altar Valley. Dad, you can bet that made me wild. That was Dick's plan, his discovery, and here were surveyors on Laddy's claim.

"Then I told him that he was working on private land and he'd better get off. He seemed to forget his flirty proclivities in amazement. Then he looked cunning. I read his mind. It was news to him that all the land along the valley had been taken up.

"He said something about not seeing any squatters on the land, and then he shut up tight on that score. But he began to be flirty again. He got hold of Jose's bridle, and before I could catch my breath he said I was a peach, and that he wanted to make a date with me, that his name was Chase, that he owned a gold mine in Mexico. He said a lot more I didn't gather, but when he called me 'Dearie' I—well, I lost my temper.

"I jerked on the bridle and told him to let go. He held on and rolled his eyes at me. I dare say he imagined he was a gentlemen to be infatuated with. He seemed sure of conquest. One thing certain, he didn't know the least bit about horses. It scared me the way he got in front of Jose. I thanked my stars I wasn't up on Blanco Diablo. Well, Dad, I'm a little ashamed now, but I was mad. I slashed him across the face with my quirt. Jose jumped and knocked Mr. Chase into the sand. I didn't get the horse under control till I was out of sight of those surveyors, and then I let him run home."

"Nell, I guess you punished the fellow enough. Maybe he's only a conceited softy. But I don't like that sort of thing. It isn't Western. I guess he won't be so smart next time. Any fellow would remember being hit by Blanco Jose. If you'd been up on Diablo we'd have to bury Mr. Chase."

"Thank goodness I wasn't! I'm sorry now, Dad. Perhaps the fellow was hurt. But what could I do? Let's forget all about it, and I'll be careful where I ride in the future.... Dad, what does it mean, this surveying around Forlorn River?"

"I don't know, Nell," replied Belding, thoughtfully. "It worries me. It looks good for Forlorn River, but bad for Dick's plan to irrigate the valley. Lord, I'd hate to have some one forestall Dick on that!"

"No, no, we won't let anybody have Dick's rights," declared Nell.

"Where have I been keeping myself not to know about these surveyors?" muttered Belding. "They must have just come."

"Go see Mrs. Cater. She told me there were strangers in town, Americans, who had mining interests in Sonora, and were run out by Orozco. Find out what they're doing, Dad."

Belding discovered that he was, indeed, the last man of consequence in Forlorn River to learn of the arrival of Ben Chase and son, mineowners and operators in Sonora. They, with a force of miners, had been besieged by rebels and finally driven off their property. This property was not destroyed, but held for ransom. And the Chases, pending developments, had packed outfits and struck for the border. Casita had been their objective point, but, for some reason which Belding did not learn, they had arrived instead at Forlorn River. It had taken Ben Chase just one day to see the possibilities of Altar Valley, and in three days he had men at work.

Belding returned home without going to see the Chases and their operations. He wanted to think over the situation. Next morning he went out to the valley to see for himself. Mexicans were hastily erecting adobe houses upon Ladd's one hundred and sixty acres, upon Dick Gale's, upon Jim Lash's and Thorne's. There were men staking the valley floor and the river bed. That was sufficient for Belding. He turned back toward town and headed for the camp of these intruders.

In fact, the surroundings of Forlorn River, except on the river side, reminded Belding of the mushroom growth of a newly discovered mining camp. Tents were everywhere; adobe shacks were in all stages of construction; rough clapboard houses were going up. The latest of this work was new and surprising to Belding, all because he was a busy man, with no chance to hear village gossip. When he was directed to the headquarters of the Chase Mining Company he went thither in slow-growing wrath.

He came to a big tent with a huge canvas fly stretched in front, under which sat several men in their shirt sleeves. They were talking and smoking.

"My name's Belding. I want to see this Mr. Chase," said Belding, gruffly.

Slow-witted as Belding was, and absorbed in his own feelings, he yet saw plainly that his advent was disturbing to these men. They looked alarmed, exchanged glances, and then quickly turned to him. One of them, a tall, rugged man with sharp face and shrewd eyes and white hair, got up and offered his hand.

"I'm Chase, senior," he said. "My son Radford Chase is here somewhere. You're Belding, the line inspector, I take it? I meant to call on you."

He seemed a rough-and-ready, loud-spoken man, withal cordial enough.

"Yes, I'm the inspector," replied Belding, ignoring the proffered hand, "and I'd like to know what in the hell you mean by taking up land claims—staked ground that belongs to my rangers?"

"Land claims?" slowly echoed Chase, studying his man. "We're taking up only unclaimed land."

"That's a lie. You couldn't miss the stakes."

"Well, Mr. Belding, as to that, I think my men did run across some staked ground. But we recognize only squatters. If your rangers think they've got property just because they drove a few stakes in the ground they're much mistaken. A squatter has to build a house and live on his land so long, according to law, before he owns it."

This argument was unanswerable, and Belding knew it.

"According to law!" exclaimed Belding. "Then you own up; you've jumped our claims."

"Mr. Belding, I'm a plain business man. I come along. I see a good opening. Nobody seems to have tenable grants. I stake out claims, locate squatters, start to build. It seems to me your rangers have overlooked certain precautions. That's unfortunate for them. I'm prepared to hold my claim and to back all the squatters who work for me. If you don't like it you can carry the matter to Tucson. The law will uphold me."

"The law? Say, on this southwest border we haven't any law except a man's word and a gun."

"Then you'll find United States law has come along with Ben Chase," replied the other, snapping his fingers. He was still smooth, outspoken, but his mask had fallen.

"You're not a Westerner?" queried Belding.

"No, I'm from Illinois."

"I thought the West hadn't bred you. I know your kind. You'd last a long time on the Texas border; now, wouldn't you? You're one of the land and water hogs that has come to root in the West. You're like the timber sharks—take it all and leave none for those who follow. Mr. Chase, the West would fare better and last longer if men like you were driven out."

"You can't drive me out."

"I'm not so sure of that. Wait till my rangers come back. I wouldn't be in your boots. Don't mistake me. I don't suppose you could be accused of stealing another man's ideas or plan, but sure you've stolen these four claims. Maybe the law might uphold you. But the spirit, not the letter, counts with us bordermen."

"See here, Belding, I think you're taking the wrong view of the matter. I'm going to develop this valley. You'd do better to get in with me. I've a proposition to make you about that strip of land of yours facing the river."

"You can't make any deals with me. I won't have anything to do with you."

Belding abruptly left the camp and went home. Nell met him, probably intended to question him, but one look into his face confirmed her fears. She silently turned away. Belding realized he was powerless to stop Chase, and he was sick with disappointment for the ruin of Dick's hopes and his own.

XIV A LOST SON

TIME passed. The population of Forlorn River grew apace. Belding, who had once been the head of the community, found himself a person of little consequence. Even had he desired it he would not have had any voice in the selection of postmaster, sheriff, and a few other officials. The Chases divided their labors between Forlorn River and their Mexican gold mine, which had been restored to them. The desert trips between these two places were taken in automobiles. A month's time made the motor cars almost as familiar a sight in Forlorn River as they had been in Casita before the revolution.

Belding was not so busy as he had been formerly. As he lost ambition he began to find less work to do. His wrath at the usurping Chases increased as he slowly realized his powerlessness to cope with such men. They were promoters, men of big interests and wide influence in the Southwest. The more they did for Forlorn River the less reason there seemed to be for his own grievance. He had to admit that it was personal; that he and Gale and the rangers would never have been able to develop the resources of the valley as these men were doing it.

All day long he heard the heavy booming blasts and the rumble of avalanches up in the gorge. Chase's men were dynamiting the cliffs in the narrow box canyon. They were making the dam just as Gale had planned to make it. When this work of blasting was over Belding experienced a relief. He would not now be continually reminded of his and Gale's loss. Resignation finally came to him. But he could not reconcile himself to misfortune for Gale.

Moreover, Belding had other worry and strain. April arrived with no news of the rangers. From Casita came vague reports of raiders in the Sonoyta country—reports impossible to verify until his Mexican rangers returned. When these men rode in, one of them, Gonzales, an intelligent and reliable halfbreed, said he had met prospectors at the oasis. They had just come in on the Camino del Diablo, reported a terrible trip of heat and drought, and not a trace of the Yaqui's party.

"That settles it," declared Belding. "Yaqui never went to Sonoyta. He's circled round to the Devil's Road, and the rangers, Mercedes, Thorne, the horses—they—I'm afraid they have been lost in the desert. It's an old story on Camino del Diablo."

He had to tell Nell that, and it was an ordeal which left him weak.

XIV A LOST SON

Mrs. Belding listened to him, and was silent for a long time while she held the stricken Nell to her breast. Then she opposed his convictions with that quiet strength so characteristic of her arguments.

"Well, then," decided Belding, "Rojas headed the rangers at Papago Well or the Tanks."

"Tom, when you are down in the mouth you use poor judgment," she went on. "You know only by a miracle could Rojas or anybody have headed those white horses. Where's your old stubborn confidence? Yaqui was up on Diablo. Dick was up on Sol. And there were the other horses. They could not have been headed or caught. Miracles don't happen."

"All right, mother, it's sure good to hear you," said Belding. She always cheered him, and now he grasped at straws. "I'm not myself these days, don't mistake that. Tell us what you think. You always say you feel things when you really don't know them."

"I can say little more than what you said yourself the night Mercedes was taken away. You told Laddy to trust Yaqui, that he was a godsend. He might go south into some wild Sonora valley. He might lead Rojas into a trap. He would find water and grass where no Mexican or American could."

"But mother, they're gone seven weeks. Seven weeks! At the most I gave them six weeks. Seven weeks in the desert!"

"How do the Yaquis live?" she asked.

Belding could not reply to that, but hope revived in him. He had faith in his wife, though he could not in the least understand what he imagined was something mystic in her.

"Years ago when I was searching for my father I learned many things about this country," said Mrs. Belding. "You can never tell how long a man may live in the desert. The fiercest, most terrible and inaccessible places often have their hidden oasis. In his later years my father became a prospector. That was strange to me, for he never cared for gold or money. I learned that he was often gone in the desert for weeks, once for months. Then the time came when he never came back. That was years before I reached the southwest border and heard of him. Even then I did not for long give up hope of his coming back, I know now—something tells me—indeed, it seems his spirit tells me—he was lost. But I don't have that feeling for Yaqui and his party. Yaqui has given Rojas the slip or has ambushed him in some trap. Probably that took time and a long journey into Sonora. The Indian is too wise to start back now over dry trails. He'll curb the rangers; he'll wait. I seem to know this, dear Nell, so be brave, patient. Dick Gale will come back to you."

"Oh, mother!" cried Nell. "I can't give up hope while I have you."

That talk with the strong mother worked a change in Nell and Belding. Nell, who had done little but brood and watch the west and take violent rides, seemed to settle into a waiting patience that was sad, yet serene. She helped her mother more than ever; she was a comfort to Belding; she began to take active interest in the affairs of the growing village. Belding, who had been breaking under the strain of worry, recovered himself so that to outward appearance he was his old self. He alone knew, however, that his humor was forced, and that the slow burning wrath he felt for the Chases was flaming into hate.

Belding argued with himself that if Ben Chase and his son, Radford, had turned out to be big men in other ways than in the power to carry on great enterprises he might have become reconciled to them. But the father was greedy, grasping, hard, cold; the son added to those traits an overbearing disposition to rule, and he showed a fondness for drink and cards. These men were developing the valley, to be sure, and a horde of poor Mexicans and many Americans were benefiting from that development; nevertheless, these Chases were operating in a way which proved they cared only for themselves.

Belding shook off a lethargic spell and decided he had better set about several by no means small tasks, if he wanted to get them finished before the hot months. He made a trip to the Sonoyta Oasis. He satisfied himself that matters along the line were favorable, and that there was absolutely no trace of his rangers. Upon completing this trip he went to Casita with a number of his white thoroughbreds and shipped them to ranchers and horse-breeders in Texas. Then, being near the railroad, and having time, he went up to Tucson. There he learned some interesting particulars about the Chases. They had an office in the city; influential friends in the Capitol. They were powerful men in the rapidly growing finance of the West. They had interested the Southern Pacific Railroad, and in the near future a branch line was to be constructed from San Felipe to Forlorn River. These details of the Chase development were insignificant when compared to a matter striking close home to Belding. His responsibility had been subtly attacked. A doubt had been cast upon his capability of executing the duties of immigration inspector to the best advantage of the state. Belding divined that this was only an entering wedge. The Chases were bent upon driving him out of Forlorn River; but perhaps to serve better their own ends, they were proceeding at leisure. Belding returned home consumed by rage. But he controlled it. For the first time in his life he was afraid of himself. He had his wife and Nell to think of; and the old law of the West had gone forever.

"Dad, there's another Rojas round these diggings," was Nell's remark, after the greetings were over and the usual questions and answers passed.

Belding's exclamation was cut short by Nell's laugh. She was serious with a kind of amused contempt.

"Mr. Radford Chase!"

"Now Nell, what the—" roared Belding.

"Hush, Dad! Don't swear," interrupted Nell. "I only meant to tease you."

"Humph! Say, my girl, that name Chase makes me see red. If you must tease me hit on some other way. Sabe, senorita?"

"Si, si, Dad."

"Nell, you may as well tell him and have it over," said Mrs. Belding, quietly.

"You promised me once, Dad, that you'd not go packing a gun off down there, didn't you?"

"Yes, I remember," replied Belding; but he did not answer her smile.

"Will you promise again?" she asked, lightly. Here was Nell with arch eyes, yet not the old arch eyes, so full of fun and mischief. Her lips were tremulous; her cheeks seemed less round.

"Yes," rejoined Belding; and he knew why his voice was a little thick.

"Well, if you weren't such a good old blind Dad you'd have seen long ago the way Mr. Radford Chase ran round after me. At first it was only annoying, and I did not want to add to your worries. But these two weeks you've been gone I've been more than annoyed. After that time I struck Mr. Chase with my quirt he made all possible efforts to meet me. He did meet me wherever I went. He sent me letters till I got tired of sending them back.

"When you left home on your trips I don't know that he grew bolder, but he had more opportunity. I couldn't stay in the house all the time. There were mama's errands and sick people and my Sunday school, and what not. Mr. Chase waylaid me every time I went out. If he works any more I don't know when, unless it's when I'm asleep. He followed me until it was less embarassing for me to let him walk with me and talk his head off. He made love to me. He begged me to marry him. I told him I was already in love and engaged to be married. He said that didn't make any difference. Then I called him a fool.

"Next time he saw me he said he must explain. He meant I was being true to a man who, everybody on the border knew, had been lost in the desert. That—that hurt. Maybe—maybe it's true. Sometimes it seems terribly true. Since then, of course, I have stayed in the house to avoid being hurt again.

"But, Dad, a little thing like a girl sticking close to her mother and room doesn't stop Mr. Chase. I think he's crazy. Anyway, he's a most persistent fool. I want to be charitable, because the man swears he loves me, and maybe he does, but he is making me nervous. I don't sleep. I'm afraid to be in my room at night. I've gone to mother's room. He's always hanging round. Bold! Why, that isn't the thing to call Mr. Chase. He's absolutely without a sense of decency. He bribes our servants. He comes into our patio. Think of that! He makes the most ridiculous excuses. He bothers mother to death. I feel like a poor little rabbit holed by a hound. And I daren't peep out."

Somehow the thing struck Belding as funny, and he laughed. He had not had a laugh for so long that it made him feel good. He stopped only at sight of Nell's surprise and pain. Then he put his arms round her.

"Never mind, dear. I'm an old bear. But it tickled me, I guess. I sure hope Mr. Radford Chase has got it bad... Nell, it's only the old story. The fellows fall in love with you. It's your good looks, Nell. What a price women like you and Mercedes have to pay for beauty! I'd a d—— a good deal rather be ugly as a mud fence."

"So would I, Dad, if—if Dick would still love me."

"He wouldn't, you can gamble on that, as Laddy says. ... Well, the first time I catch this locoed Romeo sneaking round here I'll—I'll—"

"Dad, you promised."

"Confound it, Nell, I promised not to pack a gun. That's all. I'll only shoo this fellow off the place, gently, mind you, gently. I'll leave the rest for Dick Gale!"

"Oh, Dad!" cried Nell; and she clung to him wistful, frightened, yet something more.

"Don't mistake me, Nell. You have your own way, generally. You pull the wool over mother's eyes, and you wind me round your little finger. But you can't do either with Dick Gale. You're tender-hearted; you overlook the doings of this hound, Chase. But when Dick comes back, you just make up your mind to a little hell in the Chase camp. Oh, he'll find it out. And I sure want to be round when Dick hands Mr. Radford the same as he handed Rojas!"

Belding kept a sharp lookout for young Chase, and then, a few days later, learned that both son and father had gone off upon one of their frequent trips to Casa Grandes, near where their mines were situated.

April grew apace, and soon gave way to May. One morning Belding was called from some garden work by the whirring of an automobile and a "Holloa!" He went forward to the front yard and there saw a car he thought resembled one he had seen in Casita. It contained a familiar-looking driver, but the three figures in gray coats and veils were strange to him. By the time he had gotten to the road he decided two were women and the other a man. At the moment their faces were emerging from dusty veils. Belding saw an elderly, sallow-faced, rather frail-appearing man who was an entire stranger to him; a handsome dark-eyed woman whose hair showed white through her veil; and a superbly built girl, whose face made Belding at once think of Dick Gale.

"Is this Mr. Tom Belding, inspector of immigration?" inquired the gentleman, courteously.

"I'm Belding, and I know who you are," replied Belding in hearty amaze, as he stretched forth his big hand. "You're Dick Gale's Dad—the Governor, Dick used to say. I'm sure glad to meet you."

"Thank you. Yes, I'm Dick's governor, and here, Mr. Belding—Dick's mother and his sister Elsie."

Beaming his pleasure, Belding shook hands with the ladies, who showed their agitation clearly.

"Mr. Belding, I've come west to look up my lost son," said Mr. Gale. "His sister's letters were unanswered. We haven't heard from him in months. Is he still here with you?"

"Well, now, sure I'm awful sorry," began Belding, his slow mind at work. "Dick's away just now—been away for a considerable spell. I'm expecting him back any day.... Won't you come in? You're all dusty and hot and tired. Come in, and let mother and Nell make you comfortable. Of course you'll stay. We've a big house. You must stay till Dick comes back. Maybe that 'll be— Aw, I guess it won't be long.... Let me handle the baggage, Mr. Gale.... Come in. I sure am glad to meet you all."

Eager, excited, delighted, Belding went on talking as he ushered the Gales into the sitting-room, presenting them in his hearty way to the astounded Mrs. Belding and Nell. For the space of a few moments his wife and daughter were bewildered. Belding did not recollect any other occasion when a few callers had thrown them off their balance. But of course this was different. He was a little flustered himself—a circumstance that dawned upon him with surprise. When the Gales had been shown to rooms, Mrs. Belding gained the poise momentarily lost; but Nell came rushing back, wilder than a deer, in a state of excitement strange even for her.

"Oh! Dick's mother, his sister!" whispered Nell.

Belding observed the omission of the father in Nell's exclamation of mingled delight and alarm.

"His mother!" went on Nell. "Oh, I knew it! I always guessed it! Dick's people are proud, rich; they're somebody. I thought I'd faint when she looked at me. She was just curious—curious, but so cold and proud. She was wondering about me. I'm wearing his ring. It was his mother's, he said. I won't—I can't take it off. And I'm scared.... But the sister—oh, she's lovely and sweet—proud, too. I felt warm all over when she looked at me. I—I wanted to kiss her. She looks like Dick when he first came to us. But he's changed. They'll hardly recognize him.... To think they've come! And I had to be looking a fright, when of all times on earth I'd want to look my best."

Nell, out of breath, ran away evidently to make herself presentable, according to her idea of the exigency of the case. Belding caught a glimpse of his wife's face as she went out, and it wore a sad, strange, anxious expression. Then Belding sat alone, pondering the contracting emotions of his wife and daughter. It was beyond his understanding. Women were creatures of feeling. Belding saw reason to be delighted to entertain Dick's family; and for the time being no disturbing thought entered his mind.

Presently the Gales came back into the sitting-room, looking very different without the long gray cloaks and veils. Belding saw distinction and elegance. Mr. Gale seemed a grave, troubled, kindly person, ill in body and mind. Belding received the same impression of power that Ben Chase had given him, only here it was minus any harshness or hard quality. He gathered that Mr. Gale was a man of authority. Mrs. Gale rather frightened Belding, but he could not have told why. The girl was just like Dick as he used to be.

Their manner of speaking also reminded Belding of Dick. They talked of the ride from Ash Fork down to the border, of the ugly and torn-up Casita, of the heat and dust and cactus along the trail. Presently Nell came in, now cool and sweet in white, with a red rose at her breast. Belding had never been so proud of her. He saw that she meant to appear well in the eyes of Dick's people, and began to have a faint perception of what the ordeal was for her. Belding imagined the sooner the Gales were told that Dick was to marry Nell the better for all concerned, and especially for Nell. In the general conversation that ensued he sought for an opening in which to tell this important news, but he was kept so busy answering questions about his position on the border, the kind of place Forlorn River was, the reason for so many tents, etc., that he was unable to find opportunity.

"It's very interesting, very interesting," said Mr. Gale. "At another time I want to learn all you'll tell me about the West. It's new to me. I'm surprised, amazed, sir, I may say.... But, Mr. Belding, what I want to know most is about my son. I'm broken in health. I've worried myself ill over him. I don't mind telling you, sir, that we quarreled. I laughed at his threats. He went away. And I've come to see that I didn't know Richard. I was wrong to upbraid him. For a year we've known nothing of his doings, and now for almost six months we've not heard from him at all. Frankly, Mr. Belding, I weakened first, and I've come to hunt him up. My fear is that I didn't start soon enough. The boy will have a great position some day—God knows, perhaps soon! I should not have allowed him to run over this wild country for so long. But I hoped, though I hardly believed, that he might find himself. Now I'm afraid he's—"

Mr. Gale paused and the white hand he raised expressively shook a little.

Belding was not so thick-witted where men were concerned. He saw how the matter lay between Dick Gale and his father.

"Well, Mr. Gale, sure most young bucks from the East go to the bad out here," he said, bluntly.

"I've been told that," replied Mr. Gale; and a shade overspread his worn face.

"They blow their money, then go punching cows, take to whiskey."

"Yes," rejoined Mr. Gale, feebly nodding.

"Then they get to gambling, lose their jobs," went on Belding.

Mr. Gale lifted haggard eyes.

"Then it's bumming around, regular tramps, and to the bad generally." Belding spread wide his big arms, and when one of them dropped round Nell, who sat beside him, she squeezed his hand tight. "Sure, it's the regular thing," he concluded, cheerfully.

He rather felt a little glee at Mr. Gale's distress, and Mrs. Gale's crushed I-told-you-so woe in no wise bothered him; but the look in the big, dark eyes of Dick's sister was too much for Belding.

He choked off his characteristic oath when excited and blurted out, "Say, but Dick Gale never went to the bad!... Listen!"

Belding had scarcely started Dick Gale's story when he perceived that never in his life had he such an absorbed and breathless audience. Presently they were awed, and at the conclusion of that story they sat white-faced, still, amazed beyond speech. Dick Gale's advent in Casita, his rescue of Mercedes, his life as a border ranger certainly lost no picturesque or daring or even noble detail in Belding's telling. He kept back nothing but the present doubt of Dick's safety.

Dick's sister was the first of the three to recover herself.

"Oh, father!" she cried; and there was a glorious light in her eyes. "Deep down in my heart I knew Dick was a man!"

Mr. Gale rose unsteadily from his chair. His frailty was now painfully manifest.

"Mr. Belding, do you mean my son—Richard Gale—has done all that you told us?" he asked, incredulously.

"I sure do," replied Belding, with hearty good will.

"Martha, do you hear?" Mr. Gale turned to question his wife. She could not answer. Her face had not yet regained its natural color.

"He faced that bandit and his gang alone—he fought them?" demanded Mr. Gale, his voice stronger.

"Dick mopped up the floor with the whole outfit!"

"He rescued a Spanish girl, went into the desert without food, weapons, anything but his hands? Richard Gale, whose hands were always useless?"

Belding nodded with a grin.

"He's a ranger now—riding, fighting, sleeping on the sand, preparing his own food?"

"Well, I should smile," rejoined Belding.

"He cares for his horse, with his own hands?" This query seemed to be the climax of Mr. Gale's strange hunger for truth. He had raised his head a little higher, and his eye was brighter.

Mention of a horse fired Belding's blood.

"Does Dick Gale care for his horse? Say, there are not many men as well loved as that white horse of Dick's. Blanco Sol he is, Mr. Gale. That's Mex for White Sun. Wait till you see Blanco Sol! Bar one, the whitest, biggest, strongest, fastest, grandest horse in the Southwest!"

"So he loves a horse! I shall not know my own son.... Mr. Belding, you say Richard works for you. May I ask, at what salary?"

"He gets forty dollars, board and outfit," replied Belding, proudly.

"Forty dollars?" echoed the father. "By the day or week?"

"The month, of course," said Belding, somewhat taken aback.

"Forty dollars a month for a young man who spent five hundred in the same time when he was at college, and who ran it into thousands when he got out!"

Mr. Gale laughed for the first time, and it was the laugh of a man who wanted to believe what he heard yet scarcely dared to do it.

"What does he do with so much money—money earned by peril, toil, sweat, and blood? Forty dollars a month!"

"He saves it," replied Belding.

Evidently this was too much for Dick Gale's father, and he gazed at his wife in sheer speechless astonishment. Dick's sister clapped her hands like a little child.

Belding saw that the moment was propitious.

"Sure he saves it. Dick's engaged to marry Nell here. My stepdaughter, Nell Burton."

"Oh-h, Dad!" faltered Nell; and she rose, white as her dress.

How strange it was to see Dick's mother and sister rise, also, and turn to Nell with dark, proud, searching eyes. Belding vaguely realized some blunder he had made. Nell's white, appealing face gave him a pang. What had he done? Surely this family of Dick's ought to know his relation to Nell. There was a silence that positively made Belding nervous.

Then Elsie Gale stepped close to Nell.

"Miss Burton, are you really Richard's betrothed?"

Nell's tremulous lips framed an affirmative, but never uttered it. She held out her hand, showing the ring Dick had given her. Miss Gale's recognition was instant, and her response was warm, sweet, gracious.

"I think I am going to be very, very glad," she said, and kissed Nell.

"Miss Burton, we are learning wonderful things about Richard," added Mr. Gale, in an earnest though shaken voice. "If you have had to do with making a man of him—and now I begin to see, to believe so—may God bless you!... My dear girl, I have not really looked at you. Richard's fiancee!... Mother, we have not found him yet, but I think we've found his secret. We believed him a lost son. But here is his sweetheart!"

It was only then that the pride and hauteur of Mrs. Gale's face broke into an expression of mingled pain and joy. She opened her arms. Nell, uttering a strange little stifled cry, flew into them.

Belding suddenly discovered an unaccountable blur in his sight. He could not see perfectly, and that was why, when Mrs. Belding entered the sitting-room, he was not certain that her face was as sad and white as it seemed.

XV BOUND IN THE DESERT

FAR away from Forlorn River Dick Gale sat stunned, gazing down into the purple depths where Rojas had plunged to his death. The Yaqui stood motionless upon the steep red wall of lava from which he had cut the bandit's hold. Mercedes lay quietly where she had fallen. From across the depths there came to Gale's ear the Indian's strange, wild cry.

Then silence, hollow, breathless, stony silence enveloped the great abyss and its upheaved lava walls. The sun was setting. Every instant the haze reddened and thickened.

Action on the part of the Yaqui loosened the spell which held Gale as motionless as his surroundings. The Indian was edging back toward the ledge. He did not move with his former lithe and sure freedom. He crawled, slipped, dragged himself, rested often, and went on again. He had been wounded. When at last he reached the ledge where Mercedes lay Gale jumped to his feet, strong and thrilling, spurred to meet the responsibility that now rested upon him.

Swiftly he turned to where Thorne lay. The cavalryman was just returning to consciousness. Gale ran for a canteen, bathed his face, made him drink. The look in Thorne's eyes was hard to bear.

"Thorne! Thorne! it's all right, it's all right!" cried Gale, in piercing tones. "Mercedes is safe! Yaqui saved her! Rojas is done for! Yaqui jumped down the wall and drove the bandit off the ledge. Cut him loose from the wall, foot by foot, hand by hand! We've won the fight, Thorne."

For Thorne these were marvelous strength-giving words. The dark horror left his eyes, and they began to dilate, to shine. He stood up, dizzily but unaided, and he gazed across the crater. Yaqui had reached the side of Mercedes, was bending over her. She stirred. Yaqui lifted her to her feet. She appeared weak, unable to stand alone. But she faced across the crater and waved her hand. She was unharmed. Thorne lifted both arms above head, and from his lips issued a cry. It was neither call nor holloa nor welcome nor answer. Like the Yaqui's, it could scarcely be named. But it was deep, husky, prolonged, terribly human in its intensity. It made Gale shudder and made his heart beat like a trip hammer. Mercedes again waved a white hand. The Yaqui waved, too, and Gale saw in the action an urgent signal.

Hastily taking up canteen and rifles, Gale put a supporting arm around Thorne.

"Come, old man. Can you walk? Sure you can walk! Lean on me, and we'll soon get out of this. Don't look across. Look where you step. We've not much time before dark. Oh, Thorne, I'm afraid Jim has cashed in! And the last I saw of Laddy he was badly hurt."

Gale was keyed up to a high pitch of excitement and alertness. He seemed to be able to do many things. But once off the ragged notched lava into the trail he had not such difficulty with Thorne, and could keep his keen gaze shifting everywhere for sight of enemies.

"Listen, Thorne! What's that?" asked Gale, halting as they came to a place where the trail led down through rough breaks in the lava. The silence was broken by a strange sound, almost unbelieveable considering the time and place. A voice was droning: "Turn the lady, turn! Turn the lady, turn! Alamon left. All swing; turn the lady, turn!"

"Hello, Jim," called Gale, dragging Thorne round the corner of lava. "Where are you? Oh, you son of a gun! I thought you were dead. Oh, I'm glad to see you! Jim, are you hurt?"

Jim Lash stood in the trail leaning over the butt of his rifle, which evidently he was utilizing as a crutch. He was pale but smiling. His hands were bloody. A scarf had been bound tightly round his left leg just above the knee. The leg hung limp, and the foot dragged.

"I reckon I ain't injured much," replied Him. "But my leg hurts like hell, if you want to know."

"Laddy! Oh, where's Laddy?"

"He's just across the crack there. I was trying to get to him. We had it hot an' heavy down here. Laddy was pretty bad shot up before he tried to head Rojas off the trail.... Dick, did you see the Yaqui go after Rojas?"

"Did I!" exclaimed Gale, grimly.

"The finish was all that saved me from runnin' loco plumb over the rim. You see I was closer'n you to where Mercedes was hid. When Rojas an' his last Greaser started across, Laddy went after them, but I couldn't. Laddy did for Rojas's man, then went down himself. But he got up an' fell, got up, went on, an' fell again. Laddy kept doin' that till he dropped for good. I reckon our chances are against findin' him alive.... I tell you, boys, Rojas was hell-bent. An' Mercedes was game. I saw her shoot him. But mebbe bullets couldn't stop him then. If I didn't sweat blood when Mercedes was fightin' him on the cliff! Then the finish! Only a Yaqui could have done that.... Thorne, you didn't miss it?"

"Yes, I was down and out," replied the cavalryman.

"It's a shame. Greatest stunt I ever seen! Thorne, you're standin' up pretty fair. How about you? Dick, is he bad hurt?"

"No, he's not. A hard knock on the skull and a scalp wound," replied Dick. "Here, Jim, let me help you over this place."

Step by step Gale got the two injured men down the uneven declivity and then across the narrow lava bridge over the fissure. Here he bade them rest while he went along the trail on that side to search for Laddy. Gale found the ranger stretched out, face downward, a reddened hand clutching a gun. Gale thought he was dead. Upon examination, however, it was found that Ladd still lived, though he had many wounds. Gale lifted him and carried him back to the others.

"He's alive, but that's all," said Dick, as he laid the ranger down. "Do what you can. Stop the blood. Laddy's tough as cactus, you know. I'll hurry back for Mercedes and Yaqui."

Gale, like a fleet, sure-footed mountain sheep, ran along the trail. When he came across the Mexican, Rojas's last ally, Gale had evidence of the terrible execution of the .405. He did not pause. On the first part of that descent he made faster time than had Rojas. But he exercised care along the hard, slippery, ragged slope leading to the ledge. Presently he came upon Mercedes and the Yaqui. She ran right into Dick's arms, and there her strength, if not her courage, broke, and she grew lax.

"Mercedes, you're safe! Thorne's safe. It's all right now."

"Rojas!" she whispered.

"Gone! To the bottom of the crater! A Yaqui's vengeance, Mercedes."

He heard the girl whisper the name of the Virgin. Then he gathered her up in his arms.

"Come, Yaqui."

The Indian grunted. He had one hand pressed close over a bloody place in his shoulder. Gale looked keenly at him. Yaqui was inscrutable, as of old, yet Gale somehow knew that wound meant little to him. The Indian followed him.

Without pausing, moving slowly in some places, very carefully in others, and swiftly on the smooth part of the trail, Gale carried Mercedes up to the rim and along to the the others. Jim Lash worked awkwardly over Ladd. Thorne was trying to assist. Ladd, himself, was conscious, but he was a pallid, apparently a death-stricken man. The greeting between Mercedes and Thorne was calm—strangely so, it seemed to Gale. But he was calm himself. Ladd smiled at him, and evidently would have spoken had he the power. Yaqui then joined the group, and his piercing eyes roved from one to the other, lingering longest over Ladd.

"Dick, I'm figger'n hard," said Jim, faintly. "In a minute it 'll be up to you an' Mercedes. I've about shot my bolt.... Reckon you'll do— best by bringin' up blankets—water—salt—firewood. Laddy's got—one chance—in a hundred. Fix him up—first. Use hot salt water. If my leg's broke—set it best you can. That hole in Yaqui—only 'll bother him a day. Thorne's bad hurt... Now rustle—Dick, old—boy."

Lash's voice died away in a husky whisper, and he quietly lay back, stretching out all but the crippled leg. Gale examined it, assured himself the bones had not been broken, and then rose ready to go down the trail.

"Mercedes, hold Thorne's head up, in your lap—so. Now I'll go."

On the moment Yaqui appeared to have completed the binding of his wounded shoulder, and he started to follow Gale. He paid no attention to Gale's order for him to stay back. But he was slow, and gradually Gale forged ahead. The lingering brightness of the sunset lightened the trail, and the descent to the arroyo was swift and easy. Some of the white horses had come in for water. Blanco Sol spied Gale and whistled and came pounding toward him. It was twilight down in the arroyo. Yaqui appeared and began collecting a bundle of mesquite sticks. Gale hastily put together the things he needed; and, packing them all in a tarpaulin, he turned to retrace his steps up the trail.

Darkness was setting in. The trail was narrow, exceedingly steep, and in some places fronted on precipices. Gale's burden was not very heavy, but its bulk made it unwieldy, and it was always overbalancing him or knocking against the wall side of the trail. Gale found it necessary to wait for Yaqui to take the lead. The Indian's eyes must have seen as well at night as by day. Gale toiled upward, shouldering, swinging, dragging the big pack; and, though the ascent of the slope was not really long, it seemed endless. At last they reached a level, and were soon on the spot with Mercedes and the injured men.

Gale then set to work. Yaqui's part was to keep the fire blazing and the water hot, Mercedes's to help Gale in what way she could. Gale found Ladd had many wounds, yet not one of them was directly in a vital place. Evidently, the ranger had almost bled to death. He remained unconscious through Gale's operations. According to Jim Lash, Ladd had one chance in a hundred, but Gale considered it one in a thousand. Having done all that was possible for the ranger, Gale slipped blankets under and around him, and then turned his attention to Lash.

Jim came out of his stupor. A mushrooming bullet had torn a great hole in his leg. Gale, upon examination, could not be sure the bones had been missed, but there was no bad break. The application of hot salt water made Jim groan. When he had been bandaged and laid beside Ladd, Gale went on to the cavalryman. Thorne was very weak and scarcely conscious. A furrow had been plowed through his scalp down to the bone. When it had been dressed, Mercedes collapsed. Gale laid her with the three in a row and covered them with blankets and the tarpaulin.

Then Yaqui submitted to examination. A bullet had gone through the Indian's shoulder. To Gale it appeared serious. Yaqui said it was a flea bite. But he allowed Gale to bandage it, and obeyed when he was told to lie quiet in his blanket beside the fire.

Gale stood guard. He seemed still calm, and wondered at what he considered a strange absence of poignant feeling. If he had felt weariness it was now gone. He coaxed the fire with as little wood as would keep it burning; he sat beside it; he walked to and fro close by; sometimes he stood over the five sleepers, wondering if two of them, at least, would ever awaken.

Time had passed swiftly, but as the necessity for immediate action had gone by, the hours gradually assumed something of their normal length. The night wore on. The air grew colder, the stars brighter, the sky bluer, and, if such could be possible, the silence more intense. The fire burned out, and for lack of wood could not be rekindled. Gale patrolled his short beat, becoming colder and damper as dawn approached. The darkness grew so dense that he could not see the pale faces of the sleepers. He dreaded the gray dawn and the light. Slowly the heavy black belt close to the lava changed to a pale gloom, then to gray, and after that morning came quickly.

The hour had come for Dick Gale to face his great problem. It was natural that he hung back a little at first; natural that when he went forward to look at the quiet sleepers he did so with a grim and stern force urging him. Yaqui stirred, roused, yawned, got up; and, though he did not smile at Gale, a light shone swiftly across his dark face. His shoulder drooped and appeared stiff, otherwise he was himself. Mercedes lay in deep slumber. Thorne had a high fever, and was beginning to show signs of restlessness. Ladd seemed just barely alive. Jim Lash slept as if he was not much the worse for his wound.

Gale rose from his examination with a sharp breaking of his cold mood. While there was life in Thorne and Ladd there was hope for them. Then he faced his problem, and his decision was instant.

He awoke Mercedes. How wondering, wistful, beautiful was that first opening flash of her eyes! Then the dark, troubled thought came. Swiftly she sat up.

"Mercedes—come. Are you all right? Laddy is alive Thorne's not—not so bad. But we've got a job on our hands! You must help me."

She bent over Thorne and laid her hands on his hot face. Then she rose—a woman such as he had imagined she might be in an hour of trial.

Gale took up Ladd as carefully and gently as possible.

"Mercedes, bring what you can carry and follow me," he said. Then, motioning for Yaqui to remain there, he turned down the slope with Ladd in his arms.

Neither pausing nor making a misstep nor conscious of great effort, Gale carried the wounded man down into the arroyo. Mercedes kept at his heels, light, supple, lithe as a panther. He left her with Ladd and went back. When he had started off with Thorne in his arms he felt the tax on his strength. Surely and swiftly, however, he bore the cavalryman down the trail to lay him beside Ladd. Again he started back, and when he began to mount the steep lava steps he was hot, wet, breathing hard. As he reached the scene of that night's camp a voice greeted him. Jim Lash was sitting up.

"Hello, Dick. I woke some late this mornin'. Where's Laddy? Dick, you ain't a-goin' to say—"

"Laddy's alive—that's about all," replied Dick.

"Where's Thorne an' Mercedes? Look here, man. I reckon you ain't packin' this crippled outfit down that awful trail?"

"Had to, Jim. An hour's sun—would kill—both Laddy and Thorne. Come on now."

For once Jim Lash's cool good nature and careless indifference gave precedence to amaze and concern.

"Always knew you was a husky chap. But, Dick, you're no hoss! Get me a crutch an' give me a lift on one side."

"Come on," replied Gale. "I've no time to monkey."

He lifted the ranger, called to Yaqui to follow with some of the camp outfit, and once more essayed the steep descent. Jim Lash was the heaviest man of the three, and Gale's strength was put to enormous strain to carry him on that broken trail. Nevertheless, Gale went down, down, walking swiftly and surely over the bad places; and at last he staggered into the arroyo with bursting heart and red-blinded eyes. When he had recovered he made a final trip up the slope for the camp effects which Yaqui had been unable to carry.

Then he drew Jim and Mercedes and Yaqui, also, into an earnest discussion of ways and means whereby to fight for the life of Thorne. Ladd's case Gale now considered hopeless, though he meant to fight for him, too, as long as he breathed.

In the labor of watching and nursing it seemed to Gale that two days and two nights slipped by like a few hours. During that time the Indian recovered from his injury, and became capable of performing all except heavy tasks. Then Gale succumbed to weariness. After his much-needed rest he relieved Mercedes of the care and watch over Thorne which, up to that time, she had absolutely refused to relinquish. The cavalryman had high fever, and Gale feared he had developed blood poisoning. He required constant attention. His condition slowly grew worse, and there came a day which Gale thought surely was the end. But that day passed, and the night, and the next day, and Thorne lived on, ghastly, stricken, raving. Mercedes hung over him with jealous, passionate care and did all that could have been humanly done for a man. She grew wan, absorbed, silent. But suddenly, and to Gale's amaze and thanksgiving, there came an abatement of Thorne's fever. With it some of the heat and redness of the inflamed wound disappeared. Next morning he was conscious, and Gale grasped some of the hope that Mercedes had never abandoned. He forced her to rest while he attended to Thorne. That day he saw that the crisis was past. Recovery for Thorne was now possible, and would perhaps depend entirely upon the care he received.

Jim Lash's wound healed without any aggravating symptoms. It would be only a matter of time until he had the use of his leg again. All these days, however, there was little apparent change in Ladd's condition unless it was that he seemed to fade away as he lingered. At first his wounds remained open; they bled a little all the time outwardly, perhaps internally also; the blood did not seem to clot, and so the bullet holes did not close. Then Yaqui asked for the care of Ladd. Gale yielded it with opposing thoughts—that Ladd would waste slowly away till life ceased, and that there never was any telling what might lie in the power of this strange Indian. Yaqui absented himself from camp for a while, and when he returned he carried the roots and leaves of desert plants unknown to Gale. From these the Indian brewed an ointment. Then he stripped the bandages from Ladd and applied the mixture to his wounds. That done, he let him lie with the wounds exposed to the air, at night covering him. Next day he again exposed the wounds to the warm, dry air. Slowly they closed, and Ladd ceased to bleed externally.

Days passed and grew into what Gale imagined must have been weeks. Yaqui recovered fully. Jim Lash began to move about on a crutch; he shared the Indian's watch over Ladd. Thorne lay haggard, emaciated ghost of his rugged self, but with life in the eyes that turned always toward Mercedes. Ladd lingered and lingered. The life seemingly would not leave his bullet-pierced body. He faded, withered, shrunk till he was almost a skeleton. He knew those who worked and watched over him, but he had no power of speech. His eyes and eyelids moved; the rest of him seemed stone. All those days nothing except water was given him. It was marvelous how tenaciously, however feebly, he clung to life. Gale imagined it was the Yaqui's spirit that held back death. That tireless, implacable, inscrutable savage was ever at the ranger's side. His great somber eyes burned. At length he went to Gale, and, with that strange light flitting across the hard bronzed face, he said Ladd would live.

The second day after Ladd had been given such thin nourishment as he could swallow he recovered the use of his tongue.

"Shore—this's—hell," he whispered.

That was a characteristic speech for the ranger, Gale thought; and indeed it made all who heard it smile while their eyes were wet.

From that time forward Ladd gained, but he gained so immeasurably slowly that only the eyes of hope could have seen any improvement. Jim Lash threw away his crutch, and Thorne was well, if still somewhat weak, before Ladd could lift his arm or turn his head. A kind of long, immovable gloom passed, like a shadow, from his face. His whispers grew stronger. And the day arrived when Gale, who was perhaps the least optimistic, threw doubt to the winds and knew the ranger would get well. For Gale that joyous moment of realization was one in which he seemed to return to a former self long absent. He experienced an elevation of soul. He was suddenly overwhelmed with gratefulness, humility, awe. A gloomy black terror had passed by. He wanted to thank the faithful Mercedes, and Thorne for getting well, and the cheerful Lash, and Ladd himself, and that strange and wonderful Yaqui, now such a splendid figure. He thought of home and Nell. The terrible encompassing red slopes lost something of their fearsomeness, and there was a good spirit hovering near.

"Boys, come round," called Ladd, in his low voice. "An' you, Mercedes. An' call the Yaqui."

Ladd lay in the shade of the brush shelter that had been erected. His head was raised slightly on a pillow. There seemed little of him but long lean lines, and if it had not been for his keen, thoughtful, kindly eyes, his face would have resembled a death mask of a man starved.

"Shore I want to know what day is it an' what month?" asked Ladd.

Nobody could answer him. The question seemed a surprise to Gale, and evidently was so to the others.

"Look at that cactus," went on Ladd.

Near the wall of lava a stunted saguaro lifted its head. A few shriveled blossoms that had once been white hung along the fluted column.

"I reckon according to that giant cactus it's somewheres along the end of March," said Jim Lash, soberly.

"Shore it's April. Look where the sun is. An' can't you feel it's gettin' hot?"

"Supposin' it is April?" queried Lash slowly.

"Well, what I'm drivin' at is it's about time you all was hittin' the trail back to Forlorn River, before the waterholes dry out."

"Laddy, I reckon we'll start soon as you're able to be put on a hoss."

"Shore that 'll be too late."

A silence ensued, in which those who heard Ladd gazed fixedly at him and then at one another. Lash uneasily shifted the position of his lame leg, and Gale saw him moisten his lips with his tongue.

"Charlie Ladd, I ain't reckonin' you mean we're to ride off an' leave you here?"

"What else is there to do? The hot weather's close. Pretty soon most of the waterholes will be dry. You can't travel then.... I'm on my back here, an' God only knows when I could be packed out. Not for weeks, mebbe. I'll never be any good again, even if I was to get out alive.... You see, shore this sort of case comes round sometimes in the desert. It's common enough. I've heard of several cases where men had to go an' leave a feller behind. It's reasonable. If you're fightin' the desert you can't afford to be sentimental... Now, as I said, I'm all in. So what's the sense of you waitin' here, when it means the old desert story? By goin' now mebbe you'll get home. If you wait on a chance of takin' me, you'll be too late. Pretty soon this lava 'll be one roastin' hell. Shore now, boys, you'll see this the right way? Jim, old pard?"

"No, Laddy, an' I can't figger how you could ever ask me."

"Shore then leave me here with Yaqui an' a couple of the hosses. We can eat sheep meat. An' if the water holds out—"

"No!" interrupted Lash, violently.

Ladd's eyes sought Gale's face.

"Son, you ain't bull-headed like Jim. You'll see the sense of it. There's Nell a-waitin' back at Forlorn River. Think what it means to her! She's a damn fine girl, Dick, an' what right have you to break her heart for an old worn-out cowpuncher? Think how she's watchin' for you with that sweet face all sad an' troubled, an' her eyes turnin' black. You'll go, son, won't you?"

Dick shook his head.

The ranger turned his gaze upon Thorne, and now the keen, glistening light in his gray eyes had blurred.

"Thorne, it's different with you. Jim's a fool, an' young Gale has been punctured by *choya* thorns. He's got the desert poison in his blood. But you now—you've no call to stick—you can find that trail out. It's easy to follow, made by so many shod hosses. Take your wife an' go.... Shore you'll go, Thorne?"

Deliberately and without an instant's hesitation the cavalryman replied "No."

Ladd then directed his appeal to Mercedes. His face was now convulsed, and his voice, though it had sunk to a whisper, was clear, and beautiful with some rich quality that Gale had never heard in it.

"Mercedes, you're a woman. You're the woman we fought for. An' some of us are shore goin' to die for you. Don't make it all for nothin'. Let us feel we saved the woman. Shore you can make Thorne go. He'll have to go if you say. They'll all have to go. Think of the years of love an' happiness in store for you. A week or so an' it 'll be too late. Can you stand for me seein' you?... Let me tell you, Mercedes, when the summer heat hits the lava we'll all wither an' curl up like shavin's near a fire. A wind of hell will blow up this slope. Look at them mesquites. See the twist in them. That's the torture of heat an' thirst. Do you want me or all us men seein' you like that?... Mercedes, don't make it all for nothin'. Say you'll persuade Thorne, if not the others."

For all the effect his appeal had to move her Mercedes might have possessed a heart as hard and fixed as the surrounding lava.

"Never!"

White-faced, with great black eyes flashing, the Spanish girl spoke the word that bound her and her companions in the desert.

The subject was never mentioned again. Gale thought that he read a sinister purpose in Ladd's mind. To his astonishment, Lash came to him with the same fancy. After that they made certain there never was a gun within reach of Ladd's clutching, clawlike hands.

Gradually a somber spell lifted from the ranger's mind. When he was entirely free of it he began to gather strength daily. Then it was as if he had never known patience—he who had shown so well how to wait. He was in a frenzy to get well. He appetite could not be satisfied.

The sun climbed higher, whiter, hotter. At midday a wind from gulfward roared up the arroyo, and now only palos verdes and the few saguaros were green. Every day the water in the lava hole sank an inch.

The Yaqui alone spent the waiting time in activity. He made trips up on the lava slope, and each time he returned with guns or boots or sombreros, or something belonging to the bandits that had fallen. He never fetched in a saddle or bridle, and from that the rangers concluded Rojas's horses had long before taken their back trail. What speculation, what consternation those saddled horses would cause if they returned to Forlorn River!

As Ladd improved there was one story he had to hear every day. It was the one relating to what he had missed—the sight of Rojas pursued and plunged to his doom. The thing had a morbid fascination for the sick ranger. He reveled in it. He tortured Mercedes. His gentleness and consideration, heretofore so marked, were in abeyance to some sinister, ghastly joy. But to humor him Mercedes racked her soul with the sensations she had suffered when Rojas hounded her out on the ledge; when she shot him; when she sprang to throw herself over the precipice; when she fought him; when with half-blinded eyes she looked up to see the merciless Yaqui reaching for the bandit. Ladd fed his cruel longing with Thorne's poignant recollections, with the keen, clear, never-to-be-forgotten shocks to Gale's eye and ear. Jim Lash, for one at least, never tired of telling how he had seen and heard the tragedy, and every time in the telling it gathered some more tragic and gruesome detail. Jim believed in satiating the ranger. Then in the twilight, when the campfire burned, Ladd would try to get the Yaqui to tell his side of the story. But this the Indian would never do. There was only the expression of his fathomless eyes and the set passion of his massive face.

Those waiting days grew into weeks. Ladd gained very slowly. Nevertheless, at last he could walk about, and soon he averred that, strapped to a horse, he could last out the trip to Forlorn River.

There was rejoicing in camp, and plans were eagerly suggested. The Yaqui happened to be absent. When he returned the rangers told him they were now ready to undertake the journey back across lava and cactus.

Yaqui shook his head. They declared again their intention.

"No!" replied the Indian, and his deep, sonorous voice rolled out upon the quiet of the arroyo. He spoke briefly then. They had waited too long. The smaller waterholes back in the trail were dry. The hot summer was upon them. There could be only death waiting down in the burning valley. Here was water and grass and wood and shade from the sun's rays, and sheep to be killed on the peaks. The water would hold unless the season was that dreaded ano seco of the Mexicans.

"Wait for rain," concluded Yaqui, and now as never before he spoke as one with authority. "If no rain—" Silently he lifted his hand.

XVI MOUNTAIN SHEEP

WHAT Gale might have thought an appalling situation, if considered from a safe and comfortable home away from the desert, became, now that he was shut in by the red-ribbed lava walls and great dry wastes, a matter calmly accepted as inevitable. So he imagined it was accepted by the others. Not even Mercedes uttered a regret. No word was spoken of home. If there was thought of loved one, it was locked deep in their minds. In Mercedes there was no change in womanly quality, perhaps because all she had to love was there in the desert with her.

Gale had often pondered over this singular change in character. He had trained himself, in order to fight a paralyzing something in the desert's influence, to oppose with memory and thought an insidious primitive retrogression to what was scarcely consciousness at all, merely a savage's instinct of sight and sound. He felt the need now of redoubled effort. For there was a sheer happiness in drifting. Not only was it easy to forget, it was hard to remember. His idea was that a man laboring under a great wrong, a great crime, a great passion might find the lonely desert a fitting place for either remembrance or oblivion, according to the nature of his soul. But an ordinary, healthy, reasonably happy mortal who loved the open with its blaze of sun and sweep of wind would have a task to keep from going backward to the natural man as he was before civilization.

By tacit agreement Ladd again became the leader of the party. Ladd was a man who would have taken all the responsibility whether or not it was given him. In moments of hazard, of uncertainty, Lash and Gale, even Belding, unconsciously looked to the ranger. He had that kind of power.

The first thing Ladd asked was to have the store of food that remained spread out upon a tarpaulin. Assuredly, it was a slender enough supply. The ranger stood for long moments gazing down at it. He was groping among past experiences, calling back from his years of life on range and desert that which might be valuable for the present issue. It was impossible to read the gravity of Ladd's face, for he still looked like a dead man, but the slow shake of his head told Gale much. There was a grain of hope, however, in the significance with which he touched the bags of salt and said, "Shore it was sense packin' all that salt!"

Then he turned to face his comrades.

"That's little grub for six starvin' people corralled in the desert. But the grub end ain't worryin' me. Yaqui can get sheep up the slopes. Water! That's the beginnin' and middle an' end of our case."

"Laddy, I reckon the waterhole here never goes dry," replied Jim.

"Ask the Indian."

Upon being questioned, Yaqui repeated what he had said about the dreaded ano seco of the Mexicans. In a dry year this waterhole failed.

"Dick, take a rope an' see how much water's in the hole."

Gale could not find bottom with a thirty foot lasso. The water was as cool, clear, sweet as if it had been kept in a shaded iron receptacle.

Ladd welcomed this information with surprise and gladness.

"Let's see. Last year was shore pretty dry. Mebbe this summer won't be. Mebbe our wonderful good luck'll hold. Ask Yaqui if he thinks it 'll rain."

Mercedes questioned the Indian.

"He says no man can tell surely. But he thinks the rain will come," she replied.

"Shore it 'll rain, you can gamble on that now," continued Ladd. "If there's only grass for the hosses! We can't get out of here without hosses. Dick, take the Indian an' scout down the arroyo. To-day I seen the hosses were gettin' fat. Gettin' fat in this desert! But mebbe they've about grazed up all the grass. Go an' see, Dick. An' may you come back with more good news!"

Gale, upon the few occasions when he had wandered down the arroyo, had never gone far. The Yaqui said there was grass for the horses, and until now no one had given the question more consideration. Gale found that the arroyo widened as it opened. Near the head, where it was narrow, the grass lined the course of the dry stream bed. But farther down this stream bed spread out. There was every indication that at flood seasons the water covered the floor of the arroyo. The farther Gale went the thicker and larger grew the gnarled mesquites and palo verdes, the more cactus and greasewood there were, and other desert growths. Patches of gray grass grew everywhere. Gale began to wonder where the horses were. Finally the trees and brush thinned out, and a mile-wide gray plain stretched down to reddish sand dunes. Over to one side were the white horses, and even as Gale saw them both Blanco Diablo and Sol lifted their heads and, with white manes tossing in the wind, whistled clarion calls. Here was grass enough for many horses; the arroyo was indeed an oasis.

Ladd and the others were awaiting Gale's report, and they received it with calmness, yet with a joy no less evident because it was restrained. Gale, in his keen observation at the moment, found that he and his comrades turned with glad eyes to the woman of the party.

"Senor Laddy, you think—you believe—we shall—" she faltered, and her voice failed. It was the woman in her, weakening in the light of real hope, of the happiness now possible beyond that desert barrier.

"Mercedes, no white man can tell what'll come to pass out here," said Ladd, earnestly. "Shore I have hopes now I never dreamed of. I was pretty near a dead man. The Indian saved me. Queer notions have come into my head about Yaqui. I don't understand them. He seems when you look at him only a squalid, sullen, vengeful savage. But Lord! that's far from the truth. Mebbe Yaqui's different from most Indians. He looks the same, though. Mebbe the trouble is we white folks never knew the Indian. Anyway, Beldin' had it right. Yaqui's our godsend. Now as to the future, I'd like to know mebbe as well as you if we're ever to get home. Only bein' what I am, I say, Quien sabe? But somethin' tells me Yaqui knows. Ask him, Mercedes. Make him tell. We'll all be the better for knowin'. We'd be stronger for havin' more'n our faith in him. He's silent Indian, but make him tell."

Mercedes called to Yaqui. At her bidding there was always a suggestion of hurry, which otherwise was never manifest in his actions. She put a hand on his bared muscular arm and began to speak in Spanish. Her voice was low, swift, full of deep emotion, sweet as the sound of a bell. It thrilled Gale, though he understood scarcely a word she said. He did not need translation to know that here spoke the longing of a woman for life, love, home, the heritage of a woman's heart.

Gale doubted his own divining impression. It was that the Yaqui understood this woman's longing. In Gale's sight the Indian's stoicism, his inscrutability, the lavalike hardness of his face, although they did not change, seemed to give forth light, gentleness, loyalty. For an instant Gale seemed to have a vision; but it did not last, and he failed to hold some beautiful illusive thing.

"Si!" rolled out the Indian's reply, full of power and depth.

Mercedes drew a long breath, and her hand sought Thorne's.

"He says yes," she whispered. "He answers he'll save us; he'll take us all back—he knows!"

The Indian turned away to his tasks, and the silence that held the little group was finally broken by Ladd.

"Shore I said so. Now all we've got to do is use sense. Friends, I'm the commissary department of this outfit, an' what I say goes. You all won't eat except when I tell you. Mebbe it'll not be so hard to keep our health. Starved beggars don't get sick. But there's the heat comin', an' we can all go loco, you know. To pass the time! Lord, that's our problem. Now if you all only had a hankerin' for checkers. Shore I'll make a board an' make you play. Thorne, you're the luckiest. You've got your girl, an' this can be a honeymoon. Now with a few tools an' little material see what a grand house you can build for your wife. Dick, you're lucky, too. You like to hunt, an' up there you'll find the finest bighorn huntin' in the West. Take Yaqui and the .405. We need the meat, but while you're gettin' it have your sport. The same chance will never come again. I wish we all was able to go. But crippled men can't climb the lava. Shore you'll see some country from the peaks. There's no wilder place on earth, except the poles. An' when you're older, you an' Nell, with a couple of fine boys, think what it'll be to tell them about bein' lost in the lava, an' huntin' sheep with a Yaqui. Shore I've hit it. You can take yours out in huntin' an' thinkin'. Now if I had a girl like Nell I'd never go crazy. That's your game, Dick. Hunt, an' think of Nell, an' how you'll tell those fine boys about it all, an' about the old cowman you knowed, Laddy, who'll by then be long past the divide. Rustle now, son. Get some enthusiasm. For shore you'll need it for yourself an' us."

Gale climbed the lava slope, away round to the right of the arroyo, along an old trail that Yaqui said the Papagos had made before his own people had hunted there. Part way it led through spiked, crested, upheaved lava that would have been almost impassable even without its silver coating of *choya* cactus. There were benches and ledges and ridges bare and glistening in the sun. From the crests of these Yaqui's searching falcon gaze roved near and far for signs of sheep, and Gale used his glass on the reaches of lava that slanted steeply upward to the corrugated peaks, and down over endless heave and roll and red-waved slopes. The heat smoked up from the lava, and this, with the red color and the shiny *choyas*, gave the impression of a world of smoldering fire.

Farther along the slope Yaqui halted and crawled behind projections to a point commanding a view over an extraordinary section of country. The peaks were off to the left. In the foreground were gullies, ridges, and canyons, arroyos, all glistening with *choyas* and some other and more numerous white bushes, and here and there towered a green cactus. This region was only a splintered and more devastated part of the volcanic slope, but it was miles in extent. Yaqui peeped over the top of a blunt block of lava and searched the sharp-billowed wilderness. Suddenly he grasped Gale and pointed across a deep wide gully.

With the aid of his glass Gale saw five sheep. They were much larger than he had expected, dull brown in color, and two of them were rams with great curved horns. They were looking in his direction. Remembering what he had heard about the wonderful eyesight of these mountain animals, Gale could only conclude that they had seen the hunters.

Then Yaqui's movements attracted and interested him. The Indian had brought with him a red scarf and a mesquite branch. He tied the scarf to the stick, and propped this up in a crack of the lava. The scarf waved in the wind. That done, the Indian bade Gale watch.

Once again he leveled the glass at the sheep. All five were motionless, standing like statues, heads pointed across the gully. They were more than a mile distant. When Gale looked without his glass they merged into the roughness of the lava. He was intensely interested. Did the sheep see the red scarf? It seemed incredible, but nothing else could account for that statuesque alertness. The sheep held this rigid position for perhaps fifteen minutes. Then the leading ram started to approach. The others followed. He took a few steps, then halted. Always he held his head up, nose pointed.

"By George, they're coming!" exclaimed Gale. "They see that flag. They're hunting us. They're curious. If this doesn't beat me!"

Evidently the Indian understood, for he grunted.

Gale found difficulty in curbing his impatience. The approach of the sheep was slow. The advances of the leader and the intervals of watching had a singular regularity. He worked like a machine. Gale followed him down the opposite wall, around holes, across gullies, over ridges. Then Gale shifted the glass back to find the others. They were coming also, with exactly the same pace and pause of their leader. What steppers they were! How sure-footed! What leaps they made! It was thrilling to watch them. Gale forgot he had a rifle. The Yaqui pressed a heavy hand down upon his shoulder. He was to keep well hidden and to be quiet. Gale suddenly conceived the idea that the sheep might come clear across to investigate the puzzling red thing fluttering in the breeze. Strange, indeed, would that be for the wildest creatures in the world.

The big ram led on with the same regular persistence, and in half an hour's time he was in the bottom of the great gulf, and soon he was facing up the slope. Gale knew then that the alluring scarf had fascinated him. It was no longer necessary now for Gale to use his glass. There was a short period when an intervening crest of lava hid the sheep from view. After that the two rams and their smaller followers were plainly in sight for perhaps a quarter of an hour. Then they disappeared behind another ridge. Gale kept watching sure they would come out farther on. A tense period of waiting passed, then a suddenly electrifying pressure of Yaqui's hand made Gale tremble with excitement.

Very cautiously he shifted his position. There, not fifty feet distant upon a high mound of lava, stood the leader of the sheep. His size astounded Gale. He seemed all horns. But only for a moment did the impression of horns overbalancing body remain with Gale. The sheep was graceful, sinewy, slender, powerfully built, and in poise magnificent. As Gale watched, spellbound, the second ram leaped lightly upon the mound, and presently the three others did likewise.

Then, indeed, Gale feasted his eyes with a spectacle for a hunter. It came to him suddenly that there had been something he expected to see in this Rocky Mountain bighorn, and it was lacking. They were beautiful, as wonderful as even Ladd's encomiums had led him to suppose. He thought perhaps it was the contrast these soft, sleek, short-furred, graceful animals afforded to what he imagined the barren, terrible lava mountains might develop.

The splendid leader stepped closer, his round, protruding amber eyes, which Gale could now plainly see, intent upon that fatal red flag. Like automatons the other four crowded into his tracks. A few little slow steps, then the leader halted.

At this instant Gale's absorbed attention was directed by Yaqui to the rifle, and so to the purpose of the climb. A little cold shock affronted Gale's vivid pleasure. With it dawned a realization of what he had imagined was lacking in these animals. They did not look wild! The so-called wildest of wild creatures appeared tamer than sheep he had followed on a farm. It would be little less than murder to kill them. Gale regretted the need of slaughter. Nevertheless, he could not resist the desire to show himself and see how tame they really were.

He reached for the .405, and as he threw a shell into the chamber the slight metallic click made the sheep jump. Then Gale rose quickly to his feet.

The noble ram and his band simply stared at Gale. They had never seen a man. They showed not the slightest indication of instinctive fear. Curiosity, surprise, even friendliness, seemed to mark their attitude of attention. Gale imagined that they were going to step still closer. He did not choose to wait to see if this were true. Certainly it already took a grim resolution to raise the heavy .405.

His shot killed the big leader. The others bounded away with remarkable nimbleness. Gale used up the remaining four shells to drop the second ram, and by the time he had reloaded the others were out of range.

The Yaqui's method of hunting was sure and deadly and saving of energy, but Gale never would try it again. He chose to stalk the game. This entailed a great expenditure of strength, the eyes and lungs of a mountaineer, and, as Gale put it to Ladd, the need of seven-league boots. After being hunted a few times and shot at, the sheep became exceedingly difficult to approach. Gale learned to know that their fame as the keenest-eyed of all animals was well founded. If he worked directly toward a flock, crawling over the sharp lava, always a sentinel ram espied him before he got within range. The only method of attack that he found successful was to locate sheep with his glass, work round to windward of them, and then, getting behind a ridge or buttress, crawl like a lizard to a vantage point. He failed often. The stalk called forth all that was in him of endurance, cunning, speed. As the days grew hotter he hunted in the early morning hours and a while before the sun went down. More than one night he lay out on the lava, with the great stars close overhead and the immense void all beneath him. This pursuit he learned to love. Upon those scarred and blasted slopes the wild spirit that was in him had free rein. And like a shadow the faithful Yaqui tried ever to keep at his heels.

One morning the rising sun greeted him as he surmounted the higher cone of the volcano. He saw the vastness of the east aglow with a glazed rosy whiteness, like the changing hue of an ember. At this height there was a sweeping wind, still cool. The western slopes of lava lay dark, and all that world of sand and gulf and mountain barrier beyond was shrouded in the mystic cloud of distance. Gale had assimilated much of the loneliness and the sense of ownership and the love of lofty heights that might well belong to the great condor of the peak. Like this wide-winged bird, he had an unparalleled range of vision. The very corners whence came the winds seemed pierced by Gale's eyes.

Yaqui spied a flock of sheep far under the curved broken rim of the main crater. Then began the stalk. Gale had taught the Yaqui something—that speed might win as well as patient cunning. Keeping out of sight, Gale ran over the spike-crusted lava, leaving the Indian far behind. His feet were magnets, attracting supporting holds and he passed over them too fast to fall. The wind, the keen air of the heights, the red lava, the boundless surrounding blue, all seemed to have something to do with his wildness. Then, hiding, slipping, creeping, crawling, he closed in upon his quarry until the long rifle grew like stone in his grip, and the whipping "spang" ripped the silence, and the strange echo boomed deep in the crater, and rolled around, as if in hollow mockery at the hopelessness of escape.

Gale's exultant yell was given as much to free himself of some bursting joy of action as it was to call the slower Yaqui. Then he liked the strange echoes. It was a maddening whirl of sound that bored deeper and deeper along the whorled and caverned walls of the crater. It was as if these aged walls resented the violating of their silent sanctity. Gale felt himself a man, a thing alive, something superior to all this savage, dead, upflung world of iron, a master even of all this grandeur and sublimity because he had a soul.

He waited beside his quarry, and breathed deep, and swept the long slopes with searching eyes of habit.

When Yaqui came up they set about the hardest task of all, to pack the best of that heavy sheep down miles of steep, ragged, *choya*-covered lava. But even in this Gale rejoiced. The heat was nothing, the millions of little pits which could hold and twist a foot were nothing; the blade-edged crusts and the deep fissures and the choked canyons and the tangled, dwarfed mesquites, all these were as nothing but obstacles to be cheerfully overcome. Only the *choya* hindered Dick Gale.

When his heavy burden pulled him out of sure-footedness, and he plunged into a *choya*, or when the strange, deceitful, uncanny, almost invisible frosty thorns caught and pierced him, then there was call for all of fortitude and endurance. For this cactus had a malignant power of torture. Its pain was a stinging, blinding, burning, sickening poison in the blood. If thorns pierced his legs he felt the pain all over his body; if his hands rose from a fall full of the barbed joints, he was helpless and quivering till Yaqui tore them out.

But this one peril, dreaded more than dizzy height of precipice or sunblindness on the glistening peak, did not daunt Gale. His teacher was the Yaqui, and always before him was an example that made him despair of a white man's equality. Color, race, blood, breeding—what were these in the wilderness? Verily, Dick Gale had come to learn the use of his hands.

So in a descent of hours he toiled down the lava slope, to stalk into the arroyo like a burdened giant, wringing wet, panting, clear-eyed and dark-faced, his ragged clothes and boots white with *choya* thorns.

The gaunt Ladd rose from his shaded seat, and removed his pipe from smiling lips, and turned to nod at Jim, and then looked back again.

The torrid summer heat came imperceptibly, or it could never have been borne by white men. It changed the lives of the fugitives, making them partly nocturnal in habit. The nights had the balmy coolness of spring, and would have been delightful for sleep, but that would have made the blazing days unendurable.

The sun rose in a vast white flame. With it came the blasting, withering wind from the gulf. A red haze, like that of earlier sunsets, seemed to come sweeping on the wind, and it roared up the arroyo, and went bellowing into the crater, and rushed on in fury to lash the peaks.

During these hot, windy hours the desert-bound party slept in deep recesses in the lava; and if necessity brought them forth they could not remain out long. The sand burned through boots, and a touch of bare hand on lava raised a blister.

A short while before sundown the Yaqui went forth to build a campfire, and soon the others came out, heat-dazed, half blinded, with parching throats to allay and hunger that was never satisfied. A little action and a cooling of the air revived them, and when night set in they were comfortable round the campfire.

As Ladd had said, one of their greatest problems was the passing of time. The nights were interminably long, but they had to be passed in work or play or dream—anything except sleep. That was Ladd's most inflexible command. He gave no reason. But not improbably the ranger thought that the terrific heat of the day spend in slumber lessened a wear and strain, if not a real danger of madness.

Accordingly, at first the occupations of this little group were many and various. They worked if they had something to do, or could invent a pretext. They told and retold stories until all were wearisome. They sang songs. Mercedes taught Spanish. They played every game they knew. They invented others that were so trivial children would scarcely have been interested, and these they played seriously. In a word, with intelligence and passion, with all that was civilized and human, they fought the ever-infringing loneliness, the savage solitude of their environment.

But they had only finite minds. It was not in reason to expect a complete victory against this mighty Nature, this bounding horizon of death and desolation and decay. Gradually they fell back upon fewer and fewer occupations, until the time came when the silence was hard to break.

Gale believed himself the keenest of the party, the one who thought most, and he watched the effect of the desert upon his companions. He imagined that he saw Ladd grow old sitting round the campfire. Certain it was that the ranger's gray hair had turned white. What had been at times hard and cold and grim about him had strangely vanished in sweet temper and a vacant-mindedness that held him longer as the days passed. For hours, it seemed, Ladd would bend over his checkerboard and never make a move. It mattered not now whether or not he had a partner. He was always glad of being spoken to, as if he were called back from vague region of mind. Jim Lash, the calmest, coolest, most nonchalant, best-humored Westerner Gale had ever met, had by slow degrees lost that cheerful character which would have been of such infinite good to his companions, and always he sat brooding, silently brooding. Jim had no ties, few memories, and the desert was claiming him.

Thorne and Mercedes, however, were living, wonderful proof that spirit, mind, and heart were free—free to soar in scorn of the colossal barrenness and silence and space of that terrible hedging prison of lava. They were young; they loved; they were together; and the oasis was almost a paradise. Gale believe he helped himself by watching them. Imagination had never pictured real happiness to him. Thorne and Mercedes had forgotten the outside world. If they had been existing on the burned-out desolate moon they could hardly have been in a harsher, grim-reports have come to Linrock that soon as he could get round to it he'd ride down d rid the community of that botherso

Mercedes grew thinner, until she was a slender shadow of her former self. She became hard, brown as the rangers, lithe and quick as a panther. She seemed to live on water and the air—perhaps, indeed, on love. For of the scant fare, the best of which was continually urged upon her, she partook but little. She reminded Gale of a wild brown creature, free as the wind on the lava slopes. Yet, despite the great change, her beauty remained undiminished. Her eyes, seeming so much larger now in her small face, were great black, starry gulfs. She was the life of that camp. Her smiles, her rapid speech, her low laughter, her quick movements, her playful moods with the rangers, the dark and passionate glance, which rested so often on her lover, the whispers in the dusk as hand in hand they paced the campfire beat—these helped Gale to retain his loosening hold on reality, to resist the lure of a strange beckoning life where a man stood free in the golden open, where emotion was not, nor trouble, nor sickness, nor anything but the savage's rest and sleep and action and dream.

Although the Yaqui was as his shadow, Gale reached a point when he seemed to wander alone at twilight, in the night, at dawn. Far down the arroyo, in the deepening red twilight, when the heat rolled away on slow-dying wind, Blanco Sol raised his splendid head and whistled for his master. Gale reproached himself for neglect of the noble horse. Blanco Sol was always the same. He loved four things—his master, a long drink of cool water, to graze at will, and to run. Time and place, Gale thought, meant little to Sol if he could have those four things. Gale put his arm over the great arched neck and laid his cheek against the long white mane, and then even as he stood there forgot the horse. What was the dull, red-tinged, horizon-wide mantle creeping up the slope? Through it the copper sun glowed, paled, died. Was it only twilight? Was it gloom? If he thought about it he had a feeling that it was the herald of night and the night must be a vigil, and that made him tremble.

At night he had formed a habit of climbing up the lava slope as far as the smooth trail extended, and there on a promontory he paced to and fro, and watched the stars, and sat stone-still for hours looking down at the vast void with its moving, changing shadows. From that promontory he gazed up at a velvet-blue sky, deep and dark, bright with millions of cold, distant, blinking stars, and he grasped a little of the meaning of infinitude. He gazed down into the shadows, which, black as they were and impenetrable, yet have a conception of immeasurable space.

Then the silence! He was dumb, he was awed, he bowed his head, he trembled, he marveled at the desert silence. It was the one thing always present. Even when the wind roared there seemed to be silence. But at night, in this lava world of ashes and canker, he waited for this terrible strangeness of nature to come to him with the secret. He seemed at once a little child and a strong man, and something very old. What tortured him was the incomprehensibility that the vaster the space the greater the silence! At one moment Gale felt there was only death here, and that was the secret; at another he heard the slow beat of a mighty heart.

He came at length to realize that the desert was a teacher. He did not realize all that he had learned, but he was a different man. And when he decided upon that, he was not thinking of the slow, sure call to the primal instincts of man; he was thinking that the desert, as much as he had experienced and no more, would absolutely overturn the whole scale of a man's values, break old habits, form new ones, remake him. More of desert experience, Gale believe, would be too much for intellect. The desert did not breed civilized man, and that made Gale ponder over a strange thought: after all, was the civilized man inferior to the savage?

Yaqui was the answer to that. When Gale acknowledged this he always remembered his present strange manner of thought. The past, the old order of mind, seemed as remote as this desert world was from the haunts of civilized men. A man must know a savage as Gale knew Yaqui before he could speak authoritatively, and then something stilled his tongue. In the first stage of Gale's observation of Yaqui he had marked tenaciousness of life, stoicism, endurance, strength. These were the attributes of the desert. But what of that second stage wherein the Indian had loomed up a colossal figure of strange honor, loyalty, love? Gale doubted his convictions and scorned himself for doubting.

There in the gloom sat the silent, impassive, inscrutable Yaqui. His dark face, his dark eyes were plain in the light of the stars. Always he was near Gale, unobtrusive, shadowy, but there. Why? Gale absolutely could not doubt that the Indian had heart as well as mind. Yaqui had from the very first stood between Gale and accident, toil, peril. It was his own choosing. Gale could not change him or thwart him. He understood the Indian's idea of obligation and sacred duty. But there was more, and that baffled Gale. In the night hours, alone on the slope, Gale felt in Yaqui, as he felt the mighty throb of that desert pulse, a something that drew him irresistibly to the Indian. Sometimes he looked around to find the Indian, to dispel these strange, pressing thoughts of unreality, and it was never in vain.

Thus the nights passed, endlessly long, with Gale fighting for his old order of thought, fighting the fascination of the infinite sky, and the gloomy insulating whirl of the wide shadows, fighting for belief, hope, prayer, fighting against that terrible ever-recurring idea of being lost, lost, lost in the desert, fighting harder than any other thing the insidious, penetrating, tranquil, unfeeling self that was coming between him and his memory.

He was losing the battle, losing his hold on tangible things, losing his power to stand up under this ponderous, merciless weight of desert space and silence.

He acknowledged it in a kind of despair, and the shadows of the night seemed whirling fiends. Lost! Lost! Lost! What are you waiting for? Rain!... Lost! Lost! Lost in the desert! So the shadows seemed to scream in voiceless mockery.

At the moment he was alone on the promontory. The night was far spent. A ghastly moon haunted the black volcanic spurs. The winds blew silently. Was he alone? No, he did not seem to be alone. The Yaqui was there. Suddenly a strange, cold sensation crept over Gale. It was new. He felt a presence. Turning, he expected to see the Indian, but instead, a slight shadow, pale, almost white, stood there, not close nor yet distant. It seemed to brighten. Then he saw a woman who resembled a girl he had seemed to know long ago. She was white-faced, golden-haired, and her lips were sweet, and her eyes were turning black. Nell! He had forgotten her. Over him flooded a torrent of memory. There was tragic woe in this sweet face. Nell was holding out her arms—she was crying aloud to him across the sand and the cactus and the lava. She was in trouble, and he had been forgetting.

That night he climbed the lava to the topmost cone, and never slipped on a ragged crust nor touched a *choya* thorn. A voice called to him. He saw Nell's eyes in the stars, in the velvet blue of sky, in the blackness of the engulfing shadows. She was with him, a slender shape, a spirit, keeping step with him, and memory was strong, sweet, beating, beautiful. Far down in the west, faintly golden with light of the sinking moon, he saw a cloud that resembled her face. A cloud on the desert horizon! He gazed and gazed. Was that a spirit face like the one by his side? No—he did not dream.

In the hot, sultry morning Yaqui appeared at camp, after long hours of absence, and he pointed with a long, dark arm toward the west. A bank of clouds was rising above the mountain barrier.

"Rain!" he cried; and his sonorous voice rolled down the arroyo.

Those who heard him were as shipwrecked mariners at sight of a distant sail.

Dick Gale, silent, grateful to the depths of his soul, stood with arm over Blanco Sol and watched the transforming west, where clouds of wonderous size and hue piled over one another, rushing, darkening, spreading, sweeping upward toward that white and glowing sun.

When they reached the zenith and swept round to blot out the blazing orb, the earth took on a dark, lowering aspect. The red of sand and lava changed to steely gray. Vast shadows, like ripples on water, sheeted in from the gulf with a low, strange moan. Yet the silence was like death. The desert was awaiting a strange and hated visitation—storm! If all the endless torrid days, the endless mystic nights had seemed unreal to Gale, what, then, seemed this stupendous spectacle?

"Oh! I felt a drop of rain on my face!" cried Mercedes; and whispering the name of a saint, she kissed her husband.

The white-haired Ladd, gaunt, old, bent, looked up at the maelstrom of clouds, and he said, softly, "Shore we'll get in the hosses, an' pack light, an' hit the trail, an' make night marches!"

Then up out of the gulf of the west swept a bellowing wind and a black pall and terrible flashes of lightning and thunder like the end of the world—fury, blackness, chaos, the desert storm.

XVII THE WHISTLE OF A HORSE

AT the ranch-house at Forlorn River Belding stood alone in his darkened room. It was quiet there and quiet outside; the sickening midsummer heat, like a hot heavy blanket, lay upon the house.

He took up the gun belt from his table and with slow hands buckled it around his waist. He seemed to feel something familiar and comfortable and inspiring in the weight of the big gun against his hip. He faced the door as if to go out, but hesitated, and then began a slow, plodding walk up and down the length of the room. Presently he halted at the table, and with reluctant hands he unbuckled the gun belt and laid it down.

The action did not have an air of finality, and Belding knew it. He had seen border life in Texas in the early days; he had been a sheriff when the law in the West depended on a quickness of wrist; he had seen many a man lay down his gun for good and all. His own action was not final. Of late he had done the same thing many times and this last time it seemed a little harder to do, a little more indicative of vacillation. There were reasons why Belding's gun held for him a gloomy fascination.

The Chases, those grasping and conscienceless agents of a new force in the development of the West, were bent upon Belding's ruin, and so far as his fortunes at Forlorn River were concerned, had almost accomplished it. One by one he lost points for which he contended with them. He carried into the Tucson courts the matter of the staked claims, and mining claims, and water claims, and he lost all. Following that he lost his government position as inspector of immigration; and this fact, because of what he considered its injustice, had been a hard blow. He had been made to suffer a humiliation equally as great. It came about that he actually had to pay the Chases for water to irrigate his alfalfa fields. The never-failing spring upon his land answered for the needs of household and horses, but no more.

These matters were unfortunate for Belding, but not by any means wholly accountable for his worry and unhappiness and brooding hate. He believed Dick Gale and the rest of the party taken into the desert by the Yaqui had been killed or lost. Two months before a string of Mexican horses, riderless, saddled, starved for grass and wild for water, had come in to Forlorn River. They were a part of the horses belonging to Rojas and his band. Their arrival complicated the mystery and strengthened convictions of the loss of both pursuers and pursued. Belding was wont to say that he had worried himself gray over the fate of his rangers.

Belding's unhappiness could hardly be laid to material loss. He had been rich and was now poor, but change of fortune such as that could not have made him unhappy. Something more somber and mysterious and sad than the loss of Dick Gale and their friends had come into the lives of his wife and Nell. He dated the time of this change back to a certain day when Mrs. Belding recognized in the elder Chase an old schoolmate and a rejected suitor. It took time for slow-thinking Belding to discover anything wrong in his household, especially as the fact of the Gales lingering there made Mrs. Belding and Nell, for the most part, hide their real and deeper feelings. Gradually, however, Belding had forced on him the fact of some secret cause for grief other than Gale's loss. He was sure of it when his wife signified her desire to make a visit to her old home back in Peoria. She did not give many reasons, but she did show him a letter that had found its way from old friends. This letter contained news that may or may not have been authentic; but it was enough, Belding thought, to interest his wife. An old prospector had returned to Peoria, and he had told relatives of meeting Robert Burton at the Sonoyta Oasis fifteen years before, and that Burton had gone into the desert never to return. To Belding this was no surprise, for he had heard that before his marriage. There appeared to have been no doubts as to the death of his wife's first husband. The singular thing was that both Nell's father and grandfather had been lost somewhere in the Sonora Desert.

Belding did not oppose his wife's desire to visit her old home. He thought it would be a wholesome trip for her, and did all in his power to persuade Nell to accompany her. But Nell would not go.

It was after Mrs. Belding's departure that Belding discovered in Nell a condition of mind that amazed and distressed him. She had suddenly become strangely wretched, so that she could not conceal it from even the Gales, who, of all people, Belding imagined, were the ones to make Nell proud. She would tell him nothing. But after a while, when he had thought it out, he dated this further and more deplorable change in Nell back to a day on which he had met Nell with Radford Chase. This indefatigable wooer had not in the least abandoned his suit. Something about the fellow made Belding grind his teeth. But Nell grew not only solicitously, but now strangely, entreatingly earnest in her importunities to Belding not to insult or lay a hand on Chase. This had bound Belding so far; it had made him think and watch. He had never been a man to interfere with his women folk. They could do as they liked, and usually that pleased him. But a slow surprise gathered and grew upon him when he saw that Nell, apparently, was accepting young Chase's attentions. At least, she no longer hid from him. Belding could not account for this, because he was sure Nell cordially despised the fellow. And toward the end he divined, if he did not actually know, that these Chases possessed some strange power over Nell, and were using it. That stirred a hate in Belding—a hate he had felt at the very first and had manfully striven against, and which now gave him over to dark brooding thoughts.

Midsummer passed, and the storms came late. But when they arrived they made up for tardiness. Belding did not remember so terrible a storm of wind and rain as that which broke the summer's drought.

In a few days, it seemed, Altar Valley was a bright and green expanse, where dust clouds did not rise. Forlorn River ran, a slow, heavy, turgid torrent. Belding never saw the river in flood that it did not give him joy; yet now, desert man as he was, he suffered a regret when he thought of the great Chase reservoir full and overflowing. The dull thunder of the spillway was not pleasant. It was the first time in his life that the sound of falling water jarred upon him.

Belding noticed workmen once more engaged in the fields bounding his land. The Chases had extended a main irrigation ditch down to Belding's farm, skipped the width of his ground, then had gone on down through Altar Valley. They had exerted every influence to obtain right to connect these ditches by digging through his land, but Belding had remained obdurate. He refused to have any dealings with them. It was therefore with some curiosity and suspicion that he saw a gang of Mexicans once more at work upon these ditches.

At daylight next morning a tremendous blast almost threw Belding out of his bed. It cracked the adobe walls of his house and broke windows and sent pans and crockery to the floor with a crash. Belding's idea was that the store of dynamite kept by the Chases for blasting had blown up. Hurriedly getting into his clothes, he went to Nell's room to reassure her; and, telling her to have a thought for their guests, he went out to see what had happened.

The villagers were pretty badly frightened. Many of the poorly constructed adobe huts had crumbled almost into dust. A great yellow cloud, like smoke, hung over the river. This appeared to be at the upper end of Belding's plot, and close to the river. When he reached his fence the smoke and dust were so thick he could scarcely breathe, and for a little while he was unable to see what had happened. Presently he made out a huge hole in the sand just about where the irrigation ditch had stopped near his line. For some reason or other, not clear to Belding, the Mexicans had set off an extraordinarily heavy blast at that point.

Belding pondered. He did not now for a moment consider an accidental discharge of dynamite. But why had this blast been set off? The loose sandy soil had yielded readily to shovel; there were no rocks; as far as construction of a ditch was concerned such a blast would have done more harm than good.

Slowly, with reluctant feet, Belding walked toward a green hollow, where in a cluster of willows lay the never-failing spring that his horses loved so well, and, indeed, which he loved no less. He was actually afraid to part the drooping willows to enter the little cool, shady path that led to the spring. Then, suddenly seized by suspense, he ran the rest of the way.

He was just in time to see the last of the water. It seemed to sink as in quicksand. The shape of the hole had changed. The tremendous force of the blast in the adjoining field had obstructed or diverted the underground stream of water.

Belding's never-failing spring had been ruined. What had made this little plot of ground green and sweet and fragrant was now no more. Belding's first feeling was for the pity of it. The pale Ajo lilies would bloom no more under those willows. The willows themselves would soon wither and die. He thought how many times in the middle of hot summer nights he had come down to the spring to drink. Never again!

Suddenly he thought of Blanco Diablo. How the great white thoroughbred had loved this spring! Belding straightened up and looked with tear-blurred eyes out over the waste of desert to the west. Never a day passed that he had not thought of the splendid horse; but this moment, with its significant memory, was doubly keen, and there came a dull pang in his breast.

"Diablo will never drink here again!" muttered Belding.

The loss of Blanco Diablo, though admitted and mourned by Belding, had never seemed quite real until this moment.

The pall of dust drifting over him, the din of the falling water up at the dam, diverted Belding's mind to the Chases. All at once he was in the harsh grip of a cold certainty. The blast had been set off intentionally to ruin his spring. What a hellish trick! No Westerner, no Indian or Mexican, no desert man could have been guilty of such a crime. To ruin a beautiful, clear, cool, never-failing stream of water in the desert!

It was then that Belding's worry and indecision and brooding were as if they had never existed. As he strode swiftly back to the house, his head, which had long been bent thoughtfully and sadly, was held erect. He went directly to his room, and with an air that was now final he buckled on his gun belt. He looked the gun over and tried the action. He squared himself and walked a little more erect. Some long-lost individuality had returned to Belding.

"Let's see," he was saying. "I can get Carter to send the horses I've left back to Waco to my brother. I'll make Nell take what money there is and go hunt up her mother. The Gales are ready to go—to-day, if I say the word. Nell can travel with them part way East. That's your game, Tom Belding, don't mistake me."

As he went out he encountered Mr. Gale coming up the walk. The long sojourn at Forlorn River, despite the fact that it had been laden with a suspense which was gradually changing to a sad certainty, had been of great benefit to Dick's father. The dry air, the heat, and the quiet had made him, if not entirely a well man, certainly stronger than he had been in many years.

"Belding, what was that terrible roar?" asked Mr. Gale. "We were badly frightened until Miss Nell came to us. We feared it was an earthquake."

"Well, I'll tell you, Mr. Gale, we've had some quakes here, but none of them could hold a candle to this jar we just had."

Then Belding explained what had caused the explosion, and why it had been set off so close to his property.

"It's an outrage, sir, an unspeakable outrage," declared Mr. Gale, hotly. "Such a thing would not be tolerated in the East. Mr. Belding, I'm amazed at your attitude in the face of all this trickery."

"You see—there was mother and Nell," began Belding, as if apologizing. He dropped his head a little and made marks in the sand with the toe of his boot.

"Mr. Gale, I've been sort of half hitched, as Laddy used to say. I'm planning to have a little more elbow room round this ranch. I'm going to send Nell East to her mother. Then I'll— See here, Mr. Gale, would you mind having Nell with you part way when you go home?"

"We'd all be delighted to have her go all the way and make us a visit," replied Mr. Gale.

"That's fine. And you'll be going soon? Don't take that as if I wanted to—" Belding paused, for the truth was that he did want to hurry them off.

"We would have been gone before this, but for you," said Mr. Gale. "Long ago we gave up hope of—of Richard ever returning. And I believe, now we're sure he was lost, that we'd do well to go home at once. You wished us to remain until the heat was broken—till the rains came to make traveling easier for us. Now I see no need for further delay. My stay here has greatly benefited my health. I shall never forget your hospitality. This Western trip would have made me a new man if—only—Richard—"

"Sure. I understand," said Belding, gruffly. "Let's go in and tell the women to pack up."

Nell was busy with the servants preparing breakfast. Belding took her into the sitting-room while Mr. Gale called his wife and daughter.

"My girl, I've some news for you," began Belding. "Mr. Gale is leaving to-day with his family. I'm going to send you with them—part way, anyhow. You're invited to visit them. I think that 'd be great for you—help you to forget. But the main thing is—you're going East to join mother."

Nell gazed at him, white-faced, without uttering a word.

"You see, Nell, I'm about done in Forlorn River," went on Belding. "That blast this morning sank my spring. There's no water now. It was the last straw. So we'll shake the dust of Forlorn River. I'll come on a little later—that's all."

"Dad, you're packing your gun!" exclaimed Nell, suddenly pointing with a trembling finger. She ran to him, and for the first time in his life Belding put her away from him. His movements had lost the old slow gentleness.

"Why, so I am," replied Belding, coolly, as his hand moved down to the sheath swinging at his hip. "Nell, I'm that absent-minded these days!"

"Dad!" she cried.

"That'll do from you," he replied, in a voice he had never used to her. "Get breakfast now, then pack to leave Forlorn River."

"Leave Forlorn River!" whispered Nell, with a thin white hand stealing up to her breast. How changed the girl was! Belding reproached himself for his hardness, but did not speak his thought aloud. Nell was fading here, just as Mercedes had faded before the coming of Thorne.

Nell turned away to the west window and looked out across the desert toward the dim blue peaks in the distance. Belding watched her; likewise the Gales; and no one spoke. There ensued a long silence. Belding felt a lump rise in his throat. Nell laid her arm against the window frame, but gradually it dropped, and she was leaning with her face against the wood. A low sob broke from her. Elsie Gale went to her, embraced her, took the drooping head on her shoulder.

"We've come to be such friends," she said. "I believe it'll be good for you to visit me in the city. Here—all day you look out across that awful lonely desert.... Come, Nell."

Heavy steps sounded outside on the flagstones, then the door rattled under a strong knock. Belding opened it. The Chases, father and son, stood beyond the threshold.

"Good morning, Belding," said the elder Chase. "We were routed out early by that big blast and came up to see what was wrong. All a blunder. The Greaser foreman was drunk yesterday, and his ignorant men made a mistake. Sorry if the blast bothered you."

"Chase, I reckon that's the first of your blasts I was ever glad to hear," replied Belding, in a way that made Chase look blank.

"So? Well, I'm glad you're glad," he went on, evidently puzzled. "I was a little worried—you've always been so touchy—we never could get together. I hurried over, fearing maybe you might think the blast—you see, Belding—"

"I see this, Mr. Ben Chase," interrupted Belding, in curt and ringing voice. "That blast was a mistake, the biggest you ever made in your life."

"What do you mean?" demanded Chase.

"You'll have to excuse me for a while, unless you're dead set on having it out right now. Mr. Gale and his family are leaving, and my daughter is going with them. I'd rather you'd wait a little."

"Nell going away!" exclaimed Radford Chase. He reminded Belding of an overgrown boy in disappointment.

"Yes. But—Miss Burton to you, young man—"

"Mr. Belding, I certainly would prefer a conference with you right now," interposed the elder Chase, cutting short Belding's strange speech. "There are other matters—important matters to discuss. They've got to be settled. May we step in, sir?"

"No, you may not," replied Belding, bluntly. "I'm sure particular who I invite into my house. But I'll go with you."

Belding stepped out and closed the door. "Come away from the house so the women won't hear the—the talk."

The elder Chase was purple with rage, yet seemed to be controlling it. The younger man looked black, sullen, impatient. He appeared not to have a thought of Belding. He was absolutely blind to the situation, as considered from Belding's point of view. Ben Chase found his voice about the time Belding halted under the trees out of earshot from the house.

"Sir, you've insulted me—my son. How dare you? I want you to understand that you're—"

"Chop that kind of talk with me, you ——— ——— ——— ———!" interrupted Belding. He had always been profane, and now he certainly did not choose his language. Chase turned livid, gasped, and seemed about to give way to fury. But something about Belding evidently exerted a powerful quieting influence. "If you talk sense I'll listen," went on Belding.

Belding was frankly curious. He did not think any argument or inducement offered by Chase could change his mind on past dealings or his purpose of the present. But he believed by listening he might get some light on what had long puzzled him. The masterly effort Chase put forth to conquer his aroused passions gave Belding another idea of the character of this promoter.

"I want to make a last effort to propitiate you," began Chase, in his quick, smooth voice. That was a singular change to Belding—the dropping instantly into an easy flow of speech. "You've had losses here, and naturally you're sore. I don't blame you. But you can't see this thing from my side of the fence. Business is business. In business the best man wins. The law upheld those transactions of mine the honesty of which you questioned. As to mining and water claims, you lost on this technical point—that you had nothing to prove you had held them for five years. Five years is the time necessary in law. A dozen men might claim the source of Forlorn River, but if they had no house or papers to prove their squatters' rights any man could go in and fight them for the water. .... Now I want to run that main ditch along the river, through your farm. Can't we make a deal? I'm ready to be liberal—to meet you more than halfway. I'll give you an interest in the company. I think I've influence enough up at the Capitol to have you reinstated as inspector. A little reasonableness on your part will put you right again in Forlorn River, with a chance of growing rich. There's a big future here.... My interest, Belding, has become personal. Radford is in love with your step-daughter. He wants to marry her. I'll admit now if I had foreseen this situation I wouldn't have pushed you so hard. But we can square the thing. Now let's get together not only in business, but in a family way. If my son's happiness depends upon having this girl, you may rest assured I'll do all I can to get her for him. I'll absolutely make good all your losses. Now what do you say?"

"No," replied Belding. "Your money can't buy a right of way across my ranch. And Nell doesn't want your son. That settles that."

"But you could persuade her."

"I won't, that's all."

"May I ask why?" Chases's voice was losing its suave quality, but it was even swifter than before.

"Sure. I don't mind your asking," replied Belding in slow deliberation. "I wouldn't do such a low-down trick. Besides, if I would, I'd want it to be a man I was persuading for. I know Greasers—I know a Yaqui I'd rather give Nell to than your son."

Radford Chase began to roar in inarticulate rage. Belding paid no attention to him; indeed, he never glanced at the young man. The elder Chase checked a violent start. He plucked at the collar of his gray flannel shirt, opened it at the neck.

"My son's offer of marriage is an honor—more an honor, sir, than you perhaps are aware of."

Belding made no reply. His steady gaze did not turn from the long lane that led down to the river. He waited coldly, sure of himself.

"Mrs. Belding's daughter has no right to the name of Burton," snapped Chase. "Did you know that?"

"I did not," replied Belding, quietly.

"Well, you know it now," added Chase, bitingly.

"Sure you can prove what you say?" queried Belding, in the same cool, unemotional tone. It struck him strangely at the moment what little knowledge this man had of the West and of Western character.

"Prove it? Why, yes, I think so, enough to make the truth plain to any reasonable man. I come from Peoria—was born and raised there. I went to school with Nell Warren. That was your wife's maiden name. She was a beautiful, gay girl. All the fellows were in love with her. I knew Bob Burton well. He was a splendid fellow, but wild. Nobody ever knew for sure, but we all supposed he was engaged to marry Nell. He left Peoria, however, and soon after that the truth about Nell came out. She ran away. It was at least a couple of months before Burton showed up in Peoria. He did not stay long. Then for years nothing was heard of either of them. When word did come Nell was in Oklahoma, Burton was in Denver. There's chance, of course, that Burton followed Nell and married her. That would account for Nell Warren taking the name of Burton. But it isn't likely. None of us ever heard of such a thing and wouldn't have believed it if we had. The affair seemed destined to end unfortunately. But Belding, while I'm at it, I want to say that Nell Warren was one of the sweetest, finest, truest girls in the world. If she drifted to the Southwest and kept her past a secret that was only natural. Certainly it should not be held against her. Why, she was only a child—a girl—seventeen—eighteen years old.... In a moment of amazement—when I recognized your wife as an old schoolmate—I blurted the thing out to Radford. You see now how little it matters to me when I ask your stepdaughter's hand in marriage for my son."

Belding stood listening. The genuine emotion in Chase's voice was as strong as the ring of truth. Belding knew truth when he heard it. The revelation did not surprise him. Belding did not soften, for he devined that Chase's emotion was due to the probing of an old wound, the recalling of a past both happy and painful. Still, human nature was so strange that perhaps kindness and sympathy might yet have a place in this Chase's heart. Belding did not believe so, but he was willing to give Chase the benefit of the doubt.

"So you told my wife you'd respect her secret—keep her dishonor from husband and daughter?" demanded Belding, his dark gaze sweeping back from the lane.

"What! I—I" stammered Chase.

"You made your son swear to be a man and die before he'd hint the thing to Nell?" went on Belding, and his voice rang louder.

Ben Chase had no answer. The red left his face. His son slunk back against the fence.

"I say you never held this secret over the heads of my wife and her daughter?" thundered Belding.

He had his answer in the gray faces, in the lips that fear made mute. Like a flash Belding saw the whole truth of Mrs. Belding's agony, the reason for her departure; he saw what had been driving Nell; and it seemed that all the dogs of hell were loosed within his heart. He struck out blindly, instinctively in his pain, and the blow sent Ben Chase staggering into the fence corner. Then he stretched forth a long arm and whirled Radford Chase back beside his father.

"I see it all now," went on Belding, hoarsely. "You found the woman's weakness—her love for the girl. You found the girl's weakness—her pride and fear of shame. So you drove the one and hounded the other. God, what a base thing to do! To tell the girl was bad enough, but to threaten her with betrayal; there's no name for that!"

Belding's voice thickened, and he paused, breathing heavily. He stepped back a few paces; and this, an ominous action for an armed man of his kind, instead of adding to the fear of the Chases, seemed to relieve them. If there had been any pity in Belding's heart he would have felt it then.

"And now, gentlemen," continued Belding, speaking low and with difficulty, "seeing I've turned down your proposition, I suppose you think you've no more call to keep your mouths shut?"

The elder Chase appeared fascinated by something he either saw or felt in Belding, and his gray face grew grayer. He put up a shaking hand. Then Radford Chase, livid and snarling, burst out: "I'll talk till I'm black in the face. You can't stop me!"

"You'll go black in the face, but it won't be from talking," hissed Belding.

His big arm swept down, and when he threw it up the gun glittered in his hand. Simultaneously with the latter action pealed out a shrill, penetrating whistle.

The whistle of a horse! It froze Belding's arm aloft. For an instant he could not move even his eyes. The familiarity of that whistle was terrible in its power to rob him of strength. Then he heard the rapid, heavy pound of hoofs, and again the piercing whistle.

"Blanco Diablo!" he cried, huskily.

He turned to see a huge white horse come thundering into the yard. A wild, gaunt, terrible horse; indeed, the loved Blanco Diablo. A bronzed, long-haired Indian bestrode him. More white horses galloped into the yard, pounded to a halt, whistling home. Belding saw a slim shadow of a girl who seemed all great black eyes.

Under the trees flashed Blanco Sol, as dazzling white, as beautiful as if he had never been lost in the desert. He slid to a halt, then plunged and stamped. His rider leaped, throwing the bridle. Belding saw a powerful, spare, ragged man, with dark, gaunt face and eyes of flame.

Then Nell came running from the house, her golden hair flying, her hands outstretched, her face wonderful.

"Dick! Dick! Oh-h-h, Dick!" she cried. Her voice seemed to quiver in Belding's heart.

Belding's eyes began to blur. He was not sure he saw clearly. Whose face was this now close before him—a long thin, shrunken face, haggard, tragic in its semblance of torture, almost of death? But the eyes were keen and kind. Belding thought wildly that they proved he was not dreaming.

"I shore am glad to see you all," said a well-remembered voice in a slow, cool drawl.

XVIII REALITY AGAINST DREAMS

LADD, Lash, Thorne, Mercedes, they were all held tight in Belding's arms. Then he ran to Blanco Diablo. For once the great horse was gentle, quiet, glad. He remembered this kindest of masters and reached for him with warm, wet muzzle.

Dick Gale was standing bowed over Nell's slight form, almost hidden in his arms. Belding hugged them both. He was like a boy. He saw Ben Chase and his son slip away under the trees, but the circumstances meant nothing to him then.

"Dick! Dick!" he roared. "Is it you?... Say, who do you think's here—here, in Forlorn River?"

Gale gripped Belding with a hand as rough and hard as a file and as strong as a vise. But he did not speak a word. Belding thought Gale's eyes would haunt him forever.

It was then three more persons came upon the scene—Elsie Gale, running swiftly, her father assisting Mrs. Gale, who appeared about to faint.

"Belding! Who on earth's that?" cried Dick hoarsely.

"Quien sabe, my son," replied Belding; and now his voice seemed a little shaky. "Nell, come here. Give him a chance."

Belding slipped his arm round Nell, and whispered in her ear. "This 'll be great!"

Elsie Gale's face was white and agitated, a face expressing extreme joy.

"Oh, brother! Mama saw you—Papa saw you, and never knew you! But I knew you when you jumped quick—that way—off your horse. And now I don't know you. You wild man! You giant! You splendid barbarian!... Mama, Papa, hurry! It is Dick! Look at him. Just look at him! Oh-h, thank God!"

Belding turned away and drew Nell with him. In another second she and Mercedes were clasped in each other's arms. Then followed a time of joyful greetings all round.

The Yaqui stood leaning against a tree watching the welcoming home of the lost. No one seemed to think of him, until Belding, ever mindful of the needs of horses, put a hand on Blanco Diablo and called to Yaqui to bring the others. They led the string of whites down to the barn, freed them of wet and dusty saddles and packs, and turned them loose in the alfalfa, now breast-high. Diablo found his old spirit; Blanco Sol tossed his head and whistled his satisfaction; White Woman pranced to and fro; and presently they all settled down to quiet grazing. How good it was for Belding to see those white shapes against the rich background of green! His eyes glistened. It was a sight he had never expected to see again. He lingered there many moments when he wanted to hurry back to his rangers.

At last he tore himself away from watching Blanco Diablo and returned to the house. It was only to find that he might have spared himself the hurry. Jim and Ladd were lying on the beds that had not held them for so many months. Their slumber seemed as deep and quiet as death. Curiously Belding gazed down upon them. They had removed only boots and chaps. Their clothes were in tatters. Jim appeared little more than skin and bones, a long shape, dark and hard as iron. Ladd's appearance shocked Belding. The ranger looked an old man, blasted, shriveled, starved. Yet his gaunt face, though terrible in its records of tortures, had something fine and noble, even beautiful to Belding, in its strength, its victory.

Thorne and Mercedes had disappeared. The low murmur of voices came from Mrs. Gale's room, and Belding concluded that Dick was still with his family. No doubt he, also, would soon seek rest and sleep. Belding went through the patio and called in at Nell's door. She was there sitting by her window. The flush of happiness had not left her face, but she looked stunned, and a shadow of fear lay dark in her eyes. Belding had intended to talk. He wanted some one to listen to him. The expression in Nell's eyes, however, silenced him. He had forgotten. Nell read his thought in his face, and then she lost all her color and dropped her head. Belding entered, stood beside her with a hand on hers. He tried desperately hard to think of the right thing to say, and realized so long as he tried that he could not speak at all.

"Nell—Dick's back safe and sound," he said, slowly. "That's the main thing. I wish you could have seen his eyes when he held you in his arms out there.... Of course, Dick's coming knocks out your trip East and changes plans generally. We haven't had the happiest time lately. But now it'll be different. Dick's as true as a Yaqui. He'll chase that Chase fellow, don't mistake me.... Then mother will be home soon. She'll straighten out this—this mystery. And Nell—however it turns out—I know Dick Gale will feel just the same as I feel. Brace up now, girl."

Belding left the patio and traced thoughtful steps back toward the corrals. He realized the need of his wife. If she had been at home he would not have come so close to killing two men. Nell would never have fallen so low in spirit. Whatever the real truth of the tragedy of his wife's life, it would not make the slightest difference to him. What hurt him was the pain mother and daughter had suffered, were suffering still. Somehow he must put an end to that pain.

He found the Yaqui curled up in a corner of the barn in as deep a sleep as that of the rangers. Looking down at him, Belding felt again the rush of curious thrilling eagerness to learn all that had happened since the dark night when Yaqui had led the white horses away into the desert. Belding curbed his impatience and set to work upon tasks he had long neglected. Presently he was interrupted by Mr. Gale, who came out, beside himself with happiness and excitement. He flung a hundred questions at Belding and never gave him time to answer one, even if that had been possible. Finally, when Mr. Gale lost his breath, Belding got a word in. "See here, Mr. Gale, you know as much as I know. Dick's back. They're all back—a hard lot, starved, burned, torn to pieces, worked out to the limit I never saw in desert travelers, but they're alive—alive and well, man! Just wait. Just gamble I won't sleep or eat till I hear that story. But they've got to sleep and eat."

Belding gathered with growing amusement that besides the joy, excitement, anxiety, impatience expressed by Mr. Gale there was something else which Belding took for pride. It pleased him. Looking back, he remembered some of the things Dick had confessed his father thought of him. Belding's sympathy had always been with the boy. But he had learned to like the old man, to find him kind and wise, and to think that perhaps college and business had not brought out the best in Richard Gale. The West had done that, however, as it had for many a wild youngster; and Belding resolved to have a little fun at the expense of Mr. Gale. So he began by making a few remarks that appeared to rob Dick's father of both speech and breath.

"And don't mistake me," concluded Belding, "just keep out of earshot when Laddy tells us the story of that desert trip, unless you're hankering to have your hair turn pure white and stand curled on end and freeze that way."

About the middle of the forenoon on the following day the rangers hobbled out of the kitchen to the porch.

"I'm a sick man, I tell you," Ladd was complaining, "an' I gotta be fed. Soup! Beef tea! That ain't so much as wind to me. I want about a barrel of bread an' butter, an' a whole platter of mashed potatoes with gravy an' green stuff—all kinds of green stuff—an' a whole big apple pie. Give me everythin' an' anythin' to eat but meat. Shore I never, never want to taste meat again, an' sight of a piece of sheep meat would jest about finish me.... Jim, you used to be a human bein' that stood up for Charlie Ladd."

"Laddy, I'm lined up beside you with both guns," replied Jim, plaintively. "Hungry? Say, the smell of breakfast in that kitchen made my mouth water so I near choked to death. I reckon we're gettin' most onhuman treatment."

"But I'm a sick man," protested Ladd, "an' I'm agoin' to fall over in a minute if somebody doesn't feed me. Nell, you used to be fond of me."

"Oh, Laddy, I am yet," replied Nell.

"Shore I don't believe it. Any girl with a tender heart just couldn't let a man starve under her eyes... Look at Dick, there. I'll bet he's had something to eat, mebbe potatoes an' gravy, an' pie an'—"

"Laddy, Dick has had no more than I gave you—indeed, not nearly so much."

"Shore he's had a lot of kisses then, for he hasn't hollered onct about this treatment."

"Perhaps he has," said Nell, with a blush; "and if you think that—they would help you to be reasonable I might—I'll—"

"Well, powerful fond as I am of you, just now kisses 'll have to run second to bread an' butter."

"Oh, Laddy, what a gallant speech!" laughed Nell. "I'm sorry, but I've Dad's orders."

"Laddy," interrupted Belding, "you've got to be broke in gradually to eating. Now you know that. You'd be the severest kind of a boss if you had some starved beggars on your hands."

"But I'm sick—I'm dyin'," howled Ladd.

"You were never sick in your life, and if all the bullet holes I see in you couldn't kill you, why, you never will die."

"Can I smoke?" queried Ladd, with sudden animation. "My Gawd, I used to smoke. Shore I've forgot. Nell, if you want to be reinstated in my gallery of angels, just find me a pipe an' tobacco."

"I've hung onto my pipe," said Jim, thoughtfully. "I reckon I had it empty in my mouth for seven years or so, wasn't it, Laddy? A long time! I can see the red lava an' the red haze, an' the red twilight creepin' up. It was hot an' some lonely. Then the wind, and always that awful silence! An' always Yaqui watchin' the west, an' Laddy with his checkers, an' Mercedes burnin' up, wastin' away to nothin' but eyes! It's all there—I'll never get rid—"

"Chop that kind of talk," interrupted Belding, bluntly. "Tell us where Yaqui took you—what happened to Rojas—why you seemed lost for so long."

"I reckon Laddy can tell all that best; but when it comes to Rojas's finish I'll tell what I seen, an' so'll Dick an' Thorne. Laddy missed Rojas's finish. Bar none, that was the—"

"I'm a sick man, but I can talk," put in Ladd, "an' shore I don't want the whole story exaggerated none by Jim."

Ladd filled the pipe Nell brought, puffed ecstatically at it, and settled himself upon the bench for a long talk. Nell glanced appealingly at Dick, who tried to slip away. Mercedes did go, and was followed by Thorne. Mr. Gale brought chairs, and in subdued excitement called his wife and daughter. Belding leaned forward, rendered all the more eager by Dick's reluctance to stay, the memory of the quick tragic change in the expression of Mercedes's beautiful eyes, by the strange gloomy cast stealing over Ladd's face.

The ranger talked for two hours—talked till his voice weakened to a husky whisper. At the conclusion of his story there was an impressive silence. Then Elsie Gale stood up, and with her hand on Dick's shoulder, her eyes bright and warm as sunlight, she showed the rangers what a woman thought of them and of the Yaqui. Nell clung to Dick, weeping silently. Mrs. Gale was overcome, and Mr. Gale, very white and quiet, helped her up to her room.

"The Indian! the Indian!" burst out Belding, his voice deep and rolling. "What did I tell you? Didn't I say he'd be a godsend? Remember what I said about Yaqui and some gory Aztec knifework? So he cut Rojas loose from that awful crater wall, foot by foot, finger by finger, slow and terrible? And Rojas didn't hang long on the *choya* thorns? Thank the Lord for that!... Laddy, no story of Camino del Diablo can hold a candle to yours. The flight and the fight were jobs for men.

But living through this long hot summer and coming out—that's a miracle. Only the Yaqui could have done it. The Yaqui! The Yaqui!"

"Shore. Charlie Ladd looks up at an Indian these days. But Beldin', as for the comin' out, don't forget the hosses. Without grand old Sol an' Diablo, who I don't hate no more, an' the other Blancos, we'd never have got here. Yaqui an' the hosses, that's my story!"

Early in the afternoon of the next day Belding encountered Dick at the water barrel.

"Belding, this is river water, and muddy at that," said Dick. "Lord knows I'm not kicking. But I've dreamed some of our cool running spring, and I want a drink from it."

"Never again, son. The spring's gone, faded, sunk, dry as dust."

"Dry!" Gale slowly straightened. "We've had rains. The river's full. The spring ought to be overflowing. What's wrong? Why is it dry?"

"Dick, seeing you're interested, I may as well tell you that a big charge of nitroglycerin choked my spring."

"Nitroglycerin?" echoed Gale. Then he gave a quick start. "My mind's been on home, Nell, my family. But all the same I felt something was wrong here with the ranch, with you, with Nell... Belding, that ditch there is dry. The roses are dead. The little green in that grass has come with the rains. What's happened? The ranch's run down. Now I look around I see a change."

"Some change, yes," replied Belding, bitterly. "Listen, son."

Briefly, but not the less forcibly for that, Belding related his story of the operations of the Chases.

Astonishment appeared to be Gale's first feeling. "Our water gone, our claims gone, our plans forestalled! Why, Belding, it's unbelievable. Forlorn River with promoters, business, railroad, bank, and what not!"

Suddenly he became fiery and suspicious. "These Chases—did they do all this on the level?"

"Barefaced robbery! Worse than a Greaser holdup," replied Belding, grimly.

"You say the law upheld them?"

"Sure. Why, Ben Chase has a pull as strong as Diablo's on a down grade. Dick, we're jobbed, outfigured, beat, tricked, and we can't do a thing."

"Oh, I'm sorry, Belding, most of all for Laddy," said Gale, feelingly. "He's all in. He'll never ride again. He wanted to settle down here on the farm he thought he owned, grow grass and raise horses, and take it easy. Oh, but it's tough! Say, he doesn't know it yet. He was just telling me he'd like to go out and look the farm over. Who's going to tell him? What's he going to do when he finds out about this deal?"

"Son, that's made me think some," replied Belding, with keen eyes fast upon the young man. "And I was kind of wondering how you'd take it."

"I? Well, I'll call on the Chases. Look here, Belding, I'd better do some forestalling myself. If Laddy gets started now there'll be blood spilled. He's not just right in his mind yet. He talks in his sleep sometimes about how Yaqui finished Rojas. If it's left to him—he'll kill these men. But if I take it up—"

"You're talking sense, Dick. Only here, I'm not so sure of you. And there's more to tell. Son, you've Nell to think of and your mother."

Belding's ranger gave him a long and searching glance.

"You can be sure of me," he said.

"All right, then; listen," began Belding. With deep voice that had many a beak and tremor he told Gale how Nell had been hounded by Radford Chase, how her mother had been driven by Ben Chase—the whole sad story.

"So that's the trouble! Poor little girl!" murmured Gale, brokenly. "I felt something was wrong. Nell wasn't natural, like her old self. And when I begged her to marry me soon, while Dad was here, she couldn't talk. She could only cry."

"It was hard on Nell," said Belding, simply. "But it 'll be better now you're back. Dick, I know the girl. She'll refuse to marry you and you'll have a hard job to break her down, as hard as the one you just rode in off of. I think I know you, too, or I wouldn't be saying—"

"Belding, what 're you hinting at?" demanded Gale. "Do you dare insinuate that—that—if the thing were true it'd make any difference to me?"

"Aw, come now, Dick; I couldn't mean that. I'm only awkward at saying things. And I'm cut pretty deep—"

"For God's sake, you don't believe what Chase said?" queried Gale, in passionate haste. "It's a lie. I swear it's a lie. I know it's a lie. And I've got to tell Nell this minute. Come on in with me. I want you, Belding. Oh, why didn't you tell me sooner?"

Belding felt himself dragged by an iron arm into the sitting-room out into the patio, and across that to where Nell sat in her door. At sight of them she gave a little cry, drooped for an instant, then raised a pale, still face, with eyes beginning to darken.

"Dearest, I know now why you are not wearing my mother's ring," said Gale, steadily and low-voiced.

"Dick, I am not worthy," she replied, and held out a trembling hand with the ring lying in the palm.

Swift as light Gale caught her hand and slipped the ring back upon the third finger.

"Nell! Look at me. It is your engagement ring.... Listen. I don't believe this—this thing that's been torturing you. I know it's a lie. I am absolutely sure your mother will prove it a lie. She must have suffered once—perhaps there was a sad error—but the thing you fear is not true. But, hear me, dearest; even if it was true it wouldn't make the slightest difference to me. I'd promise you on my honor I'd never think of it again. I'd love you all the more because you'd suffered. I want you all the more to be my wife—to let me make you forget—to—"

She rose swiftly with the passionate abandon of a woman stirred to her depths, and she kissed him.

"Oh, Dick, you're good—so good! You'll never know—just what those words mean to me. They've saved me—I think."

"Then, dearest, it's all right?" Dick questioned, eagerly. "You will keep your promise? You will marry me?"

The glow, the light faded out of her face, and now the blue eyes were almost black. She drooped and shook her head.

"Nell!" exclaimed Gale, sharply catching his breath.

"Don't ask me, Dick. I—I won't marry you."

"Why?"

"You know. It's true that I—"

"It's a lie," interrupted Gale, fiercely. "But even if it's true—why—why won't you marry me? Between you and me love is the thing. Love, and nothing else! Don't you love me any more?"

They had forgotten Belding, who stepped back into the shade.

"I love you with my whole heart and soul. I'd die for you," whispered Nell, with clenching hands. "But I won't disgrace you."

"Dear, you have worried over this trouble till you're morbid. It has grown out of all proportion. I tell you that I'll not only be the happiest man on earth, but the luckiest, if you marry me."

"Dick, you give not one thought to your family. Would they receive me as your wife?"

"They surely would," replied Gale, steadily.

"No! oh no!"

"You're wrong, Nell. I'm glad you said that. You give me a chance to prove something. I'll go this minute and tell them all. I'll be back here in less than—"

"Dick, you will not tell her—your mother?" cried Nell, with her eyes streaming. "You will not? Oh, I can't bear it! She's so proud! And Dick, I love her. Don't tell her! Please, please don't! She'll be going soon. She needn't ever know—about me. I want her always to think well of me. Dick, I beg of you. Oh, the fear of her knowing has been the worst of all! Please don't go!"

"Nell, I'm sorry. I hate to hurt you. But you're wrong. You can't see things clearly. This is your happiness I'm fighting for. And it's my life.... Wait here, dear. I won't be long."

Gale ran across the patio and disappeared. Nell sank to the doorstep, and as she met the question in Belding's eyes she shook her head mournfully. They waited without speaking. It seemed a long while before Gale returned. Belding thrilled at sight of him. There was more boy about him than Belding had ever seen. Dick was coming swiftly, flushed, glowing, eager, erect, almost smiling.

"I told them. I swore it was a lie, but I wanted them to decide as if it were true. I didn't have to waste a minute on Elsie. She loves you, Nell. The Governor is crazy about you. I didn't have to waste two minutes on him. Mother used up the time. She wanted to know all there was to tell. She is proud, yes; but, Nell, I wish you could have seen how she took the—the story about you. Why, she never thought of me at all, until she had cried over you. Nell, she loves you, too. They all love you. Oh, it's so good to tell you. I think mother realizes the part you have had in the—what shall I call it?—the regeneration of Richard Gale. Doesn't that sound fine? Darling, mother not only consents, she wants you to be my wife. Do you hear that? And listen—she had me in a corner and, of course, being my mother, she put on the screws. She made me promise that we'd live in the East half the year. That means Chicago, Cape May, New York—you see, I'm not exactly the lost son any more. Why, Nell, dear, you'll have to learn who Dick Gale really is. But I always want to be the ranger you helped me become, and ride Blanco Sol, and see a little of the desert. Don't let the idea of big cities frighten you. W'ell always love the open places best. Now, Nell, say you'll forget this trouble. I know it'll come all right. Say you'll marry me soon.... Why, dearest, you're crying.... Nell!"

"My—heart—is broken," sobbed Nell, "for—I—I—can't marry you."

The boyish brightness faded out of Gale's face. Here, Belding saw, was the stern reality arrayed against his dreams.

"That devil Radford Chase—he'll tell my secret," panted Nell. "He swore if you ever came back and married me he'd follow us all over the world to tell it."

Belding saw Gale grow deathly white and suddenly stand stock-still.

"Chase threatened you, then?" asked Dick; and the forced naturalness of his voice struck Belding.

"Threatened me? He made my life a nightmare," replied Nell, in a rush of speech. "At first I wondered how he was worrying mother sick. But she wouldn't tell me. Then when she went away he began to hint things. I hated him all the more. But when he told me—I was frightened, shamed. Still I did not weaken. He was pretty decent when he was sober. But when he was half drunk he was the devil. He laughed at me and my pride. I didn't dare shut the door in his face. After a while he found out that your mother loved me and that I loved her. Then he began to threaten me. If I didn't give in to him he'd see she learned the truth. That made me weaken. It nearly killed me. I simply could not bear the thought of Mrs. Gale knowing. But I couldn't marry him. Besides, he got so half the time, when he was drunk, he didn't want or ask me to be his wife. I was about ready to give up and go mad when you—you came home."

She ended in a whisper, looking up wistfully and sadly at him. Belding was a raging fire within, cold without. He watched Gale, and believed he could foretell that young man's future conduct. Gale gathered Nell up into his arms and held her to his breast for a long moment.

"Dear Nell, I'm sure the worst of your trouble is over," he said gently. "I will not give you up. Now, won't you lie down, try to rest and calm yourself. Don't grieve any more. This thing isn't so bad as you make it. Trust me. I'll shut Mr. Radford Chase's mouth."

As he released her she glanced quickly up at him, then lifted appealing hands.

"Dick, you won't hunt for him—go after him?"

Gale laughed, and the laugh made Belding jump.

"Dick, I beg of you. Please don't make trouble. The Chases have been hard enough on us. They are rich, powerful. Dick, say you will not make matters worse. Please promise me you'll not go to him."

"You ask me that?" he demanded.

"Yes. Oh yes!"

"But you know it's useless. What kind of a man do you want me to be?"

"It's only that I'm afraid. Oh, Dick, he'd shoot you in the back."

"No, Nell, a man of his kind wouldn't have nerve enough even for that."

"You'll go?" she cried wildly.

Gale smiled, and the smile made Belding cold.

"Dick, I cannot keep you back?"

"No," he said.

Then the woman in her burst through instinctive fear, and with her eyes blazing black in her white face she lifted parted quivering lips and kissed him.

Gale left the patio, and Belding followed closely at his heels. They went through the sitting-room. Outside upon the porch sat the rangers, Mr. Gale, and Thorne. Dick went into his room without speaking.

"Shore somethin's comin' off," said Ladd, sharply; and he sat up with keen eyes narrowing.

Belding spoke a few words; and, remembering an impression he had wished to make upon Mr. Gale, he made them strong. But now it was with grim humor that he spoke.

"Better stop that boy," he concluded, looking at Mr. Gale. "He'll do some mischief. He's wilder'n hell."

"Stop him? Why, assuredly," replied Mr. Gale, rising with nervous haste.

Just then Dick came out of his door. Belding eyed him keenly. The only change he could see was that Dick had put on a hat and a pair of heavy gloves.

"Richard, where are you going?" asked his father.

"I'm going over here to see a man."

"No. It is my wish that you remain. I forbid you to go," said Mr. Gale, with a hand on his son's shoulder.

Dick put Mr. Gale aside gently, respectfully, yet forcibly. The old man gasped.

"Dad, I haven't gotten over my bad habit of disobeying you. I'm sorry. Don't interfere with me now. And don't follow me. You might see something unpleasant."

"But my son! What are you going to do?"

"I'm going to beat a dog."

Mr. Gale looked helplessly from this strangely calm and cold son to the restless Belding. Then Dick strode off the porch.

"Hold on!" Ladd's voice would have stopped almost any man. "Dick, you wasn't agoin' without me?"

"Yes, I was. But I'm thoughtless just now, Laddy."

"Shore you was. Wait a minute, Dick. I'm a sick man, but at that nobody can pull any stunts round here without me."

He hobbled along the porch and went into his room. Jim Lash knocked the ashes out of his pipe, and, humming his dance tune, he followed Ladd. In a moment the rangers appeared, and both were packing guns.

Not a little of Belding's grim excitement came from observation of Mr. Gale. At sight of the rangers with their guns the old man turned white and began to tremble.

"Better stay behind," whispered Belding. "Dick's going to beat that two-legged dog, and the rangers get excited when they're packing guns."

"I will not stay behind," replied Mr. Gale, stoutly. "I'll see this affair through. Belding, I've guessed it. Richard is going to fight the Chases, those robbers who have ruined you."

"Well, I can't guarantee any fight on their side," returned Belding, dryly. "But maybe there'll be Greasers with a gun or two."

Belding stalked off to catch up with Dick, and Mr. Gale came trudging behind with Thorne.

"Where will we find these Chases?" asked Dick of Belding.

"They've got a place down the road adjoining the inn. They call it their club. At this hour Radford will be there sure. I don't know about the old man. But his office is now just across the way."

They passed several houses, turned a corner into the main street, and stopped at a wide, low adobe structure. A number of saddled horses stood haltered to posts. Mexicans lolled around the wide doorway.

"There's Ben Chase now over on the corner," said Belding to Dick. "See, the tall man with the white hair, and leather band on his hat. He sees us. He knows there's something up. He's got men with him. They'll come over. We're after the young buck, and sure he'll be in here."

They entered. The place was a hall, and needed only a bar to make it a saloon. There were two rickety pool tables. Evidently Chase had fitted up this amusement room for his laborers as well as for the use of his engineers and assistants, for the crowd contained both Mexicans and Americans. A large table near a window was surrounded by a noisy, smoking, drinking circle of card-players.

"Point out this Radford Chase to me," said Gale.

"There! The big fellow with the red face. His eyes stick out a little. See! He's dropped his cards and his face isn't red any more."

Dick strode across the room.

Belding grasped Mr. Gale and whispered hoarsely: "Don't miss anything. It'll be great. Watch Dick and watch Laddy! If there's any gun play, dodge behind me."

Belding smiled with a grim pleasure as he saw Mr. Gales' face turn white.

Dick halted beside the table. His heavy boot shot up, and with a crash the table split, and glasses, cards, chips flew everywhere. As they rattled down and the chairs of the dumfounded players began to slide Dick called out: "My name is Gale. I'm looking for Mr. Radford Chase."

A tall, heavy-shouldered fellow rose, boldly enough, even swaggeringly, and glowered at Gale.

"I'm Radford Chase," he said. His voice betrayed the boldness of his action.

It was over in a few moments. The tables and chairs were tumbled into a heap; one of the pool tables had been shoved aside; a lamp lay shattered, with oil running dark upon the floor. Ladd leaned against a post with a smoking gun in his hand. A Mexican crouched close to the wall moaning over a broken arm. In the far corner upheld by comrades another wounded Mexican cried out in pain. These two had attempted to draw weapons upon Gale, and Ladd had crippled them.

In the center of the room lay Radford Chase, a limp, torn, hulking, bloody figure. He was not seriously injured. But he was helpless, a miserable beaten wretch, who knew his condition and felt the eyes upon him. He sobbed and moaned and howled. But no one offered to help him to his feet.

Backed against the door of the hall stood Ben Chase, for once stripped of all authority and confidence and courage. Gale confronted him, and now Gale's mien was in striking contrast to the coolness with which he had entered the place. Though sweat dripped from his face, it was as white as chalk. Like dark flames his eyes seemed to leap and dance and burn. His lean jaw hung down and quivered with passion. He shook a huge gloved fist in Chase's face.

"Your gray hairs save you this time. But keep out of my way! And when that son of yours comes to, tell him every time I meet him I'll add some more to what he got to-day!"

XIX THE SECRET OF FORLORN RIVER

IN the early morning Gale, seeking solitude where he could brood over his trouble, wandered alone. It was not easy for him to elude the Yaqui, and just at the moment when he had cast himself down in a secluded shady corner the Indian appeared, noiseless, shadowy, mysterious as always.

"Malo," he said, in his deep voice.

"Yes, Yaqui, it's bad—very bad," replied Gale.

The Indian had been told of the losses sustained by Belding and his rangers.

"Go—me!" said Yaqui, with an impressive gesture toward the lofty lilac-colored steps of No Name Mountains.

He seemed the same as usual, but a glance on Gale's part, a moment's attention, made him conscious of the old strange force in the Yaqui. "Why does my brother want me to climb the nameless mountains with him?" asked Gale.

"Lluvia d'oro," replied Yaqui, and he made motions that Gale found difficult of interpretation.

"Shower of Gold," translated Gale. That was the Yaqui's name for Nell. What did he mean by using it in connection with a climb into the mountains? Were his motions intended to convey an idea of a shower of golden blossoms from that rare and beautiful tree, or a golden rain? Gale's listlessness vanished in a flash of thought. The Yaqui meant gold. Gold! He meant he could retrieve the fallen fortunes of the white brother who had saved his life that evil day at the Papago Well. Gale thrilled as he gazed piercingly into the wonderful eyes of this Indian. Would Yaqui never consider his debt paid?

"Go—me?" repeat the Indian, pointing with the singular directness that always made this action remarkable in him.

"Yes, Yaqui."

Gale ran to his room, put on hobnailed boots, filled a canteen, and hurried back to the corral. Yaqui awaited him. The Indian carried a coiled lasso and a short stout stick. Without a word he led the way down the lane, turned up the river toward the mountains. None of Belding's household saw their departure.

What had once been only a narrow mesquite-bordered trail was now a well-trodden road. A deep irrigation ditch, full of flowing muddy water, ran parallel with the road. Gale had been curious about the operations of the Chases, but bitterness he could not help had kept him from going out to see the work. He was not surprised to find that the engineers who had constructed the ditches and dam had anticipated him in every particular. The dammed-up gulch made a magnificent reservoir, and Gale could not look upon the long narrow lake without a feeling of gladness. The dreaded ano seco of the Mexicans might come again and would come, but never to the inhabitants of Forlorn River. That stone-walled, stone-floored gulch would never leak, and already it contained water enough to irrigate the whole Altar Valley for two dry seasons.

Yaqui led swiftly along the lake to the upper end, where the stream roared down over unscalable walls. This point was the farthest Gale had ever penetrated into the rough foothills, and he had Belding's word for it that no white man had ever climbed No Name Mountains from the west.

But a white man was not an Indian. The former might have stolen the range and valley and mountain, even the desert, but his possessions would ever remain mysteries. Gale had scarcely faced the great gray ponderous wall of cliff before the old strange interest in the Yaqui seized him again. It recalled the tie that existed between them, a tie almost as close as blood. Then he was eager and curious to see how the Indian would conquer those seemingly insurmountable steps of stone.

Yaqui left the gulch and clambered up over a jumble of weathered slides and traced a slow course along the base of the giant wall. He looked up and seemed to select a point for ascent. It was the last place in that mountainside where Gale would have thought climbing possible. Before him the wall rose, leaning over him, shutting out the light, a dark mighty mountain mass. Innumerable cracks and crevices and caves roughened the bulging sides of dark rock.

Yaqui tied one end of his lasso to the short, stout stick and, carefully disentangling the coils, he whirled the stick round and round and threw it almost over the first rim of the shelf, perhaps thirty feet up. The stick did not lodge. Yaqui tried again. This time it caught in a crack. He pulled hard. Then, holding to the lasso, he walked up the steep slant, hand over hand on the rope. When he reached the shelf he motioned for Gale to follow. Gale found that method of scaling a wall both quick and easy. Yaqui pulled up the lasso, and threw the stick aloft into another crack. He climbed to another shelf, and Gale followed him. The third effort brought them to a more rugged bench a hundred feet above the slides. The Yaqui worked round to the left, and turned into a dark fissure. Gale kept close to his heels. They came out presently into lighter space, yet one that restricted any extended view. Broken sections of cliff were on all sides.

Here the ascent became toil. Gale could distance Yaqui going downhill; on the climb, however, he was hard put to it to keep the Indian in sight. It was not a question of strength or lightness of foot. These Gale had beyond the share of most men. It was a matter of lung power, and the Yaqui's life had been spent scaling the desert heights. Moreover, the climbing was infinitely slow, tedious, dangerous. On the way up several times Gale imagined he heard a dull roar of falling water. The sound seemed to be under him, over him to this side and to that. When he was certain he could locate the direction from which it came then he heard it no more until he had gone on. Gradually he forgot it in the physical sensations of the climb. He burned his hands and knees. He grew hot and wet and winded. His heart thumped so that it hurt, and there were instants when his sight was blurred. When at last he had toiled to where the Yaqui sat awaiting him upon the rim of that great wall, it was none too soon.

Gale lay back and rested for a while without note of anything except the blue sky. Then he sat up. He was amazed to find that after that wonderful climb he was only a thousand feet or so above the valley. Judged by the nature of his effort, he would have said he had climbed a mile. The village lay beneath him, with its new adobe structures and tents and buildings in bright contrast with the older habitations. He saw the green alfalfa fields, and Belding's white horses, looking very small and motionless. He pleased himself by imagining he could pick out Blanco Sol. Then his gaze swept on to the river.

Indeed, he realized now why some one had named it Forlorn River. Even at this season when it was full of water it had a forlorn aspect. It was doomed to fail out there on the desert—doomed never to mingle with the waters of the Gulf. It wound away down the valley, growing wider and shallower, encroaching more and more on the gray flats, until it disappeared on its sad journey toward Sonoyta. That vast shimmering, sun-governed waste recognized its life only at this flood season, and was already with parched tongue and insatiate fire licking and burning up its futile waters.

Yaqui put a hand on Gale's knee. It was a bronzed, scarred, powerful hand, always eloquent of meaning. The Indian was listening. His bent head, his strange dilating eyes, his rigid form, and that close-pressing hand, how these brought back to Gale the terrible lonely night hours on the lava!

"What do you hear, Yaqui?" asked Gale. He laughed a little at the mood that had come over him. But the sound of his voice did not break the spell. He did not want to speak again. He yielded to Yaqui's subtle nameless influence. He listened himself, heard nothing but the scream of an eagle. Often he wondered if the Indian could hear things that made no sound. Yaqui was beyond understanding.

Whatever the Indian had listened to or for, presently he satisfied himself, and, with a grunt that might mean anything, he rose and turned away from the rim. Gale followed, rested now and eager to go on. He saw that the great cliff they had climbed was only a stairway up to the huge looming dark bulk of the plateau above.

Suddenly he again heard the dull roar of falling water. It seemed to have cleared itself of muffled vibrations. Yaqui mounted a little ridge and halted. The next instant Gale stood above a bottomless cleft into which a white stream leaped. His astounded gaze swept backward along this narrow swift stream to its end in a dark, round, boiling pool. It was a huge spring, a bubbling well, the outcropping of an underground river coming down from the vast plateau above.

Yaqui had brought Gale to the source of Forlorn River.

Flashing thoughts in Gale's mind were no swifter than the thrills that ran over him. He would stake out a claim here and never be cheated out of it. Ditches on the benches and troughs on the steep walls would carry water down to the valley. Ben Chase had build a great dam which would be useless if Gale chose to turn Forlorn River from its natural course. The fountain head of that mysterious desert river belonged to him.

His eagerness, his mounting passion, was checked by Yaqui's unusual action. The Indian showed wonder, hesitation, even reluctance. His strange eyes surveyed this boiling well as if they could not believe the sight they saw. Gale divined instantly that Yaqui had never before seen the source of Forlorn River. If he had ever ascended to this plateau, probably it had been to some other part, for the water was new to him. He stood gazing aloft at peaks, at lower ramparts of the mountain, and at nearer landmarks of prominence. Yaqui seemed at fault. He was not sure of his location.

Then he strode past the swirling pool of dark water and began to ascend a little slope that led up to a shelving cliff. Another object halted the Indian. It was a pile of stones, weathered, crumbled, fallen into ruin, but still retaining shape enough to prove it had been built there by the hands of men. Round and round this the Yaqui stalked, and his curiosity attested a further uncertainty. It was as if he had come upon something surprising. Gale wondered about the pile of stones. Had it once been a prospector's claim?

"Ugh!" grunted the Indian; and, though his exclamation expressed no satisfaction, it surely put an end to doubt. He pointed up to the roof of the sloping yellow shelf of stone. Faintly outlined there in red were the imprints of many human hands with fingers spread wide. Gale had often seen such paintings on the walls of the desert caverns. Manifestly these told Yaqui he had come to the spot for which he had aimed.

Then his actions became swift—and Yaqui seldom moved swiftly. The fact impressed Gale. The Indian searched the level floor under the shelf. He gathered up handfuls of small black stones, and thrust them at Gale. Their weight made Gale start, and then he trembled. The Indian's next move was to pick up a piece of weathered rock and throw it against the wall. It broke. He snatched up parts, and showed the broken edges to Gale. They contained yellow steaks, dull glints, faint tracings of green. It was gold.

Gale found his legs shaking under him; and he sat down, trying to take all the bits of stone into his lap. His fingers were all thumbs as with knife blade he dug into the black pieces of rock. He found gold. Then he stared down the slope, down into the valley with its river winding forlornly away into the desert. But he did not see any of that. Here was reality as sweet, as wonderful, as saving as a dream come true. Yaqui had led him to a ledge of gold. Gale had learned enough about mineral to know that this was a rich strike. All in a second he was speechless with the joy of it. But his mind whirled in thought about this strange and noble Indian, who seemed never to be able to pay a debt. Belding and the poverty that had come to him! Nell, who had wept over the loss of a spring! Laddy, who never could ride again! Jim Lash, who swore he would always look after his friend! Thorne and Mercedes! All these people, who had been good to him and whom he loved, were poor. But now they would be rich. They would one and all be his partners. He had discovered the source of Forlorn River, and was rich in water. Yaqui had made him rich in gold. Gale wanted to rush down the slope, down into the valley, and tell his wonderful news.

Suddenly his eyes cleared and he saw the pile of stones. His blood turned to ice, then to fire. That was the mark of a prospector's claim. But it was old, very old. The ledge had never been worked, the slope was wild. There was not another single indication that a prospector had ever been there. Where, then, was he who had first staked this claim? Gale wondered with growing hope, with the fire easing, with the cold passing.

The Yaqui uttered the low, strange, involuntary cry so rare with him, a cry somehow always associated with death. Gale shuddered.

The Indian was digging in the sand and dust under the shelving wall. He threw out an object that rang against the stone. It was a belt buckle. He threw out old shrunken, withered boots. He came upon other things, and then he ceased to dig.

The grave of desert prospectors! Gale had seen more than one. Ladd had told him many a story of such gruesome finds. It was grim, hard fact.

Then the keen-eyed Yaqui reached up to a little projecting shelf of rock and took from it a small object. He showed no curiosity and gave the thing to Gale.

How strangely Gale felt when he received into his hands a flat oblong box! Was it only the influence of the Yaqui, or was there a nameless and unseen presence beside that grave? Gale could not be sure. But he knew he had gone back to the old desert mood. He knew something hung in the balance. No accident, no luck, no debt-paying Indian could account wholly for that moment. Gale knew he held in his hands more than gold.

The box was a tin one, and not all rusty. Gale pried open the reluctant lid. A faint old musty odor penetrated his nostrils. Inside the box lay a packet wrapped in what once might have been oilskin. He took it out and removed this covering. A folded paper remained in his hands.

It was growing yellow with age. But he descried a dim tracery of words. A crabbed scrawl, written in blood, hard to read! He held it more to the light, and slowly he deciphered its content.

> "We, Robert Burton and Jonas Warren, give half of this gold claim to the man who finds it and half to Nell Burton, daughter and granddaughter."

Gasping, with a bursting heart, overwhelmed by an unutterable joy of divination, Gale fumbled with the paper until he got it open.

It was a certificate twenty-one years old, and recorded the marriage of Robert Burton and Nellie Warren.

XX DESERT GOLD

A SUMMER day dawned on Forlorn River, a beautiful, still, hot, golden day with huge sail clouds of white motionless over No Name Peaks and the purple of clear air in the distance along the desert horizon.

Mrs. Belding returned that day to find her daughter happy and the past buried forever in two lonely graves. The haunting shadow left her eyes. Gale believed he would never forget the sweetness, the wonder, the passion of her embrace when she called him her boy and gave him her blessing.

The little wrinkled padre who married Gale and Nell performed the ceremony as he told his beads, without interest or penetration, and went his way, leaving happiness behind.

"Shore I was a sick man," Ladd said, "an' darn near a dead one, but I'm agoin' to get well. Mebbe I'll be able to ride again someday. Nell, I lay it to you. An' I'm agoin' to kiss you an' wish you all the joy there is in this world. An', Dick, as Yaqui says, she's shore your Shower of Gold."

He spoke of Gale's finding love—spoke of it with the deep and wistful feeling of the lonely ranger who had always yearned for love and had never known it. Belding, once more practical, and important as never before with mining projects and water claims to manage, spoke of Gale's great good fortune in finding of gold—he called it desert gold.

"Ah, yes. Desert Gold!" exclaimed Dick's father, softly, with eyes of pride. Perhaps he was glad Dick had found the rich claim; surely he was happy that Dick had won the girl he loved. But it seemed to Dick himself that his father meant something very different from love and fortune in his allusion to desert gold.

That beautiful happy day, like life or love itself, could not be wholly perfect.

Yaqui came to Dick to say good-by. Dick was startled, grieved, and in his impulsiveness forgot for a moment the nature of the Indian. Yaqui was not to be changed.

Belding tried to overload him with gifts. The Indian packed a bag of food, a blanket, a gun, a knife, a canteen, and no more. The whole household went out with him to the corrals and fields from which Belding bade him choose a horse—any horse, even the loved Blanco Diablo. Gale's heart was in his throat for fear the Indian might choose Blanco Sol, and Gale hated himself for a selfishness he could not help. But without a word he would have parted with the treasured Sol.

Yaqui whistled the horses up—for the last time. Did he care for them? It would have been hard to say. He never looked at the fierce and haughty Diablo, nor at Blanco Sol as he raised his noble head and rang his piercing blast. The Indian did not choose one of Belding's whites. He caught a lean and wiry broncho, strapped a blanket on him, and fastened on the pack.

Then he turned to these friends, the same emotionless, inscrutable dark and silent Indian that he had always been. This parting was nothing to him. He had stayed to pay a debt, and now he was going home.

He shook hands with the men, swept a dark fleeting glance over Nell, and rested his strange eyes upon Mercedes's beautiful and agitated face. It must have been a moment of intense feeling for the Spanish girl. She owed it to him that she had life and love and happiness. She held out those speaking slender hands. But Yaqui did not touch them. Turning away, he mounted the broncho and rode down the trail toward the river.

"He's going home," said Belding.

"Home!" whispered Ladd; and Dick knew the ranger felt the resurging tide of memory. Home—across the cactus and lava, through solemn lonely days, the silent, lonely nights, into the vast and red-hazed world of desolation.

"Thorne, Mercedes, Nell, let's climb the foothill yonder and watch him out of sight," said Dick.

They climbed while the others returned to the house. When they reached the summit of the hill Yaqui was riding up the far bank of the river.

"He will turn to look—to wave good-by?" asked Nell.

"Dear he is an Indian," replied Gale.

From that height they watched him ride through the mesquites, up over the river bank to enter the cactus. His mount showed dark against the green and white, and for a long time he was plainly in sight. The sun hung red in a golden sky. The last the watchers saw of Yaqui was when he rode across a ridge and stood silhouetted against the gold of desert sky—a wild, lonely, beautiful picture. Then he was gone.

Strangely it came to Gale then that he was glad. Yaqui had returned to his own—the great spaces, the desolation, the solitude—to the trails he had trodden when a child, trails haunted now by ghosts of his people, and ever by his gods. Gale realized that in the Yaqui he had known the spirit of the desert, that this spirit had claimed all which was wild and primitive in him.

Tears glistened in Mercedes's magnificent black eyes, and Thorne kissed them away—kissed the fire back to them and the flame to her cheeks.

That action recalled Gale's earlier mood, the joy of the present, and he turned to Nell's sweet face. The desert was there, wonderful, constructive, ennobling, beautiful, terrible, but it was not for him as it was for the Indian. In the light of Nell's tremulous returning smile that strange, deep, clutching shadow faded, lost its hold forever; and he leaned close to her, whispering: "Lluvia d'oro"—"Shower of Gold."

THE RUSTLERS OF PECOS COUNTY

CHAPTER 1 VAUGHN STEELE AND RUSS SITTELL

In the morning, after breakfasting early, I took a turn up and down the main street of Sanderson, made observations and got information likely to serve me at some future day, and then I returned to the hotel ready for what might happen.

The stage-coach was there and already full of passengers. This stage did not go to Linrock, but I had found that another one left for that point three days a week.

Several cowboy broncos stood hitched to a railing and a little farther down were two buckboards, with horses that took my eye. These probably were the teams Colonel Sampson had spoken of to George Wright.

As I strolled up, both men came out of the hotel. Wright saw me, and making an almost imperceptible sign to Sampson, he walked toward me.

"You're the cowboy Russ?" he asked.

I nodded and looked him over. By day he made as striking a figure as I had noted by night, but the light was not generous to his dark face.

"Here's your pay," he said, handing me some bills. "Miss Sampson won't need you out at the ranch any more."

"What do you mean? This is the first I've heard about that."

"Sorry, kid. That's it," he said abruptly. "She just gave me the money—told me to pay you off. You needn't bother to speak with her about it."

He might as well have said, just as politely, that my seeing her, even to say good-by, was undesirable.

As my luck would have it, the girls appeared at the moment, and I went directly up to them, to be greeted in a manner I was glad George Wright could not help but see.

In Miss Sampson's smile and "Good morning, Russ," there was not the slightest discoverable sign that I was not to serve her indefinitely.

It was as I had expected—she knew nothing of Wright's discharging me in her name.

"Miss Sampson," I said, in dismay, "what have I done? Why did you let me go?"

She looked astonished.

"Russ, I don't understand you."

"Why did you discharge me?" I went on, trying to look heart-broken. "I haven't had a chance yet. I wanted so much to work for you—Miss Sally, what have I done? Why did she discharge me?"

"I did not," declared Miss Sampson, her dark eyes lighting.

"But look here—here's my pay," I went on, exhibiting the money. "Mr. Wright just came to me—said you sent this money—that you wouldn't need me out at the ranch."

It was Miss Sally then who uttered a little exclamation. Miss Sampson seemed scarcely to have believed what she had heard.

"My cousin Mr. Wright said that?"

I nodded vehemently.

At this juncture Wright strode before me, practically thrusting me aside.

"Come girls, let's walk a little before we start," he said gaily. "I'll show you Sanderson."

"Wait, please," Miss Sampson replied, looking directly at him. "Cousin George, I think there's a mistake—perhaps a misunderstanding. Here's the cowboy I've engaged—Mr. Russ. He declares you gave him money—told him I discharged him."

"Yes, cousin, I did," he replied, his voice rising a little. There was a tinge of red in his cheek. "We—you don't need him out at the ranch. We've any numbers of boys. I just told him that—let him down easy—didn't want to bother you."

Certain it was that George Wright had made a poor reckoning. First she showed utter amaze, then distinct disappointment, and then she lifted her head with a kind of haughty grace. She would have addressed him then, had not Colonel Sampson come up.

"Papa, did you instruct Cousin George to discharge Russ?" she asked.

"I sure didn't," declared the colonel, with a laugh. "George took that upon his own hands."

"Indeed! I'd like my cousin to understand that I'm my own mistress. I've been accustomed to attending to my own affairs and shall continue doing so. Russ, I'm sorry you've been treated this way. Please, in future, take your orders from me."

"Then I'm to go to Linrock with you?" I asked.

"Assuredly. Ride with Sally and me to-day, please."

She turned away with Sally, and they walked toward the first buckboard.

Colonel Sampson found a grim enjoyment in Wright's discomfiture.

"Diane's like her mother was, George," he said. "You've made a bad start with her."

Here Wright showed manifestation of the Sampson temper, and I took him to be a dangerous man, with unbridled passions.

"Russ, here's my own talk to you," he said, hard and dark, leaning toward me. "Don't go to Linrock."

"Say, Mr. Wright," I blustered for all the world like a young and frightened cowboy, "If you threaten me I'll have you put in jail!"

Both men seemed to have received a slight shock. Wright hardly knew what to make of my boyish speech. "Are you going to Linrock?" he asked thickly.

I eyed him with an entirely different glance from my other fearful one.

"I should smile," was my reply, as caustic as the most reckless cowboy's, and I saw him shake.

Colonel Sampson laid a restraining hand upon Wright. Then they both regarded me with undisguised interest. I sauntered away.

"George, your temper'll do for you some day," I heard the colonel say. "You'll get in bad with the wrong man some time. Hello, here are Joe and Brick!"

Mention of these fellows engaged my attention once more.

I saw two cowboys, one evidently getting his name from his brick-red hair. They were the roistering type, hard drinkers, devil-may-care fellows, packing guns and wearing bold fronts—a kind that the Rangers always called four-flushes.

However, as the Rangers' standard of nerve was high, there was room left for cowboys like these to be dangerous to ordinary men.

The little one was Joe, and directly Wright spoke to him he turned to look at me, and his thin mouth slanted down as he looked. Brick eyed me, too, and I saw that he was heavy, not a hard-riding cowboy.

Here right at the start were three enemies for me—Wright and his cowboys. But it did not matter; under any circumstances there would have been friction between such men and me.

I believed there might have been friction right then had not Miss Sampson called for me.

"Get our baggage, Russ," she said.

I hurried to comply, and when I had fetched it out Wright and the cowboys had mounted their horses, Colonel Sampson was in the one buckboard with two men I had not before observed, and the girls were in the other.

The driver of this one was a tall, lanky, tow-headed youth, growing like a Texas weed. We had not any too much room in the buckboard, but that fact was not going to spoil the ride for me.

We followed the leaders through the main street, out into the open, on to a wide, hard-packed road, showing years of travel. It headed northwest.

To our left rose the range of low, bleak mountains I had noted yesterday, and to our right sloped the mesquite-patched sweep of ridge and flat.

The driver pushed his team to a fast trot, which gait surely covered ground rapidly. We were close behind Colonel Sampson, who, from his vehement gestures, must have been engaged in very earnest colloquy with his companions.

The girls behind me, now that they were nearing the end of the journey, manifested less interest in the ride, and were speculating upon Linrock, and what it would be like. Occasionally I asked the driver a question, and sometimes the girls did likewise; but, to my disappointment, the ride seemed not to be the same as that of yesterday.

Every half mile or so we passed a ranch house, and as we traveled on these ranches grew further apart, until, twelve or fifteen miles out of Sanderson, they were so widely separated that each appeared alone on the wild range.

We came to a stream that ran north and I was surprised to see a goodly volume of water. It evidently flowed down from the mountain far to the west.

Tufts of grass were well scattered over the sandy ground, but it was high and thick, and considering the immense area in sight, there was grazing for a million head of stock.

We made three stops in the forenoon, one at a likely place to water the horses, the second at a chuckwagon belonging to cowboys who were riding after stock, and the third at a small cluster of adobe and stone houses, constituting a hamlet the driver called Sampson, named after the Colonel. From that point on to Linrock there were only a few ranches, each one controlling great acreage.

Early in the afternoon from a ridgetop we sighted Linrock, a green path in the mass of gray. For the barrens of Texas it was indeed a fair sight.

But I was more concerned with its remoteness from civilization than its beauty. At that time in the early 'seventies, when the vast western third of Texas was a wilderness, the pioneer had done wonders to settle there and establish places like Linrock.

As we rolled swiftly along, the whole sweeping range was dotted with cattle, and farther on, within a few miles of town, there were droves of horses that brought enthusiastic praise from Miss Sampson and her cousin.

"Plenty of room here for the long rides," I said, waving a hand at the gray-green expanse. "Your horses won't suffer on this range."

She was delighted, and her cousin for once seemed speechless.

"That's the ranch," said the driver, pointing with his whip.

It needed only a glance for me to see that Colonel Sampson's ranch was on a scale fitting the country.

The house was situated on the only elevation around Linrock, and it was not high, nor more than a few minutes' walk from the edge of town.

It was a low, flat-roofed structure, made of red adobe bricks and covered what appeared to be fully an acre of ground. All was green about it except where the fenced corrals and numerous barns or sheds showed gray and red.

Wright and the cowboys disappeared ahead of us in the cottonwood trees. Colonel Sampson got out of the buckboard and waited for us. His face wore the best expression I had seen upon it yet. There was warmth and love, and something that approached sorrow or regret.

His daughter was agitated, too. I got out and offered my seat, which Colonel Sampson took.

It was scarcely a time for me to be required, or even noticed at all, and I took advantage of it and turned toward the town.

Ten minutes of leisurely walking brought me to the shady outskirts of Linrock and I entered the town with mingled feelings of curiosity, eagerness, and expectation.

CHAPTER 1 VAUGHN STEELE AND RUSS SITTELL

The street I walked down was not a main one. There were small, red houses among oaks and cottonwoods.

I went clear through to the other side, probably more than half a mile. I crossed a number of intersecting streets, met children, nice-looking women, and more than one dusty-booted man.

Half-way back this street I turned at right angles and walked up several blocks till I came to a tree-bordered plaza. On the far side opened a broad street which for all its horses and people had a sleepy look.

I walked on, alert, trying to take in everything, wondering if I would meet Steele, wondering how I would know him if we did meet. But I believed I could have picked that Ranger out of a thousand strangers, though I had never seen him.

Presently the residences gave place to buildings fronting right upon the stone sidewalk. I passed a grain store, a hardware store, a grocery store, then several unoccupied buildings and a vacant corner.

The next block, aside from the rough fronts of the crude structures, would have done credit to a small town even in eastern Texas. Here was evidence of business consistent with any prosperous community of two thousand inhabitants.

The next block, on both sides of the street, was a solid row of saloons, resorts, hotels. Saddled horses stood hitched all along the sidewalk in two long lines, with a buckboard and team here and there breaking the continuity. This block was busy and noisy.

From all outside appearances, Linrock was no different from other frontier towns, and my expectations were scarcely realized.

As the afternoon was waning I retraced my steps and returned to the ranch. The driver boy, whom I had heard called Dick, was looking for me, evidently at Miss Sampson's order, and he led me up to the house.

It was even bigger than I had conceived from a distance, and so old that the adobe bricks were worn smooth by rain and wind. I had a glimpse in at several doors as we passed by.

There was comfort here that spoke eloquently of many a freighter's trip from Del Rio. For the sake of the young ladies, I was glad to see things little short of luxurious for that part of the country.

At the far end of the house Dick conducted me to a little room, very satisfactory indeed to me. I asked about bunk-houses for the cowboys, and he said they were full to overflowing.

"Colonel Sampson has a big outfit, eh?"

"Reckon he has," replied Dick. "Don' know how many cowboys. They're always comin' an' goin'. I ain't acquainted with half of them."

"Much movement of stock these days?"

"Stock's always movin'," he replied with a queer look.

"Rustlers?"

But he did not follow up that look with the affirmative I expected.

"Lively place, I hear—Linrock is?"

"Ain't so lively as Sanderson, but it's bigger."

"Yes, I heard it was. Fellow down there was talking about two cowboys who were arrested."

"Sure. I heerd all about thet. Joe Bean an' Brick Higgins—they belong heah, but they ain't heah much."

I did not want Dick to think me overinquisitive, so I turned the talk into other channels. It appeared that Miss Sampson had not left any instructions for me, so I was glad to go with Dick to supper, which we had in the kitchen.

Dick informed me that the cowboys prepared their own meals down at the bunks; and as I had been given a room at the ranch-house he supposed I would get my meals there, too.

After supper I walked all over the grounds, had a look at the horses in the corrals, and came to the conclusion that it would be strange if Miss Sampson did not love her new home, and if her cousin did not enjoy her sojourn there. From a distance I saw the girls approaching with Wright, and not wishing to meet them I sheered off.

When the sun had set I went down to the town with the intention of finding Steele.

This task, considering I dared not make inquiries and must approach him secretly, might turn out to be anything but easy.

While it was still light, I strolled up and down the main street. When darkness set in I went into a hotel, bought cigars, sat around and watched, without any clue.

Then I went into the next place. This was of a rough crude exterior, but the inside was comparatively pretentious, and ablaze with lights.

It was full of men, coming and going—a dusty-booted crowd that smelled of horses and smoke.

I sat down for a while, with wide eyes and open ears. Then I hunted up a saloon, where most of the guests had been or were going. I found a great square room lighted by six huge lamps, a bar at one side, and all the floor space taken up by tables and chairs.

This must have been the gambling resort mentioned in the Ranger's letter to Captain Neal and the one rumored to be owned by the mayor of Linrock. This was the only gambling place of any size in southern Texas in which I had noted the absence of Mexicans. There was some card playing going on at this moment.

I stayed in there for a while, and knew that strangers were too common in Linrock to be conspicuous. But I saw no man whom I could have taken for Steele.

Then I went out.

It had often been a boast of mine that I could not spend an hour in a strange town, or walk a block along a dark street, without having something happen out of the ordinary.

Mine was an experiencing nature. Some people called this luck. But it was my private opinion that things gravitated my way because I looked and listened for them.

However, upon the occasion of my first day and evening in Linrock it appeared, despite my vigilance and inquisitiveness, that here was to be an exception.

This thought came to me just before I reached the last lighted place in the block, a little dingy restaurant, out of which at the moment, a tall, dark form passed. It disappeared in the gloom. I saw a man sitting on the low steps, and another standing in the door.

"That was the fellow the whole town's talkin' about—the Ranger," said one man.

Like a shot I halted in the shadow, where I had not been seen.

"Sho! Ain't boardin' heah, is he?" said the other.

"Yes."

"Reckon he'll hurt your business, Jim."

The fellow called Jim emitted a mirthless laugh. "Wal, he's been *all* my business these days. An' he's offered to rent that old 'dobe of mine just out of town. You know, where I lived before movin' in heah. He's goin' to look at it tomorrow."

"Lord! does he expect to *stay*?"

"Say so. An' if he ain't a stayer I never seen none. Nice, quiet, easy chap, but he just looks deep."

"Aw, Jim, he can't hang out heah. He's after some feller, that's all."

"I don't know his game. But he says he was heah for a while. An' he impressed me some. Just now he says: 'Where does Sampson live?' I asked him if he was goin' to make a call on our mayor, an' he says yes. Then I told him how to go out to the ranch. He went out, headed that way."

"The hell he did!"

I gathered from this fellow's exclamation that he was divided between amaze and mirth. Then he got up from the steps and went into the restaurant and was followed by the man called Jim. Before the door was closed he made another remark, but it was unintelligible to me.

As I passed on I decided I would scrape acquaintance with this restaurant keeper.

The thing of most moment was that I had gotten track of Steele. I hurried ahead. While I had been listening back there moments had elapsed and evidently he had walked swiftly.

I came to the plaza, crossed it, and then did not know which direction to take. Concluding that it did not matter I hurried on in an endeavor to reach the ranch before Steele. Although I was not sure, I believed I had succeeded.

The moon shone brightly. I heard a banjo in the distance and a cowboy sing. There was not a person in sight in the wide courts or on the porch. I did not have a well-defined idea about the inside of the house.

Peeping in at the first lighted window I saw a large room. Miss Sampson and Sally were there alone. Evidently this was a parlor or a sitting room, and it had clean white walls, a blanketed floor, an open fireplace with a cheery blazing log, and a large table upon which were lamp, books, papers. Backing away I saw that this corner room had a door opening on the porch and two other windows.

I listened, hoping to hear Steele's footsteps coming up the road. But I heard only Sally's laugh and her cousin's mellow voice.

Then I saw lighted windows down at the other end of the front part of the house. I walked down. A door stood open and through it I saw a room identical with that at the other corner; and here were Colonel Sampson, Wright, and several other men, all smoking and talking.

It might have been interesting to tarry there within ear-shot, but I wanted to get back to the road to intercept Steele. Scarcely had I retraced my steps and seated myself on the porch steps when a very tall dark figure loomed up in the moonlit road.

Steele! I wanted to yell like a boy. He came on slowly, looking all around, halted some twenty paces distant, surveyed the house, then evidently espying me, came on again.

My first feeling was, What a giant! But his face was hidden in the shadow of a sombrero.

I had intended, of course, upon first sight to blurt out my identity. Yet I did not. He affected me strangely, or perhaps it was my emotion at the thought that we Rangers, with so much in common and at stake, had come together.

"Is Sampson at home?" he asked abruptly.

I said, "Yes."

"Ask him if he'll see Vaughn Steele, Ranger."

"Wait here," I replied. I did not want to take up any time then explaining my presence there.

Deliberately and noisily I strode down the porch and entered the room with the smoking men.

I went in farther than was necessary for me to state my errand. But I wanted to see Sampson's face, to see into his eyes.

As I entered, the talking ceased. I saw no face except his and that seemed blank.

"Vaughn Steele, Ranger—come to see you, sir." I announced.

Did Sampson start—did his eyes show a fleeting glint—did his face almost imperceptibly blanch? I could not have sworn to either. But there was a change, maybe from surprise.

The first sure effect of my announcement came in a quick exclamation from Wright, a sibilant intake of breath, that did not seem to denote surprise so much as certainty. Wright might have emitted a curse with less force.

Sampson moved his hand significantly and the action was a voiceless command for silence as well as an assertion that he would attend to this matter. I read him clearly so far. He had authority, and again I felt his power.

"Steele to see me. Did he state his business?"

"No, sir." I replied.

"Russ, say I'm not at home," said Sampson presently, bending over to relight his pipe.

I went out. Someone slammed the door behind me.

As I strode back across the porch my mind worked swiftly; the machinery had been idle for a while and was now started.

"Mr. Steele," I said, "Colonel Sampson says he's not at home. Tell your business to his daughter."

Without waiting to see the effect of my taking so much upon myself, I knocked upon the parlor door. Miss Sampson opened it. She wore white. Looking at her, I thought it would be strange if Steele's well-known indifference to women did not suffer an eclipse.

"Miss Sampson, here is Vaughn Steele to see you," I said.

"Won't you come in?" she said graciously.

Steele had to bend his head to enter the door. I went in with him, an intrusion, perhaps, that in the interest of the moment she appeared not to notice.

Steele seemed to fill the room with his giant form. His face was fine, stern, clear cut, with blue or gray eyes, strangely penetrating. He was coatless, vestless. He wore a gray flannel shirt, corduroys, a big gun swinging low, and top boots reaching to his knees.

He was the most stalwart son of Texas I had seen in many a day, but neither his great stature nor his striking face accounted for something I felt—a something spiritual, vital, compelling, that drew me.

"Mr. Steele, I'm pleased to meet you," said Miss Sampson. "This is my cousin, Sally Langdon. We just arrived—I to make this my home, she to visit me."

Steele smiled as he bowed to Sally. He was easy, with a kind of rude grace, and showed no sign of embarrassment or that beautiful girls were unusual to him.

"Mr. Steele, we've heard of you in Austin," said Sally with her eyes misbehaving.

I hoped I would not have to be jealous of Steele. But this girl was a little minx if not altogether a flirt.

"I did not expect to be received by ladies," replied Steele. "I called upon Mr. Sampson. He would not see me. I was to tell my business to his daughter. I'm glad to know you, Miss Sampson and your cousin, but sorry you've come to Linrock now."

"Why?" queried both girls in unison.

"Because it's—oh, pretty rough—no place for girls to walk and ride."

"Ah! I see. And your business has to do with rough places," said Miss Sampson. "Strange that papa would not see you. Stranger that he should want me to hear your business. Either he's joking or wants to impress me.

"Papa tried to persuade me not to come. He tried to frighten me with tales of this—this roughness out here. He knows I'm in earnest, how I'd like to help somehow, do some little good. Pray tell me this business."

"I wished to get your father's cooperation in my work."

"Your work? You mean your Ranger duty—the arresting of rough characters?"

"That, yes. But that's only a detail. Linrock is bad internally. My job is to make it good."

"A splendid and worthy task," replied Miss Sampson warmly. "I wish you success. But, Mr. Steele, aren't you exaggerating Linrock's wickedness?"

"No," he answered forcibly.

"Indeed! And papa refused to see you—presumably refused to cooperate with you?" she asked thoughtfully.

"I take it that way."

"Mr. Steele, pray tell me what is the matter with Linrock and just what the work is you're called upon to do?" she asked seriously. "I heard papa say that he was the law in Linrock. Perhaps he resents interference. I know he'll not tolerate any opposition to his will. Please tell me. I may be able to influence him."

I listened to Steele's deep voice as he talked about Linrock. What he said was old to me, and I gave heed only to its effect.

Miss Sampson's expression, which at first had been earnest and grave, turned into one of incredulous amaze. She, and Sally too, watched Steele's face in fascinated attention.

When it came to telling what he wanted to do, the Ranger warmed to his subject; he talked beautifully, convincingly, with a certain strange, persuasive power that betrayed how he worked his way; and his fine face, losing its stern, hard lines, seemed to glow and give forth a spirit austere, yet noble, almost gentle, assuredly something vastly different from what might have been expected in the expression of a gun-fighting Ranger. I sensed that Miss Sampson felt this just as I did.

"Papa said you were a hounder of outlaws—a man who'd rather kill than save!" she exclaimed.

The old stern cast returned to Steele's face. It was as if he had suddenly remembered himself.

"My name is infamous, I am sorry to say," he replied.

"You have killed men?" she asked, her dark eyes dilating.

Had any one ever dared ask Steele that before? His face became a mask. It told truth to me, but she could not see, and he did not answer.

"Oh, you are above that. Don't—don't kill any one here!"

"Miss Sampson, I hope I won't." His voice seemed to check her. I had been right in my estimate of her character—young, untried, but all pride, fire, passion. She was white then, and certainly beautiful.

Steele watched her, could scarcely have failed to see the white gleam of her beauty, and all that evidence of a quick and noble heart.

"Pardon me, please, Mr. Steele," she said, recovering her composure. "I am—just a little overexcited. I didn't mean to be inquisitive. Thank you for your confidence. I've enjoyed your call, though your news did distress me. You may rely upon me to talk to papa."

That appeared to be a dismissal, and, bowing to her and Sally, the Ranger went out. I followed, not having spoken.

At the end of the porch I caught up with Steele and walked out into the moonlight beside him.

Just why I did not now reveal my identity I could not say, for certainly I was bursting with the desire to surprise him, to earn his approval. He loomed dark above me, appearing not to be aware of my presence. What a cold, strange proposition this Ranger was!

Still, remembering the earnestness of his talk to Miss Sampson, I could not think him cold. But I must have thought him so to any attraction of those charming girls.

Suddenly, as we passed under the shade of cottonwoods, he clamped a big hand down on my shoulder.

"My God, Russ, isn't she lovely!" he ejaculated.

In spite of my being dumbfounded I had to hug him. He knew me!

"Thought you didn't swear!" I gasped.

Ridiculously those were my first words to Vaughn Steele.

"My boy, I saw you parading up and down the street looking for me," he said. "I intended to help you find me to-morrow."

We gripped hands, and that strong feel and clasp meant much.

"Yes, she's lovely, Steele," I said. "But did you look at the cousin, the little girl with the eyes?"

Then we laughed and loosed hands.

"Come on, let's get out somewhere. I've a million things to tell you."

We went away out into the open where some stones gleamed white in the moonlight, and there, sitting in the sand, our backs against a rest, and with all quiet about us, we settled down for a long conference.

I began with Neal's urgent message to me, then told of my going to the capitol—what I had overheard when Governor Smith was in the adjutant's office; of my interview with them; of the spying on Colonel Sampson; Neal's directions, advice, and command; the ride toward San Antonio; my being engaged as cowboy by Miss Sampson; of the further ride on to Sanderson and the incident there; and finally how I had approached Sampson and then had thought it well to get his daughter into the scheme of things.

It was a long talk, even for me, and my voice sounded husky.

"I told Neal I'd be lucky to get you," said Steele, after a silence.

That was the only comment on my actions, the only praise, but the quiet way he spoke it made me feel like a boy undeserving of so much.

"Here, I forgot the money Neal sent," I went on, glad to be rid of the huge roll of bills.

The Ranger showed surprise. Besides, he was very glad.

"The Captain loves the service," said Steele. "He alone knows the worth of the Rangers. And the work he's given his life to—the *good* that *service* really does—all depends on you and me, Russ!"

I assented, gloomily enough. Then I waited while he pondered.

The moon soared clear; there was a cool wind rustling the greasewood; a dog bayed a barking coyote; lights twinkled down in the town.

I looked back up at the dark hill and thought of Sally Langdon. Getting here to Linrock, meeting Steele had not changed my feelings toward her, only somehow they had removed me far off in thought, out of possible touch, it seemed.

"Well, son, listen," began Steele. His calling me that was a joke, yet I did not feel it. "You've made a better start than I could have figured. Neal said you were lucky. Perhaps. But you've got brains.

"Now, here's your cue for the present. Work for Miss Sampson. Do your best for her as long as you last. I don't suppose you'll last long. You have got to get in with this gang in town. Be a flash cowboy. You don't need to get drunk, but you're to pretend it.

"Gamble. Be a good fellow. Hang round the barrooms. I don't care how you play the part, so long as you make friends, learn the ropes. We can meet out here at nights to talk and plan.

"You're to take sides with those who're against me. I'll furnish you with the money. You'd better appear to be a winning gambler, even if you're not. How's this plan strike you?"

"Great—except for one thing," I replied. "I hate to lie to Miss Sampson. She's true blue, Steele."

"Son, you haven't got soft on her?"

"Not a bit. Maybe I'm soft on the little cousin. But I just like Miss Sampson—think she's fine—could look up to her. And I hate to be different from what she thinks."

"I understand, Russ," he replied in his deep voice that had such quality to influence a man. "It's no decent job. You'll be ashamed before her. So would I. But here's our work, the hardest ever cut out for Rangers. Think what depends upon it. And—"

"There's something wrong with Miss Sampson's father," I interrupted.

"Something strange if not wrong. No man in this community is beyond us, Russ, or above suspicion. You've a great opportunity. I needn't say use your eyes and ears as never before."

"I hope Sampson turns out to be on the square," I replied. "He might be a lax mayor, too good-natured to uphold law in a wild country. And his Southern pride would fire at interference. I don't like him, but for his daughter's sake I hope we're wrong."

Steele's eyes, deep and gleaming in the moonlight, searched my face.

"Son, sure you're not in love with her—you'll not fall in love with her?"

"No. I am positive. Why?"

"Because in either case I'd likely have need of a new man in your place," he said.

"Steele, you know something about Sampson—something more!" I exclaimed swiftly.

"No more than you. When I meet him face to face I may know more. Russ, when a fellow has been years at this game he has a sixth sense. Mine seldom fails me. I never yet faced the criminal who didn't somehow betray fear—not so much fear of me, but fear of himself—his life, his deeds. That's conscience, or if not, just realization of fate."

Had that been the thing I imagined I had seen in Sampson's face?

"I'm sorry Diane Sampson came out here," I said impulsively.

Steele did not say he shared that feeling. He was looking out upon the moon-blanched level.

Some subtle thing in his face made me divine that he was thinking of the beautiful girl to whom he might bring disgrace and unhappiness.

CHAPTER 2 A KISS AND AN ARREST

A month had passed, a swift-flying time full of new life. Wonderful it was for me to think I was still in Diane Sampson's employ.

It was the early morning hour of a day in May. The sun had not yet grown hot. Dew like diamond drops sparkled on the leaves and grass. The gentle breeze was clear, sweet, with the song of larks upon it.

And the range, a sea of gray-green growing greener, swept away westward in rolling ridges and hollows, like waves to meet the dark, low hills that notched the horizon line of blue.

I was sitting on the top bar of the corral fence and before me stood three saddled horses that would have gladdened any eye. I was waiting to take the young ladies on their usual morning ride.

Once upon a time, in what seemed the distant past to this eventful month, I had flattered myself there had been occasions for thought, but scornfully I soliloquized that in those days I had no cue for thought such as I had now.

This was one of the moments when my real self seemed to stand off and skeptically regard the fictitious cowboy.

This gentleman of the range wore a huge sombrero with an ornamented silver band, a silken scarf of red, a black velvet shirt, much affected by the Indians, an embroidered buckskin vest, corduroys, and fringed chaps with silver buttons, a big blue gun swinging low, high heeled boots, and long spurs with silver rowels.

A flash cowboy! Steele vowed I was a born actor.

But I never divulged the fact that had it not been for my infatuation for Sally, I never could have carried on that part, not to save the Ranger service, or the whole State of Texas.

The hardest part had not been the establishing of a reputation. The scorn of cowboys, the ridicule of gamblers, the badinage of the young bucks of the settlement—these I had soon made dangerous procedures for any one. I was quick with tongue and fist and gun.

There had been fights and respect was quickly earned, though the constant advent of strangers in Linrock always had me in hot water.

Moreover, instead of being difficult, it was fun to spend all the time I could in the hotels and resorts, shamming a weakness for drink, gambling, lounging, making friends among the rough set, when all the time I was a cool, keen registering machine.

The hard thing was the lie I lived in the eyes of Diane Sampson and Sally Langdon.

I had indeed won the sincere regard of my employer. Her father, her cousin George, and new-made friends in town had come to her with tales of my reckless doings, and had urged my dismissal.

But she kept me and all the time pleaded like a sister to have me mend my vicious ways. She believed what she was told about me, but had faith in me despite that.

As for Sally, I had fallen hopelessly in love with her. By turns Sally was indifferent to me, cold, friendly like a comrade, and dangerously sweet.

Somehow she saw through me, knew I was not just what I pretended to be. But she never breathed her conviction. She championed me. I wanted to tell her the truth about myself because I believed the doubt of me alone stood in the way of my winning her.

Still that might have been my vanity. She had never said she cared for me although she had looked it.

This tangle of my personal life, however, had not in the least affected my loyalty and duty to Vaughn Steele. Day by day I had grown more attached to him, keener in the interest of our work.

It had been a busy month—a month of foundation building. My vigilance and my stealthy efforts had not been rewarded by anything calculated to strengthen our suspicions of Sampson. But then he had been absent from the home very often, and was difficult to watch when he was there.

George Wright came and went, too, presumably upon stock business. I could not yet see that he was anything but an honest rancher, deeply involved with Sampson and other men in stock deals; nevertheless, as a man he had earned my contempt.

He was a hard drinker, cruel to horses, a gambler not above stacking the cards, a quick-tempered, passionate Southerner.

He had fallen in love with Diane Sampson, was like her shadow when at home. He hated me; he treated me as if I were the scum of the earth; if he had to address me for something, which was seldom, he did it harshly, like ordering a dog. Whenever I saw his sinister, handsome face, with its dark eyes always half shut, my hand itched for my gun, and I would go my way with something thick and hot inside my breast.

In my talks with Steele we spent time studying George Wright's character and actions. He was Sampson's partner, and at the head of a small group of Linrock ranchers who were rich in cattle and property, if not in money.

Steele and I had seen fit to wait before we made any thorough investigation into their business methods. Ours was a waiting game, anyway.

Right at the start Linrock had apparently arisen in resentment at the presence of Vaughn Steele. But it was my opinion that there were men in Linrock secretly glad of the Ranger's presence.

What he intended to do was food for great speculation. His fame, of course, had preceded him. A company of militia could not have had the effect upon the wild element of Linrock that Steele's presence had.

A thousand stories went from lip to lip, most of which were false. He was lightning swift on the draw. It was death to face him. He had killed thirty men—wildest rumor of all.

He had the gun skill of Buck Duane, the craft of Cheseldine, the deviltry of King Fisher, the most notorious of Texas desperadoes. His nerve, his lack of fear—those made him stand out alone even among a horde of bold men.

At first there had not only been great conjecture among the vicious element, with which I had begun to affiliate myself, but also a very decided checking of all kinds of action calculated to be conspicuous to a keen eyed Ranger.

Steele did not hide, but during these opening days of his stay in Linrock he was not often seen in town. At the tables, at the bars and lounging places remarks went the rounds:

"Who's thet Ranger after? What'll he do fust off? Is he waitin' fer somebody? Who's goin' to draw on him fust—an' go to hell? Jest about how soon will he be found somewhere full of lead?"

Those whom it was my interest to cultivate grew more curious, more speculative and impatient as time went by. When it leaked out somewhere that Steele was openly cultivating the honest stay-at-home citizens, to array them in time against the other element, then Linrock showed its wolf teeth hinted of in the letters to Captain Neal.

Several times Steele was shot at in the dark and once slightly injured. Rumor had it that Jack Blome, the gunman of those parts, was coming in to meet Steele. Part of Linrock awakened and another part, much smaller, became quieter, more secluded.

Strangers upon whom we could get no line mysteriously came and went. The drinking, gambling, fighting in the resorts seemed to gather renewed life. Abundance of money floated in circulation.

And rumors, vague and unfounded, crept in from Sanderson and other points, rumors of a gang of rustlers off here, a hold-up of the stage off here, robbery of a rancher at this distant point, and murder done at another.

This was Texas and New Mexico life in these frontier days but, strangely neither Steele nor I had yet been able to associate any rumor or act with a possible gang of rustlers in Linrock.

Nevertheless we had not been discouraged. After three weeks of waiting we had become alive to activity around us, and though it was unseen, we believed we would soon be on its track.

My task was the busier and the easier. Steele had to have a care for his life. I never failed to caution him of this.

CHAPTER 2 A KISS AND AN ARREST

My long reflection on the month's happenings and possibilities was brought to an end by the appearance of Miss Sampson and Sally.

My employer looked worried. Sally was in a regular cowgirl riding costume, in which her trim, shapely figure showed at its best, and her face was saucy, sparkling, daring.

"Good morning, Russ," said Miss Sampson and she gazed searchingly at me. I had dropped off the fence, sombrero in hand. I knew I was in for a lecture, and I put on a brazen, innocent air.

"Did you break your promise to me?" she asked reproachfully.

"Which one?" I asked. It was Sally's bright eyes upon me, rather than Miss Sampson's reproach, that bothered me.

"About getting drunk again," she said.

"I didn't break *that* one."

"My cousin George saw you in the Hope So gambling place last night, drunk, staggering, mixing with that riffraff, on the verge of a brawl."

"Miss Sampson, with all due respect to Mr. Wright, I want to say that he has a strange wish to lower me in the eyes of you ladies," I protested with a fine show of spirit.

"Russ, *were* you drunk?" she demanded.

"No. I should think you needn't ask me that. Didn't you ever see a man the morning after a carouse?"

Evidently she had. And there I knew I stood, fresh, clean-shaven, clear-eyed as the morning.

Sally's saucy face grew thoughtful, too. The only thing she had ever asked of me was not to drink. The habit had gone hard with the Sampson family.

"Russ, you look just as—as nice as I'd want you to," Miss Sampson replied. "I don't know what to think. They tell me things. You deny. Whom shall I believe? George swore he saw you."

"Miss Sampson, did I ever lie to you?"

"Not to my knowledge."

Then I looked at her, and she understood what I meant.

"George has lied to me. That day at Sanderson. And since, too, I fear. Do you say he lies?"

"Miss Sampson, I would not call your cousin a liar."

Here Sally edged closer, with the bridle rein of her horse over her arm.

"Russ, cousin George isn't the only one who saw you. Burt Waters told me the same," said Sally nervously. I believed she hoped I was telling the truth.

"Waters! So he runs me down behind my back. All right, I won't say a word about him. But do you believe I was drunk when I say no?"

"I'm afraid I do, Russ," she replied in reluctance. Was she testing me?

"See here, Miss Sampson," I burst out. "Why don't you discharge me? Please let me go. I'm not claiming much for myself, but you don't believe even that. I'm pretty bad. I never denied the scraps, the gambling—all that. But I did do as Miss

Sally asked me—I did keep my promise to you. Now, discharge me. Then I'll be free to call on Mr. Burt Waters."

Miss Sampson looked alarmed and Sally turned pale, to my extreme joy.

Those girls believed I was a desperate devil of a cowboy, who had been held back from spilling blood solely through their kind relation to me.

"Oh, no!" exclaimed Sally. "Diane, don't let him go!"

"Russ, pray don't get angry," replied Miss Sampson and she put a soft hand on me that thrilled me, while it made me feel like a villain. "I won't discharge you. I need you. Sally needs you. After all, it's none of my business what you do away from here. But I hoped I would be so happy to—to reclaim you from—Didn't you ever have a sister, Russ?"

I kept silent for fear that I would perjure myself anew. Yet the situation was delicious, and suddenly I conceived a wild idea.

"Miss Sampson," I began haltingly, but with brave front, "I've been wild in the past. But I've been tolerably straight here, trying to please you. Lately I have been going to the bad again. Not drunk, but leaning that way. Lord knows what I'll do soon if—if my trouble isn't cured."

"Russ! What trouble?"

"You know what's the matter with me," I went on hurriedly. "Anybody could see that."

Sally turned a flaming scarlet. Miss Sampson made it easier for me by reason of her quick glance of divination.

"I've fallen in love with Miss Sally. I'm crazy about her. Here I've got to see these fellows flirting with her. And it's killing me. I've—"

"If you are crazy about me, you don't have to tell!" cried Sally, red and white by turns.

"I want to stop your flirting one way or another. I've been in earnest. I wasn't flirting. I begged you to—to..."

"You never did," interrupted Sally furiously. That hint had been a spark.

"I couldn't have dreamed it," I protested, in a passion to be earnest, yet tingling with the fun of it. "That day when I—didn't I ask..."

"If my memory serves me correctly, you didn't ask anything," she replied, with anger and scorn now struggling with mirth.

"But, Sally, I meant to. You understood me? Say you didn't believe I could take that liberty without honorable intentions."

That was too much for Sally. She jumped at her horse, made the quickest kind of a mount, and was off like a flash.

"Stop me if you can," she called back over her shoulder, her face alight and saucy.

"Russ, go after her," said Miss Sampson. "In that mood she'll ride to Sanderson. My dear fellow, don't stare so. I understand many things now. Sally is a flirt. She would drive any man mad. Russ, I've grown in a short time to like you. If you'll be a man—give up drinking and gambling—maybe you'll have a chance with her. Hurry now—go after her."

CHAPTER 2 A KISS AND AN ARREST

I mounted and spurred my horse after Sally's. She was down on the level now, out in the open, and giving her mount his head. Even had I wanted to overhaul her at once the matter would have been difficult, well nigh impossible under five miles.

Sally had as fast a horse as there was on the range; she made no weight in the saddle, and she could ride. From time to time she looked back over her shoulder.

I gained enough to make her think I was trying to catch her. Sally loved a horse; she loved a race; she loved to win.

My good fortune had given me more than one ride alone with Sally. Miss Sampson enjoyed riding, too; but she was not a madcap, and when she accompanied us there was never any race.

When Sally got out alone with me she made me ride to keep her from disappearing somewhere on the horizon. This morning I wanted her to enjoy to the fullest her utter freedom and to feel that for once I could not catch her.

Perhaps my declaration to Miss Sampson had liberated my strongest emotions.

However that might be, the fact was that no ride before had ever been like this one—no sky so blue, no scene so open, free, and enchanting as that beautiful gray-green range, no wind so sweet. The breeze that rushed at me might have been laden with the perfume of Sally Langdon's hair.

I sailed along on what seemed a strange ride. Grazing horses pranced and whistled as I went by; jack-rabbits bounded away to hide in the longer clumps of grass; a prowling wolf trotted from his covert near a herd of cattle.

Far to the west rose the low, dark lines of bleak mountains. They were always mysterious to me, as if holding a secret I needed to know.

It was a strange ride because in the back of my head worked a haunting consciousness of the deadly nature of my business there on the frontier, a business in such contrast with this dreaming and dallying, this longing for what surely was futile.

Any moment I might be stripped of my disguise. Any moment I might have to be the Ranger.

Sally kept the lead across the wide plain, and mounted to the top of a ridge, where tired out, and satisfied with her victory, she awaited me. I was in no hurry to reach the summit of the long, slow-sloping ridge, and I let my horse walk.

Just how would Sally Langdon meet me now, after my regretted exhibition before her cousin? There was no use to conjecture, but I was not hopeful.

When I got there to find her in her sweetest mood, with some little difference never before noted—a touch of shyness—I concealed my surprise.

"Russ, I gave you a run that time," she said. "Ten miles and you never caught me!"

"But look at the start you had. I've had my troubles beating you with an even break."

Sally was susceptible to flattery in regard to her riding, a fact that I made subtle use of.

"But in a long race I was afraid you'd beat me. Russ, I've learned to ride out here. Back home I never had room to ride a horse. Just look. Miles and miles of level, of green. Little hills with black bunches of trees. Not a soul in sight. Even the town hidden in the green. All wild and lonely. Isn't it glorious, Russ?"

"Lately it's been getting to me," I replied soberly.

We both gazed out over the sea of gray-green, at the undulating waves of ground in the distance. On these rides with her I had learned to appreciate the beauty of the lonely reaches of plain.

But when I could look at her I seldom wasted time on scenery. Looking at her now I tried to get again that impression of a difference in her. It eluded me.

Just now with the rose in her brown cheeks, her hair flying, her eyes with grave instead of mocking light, she seemed only prettier than usual. I got down ostensibly to tighten the saddle girths on her horse. But I lingered over the task.

Presently, when she looked down at me, I received that subtle impression of change, and read it as her soft mood of dangerous sweetness that came so seldom, mingled with something deeper, more of character and womanliness than I had ever sensed in her.

"Russ, it wasn't nice to tell Diane that," she said.

"Nice! It was—oh, I'd like to swear!" I ejaculated. "But now I understand my miserable feeling. I was jealous, Sally, I'm sorry. I apologize."

She had drawn off her gloves, and one little hand, brown, shapely, rested upon her knee very near to me. I took it in mine. She let it stay, though she looked away from me, the color rich in her cheeks.

"I can forgive that," she murmured. "But the lie. Jealousy doesn't excuse a lie."

"You mean—what I intimated to your cousin," I said, trying to make her look at me. "That was the devil in me. Only it's true."

"How can it be true when you never asked—said a word—you hinted of?" she queried. "Diane believed what you said. I know she thinks me horrid."

"No she doesn't. As for what I said, or meant to say, which is the same thing, how'd you take my actions? I hope not the same as you take Wright's or the other fellow's."

Sally was silent, a little pale now, and I saw that I did not need to say any more about the other fellows. The change, the difference was now marked. It drove me to give in wholly to this earnest and passionate side of myself.

"Sally, I do love you. I don't know how you took my actions. Anyway, now I'll make them plain. I was beside myself with love and jealousy. Will you marry me?"

She did not answer. But the old willful Sally was not in evidence. Watching her face I gave her a slow and gentle pull, one she could easily resist if she cared to, and she slipped from her saddle into my arms.

Then there was one wildly sweet moment in which I had the blissful certainty that she kissed me of her own accord. She was abashed, yet yielding; she let herself go, yet seemed not utterly unstrung. Perhaps I was rough, held her too hard, for she cried out a little.

"Russ! Let me go. Help me—back."

I righted her in the saddle, although not entirely releasing her.

"But, Sally, you haven't told me anything," I remonstrated tenderly. "Do you love me?"

"I think so," she whispered.

"Sally, will you marry me?"

She disengaged herself then, sat erect and faced away from me, with her breast heaving.

"No, Russ," she presently said, once more calm.

"But Sally—if you love me—" I burst out, and then stopped, stilled by something in her face.

"I can't help—loving you, Russ," she said. "But to promise to marry you, that's different. Why, Russ, I know nothing about you, not even your last name. You're not a—a steady fellow. You drink, gamble, fight. You'll kill somebody yet. Then I'll *not* love you. Besides, I've always felt you're not just what you seemed. I can't trust you. There's something wrong about you."

I knew my face darkened, and perhaps hope and happiness died in it. Swiftly she placed a kind hand on my shoulder.

"Now, I've hurt you. Oh, I'm sorry. Your asking me makes such a difference. *They* are not in earnest. But, Russ, I had to tell you why I couldn't be engaged to you."

"I'm not good enough for you. I'd no right to ask you to marry me," I replied abjectly.

"Russ, don't think me proud," she faltered. "I wouldn't care who you were if I could only—only respect you. Some things about you are splendid, you're such a man, that's why I cared. But you gamble. You drink—and I *hate* that. You're dangerous they say, and I'd be, I *am* in constant dread you'll kill somebody. Remember, Russ, I'm no Texan."

This regret of Sally's, this faltering distress at giving me pain, was such sweet assurance that she did love me, better than she knew, that I was divided between extremes of emotion.

"Will you wait? Will you trust me a little? Will you give me a chance? After all, maybe I'm not so bad as I seem."

"Oh, if you weren't! Russ, are you asking me to trust you?"

"I beg you to—dearest. Trust me and wait."

"Wait? What for? Are you really on the square, Russ? Or are you what George calls you—a drunken cowboy, a gambler, sharp with the cards, a gun-fighter?"

My face grew cold as I felt the blood leave it. At that moment mention of George Wright fixed once for all my hate of him.

Bitter indeed was it that I dared not give him the lie. But what could I do? The character Wright gave me was scarcely worse than what I had chosen to represent. I had to acknowledge the justice of his claim, but nevertheless I hated him.

"Sally, I ask you to trust me in spite of my reputation."

"You ask me a great deal," she replied.

"Yes, it's too much. Let it be then only this—you'll wait. And while you wait, promise not to flirt with Wright and Waters."

"Russ, I'll not let George or any of them so much as dare touch me," she declared in girlish earnestness, her voice rising. "I'll promise if you'll promise me not to go into those saloons any more."

One word would have brought her into my arms for good and all. The better side of Sally Langdon showed then in her appeal. That appeal was as strong as the drawing power of her little face, all eloquent with its light, and eyes dark with tears, and lips wanting to smile.

My response should have been instant. How I yearned to give it and win the reward I imagined I saw on her tremulous lips! But I was bound. The grim, dark nature of my enterprise there in Linrock returned to stultify my eagerness, dispel my illusion, shatter my dream.

For one instant it flashed through my mind to tell Sally who I was, what my errand was, after the truth. But the secret was not mine to tell. And I kept my pledges.

The hopeful glow left Sally's face. Her disappointment seemed keen. Then a little scorn of certainty was the bitterest of all for me to bear.

"That's too much to promise all at once," I protested lamely, and I knew I would have done better to keep silence.

"Russ, a promise like that is nothing—if a man loves a girl," she retorted. "Don't make any more love to me, please, unless you want me to laugh at you. And don't feel such terrible trouble if you happen to see me flirting occasionally."

She ended with a little mocking laugh. That was the perverse side of her, the cat using her claws. I tried not to be angry, but failed.

"All right. I'll take my medicine," I replied bitterly. "I'll certainly never make love to you again. And I'll stand it if I happen to see Waters kiss you, or any other decent fellow. But look out how you let that damned backbiter Wright fool around you!"

I spoke to her as I had never spoken before, in quick, fierce meaning, with eyes holding hers.

She paled. But even my scarce-veiled hint did not chill her anger. Tossing her head she wheeled and rode away.

I followed at a little distance, and thus we traveled the ten miles back to the ranch. When we reached the corrals she dismounted and, turning her horse over to Dick, she went off toward the house without so much as a nod or good-by to me.

I went down to town for once in a mood to live up to what had been heretofore only a sham character.

But turning a corner into the main street I instantly forgot myself at the sight of a crowd congregated before the town hall. There was a babel of voices and an air of excitement that I immediately associated with Sampson, who as mayor of Linrock, once in a month of moons held court in this hall.

CHAPTER 2 A KISS AND AN ARREST

It took slipping and elbowing to get through the crowd. Once inside the door I saw that the crowd was mostly outside, and evidently not so desirous as I was to enter.

The first man I saw was Steele looming up; the next was Sampson chewing his mustache—the third, Wright, whose dark and sinister face told much. Something was up in Linrock. Steele had opened the hall.

There were other men in the hall, a dozen or more, and all seemed shouting excitedly in unison with the crowd outside. I did not try to hear what was said. I edged closer in, among the men to the front.

Sampson sat at a table up on a platform. Near him sat a thick-set grizzled man, with deep eyes; and this was Hanford Owens, county judge.

To the right stood a tall, angular, yellow-faced fellow with a drooping, sandy mustache. Conspicuous on his vest was a huge silver shield. This was Gorsech, one of Sampson's sheriffs.

There were four other men whom I knew, several whose faces were familiar, and half a dozen strangers, all dusty horsemen.

Steele stood apart from them, a little to one side, so that he faced them all. His hair was disheveled, and his shirt open at the neck. He looked cool and hard.

When I caught his eye I realized in an instant that the long deferred action, the beginning of our real fight was at hand.

Sampson pounded hard on the table to be heard. Mayor or not, he was unable at once to quell the excitement.

Gradually, however, it subsided and from the last few utterances before quiet was restored I gathered that Steele had intruded upon some kind of a meeting in the hall.

"Steele, what'd you break in here for?" demanded Sampson.

"Isn't this court? Aren't you the mayor of Linrock?" interrogated Steele. His voice was so clear and loud, almost piercing, that I saw at once that he wanted all those outside to hear.

"Yes," replied Sampson. Like flint he seemed, yet I felt his intense interest.

I had no doubt then that Steele intended to make him stand out before this crowd as the real mayor of Linrock or as a man whose office was a sham.

"I've arrested a criminal," said Steele. "Bud Snell. I charge him with assault on Jim Hoden and attempted robbery—if not murder. Snell had a shady past here, as the court will know if it keeps a record."

Then I saw Snell hunching down on a bench, a nerveless and shaken man if there ever was one. He had been a hanger-on round the gambling dens, the kind of sneak I never turned my back to.

Jim Hoden, the restaurant keeper, was present also, and on second glance I saw that he was pale. There was blood on his face. I knew Jim, liked him, had tried to make a friend of him.

I was not dead to the stinging interrogation in the concluding sentence of Steele's speech. Then I felt sure I had correctly judged Steele's motive. I began to warm to the situation.

"What's this I hear about you, Bud? Get up and speak for yourself," said Sampson, gruffly.

Snell got up, not without a furtive glance at Steele, and he had shuffled forward a few steps toward the mayor. He had an evil front, but not the boldness even of a rustler.

"It ain't so, Sampson," he began loudly. "I went in Hoden's place fer grub. Some feller I never seen before come in from the hall an' hit him an' wrastled him on the floor. Then this big Ranger grabbed me an' fetched me here. I didn't do nothin'. This Ranger's hankerin' to arrest somebody. Thet's my hunch, Sampson."

"What have you to say about this, Hoden?" sharply queried Sampson. "I call to your mind the fact that you once testified falsely in court, and got punished for it."

Why did my sharpened and experienced wits interpret a hint of threat or menace in Sampson's reminder? Hoden rose from the bench and with an unsteady hand reached down to support himself.

He was no longer young, and he seemed broken in health and spirit. He had been hurt somewhat about the head.

"I haven't much to say," he replied. "The Ranger dragged me here. I told him I didn't take my troubles to court. Besides, I can't swear it was Snell who hit me."

Sampson said something in an undertone to Judge Owens, and that worthy nodded his great, bushy head.

"Bud, you're discharged," said Sampson bluntly. "Now, the rest of you clear out of here."

He absolutely ignored the Ranger. That was his rebuff to Steele's advances, his slap in the face to an interfering Ranger Service.

If Sampson was crooked he certainly had magnificent nerve. I almost decided he was above suspicion. But his nonchalance, his air of finality, his authoritative assurance—these to my keen and practiced eyes were in significant contrast to a certain tenseness of line about his mouth and a slow paling of his olive skin.

He had crossed the path of Vaughn Steele; he had blocked the way of this Texas Ranger. If he had intelligence and remembered Steele's fame, which surely he had, then he had some appreciation of what he had undertaken.

In that momentary lull my scrutiny of Sampson gathered an impression of the man's intense curiosity.

Then Bud Snell, with a cough that broke the silence, shuffled a couple of steps toward the door.

"Hold on!" called Steele.

It was a bugle-call. It halted Snell as if it had been a bullet. He seemed to shrink.

"Sampson, I *saw* Snell attack Hoden," said Steele, his voice still ringing. "What has the court to say to that?"

The moment for open rupture between Ranger Service and Sampson's idea of law was at hand. Sampson showed not the slightest hesitation.

"The court has to say this: West of the Pecos we'll not aid or abet or accept any Ranger Service. Steele, we don't want you out here. Linrock doesn't need you."

"That's a lie, Sampson," retorted Steele. "I've a pocket full of letters from Linrock citizens, all begging for Ranger Service."

Sampson turned white. The veins corded at his temples. He appeared about to burst into rage. He was at a loss for a quick reply.

Steele shook a long arm at the mayor.

"I need your help. You refuse. Now, I'll work alone. This man Snell goes to Del Rio in irons."

George Wright rushed up to the table. The blood showed black and thick in his face; his utterance was incoherent, his uncontrollable outbreak of temper seemed out of all proportion to any cause he should reasonably have had for anger.

Sampson shoved him back with a curse and warning glare.

"Where's your warrant to arrest Snell?" shouted Sampson. "I won't give you one. You can't take him without a warrant."

"I don't need warrants to make arrests. Sampson, you're ignorant of the power of Texas Rangers."

"You'll take Snell without papers?" bellowed Sampson.

"He goes to Del Rio to jail," answered Steele.

"He won't. You'll pull none of your damned Ranger stunts out here. I'll block you, Steele."

That passionate reply of Sampson's appeared to be the signal Steele had been waiting for.

He had helped on the crisis. I believed I saw how he wanted to force Sampson's hand and show the town his stand.

Steele backed clear of everybody and like two swift flashes of light his guns leaped forth. He was transformed. My wish was fulfilled.

Here was Steele, the Ranger, in one of his lone lion stands. Not exactly alone either, for my hands itched for my guns!

"Men! I call on you all!" cried Steele, piercingly. "I call on you to witness the arrest of a criminal opposed by Sampson, mayor of Linrock. It will be recorded in the report sent to the Adjutant General at Austin. Sampson, I warn you—don't follow up your threat."

Sampson sat white with working jaw.

"Snell, come here," ordered Steele.

The man went as if drawn and appeared to slink out of line with the guns. Steele's cold gray glance held every eye in the hall.

"Take the handcuffs out of my pocket. This side. Go over to Gorsech with them. Gorsech, snap those irons on Snell's wrists. Now, Snell, back here to the right of me."

It was no wonder to me to see how instantly Steele was obeyed. He might have seen more danger in that moment than was manifest to me; on the other hand he might have wanted to drive home hard what he meant.

It was a critical moment for those who opposed him. There was death in the balance.

This Ranger, whose last resort was gun-play, had instantly taken the initiative, and his nerve chilled even me. Perhaps though, he read this crowd differently from me and saw that intimidation was his cue. I forgot I was not a spectator, but an ally.

"Sampson, you've shown your hand," said Steele, in the deep voice that carried so far and held those who heard. "Any honest citizen of Linrock can now see what's plain—yours is a damn poor hand!

"You're going to hear me call a spade a spade. Your office is a farce. In the two years you've been mayor you've never arrested one rustler. Strange, when Linrock's a nest for rustlers! You've never sent a prisoner to Del Rio, let alone to Austin. You have no jail.

"There have been nine murders since you took office, innumerable street fights and hold-ups. *Not one arrest!* But you have ordered arrests for trivial offenses, and have punished these out of all proportion.

"There have been law-suits in your court—suits over water rights, cattle deals, property lines. Strange how in these law-suits, you or Wright or other men close to you were always involved! Stranger how it seems the law was stretched to favor your interests!"

Steele paused in his cold, ringing speech. In the silence, both outside and inside the hall, could be heard the deep breathing of agitated men.

I would have liked to search for possible satisfaction on the faces of any present, but I was concerned only with Sampson. I did not need to fear that any man might draw on Steele.

Never had I seen a crowd so sold, so stiff, so held! Sampson was indeed a study. Yet did he betray anything but rage at this interloper?

"Sampson, here's plain talk for you and Linrock to digest," went on Steele. "I don't accuse you and your court of dishonesty. I say—*strange*! Law here has been a farce. The motive behind all this laxity isn't plain to me—yet. But I call your hand!"

CHAPTER 3 SOUNDING THE TIMBER

When Steele left the hall, pushing Snell before him, making a lane through the crowd, it was not any longer possible to watch everybody.

Yet now he seemed to ignore the men behind him. Any friend of Snell's among the vicious element might have pulled a gun. I wondered if Steele knew how I watched those men at his back—how fatal it would have been for any of them to make a significant move.

No—I decided that Steele trusted to the effect his boldness had created. It was this power to cow ordinary men that explained so many of his feats; just the same it was his keenness to read desperate men, his nerve to confront them, that made him great.

The crowd followed Steele and his captive down the middle of the main street and watched him secure a team and buckboard and drive off on the road to Sanderson.

Only then did that crowd appear to realize what had happened. Then my long-looked-for opportunity arrived. In the expression of silent men I found something which I had sought; from the hurried departure of others homeward I gathered import; on the husky, whispering lips of yet others I read words I needed to hear.

The other part of that crowd—to my surprise, the smaller part—was the roaring, threatening, complaining one.

Thus I segregated Linrock that was lawless from Linrock that wanted law, but for some reason not yet clear the latter did not dare to voice their choice.

How could Steele and I win them openly to our cause? If that could be done long before the year was up Linrock would be free of violence and Captain Neal's Ranger Service saved to the State.

I went from place to place, corner to corner, bar to bar, watching, listening, recording; and not until long after sunset did I go out to the ranch.

The excitement had preceded me and speculation was rife. Hurrying through my supper, to get away from questions and to go on with my spying, I went out to the front of the house.

The evening was warm; the doors were open; and in the twilight the only lamps that had been lit were in Sampson's big sitting room at the far end of the house. Neither Sampson nor Wright had come home to supper.

I would have given much to hear their talk right then, and certainly intended to try to hear it when they did come home.

When the buckboard drove up and they alighted I was well hidden in the bushes, so well screened that I could get but a fleeting glimpse of Sampson as he went in.

For all I could see, he appeared to be a calm and quiet man, intense beneath the surface, with an air of dignity under insult. My chance to observe Wright was lost.

They went into the house without speaking, and closed the door.

At the other end of the porch, close under a window, was an offset between step and wall, and there in the shadow I hid. If Sampson or Wright visited the girls that evening I wanted to hear what was said about Steele.

It seemed to me that it might be a good clue for me—the circumstance whether or not Diane Sampson was told the truth. So I waited there in the darkness with patience born of many hours of like duty.

Presently the small lamp was lit—I could tell the difference in light when the big one was burning—and I heard the swish of skirts.

"Something's happened, surely, Sally," I heard Miss Sampson say anxiously. "Papa just met me in the hall and didn't speak. He seemed pale, worried."

"Cousin George looked like a thundercloud," said Sally. "For once, he didn't try to kiss me. Something's happened. Well, Diane, this has been a bad day for me, too."

Plainly I heard Sally's sigh, and the little pathetic sound brought me vividly out of my sordid business of suspicion and speculation. So she was sorry.

"Bad for you, too?" replied Diane in amused surprise. "Oh, I see—I forgot. You and Russ had it out."

"Out? We fought like the very old deuce. I'll never speak to him again."

"So your little—affair with Russ is all over?"

"Yes." Here she sighed again.

"Well, Sally, it began swiftly and it's just as well short," said Diane earnestly. "We know nothing at all of Russ."

"Diane, after to-day I respect him in—in spite of things—even though he seems no good. I—I cared a lot, too."

"My dear, your loves are like the summer flowers. I thought maybe your flirting with Russ might amount to something. Yet he seems so different now from what he was at first. It's only occasionally I get the impression I had of him after that night he saved me from violence. He's strange. Perhaps it all comes of his infatuation for you. He is in love with you. I'm afraid of what may come of it."

"Diane, he'll do something dreadful to George, mark my words," whispered Sally. "He swore he would if George fooled around me any more."

"Oh, dear. Sally, what can we do? These are wild men. George makes life miserable for me. And he teases you unmer..."

"I don't call it teasing. George wants to spoon," declared Sally emphatically. "He'd run after any woman."

"A fine compliment to me, Cousin Sally," laughed Diane.

"I don't agree," replied Sally stubbornly. "It's so. He's spoony. And when he's been drinking and tries to kiss me, I hate him."

"Sally, you look as if you'd rather like Russ to do something dreadful to George," said Diane with a laugh that this time was only half mirth.

"Half of me would and half of me would not," returned Sally. "But all of me would if I weren't afraid of Russ. I've got a feeling—I don't know what—something will happen between George and Russ some day."

There were quick steps on the hall floor, steps I thought I recognized.

"Hello, girls!" sounded out Wright's voice, minus its usual gaiety. Then ensued a pause that made me bring to mind a picture of Wright's glum face.

"George, what's the matter?" asked Diane presently. "I never saw papa as he is to-night, nor you so—so worried. Tell me, what has happened?"

"Well, Diane, we had a jar to-day," replied Wright, with a blunt, expressive laugh.

"Jar?" echoed both the girls curiously.

"Jar? We had to submit to a damnable outrage," added Wright passionately, as if the sound of his voice augmented his feeling. "Listen, girls. I'll tell you all about it."

He coughed, clearing his throat in a way that betrayed he had been drinking.

I sunk deeper in the shadow of my covert, and stiffening my muscles for a protracted spell of rigidity, prepared to listen with all acuteness and intensity.

Just one word from this Wright, inadvertently uttered in a moment of passion, might be the word Steele needed for his clue.

"It happened at the town hall," began Wright rapidly. "Your father and Judge Owens and I were there in consultation with three ranchers from out of town. First we were disturbed by gunshots from somewhere, but not close at hand. Then we heard the loud voices outside.

"A crowd was coming down street. It stopped before the hall. Men came running in, yelling. We thought there was a fire. Then that Ranger, Steele, stalked in, dragging a fellow by the name of Snell. We couldn't tell what was wanted because of the uproar. Finally your father restored order.

"Steele had arrested Snell for alleged assault on a restaurant keeper named Hoden. It developed that Hoden didn't accuse anybody, didn't know who attacked him. Snell, being obviously innocent, was discharged. Then this—this gun fighting Ranger pulled his guns on the court and halted the proceedings."

When Wright paused I plainly heard his intake of breath. Far indeed was he from calm.

"Steele held everybody in that hall in fear of death, and he began shouting his insults. Law was a farce in Linrock. The court was a farce. There was no law. Your father's office as mayor should be impeached. He made arrests only for petty offenses. He was afraid of the rustlers, highwaymen, murderers. He was afraid or—he just let them alone. He used his office to cheat ranchers and cattlemen in law-suits.

"All of this Steele yelled for everyone to hear. A damnable outrage! Your father, Diane, insulted in his own court by a rowdy Ranger! Not only insulted, but threatened with death—two big guns thrust almost in his face!"

"Oh! How horrible!" cried Diane, in mingled distress and anger.

"Steele's a Ranger. The Ranger Service wants to rule western Texas," went on Wright. "These Rangers are all a low set, many of them worse than the outlaws they hunt. Some of them were outlaws and gun fighters before they became Rangers.

"This Steele is one of the worst of the lot. He's keen, intelligent, smooth, and that makes him more to be feared. For he is to be feared. He wanted to kill. He meant to kill. If your father had made the least move Steele would have shot him. He's a cold-nerved devil—the born gunman. My God, any instant I expected to see your father fall dead at my feet!"

"Oh, George! The—the unspeakable ruffian!" cried Diane, passionately.

"You see, Diane, this fellow Steele has failed here in Linrock. He's been here weeks and done nothing. He must have got desperate. He's infamous and he loves his name. He seeks notoriety. He made that play with Snell just for a chance to rant against your father. He tried to inflame all Linrock against him. That about law-suits was the worst! Damn him! He'll make us enemies."

"What do you care for the insinuations of such a man?" said Diane Sampson, her voice now deep and rich with feeling. "After a moment's thought no one will be influenced by them. Do not worry, George, tell papa not to worry. Surely after all these years he can't be injured in reputation by—by an adventurer."

"Yes, he can be injured," replied George quickly. "The frontier is a queer place. There are many bitter men here, men who have failed at ranching. And your father has been wonderfully successful. Steele has dropped some poison, and it'll spread."

Then followed a silence, during which, evidently, the worried Wright bestrode the floor.

"Cousin George, what became of Steele and his prisoner?" suddenly asked Sally.

How like her it was, with her inquisitive bent of mind and shifting points of view, to ask a question the answering of which would be gall and wormwood to Wright!

It amused while it thrilled me. Sally might be a flirt, but she was no fool.

"What became of them? Ha! Steele bluffed the whole town—at least all of it who had heard the mayor's order to discharge Snell," growled Wright. "He took Snell—rode off for Del Rio to jail him."

"George!" exclaimed Diane. "Then, after all, this Ranger was able to arrest Snell, the innocent man father discharged, and take him to jail?"

"Exactly. That's the toughest part...." Wright ended abruptly, and then broke out fiercely: "But, by God, he'll never come back!"

Wright's slow pacing quickened and he strode from the parlor, leaving behind him a silence eloquent of the effect of his sinister prediction.

"Sally, what did he mean?" asked Diane in a low voice.

"Steele will be killed," replied Sally, just as low-voiced.

"Killed! That magnificent fellow! Ah, I forgot. Sally, my wits are sadly mixed. I ought to be glad if somebody kills my father's defamer. But, oh, I can't be!

"This bloody frontier makes me sick. Papa doesn't want me to stay for good. And no wonder. Shall I go back? I hate to show a white feather.

"Do you know, Sally, I was—a little taken with this Texas Ranger. Miserably, I confess. He seemed so like in spirit to the grand stature of him. How can so splendid a man be so bloody, base at heart? It's hideous. How little we know of men! I had my dream about Vaughn Steele. I confess because it shames me—because I hate myself!"

Next morning I awakened with a feeling that I was more like my old self. In the experience of activity of body and mind, with a prospect that this was merely the forerunner of great events, I came round to my own again.

Sally was not forgotten; she had just become a sorrow. So perhaps my downfall as a lover was a precursor of better results as an officer.

I held in abeyance my last conclusion regarding Sampson and Wright, and only awaited Steele's return to have fixed in mind what these men were.

Wright's remark about Steele not returning did not worry me. I had heard many such dark sayings in reference to Rangers.

Rangers had a trick of coming back. I did not see any man or men on the present horizon of Linrock equal to the killing of Steele.

As Miss Sampson and Sally had no inclination to ride, I had even more freedom. I went down to the town and burst, cheerily whistling, into Jim Hoden's place.

Jim always made me welcome there, as much for my society as for the money I spent, and I never neglected being free with both. I bought a handful of cigars and shoved some of them in his pocket.

"How's tricks, Jim?" I asked cheerily.

"Reckon I'm feelin' as well as could be expected," replied Jim. His head was circled by a bandage that did not conceal the lump where he had been struck. Jim looked a little pale, but he was bright enough.

"That was a hell of a biff Snell gave you, the skunk," I remarked with the same cheery assurance.

"Russ, I ain't accusin' Snell," remonstrated Jim with eyes that made me thoughtful.

"Sure, I know you're too good a sport to send a fellow up. But Snell deserved what he got. I saw his face when he made his talk to Sampson's court. Snell lied. And I'll tell you what, Jim, if it'd been me instead of that Ranger, Bud Snell would have got settled."

Jim appeared to be agitated by my forcible intimation of friendship.

"Jim, that's between ourselves," I went on. "I'm no fool. And much as I blab when I'm hunky, it's all air. Maybe you've noticed that about me. In some parts of

Texas it's policy to be close-mouthed. Policy and healthy. Between ourselves, as friends, I want you to know I lean some on Steele's side of the fence."

As I lighted a cigar I saw, out of the corner of my eye, how Hoden gave a quick start. I expected some kind of a startling idea to flash into his mind.

Presently I turned and frankly met his gaze. I had startled him out of his habitual set taciturnity, but even as I looked the light that might have been amaze and joy faded out of his face, leaving it the same old mask.

Still I had seen enough. Like a bloodhound, I had a scent. "Thet's funny, Russ, seein' as you drift with the gang Steele's bound to fight," remarked Hoden.

"Sure. I'm a sport. If I can't gamble with gentlemen I'll gamble with rustlers."

Again he gave a slight start, and this time he hid his eyes.

"Wal, Russ, I've heard you was slick," he said.

"You tumble, Jim. I'm a little better on the draw."

"On the draw? With cards, an' gun, too, eh?"

"Now, Jim, that last follows natural. I haven't had much chance to show how good I am on the draw with a gun. But that'll come soon."

"Reckon thet talk's a little air," said Hoden with his dry laugh. "Same as you leanin' a little on the Ranger's side of the fence."

"But, Jim, wasn't he game? What'd you think of that stand? Bluffed the whole gang! The way he called Sampson—why, it was great! The justice of that call doesn't bother me. It was Steele's nerve that got me. That'd warm any man's blood."

There was a little red in Hoden's pale cheeks and I saw him swallow hard. I had struck deep again.

"Say, don't you work for Sampson?" he queried.

"Me? I *guess* not. I'm Miss Sampson's man. He and Wright have tried to fire me many a time."

"Thet so?" he said curiously. "What for?"

"Too many silver trimmings on me, Jim. And I pack my gun low down."

"Wal, them two don't go much together out here," replied Hoden. "But I ain't seen thet anyone has shot off the trimmin's."

"Maybe it'll commence, Jim, as soon as I stop buying drinks. Talking about work—who'd you say Snell worked for?"

"I didn't say."

"Well, say so now, can't you? Jim, you're powerful peevish to-day. It's the bump on your head. Who does Snell work for?"

"When he works at all, which sure ain't often, he rides for Sampson."

"Humph! Seems to me, Jim, that Sampson's the whole circus round Linrock. I was some sore the other day to find I was losing good money at Sampson's faro game. Sure if I'd won I wouldn't have been sorry, eh? But I was surprised to hear some scully say Sampson owned the Hope So dive."

"I've heard he owned considerable property hereabouts," replied Jim constrainedly.

"Humph again! Why, Jim, you *know* it, only like every other scully you meet in this town, you're afraid to open your mug about Sampson. Get me straight, Jim Hoden. I don't care a damn for Colonel Mayor Sampson. And for cause I'd throw a gun on him just as quick as on any rustler in Pecos."

"Talk's cheap, my boy," replied Hoden, making light of my bluster, but the red was deep in his face.

"Sure, I know that," I said, calming down. "My temper gets up, Jim. Then it's not well known that Sampson owns the Hope So?"

"Reckon it's known in Pecos, all right. But Sampson's name isn't connected with the Hope So. Blandy runs the place."

"That Blandy—I've got no use for him. His faro game's crooked, or I'm locoed bronc. Not that we don't have lots of crooked faro dealers. A fellow can stand for them. But Blandy's mean, back handed, never looks you in the eyes. That Hope So place ought to be run by a good fellow like you, Hoden."

"Thanks, Russ," replied he, and I imagined his voice a little husky. "Didn't you ever hear *I* used to run it?"

"No. Did you?" I said quickly.

"I reckon. I built the place, made additions twice, owned it for eleven years."

"Well, I'll be doggoned!"

It was indeed my turn to be surprised, and with the surprise came glimmering.

"I'm sorry you're not there now, Jim. Did you sell out?"

"No. Just lost the place."

Hoden was bursting for relief now—to talk—to tell. Sympathy had made him soft. I did not need to ask another question.

"It was two years ago—two years last March," he went on. "I was in a big cattle deal with Sampson. We got the stock, an' my share, eighteen hundred head, was rustled off. I owed Sampson. He pressed me. It come to a lawsuit, an' I—was ruined."

It hurt me to look at Hoden. He was white, and tears rolled down his cheeks.

I saw the bitterness, the defeat, the agony of the man. He had failed to meet his obligation; nevertheless he had been swindled.

All that he suppressed, all that would have been passion had the man's spirit not been broken, lay bare for me to see. I had now the secret of his bitterness.

But the reason he did not openly accuse Sampson, the secret of his reticence and fear—these I thought best to try to learn at some later time, after I had consulted with Steele.

"Hard luck! Jim, it certainly was tough," I said. "But you're a good loser. And the wheel turns!

"Now, Jim, here's what I come particular to see you for. I need your advice. I've got a little money. Between you and me, as friends, I've been adding some to that roll all the time. But before I lose it I want to invest some. Buy some stock or buy an interest in some rancher's herd.

"What I want you to steer me on is a good, square rancher. Or maybe a couple of ranchers if there happen to be two honest ones in Pecos. Eh? No deals with ranchers who ride in the dark with rustlers! I've a hunch Linrock's full of them.

"Now, Jim, you've been here for years. So you must know a couple of men above suspicion."

"Thank God I do, Russ," he replied feelingly. "Frank Morton an' Si Zimmer, my friends an' neighbors all my prosperous days. An' friends still. You can gamble on Frank and Si. But Russ, if you want advice from me, don't invest money in stock now."

"Why?"

"Because any new feller buyin' stock in Pecos these days will be rustled quicker'n he can say Jack Robinson. The pioneers, the new cattlemen—these are easy pickin'. But the new fellers have to learn the ropes. They don't know anythin' or anybody. An' the old ranchers are wise an' sore. They'd fight if they...."

"What?" I put in as he paused. "If they knew who was rustling the stock?"

"Nope."

"If they had the nerve?"

"Not thet so much."

"What then? What'd make them fight?"

"A leader!"

I went out of Hoden's with that word ringing in my ears. A leader! In my mind's eye I saw a horde of dark faced, dusty-booted cattlemen riding grim and armed behind Vaughn Steele.

More thoughtful than usual, I walked on, passing some of my old haunts, and was about to turn in front of a feed and grain store when a hearty slap on my back disturbed my reflection.

"Howdy thar, cowboy," boomed a big voice.

It was Morton, the rancher whom Jim had mentioned, and whose acquaintance I had made. He was a man of great bulk, with a ruddy, merry face.

"Hello, Morton. Let's have a drink," I replied.

"Gotta rustle home," he said. "Young feller, I've a ranch to work."

"Sell it to me, Morton."

He laughed and said he wished he could. His buckboard stood at the rail, the horses stamping impatiently.

"Cards must be runnin' lucky," he went on, with another hearty laugh.

"Can't kick on the luck. But I'm afraid it will change. Morton, my friend Hoden gave me a hunch you'd be a good man to tie to. Now, I've a little money, and before I lose it I'd like to invest it in stock."

He smiled broadly, but for all his doubt of me he took definite interest.

"I'm not drunk, and I'm on the square," I said bluntly. "You've taken me for a no-good cow puncher without any brains. Wake up, Morton. If you never size up your neighbors any better than you have me—well, you won't get any richer."

It was sheer enjoyment for me to make my remarks to these men, pregnant with meaning. Morton showed his pleasure, his interest, but his faith held aloof.

"I've got some money. I had some. Then the cards have run lucky. Will you let me in on some kind of deal? Will you start me up as a stockman, with a little herd all my own?"

"Russ, this's durn strange, comin' from Sampson's cowboy," he said.

"I'm not in his outfit. My job's with Miss Sampson. She's fine, but the old man? Nit! He's been after me for weeks. I won't last long. That's one reason why I want to start up for myself."

"Hoden sent you to me, did he? Poor ol' Jim. Wal, Russ, to come out flat-footed, you'd be foolish to buy cattle now. I don't want to take your money an' see you lose out. Better go back across the Pecos where the rustlers ain't so strong. I haven't had more'n twenty-five-hundred head of stock for ten years. The rustlers let me hang on to a breedin' herd. Kind of them, ain't it?"

"Sort of kind. All I hear is rustlers." I replied with impatience. "You see, I haven't ever lived long in a rustler-run county. Who heads the gang anyway?"

Frank Morton looked at me with a curiously-amused smile.

"I hear lots about Jack Blome and Snecker. Everybody calls them out and out bad. Do they head this mysterious gang?"

"Russ, I opine Blome an' Snecker parade themselves off boss rustlers same as gun throwers. But thet's the love such men have for bein' thought hell. That's brains headin' the rustler gang hereabouts."

"Maybe Blome and Snecker are blinds. Savvy what I mean, Morton? Maybe there's more in the parade than just the fame of it."

Morton snapped his big jaw as if to shut in impulsive words.

"Look here, Morton. I'm not so young in years even if I am young west of the Pecos. I can figure ahead. It stands to reason, no matter how damn strong these rustlers are, how hidden their work, however involved with supposedly honest men—they can't last."

"They come with the pioneers an' they'll last as long as thar's a single steer left," he declared.

"Well, if you take that view of circumstances I just figure you as one of the rustlers!"

Morton looked as if he were about to brain me with the butt of his whip. His anger flashed by then as unworthy of him, and, something striking him as funny, he boomed out a laugh.

"It's not so funny," I went on. "If you're going to pretend a yellow streak, what else will I think?"

"Pretend?" he repeated.

"Sure. You can't fool me, Morton. I know men of nerve. And here in Pecos they're not any different from those in other places. I say if you show anything like a lack of sand it's all bluff.

"By nature you've got nerve. There are a lot of men round Linrock who're afraid of their shadows, afraid to be out after dark, afraid to open their mouths. But you're not one.

"So, I say, if you claim these rustlers will last, you're pretending lack of nerve just to help the popular idea along. For they can't last.

"Morton, I don't want to be a hard-riding cowboy all my days. Do you think I'd let fear of a gang of rustlers stop me from going in business with a rancher? Nit! What you need out here in Pecos is some new blood—a few youngsters like me to get you old guys started. Savvy what I mean?"

"Wal, I reckon I do," he replied, looking as if a storm had blown over him.

I gauged the hold the rustler gang had on Linrock by the difficult job it was to stir this really courageous old cattleman. He had grown up with the evil. To him it must have been a necessary one, the same as dry seasons and cyclones.

"Russ, I'll look you up the next time I come to town," he said soberly.

We parted, and I, more than content with the meeting, retraced my steps down street to the Hope So saloon.

Here I entered, bent on tasks as sincere as the ones just finished, but displeasing, because I had to mix with a low, profane set, to cultivate them, to drink occasionally despite my deftness at emptying glasses on the floor, to gamble with them and strangers, always playing the part of a flush and flashy cowboy, half drunk, ready to laugh or fight.

On the night of the fifth day after Steele's departure, I went, as was my habit, to the rendezvous we maintained at the pile of rocks out in the open.

The night was clear, bright starlight, without any moon, and for this latter fact safer to be abroad. Often from my covert I had seen dark figures skulking in and out of Linrock.

It would have been interesting to hold up these mysterious travelers; so far, however, this had not been our game. I had enough to keep my own tracks hidden, and my own comings and goings.

I liked to be out in the night, with the darkness close down to the earth, and the feeling of a limitless open all around. Not only did I listen for Steele's soft step, but for any sound—the yelp of coyote or mourn of wolf, the creak of wind in the dead brush, the distant clatter of hoofs, a woman's singing voice faint from the town.

This time, just when I was about to give up for that evening, Steele came looming like a black giant long before I heard his soft step. It was good to feel his grip, even if it hurt, because after five days I had begun to worry.

"Well, old boy, how's tricks?" he asked easily.

"Well, old man, did you land that son of a gun in jail?"

"You bet I did. And he'll stay there for a while. Del Rio rather liked the idea, Russ. All right there. I side-stepped Sanderson on the way back. But over here at the little village—Sampson they call it—I was held up. Couldn't help it, because there wasn't any road around."

"Held up?" I queried.

"That's it, the buckboard was held up. I got into the brush in time to save my bacon. They began to shoot too soon."

"Did you get any of them?"

"Didn't stay to see," he chuckled. "Had to hoof it to Linrock, and it's a good long walk."

"Been to your 'dobe yet to-night?"

"I slipped in at the back. Russ, it bothered me some to make sure no one was laying for me in the dark."

"You'll have to get a safer place. Why not take to the open every night?"

"Russ, that's well enough on a trail. But I need grub, and I've got to have a few comforts. I'll risk the 'dobe yet a little."

Then I narrated all that I had seen and done and heard during his absence, holding back one thing. What I did tell him sobered him at once, brought the quiet, somber mood, the thoughtful air.

"So that's all. Well, it's enough."

"All pertaining to our job, Vaughn," I replied. "The rest is sentiment, perhaps. I had a pretty bad case of moons over the little Langdon girl. But we quarreled. And it's ended now. Just as well, too, because if she'd...."

"Russ, did you honestly care for her? The real thing, I mean?"

"I—I'm afraid so. I'm sort of hurt inside. But, hell! There's one thing sure, a love affair might have hindered me, made me soft. I'm glad it's over."

He said no more, but his big hand pressing on my knee told me of his sympathy, another indication that there was nothing wanting in this Ranger.

"The other thing concerns you," I went on, somehow reluctant now to tell this. "You remember how I heard Wright making you out vile to Miss Sampson? Swore you'd never come back? Well, after he had gone, when Sally said he'd meant you'd be killed, Miss Sampson felt bad about it. She said she ought to be glad if someone killed you, but she couldn't be. She called you a bloody ruffian, yet she didn't want you shot.

"She said some things about the difference between your hideous character and your splendid stature. Called you a magnificent fellow—that was it. Well, then she choked up and confessed something to Sally in shame and disgrace."

"Shame—disgrace?" echoed Steele, greatly interested. "What?"

"She confessed she had been taken with you—had her little dream about you. And she hated herself for it."

Never, I thought, would I forget Vaughn Steele's eyes. It did not matter that it was dark; I saw the fixed gleam, then the leaping, shadowy light.

"Did she say that?" His voice was not quite steady. "Wonderful! Even if it only lasted a minute! She might—we might—If it wasn't for this hellish job! Russ, has it dawned on you yet, what I've got to do to Diane Sampson?"

"Yes," I replied. "Vaughn, you haven't gone sweet on her?"

What else could I make of that terrible thing in his eyes? He did not reply to that at all. I thought my arm would break in his clutch.

"You said you knew what I've got to do to Diane Sampson," he repeated hoarsely.

"Yes, you've got to ruin her happiness, if not her life."

"Why? Speak out, Russ. All this comes like a blow. There for a little I hoped you had worked out things differently from me. No hope. Ruin her life! Why?"

I could explain this strange agitation in Steele in no other way except that realization had brought keen suffering as incomprehensible as it was painful. I could not tell if it came from suddenly divined love for Diane Sampson equally with a poignant conviction that his fate was to wreck her. But I did see that he needed to speak out the brutal truth.

"Steele, old man, you'll ruin Diane Sampson, because, as arrest looks improbable to me, you'll have to kill her father."

"My God! Why, why? Say it!"

"Because Sampson is the leader of the Linrock gang of rustlers."

That night before we parted we had gone rather deeply into the plan of action for the immediate future.

First I gave Steele my earnest counsel and then as stiff an argument as I knew how to put up, all anent the absolute necessity of his eternal vigilance. If he got shot in a fair encounter with his enemies—well, that was a Ranger's risk and no disgrace. But to be massacred in bed, knifed, in the dark, shot in the back, ambushed in any manner—not one of these miserable ends must be the last record of Vaughn Steele.

He promised me in a way that made me wonder if he would ever sleep again or turn his back on anyone—made me wonder too, at the menace in his voice. Steele seemed likely to be torn two ways, and already there was a hint of future desperation.

It was agreed that I make cautious advances to Hoden and Morton, and when I could satisfy myself of their trustworthiness reveal my identity to them. Through this I was to cultivate Zimmer, and then other ranchers whom we should decide could be let into the secret.

It was not only imperative that we learn through them clues by which we might eventually fix guilt on the rustler gang, but also just as imperative that we develop a band of deputies to help us when the fight began.

Steele, now that he was back in Linrock, would have the center of the stage, with all eyes upon him. We agreed, moreover, that the bolder the front now the better the chance of ultimate success. The more nerve he showed the less danger of being ambushed, the less peril in facing vicious men.

But we needed a jail. Prisoners had to be corraled after arrest, or the work would be useless, almost a farce, and there was no possibility of repeating trips to Del Rio.

We could not use an adobe house for a jail, because that could be easily cut out of or torn down.

Finally I remembered an old stone house near the end of the main street; it had one window and one door, and had been long in disuse. Steele would rent it, hire men to guard and feed his prisoners; and if these prisoners bribed or fought their way to freedom, that would not injure the great principle for which he stood.

CHAPTER 3 SOUNDING THE TIMBER

Both Steele and I simultaneously, from different angles of reasoning, had arrived at a conviction of Sampson's guilt. It was not so strong as realization; rather a divination.

Long experience in detecting, in feeling the hidden guilt of men, had sharpened our senses for that particular thing. Steele acknowledged a few mistakes in his day; but I, allowing for the same strength of conviction, had never made a single mistake.

But conviction was one thing and proof vastly another. Furthermore, when proof was secured, then came the crowning task—that of taking desperate men in a wild country they dominated.

Verily, Steele and I had our work cut out for us. However, we were prepared to go at it with infinite patience and implacable resolve. Steele and I differed only in the driving incentive; of course, outside of that one binding vow to save the Ranger Service.

He had a strange passion, almost an obsession, to represent the law of Texas, and by so doing render something of safety and happiness to the honest pioneers.

Beside Steele I knew I shrunk to a shadow. I was not exactly a heathen, and certainly I wanted to help harassed people, especially women and children; but mainly with me it was the zest, the thrill, the hazard, the matching of wits—in a word, the adventure of the game.

Next morning I rode with the young ladies. In the light of Sally's persistently flagrant advances, to which I was apparently blind, I saw that my hard-won victory over self was likely to be short-lived.

That possibility made me outwardly like ice. I was an attentive, careful, reliable, and respectful attendant, seeing to the safety of my charges; but the one-time gay and debonair cowboy was a thing of the past.

Sally, womanlike, had been a little—a very little—repentant; she had showed it, my indifference had piqued her; she had made advances and then my coldness had roused her spirit. She was the kind of girl to value most what she had lost, and to throw consequences to the winds in winning it back.

When I divined this I saw my revenge. To be sure, when I thought of it I had no reason to want revenge. She had been most gracious to me.

But there was the catty thing she had said about being kissed again by her admirers. Then, in all seriousness, sentiment aside, I dared not make up with her.

So the cold and indifferent part I played was imperative.

We halted out on the ridge and dismounted for the usual little rest. Mine I took in the shade of a scrubby mesquite. The girls strolled away out of sight. It was a drowsy day, and I nearly fell asleep.

Something aroused me—a patter of footsteps or a rustle of skirts. Then a soft thud behind me gave me at once a start and a thrill. First I saw Sally's little brown hands on my shoulders. Then her head, with hair all shiny and flying and fragrant, came round over my shoulder, softly smoothing my cheek, until her sweet, saucy, heated face was right under my eyes.

"Russ, don't you love me any more?" she whispered.

CHAPTER 4 STEELE BREAKS UP THE PARTY

That night, I saw Steele at our meeting place, and we compared notes and pondered details of our problem.

Steele had rented the stone house to be used as a jail. While the blacksmith was putting up a door and window calculated to withstand many onslaughts, all the idlers and strangers in town went to see the sight. Manifestly it was an occasion for Linrock. When Steele let it be known that he wanted to hire a jailer and a guard this caustically humorous element offered itself *en masse*. The men made a joke out of it.

When Steele and I were about to separate I remembered a party that was to be given by Miss Sampson, and I told him about it. He shook his head sadly, almost doubtfully.

Was it possible that Sampson could be a deep eyed, cunning scoundrel, the true leader of the cattle rustlers, yet keep that beautiful and innocent girl out on the frontier and let her give parties to sons and daughters of a community he had robbed? To any but remorseless Rangers the idea was incredible.

Thursday evening came in spite of what the girls must have regarded as an interminably dragging day.

It was easy to differentiate their attitudes toward this party. Sally wanted to look beautiful, to excell all the young ladies who were to attend, to attach to her train all the young men, and have them fighting to dance with her. Miss Sampson had an earnest desire to open her father's house to the people of Linrock, to show that a daughter had come into his long cheerless home, to make the evening one of pleasure and entertainment.

I happened to be present in the parlor, was carrying in some flowers for final decoration, when Miss Sampson learned that her father had just ridden off with three horsemen whom Dick, who brought the news, had not recognized.

In her keen disappointment she scarcely heard Dick's concluding remark about the hurry of the colonel. My sharp ears, however, took this in and it was thought-provoking. Sampson was known to ride off at all hours, yet this incident seemed unusual.

At eight o'clock the house and porch and patio were ablaze with lights. Every lantern and lamp on the place, together with all that could be bought and borrowed, had been brought into requisition.

CHAPTER 4 STEELE BREAKS UP THE PARTY

The cowboys arrived first, all dressed in their best, clean shaven, red faced, bright eyed, eager for the fun to commence. Then the young people from town, and a good sprinkling of older people, came in a steady stream.

Miss Sampson received them graciously, excused her father's absence, and bade them be at home.

The music, or the discordance that went by that name, was furnished by two cowboys with banjos and an antediluvian gentleman with a fiddle. Nevertheless, it was music that could be danced to, and there was no lack of enthusiasm.

I went from porch to parlor and thence to patio, watching and amused. The lights and the decorations of flowers, the bright dresses and the flashy scarfs of the cowboys furnished a gay enough scene to a man of lonesome and stern life like mine. During the dance there was a steady, continuous shuffling tramp of boots, and during the interval following a steady, low hum of merry talk and laughter.

My wandering from place to place, apart from my usual careful observation, was an unobtrusive but, to me, a sneaking pursuit of Sally Langdon.

She had on a white dress I had never seen with a low neck and short sleeves, and she looked so sweet, so dainty, so altogether desirable, that I groaned a hundred times in my jealousy. Because, manifestly, Sally did not intend to run any risk of my not seeing her in her glory, no matter where my eyes looked.

A couple of times in promenading I passed her on the arm of some proud cowboy or gallant young buck from town, and on these occasions she favored her escort with a languishing glance that probably did as much damage to him as to me.

Presently she caught me red-handed in my careless, sauntering pursuit of her, and then, whether by intent or from indifference, she apparently deigned me no more notice. But, quick to feel a difference in her, I marked that from that moment her gaiety gradually merged into coquettishness, and soon into flirtation.

Then, just to see how far she would go, perhaps desperately hoping she would make me hate her, I followed her shamelessly from patio to parlor, porch to court, even to the waltz.

To her credit, she always weakened when some young fellow got her in a corner and tried to push the flirting to extremes. Young Waters was the only one lucky enough to kiss her, and there was more of strength in his conquest of her than any decent fellow could be proud of.

When George Wright sought Sally out there was added to my jealousy a real anxiety. I had brushed against Wright more than once that evening. He was not drunk, yet under the influence of liquor.

Sally, however, evidently did not discover that, because, knowing her abhorrence of drink, I believed she would not have walked out with him had she known. Anyway, I followed them, close in the shadow.

Wright was unusually gay. I saw him put his arm around her without remonstrance. When the music recommenced they went back to the house. Wright danced with Sally, not ungracefully for a man who rode a horse as much as he.

After the dance he waved aside Sally's many partners, not so gaily as would have been consistent with good feeling, and led her away. I followed. They ended up that walk at the extreme corner of the patio, where, under gaily colored lights, a little arbor had been made among the flowers and vines.

Sally seemed to have lost something of her vivacity. They had not been out of my sight for a moment before Sally cried out. It was a cry of impatience or remonstrance, rather than alarm, but I decided that it would serve me an excuse.

I dashed back, leaped to the door of the arbor, my hand on my gun.

Wright was holding Sally. When he heard me he let her go. Then she uttered a cry that was one of alarm. Her face blanched; her eyes grew strained. One hand went to her breast. She thought I meant to kill Wright.

"Excuse me," I burst out frankly, turning to Wright. I never saw a hyena, but he looked like one. "I heard a squeal. Thought a girl was hurt, or something. Miss Sampson gave me orders to watch out for accidents, fire, anything. So excuse me, Wright."

As I stepped back, to my amazement, Sally, excusing herself to the scowling Wright, hurriedly joined me.

"Oh, it's our dance, Russ!"

She took my arm and we walked through the patio.

"I'm afraid of him, Russ," she whispered. "You frightened me worse though. You didn't mean to—to—"

"I made a bluff. Saw he'd been drinking, so I kept near you."

"You return good for evil," she replied, squeezing my arm. "Russ, let me tell you—whenever anything frightens me since we got here I think of you. If you're only near I feel safe."

We paused at the door leading into the big parlor. Couples were passing. Here I could scarcely distinguish the last words she said. She stood before me, eyes downcast, face flushed, as sweet and pretty a lass as man could want to see, and with her hand she twisted round and round a silver button on my buckskin vest.

"Dance with me, the rest of this," she said. "George shooed away my partner. I'm glad for the chance. Dance with me, Russ—not gallantly or dutifully because I ask you, but because you *want* to. Else not at all."

There was a limit to my endurance. There would hardly be another evening like this, at least, for me, in that country. I capitulated with what grace I could express.

We went into the parlor, and as we joined the dancers, despite all that confusion I heard her whisper: "I've been a little beast to you."

That dance seemingly lasted only a moment—a moment while she was all airy grace, radiant, and alluring, floating close to me, with our hands clasped. Then it appeared the music had ceased, the couples were finding seats, and Sally and I were accosted by Miss Sampson.

She said we made a graceful couple in the dance. And Sally said she did not have to reach up a mile to me—I was not so awfully tall.

And I, tongue-tied for once, said nothing.

CHAPTER 4 STEELE BREAKS UP THE PARTY

Wright had returned and was now standing, cigarette between lips, in the door leading out to the patio. At the same moment that I heard a heavy tramp of boots, from the porch side I saw Wright's face change remarkably, expressing amaze, consternation, then fear.

I wheeled in time to see Vaughn Steele bend his head to enter the door on that side. The dancers fell back.

At sight of him I was again the Ranger, his ally. Steele was pale, yet heated. He panted. He wore no hat. He had his coat turned up and with left hand he held the lapels together.

In a quick ensuing silence Miss Sampson rose, white as her dress. The young women present stared in astonishment and their partners showed excitement.

"Miss Sampson, I came to search your house!" panted Steele, courteously, yet with authority.

I disengaged myself from Sally, who was clinging to my hands, and I stepped forward out of the corner. Steele had been running. Why did he hold his coat like that? I sensed action, and the cold thrill animated me.

Miss Sampson's astonishment was succeeded by anger difficult to control.

"In the absence of my father I am mistress here. I will not permit you to search my house."

"Then I regret to say I must do so without your permission," he said sternly.

"Do not dare!" she flashed. She stood erect, her bosom swelling, her eyes magnificently black with passion. "How dare you intrude here? Have you not insulted us enough? To search my house to-night—to break up my party—oh, it's worse than outrage! Why on earth do you want to search here? Ah, for the same reason you dragged a poor innocent man into my father's court! Sir, I forbid you to take another step into this house."

Steele's face was bloodless now, and I wondered if it had to do with her scathing scorn or something that he hid with his hand closing his coat that way.

"Miss Sampson, I don't need warrants to search houses," he said. "But this time I'll respect your command. It would be too bad to spoil your party. Let me add, perhaps you do me a little wrong. God knows I hope so. I was shot by a rustler. He fled. I chased him here. He has taken refuge here—in your father's house. He's hidden somewhere."

Steele spread wide his coat lapels. He wore a light shirt, the color of which in places was white. The rest was all a bloody mass from which dark red drops fell to the floor.

"Oh!" cried Miss Sampson.

Scorn and passion vanished in the horror, the pity, of a woman who imagined she saw a man mortally wounded. It was a hard sight for a woman's eyes, that crimson, heaving breast.

"Surely I didn't see that," went on Steele, closing his coat. "You used unforgettable words, Miss Sampson. From you they hurt. For I stand alone. My fight is to make Linrock safer, cleaner, a better home for women and children. Some day you will remember what you said."

How splendid he looked, how strong against odds. How simple a dignity fitted his words. Why, a woman far blinder than Diane Sampson could have seen that here stood a man.

Steele bowed, turned on his heel, and strode out to vanish in the dark.

Then while she stood bewildered, still shocked, I elected to do some rapid thinking.

How seriously was Steele injured? An instant's thought was enough to tell me that if he had sustained any more than a flesh wound he would not have chased his assailant, not with so much at stake in the future.

Then I concerned myself with a cold grip of desire to get near the rustler who had wounded Steele. As I started forward, however, Miss Sampson defeated me. Sally once more clung to my hands, and directly we were surrounded by an excited circle.

It took a moment or two to calm them.

"Then there's a rustler—here—hiding?" repeated Miss Sampson.

"Miss Sampson, I'll find him. I'll rout him out," I said.

"Yes, yes, find him, Russ, but don't use violence," she replied. "Send him away—no, give him over to—"

"Nothing of the kind," interrupted George Wright, loud-voiced. "Cousin, go on with your dance. I'll take a couple of cowboys. I'll find this—this rustler, if there's one here. But I think it's only another bluff of Steele's."

This from Wright angered me deeply, and I strode right for the door.

"Where are you going?" he demanded.

"I've Miss Sampson's orders. She wants me to find this hidden man. She trusts me not to allow any violence."

"Didn't I say I'd see to that?" he snarled.

"Wright, I don't care what you say," I retorted. "But I'm thinking you might not want me to find this rustler."

Wright turned black in the face. Verily, if he had worn a gun he would have pulled it on me. As it was, Miss Sampson's interference probably prevented more words, if no worse.

"Don't quarrel," she said. "George, you go with Russ. Please hurry. I'll be nervous till the rustler's found or you're sure there's not one."

We started with several cowboys to ransack the house. We went through the rooms, searching, calling out, flashing our lanterns in dark places.

It struck me forcibly that Wright did all the calling. He hurried, too, tried to keep in the lead. I wondered if he knew his voice would be recognized by the hiding man.

Be that as it might, it was I who peered into a dark corner, and then with a cocked gun leveled I said: "Come out!"

He came forth into the flare of lanterns, a tall, slim, dark-faced youth, wearing dark sombrero, blouse and trousers. I collared him before any of the others could move, and I held the gun close enough to make him shrink.

But he did not impress me as being frightened just then; nevertheless, he had a clammy face, the pallid look of a man who had just gotten over a shock. He peered into my face, then into that of the cowboy next to me, then into Wright's and if ever in my life I beheld relief I saw it then.

That was all I needed to know, but I meant to find out more if I could.

"Who're you?" I asked quietly.

He gazed rather arrogantly down at me. It always irritated me to be looked down at that way.

"Say, don't be gay with me or you'll get it good," I yelled, prodding him in the side with the cocked gun. "Who are you? Quick!"

"Bo Snecker," he said.

"Any relation to Bill Snecker?"

"His son."

"What'd you hide here for?"

He appeared to grow sullen.

"Reckoned I'd be as safe in Sampson's as anywheres."

"Ahuh! You're taking a long chance," I replied, and he never knew, or any of the others, just how long a chance that was.

Sight of Steele's bloody breast remained with me, and I had something sinister to combat. This was no time for me to reveal myself or to show unusual feeling or interest for Steele.

As Steele had abandoned his search, I had nothing to do now but let the others decide what disposition was to be made of Snecker.

"Wright, what'll you do with him?" I queried, as if uncertain, now the capture was made. I let Snecker go and sheathed my weapon.

That seemed a signal for him to come to life. I guessed he had not much fancied the wide and somewhat variable sweep of that cocked gun.

"I'll see to that," replied Wright gruffly, and he pushed Snecker in front of him into the hall. I followed them out into the court at the back of the house.

As I had very little further curiosity I did not wait to see where they went, but hurried back to relieve Miss Sampson and Sally.

I found them as I had left them—Sally quiet, pale, Miss Sampson nervous and distressed. I soon calmed their fears of any further trouble or possible disturbance. Miss Sampson then became curious and wanted to know who the rustler was.

"How strange he should come here," she said several times.

"Probably he'd run this way or thought he had a better chance to hide where there was dancing and confusion," I replied glibly.

I wondered how much longer I would find myself keen to shunt her mind from any channel leading to suspicion.

"Would papa have arrested him?" she asked.

"Colonel Sampson might have made it hot for him," I replied frankly, feeling that if what I said had a double meaning it still was no lie.

"Oh, I forgot—the Ranger!" she exclaimed suddenly. "That awful sight—the whole front of him bloody! Russ, how could he stand up under such a wound? Do you think it'll kill him?"

"That's hard to say. A man like Steele can stand a lot."

"Russ, please go find him! See how it is with him!" she said, almost pleadingly.

I started, glad of the chance and hurried down toward the town.

There was a light in the little adobe house where he lived, and proceeding cautiously, so as to be sure no one saw me, I went close and whistled low in a way he would recognize. Then he opened the door and I went in.

"Hello, son!" he said. "You needn't have worried. Sling a blanket over that window so no one can see in."

He had his shirt off and had been in the act of bandaging a wound that the bullet had cut in his shoulder.

"Let me tie that up," I said, taking the strips of linen. "Ahuh! Shot you from behind, didn't he?"

"How else, you locoed lady-charmer? It's a wonder I didn't have to tell you that."

"Tell me about it."

Steele related a circumstance differing little from other attempts at his life, and concluded by saying that Snecker was a good runner if he was not a good shot.

I finished the bandaging and stood off, admiring Steele's magnificent shoulders. I noted, too, on the fine white skin more than one scar made by bullets. I got an impression that his strength and vitality were like his spirit—unconquerable!

"So you knew it was Bill Snecker's son?" I asked when I had told him about finding the rustler.

"Sure. Jim Hoden pointed him out to me yesterday. Both the Sneckers are in town. From now on we're going to be busy, Russ."

"It can't come too soon for me," I replied. "Shall I chuck my job? Come out from behind these cowboy togs?"

"Not yet. We need proof, Russ. We've got to be able to prove things. Hang on at the ranch yet awhile."

"This Bo Snecker was scared stiff till he recognized Wright. Isn't that proof?"

"No, that's nothing. We've got to catch Sampson and Wright red-handed."

"I don't like the idea of you trailing along alone," I protested. "Remember what Neal told me. I'm to kick. It's time for me to hang round with a couple of guns. You'll never use one."

"The hell I won't," he retorted, with a dark glance of passion. I was surprised that my remark had angered him. "You fellows are all wrong. I know *when* to throw a gun. You ought to remember that Rangers have a bad name for wanting to shoot. And I'm afraid it's deserved."

"Did you shoot at Snecker?" I queried.

"I could have got him in the back. But that wouldn't do. I shot three times at his legs—tried to let him down. I'd have made him tell everything he knew, but he ran. He was too fast for me."

"Shooting at his legs! No wonder he ran. He savvied your game all right. It's funny, Vaughn, how these rustlers and gunmen don't mind being killed. But to cripple them, rope them, jail them—that's hell to them! Well, I'm to go on, up at the ranch, falling further in love with that sweet kid instead of coming out straight to face things with you?"

Steele had to laugh, yet he was more thoughtful of my insistence.

"Russ, you think you have patience, but you don't know what patience is. I won't be hurried on this job. But I'll tell you what: I'll hang under cover most of the time when you're not close to me. See? That can be managed. I'll watch for you when you come in town. We'll go in the same places. And in case I get busy you can stand by and trail along after me. That satisfy you?"

"Fine!" I said, both delighted and relieved. "Well, I'll have to rustle back now to tell Miss Sampson you're all right."

Steele had about finished pulling on a clean shirt, exercising care not to disarrange the bandages; and he stopped short to turn squarely and look at me with hungry eyes.

"Russ, did she—show sympathy?"

"She was all broken up about it. Thought you were going to die."

"Did she send you?"

"Sure. And she said hurry," I replied.

I was not a little gleeful over the apparent possibility of Steele being in the same boat with me.

"Do you think she would have cared if—if I had been shot up bad?"

The great giant of a Ranger asked this like a boy, hesitatingly, with color in his face.

"Care! Vaughn, you're as thickheaded as you say I'm locoed. Diane Sampson has fallen in love with you! That's all. Love at first sight! She doesn't realize it. But I know."

There he stood as if another bullet had struck him, this time straight through the heart. Perhaps one had—and I repented a little of my overconfident declaration.

Still, I would not go back on it. I believed it.

"Russ, for God's sake! What a terrible thing to say!" he ejaculated hoarsely.

"No. It's not terrible to *say* it—only the fact is terrible," I went on. I may be wrong. But I swear I'm right. When you opened your coat, showed that bloody breast—well, I'll never forget her eyes.

"She had been furious. She showed passion—hate. Then all in a second something wonderful, beautiful broke through. Pity, fear, agonized thought of your death! If that's not love, if—if she did not betray love, then I never saw it. She thinks she hates you. But she loves you."

"Get out of here," he ordered thickly.

I went, not forgetting to peep out at the door and to listen a moment, then I hurried into the open, up toward the ranch.

The stars were very big and bright, so calm, so cold, that it somehow hurt me to look at them. Not like men's lives, surely!

What had fate done to Vaughn Steele and to me? I had a moment of bitterness, an emotion rare with me.

Most Rangers put love behind them when they entered the Service and seldom found it after that. But love had certainly met me on the way, and I now had confirmation of my fear that Vaughn was hard hit.

Then the wildness, the adventurer in me stirred to the wonder of it all. It was in me to exult even in the face of fate. Steele and I, while balancing our lives on the hair-trigger of a gun, had certainly fallen into a tangled web of circumstances not calculated in the role of Rangers.

I went back to the ranch with regret, remorse, sorrow knocking at my heart, but notwithstanding that, tingling alive to the devilish excitement of the game.

I knew not what it was that prompted me to sow the same seed in Diane Sampson's breast that I had sown in Steele's; probably it was just a propensity for sheer mischief, probably a certainty of the truth and a strange foreshadowing of a coming event.

If Diane Sampson loved, through her this event might be less tragic. Somehow love might save us all.

That was the shadowy portent flitting in the dark maze of my mind.

At the ranch dancing had been resumed. There might never have been any interruption of the gaiety. I found Miss Sampson on the lookout for me and she searched my face with eyes that silenced my one last qualm of conscience.

"Let's go out in the patio," I suggested. "I don't want any one to hear what I say."

Outside in the starlight she looked white and very beautiful. I felt her tremble. Perhaps my gravity presaged the worst. So it did in one way—poor Vaughn!

"I went down to Steele's 'dobe, the little place where he lives." I began, weighing my words. "He let me in—was surprised. He had been shot high in the shoulder, not a dangerous wound. I bandaged it for him. He was grateful—said he had no friends."

"Poor fellow! Oh, I'm glad it—it isn't bad," said Miss Sampson. Something glistened in her eyes.

"He looked strange, sort of forlorn. I think your words—what you said hurt him more than the bullet. I'm sure of that, Miss Sampson."

"Oh, I saw that myself! I was furious. But I—I meant what I said."

"You wronged Steele. I happen to know. I know his record along the Rio Grande. It's scarcely my place, Miss Sampson, to tell you what you'll find out for yourself, sooner or later."

"What shall I find out?" she demanded.

"I've said enough."

"No. You mean my father and cousin George are misinformed or wrong about Steele? I've feared it this last hour. It was his look. That pierced me. Oh, I'd hate to be unjust. You say I wronged him, Russ? Then you take sides with him against my father?"

"Yes," I replied very low.

She was keenly hurt and seemed, despite an effort, to shrink from me.

"It's only natural you should fight for your father," I went on. "Perhaps you don't understand. He has ruled here for long. He's been—well, let's say, easy with the evil-doers. But times are changing. He opposed the Ranger idea, which is also natural, I suppose. Still, he's wrong about Steele, terribly wrong, and it means trouble."

"Oh, I don't know what to believe!"

"It might be well for you to think things out for yourself."

"Russ, I feel as though I couldn't. I can't make head or tail of life out here. My father seems so strange. Though, of course, I've only seen him twice a year since I was a little girl. He has two sides to him. When I come upon that strange side, the one I never knew, he's like a man I never saw.

"I want to be a good and loving daughter. I want to help him fight his battles. But he doesn't—he doesn't *satisfy* me. He's grown impatient and wants me to go back to Louisiana. That gives me a feeling of mystery. Oh, it's *all* mystery!"

"True, you're right," I replied, my heart aching for her. "It's all mystery—and trouble for you, too. Perhaps you'd do well to go home."

"Russ, you suggest I leave here—leave my father?" she asked.

"I advise it. You struck a—a rather troublesome time. Later you might return if—"

"Never. I came to stay, and I'll stay," she declared, and there her temper spoke.

"Miss Sampson," I began again, after taking a long, deep breath, "I ought to tell you one thing more about Steele."

"Well, go on."

"Doesn't he strike you now as being the farthest removed from a ranting, brutal Ranger?"

"I confess he was at least a gentleman."

"Rangers don't allow anything to interfere with the discharge of their duty. He was courteous after you defamed him. He respected your wish. He did not break up the dance.

"This may not strike you particularly. But let me explain that Steele was chasing an outlaw who had shot him. Under ordinary circumstances he would have searched your house. He would have been like a lion. He would have torn the place down around our ears to get that rustler.

"But his action was so different from what I had expected, it amazed me. Just now, when I was with him, I learned, I guessed, what stayed his hand. I believe you ought to know."

"Know what?" she asked. How starry and magnetic her eyes! A woman's divining intuition made them wonderful with swift-varying emotion.

They drew me on to the fatal plunge. What was I doing to her—to Vaughn? Something bound my throat, making speech difficult.

"He's fallen in love with you," I hurried on in a husky voice. "Love at first sight! Terrible! Hopeless! I saw it—felt it. I can't explain how I know, but I do know.

"That's what stayed his hand here. And that's why I'm on his side. He's alone. He has a terrible task here without any handicaps. Every man is against him. If he fails, you might be the force that weakened him. So you ought to be kinder in your thought of him. Wait before you judge him further.

"If he isn't killed, time will prove him noble instead of vile. If he is killed, which is more than likely, you'll feel the happier for a generous doubt in favor of the man who loved you."

Like one stricken blind, she stood an instant; then, with her hands at her breast, she walked straight across the patio into the dark, open door of her room.

CHAPTER 5 CLEANING OUT LINROCK

Not much sleep visited me that night. In the morning, the young ladies not stirring and no prospects of duty for me, I rode down to town.

Sight of the wide street, lined by its hitching posts and saddled horses, the square buildings with their ugly signs, unfinished yet old, the lounging, dust-gray men at every corner—these awoke in me a significance that had gone into oblivion overnight.

That last talk with Miss Sampson had unnerved me, wrought strangely upon me. And afterward, waking and dozing, I had dreamed, lived in a warm, golden place where there were music and flowers and Sally's spritelike form leading me on after two tall, beautiful lovers, Diane and Vaughn, walking hand in hand.

Fine employment of mind for a Ranger whose single glance down a quiet street pictured it with darkgarbed men in grim action, guns spouting red, horses plunging!

In front of Hoden's restaurant I dismounted and threw my bridle. Jim was unmistakably glad to see me.

"Where've you been? Morton was in an' powerful set on seein' you. I steered him from goin' up to Sampson's. What kind of a game was you givin' Frank?"

"Jim, I just wanted to see if he was a safe rancher to make a stock deal for me."

"He says you told him he didn't have no yellow streak an' that he was a rustler. Frank can't git over them two hunches. When he sees you he's goin' to swear he's no rustler, but he *has* got a yellow streak, unless..."

This little, broken-down Texan had eyes like flint striking fire.

"Unless?" I queried sharply.

Jim breathed a deep breath and looked around the room before his gaze fixed again on mine.

"Wal," he replied, speaking low, "Me and Frank allows you've picked the right men. It was me that sent them letters to the Ranger captain at Austin. Now who in hell are you?"

It was my turn to draw a deep breath.

I had taken six weeks to strike fire from a Texan whom I instinctively felt had been prey to the power that shadowed Linrock. There was no one in the room except us, no one passing, nor near.

Reaching into the inside pocket of my buckskin vest, I turned the lining out. A star-shaped, bright, silver object flashed as I shoved it, pocket and all, under Jim's hard eyes.

He could not help but read; United States Deputy Marshall.

"By golly," he whispered, cracking the table with his fist. "Russ, you sure rung true to me. But never as a cowboy!"

"Jim, the woods is full of us!"

Heavy footsteps sounded on the walk. Presently Steele's bulk darkened the door.

"Hello," I greeted. "Steele, shake hands with Jim Hoden."

"Hello," replied Steele slowly. "Say, I reckon I know Hoden."

"Nit. Not this one. He's the old Hoden. He used to own the Hope So saloon. It was on the square when he ran it. Maybe he'll get it back pretty soon. Hope so!"

I laughed at my execrable pun. Steele leaned against the counter, his gray glance studying the man I had so oddly introduced.

Hoden in one flash associated the Ranger with me—a relation he had not dreamed of. Then, whether from shock or hope or fear I know not, he appeared about to faint.

"Hoden, do you know who's boss of this secret gang of rustlers hereabouts?" asked Steele bluntly.

It was characteristic of him to come sharp to the point. His voice, something deep, easy, cool about him, seemed to steady Hoden.

"No," replied Hoden.

"Does anybody know?" went on Steele.

"Wal, I reckon there's not one honest native of Pecos who *knows*."

"But you have your suspicions?"

"We have."

"You can keep your suspicions to yourself. But you can give me your idea about this crowd that hangs round the saloons, the regulars."

"Jest a bad lot," replied Hoden, with the quick assurance of knowledge. "Most of them have been here years. Others have drifted in. Some of them work odd times. They rustle a few steer, steal, rob, anythin' for a little money to drink an' gamble. Jest a bad lot!

"But the strangers as are always comin' an' goin'—strangers that never git acquainted—some of them are likely to be *the* rustlers. Bill an' Bo Snecker are in town now. Bill's a known cattle-thief. Bo's no good, the makin' of a gun-fighter. He heads thet way.

"They might be rustlers. But the boy, he's hardly careful enough for this gang. Then there's Jack Blome. He comes to town often. He lives up in the hills. He always has three or four strangers with him. Blome's the fancy gun fighter. He shot a gambler here last fall. Then he was in a fight in Sanderson lately. Got two cowboys then.

"Blome's killed a dozen Pecos men. He's a rustler, too, but I reckon he's not the brains of thet secret outfit, if he's in it at all."

Steele appeared pleased with Hoden's idea. Probably it coincided with the one he had arrived at himself.

"Now, I'm puzzled over this," said Steele. "Why do men, apparently honest men, seem to be so close-mouthed here? Is that a fact or only my impression?"

"It's sure a fact," replied Hoden darkly. "Men have lost cattle an' property in Linrock—lost them honestly or otherwise, as hasn't been proved. An' in some cases when they talked—hinted a little—they was found dead. Apparently held up an' robbed. But dead. Dead men don't talk. Thet's why we're close-mouthed."

Steele's face wore a dark, somber sternness.

Rustling cattle was not intolerable. Western Texas had gone on prospering, growing in spite of the horde of rustlers ranging its vast stretches; but this cold, secret, murderous hold on a little struggling community was something too strange, too terrible for men to stand long.

It had waited for a leader like Steele, and now it could not last. Hoden's revived spirit showed that.

The ranger was about to speak again when the clatter of hoofs interrupted him. Horses halted out in front.

A motion of Steele's hand caused me to dive through a curtained door back of Hoden's counter. I turned to peep out and was in time to see George Wright enter with the red-headed cowboy called Brick.

That was the first time I had ever seen Wright come into Hoden's. He called for tobacco.

If his visit surprised Jim he did not show any evidence. But Wright showed astonishment as he saw the Ranger, and then a dark glint flitted from the eyes that shifted from Steele to Hoden and back again.

Steele leaned easily against the counter, and he said good morning pleasantly. Wright deigned no reply, although he bent a curious and hard scrutiny upon Steele. In fact, Wright evinced nothing that would lead one to think he had any respect for Steele as a man or as a Ranger.

"Steele, that was the second break of yours last night," he said finally. "If you come fooling round the ranch again there'll be hell!"

It seemed strange that a man who had lived west of the Pecos for ten years could not see in Steele something which forbade that kind of talk.

It certainly was not nerve Wright showed; men of courage were seldom intolerant; and with the matchless nerve that characterized Steele or the great gunmen of the day there went a cool, unobtrusive manner, a speech brief, almost gentle, certainly courteous. Wright was a hot-headed Louisianian of French extraction; a man evidently who had never been crossed in anything, and who was strong, brutal, passionate, which qualities, in the face of a situation like this, made him simply a fool!

The way Steele looked at Wright was joy to me. I hated this smooth, dark-skinned Southerner. But, of course, an ordinary affront like Wright's only earned silence from Steele.

"I'm thinking you used your Ranger bluff just to get near Diane Sampson," Wright sneered. "Mind you, if you come up there again there'll be hell!"

"You're damn right there'll be hell!" retorted Steele, a kind of high ring in his voice. I saw thick, dark red creep into his face.

Had Wright's incomprehensible mention of Diane Sampson been an instinct of love—of jealousy? Verily, it had pierced into the depths of the Ranger, probably as no other thrust could have.

"Diane Sampson wouldn't stoop to know a dirty blood-tracker like you," said Wright hotly. His was not a deliberate intention to rouse Steele; the man was simply rancorous. "I'll call you right, you cheap bluffer! You four-flush! You damned interfering conceited Ranger!"

Long before Wright ended his tirade Steele's face had lost the tinge of color, so foreign to it in moments like this; and the cool shade, the steady eyes like ice on fire, the ruthless lips had warned me, if they had not Wright.

"Wright, I'll not take offense, because you seem to be championing your beautiful cousin," replied Steele in slow speech, biting. "But let me return your compliment. You're a fine Southerner! Why, you're only a cheap four-flush—damned bull-headed—*rustler*"

Steele hissed the last word. Then for him—for me—for Hoden—there was the truth in Wright's working passion-blackened face.

Wright jerked, moved, meant to draw. But how slow! Steele lunged forward. His long arm swept up.

And Wright staggered backward, knocking table and chairs, to fall hard, in a half-sitting posture, against the wall.

"Don't draw!" warned Steele.

"Wright, get away from your gun!" yelled the cowboy Brick.

But Wright was crazed by fury. He tugged at his hip, his face corded with purple welts, malignant, murderous, while he got to his feet.

I was about to leap through the door when Steele shot. Wright's gun went ringing to the floor.

Like a beast in pain Wright screamed. Frantically he waved a limp arm, flinging blood over the white table-cloths. Steele had crippled him.

"Here, you cowboy," ordered Steele; "take him out, quick!"

Brick saw the need of expediency, if Wright did not realize it, and he pulled the raving man out of the place. He hurried Wright down the street, leaving the horses behind.

Steele calmly sheathed his gun.

"Well, I guess that opens the ball," he said as I came out.

Hoden seemed fascinated by the spots of blood on the table-cloths. It was horrible to see him rubbing his hands there like a ghoul!

"I tell you what, fellows," said Steele, "we've just had a few pleasant moments with the man who has made it healthy to keep close-mouthed in Linrock."

Hoden lifted his shaking hands.

"What'd you wing him for?" he wailed. "He was drawin' on you. Shootin' arms off men like him won't do out here."

I was inclined to agree with Hoden.

"That bull-headed fool will roar and butt himself with all his gang right into our hands. He's just the man I've needed to meet. Besides, shooting him would have been murder for me!"

"Murder!" exclaimed Hoden.

"He was a fool, and slow at that. Under such circumstances could I kill him when I didn't have to?"

"Sure it'd been the trick." declared Jim positively. "I'm not allowin' for whether he's really a rustler or not. It just won't do, because these fellers out here ain't go-in' to be afraid of you."

"See here, Hoden. If a man's going to be afraid of me at all, that trick will make him more afraid of me. I know it. It works out. When Wright cools down he'll remember, he'll begin to think, he'll realize that I could more easily have killed him than risk a snapshot at his arm. I'll bet you he goes pale to the gills next time he even sees me."

"That may be true, Steele. But if Wright's the man you think he is he'll begin that secret underground bizness. It's been tolerable healthy these last six months. You can gamble on this. If thet secret work does commence you'll have more reason to suspect Wright. I won't feel very safe from now on.

"I heard you call him rustler. He knows thet. Why, Wright won't sleep at night now. He an' Sampson have always been after me."

"Hoden, what are your eyes for?" demanded Steele. "Watch out. And now here. See your friend Morton. Tell him this game grows hot. Together you approach four or five men you know well and can absolutely trust.

"Hello, there's somebody coming. You meet Russ and me to-night, out in the open a quarter of a mile, straight from the end of this street. You'll find a pile of stones. Meet us there to-night at ten o'clock."

The next few days, for the several hours each day that I was in town, I had Steele in sight all the time or knew that he was safe under cover.

Nothing happened. His presence in the saloons or any place where men congregated was marked by a certain uneasy watchfulness on the part of almost everybody, and some amusement on the part of a few.

It was natural to suppose that the lawless element would rise up in a mass and slay Steele on sight. But this sort of thing never happened. It was not so much that these enemies of the law awaited his next move, but just a slowness peculiar to the frontier.

The ranger was in their midst. He was interesting, if formidable. He would have been welcomed at card tables, at the bars, to play and drink with the men who knew they were under suspicion.

There was a rude kind of good humor even in their open hostility.

Besides, one Ranger, or a company of Rangers could not have held the undivided attention of these men from their games and drinks and quarrels except by some decided move. Excitement, greed, appetite were rife in them.

I marked, however, a striking exception to the usual run of strangers I had been in the habit of seeing. The Sneckers had gone or were under cover. Again I caught a vague rumor of the coming of Jack Blome, yet he never seemed to arrive.

Moreover, the goings-on among the habitues of the resorts and the cowboys who came in to drink and gamble were unusually mild in comparison with former conduct.

This lull, however, did not deceive Steele and me. It could not last. The wonder was that it had lasted so long.

There was, of course, no post office in Linrock. A stage arrived twice a week from Sanderson, if it did not get held up on the way, and the driver usually had letters, which he turned over to the elderly keeper of a little store.

This man's name was Jones, and everybody liked him. On the evenings the stage arrived there was always a crowd at his store, which fact was a source of no little revenue to him.

One night, so we ascertained, after the crowd had dispersed, two thugs entered his store, beat the old man and robbed him. He made no complaint; however, when Steele called him he rather reluctantly gave not only descriptions of his assailants, but their names.

Steele straightaway went in search of the men and came across them in Lerett's place. I was around when it happened.

Steele strode up to a table which was surrounded by seven or eight men and he tapped Sim Bass on the shoulder.

"Get up, I want you," he said.

Bass looked up only to see who had accosted him.

"The hell you say!" he replied impudently.

Steele's big hand shifted to the fellow's collar. One jerk, seemingly no effort at all, sent Bass sliding, chair and all, to crash into the bar and fall in a heap. He lay there, wondering what had struck him.

"Miller, I want you. Get up," said Steele.

Miller complied with alacrity. A sharp kick put more life and understanding into Bass.

Then Steele searched these men right before the eyes of their comrades, took what money and weapons they had, and marched them out, followed by a crowd that gathered more and more to it as they went down the street. Steele took his prisoners into Jones' store, had them identified; returned the money they had stolen, and then, pushing the two through the gaping crowd, he marched them down to his stone jail and locked them up.

Obviously the serious side of this incident was entirely lost upon the highly entertained audience. Many and loud were the coarse jokes cracked at the expense of Bass and Miller and after the rude door had closed upon them similar remarks were addressed to Steele's jailer and guard, who in truth, were just as disreputable looking as their prisoners.

Then the crowd returned to their pastimes, leaving their erstwhile comrades to taste the sweets of prison life.

When I got a chance I asked Steele if he could rely on his hired hands, and with a twinkle in his eye which surprised me as much as his reply, he said Miller and Bass would have flown the coop before morning.

He was right. When I reached the lower end of town next morning, the same old crowd, enlarged by other curious men and youths, had come to pay their respects to the new institution.

Jailer and guard were on hand, loud in their proclamations and explanations. Naturally they had fallen asleep, as all other hard working citizens had, and while they slept the prisoners made a hole somewhere and escaped.

Steele examined the hole, and then engaged a stripling of a youth to see if he could crawl through. The youngster essayed the job, stuck in the middle, and was with difficulty extricated.

Whereupon the crowd evinced its delight.

Steele, without more ado, shoved his jailer and guard inside his jail, deliberately closed, barred and chained the iron bolted door, and put the key in his pocket. Then he remained there all day without giving heed to his prisoners' threats.

Toward evening, having gone without drink infinitely longer than was customary, they made appeals, to which Steele was deaf.

He left the jail, however, just before dark, and when we met he told me to be on hand to help him watch that night. We went around the outskirts of town, carrying two heavy double-barreled shotguns Steele had gotten somewhere and taking up a position behind bushes in the lot adjoining the jail; we awaited developments.

Steele was not above paying back these fellows.

All the early part of the evening, gangs of half a dozen men or more came down the street and had their last treat at the expense of the jail guard and jailer. These prisoners yelled for drink—not water but drink, and the more they yelled the more merriment was loosed upon the night air.

About ten o'clock the last gang left, to the despair of the hungry and thirsty prisoners.

Steele and I had hugely enjoyed the fun, and thought the best part of the joke for us was yet to come. The moon had arisen, and though somewhat hazed by clouds, had lightened the night. We were hidden about sixty paces from the jail, a little above it, and we had a fine command of the door.

About eleven o'clock, when all was still, we heard soft steps back of the jail, and soon two dark forms stole round in front. They laid down something that gave forth a metallic clink, like a crowbar. We heard whisperings and then, low, coarse laughs.

Then the rescuers, who undoubtedly were Miller and Bass, set to work to open the door. Softly they worked at first, but as that door had been put there to stay, and they were not fond of hard work, they began to swear and make noises.

Steele whispered to me to wait until the door had been opened, and then when all four presented a good target, to fire both barrels. We could easily have slipped down and captured the rescuers, but that was not Steele's game.

A trick met by a trick; cunning matching craft would be the surest of all ways to command respect.

Four times the workers had to rest, and once they were so enraged at the insistence of the prisoners, who wanted to delay proceedings to send one of them after a bottle, that they swore they would go away and cut the job altogether.

But they were prevailed upon to stay and attack the stout door once more. Finally it yielded, with enough noise to have awakened sleepers a block distant, and forth into the moonlight came rescuers and rescued with low, satisfied grunts of laughter.

Just then Steele and I each discharged both barrels, and the reports blended as one in a tremendous boom.

That little compact bunch disintegrated like quicksilver. Two stumbled over; the others leaped out, and all yelled in pain and terror. Then the fallen ones scrambled up and began to hobble and limp and jerk along after their comrades.

Before the four of them got out of sight they had ceased their yells, but were moving slowly, hanging on to one another in a way that satisfied us they would be lame for many a day.

Next morning at breakfast Dick regaled me with an elaborate story about how the Ranger had turned the tables on the jokers. Evidently in a night the whole town knew it.

Probably a desperate stand of Steele's even to the extreme of killing men, could not have educated these crude natives so quickly into the realization that the Ranger was not to be fooled with.

That morning I went for a ride with the girls, and both had heard something and wanted to know everything. I had become a news-carrier, and Miss Sampson never thought of questioning me in regard to my fund of information.

She showed more than curiosity. The account I gave of the jail affair amused her and made Sally laugh heartily.

Diane questioned me also about a rumor that had come to her concerning George Wright.

He had wounded himself with a gun, it seemed, and though not seriously injured, was not able to go about. He had not been up to the ranch for days.

"I asked papa about him," said, Diane, "and papa laughed like—well, like a regular hyena. I was dumbfounded. Papa's so queer. He looked thunder-clouds at me.

"When I insisted, for I wanted to know, he ripped out: 'Yes, the damn fool got himself shot, and I'm sorry it's not worse.'

"Now, Russ, what do you make of my dad? Cheerful and kind, isn't he?"

CHAPTER 5 CLEANING OUT LINROCK

I laughed with Sally, but I disclaimed any knowledge of George's accident. I hated the thought of Wright, let alone anything concerning the fatal certainty that sooner or later these cousins of his were to suffer through him.

Sally did not make these rides easy for me, for she was sweeter than anything that has a name. Since the evening of the dance I had tried to avoid her. Either she was sincerely sorry for her tantrum or she was bent upon utterly destroying my peace.

I took good care we were never alone, for in that case, if she ever got into my arms again I would find the ground slipping from under me.

Despite, however, the wear and constant strain of resisting Sally, I enjoyed the ride. There was a charm about being with these girls.

Then perhaps Miss Sampson's growing unconscious curiosity in regard to Steele was no little satisfaction to me.

I pretended a reluctance to speak of the Ranger, but when I did it was to drop a subtle word or briefly tell of an action that suggested such.

I never again hinted the thing that had been such a shock to her. What was in her mind I could not guess; her curiosity, perhaps the greater part, was due to a generous nature not entirely satisfied with itself. She probably had not abandoned her father's estimate of the Ranger but absolute assurance that this was just did not abide with her. For the rest she was like any other girl, a worshipper of the lion in a man, a weaver of romance, ignorant of her own heart.

Not the least talked of and speculated upon of all the details of the jail incident was the part played by Storekeeper Jones, who had informed upon his assailants. Steele and I both awaited results of this significant fact.

When would the town wake up, not only to a little nerve, but to the usefulness of a Ranger?

Three days afterward Steele told me a woman accosted him on the street. She seemed a poor, hardworking person, plain spoken and honest.

Her husband did not drink enough to complain of, but he liked to gamble and he had been fleeced by a crooked game in Jack Martin's saloon. Other wives could make the same complaints. It was God's blessing for such women that Ranger Steele had come to Linrock.

Of course, he could not get back the lost money, but would it be possible to close Martin's place, or at least break up the crooked game?

Steele had asked this woman, whose name was Price, how much her husband had lost, and, being told, he assured her that if he found evidence of cheating, not only would he get back the money, but also he would shut up Martin's place.

Steele instructed me to go that night to the saloon in question and get in the game. I complied, and, in order not to be overcarefully sized up by the dealer, I pretended to be well under the influence of liquor.

By nine o'clock, when Steele strolled in, I had the game well studied, and a more flagrantly crooked one I had never sat in. It was barefaced robbery.

Steele and I had agreed upon a sign from me, because he was not so adept in the intricacies of gambling as I was. I was not in a hurry, however, for there was a little frecklefaced cattleman in the game, and he had been losing, too. He had sold a bunch of stock that day and had considerable money, which evidently he was to be deprived of before he got started for Del Rio.

Steele stood at our backs, and I could feel his presence. He thrilled me. He had some kind of effect on the others, especially the dealer, who was honest enough while the Ranger looked on.

When, however, Steele shifted his attention to other tables and players our dealer reverted to his crooked work. I was about to make a disturbance, when the little cattleman, leaning over, fire in his eye and gun in hand, made it for me.

Evidently he was a keener and nervier gambler than he had been taken for. There might have been gun-play right then if Steele had not interfered.

"Hold on!" he yelled, leaping for our table. "Put up your gun!"

"Who are you?" demanded the cattleman, never moving. "Better keep out of this."

"I'm Steele. Put up your gun."

"You're thet Ranger, hey?" replied the other. "All right! But just a minute. I want this dealer to sit quiet. I've been robbed. And I want my money back."

Certainly the dealer and everyone else round the table sat quiet while the cattleman coolly held his gun leveled.

"Crooked game?" asked Steele, bending over the table. "Show me."

It did not take the aggrieved gambler more than a moment to prove his assertion. Steele, however, desired corroboration from others beside the cattleman, and one by one he questioned them.

To my surprise, one of the players admitted his conviction that the game was not straight.

"What do you say?" demanded Steele of me.

"Worse'n a hold-up, Mr. Ranger," I burst out. "Let me show you."

Deftly I made the dealer's guilt plain to all, and then I seconded the cattleman's angry claim for lost money. The players from other tables gathered round, curious, muttering.

And just then Martin strolled in. His appearance was not prepossessing.

"What's this holler?" he asked, and halted as he saw the cattleman's gun still in line with the dealer.

"Martin, you know what it's for," replied Steele. "Take your dealer and dig—unless you want to see me clean out your place."

Sullen and fierce, Martin stood looking from Steele to the cattleman and then the dealer. Some men in the crowd muttered, and that was a signal for Steele to shove the circle apart and get out, back to the wall.

The cattleman rose slowly in the center, pulling another gun, and he certainly looked business to me.

"Wal, Ranger, I reckon I'll hang round an' see you ain't bothered none," he said. "Friend," he went on, indicating me with a slight wave of one extended gun, "jest rustle the money in sight. We'll square up after the show."

I reached out and swept the considerable sum toward me, and, pocketing it, I too rose, ready for what might come.

"You-all give me elbow room!" yelled Steele at Martin and his cowed contingent.

Steele looked around, evidently for some kind of implement, and, espying a heavy ax in a corner, he grasped it, and, sweeping it to and fro as if it had been a buggy-whip, he advanced on the faro layout. The crowd fell back, edging toward the door.

One crashing blow wrecked the dealer's box and table, sending them splintering among the tumbled chairs. Then the giant Ranger began to spread further ruin about him.

Martin's place was rough and bare, of the most primitive order, and like a thousand other dens of its kind, consisted of a large room with adobe walls, a rude bar of boards, piles of kegs in a corner, a stove, and a few tables with chairs.

Steele required only one blow for each article he struck, and he demolished it. He stove in the head of each keg.

When the dark liquor gurgled out, Martin cursed, and the crowd followed suit. That was a loss!

The little cattleman, holding the men covered, backed them out of the room, Martin needing a plain, stern word to put him out entirely. I went out, too, for I did not want to miss any moves on the part of that gang.

Close behind me came the cattleman, the kind of cool, nervy Texan I liked. He had Martin well judged, too, for there was no evidence of any bold resistance.

But there were shouts and loud acclamations; and these, with the crashing blows of Steele's ax, brought a curious and growing addition to the crowd.

Soon sodden thuds from inside the saloon and red dust pouring out the door told that Steele was attacking the walls of Martin's place. Those adobe bricks when old and crumbly were easily demolished.

Steele made short work of the back wall, and then he smashed out half of the front of the building. That seemed to satisfy him.

When he stepped out of the dust he was wet with sweat, dirty, and disheveled, hot with his exertion—a man whose great stature and muscular development expressed a wonderful physical strength and energy. And his somber face, with the big gray eyes, like open furnaces, expressed a passion equal to his strength.

Perhaps only then did wild and lawless Linrock grasp the real significance of this Ranger.

Steele threw the ax at Martin's feet.

"Martin, don't reopen here," he said curtly. "Don't start another place in Linrock. If you do—jail at Austin for years."

Martin, livid and scowling, yet seemingly dazed with what had occurred, slunk away, accompanied by his cronies. Steele took the money I had appropriated, returned to me what I had lost, did likewise with the cattleman, and then, taking out the sum named by Mrs. Price, he divided the balance with the other players who had been in the game.

Then he stalked off through the crowd as if he knew that men who slunk from facing him would not have nerve enough to attack him even from behind.

"Wal, damn me!" ejaculated the little cattleman in mingled admiration and satisfaction. "So thet's that Texas Ranger, Steele, hey? Never seen him before. All Texas, thet Ranger!"

I lingered downtown as much to enjoy the sensation as to gain the different points of view.

No doubt about the sensation! In one hour every male resident of Linrock and almost every female had viewed the wreck of Martin's place. A fire could not have created half the excitement.

And in that excitement both men and women gave vent to speech they might not have voiced at a calmer moment. The women, at least, were not afraid to talk, and I made mental note of the things they said.

"Did he do it all alone?"

"Thank God a *man's* come to Linrock."

"Good for Molly Price!"

"Oh, it'll make bad times for Linrock."

It almost seemed that all the women were glad, and this was in itself a vindication of the Ranger's idea of law.

The men, however—Blandy, proprietor of the Hope So, and others of his ilk, together with the whole brood of idle gaming loungers, and in fact even storekeepers, ranchers, cowboys—all shook their heads sullenly or doubtfully.

Striking indeed now was the absence of any joking. Steele had showed his hand, and, as one gambler said: "It's a hard hand to call."

The truth was, this Ranger Service was hateful to the free-and-easy Texan who lived by anything except hard and honest work, and it was damnably hateful to the lawless class. Steele's authority, now obvious to all, was unlimited; it could go as far as he had power to carry it.

From present indications that power might be considerable. The work of native sheriffs and constables in western Texas had been a farce, an utter failure. If an honest native of a community undertook to be a sheriff he became immediately a target for rowdy cowboys and other vicious elements.

Many a town south and west of San Antonio owed its peace and prosperity to Rangers, and only to them. They had killed or driven out the criminals. They interpreted the law for themselves, and it was only such an attitude toward law—the stern, uncompromising, implacable extermination of the lawless—that was going to do for all Texas what it had done for part.

Steele was the driving wedge that had begun to split Linrock—split the honest from dominance by the dishonest. To be sure, Steele might be killed at any moment, and that contingency was voiced in the growl of one sullen man who said: "Wot the hell are we up against? Ain't somebody goin' to plug this Ranger?"

It was then that the thing for which Steele stood, the Ranger Service—to help, to save, to defend, to punish, with such somber menace of death as seemed embodied in his cold attitude toward resistance—took hold of Linrock and sunk deep into both black and honest hearts.

It was what was behind Steele that seemed to make him more than an officer—a man.

I could feel how he began to loom up, the embodiment of a powerful force—the Ranger Service—the fame of which, long known to this lawless Pecos gang, but scouted as a vague and distant thing, now became an actuality, a Ranger in the flesh, whose surprising attributes included both the law and the enforcement of it.

When I reached the ranch the excitement had preceded me. Miss Sampson and Sally, both talking at once, acquainted me with the fact that they had been in a store on the main street a block or more from Martin's place.

They had seen the crowd, heard the uproar; and, as they had been hurriedly started toward home by their attendant Dick, they had encountered Steele stalking by.

"He looked grand!" exclaimed Sally.

Then I told the girls the whole story in detail.

"Russ, is it true, just as you tell it?" inquired Diane earnestly.

"Absolutely. I know Mrs. Price went to Steele with her trouble. I was in Martin's place when he entered. Also I was playing in the crooked game. And I saw him wreck Martin's place. Also, I heard him forbid Martin to start another place in Linrock."

"Then he does do splendid things," she said softly, as if affirming to herself.

I walked on then, having gotten a glimpse of Colonel Sampson in the background. Before I reached the corrals Sally came running after me, quite flushed and excited.

"Russ, my uncle wants to see you," she said. "He's in a bad temper. Don't lose yours, please."

She actually took my hand. What a child she was, in all ways except that fatal propensity to flirt. Her statement startled me out of any further thought of her. Why did Sampson want to see me? He never noticed me. I dreaded facing him—not from fear, but because I must see more and more of the signs of guilt in Diane's father.

He awaited me on the porch. As usual, he wore riding garb, but evidently he had not been out so far this day. He looked worn. There was a furtive shadow in his eyes. The haughty, imperious temper, despite Sally's conviction, seemed to be in abeyance.

"Russ, what's this I hear about Martin's saloon being cleaned out?" he asked. "Dick can't give particulars."

Briefly and concisely I told the colonel exactly what had happened. He chewed his cigar, then spat it out with an unintelligible exclamation.

"Martin's no worse than others," he said. "Blandy leans to crooked faro. I've tried to stop that, anyway. If Steele can, more power to him!"

Sampson turned on his heel then and left me with a queer feeling of surprise and pity.

He had surprised me before, but he had never roused the least sympathy. It was probably that Sampson was indeed powerless, no matter what his position.

I had known men before who had become involved in crime, yet were too manly to sanction a crookedness they could not help.

Miss Sampson had been standing in her door. I could tell she had heard; she looked agitated. I knew she had been talking to her father.

"Russ, he hates the Ranger," she said. "That's what I fear. It'll bring trouble on us. Besides, like everybody here, he's biased. He can't see anything good in Steele. Yet he says: 'More power to him!' I'm mystified, and, oh, I'm between two fires!"

Steele's next noteworthy achievement was as new to me as it was strange to Linrock. I heard a good deal about it from my acquaintances, some little from Steele, and the concluding incident I saw and heard myself.

Andy Vey was a broken-down rustler whose activity had ceased and who spent his time hanging on at the places frequented by younger and better men of his kind. As he was a parasite, he was often thrown out of the dens.

Moreover, it was an open secret that he had been a rustler, and the men with whom he associated had not yet, to most of Linrock, become known as such.

One night Vey had been badly beaten in some back room of a saloon and carried out into a vacant lot and left there. He lay there all that night and all the next day. Probably he would have died there had not Steele happened along.

The Ranger gathered up the crippled rustler, took him home, attended to his wounds, nursed him, and in fact spent days in the little adobe house with him.

During this time I saw Steele twice, at night out in our rendezvous. He had little to communicate, but was eager to hear when I had seen Jim Hoden, Morton, Wright, Sampson, and all I could tell about them, and the significance of things in town.

Andy Vey recovered, and it was my good fortune to be in the Hope So when he came in and addressed a crowd of gamesters there.

"Fellers," he said, "I'm biddin' good-by to them as was once my friends. I'm leavin' Linrock. An' I'm askin' some of you to take thet good-by an' a partin' word to them as did me dirt.

"I ain't a-goin' to say if I'd crossed the trail of this Ranger years ago thet I'd of turned round an' gone straight. But mebbe I would—mebbe. There's a hell of a lot a man doesn't know till too late. I'm old now, ready fer the bone pile, an' it doesn't matter. But I've got a head on me yet, an' I want to give a hunch to thet gang who done me. An' that hunch wants to go around an' up to the big guns of Pecos.

"This Texas Star Ranger was the feller who took me in. I'd of died like a poisoned coyote but fer him. An' he talked to me. He gave me money to git out of Pecos. Mebbe everybody'll think he helped me because he wanted me to squeal. To squeal who's who round these rustler diggin's. Wal, he never asked me. Mebbe he seen I wasn't a squealer. But I'm thinkin' he wouldn't ask a feller thet nohow.

"An' here's my hunch. Steele has spotted the outfit. Thet ain't so much, mebbe. But I've been with him, an' I'm old figgerin' men. Jest as sure as God made little apples he's a goin' to put thet outfit through—or he's a-goin' to kill them!"

CHAPTER 6 ENTER JACK BLOME

Strange that the narrating of this incident made Diane Sampson unhappy.

When I told her she exhibited one flash of gladness, such as any woman might have shown for a noble deed and then she became thoughtful, almost gloomy, sad. I could not understand her complex emotions. Perhaps she contrasted Steele with her father; perhaps she wanted to believe in Steele and dared not; perhaps she had all at once seen the Ranger in his true light, and to her undoing.

She bade me take Sally for a ride and sought her room. I had my misgivings when I saw Sally come out in that trim cowgirl suit and look at me as if to say this day would be my Waterloo.

But she rode hard and long ahead of me before she put any machinations into effect. The first one found me with a respectful demeanor but an internal conflict.

"Russ, tighten my cinch," she said when I caught up with her.

Dismounting, I drew the cinch up another hole and fastened it.

"My boot's unlaced, too," she added, slipping a shapely foot out of the stirrup.

To be sure, it was very much unlaced. I had to take off my gloves to lace it up, and I did it heroically, with bent head and outward calm, when all the time I was mad to snatch the girl out of the saddle and hold her tight or run off with her or do some other fool thing.

"Russ, I believe Diane's in love with Steele," she said soberly, with the sweet confidence she sometimes manifested in me.

"Small wonder. It's in the air," I replied.

She regarded me doubtfully.

"It was," she retorted demurely.

"The fickleness of women is no new thing to me. I didn't expect Waters to last long."

"Certainly not when there are nicer fellows around. One, anyway, when he cares."

A little brown hand slid out of its glove and dropped to my shoulder.

"Make up. You've been hateful lately. Make up with me."

It was not so much what she said as the sweet tone of her voice and the nearness of her that made a tumult within me. I felt the blood tingle to my face.

"Why should I make up with you?" I queried in self defense. "You are only flirting. You won't—you can't ever be anything to me, really."

Sally bent over me and I had not the nerve to look up.

"Never mind things—really," she replied. "The future's far off. Let it alone. We're together. I—I like you, Russ. And I've got to be—to be loved. There. I never confessed that to any other man. You've been hateful when we might have had such fun. The rides in the sun, in the open with the wind in our faces. The walks at night in the moonlight. Russ, haven't you missed something?"

The sweetness and seductiveness of her, the little luring devil of her, irresistible as they were, were no more irresistible than the naturalness, the truth of her.

I trembled even before I looked up into her flushed face and arch eyes; and after that I knew if I could not frighten her out of this daring mood I would have to yield despite my conviction that she only trifled. As my manhood, as well as duty to Steele, forced me to be unyielding, all that was left seemed to be to frighten her.

The instant this was decided a wave of emotion—love, regret, bitterness, anger—surged over me, making me shake. I felt the skin on my face tighten and chill. I grasped her with strength that might have need to hold a plunging, unruly horse. I hurt her. I held her as in a vise.

And the action, the feel of her, her suddenly uttered cry wrought against all pretense, hurt me as my brutality hurt her, and then I spoke what was hard, passionate truth.

"Girl, you're playing with fire!" I cried out hoarsely. "I love you—love you as I'd want my sister loved. I asked you to marry me. That was proof, if it was foolish. Even if you were on the square, which you're not, we couldn't ever be anything to each other. Understand? There's a reason, besides your being above me. I can't stand it. Stop playing with me or I'll—I'll..."

Whatever I meant to say was not spoken, for Sally turned deathly white, probably from my grasp and my looks as well as my threat.

I let go of her, and stepping back to my horse choked down my emotion.

"Russ!" she faltered, and there was womanliness and regret trembling with the fear in her voice. "I—I am on the square."

That had touched the real heart of the girl.

"If you are, then play the game square," I replied darkly.

"I will, Russ, I promise. I'll never tease or coax you again. If I do, then I'll deserve what you—what I get. But, Russ, don't think me a—a four-flush."

All the long ride home we did not exchange another word. The traveling gait of Sally's horse was a lope, that of mine a trot; and therefore, to my relief, she was always out in front.

As we neared the ranch, however, Sally slowed down until I caught up with her; and side by side we rode the remainder of the way. At the corrals, while I unsaddled, she lingered.

"Russ, you didn't tell me if you agreed with me about Diane," she said finally.

"Maybe you're right. I hope she's fallen in love with Steele. Lord knows I hope so," I blurted out.

I bit my tongue. There was no use in trying to be as shrewd with women as I was with men. I made no reply.

"Misery loves company. Maybe that's why," she added. "You told me Steele lost his head over Diane at first sight. Well, we all have company. Good night, Russ."

That night I told Steele about the singular effect the story of his treatment of Vey had upon Miss Sampson. He could not conceal his feelings. I read him like an open book.

If she was unhappy because he did something really good, then she was unhappy because she was realizing she had wronged him.

Steele never asked questions, but the hungry look in his eyes was enough to make even a truthful fellow exaggerate things.

I told him how Diane was dressed, how her face changed with each emotion, how her eyes burned and softened and shadowed, how her voice had been deep and full when she admitted her father hated him, how much she must have meant when she said she was between two fires. I divined how he felt and I tried to satisfy in some little measure his craving for news of her.

When I had exhausted my fund and stretched my imagination I was rewarded by being told that I was a regular old woman for gossip.

Much taken back by this remarkable statement I could but gape at my comrade. Irritation had followed shortly upon his curiosity and pleasure, and then the old sane mind reasserted itself, the old stern look, a little sad now, replaced the glow, the strange eagerness of youth on his face.

"Son, I beg your pardon," he said, with his hand on my shoulder. "We're Rangers, but we can't help being human. To speak right out, it seems two sweet and lovable girls have come, unfortunately for us all, across the dark trail we're on. Let us find what solace we can in the hope that somehow, God only knows how, in doing our duty as Rangers we may yet be doing right by these two innocent girls. I ask you, as my friend, please do not speak again to me of—Miss Sampson."

I left him and went up the quiet trail with the thick shadows all around me and the cold stars overhead; and I was sober in thought, sick at heart for him as much as for myself, and I tortured my mind in fruitless conjecture as to what the end of this strange and fateful adventure would be.

I discovered that less and less the old wild spirit abided with me and I become conscious of a dull, deep-seated ache in my breast, a pang in the bone.

From that day there was a change in Diane Sampson. She became feverishly active. She wanted to ride, to see for herself what was going on in Linrock, to learn of that wild Pecos county life at first hand.

She made such demands on my time now that I scarcely ever found an hour to be with or near Steele until after dark. However, as he was playing a waiting game on the rustlers, keeping out of the resorts for the present, I had not great cause for worry. Hoden was slowly gathering men together, a band of trustworthy ones, and until this organization was complete and ready, Steele thought better to go slow.

It was of little use for me to remonstrate with Miss Sampson when she refused to obey a distracted and angry father. I began to feel sorry for Sampson. He was an unscrupulous man, but he loved this daughter who belonged to another and better and past side of his life.

I heard him appeal to her to go back to Louisiana; to let him take her home, giving as urgent reason the probability of trouble for him. She could not help, could only handicap him.

She agreed to go, provided he sold his property, took the best of his horses and went with her back to the old home to live there the rest of their lives. He replied with considerable feeling that he wished he could go, but it was impossible. Then that settled the matter for her, she averred.

Failing to persuade her to leave Linrock, he told her to keep to the ranch. Naturally, in spite of his anger, Miss Sampson refused to obey; and she frankly told him that it was the free, unfettered life of the country, the riding here and there that appealed so much to her.

Sampson came to me a little later and his worn face showed traces of internal storm.

"Russ, for a while there I wanted to get rid of you," he said. "I've changed. Diane always was a spoiled kid. Now she's a woman. Something's fired her blood. Maybe it's this damned wild country. Anyway, she's got the bit between her teeth. She'll run till she's run herself out.

"Now, it seems the safety of Diane, and Sally, too, has fallen into your hands. The girls won't have one of my cowboys near them. Lately they've got shy of George, too. Between you and me I want to tell you that conditions here in Pecos are worse than they've seemed since you-all reached the ranch. But bad work will break out again—it's coming soon.

"I can't stop it. The town will be full of the hardest gang in western Texas. My daughter and Sally would not be safe if left alone to go anywhere. With you, perhaps, they'll be safe. Can I rely on you?"

"Yes, Sampson, you sure can," I replied. "I'm on pretty good terms with most everybody in town. I think I can say none of the tough set who hang out down there would ever made any move while I'm with the girls. But I'll be pretty careful to avoid them, and particularly strange fellows who may come riding in.

"And if any of them do meet us and start trouble, I'm going for my gun, that's all. There won't be any talk."

"Good! I'll back you," Sampson replied. "Understand, Russ, I didn't want you here, but I always had you sized up as a pretty hard nut, a man not to be trifled with. You've got a bad name. Diane insists the name's not deserved. She'd trust you with herself under any circumstances. And the kid, Sally, she'd be fond of you if it wasn't for the drink. Have you been drunk a good deal? Straight now, between you and me."

"Not once," I replied.

"George's a liar then. He's had it in for you since that day at Sanderson. Look out you two don't clash. He's got a temper, and when he's drinking he's a devil. Keep out of his way."

"I've stood a good deal from Wright, and guess I can stand more."

"All right, Russ," he continued, as if relieved. "Chuck the drink and cards for a while and keep an eye on the girls. When my affairs straighten out maybe I'll make you a proposition."

Sampson left me material for thought. Perhaps it was not only the presence of a Ranger in town that gave him concern, nor the wilfulness of his daughter. There must be internal strife in the rustler gang with which we had associated him.

Perhaps a menace of publicity, rather than risk, was the cause of the wearing strain on him. I began to get a closer insight into Sampson, and in the absence of any conclusive evidence of his personal baseness I felt pity for him.

In the beginning he had opposed me just because I did not happen to be a cowboy he had selected. This latest interview with me, amounting in some instances to confidence, proved absolutely that he had not the slightest suspicion that I was otherwise than the cowboy I pretended to be.

Another interesting deduction was that he appeared to be out of patience with Wright. In fact, I imagined I sensed something of fear and distrust in this spoken attitude toward his relative. Not improbably here was the internal strife between Sampson and Wright, and there flashed into my mind, absolutely without reason, an idea that the clash was over Diane Sampson.

I scouted this intuitive idea as absurd; but, just the same, it refused to be dismissed.

As I turned my back on the coarse and exciting life in the saloons and gambling hells, and spent all my time except when sleeping, out in the windy open under blue sky and starry heaven, my spirit had an uplift.

I was glad to be free of that job. It was bad enough to have to go into these dens to arrest men, let alone living with them, almost being one.

Diane Sampson noted a change in me, attributed it to the absence of the influence of drink, and she was glad. Sally made no attempt to conceal her happiness; and to my dismay, she utterly failed to keep her promise not to tease or tempt me further.

She was adorable, distracting.

We rode every day and almost all day. We took our dinner and went clear to the foothills to return as the sun set. We visited outlying ranches, water-holes, old adobe houses famous in one way or another as scenes of past fights of rustlers and ranchers.

We rode to the little village of Sampson, and half-way to Sanderson, and all over the country.

There was no satisfying Miss Sampson with rides, new places, new faces, new adventures. And every time we rode out she insisted on first riding through Linrock; and every time we rode home she insisted on going back that way.

CHAPTER 6 ENTER JACK BLOME

We visited all the stores, the blacksmith, the wagon shop, the feed and grain houses—everywhere that she could find excuse for visiting. I had to point out to her all the infamous dens in town, and all the lawless and lounging men we met.

She insisted upon being shown the inside of the Hope So, to the extreme confusion of that bewildered resort.

I pretended to be blind to this restless curiosity. Sally understood the cause, too, and it divided her between a sweet gravity and a naughty humor.

The last, however, she never evinced in sight or hearing of Diane.

It seemed that we were indeed fated to cross the path of Vaughn Steele. We saw him working round his adobe house; then we saw him on horseback. Once we met him face to face in a store.

He gazed steadily into Diane Sampson's eyes and went his way without any sign of recognition. There was red in her face when he passed and white when he had gone.

That day she rode as I had never seen her, risking her life, unmindful of her horse.

Another day we met Steele down in the valley, where, inquiry discovered to us, he had gone to the home of an old cattleman who lived alone and was ill.

Last and perhaps most significant of all these meetings was the one when we were walking tired horses home through the main street of Linrock and came upon Steele just in time to see him in action.

It happened at a corner where the usual slouchy, shirt-sleeved loungers were congregated. They were in high glee over the predicament of one ruffian who had purchased or been given a poor, emaciated little burro that was on his last legs. The burro evidently did not want to go with its new owner, who pulled on a halter and then viciously swung the end of the rope to make welts on the worn and scarred back.

If there was one thing that Diane Sampson could not bear it was to see an animal in pain. She passionately loved horses, and hated the sight of a spur or whip.

When we saw the man beating the little burro she cried out to me:

"Make the brute stop!"

I might have made a move had I not on the instant seen Steele heaving into sight round the corner.

Just then the fellow, whom I now recognized to be a despicable character named Andrews, began to bestow heavy and brutal kicks upon the body of the little burro. These kicks sounded deep, hollow, almost like the boom of a drum.

The burro uttered the strangest sound I ever heard issue from any beast and it dropped in its tracks with jerking legs that told any horseman what had happened. Steele saw the last swings of Andrews' heavy boot. He yelled. It was a sharp yell that would have made anyone start. But it came too late, for the burro had dropped.

Steele knocked over several of the jeering men to get to Andrews. He kicked the fellow's feet from under him, sending him hard to the ground.

Then Steele picked up the end of the halter and began to swing it powerfully. Resounding smacks mingled with hoarse bellows of fury and pain. Andrews flopped here and there, trying to arise, but every time the heavy knotted halter beat him down.

Presently Steele stopped. Andrews rose right in front of the Ranger, and there, like the madman he was, he went for his gun.

But it scarcely leaped from its holster when Steele's swift hand intercepted it. Steele clutched Andrews' arm.

Then came a wrench, a cracking of bones, a scream of agony.

The gun dropped into the dust; and in a moment of wrestling fury Andrews, broken, beaten down, just able to moan, lay beside it.

Steele, so cool and dark for a man who had acted with such passionate swiftness, faced the others as if to dare them to move. They neither moved nor spoke, and then he strode away.

Miss Sampson did not speak a word while we were riding the rest of the way home, but she was strangely white of face and dark of eye. Sally could not speak fast enough to say all she felt.

And I, of course, had my measure of feelings. One of them was that as sure as the sun rose and set it was written that Diane Sampson was to love Vaughn Steele.

I could not read her mind, but I had a mind of my own.

How could any woman, seeing this maligned and menaced Ranger, whose life was in danger every moment he spent on the streets, in the light of his action on behalf of a poor little beast, help but wonder and brood over the magnificent height he might reach if he had love—passion—a woman for his inspiration?

It was the day after this incident that, as Sally, Diane, and I were riding homeward on the road from Sampson, I caught sight of a group of dark horses and riders swiftly catching up with us.

We were on the main road, in plain sight of town and passing by ranches; nevertheless, I did not like the looks of the horsemen and grew uneasy. Still, I scarcely thought it needful to race our horses just to reach town a little ahead of these strangers.

Accordingly, they soon caught up with us.

They were five in number, all dark-faced except one, dark-clad and superbly mounted on dark bays and blacks. They had no pack animals and, for that matter, carried no packs at all.

Four of them, at a swinging canter, passed us, and the fifth pulled his horse to suit our pace and fell in between Sally and me.

"Good day," he said pleasantly to me. "Don't mind my ridin' in with you-all, I hope?"

Considering his pleasant approach, I could not but be civil.

He was a singularly handsome fellow, at a quick glance, under forty years, with curly, blond hair, almost gold, a skin very fair for that country, and the keenest, clearest, boldest blue eyes I had ever seen in a man.

"You're Russ, I reckon," he said. "Some of my men have seen you ridin' round with Sampson's girls. I'm Jack Blome."

He did not speak that name with any flaunt or flourish. He merely stated it.

Blome, the rustler! I grew tight all over.

Still, manifestly there was nothing for me to do but return his pleasantry. I really felt less uneasiness after he had made himself known to me. And without any awkwardness, I introduced him to the girls.

He took off his sombrero and made gallant bows to both.

Miss Sampson had heard of him and his record, and she could not help a paleness, a shrinking, which, however, he did not appear to notice. Sally had been dying to meet a real rustler, and here he was, a very prince of rascals.

But I gathered that she would require a little time before she could be natural. Blome seemed to have more of an eye for Sally than for Diane. "Do you like Pecos?" he asked Sally.

"Out here? Oh, yes, indeed!" she replied.

"Like ridin'?"

"I love horses."

Like almost every man who made Sally's acquaintance, he hit upon the subject best calculated to make her interesting to free-riding, outdoor Western men.

That he loved a thoroughbred horse himself was plain. He spoke naturally to Sally with interest, just as I had upon first meeting her, and he might not have been Jack Blome, for all the indication he gave of the fact in his talk.

But the look of the man was different. He was a desperado, one of the dashing, reckless kind—more famous along the Pecos and Rio Grande than more really desperate men. His attire proclaimed a vanity seldom seen in any Westerner except of that unusual brand, yet it was neither gaudy or showy.

One had to be close to Blome to see the silk, the velvet, the gold, the fine leather. When I envied a man's spurs then they were indeed worth coveting.

Blome had a short rifle and a gun in saddle-sheaths. My sharp eye, running over him, caught a row of notches on the bone handle of the big Colt he packed.

It was then that the marshal, the Ranger in me, went hot under the collar. The custom that desperadoes and gun-fighters had of cutting a notch on their guns for every man killed was one of which the mere mention made my gorge rise.

At the edge of town Blome doffed his sombrero again, said "*Adios*," and rode on ahead of us. And it was then I was hard put to it to keep track of the queries, exclamations, and other wild talk of two very much excited young ladies. I wanted to think; I *needed* to think.

"Wasn't he lovely? Oh, I could adore him!" rapturously uttered Miss Sally Langdon several times, to my ultimate disgust.

Also, after Blome had ridden out of sight, Miss Sampson lost the evident effect of his sinister presence, and she joined Miss Langdon in paying the rustler compliments, too. Perhaps my irritation was an indication of the quick and subtle shifting of my mind to harsher thought.

"Jack Blome!" I broke in upon their adulations. "Rustler and gunman. Did you see the notches on his gun? Every notch for a man he's killed! For weeks reports have come to Linrock that soon as he could get round to it he'd ride down and rid the community of that bothersome fellow, that Texas Ranger! He's come to kill Vaughn Steele!"

CHAPTER 7 DIANE AND VAUGHN

Then as gloom descended on me with my uttered thought, my heart smote me at Sally's broken: "Oh, Russ! No! No!" Diane Sampson bent dark, shocked eyes upon the hill and ranch in front of her; but they were sightless, they looked into space and eternity, and in them I read the truth suddenly and cruelly revealed to her—she loved Steele!

I found it impossible to leave Miss Sampson with the impression I had given. My own mood fitted a kind of ruthless pleasure in seeing her suffer through love as I had intimation I was to suffer.

But now, when my strange desire that she should love Steele had its fulfilment, and my fiendish subtleties to that end had been crowned with success, I was confounded in pity and the enormity of my crime. For it had been a crime to make, or help to make, this noble and beautiful woman love a Ranger, the enemy of her father, and surely the author of her coming misery. I felt shocked at my work. I tried to hang an excuse on my old motive that through her love we might all be saved. When it was too late, however, I found that this motive was wrong and perhaps without warrant.

We rode home in silence. Miss Sampson, contrary to her usual custom of riding to the corrals or the porch, dismounted at a path leading in among the trees and flowers. "I want to rest, to think before I go in," she said.

Sally accompanied me to the corrals. As our horses stopped at the gate I turned to find confirmation of my fears in Sally's wet eyes.

"Russ," she said, "it's worse than we thought."

"Worse? I should say so," I replied.

"It'll about kill her. She never cared that way for any man. When the Sampson women love, they love."

"Well, you're lucky to be a Langdon," I retorted bitterly.

"I'm Sampson enough to be unhappy," she flashed back at me, "and I'm Langdon enough to have some sense. You haven't any sense or kindness, either. Why'd you want to blurt out that Jack Blome was here to kill Steele?"

"I'm ashamed, Sally," I returned, with hanging head. "I've been a brute. I've wanted her to love Steele. I thought I had a reason, but now it seems silly. Just now I wanted to see how much she did care.

"Sally, the other day you said misery loved company. That's the trouble. I'm sore—bitter. I'm like a sick coyote that snaps at everything. I've wanted you to go into the very depths of despair. But I couldn't send you. So I took out my spite on poor Miss Sampson. It was a damn unmanly thing for me to do."

"Oh, it's not so bad as all that. But you might have been less abrupt. Russ, you seem to take an—an awful tragic view of your—your own case."

"Tragic? Hah!" I cried like the villain in the play. "What other way could I look at it? I tell you I love you so I can't sleep or do anything."

"That's not tragic. When you've no chance, *then* that's tragic."

Sally, as swiftly as she had blushed, could change into that deadly sweet mood. She did both now. She seemed warm, softened, agitated. How could this be anything but sincere? I felt myself slipping; so I laughed harshly.

"Chance! I've no chance on earth."

"Try!" she whispered.

But I caught myself in time. Then the shock of bitter renunciation made it easy for me to simulate anger.

"You promised not to—not to—" I began, choking. My voice was hoarse and it broke, matters surely far removed from pretense.

I had seen Sally Langdon in varying degrees of emotion, but never as she appeared now. She was pale and she trembled a little. If it was not fright, then I could not tell what it was. But there were contrition and earnestness about her, too.

"Russ, I know. I promised not to—to tease—to tempt you anymore," she faltered. "I've broken it. I'm ashamed. I haven't played the game square. But I couldn't—I can't help myself. I've got sense enough not to engage myself to you, but I can't keep from loving you. I can't let you alone. There—if you want it on the square! What's more, I'll go on as I have done unless you keep away from me. I don't care what I deserve—what you do—I will—I will!"

She had begun falteringly and she ended passionately.

Somehow I kept my head, even though my heart pounded like a hammer and the blood drummed in my ears. It was the thought of Steele that saved me. But I felt cold at the narrow margin. I had reached a point, I feared, where a kiss, one touch from this bewildering creature of fire and change and sweetness would make me put her before Steele and my duty.

"Sally, if you dare break your promise again, you'll wish you never had been born," I said with all the fierceness at my command.

"I wish that now. And you can't bluff me, Mr. Gambler. I may have no hand to play, but you can't make me lay it down," she replied.

Something told me Sally Langdon was finding herself; that presently I could not frighten her, and then—then I would be doomed.

"Why, if I got drunk, I might do anything," I said cool and hard now. "Cut off your beautiful chestnut hair for bracelets for my arms."

Sally laughed, but she was still white. She was indeed finding herself. "If you ever get drunk again you can't kiss me any more. And if you don't—you can."

I felt myself shake and, with all of the iron will I could assert, I hid from her the sweetness of this thing that was my weakness and her strength.

"I might lasso you from my horse, drag you through the cactus," I added with the implacability of an Apache.

"Russ!" she cried. Something in this last ridiculous threat had found a vital mark. "After all, maybe those awful stories Joe Harper told about you were true."

"They sure were," I declared with great relief. "And now to forget ourselves. I'm more than sorry I distressed Miss Sampson; more than sorry because what I said wasn't on the square. Blome, no doubt, has come to Linrock after Steele. His intention is to kill him. I said that—let Miss Sampson think it all meant fatality to the Ranger. But, Sally, I don't believe that Blome can kill Steele any more than—than you can."

"Why?" she asked; and she seemed eager, glad.

"Because he's not man enough. That's all, without details. You need not worry; and I wish you'd go tell Miss Sampson—"

"Go yourself," interrupted Sally. "I think she's afraid of my eyes. But she won't fear you'd guess her secret.

"Go to her, Russ. Find some excuse to tell her. Say you thought it over, believed she'd be distressed about what might never happen. Go—and afterward pray for your sins, you queer, good-natured, love-meddling cowboy-devil, you!"

For once I had no retort ready for Sally. I hurried off as quickly as I could walk in chaps and spurs.

I found Miss Sampson sitting on a bench in the shade of a tree. Her pallor and quiet composure told of the conquering and passing of the storm. Always she had a smile for me, and now it smote me, for I in a sense, had betrayed her.

"Miss Sampson," I began, awkwardly yet swiftly, "I—I got to thinking it over, and the idea struck me, maybe you felt bad about this gun-fighter Blome coming down here to kill Steele. At first I imagined you felt sick just because there might be blood spilled. Then I thought you've showed interest in Steele—naturally his kind of Ranger work is bound to appeal to women—you might be sorry it couldn't go on, you might care."

"Russ, don't beat about the bush," she said interrupting my floundering. "You know I care."

How wonderful her eyes were then—great dark, sad gulfs with the soul of a woman at the bottom! Almost I loved her myself; I did love her truth, the woman in her that scorned any subterfuge.

Instantly she inspired me to command over myself. "Listen," I said. "Jack Blome has come here to meet Steele. There will be a fight. But Blome can't kill Steele."

"How is that? Why can't he? You said this Blome was a killer of men. You spoke of notches on his gun. I've heard my father and my cousin, too, speak of Blome's record. He must be a terrible ruffian. If his intent is evil, why will he fail in it?"

"Because, Miss Sampson, when it comes to the last word, Steele will be on the lookout and Blome won't be quick enough on the draw to kill him. That's all."

"Quick enough on the draw? I understand, but I want to know more."

"I doubt if there's a man on the frontier to-day quick enough to kill Steele in an even break. That means a fair fight. This Blome is conceited. He'll make the meeting fair enough. It'll come off about like this, Miss Sampson.

"Blome will send out his bluff—he'll begin to blow—to look for Steele. But Steele will avoid him as long as possible—perhaps altogether, though that's improbable. If they do meet, then Blome must force the issue. It's interesting to figure on that. Steele affects men strangely. It's all very well for this Blome to rant about himself and to hunt Steele up. But the test'll come when he faces the Ranger. He never saw Steele. He doesn't know what he's up against. He knows Steele's reputation, but I don't mean that. I mean Steele in the flesh, his nerve, the something that's in his eyes.

"Now, when it comes to handling a gun the man doesn't breathe who has anything on Steele. There was an outlaw, Duane, who might have killed Steele, had they ever met. I'll tell you Duane's story some day. A girl saved him, made a Ranger of him, then got him to go far away from Texas."

"That was wise. Indeed, I'd like to hear the story," she replied. "Then, after all, Russ, in this dreadful part of Texas life, when man faces man, it's all in the quickness of hand?"

"Absolutely. It's the draw. And Steele's a wonder. See here. Look at this."

I stepped back and drew my gun.

"I didn't see how you did that," she said curiously. "Try it again."

I complied, and still she was not quick enough of eye to see my draw. Then I did it slowly, explaining to her the action of hand and then of finger. She seemed fascinated, as a woman might have been by the striking power of a rattlesnake.

"So men's lives depend on that! How horrible for me to be interested—to ask about it—to watch you! But I'm out here on the frontier now, caught somehow in its wildness, and I feel a relief, a gladness to know Vaughn Steele has the skill you claim. Thank you, Russ."

She seemed about to dismiss me then, for she rose and half turned away. Then she hesitated. She had one hand at her breast, the other on the bench. "Have you been with him—talked to him lately?" she asked, and a faint rose tint came into her cheeks. But her eyes were steady, dark, and deep, and peered through and far beyond me.

"Yes, I've met him a few times, around places."

"Did he ever speak of—of me?"

"Once or twice, and then as if he couldn't help it."

"What did he say?"

"Well, the last time he seemed hungry to hear something about you. He didn't exactly ask, but, all the same, he was begging. So I told him."

"What?"

"Oh, how you were dressed, how you looked, what you said, what you did—all about you. Don't be offended with me, Miss Sampson. It was real charity. I talk too much. It's my weakness. Please don't be offended."

She never heard my apology or my entreaty. There was a kind of glory in her eyes. Looking at her, I found a dimness hazing my sight, and when I rubbed it away it came back.

"Then—what did he say?" This was whispered, almost shyly, and I could scarcely believe the proud Miss Sampson stood before me.

"Why, he flew into a fury, called me an—" Hastily I caught myself. "Well, he said if I wanted to talk to him any more not to speak of you. He was sure unreasonable."

"Russ—you think—you told me once—he—you think he still—" She was not facing me at all now. She had her head bent. Both hands were at her breast, and I saw it heave. Her cheek was white as a flower, her neck darkly, richly red with mounting blood.

I understood. And I pitied her and hated myself and marveled at this thing, love. It made another woman out of Diane Sampson. I could scarcely comprehend that she was asking me, almost beseechingly, for further assurance of Steele's love. I knew nothing of women, but this seemed strange. Then a thought sent the blood chilling back to my heart. Had Diane Sampson guessed the guilt of her father? Was it more for his sake than for her own that she hoped—for surely she hoped—that Steele loved her?

Here was more mystery, more food for reflection. Only a powerful motive or a self-leveling love could have made a woman of Diane Sampson's pride ask such a question. Whatever her reason, I determined to assure her, once and forever, what I knew to be true. Accordingly, I told her in unforgettable words, with my own regard for her and love for Sally filling my voice with emotion, how I could see that Steele loved her, how madly he was destined to love her, how terribly hard that was going to make his work in Linrock.

There was a stillness about her then, a light on her face, which brought to my mind thought of Sally when I had asked her to marry me.

"Russ, I beg you—bring us together," said Miss Sampson. "Bring about a meeting. You are my friend." Then she went swiftly away through the flowers, leaving me there, thrilled to my soul at her betrayal of herself, ready to die in her service, yet cursing the fatal day Vaughn Steele had chosen me for his comrade in this tragic game.

That evening in the girls' sitting-room, where they invited me, I was led into a discourse upon the gun-fighters, outlaws, desperadoes, and bad men of the frontier. Miss Sampson and Sally had been, before their arrival in Texas, as ignorant of such characters as any girls in the North or East. They were now peculiarly interested, fascinated, and at the same time repelled.

Miss Sampson must have placed the Rangers in one of those classes, somewhat as Governor Smith had, and her father, too. Sally thought she was in love with a cowboy whom she had been led to believe had as bad a record as any.

They were certainly a most persuasive and appreciative audience. So as it was in regard to horses, if I knew any subject well, it was this one of dangerous and bad men. Texas, and the whole developing Southwest, was full of such characters. It was a very difficult thing to distinguish between fighters who were bad men and fighters who were good men. However, it was no difficult thing for one of my calling to tell the difference between a real bad man and the imitation "four-flush."

Then I told the girls the story of Buck Duane, famous outlaw and Ranger. And I narrated the histories of Murrell, most terrible of blood-spillers ever known to Texas; of Hardin, whose long career of crime ended in the main street in Huntsville when he faced Buck Duane; of Sandobal, the Mexican terror; of Cheseldine, Bland, Alloway, and other outlaws of the Rio Grande; of King Fisher and Thompson and Sterrett, all still living and still busy adding notches to their guns.

I ended my little talk by telling the story of Amos Clark, a criminal of a higher type than most bad men, yet infinitely more dangerous because of that. He was a Southerner of good family. After the war he went to Dimmick County and there developed and prospered with the country. He became the most influential citizen of his town and the richest in that section. He held offices. He was energetic in his opposition to rustlers and outlaws. He was held in high esteem by his countrymen. But this Amos Clark was the leader of a band of rustlers, highwaymen, and murderers.

Captain Neal and some of his Rangers ferreted out Clark's relation to this lawless gang, and in the end caught him red-handed. He was arrested and eventually hanged. His case was unusual, and it furnished an example of what was possible in that wild country. Clark had a son who was honest and a wife whom he dearly loved, both of whom had been utterly ignorant of the other and wicked side of life. I told this last story deliberately, yet with some misgivings. I wanted to see—I convinced myself it was needful for me to see—if Miss Sampson had any suspicion of her father. To look into her face then was no easy task. But when I did I experienced a shock, though not exactly the kind I had prepared myself for.

She knew something; maybe she knew actually more than Steele or I; still, if it were a crime, she had a marvelous control over her true feelings.

Jack Blome and his men had been in Linrock for several days; old Snecker and his son Bo had reappeared, and other hard-looking customers, new to me if not to Linrock. These helped to create a charged and waiting atmosphere. The saloons did unusual business and were never closed. Respectable citizens of the town were awakened in the early dawn by rowdies carousing in the streets.

Steele kept pretty closely under cover. He did not entertain the opinion, nor did I, that the first time he walked down the street he would be a target for Blome and his gang. Things seldom happened that way, and when they did happen so it was more accident than design. Blome was setting the stage for his little drama.

Meanwhile Steele was not idle. He told me he had met Jim Hoden, Morton and Zimmer, and that these men had approached others of like character; a secret club had been formed and all the members were ready for action. Steele also told me that he had spent hours at night watching the house where George Wright stayed when he was not up at Sampson's. Wright had almost recovered from the injury to his arm, but he still remained most of the time indoors. At night he was visited, or at least his house was, by strange men who were swift, stealthy, mysterious—all men who formerly would not have been friends or neighbors.

Steele had not been able to recognize any of these night visitors, and he did not think the time was ripe for a bold holding up of one of them.

Jim Hoden had forcibly declared and stated that some deviltry was afoot, something vastly different from Blome's open intention of meeting the Ranger.

Hoden was right. Not twenty-four hours after his last talk with Steele, in which he advised quick action, he was found behind the little room of his restaurant, with a bullet hole in his breast, dead. No one could be found who had heard a shot.

It had been deliberate murder, for behind the bar had been left a piece of paper rudely scrawled with a pencil:

"All friends of Ranger Steele look for the same."

Later that day I met Steele at Hoden's and was with him when he looked at the body and the written message which spoke so tersely of the enmity toward him. We left there together, and I hoped Steele would let me stay with him from that moment.

"Russ, it's all in the dark," he said. "I feel Wright's hand in this."

I agreed. "I remember his face at Hoden's that day you winged him. Because Jim swore you were wrong not to kill instead of wing him. You were wrong."

"No, Russ, I never let feeling run wild with my head. We can't prove a thing on Wright."

"Come on; let's hunt him up. I'll bet I can accuse him and make him show his hand. Come on!"

That Steele found me hard to resist was all the satisfaction I got for the anger and desire to avenge Jim Hoden that consumed me.

"Son, you'll have your belly full of trouble soon enough," replied Steele. "Hold yourself in. Wait. Try to keep your eye on Sampson at night. See if anyone visits him. Spy on him. I'll watch Wright."

"Don't you think you'd do well to keep out of town, especially when you sleep?"

"Sure. I've got blankets out in the brush, and I go there every night late and leave before daylight. But I keep a light burning in the 'dobe house and make it look as if I were there."

"Good. That worried me. Now, what's this murder of Jim Hoden going to do to Morton, Zimmer, and their crowd?"

"Russ, they've all got blood in their eyes. This'll make them see red. I've only to say the word and we'll have all the backing we need."

"Have you run into Blome?"

"Once. I was across the street. He came out of the Hope So with some of his gang. They lined up and watched me. But I went right on."

"He's here looking for trouble, Steele."

"Yes; and he'd have found it before this if I just knew his relation to Sampson and Wright."

"Do you think Blome a dangerous man to meet?"

"Hardly. He's a genuine bad man, but for all that he's not much to be feared. If he were quietly keeping away from trouble, then that'd be different. Blome will probably die in his boots, thinking he's the worst man and the quickest one on the draw in the West."

That was conclusive enough for me. The little shadow of worry that had haunted me in spite of my confidence vanished entirely.

"Russ, for the present help me do something for Jim Hoden's family," went on Steele. "His wife's in bad shape. She's not a strong woman. There are a lot of kids, and you know Jim Hoden was poor. She told me her neighbors would keep shy of her now. They'd be afraid. Oh, it's tough! But we can put Jim away decently and help his family."

Several days after this talk with Steele I took Miss Sampson and Sally out to see Jim Hoden's wife and children. I knew Steele would be there that afternoon, but I did not mention this fact to Miss Sampson. We rode down to the little adobe house which belonged to Mrs. Hoden's people, and where Steele and I had moved her and the children after Jim Hoden's funeral. The house was small, but comfortable, and the yard green and shady.

If this poor wife and mother had not been utterly forsaken by neighbors and friends it certainly appeared so, for to my knowledge no one besides Steele and me visited her. Miss Sampson had packed a big basket full of good things to eat, and I carried this in front of me on the pommel as we rode. We hitched our horses to the fence and went round to the back of the house. There was a little porch with a stone flooring, and here several children were playing. The door stood open. At my knock Mrs. Hoden bade me come in. Evidently Steele was not there, so I went in with the girls.

"Mrs. Hoden, I've brought Miss Sampson and her cousin to see you," I said cheerfully.

The little room was not very light, there being only one window and the door; but Mrs. Hoden could be seen plainly enough as she lay, hollow-cheeked and haggard, on a bed. Once she had evidently been a woman of some comeliness. The ravages of trouble and grief were there to read in her worn face; it had not, however, any of the hard and bitter lines that had characterized her husband's.

I wondered, considering that Sampson had ruined Hoden, how Mrs. Hoden was going to regard the daughter of an enemy.

"So you're Roger Sampson's girl?" queried the woman, with her bright black eyes fixed on her visitor.

"Yes," replied Miss Sampson, simply. "This is my cousin, Sally Langdon. We've come to nurse you, take care of the children, help you in any way you'll let us."

There was a long silence.

"Well, you look a little like Sampson," finally said Mrs. Hoden, "but you're not at all like him. You must take after your mother. Miss Sampson, I don't know if I can—if I *ought* to accept anything from you. Your father ruined my husband."

"Yes, I know," replied the girl sadly. "That's all the more reason you should let me help you. Pray don't refuse. It will—mean so much to me."

If this poor, stricken woman had any resentment it speedily melted in the warmth and sweetness of Miss Sampson's manner. My idea was that the impression of Diane Sampson's beauty was always swiftly succeeded by that of her generosity and nobility. At any rate, she had started well with Mrs. Hoden, and no sooner had she begun to talk to the children than both they and the mother were won.

The opening of that big basket was an event. Poor, starved little beggars! I went out on the porch to get away from them. My feelings seemed too easily aroused. Hard indeed would it have gone with Jim Hoden's slayer if I could have laid my eyes on him then. However, Miss Sampson and Sally, after the nature of tender and practical girls, did not appear to take the sad situation to heart. The havoc had already been wrought in that household. The needs now were cheerfulness, kindness, help, action, and these the girls furnished with a spirit that did me good.

"Mrs. Hoden, who dressed this baby?" presently asked Miss Sampson. I peeped in to see a dilapidated youngster on her knees. That sight, if any other was needed, completed my full and splendid estimate of Diane Sampson.

"Mr. Steele," replied Mrs. Hoden.

"Mr. Steele!" exclaimed Miss Sampson.

"Yes; he's taken care of us all since—since—" Mrs. Hoden choked.

"Oh, so you've had no help but his," replied Miss Sampson hastily. "No women? Too bad! I'll send someone, Mrs. Hoden, and I'll come myself."

"It'll be good of you," went on the older woman. "You see, Jim had few friends—that is, right in town. And they've been afraid to help us—afraid they'd get what poor Jim—"

"That's awful!" burst out Miss Sampson passionately. "A brave lot of friends! Mrs. Hoden, don't you worry any more. We'll take care of you. Here, Sally help me. Whatever is the matter with baby's dress?" Manifestly Miss Sampson had some difficulty in subduing her emotion.

"Why, it's on hind side before," declared Sally. "I guess Mr. Steele hasn't dressed many babies."

"He did the best he could," said Mrs. Hoden. "Lord only knows what would have become of us! He brought your cowboy, Russ, who's been very good too."

"Mr. Steele, then is—is something more than a Ranger?" queried Miss Sampson, with a little break in her voice.

"He's more than I can tell," replied Mrs. Hoden. "He buried Jim. He paid our debts. He fetched us here. He bought food for us. He cooked for us and fed us. He washed and dressed the baby. He sat with me the first two nights after Jim's death, when I thought I'd die myself.

"He's so kind, so gentle, so patient. He has kept me up just by being near. Sometimes I'd wake from a doze an', seeing him there, I'd know how false were all these tales Jim heard about him and believed at first. Why, he plays with the children just—just like any good man might. When he has the baby up I just can't believe he's a bloody gunman, as they say.

"He's good, but he isn't happy. He has such sad eyes. He looks far off sometimes when the children climb round him. They love him. I think he must have loved some woman. His life is sad. Nobody need tell me—he sees the good in things. Once he said somebody had to be a Ranger. Well, I say, thank God for a Ranger like him!"

After that there was a long silence in the little room, broken only by the cooing of the baby. I did not dare to peep in at Miss Sampson then.

Somehow I expected Steele to arrive at that moment, and his step did not surprise me. He came round the corner as he always turned any corner, quick, alert, with his hand down. If I had been an enemy waiting there with a gun I would have needed to hurry. Steele was instinctively and habitually on the defense.

"Hello, son! How are Mrs. Hoden and the youngster to-day?" he asked.

"Hello yourself! Why, they're doing fine! I brought the girls down—"

Then in the semishadow of the room, across Mrs. Hoden's bed, Diane Sampson and Steele faced each other.

That was a moment! Having seen her face then I would not have missed sight of it for anything I could name; never so long as memory remained with me would I forget. She did not speak. Sally, however, bowed and spoke to the Ranger. Steele, after the first start, showed no unusual feeling. He greeted both girls pleasantly.

"Russ, that was thoughtful of you," he said. "It was womankind needed here. I could do so little—Mrs. Hoden, you look better to-day. I'm glad. And here's baby, all clean and white. Baby, what a time I had trying to puzzle out the way your clothes went on! Well, Mrs. Hoden, didn't I tell you friends would come? So will the brighter side."

"Yes; I've more faith than I had," replied Mrs. Hoden. "Roger Sampson's daughter has come to me. There for a while after Jim's death I thought I'd sink. We have nothing. How could I ever take care of my little ones? But I'm gaining courage."

"Mrs. Hoden, do not distress yourself any more," said Miss Sampson. "I shall see you are well cared for. I promise you."

"Miss Sampson, that's fine!" exclaimed Steele, with a ring in his voice. "It's what I'd have hoped—expected of you..."

It must have been sweet praise to her, for the whiteness of her face burned in a beautiful blush.

"And it's good of you, too, Miss Langdon, to come," added Steele. "Let me thank you both. I'm glad I have you girls as allies in part of my lonely task here. More than glad, for the sake of this good woman and the little ones. But both of you be careful. Don't stir without Russ. There's risk. And now I'll be going. Good-by. Mrs. Hoden, I'll drop in again to-night. Good-by!"

Steele backed to the door, and I slipped out before him.

"Mr. Steele—wait!" called Miss Sampson as he stepped out. He uttered a little sound like a hiss or a gasp or an intake of breath, I did not know what; and then the incomprehensible fellow bestowed a kick upon me that I thought about broke my leg. But I understood and gamely endured the pain. Then we were looking at Diane Sampson. She was white and wonderful. She stepped out of the door, close to Steele. She did not see me; she cared nothing for my presence. All the world would not have mattered to her then.

"I have wronged you!" she said impulsively.

Looking on, I seemed to see or feel some slow, mighty force gathering in Steele to meet this ordeal. Then he appeared as always—yet, to me, how different!

"Miss Sampson, how can you say that?" he returned.

"I believed what my father and George Wright said about you—that bloody, despicable record! Now I do *not* believe. I see—I wronged you."

"You make me very glad when you tell me this. It was hard to have you think so ill of me. But, Miss Sampson, please don't speak of wronging me. I am a Ranger, and much said of me is true. My duty is hard on others—sometimes on those who are innocent, alas! But God knows that duty is hard, too, on me."

"I did wrong you. In thought—in word. I ordered you from my home as if you were indeed what they called you. But I was deceived. I see my error. If you entered my home again I would think it an honor. I—"

"Please—please don't, Miss Sampson," interrupted poor Steele. I could see the gray beneath his bronze and something that was like gold deep in his eyes.

"But, sir, my conscience flays me," she went on. There was no other sound like her voice. If I was all distraught with emotion, what must Steele have been? "I make amends. Will you take my hand? Will you forgive me?" She gave it royally, while the other was there pressing at her breast.

Steele took the proffered hand and held it, and did not release it. What else could he have done? But he could not speak. Then it seemed to dawn upon Steele there was more behind this white, sweet, noble intensity of her than just making amends for a fancied or real wrong. For myself, I thought the man did not live on earth who could have resisted her then. And there was resistance; I felt it; she must have felt it. It was poor Steele's hard fate to fight the charm and eloquence and sweetness of this woman when, for some reason unknown to him, and only guessed at by me, she was burning with all the fire and passion of her soul.

"Mr. Steele, I honor you for your goodness to this unfortunate woman," she said, and now her speech came swiftly. "When she was all alone and helpless you were her friend. It was the deed of a man. But Mrs. Hoden isn't the only unfortunate woman in the world. I, too, am unfortunate. Ah, how I may soon need a friend!

"Vaughn Steele, the man whom I need most to be my friend—want most to lean upon—is the one whose duty is to stab me to the heart, to ruin me. You! Will you be my friend? If you knew Diane Sampson you would know she would never ask you to be false to your duty. Be true to us both! I'm so alone—no one but Sally loves me. I'll need a friend soon—soon.

"Oh, I know—I know what you'll find out sooner or later. I know *now*! I want to help you. Let us save life, if not honor. Must I stand alone—all alone? Will you—will you be—"

Her voice failed. She was swaying toward Steele. I expected to see his arms spread wide and enfold her in their embrace.

"Diane Sampson, I love you!" whispered Steele hoarsely, white now to his lips. "I must be true to my duty. But if I can't be true to you, then by God, I want no more of life!" He kissed her hand and rushed away.

She stood a moment as if blindly watching the place where he had vanished, and then as a sister might have turned to a brother, she reached for me.

CHAPTER 8 THE EAVESDROPPER

We silently rode home in the gathering dusk. Miss Sampson dismounted at the porch, but Sally went on with me to the corrals. I felt heavy and somber, as if a catastrophe was near at hand.

"Help me down," said Sally. Her voice was low and tremulous.

"Sally, did you hear what Miss Sampson said to Steele?" I asked.

"A little, here and there. I heard Steele tell her he loved her. Isn't this a terrible mix?"

"It sure is. Did you hear—do you understand why she appealed to Steele, asked him to be her friend?"

"Did she? No, I didn't hear that. I heard her say she had wronged him. Then I tried not to hear any more. Tell me."

"No Sally; it's not my secret. I wish I could do something—help them somehow. Yes, it's sure a terrible mix. I don't care so much about myself."

"Nor me," Sally retorted.

"You! Oh, you're only a shallow spoiled child! You'd cease to love anything the moment you won it. And I—well, I'm no good, you say. But their love! My God, what a tragedy! You've no idea, Sally. They've hardly spoken to each other, yet are ready to be overwhelmed."

Sally sat so still and silent that I thought I had angered or offended her. But I did not care much, one way or another. Her coquettish fancy for me and my own trouble had sunk into insignificance. I did not look up at her, though she was so close I could feel her little, restless foot touching me. The horses in the corrals were trooping up to the bars. Dusk had about given place to night, although in the west a broad flare of golden sky showed bright behind dark mountains.

"So I say you're no good?" asked Sally after a long silence. Then her voice and the way her hand stole to my shoulder should have been warning for me. But it was not, or I did not care.

"Yes, you said that, didn't you?" I replied absently.

"I can change my mind, can't I? Maybe you're only wild and reckless when you drink. Mrs. Hoden said such nice things about you. They made me feel so good."

I had no reply for that and still did not look up at her. I heard her swing herself around in the saddle. "Lift me down," she said.

Perhaps at any other time I would have remarked that this request was rather unusual, considering the fact that she was very light and sure of action, extremely proud of it, and likely to be insulted by an offer of assistance. But my spirit was dead. I reached for her hands, but they eluded mine, slipped up my arms as she came sliding out of the saddle, and then her face was very close to mine. "Russ!" she whispered. It was torment, wistfulness, uncertainty, and yet tenderness all in one little whisper. It caught me off guard or indifferent to consequences. So I kissed her, without passion, with all regret and sadness. She uttered a little cry that might have been mingled exultation and remorse for her victory and her broken faith. Certainly the instant I kissed her she remembered the latter. She trembled against me, and leaving unsaid something she had meant to say, she slipped out of my arms and ran. She assuredly was frightened, and I thought it just as well that she was.

Presently she disappeared in the darkness and then the swift little clinks of her spurs ceased. I laughed somewhat ruefully and hoped she would be satisfied. Then I put away the horses and went in for my supper.

After supper I noisily bustled around my room, and soon stole out for my usual evening's spying. The night was dark, without starlight, and the stiff wind rustled the leaves and tore through the vines on the old house. The fact that I had seen and heard so little during my constant vigilance did not make me careless or the task monotonous. I had so much to think about that sometimes I sat in one place for hours and never knew where the time went.

This night, the very first thing, I heard Wright's well-known footsteps, and I saw Sampson's door open, flashing a broad bar of light into the darkness. Wright crossed the threshold, the door closed, and all was dark again outside. Not a ray of light escaped from the window. This was the first visit of Wright for a considerable stretch of time. Little doubt there was that his talk with Sampson would be interesting to me.

I tiptoed to the door and listened, but I could hear only a murmur of voices. Besides, that position was too risky. I went round the corner of the house. Some time before I had made a discovery that I imagined would be valuable to me. This side of the big adobe house was of much older construction than the back and larger part. There was a narrow passage about a foot wide between the old and new walls, and this ran from the outside through to the patio. I had discovered the entrance by accident, as it was concealed by vines and shrubbery. I crawled in there, upon an opportune occasion, with the intention of boring a small hole through the adobe bricks. But it was not necessary to do that, for the wall was cracked; and in one place I could see into Sampson's room. This passage now afforded me my opportunity, and I decided to avail myself of it in spite of the very great danger. Crawling on my hands and knees very stealthily, I got under the shrubbery to the entrance of the passage. In the blackness a faint streak of light showed the location of the crack in the wall.

I had to slip in sidewise. It was a tight squeeze, but I entered without the slightest sound. If my position were to be betrayed it would not be from noise. As

I progressed the passage grew a very little wider in that direction, and this fact gave rise to the thought that in case of a necessary and hurried exit I would do best by working toward the patio. It seemed a good deal of time was consumed in reaching my vantage-point. When I did get there the crack was a foot over my head. If I had only been tall like Steele! There was nothing to do but find toe-holes in the crumbling walls, and by bracing knees on one side, back against the other, hold myself up to the crack.

Once with my eye there I did not care what risk I ran. Sampson appeared disturbed; he sat stroking his mustache; his brow was clouded. Wright's face seemed darker, more sullen, yet lighted by some indomitable resolve.

"We'll settle both deals to-night," Wright was saying. "That's what I came for. That's why I've asked Snecker and Blome to be here."

"But suppose I don't choose to talk here?" protested Sampson impatiently. "I never before made my house a place to—"

"We've waited long enough. This place's as good as any. You've lost your nerve since that Ranger hit the town. First, now, will you give Diane to me?"

"George, you talk like a spoiled boy. Give Diane to you! Why, she's a woman and I'm finding out that she's got a mind of her own. I told you I was willing for her to marry you. I tried to persuade her. But Diane hasn't any use for you now. She liked you at first; but now she doesn't. So what can I do?"

"You can make her marry me," replied Wright.

"Make that girl do what she doesn't want to? It couldn't be done, even if I tried. And I don't believe I'll try. I haven't the highest opinion of you as a prospective son-in-law, George. But if Diane loved you I would consent. We'd all go away together before this damned miserable business is out. Then she'd never know. And maybe you might be more like you used to be before the West ruined you. But as matters stand you fight your own game with her; and I'll tell you now, you'll lose."

"What'd you want to let her come out here for?" demanded Wright hotly. "It was a dead mistake. I've lost my head over her. I'll have her or die. Don't you think if she was my wife I'd soon pull myself together? Since she came we've none of us been right. And the gang has put up a holler. No, Sampson, we've got to settle things to-night."

"Well, we can settle what Diane's concerned in right now," replied Sampson, rising. "Come on; we'll go ask her. See where you stand."

They went out, leaving the door open. I dropped down to rest myself and to wait. I would have liked to hear Miss Sampson's answer to him. But I could guess what it would be. Wright appeared to be all I had thought of him, and I believed I was going to find out presently that he was worse. Just then I wanted Steele as never before. Still, he was too big to worm his way into this place.

The men seemed to be absent a good while, though that feeling might have been occasioned by my interest and anxiety. Finally I heard heavy steps. Wright came in alone. He was leaden-faced, humiliated. Then something abject in him gave place to rage. He strode the room; he cursed.

Sampson returned, now appreciably calmer. I could not but decide that he felt relief at the evident rejection of Wright's proposal. "Don't fume about it, George," he said. "You see I can't help it. We're pretty wild out here, but I can't rope my daughter and give her to you as I would an unruly steer."

"Sampson, I can *make* her marry me," declared Wright thickly.

"How?"

"You know the hold I got on you—the deal that made you boss of this rustler gang?"

"It isn't likely I'd forget," replied Sampson grimly.

"I can go to Diane—tell her that—make her believe I'd tell it broadcast, tell this Ranger Steele, unless she'd marry me!" Wright spoke breathlessly, with haggard face and shadowed eyes. He had no shame. He was simply in the grip of passion. Sampson gazed with dark, controlled fury at his relative. In that look I saw a strong, unscrupulous man fallen into evil ways, but still a man. It betrayed Wright to be the wild and passionate weakling.

I seemed to see also how, during all the years of association, this strong man had upheld the weak one. But that time had gone forever, both in intent on Sampson's part and in possibility. Wright, like the great majority of evil and unrestrained men on the border, had reached a point where influence was futile. Reason had degenerated. He saw only himself.

"But, George, Diane's the one person on earth who must never know I'm a rustler, a thief, a red-handed ruler of the worst gang on the border," replied Sampson impressively.

George bowed his head at that, as if the significance had just occurred to him. But he was not long at a loss. "She's going to find it out sooner or later. I tell you she knows now there's something wrong out here. She's got eyes. And that meddling cowboy of hers is smarter than you give him credit for. They're always together. You'll regret the day Russ ever straddled a horse on this ranch. Mark what I say."

"Diane's changed, I know; but she hasn't any idea yet that her daddy's a boss rustler. Diane's concerned about what she calls my duty as mayor. Also I think she's not satisfied with my explanations in regard to certain property."

Wright halted in his restless walk and leaned against the stone mantelpiece. He squared himself as if this was his last stand. He looked desperate, but on the moment showed an absence of his usual nervous excitement. "Sampson, that may well be true," he said. "No doubt all you say is true. But it doesn't help me. I want the girl. If I don't get her I reckon we'll all go to hell!" He might have meant anything, probably meant the worst. He certainly had something more in mind.

Sampson gave a slight start, barely perceptible like the twitch of an awakening tiger. He sat there, head down, stroking his mustache. Almost I saw his thought. I had long experience in reading men under stress of such emotion. I had no means to vindicate my judgment, but my conviction was that Sampson right then and there decided that the thing to do was to kill Wright. For my part, I wondered that he had not come to such a conclusion before. Not improbably the advent of his daughter had put Sampson in conflict with himself.

Suddenly he threw off a somber cast of countenance and began to talk. He talked swiftly, persuasively, yet I imagined he was talking to smooth Wright's passion for the moment. Wright no more caught the fateful significance of a line crossed, a limit reached, a decree decided, than if he had not been present. He was obsessed with himself.

How, I wondered, had a man of his mind ever lived so long and gone so far among the exacting conditions of Pecos County? The answer was perhaps, that Sampson had guided him, upheld him, protected him. The coming of Diane Sampson had been the entering wedge of dissension.

"You're too impatient," concluded Sampson. "You'll ruin any chance of happiness if you rush Diane. She might be won. If you told her who I am she'd hate you forever. She might marry you to save me, but she'd hate you.

"That isn't the way. Wait. Play for time. Be different with her. Cut out your drinking. She despises that. Let's plan to sell out here, stock, ranch, property, and leave the country. Then you'd have a show with her."

"I told you we've got to stick," growled Wright. "The gang won't stand for our going. It can't be done unless you want to sacrifice everything."

"You mean double-cross the men? Go without their knowing? Leave them here to face whatever comes?"

"I mean just that."

"I'm bad enough, but not that bad," returned Sampson. "If I can't get the gang to let me off I'll stay and face the music. All the same, Wright, did it ever strike you that most of our deals the last few years have been yours?"

"Yes. If I hadn't rung them in, there wouldn't have been any. You've had cold feet, Owens says, especially since this Ranger Steele has been here."

"Well, call it cold feet if you like. But I call it sense. We reached our limit long ago. We began by rustling a few cattle at a time when rustling was laughed at. But as our greed grew so did our boldness. Then came the gang, the regular trips, and one thing and another till, before we knew it—before *I* knew it, we had shady deals, hold-ups, and murders on our record. Then we had to go on. Too late to turn back!"

"I reckon we've all said that. None of the gang wants to quit. They all think, and I think, we can't be touched. We may be blamed, but nothing can be proved. We're too strong."

"There's where you're dead wrong," rejoined Sampson, emphatically. "I imagined that once, not long ago. I was bull-headed. Who would ever connect Roger Sampson with a rustler gang? I've changed my mind. I've begun to think. I've reasoned out things. We're crooked and we can't last. It's the nature of life, even in wild Pecos, for conditions to grow better. The wise deal for us would be to divide equally and leave the country, all of us."

"But you and I have all the stock—all the gain," protested Wright.

"I'll split mine."

"I won't—that settles that," added Wright instantly.

Sampson spread wide his hands as if it was useless to try to convince this man. Talking had not increased his calmness, and he now showed more than impatience. A dull glint gleamed deep in his eyes. "Your stock and property will last a long time—do you lots of good when Steele—"

"Bah!" hoarsely croaked Wright. The Ranger's name was a match applied to powder. "Haven't I told you he'd be dead soon same as Hoden is?"

"Yes, you mentioned the supposition," replied Sampson sarcastically. "I inquired, too just how that very desired event was to be brought about."

"Blome's here to kill Steele."

"Bah!" retorted Sampson in turn. "Blome can't kill this Ranger. He can't face him with a ghost of a show—he'll never get a chance at Steele's back. The man don't live on this border who's quick and smart enough to kill Steele."

"I'd like to know why?" demanded Wright sullenly.

"You ought to know. You've seen the Ranger pull a gun."

"Who told you?" queried Wright, his face working.

"Oh, I guessed it, if that'll do you."

"If Jack doesn't kill this damned Ranger I will," replied Wright, pounding the table.

Sampson laughed contemptuously. "George, don't make so much noise. And don't be a fool. You've been on the border for ten years. You've packed a gun and you've used it. You've been with Blome and Snecker when they killed their men. You've been present at many fights. But you never saw a man like Steele. You haven't got sense enough to see him right if you had a chance. Neither has Blome. The only way to get rid of Steele is for the gang to draw on him, all at once. And even then he's going to drop some of them."

"Sampson, you say that like a man who wouldn't care much if Steele did drop some of them," declared Wright, and now he was sarcastic.

"To tell you the truth I wouldn't," returned the other bluntly. "I'm pretty sick of this mess."

Wright cursed in amaze. His emotions were out of all proportion to his intelligence. He was not at all quick-witted. I had never seen a vainer or more arrogant man. "Sampson, I don't like your talk," he said.

"If you don't like the way I talk you know what you can do," replied Sampson quickly. He stood up then, cool and quiet, with flash of eyes and set of lips that told me he was dangerous.

"Well, after all, that's neither here nor there," went on Wright, unconsciously cowed by the other. "The thing is, do I get the girl?"

"Not by any means, except her consent."

"You'll not make her marry me?"

"No. No," replied Sampson, his voice still cold, low-pitched.

"All right. Then I'll make her."

CHAPTER 8 THE EAVESDROPPER

Evidently Sampson understood the man before him so well that he wasted no more words. I knew what Wright never dreamed of, and that was that Sampson had a gun somewhere within reach and meant to use it.

Then heavy footsteps sounded outside, tramping upon the porch. I might have been mistaken, but I believed those footsteps saved Wright's life.

"There they are," said Wright, and he opened the door. Five masked men entered. About two of them I could not recognize anything familiar. I thought one had old Snecker's burly shoulders and another Bo Snecker's stripling shape. I did recognize Blome in spite of his mask, because his fair skin and hair, his garb and air of distinction made plain his identity. They all wore coats, hiding any weapons. The big man with burly shoulders shook hands with Sampson and the others stood back.

The atmosphere of that room had changed. Wright might have been a nonentity for all he counted. Sampson was another man—a stranger to me. If he had entertained a hope of freeing himself from his band, of getting away to a safer country, he abandoned it at the very sight of these men. There was power here and he was bound.

The big man spoke in low, hoarse whispers, and at this all the others gathered round him, close to the table. There were evidently some signs of membership not plain to me. Then all the heads were bent over the table. Low voices spoke, queried, answered, argued. By straining my ears I caught a word here and there. They were planning. I did not attempt to get at the meaning of the few words and phrases I distinguished, but held them in mind so to piece all together afterward. Before the plotters finished conferring I had an involuntary flashed knowledge of much and my whirling, excited mind made reception difficult.

When these rustlers finished whispering I was in a cold sweat. Steele was to be killed as soon as possible by Blome, or by the gang going to Steele's house at night. Morton had been seen with the Ranger. He was to meet the same fate as Hoden, dealt by Bo Snecker, who evidently worked in the dark like a ferret. Any other person known to be communing with Steele, or interested in him, or suspected of either, was to be silenced. Then the town was to suffer a short deadly spell of violence, directed anywhere, for the purpose of intimidating those people who had begun to be restless under the influence of the Ranger. After that, big herds of stock were to be rustled off the ranches to the north and driven to El Paso.

Then the big man, who evidently was the leader of the present convention, got up to depart. He went as swiftly as he had come, and was followed by the slender fellow. As far as it was possible for me to be sure, I identified these two as Snecker and his son. The others, however, remained. Blome removed his mask, which action was duplicated by the two rustlers who had stayed with him. They were both young, bronzed, hard of countenance, not unlike cowboys. Evidently this was now a social call on Sampson. He set out cigars and liquors for his guests, and a general conversation ensued, differing little from what might have been indulged in by neighborly ranchers. There was not a word spoken that would have caused suspicion.

Blome was genial, gay, and he talked the most. Wright alone seemed uncommunicative and unsociable. He smoked fiercely and drank continually. All at once he straightened up as if listening. "What's that?" he called suddenly.

The talking and laughter ceased. My own strained ears were pervaded by a slight rustling sound.

"Must be a rat," replied Sampson in relief. Strange how any sudden or unknown thing weighed upon him.

The rustling became a rattle.

"Sounds like a rattlesnake to me," said Blome.

Sampson got up from the table and peered round the room. Just at that instant I felt an almost inappreciable movement of the adobe wall which supported me. I could scarcely credit my senses. But the rattle inside Sampson's room was mingling with little dull thuds of falling dirt. The adobe wall, merely dried mud was crumbling. I distinctly felt a tremor pass through it. Then the blood gushed with sickening coldness back to my heart and seemingly clogged it.

"What in the hell!" exclaimed Sampson.

"I smell dust," said Blome sharply.

That was the signal for me to drop down from my perch, yet despite my care I made a noise.

"Did you hear a step?" queried Sampson.

Then a section of the wall fell inward with a crash. I began to squeeze my body through the narrow passage toward the patio.

"Hear him!" yelled Wright. "This side."

"No, he's going that way," yelled someone else. The tramp of heavy boots lent me the strength and speed of desperation. I was not shirking a fight, but to be cornered like a trapped coyote was another matter. I almost tore my clothes off in that passage. The dust nearly stifled me.

When I burst into the patio it was not one single instant too soon. But one deep gash of breath revived me, and I was up, gun in hand, running for the outlet into the court. Thumping footsteps turned me back. While there was a chance to get away I did not want to meet odds in a fight. I thought I heard some one running into the patio from the other end. I stole along, and coming to a door, without any idea of where it might lead, I softly pushed it open a little way and slipped in.

CHAPTER 9 IN FLAGRANTE DELICTO

A low cry greeted me. The room was light. I saw Sally Langdon sitting on her bed in her dressing gown. Shaking my gun at her with a fierce warning gesture to be silent, I turned to close the door. It was a heavy door, without bolt or bar, and when I had shut it I felt safe only for the moment. Then I gazed around the room. There was one window with blind closely drawn. I listened and seemed to hear footsteps retreating, dying away. Then I turned to Sally. She had slipped off the bed to her knees and was holding out trembling hands as if both to supplicate mercy and to ward me off. She was as white as the pillow on her bed. She was terribly frightened. Again with warning hand commanding silence I stepped softly forward, meaning to reassure her.

"Russ! Russ!" she whispered wildly, and I thought she was going to faint. When I got close and looked into her eyes I understood the strange dark expression in them. She was terrified because she believed I meant to kill her, or do worse, probably worse. She had believed many a hard story about me and had cared for me in spite of them. I remembered, then, that she had broken her promise, she had tempted me, led me to kiss her, made a fool out of me. I remembered, also how I had threatened her. This intrusion of mine was the wild cowboy's vengeance.

I verily believed she thought I was drunk. I must have looked pretty hard and fierce, bursting into her room with that big gun in hand. My first action then was to lay the gun on her bureau.

"You poor kid!" I whispered, taking her hands and trying to raise her. But she stayed on her knees and clung to me.

"Russ! It was vile of me," she whispered. "I know it. I deserve anything—anything! But I am only a kid. Russ, I didn't break my word—I didn't make you kiss me just for, vanity's sake. I swear I didn't. I wanted you to. For I care, Russ, I can't help it. Please forgive me. Please let me off this time. Don't—don't—"

"Will you shut up!" I interrupted, half beside myself. And I used force in another way than speech. I shook her and sat her on the bed. "You little fool, I didn't come in here to kill you or do some other awful thing, as you think. For God's sake, Sally, what do you take me for?"

"Russ, you swore you'd do something terrible if I tempted you anymore," she faltered. The way she searched my face with doubtful, fearful eyes hurt me.

"Listen," and with the word I seemed to be pervaded by peace. "I didn't know this was your room. I came in here to get away—to save my life. I was pursued. I was spying on Sampson and his men. They heard me, but did not see me. They don't know who was listening. They're after me now. I'm Special United States Deputy Marshal Sittell—Russell Archibald Sittell. I'm a Ranger. I'm here as secret aid to Steele."

Sally's eyes changed from blank gulfs to dilating, shadowing, quickening windows of thought. "Russ-ell Archi-bald Sittell," she echoed. "Ranger! Secret aid to Steele!"

"Yes."

"Then you're no cowboy?"

"No."

"Only a make-believe one?"

"Yes."

"And the drinking, the gambling, the association with those low men—that was all put on?"

"Part of the game, Sally. I'm not a drinking man. And I sure hate those places I had to go in, and all that pertains to them."

"Oh, so *that's* it! I knew there was something. How glad—how glad I am!" Then Sally threw her arms around my neck, and without reserve or restraint began to kiss me and love me. It must have been a moment of sheer gladness to feel that I was not disreputable, a moment when something deep and womanly in her was vindicated. Assuredly she was entirely different from what she had ever been before.

There was a little space of time, a sweet confusion of senses, when I could not but meet her half-way in tenderness. Quite as suddenly, then she began to cry. I whispered in her ear, cautioning her to be careful, that my life was at stake; and after that she cried silently, with one of her arms round my neck, her head on my breast, and her hand clasping mine. So I held her for what seemed a long time. Indistinct voices came to me and footsteps seemingly a long way off. I heard the wind in the rose-bush outside. Some one walked down the stony court. Then a shrill neigh of a horse pierced the silence. A rider was mounting out there for some reason. With my life at stake I grasped all the sweetness of that situation. Sally stirred in my arms, raised a red, tear-stained yet happy face, and tried to smile. "It isn't any time to cry," she whispered. "But I had to. You can't understand what it made me feel to learn you're no drunkard, no desperado, but a *man*—a man like that Ranger!" Very sweetly and seriously she kissed me again. "Russ, if I didn't honestly and truly love you before, I do now."

Then she stood up and faced me with the fire and intelligence of a woman in her eyes. "Tell me now. You were spying on my uncle?"

Briefly I told her what had happened before I entered her room, not omitting a terse word as to the character of the men I had watched.

"My God! So it's Uncle Roger! I knew something was very wrong here—with him, with the place, the people. And right off I hated George Wright. Russ, does Diane know?"

"She knows something. I haven't any idea how much."

"This explains her appeal to Steele. Oh, it'll kill her! You don't know how proud, how good Diane is. Oh, it'll kill her!"

"Sally, she's no baby. She's got sand, that girl—"

The sound of soft steps somewhere near distracted my attention, reminded me of my peril, and now, what counted more with me, made clear the probability of being discovered in Sally's room. "I'll have to get out of here," I whispered.

"Wait," she replied, detaining me. "Didn't you say they were hunting for you?"

"They sure are," I returned grimly.

"Oh! Then you mustn't go. They might shoot you before you got away. Stay. If we hear them you can hide under my bed. I'll turn out the light. I'll meet them at the door. You can trust me. Stay, Russ. Wait till all quiets down, if we have to wait till morning. Then you can slip out."

"Sally, I oughtn't to stay. I don't want to—I won't," I replied perplexed and stubborn.

"But you must. It's the only safe way. They won't come here."

"Suppose they should? It's an even chance Sampson'll search every room and corner in this old house. If they found me here I couldn't start a fight. You might be hurt. Then—the fact of my being here—" I did not finish what I meant, but instead made a step toward the door.

Sally was on me like a little whirlwind, white of face and dark of eye, with a resoluteness I could not have deemed her capable of. She was as strong and supple as a panther, too. But she need not have been either resolute or strong, for the clasp of her arms, the feel of her warm breast as she pressed me back were enough to make me weak as water. My knees buckled as I touched the chair, and I was glad to sit down. My face was wet with perspiration and a kind of cold ripple shot over me. I imagined I was losing my nerve then. Proof beyond doubt that Sally loved me was so sweet, so overwhelming a thing, that I could not resist, even to save her disgrace.

"Russ, the fact of your being here is the very thing to save you—if they come," Sally whispered softly. "What do I care what they think?" She put her arms round my neck. I gave up then and held her as if she indeed were my only hope. A noise, a stealthy sound, a step, froze that embrace into stone.

"Up yet, Sally?" came Sampson's clear voice, too strained, too eager to be natural.

"No. I'm in bed, reading. Good night, Uncle," instantly replied Sally, so calmly and naturally that I marveled at the difference between man and woman. Perhaps that was the difference between love and hate.

"Are you alone?" went on Sampson's penetrating voice, colder now.

"Yes," replied Sally.

The door swung inward with a swift scrape and jar. Sampson half entered, haggard, flaming-eyed. His leveled gun did not have to move an inch to cover me. Behind him I saw Wright and indistinctly, another man.

"Well!" gasped Sampson. He showed amazement. "Hands up, Russ!"

I put up my hands quickly, but all the time I was calculating what chance I had to leap for my gun or dash out the light. I was trapped. And fury, like the hot teeth of a wolf, bit into me. That leveled gun, the menace in Sampson's puzzled eyes, Wright's dark and hateful face, these loosened the spirit of fight in me. If Sally had not been there I would have made some desperate move.

Sampson barred Wright from entering, which action showed control as well as distrust.

"You lied!" said Sampson to Sally. He was hard as flint, yet doubtful and curious, too.

"Certainly I lied," snapped Sally in reply. She was cool, almost flippant. I awakened to the knowledge that she was to be reckoned with in this situation. Suddenly she stepped squarely between Sampson and me.

"Move aside," ordered Sampson sternly.

"I won't! What do I care for your old gun? You shan't shoot Russ or do anything else to him. It's my fault he's here in my room. I coaxed him to come."

"You little hussy!" exclaimed Sampson, and he lowered the gun.

If I ever before had occasion to glory in Sally I had it then. She betrayed not the slightest fear. She looked as if she could fight like a little tigress. She was white, composed, defiant.

"How long has Russ been in here?" demanded Sampson.

"All evening. I left Diane at eight o'clock. Russ came right after that."

"But you'd undressed for bed!" ejaculated the angry and perplexed uncle.

"Yes." That simple answer was so noncommittal, so above subterfuge, so innocent, and yet so confounding in its provocation of thought that Sampson just stared his astonishment. But I started as if I had been struck.

"See here Sampson—" I began, passionately.

Like a flash Sally whirled into my arms and one hand crossed my lips. "It's my fault. I will take the blame," she cried, and now the agony of fear in her voice quieted me. I realized I would be wise to be silent. "Uncle," began Sally, turning her head, yet still clinging to me, "I've tormented Russ into loving me. I've flirted with him—teased him—tempted him. We love each other now. We're engaged. Please—please don't—" She began to falter and I felt her weight sag a little against me.

"Well, let go of him," said Sampson. "I won't hurt him. Sally, how long has this affair been going on?"

"For weeks—I don't know how long."

"Does Diane know?"

"She knows we love each other, but not that we met—did this—" Light swift steps, the rustle of silk interrupted Sampson, and made my heart sink like lead.

CHAPTER 9 IN FLAGRANTE DELICTO

"Is that you, George?" came Miss Sampson's deep voice, nervous, hurried. "What's all this commotion? I hear—"

"Diane, go on back," ordered Sampson.

Just then Miss Sampson's beautiful agitated face appeared beside Wright. He failed to prevent her from seeing all of us.

"Papa! Sally!" she exclaimed, in consternation. Then she swept into the room. "What has happened?"

Sampson, like the devil he was, laughed when it was too late. He had good impulses, but they never interfered with his sardonic humor. He paced the little room, shrugging his shoulders, offering no explanation. Sally appeared about ready to collapse and I could not have told Sally's lie to Miss Sampson to save my life.

"Diane, your father and I broke in on a little Romeo and Juliet scene," said George Wright with a leer. Then Miss Sampson's dark gaze swept from George to her father, then to Sally's attire and her shamed face, and finally to me. What effect the magnificent wrath and outraged trust in her eyes had upon me!

"Russ, do they dare insinuate you came to Sally's room?" For myself I could keep silent, but for Sally I began to feel a hot clamoring outburst swelling in my throat.

"Sally confessed it, Diane," replied Wright.

"Sally!" A shrinking, shuddering disbelief filled Miss Sampson's voice.

"Diane, I told you I loved him—didn't I?" replied Sally. She managed to hold up her head with a ghost of her former defiant spirit.

"Miss Sampson, it's a—" I burst out.

Then Sally fainted. It was I who caught her. Miss Sampson hurried to her side with a little cry of distress.

"Russ, your hand's called," said Sampson. "Of course you'll swear the moon's green cheese. And I like you the better for it. But we know now, and you can save your breath. If Sally hadn't stuck up so gamely for you I'd have shot you. But at that I wasn't looking for you. Now clear out of here." I picked up my gun from the bureau and dropped it in its sheath. For the life of me I could not leave without another look at Miss Sampson. The scorn in her eyes did not wholly hide the sadness. She who needed friends was experiencing the bitterness of misplaced trust. That came out in the scorn, but the sadness—I knew what hurt her most was her sorrow.

I dropped my head and stalked out.

CHAPTER 10 A SLAP IN THE FACE

When I got out into the dark, where my hot face cooled in the wind, my relief equaled my other feelings. Sampson had told me to clear out, and although I did not take that as a dismissal I considered I would be wise to leave the ranch at once. Daylight might disclose my footprints between the walls, but even if it did not, my work there was finished. So I went to my room and packed my few belongings.

The night was dark, windy, stormy, yet there was no rain. I hoped as soon as I got clear of the ranch to lose something of the pain I felt. But long after I had tramped out into the open there was a lump in my throat and an ache in my breast. And all my thought centered round Sally.

What a game and loyal little girl she had turned out to be! I was absolutely at a loss concerning what the future held in store for us. I seemed to have a vague but clinging hope that, after the trouble was over, there might be—there *must* be—something more between us.

Steele was not at our rendezvous among the rocks. The hour was too late. Among the few dim lights flickering on the outskirts of town I picked out the one of his little adobe house but I knew almost to a certainty that he was not there. So I turned my way into the darkness, not with any great hope of finding Steele out there, but with the intention of seeking a covert for myself until morning.

There was no trail and the night was so black that I could see only the lighter sandy patches of ground. I stumbled over the little clumps of brush, fell into washes, and pricked myself on cactus. By and by mesquites and rocks began to make progress still harder for me. I wandered around, at last getting on higher ground and here in spite of the darkness, felt some sense of familiarity with things. I was probably near Steele's hiding place.

I went on till rocks and brush barred further progress, and then I ventured to whistle. But no answer came. Whereupon I spread my blanket in as sheltered a place as I could find and lay down. The coyotes were on noisy duty, the wind moaned and rushed through the mesquites. But despite these sounds and worry about Steele, and the never-absent haunting thought of Sally, I went to sleep.

A little rain had fallen during the night, as I discovered upon waking; still it was not enough to cause me any discomfort. The morning was bright and beautiful, yet somehow I hated it. I had work to do that did not go well with that golden wave of grass and brush on the windy open.

I climbed to the highest rock of that ridge and looked about. It was a wild spot, some three miles from town. Presently I recognized landmarks given to me by Steele and knew I was near his place. I whistled, then halloed, but got no reply. Then by working back and forth across the ridge I found what appeared to be a faint trail. This I followed, lost and found again, and eventually, still higher up on another ridge, with a commanding outlook, I found Steele's hiding place. He had not been there for perhaps forty-eight hours. I wondered where he had slept.

Under a shelving rock I found a pack of food, carefully protected by a heavy slab. There was also a canteen full of water. I lost no time getting myself some breakfast, and then, hiding my own pack, I set off at a rapid walk for town.

But I had scarcely gone a quarter of a mile, had, in fact, just reached a level, when sight of two horsemen halted me and made me take to cover. They appeared to be cowboys hunting for a horse or a steer. Under the circumstances, however, I was suspicious, and I watched them closely, and followed them a mile or so round the base of the ridges, until I had thoroughly satisfied myself they were not tracking Steele. They were a long time working out of sight, which further retarded my venturing forth into the open.

Finally I did get started. Then about half-way to town more horsemen in the flat caused me to lie low for a while, and make a wide detour to avoid being seen.

Somewhat to my anxiety it was afternoon before I arrived in town. For my life I could not have told why I knew something had happened since my last visit, but I certainly felt it; and was proportionately curious and anxious.

The first person I saw whom I recognized was Dick, and he handed me a note from Sally. She seemed to take it for granted that I had been wise to leave the ranch. Miss Sampson had softened somewhat when she learned Sally and I were engaged, and she had forgiven my deceit. Sally asked me to come that night after eight, down among the trees and shrubbery, to a secluded spot we knew. It was a brief note and all to the point. But there was something in it that affected me strangely. I had imagined the engagement an invention for the moment. But after danger to me was past Sally would not have carried on a pretense, not even to win back Miss Sampson's respect. The fact was, Sally meant that engagement. If I did the right thing now I would not lose her.

But what was the right thing?

I was sorely perplexed and deeply touched. Never had I a harder task than that of the hour—to put her out of my mind. I went boldly to Steele's house. He was not there. There was nothing by which I could tell when he had been there. The lamp might have been turned out or might have burned out. The oil was low. I saw a good many tracks round in the sandy walks. I did not recognize Steele's.

As I hurried away I detected more than one of Steele's nearest neighbors peering at me from windows and doors. Then I went to Mrs. Hoden's. She was up and about and cheerful. The children were playing, manifestly well cared for and content. Mrs. Hoden had not seen Steele since I had. Miss Samson had sent her servant. There was a very decided change in the atmosphere of Mrs. Hoden's home, and I saw that for her the worst was past, and she was bravely, hopefully facing the future.

From there, I hurried to the main street of Linrock and to that section where violence brooded, ready at any chance moment to lift its hydra head. For that time of day the street seemed unusually quiet. Few pedestrians were abroad and few loungers. There was a row of saddled horses on each side of the street, the full extent of the block.

I went into the big barroom of the Hope So. I had never seen the place so full, nor had it ever seemed so quiet. The whole long bar was lined by shirt-sleeved men, with hats slouched back and vests flapping wide. Those who were not drinking were talking low. Half a dozen tables held as many groups of dusty, motley men, some silent, others speaking and gesticulating, all earnest.

At first glance I did not see any one in whom I had especial interest. The principal actors of my drama did not appear to be present. However, there were rough characters more in evidence than at any other time I had visited the saloon. Voices were too low for me to catch, but I followed the direction of some of the significant gestures. Then I saw that these half dozen tables were rather closely grouped and drawn back from the center of the big room. Next my quick sight took in a smashed table and chairs, some broken bottles on the floor, and then a dark sinister splotch of blood.

I had no time to make inquiries, for my roving eye caught Frank Morton in the doorway, and evidently he wanted to attract my attention. He turned away and I followed. When I got outside, he was leaning against the hitching-rail. One look at this big rancher was enough for me to see that he had been told my part in Steele's game, and that he himself had roused to the Texas fighting temper. He had a clouded brow. He looked somber and thick. He seemed slow, heavy, guarded.

"Howdy, Russ," he said. "We've been wantin' you."

"There's ten of us in town, all scattered round, ready. It's goin' to start to-day."

"Where's Steele?" was my first query.

"Saw him less'n hour ago. He's somewhere close. He may show up any time."

"Is he all right?"

"Wal, he was pretty fit a little while back," replied Morton significantly.

"What's come off? Tell me all."

"Wal, the ball opened last night, I reckon. Jack Blome came swaggerin' in here askin' for Steele. We all knew what he was in town for. But last night he came out with it. Every man in the saloons, every man on the streets heard Blome's loud an' longin' call for the Ranger. Blome's pals took it up and they all enjoyed themselves some."

"Drinking hard?" I queried.

"Nope—they didn't hit it up very hard. But they laid foundations." Of course, Steele was not to be seen last night. This morning Blome and his gang were out pretty early. But they traveled alone. Blome just strolled up and down by himself.

I watched him walk up this street on one side and then down the other, just a matter of thirty-one times. I counted them. For all I could see maybe Blome did not take a drink. But his gang, especially Bo Snecker, sure looked on the red liquor.

"By eleven o'clock everybody in town knew what was coming off. There was no work or business, except in the saloons. Zimmer and I were together, and the rest of our crowd in pairs at different places. I reckon it was about noon when Blome got tired parading up and down. He went in the Hope So, and the crowd followed. Zimmer stayed outside so to give Steele a hunch in case he came along. I went in to see the show.

"Wal, it was some curious to me, and I've lived all my life in Texas. But I never before saw a gunman on the job, so to say. Blome's a handsome fellow, an' he seemed different from what I expected. Sure, I thought he'd yell an' prance round like a drunken fool. But he was cool an' quiet enough. The blowin' an' drinkin' was done by his pals. But after a little while it got to me that Blome gloried in this situation. I've seen a man dead-set to kill another, all dark, sullen, restless. But Blome wasn't that way. He didn't seem at all like a bloody devil. He was vain, cocksure. He was revelin' in the effect he made. I had him figured all right.

"Blome sat on the edge of a table an' he faced the door. Of course, there was a pard outside, ready to pop in an' tell him if Steele was comin'. But Steele didn't come in that way. He wasn't on the street just before that time, because Zimmer told me afterward. Steele must have been in the Hope So somewhere. Any way, just like he dropped from the clouds he came through the door near the bar. Blome didn't see him come. But most of the gang did, an' I want to tell you that big room went pretty quiet.

"'Hello Blome, I hear you're lookin' for me,' called out Steele.

"I don't know if he spoke ordinary or not, but his voice drew me up same as it did the rest, an' damn me! Blome seemed to turn to stone. He didn't start or jump. He turned gray. An' I could see that he was tryin' to think in a moment when thinkin' was hard. Then Blome turned his head. Sure he expected to look into a six-shooter. But Steele was standin' back there in his shirt sleeves, his hands on his hips, and he looked more man than any one I ever saw. It's easy to remember the look of him, but how he made me feel, that isn't easy.

"Blome was at a disadvantage. He was half sittin' on a table, an' Steele was behind an' to the left of him. For Blome to make a move then would have been a fool trick. He saw that. So did everybody. The crowd slid back without noise, but Bo Snecker an' a rustler named March stuck near Blome. I figured this Bo Snecker as dangerous as Blome, an' results proved I was right.

"Steele didn't choose to keep his advantage, so far as position in regard to Blome went. He just walked round in front of the rustler. But this put all the crowd in front of Steele, an' perhaps he had an eye for that.

"'I hear you've been looking for me,' repeated the Ranger.

"Blome never moved a muscle but he seemed to come to life. It struck me that Steele's presence had made an impression on Blome which was new to the rustler.

"'Yes, I have,' replied Blome.

"'Well, here I am. What do you want?'

"When everybody knew what Blome wanted and had intended, this question of Steele's seemed strange on one hand. An' yet on the other, now that the Ranger stood there, it struck me as natural enough.

"'If you heard I was lookin' for you, you sure heard what for,' replied Blome.

"'Blome, my experience with such men as you is that you all brag one thing behind my back an' you mean different when I show up. I've called you now. What do you mean?'

"'I reckon you know what Jack Blome means.'

"'Jack Blome! That name means nothin' to me. Blome, you've been braggin' around that you'd meet me—kill me! You thought you meant it, didn't you?'

"'Yes—I did mean it.'

"'All right. Go ahead!'

"The barroom became perfectly still, except for the slow breaths I heard. There wasn't any movement anywhere. That queer gray came to Blome's face again. He might again have been stone. I thought, an' I'll gamble every one else watchin' thought, Blome would draw an' get killed in the act. But he never moved. Steele had cowed him. If Blome had been heated by drink, or mad, or anythin' but what he was just then, maybe he might have throwed a gun. But he didn't. I've heard of really brave men gettin' panicked like that, an' after seein' Steele I didn't wonder at Blome.

"'You see, Blome, you don't want to meet me, for all your talk,' went on the Ranger. 'You thought you did, but that was before you faced the man you intended to kill. Blome, you're one of these dandy, cock-of-the-walk four-flushers. I'll tell you how I know. Because I've met the real gun-fighters, an' there never was one of them yet who bragged or talked. Now don't you go round blowin' any more.'

"Then Steele deliberately stepped forward an' slapped Blome on one side of his face an' again on the other.

"'Keep out of my way after this or I'm liable to spoil some of your dandy looks.'

"Blome got up an' walked straight out of the place. I had my eyes on him, kept me from seein' Steele. But on hearin' somethin', I don't know what, I turned back an' there Steele had got a long arm on Bo Snecker, who was tryin' to throw a gun.

"But he wasn't quick enough. The gun banged in the air an' then it went spinnin' away, while Snecker dropped in a heap on the floor. The table was overturned, an' March, the other rustler, who was on that side, got up, pullin' his gun. But somebody in the crowd killed him before he could get goin'. I didn't see who fired that shot, an' neither did anybody else. But the crowd broke an' run. Steele dragged Bo Snecker down to jail an' locked him up."

Morton concluded his narrative, and then evidently somewhat dry of tongue, he produced knife and tobacco and cut himself a huge quid. "That's all, so far, today, Russ, but I reckon you'll agree with me on the main issue—Steele's game's opened."

CHAPTER 10 A SLAP IN THE FACE

I had felt the rush of excitement, the old exultation at the prospect of danger, but this time there was something lacking in them. The wildness of the boy that had persisted in me was gone.

"Yes, Steele has opened it and I'm ready to boost the game along. Wait till I see him! But Morton, you say someone you don't know played a hand in here and killed March."

"I sure do. It wasn't any of our men. Zimmer was outside. The others were at different places."

"The fact is, then, Steele has more friends than we know, perhaps more than he knows himself."

"Right. An' it's got the gang in the air. There'll be hell to-night."

"Steele hardly expects to keep Snecker in jail, does he?"

"I can't say. Probably not. I wish Steele had put both Blome and Snecker out of the way. We'd have less to fight."

"Maybe. I'm for the elimination method myself. But Steele doesn't follow out the gun method. He will use one only when he's driven. It's hard to make him draw. You know, after all, these desperate men aren't afraid of guns or fights. Yet they are afraid of Steele. Perhaps it's his nerve, the way he faces them, the things he says, the fact that he has mysterious allies."

"Russ, we're all with him, an' I'll gamble that the honest citizens of Linrock will flock to him in another day. I can see signs of that. There were twenty or more men on Hoden's list, but Steele didn't want so many."

"We don't need any more. Morton, can you give me any idea where Steele is?"

"Not the slightest."

"All right. I'll hunt for him. If you see him tell him to hole up, and then you come after me. Tell him I've got our men spotted."

"Russ, if you Ranger fellows ain't wonders!" exclaimed Morton, with shining eyes.

Steele did not show himself in town again that day. Here his cunning was manifest. By four o'clock that afternoon Blome was drunk and he and his rustlers went roaring up and down the street. There was some shooting, but I did not see or hear that any one got hurt. The lawless element, both native to Linrock and the visitors, followed in Blome's tracks from saloon to saloon. How often had I seen this sort of procession, though not on so large a scale, in many towns of wild Texas!

The two great and dangerous things in Linrock at the hour were whisky and guns. Under such conditions the rustlers were capable of any mad act of folly.

Morton and his men sent word flying around town that a fight was imminent and all citizens should be prepared to defend their homes against possible violence. But despite his warning I saw many respectable citizens abroad whose quiet, unobtrusive manner and watchful eyes and hard faces told me that when trouble began they wanted to be there. Verily Ranger Steele had built his house of service upon a rock. It did not seem too much to say that the next few days, perhaps hours, would see a great change in the character and a proportionate decrease in number of the inhabitants of this corner of Pecos County.

Morton and I were in the crowd that watched Blome, Snecker, and a dozen other rustlers march down to Steele's jail. They had crowbars and they had cans of giant powder, which they had appropriated from a hardware store. If Steele had a jailer he was not in evidence. The door was wrenched off and Bo Snecker, evidently not wholly recovered, brought forth to his cheering comrades. Then some of the rustlers began to urge back the pressing circle, and the word given out acted as a spur to haste. The jail was to be blown up.

The crowd split and some men ran one way, some another. Morton and I were among those who hurried over the vacant ground to a little ridge that marked the edge of the open country. From this vantage point we heard several rustlers yell in warning, then they fled for their lives.

It developed that they might have spared themselves such headlong flight. The explosion appeared to be long in coming. At length we saw the lifting of the roof in a cloud of red dust, and then heard an exceedingly heavy but low detonation. When the pall of dust drifted away all that was left of Steele's jail was a part of the stone walls. The building that stood nearest, being constructed of adobe, had been badly damaged.

However, this wreck of the jail did not seem to satisfy Blome and his followers, for amid wild yells and huzzahs they set to work with crowbars and soon laid low every stone. Then with young Snecker in the fore they set off up town; and if this was not a gang in fit mood for any evil or any ridiculous celebration I greatly missed my guess.

It was a remarkable fact, however, and one that convinced me of deviltry afoot, that the crowd broke up, dispersed, and actually disappeared off the streets of Linrock. The impression given was that they were satisfied. But this impression did not remain with me. Morton was scarcely deceived either. I told him that I would almost certainly see Steele early in the evening and that we would be out of harm's way. He told me that we could trust him and his men to keep sharp watch on the night doings of Blome's gang. Then we parted.

It was almost dark. By the time I had gotten something to eat and drink at the Hope So, the hour for my meeting with Sally was about due. On the way out I did not pass a lighted house until I got to the end of the street; and then strange to say, that one was Steele's. I walked down past the place, and though I was positive he would not be there I whistled low. I halted and waited. He had two lights lit, one in the kitchen, and one in the big room. The blinds were drawn. I saw a long, dark shadow cross one window and then, a little later, cross the other. This would have deceived me had I not remembered Steele's device for casting the shadow. He had expected to have his house attacked at night, presumably while he was at home; but he had felt that it was not necessary for him to stay there to make sure. Lawless men of this class were sometimes exceedingly simple and gullible.

Then I bent my steps across the open, avoiding road and path, to the foot of the hill upon which Sampson's house stood. It was dark enough under the trees. I could hardly find my way to the secluded nook and bench where I had been directed to come. I wondered if Sally would be able to find it. Trust that girl! She might have a few qualms and come shaking a little, but she would be there on the minute.

I had hardly seated myself to wait when my keen ears detected something, then slight rustlings, then soft steps, and a dark form emerged from the blackness into the little starlit glade. Sally came swiftly towards me and right into my arms. That was sure a sweet moment. Through the excitement and dark boding thoughts of the day, I had forgotten that she would do just this thing. And now I anticipated tears, clingings, fears. But I was agreeably surprised.

"Russ, are you all right?" she whispered.

"Just at this moment I am," I replied.

Sally gave me another little hug, and then, disengaging herself from my arms, she sat down beside me.

"I can only stay a minute. Oh, it's safe enough. But I told Diane I was to meet you and she's waiting to hear if Steele is—is—"

"Steele's safe so far," I interrupted.

"There were men coming and going all day. Uncle Roger never appeared at meals. He didn't eat, Diane said. George tramped up and down, smoking, biting his nails, listening for these messengers. When they'd leave he'd go in for another drink. We heard him roar some one had been shot and we feared it might be Steele."

"No," I replied, steadily.

"Did Steele shoot anybody?"

"No. A rustler named March tried to draw on Steele, and someone in the crowd killed March."

"Someone? Russ, was it you?"

"It sure wasn't. I didn't happen to be there."

"Ah! Then Steele has other men like you around him. I might have guessed that."

"Sally, Steele makes men his friends. It's because he's on the side of justice."

"Diane will be glad to hear that. She doesn't think only of Steele's life. I believe she has a secret pride in his work. And I've an idea what she fears most is some kind of a clash between Steele and her father."

"I shouldn't wonder. Sally, what does Diane know about her father?"

"Oh, she's in the dark. She got hold of papers that made her ask him questions. And his answers made her suspicious. She realizes he's not what he has pretended to be all these years. But she never dreams her father is a rustler chief. When she finds that out—" Sally broke off and I finished the sentence in thought.

"Listen, Sally," I said, suddenly. "I've an idea that Steele's house will be attacked by the gang to-night, and destroyed, same as the jail was this afternoon. These rustlers are crazy. They'll expect to kill him while he's there. But he won't be there. If you and Diane hear shooting and yelling to-night don't be frightened. Steele and I will be safe."

"Oh, I hope so. Russ, I must hurry back. But, first, can't you arrange a meeting between Diane and Steele? It's her wish. She begged me to. She must see him."

"I'll try," I promised, knowing that promise would be hard to keep.

"We could ride out from the ranch somewhere. You remember we used to rest on the high ridge where there was a shady place—such a beautiful outlook? It was there I—I—"

"My dear, you needn't bring up painful memories. I remember where."

Sally laughed softly. She could laugh in the face of the gloomiest prospects. "Well, to-morrow morning, or the next, or any morning soon, you tie your red scarf on the dead branch of that high mesquite. I'll look every morning with the glass. If I see the scarf, Diane and I will ride out."

"That's fine. Sally, you have ideas in your pretty little head. And once I thought it held nothing but—" She put a hand on my mouth. "I must go now," she said and rose. She stood close to me and put her arms around my neck. "One thing more, Russ. It—it was dif—difficult telling Diane we—we were engaged. I lied to Uncle. But what else could I have told Diane? I—I—Oh—was it—" She faltered.

"Sally, you lied to Sampson to save me. But you must have accepted me before you could have told Diane the truth."

"Oh, Russ, I had—in my heart! But it has been some time since you asked me—and—and—"

"You imagined my offer might have been withdrawn. Well, it stands."

She slipped closer to me then, with that soft sinuousness of a woman, and I believed she might have kissed me had I not held back, toying with my happiness.

"Sally, do you love me?"

"Ever so much. Since the very first."

"I'm a marshal, a Ranger like Steele, a hunter of criminals. It's a hard life. There's spilling of blood. And any time I—I might—All the same, Sally—will you be my wife?"

"Oh, Russ! Yes. But let me tell you when your duty's done here that I will have a word to say about your future. It'll be news to you to learn I'm an orphan. And I'm not a poor one. I own a plantation in Louisiana. I'll make a planter out of you. There!"

"Sally! You're rich?" I exclaimed.

"I'm afraid I am. But nobody can ever say you married me for my money."

"Well, no, not if you tell of my abject courtship when I thought you a poor relation on a visit. My God! Sally, if I only could see this Ranger job through safely and to success!"

"You will," she said softly.

Then I took a ring from my little finger and slipped it on hers. "That was my sister's. She's dead now. No other girl ever wore it. Let it be your engagement ring. Sally, I pray I may somehow get through this awful Ranger deal to make you happy, to become worthy of you!"

"Russ, I fear only one thing," she whispered.

"And what's that?"

"There will be fighting. And you—oh, I saw into your eyes the other night when you stood with your hands up. You would kill anybody, Russ. It's awful!

But don't think me a baby. I can conceive what your work is, what a man you must be. I can love you and stick to you, too. But if you killed a blood relative of mine I would have to give you up. I'm a Southerner, Russ, and blood is thick. I scorn my uncle and I hate my cousin George. And I love you. But don't you kill one of my family, I—Oh, I beg of you go as far as you dare to avoid that!"

I could find no voice to answer her, and for a long moment we were locked in an embrace, breast to breast and lips to lips, an embrace of sweet pain.

Then she broke away, called a low, hurried good-by, and stole like a shadow into the darkness.

An hour later I lay in the open starlight among the stones and brush, out where Steele and I always met. He lay there with me, but while I looked up at the stars he had his face covered with his hands. For I had given him my proofs of the guilt of Diane Sampson's father.

Steele had made one comment: "I wish to God I'd sent for some fool who'd have bungled the job!"

This was a compliment to me, but it showed what a sad pass Steele had come to. My regret was that I had no sympathy to offer him. I failed him there. I had trouble of my own. The feel of Sally's clinging arms around my neck, the warm, sweet touch of her lips remained on mine. What Steele was enduring I did not know, but I felt that it was agony.

Meanwhile time passed. The blue, velvety sky darkened as the stars grew brighter. The wind grew stronger and colder. I heard sand blowing against the stones like the rustle of silk. Otherwise it was a singularly quiet night. I wondered where the coyotes were and longed for their chorus. By and by a prairie wolf sent in his lonely lament from the distant ridges. That mourn was worse than the silence. It made the cold shudders creep up and down my back. It was just the cry that seemed to be the one to express my own trouble. No one hearing that long-drawn, quivering wail could ever disassociate it from tragedy. By and by it ceased, and then I wished it would come again. Steele lay like the stone beside him. Was he ever going to speak? Among the vagaries of my mood was a petulant desire to have him sympathize with me.

I had just looked at my watch, making out in the starlight that the hour was eleven, when the report of a gun broke the silence.

I jumped up to peer over the stone. Steele lumbered up beside me, and I heard him draw his breath hard.

CHAPTER 11 THE FIGHT IN THE HOPE SO

I could plainly see the lights of his adobe house, but of course, nothing else was visible. There were no other lighted houses near. Several flashes gleamed, faded swiftly, to be followed by reports, and then the unmistakable jingle of glass.

"I guess the fools have opened up, Steele," I said. His response was an angry grunt. It was just as well, I concluded, that things had begun to stir. Steele needed to be roused.

Suddenly a single sharp yell pealed out. Following it came a huge flare of light, a sheet of flame in which a great cloud of smoke or dust shot up. Then, with accompanying darkness, burst a low, deep, thunderous boom. The lights of the house went out, then came a crash. Points of light flashed in a half-circle and the reports of guns blended with the yells of furious men, and all these were swallowed up in the roar of a mob.

Another and a heavier explosion momentarily lightened the darkness and then rent the air. It was succeeded by a continuous volley and a steady sound that, though composed of yells, screams, cheers, was not anything but a hideous roar of hate. It kept up long after there could have been any possibility of life under the ruins of that house. It was more than hate of Steele. All that was wild and lawless and violent hurled this deed at the Ranger Service.

Such events had happened before in Texas and other states; but, strangely, they never happened more than once in one locality. They were expressions, perhaps, that could never come but once.

I watched Steele through all that hideous din, that manifestation of insane rage at his life and joy at his death, and when silence once more reigned and he turned his white face to mine, I had a sensation of dread. And dread was something particularly foreign to my nature.

"So Blome and the Sneckers think they've done for me," he muttered.

"Pleasant surprise for them to-morrow, eh, old man?" I queried.

"To-morrow? Look, Russ, what's left of my old 'dobe house is on fire. The ruins can't be searched soon. And I was particular to fix things so it'd look like I was home. I just wanted to give them a chance. It's incomprehensible how easy men like them can be duped. Whisky-soaked! Yes, they'll be surprised!"

He lingered a while, watching the smoldering fire and the dim columns of smoke curling up against the dark blue. "Russ, do you suppose they heard up at the ranch and think I'm—"

"They heard, of course," I replied. "But the girls know you're safe with me."

"Safe? I—I almost wish to God I was there under that heap of ruins, where the rustlers think they've left me."

"Well, Steele, old fellow, come on. We need some sleep." With Steele in the lead, we stalked away into the open.

Two days later, about the middle of the forenoon, I sat upon a great flat rock in the shade of a bushy mesquite, and, besides enjoying the vast, clear sweep of gold and gray plain below, I was otherwise pleasantly engaged. Sally sat as close to me as she could get, holding to my arm as if she never intended to let go. On the other side Miss Sampson leaned against me, and she was white and breathless, partly from the quick ride out from the ranch, partly from agitation. She had grown thinner, and there were dark shadows under her eyes, yet she seemed only more beautiful. The red scarf with which I had signaled the girls waved from a branch of the mesquite. At the foot of the ridge their horses were halted in a shady spot.

"Take off your sombrero," I said to Sally. "You look hot. Besides, you're prettier with your hair flying." As she made no move, I took it off for her. Then I made bold to perform the same office for Miss Sampson. She faintly smiled her thanks. Assuredly she had forgotten all her resentment. There were little beads of perspiration upon her white brow. What a beautiful mass of black-brown hair, with strands of red or gold! Pretty soon she would be bending that exquisite head and face over poor Steele, and I, who had schemed this meeting, did not care what he might do to me.

Pretty soon, also, there was likely to be an interview that would shake us all to our depths, and naturally, I was somber at heart. But though my outward mood of good humor may have been pretense, it certainly was a pleasure to be with the girls again way out in the open. Both girls were quiet, and this made my task harder, and perhaps in my anxiety to ward off questions and appear happy for their own sakes I made an ass of myself with my silly talk and familiarity. Had ever a Ranger such a job as mine?

"Diane, did Sally show you her engagement ring?" I went on, bound to talk.

Miss Sampson either did not notice my use of her first name or she did not object. She seemed so friendly, so helplessly wistful. "Yes. It's very pretty. An antique. I've seen a few of them," she replied.

"I hope you'll let Sally marry me soon."

"*Let* her? Sally Langdon? You haven't become acquainted with your fiancee. But when—"

"Oh, next week, just as soon—"

"Russ!" cried Sally, blushing furiously.

"What's the matter?" I queried innocently.

"You're a little previous."

"Well, Sally, I don't presume to split hairs over dates. But, you see, you've become extremely more desirable—in the light of certain revelations. Diane, wasn't Sally the deceitful thing? An heiress all the time! And I'm to be a planter and smoke fine cigars and drink mint juleps! No, there won't be any juleps."

"Russ, you're talking nonsense," reproved Sally. "Surely it's no time to be funny."

"All right," I replied with resignation. It was no task to discard that hollow mask of humor. A silence ensued, and I waited for it to be broken.

"Is Steele badly hurt?" asked Miss Sampson presently.

"No. Not what he or I'd call hurt at all. He's got a scalp wound, where a bullet bounced off his skull. It's only a scratch. Then he's got another in the shoulder; but it's not bad, either."

"Where is he now?"

"Look across on the other ridge. See the big white stone? There, down under the trees, is our camp. He's there."

"When may—I see him?" There was a catch in her low voice.

"He's asleep now. After what happened yesterday he was exhausted, and the pain in his head kept him awake till late. Let him sleep a while yet. Then you can see him."

"Did he know we were coming?"

"He hadn't the slightest idea. He'll be overjoyed to see you. He can't help that. But he'll about fall upon me with harmful intent."

"Why?"

"Well, I know he's afraid to see you."

"Why?"

"Because it only makes his duty harder."

"Ah!" she breathed.

It seemed to me that my intelligence confirmed a hope of hers and gave her relief. I felt something terrible in the balance for Steele. And I was glad to be able to throw them together. The catastrophe must fall, and now the sooner it fell the better. But I experienced a tightening of my lips and a tugging at my heart-strings.

"Sally, what do you and Diane know about the goings-on in town yesterday?" I asked.

"Not much. George was like an insane man. I was afraid to go near him. Uncle wore a sardonic smile. I heard him curse George—oh, terribly! I believe he hates George. Same as day before yesterday, there were men riding in and out. But Diane and I heard only a little, and conflicting statements at that. We knew there was fighting. Dick and the servants, the cowboys, all brought rumors. Steele was killed at least ten times and came to life just as many.

"I can't recall, don't want to recall, all we heard. But this morning when I saw the red scarf flying in the wind—well, Russ, I was so glad I could not see through the glass any more. We knew then Steele was all right or you wouldn't have put up the signal."

"Reckon few people in Linrock realize just what *did* come off," I replied with a grim chuckle.

"Russ, I want you to tell me," said Miss Sampson earnestly.

"What?" I queried sharply.

"About yesterday—what Steele did—what happened."

"Miss Sampson, I could tell you in a few short statements of fact or I could take two hours in the telling. Which do you prefer?"

"I prefer the long telling. I want to know all about him."

"But why, Miss Sampson? Consider. This is hardly a story for a sensitive woman's ears."

"I am no coward," she replied, turning eyes to me that flashed like dark fire.

"But why?" I persisted. I wanted a good reason for calling up all the details of the most strenuous and terrible day in my border experience. She was silent a moment. I saw her gaze turn to the spot where Steele lay asleep, and it was a pity he could not see her eyes then. "Frankly, I don't want to tell you," I added, and I surely would have been glad to get out of the job.

"I want to hear—because I glory in his work," she replied deliberately.

I gathered as much from the expression of her face as from the deep ring of her voice, the clear content of her statement. She loved the Ranger, but that was not all of her reason.

"His work?" I echoed. "Do you want him to succeed in it?"

"With all my heart," she said, with a white glow on her face.

"My God!" I ejaculated. I just could not help it. I felt Sally's small fingers clutching my arm like sharp pincers. I bit my lips to keep them shut. What if Steele had heard her say that? Poor, noble, justice-loving, blind girl! She knew even less than I hoped. I forced my thought to the question immediately at hand. She gloried in the Ranger's work. She wanted with all her heart to see him succeed in it. She had a woman's pride in his manliness. Perhaps, with a woman's complex, incomprehensible motive, she wanted Steele to be shown to her in all the power that made him hated and feared by lawless men. She had finally accepted the wild life of this border as something terrible and inevitable, but passing. Steele was one of the strange and great and misunderstood men who were making that wild life pass.

For the first time I realized that Miss Sampson, through sharpened eyes of love, saw Steele as he really was—a wonderful and necessary violence. Her intelligence and sympathy had enabled her to see through defamation and the false records following a Ranger; she had had no choice but to love him; and then a woman's glory in a work that freed men, saved women, and made children happy effaced forever the horror of a few dark deeds of blood.

"Miss Sampson, I must tell you first," I began, and hesitated—"that I'm not a cowboy. My wild stunts, my drinking and gaming—these were all pretense."

"Indeed! I am very glad to hear it. And was Sally in your confidence?"

"Only lately. I am a United States deputy marshal in the service of Steele."

She gave a slight start, but did not raise her head.

"I have deceived you. But, all the same, I've been your friend. I ask you to respect my secret a little while. I'm telling you because otherwise my relation to Steele yesterday would not be plain. Now, if you and Sally will use this blanket, make yourselves more comfortable seats, I'll begin my story."

Miss Sampson allowed me to arrange a place for her where she could rest at ease, but Sally returned to my side and stayed there. She was an enigma to-day—pale, brooding, silent—and she never looked at me except when my face was half averted.

"Well," I began, "night before last Steele and I lay hidden among the rocks near the edge of town, and we listened to and watched the destruction of Steele's house. It had served his purpose to leave lights burning, to have shadows blow across the window-blinds, and to have a dummy in his bed. Also, he arranged guns to go off inside the house at the least jar. Steele wanted evidence against his enemies. It was not the pleasantest kind of thing to wait there listening to that drunken mob. There must have been a hundred men. The disturbance and the intent worked strangely upon Steele. It made him different. In the dark I couldn't tell how he looked, but I felt a mood coming in him that fairly made me dread the next day.

"About midnight we started for our camp here. Steele got in some sleep, but I couldn't. I was cold and hot by turns, eager and backward, furious and thoughtful. You see, the deal was such a complicated one, and to-morrow certainly was nearing the climax. By morning I was sick, distraught, gloomy, and uncertain. I had breakfast ready when Steele awoke. I hated to look at him, but when I did it was like being revived.

"He said: 'Russ, you'll trail alongside me to-day and through the rest of this mess.'

"That gave me another shock. I want to explain to you girls that this was the first time in my life I was backward at the prospects of a fight. The shock was the jump of my pulse. My nerve came back. To line up with Steele against Blome and his gang—that would be great!

"'All right, old man,' I replied. 'We're going after them, then?'

"He only nodded.

"After breakfast I watched him clean and oil and reload his guns. I didn't need to ask him if he expected to use them. I didn't need to urge upon him Captain Neal's command.

"'Russ,' said Steele, 'we'll go in together. But before we get to town I'll leave you and circle and come in at the back of the Hope So. You hurry on ahead, post Morton and his men, get the lay of the gang, if possible, and then be at the Hope So when I come in.'

"I didn't ask him if I had a free hand with my gun. I intended to have that. We left camp and hurried toward town. It was near noon when we separated.

"I came down the road, apparently from Sampson's ranch. There was a crowd around the ruins of Steele's house. It was one heap of crumbled 'dobe bricks and burned logs, still hot and smoking. No attempt had been made to dig into the ruins. The curious crowd was certain that Steele lay buried under all that stuff. One feature of that night assault made me ponder. Daylight discovered the bodies of three dead men, rustlers, who had been killed, the report went out, by random shots. Other participants in the affair had been wounded. I believed Morton and his men, under cover of the darkness and in the melee, had sent in some shots not calculated upon the program.

"From there I hurried to town. Just as I had expected, Morton and Zimmer were lounging in front of the Hope So. They had company, disreputable and otherwise. As yet Morton's crowd had not come under suspicion. He was wild for news of Steele, and when I gave it, and outlined the plan, he became as cool and dark and grim as any man of my kind could have wished. He sent Zimmer to get the others of their clique. Then he acquainted me with a few facts, although he was noncommittal in regard to my suspicion as to the strange killing of the three rustlers.

"Blome, Bo Snecker, Hilliard, and Pickens, the ringleaders, had painted the town in celebration of Steele's death. They all got gloriously drunk except old man Snecker. He had cold feet, they said. They were too happy to do any more shooting or mind what the old rustler cautioned. It was two o'clock before they went to bed.

"This morning, after eleven, one by one they appeared with their followers. The excitement had died down. Ranger Steele was out of the way and Linrock was once more wide open, free and easy. Blome alone seemed sullen and spiritless, unresponsive to his comrades and their admirers. And now, at the time of my arrival, the whole gang, with the exception of old Snecker, were assembled in the Hope So.

"'Zimmer will be clever enough to drift his outfit along one or two at a time?' I asked Morton, and he reassured me. Then we went into the saloon.

"There were perhaps sixty or seventy men in the place, more than half of whom were in open accord with Blome's gang. Of the rest there were many of doubtful repute, and a few that might have been neutral, yet all the time were secretly burning to help any cause against these rustlers. At all events, I gathered that impression from the shadowed faces, the tense bodies, the too-evident indication of anything but careless presence there. The windows were open. The light was clear. Few men smoked, but all had a drink before them. There was the ordinary subdued hum of conversation. I surveyed the scene, picked out my position so as to be close to Steele when he entered, and sauntered round to it. Morton aimlessly leaned against a post.

"Presently Zimmer came in with a man and they advanced to the bar. Other men entered as others went out. Blome, Bo Snecker, Hilliard, and Pickens had a table full in the light of the open windows. I recognized the faces of the two last-named, but I had not, until Morton informed me, known who they were. Pickens was little, scrubby, dusty, sandy, mottled, and he resembled a rattlesnake. Hilliard was big, gaunt, bronzed, with huge mustache and hollow, fierce eyes. I never had seen a grave-robber, but I imagined one would be like Hilliard. Bo Snecker was a sleek, slim, slender, hard-looking boy, marked dangerous, because he was too young and too wild to have caution or fear. Blome, the last of the bunch, showed the effects of a bad night.

"You girls remember how handsome he was, but he didn't look it now. His face was swollen, dark, red, and as it had been bright, now it was dull. Indeed, he looked sullen, shamed, sore. He was sober now. Thought was written on his clouded brow. He was awakening now to the truth that the day before had branded him a coward and sent him out to bolster up courage with drink. His vanity had begun to bleed. He knew, if his faithful comrades had not awakened to it yet, that his prestige had been ruined. For a gunman, he had suffered the last degradation. He had been bidden to draw and he had failed of the nerve.

"He breathed heavily; his eyes were not clear; his hands were shaky. Almost I pitied this rustler who very soon must face an incredibly swift and mercilessly fatal Ranger. Face him, too, suddenly, as if the grave had opened to give up its dead.

"Friends and comrades of this center group passed to and fro, and there was much lazy, merry, though not loud, talk. The whole crowd was still half-asleep. It certainly was an auspicious hour for Steele to confront them, since that duty was imperative. No man knew the stunning paralyzing effect of surprise better than Steele. I, of course, must take my cue from him, or the sudden development of events.

"But Jack Blome did not enter into my calculations. I gave him, at most, about a minute to live after Steele entered the place. I meant to keep sharp eyes all around. I knew, once with a gun out, Steele could kill Blome's comrades at the table as quick as lightning, if he chose. I rather thought my game was to watch his outside partners. This was right, and as it turned out, enabled me to save Steele's life.

"Moments passed and still the Ranger did not come. I began to get nervous. Had he been stopped? I scouted the idea. Who could have stopped him, then? Probably the time seemed longer than it really was. Morton showed the strain, also. Other men looked drawn, haggard, waiting as if expecting a thunderbolt. Once in my roving gaze I caught Blandy's glinty eye on me. I didn't like the gleam. I said to myself I'd watch him if I had to do it out of the back of my head. Blandy, by the way, is—was—I should say, the Hope So bartender." I stopped to clear my throat and get my breath.

"Was," whispered Sally. She quivered with excitement. Miss Sampson bent eyes upon me that would have stirred a stone man.

"Yes, he was once," I replied ambiguously, but mayhap my grimness betrayed the truth. "Don't hurry me, Sally. I guarantee you'll be sick enough presently.

"Well, I kept my eyes shifty. And I reckon I'll never forget that room. Likely I saw what wasn't really there. In the excitement, the suspense, I must have made shadows into real substance. Anyway, there was the half-circle of bearded, swarthy men around Blome's table. There were the four rustlers—Blome brooding, perhaps vaguely, spiritually, listening to a knock; there was Bo Snecker, reckless youth, fondling a flower he had, putting the stem in his glass, then to his lips, and lastly into the buttonhole of Blome's vest; there was Hilliard, big, gloomy, maybe with his cavernous eyes seeing the hell where I expected he'd soon be; and last, the little dusty, scaly Pickens, who looked about to leap and sting some one.

"In the lull of the general conversation I heard Pickens say: 'Jack, drink up an' come out of it. Every man has an off day. You've gambled long enough to know every feller gits called. An' as Steele has cashed, what the hell do you care?

"Hilliard nodded his ghoul's head and blinked his dead eyes. Bo Snecker laughed. It wasn't any different laugh from any other boy's. I remembered then that he killed Hoden. I began to sweat fire. Would Steele ever come?

"'Jim, the ole man hed cold feet an' he's give 'em to Jack,' said Bo. 'It ain't nothin' to lose your nerve once. Didn't I run like a scared jack-rabbit from Steele? Watch me if he comes to life, as the ole man hinted!'

"'About mebbe Steele wasn't in the 'dobe at all. Aw, thet's a joke! I seen him in bed. I seen his shadder. I heard his shots comin' from the room. Jack, you seen an' heerd same as me.'

"'Sure. I know the Ranger's cashed,' replied Blome. 'It's not that. I'm sore, boys.'

"'Deader 'n a door-nail in hell!' replied Pickens, louder, as he lifted his glass. 'Here's to Lone Star Steele's ghost! An' if I seen it this minnit I'd ask it to waltz with me!'

"The back door swung violently, and Steele, huge as a giant, plunged through and leaped square in front of that table.

"Some one of them let out a strange, harsh cry. It wasn't Blome or Snecker—probably Pickens. He dropped the glass he had lifted. The cry had stilled the room, so the breaking of the glass was plainly heard. For a space that must have been short, yet seemed long, everybody stood tight. Steele with both hands out and down, leaned a little, in a way I had never seen him do. It was the position of a greyhound, but that was merely the body of him. Steele's nerve, his spirit, his meaning was there, like lightning about to strike. Blome maintained a ghastly, stricken silence.

"Then the instant was plain when he realized this was no ghost of Steele, but the Ranger in the flesh. Blome's whole frame rippled as thought jerked him out of his trance. His comrades sat stone-still. Then Hilliard and Pickens dived without rising from the table. Their haste broke the spell.

"I wish I could tell it as quick as it happened. But Bo Snecker, turning white as a sheet, stuck to Blome. All the others failed him, as he had guessed they would fail. Low curses and exclamations were uttered by men sliding and pressing back, but the principals were mute. I was thinking hard, yet I had no time to get to Steele's side. I, like the rest, was held fast. But I kept my eyes sweeping around, then back again to that center pair.

"Blome slowly rose. I think he did it instinctively. Because if he had expected his first movement to start the action he never would have moved. Snecker sat partly on the rail of his chair, with both feet square on the floor, and he never twitched a muscle. There was a striking difference in the looks of these two rustlers. Snecker had burning holes for eyes in his white face. At the last he was staunch, defiant, game to the core. He didn't think. But Blome faced death and knew it. It was infinitely more than the facing of foes, the taking of stock, preliminary to the even break. Blome's attitude was that of a trapped wolf about to start into savage action; nevertheless, equally it was the pitifully weak stand of a ruffian against ruthless and powerful law.

"The border of Pecos County could have had no greater lesson than this—Blome face-to-face with the Ranger. That part of the border present saw its most noted exponent of lawlessness a coward, almost powerless to go for his gun, fatally sure of his own doom.

"But that moment, seeming so long, really so short, had to end. Blome made a spasmodic upheaval of shoulder and arm. Snecker a second later flashed into movement.

"Steele blurred in my sight. His action couldn't be followed. But I saw his gun, waving up, flame red once—twice—and the reports almost boomed together.

"Blome bent forward, arm down, doubled up, and fell over the table and slid to the floor.

"But Snecker's gun cracked with Steele's last shot. I heard the bullet strike Steele. It made me sick as if it had hit me. But Steele never budged. Snecker leaped up, screaming, his gun sputtering to the floor. His left hand swept to his right arm, which had been shattered by Steele's bullet.

"Blood streamed everywhere. His screams were curses, and then ended, testifying to a rage hardly human. Then, leaping, he went down on his knees after the gun.

"Don't pick it up," called Steele; his command would have checked anyone save an insane man. For an instant it even held Snecker. On his knees, right arm hanging limp, left extended, and face ghastly with agony and fiendish fury, he was certainly an appalling sight.

"'Bo, you're courtin' death,' called a hard voice from the crowd.

"'Snecker, wait. Don't make me kill you!' cried Steele swiftly. 'You're still a boy. Surrender! You'll outlive your sentence many years. I promise clemency. Hold, you fool!'

"But Snecker was not to be denied the last game move. He scrabbled for his gun. Just then something, a breathtaking intuition—I'll never know what—made me turn my head. I saw the bartender deliberately aim a huge gun at Steele. If he had not been so slow, I would have been too late. I whirled and shot. Talk about nick of time! Blandy pulled trigger just as my bullet smashed into his head.

"He dropped dead behind the bar and his gun dropped in front. But he had hit Steele.

"The Ranger staggered, almost fell. I thought he was done, and, yelling, I sped to him.

"But he righted himself. Then I wheeled again. Someone in the crowd killed Bo Snecker as he wobbled up with his gun. That was the signal for a wild run for outdoors, for cover. I heard the crack of guns and whistle of lead. I shoved Steele back of the bar, falling over Blandy as I did so.

"When I got up Steele was leaning over the bar with a gun in each hand. There was a hot fight then for a minute or so, but I didn't fire a shot. Morton and his crowd were busy. Men ran everywhere, shooting, ducking, cursing. The room got blue with smoke till you couldn't see, and then the fight changed to the street.

"Steele and I ran out. There was shooting everywhere. Morton's crowd appeared to be in pursuit of rustlers in all directions. I ran with Steele, and did not observe his condition until suddenly he fell right down in the street. Then he looked so white and so bloody I thought he'd stopped another bullet and—"

Here Miss Sampson's agitation made it necessary for me to halt my story, and I hoped she had heard enough. But she was not sick, as Sally appeared to me; she simply had been overcome by emotion. And presently, with a blaze in her eyes that showed how her soul was aflame with righteous wrath at these rustlers and ruffians, and how, whether she knew it or not, the woman in her loved a fight, she bade me go on. So I persevered, and, with poor little Sally sagging against me, I went on with the details of that fight.

I told how Steele rebounded from his weakness and could no more have been stopped than an avalanche. For all I saw, he did not use his guns again. Here, there, everywhere, as Morton and his squad cornered a rustler, Steele would go in, ordering surrender, promising protection. He seemed to have no thoughts of bullets. I could not hold him back, and it was hard to keep pace with him. How many times he was shot at I had no idea, but it was many. He dragged forth this and that rustler, and turned them all over to Morton to be guarded. More than once he protected a craven rustler from the summary dealing Morton wanted to see in order.

I told Miss Sampson particularly how Steele appeared to me, what his effect was on these men, how toward the end of the fight rustlers were appealing to him to save them from these new-born vigilantes. I believed I drew a picture of the Ranger that would live forever in her heart of hearts. If she were a hero-worshiper she would have her fill.

One thing that was strange to me—leaving fight, action, blood, peril out of the story—the singular exultation, for want of some better term, that I experienced in recalling Steele's look, his wonderful cold, resistless, inexplicable presence, his unquenchable spirit which was at once deadly and merciful. Other men would have killed where he saved. I recalled this magnificent spiritual something about him, remembered it strongest in the ring of his voice as he appealed to Bo Snecker not to force him to kill. Then I told how we left a dozen prisoners under guard and went back to the Hope So to find Blome where he had fallen. Steele's bullet had cut one of the petals of the rose Snecker had playfully put in the rustler's buttonhole. Bright and fatal target for an eye like Steele's! Bo Snecker lay clutching his gun, his face set rigidly in that last fierce expression of his savage nature.

There were five other dead men on the floor, and, significant of the work of Steele's unknown allies, Hilliard and Pickens were among them.

"Steele and I made for camp then," I concluded. "We didn't speak a word on the way out. When we reached camp all Steele said was for me to go off and leave him alone. He looked sick. I went off, only not very far. I knew what was wrong with him, and it wasn't bullet-wounds. I was near when he had his spell and fought it out.

"Strange how spilling blood affects some men! It never bothered me much. I hope I'm human, too. I certainly felt an awful joy when I sent that bullet into Blandy's bloated head in time. And I'll always feel that way about it. But Steele's different."

CHAPTER 12 TORN TWO WAYS

Steele lay in a shady little glade, partly walled by the masses of upreared rocks that we used as a lookout point. He was asleep, yet far from comfortable. The bandage I had put around his head had been made from strips of soiled towel, and, having collected sundry bloody spots, it was an unsightly affair. There was a blotch of dried blood down one side of Steele's face. His shirt bore more dark stains, and in one place was pasted fast to his shoulder where a bandage marked the location of his other wound. A number of green flies were crawling over him and buzzing around his head. He looked helpless, despite his giant size; and certainly a great deal worse off than I had intimated, and, in fact, than he really was.

Miss Sampson gasped when she saw him and both her hands flew to her breast.

"Girls, don't make any noise," I whispered. "I'd rather he didn't wake suddenly to find you here. Go round behind the rocks there. I'll wake him, and call you presently."

They complied with my wish, and I stepped down to Steele and gave him a little shake. He awoke instantly.

"Hello!" I said, "Want a drink?"

"Water or champagne?" he inquired.

I stared at him. "I've some champagne behind the rocks," I added.

"Water, you locoed son of a gun!"

He looked about as thirsty as a desert coyote; also, he looked flighty. I was reaching for the canteen when I happened to think what pleasure it would be to Miss Sampson to minister to him, and I drew back. "Wait a little." Then with an effort I plunged. "Vaughn, listen. Miss Sampson and Sally are here."

I thought he was going to jump up, he started so violently, and I pressed him back.

"She—Why, she's been here all the time—Russ, you haven't double-crossed me?"

"Steele!" I exclaimed. He was certainly out of his head.

"Pure accident, old man."

He appeared to be half stunned, yet an eager, strange, haunting look shone in his eyes. "Fool!" he exclaimed.

"Can't you make the ordeal easier for her?" I asked.

"This'll be hard on Diane. She's got to be told things!"

"Ah!" breathed Steele, sinking back. "Make it easier for her—Russ, you're a damned schemer. You have given me the double-cross. You have and she's going to."

"We're in bad, both of us," I replied thickly. "I've ideas, crazy enough maybe. I'm between the devil and the deep sea, I tell you. I'm about ready to show yellow. All the same, I say, see Miss Sampson and talk to her, even if you can't talk straight."

"All right, Russ," he replied hurriedly. "But, God, man, don't I look a sight! All this dirt and blood!"

"Well, old man, if she takes that bungled mug of yours in her lap, you can be sure you're loved. You needn't jump out of your boots! Brace up now, for I'm going to bring the girls." As I got up to go I heard him groan. I went round behind the stones and found the girls. "Come on," I said. "He's awake now, but a little queer. Feverish. He gets that way sometimes. It won't last long." I led Miss Sampson and Sally back into the shade of our little camp glade.

Steele had gotten worse all in a moment. Also, the fool had pulled the bandage off his head; his wound had begun to bleed anew, and the flies were paying no attention to his weak efforts to brush them away. His head rolled as we reached his side, and his eyes were certainly wild and wonderful and devouring enough. "Who's that?" he demanded.

"Easy there, old man," I replied. "I've brought the girls." Miss Sampson shook like a leaf in the wind.

"So you've come to see me die?" asked Steele in a deep and hollow voice. Miss Sampson gave me a lightning glance of terror.

"He's only off his head," I said. "Soon as we wash and bathe his head, cool his temperature, he'll be all right."

"Oh!" cried Miss Sampson, and dropped to her knees, flinging her gloves aside. She lifted Steele's head into her lap. When I saw her tears falling upon his face I felt worse than a villain. She bent over him for a moment, and one of the tender hands at his cheeks met the flow of fresh blood and did not shrink. "Sally," she said, "bring the scarf out of my coat. There's a veil too. Bring that. Russ, you get me some water—pour some in the pan there."

"Water!" whispered Steele.

She gave him a drink. Sally came with the scarf and veil, and then she backed away to the stone, and sat there. The sight of blood had made her a little pale and weak. Miss Sampson's hands trembled and her tears still fell, but neither interfered with her tender and skillful dressing of that bullet wound.

Steele certainly said a lot of crazy things. "But why'd you come—why're you so good—when you don't love me?"

"Oh, but—I do—love you," whispered Miss Sampson brokenly.

"How do I know?"

"I am here. I tell you."

There was a silence, during which she kept on bathing his head, and he kept on watching her. "Diane!" he broke out suddenly.

"Yes—yes."

"That won't stop the pain in my head."

"Oh, I hope so."

"Kiss me—that will," he whispered. She obeyed as a child might have, and kissed his damp forehead close to the red furrow where the bullet cut.

"Not there," Steele whispered.

Then blindly, as if drawn by a magnet, she bent to his lips. I could not turn away my head, though my instincts were delicate enough. I believe that kiss was the first kiss of love for both Diane Sampson and Vaughn Steele. It was so strange and so long, and somehow beautiful. Steele looked rapt. I could only see the side of Diane's face, and that was white, like snow. After she raised her head she seemed unable, for a moment, to take up her task where it had been broken off, and Steele lay as if he really were dead. Here I got up, and seating myself beside Sally, I put an arm around her. "Sally dear, there are others," I said.

"Oh, Russ—what's to come of it all?" she faltered, and then she broke down and began to cry softly. I would have been only too glad to tell her what hung in the balance, one way or another, had I known. But surely, catastrophe! Then I heard Steele's voice again and its huskiness, its different tone, made me fearful, made me strain my ears when I tried, or thought I tried, not to listen.

"Diane, you know how hard my duty is, don't you?"

"Yes, I know—I think I know."

"You've guessed—about your father?"

"I've seen all along you must clash. But it needn't be so bad. If I can only bring you two together—Ah! please don't speak any more. You're excited now, just not yourself."

"No, listen. We must clash, your father and I. Diane, he's not—"

"Not what he seems! Oh, I know, to my sorrow."

"What do you know?" She seemed drawn by a will stronger than her own. "To my shame I know. He has been greedy, crafty, unscrupulous—dishonest."

"Diane, if he were only that! That wouldn't make my duty torture. That wouldn't ruin your life. Dear, sweet girl, forgive me—your father's—"

"Hush, Vaughn. You're growing excited. It will not do. Please—please—"

"Diane, your father's—chief of this—gang that I came to break up."

"My God, hear him! How dare you—Oh, Vaughn, poor, poor boy, you're out of your mind! Sally, Russ, what shall we do? He's worse. He's saying the most dreadful things! I—I can't bear to hear him!"

Steele heaved a sigh and closed his eyes. I walked away with Sally, led her to and fro in a shady aisle beyond the rocks, and tried to comfort her as best I could. After a while, when we returned to the glade, Miss Sampson had considerable color in her cheeks, and Steele was leaning against the rock, grave and sad. I saw that he had recovered and he had reached the critical point. "Hello, Russ," he said. "Sprung a surprise on me, didn't you? Miss Sampson says I've been a little flighty while she bandaged me up. I hope I wasn't bad. I certainly feel better now. I seem to—to have dreamed."

Miss Sampson flushed at his concluding words. Then silence ensued. I could not think of anything to say and Sally was dumb. "You all seem very strange," said Miss Sampson.

When Steele's face turned gray to his lips I knew the moment had come. "No doubt. We all feel so deeply for you," he said.

"Me? Why?"

"Because the truth must no longer be concealed."

It was her turn to blanch, and her eyes, strained, dark as night, flashed from one of us to the other.

"The truth! Tell it then." She had more courage than any of us.

"Miss Sampson, your father is the leader of this gang of rustlers I have been tracing. Your cousin George Wright, is his right-hand man."

Miss Sampson heard, but she did not believe.

"Tell her, Russ," Steele added huskily, turning away. Wildly she whirled to me. I would have given anything to have been able to lie to her. As it was I could not speak. But she read the truth in my face. And she collapsed as if she had been shot. I caught her and laid her on the grass. Sally, murmuring and crying, worked over her. I helped. But Steele stood aloof, dark and silent, as if he hoped she would never return to consciousness.

When she did come to, and began to cry, to moan, to talk frantically, Steele staggered away, while Sally and I made futile efforts to calm her. All we could do was to prevent her doing herself violence. Presently, when her fury of emotion subsided, and she began to show a hopeless stricken shame, I left Sally with her and went off a little way myself. How long I remained absent I had no idea, but it was no inconsiderable length of time. Upon my return, to my surprise and relief, Miss Sampson had recovered her composure, or at least, self-control. She stood leaning against the rock where Steele had been, and at this moment, beyond any doubt, she was supremely more beautiful than I had ever seen her. She was white, tragic, wonderful. "Where is Mr. Steele?" she asked. Her tone and her look did not seem at all suggestive of the mood I expected to find her in—one of beseeching agony, of passionate appeal to Steele not to ruin her father.

"I'll find him," I replied turning away.

Steele was readily found and came back with me. He was as unlike himself as she was strange. But when they again faced each other, then they were indeed new to me.

"I want to know—what you must do," she said. Steele told her briefly, and his voice was stern.

"Those—those criminals outside of my own family don't concern me now. But can my father and cousin be taken without bloodshed? I want to know the absolute truth." Steele knew that they could not be, but he could not tell her so. Again she appealed to me. Thus my part in the situation grew harder. It hurt me so that it made me angry, and my anger made me cruelly frank.

"No. It can't be done. Sampson and Wright will be desperately hard to approach, which'll make the chances even. So, if you must know the truth, it'll be your father and cousin to go under, or it'll be Steele or me, or any combination luck breaks—or all of us!"

Her self-control seemed to fly to the four winds. Swift as light she flung herself down before Steele, against his knees, clasped her arms round him. "Good God! Miss Sampson, you mustn't do that!" implored Steele. He tried to break her hold with shaking hands, but he could not.

"Listen! Listen!" she cried, and her voice made Steele, and Sally and me also, still as the rock behind us. "Hear me! Do you think I beg you to let my father go, for his sake? No! No! I have gloried in your Ranger duty. I have loved you because of it. But some awful tragedy threatens here. Listen, Vaughn Steele. Do not you deny me, as I kneel here. I love you. I never loved any other man. But not for my love do I beseech you.

"There is no help here unless you forswear your duty. Forswear it! Do not kill my father—the father of the woman who loves you. Worse and more horrible it would be to let my father kill you! It's I who make this situation unnatural, impossible. You must forswear your duty. I can live no longer if you don't. I pray you—" Her voice had sunk to a whisper, and now it failed. Then she seemed to get into his arms, to wind herself around him, her hair loosened, her face upturned, white and spent, her arms blindly circling his neck. She was all love, all surrender, all supreme appeal, and these, without her beauty, would have made her wonderful. But her beauty! Would not Steele have been less than a man or more than a man had he been impervious to it? She was like some snow-white exquisite flower, broken, and suddenly blighted. She was a woman then in all that made a woman helpless—in all that made her mysterious, sacred, absolutely and unutterably more than any other thing in life. All this time my gaze had been riveted on her only. But when she lifted her white face, tried to lift it, rather, and he drew her up, and then when both white faces met and seemed to blend in something rapt, awesome, tragic as life—then I saw Steele.

I saw a god, a man as beautiful as she was. They might have stood, indeed, they did stand alone in the heart of a desert—alone in the world—alone with their love and their agony. It was a solemn and profound moment for me. I faintly realized how great it must have been for them, yet all the while there hammered at my mind the vital thing at stake. Had they forgotten, while I remembered? It might have been only a moment that he held her. It might have been my own agitation that conjured up such swift and whirling thoughts. But if my mind sometimes played me false my eyes never had. I thought I saw Diane Sampson die in Steele's arms; I could have sworn his heart was breaking; and mine was on the point of breaking, too.

How beautiful they were! How strong, how mercifully strong, yet shaken, he seemed! How tenderly, hopelessly, fatally appealing she was in that hour of her broken life! If I had been Steele I would have forsworn my duty, honor, name, service for her sake. Had I mind enough to divine his torture, his temptation, his narrow escape? I seemed to feel them, at any rate, and while I saw him with a beautiful light on his face, I saw him also ghastly, ashen, with hands that shook as they groped around her, loosing her, only to draw her convulsively back again. It was the saddest sight I had ever seen. Death was nothing to it. Here was the death of happiness. He must wreck the life of the woman who loved him and whom he loved. I was becoming half frantic, almost ready to cry out the uselessness of this scene, almost on the point of pulling them apart, when Sally dragged me away. Her clinging hold then made me feel perhaps a little of what Miss Sampson's must have been to Steele.

How different the feeling when it was mine! I could have thrust them apart, after all my schemes and tricks, to throw them together, in vague, undefined fear of their embrace. Still, when love beat at my own pulses, when Sally's soft hand held me tight and she leaned to me—that was different. I was glad to be led away—glad to have a chance to pull myself together. But was I to have that chance? Sally, who in the stife of emotion had been forgotten, might have to be reckoned with. Deep within me, some motive, some purpose, was being born in travail. I did not know what, but instinctively I feared Sally. I feared her because I loved her. My wits came back to combat my passion. This hazel-eyed girl, soft, fragile creature, might be harder to move than the Ranger. But could she divine a motive scarcely yet formed in my brain? Suddenly I became cool, with craft to conceal.

"Oh, Russ! What's the matter with you?" she queried quickly. "Can't Diane and Steele, you and I ride away from this bloody, bad country? Our own lives, our happiness, come first, do they not?"

"They ought to, I suppose," I muttered, fighting against the insidious sweetness of her. I knew then I must keep my lips shut or betray myself.

"You look so strange. Russ, I wouldn't want you to kiss me with that mouth. Thin, shut lips—smile! Soften and kiss me! Oh, you're so cold, strange! You chill me!"

"Dear child, I'm badly shaken," I said. "Don't expect me to be natural yet. There are things you can't guess. So much depended upon—Oh, never mind! I'll go now. I want to be alone, to think things out. Let me go, Sally."

She held me only the tighter, tried to pull my face around. How intuitively keen women were. She felt my distress, and that growing, stern, and powerful thing I scarcely dared to acknowledge to myself. Strangely, then, I relaxed and faced her. There was no use trying to foil these feminine creatures. Every second I seemed to grow farther from her. The swiftness of this mood of mine was my only hope. I realized I had to get away quickly, and make up my mind after that what I intended to do. It was an earnest, soulful, and loving pair of eyes that I met. What did she read in mine? Her hands left mine to slide to my shoulders, to slip behind my neck, to lock there like steel bands. Here was my ordeal. Was it to be as terrible as Steele's had been? I thought it would be, and I swore by all that was rising grim and cold in me that I would be strong. Sally gave a little cry that cut like a blade in my heart, and then she was close-pressed upon me, her quivering breast beating against mine, her eyes, dark as night now, searching my soul.

She saw more than I knew, and with her convulsive clasp of me confirmed my half-formed fears. Then she kissed me, kisses that had no more of girlhood or coquetry or joy or anything but woman's passion to blind and hold and tame. By their very intensity I sensed the tiger in me. And it was the tiger that made her new and alluring sweetness fail of its intent. I did not return one of her kisses. Just one kiss given back—and I would be lost.

"Oh, Russ, I'm your promised wife!" she whispered at my lips. "Soon, you said! I want it to be soon! To-morrow!" All the subtlety, the intelligence, the cunning, the charm, the love that made up the whole of woman's power, breathed in her pleading. What speech known to the tongue could have given me more torture? She chose the strongest weapon nature afforded her. And had the calamity to consider been mine alone, I would have laughed at it and taken Sally at her word. Then I told her in short, husky sentences what had depended on Steele: that I loved the Ranger Service, but loved him more; that his character, his life, embodied this Service I loved; that I had ruined him; and now I would forestall him, do his work, force the issue myself or die in the attempt.

"Dearest, it's great of you!" she cried. "But the cost! If you kill one of my kin I'll—I'll shrink from you! If you're killed—Oh, the thought is dreadful! You've done your share. Let Steele—some other Ranger finish it. I swear I don't plead for my uncle or my cousin, for their sakes. If they are vile, let them suffer. Russ, it's you I think of! Oh, my pitiful little dreams! I wanted so to surprise you with my beautiful home—the oranges, the mossy trees, the mocking-birds. Now you'll never, never come!"

"But, Sally, there's a chance—a mere chance I can do the job without—"

Then she let go of me. She had given up. I thought she was going to drop, and drew her toward the stone. I cursed the day I ever saw Neal and the service. Where, now, was the arch prettiness, the gay, sweet charm of Sally Langdon? She looked as if she were suffering from a desperate physical injury. And her final breakdown showed how, one way or another, I was lost to her.

As she sank on the stone I had my supreme wrench, and it left me numb, hard, in a cold sweat. "Don't betray me! I'll forestall him! He's planned nothing for to-day," I whispered hoarsely. "Sally—you dearest, gamest little girl in the world! Remember I loved you, even if I couldn't prove it your way. It's for his sake. I'm to blame for their love. Some day my act will look different to you. Good-by!"

CHAPTER 13 RUSS SITTELL IN ACTION

I ran like one possessed of devils down that rough slope, hurdling the stones and crashing through the brush, with a sound in my ears that was not all the rush of the wind. When I reached a level I kept running; but something dragged at me. I slowed down to a walk. Never in my life had I been victim of such sensation. I must flee from something that was drawing me back. Apparently one side of my mind was unalterably fixed, while the other was a hurrying conglomeration of flashes of thought, reception of sensations. I could not get calm.

By and by, almost involuntarily, with a fleeting look backward as if in expectation of pursuit, I hurried faster on. Action seemed to make my state less oppressive; it eased the weight upon me. But the farther I went on, the harder it was to continue. I was turning my back upon love, happiness, success in life, perhaps on life itself. I was doing that, but my decision had not been absolute. There seemed no use to go on farther until I was absolutely sure of myself. I received a clear warning thought that such work as seemed haunting and driving me could never be carried out in the mood under which I labored. I hung on to that thought. Several times I slowed up, then stopped, only to tramp on again.

At length, as I mounted a low ridge, Linrock lay bright and green before me, not faraway, and the sight was a conclusive check. There were mesquites on the ridge, and I sought the shade beneath them. It was the noon hour, with hot, glary sun and no wind. Here I had to have out my fight. If ever in my varied life of exciting adventure I strove to think, to understand myself, to see through difficulties, I assuredly strove then. I was utterly unlike myself; I could not bring the old self back; I was not the same man I once had been. But I could understand why. It was because of Sally Langdon, the gay and roguish girl who had bewitched me, the girl whom love had made a woman—the kind of woman meant to make life beautiful for me.

I saw her changing through all those weeks, holding many of the old traits and graces, acquiring new character of mind and body, to become what I had just fled from—a woman sweet, fair, loyal, loving, passionate.

Temptation assailed me. To have her to-morrow—my wife! She had said it. Just twenty-four little hours, and she would be mine—the only woman I had ever really coveted, the only one who had ever found the good in me. The thought was alluring. I followed it out, a long, happy stage-ride back to Austin, and then by train to her home where, as she had said, the oranges grew and the trees waved with streamers of gray moss and the mocking-birds made melody. I pictured that home. I wondered that long before I had not associated wealth and luxury with her family. Always I had owned a weakness for plantations, for the agricultural life with its open air and freedom from towns.

I saw myself riding through the cotton and rice and cane, home to the stately old mansion, where long-eared hounds bayed me welcome and a woman looked for me and met me with happy and beautiful smiles. There might—there *would* be children. And something new, strange, confounding with its emotion, came to life deep in my heart. There would be children! Sally their mother; I their father! The kind of life a lonely Ranger always yearned for and never had! I saw it all, felt it keenly, lived its sweetness in an hour of temptation that made me weak physically and my spirit faint and low.

For what had I turned my back on this beautiful, all-satisfying prospect? Was it to arrest and jail a few rustlers? Was it to meet that mocking Sampson face to face and show him my shield and reach for my gun? Was it to kill that hated Wright? Was it to save the people of Linrock from further greed, raids, murder? Was it to please and aid my old captain, Neal of the Rangers? Was it to save the Service to the State?

No—a thousand times no. It was for the sake of Steele. Because he was a wonderful man! Because I had been his undoing! Because I had thrown Diane Sampson into his arms! That had been my great error. This Ranger had always been the wonder and despair of his fellow officers, so magnificent a machine, so sober, temperate, chaste, so unremittingly loyal to the Service, so strangely stern and faithful to his conception of the law, so perfect in his fidelity to duty. He was the model, the inspiration, the pride of all of us. To me, indeed, he represented the Ranger Service. He was the incarnation of that spirit which fighting Texas had developed to oppose wildness and disorder and crime. He would carry through this Linrock case; but even so, if he were not killed, his career would be ruined. He might save the Service, yet at the cost of his happiness. He was not a machine; he was a man. He might be a perfect Ranger; still he was a human being.

The loveliness, the passion, the tragedy of a woman, great as they were, had not power to shake him from his duty. Futile, hopeless, vain her love had been to influence him. But there had flashed over me with subtle, overwhelming suggestion that not futile, not vain was *my* love to save him! Therefore, beyond and above all other claims, and by reason of my wrong to him, his claim came first.

It was then there was something cold and deathlike in my soul; it was then I bade farewell to Sally Langdon. For I knew, whatever happened, of one thing I was sure—I would have to kill either Sampson or Wright. Snecker could be managed; Sampson might be trapped into arrest; but Wright had no sense, no control, no fear. He would snarl like a panther and go for his gun, and he would have to be killed. This, of all consummations, was the one to be calculated upon. And, of course, by Sally's own words, that contingency would put me forever outside the pale for her.

I did not deceive myself; I did not accept the slightest intimation of hope; I gave her up. And then for a time regret, remorse, pain, darkness worked their will with me.

I came out of it all bitter and callous and sore, in the most fitting of moods to undertake a difficult and deadly enterprise. Miss Sampson completely slipped my mind; Sally became a wraith as of some one dead; Steele began to fade. In their places came the bushy-bearded Snecker, the olive-skinned Sampson with his sharp eyes, and dark, evil faced Wright. Their possibilities began to loom up, and with my speculation returned tenfold more thrilling and sinister the old strange zest of the man-hunt.

It was about one o'clock when I strode into Linrock. The streets for the most part were deserted. I went directly to the hall where Morton and Zimmer, with their men, had been left by Steele to guard the prisoners. I found them camping out in the place, restless, somber, anxious. The fact that only about half the original number of prisoners were left struck me as further indication of Morton's summary dealing. But when I questioned him as to the decrease in number, he said bluntly that they had escaped. I did not know whether or not to believe him. But that didn't matter. I tried to get in some more questions, only I found that Morton and Zimmer meant to be heard first. "Where's Steele?" they demanded.

"He's out of town, in a safe place," I replied. "Too bad hurt for action. I'm to rush through with the rest of the deal."

"That's good. We've waited long enough. This gang has been split, an' if we hurry they'll never get together again. Old man Snecker showed up to-day. He's drawin' the outfit in again. Reckon he's waitin' for orders. Sure he's ragin' since Bo was killed. This old fox will be dangerous if he gets goin'."

"Where is he now?" I queried.

"Over at the Hope So. Must be a dozen of the gang there. But he's the only leader left we know of. If we get him, the rustler gang will be broken for good. He's sent word down here for us to let our prisoners go or there'd be a damn bloody fight. We haven't sent our answer yet. Was hopin' Steele would show up. An' now we're sure glad you're back."

"Morton, I'll take the answer," I replied quickly. "Now there're two things. Do you know if Sampson and Wright are at the ranch?"

"They were an hour ago. We had word. Zimmer saw Dick."

"All right. Have you any horses handy?"

"Sure. Those hitched outside belong to us."

"I want you to take a man with you, in a few moments, and ride round the back roads and up to Sampson's house. Get off and wait under the trees till you hear me shoot or yell, then come fast."

Morton's breast heaved; he whistled as he breathed; his neck churned. "God Almighty! So *there* the scent leads! We always wondered—half believed. But no one spoke—no one had any nerve." Morton moistened his lips; his face was livid; his big hands shook. "Russ, you can gamble on me."

"Good. Well, that's all. Come out and get me a horse."

CHAPTER 13 RUSS SITTELL IN ACTION

When I had mounted and was half-way to the Hope So, my plan, as far as Snecker was concerned, had been formed. It was to go boldy into the saloon, ask for the rustler, first pretend I had a reply from Morton and then, when I had Snecker's ear, whisper a message supposedly from Sampson. If Snecker was too keen to be decoyed I could at least surprise him off his guard and kill him, then run for my horse. The plan seemed clever to me. I had only one thing to fear, and that was a possibility of the rustlers having seen my part in Steele's defense the other day. That had to be risked. There were always some kind of risks to be faced.

It was scarcely a block and a half to the Hope So. Before I arrived I knew I had been seen. When I dismounted before the door I felt cold, yet there was an exhilaration in the moment. I never stepped more naturally and carelessly into the saloon. It was full of men. There were men behind the bar helping themselves. Evidently Blandy's place had not been filled. Every face near the door was turned toward me; dark, intent, scowling, malignant they were, and made me need my nerve.

"Say, boys, I've a word for Snecker," I called, quite loud. Nobody stirred. I swept my glance over the crowd, but did not see Snecker. "I'm in some hurry," I added.

"Bill ain't here," said a man at the table nearest me. "Air you comin' from Morton?"

"Nit. But I'm not yellin' this message."

The rustler rose, and in a few long strides confronted me.

"Word from Sampson!" I whispered, and the rustler stared. "I'm in his confidence. He's got to see Bill at once. Sampson sends word he's quit—he's done—he's through. The jig is up, and he means to hit the road out of Linrock."

"Bill'll kill him surer 'n hell," muttered the rustler. "But we all said it'd come to thet. An' what'd Wright say?"

"Wright! Why, he's cashed in. Didn't you-all hear? Reckon Sampson shot him."

The rustler cursed his amaze and swung his rigid arm with fist clenched tight. "When did Wright get it?"

"A little while ago. I don't know how long. Anyway, I saw him lyin' dead on the porch. An' say, pard, I've got to rustle. Send Bill up quick as he comes. Tell him Sampson wants to turn over all his stock an' then light out."

I backed to the door, and the last I saw of the rustler he was standing there in a scowling amaze. I had fooled him all right. If only I had the luck to have Snecker come along soon. Mounting, I trotted the horse leisurely up the street. Business and everything else was at a standstill in Linrock these days. The doors of the stores were barricaded. Down side streets, however, I saw a few people, a buckboard, and stray cattle.

When I reached the edge of town I turned aside a little and took a look at the ruins of Steele's adobe house. The walls and debris had all been flattened, scattered about, and if anything of, value had escaped destruction it had disappeared.

Steele, however, had left very little that would have been of further use to him. Turning again, I continued on my way up to the ranch. It seemed that, though I was eager rather than backward, my mind seized avidly upon suggestion or attraction, as if to escape the burden of grim pondering. When about half-way across the flat, and perhaps just out of gun-shot sound of Sampson's house, I heard the rapid clatter of hoofs on the hard road. I wheeled, expecting to see Morton and his man, and was ready to be chagrined at their coming openly instead of by the back way. But this was only one man, and it was not Morton. He seemed of big build, and he bestrode a fine bay horse. There evidently was reason for hurry, too. At about one hundred yards, when I recognized Snecker, complete astonishment possessed me.

Well it was I had ample time to get on my guard! In wheeling my horse I booted him so hard that he reared. As I had been warm I had my sombrero over the pommel of the saddle. And when the head of my horse blocked any possible sight of movement of my hand, I pulled my gun and held it concealed under my sombrero. This rustler had bothered me in my calculations. And here he came galloping, alone. Exultation would have been involuntary then but for the sudden shock, and then the cold settling of temper, the breathless suspense. Snecker pulled his huge bay and pounded to halt abreast of me. Luck favored me. Had I ever had anything but luck in these dangerous deals?

Snecker seemed to fume; internally there was a volcano. His wide sombrero and bushy beard hid all of his face except his eyes, which were deepset furnaces. He, too, like his lieutenant, had been carried completely off balance by the strange message apparently from Sampson. It was Sampson's name that had fooled and decoyed these men. "Hey! You're the feller who jest left word fer some one at the Hope So?" he asked.

"Yes," I replied, while with my left hand I patted the neck of my horse, holding him still.

"Sampson wants me bad, eh?"

"Reckon there's only one man who wants you more."

Steadily, I met his piercing gaze. This was a rustler not to be long victim to any ruse. I waited in cold surety.

"You thet cowboy, Russ?" he asked.

"I was—and I'm not!" I replied significantly.

The violent start of this violent outlaw was a rippling jerk of passion. "What'n hell!" he ejaculated.

"Bill, you're easy."

"Who're you?" he uttered hoarsely.

I watched Snecker with hawk-like keenness. "United States deputy marshal. Bill, you're under arrest!"

He roared a mad curse as his hand clapped down to his gun. Then I fired through my sombrero. Snecker's big horse plunged. The rustler fell back, and one of his legs pitched high as he slid off the lunging steed. His other foot caught in the stirrup. This fact terribly frightened the horse. He bolted, dragging the rustler for a dozen jumps. Then Snecker's foot slipped loose. He lay limp and still and shapeless in the road. I did not need to go back to look him over.

But to make assurance doubly sure, I dismounted, and went back to where he lay. My bullet had gone where it had been aimed. As I rode up into Sampson's court-yard and turned in to the porch I heard loud and angry voices. Sampson and Wright were quarrelling again. How my lucky star guided me! I had no plan of action, but my brain was equal to a hundred lightning-swift evolutions. The voices ceased. The men had heard the horse. Both of them came out on the porch. In an instant I was again the lolling impudent cowboy, half under the influence of liquor.

"It's only Russ and he's drunk," said George Wright contemptuously.

"I heard horses trotting off there," replied Sampson. "Maybe the girls are coming. I bet I teach them not to run off again—Hello, Russ."

He looked haggard and thin, but seemed amiable enough. He was in his shirt-sleeves and he had come out with a gun in his hand. This he laid on a table near the wall. He wore no belt. I rode right up to the porch and, greeting them laconically, made a show of a somewhat tangle-footed cowboy dismounting. The moment I got off and straightened up, I asked no more. The game was mine. It was the great hour of my life and I met it as I had never met another. I looked and acted what I pretended to be, though a deep and intense passion, an almost ungovernable suspense, an icy sickening nausea abided with me. All I needed, all I wanted was to get Sampson and Wright together, or failing that, to maneuver into such position that I had any kind of a chance. Sampson's gun on the table made three distinct objects for me to watch and two of them could change position.

"What do you want here?" demanded Wright. He was red, bloated, thick-lipped, all fiery and sweaty from drink, though sober on the moment, and he had the expression of a desperate man in his last stand. It *was* his last stand, though he was ignorant of that.

"Me—Say, Wright, I ain't fired yet," I replied, in slow-rising resentment.

"Well, you're fired now," he replied insolently.

"Who fires me, I'd like to know?" I walked up on the porch and I had a cigarette in one hand, a match in the other. I struck the match.

"I do," said Wright.

I studied him with apparent amusement. It had taken only one glance around for me to divine that Sampson would enjoy any kind of a clash between Wright and me. "Huh! You fired me once before an' it didn't go, Wright. I reckon you don't stack up here as strong as you think."

He was facing the porch, moody, preoccupied, somber, all the time. Only a little of his mind was concerned with me. Manifestly there were strong forces at work. Both men were strained to a last degree, and Wright could be made to break at almost a word. Sampson laughed mockingly at this sally of mine, and that stung Wright. He stopped his pacing and turned his handsome, fiery eyes on me. "Sampson, I won't stand this man's impudence."

"Aw, Wright, cut that talk. I'm not impudent. Sampson knows I'm a good fellow, on the square, and I have you sized up about O.K."

"All the same, Russ, you'd better dig out," said Sampson. "Don't kick up any fuss. We're busy with deals to-day. And I expect visitors."

"Sure. I won't stay around where I ain't wanted," I replied. Then I lit my cigarette and did not move an inch out of my tracks.

Sampson sat in a chair near the door; the table upon which lay his gun stood between him and Wright. This position did not invite me to start anything. But the tension had begun to be felt. Sampson had his sharp gaze on me. "What'd you come for, anyway?" he asked suddenly.

"Well, I had some news I was asked to fetch in."

"Get it out of you then."

"See here now, Mr. Sampson, the fact is I'm a tender-hearted fellow. I hate to hurt people's feelin's. And if I was to spring this news in Mr. Wright's hearin', why, such a sensitive, high-tempered gentleman as he would go plumb off his nut." Unconcealed sarcasm was the dominant note in that speech. Wright flared up, yet he was eagerly curious. Sampson, probably, thought I was only a little worse for drink, and but for the way I rubbed Wright he would not have tolerated me at all.

"What's this news? You needn't be afraid of my feelings," said Wright.

"Ain't so sure of that," I drawled. "It concerns the lady you're sweet on, an' the ranger you ain't sweet on."

Sampson jumped up. "Russ, had Diane gone out to meet Steele?" he asked angrily.

"Sure she had," I replied.

I thought Wright would choke. He was thick-necked anyway, and the gush of blood made him tear at the soft collar of his shirt. Both men were excited now, moving about, beginning to rouse. I awaited my chance, patient, cold, all my feelings shut in the vise of my will.

"How do you know she met Steele?" demanded Sampson.

"I was there. I met Sally at the same time."

"But why should my daughter meet this Ranger?"

"She's in love with him and he's in love with her."

The simple statement might have had the force of a juggernaut. I reveled in Wright's state, but I felt sorry for Sampson. He had not outlived his pride. Then I saw the leaping thought—would this daughter side against him? Would she help to betray him? He seemed to shrivel up, to grow old while I watched him.

Wright, finding his voice, cursed Diane, cursed the Ranger, then Sampson, then me.

"You damned, selfish fool!" cried Sampson, in deep, bitter scorn. "All you think of is yourself. Your loss of the girl! Think once of me—my home—my life!"

Then the connection subtly put out by Sampson apparently dawned upon the other. Somehow, through this girl, her father and cousin were to be betrayed. I got that impression, though I could not tell how true it was. Certainly, Wright's jealousy was his paramount emotion.

Sampson thrust me sidewise off the porch. "Go away," he ordered. He did not look around to see if I came back. Quickly I leaped to my former position. He confronted Wright. He was beyond the table where the gun lay. They were close together. My moment had come. The game was mine—and a ball of fire burst in my brain to race all over me.

"To hell with you!" burst out Wright incoherently. He was frenzied. "I'll have her or nobody else will!"

"You never will," returned Sampson stridently. "So help me God, I'd rather see her Ranger Steele's wife than yours!"

While Wright absorbed that shock Sampson leaned toward him, all of hate and menace in his mien. They had forgotten the half-drunken cowboy. "Wright, you made me what I am," continued Sampson. "I backed you, protected you, finally I went in with you. Now it's ended. I quit you. I'm done!" Their gray, passion-corded faces were still as stones.

"Gentlemen," I called in clear, high, far-reaching voice, the intonation of authority, "you're both done!"

They wheeled to confront me, to see my leveled gun. "Don't move! Not a muscle! Not a finger!" I warned. Sampson read what Wright had not the mind to read. His face turned paler gray, to ashen.

"What d'ye mean?" yelled Wright fiercely, shrilly. It was not in him to obey my command, to see impending death. All quivering and strung, yet with perfect control, I raised my left hand to turn back a lapel of my open vest. The silver shield flashed brightly.

"United States deputy marshal in service of Ranger Steele!"

Wright howled like a dog. With barbarous and insane fury, with sheer, impotent folly, he swept a clawing hand for his gun. My shot broke his action as it cut short his life. Before Wright even tottered, before he loosed the gun, Sampson leaped behind him, clasped him with his left arm, quick as lightning jerked the gun from both clutching fingers and sheath. I shot at Sampson, then again, then a third time. All my bullets sped into the upheld nodding Wright. Sampson had protected himself with the body of the dead man. I had seen red flashes, puffs of smoke, had heard quick reports. Something stung my left arm. Then a blow like wind, light of sound yet shocking in impact, struck me, knocked me flat. The hot rend of lead followed the blow. My heart seemed to explode, yet my mind kept extraordinarily clear and rapid.

I raised myself, felt a post at my shoulder, leaned on it. I heard Sampson work the action of Wright's gun. I heard the hammer click, fall upon empty shells. He had used up all the loads in Wright's gun. I heard him curse as a man cursed at defeat. I waited, cool and sure now, for him to show his head or other vital part from behind his bolster. He tried to lift the dead man, to edge him closer toward the table where the gun lay. But, considering the peril of exposing himself, he found the task beyond him. He bent, peering at me under Wright's arm. Sampson's eyes were the eyes of a man who meant to kill me. There was never any mistaking the strange and terrible light of eyes like those.

More than once I had a chance to aim at them, at the top of Sampson's head, at a strip of his side. But I had only two shells left. I wanted to make sure. Suddenly I remembered Morton and his man. Then I pealed out a cry—hoarse, strange, yet far-reaching. It was answered by a shout. Sampson heard it. It called forth all that was in the man. He flung Wright's body off. But even as it dropped, before Sampson could recover to leap as he surely intended for the gun, I covered him, called piercingly to him. I could kill him there or as he moved. But one chance I gave him.

"Don't jump for the gun! Don't! I'll kill you! I've got two shells left! Sure as God, I'll kill you!"

He stood perhaps ten feet from the table where his gun lay. I saw him calculating chances. He was game. He had the courage that forced me to respect him. I just saw him measure the distance to that gun. He was magnificent. He meant to do it. I would have to kill him.

"Sampson, listen!" I cried, very swiftly. "The game's up! You're done! But think of your daughter! I'll spare your life, I'll give you freedom on one condition. For her sake! I've got you nailed—all the proofs. It was I behind the wall the other night. Blome, Hilliard, Pickens, Bo Snecker, are dead. I killed Bo Snecker on the way up here. There lies Wright. You're alone. And here comes Morton and his men to my aid.

"Give up! Surrender! Consent to demands and I'll spare you. You can go free back to your old country. It's for Diane's sake! Her life, perhaps her happiness, can be saved! Hurry, man! Your answer!"

"Suppose I refuse?" he queried, with a dark and terrible earnestness.

"Then I'll kill you in your tracks! You can't move a hand! Your word or death! Hurry, Sampson! I can't last much longer. But I can kill you before I drop. Be a man! For her sake! Quick! Another second now—By God, I'll kill you!"

"All right, Russ! I give my word," he said, and deliberately walked to the chair and fell into it, just as Morton came running up with his man.

"Put away your gun," I ordered them. "The game's up. Snecker and Wright are dead. Sampson is my prisoner. He has my word he'll be protected. It's for you to draw up papers with him. He'll divide all his property, every last acre, every head of stock as you and Zimmer dictate. He gives up all. Then he's free to leave the country, and he's never to return."

CHAPTER 14 THROUGH THE VALLEY

Sampson looked strangely at the great bloody blot on my breast and his look made me conscious of a dark hurrying of my mind. Morton came stamping up the steps with blunt queries, with anxious mien. When he saw the front of me he halted, threw wide his arms.

"There come the girls!" suddenly exclaimed Sampson. "Morton, help me drag Wright inside. They mustn't see him."

I was facing down the porch toward the court and corrals. Miss Sampson and Sally had come in sight, were swiftly approaching, evidently alarmed. Steele, no doubt, had remained out at the camp. I was watching them, wondering what they would do and say presently, and then Sampson and Johnson came to carry me indoors. They laid me on the couch in the parlor where the girls used to be so often.

"Russ, you're pretty hard hit," said Sampson, bending over me, with his hands at my breast. The room was bright with sunshine, yet the light seemed to be fading.

"Reckon I am," I replied.

"I'm sorry. If only you could have told me sooner! Wright, damn him! Always I've split over him!"

"But the last time, Sampson."

"Yes, and I came near driving you to kill me, too. Russ, you talked me out of it. For Diane's sake! She'll be in here in a minute. This'll be harder than facing a gun."

"Hard now. But it'll—turn out—O.K."

"Russ, will you do me a favor?" he asked, and he seemed shamefaced.

"Sure."

"Let Diane and Sally think Wright shot you. He's dead. It can't matter. And you're hard hit. The girls are fond of you. If—if you go under—Russ, the old side of my life is coming back. It's *been* coming. It'll be here just about when she enters this room. And by God, I'd change places with you if I could."

"Glad you—said that, Sampson," I replied. "And sure—Wright plugged me. It's our secret. I've a reason, too, not—that—it—matters—much—now."

The light was fading. I could not talk very well. I felt dumb, strange, locked in ice, with dull little prickings of my flesh, with dim rushing sounds in my ears. But my mind was clear. Evidently there was little to be done. Morton came in, looked at me, and went out. I heard the quick, light steps of the girls on the porch, and murmuring voices.

"Where'm I hit?" I whispered.

"Three places. Arm, shoulder, and a bad one in the breast. It got your lung, I'm afraid. But if you don't go quick, you've a chance."

"Sure I've a chance."

"Russ, I'll tell the girls, do what I can for you, then settle with Morton and clear out."

Just then Diane and Sally entered the room. I heard two low cries, so different in tone, and I saw two dim white faces. Sally flew to my side and dropped to her knees. Both hands went to my face, then to my breast. She lifted them, shaking. They were red. White and mute she gazed from them to me. But some woman's intuition kept her from fainting.

"Papa!" cried Diane, wringing her hands.

"Don't give way," he replied. "Both you girls will need your nerve. Russ is badly hurt. There's little hope for him."

Sally moaned and dropped her face against me, clasping me convulsively. I tried to reach a hand out to touch her, but I could not move. I felt her hair against my face. Diane uttered a low heart-rending cry, which both Sampson and I understood.

"Listen, let me tell it quick," he said huskily. "There's been a fight. Russ killed Snecker and Wright. They resisted arrest. It—it was Wright—it was Wright's gun that put Russ down. Russ let me off. In fact, Diane, he saved me. I'm to divide my property—return so far as possible what I've stolen—leave Texas at once and forever. You'll find me back in old Louisiana—if—if you ever want to come home."

As she stood there, realizing her deliverance, with the dark and tragic glory of her eyes passing from her father to me, my own sight shadowed, and I thought if I were dying then, it was not in vain.

"Send—for—Steele," I whispered.

Silently, swiftly, breathlessly they worked over me. I was exquisitely sensitive to touch, to sound, but I could not see anything. By and by all was quiet, and I slipped into a black void. Familiar heavy swift footsteps, the thump of heels of a powerful and striding man, jarred into the blackness that held me, seemed to split it to let me out; and I opened my eyes in a sunlit room to see Sally's face all lined and haggard, to see Miss Sampson fly to the door, and the stalwart Ranger bow his lofty head to enter. However far life had ebbed from me, then it came rushing back, keen-sighted, memorable, with agonizing pain in every nerve. I saw him start, I heard him cry, but I could not speak. He bent over me and I tried to smile. He stood silent, his hand on me, while Diane Sampson told swiftly, brokenly, what had happened.

How she told it! I tried to whisper a protest. To any one on earth except Steele I might have wished to appear a hero. Still, at that moment I had more dread of him than any other feeling. She finished the story with her head on his shoulder, with tears that certainly were in part for me. Once in my life, then, I saw him stunned. But when he recovered it was not Diane that he thought of first, nor of the end of Sampson's power. He turned to me.

"Little hope?" he cried out, with the deep ring in his voice. "No! There's every hope. No bullet hole like that could ever kill this Ranger. Russ!"

I could not answer him. But this time I did achieve a smile. There was no shadow, no pain in his face such as had haunted me in Sally's and Diane's. He could fight death the same as he could fight evil. He vitalized the girls. Diane began to hope; Sally lost her woe. He changed the atmosphere of that room. Something filled it, something like himself, big, virile, strong. The very look of him made me suddenly want to live; and all at once it seemed I felt alive. And that was like taking the deadened ends of nerves to cut them raw and quicken them with fiery current.

From stupor I had leaped to pain, and that tossed me into fever. There were spaces darkened, mercifully shutting me in; there were others of light, where I burned and burned in my heated blood. Sally, like the wraith she had become in my mind, passed in and out; Diane watched and helped in those hours when sight was clear. But always the Ranger was with me. Sometimes I seemed to feel his spirit grappling with mine, drawing me back from the verge. Sometimes, in strange dreams, I saw him there between me and a dark, cold, sinister shape.

The fever passed, and with the first nourishing drink given me I seemed to find my tongue, to gain something.

"Hello, old man," I whispered to Steele.

"Oh, Lord, Russ, to think you would double-cross me the way you did!"

That was his first speech to me after I had appeared to face round from the grave. His good-humored reproach told me more than any other thing how far from his mind was thought of death for me. Then he talked a little to me, cheerfully, with that directness and force characteristic of him always, showing me that the danger was past, and that I would now be rapidly on the mend. I discovered that I cared little whether I was on the mend or not. When I had passed the state of somber unrealities and then the hours of pain and then that first inspiring flush of renewed desire to live, an entirely different mood came over me. But I kept it to myself. I never even asked why, for three days, Sally never entered the room where I lay. I associated this fact, however, with what I had imagined her shrinking from me, her intent and pale face, her singular manner when occasion made it necessary or unavoidable for her to be near me.

No difficulty was there in associating my change of mood with her absence. I brooded. Steele's keen insight betrayed me to him, but all his power and his spirit availed nothing to cheer me. I pretended to be cheerful; I drank and ate anything given me; I was patient and quiet. But I ceased to mend.

Then, one day she came back, and Steele, who was watching me as she entered, quietly got up and without a word took Diane out of the room and left me alone with Sally.

"Russ, I've been sick myself—in bed for three days," she said. "I'm better now. I hope you are. You look so pale. Do you still think, brood about that fight?"

"Yes, I can't forget. I'm afraid it cost me more than life."

Sally was somber, bloomy, thoughtful. "You weren't driven to kill George?" she asked.

"How do you mean?"

"By that awful instinct, that hankering to kill, you once told me these gunmen had."

"No, I can swear it wasn't that. I didn't want to kill him. But he forced me. As I had to go after these two men it was a foregone conclusion about Wright. It was premeditated. I have no excuse."

"Hush—Tell me, if you confronted them, drew on them, then you had a chance to kill my uncle?"

"Yes. I could have done it easily."

"Why, then, didn't you?"

"It was for Diane's sake. I'm afraid I didn't think of you. I had put you out of my mind."

"Well, if a man can be noble at the same time he's terrible, you've been, Russ—I don't know how I feel. I'm sick and I can't think. I see, though, what you saved Diane and Steele. Why, she's touching happiness again, fearfully, yet really. Think of that! God only knows what you did for Steele. If I judged it by his suffering as you lay there about to die it would be beyond words to tell. But, Russ, you're pale and shaky now. Hush! No more talk!"

With all my eyes and mind and heart and soul I watched to see if she shrank from me. She was passive, yet tender as she smoothed my pillow and moved my head. A dark abstraction hung over her, and it was so strange, so foreign to her nature. No sensitiveness on earth could have equaled mine at that moment. And I saw and felt and knew that she did not shrink from me. Thought and feeling escaped me for a while. I dozed. The old shadows floated to and fro.

When I awoke Steele and Diane had just come in. As he bent over me I looked up into his keen gray eyes and there was no mask on my own as I looked up to him.

"Son, the thing that was needed was a change of nurses," he said gently. "I intend to make up some sleep now and leave you in better care."

From that hour I improved. I slept, I lay quietly awake, I partook of nourishing food. I listened and watched, and all the time I gained. But I spoke very little, and though I tried to brighten when Steele was in the room I made only indifferent success of it. Days passed. Sally was almost always with me, yet seldom alone. She was grave where once she had been gay. How I watched her face, praying for that shade to lift! How I listened for a note of the old music in her voice! Sally Langdon had sustained a shock to her soul almost as dangerous as had been the blow at my life. Still I hoped. I had seen other women's deadened and darkened spirits rebound and glow once more. It began to dawn upon me, however, that more than time was imperative if she were ever to become her old self again.

Studying her closer, with less thought of myself and her reaction to my presence, I discovered that she trembled at shadows, seemed like a frightened deer with a step always on its trail, was afraid of the dark. Then I wondered why I had not long before divined one cause of her strangeness. The house where I had killed one of her kin would ever be haunted for her. She had said she was a Southerner and that blood was thick. When I had thought out the matter a little further, I deliberately sat up in bed, scaring the wits out of all my kind nurses.

"Steele, I'll never get well in this house. I want to go home. When can you take me?"

They remonstrated with me and pleaded and scolded, all to little avail. Then they were persuaded to take me seriously, to plan, providing I improved, to start in a few days. We were to ride out of Pecos County together, back along the stage trail to civilization. The look in Sally's eyes decided my measure of improvement. I could have started that very day and have borne up under any pain or distress. Strange to see, too, how Steele and Diane responded to the stimulus of my idea, to the promise of what lay beyond the wild and barren hills!

He told me that day about the headlong flight of every lawless character out of Linrock, the very hour that Snecker and Wright and Sampson were known to have fallen. Steele expressed deep feeling, almost mortification, that the credit of that final coup had gone to him, instead of me. His denial and explanation had been only a few soundless words in the face of a grateful and clamorous populace that tried to reward him, to make him mayor of Linrock. Sampson had made restitution in every case where he had personally gained at the loss of farmer or rancher; and the accumulation of years went far toward returning to Linrock what it had lost in a material way. He had been a poor man when he boarded the stage for Sanderson, on his way out of Texas forever.

Not long afterward I heard Steele talking to Miss Sampson, in a deep and agitated voice. "You must rise above this. When I come upon you alone I see the shadow, the pain in your face. How wonderfully this thing has turned out when it might have ruined you! I expected it to ruin you. Who, but that wild boy in there could have saved us all? Diane, you have had cause for sorrow. But your father is alive and will live it down. Perhaps, back there in Louisiana, the dishonor will never be known. Pecos County is far from your old home. And even in San Antonio and Austin, a man's evil repute means little.

"Then the line between a rustler and a rancher is hard to draw in these wild border days. Rustling is stealing cattle, and I once heard a well-known rancher say that all rich cattlemen had done a little stealing. Your father drifted out here, and like a good many others, he succeeded. It's perhaps just as well not to split hairs, to judge him by the law and morality of a civilized country. Some way or other he drifted in with bad men. Maybe a deal that was honest somehow tied his hands and started him in wrong.

"This matter of land, water, a few stray head of stock had to be decided out of court. I'm sure in his case he never realized where he was drifting. Then one thing led to another, until he was face to face with dealing that took on crooked form.

To protect himself he bound men to him. And so the gang developed. Many powerful gangs have developed that way out here. He could not control them. He became involved with them.

"And eventually their dealings became deliberately and boldly dishonest. That meant the inevitable spilling of blood sooner or later, and so he grew into the leader because he was the strongest. Whatever he is to be judged for I think he could have been infinitely worse."

When he ceased speaking I had the same impulse that must have governed Steele—somehow to show Sampson not so black as he was painted, to give him the benefit of a doubt, to arraign him justly in the eyes of Rangers who knew what wild border life was.

"Steele, bring Diane in!" I called. "I've something to tell her." They came quickly, concerned probably at my tone. "I've been hoping for a chance to tell you something, Miss Sampson. That day I came here your father was quarreling with Wright. I had heard them do that before. He hated Wright. The reason came out just before we had the fight. It was my plan to surprise them. I did. I told them you went out to meet Steele—that you two were in love with each other. Wright grew wild. He swore no one would ever have you. Then Sampson said he'd rather have you Steele's wife than Wright's.

"I'll not forget that scene. There was a great deal back of it, long before you ever came out to Linrock. Your father said that he had backed Wright, that the deal had ruined him, made him a rustler. He said he quit; he was done. Now, this is all clear to me, and I want to explain, Miss Sampson. It was Wright who ruined your father. It was Wright who was the rustler. It was Wright who made the gang necessary. But Wright had not the brains or the power to lead men. Because blood is thick, your father became the leader of that gang. At heart he was never a criminal.

"The reason I respected him was because he showed himself a man at the last. He faced me to be shot, and I couldn't do it. As Steele said, you've reason for sorrow. But you must get over it. You mustn't brood. I do not see that you'll be disgraced or dishonored. Of course, that's not the point. The vital thing is whether or not a woman of your high-mindedness had real and lasting cause for shame. Steele says no. I say no."

Then, as Miss Sampson dropped down beside me, her eyes shining and wet, Sally entered the room in time to see her cousin bend to kiss me gratefully with sisterly fervor. Yet it was a woman's kiss, given for its own sake. Sally could not comprehend; it was too sudden, too unheard-of, that Diane Sampson should kiss me, the man she did not love. Sally's white, sad face changed, and in the flaming wave of scarlet that dyed neck and cheek and brow I read with mighty pound of heart that, despite the dark stain between us, she loved me still.

CHAPTER 15 CONVALESCENCE

Four mornings later we were aboard the stage, riding down the main street, on the way out of Linrock. The whole town turned out to bid us farewell. The cheering, the clamor, the almost passionate fervor of the populace irritated me, and I could not see the incident from their point of view. Never in my life had I been so eager to get out of a place. But then I was morbid, and the whole world hinged on one thing. Morton insisted on giving us an escort as far as Del Rio. It consisted of six cowboys, mounted, with light packs, and they rode ahead of the stage.

We had the huge vehicle to ourselves. A comfortable bed had been rigged up for me by placing boards across from seat to seat, and furnishing it with blankets and pillows. By some squeezing there was still room enough inside for my three companions; but Steele expressed an intention of riding mostly outside, and Miss Sampson's expression betrayed her. I was to be alone with Sally. The prospect thrilled while it saddened me. How different this ride from that first one, with all its promise of adventure and charm!

"It's over!" said Steele thickly. "It's done! I'm glad, for their sakes—glad for ours. We're out of town."

I had been quick to miss the shouts and cheers. And I had been just as quick to see, or to imagine, a subtle change in Sally Langdon's face. We had not traveled a mile before the tension relaxed about her lips, the downcast eyelids lifted, and I saw, beyond any peradventure of doubt, a lighter spirit. Then I relaxed myself, for I had keyed up every nerve to make myself strong for this undertaking. I lay back with closed eyes, weary, aching, in more pain than I wanted them to discover. And I thought and thought.

Miss Sampson had said to me: "Russ, it'll all come right. I can tell you now what you never guessed. For years Sally had been fond of our cousin, George Wright. She hadn't seen him since she was a child. But she remembered. She had an only brother who was the image of George. Sally devotedly loved Arthur. He was killed in the Rebellion. She never got over it. That left her without any family. George and I were her nearest kin.

"How she looked forward to meeting George out here! But he disappointed her right at the start. She hates a drinking man. I think she came to hate George, too. But he always reminded her of Arthur, and she could never get over that. So, naturally, when you killed George she was terribly shocked. There were nights when she was haunted, when I had to stay with her. Vaughn and I have studied her, talked about her, and we think she's gradually recovering. She loved you, too; and Sally doesn't change. Once with her is for always. So let me say to you what you said to me—do not brood. All will yet be well, thank God!"

Those had been words to remember, to make me patient, to lessen my insistent fear. Yet, what did I know of women? Had not Diane Sampson and Sally Langdon amazed and nonplused me many a time, at the very moment when I had calculated to a nicety my conviction of their action, their feeling? It was possible that I had killed Sally's love for me, though I could not believe so; but it was very possible that, still loving me, she might never break down the barrier between us. The beginning of that journey distressed me physically; yet, gradually, as I grew accustomed to the roll of the stage and to occasional jars, I found myself easier in body. Fortunately there had been rain, which settled the dust; and a favorable breeze made riding pleasant, where ordinarily it would have been hot and disagreeable.

We tarried long enough in the little hamlet of Sampson for Steele to get letters from reliable ranchers. He wanted a number of references to verify the Ranger report he had to turn in to Captain Neal. This precaution he took so as to place in Neal's hands all the evidence needed to convince Governor Smith. And now, as Steele returned to us and entered the stage, he spoke of this report. "It's the longest and the best I ever turned in," he said, with a gray flame in his eyes. "I shan't let Russ read it. He's peevish because I want his part put on record. And listen, Diane. There's to be a blank line in this report. Your father's name will never be recorded. Neither the Governor, nor the adjutant-general, nor Captain Neal, nor any one back Austin way will ever know who this mysterious leader of the Pecos gang might have been.

"Even out here very few know. Many supposed, but few knew. I've shut the mouths of those few. That blank line in the report is for a supposed and mysterious leader who vanished. Jack Blome, the reputed leader, and all his lawless associates are dead. Linrock is free and safe now, its future in the hands of roused, determined, and capable men."

We were all silent after Steele ceased talking. I did not believe Diane could have spoken just then. If sorrow and joy could be perfectly blended in one beautiful expression, they were in her face. By and by I dared to say: "And Vaughn Steele, Lone Star Ranger, has seen his last service!"

"Yes," he replied with emotion.

Sally stirred and turned a strange look upon us all. "In that case, then, if I am not mistaken, there were two Lone Star Rangers—and both have seen their last service!" Sally's lips were trembling, the way they trembled when it was impossible to tell whether she was about to laugh or cry. The first hint of her old combative spirit or her old archness! A wave of feeling rushed over me, too much for me in my weakened condition. Dizzy, racked with sudden shooting pains, I closed my eyes; and the happiness I embraced was all the sweeter for the suffering it entailed. Something beat into my ears, into my brain, with the regularity and rapid beat of pulsing blood—not too late! Not too late!

From that moment the ride grew different, even as I improved with leaps and bounds. Sanderson behind us, the long gray barren between Sanderson and the Rio Grande behind us, Del Rio for two days, where I was able to sit up, all behind us—and the eastward trail to Uvalde before us! We were the only passengers on the stage from Del Rio to Uvalde. Perhaps Steele had so managed the journey. Assuredly he had become an individual with whom traveling under the curious gaze of strangers would have been embarrassing. He was most desperately in love. And Diane, all in a few days, while riding these long, tedious miles, ordinarily so fatiguing, had renewed her bloom, had gained what she had lost. She, too, was desperately in love, though she remembered her identity occasionally, and that she was in the company of a badly shot-up young man and a broken-hearted cousin.

Most of the time Diane and Steele rode on top of the stage. When they did ride inside their conduct was not unbecoming; indeed, it was sweet to watch; yet it loosed the fires of jealous rage and longing in me; and certainly had some remarkable effect upon Sally. Gradually she had been losing that strange and somber mood she had acquired, to brighten and change more and more. Perhaps she divined something about Diane and Steele that escaped me. Anyway, all of a sudden she was transformed. "Look here, if you people want to spoon, please get out on top," she said.

If that was not the old Sally Langdon I did not know who it was. Miss Sampson tried to appear offended, and Steele tried to look insulted, but they both failed. They could not have looked anything but happy. Youth and love were too strong for this couple, whom circumstances might well have made grave and thoughtful. They were magnet and steel, powder and spark. Any moment, right before my eyes, I expected them to rush right into each other's arms. And when they refrained, merely substituting clasped hands for a dearer embrace, I closed my eyes and remembered them, as they would live in my memory forever, standing crushed together on the ridge that day, white lips to white lips, embodying all that was beautiful, passionate and tragic.

And I, who had been their undoing, in the end was their salvation. How I hugged that truth to my heart!

It seemed, following Sally's pert remark, that after an interval of decent dignity, Diane and Steele did go out upon the top of the stage. "Russ," whispered Sally, "they're up to something. I heard a few words. I bet you they're going to get married in San Antonio."

"Well, it's about time," I replied.

"But oughtn't they take us into their confidence?"

"Sally, they have forgotten we are upon the earth."

"Oh, I'm so glad they're happy!"

Then there was a long silence. It was better for me to ride lying down, in which position I was at this time. After a mile Sally took my hand and held it without speaking. My heart leaped, but I did not open my eyes or break that spell even with a whisper. "Russ, I must say—tell you—"

She faltered, and still I kept my eyes closed. I did not want to wake up from that dream. "Have I been very—very sad?" she went on.

"Sad and strange, Sally. That was worse than my bullet-holes." She gripped my hand. I felt her hair on my brow, felt her breath on my cheek.

"Russ, I swore—I'd hate you if you—if you—"

"I know. Don't speak of it," I interposed hurriedly.

"But I don't hate you. I—I love you. And I can't give you up!"

"Darling! But, Sally, can you get over it—can you forget?"

"Yes. That horrid black spell had gone with the miles. Little by little, mile after mile, and now it's gone! But I had to come to the point. To go back on my word! To tell you. Russ, you never, *never* had any sense!"

Then I opened my eyes and my arms, too, and we were reunited. It must have been a happy moment, so happy that it numbed me beyond appreciation. "Yes, Sally," I agreed; "but no man ever had such a wonderful girl."

"Russ, I never—took off your ring," she whispered.

"But you hid your hand from my sight," I replied quickly.

"Oh dear Russ, we're crazy—as crazy as those lunatics outside. Let's think a little."

I was very content to have no thought at all, just to see and feel her close to me.

"Russ, will you give up the Ranger Service for me?" she asked.

"Indeed I will."

"And leave this fighting Texas, never to return till the day of guns and Rangers and bad men and even-breaks is past?"

"Yes."

"Will you go with me to my old home? It was beautiful once, Russ, before it was let run to rack and ruin. A thousand acres. An old stone house. Great mossy oaks. A lake and river. There are bear, deer, panther, wild boars in the breaks. You can hunt. And ride! I've horses, Russ, such horses! They could run these scrubby broncos off their legs. Will you come?"

"Come! Sally, I rather think I will. But, dearest, after I'm well again I must work," I said earnestly. "I've got to have a job."

"You're indeed a poor cowboy out of a job! Remember your deceit. Oh, Russ! Well, you'll have work, never fear."

"Sally, is this old home of yours near the one Diane speaks of so much?" I asked.

"Indeed it is. But hers has been kept under cultivation and in repair, while mine has run down. That will be our work, to build it up. So it's settled then?"

"Almost. There are certain—er—formalities—needful in a compact of this kind." She looked inquiringly at me, with a soft flush. "Well, if you are so dense, try to bring back that Sally Langdon who used to torment me. How you broke your promises! How you leaned from your saddle! Kiss me, Sally!"

CHAPTER 15 CONVALESCENCE

Later, as we drew close to Uvalde, Sally and I sat in one seat, after the manner of Diane and Vaughn, and we looked out over the west where the sun was setting behind dim and distant mountains. We were fast leaving the wild and barren border. Already it seemed far beyond that broken rugged horizon with its dark line silhouetted against the rosy and golden sky. Already the spell of its wild life and the grim and haunting faces had begun to fade out of my memory. Let newer Rangers, with less to lose, and with the call in their hearts, go on with our work 'till soon that wild border would be safe!

The great Lone Star State must work out its destiny. Some distant day, in the fulness of time, what place the Rangers had in that destiny would be history.

The Scarlet Pimpernel Omnibus - Unabridged - The Scarlet Pimpernel, I Will Repay, Eldorado, Sir Percy Hits Back
Baroness Orczy
Oxford City Press, 2012
824 pages
ISBN: 978-1-78139-228-7

Available from www.amazon.com, www.amazon.co.uk

The Scarlet Pimpernel appears in a play and a series of novels and short stories by Baroness Emmuska Orczy. They are set at the start of the French Revolution, Pimpernel being a master of disguise and a precursor to other heroes such as Zorro and Batman. The play and the tales brought Orczy international acclaim, being translated into sixteen languages. This omnibus edition includes the following unabridged stories: The Scarlet Pimpernel, I Will Repay, Eldorado, and Sir Percy Hits Back

The Gallant Pimpernel - Unabridged - Lord Tony's Wife, The Way of the Scarlet Pimpernel, Sir Percy Leads the Band, The Triumph of the Scarlet Pimpernel
Baroness Orczy
Oxford City Press, 2012
804 pages
ISBN: 978-1-78139-227-0

Available from www.amazon.com, www.amazon.co.uk

The Scarlet Pimpernel appears in a play and a series of novels and short stories by Baroness Emmuska Orczy. They are set at the start of the French Revolution, Pimpernel being a master of disguise and a precursor to other heroes such as Zorro and Batman. The play and the tales brought Orczy international acclaim, being translated into sixteen languages. This omnibus edition includes the following unabridged stories: Lord Tony's Wife, The Way of the Scarlet Pimpernel, Sir Percy Leads the Band, and The Triumph of the Scarlet Pimpernel.

The Elusive Pimpernel with A Child of the Revolution, Mam'zelle Guillotine, The League of the Scarlet Pimpernel and The Adventures of the Scarlet Pimpernel - unabridged
Baroness Orczy
Oxford City Press, 2012
882 pages
ISBN: 978-1-78139-284-3

Available from www.amazon.com, www.amazon.co.uk

The Scarlet Pimpernel appears in a play and a series of novels and short stories by Baroness Emmuska Orczy. They are set at the start of the French Revolution, Pimpernel being a master of disguise and a precursor to other heroes such as Zorro and Batman. The play and the tales brought Orczy international acclaim, being translated into sixteen languages. This omnibus edition includes the following unabridged novels: The Elusive Pimpernel, A child of the Revolution, Mam'zelle Guillotine and the following collections of short stories: The League of the Scarlet Pimpernel and The Adventures of the Scarlet Pimpernel.

Anthony Hope Omnibus, containing Dolly Dialogues, The Prisoner of Zenda, Rupert of Hentzau, Simon Dale, The King's Mirror and Quisanté (all unabridged)
Anthony Hope
Benediction Classics, 2012
1032 pages
ISBN: 978-1-78139-255-3

Available from www.amazon.com, www.amazon.co.uk

This Omnibus edition contains: Dolly Dialogues, The Prisoner of Zenda, Rupert of Hentzau, Simon Dale, The King's Mirror, Quisanté. Anthony Hope (1863 - 1933), more fully Sir Anthony Hope Hawkins was an English novelist and playwright. He was a prolific writer of adventure novels and his stories

Also from Benediction Books …

Wandering Between Two Worlds: Essays on Faith and Art
Anita Mathias
Benediction Books, 2007
152 pages
ISBN: 0955373700

Available from www.amazon.com, www.amazon.co.uk

In these wide-ranging lyrical essays, Anita Mathias writes, in lush, lovely prose, of her naughty Catholic childhood in Jamshedpur, India; her large, eccentric family in Mangalore, a sea-coast town converted by the Portuguese in the sixteenth century; her rebellion and atheism as a teenager in her Himalayan boarding school, run by German missionary nuns, St. Mary's Convent, Nainital; and her abrupt religious conversion after which she entered Mother Teresa's convent in Calcutta as a novice. Later rich, elegant essays explore the dualities of her life as a writer, mother, and Christian in the United States-- Domesticity and Art, Writing and Prayer, and the experience of being "an alien and stranger" as an immigrant in America, sensing the need for roots.

About the Author

Anita Mathias is the author of *Wandering Between Two Worlds: Essays on Faith and Art*. She has a B.A. and M.A. in English from Somerville College, Oxford University, and an M.A. in Creative Writing from the Ohio State University, USA. Anita won a National Endowment of the Arts fellowship in Creative Non-fiction in 1997. She lives in Oxford, England with her husband, Roy, and her daughters, Zoe and Irene.

Anita's website:
http://www.anitamathias.com, and
Anita's blog Dreaming Beneath the Spires:
http://dreamingbeneaththespires.blogspot.com

The Church That Had Too Much
Anita Mathias
Benediction Books, 2010
52 pages
ISBN: 9781849026567

Available from www.amazon.com, www.amazon.co.uk

The Church That Had Too Much was very well-intentioned. She wanted to love God, she wanted to love people, but she was both hampered by her muchness and the abundance of her possessions, and beset by ambition, power struggles and snobbery. Read about the surprising way The Church That Had Too Much began to resolve her problems in this deceptively simple and enchanting fable.

About the Author

Anita Mathias is the author of *Wandering Between Two Worlds: Essays on Faith and Art*. She has a B.A. and M.A. in English from Somerville College, Oxford University, and an M.A. in Creative Writing from the Ohio State University, USA. Anita won a National Endowment of the Arts fellowship in Creative Non-fiction in 1997. She lives in Oxford, England with her husband, Roy, and her daughters, Zoe and Irene.

Anita's website:
    http://www.anitamathias.com, and
Anita's blog Dreaming Beneath the Spires:
    http://dreamingbeneaththespires.blogspot.com

www.ingramcontent.com/pod-product-compliance
Lightning Source LLC
Chambersburg PA
CBHW081129300726
48982CB00005B/905
* 9 7 8 1 7 8 1 3 9 4 7 8 6 *